D1000260

MAURIER DAPHNE DU MAURIER DAPHNE DU MA
AURIER DAPHNE DU MAURIER DAPHNE DU MA
MAURIER DAPHNE DU MAURIER DAPHNE DU MA
AURIER DAPHNE DU MAURIER DAPHNE DU MA
MAURIER DAPHNE DU MAURIER DAPHNE DU MA
AURIER DAPHNE DU MAURIER DAPHNE DU MAU
MAURIER DAPHNE DU MAURIER DAPHNE DU MA
AURIER DAPHNE DU MAURIER DAPHNE DU MAUI
MAURIER DAPHNE DU MAURIER DAPHNE DU MA
AURIER DAPHNE DU MAURIER DAPHNE DU MAUI
MAURIER DAPHNE DU MAURIER DAPHNE DU MA
AURIER DAPHNE DU MAURIER DAPHNE DU MAUI
MAURIER DAPHNE DU MAURIER DAPHNE DU MA
AURIER DAPHNE DU MAURIER DAPHNE DU MAUI
MAURIER DAPHNE DU MAURIER DAPHNE DU MA
AURIER DAPHNE DU MAURIER DAPHNE DU MAUI
MAURIER DAPHNE DU MAURIER DAPHNE DU MA
AURIER DAPHNE DU MAURIER DAPHNE DU MAUI
MAURIER DAPHNE DU MAURIER DAPHNE DU MA
AURIER DAPHNE DU MAURIER DAPHNE DU MAUI
MAURIER DAPHNE DU MAURIER DAPHNE DU MA
AURIER DAPHNE DU MAURIER DAPHNE DU MAUI
MAURIER DAPHNE DU MAURIER DAPHNE DU MA
AURIER DAPHNE DU MAURIER DAPHNE DU MAUI
MAURIER DAPHNE DU MAURIER DAPHNE DU MA
AURIER DAPHNE DU MAURIER DAPHNE DU MAUI
MAURIER DAPHNE DU MAURIER DAPHNE DU MA
AURIER DAPHNE DU MAURIER DAPHNE DU MAUI
MAURIER DAPHNE DU MAURIER DAPHNE DU MA
AURIER DAPHNE DU MAURIER DAPHNE DU MAUI

Daphne du Maurier

Rebecca

Jamaica Inn

Frenchman's Creek

My Cousin Rachel

Daphne du Maurier

Octopus / Heinemann

Rebecca was first published in the United States by Doubleday & Company, Inc
in 1938; in Great Britain by Victor Gollancz Ltd in 1938
Jamaica Inn was first published in the United States by Doubleday & Company, Inc
in 1936; in Great Britain by Victor Gollancz Ltd in 1936
Frenchman's Creek was first published in the United States by Doubleday & Company, Inc
in 1942; in Great Britain by Victor Gollancz Ltd in 1941
My Cousin Rachel was first published in the United States by Doubleday & Company, Inc
in 1952; in Great Britain by Victor Gollancz Ltd in 1951

This edition first published in the United States of America
by arrangement with Doubleday & Company, Inc
in 1980 jointly by

William Heinemann Inc
450 Park Avenue, New York, NY 10022

and

Octopus Books Inc
747 Third Avenue, New York, NY 10017

ISBN 0 905712 48 X

Frenchman's Creek © Daphne du Maurier Browning 1941
My Cousin Rachel © Daphne du Maurier 1951

Printed in the United States of America
by R. R. Donnelley and Sons Company

Contents

Daphne
du Maurier

Rebecca

Daphne du Maurier

Chapter One

Last night I dreamt I went to Manderley again. It seemed to me I stood by the iron gate leading to the drive, and for a while I could not enter for the way was barred to me. There was a padlock and a chain upon the gate. I called in my dream to the lodge-keeper, and had no answer, and peering closer through the rusted spokes of the gate I saw that the lodge was uninhabited.

No smoke came from the chimney, and the little lattice windows gaped forlorn. Then, like all dreamers, I was possessed of a sudden with supernatural powers and passed like a spirit through the barrier before me. The drive wound away in front of me, twisting and turning as it had always done, but as I advanced I was aware that a change had come upon it; it was narrow and unkept, not the drive that we had known. At first I was puzzled and did not understand, and it was only when I bent my head to avoid the low swinging branch of a tree that I realised what had happened. Nature had come into her own again and, little by little, in her stealthy, insidious way had encroached upon the drive with long, tenacious fingers. The woods, always a menace even in the past, had triumphed in the end. They crowded, dark and uncontrolled, to the borders of the drive. The beeches with white, naked limbs leant close to one another, their branches intermingled in a strange embrace, making a vault above my head like the archway of a church. And there were other trees as well, trees that I did not recognise, squat oaks and tortured elms that straggled cheek by jowl with the beeches, and had thrust themselves out of the quiet earth, along with monster shrubs and plants, none of which I remembered.

The drive was a ribbon now, a thread of its former self, with gravel surface gone, and choked with grass and moss. The trees had thrown out low branches, making an impediment to progress; the gnarled roots looked like skeleton claws. Scattered here and again amongst this jungle growth I would recognise shrubs that had been landmarks in our time, things of culture and of grace, hydrangeas whose blue heads had been famous. No hand had checked their progress, and they had gone native now, rearing to monster height without a bloom, black and ugly as the nameless parasites that grew beside them.

On and on, now east now west, wound the poor thread that once had been our drive. Sometimes I thought it lost, but it appeared again, beneath a fallen tree perhaps, or struggling on the other side of a muddied ditch created by the winter rains. I had not thought the way so long. Surely the miles had multiplied, even as the trees had done, and this path led but to a labyrinth,

some choked wilderness, and not to the house at all. I came upon it suddenly;
the approach masked by the unnatural growth of a vast shrub that spread
in all directions, and I stood, my heart thumping in my breast, the strange
prick of tears behind my eyes.

There was Manderley, our Manderley, secretive and silent as it had
always been, the grey stone shining in the moonlight of my dream, the
mullioned windows reflecting the green lawns and the terrace. Time could
not wreck the perfect symmetry of those walls, nor the site itself, a jewel in
the hollow of a hand.

The terrace sloped to the lawns, and the lawns stretched to the sea, and
turning I could see the sheet of silver, placid under the moon, like a lake
undisturbed by wind or storm. No waves would come to ruffle this dream
water, and no bulk of cloud, wind-driven from the west, obscure the clarity
of this pale sky. I turned again to the house, and though it stood inviolate,
untouched, as though we ourselves had left but yesterday, I saw that the
garden had obeyed the jungle law, even as the woods had done. The
rhododendrons stood fifty feet high, twisted and entwined with bracken, and
they had entered into alien marriage with a host of nameless shrubs, poor,
bastard things that clung about their roots as though conscious of their
spurious origin. A lilac had mated with a copper beech, and to bind them
yet more closely to one another the malevolent ivy, always an enemy to grace,
had thrown her tendrils about the pair and made them prisoners. Ivy held
prior place in this lost garden, the long strands crept across the lawns, and
soon would encroach upon the house itself. There was another plant too,
some half-breed from the woods, whose seed had been scattered long ago
beneath the trees and then forgotten, and now, marching in unison with the
ivy, thrust its ugly form like a giant rhubarb towards the soft grass where
the daffodils had blown.

Nettles were everywhere, the vanguard of the army. They choked the
terrace, they sprawled about the paths, they leant, vulgar and lanky, against
the very windows of the house. They made indifferent sentinels, for in many
places their ranks had been broken by the rhubarb plant, and they lay with
crumpled heads and listless stems, making a pathway for the rabbits. I left
the drive and went on to the terrace, for the nettles were no barrier to me,
a dreamer, I walked enchanted, and nothing held me back.

Moonlight can play odd tricks upon the fancy, even upon a dreamer's
fancy. As I stood there, hushed and still, I could swear that the house was
not an empty shell but lived and breathed as it had lived before.

Light came from the windows, the curtains blew softly in the night air,
and there, in the library, the door would stand half open as we had left it,
with my handkerchief on the table beside the bowl of autumn roses.

The room would bear witness to our presence. The little heap of library
books marked ready to return, and the discarded copy of *The Times*. Ash-
trays, with the stub of a cigarette; cushions, with the imprint of our heads
upon them, lolling in the chairs; the charred embers of our log fire still
smouldering against the morning. And Jasper, dear Jasper, with his soulful

eyes and great, sagging jowl, would be stretched upon the floor, his tail a-thump when he heard his master's footsteps.

A cloud, hitherto unseen, came upon the moon, and hovered an instant like a dark hand before a face. The illusion went with it, and the lights in the windows were extinguished. I looked upon a desolate shell, soulless at last, unhaunted, with no whisper of the past about its staring walls.

The house was a sepulchre, our fear and suffering lay buried in the ruins. There would be no resurrection. When I thought of Manderley in my waking hours I would not be bitter. I should think of it as it might have been, could I have lived there without fear. I should remember the rose-garden in summer, and the birds that sang at dawn. Tea under the chestnut tree, and the murmur of the sea coming up to us from the lawns below.

I would think of the blown lilac, and the Happy Valley. These things were permanent, they could not be dissolved. They were memories that cannot hurt. All this I resolved in my dream, while the clouds lay across the face of the moon, for like most sleepers I knew that I dreamed. In reality I lay many hundred miles away in an alien land, and would wake, before many seconds had passed, in the bare little hotel bedroom, comforting in its very lack of atmosphere. I would sigh a moment, stretch myself and turn, and opening my eyes, be bewildered at that glittering sun, that hard, clean sky, so different from the soft moonlight of my dream. The day would lie before us both, long no doubt, and uneventful, but fraught with a certain stillness, a dear tranquillity we had not known before. We would not talk of Manderley, I would not tell my dream. For Manderley was ours no longer. Manderley was no more.

Chapter Two

We can never go back again, that much is certain. The past is still too close to us. The things we have tried to forget and put behind us would stir again, and that sense of fear, of furtive unrest, struggling at length to blind unreasoning panic – now mercifully stilled, thank God – might in some manner unforeseen become a living companion, as it had been before.

He is wonderfully patient and never complains, not even when he remembers ... which happens, I think, rather more often than he would have me know.

I can tell by the way he will look lost and puzzled suddenly, all expression dying away from his dear face as though swept clean by an unseen hand, and in its place a mask will form, a sculptured thing, formal and cold, beautiful still but lifeless. He will fall to smoking cigarette after cigarette, not bothering to extinguish them, and the glowing stubs will lie around on the ground like petals. He will talk quickly and eagerly about nothing at all, snatching at any subject as a panacea to pain. I believe there is a theory that men and women emerge finer and stronger after suffering, and that to advance in this or any world we must endure ordeal by fire. This we have done in full measure, ironic though it seems. We have both known fear, and loneliness, and very great distress. I suppose sooner or later in the life of everyone comes a moment of trial. We all of us have our particular devil who rides us and torments us, and we must give battle in the end. We have conquered ours, or so we believe.

The devil does not ride us any more. We have come through our crisis, not unscathed of course. His premonition of disaster was correct from the beginning; and like a ranting actress in an indifferent play, I might say that we have paid for freedom. But I have had enough melodrama in this life, and would willingly give my five senses if they could ensure us our present peace and security. Happiness is not a possession to be prized, it is a quality of thought, a state of mind. Of course we have our moments of depression; but there are other moments too, when time, unmeasured by the clock, runs on into eternity and, catching his smile, I know we are together, we march in unison, no clash of thought or of opinion makes a barrier between us.

We have no secrets now from one another. All things are shared. Granted that our little hotel is dull, and the food indifferent, and that day after day dawns very much the same, yet we would not have it otherwise. We should meet too many of the people he knows in any of the big hotels. We both appreciate simplicity, and if we are sometimes bored – well, boredom is a pleasing antidote to fear. We live very much by routine, and I – I have developed a genius for reading aloud. The only time I have known him show impatience is when the postman lags, for it means we must wait another day before the arrival of our English mail. We have tried wireless, but the noise is such an irritant, and we prefer to store up our excitement; the result of a cricket match played many days ago means much to us.

Oh, the Test matches that have saved us from ennui, the boxing bouts, even the billiard scores. Finals of schoolboy sports, dog racing, strange little competitions in the remoter counties, all these are grist to our hungry mill. Sometimes old copies of the *Field* come my way, and I am transported from this indifferent island to the realities of an English spring. I read of chalk streams, of the mayfly, of sorrel growing in green meadows, of rooks circling above the woods as they used to do at Manderley. The smell of wet earth comes to me from those thumbed and tattered pages, the sour tang of moorland peat, the feel of soggy moss spattered white in places by a heron's droppings.

Once there was an article on wood pigeons, and as I read it aloud it seemed to me that once again I was in the deep woods at Manderley, with pigeons fluttering above my head. I heard their soft, complacent call, so comfortable and cool on a hot summer's afternoon, and there would be no disturbing of their peace until Jasper came loping through the undergrowth to find me, his damp muzzle questing the ground. Like old ladies caught at their ablutions, the pigeons would flutter from their hiding-place, shocked into silly agitation, and, making a monstrous to do with their wings, streak away from us above the tree-tops, and so out of sight and sound. When they were gone a new silence would come upon the place, and I – uneasy for no known reason – would realise that the sun no longer wove a pattern on the rustling leaves, that the branches had grown darker, the shadows longer; and back at the house there would be fresh raspberries for tea. I would rise from my bed of bracken, then, shaking the feathery dust of last year's leaves from my skirt and whistling to Jasper, set off towards the house, despising myself even as I walked for my hurrying feet, my one swift glance behind.

How strange that an article on wood pigeons could so recall the past and make me falter as I read aloud. It was the grey look on his face that made me stop abruptly, and turn the pages until I found a paragraph on cricket, very practical and dull – Middlesex batting on a dry wicket at the Oval and piling up interminable dreary runs. How I blessed those stolid, flannelled figures, for in a few minutes his face had settled back into repose, the colour had returned, and he was deriding the Surrey bowling in healthy irritation.

We were saved a retreat into the past, and I had learnt my lesson. Read English news, yes, and English sport, politics and pomposity, but in future keep the things that hurt to myself alone. They can be my secret indulgence. Colour and scent and sound, rain and the lapping of water, even the mists of autumn and the smell of the flood tide, these are memories of Manderley that will not be denied. Some people have a vice of reading Bradshaws. They plan innumerable journeys across country for the fun of linking up impossible connections. My hobby is less tedious, if as strange. I am a mine of information on the English countryside. I know the name of every owner of every British moor, yes – and their tenants too. I know how many grouse are killed, how many partridge, how many head of deer. I know where trout are rising, and where the salmon leap. I attend all meets, I follow every run. Even the names of those who walk hound puppies are familiar to me. The state of the crops, the price of fat cattle, the mysterious ailments of swine, I relish them all. A poor pastime, perhaps, and not a very intellectual one, but I breathe the air of England as I read, and can face this glittering sky with greater courage.

The scrubby vineyards and the crumbling stones become things of no account, for if I wish I can give rein to my imagination, and pick foxgloves and pale campions from a wet, streaking hedge.

Poor whims of fancy, tender and un-harsh. They are the enemy to bitterness and regret, and sweeten this exile we have brought upon ourselves.

Because of them I can enjoy my afternoon, and return, smiling and refreshed, to face the little ritual of our tea. The order never varies. Two slices of bread and butter each, and China tea. What a hide-bound couple we must seem, clinging to custom because we did so in England. Here, on this clean balcony, white and impersonal with centuries of sun, I think of half-past four at Manderley, and the table drawn before the library fire. The door flung open, punctual to the minute, and the performance, never-varying, of the laying of the tea, the silver tray, the kettle, the snowy cloth.

While Jasper, his spaniel ears a-droop, feigns indifference to the arrival of the cakes. That feast was laid before us always, and yet we ate so little.

Those dripping crumpets, I can see them now. Tiny crisp wedges of toast, and piping-hot, floury scones. Sandwiches of unknown nature, mysteriously flavoured and quite delectable, and that very special gingerbread. Angel cake, that melted in the mouth, and his rather stodgier companion, bursting with peel and raisins. There was enough food there to keep a starving family for a week. I never knew what happened to it all, and the waste used to worry me sometimes.

But I never dared ask Mrs. Danvers what she did about it. She would have looked at me in scorn, smiling that freezing, superior smile of hers, and I can imagine her saying: 'There were never any complaints when Mrs. de Winter was alive.' Mrs. Danvers. I wonder what she is doing now. She and Favell. I think it was the expression on her face that gave me my first feeling of unrest. Instinctively I thought, 'She is comparing me to Rebecca'; and sharp as a sword the shadow came between us. . . .

Well, it is over now, finished and done with. I ride no more tormented, and both of us are free. Even my faithful Jasper has gone to the happy hunting grounds, and Manderley is no more. It lies like an empty shell amidst the tangle of the deep woods, even as I saw it in my dream. A multitude of weeds, a colony of birds. Sometimes perhaps a tramp will wander there, seeking shelter from a sudden shower of rain and, if he is stout-hearted, he may walk there with impunity. But your timid fellow, your nervous poacher – the woods of Manderley are not for him. He might stumble upon the little cottage in the cove and he would not be happy beneath its tumbled roof, the thin rain beating a tattoo. There might linger there still a certain atmosphere of stress. . . . That corner in the drive, too, where the trees encroach upon the gravel, is not a place in which to pause, not after the sun has set. When the leaves rustle, they sound very much like the stealthy movement of a woman in evening dress, and when they shiver suddenly, and fall, and scatter away along the ground, they might be the patter, patter, of a woman's hurrying footstep, and the mark in the gravel the imprint of a high-heeled satin shoe.

It is when I remember these things that I turn with relief to the prospect from our balcony. No shadows steal upon this hard glare, the stony vineyards shimmer in the sun and the bougainvillaea is white with dust. I may one day look upon it with affection. At the moment it inspires me, if not with love, at least with confidence. And confidence is a quality I prize, although it has come to me a little late in the day. I suppose it is his dependence upon me that has made me bold at last. At any rate I have lost my diffidence, my timidity, my shyness with strangers. I am very different from that self who drove to Manderley for the first time, hopeful and eager, handicapped by a rather desperate gaucherie and filled with an intense desire to please. It was my lack of poise of course that made such a bad impression on people like Mrs. Danvers. What must I have seemed like after Rebecca? I can see myself now, memory spanning the years like a bridge, with straight, bobbed hair and youthful, unpowdered face, dressed in an ill-fitting coat and skirt and a jumper of my own creation, trailing in the wake of Mrs. Van Hopper like a shy, uneasy colt. She would precede me in to lunch, her short body ill-balanced upon tottering, high heels, her fussy, frilly blouse a complement to her large bosom and swinging hips, her new hat pierced with a monster quill aslant upon her head, exposing a wide expanse of forehead bare as a schoolboy's knee. One hand carried a gigantic bag, the kind that holds passports, engagement diaries, and bridge scores, while the other hand toyed with that inevitable lorgnette, the enemy to other people's privacy.

She would make for her usual table in the corner of the restaurant, close to the window, and lifting her lorgnette to her small pig's eyes survey the scene to right and left of her, then she would let the lorgnette fall at length upon its black ribbon and utter a little exclamation of disgust: 'Not a single well-known personality, I shall tell the management they must make a reduction on my bill. What do they think I come here for? To look at the page boys?' And she would summon the waiter to her side, her voice sharp and staccato, cutting the air like a saw.

How different the little restaurant where we eat to-day to that vast dining-room, ornate and ostentatious, the hotel Côte d'Azur at Monte Carlo; and how different my present companion, his steady, well-shaped hands peeling a mandarin in quiet, methodical fashion, looking up now and again from his task to smile at me, compared to Mrs. Van Hopper, her fat, bejewelled fingers questing a plate heaped high with ravioli, her eyes darting suspiciously from her plate to mine for fear I should have made the better choice. She need not have disturbed herself, for the waiter, with the uncanny swiftness of his kind, had long sensed my position as inferior and subservient to hers, and had placed before me a plate of ham and tongue that somebody had sent back to the cold buffet half an hour before as badly carved. Odd, that resentment of servants, and their obvious impatience. I remember staying once with Mrs. Van Hopper in a country house, and the maid never answered my timid bell, or brought up my shoes, and early morning tea, stone cold, was dumped outside my bedroom door. It was the same at the Côte d'Azur, though to a lesser degree, and sometimes the studied indifference turned to familiarity, smirking and offensive, which made buying stamps from the reception clerk an ordeal I would avoid. How young and inexperienced I must have seemed, and how I felt it, too. One was too sensitive, too raw, there were thorns and pin-pricks in so many words that in reality fell lightly on the air.

I remember well that plate of ham and tongue. It was dry, unappetising, cut in a wedge from the outside, but I had not the courage to refuse it. We ate in silence, for Mrs. Van Hopper liked to concentrate on food, and I could tell by the way the sauce ran down her chin that her dish of ravioli pleased her.

It was not a sight that engendered into me great appetite for my own cold choice, and looking away from her I saw that the table next to ours, left vacant for three days, was to be occupied once more. The maître d'hôtel, with the particular bow reserved for his more special patrons, was ushering the new arrival to his place.

Mrs. Van Hopper put down her fork, and reached for her lorgnette. I blushed for her while she stared, and the new-comer, unconscious of her interest, cast a wandering eye over the menu. Then Mrs. Van Hopper folded her lorgnette with a snap, and leant across the table to me, her small eyes bright with excitement, her voice a shade too loud.

'It's Max de Winter,' she said, 'the man who owns Manderley. You've heard of it, of course. He looks ill, doesn't he? They say he can't get over his wife's death. . . .'

Chapter Three

I wonder what my life would be to-day, if Mrs. Van Hopper had not been a snob.

Funny to think that the course of my existence hung like a thread upon that quality of hers. Her curiosity was a disease, almost a mania. At first I had been shocked, wretchedly embarrassed; I would feel like a whipping boy who must bear his master's pains when I watched people laugh behind her back, leave a room hurriedly upon her entrance, or even vanish behind a Service door on the corridor upstairs. For many years now she had come to the Hotel Côte d'Azur, and, apart from bridge, her one pastime, which was notorious by now in Monte Carlo, was to claim visitors of distinction as her friends had she but seen them once at the other end of the post-office. Somehow she would manage to introduce herself, and before her victim had scented danger she had proffered an invitation to her suite. Her method of attack was so downright and sudden that there was seldom opportunity to escape. At the Côte d'Azur she staked a claim upon a certain sofa in the lounge, midway between the reception hall and the passage to the restaurant, and she would have her coffee there after luncheon and dinner, and all who came and went must pass her by. Sometimes she would employ me as a bait to draw her prey, and, hating my errand, I would be sent across the lounge with a verbal message, the loan of a book or paper, the address of some shop or other, the sudden discovery of a mutual friend. It seemed as though notables must be fed to her, much as invalids are spooned their jelly; and though titles were preferred by her, any face once seen in a social paper served as well. Names scattered in a gossip column, authors, artists, actors and their kind, even the mediocre ones, as long as she had learnt of them in print.

I can see her as though it were but yesterday, on that unforgettable afternoon – never mind how many years ago – when she sat at her favourite sofa in the lounge, debating her method of attack. I could tell by her abrupt manner, and the way she tapped her lorgnette against her teeth, that she was questing possibilities. I knew, too, when she had missed the sweet and rushed through dessert, that she had wished to finish luncheon before the new arrival and so install herself where he must pass. Suddenly she turned to me, her small eyes alight.

'Go upstairs quickly and find that letter from my nephew. You remember, the one written on his honeymoon, with the snapshot. Bring it down to me right away.'

I saw then that her plans were formed, and the nephew was to be the means of introduction. Not for the first time I resented the part that I must play in her schemes. Like a juggler's assistant I produced the props, then silent and attentive I waited on my cue. This new-comer would not welcome intrusion, I felt certain of that. In the little I had learnt of him at luncheon, a smattering of hearsay garnered by her ten months ago from the daily papers and stored in her memory for future use, I could imagine, in spite of my youth and inexperience of the world, that he would resent this sudden bursting in upon his solitude. Why he should have chosen to come to the Côte d'Azur at Monte Carlo was not our concern, his problems were his own, and anyone but Mrs. Van Hopper would have understood. Tact was a quality unknown to her, discretion too, and because gossip was the breath of life to her this stranger must be served for her dissection. I found the letter in a pigeon-hole in her desk, and hesitated a moment before going down again to the lounge. It seemed to me, rather senselessly, that I was allowing him a few more moments of seclusion.

I wished I had the courage to go by the Service staircase and so by a roundabout way to the restaurant, and there warn him of the ambush. Convention was too strong for me though, nor did I know how I should frame my sentence. There was nothing for it but to sit in my usual place beside Mrs. Van Hopper while she, like a large, complacent spider, spun her wide net of tedium about the stranger's person.

I had been longer than I thought, for when I returned to the lounge I saw he had already left the dining-room, and she, fearful of losing him, had not waited for the letter, but had risked a bare-faced introduction on her own. He was even now sitting beside her on the sofa. I walked across to them, and gave her the letter without a word. He rose to his feet at once, while Mrs. Van Hopper, flushed with her success, waved a vague hand in my direction and mumbled my name.

'Mr. de Winter is having coffee with us, go and ask the waiter for another cup,' she said, her tone just casual enough to warn him of my footing. It meant I was a youthful thing and unimportant, and that there was no need to include me in the conversation. She always spoke in that tone when she wished to be impressive, and her method of introduction was a form of self-protection, for once I had been taken for her daughter, an acute embarrassment for us both. This abruptness showed that I could safely be ignored, and women would give me a brief nod which served as a greeting and a dismissal in one, while men, with large relief, would realise they could sink back into a comfortable chair without offending courtesy.

It was a surprise, therefore, to find that this new-comer remained standing on his feet, and it was he who made a signal to the waiter.

'I'm afraid I must contradict you,' he said to her, 'you are both having coffee with me'; and before I knew what had happened he was sitting in my usual hard chair, and I was on the sofa beside Mrs. Van Hopper.

For a moment she looked annoyed, this was not what she had intended, but she soon composed her face, and thrusting her large self between me and the table she leant forward to his chair, talking eagerly and loudly, fluttering the letter in her hand.

'You know I recognised you just as soon as you walked into the restaurant,' she said, 'and I thought, "Why, there's Mr. de Winter, Billy's friend, I simply must show him those snaps of Billy and his bride taken on their honeymoon", and here they are. There's Dora. Isn't she just adorable? That little, slim waist, those great big eyes. Here they are sun-bathing at Palm Beach. Billy is crazy about her, you can imagine. He had not met her of course when he gave that party at Claridges, and where I saw you first. But I dare say you don't remember an old woman like me?'

This with a provocative glance, and a gleam of teeth.

'On the contrary I remember you very well,' he said, and before she could trap him into a resurrection of their first meeting he had handed her his cigarette case, and the business of lighting-up stalled her for the moment. 'I don't think I should care for Palm Beach,' he said, blowing the match, and glancing at him I thought how unreal he would look against a Florida background. He belonged to a walled city of the fifteenth century, a city of narrow, cobbled streets, and thin spires, where the inhabitants wore pointed shoes and worsted hose. His face was arresting, sensitive, medieval in some strange inexplicable way, and I was reminded of a portrait seen in a gallery, I had forgotten where, of a certain Gentleman Unknown. Could one but rob him of his English tweeds, and put him in black, with lace at his throat and wrists, he would stare down at us in our new world from a long distant past – a past where men walked cloaked at night, and stood in the shadow of old doorways, a past of narrow stairways and dim dungeons, a past of whispers in the dark, of shimmering rapier blades, of silent, exquisite courtesy.

I wished I could remember the Old Master who had painted that portrait. It stood in a corner of the gallery, and the eyes followed one from the dusky frame. . . .

They were talking, though, and I had lost the thread of conversation. 'No, not even twenty years ago,' he was saying. 'That sort of thing has never amused me.'

I heard Mrs. Van Hopper give her fat, complacent laugh. 'If Billy had a home like Manderley he would not want to play around in Palm Beach,' she said. 'I'm told it's like fairy-land, there's no other word for it.'

She paused, expecting him to smile, but he went on smoking his cigarette, and I noticed, faint as gossamer, the line between his brows.

'I've seen pictures of it, of course,' she persisted, 'and it looks perfectly enchanting. I remember Billy telling me it had all those big places beat for beauty. I wonder you can ever bear to leave it.'

His silence now was painful, and would have been patent to anyone else, but she ran on like a clumsy goat, trampling and trespassing on land that was preserved, and I felt the colour flood my face, dragged with her as I was into humiliation.

'Of course you Englishmen are all the same about your homes,' she said, her voice becoming louder and louder, 'you depreciate them so as not to seem proud. Isn't there a minstrels' gallery at Manderley, and some very valuable portraits?' She turned to me by way of explanation. 'Mr. de Winter is so modest he won't admit to it, but I believe that lovely home of his has been in his family's possession since the Conquest. They say that minstrels' gallery is a gem. I suppose your ancestors often entertained royalty at Manderley, Mr. de Winter?'

This was more than I had hitherto endured, even from her, but the swift lash of his reply was unexpected. 'Not since Ethelred,' he said, 'the one who was called Unready. In fact, it was while staying with my family that the name was given him. He was invariably late for dinner.'

She deserved it, of course, and I waited for her change of face, but incredible as it may seem his words were lost on her, and I was left to writhe in her stead, feeling like a child that had been smacked.

'Is that really so?' she blundered. 'I'd no idea. My history is very shaky, and the kings of England always muddled me. How interesting though. I must write and tell my daughter, she's a great scholar.'

There was a pause, and I felt the colour flood into my face. I was too young, that was the trouble. Had I been older I would have caught his eye and smiled, her unbelievable behaviour making a bond between us; but as it was I was stricken into shame, and endured one of the frequent agonies of youth.

I think he realised my distress, for he leant forward in his chair and spoke to me, his voice gentle, asking if I would have more coffee, and when I refused and shook my head I felt that his eyes were still upon me, puzzled, reflective. He was pondering my exact relationship to her, and wondering whether he must bracket us together in futility.

'What do you think of Monte Carlo, or don't you think of it at all?' he said. This including of me in the conversation found me at my worst, the raw ex-schoolgirl, red-elbowed and lanky-haired, and I said something obvious and idiotic about the place being artificial, but before I could finish my halting sentence Mrs. Van Hopper interrupted.

'She's spoilt, Mr. de Winter, that's her trouble. Most girls would give their eyes for the chance of seeing Monte.'

'Wouldn't that rather defeat the purpose?' he said smiling.

She shrugged her shoulders, blowing a cloud of cigarette smoke into the air. I don't think she understood him for a moment. 'I'm faithful to Monte,' she told him; 'the English winter gets me down, and my constitution just won't stand it. What brings you here? You're not one of the regulars. Are you going to play "Chemy", or have you brought your golf-clubs?'

'I have not made up my mind,' he said, 'I came away in rather a hurry.'

His own words must have jolted a memory, for his face clouded again and he frowned very slightly. She babbled on, impervious. 'Of course you miss the fogs at Manderley, it's quite another matter; the west country must be delightful in the spring.' He reached for the ash-tray, squashing his cigarette, and I noticed the subtle change in his eyes, the indefinable something that lingered there, momentarily, and I felt I had looked upon something personal to himself with which I had no concern.

'Yes,' he said shortly, 'Manderley was looking its best.'

A silence fell upon us, during a moment or two, a silence that brought something of discomfort in its train, and stealing a glance at him I was reminded more than ever of my Gentleman Unknown who, cloaked and secret, walked a corridor by night. Mrs. Van Hopper's voice pierced my dream like an electric bell.

'I suppose you know a crowd of people here, though I must say Monte is very dull this winter. One sees so few well-known faces. The Duke of Middlesex is here in his yacht, but I haven't been aboard yet.' She never had, to my knowledge. 'You know Nell Middlesex of course,' she went on. 'What a charmer she is. They always say that second child isn't his, but I don't believe it. People will say anything, won't they, when a woman is attractive? And she is so very lovely. Tell me, is it true the Caxton-Hyslop marriage is not a success?' She ran on, through a tangled fringe of gossip, never seeing that these names were alien to him, they meant nothing, and that as she prattled unaware he grew colder and more silent. Never for a moment did he interrupt or glance at his watch; it was as though he had set himself a standard of behaviour, since the original lapse when he had made a fool of her in front of me, and clung to it grimly rather than offend again. It was a page-boy in the end who released him, with the news that a dressmaker awaited Mrs. Van Hopper in the suite.

He got up at once, pushing back his chair. 'Don't let me keep you,' he said. 'Fashions change so quickly nowadays they may even have altered by the time you get upstairs.'

The sting did not touch her, she accepted it as a pleasantry. 'It's so delightful to have run into you like this, Mr. de Winter,' she said, as we went towards the lift; 'now I've been brave enough to break the ice I hope I shall see something of you. You must come and have a drink some time in the suite. I may have one or two people coming in tomorrow evening. Why not join us?' I turned away so that I should not watch him search for an excuse.

'I'm so sorry,' he said, 'to-morrow I am probably driving to Sospel, I'm not sure when I shall get back.'

Reluctantly she left it, but we still hovered at the entrance to the lift.

'I hope they've given you a good room, the place is half empty, so if you are uncomfortable mind you make a fuss. Your valet has unpacked for you, I suppose?' This familiarity was excessive, even for her, and I caught a glimpse of his expression.

'I don't possess one,' he said quietly, 'perhaps you would like to do it for me?'

This time his shaft had found its mark, for she reddened, and laughed a little awkwardly.

'Why, I hardly think . . .' she began, and then suddenly, and unbelievably, she turned upon me. 'Perhaps you could make yourself useful to Mr. de Winter, if he wants anything done. You're a capable child in many ways.'

There was a momentary pause, while I stood stricken, waiting for his answer. He looked down at us, mocking, faintly sardonic, a ghost of a smile on his lips.

'A charming suggestion,' he said, 'but I cling to the family motto. He travels the fastest who travels alone. Perhaps you have not heard of it.'

And without waiting for her answer he turned and left us.

'What a funny thing,' said Mrs. Van Hopper, as we went upstairs in the lift, 'do you suppose that sudden departure was a form of humour? Men do such extraordinary things. I remember a well-known writer once who used to dart down the Service staircase whenever he saw me coming. I suppose he had a penchant for me and wasn't sure of himself. However, I was younger then.'

The lift stopped with a jerk. We had arrived at our floor. The page-boy flung open the gates. 'By-the-way, dear,' she said, as we walked along the corridor, 'don't think I mean to be unkind, but you put yourself just a teeny bit forward this afternoon. Your efforts to monopolise the conversation quite embarrassed me, and I'm sure it did him. Men loathe that sort of thing.'

I said nothing. There seemed no possible reply. 'Oh, come, don't sulk,' she laughed, and shrugged her shoulders; 'after all, I am responsible for your behaviour here, and surely you can accept advice from a woman old enough to be your mother. Eh bien, Blaize, je viens . . .' and humming a tune she went into the bedroom where the dressmaker was waiting for her.

I knelt on the window-seat and looked out upon the afternoon. The sun shone very brightly still, and there was a gay high wind. In half an hour we should be sitting to our bridge, the windows tightly closed, the central heating turned to the full. I thought of the ash-trays I would have to clear, and how the squashed stubs, stained with lip-stick, would sprawl in company with discarded chocolate creams. Bridge does not come easily to a mind brought up on Snap and Happy Families; besides, it bored her friends to play with me.

I felt my youthful presence put a curb upon their conversation, much as a parlour-maid does until the arrival of dessert, and they could not fling themselves so easily into the melting-pot of scandal and insinuation. Her men-friends would assume a sort of forced heartiness, and ask me jocular questions about history or painting, guessing I had not long left school and that this would be my only form of conversation.

I sighed, and turned away from the window. The sun was so full of promise, and the sea was whipped white with a merry wind. I thought of that corner in Monaco which I had passed a day or two ago, and where a crooked house leant to a cobbled square. High up in the tumbled roof there was a window, narrow as a slit. It might have held a presence medieval; and, reaching to the desk for pencil and paper, I sketched in fancy with an absent mind a profile, pale and aquiline. A sombre eye, a high-bridged nose, a scornful upper lip. And I added a pointed beard and lace at the throat, as the painter had done, long ago in a different time.

Someone knocked at the door, and the lift-boy came in with a note in his hand. 'Madame is in the bedroom,' I told him, but he shook his head and said it was for me. I opened it, and found a single sheet of note-paper inside, with a few words written in an unfamiliar hand.

'Forgive me. I was very rude this afternoon.' That was all. No signature, and no beginning. But my name was on the envelope, and spelt correctly, an unusual thing.

'Is there any answer?' asked the boy.

I looked up from the scrawled words. 'No,' I said. 'No, there isn't any answer.'

When he had gone I put the note away in my pocket, and turned once more to my pencil drawing, but for no known reason it did not please me any more, the face was stiff and lifeless, and the lace collar and the beard were like props in a charade.

Chapter Four

The morning after the bridge party Mrs. Van Hopper woke with a sore throat and a temperature of a hundred and two. I rang up her doctor, who came round at once and diagnosed the usual influenza. 'You are to stay in bed until I allow you to get up,' he told her; 'I don't like the sound of that heart of yours, and it won't get better unless you keep perfectly quiet and still. I should prefer,' he went on, turning to me, 'that Mrs. Van Hopper had a trained nurse. You can't possibly lift her. It will only be for a fortnight or so.'

I thought this rather absurd, and protested, but to my surprise she agreed with him. I think she enjoyed the fuss it would create, the sympathy of people, the visits and messages from friends, and the arrival of flowers. Monte Carlo had begun to bore her, and this little illness would make a distraction.

The nurse would give her injections, and a light massage, and she would have a diet. I left her quite happy after the arrival of the nurse, propped up on pillows with a falling temperature, her best bed-jacket round her shoulders and be-ribboned boudoir cap upon her head. Rather ashamed of my light heart, I telephoned her friends, putting off the small party she had arranged for the evening, and went down to the restaurant for lunch, a good half hour before our usual time. I expected the room to be empty, nobody lunched generally before one o'clock. It was empty, except for the table next to ours. This was a contingency for which I was unprepared. I thought he had gone to Sospel. No doubt he was lunching early because he hoped to avoid us at one o'clock. I was already half-way across the room and could not go back. I had not seen him since we disappeared in the lift the day before, for wisely he had avoided dinner in the restaurant, possibly for the same reason that he lunched early now.

It was a situation for which I was ill-trained. I wish I was older, different. I went to our table, looking straight before me, and immediately paid the penalty of gaucherie by knocking over the vase of stiff anemones as I unfolded my napkin. The water soaked the cloth, and ran down on to my lap. The waiter was at the other end of the room, nor had he seen. In a second though my neighbour was by my side, dry napkin in hand.

'You can't sit at a wet tablecloth,' he said brusquely, 'it will put you off your food. Get out of the way.'

He began to mop the cloth, while the waiter, seeing the disturbance, came swiftly to the rescue.

'I don't mind,' I said, 'it doesn't matter a bit. I'm all alone.'

He said nothing, and then the waiter arrived and whipped away the vase and the sprawling flowers.

'Leave that,' he said suddenly, 'and lay another place at my table. Mademoiselle will have luncheon with me.'

I looked up in confusion. 'Oh, no,' I said, 'I couldn't possibly.'

'Why not?' he said.

I tried to think of an excuse. I knew he did not want to lunch with me. It was his form of courtesy. I should ruin his meal. I determined to be bold and speak the truth.

'Please,' I begged, 'don't be polite. It's very kind of you but I shall be quite all right if the waiter just wipes the cloth.'

'But I'm not being polite,' he insisted, 'I would like you to have luncheon with me. Even if you had not knocked over that vase so clumsily I should have asked you.' I suppose my face told him my doubt, for he smiled. 'You don't believe me,' he said, 'never mind, come and sit down. We needn't talk to each other unless we feel like it.'

We sat down, and he gave me the menu, leaving me to choose, and went on with his *hors d'oeuvre* as though nothing had happened.

His quality of detachment was peculiar to himself, and I knew that we might continue thus, without speaking, throughout the meal and it would not matter. There would be no sense of strain. He would not ask me questions on history.

'What's happened to your friend?' he said. I told him about the influenza. 'I'm so sorry,' he said, and then, after pausing a moment, 'you got my note, I suppose. I felt very much ashamed of myself. My manners were atrocious. The only excuse I can make is that I've become boorish through living alone. That's why it's so kind of you to lunch with me to-day.'

'You weren't rude,' I said, 'at least, not the sort of rudeness she would understand. That curiosity of hers – she does not mean to be offensive, but she does it to everyone. That is, everyone of importance.'

'I ought to be flattered then,' he said, 'why should she consider me of any importance?' I hesitated a moment before replying.

'I think because of Manderley,' I said.

He did not answer, and I was aware again of that feeling of discomfort, as though I had trespassed on forbidden ground. I wondered why it was that this home of his, known to so many people by hearsay, even to me, should so inevitably silence him, making as it were a barrier between him and others.

We ate for a while without talking, and I thought of a picture postcard I had bought once at a village shop, when on holiday as a child in the west country. It was the painting of a house, crudely done of course and highly coloured, but even those faults could not destroy the symmetry of the building, the wide stone steps before the terrace, the green lawns stretching to the sea. I paid twopence for the painting – half my weekly pocket money – and then asked the wrinkled shop woman what it was meant to be. She looked astonished at my ignorance.

'That's Manderley,' she said, and I remember coming out of the shop feeling rebuffed, yet hardly wiser than before.

Perhaps it was the memory of this postcard, lost long ago in some forgotten book, that made me sympathise with his defensive attitude. He resented Mrs. Van Hopper and her like with their intruding questions. Maybe there was something inviolate about Manderley that made it a place apart, it would not bear discussion. I could imagine her tramping through the rooms, perhaps paying sixpence for admission, ripping the quietude with her sharp, staccato laugh. Our minds must have run in the same channel for he began to talk about her.

'Your friend,' he began, 'she is very much older than you. Is she a relation? Have you known her long?' I saw he was still puzzled by us.

'She's not really a friend,' I told him, 'she's an employer, she's training me to be a thing called a companion, and she pays me ninety pounds a year.'

'I did not know one could buy companionship,' he said; 'it sounds a primitive idea. Rather like the eastern slave market.'

'I looked up the word companion once in the dictionary,' I admitted, 'and it said "a companion is a friend of the bosom".'

'You haven't much in common with her,' he said.

He laughed, looking quite different, younger somehow and less detached. 'What do you do it for?' he asked me.

'Ninety pounds is a lot of money to me,' I said.

'Haven't you any family?'

'No – they're dead.'

'You have a very lovely and unusual name.'

'My father was a lovely and unusual person.'

'Tell me about him,' he said.

I looked at him over my glass of citronade. It was not easy to explain my father, and usually I never talked about him. He was my secret property.

Preserved for me alone, much as Manderley was preserved for my neighbour. I had no wish to introduce him casually over a table in a Monte Carlo restaurant.

There was a strange air of unreality about that luncheon, and looking back upon it now it is invested for me with a curious glamour. There was I, so much of a school-girl still, who only the day before had sat with Mrs. Van Hopper, prim, silent and subdued, and twenty-four hours afterwards my family history was mine no longer, I shared it with a man I did not know. For some reason I felt impelled to speak, because his eyes followed me in sympathy like the Gentleman Unknown.

My shyness fell away from me, loosening as it did so my reluctant tongue, and out they all came, the little secrets of childhood, the pleasures and the pains. It seemed to me as though he understood, from my poor description, something of the vibrant personality that had been my father's, and something too of the love my mother had for him making it a vital, living force, with a spark of divinity about it, so much that when he died that desperate winter, struck down by pneumonia, she lingered behind him for five short weeks and stayed no more. I remember pausing, a little breathless, a little dazed. The restaurant was filled now with people who chatted and laughed to an orchestral background and a clatter of plates, and glancing at the clock above the door I saw that it was two o'clock. We had been sitting there an hour and a half, and the conversation had been mine alone.

I tumbled down into reality, hot-handed and self-conscious, and my face aflame, and began to stammer my apologies. He would not listen to me.

'I told you at the beginning of lunch you had a lovely and unusual name,' he said. 'I shall go further, if you will forgive me, and say that it becomes you as well as it became your father. I've enjoyed this hour with you more than I have enjoyed anything for a very long time. You've taken me out of myself, out of despondency and introspection, both of which have been my devils for a year.'

I looked at him, and believed he spoke the truth, he seemed less fettered than he had before, more modern, more human, he was not hemmed in by shadows.

'You know,' he said, 'we've got a bond in common, you and I. We are both alone in the world. Oh, I've got a sister, though we don't see much of each other, and an ancient grandmother whom I pay duty visits to three times a year, but neither of them make for companionship. I shall have to congratulate Mrs. Van Hopper. You're cheap at ninety pounds a year.'

'You forget,' I said, 'you have a home and I have none.'

The moment I spoke I regretted my words, for the secret, inscrutable look came back in his eyes again, and once again I suffered the intolerable discomfort that floods one after lack of tact. He bent his head to light a cigarette, and did not reply immediately.

'An empty house can be as lonely as a full hotel,' he said at length. 'The trouble is that it is less impersonal.' He hesitated, and for a moment I thought he was going to talk of Manderley at last, but something held him back, some phobia that struggled to the surface of his mind and won supremacy, for he blew out his match and his flash of confidence at the same time.

'So the friend of the bosom has a holiday?' he said, on a level plane again, an easy camaraderie between us. 'What does she propose to do with it?'

I thought of the cobbled square in Monaco, and the house with the narrow window. I could be off there by three o'clock with my sketch-book and pencil, and I told him as much, a little shyly perhaps, like all untalented persons with a pet hobby.

'I'll drive you there in the car,' he said, and would not listen to protests.

I remembered Mrs. Van Hoppers' warning of the night before about putting myself forward, and was embarrassed that he might think my talk of Monaco was a subterfuge to win a lift. It was so blatantly the type of thing that she would do herself, and I did not want him to bracket us together. I had already risen in importance from my lunch with him, for as we got up from the table the little maître d'hôtel rushed forward to pull away my chair. He bowed and smiled – a total change from his usual attitude of indifference – picked up my handkerchief that had fallen on the floor, and hoped 'mademoiselle had enjoyed her lunch'. Even the page-boy by the swing doors glanced at me with respect. My companion accepted it as natural, of course, he knew nothing of the ill-carved ham of yesterday. I found the change depressing, it made me despise myself. I remembered my father and his scorn of superficial snobbery.

'What are you thinking about?' We were walking along the corridor to the lounge, and looking up I saw his eyes fixed on me in curiosity.

'Has something annoyed you?' he said.

The attentions of the maître d'hôtel had opened up a train of thought, and as we drank our coffee I told him about Blaize, the dressmaker. She had been so pleased when Mrs. Van Hopper had bought three frocks, and I, taking her to the lift afterwards, had pictured her working upon them in her own small salon, behind the stuffy little shop, with a consumptive son wasting upon her sofa. I could see her, with tired eyes, threading needles, and the floor covered with snippets of material.

'Well,' he said smiling, 'wasn't your picture true?'

'I don't know,' I said, 'I never found out.' And I told him how I had rung the bell for the lift, and as I had done so she had fumbled in her bag and gave me a note for a hundred francs. 'Here,' she had whispered, her tone intimate and unpleasant, 'I want you to accept this small commission in return for bringing your patron to my shop.' When I had refused, scarlet with embarrassment, she had shrugged her shoulders disagreeably. 'Just as you like,' she had said, 'but I assure you it's quite usual. Perhaps you would rather have a frock. Come along to the shop sometime without Madame and I will fix you up without charging you a sou.' Somehow, I don't know why, I had been aware of that sick, unhealthy feeling I had experienced as a child when turning the pages of a forbidden book. The vision of the consumptive son faded, and in its stead arose the picture of myself had I been different, pocketing that greasy note with an understanding smile, and perhaps slipping round to Blaize's shop on this free afternoon and coming away with a frock I had not paid for.

I expected him to laugh, it was a stupid story, I don't know why I told him, but he looked at me thoughtfully as he stirred his coffee.

'I think you've made a big mistake,' he said, after a moment.

'In refusing that hundred francs?' I asked, revolted.

'No – good heavens, what do you take me for? I think you've made a mistake in coming here, in joining forces with Mrs. Van Hopper. You are not made for the sort of job. You're too young, for one thing, and too soft. Blaize and her commission, that's nothing. The first of many similar incidents from other Blaizes. You will either have to give in, and become a sort of Blaize yourself, or stay as you are and be broken. Who suggested you took on this thing in the first place?' It seemed natural for him to question me, nor did I mind. It was as though we had known one another for a long time, and had met again after a lapse of years.

'Have you ever thought about the future,' he asked me, 'and what this sort of thing will lead to? Supposing Mrs. Van Hopper gets tired of her "friend of the bosom", what then?'

I smiled and told him that I did not mind very much. There would be other Mrs. Van Hoppers, and I was young, and confident, and strong. But even as he spoke I remembered those advertisements seen often in good class magazines where a friendly society demands succour for young women in reduced circumstances; I thought of the type of boarding-house that answers the advertisement and gives temporary shelter, and then I saw myself, useless sketch-book in hand, without qualifications of any kind, stammering replies to stern employment agents. Perhaps I should have accepted Blaize's ten per cent.

'How old are you?' he said, and when I told him he laughed, and got up from his chair. 'I know that age, it's a particularly obstinate one, and a thousand bogies won't make you fear the future. A pity we can't change over. Go upstairs and put your hat on, and I'll have the car brought round.'

As he watched me into the lift I thought of yesterday, Mrs. Van Hopper's chattering tongue, and his cold courtesy. I had ill-judged him, he was neither hard nor sardonic, he was already my friend of many years, the brother I had never possessed. Mine was a happy mood that afternoon, and I remember it well. I can see the rippled sky, fluffy with cloud, and the white-whipped sea. I can feel again the wind on my face, and hear my laugh, and his that echoed it. It was not the Monte Carlo I had known, or perhaps the truth was that it pleased me better. There was a glamour about that had not been before. I must have looked upon it before with dull eyes. The harbour was a dancing thing, with fluttering paper boats, and the sailors on the quay were jovial, smiling fellows, merry as the wind. We passed the yacht, beloved of Mrs. Van Hopper because of its ducal owner, and snapped our fingers at the glistening brass, and looked at one another and laughed again. I can remember as though I wore it still my comfortable, ill-fitting flannel suit, and how the skirt was lighter than the coat through harder wear. My shabby hat, too broad about the brim, and my low-heeled shoes, fastened with a

single strap. A pair of gauntlet gloves clutched in a grubby hand. I had
never looked more youthful, I had never felt so old. Mrs. Van Hopper and
her influenza did not exist for me. The bridge and the cocktail parties were
forgotten, and with them my own humble status.

I was a person of importance, I was grown up at last. That girl, who,
tortured by shyness, would stand outside the sitting-room door twisting a
handkerchief in her hands, while from within came that babble of confused
chatter so unnerving to the intruder – she had gone with the wind that
afternoon. She was a poor creature, and I thought of her with scorn if I
considered her at all.

The wind was too high for sketching, it tore in cheerful gusts around the
corner of my cobbled square, and back to the car we went and drove I know
not where. The long road climbed the hills, and the car climbed with it, and
we circled in the heights like a bird in the air. How different his car to Mrs.
Van Hopper's hireling for the season, a square old-fashioned Daimler that
took us to Mentone on placid afternoons, when I, sitting on the little seat
with my back to the driver, must crane my neck to see the view. This car
had the wings of Mercury I thought, for higher yet we climbed, and
dangerously fast, and the danger pleased me because it was new to me,
because I was young.

I remember laughing aloud, and the laugh being carried by the wind away
from me; and, looking at him, I realised he laughed no longer, he was once
more silent and detached, the man of yesterday wrapped in his secret self.

I realised, too, that the car could climb no more, we had reached the
summit, and below us stretched the way that we had come, precipitous and
hollow. He stopped the car, and I could see that the edge of the road bordered
a vertical slope that crumbled into vacancy, a fall of perhaps two thousand
feet. We got out of the car and looked beneath us. This sobered me at last,
I knew that but half the car's length had lain between us and the fall. The
sea, like a crinkled chart, spread to the horizon and lapped the sharp outline
of the coast, while the houses were white shells in a rounded grotto, pricked
here and there by a great orange sun. We knew another sunlight on our hill,
and silence made it harder, more austere. A change had come upon our
afternoon, it was not the thing of gossamer it had been. The wind dropped,
and it suddenly grew cold.

When I spoke my voice was far too casual, the silly nervous voice of
someone ill at ease. 'Do you know this place?' I said. 'Have you been here
before?' He looked down at me without recognition, and I realised with a
little stab of anxiety that he must have forgotten all about me, perhaps for
some considerable time, and that he himself was so lost in the labyrinth of
his own unquiet thoughts that I did not exist. He had the face of one who
walks in his sleep, and for a wild moment the idea came to me that perhaps
he was not normal, not altogether sane. There were people who had trances,
I had surely heard of them, and they followed strange laws of which we
could know nothing, they obeyed the tangled orders of their own sub-
conscious minds. Perhaps he was one of them, and here we were within six
foot of death.

'It's getting late, shall we go home?' I said, and my careless tone, my little ineffectual smile would scarcely have deceived a child.

I had misjudged him, of course, there was nothing wrong after all, for as soon as I spoke this second time he came clear of his dream and began to apologise. I had gone white, I suppose, and he had noticed it.

'That was an unforgivable thing for me to do,' he said, and taking my arm he pushed me back towards the car, and we climbed in again, and he slammed the door. 'Don't be frightened, the turn is far easier than it looks,' he said, and while I, sick and giddy, clung to the seat with both hands, he manoeuvred the car gently, very gently, until it faced the sloping road once more.

'Then you have been here before?' I said to him, my sense of strain departing, as the car crept away down the twisting narrow road.

'Yes,' he said, and then, after pausing a moment, 'but not for many years. I wanted to see if it had changed.'

'And has it?' I asked him.

'No,' he said. 'No, it has not changed.'

I wondered what had driven him to this retreat into the past, with me an unconscious witness of his mood. What gulf of years stretched between him and that other time, what deed of thought and action, what difference in temperament? I did not want to know. I wished I had not come.

Down the twisting road we went without a check, without a word; a great ridge of cloud stretched above the setting sun, and air was cold and clean. Suddenly he began to talk about Manderley. He said nothing of his life there, no word about himself, but he told me how the sun set there, on a spring afternoon, leaving a glow upon the headland. The sea would look like slate, cold still from the long winter, and from the terrace you could hear the ripple of the coming tide washing in the little bay. The daffodils were in bloom, stirring in the evening breeze, golden heads cupped upon lean stalks, and however many you might pick there would be no thinning of the ranks, they were massed like an army, shoulder to shoulder. On a bank below the lawns, crocuses were planted, golden, pink, and mauve, but by this time they would be past their best, dropping and fading, like the pallid snowdrops. The primrose was more vulgar, a homely pleasant creature who appeared in every cranny like a weed. Too early yet for bluebells, their heads were still hidden beneath last year's leaves, but when they came, dwarfing the more humble violet, they choked the very bracken in the woods, and with their colour made a challenge to the sky.

He never would have them in the house, he said. Thrust into vases they became dank and listless, and to see them at their best you must walk in the woods in the morning, about twelve o'clock, when the sun was overhead. They had a smoky, rather bitter smell, as though a wild sap ran in their stalks, pungent and juicy. People who plucked bluebells from the woods were vandals, he had forbidden it at Manderley. Sometimes, driving in the country, he had seen bicyclists with huge bunches strapped before them on the handles, the bloom already fading from the dying heads, the ravaged stalks straggling naked and unclean.

The primrose did not mind it quite so much, although a creature of the wilds it had a leaning towards civilisation, and preened and smiled in a jam-jar in some cottage window without resentment, living quite a week if given water. No wild flowers came in the house at Manderley. He had special cultivated flowers, grown for the house alone, in the walled garden. A rose was one of the few flowers, he said, that looked better picked than growing. A bowl of roses in a drawing-room had a depth of colour and scent they had not possessed in the open. There was something rather blowsy about roses in full bloom, something shallow and raucous, like women with untidy hair. In the house they became mysterious and subtle. He had roses in the house at Manderley for eight months of the year. Did I like syringa, he asked me? There was a tree on the edge of the lawn he could smell from his bedroom window. His sister, who was a hard, rather practical person, used to complain that there were too many scents at Manderley, they made her drunk. Perhaps she was right. He did not care. It was the only form of intoxication that appealed to him. His earliest recollection was of great branches of lilac, standing in white jars, and they filled the house with a wistful, poignant smell.

The little pathway down the valley to the bay had clumps of azalea and rhododendron planted to the left of it, and if you wandered down it on a May evening after dinner it was just as though the shrubs had sweated in the air. You could stoop down and pick a fallen petal, crush it between your fingers, and you had there, in the hollow of your hand, the essence of a thousand scents, unbearable and sweet. All from a curled and crumpled petal. And you came out of the valley, heady and rather dazed, to the hard white shingle of the beach and the still water. A curious, perhaps too sudden contrast. . . .

As he spoke the car became one of many once again, dusk had fallen without my noticing it, and we were in the midst of light and sound in the streets of Monte Carlo. The clatter jagged on my nerves, and the lights were far too brilliant, far too yellow. It was a swift, unwelcome anticlimax.

Soon we would come to the hotel, and I felt for my gloves in the pocket of the car. I found them, and my fingers closed upon a book as well, whose slim covers told of poetry. I peered to read the title as the car slowed before the door of the hotel. 'You can take it and read it if you like,' he said, his voice casual and indifferent now that the drive was over, and we were back again, and Manderley was many hundreds of miles distant.

I was glad, and held it tightly with my gloves. I felt I wanted some possession of his, now that the day was finished.

'Hop out,' he said, 'I must go and put the car away. I shan't see you in the restaurant this evening as I'm dining out. But thank you for to-day.'

I went up the hotel steps alone, with all the despondency of a child whose treat is over. My afternoon had spoilt me for the hours that still remained, and I thought how long they would seem until my bed-time, how empty too my supper all alone. Somehow I could not face the bright enquiries of the nurse upstairs, or the possibilities of Mrs. Van Hopper's husky interrogation, so I sat down in the corner of the lounge behind a pillar and ordered tea.

The waiter appeared bored, seeing me alone there was no need for him to press, and anyway it was that dragging time of day, a few minutes after half-past five, when the normal tea is finished and the hour for drinks remote.

Rather forlorn, more than a little dissatisfied, I leant back in my chair and took up the book of poems. The volume was well worn, well thumbed, falling open automatically at what must be a much-frequented page.

> 'I fled Him, down the nights and down the days;
> I fled Him, down the arches of the years;
> I fled Him, down the labyrinthine ways
> Of my own mind; and in the midst of tears
> I hid from Him, and under running laughter.
>   Up vistaed slopes I sped
>   And shot, precipited
> Adown Titanic glooms or chasmed fears,
> From those strong feet that followed, followed after.'

I felt rather like someone peering through the keyhole of a locked door, and a little furtively I laid the book aside. What hound of heaven had driven him to the high hills this afternoon? I thought of his car, with half a length between it and that drop of two thousand feet, and the blank expression on his face. What footsteps echoed in his mind, what whispers, and what memories, and why, of all poems, must he keep this one in the pocket of his car? I wished he were less remote; and I anything but the creature that I was in my shabby coat and skirt, my broad-brimmed school-girl hat.

The sulky waiter brought my tea, and while I ate bread-and-butter dull as sawdust I thought of the pathway through the valley he had described to me this afternoon, the smell of the azaleas, and the white shingle of the bay. If he loved it all so much why did he seek the superficial froth of Monte Carlo? He had told Mrs. Van Hopper he had made no plans, he came away in rather a hurry. And I pictured him running down that pathway in the valley with his own hound of heaven at his heels.

I picked up the book again, and this time it opened at the title-page, and I read the dedication. 'Max – from Rebecca. May 17th', written in a curious, slanting hand. A little blob of ink marred the white page opposite, as though the writer, in impatience, had shaken her pen to make the ink flow freely. And then, as it bubbled through the nib, it came a little thick, so that the name Rebecca stood out black and strong, the tall and sloping R dwarfing the other letters.

I shut the book with a snap, and put it away under my gloves; and stretching to a near-by-chair, I took up an old copy of *L'Illustration* and turned the pages. There were some fine photographs of the chateaux of the Loire, and an article as well. I read it carefully, referring to the photographs, but when I finished I knew I had not understood a word. It was not Blois with its thin turrets and its spires that stared up at me from the printed page. It was the face of Mrs. Van Hopper in the restaurant the day before, her small pig's eyes darting to the neighbouring table, her fork, heaped high with ravioli, pausing in mid-air.

'An appalling tragedy,' she was saying, 'the papers were full of it of course. They say he never talks about it, never mentions her name. She was drowned you know, in a bay near Manderley. . . .'

Chapter Five

I am glad it cannot happen twice, the fever of first love. For it is a fever, and a burden, too, whatever the poets may say. They are not brave, the days when we are twenty-one. They are full of little cowardices, little fears without foundation, and one is so easily bruised, so swiftly wounded, one falls to the first barbed word. To-day, wrapped in the complacent armour of approaching middle age, the infinitesimal pricks of day by day brush one but lightly and are soon forgotten, but then – how a careless word would linger, becoming a fiery stigma, and how a look, a glance over a shoulder, branded themselves as things eternal. A denial heralded the thrice crowing of a cock, and an insincerity was like the kiss of Judas. The adult mind can lie with untroubled conscience and a gay composure, but in those days even a small deception scoured the tongue, lashing one against the stake itself.

'What have you been doing this morning?' I can hear her now, propped against her pillows, with all the small irritability of the patient who is not really ill, who has lain in bed too long, and I, reaching to the bedside drawer for the pack of cards, would feel the guilty flush form patches on my neck.

'I've been playing tennis with the professional,' I told her, the false words bringing me to panic, even as I spoke, for what if the professional himself should come up to the suite, then, that very afternoon, and bursting in upon her complain that I had missed my lesson now for many days?

'The trouble is with me laid up like this you haven't got enough to do,' she said, mashing her cigarette in a jar of cleansing cream, and taking the cards in her hand she mixed them in the deft, irritating shuffle of the inveterate player, shaking them in threes, snapping the backs.

'I don't know what you find to do with yourself all day,' she went on, 'you never have any sketches to show me, and when I do ask you to do some shopping for me you forget to buy my Taxol. All I can say is that I hope your tennis will improve, it will be useful to you later on. A poor player is a great bore. Do you still serve underhand?' She flipped the Queen of Spades into the pool, and the dark face stared up at me like Jezebel.

'Yes,' I said, stung by her question, thinking how just and appropriate her word. It described me well. I was underhand. I had not played tennis with the professional at all, I had not once played since she had lain in bed, and that was a little over a fortnight now. I wondered why it was I clung to this reserve, and why it was I did not tell her that every morning I drove with de Winter in his car, and lunched with him too, at his table in the restaurant.

'You must come up to the net more, you will never play a good game until you do,' she continued, and I agreed, flinching at my own hypocrisy, covering her Queen with the weak-chinned Knave of Hearts.

I have forgotten much of Monte Carlo, of those morning drives, of where we went, even our conversation; but I have not forgotten how my fingers trembled, cramming on my hat, and how I ran along the corridor and down the stairs, too impatient to wait for the slow whining of the lift, and so outside brushing the swing doors before the commissionaire could help me.

He would be there, in the driver's seat, reading a paper while he waited, and when he saw me he would smile, and toss it behind him in the back seat, and open the door, saying, 'Well, how is the friend-of-the-bosom this morning, and where does she want to go?' If he had driven round in circles it would not have mattered to me, for I was in that first flushed stage when to climb into the seat beside him, and lean forward to the wind-screen hugging my knees, was almost too much to bear. I was like a little scrubby school-boy, with a passion for a sixth-form prefect, and he kinder, and far more inaccessible.

'There's a cold wind this morning, you had better put on my coat.'

I remember that, for I was young enough to win happiness in the wearing of his clothes, playing the school-boy again who carries his hero's sweater and ties it about his throat choking with pride, and this borrowing of his coat, wearing it around my shoulders for even a few minutes at a time, was a triumph in itself, and made a glow about my morning.

Not for me the languor and the subtlety I had read about in books. The challenge and the chase. The swordplay, the swift glance, the stimulating smile. The art of provocation was unknown to me, and I would sit with his map upon my lap, the wind blowing my dull, lanky hair, happy in his silence yet eager for his words. Whether he talked or not made little difference to my mood. My only enemy was the clock on the dash-board, whose hands would move relentlessly to one o'clock. We drove east, we drove west, amidst the myriad villages that cling like limpets to the Mediterranean shore, and to-day I remember none of them.

All I remember is the feel of the leather seats, the texture of the map upon my knee, its frayed edges, its worn seams, and how one day, looking at the clock, I thought to myself, 'This moment now, at twenty past eleven, this must never be lost,' and I shut my eyes to make the experience more lasting. When I opened my eyes we were by a bend in the road, and a peasant girl in a black shawl waved to us; I can see her now, her dusty skirt, her gleaming, friendly smile and in a second we had passed the bend and could see her no more. Already she belonged to the past, she was only a memory.

I wanted to go back again, to recapture the moment that had gone, and then it came to me that if we did it would not be the same, even the sun would be changed in the sky, casting another shadow, and the peasant girl would trudge past us along the road in a different way, not waving this time, perhaps not even seeing us. There was something chilling in the thought, something a little melancholy, and looking at the clock I saw that five more minutes had gone by. Soon we would have reached our time limit, and must return to the hotel.

'If only there could be an invention,' I said impulsively, 'that bottled up a memory, like scent. And it never faded, and it never got stale. And then, when one wanted it, the bottle could be uncorked, and it would be like living the moment all over again.' I looked up at him, to see what he would say. He did not turn to me, he went on watching the road ahead.

'What particular moments in your young life do you wish uncorked?' he said. I could not tell from his voice whether he was teasing me or not. 'I'm not sure,' I began, and then blundered on, rather foolishly, not thinking of my words, 'I'd like to keep this moment and never forget it.'

'Is that meant to be a compliment to the day, or to my driving?' he said, and as he laughed, like a mocking brother, I became silent, overwhelmed suddenly by the great gulf between us, and how his very kindness to me widened it.

I knew then that I would never tell Mrs. Van Hopper about these morning expeditions, for her smile would hurt me as his laugh had done. She would not be angry, nor would she be shocked, she would raise her eyebrows very faintly, as though she did not altogether believe my story, and then with a tolerant shrug of the shoulder she would say, 'My dear child, it's extremely sweet and kind of him to take you driving, the only thing is – are you sure it does not bore him dreadfully?' And then she would send me out to buy Taxol, patting me on the shoulder. What degradation lay in being young, I thought, and fell to tearing at my nails.

'I wish,' I said savagely, still mindful of his laugh and throwing discretion to the wind, 'I wish I was a woman of about thirty-six dressed in black satin with a string of pearls.'

'You would not be in this car with me if you were,' he said, 'and stop biting those nails, they are ugly enough already.'

'You'll think me impertinent and rude I dare say,' I went on, 'but I would like to know why you ask me to come out in the car, day after day. You are being kind, that's obvious, but why do you choose me for your charity?'

I sat up stiff and straight in my seat with all the poor pomposity of youth.

'I ask you,' he said gravely, 'because you are not dressed in black satin, with a string of pearls, nor are you thirty-six.' His face was without expression, I could not tell whether he laughed inwardly or not.

'It's all very well,' I said, 'you know everything there is to know about me. There's not much, I admit, because I have not been alive for very long and nothing much has happened to me, except people dying, but you – I know nothing more about you than I did the first day we met.'

'And what did you know then?' he asked.

'Why, that you lived at Manderley and – and that you had lost your wife.' There, I had said it at last, the word that had hovered on my tongue for days. Your wife. It came out with ease, without reluctance, as though the mere mention of her must be the most casual thing in all the world. Your wife. The word lingered in the air once I had uttered it, dancing before me, and because he received it silently, making no comment, the word magnified itself into something heinous and appalling, a forbidden word, unnatural to the tongue. And I could not call it back, it could never be unsaid. Once again I saw the inscription on the fly-leaf of that book of poems, and the curious slanting R. I felt sick at heart and cold. He would never forgive me, and this would be the end of our friendship.

I remember staring straight in front of me at the windscreen, seeing nothing of the flying road, my ears still tingling with that spoken word. The silence became minutes, and the minutes became miles, and everything is over now, I thought, I shall never drive with him again. To-morrow he will go away. And Mrs. Van Hopper will be up again. She and I will walk along the terrace as we did before. The porter will bring down his trunks, I shall catch a glimpse of them in the luggage lift, with new-plastered labels. The bustle and finality of departure. The sound of the car changing gear as it turned the corner, and then even that sound merging into the common traffic, and being lost, and so absorbed forever.

I was so deep in my picture, I even saw the porter pocketing his tip and going back through the swing-door of the hotel, saying something over his shoulder to the commissionaire, that I did not notice the slowing-down of the car, and it was only when we stopped, drawing up by the side of the road, that I brought myself back to the present once again. He sat motionless, looking without his hat and with his white scarf round his neck, more than ever like someone medieval who lived within a frame. He did not belong to the bright landscape, he should be standing on the steps of a gaunt cathedral, his cloak flung back, while a beggar at his feet scrambled for gold coins.

The friend had gone, with his kindliness and his easy camaraderie, and the brother too, who had mocked me for nibbling at my nails. This man was a stranger. I wondered why I was sitting beside him in the car.

Then he turned to me and spoke. 'A little while ago you talked about an invention,' he said, 'some scheme for capturing a memory. You would like, you told me, at a chosen moment to live the past again. I'm afraid I think rather differently from you. All memories are bitter, and I prefer to ignore them. Something happened a year ago that altered my whole life, and I want to forget every phase in my existence up to that time. Those days are finished. They are blotted out. I must begin living all over again. The first day we met, your Mrs. Van Hopper asked me why I came to Monte Carlo. It put a stopper on those memories you would like to resurrect. It does not always work, of course, sometimes the scent is too strong for the bottle, and too strong for me. And then the devil in one, like a furtive peeping Tom, tries to draw the cork. I did that in the first drive we took together. When we climbed the hills and looked down over the precipice. I was there some years ago, with my wife. You asked me if it was still the same, if it had changed at all. It was just the same, but – I was thankful to realise – oddly impersonal. There was no suggestion of the other time. She and I had left no record. It may have been because you were with me. You have blotted out the past for me, you know, far more effectively than all the bright lights of Monte Carlo. But for you I should have left long ago, gone on to Italy, and Greece, and further still perhaps. You have spared me all those wanderings. Damn your puritanical little tight-lipped speech to me. Damn your idea of my kindness and my charity. I ask you to come with me because I want you and your company, and if you don't believe me you can leave the car now and find your own way home. Go on, open the door, and get out.'

I sat still, my hands in my lap, not knowing whether he meant it or not.

'Well,' he said, 'what are you going to do about it?'

Had I been a year or two younger I think I should have cried. Children's tears are very near the surface, and come at the first crisis. As it was I felt them prick behind my eyes, felt the ready colour flood my face, and catching a sudden glimpse of myself in the glass above the wind-screen saw in full the sorry spectacle that I made, with troubled eyes and scarlet cheeks, lank hair flopping under broad felt hat.

'I want to go home,' I said, my voice perilously near to trembling, and without a word he started up the engine, let in the clutch, and turned the car round the way that we had come.

Swiftly we covered the ground, far too swiftly, I thought, far too easily, and the callous countryside watched us with indifference. We came to the bend in the road that I had wished to imprison as a memory, and the peasant girl was gone, and the colour was flat, and it was no more after all than any bend in any road passed by a hundred motorists. The glamour of it had gone with my happy mood, and at the thought of it my frozen face quivered into feeling, my adult pride was lost, and those despicable tears rejoicing at their conquest welled into my eyes and strayed upon my cheeks.

I could not check them, for they came unbidden, and had I reached in my pocket for a handkerchief he would have seen. I must let them fall untouched, and suffer the bitter salt upon my lips, plumbing the depths of humiliation. Whether he had turned his head to look at me I do not know, for I watched the road ahead with blurred and steady stare, but suddenly he put out his hand and took hold of mine, and kissed it, still saying nothing, and then he threw his handkerchief on my lap, which I was too ashamed to touch.

I thought of all those heroines of fiction who looked pretty when they cried, and what a contrast I must make with blotched and swollen face, and red rims to my eyes. It was a dismal finish to my morning, and the day that stretched ahead of me was long. I had to lunch with Mrs. Van Hopper in her room, because the nurse was going out, and afterwards she would make me play bezique with all the tireless energy of the convalescent. I knew I should stifle in that room. There was something sordid about the tumbled sheets, the sprawling blankets and the thumped pillows, and that bed-side table dusty with powder, spilt scent, and melting liquid rouge. Her bed would be littered with the separated sheets of the daily papers folded anyhow, while French novels with curling edges and the covers torn kept company with American magazines. The mashed stubs of cigarettes lay everywhere, in cleansing cream, in a dish of grapes, and on the floor beneath the bed.

Visitors were lavish with their flowers, and the vases stood cheek-by-jowl in any fashion, hot-house exotics crammed beside mimosa, while a great beribboned casket crowned them all, with tier upon tier of crystallised fruit. Later her friends would come in for a drink, which I must mix for them, hating my task, shy and ill-at-ease in my corner hemmed in by their parrot chatter, and I would be a whipping-boy again, blushing for her when, excited by her little crowd, she must sit up in bed and talk too loudly, laugh too long, reach to the portable gramophone and start a record, shrugging her large shoulders to the tune. I preferred her irritable and snappy, her hair done up in pins, scolding me for forgetting her Taxol. All this awaited me in the suite, while he, once he had left me at the hotel, would go away somewhere alone, towards the sea perhaps, feel the wind on his cheek, follow the sun; and it might happen that he would lose himself in those memories that I knew nothing of, that I could not share, he would wander down the years that were gone.

The gulf that lay between us was wider now than it had ever been, and he stood away from me, with his back turned, on the further shore. I felt young and small and very much alone, and now, in spite of my pride, I found his handkerchief and blew my nose, throwing my drab appearance to the winds. It could never matter.

'To hell with this,' he said suddenly, as though angry, as though bored, and he pulled me beside him, and put his arm round my shoulder, still looking straight ahead of him, his right hand on the wheel. He drove, I remember, even faster than before. 'I suppose you are young enough to be my daughter, and I don't know how to deal with you,' he said. The road narrowed then to a corner, and he had to swerve to avoid a dog. I thought he would release me, but he went on holding me beside him, and when the corner was passed, and the road came straight again he did not let me go. 'You can forget all I said to you this morning,' he said, 'that's all finished and done with. Don't let's ever think of it again. My family always call me Maxim, I'd like you to do the same. You've been formal with me long enough.' He felt for the brim of my hat, and took hold of it, throwing it over his shoulder to the back seat, and then bent down and kissed the top of my head. 'Promise me you will never wear black satin,' he said. I smiled then, and he laughed back at me, and the morning was gay again, the morning was a shining thing. Mrs. Van Hopper and the afternoon did not matter a flip of the finger. It would pass so quickly, and there would be to-night, and another day to-morrow. I was cocksure, jubilant, at that moment I almost had the courage to claim equality. I saw myself strolling into Mrs. Van Hopper's bedroom rather late for my bezique, and when questioned by her yawning carelessly, saying, 'I forgot the time. I've been lunching with Maxim.'

I was still child enough to consider a Christian name like a plume in the hat, though from the very first he had called me by mine. The morning, for all its shadowed moments, and promoted me to a new level of friendship, I did not lag so far behind as I had thought. He had kissed me too, a natural business, comforting and quiet. Not dramatic as in books. Not embarrassing.

It seemed to bring about an ease in our relationship, it made everything more simple. The gulf between us had been bridged after all. I was to call him Maxim. And that afternoon playing bezique with Mrs. Van Hopper was not so tedious as it might have been, though my courage failed me and I said nothing of my morning. For when, gathering her cards together at the end, and reaching for the box, she said casually, 'Tell me, is Max de Winter still in the hotel?' I hesitated a moment, like a diver on the brink, then lost my nerve and my tutored self-possession, saying, 'Yes, I believe so – he comes into the restaurant for his meals.'

Someone has told her, I thought, someone has seen us together, the tennis professional has complained, the manager has sent a note, and I waited for her attack. But she went on putting the cards back into the box, yawning a little, while I straightened the tumbled bed. I gave her the bowl of powder, the rouge compact, and the lip-stick, and she put away the cards and took up the hand glass from the table by her side. 'Attractive creature,' she said, 'but queer-tempered I should think, difficult to know. I thought he might have made some gesture of asking one to Manderley that day in the lounge, but he was very close.'

I said nothing. I watched her pick up the lip-stick and outline a bow upon her hard mouth. 'I never saw her,' she said, holding the glass away to see the effect, 'but I believe she was very lovely. Exquisitely turned out, and brilliant in every way. They used to give tremendous parties at Manderley. It was all very sudden and tragic, and I believe he adored her. I need the darker shade of powder with this brilliant red, my dear, fetch it will you, and put this box back in the drawer?'

And we were busy then with powder, scent, and rouge, until the bell rang and her visitors came in. I handed them their drinks, dully, saying little; I changed the records on the gramophone, I threw away the stubs of cigarettes.

'Been doing any sketching lately, little lady?' The forced heartiness of an old banker, his monocle dangling on a string, and my bright smile of insincerity: 'No, not very lately; will you have another cigarette?'

It was not I that answered, I was not there at all. I was following a phantom in my mind, whose shadowy form had taken shape at last. Her features were blurred, her colouring indistinct, the setting of her eyes and the texture of her hair was still uncertain, still to be revealed.

She had beauty that endured, and a smile that was not forgotten. Somewhere her voice still lingered, and the memory of her words. There were places she had visited, and things that she had touched. Perhaps in cupboards there were clothes that she had worn, with the scent about them still. In my bedroom, under my pillow, I had a book that she had taken in her hands, and I could see her turning to that first white page, smiling as she wrote, and shaking the bent nib. Max from Rebecca. It must have been his birthday, and she had put it amongst her other presents on the breakfast table. And they had laughed together as he tore off the paper and the string. She leant, perhaps, over his shoulder, while he read. Max. She called him Max. It was familiar, gay, and easy on the tongue. The family could call him Maxim if they liked. Grandmothers and aunts. And people like myself, quiet and dull and youthful, who did not matter. Max was her choice, the word was her possession, she had written it with so great a confidence on the fly-leaf of that book. That bold, slanting hand, stabbing the white paper, the symbol of herself, so certain, so assured.

How many times she must have written to him thus, in how many varied moods.

Little notes, scrawled on half-sheets of paper, and letters, when he was away, page after page, intimate, *their* news. Her voice, echoing through the house, and down the garden, careless and familiar like the writing in the book.

And I had to call him Maxim.

Chapter Six

Packing up. The nagging worry of departure. Lost keys, unwritten labels, tissue paper lying on the floor. I hate it all. Even now, when I have done so much of it, when I live, as the saying goes, in my boxes. Even to-day, when shutting drawers and flinging wide a hotel wardrobe, or the impersonal shelves of a furnished villa, is a methodical matter of routine, I am aware of sadness, of a sense of loss. Here, I say, we have lived, we have been happy. This has been ours, however brief the time. Though two nights only have been spent beneath a roof, yet we leave something of ourselves behind. Nothing material, not a hair-pin on a dressing-table, not an empty bottle of Aspirin tablets, not a handkerchief beneath a pillow, but something indefinable, a moment of our lives, a thought, a mood.

This house sheltered us, we spoke, we loved within those walls. That was yesterday. To-day we pass on, we see it no more, and we are different, changed in some infinitesimal way. We can never be quite the same again. Even stopping for luncheon at a way-side inn, and going to a dark, unfamiliar room to wash my hands, the handle of the door unknown to me, the wall-paper peeling in strips, a funny little cracked mirror above the basin, for this moment, it is mine, it belongs to me. We know one another. This is the present. There is no past and no future. Here I am washing my hands and the cracked mirror shows me to myself, suspended, as it were, in time; this is me, this moment will not pass.

And then I open the door and go to the dining-room, where he is sitting waiting for me at a table, and I think how in that moment I have aged, and passed on, how I have advanced one step towards an unknown destiny.

We smile, we choose our lunch, we speak of this and that, but - I say to myself – I am not she who left him five minutes ago. She has stayed behind. I am another woman, older, more mature. . . .

I saw in a paper the other day that the hotel Côte d'Azur at Monte Carlo had gone to new management, and had a different name. The rooms had been re-decorated, and the whole interior changed. Perhaps Mrs. Van Hopper's suite on the first floor exists no more. Perhaps there is no trace of the small bedroom that was mine. I knew I should never go back, that day I knelt on the floor and fumbled with the awkward catch of her trunk.

The episode was finished, with the snapping of the lock. I glanced out of the window, and it was like turning the page of a photograph album. Those roof tops and that sea were mine no more. They belonged to yesterday, to the past. The rooms already wore an empty air, stripped of our possessions, and there was something hungry about the suite, as though it wished us gone, and the new arrivals, who would come to-morrow, in our place. The heavy luggage stood ready strapped and locked in the corridor outside. The smaller stuff would be finished later. Waste-paper baskets groaned under litter. All her half-empty medicine bottles and discarded face-cream jars, with torn-up bills and letters. Drawers in tables gaped, the bureau was stripped bare.

She had flung a letter at me the morning before, as I poured out her coffee at breakfast. 'Helen is sailing for New York on Saturday. Little Nancy has a threatened appendix, and they've cabled her to go home. That's decided me. We're going too. I'm tired to death of Europe, and we can come back in the early fall. How d'you like the idea of seeing New York?'

The thought was worse than prison. Something of my misery must have shown in my face, for at first she looked astonished, then annoyed.

'What an odd, unsatisfactory child you are. I can't make you out. Don't you realise that at home girls of your position without any money can have the grandest fun? Plenty of boys and excitement. All in your own class. You can have your own little set of friends, and needn't be at my beck and call as much as you are here. I thought you didn't care for Monte?'

'I've got used to it,' I said lamely, wretchedly, my mind a conflict.

'Well, you'll just have to get used to New York, that's all. We're going to catch that boat of Helen's, and it means seeing about our passage at once. Go down to the reception office right away, and make that young clerk show some sign of efficiency. Your day will be so full that you won't have time to have any pangs about leaving Monte!' She laughed disagreeably, squashing her cigarette in the butter, and went to the telephone to ring up all her friends.

I could not face the office right away. I went into the bathroom and locked the door, and sat down on the cork mat, my head in my hands. It had happened at last, the business of going away. It was all over. To-morrow evening I should be in the train, holding her jewel case and her rug, like a maid, and she in that monstrous new hat with the single quill, dwarfed in her fur-coat, sitting opposite me in the wagon-lit. We would wash and clean our teeth in that stuffy little compartment with the rattling doors, the splashed basin, the damp towel, the soap with a single hair on it, the carafe half-filled with water, the inevitable notice on the wall '*Sous le lavabo se trouve une vase*', while every rattle, every throb and jerk of the screaming train would tell me that the miles carried me away from him, sitting alone in the restaurant of the hotel, at the table I had known, reading a book, not minding, not thinking.

I should say good-bye to him in the lounge, perhaps, before we left. A furtive, scrambled farewell, because of her, and there would be a pause, and a smile, and words like 'Yes, of course, do write', and 'I've never thanked you properly for being so kind', and 'You must forward those snapshots', 'What about your address?' 'Well, I'll have to let you know'. And he would light a cigarette casually, asking a passing waiter for a light, while I thought, 'Four and a half more minutes to go. I shall never see him again.'

Because I was going, because it was over, there would suddenly be nothing more to say, we would be strangers, meeting for the last and only time, while my mind clamoured painfully, crying 'I love you so much. I'm terribly unhappy. This has never come to me before, and never will again'. My face would be set in a prim, conventional smile, my voice would be saying, 'Look at that funny old man over there, I wonder who he is, he must be new here.' And because we were already strangers to one another. 'I hope the snapshots come out well', repeating oneself in desperation, and he 'Yes, that one of the square ought to be good, the light was just right'. Having both of us gone into all that at the time, having agreed upon it, and anyway I would not care if the result was fogged and black, because this was the last moment, the final good-bye had been attained.

'Well,' my dreadful smile stretching across my face, 'thanks most awfully once again, it's been so ripping. . . .' using words I had never used before. Ripping: what did it mean? – God knows, I did not care; it was the sort of word that school-girls had for hockey, wildly inappropriate to those past weeks of misery and exultation. Then the doors of the lift would open upon Mrs. Van Hopper and I would cross the lounge to meet her, and he would stroll back again to his corner and pick up a paper.

Sitting there, ridiculously, on the cork mat of the bathroom floor I lived it all, and our journey too, and our arrival in New York. The shrill voice of Helen a narrower edition of her mother, and Nancy, her horrid little child. The college boys that Mrs. Van Hopper would have me know, and the young bank clerks, suitable to my station, 'Let's make Wednesday night a date.' 'D'you like Hot music?' Snub-nosed boys, with shiny faces. Having to be polite. And wanting to be alone with my own thoughts as I was now, locked behind the bathroom door. . . .

She came and rattled on the door. 'What are you doing?'

'All right – I'm sorry, I'm coming now,' and I made a pretence of turning on the tap, of bustling about and folding a towel on a rail.

She glanced at me curiously as I opened the door. 'What a time you've been. You can't afford to dream this morning, you know, there's too much to be done.'

He would go back to Manderley, of course, in a few weeks, I felt certain of that. There would be a great pile of letters waiting for him in the hall, and mine amongst them, scribbled on the boat. A forced letter, trying to amuse, describing my fellow passengers. It would lie about inside his blotter, and he would answer it weeks later, one Sunday morning in a hurry, before lunch, having come across it when he paid some bills. And then no more. Nothing until the final degradation of the Christmas card. Manderley itself perhaps, against a frosted background. The message printed, saying 'A happy Christmas and a prosperous New Year from Maximilian de Winter'. Gold lettering. But to be kind he would have run his pen through the printed name and written in ink underneath 'from Maxim', as a sort of sop, and if there was space, a message, 'I hope you are enjoying New York'. A lick of the envelope, a stamp, and tossed in a pile of a hundred others.

'It's too bad you are leaving to-morrow,' said the reception clerk, telephone in hand, 'the Ballet starts next week you know. Does Mrs. Van Hopper know?' I dragged myself back from Christmas at Manderley to the realities of the wagon-lit.

Mrs Van Hopper lunched in the restaurant for the first time since her influenza, and I had a pain in the pit of my stomach as I followed her into the room. He had gone to Cannes for the day, that much I knew, for he had warned me the day before, but I kept thinking the waiter might commit an indiscretion and say: 'Will Mademoiselle be dining with Monsieur to-night as usual?' I felt a little sick whenever he came near the table, but he said nothing.

The day was spent in packing, and in the evening people came to say goodbye. We dined in the sitting-room, and she went to bed directly afterwards. Still I had not seen him. I went down to the lounge about half-past nine on the pretext of getting luggage labels and he was not there. The odious reception clerk smiled when he saw me. 'If you are looking for Mr. de Winter we had a message from Cannes to say he would not be back before midnight.'

'I want a packet of luggage labels,' I said, but I saw by his eye that he was not deceived. So there would be no last evening after all. The hour I had looked forward to all day must be spent by myself alone, in my own bedroom, gazing at my Revelation suit-case and the stout hold-all. Perhaps it was just as well, for I should have made a poor companion, and he must have read my face.

I know I cried that night, bitter youthful tears that could not come from me to-day. That kind of crying, deep into a pillow, does not happen after we are twenty-one. The throbbing head, the swollen eyes, the tight contracted throat. And the wild anxiety in the morning to hide all traces from the world, sponging with cold water, dabbing eau-de-Cologne, the furtive dash of powder that is significant in itself. The panic, too, that one might cry again, the tears swelling without control, and a fatal trembling of the mouth lead one to disaster. I remember opening wide my window and leaning out, hoping the fresh morning air would blow away the tell-tale pink under the powder, and the sun had never seemed so bright, nor the day so full of promise. Monte Carlo was suddenly full of kindliness and charm, the one place in the world that held sincerity. I loved it. Affection overwhelmed me.

I wanted to live there all my life. And I was leaving to-day. This is the last time I shall brush my hair before the looking-glass, the last time I shall clean my teeth into the basin. Never again sleep in that bed. Never more turn off the switch of that electric light. There I was, padding about in a dressing-gown, making a slough of sentiment out of a commonplace hotel bedroom.

'You haven't started a cold, have you?' she said at breakfast.

'No,' I told her, 'I don't think so,' clutching at a straw, for this might serve as an excuse later, if I was over-pink about the eyes.

'I hate hanging about once everything is packed,' she grumbled; 'we ought to have decided on the earlier train. We could get it if we made the effort, and then have longer in Paris. Wire Helen not to meet us, but arrange another rendezvous. I wonder' – she glanced at her watch – 'I suppose they could change the reservations. Anyway it's worth trying. Go down to the office and see.'

'Yes,' I said, a dummy to her moods, going into my bedroom and flinging off my dressing-gown, fastening my inevitable flannel skirt and stretching my home-made jumper over my head. My indifference to her turned to hatred. This was the end then, even my morning must be taken from me. No last half-hour on the terrace, not even ten minutes perhaps to say good-bye. Because she had finished breakfast earlier than she expected, because she was bored. Well then, I would fling away restraint and modesty, I would not be proud any more. I slammed the door of the sitting-room and ran along the passage. I did not wait for the lift, I climbed the stairs, three at a time, up to the third floor. I knew the number of his room, 148, and I hammered at the door, very flushed in the face and breathless.

'Come in,' he shouted, and I opened the door, repenting already, my nerve failing me, for perhaps he had only just woken up, having been late last night, and would be still in bed, tousled in the head and irritable.

He was shaving by the open window, a camel-hair jacket over his pyjamas, and I in my flannel suit and heavy shoes felt clumsy and overdressed. I was merely foolish, when I had felt myself dramatic.

'What do you want,' he said, 'is something the matter?'

'I've come to say good-bye,' I said, 'we're going this morning.'

He stared at me, then put his razor down on the washstand. 'Shut the door,' he said.

I closed it behind me, and stood there, rather self-conscious, my hands hanging by my side. 'What on earth are you talking about?' he asked.

'It's true, we're leaving to-day. We were going by the later train, and now she wants to catch the earlier one, and I was afraid I shouldn't see you again. I felt I must see you before I left, to thank you.'

They tumbled out, the idiotic words, just as I had imagined them. I was stiff and awkward, in a moment I should say he had been ripping.

'Why didn't you tell me about this before?' he said.

'She only decided yesterday. It was all done in a hurry. Her daughter sails for New York on Saturday, and we are going with her. We're joining her in Paris, and going through to Cherbourg.'

'She's taking you with her to New York?'

'Yes, and I don't want to go. I shall hate it; I shall be miserable.'

'Why in heaven's name go with her then?'

'I have to, you know that. I work for a salary. I can't afford to leave her.' He picked up his razor again, and took the soap off his face. 'Sit down,' he said. 'I shan't be long. I'll dress in the bathroom, and be ready in five minutes.'

He took his clothes off the chair and threw them on the bathroom floor, and went inside, slamming the door. I sat down on the bed and began biting my nails. The situation was unreal, and I felt like a lay-figure. I wondered what he was thinking, what he was going to do. I glanced round the room, and it was the room of any man, untidy and impersonal. Lots of shoes, more than were ever needed, and strings of ties. The dressing-table was bare, except for a large bottle of hair-wash and a pair of ivory hair-brushes. No photographs. No snapshots. Nothing like that. Instinctively I had looked for them, thinking there would be one photograph at least beside his bed, or in the middle of the mantelpiece. One large one, in a leather frame. There were only books though, and a box of cigarettes.

He was ready, as he had promised, in five minutes. 'Come down to the terrace while I eat my breakfast,' he said.

I looked at my watch. 'I haven't time,' I told him. 'I ought to be in the office now, changing the reservations.'

'Never mind about that, I've got to talk to you,' he said.

We walked down the corridor and he rang for the lift. He can't realise, I thought, that the early train leaves in about an hour and a half. Mrs. Van Hopper will ring up the office, in a moment, and ask if I am there. We went down in the lift, not talking, and so out to the terrace, where the tables were laid for breakfast.

'What are you going to have?' he said.

'I've had mine already,' I told him, 'and I can only stay four minutes anyway.'

'Bring me coffee, a boiled egg, toast, marmalade, and a tangerine,' he said to the waiter. And he took an emery board out of his pocket and began filing his nails.

'So Mrs. Van Hopper has had enough of Monte Carlo,' he said, 'and now she wants to go home. So do I. She to New York and I to Manderley. Which would you prefer? You can take your choice.'

'Don't make a joke about it, it's unfair,' I said, 'and I think I had better see about those tickets, and say good-bye now.'

'If you think I'm one of the people who try to be funny at breakfast you're wrong,' he said. 'I'm invariably ill-tempered in the early morning. I repeat to you, the choice is open to you. Either you go to America with Mrs. Van Hopper or you come home to Manderley with me.'

'Do you mean you want a secretary or something?'

'No, I'm asking you to marry me, you little fool.'

The waiter came with the breakfast, and I sat with my hands in my lap, watching while he put down the pot of coffee and the jug of milk.

'You don't understand,' I said, when the waiter had gone, 'I'm not the sort of person men marry.'

'What the devil do you mean?' he said, staring at me, laying down his spoon.

I watched a fly settle on the marmalade, and he brushed it away impatiently.

'I'm not sure,' I said slowly. 'I don't think I know how to explain. I don't belong to your sort of world for one thing.'

'What is my world?'

'Well – Manderley. You know what I mean.'

He picked up his spoon again and helped himself to marmalade.

'You are almost as ignorant as Mrs. Van Hopper, and just as unintelligent. What do you know of Manderley? I'm the person to judge that, whether you would belong there or not. You think I ask you this on the spur of the moment, don't you? Because you say you don't want to go to New York. You think I ask you to marry me for the same reason you believed I drove you about in the car, yes, and gave you dinner that first evening. To be kind. Don't you?'

'Yes,' I said.

'One day,' he went on, spreading his toast thick, 'you may realise that philanthropy is not my strongest quality. At the moment I don't think you realise anything at all. You haven't answered my question. Are you going to marry me?'

I don't believe, even in my fiercest moments, I had considered this possibility. I had once, when driving with him and we had been silent for many miles, started a rambling story in my head about him being very ill, delirious I think, and sending for me and I having to nurse him. I had reached the point in my story where I was putting eau-de-Cologne on his head when we arrived at the hotel, and so it finished there. And another time I had imagined living in a lodge in the grounds of Manderley, and how he would visit me sometimes, and sit in front of the fire. This sudden talk of marriage bewildered me, even shocked me I think. It was as though the King asked one. It did not ring true. And he went on eating his marmalade as though everything were natural. In books men knelt to women, and it would be moonlight. Not at breakfast, not like this.

'My suggestion doesn't seem to have gone too well,' he said. 'I'm sorry. I rather thought you loved me. A fine blow to my conceit.'

'I do love you,' I said. 'I love you dreadfully. You've made me very unhappy and I've been crying all night because I thought I should never see you again.'

When I said this I remember he laughed, and stretched his hand to me across the breakfast table. 'Bless you for that,' he said; 'one day, when you reach that exalted age of thirty-five which you told me was your ambition, I'll remind you of this moment. And you won't believe me. It's a pity you have to grow up.'

I was ashamed already, and angry with him for laughing. So women did not make those confessions to men. I had a lot to learn.

'So that's settled, isn't it?' he said, going on with his toast and marmalade; 'instead of being companion to Mrs. Van Hopper you become mine, and your duties will be almost exactly the same. I also like new library books, and flowers in the drawing-room, and bezique after dinner. And someone to pour out my tea. The only difference is that I don't take Taxol, I prefer Eno's, and you must never let me run out of my particular brand of tooth-paste.'

I drummed with my fingers on the table, uncertain of myself and of him. Was he still laughing at me, was it all a joke? He looked up, and saw the anxiety on my face. 'I'm being rather a brute to you, aren't I?' he said; 'this isn't your idea of a proposal. We ought to be in a conservatory, you in a white frock with a rose in your hand, and a violin playing a waltz in the distance. And I should make violent love to you behind a palm tree. You would feel then you were getting your money's worth. Poor darling, what a shame. Never mind, I'll take you to Venice for our honeymoon and we'll hold hands in the gondola. But we won't stay too long, because I want to show you Manderley.'

He wanted to show me Manderley. . . . And suddenly I realised that it would all happen, I would be his wife, we would walk in the garden together, we would stroll down that path in the valley to the shingle beach. I knew how I would stand on the steps after breakfast, looking at the day, throwing crumbs to the birds, and later wander out in a shady hat with long scissors in my hand, and cut flowers for the house. I knew now why I had bought that picture postcard as a child, it was a premonition, a blank step into the future.

He wanted to show me Manderley . . . My mind ran riot then, figures came before me and picture after picture – and all the while he ate his tangerine, giving me a piece now and then, and watching me. We would be in a crowd of people, and he would say, 'I don't think you have met my wife'. Mrs. de Winter. I would be Mrs. de Winter. I considered my name, and the signature on cheques, to tradesmen, and in letters asking people to dinner. I heard myself talking on the telephone 'Why not come down to Manderley next week-end?' People, always a throng of people. 'Oh, but she's simply charming, you must meet her – ' This about me, a whisper on the fringe of a crowd, and I would turn away, pretending I had not heard.

Going down to the lodge with a basket on my arm, grapes and peaches for the old lady who was sick. Her hands stretched out to me, 'The Lord .bless you, Madam, for being so good', and my saying 'Just send up to the house for anything you want'. Mrs. de Winter. I would be Mrs. de Winter. I saw the polished table in the dining-room, and the long candles. Maxim sitting at the end. A party of twenty-four. I had a flower in my hair. Everyone looked towards me, holding up his glass. 'We must drink the health of the bride', and Maxim saying afterwards 'I have never seen you look so lovely'. Great cool rooms, filled with flowers. My bedroom, with a fire in the winter, someone knocking at the door. And a woman comes in, smiling, she is Maxim's sister, and she is saying, 'It's really wonderful how happy you have made him, everyone is so pleased, you are such a success'. Mrs. de Winter. I would be Mrs. de Winter.

'The rest of the tangerine is sour, I shouldn't eat it,' he said, and I stared at him, the words going slowly to my head, then looked down at the fruit on my plate. The quarter was hard and pale. He was right. The tangerine was very sour. I had a sharp, bitter taste in my mouth, and I had only just noticed it.

'Am I going to break the news to Mrs. Van Hopper or are you?' he said.

He was folding up his napkin, pushing back his plate, and I wondered how it was he spoke so casually, as though the matter was of little consequence, a mere adjustment of plans. Whereas to me it was a bombshell, exploding in a thousand fragments.

'You tell her,' I said, 'she'll be so angry.'

We got up from the table, I excited and flushed, trembling already in anticipation. I wondered if he would tell the waiter, take my arm smilingly and say, 'You must congratulate us, Mademoiselle and I are going to be married'. And all the other waiters would hear, would bow to us, would smile, and we would pass into the lounge, a wave of excitement following us, a flutter of expectation. But he said nothing. He left the terrace without a word, and I followed him to the lift. We passed the reception desk and no one even looked at us. The clerk was busy with a sheaf of papers, he was talking over his shoulder to his junior. He does not know, I thought, that I am going to be Mrs. de Winter. I am going to live at Manderley. Manderley will belong to me. We went up in the lift to the first floor, and so along the passage. He took my hand and swung it as we went along. 'Does forty-two seem very old to you?' he said.

'Oh, no,' I told him, quickly, too eagerly perhaps. 'I don't like young men.'

'You've never known any,' he said.

We came to the door of the suite. 'I think I had better deal with this alone,' he said; 'tell me something – do you mind how soon you marry me? You don't want a trousseau, do you, or any of that nonsense? Because the whole thing can be so easily arranged in a few days. Over a desk, with a licence, and then off in the car to Venice or anywhere you fancy.'

'Not in a church?' I asked. 'Not in white, with bridesmaids, and bells, and choir boys? What about your relations, and all your friends?'

'You forget,' he said, 'I had that sort of wedding before.'

We went on standing in front of the door of the suite, and I noticed that the daily paper was still thrust through the letter-box. We had been too busy to read it at breakfast.

'Well,' he said, 'what about it?'

'Of course,' I answered, 'I was thinking for the moment we would be married at home. Naturally I don't expect a church, or people, or anything like that.'

And I smiled at him. I made a cheerful face. 'Won't it be fun?' I said.

He had turned to the door though, and opened it, and we were inside the suite in the little entrance passage.

'Is that you?' called Mrs. Van Hopper from the sitting-room. 'What in the name of Mike have you been doing? I've rang the office three times and they said they hadn't seen you.'

I was seized with a sudden desire to laugh, to cry, to do both, and I had a pain, too, at the pit of my stomach. I wished, for one wild moment, that none of this had happened, that I was alone somewhere, going for a walk, and whistling.

'I'm afraid it's all my fault,' he said, going into the sitting-room, shutting the door behind him, and I heard her exclamation of surprise.

Then I went into my bedroom and sat down by the open window. It was like waiting in the ante-room at a doctor's. I ought to turn over the pages of a magazine, look at photographs that did not matter and read articles I should never remember, until the nurse came, bright and efficient, all humanity washed away by years of disinfectant: 'It's all right, the operation was quite successful. There is no need to worry at all. I should go home and have some sleep.'

The walls of the suite were thick, I could hear no hum of voices. I wondered what he was saying to her, how he phrased his words. Perhaps he said, 'I fell in love with her, you know, the very first time we met. We've been seeing one another every day.' And she in answer, 'Why, Mr. de Winter, it's quite the most romantic thing I've ever heard'. Romantic, that was the word I had tried to remember coming up in the lift. Yes, of course. Romantic. That was what people would say. It was all very sudden and romantic. They suddenly decided to get married and there it was. Such an adventure. I smiled to myself as I hugged my knees on the window-seat, thinking how wonderful it was, how happy I was going to be. I was to marry the man I loved. I was to be Mrs. de Winter. It was foolish to go on having that pain in the pit of my stomach when I was so happy. Nerves of course. Waiting like this; the doctor's ante-room. It would have been better, after all, more natural surely to have gone into the sitting-room hand in hand, laughing, smiling at one another and for him to say 'We're going to be married, we're very much in love'.

In love. He had not said anything yet about being in love. No time perhaps. It was all so hurried at the breakfast table. Marmalade, and coffee. and that tangerine. No time. The tangerine was very bitter. No, he had not said anything about being in love. Just that we would be married. Short and definite, very original. Original proposals were much better. More genuine. Not like other people. Not like younger men who talked nonsense probably, not meaning half they said. Not like younger men being very incoherent, very passionate, swearing impossibilities. Not like him the first time, asking Rebecca. . . . I must not think of that. Put it away. A thought forbidden, prompted by demons. Get thee behind me, Satan. I must never think about that, never, never, never. He loves me, he wants to show me Manderley. Would they ever have done with their talking, would they ever call me into the room?

There was the book of poems lying beside my bed. He had forgotten he had ever lent them to me. They could not mean much to him then. 'Go on,' whispered the demon, 'open the title-page, that's what you want to do, isn't it? Open the title page.' Nonsense, I said, I'm only going to put the book with the rest of the things. I yawned, I wandered to the table beside the bed. I picked up the book. I caught my foot in the flex of the bedside lamp, and stumbled, the book falling from my hands on to the floor. It fell open, at the title page. 'Max from Rebecca.' She was dead, and one must not have thoughts about the dead. They slept in peace, the grass grew over their graves. How alive was her writing though, how full of force. Those curious, sloping letters. The blob of ink. Done yesterday. It was just as if it had been written yesterday. I took my nail scissors from the dressing-case and cut the page, looking over my shoulder like a criminal.

I cut the page right out of the book. I left no jagged edges, and the book looked white and clean when the page was gone. A new book, that had not been touched. I tore the page up in many little fragments and threw them into the waste-paper basket. Then I went and sat on the window-seat again. But I kept thinking of the torn scraps in the basket, and after a moment I had to get up and look in the basket once more. Even now the ink stood up on the fragments thick and black, the writing was not destroyed. I took a box of matches and set fire to the fragments. The flame had a lovely light, staining the paper, curling the edges, making the slanting writing impossible to distinguish. The fragments fluttered to grey ashes. The letter R was the last to go, it twisted in the flame, it curled outwards for a moment, becoming larger than ever. Then it crumpled too; the flame destroyed it. It was not ashes even, it was feathery dust. . . . I went and washed my hands in the basin. I felt better, much better. I had the clean, new feeling that one has when the calendar is hung on the wall at the beginning of the year. January the 1st. I was aware of the same freshness, the same gay confidence. The door opened and he came into the room.

'All's well,' he said; 'shock made her speechless at first, but she's beginning to recover, so I'm going downstairs to the office, to make certain she will catch the first train. For a moment she wavered, I think she had hopes of acting witness at the wedding, but I was very firm. Go and talk to her.'

He said nothing about being glad, about being happy. He did not take my arm and go into the sitting-room with me. He smiled, and waved his hand, and went off down the corridor alone. I went to Mrs. Van Hopper, uncertain, rather self-conscious, like a maid who has handed in her notice through a friend.

She was standing by the window, smoking a cigarette, an odd, dumpy little figure I should not see again, her coat stretched tight over her large breasts, her ridiculous hat perched sideways on her head.

'Well,' she said, her voice dry and hard, not the voice she would have used to him, 'I suppose I've got to hand it to you for a double-time worker. Still waters certainly run deep in your case. How did you manage it?'

I did not know what to answer. I did not like her smile.

'It was a lucky thing for you I had the influenza,' she said. 'I realise now how you spent your days, and why you were so forgetful. Tennis lessons my eye. You might have told me, you know.'

'I'm sorry,' I said.

She looked at me curiously, she ran her eyes over my figure. 'And he tells me he wants to marry you in a few days. Lucky again for you that you haven't a family to ask questions. Well, it's nothing to do with me any more, I wash my hands of the whole affair. I rather wonder what his friends will think, but I suppose that's up to him. You realise he's years older than you?'

'He's only forty-two,' I said, 'and I'm old for my age.'

She laughed, she dropped cigarette ash on the floor. 'You certainly are.' She went on looking at me in a way she had never done before. Appraising me, running her eyes over my points like a judge at a cattle show. There was something inquisitive about her eyes, something unpleasant.

'Tell me,' she said, intimate, a friend to a friend, 'have you been doing anything you shouldn't?'

She was like Blaize, the dressmaker, who had offered me that ten per cent.

'I don't know what you mean,' I said.

She laughed, she shrugged her shoulders. 'Oh, well . . . never mind. But I always said English girls were dark horses, for all their hockey-playing attitude. So I'm supposed to travel to Paris alone, and leave you here while your beau gets a marriage licence? I notice he doesn't ask me to the wedding.'

'I don't think he wants anyone, and anyway you would have sailed,' I said.

'H'm, h'm,' she said. She took out her vanity case and began powdering her nose. 'I suppose you really do know your own mind,' she went on; 'after all, the whole thing hàs been very hurried, hasn't it? A matter of a few weeks. I don't suppose he's too easy, and you'll have to adapt yourself to his ways. You've led an extremely sheltered life up to now, you know, and you can't say that I've run you off your feet. You will have your work cut out as mistress of Manderley. To be perfectly frank, my dear, I simply can't see you doing it.'

Her words sounded like the echo of my own an hour before.

'You haven't the experience,' she continued, 'you don't know that milieu. You can scarcely string two sentences together at my bridge teas, what are you going to say to all his friends? The Manderley parties were famous when she was alive. Of course he's told you all about them?'

I hesitated, but she went on, thank heaven, not waiting for my answer.

'Naturally one wants you to be happy, and I grant you he's a very attractive creature but – well, I'm sorry; and personally I think you are making a big mistake – one you will bitterly regret.'

She put down the box of powder, and looked at me over her shoulder. Perhaps she was being sincere at last, but I did not want that sort of honesty. I did not say anything. I looked sullen, perhaps, for she shrugged her shoulders and wandered to the looking-glass, straightening her little mushroom hat. I was glad she was going, glad I should not see her again. I grudged the months I had spent with her, employed by her, taking her money, trotting in her wake like a shadow, drab and dumb. Of course I was inexperienced, of course I was idiotic, shy and young. I knew all that. She did not have to tell me. I supposed her attitude was deliberate, and for some odd feminine reason she resented this marriage, her scale of values had received a shock.

Well, I would not care, I would forget her and her barbed words. A new confidence had been born in me when I burnt that page and scattered the fragments. The past would not exist for either of us, we were starting afresh, he and I. The past had blown away like the ashes in the waste paper basket. I was going to be Mrs. de Winter. I was going to live at Manderley.

Soon she would be gone, rattling alone in the wagon-lit without me, and he and I would be together in the dining-room of the hotel, lunching at the same table, planning the future. The brink of a big adventure. Perhaps, once she had gone, he would talk to me at last, about loving me, about being happy. Up to now there had been no time, and anyway those things are not easily said, they must wait their moment. I looked up, and caught her reflection in the looking-glass. She was watching me, a little tolerant smile on her lips. I thought she was going to be generous after all, hold out her hand and wish me luck, give me encouragement and tell me that everything was going to be all right. But she went on smiling, twisting a stray hair into place beneath her hat.

'Of course,' she said, 'you know why he is marrying you, don't you? You haven't flattered yourself he's in love with you? The fact is that empty house got on his nerves to such an extent he nearly went off his head. He admitted as much before you came into the room. He just can't go on living there alone. . . .'

Chapter Seven

We came to Manderley in early May, arriving so Maxim said, with the first swallows and the bluebells. It would be the best moment, before the full flush of summer, and in the valley the azaleas would be prodigal of scent, and the blood-red rhododendrons in bloom. We motored, I remember, leaving London in the morning in a heavy shower of rain, coming to Manderley about five o'clock, in time for tea. I can see myself now, unsuitably dressed as usual, although a bride of seven weeks, in a tan-coloured stockinette frock, a small fur known as a stone marten round my neck, and over all a shapeless mackintosh, far too big for me and dragging to my ankles. It was, I thought, a gesture to the weather, and the length added inches to my height. I clutched a pair of gauntlet gloves in my hands, and carried a large leather handbag.

'This is London rain,' said Maxim when we left, 'you wait, the sun will be shining for you when we come to Manderley'; and he was right, for the clouds left us at Exeter, they rolled away behind us, leaving a great blue sky above our heads and a white road in front of us.

I was glad to see the sun, for in superstitious fashion I looked upon rain as an omen of ill-will, and the leaden skies of London had made me silent.

'Feeling better?' said Maxim, and I smiled at him, taking his hand, thinking how easy it was for him, going to his own home, wandering into the hall, picking up letters, ringing a bell for tea, and I wondered how much he guessed of my nervousness, and whether his question 'Feeling better?' meant that he understood. 'Never mind, we'll soon be there. I expect you want your tea,' he said, and he let go my hand because we had reached a bend in the road and must slow down.

I knew then that he had mistaken my silence for fatigue, and it had not occurred to him I dreaded this arrival at Manderley as much as I had longed for it in theory. Now the moment was upon me I wished it delayed. I wanted to draw up at some wayside inn and stay there, in a coffee-room, by an impersonal fire. I wanted to be a traveller on the road, a bride in love with her husband. Not myself coming to Manderley for the first time, the wife of Maxim de Winter. We passed many friendly villages where the cottage windows had a kindly air. A woman, holding a baby in her arms, smiled at me from a doorway, while a man clanked across a road to a well, carrying a pail.

I wished we could have been one with them, perhaps their neighbours, and that Maxim could lean over a cottage gate in the evenings, smoking a pipe, proud of a very tall hollyhock he had grown himself, while I bustled in my kitchen, clean as a pin, laying the table for supper. There would be an alarm clock on the dresser ticking loudly, and a row of shining plates, while after supper Maxim would read his paper, boots on the fender, and I reach for a great pile of mending in the dresser drawer. Surely it would be peaceful and steady, that way of living, and easier, too, demanding no set standard?

'Only two miles further,' said Maxim; 'you see that great belt of trees on the brow of the hill there, sloping to the valley, with a scrap of sea beyond? That's Manderley, in there. Those are the woods.'

I forced a smile, and did not answer him, aware now of a stab of panic, an uneasy sickness that could not be controlled. Gone was my glad excitement, vanished my happy pride. I was like a child brought to her first school, or a little untrained maid who has never left home before, seeking a situation. Any measure of self-possession I had gained hitherto, during the brief seven weeks of marriage, was like a rag now, fluttering before the wind; it seemed to me that even the most elementary knowledge of behaviour was unknown to me now, I should not know my right hand from my left, whether to stand or sit, what spoons and forks to use at dinner.

'I should shed that mackintosh,' he said, glancing down at me, 'it has not rained down here at all, and put your funny little fur straight. Poor lamb, I've bustled you down here like this, and you probably ought to have bought a lot of clothes in London.'

'It doesn't matter to me, as long as you don't mind,' I said.

'Most women think of nothing but clothes,' he said absently, and turning a corner we came to a cross-road, and the beginning of a high wall.

'Here we are,' he said, a new note of excitement in his voice, and I gripped the leather seat of the car with my two hands.

The road curved, and before us, on the left, were two high iron gates beside a lodge, open wide to the long drive beyond. As we drove through I saw faces peering through the dark window of the lodge, and a child ran round from the back, staring curiously. I shrank back against the seat, my heart beating quickly, knowing why the faces were at the window, and why the child stared.

They wanted to see what I was like. I could imagine them now, talking excitedly, laughing in the little kitchen. 'Only caught sight of the top of her hat,' they would say, 'she wouldn't show her face. Oh, well, we'll know by to-morrow. Word will come from the house.' Perhaps he guessed something of my shyness at last for he took my hand, and kissed it, and laughed a little, even as he spoke.

'You mustn't mind if there's a certain amount of curiosity,' he said, 'everyone will want to know what you are like. They have probably talked of nothing else for weeks. You've only got to be yourself and they will all adore you. And you don't have to worry about the house, Mrs. Danvers does everything. Just leave it all to her. She'll be stiff with you at first, I dare say, she's an extraordinary character, but you mustn't let it worry you. It's just her manner. See those shrubs? It's like a blue wall along here when the hydrangeas are in bloom.'

I did not answer him, for I was thinking of that self who long ago bought a picture post-card in a village shop, and came out into the bright sunlight twisting it in her hands, pleased with her purchase, thinking 'This will do for my album, "Manderley", what a lovely name'. And now I belonged here, this was my home, I would write letters to people saying, 'We shall be down at Manderley all the summer, you must come and see us', and I would walk along this drive, strange and unfamiliar to me now, with perfect knowledge, conscious of every twist and turn, marking and approving where the gardeners had worked, here a cutting back of the shrubs, there a lopping of a branch, calling at the lodge by the iron gates on some friendly errand, saying, 'Well, how's the leg to-day?' while the old woman, curious no longer, bade me welcome to her kitchen. I envied Maxim, careless and at ease, and the little smile on his lips which meant he was happy to be coming home.

It seemed remote to me, and far too distant, the time when I too should smile and be at ease, and I wished it could come quickly, that I could be old even, with grey hair, and slow of step, having lived here many years, anything but the timid, foolish creature I felt myself to be.

The gates had shut to with a crash behind us, the dusty high-road was out of sight, and I became aware that this was not the drive I had imagined would be Manderley's, this was not a broad and spacious thing of gravel, flanked with neat turf at either side, kept smooth with rake and brush.

This drive twisted and turned as a serpent, scarce wider in places than a path, and above our heads was a great colonnade of trees, whose branches nodded and intermingled with one another, making an archway for us, like the roof of a church. Even the midday sun would not penetrate the interlacing of those green leaves, they were too thickly entwined, one with another, and only little flickering patches of warm light would come in intermittent waves to dapple the drive with gold. It was very silent, very still. On the high-road there had been a gay west wind blowing in my face, making the grass on the hedges dance in unison, but here there was no wind. Even the engine of the car had taken on a new note, throbbing low, quieter than before. As the drive descended to the valley so the trees came in upon us, great beeches with lovely smooth white stems, lifting their myriad branches to one another, and other trees, trees I could not name, coming close, so close that I could touch them with my hands. On we went, over a little bridge that spanned a narrow stream, and still this drive that was no drive twisted and turned like an enchanted ribbon through the dark and silent woods, penetrating even deeper to the very heart surely of the forest itself, and still there was no clearing, no space to hold a house.

The length of it began to nag at my nerves, it must be this turn, I thought, or round that further bend, but as I leant forward in my seat I was forever disappointed, there was no house, no field, no broad and friendly garden, nothing but the silence and deep woods. The lodge gates were a memory, and the high-road something belonging to another time, another world.

Suddenly I saw a clearing in the dark drive ahead, and a patch of sky, and in a moment the dark trees had thinned, the nameless shrubs had disappeared, and on either side of us was a wall of colour, blood-red, reaching far above our heads. We were amongst the rhododendrons. There was something bewildering, even shocking, about the suddenness of their discovery. The woods had not prepared me for them. They startled me with their crimson faces, massed one upon the other in incredible profusion, showing no leaf, no twig, nothing but the slaughterous red, luscious and fantastic, unlike any rhododendron plant I had seen before.

I glanced at Maxim. He was smiling. 'Like them?' he said.

I told him 'Yes', a little breathlessly, uncertain whether I was speaking the truth or not, for to me a rhododendron was a homely, domestic thing, strictly conventional, mauve or pink in colour, standing one beside the other in a neat round bed. And these were monsters, rearing to the sky, massed like a battalion, too beautiful I thought, too powerful, they were not plants at all.

We were not far from the house now, I saw the drive broaden to the sweep I had expected, and the the blood-red wall still flanking us on either side, we turned the last corner, and so came to Manderley. Yes, there it was, the Manderley I had expected, the Manderley of my picture post-card long ago. A thing of grace and beauty, exquisite and faultless, lovelier even than I had ever dreamed, built in its hollow of smooth grass-land and mossy lawns, the terraces sloping to the gardens, and the gardens to the sea. As we drove up to the wide stone steps and stopped before the open door, I saw through one of the mullioned windows that the hall was full of people, and I heard Maxim swear under his breath. 'Damn that woman,' he said, 'she knows perfectly well I did not want this sort of thing,' and he put on the brakes with a jerk.

'What's the matter?' I said. 'Who are all those people?'

'I'm afraid you will have to face it now,' he said, in irritation. 'Mrs. Danvers has collected the whole damned staff in the house and on the estate to welcome us. It's all right, you won't have to say anything, I'll do it all.'

I fumbled for the handle of the door, feeling slightly sick, and cold now too from the long drive, and as I fumbled with the catch the butler came down the steps, followed by a footman, and he opened the door for me.

He was old, he had a kind face, and I smiled up at him, holding out my hand, but I don't think he could have seen, for he took the rug instead, and my small dressing-case, and turned to Maxim, helping me from the car at the same time.

'Well, here we are, Frith,' said Maxim, taking off his gloves, 'it was raining when we left London. You don't seem to have had it here. Everyone well?'

'Yes, sir, thank you, sir. No, we have had a dry month on the whole. Glad to see you home, and hope you have been keeping well. And Madam too.'

'Yes, we are both well, thank you, Frith. Rather tired from the drive, and wanting our tea. I didn't expect this business.' He jerked his head to the hall.

'Mrs. Danvers's orders, sir,' said the man, his face expressionless.

'I might have guessed it,' said Maxim abruptly, 'come on,' he turned to me, 'it won't take long, and then you shall have your tea.'

We went together up the flight of steps, Frith and the footman following with the rug and my mackintosh, and I was aware of a little pain at the pit of my stomach, and a nervous contraction of my throat.

I can close my eyes now, and look back on it, and see myself as I must have been, standing on the threshold of the house, a slim, awkward figure in my stockinette dress, clutching in my sticky hands a pair of gauntlet gloves. I can see the great stone hall, the wide doors open to the library, the Peter Lelys and the Vandykes on the walls, the exquisite staircase leading to the minstrel's gallery, and there, ranged one behind the other in the hall, over-flowing to the stone passages beyond, and to the dining-room, a sea of faces, open-mouthed and curious, gazing at me as though they were the watching crowd about the block, and I the victim with my hands behind my back. Someone advanced from the sea of faces, someone tall and gaunt, dressed in deep black, whose prominent cheek-bones and great, hollow eyes gave her a skull's face, parchment-white, set on a skeleton's frame.

She came towards me, and I held out my hand, envying her for her dignity and her composure; but when she took my hand hers was limp and heavy, deathly cold, and it lay in mine like a lifeless thing.

'This is Mrs. Danvers,' said Maxim, and she began to speak, still leaving that dead hand in mine, her hollow eyes never leaving my eyes, so that my own wavered and would not meet hers, and as they did so her hand moved in mine, the life returned to it, and I was aware of a sensation of discomfort and of shame.

I cannot remember her words now, but I know that she bade me welcome to Manderley, in the name of herself and the staff, a stiff, conventional speech rehearsed for the occasion, spoken in a voice as cold and lifeless as her hands had been. When she had finished she waited, as though for a reply, and I remember blushing scarlet, stammering some sort of thanks in return, and dropping both my gloves in my confusion. She stooped to pick them up, and as she handed them to me I saw a little smile of scorn upon her lips, and I guessed at once she considered me ill-bred. Something, in the expression of her face, gave me a feeling of unrest, and even when she had stepped back, and taken her place amongst the rest, I could see that black figure standing out alone, individual and apart, and for all her silence I knew her eye to be upon me. Maxim took my arm and made a little speech of thanks, perfectly easy and free from embarrassment, as though the making of it was no effort to him at all, and then he bore me off to the library to tea, closing the doors behind us, and we were alone again.

Two cocker spaniels came from the fireside to greet us. They pawed at Maxim, their long, silken ears strained back with affection, their noses questing his hands, and then they left him and came to me, sniffing at my heels, rather uncertain, rather suspicious. One was the mother, blind in one eye, and soon she had enough of me, and took herself with a grunt to the fire again, but Jasper, the younger, put his nose into my hand, and laid a chin upon my knee, his eyes deep with meaning, his tail a-thump when I stroked his silken ears.

I felt better when I had taken my hat off, and my wretched little fur, and thrown them both beside my gloves and my bag on the window-seat. It was a deep, comfortable room, with books lining the walls to the ceiling, the sort of room a man would move from never, did he live alone, solid chairs beside a great open fire-place, baskets for the two dogs in which I felt they never sat, for the hollows in the chairs had tell-tale marks. The long windows looked out upon the lawns, and beyond the lawns to the distant shimmer of the sea.

There was an old quiet smell about the room, as though the air in it was little changed, for all the sweet lilac scent and the roses brought to it throughout the early summer. Whatever air came to this room, whether from the garden or from the sea, would lose its first freshness, becoming part of the unchanging room itself, one with the books, musty and never read, one with the scrolled ceiling, the dark panelling, the heavy curtains.

It was an ancient mossy smell, the smell of a silent church where services are seldom held, where rusty lichen grows upon the stones and ivy tendrils creep to the very windows. A room for peace, a room for meditation.

Soon tea was brought to us, a stately little performance enacted by Frith and the young footman, in which I played no part until they had gone, and while Maxim glanced through his great pile of letters I played with two dripping crumpets, crumbled cake with my hands, and swallowed my scalding tea.

Now and again he looked up at me and smiled, and then returned to his letters, the accumulation of the last months I supposed, and I thought how little I knew of his life here at Manderley, of how it went, day by day, of the people he knew, of his friends, men and women, of what bills he paid, what orders he gave about his household. The last weeks had gone so swiftly, and I – driving by his side through France and Italy – thought only of how I loved him, seeing Venice with his eyes, echoing his words, asking no questions of the past and future, content with the little glory of the living present.

For he was gayer than I had thought, more tender than I had dreamed, youthful and ardent in a hundred happy ways, not the Maxim I had first met, not the stranger who sat alone at the table in the restaurant, staring before him, wrapped in his secret self. My Maxim laughed and sang, threw stones into the water, took my hand, wore no frown between his eyes, carried no burden on his shoulder. I knew him as a lover, as a friend, and during those weeks I had forgotten that he had a life, orderly, methodical, a life which must be taken up again, continued as before, making vanished weeks a brief discarded holiday.

I watched him read his letters, saw him frown at one, smile at another, dismiss the next with no expression, and but for the grace of God, I thought, my letter would be lying there, written from New York, and he would read it in the same indifferent fashion, puzzled at first perhaps by the signature, and then tossing it with a yawn to the pile of others in the basket, reaching for his cup of tea. The knowledge of this chilled me, how narrow a chance had stood between me and what might-have-been, for he would have sat there to his tea, as he sat now, continuing his home life as he would in any case, and perhaps he would not have thought of me much, not with regret anyway, while I, in New York, playing bridge with Mrs. Van Hopper would wait day after day for a letter that never came.

I leant back in my chair, glancing about the room, trying to instil into myself some measure of confidence, some genuine realisation that I was here, at Manderley, the house of the picture post-card, the Manderley that was famous. I had to teach myself that all this was mine now, mine as much as his, the deep chair I was sitting in, that mass of books stretching to the ceiling, the pictures on the walls, the gardens, the woods, the Manderley I had read about, all of this was mine now because I was married to Maxim.

We should grow old here together, we should sit like this to our tea as old people, Maxim and I, with other dogs, the successors of these, and the library would wear the same ancient musty smell that it did now. It would know a period of glorious shabbiness and wear when the boys were young – our boys – for I saw them sprawling on the sofa with muddy boots, bringing with them always a litter of rods, and cricket bats, great clasp-knives, bows and arrows.

On the table there, polished now and plain, an ugly case would stand containing butterflies and moths, and another one with birds' eggs, wrapped in cotton wool. 'Not all this junk in here,' I would say, 'take them to the schoolroom, darlings', and they would run off, shouting, calling to one another, but the little one staying behind, pottering on his own, quieter than the others.

My vision was disturbed by the opening of the door, and Frith came in with the footman to clear the tea. 'Mrs. Danvers wondered, Madam, whether you would like to see your room,' he said to me, when the tea had been taken away.

Maxim glanced up from his letters. 'What sort of job have they made of the east wing?' he said.

'Very nice indeed, sir, it seems to me; the men made a mess when they were working, of course, and for a time Mrs. Danvers was rather afraid it would not be finished by your return. But they cleared out last Monday. I should imagine you would be very comfortable there, sir, it's a lot lighter of course on that side of the house.'

'Have you been making alterations?' I asked.

'Oh, nothing much,' said Maxim briefly, 'only redecorating and painting the suite in the east wing, which I thought we would use for ours. As Frith says it's much more cheerful on that side of the house, and it has a lovely view of the rose-garden. It was the visitor's wing when my mother was alive. I'll just finish these letters and then I'll come up and join you. Run along and make friends with Mrs. Danvers, it's a good opportunity.'

I got up slowly, my old nervousness returning, and went out into the hall. I wished I could have waited for him, and then, taking his arm, seen the rooms together. I did not want to go alone, with Mrs. Danvers. How vast the great hall looked now that it was empty. My feet rang on the flagged stones, echoing to the ceiling, and I felt guilty at the sound, as one does in church, self-conscious, aware of the same constraint. My feet made a stupid pitter-patter as I walked, and I thought that Frith, with his felt soles, must have thought me foolish.

'It's very big, isn't it?' I said, too brightly, too forced, a school-girl still, but he answered me in all solemnity. 'Yes, Madam, Manderley is a big place. Not so big as some, of course, but big enough. This was the old banqueting hall, in old days. It is used still on great occasions, such as a big dinner, or a ball. And the public are admitted here, you know, once a week.'

'Yes,' I said, still aware of my loud footsteps, feeling, as I followed him, that he considered me as he would one of the public visitors, and I behaved like a visitor too, glancing politely to right and left, taking in the weapons on the wall, and the pictures, touching the carved staircase with my hands.

A black figure stood waiting for me at the head of the stairs, the hollow eyes watching me intently from the white skull's face. I looked round for the solid Frith, but he had passed along the hall and into the further corridor.

I was alone now with Mrs. Danvers. I went up the great stairs towards her, and she waited motionless, her hands folded before her, her eyes never leaving my face. I summoned a smile, which was not returned, nor did I blame her, for there was no purpose to the smile, it was a silly thing, bright and artificial. 'I hope I haven't kept you waiting,' I said.

'It's for you to make your own time, Madam,' she answered. 'I'm here to carry out your orders,' and then she turned, through the archway of the gallery, to the corridor beyond. We went along a broad, carpeted passage, and then turned left, through an oak door, and down a narrow flight of stairs and up a corresponding flight, and so to another door. This she flung open, standing aside to let me pass, and I came to a little ante-room, or boudoir, furnished with a sofa, chairs, and writing-desk, which opened out to a large double bedroom with wide windows, and a bathroom beyond. I went at once to the window, and looked out. The rose-garden lay below, and the eastern part of the terrace, while beyond the rose-garden rose a smooth grass bank, stretching to the near woods.

'You can't see the sea from here then,' I said, turning to Mrs. Danvers.

'No, not from this wing,' she answered, 'you can't even hear it, either. You would not know the sea was anywhere near, not from this wing.'

She spoke in a peculiar way, as though something lay behind her words, and she laid an emphasis on the words, 'this wing', as if suggesting that the suite where we stood now held some inferiority.

'I'm sorry about that, I like the sea,' I said.

She did not answer, she just went on staring at me, her hands folded before her.

'However, it's a very charming room,' I said, 'and I'm sure I shall be comfortable. I understand that it's been done up for our return.'

'Yes,' she said.

'What was it like before?' I asked.

'It had a mauve paper, and different hangings; Mr. de Winter did not think it very cheerful. It was never much used, except for occasional visitors. But Mr. de Winter gave special orders in his letter that you would have this room.'

'Then this was not his bedroom originally?' I said.

'No, Madam, he's never used the rooms in this wing before.'

'Oh,' I said, 'he didn't tell me that,' and I wandered to the dressing-table and began combing my hair. My things were already unpacked, my brushes and comb upon the tray. I was glad Maxim had given me a set of brushes, and that they were laid out there, upon the dressing-table, for Mrs. Danvers to see. They were new, they had cost money, I need not be ashamed of them.

'Alice has unpacked for you and will look after you until your maid arrives,' said Mrs. Danvers. I smiled at her again, I put down the brush upon the dressing-table.

'I don't have a maid,' I said awkwardly, 'I'm sure Alice, if she is the housemaid, will look after me all right.'

She wore the same expression that she had done on our first meeting, when I dropped my gloves so gauchely on the floor.

'I'm afraid that would not do for very long,' she said, 'it's usual, you know, for ladies in your position, to have a personal maid.'

I flushed, and reached for my brush again. There was a sting in her words I understood too well. 'If you think it necessary perhaps you would see about it for me,' I said, avoiding her eyes, 'some young girl perhaps, wanting to train.'

'If you wish,' she said. 'It's for you to say.'

There was silence between us, I wished she would go away. I wondered why she must go on standing there, watching me, her hands folded on her black dress.

'I suppose you have been at Manderley for many years,' I said, making a fresh effort, 'longer than anyone else?'

'Not so long as Frith,' she said, and I thought how lifeless her voice was, and cold, like her hand when it had lain in mine; 'Frith was here when the old gentleman was living, when Mr. de Winter was a boy.'

'I see,' I said, 'so you did not come till after that?'

'No,' she said, 'not till after that.'

Once more I glanced up at her, and once more I met her eyes, dark and sombre, in that white face of hers, instilling into me, I knew not why, a strange feeling of disquiet, of foreboding. I tried to smile, and could not, I found myself held by those eyes, that had no light, no flicker of sympathy towards me.

'I came here when the first Mrs. de Winter was a bride,' she said, and her voice, which had hitherto, as I said, been dull and toneless, was harsh now with unexpected animation, with life and meaning, and there was a spot of colour on the gaunt cheek bones.

The change was so sudden that I was shocked, and a little scared. I did not know what to do, or what to say. It was as though she had spoken words that were forbidden, words that she had hidden within herself for a long time and now would be repressed no longer. Still her eyes never left my face, they looked upon me with a curious mixture of pity and of scorn, until I felt myself to be even younger and more untutored to the ways of life than I had believed.

I could see she despised me, marking with all the snobbery of her class that I was no great lady, that I was humble, shy, and diffident. Yet there was something beside scorn in those eyes of hers, something surely of positive dislike, or actual malice?

I had to say something, I could not go on sitting there, playing with my hair brush, letting her see how much I feared and mistrusted her.

'Mrs. Danvers,' I heard myself saying, 'I hope we shall be friends and come to understand one another. You must have patience with me, you know, because this sort of life is new to me, I've lived rather differently. And I do want to make a success of it, and above all to make Mr. de Winter happy. I know I can leave all household arrangements to you, Mr. de Winter said so, and you must just run things as they have always been run, I shan't want to make any changes.'

I stopped, a little breathless, still uncertain of myself and whether I was saying the right thing, and when I looked up again I saw that she had moved, and was standing with her hand on the handle of the door.

'Very good,' she said; 'I hope I shall do everything to your satisfaction. The house has been in my charge now for more than a year, and Mr. de Winter has never complained. It was very different of course when the late Mrs. de Winter was alive, there was a lot of entertaining then, a lot of parties, and though I managed for her she liked to supervise things herself.'

Once again I had the impression that she chose her words with care, that she was feeling her way, as it were, into my mind, and watching for the effect upon my face.

'I would rather leave it to you,' I repeated, 'much rather,' and into her face came the same expression I had noticed before, when first I had shaken hands with her in the hall, a look surely of derision, of definite contempt. She knew that I would never withstand her, and that I feared her too.

'Can I do anything more for you?' she said, and I pretended to glance round the room. 'No,' I said. 'No, I think I have everything. I shall be very comfortable here. You have made the room so charming' – this last a final crawling sop to win her approval. She shrugged her shoulders, and still she did not smile. 'I only followed out Mr. de Winter's instructions,' she said.

She hesitated by the doorway, her hand on the handle of the open door. It was as though she still had something to say to me, and could not decide upon the words, yet waited there, for me to give her opportunity.

I wished she would go, she was like a shadow standing there, watching me, appraising me with her hollow eyes, set in that dead skull's face.

'If you find anything not to your liking you will tell me at once?' she asked.

'Yes,' I said. 'Yes, of course, Mrs. Danvers,' but I knew this was not what she had meant to say, and silence fell between us once again.

'If Mr. de Winter asks for his big wardrobe,' she said suddenly, 'you must tell him it was impossible to move. We tried, but we could not get it through these narrow doorways. These are smaller rooms than those in the west wing. If he doesn't like the arrangement of this suite he must tell me. It was difficult to know how to furnish these rooms.'

'Please don't worry, Mrs. Danvers,' I said, 'I'm sure he will be pleased with everything. But I'm sorry it's given you so much trouble. I had no idea he was having rooms re-decorated and furnished, he shouldn't have bothered. I'm sure I should have been just as happy and comfortable in the west wing.'

She looked at me curiously, and began twisting the handle of the door. 'Mr. de Winter said you would prefer to be on this side,' she said, 'the rooms in the west wing are very old. The bedroom in the big suite is twice as large as this, a very beautiful room too, with a scrolled ceiling. The tapestry chairs are very valuable, and so is the carved mantelpiece. It's the most beautiful room in the house. And the windows look down across the lawns to the sea.'

I felt uncomfortable, a little shy. I did not know why she must speak with such an undercurrent of resentment, implying as she did at the same time that this room, where I found myself to be installed, was something inferior, not up to Manderley standard, a second-rate room, as it were, for a second-rate person.

'I suppose Mr. de Winter keeps the most beautiful room to show the public,' I said. She went on twisting the handle of the door, and then looked up at me again, watching my eyes, hesitating before replying, and when she spoke her voice was quieter even, and more toneless, than it had been before.

'The bedrooms are never shown to the public,' she said, 'only the hall and the gallery, and the rooms below.' She paused an instant, feeling me with her eyes. 'They used to live in the west wing and use those rooms when Mrs. de Winter was alive. That big room, I was telling you about, that looked down to the sea, was Mrs. de Winter's bedroom.'

Then I saw a shadow flit across her face, and she drew back against the wall, effacing herself, as a step sounded outside and Maxim came into the room.

'How is it?' he said to me. 'All right? Do you think you'll like it?'

He looked round with enthusiasm, pleased as a schoolboy. 'I always thought this a most attractive room,' he said. 'It was wasted all those years as a guest-room, but I always thought it had possibilities. You've made a great success of it, Mrs. Danvers, I give you full marks.'

'Thank you, sir,' she said, her face expressionless, and then she turned, and went out of the room, closing the door softly behind her.

Maxim went and leant out of the window. 'I love the rose-garden,' he said; 'one of the first things I remember is walking after my mother, on very small, unsteady legs, while she picked off the dead heads of the roses. There's something peaceful and happy about this room, and it's quiet too. You could never tell you were within five minutes of the sea, from this room.'

'That's what Mrs. Danvers said,' I told him.

He came away from the window, he prowled about the room, touching things, looking at the pictures, opening wardrobes, fingering my clothes, already unpacked.

'How did you get on with old Danvers?' he said abruptly.

I turned away, and began combing my hair again before the looking glass. 'She seems just a little bit stiff,' I said, after a moment or two, 'perhaps she thought I was going to interfere with the running of the house.'

'I don't think she would mind your doing that,' he said. I looked up and saw him watching my reflection in the looking-glass, and then he turned away and went over to the window again, whistling quietly, under his breath, rocking backwards and forwards on his heels.

'Don't mind her,' he said, 'she's an extraordinary character in many ways, and possibly not very easy for another woman to get on with. You mustn't worry about it. If she really makes herself a nuisance we'll get rid of her. But she's efficient, you know, and will take all housekeeping worries off your hands. I dare say she's a bit of a bully to the staff. She doesn't dare bully me though. I'd have given her the sack long ago if she had tried.'

'I expect we shall get on very well when she knows me better,' I said quickly, 'after all, it's natural enough that she should resent me a bit at first.'

'Resent you, why resent you? What the devil do you mean?' he said.

He turned from the window, frowning, an odd, half angry expression on his face. I wondered why he should mind, and wished I had said something else.

'I mean, it must be much easier for a housekeeper to look after a man alone,' I said. 'I dare say she had got into the way of doing it, and perhaps she was afraid I should be very overbearing.'

'Overbearing, my God . . .' he began, 'if you think . . .' and then he stopped, and came across to me, and kissed me on the top of my head.

'Let's forget about Mrs. Danvers,' he said; 'she doesn't interest me very much I'm afraid. Come along, and let me show you something of Manderley.'

I did not see Mrs. Danvers again that evening, and we did not talk about her any more. I felt happier, when I had dismissed her from my thoughts, less of an interloper, and as we wandered about the rooms downstairs, and looked at the pictures, and Maxim put his arm round my shoulder, I began to feel more like the self I wanted to become, the self I had pictured in my dreams, who made Manderley her home.

My footsteps no longer sounded foolish on the stone flags of the hall, for Maxim's nailed shoes made far more noise than mine, and the pattering feet of the two dogs was a comfortable, pleasing note.

I was glad, too, because it was the first evening, and we had only been back a little while, and the showing of the pictures had taken time, when Maxim, looking at the clock, said it was too late to change for dinner, so that I was spared the embarrassment of Alice, the maid, asking what I should wear, and of her helping me to dress, and myself walking down that long flight of stairs to the hall, cold, with bare shoulders, in a dress that Mrs. Van Hopper had given me because it did not suit her daughter. I had dreaded the formality of dinner in that austere dining-room, and now, because of the little fact that we had not changed, it was quite all right, quite easy, just the same as when we had dined together in restaurants. I was comfortable in my stockinette dress, I laughed and talked about things we had seen in Italy and France, we even had the snapshots on the table, and Frith and the footman were impersonal people, as the waiters had been, they did not stare at me as Mrs. Danvers had done.

We sat in the library after dinner, and presently the curtains were drawn, and more logs thrown on to the fire, it was cool for May, I was thankful for the warmth that came from the steady burning logs.

It was new for us to sit together like this, after dinner, for in Italy we had wandered about, walked or driven, gone into little cafés, leant over bridges. Maxim made instinctively now for the chair on the left of the open fireplace, and stretched out his hand for the papers. He settled one of the broad cushions behind his head, and lit a cigarette. 'This is his routine,' I thought, 'this is what he always does, this has been his custom for years.'

He did not look at me, he went on reading his paper, contented, comfortable, having assumed his way of living, the master of his house. And as I sat there, brooding, my chin in my hands, fondling the soft ears of one of the spaniels, it came to me that I was not the first one to lounge there in possession of the chair, someone had been before me, had surely left an imprint of her person on the cushions, and on the arm where her hand had rested. Another one had poured the coffee from that same silver coffee pot, had placed the cup to her lips, had bent down to the dog, even as I was doing.

Unconsciously I shivered, as though someone had opened the door behind me, and let a draught into the room. I was sitting in Rebecca's chair, I was leaning against Rebecca's cushion, and the dog had come to me and laid his head upon my knee because that had been his custom, and he remembered, in the past, she had given sugar to him there.

Chapter Eight

I had never realised, of course, that life at Manderley would be so orderly and planned. I remember now, looking back, how on that first morning Maxim was up and dressed and writing letters, even before breakfast, and when I got downstairs, rather after nine o'clock, a little flurried by the booming summons of the gong, I found he had nearly finished, he was already peeling his fruit.

He looked up at me and smiled. 'You mustn't mind,' he said, 'this is something you will have to get used to. I've no time to hang about at this hour of the day. Running a place like Manderley, you know, is a full-time job. The coffee and the hot dishes are on the side-board. We always help ourselves at breakfast.' I said something about my clock being slow, about having been too long in the bath, but he did not listen, he was looking down at a letter, frowning at something.

How impressed I was, I remember well; impressed and a little over-awed by the magnificence of the breakfast offered to us. There was tea, in a great silver urn, and coffee too, and on the heater, piping hot, dishes of scrambled eggs, of bacon, and another of fish. There was a little clutch of boiled eggs as well, in their own special heater, and porridge, in a silver porringer. On another side-board was a ham, and a great piece of cold bacon. There were scones too, on the table, and toast, and various pots of jam, marmalade, and honey, while dessert dishes, piled high with fruit, stood at either end. It seemed strange to me that Maxim, who in Italy and France had eaten a *croissant* and fruit only, and drunk a cup of coffee, should sit down to this breakfast at home, enough for a dozen people, day after day probably, year after year, seeing nothing ridiculous about it, nothing wasteful.

I noticed he had eaten a small piece of fish. I took a boiled egg. And I wondered what happened to the rest, all those scrambled eggs, that crisp bacon, the porridge, the remains of the fish. Were there menials, I wondered, whom I should never know, never see, waiting behind kitchen doors for the gift of our breakfast? Or was it all thrown away, shovelled into dustpans? I would never know, of course, I would never dare to ask.

'Thank the Lord I haven't a great crowd of relations to inflict upon you,' said Maxim, 'a sister I very rarely see, and a grandmother who is nearly blind. Beatrice, by the way, asks herself over to lunch. I half expected she would. I suppose she wants to have a look at you.'

'To-day?' I said, my spirits sinking to zero.

'Yes, according to the letter I got this morning. She won't stay long. You'll like her, I think. She's very direct, believes in speaking her mind. No humbug at all. If she doesn't like you she'll tell you so, to your face.'

I found this hardly comforting, and wondered if there was not some virtue in the quality of insincerity. Maxim got up from his chair, and lit a cigarette. 'I've a mass of things to see to this morning, do you think you can amuse yourself?' he said. 'I'd like to have taken you round the garden, but I must see Crawley, my agent. I've been away from things too long. He'll be in to lunch, too, by the way. You don't mind, do you, you will be all right?'

'Of course,' I said, 'I shall be quite happy.'

Then he picked up his letters, and went out of the room, and I remember thinking this was not how I had imagined my first morning; I had seen us walking together, arms linked, to the sea, coming back rather late and tired and happy to a cold lunch, alone, and sitting afterwards under that chestnut tree I could see from the library window.

I lingered long over my first breakfast, spinning out the time, and it was not until I saw Frith come in and look at me, from behind the service screen, that I realised it was after ten o'clock. I sprang to my feet at once, feeling guilty, and apologised for sitting there so late, and he bowed, saying nothing, very polite, very correct, but I caught a flicker of surprise in his eyes. I wondered if I had said the wrong thing. Perhaps it did not do to apologise. Perhaps it lowered me in his estimation. I wished I knew what to say, what to do. I wondered if he suspected, as Mrs. Danvers had done, that poise, and grace, and assurance were not qualities inbred in me, but were things to be acquired, painfully perhaps, and slowly, costing me many bitter moments.

As it was, leaving the room, I stumbled, not looking where I was going, catching my foot on the step by the door, and Frith came forward to help me, picking up my handkerchief, while Robert, the young footman, who was standing behind the screen, turned away to hide his smile.

I heard the murmur of their voices as I crossed the hall, and one of them laughed, Robert, I supposed. Perhaps they were laughing at me. I went upstairs again, to the privacy of my bedroom, but when I opened the door I found the housemaids in there doing the room, one was sweeping the floor, the other dusting the dressing-table. They looked at me in surprise. I quickly went out again. It could not be right then, for me to go to my room at that hour in the morning. It was not expected of me. It broke the household routine. I crept downstairs once more, silently, thankful of my slippers that made no sound on the stone flags, and so into the library which was chilly, the windows flung wide open, the fire laid but not lit.

I shut the windows, and looked round for a box of matches. I could not find one. I wondered what I should do. I did not like to ring. But the library, so snug and warm last night with the burning logs was like an ice-house now, in the early morning. There were matches upstairs in the bedroom, but I did not like to go for them because it would mean disturbing the housemaids at their work. I could not bear their moon faces staring at me again. I decided that when Frith and Robert had left the dining-room I would fetch the matches from the side-board. I tiptoed out into the hall and listened. They were still clearing, I could hear the sound of voices, and the movement of trays. Presently all was silent, they must have gone through the service doors into the kitchen quarters, so I went across the hall and into the dining-room once more. Yes, there was a box of matches on the side-board, as I expected. I crossed the room quickly, and picked them up, and as I did so Frith came back into the room. I tried to cram the box furtively into my pocket, but I saw him glance at my hand in surprise.

'Did you require anything, Madam?' he said.

'Oh, Frith,' I said awkwardly. 'I could not find any matches.' He at once proffered me another box, handing me the cigarettes too, at the same time. This was another embarrassment, for I did not smoke.

'No, the fact is,' I said, 'I felt rather cool in the library, I suppose the weather seems chilly to me, after being abroad, and I thought perhaps I would just put a match to the fire.'

'The fire in the library is not usually lit until the afternoon, Madam,' he said. 'Mrs. de Winter always used the morning-room. There is a good fire in there. Of course if you should wish to have the fire in the library as well I will give orders for it to be lit.'

'Oh, no,' I said, 'I would not dream of it. I will go into the morning-room. Thank you, Frith.'

'You will find writing-paper, and pens, and ink, in there, Madam,' he said. 'Mrs. de Winter always did her correspondence and telephoning in the morning-room, after breakfast. The house telephone is also there, should you wish to speak to Mrs. Danvers.'

'Thank you, Frith,' I said.

I turned away into the hall again, humming a little tune to give me an air of confidence. I could not tell him that I had never seen the morning room, that Maxim had not shown it to me the night before. I knew he was standing in the entrance to the dining-room, watching me, as I went across the hall, and that I must make some show of knowing my way. There was a door to the left of the great staircase, and I went recklessly towards it, praying in my heart that it would take me to my goal, but when I came to it and opened it I saw it was a garden room, a place for odds and ends, there was a table where flowers were done, there were basket chairs stacked against the wall, and a couple of mackintoshes too, hanging on a peg. I came out, a little defiantly, glancing across the hall, and saw Frith still standing there. I had not deceived him though, not for a moment.

'You go through the drawing-room to the morning-room, Madam,' he said, 'through the door there, on your right, this side of the staircase. You go straight through the double drawing-room, and turn to your left.'

'Thank you, Frith,' I said humbly, pretending no longer.

I went through the long drawing-room, as he had directed, a lovely room this, beautifully proportioned, looking out upon the lawns down to the sea. The public would see this room, I supposed, and Frith, if he showed them round, would know the history of the pictures on the wall, and the period of the furniture. It was beautiful of course, I knew that, and those chairs and tables probably without price, but for all that I had no wish to linger there, I could not see myself sitting ever in those chairs, standing before that carved mantelpiece, throwing books down on to the tables. It had all the formality of a room in a museum, where alcoves were roped off, and a guardian, in cloak and hat like the guides in the French châteaux, sat in a chair beside the door. I went through then, and turned to the left, and so on to the little morning-room I had not seen before.

I was glad to see the dogs there, sitting before the fire, and Jasper, the younger, came over to me at once, his tail wagging, and thrust his nose into my hand. The old one lifted her muzzle at my approach, and gazed in my direction with her blind eyes, but when she had sniffed the air a moment, and found I was not the one she sought, she turned her head away with a grunt, and looked steadily into the fire again. Then Jasper left me, too, and settled himself by the side of his companion, licking his side. This was their routine. They knew, even as Frith had known, that the library fire was not lit until the afternoon. They came to the morning-room from long custom. Somehow I guessed, before going to the window, that the room looked out upon the rhododendrons. Yes, there they were, blood-red and luscious, as I had seen them in the evening before, great bushes of them, massed beneath the open window, encroaching on to the sweep of the drive itself. There was a little clearing too, between the bushes, like a miniature lawn, the grass a smooth carpet of moss, and in the centre of this, the tiny statue of a naked faun, his pipes to his lips.

The crimson rhododendrons made his background, and the clearing itself was like a little stage, where he would dance, and play his part. There was no musty smell about this room, as there had been in the library. There were no old well-worn chairs, no tables littered with magazines and papers, seldom if ever read, but left there from long custom, because Maxim's father, or even grandfather perhaps, had wished it so.

This was a woman's room, graceful, fragile, the room of someone who had chosen every particle of furniture with great care, so that each chair, each vase, each small, infinitesimal thing should be in harmony with one another, and with her own personality. It was as though she who had arranged this room had said: 'This I will have, and this, and this', taking piece by piece from the treasures in Manderley each object that pleased her best, ignoring the second-rate, the mediocre, laying her hand with sure and certain instinct only upon the best. There was no intermingling of style, no confusing of period, and the result was perfection in a strange and startling way, not coldly formal like the drawing-room shown to the public, but vividly alive, having something of the same glow and brilliance that the rhododendrons had, massed there, beneath the window. And I noticed then that the rhododendrons, not content with forming their theatre on the little lawn outside the window, had been permitted to the room itself. Their great warm faces looked down upon me from the mantelpiece, they floated in a bowl upon the table by the sofa, they stood, lean and graceful, on the writing desk beside the golden candlesticks.

The room was filled with them, even the walls took colour from them, becoming rich and glowing in the morning sun. They were the only flowers in the room, and I wondered if there was some purpose in it, whether the room had been arranged originally with this one end in view, for nowhere else in the house did the rhododendrons obtrude. There were flowers in the dining-room, flowers in the library, but orderly and trim, rather in the background, not like this, not in profusion. I went and sat down at the writing-desk, and I thought how strange it was that this room, so lovely and so rich in colour, should be, at the same time, so business-like and purposeful. Somehow I should have expected that a room furnished as this was in such exquisite taste, for all the exaggeration of the flowers, would be a place of decoration only, languorous and intimate.

But this writing-table, beautiful as it was, was no pretty toy where a woman would scribble little notes, nibbling the end of a pen, leaving it, day after day, in carelessness, the blotter a little askew. The pigeon-holes were docketed, 'letters-unanswered', 'letters-to-keep', 'household', 'estate', 'menus', 'miscellaneous', 'addresses'; each ticket written in that same scrawling pointed hand that I knew already. And it shocked me, even startled me, to recognise it again, for I had not seen it since I had destroyed the page from the book of poems, and I had not thought to see it again.

I opened a drawer at hazard, and there was the writing once more, this time in an open leather book, whose heading 'Guests at Manderley' showed at once, divided into weeks and months, what visitors had come and gone, the rooms they had used, the food they had eaten. I turned over the pages, and saw that the book was a complete record of a year, so that the hostess, glancing back, would know to the day, almost to the hour, what guest had passed what night under her roof, and where he had slept, and what she had given him to eat. There was note-paper also in the drawer, thick white sheets, for rough writing, and the note-paper of the house, with the crest, and the address, and visiting cards, ivory white, in little boxes.

I took one out and looked at it, unwrapped it from its thin tissue of paper. 'Mrs. M. de Winter' it said, and in the corner 'Manderley'. I put it back in the box again, and shut the drawer, feeling guilty suddenly, and deceitful, as though I were staying in somebody else's house and my hostess had said to me, 'Yes, of course, write letters at my desk', and I had unforgivably, in a stealthy manner, peeped at her correspondence. At any moment she might come back into the room, and she would see me there, sitting before her open drawer, which I had no right to touch.

And when the telephone rang, suddenly, alarmingly, on the desk in front of me, my heart leapt and I started up in terror, thinking I had been discovered. I took the receiver off with trembling hands, and 'Who is it?' I said, 'who do you want?' There was a strange buzzing at the end of the line, and then a voice came, low and rather harsh, whether that of a woman or a man I could not tell, and 'Mrs. de Winter?' it said. 'Mrs. de Winter?'

'I'm afraid you have made a mistake,' I said, 'Mrs. de Winter has been dead for over a year.' I sat there waiting, staring stupidly into the mouthpiece, and it was not until the name was repeated again, the voice incredulous, slightly raised, that I became aware, with a rush of colour to my face, that I had blundered irretrievably, and could not take back my words. 'It's Mrs. Danvers, Madam,' said the voice, 'I'm speaking to you on the house telephone.' My faux-pas was so palpably obvious, so idiotic and unpardonable, that to ignore it would show me to be an even greater fool, if possible, than I was already.

'I'm sorry, Mrs. Danvers,' I said stammering, my words tumbling over one another, 'the telephone startled me, I didn't know what I was saying, I didn't realise the call was for me, and I never noticed I was speaking on the house telephone.'

'I'm sorry to have disturbed you, Madam,' she said, and she knows, I thought, she guesses I have been looking through the desk, 'I only wondered whether you wished to see me, and whether you approved of the menus for to-day.'

'Oh,' I said. 'Oh, I'm sure I do, that is, I'm sure I approve of the menus, just order what you like, Mrs. Danvers, you needn't bother to ask me.'

'It would be better I think if you read the list,' continued the voice, 'you will find the menu of the day on the blotter, beside you.'

I searched feverishly about me on the desk, and found at last a sheet of paper I had not noticed before. I glanced hurriedly through it, curried prawns, roast veal, asparagus, cold chocolate mousse – was this lunch or dinner, I could not see, lunch I suppose.

'Yes, Mrs. Danvers,' I said, 'very suitable, very nice indeed.'

'If you wish anything changed please say so,' she answered, 'and I will give orders at once. You will notice I have left a blank space beside the sauce, for you to mark your preference. I was not sure what sauce you are used to having served with the roast veal. Mrs. de Winter was most particular about her sauces, and I always had to refer to her.'

'Oh,' I said. 'Oh, well . . . let me see, Mrs. Danvers, I hardly know; I think we had better have what you usually have, whatever you think Mrs. de Winter would have ordered.'

'You have no preference, Madam?'

'No,' I said. 'No, really, Mrs. Danvers.'

'I rather think Mrs. de Winter would have ordered a wine sauce, Madam.'

'We will have the same then, of course,' I said.

'I'm very sorry I disturbed you while you were writing, Madam.'

'You didn't disturb me at all,' I said, 'please don't apologise.'

'The post leaves at midday, and Robert will come for your letters, and stamp them himself,' she said; 'all you have to do is to ring through to him, on the telephone, if you have anything urgent to be sent, and he will give orders for them to be taken in to the post-office immediately.'

'Thank you, Mrs. Danvers,' I said. I listened for a moment, but she said no more, and then I heard a little click at the end of the telephone, which meant she had replaced the receiver. I did the same. Then I looked down again at the desk, and the note-paper, ready for use, upon the blotter. In front of me stared the ticketed pigeon-holes, and the words upon them, 'letters-unanswered', 'estate', 'miscellaneous', were like a reproach to me for my idleness. She who sat here before me had not wasted her time, as I was doing. She had reached out for the house telephone and given her orders for the day, swiftly, efficiently, and run her pencil perhaps through an item in the menu that had not pleased her. She had not said 'Yes, Mrs. Danvers', and 'Of course, Mrs. Danvers', as I had done. And then, when she had finished, she began her letters, five, six, seven perhaps to be answered, all written in that same curious, slanting hand I knew so well. She would tear off sheet after sheet of that smooth white paper, using it extravagantly, because of the long strokes she made when she wrote, and at the end of each of her personal letters she put her signature, 'Rebecca', that tall sloping R dwarfing its fellows.

I drummed with my fingers on the desk. The pigeon-holes were empty now. There were no 'letters-unanswered' waiting to be dealt with, no bills to pay that I knew anything about. If I had anything urgent, Mrs. Danvers said, I must telephone through to Robert and he would give orders for it to be taken to the post. I wondered how many urgent letters Rebecca used to write, and who they were written to. Dressmakers perhaps – 'I must have the white satin on Tuesday, without fail', or to her hair-dresser – 'I shall be coming up next Friday, and want an appointment at three o'clock with Monsieur Antoine himself. Shampoo, massage, set, and manicure.' No, letters of that type would be a waste of time. She would have a call put through to London, Frith would do it. Frith would say 'I am speaking for Mrs. de Winter'. I went on drumming with my fingers on the desk. I could think of nobody to write to. Only Mrs. Van Hopper. And there was something foolish, rather ironical, in the realisation that here I was sitting at my own desk in my own home with nothing better to do than to write a letter to Mrs. Van Hopper, a woman I disliked, whom I should never see again. I pulled a sheet of note-paper towards me. I took up the narrow, slender pen, with the bright pointed nib. 'Dear Mrs. Van Hopper,' I began. And as I wrote, in halting, laboured fashion, saying I hoped the voyage had been good, that she had found her daughter better, that the weather in New York was fine and warm, I noticed for the first time how cramped and unformed was my own hand-writing, without individuality, without style, uneducated even, the writing of an indifferent pupil taught in a second-rate school.

Chapter Nine

When I heard the sound of the car in the drive I got up in sudden panic, glancing at the clock, for I knew that it meant Beatrice and her husband had arrived. It was only just gone twelve, they were much earlier than I expected. And Maxim was not yet back. I wondered if it would be possible to hide, to get out of the window into the garden, so that Frith, bringing them to the morning-room would say 'Madam must have gone out', and it would seem quite natural, they would take it as a matter of course. The dogs looked up enquiringly as I ran to the window, and Jasper followed me, wagging his tail.

The window opened out on to the terrace and the little grass clearing beyond, but as I prepared to brush past the rhododendrons the sound of voices came close, and I backed again into the room. They were coming to the house by way of the garden, Frith having told them doubtless that I was in the morning-room. I went quickly into the big drawing-room, and made for a door near me on the left. It led into a long stone passage, and I ran along it, fully aware of my stupidity, despising myself for this sudden attack of nerves, but I knew I could not face these people, not for a moment anyway. The passage seemed to be taking me to the back regions, and as I turned the corner, coming upon another staircase, I met a servant I had not seen before, a scullery-maid perhaps, she carried a mop and a pail in her hands. She stared at me in wonder, as though I were a vision, unexpected in this part of the house, and 'Good morning', I said, in great confusion, making for the stairway, and 'Good morning, Madam', she returned, her mouth open, her round eyes inquisitive as I climbed the stairs.

They would lead me, I supposed, to the bedrooms, and I could find my suite in the east wing, and sit up there a little while, until I judged it nearly time for lunch, when good manners would compel me to come down again.

I must have lost my bearings, for passing through a door at the head of the stairs I came to a long corridor that I had not seen before, similar in some ways to the one in the east wing, but broader and darker – dark owing to the panelling of the walls.

I hesitated, then turned left, coming upon a broad landing and another staircase. It was very quiet and dark. No one was about. If there had been housemaids here, during the morning, they had finished their work by now and gone downstairs. There was no trace of their presence, no lingering dust smell of carpets lately swept, and I thought, as I stood there, wondering

which way to turn, that the silence was unusual, holding something of the
same oppression as an empty house does, when the owners have gone away.

I opened a door at hazard, and found a room in total darkness, no chink
of light coming through the closed shutters, while I could see dimly, in the
centre of the room, the outline of furniture swathed in white dust-sheets.
The room smelt close and stale, the smell of a room seldom if ever used,
whose ornaments are herded together in the centre of a bed and left there,
covered with a sheet. It might be too that the curtains had not been drawn
from the window since some preceding summer, and if one crossed there
now and pulled them aside, opening the creaking shutters, a dead moth who
had been imprisoned behind them for many months would fall to the carpet
and lie there, beside a forgotten pin, and a dried leaf blown there before the
windows were closed for the last time. I shut the door softly, and went
uncertainly along the corridor, flanked on either side by doors, all of them
closed, until I came to a little alcove, set in an outside wall, where a broad
window gave me light at last. I looked out, and I saw below me the smooth
grass lawns stretching to the sea, and the sea itself, bright green with white-
topped crests, whipped by a westerly wind and scudding from the shore.

It was closer than I had thought, much closer; it ran surely, beneath that
little knot of trees below the lawns, barely five minutes away, and if I
listened now, my ear to the window, I could hear the surf breaking on the
shores of some little bay I could not see. I knew then I had made the circuit
of the house, and was standing in the corridor of the west wing. Yes, Mrs.
Danvers was right. You could hear the sea from here. You might imagine,
in the winter, it would creep up on to those green lawns and threaten the
house itself, for even now, because of the high wind, there was a mist upon
the window-glass, as though someone had breathed upon it. A mist salt-
laden, borne upwards from the sea. A hurrying cloud hid the sun for a
moment as I watched, and the sea changed colour instantly, becoming black,
and the white crests with them very pitiless suddenly, and cruel, not the gay
sparkling sea I had looked on first.

Somehow I was glad my rooms were in the east wing. I preferred the
rose-garden, after all, to the sound of the sea. I went back to the landing
then, at the head of the stairs, and as I prepared to go down, one hand upon
the banister, I heard the door behind me open, and it was Mrs. Danvers.
We stared at one another for a moment without speaking, and I could not
be certain whether it was anger I read in her eyes or curiosity, for her face
became a mask directly she saw me. Although she said nothing I felt guilty
and ashamed, as though I had been caught trespassing, and I felt the tell-
tale colour come up into my face.

'I lost my way,' I said, 'I was trying to find my room.'

'You have come to the opposite end of the house,' she said, 'this is the west
wing.'

'Yes, I know,' I said.

'Did you go into any of the rooms?' she asked me.

'No,' I said. 'No, I just opened a door, I did not go in. Everything was dark, covered up in dust-sheets. I'm sorry. I did not mean to disturb anything. I expect you like to keep all this shut up.'

'If you wish to open up the rooms I will have it done,' she said, 'you have only to tell me. The rooms are all furnished, and can be used.'

'Oh, no,' I said. 'No, I did not mean you to think that.'

'Perhaps you would like me to show you all over the west wing?' she said.

I shook my head. 'No, not now,' I said. 'No, I must go downstairs.' I began to walk down the stairs, and she came with me, by my side, as though she were a warder, and I in custody.

'Any time, when you have nothing to do, you have only to ask me, and I will show you the rooms in the west wing,' she persisted, making me vaguely uncomfortable, I knew not why. Her insistence struck a chord in my memory, reminding me of a visit to a friend's house, as a child, when the daughter of the house, older than me, took my arm and whispered in my ear, 'I know where there is a book, locked in a cupboard, in my mother's bedroom. Shall we go and look at it?' I remembered her white, excited face, and her small, beady eyes, and the way she kept pinching my arm.

'I will have the dust-sheets removed, and then you can see the rooms as they looked when they were used,' said Mrs. Danvers. 'I would have shown you this morning, but I believed you to be writing letters in the morning-room. You have only to telephone through to my room, you know, when you want me. It would only take a short while to have the rooms in readiness.'

We had come down the short flight of stairs, and she opened another door, standing aside for me to pass through, her dark eyes questing my face.

'It's very kind of you, Mrs. Danvers,' I said 'I will let you know some time.'

We passed out together on to the landing beyond, and I saw we were at the head of the main stair-case now, behind the minstrel's gallery.

'I wonder how you came to miss your way?' she said. 'The door through to the west wing is very different to this.'

'I did not come this way,' I said.

'Then you must have come up the back way, from the stone passage?' she said.

'Yes,' I said, not meeting her eyes. 'Yes, I came through a stone passage.'

She went on looking at me, as though she expected me to tell her why I left the morning-room in sudden panic, going through the back regions, and I felt suddenly that she knew, that she must have watched me, that she had seen me wandering perhaps in that west wing from the first, her eye to a crack in the door. 'Mrs. Lacy, and Major Lacy, have been here some time,' she said. 'I heard their car drive up shortly after twelve.'

'Oh!' I said. 'I had not realised that.'

'Frith will have taken them to the morning-room,' she said, 'it must be getting on for half-past twelve. You know your way now, don't you?'

'Yes, Mrs. Danvers,' I said. And I went down the big stairway into the hall, knowing she was standing there above me, her eyes watching me.

I knew I must go back now, to the morning-room, and meet Maxim's sister and her husband. I could not hide in my bedroom now. As I went into the drawing-room I glanced back, over my shoulder, and I saw Mrs. Danvers still standing there at the head of the stairs, like a black sentinel.

I stood for a moment outside the morning-room, with my hand on the door, listening to the hub of voices. Maxim had returned then, while I had been upstairs, bringing his agent with him I supposed, for it sounded to me as if the room was full of people. I was aware of the same feeling of sick uncertainty I had experienced so often as a child, when summoned to shake hands with visitors, and turning the handle of the door I blundered in, to be met at once, it seemed, with a sea of faces and a general silence.

'Here she is at last,' said Maxim. 'Where have you been hiding, we were thinking of sending out a search party? Here is Beatrice, and this is Giles, and this is Frank Crawley. Look out, you nearly trod on the dog.'

Beatrice was tall, broad-shouldered, very handsome, very much like Maxim about the eyes and jaw, but not as smart as I had expected, much tweedier; the sort of person who would nurse dogs through distemper, know about horses, shoot well. She did not kiss me. She shook hands very firmly, looking me straight in the eyes, and then she turned to Maxim, 'Quite different from what I expected. Doesn't answer to your description at all.'

Everyone laughed, and I joined in, not quite certain if the laugh was against me or not, wondering secretly what it was she had expected, and what had been Maxim's description.

And 'This is Giles,' said Maxim, prodding my arm, and Giles stretched out an enormous paw and wrung my hand, squeezing the fingers limp, genial eyes smiling from behind horn-rimmed glasses.

'Frank Crawley,' said Maxim, and I turned to the agent, a colourless, rather thin man with a prominent Adam's apple, in whose eyes I read relief as he looked upon me. I wondered why, but I had no time to think of that, because Frith had come in, and was offering me sherry, and Beatrice was talking to me again. 'Maxim tells me you only got back last night. I had not realised that, or of course we would never have thrust ourselves upon you so soon. Well, what do you think of Manderley?'

'I've scarcely seen anything of it yet,' I answered, 'it's beautiful, of course.'

She was looking me up and down, as I had expected, but in a direct, straightforward fashion, not maliciously like Mrs. Danvers, not with unfriendliness. She had a right to judge me, she was Maxim's sister, and Maxim himself came to my side now, putting his arm through mine, giving me confidence.

'You're looking better, old man,' she said to him, her head on one side, considering him, 'you've lost that fine-drawn look, thank goodness. I suppose we've got you to thank for that?' nodding at me.

'I'm always very fit,' said Maxim shortly, 'never had anything wrong with me in my life. You imagine everyone ill who doesn't look as fat as Giles.'

'Bosh,' said Beatrice, 'you know perfectly well you were a perfect wreck six months ago. Gave me the fright of my life when I came and saw you. I thought you were in for a breakdown. Giles, bear me out. Didn't Maxim look perfectly ghastly last time we came over, and didn't I say he was heading for a breakdown?'

'Well, I must say, old chap, you're looking a different person,' said Giles. 'Very good thing you went away. Doesn't he look well, Crawley?'

I could tell by the tightening of Maxim's muscles under my arm that he was trying to keep his temper. For some reason this talk about his health was not welcome to him, angered him even, and I thought it tactless of Beatrice to harp upon it in this way, making so big a point of it.

'Maxim's very sunburnt,' I said shyly, 'it hides a multitude of sins. You should have seen him in Venice, having breakfast on the balcony, trying to get brown on purpose. He thinks it makes him better-looking.'

Everyone laughed, and Mr. Crawley said, 'It must have been wonderful in Venice, Mrs. de Winter, this time of the year,' and 'Yes,' I said, 'we had really wonderful weather. Only one bad day, wasn't it, Maxim?', the conversation drawing away happily from his health, and so to Italy, safest of subjects, and the blessed topic of fine weather. Conversation was easy now, no longer an effort, Maxim and Giles and Beatrice were discussing the running of Maxim's car, and Mr. Crawley was asking if it was true there were no more gondolas in the canals now, only motor-boats. I don't think he would have cared at all had there been steamers at anchor in the Grand Canal, he was saying this to help me, it was his contribution to the little effort of steering the talk away from Maxim's health, and I was grateful to him, feeling him an ally, for all his dull appearance.

'Jasper wants exercise,' said Beatrice, stirring the dog with her foot; 'he's getting much too fat, and he's barely two years old. What do you feed him on, Maxim?'

'My dear Beatrice, he has exactly the same routine as your dogs,' said Maxim. 'Don't show off and make out you know more about animals than I do.'

'Dear old boy, how can you pretend to know what Jasper has been fed on when you've been away for a couple of months? Don't tell me Frith walks to the lodge gates with him twice a day. This dog hasn't had a run for weeks, I can tell by the condition of his coat.'

'I'd rather he looked colossal than half-starved like that half-wit dog of yours,' said Maxim.

'Not a very intelligent remark when Lion won two firsts at Crufts' last February,' said Beatrice.

The atmosphere was becoming rather strained again, I could tell by the narrow line of Maxim's mouth, and I wondered if brothers and sisters always sparred like this, making it uncomfortable for those who listened. I wished that Frith would come in and announce lunch. Or would we be summoned by a booming gong? I did not know what happened at Manderley.

'How far away from us are you?' I asked, sitting down by Beatrice. 'Did you have to make a very early start?'

'We're fifty miles away, my dear, in the next county, the other side of Trowchester. The hunting is so much better with us. You must come over and stay, when Maxim can spare you. Giles will mount you.'

'I'm afraid I don't hunt,' I confessed, 'I learnt to ride, as a child, but very feebly, I don't remember much about it.'

'You must take it up again,' she said, 'you can't possibly live in the country and not ride. You wouldn't know what to do with yourself. Maxim says you paint. That's very nice, of course, but there's no exercise in it, is there? All very well on a wet day when there's nothing better to do.'

'My dear Beatrice, we are not all such fresh-air fiends as you,' said Maxim.

'I wasn't talking to you, old boy. We all know you are perfectly happy slopping about the Manderley gardens and never breaking out of a slow walk.'

'I'm very fond of walking too,' I said swiftly, 'I'm sure I shall never get tired of rambling about Manderley. And I can bathe too, when it's warmer.'

'My dear, you are an optimist,' said Beatrice, 'I can hardly ever remember bathing here. The water is far too cold, and the beach is shingle.'

'I don't mind that,' I said. 'I love bathing. As long as the currents are not too strong. Is the bathing safe in the bay?'

Nobody answered, and I realised suddenly what I had said. My heart thumped, and I felt my cheeks go flaming red. I bent down to stroke Jasper's ear, in an agony of confusion. 'Jasper could do with a swim, and get some of that fat off,' said Beatrice, breaking the pause, 'but he'd find it a bit too much for him in the bay, wouldn't you Jasper? Good old Jasper. Nice old man.' We patted the dog together, not looking at one another.

'I say, I'm getting infernally hungry, what on earth is happening to lunch?' said Maxim.

'It's only just on one now,' said Mr. Crawley, 'according to the clock on the mantelpiece.'

'That clock was always fast,' said Beatrice.

'It's kept perfect time now for months,' said Maxim.

At that moment the door opened and Frith announced that luncheon was served. 'I say, I must have a wash,' said Giles, looking at his hands.

We all got up and wandered through the drawing-room to the hall in great relief, Beatrice and I a little ahead of the men, she taking my arm.

'Dear old Frith,' she said, 'he always looks exactly the same, and makes me feel like a girl again. You know, don't mind me saying so, but you are even younger than I expected. Maxim told me your age, but you're an absolute child. Tell me, are you very much in love with him?'

I was not prepared for this question, and she must have seen the surprise in my face for she laughed lightly, and squeezed my arm.

'Don't answer,' she said, 'I can see what you feel. I'm an interfering bore, aren't I? You mustn't mind me. I'm devoted to Maxim, you know, though we always bicker like cat and dog when we meet. I congratulate you again on his looks. We were all very worried about him this time last year, but of course you know the whole story.' We had come to the dining-room by now, and she said no more, for the servants were there and the others had joined us, but as I sat down, and unfolded my napkin, I wondered what Beatrice would say did she realise that I knew nothing of that preceding year, no details of the tragedy that had happened down there, in the bay, that Maxim kept these things to himself, that I questioned him never.

Lunch passed off better than I had dared to hope. There were few arguments, or perhaps Beatrice was exercising tact at last, at any rate she and Maxim chatted about matters concerning Manderley, her horses, the garden, mutual friends, and Frank Crawley, on my left, kept up an easy patter with me for which I was grateful, as it required no effort. Giles was more concerned with food than with the conversation, though now and again he remembered my existence and flung me a remark at hazard.

'Same cook I suppose, Maxim?' he said, when Robert had offered him the cold soufflé for the second time. 'I always tell Bee, Manderley's the only place left in England where one can get decent cooking. I remember this soufflé of old.'

'I think we change cooks periodically,' said Maxim, 'but the standard of cooking remains the same. Mrs. Danvers has all the recipes, she tells them what to do.'

'Amazing woman, that Mrs. Danvers,' said Giles, turning to me, 'don't you think so?'

'Oh, yes,' I said, 'Mrs. Danvers seems to be a wonderful person.'

'She's no oil painting though, is she?' said Giles, and he roared with laughter. Frank Crawley said nothing, and looking up I saw Beatrice was watching me. She turned away then, and began talking to Maxim.

'Do you play golf at all, Mrs. de Winter?' said Mr. Crawley.

'No, I'm afraid, I don't,' I answered, glad that the subject had been changed again, that Mrs. Danvers was forgotten, and even though I was no player, knew nothing of the game, I was prepared to listen to him as long as he pleased; there was something solid and safe and dull about golf, it could not bring us into any difficulties. We had cheese, and coffee, and I wondered whether I was supposed to make a move. I kept looking at Maxim, but he gave no sign, and then Giles embarked upon a story, rather difficult to follow, about digging a car out of a snow-drift – what had started the train of thought I could not tell – and I listened to him politely, nodding my head now and again and smiling, aware of Maxim becoming restive at his end of the table. At last he paused, and I caught Maxim's eye. He frowned very slightly, and jerked his head towards the door.

I got up at once, shaking the table clumsily as I moved my chair, and upsetting Giles's glass of port. 'Oh, dear,' I said, hovering, wondering what to do, reaching ineffectively for my napkin, but 'All right, Frith will deal with it,' said Maxim, 'don't add to the confusion. Beatrice, take her out in the garden, she's scarcely seen the place yet.'

He looked tired, rather jaded. I began to wish none of them had come. They had spoilt our day anyway. It was too much of an effort, just as we returned. I felt tired too, tired and depressed. Maxim had seemed almost irritable when he suggested we should go into the garden. What a fool I had been, upsetting that glass of port.

We went out on to the terrace and walked down on to the smooth green lawns.

'I think it's a pity you came back to Manderley so soon,' said Beatrice, 'it would have been far better to potter about in Italy for three or four months, and then come back in the middle of the summer. Done Maxim a power of good too, besides being easier from your point of view. I can't help feeling it's going to be rather a strain here for you at first.'

'Oh, I don't think so,' I said. 'I know I shall come to love Manderley.'

She did not answer, and we strolled backwards and forwards on the lawns.

'Tell me a bit about yourself,' she said at last, 'what was it you were doing in the south of France? Living with some appalling American woman, Maxim said.'

I explained about Mrs. Van Hopper, and what had led to it, and she seemed sympathetic but a little vague, as though she was thinking of something else.

'Yes,' she said, when I paused, 'it all happened very suddenly, as you say. But of course we were all delighted, my dear, and I do hope you will be happy.'

'Thank you, Beatrice,' I said, 'thank you very much.'

I wondered why she said she hoped we would be happy, instead of saying she knew we would be so. She was kind, she was sincere, I liked her very much, but there was a tiny doubt in her voice that made me afraid.

'When Maxim wrote and told me,' she went on, taking my arm, 'and said he had discovered you in the south of France, and you were very young, very pretty, I must admit it gave me a bit of a shock. Of course we all expected a social butterfly, very modern and plastered with paint, the sort of girl you expected to meet in those sort of places. When you came into the morning-room before lunch you could have knocked me down with a feather.'

She laughed, and I laughed with her. But she did not say whether or not she was disappointed in my appearance or relieved.

'Poor Maxim,' she said, 'he went through a ghastly time, and let's hope you have made him forget about it. Of course he adores Manderley.'

Part of me wanted her to continue her train of thought, to tell me more of the past, naturally and easily like this, and something else, way back in my mind, did not want to know, did not want to hear.

'We are not a bit alike, you know,' she said, 'our characters are poles apart. I show everything on my face, whether I like people or not, whether I am angry or pleased. There's no reserve about me, Maxim is entirely different. Very quiet, very reserved. You never know what's going on in that funny mind of his. I lose my temper on the slightest provocation, flare up, and then it's all over. Maxim loses his temper once or twice in a year, and when he does – my God – he *does* lose it. I don't suppose he ever will with you. I should think you are a placid little thing.'

She smiled, and pinched my arm, and I thought about being placid, how quiet and comfortable it sounded, someone with knitting on her lap, with calm unruffled brow. Someone who was never anxious, never tortured by doubt and indecision, someone who never stood as I did, hopeful, eager, frightened, tearing at bitten nails, uncertain which way to go, what star to follow.

'You won't mind me saying so, will you,' she went on, 'but I think you ought to do something to your hair. Why don't you have it waved? It's so very lanky, isn't it, like that? Must look awful under a hat. Why don't you sweep it back behind your ears?'

I did so obediently, and waited for her approval. She looked at me critically, her head on one side. 'No,' she said. 'No, I think that's worse. It's too severe, and doesn't suit you. No, all you need is a wave, just to pinch it up. I never have cared for that Joan of Arc business or whatever they call it. What does Maxim say? Does he think it suits you?'

'I don't know,' I said, 'he's never mentioned it.'

'Oh well,' she said, 'perhaps he likes it. Don't go by me. Tell me, did you get any clothes in London or Paris?'

'No,' I said, 'we had no time. Maxim was anxious to get home. And I can always send for catalogues.'

'I can tell by the way you dress that you don't care a hoot what you wear,' she said. I glanced at my flannel skirt apologetically.

'I do,' I said. 'I'm very fond of nice things. I've never had much money to spend on clothes up to now.'

'I wonder Maxim did not stay a week or so in London and get you something decent to wear,' she said. 'I must say, I think it's rather selfish of him. So unlike him too. He's generally so particular.'

'Is he?' I said. 'He's never seemed particular to me. I don't think he notices what I wear at all. I don't think he minds.'

'Oh,' she said. 'Oh, well, he must have changed then.'

She looked away from me, and whistled to Jasper, her hands in her pockets, and then stared up at the house above us.

'You're not using the west wing then,' she said.

'No,' I said. 'No, we have the suite in the east wing. It's all been done up.'

'Has it?' she said. 'I didn't know that. I wonder why.'

'It was Maxim's idea,' I said, 'he seems to prefer it.'

She said nothing, she went on looking at the windows, and whistling. 'How do you get on with Mrs. Danvers?' she said suddenly.

I bent down, and began patting Jasper's head, and stroking his ears. 'I have not seen very much of her,' I said, 'she scares me a little. I've never seen anyone quite like her before.'

'I don't suppose you have,' said Beatrice.

Jasper looked up at me with great eyes, humble, rather self-conscious. I kissed the top of his silken head, and put my hand over his black nose.

'There's no need to be frightened of her,' said Beatrice, 'and don't let her see it, whatever you do. Of course I've never had anything to do with her, and I don't think I ever want to either. However, she's always been very civil to me.' I went on patting Jasper's head.

'Did she seem friendly?' said Beatrice.

'No,' I said. 'No, not very.'

Beatrice began whistling again, and she rubbed Jasper's head with her foot. 'I shouldn't have more to do with her than you can help,' she said.

'No,' I said. 'She runs the house very efficiently, there's no need for me to interfere.'

'Oh, I don't suppose she'd mind that,' said Beatrice. That was what Maxim had said, the evening before, and I thought it odd that they should both have the same opinion. I should have imagined that interference was the one thing Mrs. Danvers did not want.

'I dare say she will get over it in time,' said Beatrice, 'but it may make things rather unpleasant for you at first. Of course she's insanely jealous. I was afraid she would be.

'Why?' I asked, looking up at her. 'Why should she be jealous? Maxim does not seem to be particularly fond of her?'

'My dear child, it's not Maxim she's thinking of,' said Beatrice, 'I think she respects him and all that, but nothing more very much. 'No, you see,' – she paused, frowning a little, looking at me uncertainly – 'she resents your being here at all, that's the trouble.'

'Why?' I said. 'Why should she resent me?'

'I thought you knew,' said Beatrice; 'I thought Maxim would have told you. She simply adored Rebecca.'

'Oh,' I said. 'Oh, I see.'

We both went on patting and stroking Jasper, who, unaccustomed to such attention, rolled over on his back in ecstasy.

'Here are the men,' said Beatrice, 'let's have some chairs out and sit under the chestnut. How fat Giles is getting, he looks quite repulsive beside Maxim. I suppose Frank will go back to the office. What a dull creature he is, never has anything interesting to say. Well, all of you. What have you been discussing? Pulling the world to bits I suppose.' She laughed, and the others strolled towards us, and we all stood about. Giles threw a twig for Jasper to retrieve. We all looked at Jasper. Mr. Crawley looked at his watch. 'I must be off,' he said, 'thank you very much for lunch, Mrs. de Winter.'

'You must come often,' I said, shaking hands.

I wondered if the others would go too. I was not sure whether they had just come over for lunch, or to spend the day. I hoped they would go. I wanted to be alone with Maxim again, and that it would be like when we were in Italy. We all went and sat down under the chestnut tree. Robert brought out chairs and rugs. Giles lay down on his back and tipped his hat over his eyes. After a while he began to snore, his mouth open.

'Shut up, Giles,' said Beatrice. 'I'm not asleep,' he muttered, opening his eyes, and shutting them again. I thought him unattractive. I wondered why Beatrice had married him. She could never have been in love with him. Perhaps that was what she was thinking about me. I caught her eye upon me now and again, puzzled, reflective, as though she was saying to herself 'What on earth does Maxim see in her?' but kind at the same time, not unfriendly. They were talking about their grandmother.

'We must go over and see the old lady,' Maxim was saying, and 'She's getting gaga,' said Beatrice, 'drops food all down her chin, poor darling.'

I listened to them both, leaning against Maxim's arm, rubbing my chin on his sleeve. He stroked my hand absently, not thinking, talking to Beatrice.

'That's what I do to Jasper,' I thought. 'I'm being like Jasper now, leaning against him. He pats me now and again, when he remembers, and

I'm pleased, I get closer to him for a moment. He likes me in the way I like Jasper.'

The wind had dropped. The afternoon was drowsy, peaceful. The grass had been new-mown, it smelt sweet and rich, like summer. A bee droned above Giles's head, and he flicked at it with his hat. Jasper sloped in to join us, too warm in the sun, his tongue lolling from his mouth. He flopped beside me, and began licking his side, his large eyes apologetic. The sun shone on the mullioned windows of the house, and I could see the green lawns and the terrace reflected in them. Smoke curled thinly from one of the near chimneys, and I wondered if the library fire had been lit according to routine.

A thrush flew across the lawn to the magnolia tree outside the dining-room window. I could smell the faint, soft magnolia scent as I sat here, on the lawn. Everything was quiet and still. Very distant now came the washing of the sea in the bay below. The tide must have gone out. The bee droned over us again, pausing to taste the chestnut blossom above our heads. 'This is what I always imagined,' I thought, 'this is how I hoped it would be, living at Manderley.'

I wanted to go on sitting there, not talking, not listening to the others, keeping the moment precious for all time, because we were peaceful all of us, we were content and drowsy even as the bee who droned above our heads. In a little while it would be different, there would come to-morrow, and the next day, and another year. And we would be changed perhaps, never sitting quite like this again. Some of us would go away, or suffer, or die, the future stretched away in front of us, unknown, unseen, not perhaps what we wanted, not what we planned. This moment was safe though, this could not be touched. Here we sat together, Maxim and I, hand-in-hand, and the past and the future mattered not at all. This was secure, this funny fragment of time he would never remember, never think about again. He would not hold it sacred, he was talking about cutting away some of the undergrowth in the drive, and Beatrice agreed, interrupting with some suggestion of her own, and throwing a piece of grass at Giles at the same time. For them it was just after lunch, quarter-past-three on a haphazard afternoon, like any hour, like any day. They did not want to hold it close, imprisoned and secure, as I did. They were not afraid.

'Well, I suppose we ought to be off,' said Beatrice, brushing the grass from her skirt. 'I don't want to be late, we've got the Cartrights dining.'

'How is old Vera?' asked Maxim.

'Oh, same as ever, always talking about her health. He's getting very old. They're sure to ask all about you both.'

'Give them my love,' said Maxim.

We got up. Giles shook the dust off his hat. Maxim yawned and stretched. The sun went in. I looked up at the sky. It had changed already, a mackerel sky. Little clouds scurrying in formation, line upon line.

'Wind's backing,' said Maxim.

'I hope we don't run into rain,' said Giles.

'I'm afraid we've had the best of the day,' said Beatrice.

We wandered slowly towards the drive and the waiting car.

'You haven't seen what's been done to the east wing,' said Maxim.

'Come upstairs,' I suggested, 'it won't take a minute.' We went into the hall, and up the big staircase, the men following behind.

It seemed strange that Beatrice had lived here for so many years. She had run down these same stairs as a little girl, with her nurse. She had been born here, bred here, she knew it all, she belonged here more than I should ever do. She must have many memories locked inside her heart. I wondered if she ever thought about the days that were gone, ever remembered the lanky pig-tailed child that she had been once, so different from the woman she had become, forty-five now, vigorous and settled in her ways, another person. . . .

We came to the rooms, and Giles, stooping under the low doorway said, 'How very jolly, this is a great improvement, isn't it, Bee?' and 'I say, old boy, you have spread yourself,' said Beatrice, 'new curtains, new beds, new everything. You remember, Giles, we had this room that time you were laid up with your leg? It was very dingy then. Of course Mother never had much idea of comfort. And then, you never put people here, did you, Maxim? Except when there was an overflow. The bachelors were always dumped here. Well, it's charming, I must say. Looks over the rose-garden too, which was always an advantage. May I powder my nose?'

The men went downstairs, and Beatrice peered in the mirror.

'Did old Danvers do all this for you?' she said.

'Yes,' I said. 'I think she's done it very well.'

'So she should, with her training,' said Beatrice. 'I wonder what on earth it cost. A pretty packet, I bet. Did you ask?'

'No, I'm afraid I did not,' I said.

'I don't suppose it worried Mrs. Danvers,' said Beatrice. 'Do you mind if I use your comb? These are nice brushes. Wedding present?'

'Maxim gave them to me.'

'H'm. I like them. We must give you something of course. What do you want?'

'Oh, I don't really know. You mustn't bother,' I said.

'My dear, don't be absurd. I'm not one to grudge you a present, even though we weren't asked to your wedding!'

'I hope you did not mind about that. Maxim wanted it to be abroad.'

'Of course not. Very sensible of you both. After all, it wasn't as though . . .' she stopped in the middle of her sentence, and dropped her bag. 'Damn, have I broken the catch? No, all is well. What was I saying? I can't remember. Oh, yes, wedding presents. We must think of something. You probably don't care for jewellery.'

I did not answer. 'It's so different from the ordinary young couple,' she said. 'The daughter of a friend of mine got married the other day, and of course they were started off in the usual way, with linen, and coffee sets, and dining-room chairs, and all that. I gave rather a nice standard lamp. Cost me a fiver at Harrods. If you do go up to London to buy clothes mind you go to my woman, Madame Carroux. She has damn good taste, and she doesn't rook you.'

She got up from the dressing-table, and pulled at her skirt.

'Do you suppose you will have a lot of people down?' she said.

'I don't know. Maxim hasn't said.'

'Funny old boy, one never quite knows with him. At one time one could not get a bed in the house, the place would be chock-a-block. I can't somehow see you . . .' she stopped abruptly, and patted my arm. 'Oh well,' she said, 'we'll see. It's a pity you don't ride or shoot, you must miss such a lot. You don't sail by any chance do you?'

'No,' I said.

'Thank God for that,' she said.

She went to the door, and I followed her down the corridor.

'Come and see us if you feel like it,' she said. 'I always expect people to ask themselves. Life is too short to send out invitations.'

'Thank you very much,' I said.

We came to the head of the stairs looking down upon the hall. The men were standing on the steps outside. 'Come on, Bee,' shouted Giles, 'I felt a spot of rain, so we've put on the cover. Maxim says the glass is falling.'

Beatrice took my hand, and bending down gave me a peck on my cheek. 'Good-bye,' she said, 'forgive me if I've asked you a lot of rude questions, my dear, and said all sorts of things I shouldn't. Tact never was my strong point, as Maxim will tell you. And, as I told you before, you're not a bit what I expected.' She looked at me direct, her lips pursed in a whistle, and then took a cigarette from her bag, and flashed her lighter.

'You see,' she said, snapping the top, and walking down the stairs, 'you are so very different from Rebecca.'

And we came out on to the steps and found the sun had gone behind a bank of cloud, a little thin rain was falling, and Robert was hurrying across the lawn to bring in the chairs.

Chapter Ten

We watched the car disappear round the sweep of the drive, and then Maxim took my arm and said, 'Thank God that's that. Get a coat quickly, and come out. Damn the rain, I want a walk. I can't stand this sitting about.' He looked white and strained, and I wondered why the entertaining of Beatrice and Giles, his own sister and brother-in-law, should have tired him so.

'Wait while I run upstairs for my coat,' I said.

'There's a heap of mackintoshes in the flower-room, get one of them,' he said impatiently, 'women are always half an hour when they go to their bedrooms. Robert, fetch a coat from the flower-room, will you, for Mrs. de Winter? There must be half a dozen raincoats hanging there, left by people at one time or another.' He was already standing in the drive, and calling to Jasper. 'Come on, you lazy little beggar, and take some of that fat off.' Jasper ran round in circles, barking hysterically at the prospect of his walk. 'Shut up, you idiot,' said Maxim, 'what on earth is Robert doing?'

Robert came running out of the hall carrying a raincoat, and I struggled into it hurriedly, fumbling with the collar. It was too big, of course, and too long, but there was no time to change it, and we set off together across the lawn to the woods, Jasper running in front.

'I find a little of my family goes a very long way,' said Maxim. 'Beatrice is one of the best people in the world, but she invariable puts her foot in it.'

I was not sure where Beatrice had blundered, and thought it better not to ask. Perhaps he still resented the chat about his health before lunch.

'What did you think of her?' he went on.

'I liked her very much,' I said, 'she was very nice to me.'

'What did she talk to you about out here, after lunch?'

'Oh, I don't know. I think I did most of the talking. I was telling her about Mrs. Van Hopper, and how you and I met, and all that. She said I was quite different to what she expected.'

'What the devil did she expect?'

'Someone much smarter, more sophisticated, I imagine. A social butterfly, she said.'

Maxim did not answer for a moment, he bent down and threw a stick for Jasper. 'Beatrice can sometimes be infernally unintelligent,' he said.

We climbed the grass bank above the lawns, and plunged into the woods. The trees grew very close together, and it was dark. We trod upon broken twigs, and last year's leaves, and here and there the fresh green stubble of the young bracken, and the shoots of the bluebells soon to blossom. Jasper was silent now, his nose to the ground. I took Maxim's arm.

'Do you like my hair?' I said.

He stared down at me in astonishment. 'Your hair?' he said. 'Why on earth do you ask? Of course I like it. What's the matter with it?'

'Oh, nothing,' I said, 'I just wondered.'

'How funny you are,' he said.

We came to a clearing in the woods, and there were two paths, going in opposite directions. Jasper took the right-hand path without hesitation.

'Not that way,' called Maxim, 'come on, old chap.'

The dog looked back at us and stood there, wagging his tail, but did not return. 'Why does he want to go that way?' I asked.

'I suppose he's used to it,' said Maxim briefly, 'it leads to a small cove, where we used to keep a boat. Come on, Jasper, old man.'

We turned into the left-hand path, not saying anything, and presently I looked over my shoulder and saw that Jasper was following us.

'This brings us to the valley I told you about,' said Maxim, 'and you shall smell the azaleas. Never mind the rain, it will bring out the scent.'

He seemed all right again now, happy and cheerful, the Maxim I knew and loved, and he began talking about Frank Crawley and what a good fellow he was, so thorough and reliable, and devoted to Manderley.

'This is better,' I thought, 'this is like it was in Italy,' and I smiled up at him, squeezing his arm, relieved that the odd strained look on his face had passed away, and while I said 'Yes', and 'Really?' and 'Fancy, darling', my thoughts wandered back to Beatrice, wondering why her presence should have disturbed him, what she had done; and I thought too of all she had said about his temper, how he lost it, she told me, about once or twice a year.

She must know him, of course; she was his sister. But it was not what I had thought; it was not my idea of Maxim. I could see him moody, difficult, irritable perhaps, but not angry as she had inferred, not passionate. Perhaps she had exaggerated; people very often were wrong about their relatives.

'There,' said Maxim suddenly, 'take a look at that.'

We stood on a slope of a wooded hill, and the path wound away before us to a valley, by the side of a running stream. There were no dark trees here, no tangled undergrowth, but on either side of the narrow path stood azaleas and rhododendrons, not blood-coloured like the giants in the drive, but salmon, white, and gold, things of beauty and of grace, drooping their lovely, delicate heads in the soft summer rain.

The air was full of their scent, sweet and heady, and it seemed to me as though their very essence had mingled with the running waters of the stream, and become one with the falling rain and the dank rich moss beneath our feet. There was no sound here but the tumbling of the little stream, and the quiet rain. When Maxim spoke, his voice was hushed too, gentle and low, as if he had no wish to break upon the silence.

'We call it the Happy Valley,' he said.

We stood quite still, not speaking, looking down upon the clear white faces of the flowers closest to us, and Maxim stooped, and picked up a fallen petal and gave it to me. It was crushed and bruised, and turning brown at the curled edge, but as I rubbed it across my hand the scent rose to me sweet and strong, vivid as the living tree from which it came.

Then the birds began. First a blackbird, his note clear and cool above the running stream, and after a moment he had answer, from his fellow hidden in the woods behind us, and soon the still air about us was made turbulent with song, pursuing us as we wandered down into the valley, and the fragrance of the white petals followed us too. It was disturbing, like an enchanted place. I had not thought it could be as beautiful as this.

The sky, now overcast and sullen, so changed from the early afternoon, and the steady, insistent rain could not disturb the soft quietude of the valley; the rain and the rivulet mingled with one another, and the liquid note of the blackbird fell upon the damp air in harmony with them both. I brushed the dripping heads of the azaleas as I passed, so close they grew together, bordering the path. Little drops of water fell on to my hands from the soaked petals. There were petals at my feet too, brown and sodden, bearing their scent upon them still, and a richer, older scent as well, the smell of deep moss and bitter earth, the stems of bracken, and the twisted buried roots of trees. I held Maxim's hand and I had not spoken. The spell of the Happy Valley was upon me. This at last was the core of Manderley, the Manderley I would know and learn to love. The first drive was forgotten, the black, herded woods, the glaring rhododendrons, luscious and overproud. And the vast house too, the silence of that echoing hall, the uneasy stillness of the west wing, wrapped in dust-sheets. There I was an interloper, wandering in rooms that did not know me, sitting at a desk and in a chair that was not mine. Here it was different. The Happy Valley knew no trespassers. We came to the end of the path, and the flowers formed an archway above our heads. We bent down, passing underneath, and when I stood straight again, brushing the raindrops from my hair, I saw that the valley was behind us, and the azaleas, and the trees, and, as Maxim had described to me that afternoon many weeks ago in Monte Carlo, we were standing in a little narrow cove, the shingle hard and white under our feet, and the sea breaking on the shore beyond us.

Maxim smiled down at me, watching the bewilderment on my face.

'It's a shock, isn't it?' he said. 'No one ever expects it. The contrast is too sudden, it almost hurts.' He picked up a stone and flung it across the beach for Jasper. 'Fetch it, good man,' and Jasper streaked away in search of the stone, his long black ears flapping in the wind.

The enchantment was no more, the spell was broken. We were mortal again, two people playing on a beach. We threw more stones, went to the water's edge, flung ducks and drakes, and fished for driftwood. The tide had turned, and came lapping in the bay. The small rocks were covered, the seaweed washed on the stones. We rescued a big floating plank and carried it up the beach above high-water mark. Maxim turned to me, laughing, wiping the hair out of his eyes, and I unrolled the sleeves of my mackintosh caught by the sea spray. And then we looked round, and saw that Jasper had disappeared. We called and whistled, and he did not come. I looked anxiously towards the mouth of the cove where the waves were breaking upon the rocks.

'No,' said Maxim 'we should have seen him, he can't have fallen. Jasper, you idiot, where are you? Jasper, Jasper?'

'Perhaps he's gone back to the Happy Valley?' I said.

'He was by that rock a minute ago, sniffing a dead seagull,' said Maxim.

We walked up the beach towards the valley once again. 'Jasper, Jasper?' called Maxim.

In the distance, beyond the rocks to the right of the beach, I heard a short sharp bark. 'Hear that?' I said. 'He's climbed over this way.' I began to scramble up the slippery rocks in the direction of the bark.

'Come back,' said Maxim sharply, 'we don't want to go that way. The fool of a dog must look after himself.'

I hesitated, looking down from my rock. 'Perhaps he's fallen,' I said, 'poor little chap. Let me fetch him.' Jasper barked again, further away this time. 'Oh listen,' I said, 'I must get him. It's quite safe isn't it? The tide won't have cut him off?'

'He's all right,' said Maxim irritably, 'why not leave him? He knows his own way back.'

I pretended not to hear, and began scrambling over the rocks towards Jasper. Great jagged boulders screened the view, and I slipped and stumbled on the wet rocks, making my way as best I could in Jasper's direction. It was heartless of Maxim to leave Jasper, I thought, and I could not understand it. Besides, the tide was coming in. I came up beside the big boulder that had hidden the view, and looked beyond it. And I saw, to my surprise, that I was looking down into another cove, similar to the one I had left, but wider and more rounded. A small stone breakwater had been thrown out across the cove for shelter, and behind it the bay formed a tiny natural harbour. There was a buoy anchored there, but no boat. The beach in the cove was white shingle, like the one behind me, but steeper, shelving suddenly to the sea. The woods came right down to the tangle of seaweed marking high water, encroaching almost to the rocks themselves, and at the fringe of the woods was a long low building, half cottage, half boat-house, built of the same stone as the breakwater.

There was a man on the beach, a fisherman perhaps, in long boots and a sou' wester, and Jasper was barking at him, running round him in circles, darting at his boots. The man took no notice, he was bending down, and scraping in the shingle. 'Jasper,' I shouted, 'Jasper, come here.'

The dog looked up, wagging his tail, but he did not obey me. He went on baiting the solitary figure on the beach.

I looked over my shoulder. There was still no sign of Maxim. I climbed down over the rocks to the beach below. My feet made a crunching noise across the shingle, and the man looked up at the sound. I saw then that he had the small slit eyes of an idiot, and the red, wet mouth. He smiled at me, showing toothless gums.

'G'day,' he said. 'Dirty, aien't it?'

'Good afternoon,' I said. 'No, I'm afraid it's not very nice weather.'

He watched me with interest, smiling all the while. 'Diggin' for shell,' he said. 'No shell here. Been diggin' since forenoon.'

'Oh,' I said, 'I'm sorry you can't find any.'

'That's right,' he said, 'no shell here.'

'Come on, Jasper,' I said, 'it's getting late. Come on, old boy.'

But Jasper was in an infuriating mood. Perhaps the wind and sea had gone to his head, for he backed away from me, barking stupidly, and began racing round the beach after nothing at all. I saw he would never follow me, and I had no lead. I turned to the man, who had bent down again to his futile digging.

'Have you got any string?' I said.

'Eh?' he said.

'Have you got any string?' I repeated.

'No shell here,' he said, shaking his head. 'Been diggin' since forenoon.' He nodded his head at me, and wiped his pale blue watery eyes.

'I want something to tie the dog,' I said. 'He won't follow me.'

'Eh?' he said. And he smiled his poor idiot's smile.

'All right,' I said, 'it doesn't matter.' He looked at me uncertainly, and then leant forward, and poked me in the chest.

'I know that dog,' he said, 'he comes fro' the house.'

'Yes,' I said. 'I want him to come back with me now.'

'He's not yourn,' he said.

'He's Mr. de Winter's dog,' I said gently. 'I want to take him back to the house.'

'Eh?' he said.

I called Jasper once more, but he was chasing a feather blown by the wind. I wondered if there was any string in the boat-house, and I walked up the beach towards it. There must have been a garden once, but now the grass was long and overgrown, crowded with nettles. The windows were boarded up. No doubt the door was locked, and I lifted the latch without much hope. To my surprise it opened after the first stiffness, and I went inside, bending my head because of the low door. I expected to find the usual boat store, dirty and dusty with disuse, ropes and blocks and oars upon the floor. The dust was there, and the dirt too in places, but there were no ropes or blocks. The room was furnished, and ran the whole length of the cottage. There was a desk in the corner, a table, and chairs, and a bed-sofa pushed against the wall. There was a dresser too, with cups and plates. Bookshelves, the books inside them, and models of ships standing on the top of the shelves. For a moment I thought it must be inhabited – perhaps the poor man on the beach lived here – but I looked around me again, and saw no sign of recent occupation. That rusted grate knew no fire, this dusty floor no footsteps, and the china there on the dresser was blue-spotted with the damp. There was a queer musty smell about the place. Cobwebs spun threads upon the ship's models, making their own ghostly rigging. No one lived here. No one came here. The door had creaked on its hinges when I opened it. The rain pattered on the roof with a hollow sound, and tapped upon the boarded windows. The fabric of the sofa-bed had been nibbled by mice or rats. I could see the jagged holes, and the frayed edges. It was damp in the cottage, damp and chill. Dark, and oppressive. I did not like it. I had no wish to stay there. I hated the hollow sound of the rain pattering on the roof. It seemed to echo in the room itself, and I heard the water dripping too into the rusted grate.

I looked about me for some string. There was nothing that would serve my purpose, nothing at all. There was another door at the end of the room, and I went to it, and opened it, a little fearful now, a little afraid, for I had the odd, uneasy feeling that I might come upon something unawares, that I had no wish to see. Something that might harm me, that might be horrible.

It was nonsense of course, and I opened the door. It was only a boat store after all. Here were the ropes and blocks I had expected, two or three sails, fenders, a small punt, pots of paint, all the litter and junk that goes with the using of boats. A ball of twine lay on a shelf, a rusted clasp knife beside it. This would be all I needed for Jasper. I opened the knife, and cut a length of twine, and came back into the room again. The rain still fell upon the roof, and into the grate. I came out of the cottage hurriedly, not looking behind me, trying not to see the torn sofa and the mildewed china, the spun cobwebs on the model ships, and so through the creaking gate and on to the white beach.

The man was not digging any more, he was watching me, Jasper at his side.

'Come along, Jasper,' I said, 'come on, good dog.' I bent down, and this time he allowed me to touch him and pull hold of his collar. 'I found some string in the cottage,' I said to the man.

He did not answer, and I tied the string loosely round Jasper's collar.

'Good afternoon,' I said, tugging at Jasper. The man nodded, staring at me with his narrow idiot's eyes. 'I saw'ee go in yonder,' he said.

'Yes,' I said, 'it's all right. Mr. de Winter won't mind.'

'She don't go in there now,' he said.

'No,' I said, 'not now.'

'She's gone in the sea, ain't she,' he said, 'she won't come back no more?'

'No,' I said, 'she'll not come back.'

'I never said nothing, did I?' he said.

'No, of course not, don't worry,' I said.

He bent down again to his digging, muttering to himself. I went across the shingle and I saw Maxim waiting for me by the rocks, his hands in his pockets.

'I'm sorry,' I said. 'Jasper would not come. I had to get some string.'

He turned abruptly on his heel, and made towards the woods.

'Aren't we going back over the rocks?' I said.

'What's the point, we're here now,' he said briefly.

We went up past the cottage and struck into a path through the woods. 'I'm sorry I was such a time, it was Jasper's fault,' I said, 'he kept barking at the man. Who was he?'

'Only Ben,' said Maxim; 'he's quite harmless, poor devil. His old father used to be one of the keepers, they live near the home farm. Where did you get that piece of twine?'

'I found it in the cottage on the beach,' I said.

'Was the door open?' he asked.

'Yes, I pushed it open. I found the string in the other room, where the sails were, and a small boat.'

'Oh,' he said shortly. 'Oh, I see,' and then he added, after a moment or two: 'That cottage is supposed to be locked, the door has no business to be open.'

I said nothing, it was not my affair.

'Did Ben tell you the door was open?'

'No,' I said, 'he did not seem to understand anything I asked him.'

'He makes out he's worse than he is,' said Maxim. 'He can talk quite intelligibly if he wants to. He's probably been in and out of the cottage dozens of times, and did not want you to know.'

'I don't think so,' I answered; 'the place looked deserted, quite untouched. There was dust everywhere, and no footmarks. It was terribly damp. I'm afraid those books will be quite spoilt, and the chairs, and that sofa. There are rats there, too, they have eaten away some of the covers.'

Maxim did not reply. He walked at a tremendous pace, and the climb up from the beach was steep. It was very different from the Happy Valley. The trees were dark here and close together, there were no azaleas brushing the path. The rain dripped heavily from the thick branches. It splashed on my collar and trickled down my neck. I shivered, it was unpleasant, like a cold finger. My legs ached, after the unaccustomed scramble over the rocks. And Jasper lagged behind, weary from his wild scamper, his tongue hanging from his mouth.

'Come on, Jasper, for God's sake,' said Maxim. 'Make him walk up, pull at the twine or something, can't you? Beatrice was right. The dog is much too fat.'

'It's your fault,' I said, 'you walk so fast. We can't keep up with you.'

'If you had listened to me instead of rushing wildly over those rocks we would have been home by now,' said Maxim. 'Jasper knew his way back perfectly. I can't think what you wanted to go after him for.'

'I thought he might have fallen, and I was afraid of the tide,' I said.

'Is it likely I should have left the dog had there been any question of the tide?' said Maxim. 'I told you not to go on those rocks, and now you are grumbling because you are tired.'

'I'm not grumbling,' I said. 'Anyone, even if they had legs of iron, would be tired walking at this pace. I thought you would come with me when I went after Jasper anyway, instead of staying behind.'

'Why should I exhaust myself careering after the damn dog?' he said.

'It was no more exhausting careering after Jasper on the rocks than it was careering after driftwood on the beach,' I answered. 'You just say that because you have not any other excuse.'

'My good child, what am I supposed to excuse myself about?'

'Oh, I don't know,' I said wearily, 'let's stop this.'

'Not at all, you began it. What do you mean by saying I was trying to find an excuse? Excuse for what?'

'Excuse for not having come with me over the rocks, I suppose,' I said.

'Well, and why do you think I did not want to cross to the other beach?'

'Oh, Maxim, how should I know? I'm not a thought-reader. I know you did not want to, that's all. I could see it in your face.'

'See what in my face?'

'I've already told you. I could see you did not want to go. Oh, do let's have an end to it. I'm sick to death of the subject.'

'All women say that when they've lost an argument. All right, I did not want to go to the other beach. Will that please you? I never go near the bloody place, or that God-damned cottage. And if you had my memories you would not want to go there either, or talk about it, or even think about it. There. You can digest that if you like, and I hope it satisfies you.'

His face was white, and his eyes strained and wretched with that dark lost look they had had when I first met him. I put out my hand to him, I took hold of his, holding it tight.

'Please, Maxim, please,' I said.

'What's the matter?' he said roughly.

'I don't want you to look like that,' I said. 'It hurts too much. Please Maxim. Let's forget all we said. A futile silly argument. I'm sorry, darling, I'm sorry. Please let everything be all right.'

'We ought to have stayed in Italy,' he said. 'We ought never to have come back to Manderley. Oh, God, what a fool I was to come back.'

He brushed through the trees impatiently, striking even faster than before, and I had to run to keep pace with him, catching at my breath, tears very near the surface, dragging poor Jasper after me on the end of his string.

At last we came to the top of the path, and I saw its fellow branching left to the Happy Valley. We had climbed the path then that Jasper had wished to take at the beginning of the afternoon. I knew now why Jasper had turned to it. It led to the beach he knew best, and the cottage. It was his old routine.

We came out on to the lawns, and went across them to the house without a word. Maxim's face was hard, with no expression. He went straight into the hall and on to the library without looking at me. Frith was in the hall.

'We want tea at once,' said Maxim, and he shut the library door.

I fought to keep back my tears. Frith must not see them. He would think we had been quarrelling, and he would go to the servants' hall and say to them all, 'Mrs. de Winter was crying in the hall just now. It looks as though things are not going very well.' I turned away, so that Frith should not see my face. He came towards me though, he began to help me off with my mackintosh.

'I'll put your raincoat away for you in the flower-room, Madam,' he said.

'Thank you, Frith,' I replied, my face still away from him.

'Not a very pleasant afternoon for a walk I fear, Madam.'

'No,' I said. 'No, it was not very nice.'

'Your handkerchief, Madam?' he said, picking up something that had fallen on the floor. 'Thank you,' I said, putting it in my pocket.

I was wondering whether to go upstairs or whether to follow Maxim to the library. Frith took the coat to the flower-room. I stood there, hesitating, biting my nails. Frith came back again. He looked surprised to see me still there.

'There is a good fire in the library now, Madam.'

'Thank you, Frith,' I said.

I walked slowly across the hall to the library. I opened the door and went in. Maxim was sitting in his chair, Jasper at his feet, the old dog in her basket. Maxim was not reading the paper, though it lay on the arm of the chair beside him. I went and knelt down by his side and put my face close to his.

'Don't be angry with me any more,' I whispered.

He took my face in his hands, and looked down at me with his tired, strained eyes. 'I'm not angry with you,' he said.

'Yes,' I said. 'I've made you unhappy. It's the same as making you angry. You're all wounded and hurt and torn inside. I can't bear to see you like this. I love you so much.'

'Do you?' he said. 'Do you?' He held me very tight, and his eyes questioned me, dark and uncertain, the eyes of a child in pain, a child in fear.

'What is it, darling?' I said. 'Why do you look like that?'

I heard the door open before he could answer, and I sank back on my heels, pretending to reach for a log to throw on the fire, while Frith came into the room followed by Robert, and the ritual of our tea began.

The performance of the day before was repeated, the placing of the table, the laying of the snow-white cloth, the putting down of cakes and crumpets, the silver kettle of hot water placed on its little flame, while Jasper, wagging his tail, his ears stretched back in anticipation, watched my face. Five minutes must have passed before we were alone again, and when I looked at Maxim I saw the colour had come back into his face, the tired, lost look was gone, and he was reaching for a sandwich.

'Having all that crowd to lunch was the trouble,' he said. 'Poor old Beatrice always does rub me up the wrong way. We used to scrap like dogs as children. I'm so fond of her too, bless her. Such a relief though that they don't live too near. Which reminds me, we'll have to go over and see Granny some time. Pour out my tea, sweetheart, and forgive me for being a bear to you.'

It was over then. The episode was finished. We must not speak of it again. He smiled at me over his cup of tea, and then reached for the newspaper on the arm of his chair. The smile was my reward. Like a pat on the head to Jasper. Good dog then, lie down, don't worry me any more. I was Jasper again. I was back where I had been before. I took a piece of crumpet and divided it between the two dogs. I did not want it myself, I was not hungry. I felt very weary now, very tired in a dull, spent way. I looked at Maxim but he was reading his paper, he had folded it over to another page. My fingers were messy with the butter from the crumpet, and I felt in my pocket for a handkerchief. I drew it out, a tiny scrap of a thing, lace-edged. I stared at it, frowning, for it was not mine. I remembered then that Frith had picked it up from the stone floor of the hall. It must have fallen out of the pocket in the mackintosh. I turned it over in my hand. It was grubby, little bits of fluff from the pocket clung to it. It must have been in the mackintosh pocket for a long time. There was a monogram in the corner. A tall sloping R, with the letters de W interlaced. The R dwarfed the other letters, the tail of it ran down into the cambric, away from the laced edge. It was only a small handkerchief, quite a scrap of a thing. It had been rolled in a ball and put away in the pocket and forgotten.

I must have been the first person to put on that mackintosh since the handkerchief was used. She who had worn the coat then was tall, slim, broader than me about the shoulders, for I had found it big and over-long, and the sleeves had come below my wrist. Some of the buttons were missing. She had not bothered then to do it up. She had thrown it over her shoulders like a cape, or worn it loose, hanging open, her hands deep in the pocket.

There was a pink mark upon the handkerchief. The mark of lip-stick. She had rubbed her lips with the handkerchief, and then rolled it in a ball, and left it in the pocket. I wiped my fingers with the handkerchief, and as I did so I noticed that a dull scent clung about it still.

A scent I recognised, a scent I knew. I shut my eyes and tried to remember. It was something elusive, something faint and fragrant that I could not name. I had breathed it before, touched it surely, that very afternoon.

And then I knew that the vanished scent upon the handkerchief was the same as the crushed white petals of the azaleas in the Happy Valley.

Chapter Eleven

The weather was wet and cold for quite a week, as it often can be in the west country in early summer, and we did not go down to the beach again. I could see the sea from the terrace, and the lawns. It looked grey and uninviting, great rollers sweeping in to the bay past the beacon on the headland. I pictured them surging into the little cove and breaking with a roar upon the rocks, then running swift and strong to the shelving beach. If I stood on the terrace and listened I could hear the murmur of the sea below me, low and sullen. A dull, persistent sound that never ceased. And the gulls flew inland too, driven by the weather. They hovered above the house in circles, wheeling and crying, flapping their spread wings. I began to understand why some people could not bear the clamour of the sea. It has a mournful harping note sometimes, and the very persistence of it, that eternal roll and thunder and hiss, plays a jagged tune upon the nerves. I was glad our rooms were in the east wing and I could lean out of my window and look down upon the rose-garden. For sometimes I could not sleep, and getting softly out of bed in the quiet night I would wander to the window, and lean there, my arms upon the sill, and the air would be very peaceful, very still.

I could not hear the restless sea, and because I could not hear it my thoughts would be peaceful too. They would not carry me down that steep path through the woods to the grey cove and the deserted cottage. I did not want to think about the cottage. I remembered it too often in the day. The memory of it nagged at me whenever I saw the sea from the terrace. For I would see once more the blue spots on the china, the spun webs on the little masts of those model ships, and the rat holes on the sofa bed. I would remember the pattering of the rain on the roof. And I thought of Ben, too, with his narrow watery blue eyes, his sly idiot's smile. These things disturbed me, I was not happy about them. I wanted to forget them but at the same time I wanted to know why they disturbed me, why they made me uneasy and unhappy. Somewhere, at the back of my mind, there was a frightened furtive seed of curiosity that grew slowly and stealthily, for all my denial of it, and I knew all the doubt and the anxiety of the child who has been told, 'these things are not discussed, they are forbidden'.

I could not forget the white, lost look in Maxim's eyes when we came up the path through the woods, and I could not forget his words, 'Oh God, what a fool I was to come back'. It was all my fault, because I had gone down into the bay. I had opened up a road into the past again. And although Maxim had recovered, and was himself again, and we lived our lives together, sleeping, eating, walking, writing letters, driving to the village, working hour by hour through our day, I knew there was a barrier between us because of it.

He walked alone, on the other side, and I must not come to him. And I became nervous and fearful that some heedless word, some turn in a careless conversation should bring that expression back to his eyes again. I began to dread any mention of the sea, for the sea might lead to boats, to accidents, to drowning. . . . Even Frank Crawley, who came to lunch one day, put me in a little fever of fear when he said something about the sailing races in Kerrith harbour, three miles away. I looked steadily at my plate, a stab of sickness in my heart at once, but Maxim went on talking quite naturally, he did not seem to mind, while I sat in a sweat of uncertainty wondering what would happen and where the conversation would lead us.

It was during cheese, Frith had left the room, and I remember getting up and going to the side-board, and taking some more cheese, not wanting it, so as not to be at the table with them, listening; humming a little tune to myself so I could not hear. I was wrong of course, morbid, stupid, this was the hypersensitive behaviour of a neurotic, not the normal happy self I knew myself to be. But I could not help it. I did not know what to do. My shyness and gaucherie became worse, too, making me stolid and dumb when people came to the house. For we were called upon, I remember, during those first weeks, by people who lived near us in the county, and the receiving of them, and the shaking hands, and the spinning out of the formal half hour became a worse ordeal than I first anticipated, because of this new fear of mine that they would talk about something that must not be discussed. The agony of those wheels on the drive, of that pealing bell, of my own first wild rush for flight to my own room. The scrambled dab of powder on my nose, the hasty comb through my hair, and then the inevitable knock on the door and the entrance of the cards on a silver salver.

'All right. I'll be down immediately.' The clap of my heels on the stairs and across the hall, the opening of the library door or, worse still, that long, cold, lifeless drawing-room, and the strange woman waiting there, or a husband and a wife.

'How do you do? I'm so sorry, Maxim is in the garden somewhere, Frith has gone to find him.'

'We felt we must come and pay our respects to the bride.'

A little laughter, a little flurry of chat, a pause, a glance round the room.

'Manderley is looking as charming as ever. Don't you love it?'

'Oh, yes, rather . . .' And in my shyness and anxiety to please, those schoolgirl phrases would escape from me again, those words I never used except in moments like these, 'Oh, ripping'; and 'Oh, topping'; and 'absolutely'; and 'priceless'; even, I think, to one dowager who had carried a lorgnette, 'cheerio'. My relief at Maxim's arrival would be tempered by the fear they might say something indiscreet, and I became dumb at once, a set smile on my lips, my hands in my lap. They would turn to Maxim then, talking of people and places I had not met or did not know, and now and again I would find their eyes upon me, doubtful, rather bewildered.

I could picture them saying to one another as they drove away, 'My dear, what a dull girl. She scarcely opened her mouth'; and then the sentence I had first heard upon Beatrice's lips, haunting me ever since, a sentence I read in every eye, on every tongue – 'She's so different to Rebecca.'

Sometimes I would glean little snatches of information to add to my secret store. A word dropped here at random, a question, a passing phrase. And, if Maxim was not with me, the hearing of them would be a furtive, rather painful pleasure, guilty knowledge learnt in the dark.

I would return a call perhaps, for Maxim was punctilious in these matters and would not spare me, and if he did not come with me I must brave the formality alone, and there would be a pause in the conversation while I searched for something to say. 'Will you be entertaining much at Manderley, Mrs. de Winter?' they would say and my answer would come, 'I don't know, Maxim has not said much about it up to the present.' 'No, of course not, it's early yet. I believe the house was generally full of people in the old days.' Another pause. 'People from London, you know. There used to be tremendous parties.' 'Yes,' I would say. 'Yes, so I have heard.' A further pause, and then the lowered voice that is always used about the dead or in a place of worship. 'She was so tremendously popular, you know. Such a personality.' 'Yes,' I would say. 'Yes, of course.' And after a moment or so I would glance at my watch under cover of my glove, and say 'I'm afraid I ought to be going, it must be after four.'

'Won't you stay for tea? We always have it quarter past.'

'No – No, really, thanks most awfully. I promised Maxim . . .' my sentence would go trailing off into nothing, but the meaning would be understood. We would both rise to our feet, both of us knowing I was not deceived about her offer to tea nor she in my mention of a promise to Maxim. I sometimes wondered what would happen if convention were denied, if, having got into the car and waved a hand to my hostess on the doorstep, I suddenly opened it again, and said 'I don't think I'll go back after all. Let's go to your drawing-room again and sit down. I'll stay to dinner if you like or stop the night.'

I used to wonder if convention and good county manners would brave the surprise, and whether a smile of welcome would be summoned to the frozen face, 'But of course! How very delightful of you to suggest it.' I used to wish I had the courage to try. But instead the door would slam, the car would go bowling away down the smooth gravel drive, and my late hostess would wander back to her room with a sigh of relief and become herself again. It was the wife of the bishop in the neighbouring cathedral town who said to me, 'Will your husband revive the Manderley Fancy Dress ball, do you suppose? Such a lovely sight always, I shall never forget it.'

I had to smile as though I knew all about it and say, 'We have not decided. There have been so many things to do and to discuss.'

'Yes, I suppose so. But I hope it won't be dropped. You must use your influence with him. There was not one last year of course. But I remember two years ago, the bishop and I went, and it was quite enchanting. Manderley so lends itself to anything like that. The hall looked wonderful. They danced there, and had the music in the gallery; it was all so in keeping. A tremendous thing to organise but everybody appreciated it so.'

'Yes,' I said. 'Yes, I must ask Maxim about it.'

I thought of the docketed pigeon-holes in the desk in the morning-room, I pictured the stack upon stack of invitation cards, the long list of names, the addresses, and I could see a woman sitting there at the desk and putting a V beside the names she wanted, and reaching for the invitation cards, dipping her pen in the ink, writing upon them swift and sure in that long, slanting hand.

'There was a garden party, too, we went to one summer,' said the bishop's wife. 'Everything always so beautifully done. The flowers at their best. A glorious day I remember. Tea was served at little tables in the rose-garden, such an attractive original idea. Of course, she was so clever . . .'

She stopped, turning a little pink, fearing a loss of tact, but I agreed with her at once to save embarrassment, and I heard myself saying boldly, brazenly, 'Rebecca must have been a wonderful person.'

I could not believe that I had said the name at last. I waited, wondering what would happen. I had said the name. I had said the word Rebecca aloud. It was a tremendous relief. It was as though I had taken a purge and rid myself of an intolerable pain. Rebecca. I had said it aloud.

I wondered if the bishop's wife saw the flush on my face, but she went on smoothly with the conversation, and I listened to her greedily, like an eavesdropper at a shuttered window.

'You never met her then?' she asked, and when I shook my head she hesitated a moment, a little uncertain of her ground. 'We never knew her well personally, you know, the bishop was only inducted here four years ago, but of course she received us when we went to the ball and to the garden party. We dined there, too, one winter. Yes, she was a very lovely creature. So full of life.'

'She seems to have been so good at everything too,' I said, my voice just careless enough to show I did not mind, while I played with the fringe of my glove. 'It's not often you get someone who is clever and beautiful and fond of sport.'

'No, I suppose you don't,' said the bishop's wife, 'she was certainly very gifted. I can see her now, standing at the foot of the stairs on the night of the ball, shaking hands with everybody, that cloud of dark hair against the very white skin, and her costume suited her so. Yes, she was very beautiful.'

'She ran the house herself, too,' I said, smiling, as if to say, 'I am quite at my ease, I often discuss her.' 'It must have taken a lot of time and thought. I'm afraid I leave it to the housekeeper.'

'Oh, well, we can't all do everything. And you are very young, aren't you? No doubt in time, when you have settled down. Besides, you have your own hobby, haven't you? Someone told me you were fond of sketching.'

'Oh, that,' I said. 'I don't know that I can count it for much.'

'It's a nice little talent to have,' said the bishop's wife; 'it's not everyone that can sketch. You must not drop it. Manderley must be full of pretty spots to sketch.'

'Yes,' I said. 'Yes, I suppose so,' depressed by her words, having a sudden vision of myself wandering across the lawns with a camp-stool and a box of pencils under one arm, and my 'little talent', as she described it, under the other. It sounded like a pet disease.

'Do you play any games, do you ride, or shoot?' she asked.

'No,' I said, 'I don't do anything like that. I'm fond of walking,' I added, as a wretched anti-climax.

'The best exercise in the world,' she said briskly, 'the bishop and I walk a lot.' I wondered if he went round and round the cathedral, in his shovel hat and his gaiters, with her on his arm. She began to talk about a walking holiday they had taken once, years ago, in the Pennines, how they had done an average of twenty miles a day, and I nodded by head, smiling politely, wondering about the Pennines, thinking they were something like the Andes, remembering afterwards they were that chain of hills marked with a furry line in the middle of a pink England on my school atlas. And he all the time in his hat and gaiters.

The inevitable pause, the glance at the watch unnecessary, as her drawing-room clock chimed four in shrill tones, and my rise from the chair. 'I'm so glad I found you in. I hope you will come and see us.'

'We should love to. The bishop is always so busy, alas. Please remember me to your husband, and be sure and ask him to revive the ball.'

'Yes, indeed I will.' Lying, pretending I knew all about it; and in the car going home I sat in my corner, biting my thumb nail, seeing the great hall at Manderley thronged with people in fancy dress, the chatter, hum, and laughter of the moving crowd, the musicians in the gallery, supper in the drawing-room probably, long buffet tables against the wall, and I could see Maxim standing at the foot of the stairs, laughing, shaking hands, turning to someone who stood by his side, tall and slim, with dark hair, said the bishop's wife, dark hair against a white face, someone whose quick eyes saw to the comfort of her guests, who gave an order over her shoulder to a servant, someone who was never awkward, never without grace, who when she danced left a stab of perfume in the air like a white azalea.

'Will you be entertaining much at Manderley, Mrs. de Winter?' I heard the question again, suggestive, rather inquisitive, in the voice of that woman I had called on who lived the other side of Kerrith, and I saw her eye too, dubious, considering, taking in my clothes from top to toe, wondering, with that swift downward glance given to all brides, if I was going to have a baby.

I did not want to see her again. I did not want to see any of them again. They only came to call at Manderley because they were curious and prying. They liked to criticise my looks, my manners, my figure, they liked to watch how Maxim and I behaved to each other, whether we seemed fond of one another, so that they could go back afterwards and discuss us, saying, 'Very different from the old days.' They came because they wanted to compare me to Rebecca. . . . I would not return these calls any more, I decided, I should tell Maxim so. I did not mind if they thought me rude and ungracious. It would give them more to criticise, more to discuss. They could say I was ill-bred. 'I'm not surprised,' they would say, 'after all, who was she?' And then a laugh and a shrug of the shoulder. 'My dear, don't you know? He picked her up in Monte Carlo or somewhere, she hadn't a penny. She was a companion to some old woman.' More laughter, more lifting of the eyebrows. 'Nonsense, not really? How extraordinary men are. Maxim, of all people, who was so fastidious. How could he, after Rebecca?'

I did not mind. I did not care. They could say what they liked. As the car turned in at the lodge gates I leant forward in my seat to smile at the woman who lived there. She was bending down, picking flowers in the front garden. She straightened up as she heard the car, but she did not see me smile. I waved, and she stared at me blankly. I don't think she knew who I was. I leant back in my seat again. The car went on down the drive.

When we turned at one of the narrow bends I saw a man walking along the drive a little distance ahead. It was the agent, Frank Crawley. He stopped when he heard the car, and the chauffeur slowed down. Frank Crawley took off his hat and smiled when he saw me in the car. He seemed glad to see me. I smiled back at him. It was nice of him to be glad to see me. I liked Frank Crawley. I did not find him dull or uninteresting as Beatrice had done. Perhaps it was because I was dull myself. We were both dull. We neither of us had a word to say for ourselves. Like to like.

I tapped on the glass and told the chauffeur to stop.

'I think I'll get out and walk with Mr. Crawley,' I said.

He opened the door for me. 'Been paying calls, Mrs. de Winter?' he said.

'Yes, Frank,' I said. I called him Frank because Maxim did, but he would always call me Mrs. de Winter. He was that sort of person. Even if we had been thrown on a desert island together, and lived there in intimacy for the rest of our lives, I should have been Mrs. de Winter.

'I've been calling on the bishop,' I said, 'and I found the bishop out but the bishop's lady was at home. She and the bishop are very fond of walking. Sometimes they do twenty miles a day, in the Pennines.'

'I don't know that part of the world,' said Frank Crawley, 'they say the country round is very fine. An uncle of mine used to live there.'

It was the sort of remark Frank Crawley always made. Safe, conventional, very correct.

'The bishop's wife wants to know when we are going to give a Fancy Dress ball at Manderley?' I said, watching him out of the tail of my eye. 'She came to the last one, she said, and enjoyed it very much. I did not know you have Fancy Dress dances here, Frank.'

He hesitated a moment before replying. He looked a little troubled. 'Oh, yes,' he said after a moment, 'the Manderley ball was generally an annual affair. Everyone in the county came. A lot of people from London too. Quite a big show.'

'It must have taken a lot of organisation,' I said.

'Yes,' he said.

'I suppose,' I said carelessly, 'Rebecca did most of it?'

I looked straight ahead of me along the drive, but I could see his face was turned towards me, as though he wished to read my expression.

'We all of us worked pretty hard,' he said quietly.

There was a funny reserve in his manner as he said this, a certain shyness that reminded me of my own. I wondered suddenly if he had been in love with Rebecca. His voice was the sort of voice I should have used in his circumstances, had this been so. The idea opened up a new field of possibilities. Frank Crawley being so shy, so dull, he would never have told anyone, least of all Rebecca.

'I'm afraid I should not be much use if we have a dance,' I said, 'I'm no earthly use at organising anything.'

'There would be no need for you to do anything,' he said, 'you would just be yourself and look decorative.'

'That's very polite of you, Frank,' I said, 'but I'm afraid I should not be able to do that very well either.'

'I think you would do it excellently,' he said. Dear Frank Crawley, how tactful he was and considerate. I almost believed him. But he did not deceive me really.

'Will you ask Maxim about the ball?' I said.

'Why don't you ask him?' he answered.

'No,' I said. 'No, I don't like to.'

We were silent then. We went on walking along the drive. Now that I had broken down my reluctance at saying Rebecca's name, first with the bishop's wife and now with Frank Crawley, the urge to continue was strong within me. It gave me a curious satisfaction, it acted upon me like a stimulant. I knew that in a moment or two I should have to say it again. 'I was down on one of the beaches the other day,' I said, 'the one with the breakwater. Jasper was being infuriating, he kept barking at the poor man with the idiot's eyes.'

'You must mean Ben,' said Frank, his voice quite easy now, 'he always potters about on the shore. He's quite a nice fellow, you need never be frightened of him. He would not hurt a fly.'

'Oh, I wasn't frightened,' I said. I waited a moment, humming a tune to give me confidence. 'I'm afraid that cottage place is going to rack and ruin,' I said lightly. 'I had to go in, to find a piece of string or something to tie up Jasper. The china is mouldy and the books are being ruined. Why isn't something done about it? It seems such a pity.'

I knew he would not answer at once. He bent down to tie up his shoe lace.

I pretended to examine a leaf on one of the shrubs. 'I think if Maxim wanted anything done he would tell me,' he said, still fumbling with his shoe.

'Are they all Rebecca's things?' I asked.

'Yes,' he said.

I threw the leaf away and picked another, turning it over in my hands.

'What did she use the cottage for?' I asked. 'It looked quite furnished. I thought from the outside it was just a boat-house.'

'It was a boat-house originally,' he said, his voice constrained again, difficult, the voice of someone who is uncomfortable about his subject. 'Then – then she converted it like that, had furniture put, and china.'

I thought it funny the way he called her 'she.' He did not say Rebecca or Mrs. de Winter, as I expected him to do.

'Did she use it a great deal?' I asked.

'Yes,' he said. 'Yes, she did. Moonlight picnics, and – and one thing and another.'

We were walking again side by side, I still humming my little tune. 'How jolly,' I said brightly, 'moonlight picnics must be great fun. Did you ever go to them?'

'Once or twice,' he said. I pretended not to notice his manner, how quiet it had become, how reluctant to speak about these things.

'Why is the buoy there in the little harbour place?' I said.

'The boat used to be moored there,' he said.

'What boat?' I asked.

'Her boat,' he said.

A strange sort of excitement was upon me. I had to go on with my questions. He did not want to talk about it, I knew that, but although I was sorry for him and shocked at my own self I had to continue, I could not be silent.

'What happened to it?' I said. 'Was that the boat she was sailing when she was drowned?'

'Yes,' he said quietly, 'it capsized and sank. She was washed overboard.'

'What sort of size boat was it?' I asked.

'About three tons. It had a little cabin.'

'What made it capsize?' I said.

'It can be very squally in the bay,' he said.

I thought of that green sea, foam-flecked, that ran down channel beyond the headland. Did the wind come suddenly, I wondered, in a funnel from the beacon on the hill, and did the little boat heel to it, shivering, the white sail flat against a breaking sea?

'Could not someone have got out to her?' I said.

'Nobody saw the accident, nobody knew she had gone,' he said.

I was very careful not to look at him. He might have seen the surprise in my face. I had always thought it happened in a sailing race, that other boats were there, the boats from Kerrith, and that people were watching, from the cliffs. I did not know she had been alone. Quite alone, out there in the bay.

'They must have known up at the house?' I said.

'No,' he said. 'She often went out alone like that. She would come back any time of the night, and sleep at the cottage on the beach.'

'Was not she nervous?'

'Nervous?' he said. 'No, she was not nervous of anything.'

'Did – did Maxim mind her going off alone like that?'

He waited a minute, and then 'I don't know,' he said shortly. I had the impression he was being loyal to someone. Either to Maxim or to Rebecca, or perhaps even to himself. He was odd. I did not know what to make of it.

'She must have been drowned then, trying to swim to shore, after the boat sank?' I said.

'Yes,' he said.

I knew how the little boat would quiver and plunge, the water gushing into the steering well, and how the sails would press her down, suddenly, horribly, in that gust of wind. It must have been very dark out there in the bay. The shore must have seemed very far away to anyone swimming there, in the water.

'How long afterwards was it that they found her?' I said.

'About two months,' he said.

Two months. I thought drowned people were found after two days. I thought they would be washed up close to the shore, when the tide came.

'Where did they find her?' I asked.

'Near Edgecoombe, about forty miles up channel,' he said.

I had spent a holiday at Edgecoombe once, when I was seven. It was a big place, with a pier, and donkeys. I remembered riding a donkey along the sands.

'How did they know it was her, after two months, how could they tell?' I said. I wondered why he paused before each sentence, as though he weighed his words. Had he cared for her then, had he minded so much?

'Maxim went up to Edgecoombe to identify her,' he said.

Suddenly I did not want to ask him any more. I felt sick at myself, sick and disgusted. I was like a curious sight-seer standing on the fringe of a crowd after someone had been knocked down. I was like a poor person in a tenement building, when someone has died, asking if I might see the body. I hated myself. My questions had been degrading, shameful. Frank Crawley must despise me.

'It was a terrible time for all of you,' I said rapidly, 'I don't suppose you like being reminded about it. I just wondered if there was anything one could do to the cottage, that's all. It seems such a pity, all the furniture being spoilt by the damp.'

He did not say anything. I felt hot and uncomfortable. He must have sensed that it was not concern for the empty cottage that had prompted me to all these questions, and now he was silent because he was shocked at me. Ours had been a comfortable, steady sort of friendship. I had felt him an ally. Perhaps I had destroyed all this, and he would never feel the same about me again.

'What a long drive this is,' I said, 'it always reminds me of the path in the forest in a Grimm's fairy tale, where the prince gets lost, you know. It's always longer than one expects, and the trees are so dark, and close.'

'Yes, it is rather exceptional,' he said.

I could tell by his manner he was still on his guard, as though waiting for a further question from me. There was an awkwardness between us that could not be ignored. Something had to be done about it, even if it covered me with shame.

'Frank,' I said desperately, 'I know what you are thinking. You can't understand why I asked all those questions just now. You think I'm morbid, and curious, in a rather beastly way. It's not that, I promise you. It's only that – that sometimes I feel myself at such a disadvantage. It's all very strange to me, living here at Manderley. Not the sort of life I've been brought up to. When I go returning these calls, as I did this afternoon, I know people are looking me up and down, wondering what sort of success I'm going to make of it. I can imagine them saying, "What on earth does Maxim see in her?" And then, Frank, I begin to wonder myself, and I begin to doubt, and I have a fearful haunting feeling that I should never have married Maxim, that we are not going to be happy. You see, I know that all the time, whenever I meet anyone new, they are all thinking the same thing – How different she is to Rebecca.'

I stopped breathless, already a little ashamed of my outburst, feeling that now at any rate I had burnt my boats for all time. He turned to me looking very concerned and troubled.

'Mrs. de Winter, please don't think that,' he said. 'For my part I can't tell you how delighted I am that you have married Maxim. It will make all the difference to his life. I am positive that you will make a great success of it. From my point of view it's – it's very refreshing and charming to find someone like yourself who is not entirely – er –' he blushed, searching for a word 'not entirely *au fait*, shall we say, with ways at Manderley. And if the people around here give you the impression that they are criticising you, it's – well – it's most damnably offensive of them, that's all. I've never heard a word of criticism, and if I did I should take great care that it was never uttered again.'

'That's very sweet of you, Frank,' I said, 'and what you say helps enormously. I dare say I've been very stupid. I'm not good at meeting people, I've never had to do it, and all the time I keep remembering how – how it must have been at Manderley before, when there was someone there who was born and bred to it, did it all naturally and without effort. And I realise, every day, that things I lack, confidence, grace, beauty, intelligence, wit – Oh, all the qualities that mean most in a woman, – she possessed. It doesn't help, Frank, it doesn't help.'

He said nothing. He went on looking anxious, and distressed. He pulled out his handkerchief and blew his nose. 'You must not say that,' he said.

'Why not? It's true,' I said.

'You have qualities that are just as important, far more so, in fact. It's perhaps cheek of me to say so, I don't know you very well. I'm a bachelor, I don't know very much about women, I lead a quiet sort of life down here at Manderley as you know, but I should say that kindliness, and sincerity, and if I may say so – modesty – are worth far more to a man, to a husband, than all the wit and beauty in the world.'

He looked very agitated, and blew his nose again. I saw that I had upset him far more than I had upset myself, and the realisation of this calmed me and gave me a feeling of superiority. I wondered why he was making such a fuss. After all, I had not said so very much. I had only confessed my sense of insecurity, following as I did upon Rebecca. And she must have had these qualities that he presented to me as mine. She must have been kind and sincere, with all her friends, her boundless popularity. I was not sure what he meant by modesty. It was a word I had never understood. I always imagined it had something to do with minding meeting people in a passage on the way to a bathroom . . . Poor Frank. And Beatrice had called him a dull man, with never a word to say for himself.

'Well,' I said, rather embarrassed, 'well, I don't know about all that. I don't think I'm very kind, or particularly sincere, and as for being modest, I don't think I've ever had much of a chance to be anything else. It was not very modest, of course, being married hurriedly like that, down in Monte Carlo, and being alone there in that hotel, beforehand, but perhaps you don't count that?'

'My dear Mrs. de Winter, you don't think I imagine for one moment that your meeting down there was not entirely above board?' he said in a low voice.

'No, of course not,' I said gravely. Dear Frank. I think I had shocked him. What a Frank-ish expression, too, 'above board.' It made one think immediately of the sort of things that would happen below board.

'I'm sure,' he began, and hesitated, his expression still troubled, 'I'm sure that Maxim would be very worried, very distressed, if he knew how you felt. I don't think he can have any idea of it.'

'You won't tell him?' I said hastily.

'No, naturally not, what do you take me for? But you see, Mrs. de Winter, I know Maxim pretty well, and I've seen him through many . . . moods. If he thought you were worrying about – well – about the past, it would distress him more than anything on earth. I can promise you that. He's looking very well, very fit, but Mrs. Lacy was quite right the other day when she said he had been on the verge of a breakdown last year, though it was tactless of her to say so in front of him. That's why you are so good for him. You are fresh and young and – and sensible, you have nothing to do with all that time that has gone. Forget it, Mrs. de Winter, forget it, as he has done, thank heaven, and the rest of us. We none of us want to bring back the past. Maxim least of all. And it's up to you, you know, to lead us away from it. Not to take us back there again.'

He was right, of course he was right. Dear good Frank, my friend, my ally. I had been selfish and hyper-sensitive, a martyr to my own inferiority complex. 'I ought to have told you all this before,' I said.

'I wish you had,' he said, 'I might have spared you some worry.'

'I feel happier,' I said, 'much happier. And I've got you for my friend whatever happens, haven't I, Frank?'

'Yes, indeed,' he said.

We were out of the dark wooded drive and into the light again. The rhododendrons were upon us. Their hour would soon be over. Already they looked a little over-blown, a little faded. Next month the petals would fall one by one from the great faces, and the gardeners would come and sweep them away. Theirs was a brief beauty. Not lasting very long.

'Frank,' I said, 'before we put an end to this conversation, for ever let's say, will you promise to answer me one thing, quite truthfully?'

He paused, looking at me a little suspiciously. 'That's not quite fair,' he said, 'you might ask me something that I should not be able to answer, something quite impossible.'

'No,' I said, 'it's not that sort of question. It's not intimate or personal, or anything like that.'

'Very well, I'll do my best,' he said.

We came round the sweep of the drive and Manderley was before us, serene and peaceful in the hollow of the lawns, surprising me as it always did, with its perfect symmetry and grace, its great simplicity.

The sunlight flickered on the mullioned windows, and there was a soft rusted glow about the stone walls where the lichen clung. A thin column of smoke curled from the library chimney. I bit my thumb nail, watching Frank out of the tail of my eye.

'Tell me,' I said, my voice casual, not caring a bit, 'tell me, was Rebecca very beautiful?'

Frank waited a moment. I could not see his face. He was looking away from me towards the house. 'Yes,' he said slowly, 'yes, I suppose she was the most beautiful creature I ever saw in my life.'

We went up the steps then to the hall, and I rang the bell for tea.

Chapter Twelve

I did not see much of Mrs. Danvers. She kept very much to herself. She still rang the house telephone to the morning-room every day and submitted the menu to me as a matter of form, but that was the limit of our intercourse. She had engaged a maid for me, Clarice, the daughter of somebody on the estate, a nice quiet well-mannered girl, who, thank heaven, had never been in service before and had no alarming standards. I think she was the only person in the house who stood in awe of me. To her I was the mistress, I was Mrs. de Winter. The possible gossip of the others could not affect her.

She had been away for some time, brought up by an aunt fifteen miles away, and in a sense she was as new to Manderley as I was. I felt at ease with her. I did not mind saying 'Oh, Clarice, would you mend my stocking?'

The housemaid Alice had been so superior. I used to sneak my chemise and nightgowns out of my drawer and mend them myself rather than ask her to do them. I had seen her once, with one of my chemises over her arm, examining the plain material with its small edging of lace. I shall never forget her expression. She looked almost shocked, as though her own personal pride had received a blow. I had never thought about my underclothes before. As long as they were clean and neat I had not thought the material or the existence of lace mattered. Brides one read about had trousseaux, dozens of sets at a time, and I had never bothered. Alice's face taught me a lesson. I wrote quickly to a shop in London and asked for a catalogue of underlinen. By the time I had made my choice Alice was looking after me no longer and Clarice was installed instead. It seemed such a waste buying new underclothes for Clarice that I put the catalogue away in a drawer and never wrote to the shop after all.

I often wondered whether Alice told the others, and if my underclothes became a topic of conversation in the servants' hall, something rather dreadful, to be discussed in low tones when the men were nowhere about. She was too superior for it to be made a joking question. Phrases like 'Chemise to you' would never be bandied between her and Frith for instance.

No, my underclothes were more serious than that. More like a divorce case heard *in camera*.... At any rate I was glad when Alice surrendered me to Clarice. Clarice would never know real lace from false. It was considerate of Mrs. Danvers to have engaged her. She must have thought we would be fit company, one for the other. Now that I knew the reason for Mrs. Danvers' dislike and resentment it made things a little easier. I knew it was not just me personally she hated, but what I represented. She would have felt the same towards anyone who had taken Rebecca's place. At least that was what I understood from Beatrice the day she came to lunch.

'Did not you know?' she had said. 'She simply adored Rebecca.'

The words had shocked me at the time. Somehow I had not expected them. But when I thought it over I began to lose my first fear of Mrs. Danvers. I began to be sorry for her. I could imagine what she must feel. It must hurt her every time she heard me called 'Mrs. de Winter.' Every morning when she took up the house telephone and spoke to me, and I answered 'Yes, Mrs. Danvers,' she must be thinking of another voice. When she passed through the rooms and saw traces of me about the place, a beret on a window-seat, a bag of knitting on a chair, she must think of another one, who had done these things before. Even as I did. I, who had never known Rebecca. Mrs. Danvers knew how she walked and how she spoke. Mrs. Danvers knew the colour of her eyes, her smile, the texture of her hair. I knew none of these things, I had never asked about them, but sometimes I felt Rebecca was as real to me as she was to Mrs. Danvers.

Frank had told me to forget the past, and I wanted to forget it. But Frank did not have to sit in the morning-room as I did, every day, and touch the pen she had held between her fingers. He did not have to rest his hands on the blotter, and stare in front of him at her writing on the pigeon-holes. He did not have to look at the candlesticks on the mantelpiece, the clock, the vase in which the flowers stood, the pictures on the walls and remember, every day, that they belonged to her, she had chosen them, they were not mine at all. Frank did not have to sit at her place in the dining-room, hold the knife and fork that she had held, drink from her glass. He did not throw a coat over his shoulders which had been hers, nor find her handkerchief in the pocket. He did not notice, every day, as I did, the blind gaze of the old dog in its basket in the library, who lifted its head when it heard my footstep, the footstep of a woman, and sniffing the air drooped its head again, because I was not the one she sought.

Little things, meaningless and stupid in themselves, but they were there for me to see, for me to hear, for me to feel. Dear God, I did not want to think about Rebecca. I wanted to be happy, to make Maxim happy, and I wanted us to be together. There was no other wish in my heart but that. I could not help it if she came to me in thoughts, in dreams. I could not help it if I felt like a guest in Manderley, my home, walking where she had trodden, resting where she had lain. I was like a guest, biding my time, waiting for the return of the hostess. Little sentences, little reproofs reminding me every hour, every day.

'Frith,' I said, coming into the library on a summer morning, my arms full of lilac, 'Frith where can I find a tall vase for these? They are all too small in the flower-room.'

'The white alabaster vase in the drawing-room was always used for the lilac, Madam.'

'Oh, wouldn't it be spoilt? It might get broken.'

'Mrs. de Winter always used the alabaster vase, Madam.'

'Oh, oh, I see.'

Then the alabaster vase was brought for me, already filled with water, and as I put the sweet lilac in the vase and arranged the sprigs, one by one, the mauve warm scent filling the room, mingling with the smell of the new-mown lawn outside coming from the open window, I thought: 'Rebecca did this. She took the lilac, as I am doing, and put the sprigs one by one in the white vase. I'm not the first to do it. This is Rebecca's vase, this is Rebecca's lilac.' She must have wandered out into the garden as I did, in that floppy garden hat I had seen once at the back of a cupboard in the flower-room, hidden under some old cushions, and crossed the lawn to the lilac bushes, whistling perhaps, humming a tune, calling to the dogs to follow her, carrying in her hands the scissors that I carried now.

'Frith, could you move that book-stand from the table in the window, and I will put the lilac there?'

'Mrs. de Winter always had the alabaster vase on the table behind the sofa, Madam.'

'Oh, well . . . ' I hesitated, the vase in my hands, Frith's face impassive. He would obey me of course if I said I preferred to put the vase on the smaller table by the window. He would move the book-stand at once.

'All right,' I said, 'perhaps it would look better on the larger table.' And the alabaster vase stood, as it had always done, on the table behind the sofa. . . .

Beatrice remembered her promise of a wedding present. A large parcel arrived one morning, almost too large for Robert to carry. I was sitting in the morning-room, having just read the menu for the day. I have always had a childish love of parcels. I snipped the string excitedly, and tore off the dark brown paper. It looked like books. I was right. It was books. Four big volumes. *A History of Painting.* And a sheet of note-paper in the first volume saying 'I hope this is the sort of thing you like,' and signed 'Love from Beatrice.' I could see her going into the shop in Wigmore Street and buying them. Looking about her in her abrupt, rather masculine way. 'I want a set of books for someone who is keen on Art,' she would say, and the attendant would answer, 'Yes, Madam, will you come this way.' She would finger the volumes a little suspiciously. 'Yes, that's about the price. It's for a wedding present. I want them to look good. Are these all about Art?' 'Yes, this is the standard work on the subject,' the assistant would say. And then Beatrice must have written her note, and paid her cheque, and given the address 'Mrs. de Winter, Manderley.'

It was nice of Beatrice. There was something rather sincere and pathetic about her going off to a shop in London and buying me those books because she knew I was fond of painting. She imagined me, I expect, sitting down on a wet day and looking solemnly at the illustrations, and perhaps getting a sheet of drawing-paper and a paint-box and copying one of the pictures. Dear Beatrice. I had a sudden, stupid desire to cry. I gathered up the heavy volumes and looked round the morning-room for somewhere to put them. They were out of place in that fragile delicate room. Never mind, it was my room now, after all. I arranged them in a row on the top of the desk. They swayed dangerously, leaning one against the other. I stood back a bit, to watch the effect. Perhaps I moved too quickly, and it disturbed them. At any rate the foremost one fell, and the others slid after him. They upset a little china cupid who had hitherto stood alone on the desk except for the candlesticks. He fell to the ground, hitting the waste-paper basket as he did so, and broke into fragments. I glanced hurriedly at the door, like a guilty child. I knelt on the floor and swept up the pieces into my hand. I found an envelope to put them in. I hid the envelope at the back of one of the drawers in the desk. Then I took the books off to the library and found room for them on the shelves.

Maxim laughed when I showed them to him with pride.

'Dear old Bee,' he said, 'you must have had a success with her. She never opens a book if she can help it.'

'Did she say anything about – well – what she thought of me?' I asked.

'The day she came to lunch? No, I don't think so.'

'I thought she might have written or something.'

'Beatrice and I don't correspond unless there's a major event in the family. Writing letters is a waste of time,' said Maxim.

I supposed I was not a major event. Yet if I had been Beatrice, and had a brother, and the brother married, surely one would have said something, expressed an opinion, written two words? Unless of course one had taken a dislike to the wife, or thought her unsuitable. Then of course it would be different. Still, Beatrice had taken the trouble to go up to London and to buy the books for me. She would not have done that if she disliked me.

It was the following day I remember, when Frith, who had brought in the coffee after lunch to the library, waited a moment, hovering behind Maxim, and said,

'Could I speak to you, sir?' Maxim glanced up from his paper.

'Yes, Frith, what is it?' he said, rather surprised. Frith wore a stiff solemn expression, his lips pursed. I thought at once his wife had died.

'It's about Robert, sir. There has been a slight unpleasantness between him and Mrs. Danvers. Robert is very upset.'

'Oh, Lord,' said Maxim, making a face at me. I bent down to fondle Jasper, my unfailing habit in moments of embarrassment.

'Yes, sir. It appears Mrs. Danvers has accused Robert of secreting a valuable ornament from the morning-room. It is Robert's business to bring in the fresh flowers to the morning-room and place the vases. Mrs. Danvers went in this morning after the flowers had been done, and noticed one of the ornaments was missing. It was there yesterday, she said. She accused Robert of either taking the ornament or breaking it and concealing the breakage. Robert denied both accusations most emphatically, and came to me nearly in tears, sir. You may have noticed he was not himself at lunch.'

'I wondered why he handed me the cutlets without giving me a plate,' murmured Maxim. 'I did not know Robert was so sensitive. Well, I suppose someone else did it. One of the maids.'

'No, sir. Mrs. Danvers went into the room before the girl had done the room. Nobody had been there since Madam yesterday, and Robert first thing with the flowers. It makes it very unpleasant for Robert and myself, sir.'

'Yes, of course it does. Well, you had better ask Mrs. Danvers to come here and we'll get to the bottom of it. What ornament was it, anyway?'

'The china cupid, sir, that stands on the writing-table.'

'Oh! Oh, Lord. That's one of our treasures, isn't it? It will have to be found. Get hold of Mrs. Danvers at once.'

'Very good, sir.'

Frith left the room and we were alone again. 'What a confounded nuisance,' said Maxim, 'that cupid is worth a hell of a lot. How I loathe servants' rows too. I wonder why they come to me about it. That's your job, sweetheart.'

I looked up from Jasper, my face red as fire. 'Darling,' I said, 'I meant to tell you before, but – but I forgot. The fact is I broke that cupid when I was in the morning-room yesterday.'

'You broke it? Well, why the devil didn't you say so when Frith was here?'

'I don't know. I didn't like to. I was afraid he would think me a fool.'

'He'll think you much more of a fool now. You'll have to explain to him and Mrs. Danvers.'

'Oh, no, please, Maxim, you tell them. Let me go upstairs.'

'Don't be a little idiot. Anyone would think you were afraid of them.'

'I am afraid of them. At least, not afraid, but . . . '

The door opened, and Frith ushered Mrs. Danvers into the room. I looked nervously at Maxim. He shrugged his shoulders, half amused, half angry.

'It's all a mistake, Mrs. Danvers. Apparently Mrs. de Winter broke the cupid herself and forgot to say anything,' said Maxim.

They all looked at me. It was like being a child again. I was still aware of my guilty flush. 'I'm so sorry,' I said, watching Mrs. Danvers, 'I never thought Robert would get into trouble.'

'Is it possible to repair the ornament, Madam?' said Mrs. Danvers. She did not seem to be surprised that I was the culprit. She looked at me with her white skull's face and her dark eyes. I felt she had known it was me all along and had accused Robert to see if I would have the courage to confess.

'I'm afraid not,' I said, 'it smashed in little pieces.'

'What did you do with the pieces?' said Maxim.

It was like being a prisoner, giving evidence. How paltry and mean my actions sounded, even to myself. 'I put them all into an envelope,' I said.

'Well, what did you do with the envelope?' said Maxim, lighting a cigarette, his tone a mixture of amusement and exasperation.

'I put it at the back of one of the drawers in the writing-desk,' I said.

'It looks as though Mrs. de Winter thought you would put her in prison, doesn't it Mrs. Danvers?' said Maxim. 'Perhaps you would find the envelope and send the pieces up to London. If they are too far gone to mend it can't be helped. All right, Frith. Tell Robert to dry his tears.'

Mrs. Danvers lingered when Frith had gone. 'I will apologise to Robert of course,' she said, 'but the evidence pointed so strongly to him. It did not occur to me that Mrs. de Winter had broken the ornament herself. Perhaps, if such a thing should happen again, Mrs. de Winter will tell me personally, and I will have the matter attended to? It would save everybody a lot of unpleasantness.'

'Naturally,' said Maxim impatiently, 'I can't think why she didn't do so yesterday. I was just going to tell her when you came into the room.'

'Perhaps Mrs. de Winter was not aware of the value of the ornament?' said Mrs. Danvers, turning her eyes upon me.

'Yes,' I said wretchedly. 'Yes, I was afraid it was valuable. That's why I swept the pieces up so carefully.'

'And hid them at the back of a drawer where no one would find them, eh?' said Maxim, with a laugh, and a shrug of the shoulders. 'Is not that the sort of thing the between-maid is supposed to do, Mrs. Danvers?'

'The between-maid at Manderley would never be allowed to touch the valuable things in the morning-room, sir,' said Mrs. Danvers.

'No, I can't see you letting her,' said Maxim.

'It's very unfortunate,' said Mrs. Danvers, 'I don't think we have ever had any breakages in the morning-room before. We were always so particular. I've done the dusting in there myself since – last year. There was no one I could trust. When Mrs. de Winter was alive we used to do the valuables together.'

'Yes, well – it can't be helped,' said Maxim. 'All right, Mrs. Danvers.'

She went out of the room, and I sat on the window-seat, looking out of the window. Maxim picked up his paper again. Neither of us spoke.

'I'm awfully sorry, darling,' I said, after a moment, 'it was very careless of me. I can't think how it happened. I was just arranging those books on the desk, to see if they would stand, and the cupid slipped.'

'My sweet child, forget it. What does it matter?'

'It does matter. I ought to have been more careful. Mrs. Danvers must be furious with me.'

'What the devil has she got to be furious about? It's not her bit of china.'

'No, but she takes such a pride in it all. It's so awful to think nothing in there has ever been broken before. It had to be me.'

'Better you than the luckless Robert.'

'I wish it had been Robert. Mrs. Danvers will never forgive me.'

'Damn Mrs. Danvers,' said Maxim, 'she's not God Almighty, is she? I can't understand you. What do you mean by saying you are afraid of her?'

'I did not mean afraid exactly. I don't see much of her. It's not that. I can't really explain.'

'You do such extraordinary things,' said Maxim; 'fancy not getting hold of her when you broke the thing and saying, 'Here, Mrs. Danvers, get this mended.' She'd understand that. Instead of which you scrape up the remains in an envelope and hide 'em at the back of a drawer. Just like a between-maid, as I said, and not the mistress of a house.'

'I am like a between-maid,' I said slowly, 'I know I am, in lots of ways. That's why I have so much in common with Clarice. We are on the same sort of footing. And that's why she likes me. I went and saw her mother the other day. And do you know what she said? I asked her if she thought Clarice was happy with us, and she said, 'Oh yes, Mrs. de Winter. Clarice seems quite happy. She says, "It's not like being with a lady, Mum, it's like being with one of ourselves." ' Do you suppose she meant it as a compliment or not?'

'God knows,' said Maxim, 'remembering Clarice's mother I should take it as a direct insult. Her cottage is generally a shambles and smells of boiled cabbage. At one time she had nine children under eleven, and she herself used to patter about in that patch of garden with no shoes and a stocking round her head. We nearly gave her notice to quit. Why Clarice looks as neat and clean as she does I can't imagine.'

'She's been living with an aunt,' I said, feeling rather subdued. 'I know my flannel skirt has a dirty mark down the front, but I've never walked bare-foot with a stocking round my head.' I knew now why Clarice did not disdain my underclothes as Alice had done. 'Perhaps that's why I prefer calling on Clarice's mother to calling on people like the bishop's wife?' I went on. 'The bishop's wife never said I was like one of themselves.'

'If you wear that grubby skirt when you call on her I don't suppose she does,' said Maxim.

'Of course I didn't call on her in my old skirt, I wore a frock,' I said, 'and anyway I don't think much of people who just judge one by one's clothes.'

'I hardly think the bishop's wife cares twopence about clothes,' said Maxim, 'but she may have been rather surprised if you sat on the extreme edge of the chair and answered 'Yes' and 'No' like someone after a new job, which you did the only time we returned a call together.'

'I can't help being shy.'

'I know you can't sweetheart. But you don't make an effort to conquer it.'

'I think that's very unfair,' I said. 'I try every day, every time I go out or meet anyone new. I'm always making efforts. You don't understand. It's all very well for you, you're used to that sort of thing. I've not been brought up to it.'

'Rot,' said Maxim 'it's not a question of bringing up, as you put it. It's a matter of application. You don't think I like calling on people do you? It bores me stiff. But it has to be done, in this part of the world.'

'We're not talking about boredom,' I said, 'there's nothing to be afraid of in being bored. If I was just bored it would be different. I hate people looking me up and down as though I were a prize cow.'

'Who looks you up and down?'

'All the people down here. Everybody.'

'What does it matter if they do? It gives them some interest in life.'

'Why must I be the one to supply the interest, and have all the criticism?'

'Because life at Manderley is the only thing that ever interests anybody down here.'

'What a slap in the eye I must be to them then.'

Maxim did not answer. He went on looking at his paper.

'What a slap in the eye I must be to them,' I repeated. And then 'I suppose that's why you married me,' I said, 'you knew I was dull and quiet and inexperienced, so that there would never be any gossip about me.'

Maxim threw his paper on the ground and got up from his chair. 'What do you mean?' he said.

His face was dark and queer, and his voice was rough, not his voice at all.

'I – I don't know,' I said, leaning back against the window, 'I don't mean anything. Why do you look like that?'

'What do you know about any gossip down here?' he said.

'I don't, I said, scared by the way he looked at me, 'I only said it because – because of something to say. Don't look at me like that. Maxim, what have I said; what's the matter?'

'Who's been talking to you?' he said slowly.

'No one. No one at all.'

'Why did you say what you did?'

'I tell you, I don't know. It just came to my head. I was angry, cross. I do hate calling on these people, I can't help it. And you criticised me for being shy. I didn't mean it. Really, Maxim, I didn't. Please believe me.'

'It was not a particularly attractive thing to say, was it?' he said.

'No,' I said. 'No, it was rude, hateful.'

He stared at me moodily, his hands in his pockets, rocking backwards and forwards on his heels. 'I wonder if I did a very selfish thing in marrying you,' he said. He spoke slowly, thoughtfully.

I felt very cold, rather sick. 'How do you mean?' I said.

'I'm not much of a companion to you, am I?' he said. 'There are too many years between us. You ought to have waited, and then married a boy of your own age. Not someone like myself, with half his life behind him.'

'That's ridiculous,' I said hurriedly, 'you know age doesn't mean anything in marriage. Of course we are companions.'

'Are we? I don't know,' he said.

I knelt up on the window-seat and put my arms round his shoulders. 'Why do you say these things to me?' I said. 'You know I love you more than anything in the world. There has never been anyone but you. You are my father and my brother and my son. All those things.'

'It was my fault,' he said, not listening. 'I rushed you into it. I never gave you a chance to think it over.'

'I did not want to think it over,' I said, 'there was no other choice. You don't understand Maxim. When one loves a person . . . '

'Are you happy here?' he said, looking away from me, out of the window. 'I wonder sometimes. You've got thinner. Lost your colour.'

'Of course I'm happy,' I said, 'I love Manderley, I love the garden, I love everything. I don't mind calling on people. I just said that to be tiresome. I'll call on people every day, if you want me to. I don't mind what I do. I've never for one moment regretted marrying you, surely you must know that?'

He patted my cheek in his terrible absent way, and bent down, and kissed the top of my head. 'Poor lamb, you don't have much fun, do you? I'm afraid I'm very difficult to live with.'

'You're not difficult,' I said eagerly, 'you are easy, very easy. Much easier than I thought you would be. I used to think it would be dreadful to be married, that one's husband would drink, or use awful language, or grumble if the toast was soft at breakfast, and be rather unattractive altogether, smell possibly. You don't do any of those things.'

'Good God, I hope not,' said Maxim, and he smiled.

I seized advantage of his smile, I smiled too, and took his hands and kissed them. 'How absurd to say we are not companions,' I said, 'why, look how we sit here every evening, you with a book or a paper, and me with my knitting. Just like cups of tea. Just like old people, married for years and years. Of course we are companions. Of course we are happy. You talk as though you thought we had made a mistake? You don't mean it like that, do you, Maxim? You know our marriage is a success, a wonderful success?'

'If you say so, then it's all right,' he said.

'No, but you think it too, don't you darling? It's not just me? We are happy aren't we? Terribly happy?'

He did not answer. He went on staring out of the window while I held his hands. My throat felt dry and tight, and my eyes were burning. Oh, God I thought, this is like two people in a play, in a moment the curtain will come down, we shall bow to the audience, and go off to our dressing-rooms. This can't be a real moment in the lives of Maxim and myself. I sat down on the window-seat, and let go of his hands. I heard myself speaking in a hard cool voice. 'If you don't think we are happy it would be much better if you would admit it. I don't want you to pretend anything. I'd much rather go away. Not live with you any more.' It was not really happening of course. It was the girl in the play talking, not me to Maxim. I pictured the type of girl who would play the part. Tall and slim, rather nervy.

'Well, why don't you answer me?' I said.

He took my face in his hands and looked at me, just as he had before, when Frith had come into the room with tea, the day we went to the beach.

'How can I answer you?' he said. 'I don't know the answer myself. If you say we are happy, let's leave it at that. It's something I know nothing about. I take your word for it. We are happy. All right then, that's agreed!' He kissed me again, and then walked away across the room. I went on sitting by the window, stiff and straight, my hands in my lap.

'You say all this because you are disappointed in me,' I said. 'I'm gauche and awkward, I dress badly, I'm shy with people. I warned you in Monte Carlo how it would be. You think I'm not right for Manderley.'

'Don't talk nonsense,' he said. 'I've never said you dressed badly, or were gauche. It's your imagination. As for being shy, you'll get over that. I've told you so before.'

'We've argued in a circle,' I said, 'we've come right back to where we started. This all began because I broke the cupid in the morning-room. If I hadn't broken the cupid none of this would have happened. We'd have drunk our coffee, and gone out into the garden.'

'Oh, damn that infernal cupid,' said Maxim wearily. 'Do you really think I care whether it's in ten thousand pieces or not?'

'Was it very valuable?'

'Heaven knows. I suppose so. I've really forgotten.'

'Are all those things in the morning-room valuable?'

'Yes, I believe so.'

'Why were all the most valuable things put in the morning-room?'

'I don't know. I suppose because they looked well there.'

'Were they always there? When your mother was alive?'

'No. No, I don't think they were. They were scattered about the house. The chairs were in a lumber room I believe.'

'When was the morning-room furnished as it is now?'

'When I was married.'

'I suppose the cupid was put there then?'

'I suppose so.'

'Was that found in a lumber room?'

'No. No, I don't think it was. As a matter-of-fact I believe it was a wedding-present. Rebecca knew a lot about china.'

I did not look at him. I began to polish my nails. He had said the word quite naturally, quite calmly. It had been no effort to him. After a minute I glanced at him swiftly. He was standing by the mantelpiece, his hands in his pockets. He was staring straight in front of him. He is thinking about Rebecca I said to myself. He is thinking about the cupid. He is remembering who gave it to Rebecca. He is going over in his mind how the parcel came and how pleased she was. Rebecca knew a lot about china. Perhaps he came into the room, and she was kneeling on the floor, wrenching open the little crate in which the cupid was packed. She must have glanced up at him, and smiled. 'Look, Max' she would have said, 'look what we've been sent.' And she then would have plunged her hand down in to the shavings and brought out the cupid who stood on one foot, his bow in his hand. 'We'll have it in the morning-room,' she must have said, and he must have knelt down beside her, and they must have looked at the cupid together.

I went on polishing my nails. They were scrubby, like a school-boy's nails. The cuticles grew up over the half moons. The thumb was bitten nearly to the quick. I looked at Maxim again. He was still standing in front of the fireplace.

'What are you thinking about?' I said.

My voice was steady and cool. Not like my heart, thumping inside me. Not like my mind, bitter and resentful. He lit a cigarette, surely the twenty-fifth that day, and we had only just finished lunch; he threw the match into the empty grate, he picked up the paper.

'Nothing very much, why?' he said.

'Oh, I don't know,' I said, 'you looked so serious, so far away.'

He whistled a tune absently, the cigarette twisting in his fingers. 'As a matter of fact I was wondering if they had chosen the Surrey side to play Middlesex at the Oval,' he said.

He sat down in the chair again and folded the paper. I looked out of the window. Presently Jasper came to me and climbed on my lap.

Chapter Thirteen

Maxim had to go up to London at the end of June to some public dinner. A man's dinner. Something to do with the county. He was away for two days and I was left alone. I dreaded his going. When I saw the car disappear round the sweep in the drive I felt exactly as though it were to be a final parting and I should never see him again. There would be an accident of course and later on in the afternoon, when I came back from my walk, I should find Frith white and frightened waiting for me with a message. The doctor would have rung up from some cottage hospital. 'You must be very brave,' he would say, 'I am afraid you must be prepared for a great shock.'

And Frank would come, and we would go to the hospital together. Maxim would not recognise me. I went through the whole thing as I was sitting at lunch, I could see the crowd of local people clustering round the churchyard at the funeral, and myself leaning on Frank's arm. It was so real to me that I could scarcely eat any lunch, and I kept straining my ears to hear the telephone should it ring.

I sat out in the garden under the chestnut tree in the afternoon, with a book on my lap, but I scarcely read at all. When I saw Robert come across the lawn I knew it was the telephone and I felt physically sick. 'A message from the club, Madam, to say Mr. de Winter arrived ten minutes ago.'

I shut up my book. 'Thank you, Robert. How quickly he got up.'

'Yes, Madam. A very good run.'

'Did he ask to speak to me, or leave any special message?'

'No, Madam. Just that he had arrived safely. It was the porter speaking.'

'All right, Robert. Thanks very much.'

The relief was tremendous. I did not feel sick any more. The pain had gone. It was like coming ashore after a channel crossing. I began to feel rather hungry, and when Robert had gone back into the house I crept into the dining-room through the long window and stole some biscuits from the side-board. I had six of them. Bath Olivers. And then an apple as well. I had no idea I was so empty. I went and ate them in the woods, in case one of the servants should see me on the lawn from the windows, and then go and tell the cook that they did not think Mrs. de Winter cared for the food prepared in the kitchen, as they had just seen her filling herself with fruit and biscuits. The cook would be offended, and perhaps go to Mrs. Danvers.

Now that Maxim was safe in London, and I had eaten my biscuits, I felt very well and curiously happy. I was aware of a sense of freedom, as though I had no responsibilities at all. It was rather like a Saturday when one was a child. No lessons, and no prep. One could do as one liked. One put on an old skirt and a pair of sand-shoes and played Hares and Hounds on the common with the children who lived next door.

I had just the same feeling. I had not felt like this all the time I had been at Manderley. It must be because Maxim had gone to London.

I was rather shocked at myself. I could not understand it at all. I had not wanted him to go. And now this lightness of heart, this spring in my step, this childish feeling that I wanted to run across the lawn, and roll down the bank. I wiped the biscuit crumbs from my mouth and called to Jasper. Perhaps I was just feeling like this because it was a lovely day. . . .

We went through the Happy Valley to the little cove. The azaleas were finished now, the petals lay brown and crinkled on the moss. The bluebells had not faded yet, they made a solid carpet in the woods above the valley, and the young bracken was shooting up, curling and green. The moss smelt rich and deep, and the bluebells were earthy, bitter, I lay down in the long grass beside the bluebells with my hands behind my head, and Jasper at my side. He looked down at me panting, his face foolish, the saliva dripping from his tongue and his heavy jowl. There were pigeons somewhere in the trees above. It was very peaceful and quiet. I wondered why it was that places are so much lovelier when one is alone. How commonplace and stupid

it would be if I had a friend now, sitting beside me, someone I had known
at school, who would say 'By-the-way, I saw old Hilda the other day. You
remember her, the one who was so good at tennis. She's married, with two
children.' And the bluebells beside us unnoticed, and the pigeons overhead
unheard. I did not want anyone with me. Not even Maxim. If Maxim had
been there I should not be lying as I was now, chewing a piece of grass, my
eyes shut. I should have been watching him, watching his eyes, his expression.
Wondering if he liked it, if he was bored. Wondering what he was thinking.
Now I could relax, none of these things mattered. Maxim was in London.
How lovely it was to be alone again. No, I did not mean that. It was disloyal,
wicked. It was not what I meant. Maxim was my life and my world. I got
up from the bluebells and called sharply to Jasper. We set off together down
the valley to the beach. The tide was out, the sea very calm and remote. It
looked like a great placid lake out there in the bay. I could not imagine it
rough now, any more than I could imagine winter in summer. There was
no wind, and the sun shone on the lapping water where it ran into the little
pools in the rocks. Jasper scrambled up the rocks immediately, glancing back
at me, one ear blown back against his head, giving him an odd rakish
appearance.

'Not that way, Jasper,' I said.

He cared nothing for me of course. He loped off, deliberately disobedient.
'What a nuisance he is,' I said aloud, and I scrambled up the rocks after
him, pretending to myself I did not want to go to the other beach. 'Oh, well,'
I thought, 'it can't be helped. After all, Maxim is not with me. It's nothing
to do with me.'

I splashed through the pools on the rocks, humming a tune. The cove
looked different when the tide was out. Less formidable. There was only
about three foot of water in the tiny harbour. A boat would just float there
comfortably I supposed, at dead low water. The buoy was still there. It was
painted white and green, I had not noticed that before. Perhaps because it
had been raining the colouring was indistinct. There was no one on the
beach. I walked across the shingle to the other side of the cove, and climbed
the low stone wall of the jetty-arm. Jasper ran on ahead as though it was
his custom. There was a ring in the wall and an iron ladder descending to
the water. That's where the dinghy would be tied, I supposed, and one
would climb to it from the ladder. The buoy was just opposite, about thirty
feet away. There was something written on it. I craned my neck sideways
to read the lettering. 'Je Reviens'. What a funny name. Not like a boat.
Perhaps it had been a French boat though, a fishing boat. Fishing boats
sometimes had names like that, 'Happy Return', 'I'm Here', those sort of
names. 'Je Reviens' – 'I come back'. Yes, I supposed it was quite a good
name for a boat. Only it had not been right for that particular boat which
would never come back again.

It must be cold sailing out there in the bay, beyond the beacon away on
the headland. The sea was calm in the bay, but even to-day, when it was
so still, out there round the headland there was a ripple of white foam on
the surface of the water where the tide was racing. A small boat would heel

to the wind when she rounded the headland and came out of the land-locked bay. The sea would splash inboard perhaps, run down the deck. The person at the tiller would wipe the spray out of her eyes and hair, glance up at the straining mast. I wondered what colour the boat had been. Green and white perhaps, like the buoy. Not very big, Frank had said, with a little cabin.

Jasper was sniffing at the iron ladder. 'Come away,' I said. 'I don't want to go in after you.' I went back along the harbour wall to the beach. The cottage did not seem so remote and sinister at the edge of the wood as it had done before. The sun made such a difference. No rain to-day, pattering on the roof. I walked slowly up the beach towards it. After all, it was only a cottage, with nobody living in it. There was nothing to be frightened of. Nothing at all. Any place seemed damp and sinister when it had been uninhabited for a certain time. Even new bungalows and places. Besides, they had had moonlight picnics and things here. Week-end visitors probably used to come and bathe, and then go for a sail in the boat. I stood looking into the neglected garden choked with nettles. Someone ought to come and tidy it up. One of the gardeners. There was no need to leave it like this. I pushed the little gate and went to the door of the cottage. It was not entirely closed. I was certain I had closed it last time. Jasper began growling, sniffing under the door.

'Don't Jasper,' I said. He went on sniffing deeply, his nose thrust to the crack. I pushed the door open and looked inside. It was very dark. Like it had been before. Nothing was changed. The cobwebs still clung to the rigging of the model boats. The door into the boat-store at the end of the room was open though. Jasper growled again, and there was a sound of something falling. Jasper barked furiously, and darting between my legs into the room he tore to the open door of the store. I followed him, heart beating, and then stood uncertainly in the middle of the room. 'Jasper, come back, don't be a fool,' I said. He stood in the doorway, still barking furiously, an hysterical note in his voice. Something was there then, inside the store. Not a rat. He would have gone for a rat. 'Jasper, Jasper. Come here,' I said. He would not come. I went slowly to the door of the store.

'Is there anybody there?' I said.

No one answered. I bent down to Jasper, putting my hand on his collar, and looked round the edge of the door. Someone was sitting in the corner against the wall. Someone, who from his crouching position, was even more frightened than me. It was Ben. He was trying to hide behind one of the sails. 'What is the matter, do you want something?' I said. He blinked at me stupidly, his mouth slightly open.

'I'm not doing nothing,' he said.

'Quiet, Jasper,' I scolded, putting my hand over his muzzle, and I took my belt off and ran it through his collar as a leash.

'What do you want, Ben?' I said, a little bolder this time.

He did not answer. He watched me with his sly idiot's eyes.

'I think you had better come out,' I said. 'Mr. de Winter doesn't like people walking in and out of here.'

He shambled to his feet grinning furtively, wiping his nose with the back of his hand. The other hand he kept behind his back. 'What have you got, Ben?' I said. He obeyed me like a child, showing me the other hand. There was a fishing line in it. 'I'm not doing nothing,' he repeated.

'Does that line belong here?' I asked.

'Eh?' he said.

'Listen, Ben,' I said, 'you can take that line if you want to, but you mustn't do it again. It's not honest, taking people's things.'

He said nothing. He blinked at me and wriggled.

'Come along,' I said firmly. I went into the main room and he followed me. Jasper had stopped barking, and was now sniffing at Ben's heels. I did not want to stop any longer in the cottage. I walked quickly out into the sunshine, Ben shuffling behind me. Then I shut the door.

'You had better go home,' I said to Ben.

He held the fishing line clutched to his heart like a treasure. 'You won't put me to the asylum, will you?' he said.

I saw then that he was trembling with fright. His hands were shaking, and his eyes were fixed on mine in supplication, like a dumb thing.

'Of course not,' I said gently.

' I done nothing,' he repeated, 'I never told no one. I don't want to be put to the asylum.' A tear rolled down his dirty face.

'That's all right, Ben,' I said, 'no one will put you away. But you must not go to the cottage again.'

I turned away, and he came after me, pawing at my hand.

'Here,' he said. 'Here I got something for you.'

He smiled foolishly, he beckoned with his finger, and turned towards the beach. I went with him, and he bent down and picked up a flat stone by a rock. There was a little heap of shells under the stone. He chose one, and presented it to me. 'That's yourn,' he said.

'Thank you, it's very pretty,' I said.

He grinned again, rubbing his ear, his fright forgotten. 'You've got angel's eyes,' he said.

I glanced down at the shell, again, rather taken aback. I did not know what to say.

'You're not like the other one,' he said.

'Who do you mean?' I said. 'What other one?'

He shook his head. His eyes were sly again. He laid his finger against his nose. 'Tall and dark she was,' he said. 'She gave you the feeling of a snake. I seen her here with me own eyes. Be night she'd come. I seen her.' He paused, watching me intently. I did not say anything. 'I looked in on her once,' he said, 'and she turned on me, she did. "You don't know me, do you?" she said. "You've never seen me here, and you won't again. If I catch you looking at me through the windows here I'll have you put to the asylum," she said. "You wouldn't like that, would you? They're cruel to people in the asylum," she said. "I won't say nothing, M'am," I said. And I touched me cap, like this here.' He pulled at his sou'wester. 'She's gone now ain't she?' he said anxiously.

'I don't know who you mean,' I said slowly, 'no one is going to put you in the asylum. Good afternoon, Ben.'

I turned away and walked up the beach to the path dragging Jasper by his belt. Poor wretch, he was potty, of course. He did not know what he was talking about. It was hardly likely that anyone would threaten him with the asylum. Maxim had said he was quite harmless, and so had Frank. Perhaps he had heard himself discussed once, amongst his own people, and the memory of it lingered, like an ugly picture in the mind of a child. He would have a child's mentality too, regarding likes and dislikes. He would take a fancy to a person for no reason, and be friendly one day perhaps and sullen the next. He had been friendly with me because I had said he could keep the fishing line. To-morrow if I met him he might not know me. It was absurd to notice anything said by an idiot. I glanced back over my shoulder at the cove. The tide had begun to turn and was swirling slowly round the arm of the harbour wall. Ben had disappeared over the rocks. The beach was deserted again. I could just see the stone chimney of the cottage through a gap in the dark trees. I had a sudden unaccountable desire to run. I pulled at Jasper's leash and panted up the steep narrow path through the woods not looking back any more. Had I been offered all the treasures in the world I could not have turned and gone down to the cottage or the beach again. It was as though someone waited down there, in the little garden where the nettles grew. Someone who watched and listened.

Jasper barked as we ran together. He thought it was some new kind of game. He kept trying to bite the belt and worry it. I had not realised how closely the trees grew together here, their roots stretching across the path like tendrils ready to trip one. They ought to clear all this, I thought as I ran, catching my breath, Maxim should get the men on to it. There is no sense or beauty in this undergrowth. That tangle of shrubs there should be cut down to bring light to the path. It was dark, much too dark. That naked eucalyptus tree stifled by brambles looked like the white bleached limb of a skeleton, and there was a black earthy stream running beneath it, choked with the muddied rains of years, trickling silently to the beach below. The birds did not sing here as they did in the valley. It was quiet in a different way. And even as I ran and panted up the path I could hear the wash of the sea as the tide crept into the cove. I understood why Maxim disliked the path and the cove. I disliked it too. I had been a fool to come this way. I should have stayed on the other beach, on the white shingle, and come home by the Happy Valley.

I was glad to come out on to the lawn and see the house there in the hollow, solid and secure. The woods were behind me. I would ask Robert to bring me my tea under the chestnut tree. I glanced at my watch. It was earlier than I thought, not yet four. I would have to wait a bit. It was not the routine at Manderley to have tea before half-past. I was glad Frith was out. Robert would not make such a performance of bringing the tea out into the garden. As I wandered across the lawn to the terrace my eye was caught by a gleam of sunshine on something metal showing through the green of the rhododendron leaves at the turn in the drive. I shaded my eyes with my hand to see what it was. It looked like the radiator of a car. I wondered if someone had called. If they had though, they would have driven up to the house, not left their car concealed like that from the house, at the turn of the drive, by the shrubs. I went a little closer. Yes, it was a car all right. I could see the wings now and the hood. What a funny thing. Visitors never did that as a rule. And the tradesmen went round the back way by the old stables and the garage. It was not Frank's Morris. I knew that well. This was a long, low car, a sports car. I wondered what I had better do. If it was a caller Robert would have shown them into the library or the drawing-room. If the drawing-room they would be able to see me as I came across the lawn. I did not want to face a caller dressed like this. I should have to ask them to stay to tea. I hesitated, at the edge of the lawn. For no reason, perhaps because the sunlight flickered a moment on the glass, I looked up at the house, and as I did so I noticed with surprise that the shutters of one of the windows in the west wing had been opened up. Somebody stood by the window. A man. And then he must have caught sight of me because he drew back abruptly, and a figure behind him put up an arm and closed the shutters.

The arm belonged to Mrs. Danvers. I recognised the black sleeve. I wondered for a minute if it was a public day and she was showing the rooms. It could not be so though because Frith always did that, and Frith was out. Besides, the rooms in the west wing were not shown to the public. I had not even been into them myself yet. No, I knew it was not a public day. The public never came on a Tuesday. Perhaps it was something to do with a repair in one of the rooms. It was odd though the way the man had been looking out and directly he saw me he whipped back into the room and the shutters were closed. And the car too, drawn up behind the rhododendrons, so that it could not be seen from the house. Still, that was up to Mrs. Danvers. It was nothing to do with me. If she had friends she took to the west wing it was not exactly my affair. I had never known it happen before though. Odd that it should occur on the only day Maxim was from home.

I strolled rather self-consciously across the lawn to the house, aware that they might be watching me still from a chink in the shutters.

I went up the steps and through the big front door to the hall. There was no sign of a strange cap or stick, and no card on the salver. Evidently this was not an official visitor. Well, it was not my affair. I went into the flower room and washed my hands in the basin to save going upstairs. It would be awkward if I met them face to face on the stairs or somewhere. I remembered I had left my knitting in the morning-room before lunch, and I went along through the drawing-room to fetch it, the faithful Jasper at my heels. The morning-room door was open. And I noticed that my bag of knitting had been moved. I had left it on the divan, and it had been picked up and pushed behind a cushion. There was the imprint of a person on the fabric of the divan where my knitting had been before. Someone had sat down there recently, and picked up my knitting because it had been in the way. The chair by the desk had also been moved. It looked as though Mrs. Danvers entertained her visitors in the morning-room when Maxim and I were out of the way, I felt rather uncomfortable. I would rather not know. Jasper was sniffing round the divan and wagging his tail. He was not suspicious of the visitor anyway. I took my bag of knitting and went out. As I did so the door in the large drawing-room that led to the stone passage and the back premises opened, and I heard voices. I darted back into the morning-room again, just in time. I had not been seen. I waited behind the door frowning at Jasper who stood in the doorway looking at me, his tongue hanging out, wagging his tail. The little wretch would give me away. I stood very still, holding my breath.

Then I heard Mrs. Danvers speak. 'I expect she has gone to the library,' she said. 'She's come home early for some reason. If she has gone to the library you will be able to go through the hall without her seeing you. Wait here while I go and see.'

I knew they were talking about me. I began to feel more uncomfortable than ever. It was so furtive, the whole business. And I did not want to catch Mrs. Danvers in the wrong. Then Jasper turned his head sharply towards the drawing-room. He trotted out, wagging his tail.

'Hullo, you little tyke,' I heard the man say. Jasper began to bark excitedly. I looked round desperately for somewhere to hide. Hopeless of course. And then I heard a footstep quite close to my ear, and the man came into the room. He did not see me at first because I was behind the door, but Jasper made a dive at me, still barking with delight.

The man wheeled round suddenly and saw me. I have never seen anyone look more astonished. I might have been the burglar and he the master of the house.

'I beg your pardon,' he said, looking me up and down.

He was a big, hefty fellow, good-looking in a rather flashy, sunburnt way. He had the hot, blue eyes usually associated with heavy drinking and loose living. His hair was reddish like his skin. In a few years he would run to fat, his neck bulging over the back of his collar. His mouth gave him away, it was too soft, too pink. I could smell the whisky in his breath from where I stood. He began to smile. The sort of smile he would give to every woman.

'I hope I haven't startled you,' he said.

I came out from behind the door looking no doubt as big a fool as I felt. 'No, of course not,' I said, 'I heard voices, I was not quite sure who it was. I did not expect any callers this afternoon.'

'What a shame,' he said heartily, 'it's too bad of me to butt in on you like this. I hope you'll forgive me. The fact is I just popped in to see old Danny, she's a very old friend of mine.'

'Oh, of course, it's quite all right,' I said.

'Dear old Danny,' he said, 'she's so anxious, bless her, not to disturb anyone. She didn't want to worry you.'

'Oh, it does not matter at all,' I said. I was watching Jasper, who was jumping up and pawing at the man in delight.

'This little beggar hasn't forgotten me, has he?' he said. 'Grown into a jolly little beast. He was quite a youngster when I saw him last. He's too fat though. He needs more exercise.'

'I've just taken him for a long walk,' I said.

'Have you really? How sporting of you,' he said. He went on patting Jasper and smiling at me in a familiar way. Then he pulled out his cigarette case. 'Have one?' he said.

'I don't smoke,' I told him.

'Don't you really?' He took one himself and lighted it.

I never minded those things, but it seemed odd to me, in somebody else's room. It was surely rather bad manners? Not polite to me.

How's old Max?' he said.

I was surprised at his tone. It sounded as though he knew him well. It was queer, to hear Maxim talked of as Max. No one called him that.

'He's very well, thank you,' I said, 'he's gone up to London.'

'And left the bride all alone? Why, that's too bad. Isn't he afraid someone will come and carry you off?'

He laughed, opening his mouth. I did not like his laugh. There was something offensive about it. I did not like him either. Just then Mrs. Danvers came into the room. She turned her eyes upon me and I felt quite cold. Oh, God, I thought, how she must hate me.

'Hullo, Danny, there you are,' said the man, 'all your precautions were in vain. The mistress of the house was hiding behind the door.' And he laughed again. Mrs. Danvers did not say anything. She just went on looking at me. 'Well, aren't you going to introduce me?' he said. 'After all, it's the usual thing to do, isn't it, to pay one's respects to a bride?'

'This is Mr. Favell, Madam,' said Mrs. Danvers. She spoke quietly, rather unwillingly. I don't think she wanted to introduce him to me.

'How do you do,' I said, and then, with an effort to be polite, 'Won't you stay to tea?'

He looked very amused. He turned to Mrs. Danvers.

'Now isn't that a charming invitation?' he said. 'I've been asked to stay to tea? By heaven, Danny, I've a good mind to.'

I saw her flash a look of warning at him. I felt very uneasy. It was all wrong, this situation. It ought not to be happening at all.

'Well, perhaps you're right,' he said, 'it would have been a lot of fun, all the same. I suppose I had better be going, hadn't I? Come and have a look at my car.' He still spoke in a familiar rather offensive way. I did not want to go and look at his car. I felt very awkward and embarrassed. 'Come on,' he said, 'it's a jolly good little car. Much faster than anything poor old Max ever has.'

I could not think of an excuse. The whole business was so forced and stupid. I did not like it. And why did Mrs. Danvers have to stand there looking at me with that smouldering look in her eyes?

'Where is the car?' I said feebly.

'Round the bend in the drive. I didn't drive to the door, I was afraid of disturbing you. I had some idea you probably rested in the afternoon.'

I said nothing. The lie was too obvious. We all walked out through the drawing-room and into the hall. I saw him glance over his shoulder and wink at Mrs. Danvers. She did not wink in return. I hardly expected she would. She looked very hard and grim. Jasper frolicked out on to the drive. He seemed delighted with the sudden appearance of this visitor whom he appeared to know so well.

'I left my cap in the car I believe,' said the man, pretending to glance round the hall. 'As a matter-of-fact, I didn't come in this way. I slipped round and bearded Danny in her den. Coming out to see the car too?'

He looked enquiringly at Mrs. Danvers. She hesitated, watching me out of the tail of her eye.

'No,' she said. 'No, I don't think I'll come out now. Good-bye, Mr. Jack.'

He seized her hand and shook it heartily. 'Good-bye, Danny, take care of yourself. You know where to get in touch with me always. It's done me a power of good to see you again.' He walked out on to the drive, Jasper dancing at his heels, and I followed him slowly, feeling very uncomfortable still.

'Dear old Manderley,' he said, looking up at the windows, 'the place hasn't changed much. I suppose Danny sees to that. What a wonderful woman she is, eh?'

'Yes, she's very efficient,' I said.

'And what do you think of it all? Like being buried down here?'

'I'm very fond of Manderley,' I said stiffly.

'Weren't you living somewhere down in the south of France when Max met you? Monte, wasn't it? I used to know Monte well.'

'Yes, I was in Monte Carlo,' I said.

We had come to his car now. A green sports thing, typical of its owner.

'What do you think of it?' he said.

'Very nice,' I said politely.

'Come for a run to the lodge gates?' he said.

'No, I don't think I will,' I said. 'I'm rather tired.'

'You don't think it would look too good for the mistress of Manderley to be seen driving with someone like me, is that it?' he said, and he laughed, shaking his head at me.

'Oh, no,' I said, turning rather red. 'No, really.'

He went on looking me up and down in his amused way with those familiar, unpleasant blue eyes. I felt like a barmaid.

'Oh, well,' he said, 'we mustn't lead the bride astray, must we, Jasper? It wouldn't do at all.' He reached for his cap, and an enormous pair of motoring gloves. He threw his cigarette away on the drive.

'Good-bye,' he said, holding out his hand, 'it's been a lot of fun meeting you.'

'Good-bye,' I said.

'By-the-way,' he said carelessly, 'it would be very sporting and grand of you if you did not mention this little visit of mine to Max? He doesn't exactly approve of me, I'm afraid; I don't know why, and it might get poor old Danny into trouble.'

'No,' I said awkwardly. 'No, all right.'

'That's very sporting of you. Sure you won't change your mind and come for a run?'

'No, I don't think I will, if you don't mind.'

'Bye-bye, then. Perhaps I'll come and look you up one day. Get down, Jasper, you devil, you'll scratch my paint. I say, I call it a damn shame Max going up to London and leaving you alone like this?'

'I don't mind. I like being alone,' I said.

'Do you, by Jove? What an extraordinary thing. It's all wrong, you know. Against nature. How long have you been married? Three months, isn't it?'

'About that,' I said.

'I say, I wish I'd got a bride of three months waiting for me at home! I'm a poor lonesome bachelor.' He laughed again, and pulled his cap down over his eyes. 'Fare you well,' he said, starting up the engine, and the car shot down the drive snorting explosive fury from the exhaust, while Jasper stood looking after it, his ears drooping, his tail between his legs.

'Oh, come on, Jasper,' I said, 'don't be so idiotic,' I walked slowly back to the house. Mrs. Danvers had disappeared. I stood in the hall and rang the bell. Nothing happened for about five minutes. I rang. Presently Alice appeared, her face rather aggrieved. 'Yes, Madam?' she said.

'Oh, Alice,' I said, 'isn't Robert there? I rather fancied my tea out under the chestnut tree.'

'Robert went to the post this afternoon, and isn't back yet, Madam,' said Alice. 'Mrs. Danvers gave him to understand you would be late for tea. Frith is out too of course. If you want your tea now I can get it for you. I don't think it's quite half-past four yet.'

'Oh, it doesn't matter, Alice, I'll wait till Robert comes back,' I said. I supposed when Maxim was away things automatically became slack. I had never known Frith and Robert to be out at the same time. It was Frith's day of course. And Mrs. Danvers had sent Robert to the post. And I myself was understood to have gone for a long walk. That man Favell had chosen his time well to pay his call on Mrs. Danvers. It was almost too well chosen. There was something not right about it, I was certain of that. And then he had asked me not to say anything to Maxim. It was all very awkward. I did not want to get Mrs. Danvers into trouble or make any sort of scene. More important still I did not want to worry Maxim.

I wondered who he was, this man Favell. He had called Maxim 'Max.' No one ever called him Max. I had seen it written once, on the fly-leaf of a book, the letters thin and slanting, curiously pointed, the tail of the M very definite, very long. I thought there was only one person who had ever called him Max. . . .

As I stood there in the hall, undecided about my tea, wondering what to do, the thought suddenly came to me that perhaps Mrs. Danvers was dishonest, that all this time she was engaged in some business behind Maxim's back, and coming back early as I had to-day I had discovered her and this man, an accomplice, who had then bluffed his way out by pretending to be familiar with the house and with Maxim. I wondered what they had been doing in the west wing. Why had they closed the shutters when they saw me on the lawn? I was filled with vague disquiet. Frith and Robert had been away. The maids were generally in their bedrooms changing during the afternoon. Mrs. Danvers would have the run of the place. Supposing this man was a thief, and Mrs. Danvers was in his pay? There were valuable things in the west wing. I had a sudden rather terrifying impulse to creep upstairs now to the west wing and go into those rooms and see for myself.

Robert was not yet back. I would just have time before tea. I hesitated, glancing at the gallery. The house seemed very still and quiet. The servants were all in their own quarters beyond the kitchen. Jasper lapped noisily at his drinking bowl below the stairs, the sound echoing in the great stone hall. I began to walk upstairs. My heart was beating in a queer excited way.

Chapter Fourteen

I found myself in the corridor where I had stood that first morning. I had not been there since, nor had I wished to go. The sun streamed in from the window in the alcove and made gold patterns on the dark panelling.

There was no sound at all. I was aware of the same musty, unused smell that had been before. I was uncertain which way to go. The plan of the rooms was not familiar to me. I remembered then that last time Mrs. Danvers had come out of a door here, just behind me, and it seemed to me that the position of the room would make it the one I wanted, whose windows looked out upon the lawns to the sea. I turned the handle of the door and went inside. It was dark of course, because of the shutters. I felt for the electric light switch on the wall and turned it on. I was standing in a little ante-room, a dressing-room I judged, with big wardrobes round the wall, and at the end of this room was another door, open, leading to a larger room. I went through to this room, and turned on the light. My first impression was one of shock because the room was fully furnished, as though in use.

I had expected to see chairs and tables swathed in dust-sheets, and dust-sheets too over the great double bed against the wall. Nothing was covered up. There were brushes and combs on the dressing-table, scent, and powder. The bed was made up, I saw the gleam of white linen on the pillow-case, and the tip of a blanket beneath the quilted coverlet. There were flowers on the dressing-table and on the table beside the bed. Flowers too on the carved mantelpiece. A satin dressing-gown lay on a chair, and a pair of bedroom slippers beneath. For one desperate moment I thought that something had happened to my brain, that I was seeing back into Time, and looking upon the room as it used to be, before she died. . . . In a minute Rebecca herself would come back into the room, sit down before the looking-glass at her dressing-table, humming a tune, reach for her comb and run it through her hair. If she sat there I should see her reflection in the glass, and she would see me too, standing like this by the door. Nothing happened. I went on standing there, waiting for something to happen. It was the clock ticking on the wall that brought me to reality again. The hands stood at twenty-five past four. My watch said the same. There was something sane and comforting about the ticking of the clock. It reminded me of the present, and that tea would soon be ready for me on the lawn. I walked slowly into the middle of the room. No, it was not used. It was not lived in any more. Even the flowers could not destroy the musty smell. The curtains were drawn and the shutters were closed. Rebecca would never come back to the room again. Even if Mrs. Danvers did put the flowers on the mantelpiece and the sheets upon the bed, they would not bring her back. She was dead. She had been dead now for a year. She lay buried in the crypt of the church with all the other dead de Winters.

I could hear the sound of the sea very plainly. I went to the window and swung back the shutter. Yes, I was standing at the same window where Favell and Mrs. Danvers had stood, half an hour ago. The long shaft of daylight made the electric light look false and yellow. I opened the shutter a little more. The daylight cast a white beam upon the bed. It shone upon the nightdress-case, lying on the pillow. It shone on the glass top of the dressing-table, on the brushes, and on the scent bottles.

The daylight gave an even greater air of reality to the room. When the shutter was closed and it had been lit by electricity the room had more the appearance of a setting on the stage. The scene set between performances. The curtain having fallen for the night, the evening over, and the first act set for to-morrow's matinée. But the daylight made the room vivid and alive. I forgot the musty smell and the drawn curtains of the other windows. I was a guest again. An uninvited guest. I had strolled into my hostess's bedroom by mistake. Those were her brushes on the dressing-table, that was her dressing-gown and slippers laid out upon the chair.

I realised for the first time since I had come into the room that my legs were trembling, weak as straw. I sat down on the stool by the dressing-table. My heart no longer beat in a strange excited way. It felt as heavy as lead. I looked about me in the room with a sort of dumb stupidity. Yet, it was a beautiful room. Mrs. Danvers had not exaggerated that first evening. It was the most beautiful room in the house. That exquisite mantelpiece, the ceiling, the carved bedstead and the curtain hangings, even the clock on the wall and the candlesticks upon the dressing-table beside me, all were things I would have loved and almost worshipped had they been mine. They were not mine though. They belonged to somebody else. I put out my hand and touched the brushes. One was more worn than its fellow. I understood it well. There was always one brush that had the greater use. Often you forgot to use the other, and when they were taken to be washed there was one that was still quite clean and untouched. How white and thin my face looked in the glass, my hair hanging lank and straight. Did I always look like this? Surely I had more colour as a rule? The reflection stared back at me, sallow and plain.

I got up from the stool and went and touched the dressing-gown on the chair. I picked up the slippers and held them in my hand. I was aware of a growing sense of horror, of horror turning to despair. I touched the quilt on the bed, traced with my fingers the monogram on the nightdress case, R de W, interwoven and interlaced. The letters were corded and strong against the golden satin material. The nightdress was inside the case, thin as gossamer, apricot in colour. I touched it, drew it out from the case, put it against my face. It was cold, quite cold. But there was a dim mustiness about it still where the scent had been. The scent of the white azalea. I folded it, and put it back into the case, and as I did so I noticed with a sick dull aching in my heart that there were creases in the nightdress, the texture was ruffled, it had not been touched or laundered since it was last worn.

On a sudden impulse I moved away from the bed and went back to the little ante-room where I had seen the wardrobes. I opened one of them. It was as I thought. The wardrobe was full of clothes. There were evening dresses here, I caught the shimmer of silver over the top of the white bags that enfolded them. There was a piece of gold brocade. There, next to it, was velvet, wine-coloured, and soft. There was a train of white satin, dripping on the floor of the wardrobe. Peeping out from a piece of tissue paper on a shelf above was an ostrich feather fan.

The wardrobe smelt stuffy, queer. The azalea scent, so fragrant and delicate in the air, had turned stale inside the wardrobe, tarnishing the silver dresses and the brocade, and the breath of it wafted towards me now from the open doors, faded and old. I shut the doors. I went back into the bedroom once again. The gleam of light from the shutter still shone white and clear on the golden coverlet of the bed, picking out clearly and distinctly the tall sloping R of the monogram.

Then I heard a step behind me and turning round I saw Mrs. Danvers. I shall never forget the expression on her face. Triumphant, gloating, excited in a strange unhealthy way. I felt very frightened.

'Is anything the matter, Madam?' she said.

I tried to smile at her and could not. I tried to speak.

'Are you feeling unwell?' she said, coming nearer to me, speaking very softly. I backed away from her. I believe if she had come any closer to me I should have fainted. I felt her breath on my face.

'I'm all right, Mrs. Danvers,' I said, after a moment, 'I did not expect to see you. The fact is, I was looking up at the windows from the lawn. I noticed one of the shutters was not quite closed. I came up to see if I could fasten it.'

'I will fasten it,' she said, and she went silently across the room and clamped back the shutter. The daylight had gone. The room looked unreal again in the false yellow light. Unreal and ghastly.

Mrs. Danvers came back and stood beside me. She smiled, and her manner instead of being still and unbending as it usually was became startlingly familiar, fawning even.

'Why did you tell me the shutter was open?' she said. 'I closed it before I left the room. You opened it yourself, didn't you, now? You wanted to see the room. Why have you never asked me to show it to you before? I was ready to show it to you every day. You had only to ask me.'

I wanted to run away, but I could not move. I went on watching her eyes.

'Now you are here, let me show you everything,' she said, her voice ingratiating and sweet as honey, horrible, false. 'I know you want to see it all, you've wanted to for a long time, and you were too shy to ask. It's a lovely room, isn't it? The loveliest room you have ever seen.'

She took hold of my arm, and walked me towards the bed. I could not resist her, I was like a dumb thing. The touch of her hand made me shudder. And her voice was low and intimate, a voice I hated and feared.

'That was her bed. It's a beautiful bed, isn't it? I keep the golden coverlet on it always, it was her favourite. Here is her nightdress inside the case. You've been touching it, haven't you? This was the nightdress she was wearing for the last time, before she died. Would you like to touch it again?' She took the nightdress from the case and held it before me. 'Feel it, hold it,' she said, 'how soft and light it is, isn't it? I haven't washed it since she wore it for the last time. I put it out like this, and the dressing-gown and slippers, just as I put them out for her the night she never came back, the night she was drowned.' She folded up the nightgown and put it back in the case. 'I did everything for her, you know,' she said, taking my arm again, leading me to the dressing-gown and slippers. 'We tried maid after maid but not one of them suited. "You maid me better than anyone, Danny," she used to say, "I won't have anyone but you." Look, this is her dressing-gown. She was much taller than you, you can see by the length. Put it up against you. It comes down to your ankles. She had a beautiful figure. These are her slippers. "Throw me my slips, Danny," she used to say. She had little feet for her height. Put your hands inside the slippers. They are quite small and narrow, aren't they?'

She forced the slippers over my hands, smiling all the while, watching my eyes. 'You never would have thought she was so tall, would you?' she said. 'These slippers would fit a tiny foot. She was so slim too. You would forget her height, until she stood beside you. She was every bit as tall as me. But lying there in bed she looked quite a slip of a thing, with her mass of dark hair, standing out from her face like a halo.'

She put the slippers back on the floor, and laid the dressing-gown on the chair. 'You've seen her brushes, haven't you?' she said, taking me to the dressing-table. 'There they are, just as she used them, unwashed and untouched. I used to brush her hair for her every evening. "Come on, Danny, hair-drill," she would say, and I'd stand behind her by the stool here, and brush away for twenty minutes at a time. She only wore it short the last few years, you know. It came down below the waist, when she was first married. Mr. de Winter used to brush it for her then. I've come into this room time and time again and seen him, in his shirt sleeves, with the two brushes in his hand. "Harder, Max, harder," she would say, laughing up at him, and he would do as she told him. They would be dressing for dinner, you see, and the house filled with guests. "Here, I shall be late," he would say, throwing the brushes to me, and laughing back at her. He was always laughing and gay then.' She paused, her hand still resting on my arm.

'Everyone was angry with her when she cut her hair,' she said, 'but she did not care. "It's nothing to do with anyone but myself," she would say. And of course short hair was much easier for riding and sailing. She was painted on horseback, you know. A famous artist did it. The picture hung in the Academy. Did you ever see it?'

I shook my head. 'No,' I said. 'No.'

'I understood it was the picture of the year,' she went on, 'but Mr. de Winter did not care for it, and would not have it at Manderley. I don't think he considered it did her justice. You would like to see her clothes, wouldn't you?' She did not wait for my answer. She led me to the little ante-room and opened the wardrobes, one by one.

'I keep her furs in here,' she said, 'the moth have not got to them yet, and I doubt if they ever will. I'm too careful. Feel that sable wrap. That was a Christmas present from Mr. de Winter. She told me the cost once, but I've forgotten it now. This chinchilla she wore in the evenings mostly. Round her shoulders, very often, when the evenings were cold. This wardrobe here is full of her evening clothes. You opened it, didn't you? The latch is not quite closed. I believe Mr. de Winter liked her to wear silver mostly. But of course she could wear anything, stand any colour. She looked beautiful in this velvet. Put it against your face. It's soft, isn't it? You can feel it, can't you? The scent is still fresh, isn't it? You could almost imagine she had only just taken it off. I would always know when she had been before me in a room. There would be a little whiff of her scent in the room. These are her underclothes, in this drawer. This pink set here she had never worn. She was wearing slacks of course and a shirt when she died. They were torn from her body in the water though. There was nothing on the body when it was found, all those weeks afterwards.'

Her fingers tightened on my arm. She bent down to me, her skull's face close, her dark eyes searching mine. 'The rocks had battered her to bits, you know,' she whispered, 'her beautiful face unrecognisable, and both arms gone. Mr. de Winter identified her. He went up to Edgecoombe to do it. He went quite alone. He was very ill at the time but he would go. No one could stop him. Not even Mr. Crawley.'

She paused, her eyes never leaving my face. 'I shall always blame myself for the accident,' she said, 'it was my fault for being out that evening. I had gone into Kerrith for the afternoon and stayed there late, as Mrs. de Winter was up in London and not expected back until much later. That's why I did not hurry back. When I came in, about half-past nine, I heard she had returned just before seven, had her dinner, and then went out again. Down to the beach of course. I felt worried then. It was blowing up from the south-west. She would never have gone if I'd been in. She always listened to me. "I wouldn't go out this evening, it's not fit," I should have said, and she would have answered me "All right, Danny, you old fuss-pot." And we would have sat up here talking no doubt, she telling me all she had done up in London, like she always did.'

My arm was bruised and numb from the pressure of her fingers. I could see how tightly the skin was stretched across her face, showing the cheekbones. There were little patches of yellow beneath her ears.

'Mr. de Winter had been dining with Mr. Crawley down at his house,' she went on. 'I don't know what time he got back, I dare say it was after eleven. But it began to blow quite hard just before midnight, and she had not come back. I went downstairs, but there were no lights under the library door. I came upstairs again and knocked on the dressing-room door. Mr. de Winter answered at once. "Who is it, what do you want?" he said. I told him I was worried about Mrs. de Winter not being back. He waited a moment, and then he came and opened the door in his dressing-gown. "She's spending the night down at the cottage I expect," he said. "I should go to bed if I were you. She won't come back here to sleep if it goes on like this." He looked tired, and I did not like to disturb him. After all, she spent many nights at the cottage, and had sailed in every sort of weather. She might not even have gone for a sail, but just wanted the night at the cottage as a change after London. I said good night to Mr. de Winter and went back to my room. I did not sleep though. I kept wondering what she was doing.'

She paused again. I did not want to hear any more. I wanted to get away from her, away from the room.

'I sat on my bed until half-past five,' she said, 'then I couldn't wait there any longer. I got up and put on my coat and went down through the woods to the beach. It was getting light, but there was still a misty sort of rain falling, although the wind had dropped. When I got to the beach I saw the buoy there in the water and the dinghy, but the boat had gone . . .' It seemed to me that I could see the cove in the grey morning light, feel the thin drizzle on my face, and peering through the mist could make out, shadowy and indistinct, the low dark outline of the buoy.

Mrs. Danvers loosened the pressure on my arm. Her hand fell back again to her side. Her voice lost all expression, became the hard mechanical voice of every day.

'One of the life-buoys was washed up at Kerrith in the afternoon,' she said, 'and another was found the next day by some crabbers on the rocks below the headland. Bits and pieces of rigging too would come in with the tide.' She turned away from me, and closed the chest of drawers. She straightened one of the pictures on the wall. She picked up a piece of fluff from the carpet. I stood watching her, not knowing what to do.

'You know now,' she said, 'why Mr. de Winter does not use these rooms any more. Listen to the sea.'

Even with the windows closed and the shutters fastened I could hear it; a low sullen murmur as the waves broke on the white shingle in the cove. The tide would be coming in fast now and running up the beach nearly to the stone cottage.

'He has not used these rooms since the night she was drowned,' she said. 'He had his things moved out from the dressing-room. We made up one of the rooms at the end of the corridor. I don't think he slept much even there. He used to sit in the arm-chair. There would be cigarette-ash all round it in the morning. And in the daytime Frith would hear him in the library pacing up and down. Up and down, up and down.'

I too could see the ash on the floor beside the chair. I too could hear his footsteps; one, two, one two, backwards and forwards across the library. . . . Mrs. Danvers closed the door softly between the bedroom and the ante-room where we were standing, and put out the light. I could not see the bed any more, nor the nightdress case upon the pillow, nor the dressing-table, nor the slippers by the chair. She crossed the ante-room and put her hand on the knob of the door and stood waiting for me to follow her.

'I come to the rooms and dust them myself every day,' she said. 'If you want to come again you have only to tell me. Ring me on the house-telephone. I shall understand. I don't allow the maids up here. No one ever comes but me.'

Her manner was fawning again, intimate and unpleasant. The smile on her face was a false, unnatural thing. 'Sometimes when Mr. de Winter is away, and you feel lonely, you might like to come up to these rooms and sit here. You have only to tell me. They are such beautiful rooms. You would not think she had been gone now for so long, would you, not by the way the rooms are kept? You would think she had just gone out for a little while and would be back in the evening.'

I forced a smile. I could not speak. My throat felt dry and tight.

'It's not only this room,' she said. 'It's in many rooms in the house. In the morning-room, in the hall, even in the little flower-room. I feel her everywhere. You do too, don't you?'

She stared at me curiously. Her voice dropped to a whisper. 'Sometimes, when I walk along the corridor here, I fancy I hear her just behind me. That quick, light footstep. I could not mistake it anywhere. And in the minstrels' gallery above the hall. I've seen her leaning there, in the evenings in the old days, looking down at the hall below and calling to the dogs. I can fancy her there now from time to time. It's almost as though I catch the sound of her dress sweeping the stairs as she comes down to dinner.' She paused. She went on looking at me, watching my eyes. 'Do you think she can see us, talking to one another now?' she said slowly. 'Do you think the dead come back and watch the living?'

I swallowed. I dug my nails into my hands.

'I don't know,' I said. 'I don't know.' My voice sounded high-pitched and unnatural. Not my voice at all.

'Sometimes I wonder,' she whispered. 'Sometimes I wonder if she comes back here to Manderley and watches you and Mr. de Winter together.'

We stood there by the door, staring at one another. I could not take my eyes away from hers. How dark and sombre they were in the white skull's face of hers, how malevolent, how full of hatred. Then she opened the door into the corridor. 'Robert is back now,' she said. 'He came back a quarter of an hour ago. He has orders to take your tea out under the chestnut-tree.'

She stepped aside for me to pass. I stumbled out on to the corridor, not looking where I was going. I did not speak to her, I went down the stairs blindly, and turned the corner and pushed through the door that led to my own rooms in the east wing. I shut the door of my room and turned the key, and put the key in my pocket.

Then I lay down on my bed and closed my eyes. I felt deadly sick.

Chapter Fifteen

Maxim rang up the next morning to say he would be back about seven. Frith took the message. Maxim did not ask to speak to me himself. I heard the telephone ring while I was at breakfast and I thought perhaps Frith would come into the dining-room and say 'Mr. de Winter on the telephone, Madam.' I had put down my napkin and had risen to my feet. And then Frith came back into the dining-room and gave me the message.

He saw me push back my chair and go to the door. 'Mr. de Winter has rung off, Madam,' he said, 'there was no message. Just that he would be back about seven.'

I sat down in my chair again and picked up my napkin. Frith must have thought me eager and stupid rushing across the dining-room.

'All right, Frith. Thank you,' I said.

I went on eating my eggs and bacon, Jasper at my feet, the old dog in her basket in the corner. I wondered what I should do with my day. I had slept badly; perhaps because I was alone in the room. I had been restless, waking up often, and when I glanced at my clock I saw the hands had scarcely moved. When I did fall asleep I had varied, wandering dreams. We were walking through woods, Maxim and I, and he was always just a little ahead of me. I could not keep up with him. Nor could I see his face. Just his figure, striding away in front of me all the time. I must have cried while I slept, for when I woke in the morning the pillow was damp. My eyes were heavy too, when I looked in the glass. I looked plain, unattractive. I rubbed a little rouge on my cheeks in a wretched attempt to give myself colour. But it made me worse. It gave me a false clown look. Perhaps I did not know the best way to put it on. I noticed Robert staring at me as I crossed the hall and went in to breakfast.

About ten o'clock as I was crumbling some pieces for the birds on the terrace the telephone rang again. This time it was for me. Frith came and said Mrs. Lacy wanted to speak to me.

'Good morning, Beatrice,' I said.

'Well, my dear, how are you?' she said, her telephone voice typical of herself, brisk, rather masculine, standing no nonsense, and then not waiting for my answer, 'I thought of motoring over this afternoon and looking up Gran. I'm lunching with people about twenty miles from you. Shall I come and pick you up and we'll go together? It's time you met the old lady, you know.'

'I'd like to very much, Beatrice,' I said.

'Splendid. Very well, then, I'll come along for you about half-past three. Giles saw Maxim at the dinner. Poor food, he said, but excellent wine. All right, my dear, see you later.'

The click of the receiver, and she was gone. I wandered back into the garden. I was glad she had rung up and suggested the plan of going over to see the grandmother. It made something to look forward to, and broke the monotony of the day. The hours had seemed so long until seven o'clock. I did not feel in my holiday mood to-day, and I had no wish to go off with Jasper to the Happy Valley and come to the cove and throw stones in the water. The sense of freedom had departed, and the childish desire to run across the lawns in sandshoes. I went and sat down with a book and *The Times* and my knitting in the rose-garden, domestic as a matron, yawning in the warm sun while the bees hummed amongst the flowers.

I tried to concentrate on the bald newspaper columns, and later to lose myself in the racy plot of the novel in my hands. I did not want to think of yesterday afternoon and Mrs. Danvers. I tried to forget that she was in the house at this moment, perhaps looking down on me from one of the windows. And now and again, when I looked up from my book or glanced across the garden, I had the feeling I was not alone.

There were so many windows in Manderley, so many rooms that were never used by Maxim and myself that were empty now, dust-sheeted, silent, rooms that had been occupied in the old days when his father and his grandfather had been alive, when there had been much entertaining, many servants. It would be easy for Mrs. Danvers to open those doors softly, and close them again, and then steal quietly across the shrouded room and look down upon me from behind the drawn curtains.

I should not know. Even if I turned in my chair and looked up at the windows I would not see her. I remembered a game I had played as a child that my friends next-door had called 'Grandmother's Steps' and myself 'Old Witch.' You had to stand at the end of the garden with your back turned to the rest, and one by one they crept nearer to you, advancing in short furtive fashion. Every few minutes you turned to look at them, and if you saw one of them moving the offender had to retire to the back line and begin again. But there was always one a little bolder than the rest, who came up very close, whose movement was impossible to detect, and as you waited there, your back turned, counting the regulation Ten, you knew, with a fatal terrifying certainty, that before long, before even the Ten was counted, this bold player would pounce upon you from behind, unheralded, unseen, with a scream of triumph. I felt as tense and expectant as I did then. I was playing 'Old Witch' with Mrs. Danvers.

Lunch was a welcome break to the long morning. The calm efficiency of Frith, and Robert's rather foolish face, helped me more than my book and my newspaper had done. And at half-past three, punctual to the moment, I heard the sound of Beatrice's car round the sweep of the drive and pull up at the steps before the house. I ran out to meet her, ready dressed, my gloves in my hand. 'Well, my dear, here I am, what a splendid day, isn't it?' She slammed the door of the car and came up the steps to meet me. She gave me a hard swift kiss, brushing me somewhere near the ear.

'You don't look well,' she said immediately, looking me up and down, 'much too thin in the face, and no colour. What's wrong with you?'

'Nothing,' I said humbly, knowing the fault of my face too well, 'I'm not a person who ever has much colour.'

'Oh, bosh,' she replied, 'you looked quite different when I saw you before.'

'I expect the brown of Italy has worn off,' I said, getting into the car.

'H'mph,' she said shortly, 'you're as bad as Maxim. Can't stand any criticism about your health. Slam the door hard or it doesn't shut.' We started off down the drive, swerving at the corner, going rather too fast. 'You're not by any chance starting an infant, are you?' she said, turning her hawk-brown eyes upon me.

'No,' I said awkwardly. 'No, I don't think so.'

'No morning sickness or anything like that?'

'No.'

'Oh, well – of course it doesn't always follow. I never turned a hair when Roger was born. Felt as fit as a fiddle the whole nine months. I played golf the day before he arrived. There's nothing to be embarrassed about in the facts of nature, you know. If you have any suspicions you had better tell me.'

'No, really, Beatrice,' I said, 'there's nothing to tell.'

'I must say I do hope you will produce a son and heir before long. It would be so terribly good for Maxim. I hope you are doing nothing to prevent it.'

'Of course not,' I said. What an extraordinary conversation.

'Oh, don't be shocked,' she said, 'you must never mind what I say. After all, brides of to-day are up to everything. It's a damn nuisance if you want to hunt and you land yourself with an infant your first season. Quite enough to break a marriage up if you are both keen. Wouldn't matter in your case. Babies needn't interfere with sketching. How is the sketching, by-the-way?'

'I'm afraid I don't seem to do much,' I said.

'Oh, really? Nice weather, too, for sitting out of doors. You only need a camp-stool and a box of pencils, don't you? Tell me, were you interested in those books I sent you?'

'Yes, of course,' I said. 'It was a lovely present, Beatrice.'

She looked pleased. 'Glad you liked them,' she said.

The car sped along. She kept her foot permanently on the accelerator, and took every corner at an acute angle. Two motorists we passed looked out of their windows outraged as she swept by, and one pedestrian in a lane waved his stick at her. I felt rather hot for her. She did not seem to notice though. I crouched lower in my seat.

'Roger goes up to Oxford next term,' she said, 'heaven knows what he'll do with himself. Awful waste of time I think, and so does Giles, but we couldn't think what else to do with him. Of course he's just like Giles and myself. Thinks of nothing but horses. What on earth does this car in front think it's doing? Why don't you put out your hand my good man? Really, some of these people on the road to-day ought to be shot.'

We swerved into a main road, narrowly avoiding the car ahead of us. 'Had any people down to stay?' she asked.

'No, we've been very quiet,' I said.

'Much better, too,' she said, 'awful bore, I always think, those big parties. You won't find it alarming if you come to stay with us. Very nice lot of people all round, and we all know one another frightfully well. We dine in one another's houses, and have our bridge, and don't bother with outsiders. You do play bridge, don't you?'

'I'm not very good, Beatrice.'

'Oh, we shan't mind that. As long as you can play. I've no patience with people who won't learn. What on earth can one do with them between tea and dinner in the winter, and after dinner? One can't just sit and talk.'

I wondered why. However, it was simpler not to say anything.

'It's quite amusing now Roger is a reasonable age,' she went on, 'because he brings his friends to stay, and we have really good fun. You ought to have been with us last Christmas. We had charades. My dear, it was the greatest fun. Giles was in his element. He adores dressing-up, you know, and after a glass or two of champagne he's the funniest thing you've ever seen. We often say he's missed his vocation and ought to have been on the stage.' I thought of Giles, and his large moon face, his horn spectacles. I felt the sight of him being funny after champagne would embarrass me. 'He and another man, a great friend of ours, Dickie Marsh, dressed up as women and sang a duet. What exactly it had to do with the word in the charade nobody knew, but it did not matter. We all roared.'

I smiled politely. 'Fancy, how funny,' I said.

I saw them all rocking from side to side in Beatrice's drawing-room. All these friends who knew one another so well. Roger would look like Giles. Beatrice was laughing again at the memory. 'Poor Giles,' she said. 'I shall never forget his face when Dick squirted the soda syphon down his back. We were all in fits.'

I had an uneasy feeling we might be asked to spend the approaching Christmas with Beatrice. Perhaps I could have influenza.

'Of course our acting was never very ambitious,' she said. 'It was just a lot of fun amongst ourselves. At Manderley now, there is scope for a really fine show. I remember a pageant they had there, some years ago. People from London came down to do it. Of course that type of thing needs terrific organisation.'

'Yes,' I said.

She was silent for a while, and drove without speaking.

'How is Maxim?' she said, after a moment.

'Very well, thanks,' I said.

'Quite cheerful and happy?'

'Oh, yes. Yes, rather.'

A narrow village street engaged her attention. I wondered whether I should tell her about Mrs. Danvers. About the man Favell. I did not want her to make a blunder though, and perhaps tell Maxim.

'Beatrice,' I said, deciding upon it, 'have you ever heard of someone called Favell? Jack Favell?'

'Jack Favell,' she repeated. 'Yes, I do know the name. Wait a minute. Jack Favell. Of course. An awful bounder. I met him once, ages ago.'

'He came to Manderley yesterday to see Mrs. Danvers,' I said.

'Really? Oh, well, perhaps he would . . .'

'Why?' I said.

'I rather think he was Rebecca's cousin,' she said.

I was very surprised. That man her relation? It was not my idea of the sort of cousin Rebecca would have. Jack Favell her cousin. 'Oh,' I said. 'Oh, I hadn't realised that.'

'He probably used to go to Manderley a lot,' said Beatrice. 'I don't know. I couldn't tell you. I was very seldom there.' Her manner was abrupt. It gave me the impression she did not want to pursue the subject.

'I did not take to him much,' I said.

'No,' said Beatrice. 'I don't blame you.'

I waited, but she did not say any more. I thought it wiser not to tell her how Favell had asked me to keep the visit a secret. It might lead to some complication. Besides, we were just coming to our destination. A pair of white gates and a smooth gravel drive.

'Don't forget the old lady is nearly blind,' said Beatrice, 'and she's not very bright these days. I telephoned to the nurse that we were coming, so everything will be all right.'

The house was large, red-bricked, and gabled. Late Victorian I supposed. Not an attractive house. I could tell in a glance it was the sort of house that was aggressively well-kept by a big staff. And all for one old lady who was nearly blind.

A trim parlour-maid opened the door.

'Good afternoon, Norah, how are you?' said Beatrice.

'Very well, thank you, Madam. I hope you are keeping well?'

'Oh, yes, we are all flourishing. How has the old lady been, Norah?'

'Rather mixed, Madam. She has one good day, and then a bad. She's not too bad in herself, you know. She will be pleased to see you I'm sure.' She glanced curiously at me.

'This is Mrs. Maxim,' said Beatrice.

'Yes, Madam. How do you do,' said Norah.

We went through a narrow hall and a drawing-room crowded with furniture to a verandah facing a square clipped lawn. There were many bright geraniums in stone vases on the steps of the verandah. In the corner was a bath chair. Beatrice's grandmother was sitting there, propped up with pillows and surrounded by shawls. When we came close to her I saw that she had a strong, rather uncanny, resemblance to Maxim. That was what Maxim would look like, if he was very old, if he was blind. The nurse by her side got up from her chair and put a mark in the book she was reading aloud. She smiled at Beatrice.

'How are you, Mrs. Lacy?' she said.

Beatrice shook hands with her and introduced me. 'The old lady looks all right,' she said. 'I don't know how she does it, at eighty-six. Here we are, Gran,' she said, raising her voice, 'arrived safe and sound.'

The grandmother looked in our direction. 'Dear Bee,' she said, 'how sweet of you to come and visit me. We're so dull here, nothing for you to do.'

Beatrice leant over her and kissed her. 'I've brought Maxim's wife over to see you,' she said, 'she wanted to come and see you before, but she and Maxim have been so busy.'

Beatrice prodded me in the back. 'Kiss her,' she murmured. I too bent down and kissed her on the cheek.

The grandmother touched my face with her fingers. 'You nice thing,' she said, 'so good of you to come. I'm very pleased to see you, dear. You ought to have brought Maxim with you.'

'Maxim is in London,' I said, 'he's coming back to-night.'

'You must bring him next time,' she said. 'Sit down, dear, in this chair, where I can see you. And Bee, come the other side. How is dear Roger? He's a naughty boy, he doesn't come and see me.'

'He shall come during August;' shouted Beatrice; 'he's leaving Eton, you know, he's going up to Oxford.'

'Oh, dear, he'll be quite a young man, I shan't know him.'

'He's taller than Giles now,' said Beatrice.

She went on, telling her about Giles, and Roger, and the horses, and the dogs. The nurse brought out some knitting, and clicked her needles sharply. She turned to me, very bright, very cheerful.

'How are you liking Manderley, Mrs. de Winter?'

'Very much, thank you,' I said.

'It's a beautiful spot, isn't it?' she said, the needles jabbing one another. 'Of course we don't get over there now, she's not up to it. I am so sorry, I used to love our days at Manderley.'

'You must come over yourself some time,' I said.

'Thank you, I should love to. Mr. de Winter is well I suppose?'

'Yes, very well.'

'You spent your honeymoon in Italy, didn't you? We were so pleased with the picture-postcard Mr. de Winter sent.'

I wondered whether she used 'we' in the royal sense, or if she meant that Maxim's grandmother and herself were one.

'Did he send one? I don't remember.'

'Oh, yes, it was quite an excitement. We love anything like that. We keep a scrap-book you know, and paste anything to do with the family inside it. Anything pleasant, that is.'

'How nice,' I said.

I caught snatches of Beatrice's conversation on the other side. 'We had to put old Marksman down,' she was saying. 'You remember old Marksman? The best hunter I ever had.'

'Oh, dear, not old Marksman?' said her grandmother.

'Yes, poor old man. Got blind in both eyes, you know.'

'Poor Marksman,' echoed the old lady.

I thought perhaps it was not very tactful to talk about blindness, and I glanced at the nurse. She was still busy clicking her needles.

'Do you hunt, Mrs. de Winter?' she said.

'No, I'm afraid I don't,' I said.

'Perhaps you will come to it. We are all very fond of hunting in this part of the world.'

'Yes.'

'Mrs. de Winter is very keen on art,' said Beatrice to the nurse. 'I tell her there are heaps of spots in Manderley that would make very jolly pictures.'

'Oh rather,' agreed the nurse, pausing a moment from the fury of knitting. 'What a nice hobby. I had a friend who was a wonder with her pencil. We went to Provence together one Easter and she did such pretty sketches.'

'How nice,' I said.

'We're talking about sketching,' shouted Beatrice to her grandmother, 'you did not know we had an artist in the family, did you?'

'Who's an artist?' said the old lady. 'I don't know any.'

'Your new grand-daughter,' said Beatrice, 'you ask her what I gave her for a wedding-present.'

I smiled, waiting to be asked. The old lady turned her head in my direction. 'What's Bee talking about?' she said. 'I did not know you were an artist. We've never had any artists in the family.'

'Beatrice was joking,' I said; 'of course I'm not an artist really. I like drawing as a hobby. I've never had any lessons. Beatrice gave me some lovely books as a present.'

'Oh,' she said, rather bewildered. 'Beatrice gave you some books, did she? Rather like taking coals to Newcastle, wasn't it? There are so many books in the library at Manderley.' She laughed heartily. We all joined in her joke. I hoped the subject would be left at that, but Beatrice had to harp on it. 'You don't understand, Gran,' she said. 'They weren't ordinary books. They were volumes on art. Six of 'em.'

The nurse leant forward to add her tribute. 'Mrs. Lacy is trying to explain that Mrs. de Winter is very fond of sketching as a hobby. So she gave her six fine volumes all about painting as a wedding-present.'

'What a funny thing to do,' said the grandmother. 'I don't think much of books for a wedding-present. Nobody ever gave me any books when I was married. I should never have read them if they had.'

She laughed again. Beatrice looked rather offended. I smiled at her to show my sympathy. I don't think she saw. The nurse resumed her knitting.

'I want my tea,' said the old lady querulously, 'isn't it half-past four yet? Why doesn't Norah bring the tea?'

'What? Hungry again after our big lunch?' said the nurse, rising to her feet and smiling brightly at her charge.

I felt rather exhausted, and wondered, rather shocked at my callous thought, why old people were sometimes such a strain. Worse than young children or puppies because one had to be polite. I sat with my hands in my lap ready to agree with what anybody said. The nurse was thumping the pillows and arranging the shawls.

Maxim's grandmother suffered her in patience. She closed her eyes as though she too were tired. She looked more like Maxim than ever. I knew how she must have looked when she was young, tall and handsome, going round to the stables at Manderley with sugar in her pockets, holding her trailing skirt out of the mud. I pictured the nipped-in waist, the high collar, I heard her ordering the carriage for two o'clock. That was all finished now for her, all gone. Her husband had been dead for forty years, her son for fifteen. She had to live here in this bright, red gabled house with the nurse until it was time for her to die. I thought how little we know about the feelings of old people. Children we understand, their fears and hopes and make-believe. I was a child yesterday. I had not forgotten. But Maxim's grandmother, sitting there in her shawl with her poor blind eyes, what did she feel, what was she thinking? Did she know that Beatrice was yawning and glancing at her watch? Did she guess that we had come to visit her because we felt it right, it was a duty, so that when she got home afterwards Beatrice would be able to say, 'Well, that clears my conscience for three months?'

Did she ever think about Manderley? Did she remember sitting at the dining-room table, where I sat? Did she too have tea under the chestnut-tree? Or was it all forgotten and laid aside, and was there nothing left behind that calm, pale face of hers but little aches and little strange discomforts, a blurred thankfulness when the sun shone, a tremor when the wind blew cold?

I wished that I could lay my hands upon her face and take the years away. I wished I could see her young, as she was once, with colour in her cheeks and chestnut hair, alert and active as Beatrice by her side, talking as she did about hunting, hounds and horses. Not sitting there with her eyes closed while the nurse thumped the pillows behind her head.

'We've got a treat to-day, you know,' said the nurse, 'water-cress sand-wiches for tea. We love water-cress, don't we?'

'Is it water-cress day?' said Maxim's grandmother, raising her head from the pillows, and looking towards the door. 'You did not tell me that. Why does not Norah bring in the tea?'

'I wouldn't have your job, Sister, for a thousand a day,' said Beatrice *sotto voce* to the nurse.

'Oh, I'm used to it, Mrs. Lacy,' smiled the nurse; 'it's very comfortable here, you know. Of course we have our bad days but they might be a great deal worse. She's very easy, not like some patients. The staff are obliging too, that's really the main thing. Here comes Norah.'

The parlour-maid brought out a little gate-legged table and a snowy cloth.

'What a time you've been, Norah,' grumbled the old lady.

'It's only just turned the half-hour, Madam,' said Norah in a special voice, bright and cheerful like the nurse. I wondered if Maxim's grandmother realised that people spoke to her in this way. I wondered when they had done so for the first time, and if she had noticed then. Perhaps she had said to herself, 'They think I'm getting old, how very ridiculous', and then little by little she had become accustomed to it, and now it was as though they had always done so, it was part of her background. But the young woman with the chestnut hair and the narrow waist who gave sugar to the horses, where was she?

We drew our chairs to the gate-legged table and began to eat the water-cress sandwiches. The nurse prepared special ones for the old lady.

'There, now, isn't that a treat?' she said.

I saw a slow smile pass over the calm, placid face. 'I like water-cress day,' she said.

The tea was scalding, much too hot to drink. The nurse drank hers in tiny sips.

'Boiling water to-day,' she said, nodding at Beatrice. 'I have such trouble about it. They will let the tea stew. I've told them time and time again about it. They will not listen.'

'Oh, they're all the same,' said Beatrice. 'I've given it up as a bad job.' The old lady stirred hers with a spoon, her eyes very far and distant. I wished I knew what she was thinking about.

'Did you have fine weather in Italy?' said the nurse.

'Yes, it was very warm,' I said.

Beatrice turned to her grandmother. 'They had lovely weather in Italy for their honeymoon, she says. Maxim got quite sunburnt.'

'Why isn't Maxim here to-day?' said the old lady.

'We told you, darling, Maxim had to go to London,' said Beatrice impatiently. 'Some dinner you know. Giles went too.'

'Oh, I see. Why did you say Maxim was in Italy?'

'He was in Italy, Gran. In April. They're back at Manderley now.' She glanced at the nurse, shrugging her shoulders.

'Mr. and Mrs. de Winter are in Manderley now,' repeated the nurse.

'It's been lovely there this month,' I said, drawing nearer to Maxim's grandmother. 'The roses are in bloom now. I wish I had brought you some.'

'Yes, I like roses,' she said vaguely, and then peering closer at me with her dim blue eyes. 'Are you staying at Manderley too?'

I swallowed. There was a slight pause. Then Beatrice broke in with her loud, impatient voice, 'Gran, darling, you know perfectly well she lives there now. She and Maxim are married.'

I noticed the nurse put down her cup of tea and glance swiftly at the old lady. She had relaxed against the pillows, plucking at her shawl, and her mouth began to tremble. 'You talk too much, all of you. I don't understand.' Then she looked across at me, a frown on her face, and began shaking her head. 'Who are you, my dear, I haven't seen you before? I don't know your voice. I don't remember you at Manderley. Bee, who is this child? Why did not Maxim bring Rebecca? I'm so fond of Rebecca. Where is dear Rebecca?'

There was a long pause, a moment of agony. I felt my cheeks grow scarlet. The nurse got to her feet very quickly and went to the bath-chair.

'I want Rebecca,' repeated the old lady, 'what have you done with

Rebecca?' Beatrice rose clumsily from the table, shaking the cups and saucers. She too had turned very red, and her mouth twitched.

'I think you had better go, Mrs. Lacy,' said the nurse, rather pink and flustered. 'She's looking a little tired, and when she wanders like this it sometimes lasts a few hours. She does get excited like this from time to time. It's very unfortunate it should happen to-day. I'm sure you will understand, Mrs. de Winter?' She turned apologetically to me.

'Of course,' I said quickly, 'it's much better we should go.'

Beatrice and I groped for our bags and gloves. The nurse had turned to her patient again. 'Now, what's all this about? Don't you want your nice water-cress sandwich that I've cut for you?'

'Where is Rebecca? Why did not Maxim come and bring Rebecca?' replied the thin, tired, querulous voice.

We went through the drawing-room to the hall and let ourselves out of the front door. Beatrice started up the car without a word. We drove down the smooth gravel drive and out of the white gates.

I stared straight in front of me down the road. I did not mind for myself. I should not have cared if I had been alone. I minded for Beatrice.

She spoke to me when we turned out of the village. 'My dear,' she began, 'I'm so dreadfully sorry. I don't know what to say.'

'Don't be absurd, Beatrice,' I said hurriedly, 'it doesn't matter a bit. It's absolutely all right.'

'I had no idea she would do that,' said Beatrice. 'I would never have dreamt of taking you to see her. I'm so frightfully sorry.'

'There's nothing to be sorry about. Please don't say any more.'

'I can't make it out. She knew all about you. I wrote and told her, and so did Maxim. She was so interested in the wedding abroad.'

'You forget how old she is,' I said. 'Why should she remember that? She doesn't connect me with Maxim. She only connects him with Rebecca.' We went on driving in silence. It was a relief to be in the car again. I did not mind the jerky motion and the swaying corners.

'I'd forgotten she was so fond of Rebecca,' said Beatrice slowly, 'I was a fool not to expect something like this. I don't believe she ever took it in properly about the accident. Oh, Lord, what a ghastly afternoon. What on earth will you think of me?'

'Please, Beatrice, don't. I tell you I don't mind.'

'Rebecca made a great fuss of her always. And she used to have the old lady over to Manderley. Poor darling Gran was much more alert then. She used to rock with laughter at whatever Rebecca said. Of course she was always very amusing, and the old lady loved that. She had an amazing gift, Rebecca I mean, of being attractive to people; men, women, children, dogs. I suppose the old lady has never forgotten her. My dear, you won't thank me for this afternoon.'

'I don't mind, I don't mind,' I repeated mechanically. If only Beatrice could leave the subject alone. It did not interest me. What did it matter after all? What did anything matter?

'Giles will be very upset,' said Beatrice. 'He will blame me for taking you over. "What an idiotic thing to do, Bee." I can hear him saying it. I shall get into a fine row.'

'Don't say anything about it,' I said. 'I would much rather it was forgotten. The story will only get repeated and exaggerated.'

'Giles will know something is wrong from my face. I never have been able to hide anything from him.'

I was silent. I knew how the story would be tossed about in their immediate circle of friends. I could imagine the little crowd at Sunday lunch. The round eyes, the eager ears, and the gasps and exclamations –

'My Lord, how awful, what on earth did you do?' and then, 'How did she take it? How terribly embarrassing for everyone!'

The only thing that mattered to me was that Maxim should never come to hear of it. One day I might tell Frank Crawley, but not yet, not for quite a while.

It was not long before we came to the high road at the top of the hill. In the distance I could see the first grey roofs of Kerrith, while to the right, in a hollow, lay the deep woods of Manderley and the sea beyond.

'Are you in a frightful hurry to get home?' said Beatrice.

'No,' I said. 'I don't think so. Why?'

'Would you think me a perfect pig if I dropped you at the lodge gates? If I drive like hell now I shall just be in time to meet Giles by the London train, and it will save him taking the station taxi.'

'Of course,' I said. 'I can walk down the drive.'

'Thanks awfully,' she said gratefully.

I felt the afternoon had been too much for her. She wanted to be alone again, and did not want to face another belated tea at Manderley.

I got out of the car at the lodge gates and we kissed good-bye.

'Put on some weight next time I see you,' she said, 'it doesn't suit you to be so thin. Give Maxim my love, and forgive me for to-day.' She vanished in a cloud of dust and I turned in down the drive.

I wondered if it had altered much since Maxim's grandmother had driven down it in her carriage. She had ridden here as a young woman, she had smiled at the woman at the lodge as I did now. And in her day the lodge-keeper's wife had curtseyed, sweeping the path with her full wide skirt. This woman nodded to me briefly, and then called to her little boy who was grubbing with some kittens at the back. Maxim's grandmother had bowed her head to avoid the sweeping branches of the trees, and the horse had trotted down the twisting drive where I now walked. The drive had been wider then, and smoother too, better kept. The woods did not encroach upon it.

I did not think of her as she was now, lying against those pillows, with that shawl around her. I saw her when she was young, and when Manderley was her home. I saw her wandering in the gardens with a small boy, Maxim's father, clattering behind her on his hobby horse. He would wear a stiff Norfolk jacket and a round white collar. Picnics to the cove would be an expedition, a treat that was not indulged in very often. There would be a photograph somewhere, in an old album – all the family sitting very straight and rigid round a tablecloth set upon the beach, the servants in the background beside a huge lunch-basket. And I saw Maxim's grandmother when she was older too, a few years ago. Walking on the terrace at Manderley, leaning on a stick. And someone walking beside her, laughing, holding her arm. Someone tall and slim and very beautiful, who had a gift, Beatrice said, of being attractive to people. Easy to like, I supposed, easy to love.

When I came to the end of the long drive at last I saw that Maxim's car was standing in front of the house. My heart lifted, I ran quickly into the hall. His hat and gloves were lying on the table. I went towards the library, and as I came near I heard the sound of voices, one raised louder than the other, Maxim's voice. The door was shut. I hesitated a moment before going in.

'You can write and tell him from me to keep away from Manderley in future, do you hear? Never mind who told me, that's of no importance. I happen to know his car was seen here yesterday afternoon. If you want to meet him you can meet him outside Manderley. I won't have him inside the gates, do you understand? Remember, I'm warning you for the last time.'

I slipped away from the door to the stairs. I heard the door of the library open. I ran swiftly up the stairs and hid in the gallery. Mrs. Danvers came out of the library, shutting the door behind her. I crouched against the wall of the gallery so that I should not be seen. I had caught one glimpse of her face. It was grey with anger, distorted, horrible.

She passed up the stairs swiftly and silently and disappeared through the door leading to the west wing.

I waited a moment. Then I went slowly downstairs to the library. I opened the door and went in. Maxim was standing by the window, some letters in his hand. His back was turned to me. For a moment I thought of creeping out again, and going upstairs to my room and sitting there. He must have heard me though, for he swung round impatiently.

'Who is it now?' he said.

I smiled, holding out my hands. 'Hullo!' I said.

'Oh, it's you. . . .'

I could tell in a glance that something had made him very angry. His mouth was hard, his nostrils white and pinched. 'What have you been doing with yourself?' he said. He kissed the top of my head and put his arm round my shoulder. I felt as if a very long time had passed since he had left me yesterday.

'I've been to see your grandmother,' I said. 'Beatrice drove me over this afternoon.'

'How was the old lady?'

'All right.'

'What's happened to Bee?'

'She had to get back to meet Giles.'

We sat down together on the window-seat. I took his hand in mine. 'I hated you being away, I've missed you terribly,' I said.

'Have you?' he said.

We did not say anything for a bit. I just held his hand.

'Was it hot up in London?' I said.

'Yes, pretty awful. I always hate the place.'

I wondered if he would tell me what had happened just now in the library with Mrs. Danvers. I wondered who had told him about Favell.

'Are you worried about something?' I said.

'I've had a long day,' he said, 'that drive twice in twenty-four hours is too much for anyone.'

He got up and wandered away, lighting a cigarette. I knew then that he was not going to tell me about Mrs. Danvers.

'I'm tired too,' I said slowly, 'it's been a funny sort of day.'

Chapter Sixteen

It was one Sunday, I remember, when we had an invasion of visitors during the afternoon, that the subject of the fancy dress ball was first brought up. Frank Crawley had come over to lunch, and we were all three of us looking forward to a peaceful afternoon under the chestnut tree when we heard the fatal sound of a car rounding the sweep in the drive. It was too late to warn Frith, the car itself came upon us standing on the terrace with cushions and papers under our arms.

We had to come forward and welcome the unexpected guests. As it often happens in such cases, these were not to be the only visitors. Another car arrived about half-an-hour afterwards, followed by three local people who had walked from Kerrith, and we found ourselves, with the peace stripped from our day, entertaining group after group of dreary acquaintances, doing the regulation walk in the grounds, the tour of the rose-garden, the stroll across the lawns, and the formal inspection of the Happy Valley.

They stayed for tea of course, and instead of a lazy nibbling of cucumber sandwiches under the chestnut tree, we had the paraphernalia of a stiff tea in the drawing-room, which I always loathed. Frith in his element of course, directing Robert with a lift of his eyebrows, and myself rather hot and flustered with a monstrous silver tea-pot and kettle that I never knew how to manage. I found it very difficult to gauge the exact moment when it became imperative to dilute the tea with the boiling water, and more difficult still to concentrate on the small talk that was going on at my side.

Frank Crawley was invaluable at a moment like this. He took the cups from me and handed them to people, and when my answers seemed more than usually vague owing to my concentration on the silver tea-pot he quietly and unobtrusively put in his small wedge to the conversation, relieving me of responsibility. Maxim was always at the other end of the room, showing a book to a bore, or pointing out a picture, playing the perfect host in his own inimitable way, and the business of tea was a side-issue that did not matter to him. His own cup of tea grew cold, left on a side table behind some flowers, and I, steaming behind my kettle, and Frank gallantly juggling with scones and angel cake, were left to minister to the common wants of the herd. It was Lady Crowan, a tiresome gushing woman who lived in Kerrith, who introduced the matter. There was one of those pauses in conversation that happen in every tea-party, and I saw Frank's lips about to form the inevitable and idiotic remark about an angel passing overhead, when Lady Crowan, balancing a piece of cake on the edge of her saucer, looked up at Maxim who happened to be beside her.

'Oh, Mr. de Winter,' she said, 'there is something I've been wanting to ask you for ages. Now tell me, is there any chance of you reviving the Manderley fancy dress ball?' She put her head on one side as she spoke, flashing her too prominent teeth in what she supposed was a smile. I lowered my head instantly, and became very busy with the emptying of my own tea-cup, screening myself behind the cosy.

It was a moment or two before Maxim replied, and when he did his voice was quite calm and matter-of-fact. 'I haven't thought about it,' he said, 'and I don't think anyone else has.'

'Oh, but I assure you we have all thought of it so much,' continued Lady Crowan. 'It used to make the summer for all of us in this part of the world. You have no idea of the pleasure it used to give. Can't I persuade you to think about it again?'

'Well, I don't know,' said Maxim drily. 'It was all rather a business to organise. You had better ask Frank Crawley, he'd have to do it.'

'Oh, Mr. Crawley, do be on my side,' she persisted, and one or two of the others joined in. 'It would be a most popular move, you know, we all miss the Manderley gaiety.'

I heard Frank's quiet voice beside me. 'I don't mind organising the ball if Maxim has no objection to giving it. It's up to him and Mrs. de Winter. It's nothing to do with me.'

Of course I was bombarded at once. Lady Crowan moved her chair so that the cosy no longer hid me from view. 'Now, Mrs. de Winter, you get round your husband. You are the person he will listen to. He should give the ball in your honour as the bride.'

'Yes, of course,' said somebody else, a man. 'We missed the fun of the wedding you know, it's a shame to deprive us of all the excitement. Hands up for the Manderley fancy dress ball. There you see, de Winter? Carried unanimously.' There was much laughter and clapping of hands.

Maxim lit a cigarette and his eyes met mine over the tea-pot.

'What do you think about it?' he said.

'I don't know,' I said uncertainly. 'I don't mind.'

'Of course she longs to have a ball in her honour,' gushed Lady Crowan. 'What girl wouldn't? You'd look sweet, Mrs. de Winter, dressed as a little Dresden shepherdess, your hair tucked under a big three-cornered hat.'

I thought of my clumsy hands and feet and the slope of my shoulders. A fine Dresden shepherdess I should make! What an idiot the woman was. I was not surprised when nobody agreed with her, and once more I was grateful to Frank for turning the conversation away from me.

'As a matter of fact, Maxim, someone was talking about it the other day. "I suppose we shall be having some sort of celebration for the bride, shan't we, Mr. Crawley?" he said. "I wish Mr. de Winter would give a ball again. It was rare fun for all of us." It was Tucker, at the Home farm,' he added, to Lady Crowan. 'Of course they do adore a show of any kind. I don't know, I told him. Mr. de Winter hasn't said anything to me.'

'There you are,' said Lady Crowan triumphantly to the drawing-room in general. 'What did I say? Your own people are asking for a ball. If you don't care for us, surely you care about them.'

Maxim still watched me doubtfully over the tea-pot. It occurred to me that perhaps he thought I could not face it, that being shy, as he knew only too well, I should find myself unable to cope. I did not want him to think that. I did not want him to feel I should let him down.

'I think it would be rather fun,' I said.

Maxim turned away, shrugging his shoulders. 'That settles it of course,' he said. 'All right, Frank, you will have to go ahead with the arrangements. Better get Mrs. Danvers to help you. She will remember the form.'

'That amazing Mrs. Danvers is still with you then?' said Lady Crowan.

'Yes,' said Maxim shortly, 'have some more cake, will you? Or have you finished? Then let's all go into the garden.'

We wandered out on to the terrace, everyone discussing the prospect of the ball and suitable dates, and then, greatly to my relief, the car parties decided it was time to take their departure, and the walkers went too, on being offered a lift. I went back into the drawing-room and had another cup of tea which I thoroughly enjoyed now that the burden of entertaining had been taken from me, and Frank came too, and we crumbled up the remains of the scones and ate them, feeling like conspirators.

Maxim was throwing sticks for Jasper on the lawn. I wondered if it was the same in every home, this feeling of exuberance when visitors had gone. We did not say anything about the ball for a little while, and then, when I had finished my cup of tea and wiped my sticky fingers on a handkerchief, I said to Frank: 'What do you truthfully think about this fancy dress business?'

Frank hesitated, half glancing out of the window at Maxim on the lawn. 'I don't know,' he said. 'Maxim did not seem to object, did he? I thought he took the suggestion very well.'

'It was difficult for him to do anything else,' I said. 'What a tiresome person Lady Crowan is. Do you really believe all the people round here are talking and dreaming of nothing but a fancy dress ball at Manderley?'

'I think they would all enjoy a show of some sort,' said Frank. 'We're very conventional down here, you know, about these things. I don't honestly think Lady Crowan was exaggerating when she said something should be done in your honour. After all, Mrs. de Winter, you are a bride.'

How pompous and stupid it sounded. I wish Frank would not always be so terribly correct.

'I'm not a bride,' I said. 'I did not even have a proper wedding. No white dress or orange blossom or trailing bridesmaids. I don't want any silly dance given in my honour.'

'It's a very fine sight, Manderley *en fête*,' said Frank. 'You'll enjoy it, you see. You won't have to do anything alarming. You just receive the guests and there's nothing in that. Perhaps you'll give me a dance?'

Dear Frank. I loved his little solemn air of gallantry.

'You shall have as many dances as you like,' I said. 'I shan't dance with anyone except you and Maxim.'

'Oh, but that would not look right at all,' said Frank seriously. 'People would be very offended. You must dance with the people who ask you.'

I turned away to hide my smile. It was a joy to me the way he never knew when his leg had been pulled.

'Do you think Lady Crowan's suggestion about the Dresden shepherdess was a good one?' I said slyly.

He considered me solemnly without the trace of a smile. 'Yes, I do,' he said. 'I think you'd look very well indeed.'

I burst into laughter. 'Oh, Frank, dear, I do love you,' I said, and he turned rather pink, a little shocked I think at my impulsive words, and a little hurt too that I was laughing at him.

'I don't see that I've said anything funny,' he said stiffly.

Maxim came in at the window, Jasper dancing at his heels. 'What's all the excitement about?' he said.

'Frank is being so gallant,' I said. 'He thinks Lady Crowan's idea of my dressing up as a Dresden shepherdess is nothing to laugh at.'

'Lady Crowan is a damned nuisance,' said Maxim. 'If she had to write out all the invitations and organise the affair she would not be so enthusiastic. It's always been the same though. The locals look upon Manderley as if it was a pavilion on the end of a pier, and expect us to put up a turn for their benefit. I suppose we shall have to ask the whole county.'

'I've got the records in the office,' said Frank. 'It won't really entail much work. Licking the stamps is the longest job.'

'We'll give that to you to do,' said Maxim, smiling at me.

'Oh, we'll do that in the office,' said Frank. 'Mrs. de Winter need not bother her head about anything at all.'

I wondered what they would say if I suddenly announced my intention of running the whole affair. Laugh, I supposed, and then begin talking of something else. I was glad, of course, to be relieved of responsibility, but it rather added to my sense of humility to feel that I was not even capable of licking stamps. I thought of the writing-desk in the morning-room, the docketed pigeon-holes all marked in ink by that slanting pointed hand.

'What will you wear?' I said to Maxim.

'I never dress up,' said Maxim. 'It's the one perquisite allowed to the host, isn't it, Frank?'

'I can't really go as a Dresden shepherdess,' I said, 'what on earth shall I do? I'm not much good at dressing-up.'

'Put a ribbon round your hair and be Alice-in-Wonderland,' said Maxim lightly; 'you look like it now, with your finger in your mouth.'

'Don't be so rude,' I said. 'I know my hair is straight, but it isn't as straight as that. I tell you what. I'll give you and Frank the surprise of your lives, and you won't know me.'

'As long as you don't black your face and pretend to be a monkey I don't mind what you do,' said Maxim.

'All right, that's a bargain,' I said. 'I'll keep my costume a secret to the last minute, and you won't know anything about it. Come on, Jasper, we don't care what they say, do we?' I heard Maxim laughing as I went out into the garden, and he said something to Frank which I did not catch.

I wished he would not always treat me as a child, rather spoilt, rather irresponsible, someone to be petted from time to time when the mood came upon him, but more often forgotten, more often patted on the shoulder and told to run away and play. I wished something would happen to make me look wiser, more mature. Was it always going to be like this? He away ahead of me, with his own moods that I did not share, his secret troubles that I did not know? Would we never be together, he a man and I a woman, standing shoulder to shoulder, hand in hand, with no gulf between us? I did not want to be a child. I wanted to be his wife, his mother. I wanted to be old.

I stood on the terrace, biting my nails, looking down towards the sea, and as I stood there I wondered for the twentieth time that day whether it was by Maxim's orders that those rooms in the west wing were kept furnished and untouched. I wondered if he went, as Mrs. Danvers did, and touched the brushes on the dressing-table, opened the wardrobe doors and put his hands amongst the clothes.

'Come on, Jasper,' I shouted, 'run, run with me, come on, can't you?' and I tore across the grass, savagely, angrily, the bitter tears behind my eyes, with Jasper leaping at my heels and barking hysterically.

The news soon spread about the fancy dress ball. My little maid Clarice, her eyes shining with excitement, talked of nothing else. I gathered from her that the servants in general were delighted. 'Mr. Frith says it will be like old times,' said Clarice eagerly. 'I heard him saying so to Alice in the passage this morning. What will you wear, Madam?'

'I don't know, Clarice, I can't think,' I said.

'Mother said I was to be sure and tell her,' said Clarice. 'She remembers the last ball they gave at Manderley, and she has never forgotten it. Will you be hiring a costume from London, do you think?'

'I haven't made up my mind, Clarice,' I said. 'But I tell you what. When I do decide, I shall tell you and nobody else. It will be a dead secret between us both.'

'Oh, Madam, how exciting,' breathed Clarice. 'I don't know how I am going to wait for the day.'

I was curious to know Mrs. Danvers' reaction to the news. Since that afternoon I dreaded even the sound of her voice down the house telephone, and by using Robert as mediator between us I was spared this last ordeal. I could not forget the expression on her face when she left the library after that interview with Maxim. I thanked God she had not seen me crouching in the gallery. And I wondered too, if she thought that it was I who had told Maxim about Favell's visit to the house. If so, she would hate me more than ever. I shuddered now when I remembered the touch of her hand on my arm, and that dreadful soft, intimate pitch of her voice close to my ear. I did not want to remember anything about that afternoon. That was why I did not speak to her, not even on the house telephone.

The preparations went on for the ball. Everything seemed to be done down at the estate office. Maxim and Frank were down there every morning. As Frank had said, I did not have to bother my head about anything. I don't think I licked one stamp. I began to get in a panic about my costume. It seemed so feeble not to be able to think of anything, and I kept remembering all the people who would come, from Kerrith and round about, the bishop's wife who had enjoyed herself so much the last time, Beatrice and Giles, that tiresome Lady Crowan, and many more people I did not know and who had never seen me, they would every one of them have some criticism to offer, some curiosity to know what sort of effort I should make. At last, in desperation, I remembered the books that Beatrice had given me for a wedding-present, and I sat down in the library one morning turning over the pages as a last hope, passing from illustration to illustration in a sort of frenzy. Nothing seemed suitable, they were all so elaborate and pretentious, those gorgeous costumes of velvet and silk in the reproductions given of Rubens, Rembrandt and others. I got hold of a piece of paper and a pencil and copied one or two of them, but they did not please me, and I threw the sketches into the waste paper basket in disgust, thinking no more about them.

In the evening, when I was changing for dinner, there was a knock at my bedroom door. I called 'Come in,' thinking it was Clarice. The door opened and it was not Clarice. It was Mrs. Danvers. She held a piece of paper in her hand. 'I hope you will forgive me disturbing you,' she said, 'but I was not sure whether you meant to throw these drawings away. All the waste paper baskets are always brought to me to check, at the end of the day, in case of mislaying anything of value. Robert told me this was thrown into the library basket.'

I had turned quite cold all over at the sight of her, and at first I could not find my voice. She held out the paper for me to see. It was the rough drawing I had done during the morning.

'No, Mrs. Danvers,' I said, after a moment, 'it doesn't matter throwing that away. It was only a rough sketch. I don't want it.'

'Very good,' she said, 'I thought it better to enquire from you personally to save any misunderstanding.'

'Yes,' I said. 'Yes, of course.' I thought she would turn and go, but she went on standing there by the door.

'So you have not decided yet what you will wear?' she said. There was a hint of derision in her voice, a trace of odd satisfaction. I supposed she had heard of my efforts through Clarice in some way.

'No,' I said. 'No, I haven't decided.'

She continued watching me, her hand on the handle of the door.

'I wonder you don't copy one of the pictures in the gallery,' she said.

I pretended to file my nails. They were too short and too brittle, but the action gave me something to do and I did not have to look at her.

'Yes, I might think about that,' I said. I wondered privately why such an idea had never come to me before. It was an obvious and very good solution to my difficulty. I did not want her to know this though. I went on filing my nails.

'All the pictures in the gallery would make good costumes,' said Mrs. Danvers, 'especially that one of the young lady in white, with her hat in her hand. I wonder Mr. de Winter does not make it a period ball, everyone dressed more or less the same, to be in keeping. I never think it looks right to see a clown dancing with a lady in powder and patches.'

'Some people enjoy the variety,' I said. 'They think it makes it all the more amusing.'

'I don't like it myself,' said Mrs. Danvers. Her voice was surprisingly normal and friendly, and I wondered why it was she had taken the trouble to come up with my discarded sketch herself. Did she want to be friends with me at last? Or did she realise that it had not been me at all who had told Maxim about Favell, and this was her way of thanking me for my silence?

'Has not Mr. de Winter suggested a costume for you?' she said.

'No,' I said, after a moment's hesitation. 'No, I want to surprise him and Mr. Crawley. I don't want them to know anything about it.'

'It's not for me to make a suggestion, I know,' she said, 'but when you do decide, I should advise you to have your dress made in London. There is no one down here can do that sort of thing well. Voce, in Bond Street, is a good place I know.'

'I must remember that,' I said.

'Yes,' she said, and then, as she opened the door, 'I should study the pictures in the gallery, Madam, if I were you, especially the one I mentioned. And you need not think I will give you away. I won't say a word to anyone.'

'Thank you, Mrs. Danvers,' I said. She shut the door very gently behind her. I went on with my dressing, puzzled at her attitude, so different from our last encounter, and wondering whether I had the unpleasant Favell to thank for it.

Rebecca's cousin. Why should Maxim dislike Rebecca's cousin? Why had he forbidden him to come to Manderley? Beatrice had called him a bounder. She had not said much about him. And the more I considered him the more I agreed with her. Those hot blue eyes, that loose mouth, and the careless familiar laugh. Some people would consider him attractive. Girls in sweet shops giggling behind the counter, and girls who gave one programmes in a cinema. I knew how he would look at them, smiling, and half whistling a tune under his breath. The sort of look and the type of whistle that would make one feel uncomfortable. I wondered how well he knew Manderley. He seemed quite at home, and Jasper certainly recognised him, but these two facts did not fit in with Maxim's words to Mrs. Danvers. And I could not connect him with any idea of Rebecca. Rebecca, with her beauty, her charm, her breeding, why did she have a cousin like Jack Favell? It was wrong, out of all proportion. I decided he must be the skeleton in the family cupboard, and Rebecca, with her generosity, had taken pity on him from time to time and invited him to Manderley, perhaps when Maxim was from home, knowing his dislike. There had been some argument about it probably, Rebecca defending him, and ever after this perhaps a slight awkwardness whenever his name was mentioned.

As I sat down to dinner in the dining-room in my accustomed place, with Maxim at the head of the table, I pictured Rebecca sitting where I sat now, picking up her fork for the fish, and then the telephone ringing and Frith coming into the room and saying 'Mr. Favell on the 'phone, Madam, wishing to speak to you,' and Rebecca would get up from her chair with a quick glance at Maxim, who would not say anything, who would go on eating his fish. And when she came back, having finished her conversation, and sat down in her place again, Rebecca would begin talking about something different, in a gay, careless way, to cover up the little cloud between them. At first Maxim would be glum, answering in monosyllables, but little by little she would win his humour back again, telling him some story of her day, about someone she had seen in Kerrith, and when they had finished the next course he would be laughing again, looking at her and smiling, putting out his hand to her across the table.

'What the devil are you thinking about?' said Maxim.

I started, the colour flooding my face, for in that brief moment, sixty seconds in time perhaps, I had so identified myself with Rebecca that my own dull self did not exist, had never come to Manderley. I had gone back in thought and in person to the days that were gone.

'Do you know you were going through the most extraordinary antics instead of eating your fish?' said Maxim. 'First you listened, as though you heard the telephone, and then your lips moved, and you threw half a glance at me. And you shook your head, and smiled, and shrugged your shoulders. All in about a second. Are you practising your appearance for the fancy dress ball?' He looked across at me, laughing, and I wondered what he would say if he really knew my thoughts, my heart, and my mind, and that for one second he had been the Maxim of another year, and I had been Rebecca. 'You look like a little criminal,' he said, 'what is it?'

'Nothing,' I said quickly, 'I wasn't doing anything.'

'Tell me what you were thinking?'

'Why should I? You never tell me what you are thinking about.'

'I don't think you've ever asked me, have you?'

'Yes, I did once.'

'I don't remember.'

'We were in the library.'

'Very probably. What did I say?'

'You told me you were wondering who had been chosen to play for Surrey against Middlesex.'

Maxim laughed again. 'What a disappointment to you. What did you hope I was thinking?'

'Something very different.'

'What sort of thing?'

'Oh, I don't know.'

'No, I don't suppose you do. If I told you I was thinking about Surrey and Middlesex I was thinking about Surrey and Middlesex. Men are simpler than you imagine, my sweet child. But what goes on in the twisted tortuous minds of women would baffle anyone. Do you know, you did not look a bit like yourself just now? You had quite a different expression on your face.'

'I did? What sort of expression?'

'I don't know that I can explain. You looked older suddenly, deceitful. It was rather unpleasant.'

'I did not mean to.'

'No, I don't suppose you did.'

I drank some water, watching him over the rim of my glass.

'Don't you want me to look older?' I said.

'No.'

'Why not?'

'Because it would not suit you.'

'One day I shall. It can't be helped. I shall have grey hair, and lines and things.'

'I don't mind that.'

'What do you mind then?'

'I don't want you to look like you did just now. You had a twist to your mouth and a flash of knowledge in your eyes. Not the right sort of knowledge.'

I felt very curious, rather excited. 'What do you mean, Maxim? What isn't the right sort of knowledge?'

He did not answer for a moment. Frith had come back into the room and was changing the plates. Maxim waited until Frith had gone behind the screen and through the service door before speaking again.

'When I met you first you had a certain expression on your face,' he said slowly, 'and you have it still. I'm not going to define it, I don't know how to. But it was one of the reasons why I married you. A moment ago, when you were going through that curious little performance, the expression had gone. Something else had taken its place.'

'What sort of thing? Explain to me, Maxim?' I said eagerly.

He considered me a moment, his eyebrows raised, whistling softly. 'Listen, my sweet. When you were a little girl, were you ever forbidden to read certain books, and did your father put those books under lock and key?'

'Yes,' I said.

'Well, then. A husband is not so very different from a father after all. There is a certain type of knowledge I prefer you not to have. It's better kept under lock and key. So that's that. And now eat up your peaches, and don't ask me any more questions, or I shall put you in the corner.'

'I wish you would not treat me as if I was six,' I said.

'How do you want to be treated?'

'Like other men treat their wives.'

'Knock you about, do you mean?'

'Don't be absurd. Why must you make a joke of everything?'

'I'm not joking. I'm very serious.'

'No, you're not. I can tell by your eyes. You're playing with me all the time, just as if I was a silly little girl.'

'Alice-in-Wonderland. That was a good idea of mine. Have you bought your sash and your hair-ribbon yet?'

'I warn you. You'll get the surprise of your life when you do see me in my fancy dress.'

'I'm sure I shall. Get on with your peach and don't talk with your mouth full. I've got a lot of letters to write after dinner.' He did not wait for me to finish. He got up and strolled about the room, and asked Frith to bring the coffee in the library. I sat still, sullenly, being as slow as I could, hoping to keep things back and irritate him, but Frith took no notice of me and my peach, he brought the coffee at once and Maxim went off to the library by himself.

When I had finished I went upstairs to the minstrel's gallery to have a look at the pictures. I knew them well of course by now, but had never studied them with a view to reproducing one of them as a fancy-dress. Mrs. Danvers was right of course. What an idiot I had been not to think of it before. I always loved the girl in white, with a hat in her hand. It was a Raeburn, and the portrait was of Caroline de Winter, a sister of Maxim's great-great grandfather. She married a great Whig politician, and was a famous London beauty for many years, but this portrait was painted before that, when she was still unmarried. The white dress should be easy to copy. Those puffed sleeves, the flounce, and the little bodice. The hat might be rather difficult, and I should have to wear a wig. My straight hair would never curl in that way. Perhaps that Voce place in London that Mrs. Danvers had told me about would do the whole thing. I would send them a sketch of the portrait and tell them to copy it faithfully, sending my measurements.

What a relief it was to have decided at last! Quite a weight off my mind. I began almost to look forward to the ball. Perhaps I should enjoy it after all, almost as much as little Clarice.

I wrote to the shop in the morning, enclosing a sketch of the portrait, and I had a very favourable reply, full of honour at my esteemed order, and saying the work would be put in hand right away, and they would manage the wig as well.

Clarice could hardly contain herself for excitement, and I, too, began to get party fever as the great day approached. Giles and Beatrice were coming for the night, but nobody else, thank heaven, although a lot of people were expected to dinner first. I had imagined we should have to hold a large house-party for the occasion, but Maxim decided against it. 'Having the dance alone is quite enough effort,' he said; and I wondered whether he did it for my sake alone, or whether a large crowd of people really bored him as he said. I had heard so much of the Manderley parties in the old days, with people sleeping in bathrooms and on sofas because of the squash. And here we were alone in the vast house, with only Beatrice and Giles to count as guests.

The house began to wear a new, expectant air. Men came to lay the floor for dancing in the great hall, and in the drawing-room some of the furniture was moved so that the long buffet tables could be placed against the wall. Lights were put up on the terrace, and in the rose-garden too, wherever one walked there would be some sign of preparation for the ball. Workmen from the estate were everywhere, and Frank came to lunch nearly every day. The servants talked of nothing else, and Frith stalked about as though the whole of the evening would depend on him alone. Robert rather lost his head, and kept forgetting things, napkins at lunch, and handing vegetables. He wore a harassed expression, like someone who has got to catch a train. The dogs were miserable. Jasper trailed about the hall with his tail between his legs, and nipped every workman on sight. He used to stand on the terrace, barking idiotically, and then dash madly to one corner of the lawn and eat grass in a sort of frenzy. Mrs. Danvers never obtruded herself, but I was aware of her continually. It was her voice I heard in the drawing-room when they came to put the tables, it was she who gave directions for the laying of the floor in the hall. Whenever I came upon the scene she had always just disappeared; I would catch a glimpse of her skirt brushing the door, or hear the sound of her footsteps on the stairs. I was a lay-figure, no use to man or beast. I used to stand about doing nothing except get in the way. 'Excuse me, Madam,' I would hear a man say, just behind me, and he would pass, with a smile of apology, carrying two chairs on his back, his face dripping with perspiration.

'I'm awfully sorry,' I would say, getting quickly to one side, and then as a cover to my idleness, 'Can I help you? What about putting those chairs in the library?' The man would look bewildered. 'Mrs. Danvers' orders, Madam, was that we were to take the chairs round to the back, to be out of the way.'

'Oh,' I said, 'yes, of course. How silly of me. Take them round to the back, as she said.' And I would walk quickly away murmuring something about finding a piece of paper and a pencil, in a vain attempt to delude the man into thinking I was busy, while he went on across the hall, looking rather astonished, and I would feel I had not deceived him for a moment.

The great day dawned misty and over-cast, but the glass was high and we had no fears. The mist was a good sign. It cleared about eleven, as Maxim had foretold, and we had a glorious still summer's day without a cloud in the blue sky. All the morning the gardeners were bringing flowers into the house, the last of the white lilac, and great lupins and delphiniums, five foot high, roses in hundreds, and every sort of lily.

Mrs. Danvers showed herself at last; quietly, calmly, she told the gardeners where to put the flowers, and she herself arranged them, stacking the vases with quick, deft fingers. I watched her in fascination, the way she did vase after vase, carrying them herself through the flower-room to the drawing-room and the various corners of the house, massing them in just the right numbers and profusion, putting colour where colour was needed, leaving the walls bare where severity paid.

Maxim and I had lunch with Frank at his bachelor establishment next-door to the office to be out of the way. We were all three in the rather hearty, cheerful humour of people after a funeral. We made pointless jokes about nothing at all, our minds eternally on the thought of the next few hours. I felt very much the same as I did the morning I was married. The same stifled feeling that I had gone too far now to turn back.

The evening had got to be endured. Thank heaven Messrs. Voce had sent my dress in time. It looked perfect, in its folds of tissue paper. And the wig was a triumph. I had tried it on after breakfast, and was amazed at the transformation. I looked quite attractive, quite different altogether. Not me at all. Someone much more interesting, more vivid and alive. Maxim and Frank kept asking me about my costume.

'You won't know me,' I told them, 'you will both get the shock of your lives.'

'You are not going to dress up as a clown, are you?' said Maxim gloomily. 'No frightful attempt to be funny?'

'No, nothing like that,' I said, full of importance.

'I wish you had kept to Alice-in-Wonderland,' he said.

'Or Joan of Arc with your hair,' said Frank shyly.

'I never thought of that,' I said blankly, and Frank went rather pink. 'I'm sure we shall all like whatever you wear,' he said in his most pompous Frank-ish voice.

'Don't encourage her, Frank,' said Maxim. 'She's so full of her precious disguise already there's no holding her. Bee will put you in your place, that's one comfort. She'll soon tell you if she doesn't like your dress. Dear old Bee always looks just wrong on these occasions, bless her. I remember her once as Madame Pompadour and she tripped up going in to supper and her wig came adrift. "I can't stand this damned thing," she said, in that blunt voice of hers, and chucked it on a chair and went through the rest of the evening with her own cropped hair. You can imagine what it looked like, against a pale blue satin crinoline, or whatever the dress was. Poor old Giles did not cope that year. He came as a cook, and sat about in the bar all night looking perfectly miserable. I think he felt Bee had let him down.'

'No, it wasn't that,' said Frank, 'he'd lost his front teeth trying out a new mare, don't you remember, and he was so shy about it he wouldn't open his mouth.'

'Oh, was that it? Poor Giles. He generally enjoys dressing-up.'

'Beatrice says he loves playing charades,' I said. 'She told me they always have charades at Christmas.'

'I know,' said Maxim, 'that's why I've never spent Christmas with her.'

'Have some more asparagus, Mrs. de Winter, and another potato?'

'No, really, Frank, I'm not hungry, thank you.'

'Nerves,' said Maxim, shaking his head. 'Never mind, this time to-morrow it will all be over.'

'I sincerely hope so,' said Frank seriously. 'I was going to give orders that all cars should stand by for five a.m.'

I began to laugh weakly, the tears coming into my eyes. 'Oh dear,' I said, 'let's send wires to everybody not to come.'

'Come on, be brave and face it,' said Maxim. 'We need not give another one for years. Frank, I have an uneasy feeling we ought to be going up to the house. What do you think?'

Frank agreed, and I followed them unwillingly, reluctant to leave the cramped, rather uncomfortable little dining-room that was so typical of Frank's bachelor establishment, and which seemed to me to-day the embodiment of peace and quietude. When we came to the house we found that the band had arrived, and were standing about in the hall rather pink in the face and self-conscious, while Frith, more important than ever, offered refreshments. The band were to be our guests for the night, and after we had welcomed them and exchanged a few slightly obvious jokes proper to the occasion, they were borne off to their quarters to be followed by a tour of the grounds.

The afternoon dragged, like the last hours before a journey when one is packed up and keyed to departure, and I wandered from room to room almost as lost as Jasper, who trailed reproachfully at my heels.

There was nothing I could do to help, and it would have been wiser on my part to have kept clear of the house altogether and taken the dog and myself for a long walk. By the time I decided upon this it was too late, Maxim and Frank were demanding tea, and when tea was over Beatrice and Giles arrived. The evening had come upon us all too soon.

'This is like old times,' said Beatrice, kissing Maxim, and looking about her. 'Congratulations to you for remembering every detail. The flowers are exquisite,' she added, turning to me. 'Did you do them?'

'No,' I said, rather ashamed, 'Mrs. Danvers is responsible for everything.'

'Oh. Well, after all . . .' Beatrice did not finish her sentence, she accepted a light for her cigarette from Frank, and once it was lit she appeared to have forgotten what she was going to say.

'Have you got Mitchell's to do the catering as usual?' asked Giles.

'Yes,' said Maxim. 'I don't think anything has been altered, has it, Frank? We had all the records down at the office. Nothing has been forgotten, and I don't think we have left anyone out.'

'What a relief to find only ourselves,' said Beatrice. 'I remember once arriving about this time, and there were about twenty-five people in the place already. All going to stop the night.'

'What's everyone going to wear? I suppose Maxim, as always, refuses to play?'

'As always,' said Maxim.

'Such a mistake I think. The whole thing would go with much more swing if you did.'

'Have you ever known a ball at Manderley not to go with a swing?'

'No, my dear boy, the organisation is too good. But I do think the host ought to give the lead himself.'

'I think it's quite enough if the hostess makes the effort,' said Maxim. 'Why should I make myself hot and uncomfortable and a damn fool into the bargain?'

'Oh, but that's absurd. There's no need to look a fool. With your appearance, my dear Maxim, you could get away with any costume. You don't have to worry about your figure like poor Giles.'

'What is Giles going to wear to-night,' I asked, 'or is it a dead secret?'

'No, rather not,' beamed Giles, 'as a matter-of-fact, it's a pretty good effort. I got our local tailor to rig it up. I'm coming as an Arabian sheik.'

'Good God,' said Maxim.

'It's not at all bad,' said Beatrice warmly. 'He stains his face of course, and leaves off his glasses. The head-dress is authentic. We borrowed it off a friend who used to live in the East, and the rest the tailor copied from some paper. Giles looks very well in it.'

'What are you going to be, Mrs. Lacy?' said Frank.

'Oh, I'm afraid I haven't coped much,' said Beatrice. 'I've got some sort of Eastern get-up to go with Giles, but I don't pretend it's genuine. Strings of beads, you know, and a veil over my face.'

'It sounds very nice,' I said politely.

'Oh, it's not bad. Comfortable to wear, that's one blessing. I shall take off the veil if I get too hot. What are you wearing?'

'Don't ask her,' said Maxim. 'She won't tell any of us. There has never been such a secret. I believe she even wrote to London for it.'

'My dear,' said Beatrice, rather impressed, 'don't say you have gone a bust and will put us all to shame? Mine is only home-made, you know.'

'Don't worry,' I said, laughing, 'it's quite simple really. But Maxim would tease me, and I've promised to give him the surprise of his life.'

'Quite right too,' said Giles, 'Maxim is too superior altogether. The fact is he's jealous. Wishes he was dressing up like the rest of us, and doesn't like to say so.'

'Heaven forbid,' said Maxim.

'What are you doing, Crawley?' asked Giles.

Frank looked rather apologetic. 'I've been so busy I'm afraid I've left things to the last moment. I hunted up an old pair of trousers last night, and a striped football jersey, and thought of putting a patch over one eye and coming as a pirate.'

'Why on earth didn't you write to us and borrow a costume?' said Beatrice. 'There's one of a Dutchman that Roger had last winter in Switzerland. It would have suited you excellently.'

'I refuse to allow my agent to walk about as a Dutchman,' said Maxim. 'He'd never get rents out of anybody again. Let him stick to his pirate. It might frighten some of them.'

'Anything less like a pirate,' murmured Beatrice in my ear.

I pretended not to hear. Poor Frank, she was always rather down on him.

'How long will it take me to paint my face?' asked Giles.

'Two hours at least,' said Beatrice. 'I should begin thinking about it if I were you. How many shall we be at dinner?'

'Sixteen,' said Maxim, 'counting ourselves. No strangers. You know them all.'

'I'm beginning to get dress fever already,' said Beatrice. 'What fun it all is. I'm so glad you decided to do this again, Maxim.'

'You've got her to thank for it,' said Maxim, nodding at me.

'Oh, it's not true,' I said. 'It was all the fault of Lady Crowan.'

'Nonsense,' said Maxim, smiling at me, 'you know you're as excited as a child at its first party.'

'I'm not.'

'I'm longing to see your dress,' said Beatrice.

'It's nothing out of the way. Really it's not,' I insisted.

'Mrs. de Winter says we shan't know her,' said Frank.

Everybody looked at me and smiled. I felt pleased and flushed and rather happy. People were being nice. They were all so friendly. It was suddenly fun, the thought of the dance, and that I was to be the hostess.

The dance was being given for me, in my honour, because I was the bride. I sat on the table in the library, swinging my legs, while the rest of them stood round, and I had a longing to go upstairs and put on my dress, try the wig in front of the looking-glass, turn this way and that before the long mirror on the wall. It was new, this sudden unexpected sensation of being important, of having Giles, and Beatrice, and Frank and Maxim all looking at me and talking about my dress. All wondering what I was going to wear. I thought of the soft white dress in its folds of tissue paper, and how it would hide my flat dull figure, my rather sloping shoulders. I thought of my own lank hair covered by the sleek and gleaming curls.

'What's the time?' I said carelessly, yawning a little, pretending I did not care. 'I wonder if we ought to think about going upstairs . . . ?'

As we crossed the great hall on the way to our rooms I realised for the first time how the house lent itself to the occasion, and how beautiful the rooms were looking. Even the drawing-room, formal and cold to my consideration when we were alone, was a blaze of colour now, flowers in every corner, red roses in silver bowls on the white cloth of the supper table, the long windows open to the terrace, where, as soon as it was dusk, the fairy lights would shine. The band had stacked their instruments ready in the minstrel's gallery above the hall, and the hall itself wore a strange, waiting air; there was a warmth about it I had never known before, due to the night itself, so still and clear, to the flowers beneath the pictures, to our own laughter as we hovered on the wide stone stairs.

The old austerity had gone. Manderley had come alive in a fashion I would not have believed possible. It was not the still quiet Manderley I knew. There was a certain significance about it now that had not been before. A reckless air, rather triumphant, rather pleasing. It was as if the house remembered other days, long, long ago, when the hall was a banqueting hall indeed, with weapons and tapestry hanging upon the walls, and men sat at a long narrow table in the centre laughing louder than we laughed now, calling for wine, for song, throwing great pieces of meat upon the flags to the slumbering dogs. Later, in other years, it would still be gay, but with a certain grace and dignity, and Caroline de Winter, whom I should represent to-night, would walk down the wide stone stairs in her white dress to dance the minuet. I wished we could sweep away the years and see her. I wished we did not have to degrade the house with our modern jig-tunes, so out-of-place and unromantic. They would not suit Manderley. I found myself in sudden agreement with Mrs. Danvers. We should have made it a period ball, not the hotch-potch of humanity it was bound to be, with Giles, poor fellow, well-meaning and hearty in his guise of Arabian sheik. I found Clarice waiting for me in my bedroom, her round face scarlet with excitement. We giggled at one another like schoolgirls, and I bade her lock my door. There was much sound of tissue paper, rustling and mysterious. We spoke to one another softly like conspirators, we walked on tip-toe. I felt like a child again on the eve of Christmas. This padding to and fro in my room with bare feet, the little furtive bursts of laughter, the stifled exclamations, reminded me of hanging up my stocking long ago. Maxim was safe in his dressing-room, and the way through was barred against him. Clarice alone was my ally and favoured friend. The dress fitted perfectly. I stood still, hardly able to restrain my impatience while Clarice hooked me up with fumbling fingers.

'It's handsome, Madam,' she kept saying, leaning back on her heels to look at me. 'It's a dress fit for the Queen of England.'

'What about under the left shoulder there,' I said, anxiously. 'That strap of mine, is it going to show?'

'No, Madam, nothing shows.'

'How is it? How do I look?' I did not wait for her answer, I twisted and turned in front of the mirror, I frowned, I smiled. I felt different already, no longer hampered by my appearance. My own dull personality was submerged at last. 'Give me the wig,' I said excitedly, 'careful, don't crush it, the curls mustn't be flat. They are supposed to stand out from the face.' Clarice stood behind my shoulder, I saw her round face beyond mine in the reflection of the looking-glass, her eyes shining, her mouth a little open. I brushed my own hair sleek behind my ears. I took hold of the soft gleaming curls with trembling fingers, laughing under my breath, looking up at Clarice.

'Oh, Clarice,' I said, 'what will Mr. de Winter say?'

I covered my own mousy hair with the curled wig trying to hide my triumph, trying to hide my smile. Somebody came and hammered on the door.

'Who's there?' I called in panic. 'You can't come in.'

'It's me, my dear, don't alarm yourself,' said Beatrice, 'how far have you got? I want to look at you.'

'No, no,' I said, 'you can't come in, I'm not ready.'

The flustered Clarice stood beside me, her hand full of hair-pins, while I took them from her one by one, controlling the curls that had become fluffed in the box.

'I'll come down when I am ready,' I called. 'Go on down, all of you. Don't wait for me. Tell Maxim he can't come in.'

'Maxim's down,' she said. 'He came along to us. He said he hammered on your bathroom door and you never answered. Don't be too long, my dear, we are all so intrigued. Are you sure you don't want any help?'

'No,' I shouted impatiently, losing my head, 'go away, go on down.'

Why did she have to come and bother just at this moment? It fussed me, I did not know what I was doing. I jabbed with a hair-pin, flattening it against a curl. I heard no more from Beatrice, she must have gone along the passage. I wondered if she was happy in her Eastern robes and if Giles had succeeded in painting his face. How absurd it was, the whole thing. Why did we do it, I wonder, why were we such children?

I did not recognise the face that stared at me in the glass. The eyes were larger surely, the mouth narrower, the skin white and clear? The curls stood away from the head in a little cloud. I watched this self that was not me at all and then smiled; a new, slow smile.

'Oh, Clarice!' I said. 'Oh, Clarice!' I took the skirt of my dress in my hands and curtseyed to her, the flounces sweeping the ground. She giggled excitedly, rather embarrassed, flushed though, very pleased. I paraded up and down in front of my glass watching my reflection.

'Unlock the door,' I said. 'I'm going down. Run ahead and see if they are there.' She obeyed me, still giggling, and I lifted my skirts off the ground and followed her along the corridor.

She looked back at me and beckoned. 'They've gone down,' she whispered, 'Mr. de Winter, and Major and Mrs. Lacy. Mr. Crawley has just come. They are all standing in the hall.' I peered through the archway at the head of the big staircase, and looked down on the hall below.

Yes, there they were. Giles, in his white Arab dress, laughing loudly, showing the knife at his side, Beatrice swathed in an extraordinary green garment and hung about the neck with trailing beads, poor Frank self-conscious and slightly foolish in his striped jersey and sea-boots, Maxim, the only normal one of the party, in his evening clothes.

'I don't know what she's doing,' he said, 'she's been up in her bedroom for hours. What's the time, Frank? The dinner crowd will be upon us before we know where we are.'

The band were changed, and in the gallery already. One of the men was tuning his fiddle. He played a scale softly, and then plucked at a string. The light shone on the picture of Caroline de Winter.

Yes, the dress had been copied exactly from my sketch of the portrait. The puffed sleeve, the sash and the ribbon, the wide floppy hat I held in my hand. And my curls were her curls, they stood out from my face as hers did in the picture. I don't think I have ever felt so excited before, so happy and so proud. I waved my hand at the man with the fiddle, and then put my finger to my lips for silence. He smiled and bowed. He came across the gallery to the archway where I stood.

'Make the drummer announce me,' I whispered, 'make him beat the drum, you know how they do, and then call out Miss Caroline de Winter.

I want to surprise them below.' He nodded his head, he understood. My heart fluttered absurdly, and my cheeks were burning. What fun it was, what mad ridiculous childish fun! I smiled at Clarice still crouching in the corridor, I picked up my skirt in my hands. Then the sound of the drum echoed in the great hall, startling me for a moment, who had waited for it, who knew that it would come. I saw them look up surprised and bewildered from the hall below.

'Miss Caroline de Winter,' shouted the drummer.

I came forward to the head of the stairs and stood there, smiling, my hat in my hand, like the girl in the picture. I waited for the clapping and the laughter that would follow as I walked slowly down the stairs. Nobody clapped, nobody moved.

They all stared at me like dumb things. Beatrice uttered a little cry and put her hand to her mouth. I went on smiling, I put one hand on the banister.

'How do you do, Mr. de Winter,' I said.

Maxim had not moved. He stared up at me, his glass in his hand. There was no colour in his face. It was ashen white. I saw Frank go to him as though he would speak, but Maxim shook him off. I hesitated, one foot already on the stairs. Something was wrong, they had not understood. Why was Maxim looking like that? Why did they all stand like dummies, like people in a trance?

Then Maxim moved forward to the stairs, his eyes never leaving my face.

'What the hell do you think you are doing?' he said. His eyes blazed in anger. His face was still ashen white.

I could not move, I went on standing there, my hand on the banister.

'It's the picture,' I said, terrified at his eyes, at his voice. 'It's the picture, the one in the gallery.'

There was a long silence. We went on staring at each other. Nobody moved in the hall. I swallowed, my hand moved to my throat. 'What is it?' I said. 'What have I done?'

If only they would not stare at me like that with dull blank faces. If only somebody would say something. When Maxim spoke again I did not recognise his voice. It was still and quiet, icy cold, not a voice I knew.

'Go and change,' he said, 'it does not matter what you put on. Find an ordinary evening frock, anything will do. Go now, before anybody comes.'

I could not speak, I went on staring at him. His eyes were the only living things in the white mask of his face.

'What are you standing there for?' he said, his voice harsh and queer. 'Didn't you hear what I said?'

I turned and ran blindly through the archway to the corridors beyond. I caught a glimpse of the astonished face of the drummer who had announced me. I brushed past him, stumbling, not looking where I went. Tears blinded my eyes. I did not know what was happening. Clarice had gone. The corridor was deserted. I looked about me stunned and stupid like a haunted thing. Then I saw that the door leading to the west wing was open wide, and that someone was standing there.

It was Mrs. Danvers. I shall never forget the expression on her face, loathsome, triumphant. The face of an exulting devil. She stood there, smiling at me.

And then I ran from her, down the long narrow passage to my own room, tripping, stumbling over the flounces of my dress.

Chapter Seventeen

Clarice was waiting for me in my bedroom. She looked pale and scared. As soon as she saw me she burst into tears. I did not say anything. I began tearing at the hooks of my dress, ripping the stuff. I could not manage them properly, and Clarice came to help me, still crying noisily.

'It's all right, Clarice, it's not your fault,' I said, and she shook her head, the tears running down her cheeks.

'Your lovely dress, Madam,' she said, 'your lovely white dress.'

'It doesn't matter,' I said. 'Can't you find the hook? There it is, at the back. And another one somewhere, just below.'

She fumbled with the hooks, her hands trembling, making worse trouble with it than I did myself, and all the time catching at her breath.

'What will you wear instead, Madam?' she said.

'I don't know,' I said. 'I don't know.' She had managed to unfasten the hooks, and I struggled out of the dress. 'I think I'd rather like to be alone, Clarice,' I said, 'would you be a dear and leave me? Don't worry, I shall manage all right. Forget what's happened. I want you to enjoy the party.'

'Can't I press out a dress for you, Madam?' she said, looking up at me with swollen streaming eyes. 'It won't take me a moment.'

'No,' I said, 'don't bother, I'd rather you went, and Clarice . . .'

'Yes, Madam?'

'Don't – don't say anything about what's just happened.'

'No, madam.' She burst into another torrent of weeping.

'Don't let the others see you like that,' I said. 'Go to your bedroom and do something to your face. There's nothing to cry about, nothing at all.' Somebody knocked on the door. Clarice threw me a quick frightened glance.

'Who is it?' I said. The door opened and Beatrice came into the room. She came to me at once, a strange rather ludicrous figure in her Eastern drapery, the bangles jangling on her wrists.

'My dear,' she said, 'my dear,' and held out her hands to me.

Clarice slipped out of the room. I felt tired suddenly, and unable to cope. I went and sat down on the bed. I put my hand up to my head and took off the curled wig. Beatrice stood watching me.

'Are you all right?' she said. 'You look very white.'

'It's the light,' I said. 'It never gives one any colour.'

'Sit down for a few minutes and you'll be all right,' she said, 'wait, I'll get you a glass of water.'

She went into the bathroom, her bangles jangling with her every movement, and then she came back, the glass of water in her hands.

I drank some to please her, not wanting it a bit. It tasted warm from the tap; she had not let it run.

'Of course I knew at once it was just a terrible mistake,' she said. 'You could not possibly have known, why should you?'

'Know what?' I said.

'Why, the dress, you poor dear, the picture you copied of the girl in the gallery. It was what Rebecca did at the last fancy dress ball at Manderley. Identical. The same picture, the same dress. You stood there on the stairs, and for one ghastly moment I thought . . .'

She did not go on with her sentence, she patted me on the shoulder.

'You poor child, how wretchedly unfortunate, how were you to know?'

'I ought to have known,' I said stupidly, staring at her, too stunned to understand. 'I ought to have known.'

'Nonsense, how could you know? It was not the sort of thing that could possibly enter any of our heads. Only it was such a shock, you see. We none of us expected it, and Maxim . . .'

'Yes, Maxim?' I said.

'He thinks, you see, it was deliberate on your part. You had some bet that you would startle him, didn't you? Some foolish joke. And of course, he doesn't understand. It was such a frightful shock for him. I told him at once you could not have done such a thing, and that it was sheer appalling luck that you had chosen that particular picture.'

'I ought to have known,' I repeated again. 'It's all my fault, I ought to have known.'

'No, no. Don't worry, you'll be able to explain the whole thing to him quietly. Everything will be quite all right. The first lot of people were arriving just as I came upstairs to you. They are having drinks. Everything's all right. I've told Frank and Giles to make up a story about your dress not fitting, and you are very disappointed.'

I did not say anything. I went on sitting on the bed with my hands in my lap.

'What can you wear instead?' said Beatrice, going to my wardrobe and flinging open the doors. 'Here, what's this blue? It looks charming. Put this on. Nobody will mind. Quick, I'll help you.'

'No,' I said. 'No, I'm not coming down.'

Beatrice stared at me in great distress, my blue frock over her arm.

'But, my dear, you must,' she said in dismay. 'You can't possibly not appear.'

'No, Beatrice, I'm not coming down. I can't face them, not after what's happened.'

'But nobody will know about the dress,' she said. 'Frank and Giles will never breathe a word. We've got the story all arranged. The shop sent the wrong dress, and it did not fit, so you are wearing an ordinary evening dress instead. Everyone will think it perfectly natural. It won't make any difference to the evening.'

'You don't understand,' I said. 'I don't care about the dress. It's not that at all. It's what has happened, what I did. I can't come down now, Beatrice, I can't.'

'But, my dear, Giles and Frank understand perfectly. They are full of sympathy. And Maxim too. It was just the first shock. . . . I'll try and get him alone a minute, I'll explain the whole thing.'

'No!' I said. 'No!'

She put my blue frock down beside me on the bed. 'Everyone will be arriving,' she said, very worried, very upset. 'It will look so extraordinary if you don't come down. I can't say you've suddenly got a headache.'

'Why not?' I said wearily. 'What does it matter? Make anything up. Nobody will mind, they don't any of them know me.'

'Come now, my dear,' she said, patting my hand, 'try and make the effort. Put on this charming blue. Think of Maxim. You must come down for his sake.'

'I'm thinking about Maxim all the time,' I said.

'Well then, surely . . .?'

'No,' I said, tearing at my nails, rocking backwards and forwards on the bed. 'I can't, I can't.'

Somebody else knocked on the door. 'Oh, dear, who on earth is that?' said Beatrice, walking to the door. 'What is it?'

She opened the door. Giles was standing just outside. 'Everyone has turned up, Maxim sent me up to find out what's happening?' he said.

'She says she won't come down,' said Beatrice. 'What on earth are we going to say?'

I caught a sight of Giles peering at me through the open door.

'Oh, Lord, what a frightful mix-up,' he whispered. He turned away embarrassed when he noticed that I had seen him.

'What shall I say to Maxim?' he asked Beatrice. 'It's five past eight now.'

'Say she's feeling rather faint, but will try and come down later. Tell them not to wait dinner. I'll be down directly, I'll make it all right.'

'Yes, right you are.' He half glanced in my direction again, sympathetic but rather curious, wondering why I sat there on the bed, and his voice was low, as it might be after an accident, when people are waiting for the doctor.

'Is there anything else I can do?' he said.

'No,' said Beatrice, 'go down now, I'll follow in a minute.'

He obeyed her, shuffling away in his Arabian robes. This is the sort of moment, I thought, that I shall laugh at years afterwards. I shall say 'Do you remember how Giles was dressed as an Arab, and Beatrice had a veil over her face, and jangling bangles on her wrist?' And time will mellow it, make it a moment for laughter. But now it was not funny, now I did not laugh. It was not the future, it was the present. It was too vivid and too real.

I sat on the bed, plucking at the eiderdown, pulling a little feather out of a slit in one corner.

'Would you like some brandy?' said Beatrice, making a last effort. 'I know it's only Dutch courage, but it sometimes works wonders.'

'No,' I said. 'No, I don't want anything.'

'I shall have to go down. Giles says they are waiting dinner. Are you sure it's all right for me to leave you?'

'Yes. And thank you, Beatrice.'

'Oh, my dear, don't thank me. I wish I could do something.' She stooped swiftly to my looking-glass and dabbed her face with powder. 'God, what a sight I look,' she said, 'this damn veil is crooked I know. However it can't be helped.' She rustled out of the room, closing the door behind her. I felt I had forfeited her sympathy by my refusal to go down. I had shown the white feather. She had not understood. She belonged to another breed of men and women, another race than I. They had guts, the women of her race. They were not like me. If it had been Beatrice who had done this thing instead of me she would have put on her other dress and gone down again to welcome her guests. She would have stood by Giles's side, and shaken hands with people, a smile on her face. I could not do that. I had not the pride, I had not the guts. I was badly bred.

I kept seeing Maxim's eyes blazing in his white face, and behind him Giles, and Beatrice and Frank standing like dummies, staring at me.

I got up from my bed and went and looked out of the window. The gardeners were going round to the lights in the rose garden, testing them to see if they all worked. The sky was pale, with a few salmon clouds of evening streaking to the west. When it was dusk the lamps would all be lit. There were tables and chairs in the rose-garden for the couples who wanted to sit out. I could smell the roses from my window. The men were talking to one another and laughing. 'There's one here gone,' I heard a voice call out; 'can you get me another small bulb? One of the blue ones, Bill.' He fixed the light into position. He whistled a popular tune of the moment with easy confidence, and I thought how to-night perhaps the band would play the same tune in the minstrel's gallery above the hall. 'That's got it,' said the man, switching the light on and off, 'they're all right here. No others gone. We'd better have a look at those on the terrace.' They went off round the corner of the house, still whistling the song. I wished I could be the man. Later in the evening he would stand with his friend in the drive and watch the cars drive up to the house, his hands in his pockets, his cap on the back of his head. He would stand in a crowd with the other people from the estate, and then drink cider at the long table arranged for them in one corner of the terrace. 'Like the old days, isn't it?' he would say. But his friend would shake his head, puffing at his pipe. 'This new one's not like our Mrs. de Winter, she's different altogether.' And a woman next them in the crowd would agree, other people too, all saying 'That's right,' and nodding their heads.

'Where is she to-night? She's not been on the terrace once.'

'I can't say, I'm sure. I've not seen her.'

'Mrs. de Winter used to be here, there, and everywhere.'

'Aye, that's right.'

And the woman would turn to her neighbours nodding mysteriously.

'They say she's not appearing to-night at all.'

'Go on.'

''Tis true. Ask Mary here.'

'That's right. One of the servants from the house told me Mrs. de Winter hasn't come down from her room all the evening.'

'What's wrong with the maid, is she bad?'

'No, sulky I reckon. They say her dress didn't please her.'

A squeal of laughter and a murmur from the little crowd.

'Did you ever hear of such a thing? It's a shame for Mr. de Winter.'

'I wouldn't stand for it, not from a chit like her.'

'Maybe it's not true at all.'

'It's true all right. They're full of it up at the house.' One to the other. This one to the next. A smile, a wink, a shrug of the shoulder. One group, and then another group. And then spreading to the guests who walked on the terrace and strolled across the lawns. The couple who in three hours' time would sit in those chairs beneath me in the rose-garden.

'Do you suppose it's true what I heard?'

'What did you hear?'

'Why, that there's nothing wrong with her at all, they've had a colossal row, and she won't appear!'

'I say!' A lift of the eyebrows, a long whistle.

'I know. Well, it does look rather odd, don't you think? What I mean is, people don't suddenly for no reason have violent headaches. I call the whole thing jolly fishy.'

'I thought he looked a bit grim.'

'So did I.'

'Of course I have heard before the marriage is not a wild success.'

'Oh, really?'

'H'm. Several people have said so. They say he's beginning to realise he's made a big mistake. She's nothing to look at, you know.'

'No, I've heard there's nothing much to her. Who was she?'

'Oh, no one at all. Some pick-up in the south of France, a nursery gov., or something.'

'Good Lord!'

'I know. And when you think of Rebecca. . . .'

I went on staring at the empty chairs. The salmon sky had turned to grey. Above my head was the evening air. In the woods beyond the rose-garden the birds were making their last little rustling noises before nightfall. A lone gull flew across the sky. I went away from the window, back to bed again. I picked up the white dress I had left on the floor and put it back in the box with the tissue paper. I put the wig back in its box too. Then I looked in one of my cupboards for the little portable iron I used to have in Monte Carlo for Mrs. Van Hopper's dresses. It was lying at the back of a shelf with some woollen jumpers I had not worn for a long time. The iron was one of those universal kinds that go on any voltage and I fitted it to the plug in the wall. I began to iron the blue dress that Beatrice had taken from the wardrobe, slowly, methodically, as I used to iron Mrs. Van Hopper's dresses in Monte Carlo.

When I had finished I laid the dress ready on the bed. Then I cleaned the make-up off my face that I had put on for the fancy dress. I combed my hair, and washed my hands. I put on the blue dress and the shoes that went with it. I might have been my old self again, going down to the lounge of the hotel with Mrs. Van Hopper. I opened the door of my room and went along the corridor. Everything was still and silent. There might not have been a party at all. I tip-toed to the end of the passage and turned the corner. The door to the west wing was closed. There was no sound of anything at all. When I came to the archway by the gallery and the staircase I heard the murmur and hum of conversation coming from the dining-room. They were still having dinner. The great hall was deserted. There was nobody in the gallery either. The band must be having their dinner too. I did not know what arrangements had been made for them. Frank had done it – Frank or Mrs. Danvers.

From where I stood I could see the picture of Caroline de Winter facing me in the gallery. I could see the curls framing her face, and I could see the smile on her lips. I remembered the bishop's wife who had said to me that day I called, 'I shall never forget her, dressed all in white, with that cloud of dark hair.' I ought to have remembered that, I ought to have known. How queer the instruments looked in the gallery, the little stands for the music, the big drum. One of the men had left his handkerchief on a chair. I leant over the rail and looked down at the hall below. Soon it would be filled with people, like the bishop's wife had said, and Maxim would stand at the bottom of the stairs shaking hands with them, as they came into the hall. The sound of their voices would echo to the ceiling, and then the band would play from the gallery where I was leaning now, the man with the violin smiling, swaying to the music.

It would not be quiet like this any more. A board creaked in the gallery. I swung round, looking at the gallery behind me. There was nobody there. The gallery was empty, just as it had been before. A current of air blew in my face though, somebody must have left a window open in one of the passages. The hum of voices continued in the dining-room. I wondered why the board creaked when I had not moved at all. The warmth of the night perhaps, a swelling somewhere in the old wood. The draught still blew in my face though. A piece of music on one of the stands fluttered to the floor. I looked towards the archway above the stairs. The draught was coming from there. I went beneath the arch again, and when I came out on to the long corridor saw that the door to the west wing had blown open and swung back against the wall. It was dark in the west passage, none of the lights had been turned on. I could feel the wind blowing on my face from an open window. I fumbled for a switch on the wall and could not find one. I could see the window in an angle of the passage, the curtain blowing softly, backwards and forwards. The grey evening light cast queer shadows on the floor. The sound of the sea came to me through the open window, the soft hissing sound of the ebb-tide leaving the shingle.

I did not go and shut the window. I stood there shivering a moment in my thin dress, listening to the sea as it sighed and left the shore. Then I turned quickly and shut the door of the west wing behind me, and came out again through the archway by the stairs.

The murmur of voices had swollen now and was louder than before. The door of the dining-room was open. They were coming out of dinner. I could see Robert standing by the open door, and there was a scraping of chairs, a babble of conversation, and of laughter.

I walked slowly down the stairs to meet them.

When I look back at my first party at Manderley, my first and my last, I can remember little isolated things standing alone out of the vast blank canvas of the evening. The background was hazy, a sea of dim faces none of whom I knew, and there was the slow drone of the band harping out a waltz that never finished, that went on and on. The same couples swung by in rotation, with the same fixed smiles, and to me, standing with Maxim at the bottom of the stairs to welcome the late-comers, these dancing couples seemed like marionettes twisting and turning on a piece of string, held by some invisible hand.

There was a woman, I never knew her name, never saw her again, but she wore a salmon-coloured gown hooped in crinoline form, a vague gesture to some past century but whether seventeenth, eighteenth, or nineteenth I could not tell, and every time she passed me it coincided with a sweeping bar of the waltz to which she dipped and swayed, smiling as she did so in my direction. It happened again and again until it became automatic, a matter of routine, like those promenades on board ship when we meet the same people bent on exercise like ourselves, and know with deadly certainty that we will pass them by the bridge.

I can see her now, the prominent teeth, the gay spot of rouge placed high upon her cheek-bones, and her smile, vacant, happy, enjoying her evening. Later I saw her by the supper table, her keen eyes searching the food, and she heaped a plate high with salmon and lobster mayonnaise and went off into a corner. There was Lady Crowan too, monstrous in purple, disguised as I know not what romantic figure of the past, it might have been Marie Antoinette or Nell Gwynne, for all I knew, or a strange erotic combination of the two, and she kept exclaiming in excited high-pitched tones, a little higher than usual because of the champagne she had consumed, 'You all have me to thank for this, not the de Winters at all.'

I remember Robert dropping a tray of ices, and the expression on Frith's face when he saw Robert was the culprit and not one of the minions hired for the occasion. I wanted to go to Robert and stand beside him and say 'I know how you feel. I understand. I've done worse than you to-night.' I can feel now the stiff, set smile on my face that did not match the misery in my eyes. I can see Beatrice, dear friendly tactless Beatrice, watching me from her partner's arms, nodding encouragement, the bangles jangling on her wrists, the veil slipping continually from her overheated forehead. I can picture myself once more whirled round the room in a desperate dance with Giles, who with dog-like sympathy and kind warm heart would take no refusal, but must steer me through the stamping crowd as he would one of his horses at a meet. 'That's a jolly pretty dress you're wearing,' I can hear him say, 'it makes all these people look damn silly,' and I blessed him for his pathetic simple gesture of understanding and sincerity, thinking, dear Giles, that I was disappointed in my dress, that I was worrying about my appearance, that I cared.

It was Frank who brought me a plate of chicken and ham that I could not eat, and Frank who stood by my elbow with a glass of champagne I would not drink.

'I wish you would,' he said quietly, 'I think you need it,' and I took three sips of it to please him. The black patch over his eye gave him a pale odd appearance, it made him look older, different. There seemed to be lines on his face I had not seen before.

He moved amongst the guests like another host, seeing to their comfort, that they were supplied with drink, and food, and cigarettes, and he danced too in solemn painstaking fashion, walking his partners round the room with a set face. He did not wear his pirate costume with abandon, and there was something rather tragic about the side-whiskers he had fluffed under the scarlet handkerchief on his head. I thought of him standing before the looking-glass in his bare bachelor bedroom curling them round his fingers. Poor Frank. Dear Frank. I never asked, I never knew, how much he hated the last fancy dress ball ever given at Manderley.

The band played on, and the swaying couples twisted like bobbing marionettes, to and fro, to and fro, across the great hall and back again, and it was not I who watched them at all, not someone with feelings, made of flesh and blood, but a dummy-stick of a person in my stead, a prop who wore a smile screwed to its face. The figure who stood beside it was wooden too. His face was a mask, his smile was not his own. The eyes were not the eyes of the man I loved, the man I knew. They looked through me and beyond me, cold, expressionless, to some place of pain and torture I could not enter, to some private, inward hell I could not share.

He never spoke to me. He never touched me. We stood beside one another, the host and the hostess, and we were not together. I watched his courtesy to his guests. He flung a word to one, a jest to another, a smile to a third, a call over his shoulder to a fourth, and no one but myself could know that every utterance he made, every movement, was automatic and the work of a machine. We were like two performers in a play, but we were divided, we were not acting with one another. We had to endure it alone, we had to put up this show, this miserable, sham performance for the sake of all these people I did not know and did not want to see again.

'I hear your wife's frock never turned up in time,' said someone with a mottled face and a sailor's pigtail, and he laughed, and dug Maxim in the ribs. 'Damn shame, what? I should sue the shop for fraud. Same thing happened to my wife's cousin once.'

'Yes, it was unfortunate,' said Maxim.

'I tell you what,' said the sailor, turning to me, 'you ought to say you are a forget-me-not. They're blue, aren't they? Jolly little flowers, forget-me-nots. That's right, isn't it, de Winter? Tell your wife she must call herself a "forget-me-not".' He swept away, roaring with laughter, his partner in his arms. 'Pretty good idea, what? A forget-me-not.' Then Frank again hovering just behind me, another glass in his hand, lemonade this time. 'No, Frank, I'm not thirsty.'

'Why don't you dance? Or come and sit down a moment, there's a corner in the terrace.'

'No, I'm better standing. I don't want to sit down.'

'Can't I get you something, a sandwich, a peach?'

'No, I don't want anything.'

There was the salmon lady again, she forgot to smile at me this time. She was flushed after her supper. She kept looking up into her partner's face. He was very tall, very thin, he had a chin like a fiddle.

The Destiny waltz, the Blue Danube, the Merry Widow, one-two-three, one-two-three, round-and-round, one-two-three, one-two-three, round-and-round. The salmon lady, a green lady, Beatrice again, her veil pushed back off her forehead, Giles, his face streaming with perspiration, and that sailor once more, with another partner, they stopped beside me, I did not know her, she was dressed as a Tudor woman, any Tudor woman, she wore a ruffle round her throat and a black velvet dress.

'When are you coming to see us?' she said, as though we were old friends, and I answered, 'soon of course, we were talking about it the other day,' wondering why I found it so easy to lie suddenly, no effort at all. 'Such a delightful party, I do congratulate you,' she said, and 'Thank you very much,' I said. 'It's fun, isn't it?'

'I hear they sent you the wrong dress?'

'Yes, absurd, wasn't it?'

'These shops are all the same. No depending on them. But you look delightfully fresh in that pretty blue. Much more comfortable than this hot velvet. Don't forget, you must both come and dine at the Palace soon.'

'We should love to.'

What did she mean, where, what palace? Were we entertaining royalty? She swept on to the Blue Danube in the arms of the sailor, her velvet frock brushing the ground like a carpet-sweeper, and it was not until long afterwards, in the middle of some night, when I could not sleep, that I remembered the Tudor woman was the bishop's wife who liked walking in the Pennines.

What was the time? I did not know. The evening dragged on, hour after hour, the same faces and the same tunes. Now and again the bridge people crept out of the library like hermits to watch the dancers, and then returned again. Beatrice, her draperies trailing behind her, whispered in my ear.

'Why don't you sit down? You look like death.'

'I'm all right.'

Giles, the make-up running on his face, poor fellow, and stifling in his

Arab blanket came up to me and said, 'Come and watch the fireworks on the terrace.'

I remember standing on the terrace and staring up at the sky as the foolish rockets burst and fell. There was little Clarice in a corner with some boy off the estate, she was smiling happily, squealing with delight as a squib spluttered at her feet. She had forgotten her tears.

'Hullo, this will be a big'un.' Giles, his large face upturned, his mouth open. 'Here she comes. Bravo, jolly fine show.'

The slow hiss of the rocket as it sped into the air, the burst of the explosion, the stream of little emerald stars. A murmur of approval from the crowd, cries of delight, and a clapping of hands.

The salmon lady well to the front, her face eager with expectation, a remark for every star that fell. 'Oh, what a beauty . . . look at that one now, I say, how pretty. . . . Oh, that one didn't burst . . . take care, it's coming our way . . . what are those men doing over there. . . .' Even the hermits left their lair and came to join the dancers on the terrace. The lawns were black with people. The bursting stars shone on their upturned faces.

Again and again the rockets sped into the air like arrows and the sky became crimson and gold. Manderley stood out like an enchanted house, every window aflame, the grey walls coloured by the falling stars. A house bewitched, carved out of the dark woods. And when the last rocket burst and the cheering died away the night that had been fine before seemed dull and heavy in contrast, the sky became a pall. The little groups on the lawns and in the drive broke up and scattered. The guests crowded the long windows in the terrace back to the drawing-room again. It was anti-climax, the aftermath had come. We stood about with blank faces. Someone gave me a glass of champagne. I heard the sound of cars starting up in the drive.

'They're beginning to go,' I thought. 'Thank God, they're beginning to go.' The salmon lady was having some more supper. It would take time yet to clear the hall. I saw Frank make a signal to the band. I stood in the doorway between the drawing-room and the hall beside a man I did not know.

'What a wonderful party it's been,' he said.

'Yes,' I said.

'I've enjoyed every minute of it,' he said.

'I'm so glad,' I said.

'Molly was wild with fury at missing it,' he said.

'Was she?' I said.

The band began to play Auld Lang Syne. The man seized my hand and started swinging it up and down. 'Here,' he said, 'come on, some of you.' Somebody else swung my other hand, and more people joined us. We stood in a great circle singing at the top of our voices. The man who had enjoyed his evening and said Molly would be wild at missing it was dressed as a Chinese mandarin, and his false nails got caught up in his sleeve as we swung our hands up and down. He roared with laughter. We all laughed. 'Should auld acquaintance be forgot,' we sang.

The hilarious gaiety changed swiftly at the closing bars, and the drummer rattled his sticks in the inevitable prelude to God save the King. The smiles left our faces as though wiped clean by a sponge. The Mandarin sprang to attention, his hands stiff to his sides. I remember wondering vaguely if he was in the Army. How queer he looked with his long poker face, and his drooping Mandarin moustache. I caught the salmon lady's eye. God save the King had taken her unawares, she was still holding a plate heaped with chicken in aspic. She held it stiffly out in front of her like a church collection. All animation had gone from her face. As the last note of God save the King died away she relaxed again, and attacked her chicken in a sort of frenzy, chattering over her shoulder to her partner. Somebody came and wrung me by the hand.

'Don't forget, you're dining with us on the fourteenth of next month.'

'Oh, are we?' I stared at him blankly.

'Yes, we've got your sister-in-law to promise too.'

'Oh. Oh, what fun.'

'Eight-thirty, and black tie. So looking forward to seeing you.'

'Yes. Yes rather.'

People began to form up in queues to say good-bye. Maxim was at the other side of the room. I put on my smile again which had worn thin after Auld Lang Syne.

'The best evening I've spent for a long time.'

'I'm so glad.'

'Many thanks for a grand party.'

'I'm so glad.'

'Here we are, you see, staying to the bitter end.'

'Yes, I'm so glad.'

Was there no other sentence in the English language? I bowed and smiled like a dummy, my eyes searching for Maxim above their heads. He was caught up in a knot of people by the library. Beatrice too was surrounded, and Giles had led a team of stragglers to the buffet table in the drawing-room. Frank was out in the drive seeing that people got their cars. I was hemmed in by strangers.

'Good-bye, and thanks tremendously.'

'I'm so glad.'

The great hall began to empty. Already it wore that drab deserted air of a vanished evening and the dawn of a tired day. There was a grey light on the terrace, I could see the shapes of the blown firework stands taking form on the lawns.

'Good-bye, a wonderful party.'

'I'm so glad.'

Maxim had gone out to join Frank in the drive. Beatrice came up to me, pulling off her jangling bracelets. 'I can't stand these things a moment longer. Heavens, I'm dead beat. I don't believe I've missed a dance. Anyway, it was a tremendous success.'

'Was it?' I said.

'My dear, hadn't you better go to bed? You look worn out. You've been standing nearly all the evening. Where are the men?'

'Out on the drive.'

'I shall have some coffee, and eggs and bacon. What about you?'

'No, Beatrice, I don't think I will.'

'You looked very charming in your blue. Everyone said so. And nobody had an inkling about – about the other thing, so you mustn't worry.'

'No.'

'If I were you I should have a good long lie to-morrow morning. Don't attempt to get up. Have your breakfast in bed.'

'Yes, perhaps.'

'I'll tell Maxim you've gone up, shall I?'

'Please, Beatrice.'

'All right, my dear. Sleep well.' She kissed me swiftly, patting my shoulder at the same time, and then went off to find Giles in the supper room. I walked slowly up the stairs, one step at a time. The band had turned the lights off in the gallery, and had gone down to have eggs and bacon too. Pieces of music lay about the floor. One chair had been upturned. There was an ashtray full of the stubs of their cigarettes. The aftermath of the party. I went along the corridor to my room. It was getting lighter every moment, and the birds had started singing. I did not have to turn on the lights to undress. A little chill wind blew in from the open window. It was rather cold. Many people must have used the rose-garden during the evening, for all the chairs were moved, and dragged from their places. There was a tray of empty glasses on one of the tables. Someone had left a bag behind on a chair. I pulled the curtains to darken the room, but the grey morning light found its way through the gaps at the side.

I got into bed, my legs very weary, a niggling pain in the small of my back. I lay back and closed my eyes, thankful for the cool white comfort of clean sheets. I wished my mind would rest like my body, relax, and pass to sleep. Not hum round in the way it did, jigging to music, whirling in a sea of faces. I pressed my hands over my eyes but they would not go.

I wondered how long Maxim would be. The bed beside me looked stark and cold. Soon there would be no shadows in the room at all, the walls and the ceiling and the floor would be white with the morning. The birds would sing their songs, louder, gayer, less subdued. The sun would make a yellow pattern on the curtain. My little bed-side clock ticked out the minutes one by one. The hand moved round the dial. I lay on my side watching it. It came to the hour and passed it again. It started afresh on its journey. But Maxim did not come.

Chapter Eighteen

I think I fell asleep a little after seven. It was broad daylight I remember, there was no longer any pretence that the drawn curtains hid the sun. The light streamed in at the open window and made patterns on the wall. I heard the men below in the rose-garden clearing away the tables and the chairs, and taking down the chain of fairy lights. Maxim's bed was still bare and empty. I lay across my bed, my arms over my eyes, a strange, mad position and the least likely to bring sleep, but I drifted to the border-line of the unconscious and slipped over it at last. When I awoke it was past eleven, and Clarice must have come in and brought me my tea without my hearing her, for there was a tray by my side, and a stone-cold tea-pot, and my clothes had been tidied, my blue frock put away in the wardrobe.

I drank my cold tea, still blurred and stupid from my short heavy sleep, and stared at the blank wall in front of me. Maxim's empty bed brought me to realisation with a queer shock to my heart, and the full anguish of the night before was upon me once again. He had not come to bed at all. His pyjamas lay folded on the turned-down sheet untouched. I wondered what Clarice had thought when she came into the room with my tea. Had she noticed? Would she have gone out and told the other servants, and would they all discuss it over their breakfast? I wondered why I minded that, and why the thought of the servants talking about it in the kitchen should cause me such distress. It must be that I had a small mean mind, a conventional, petty hatred of gossip.

That was why I had come down last night in my blue dress and had not stayed hidden in my room. There was nothing brave or fine about it, it was a wretched tribute to convention. I had not come down for Maxim's sake, for Beatrice's, for the sake of Manderley. I had come down because I did not want the people at the ball to think I had quarrelled with Maxim. I didn't want them to go home and say, 'Of course you know they don't get on. I hear he's not at all happy.' I had come for my own sake, my own poor personal pride. As I sipped my cold tea I thought with a tired bitter feeling of despair that I would be content to live in one corner of Manderley and Maxim in the other as long as the outside world should never know. If he had no more tenderness for me, never kissed me again, did not speak to me except on matters of necessity, I believed I could bear it if I were certain that nobody knew of this but our two selves. If we could bribe servants not to tell, play our part before relations, before Beatrice, and then when we were alone sit apart in our separate rooms, leading our separate lives.

It seemed to me, as I sat there in bed, staring at the wall, at the sunlight coming in at the window, at Maxim's empty bed, that there was nothing quite so shaming, so degrading, as a marriage that had failed. Failed after three months, as mine had done. For I had no illusions left now, I no longer made any effort to pretend. Last night had shown me too well. My marriage was a failure. All the things that people would say about it if they knew, were true. We did not get on. We were not companions. We were not suited to one another. I was too young for Maxim, too inexperienced, and more important still, I was not of his world. The fact that I loved him in a sick, hurt, desperate way, like a child or a dog, did not matter. It was not the sort of love he needed. He wanted something else that I could not give him, something he had had before. I thought of the youthful almost hysterical excitement and conceit with which I had gone into this marriage, imagining I would bring happiness to Maxim who had known much greater happiness before. Even Mrs. Van Hopper, with her cheap views and common outlook, had known I was making a mistake. 'I'm afraid you will regret it,' she said. 'I believe you are making a big mistake.'

I would not listen to her, I thought her hard and cruel. But she was right. She was right in everything. That last mean thrust thrown at me before she said good-bye. 'You don't flatter yourself he's in love with you, do you? He's lonely, he can't bear that great empty house,' was the sanest, most truthful statement she had ever made in her life. Maxim was not in love with me, he had never loved me. Our honeymoon in Italy had meant nothing at all to him, nor our living here together. What I had thought was love for me, for myself as a person, was not love. It was just that he was a man, and I was his wife and was young, and he was lonely. He did not belong to me at all, he belonged to Rebecca. He still thought about Rebecca. He would never love me because of Rebecca. She was in the house still as Mrs. Danvers had said, she was in that room in the west wing, she was in the library, in the morning-room, in the gallery above the hall. Even in the little flower room, where her mackintosh still hung. And in the garden, and in the woods, and down in the stone cottage on the beach. Her footsteps sounded in the corridors, her scent lingered on the stairs. The servants obeyed her orders still, the food we ate was the food she liked. Her favourite flowers filled the rooms. Her clothes were in the wardrobes in her room, her brushes were on the table, her shoes beneath the chair, her nightdress on her bed. Rebecca was still mistress of Manderley. Rebecca was still Mrs. de Winter. I had no business here at all. I had come blundering like a poor fool on ground that was preserved. 'Where is Rebecca?' Maxim's grandmother had cried, 'I want Rebecca. What have you done with Rebecca?' She did not know me, she did not care about me. Why should she? I was a stranger to her. I did not belong to Maxim or to Manderley. And Beatrice at our first meeting, looking me up and down, frank, direct, 'You're so very different from Rebecca.' Frank, reserved, embarrassed when I spoke of her, hating those questions I had poured upon him, even as I had hated them myself, and then answering that final one as we came towards the house, his voice grave and quiet, 'Yes, she was the most beautiful creature I have ever seen.'

Rebecca, always Rebecca. Wherever I walked in Manderley, wherever I sat, even in my thoughts and in my dreams, I met Rebecca. I knew her figure now, the long slim legs, the small and narrow feet. Her shoulders, broader than mine, the capable clever hands. Hands that could steer a boat, could hold a horse. Hands that arranged flowers, made the models of ships, and wrote 'Max from Rebecca' on the fly-leaf of a book. I knew her face too, small and oval, the clear white skin, the cloud of dark hair. I knew the scent she wore, I could guess her laughter and her smile. If I heard it, even among a thousand others, I should recognise her voice. Rebecca, always Rebecca. I should never be rid of Rebecca.

Perhaps I haunted her as she haunted me; she looked down on me from the gallery as Mrs. Danvers had said, she sat beside me when I wrote my letters at her desk. That mackintosh I wore, that handkerchief I used. They were hers. Perhaps she knew and had seen me take them. Jasper had been her dog, and he ran at my heels now. The roses were hers and I cut them. Did she resent me and fear me as I resented her? Did she want Maxim alone in the house again? I could fight the living but I could not fight the dead. If there was some woman in London that Maxim loved, someone he wrote to, visited, dined with, slept with, I could fight with her. We would stand on common ground. I should not be afraid. Anger and jealousy were things that could be conquered. One day the woman would grow old or tired or different, and Maxim would not love her any more. But Rebecca would never grow old. Rebecca would always be the same. And she I could not fight. She was too strong for me.

I got out of bed and pulled the curtains. The sun streamed into the room. The men had cleared the mess away from the rose-garden. I wondered if people were talking about the ball in the way they do the day after a party.

'Did you think it quite up to their usual standard?'

'Oh, I think so.'

'The band dragged a bit I thought.'

'The supper was damn good.'

'Fireworks weren't bad.'

'Bee Lacy is beginning to look old.'

'Who wouldn't in that get-up?'

'I thought he looked rather ill.'

'He always does.'

'What did you think of the bride?'

'Not much. Rather dull.'

'I wonder if it's a success.'

'Yes, I wonder . . .'

Then I noticed for the first time there was a note under my door. I went and picked it up. I recognised the square hand of Beatrice. She had scribbled it in pencil after breakfast. '*I knocked at your door but had no answer so gather you've taken my advice and are sleeping off last night. Giles is anxious to get back early as they have rung up from home to say he's wanted to take somebody's place in a cricket match, and it starts at two. How he is going to see the ball after all the champagne he put away last night heaven only knows! I'm feeling a bit weak in the legs, but slept like a top. Frith says Maxim was down to an early breakfast, and there's now no sign of him! So please give him our love, and many thanks to you both for our evening, which we thoroughly enjoyed. Don't think any more about the dress.* (This last was heavily underlined.) *Yours affectionately, Bee,'* and a postscript, *'You must both come over and see us soon.'*

She had scribbled nine-thirty a.m. at the top of the paper, and it was now nearly half-past eleven. They had been gone about two hours. They would be home by now, Beatrice with her suit-case unpacked, going out into her garden and taking up her ordinary routine, and Giles preparing for his match, renewing the whipping on his bat.

In the afternoon Beatrice would change into a cool frock and a shady hat and watch Giles play cricket. They would have tea afterwards in a tent, Giles very hot and red in the face, Beatrice laughing and talking to her friends. 'Yes, we went over for the dance at Manderley, it was great fun. I wonder Giles was able to run a yard.' Smiling at Giles, patting him on the back. They were both middle-aged and unromantic. They had been married for twenty years and had a grown-up son who was going to Oxford. They were very happy. Their marriage was a success. It had not failed after three months as mine had done.

I could not go on sitting in my bedroom any longer. The maids would want to come and do the room. Perhaps Clarice would not have noticed about Maxim's bed after all. I rumpled it, to make it look as though he had slept there. I did not want the housemaids to know, if Clarice had not told them.

I had a bath and dressed, and went downstairs. The men had taken up the floor already in the hall and the flowers had been carried away. The music stands were gone from the gallery. The band must have caught an early train. The gardeners were sweeping the lawns and the drive clear of the spent fireworks. Soon there would be no trace left of the fancy dress ball at Manderley. How long the preparations had seemed, and how short and swift the clearance now.

I remembered the salmon lady standing by the drawing-room door with her plate of chicken, and it seemed to me a thing I must have fancied, or something that had happened very long ago. Robert was polishing the table in the dining-room. He was normal again, stolid, dull, not the fey excited creature of the past few weeks.

'Good morning, Robert,' I said.

'Good-morning, Madam.'

'Have you seen Mr. de Winter anywhere?'

'He went out soon after breakfast, Madam, before Major and Mrs. Lacy were down. He has not been in since.'

'You don't know where he went?'

'No, Madam. I could not say.'

I wandered back again into the hall. I went through the drawing-room to the morning-room. Jasper rushed at me and licked my hands in a frenzy of delight as if I had been away for a long time. He had spent the evening on Clarice's bed and I had not seen him since tea-time yesterday. Perhaps the hours had been as long for him as they had for me.

I picked up the telephone and asked for the number of the estate office. Perhaps Maxim was with Frank. I felt I must speak to him, even if it was only for two minutes. I must explain to him that I had not meant to do what I had done last night. Even if I never spoke to him again I must tell him that. The clerk answered the telephone, and told me that Maxim was not there.

'Mr. Crawley is here, Mrs. de Winter,' said the clerk, 'would you speak to him?' I would have refused, but he gave me no chance, and before I could put down the receiver I heard Frank's voice.

'Is anything the matter?' It was a funny way to begin a conversation. The thought flashed through my mind. He did not say good-morning, or did you sleep well? Why did he ask if something was the matter?

'Frank, it's me,' I said, 'where's Maxim?'

'I don't know, I haven't seen him. He's not been in this morning.'

'Not been to the office?'

'No.'

'Oh! Oh, well, it doesn't matter.'

'Did you see him at breakfast?' said Frank.

'No, I did not get up.'

'How did he sleep?'

I hesitated, Frank was the only person I did not mind knowing. 'He did not come to bed last night.'

There was silence at the other end of the line, as though Frank was thinking hard for an answer.

'Oh,' he said at last, very slowly. 'Oh, I see,' and then, after a minute, 'I was afraid something like that would happen.'

'Frank,' I cried desperately, 'what did he say last night when everyone had gone? What did you all do?'

'I had a sandwich with Giles and Mrs. Lacy,' said Frank. 'Maxim did not come. He made some excuse and went into the library. I came back home almost at once. Perhaps Mrs. Lacy can tell you.'

'She's gone,' I said, 'they went after breakfast. She sent up a note. She had not seen Maxim, she said.'

'Oh,' said Frank. I did not like it. I did not like the way he said it. It was sharp, ominous.

'Where do you think he's gone?' I said.

'I don't know,' said Frank, 'perhaps he's gone for a walk.' It was the sort of voice doctors used to relatives at a nursing-home when they came to enquire.

'Frank, I must see him,' I said. 'I've got to explain about last night.'

Frank did not answer. I could picture his anxious face, the lines on his forehead.

'Maxim thinks I did it on purpose,' I said, my voice breaking in spite of myself, and the tears that had blinded me last night and I had not shed came coursing down my cheeks sixteen hours too late. 'Maxim thinks I did it as a joke, a beastly damnable joke!'

'No,' said Frank. 'No.'

'He does, I tell you. You didn't see his eyes, as I did. You didn't stand beside him all the evening, watching him, as I did. He didn't speak to me, Frank. He never looked at me again. We stood there together the whole evening and we never spoke to one another.'

'There was no chance,' said Frank. 'All those people. Of course I saw, don't you think I know Maxim well enough for that? Look here . . .'

'I don't blame him,' I interrupted. 'If he believes I played that vile hideous joke he has a right to think what he likes of me, and never talk to me again, never see me again.'

'You mustn't talk like that,' said Frank. 'You don't know what you're saying. Let me come up and see you. I think I can explain.'

What was the use of Frank coming to see me, and us sitting in the morning-room together, Frank smoothing me down, Frank being tactful, Frank being kind? I did not want kindness from anybody now. It was too late.

'No,' I said. 'No, I don't want to go over it and over it again. It's happened, it can't be altered now. Perhaps it's a good thing, it's made me realise something I ought to have known before, that I ought to have suspected when I married Maxim.'

'What do you mean?' said Frank.

His voice was sharp, queer. I wondered why it should matter to him about Maxim not loving me. Why did he not want me to know?

'About him and Rebecca,' I said, and as I said her name it sounded strange and sour like a forbidden word, a relief to me no longer, not a pleasure, but hot and shaming as a sin confessed.

Frank did not answer for a moment. I heard him draw in his breath at the other end of the wire.

'What do you mean?' he said again, shorter and sharper than before. 'What do you mean?'

'He doesn't love me, he loves Rebecca,' I said. 'He's never forgotten her, he thinks about her still, night and day. He's never loved me, Frank. It's always Rebecca, Rebecca, Rebecca.'

I heard Frank give a startled cry but I did not care how much I shocked him now. 'Now you know how I feel,' I said, 'now you understand.'

'Look here,' he said, 'I've got to come and see you, I've got to, do you hear? It's vitally important, I can't talk to you down the telephone. Mrs. de Winter? Mrs. de Winter?'

I slammed down the receiver, and got up from the writing-desk. I did not want to see Frank. He could not help me over this. No one could help me but myself. My face was red and blotchy from crying. I walked about the room biting the corner of my handkerchief, tearing at the edge.

The feeling was strong within me that I should never see Maxim again. It was certainty, born of some strange instinct. He had gone away and would not come back. I knew in my heart that Frank believed this too and would not admit it to me on the telephone. He did not want to frighten me. If I rang him up again at the office now I should find that he had gone. The clerk would say 'Mr. Crawley has just gone out, Mrs. de Winter', and I could see Frank, hatless, climbing into his small, shabby Morris, driving off in search of Maxim.

I went and stared out of the window at the little clearing where the satyr played his pipes. The rhododendrons were all over now. They would not bloom again for another year. The tall shrubs looked dark and drab now that the colour had gone. A fog was rolling up from the sea, and I could not see the woods beyond the bank. It was very hot, very oppressive. I could imagine our guests of last night saying to one another, 'What a good thing this fog kept off for yesterday, we should never have seen the fireworks.' I went out of the morning-room and through the drawing-room to the terrace. The sun had gone in now behind a wall of mist. It was as though a blight had fallen upon Manderley taking the sky away and the light of the day. One of the gardeners passed me with a barrow full of bits of paper, and litter, and the skins of fruit left on the lawns by the people last night.

'Good-morning,' I said.

'Good-morning, Madam.'

'I'm afraid the ball last night has made a lot of work for you,' I said.

'That's all right, Madam,' he said. 'I think everyone enjoyed themselves good and hearty, and that's the main thing, isn't it?'

'Yes, I suppose so,' I said.

He looked across the lawns to the clearing in the woods where the valley sloped to the sea. The dark trees loomed thin and indistinct.

'It's coming up very thick,' he said.

'Yes,' I said.

'A good thing it wasn't like this last night,' he said.

'Yes,' I said.

He waited a moment, and then he touched his cap and went off trundling his barrow. I went across the lawns to the edge of the woods. The mist in the trees had turned to moisture and dripped upon my bare head like a thin rain. Jasper stood by my feet dejected, his tail downcast, his pink tongue hanging from his mouth. The clammy oppression of the day made him listless and heavy. I could hear the sea from where I stood, sullen and slow, as it broke in the coves below the woods. The white fog rolled on past me towards the house smelling of damp salt and seaweed. I put my hand on Jasper's coat. It was wringing wet. When I looked back at the house I could not see the chimneys or the contour of the walls, I could only see the vague substance of the house, the windows in the west wing, and the flower tubs on the terrace. The shutter had been pulled aside from the window of the large bedroom in the west wing, and someone was standing there, looking down upon the lawns. The figure was shadowy and indistinct and for one moment of shock and fear I believed it to be Maxim. Then the figure moved, I saw the arm reach up to fold the shutter, and I knew it was Mrs. Danvers. She had been watching me then as I stood at the edge of the woods bathed in that white wall of fog. She had seen me walk slowly from the terrace to the lawns. She may have listened to my conversation with Frank on the telephone from the connecting line in her own room. She would know that Maxim had not been with me last night. She would have heard my voice, known about my tears. She knew the part I had played through the long hours, standing by Maxim's side in my blue dress at the bottom of the stairs, and that he had not looked at me nor spoken to me. She knew because she had meant it to happen. This was her triumph, hers and Rebecca's.

I thought of her as I had seen her last night watching me through the open door to the west wing, and that diabolical smile on her white skull's face, and I remembered that she was a living breathing woman like myself, she was made of flesh and blood. She was not dead, like Rebecca. I could speak to her, but I could not speak to Rebecca.

I walked back across the lawns on sudden impulse to the house. I went through the hall and up the great stairs, I turned in under the archway by the gallery, I passed through the door to the west wing, and so along the dark silent corridor to Rebecca's room. I turned the handle of the door and went inside.

Mrs. Danvers was still standing by the window, and the shutter was folded back.

'Mrs. Danvers,' I said. 'Mrs. Danvers.' She turned to look at me, and I saw her eyes were red and swollen with crying, even as mine were, and there were dark shadows in her white face.

'What is it?' she said, and her voice was thick and muffled from the tears she had shed, even as mine had been.

I had not expected to find her so. I had pictured her smiling as she had smiled last night, cruel and evil. Now she was none of these things, she was an old woman who was ill and tired.

I hesitated, my hand still on the knob of the open door, and I did not know what to say to her now or what to do.

She went on staring at me with those red, swollen eyes and I could not answer her. 'I left the menu on the desk as usual,' she said. 'Do you want something changed?' Her words gave me courage, and I left the door and came to the middle of the room.

'Mrs. Danvers,' I said, 'I have not come to talk about the menu. You know that, don't you?'

She did not answer me. Her left hand opened and shut.

'You've done what you wanted, haven't you?' I said. 'You meant this to happen, didn't you? Are you pleased now, are you happy?'

She turned her head away, and looked out of the window as she had done when I first came into the room. 'Why did you ever come here?' she said. 'Nobody wanted you at Manderley. We were all right until you came. Why did not you stay where you were out in France?'

'You seem to forget I love Mr. de Winter,' I said.

'If you loved him you would never have married him,' she said.

I did not know what to say. The situation was mad, unreal. She kept talking in that choked muffled way with her head turned from me.

'I thought I hated you but I don't now,' she said, 'it seems to have spent itself, all the feeling I had.'

'Why should you hate me?' I asked. 'What have I ever done to you that you should hate me?'

'You tried to take Mrs. de Winter's place,' she said.

Still she would not look at me. She stood there sullen, her head turned from me. 'I had nothing changed.' I said. 'Manderley went on as it had always been. I gave no orders, I left everything to you. I would have been friends with you, if you had let me, but you set yourself against me from the first. I saw it in your face, the moment I shook hands with you.'

She did not answer, and her hand kept opening and shutting against her dress. 'Many people marry twice, men and women,' I said. 'There are thousands of second marriages taking place every day. You talk as though my marrying Mr. de Winter was a crime, a sacrilege against the dead. Haven't we as much right to be happy as anyone else?'

'Mr. de Winter is not happy,' she said, turning to look at me at last, 'any fool can see that. You have only to look at his eyes. He's still in hell, and he's looked like that ever since she died.'

'It's not true,' I said. 'It's not true. He was happy when we were in France together, he was younger, much younger, and laughing and gay.'

'Well, he's a man, isn't he? she said. 'No man denies himself on a honeymoon, does he? Mr. de Winter's not forty-six yet.'

She laughed contemptuously, and shrugged her shoulders.

'How dare you speak to me like that, how dare you?' I said.

I was not afraid of her any more. I went up to her, shook her by the arm. 'You made me wear that dress last night,' I said, 'I should never have thought of it but for you. You did it because you wanted to hurt Mr. de Winter, you wanted to make him suffer. Hasn't he suffered enough without your playing that vile hideous joke upon him? Do you think his agony and pain will bring Mrs. de Winter back again?'

She shook herself clear of me, the angry colour flooded her dead white face. 'What do I care for his suffering?' she said. 'He's never cared about mine. How do you think I've liked it, watching you sit in her place, walk in her footsteps, touch the things that were hers? What do you think it's meant to me all these months knowing that you wrote at her desk in the morning-room, using the very pen that she used, speaking down the house telephone where she used to speak, every morning of her life to me, ever since she first came to Manderley. What do you think it meant to me to hear Frith and Robert and the rest of the servants talking about you as "Mrs. de Winter?" "Mrs. de Winter has gone out for a walk." "Mrs. de Winter wants the car this afternoon at three o'clock," "Mrs. de Winter won't be in to tea till five o'clock." And all the while my Mrs. de Winter, my lady with her smile and her lovely face and brave ways, the real Mrs. de Winter, lying dead and cold and forgotten in the church crypt. If he suffers then he deserves to suffer, marrying a young girl like you not ten months afterwards. Well, he's paying for it now, isn't he? I've seen his face, I've seen his eyes. He's made his own hell and there's no one but himself to thank for it. He knows she sees him, he knows she comes by night and watches him. And she doesn't come kindly, not she, not my lady. She was never one to stand mute and still and be wronged. "I'll see them in hell, Danny," she'd say, "I'll see them in hell first." "That's right, my dear," I'd tell her, "no one will put upon you. You were born into this world to take what you could out of it," and she did, she didn't care, she wasn't afraid. She had all the courage and the spirit of a boy, had my Mrs. de Winter. She ought to have been a boy, I often told her that. I had the care of her as a child. You knew that, didn't you?'

'No!' I said. 'No! Mrs. Danvers, what's the use of all this? I don't want to hear any more, I don't want to know. Haven't I got feelings as well as you? Can't you understand what it means to me, to hear her mentioned, to stand here and listen while you tell me about her?'

She did not hear me, she went on raving like a mad-woman, a fanatic, her long fingers twisting and tearing the black stuff of her dress.

'She was lovely then,' she said. 'Lovely as a picture, men turning to stare at her when she passed, and she not twelve years old. She knew then, she used to wink at me like the little devil she was. "I'm going to be a beauty, aren't I, Danny?" she said, and "We'll see about that, my love, we'll see about that," I told her. She had all the knowledge then of a grown person, she'd enter into conversation with men and women as clever and full of tricks as someone of eighteen. She twisted her father round her little finger, and she'd have done the same with her mother, had she lived. Spirit, you couldn't beat my lady for spirit. She drove a four-in-hand on her fourteenth birthday, and her cousin, Mr. Jack, got up on the box beside her and tried to take the reins from her hands. They fought it out there together, for three minutes, like a couple of wild cats, and the horses galloping to glory. She won though, my lady won. She cracked her whip over his head and down he came, head-over-heels, cursing and laughing. They were a pair, I tell you, she and Mr. Jack. They sent him in the Navy, but he wouldn't stand the discipline, and I don't blame him. He had too much spirit to obey orders, like my lady.'

I watched her, fascinated, horrified; a queer ecstatic smile was on her lips making her older than ever, making her skull's face vivid and real. 'No one got the better of her, never, never,' she said. 'She did what she liked, she lived as she liked. She had the strength of a little lion too. I remember her at sixteen getting up on one of her father's horses, a big brute of an animal too, that the groom said was too hot for her to ride. She stuck to him, all right. I can see her now, with her hair flying out behind her, slashing at him, drawing blood, digging the spurs into his side, and when she got off his back he was trembling all over, full of froth and blood. "That will teach him, won't it Danny?" she said, and walked off to wash her hands as cool as you please. And that's how she went at life, when she grew up. I saw her, I was with her. She cared for nothing and for no one. And then she was beaten in the end. But it wasn't a man, it wasn't a woman. The sea got her. The sea was too strong for her. The sea got her in the end.'

She broke off, her mouth working strangely, and dragging at the corners. She began to cry noisily, harshly, her mouth open and her eyes dry.

'Mrs. Danvers,' I said. 'Mrs. Danvers.' I stood before her helplessly, not knowing what to do. I mistrusted her no longer, I was afraid of her no more, but the sight of her sobbing there, dry-eyed, made me shudder, made me ill. 'Mrs. Danvers,' I said, 'you're not well, you ought to be in bed. Why don't you go to your room and rest? Why don't you go to bed?'

She turned on me fiercely. 'Leave me alone, can't you?' she said. 'What's it to do with you if I show my grief? I'm not ashamed of it, I don't shut myself up in my room to cry. I don't walk up and down, up and down, in my room like Mr. de Winter, with the door locked on me.'

'What do you mean?' I said. 'Mr. de Winter does not do that.'

'He did,' she said, 'after she died. Up and down, up and down, in the library. I heard him. I watched him too, through the key-hole, more than once. Backwards and forwards, like an animal in a cage.'

'I don't want to hear,' I said. 'I don't want to know.'

'And then you say you made him happy on his honeymoon,' she said, 'made him happy, you, a young ignorant girl, young enough to be his daughter. What do you know about life, what do you know about men? You come here and think you can take Mrs. de Winter's place. You. You take my lady's place. Why, even the servants laughed at you when you came to Manderley. Even the little scullery-maid you met in the back passage there on your first morning. I wonder what Mr. de Winter thought when he got you back here at Manderley, after his precious honeymoon was over. I wonder what he thought when he saw you sitting at the dining-room table for the first time.'

'You'd better stop this, Mrs. Danvers,' I said; 'you'd better go to your room.'

'Go to my room,' she mimicked, 'go to my room. The mistress of the house thinks I had better go to my room. And after that, what then? You'll go running to Mr. de Winter and saying, "Mrs. Danvers has been unkind to me. Mrs. Danvers has been rude." You'll go running to him like you did before when Mr. Jack came to see me.'

'I never told him,' I said.

'That's a lie,' she said, 'who else told him, if you didn't? No one else was here, Frith and Robert were out, and none of the other servants knew. I made up my mind then I'd teach you a lesson, and him too. Let him suffer, I say. What do I care? What's his suffering to me? Why shouldn't I see Mr. Jack here at Manderley? He's the only link I have left now with Mrs. de Winter. "I'll not have him here," he said, "I'm warning you, it's the last time." He's not forgotten to be jealous, has he?'

I remembered crouching in the gallery when the library door was open. I remembered Maxim's voice raised in anger, using the words that Mrs. Danvers had just repeated. Jealous. Maxim jealous. . . .

'He was jealous while she lived, and now he's jealous when she's dead,' said Mrs. Danvers. 'He forbids Mr. Jack the house now like he did then. That shows you he's not forgotten her, doesn't it? Of course he was jealous. So was I. So was everyone who knew her. She didn't care. She only laughed. "I shall live as I please, Danny," she told me, "and the whole world won't stop me." A man had only to look at her once and be mad about her. I've seen them here, staying in the house, men she'd meet up in London and bring for week-ends. She would take them bathing from the boat, she would have a picnic supper at her cottage in the cove. They made love to her of course, who would not? She laughed, she would come back and tell me what they had said, and what they'd done. She did not mind, it was like a game to her. Like a game. Who wouldn't be jealous? They were all jealous, all mad for her. Mr. de Winter, Mr. Jack, Mr. Crawley, everyone who knew her, everyone who came to Manderley.'

'I don't want to know,' I said. 'I don't want to know.'

Mrs. Danvers came close to me, she put her face near to mine. 'It's no use, is it?' she said. 'You'll never get the better of her. She's still mistress here, even if she is dead. She's the real Mrs. de Winter, not you. It's you that's the shadow and the ghost. It's you that's forgotten and not wanted and pushed aside. Well, why don't you leave Manderley to her? Why don't you go?'

I backed away from her towards the window, my old fear and horror rising up in me again. She took my arm and held it like a vice.

'Why don't you go?' she said. 'We none of us want you. He doesn't want you, he never did. He can't forget her. He wants to be alone in the house again, with her. It's you that ought to be lying there in the church crypt, not her. It's you who ought to be dead, not Mrs. de Winter.'

She pushed me towards the open window. I could see the terrace below me grey and indistinct in the white wall of fog. 'Look down there,' she said. 'It's easy, isn't it? Why don't you jump? It wouldn't hurt, not to break your neck. It's a quick, kind way. It's not like drowning. Why don't you try it? Why don't you go?'

The fog filled the open window, damp and clammy, it stung my eyes, it clung to my nostrils. I held on to the window-sill with my hands.

'Don't be afraid,' said Mrs. Danvers. 'I won't push you. I won't stand by you. You can jump of your own accord. What's the use of your staying here at Manderley? You're not happy. Mr. de Winter doesn't love you. There's not much for you to live for, is there? Why don't you jump now and have done with it? Then you won't be unhappy any more.'

I could see the flower tubs on the terrace and the blue of the hydrangeas clumped and solid. The paved stones were smooth and grey. They were not jagged and uneven. It was the fog that made them look so far away. They were not far really, the window was not so very high.

'Why don't you jump?' whispered Mrs. Danvers. 'Why don't you try?'

The fog came thicker than before and the terrace was hidden from me. I could not see the flower tubs any more, nor the smooth paved stones. There was nothing but the white mist about me, smelling of sea-weed dank and chill. The only reality was the window-sill beneath my hands and the grip of Mrs. Danvers on my left arm. If I jumped I should not see the stones rise up to meet me, the fog would hide them from me. The pain would be sharp and sudden as she said. The fall would break my neck. It would not be slow, like drowning. It would soon be over. And Maxim did not love me. Maxim wanted to be alone again, with Rebecca.

'Go on,' whispered Mrs. Danvers. 'Go on, don't be afraid.'

I shut my eyes. I was giddy from staring down at the terrace, and my fingers ached from holding to the ledge. The mist entered my nostrils and lay upon my lips rank and sour. It was stifling, like a blanket, like an anaesthetic. I was beginning to forget about being unhappy, and about loving Maxim. I was beginning to forget Rebecca. Soon I would not have to think about Rebecca any more. . . .

As I relaxed my hands and sighed, the white mist and the silence that was part of it was shattered suddenly, was rent in two by an explosion that shook the window where we stood. The glass shivered in its frame. I opened my eyes. I stared at Mrs. Danvers. The burst was followed by another, and yet a third and fourth. The sound of the explosions stung the air and the birds rose unseen from the woods around the house and made an echo with their clamour.

'What is it?' I said stupidly. 'What has happened?'

Mrs. Danvers relaxed her grip upon my arm. She stared out of the window into fog. 'It's the rockets,' she said; 'there must be a ship gone ashore there in the bay.'

We listened, staring into the white fog together. And then we heard the sound of footsteps running on the terrace beneath us.

Chapter Nineteen

It was Maxim. I could not see him but I could hear his voice. He was shouting for Frith as he ran. I heard Frith answer from the hall and come out on to the terrace. Their figures loomed out of the mist beneath us.

'She's ashore all right,' said Maxim. 'I was watching her from the headland and I saw her come right into the bay, and head for the reef. They'll never shift her, not with these tides. She must have mistaken the bay for Kerrith harbour. It's like a wall out there, in the bay. Tell them in the house to stand by with food and drink in case these fellows want anything, and ring through to the office to Mr. Crawley and tell him what's happened. I'm going back to the cove to see if I can do anything. Get me some cigarettes, will you?'

Mrs. Danvers drew back from the window. Her face was expressionless once more, the cold white mask that I knew.

'We had better go down,' she said, 'Frith will be looking for me to make arrangements. Mr. de Winter may bring the men back to the house as he said. Be careful of your hands, I'm going to shut the window.' I stepped back into the room still dazed and stupid, not sure of myself or of her. I watched her close the window and fasten the shutters, and draw the curtains in their place.

'It's a good thing there is no sea running,' she said, 'there wouldn't have been much chance for them then. But on a day like this there's no danger. The owners will lose their ship though if she's run on the reef as Mr. de Winter said.'

She glanced round the room to make certain that nothing was disarranged or out of place. She straightened the cover on the double bed. Then she went to the door and held it open for me. 'I will tell them in the kitchen to serve cold lunch in the dining-room after all,' she said, 'and then it won't matter what time you come for it. Mr. de Winter may not want to rush back at one o'clock if he's busy down there in the cove.'

I stared at her blankly and then passed out of the open door, stiff and wooden like a dummy.

'When you see Mr. de Winter, Madam, will you tell him it will be quite all right if he wants to bring the men back from the ship. There will be a hot meal ready for them any time.'

'Yes,' I said. 'Yes, Mrs. Danvers.'

She turned her back on me and went along the corridor to the Service staircase, a weird gaunt figure in her black dress, the skirt just sweeping the ground like the full, wide skirts of thirty years ago. Then she turned the corner of the corridor and disappeared.

I walked slowly along the passage to the door by the archway, my mind still blunt and slow as though I had just woken from a long sleep. I pushed through the door and went down the stairs with no set purpose before me. Frith was crossing the hall towards the dining-room. When he saw me he stopped, and waited until I came down into the hall.

'Mr. de Winter was in a few moments ago, Madam,' he said. 'He took some cigarettes, and then went back again to the beach. It appears there is a ship gone ashore.'

'Yes,' I said.

'Did you hear the rockets, Madam?' said Frith.

'Yes, I heard the rockets,' I said.

'I was in the pantry with Robert and we both thought at first that one of the gardeners had let off a firework left over from last night,' said Frith, 'and I said to Robert "What do they want to do that for in this weather? Why don't they keep them for the kiddies on Saturday night?" And then the next one came, and then the third. "That's not fireworks," says Robert, "that's a ship in distress." "I believe you're right," I said, and I went out to the hall and there was Mr. de Winter calling me from the terrace.'

'Yes,' I said.

'Well, it's hardly to be wondered at in this fog, Madam. That's what I said to Robert just now. It's difficult to find your way on the road, let alone on the water.'

'Yes,' I said.

'If you want to catch Mr. de Winter he went straight across the lawn only two minutes ago,' said Frith.

'Thank you, Frith,' I said.

I went out on to the terrace. I could see the trees taking shape beyond the lawns. The fog was lifting, it was rising in little clouds to the sky above. It whirled above my head in wreaths of smoke. I looked up at the windows above my head. They were tightly closed, and the shutters were fastened. They looked as though they would never open, never be thrown wide.

It was by the large window in the centre that I had stood five minutes before. How high it seemed above my head, how lofty and remote. The stones were hard and solid under my feet. I looked down at my feet and then up again to the shuttered window, and as I did so I became aware suddenly that my head was swimming and I felt hot. A little trickle of perspiration ran down the back of my neck. Black dots jumped about in the air in front of me. I went into the hall again and sat down on a chair. My hands were quite wet. I sat very still, holding my knees.

'Frith,' I called, 'Frith, are you in the dining-room?'

'Yes, Madam?' He came out at once, and crossed the hall towards me.

'Don't think me very odd, Frith, but I rather think I'd like a small glass of brandy.'

'Certainly, Madam.'

I went on holding my knees and sitting very still. He came back with a liqueur glass on a silver salver.

'Do you feel a trifle unwell, Madam?' said Frith. 'Would you like me to call Clarice?'

'No, I'll be all right, Frith,' I said. 'I felt a bit hot, that's all.'

'It's a very warm morning, Madam. Very warm indeed. Oppressive, one might almost say.'

'Yes, Frith. Very oppressive.'

I drank the brandy and put the glass back on the silver salver.

'Perhaps the sound of those rockets alarmed you,' said Frith, 'they went off so very sudden.'

'Yes, they did,' I said.

'And what with the hot morning and standing about all last night you are not perhaps feeling quite like yourself, Madam,' said Frith.

'No, perhaps not,' I said.

'Will you lie down for half-an-hour? It's quite cool in the library.'

'No. No, I think I'll go out in a moment or two. Don't bother, Frith.'

'No. Very good, Madam.'

He went away and left me alone in the hall. It was quiet sitting there, quiet and cool. All trace of the party had been cleared away. It might never have happened. The hall was as it had always been, grey and silent and austere, with the portraits and the weapons on the wall. I could scarcely believe that last night I had stood there in my blue dress at the bottom of the stairs, shaking hands with five hundred people. I could not believe that there had been music stands in the minstrel's gallery, and a band playing there, a man with a fiddle, a man with a drum. I got up and went out on to the terrace again.

The fog was rising, lifting to the tops of the trees. I could see the woods at the end of the lawns. Above my head a pale sun tried to penetrate the heavy sky. It was hotter than ever. Oppressive, as Frith had said. A bee hummed by me in search of scent, bumbling, noisy, and then creeping inside a flower was suddenly silent. On the grass banks above the lawns the gardener started his mowing machine. A startled linnet fled from the whirring blades towards the rose-garden. The gardener bent to the handles of the machine and walked slowly along the bank scattering the short-tipped grass and the pin-point daisy heads. The smell of the sweet warm grass came towards me on the air, and the sun shone down upon me full and strong from out of the white mist. I whistled for Jasper but he did not come. Perhaps he had followed Maxim when he went down to the beach. I glanced at my watch. It was after half-past twelve, nearly twenty to one. This time yesterday Maxim and I were standing with Frank in the little garden in front of his house, waiting for his housekeeper to serve lunch.

Twenty-four hours ago. They were teasing me, baiting me about my dress. 'You'll both get the surprise of your lives,' I had said.

I felt sick with shame at the memory of my words. And then I realised for the first time that Maxim had not gone away as I had feared. The voice I had heard on the terrace was calm and practical. The voice I knew. Not the voice of last night when I stood at the head of the stairs. Maxim had not gone away. He was down there in the cove somewhere. He was himself, normal and sane. He had just been for a walk as Frank had said. He had been on the headland, he had seen the ship closing in towards the shore. All my fears were without foundation. Maxim was safe. Maxim was all right. I had just experienced something that was degrading and horrible and mad, something that I did not fully understand even now, that I had no wish to remember, that I wanted to bury forever more deep in the shadows of my mind with the old forgotten terrors of childhood; but even this did not matter as long as Maxim was all right.

Then I, too, went down the steep twisting path through the dark woods to the beach below.

The fog had almost gone and when I came to the cove I could see the ship at once, lying about two miles off-shore with her bows pointed towards the cliffs. I went along the breakwater and stood at the end of it, leaning against the rounded wall. There was a crowd of people on the cliffs already who must have walked along the coast-guard path from Kerrith. The cliffs and the headland were part of Manderley but the public had always used the right-of-way along the cliffs. Some of them were scrambling down the cliff face to get a closer view of the stranded ship. She lay at an awkward angle, her stern tilted, and there were a number of rowing-boats already pulling round her. The lifeboat was standing off. I saw someone stand up in her and shout through a megaphone. I could not hear what he was saying. It was still misty out in the bay, and I could not see the horizon. Another motor-boat chugged into the light with some men aboard. The motor-boat was

dark grey. I could see someone in uniform. That would be the harbour-
master from Kerrith, and the Lloyd's agent with him. Another motor-boat
followed, a party of holiday-makers from Kerrith aboard. They circled round
and round the stranded steamer chatting excitedly. I could hear their voices
echoing across the still water.

I left the breakwater and the cove and climbed up the path over the cliffs
towards the rest of the people. I did not see Maxim anywhere. Frank was
there, talking to one of the coast-guards. I hung back when I saw him,
momentarily embarrassed. Barely an hour ago I had been crying to him,
down the telephone. I was not sure what I ought to do. He saw me at once
and waved his hand. I went over to him and the coast-guard. The coast-
guard knew me.

'Come to see the fun, Mrs. de Winter?' he said smiling. 'I'm afraid it will
be a hard job. The tugs may shift her but I doubt it. She's hard and fast
where she is on that ledge.'

'What will they do?' I said.

'They'll send a diver down directly to see if she's broken her back,' he
replied. 'There's the fellow there in the red stocking cap. Like to see through
these glasses?'

I took his glasses and looked at the ship. I could see a group of men
staring over her stern. One of them was pointing at something. The man in
the lifeboat was still shouting through the megaphone.

The harbour-master from Kerrith had joined the group of men in the
stern of the stranded ship. The diver in his stocking cap was sitting in the
grey motor-boat belonging to the harbour-master.

The pleasure-boat was still circling round the ship. A woman was standing
up taking a snapshot. A group of gulls had settled on the water and were
crying foolishly, hoping for scraps.

I gave the glasses back to the coast-guard.

'Nothing seems to be happening,' I said.

'They'll send him down directly,' said the coast-guard. 'They'll argue a
bit first no doubt like all foreigners. Here come the tugs.'

'They'll never do it,' said Frank. 'Look at the angle she's lying at. It's
much shallower there than I thought.'

'That reef runs out quite a way,' said the coast-guard, 'you don't notice
it in the ordinary way, going over that piece of water in a small boat. But
a ship with her depth would touch all right.'

'I was down in the first cove by the valley when they fired the rockets,'
said Frank. 'I could scarcely see three yards in front of me where I was. And
then the things went off out of the blue.'

I thought how alike people were in a moment of common interest. Frank
was Frith all over again, giving his version of the story, as though it mattered,
as though we cared. I knew that he had gone down to the beach to look for
Maxim. I knew that he had been frightened, as I had been. And now all this
was forgotten and put aside, our conversation down the telephone, our
mutual anxiety, his insistence that he must see me. All because a ship had
gone ashore in the fog.

A small boy came running up to us. 'Will the sailors be drowned?' he asked.

'Not them. They're all right, sonny,' said the coast-guard. 'The sea's as flat as the back of my hand. No one's going to be hurt this time.'

'If it had happened last night we should never have heard them,' said Frank. 'We must have let off more than fifty rockets at our show, beside all the smaller things.'

'We'd have heard all right,' said the coast-guard. 'We'd have seen the flash and known the direction. There's the diver, Mrs. de Winter. See him putting on his helmet?'

'I want to see the diver,' said the small boy.

'There he is,' said Frank, bending and pointing, 'that chap there putting on the helmet. They're going to lower him into the water.'

'Won't he be drowned?' said the child.

'Divers don't drown,' said the coast-guard. 'They have air pumped into them all the time. Watch him disappear. There he goes.'

The surface of the water was disturbed a minute and then was clear again. 'He's gone,' said the small boy.

'Where's Maxim?' I said.

'He's taken one of the crew into Kerrith,' said Frank, 'the fellow lost his head and jumped for it apparently when the ship struck. We found him clinging on to one of the rocks here under the cliff. He was soaked to the skin of course and shaking like a jelly. Couldn't speak a word of English, of course. Maxim went down to him, and found him bleeding like a pig from a scratch on the rocks. He spoke to him in German. Then he hailed one of the motor-boats from Kerrith that was hanging around like a hungry shark, and he's gone off with him to get him bandaged by a doctor. If he's lucky he'll just catch old Phillips sitting down to lunch.'

'When did he go?' I said.

'He went just before you turned up,' said Frank, 'about five minutes ago. I wonder you didn't see the boat. He was sitting in the stern with this German fellow.'

'He must have gone while I was climbing up the cliff,' I said.

'Maxim is splendid at anything like this,' said Frank. 'He always gives a hand if he can. You'll find he will invite the whole crew back to Manderley, and feed them, and give them beds into the bargain.'

'That's right,' said the coast-guard. 'He'd give the coat off his back for any of his own people, I know that. I wish there was more like him in the county.'

'Yes, we could do with them,' said Frank.

We went on staring at the ship. The tugs were standing off still, but the life-boat had turned and gone back towards Kerrith.

'It's not their turn to-day,' said the coast-guard.

'No,' said Frank, 'and I don't think it's a job for the tugs either. It's the ship-breaker who's going to make money this time.'

The gulls wheeled overhead, mewing like hungry cats; some of them settled on the ledges of the cliff, while others, bolder, rode the surface of the water beside the ship.

The coast-guard took off his cap and mopped his forehead.

'Seems kind of airless, doesn't it?' he said.

'Yes,' I said.

The pleasure-boat with the camera people went chugging off towards Kerrith. 'They've got fed up,' said the coast-guard.

'I don't blame them,' said Frank. 'I don't suppose anything will happen for hours. The diver will have to make his report before they try and shift her.'

'That's right,' said the coast-guard.

'I don't think there's much sense in hanging about here,' said Frank, 'we can't do anything. I want my lunch.'

I did not say anything. He hesitated. I felt his eyes upon me.

'What are you going to do?' he said.

'I think I shall stay here a bit,' I said. 'I can have lunch any time. It's cold. It doesn't matter. I want to see what the diver's going to do.' Somehow I could not face Frank just at the moment. I wanted to be alone, or with someone I did not know, like the coast-guard.

'You won't see anything,' said Frank; 'there won't be anything to see. Why not come back and have some lunch with me?'

'No,' I said. 'No, really . . .'

'Oh, well,' said Frank, 'you know where to find me if you do want me. I shall be at the office all the afternoon.'

'All right,' I said.

He nodded to the coast-guard and went off down the cliff towards the cove. I wondered if I had offended him. I could not help it. All these things would be settled some day, one day. So much seemed to have happened since I spoke to him on the telephone and I did not want to think about anything any more. I just wanted to sit there on the cliff and stare at the ship.

'He's a good sort, Mr. Crawley,' said the coast-guard.

'Yes,' I said.

'He'd give his right hand for Mr. de Winter too,' he said.

'Yes, I think he would,' I said.

The small boy was still hopping round on the grass in front of us.

'When's the diver coming up again?' he said.

'Not yet, sonny,' said the coast-guard.

A woman in a pink striped frock and a hair-net came across the grass towards us. 'Charlie? Charlie? Where are you?' she called.

'Here's your mother coming to give you what-for,' said the coast-guard.

'I've seen the diver, Mum,' shouted the boy.

The woman nodded to us and smiled. She did not know me. She was a holiday-maker from Kerrith. 'The excitement all seems to be over, doesn't it?' she said. 'They are saying down on the cliff there the ship will be there for days.'

'They're waiting for the diver's report,' said the coast-guard.

'I don't know how they get them to go down under the water like that,' said the woman, 'they ought to pay them well.'

'They do that,' said the coast-guard.

'I want to be a diver, Mum,' said the small boy.

'You must ask your Daddy, dear,' said the woman, laughing at us. 'It's a lovely spot up here, isn't it?' she said to me. 'We brought a picnic lunch never thinking it would turn foggy and we'd have a wreck into the bargain. We were just thinking of going back to Kerrith when the rockets went off under our noses it seemed. I nearly jumped out of my skin. "Why, whatever's that?" I said to my husband. "That's a distress signal," he said, "let's stop and see the fun." There's no dragging him away, he's as bad as my little boy. I don't see anything in it myself.'

'No, there's not much to see now,' said the coast-guard.

'Those are nice looking woods over there, I suppose they're private,' said the woman.

The coast-guard coughed awkwardly, and glanced at me. I began eating a piece of grass, and looked away.

'Yes, that's all private in there,' he said.

'My husband says all these big estates will be chopped up in time and bungalows built,' said the woman. 'I wouldn't mind a nice little bungalow up here facing the sea. I don't know that I'd care for this part of the world in the winter though.'

'No, it's very quiet here winter times,' said the coast-guard.

I went on chewing my piece of grass. The little boy kept running round in circles. The coast-guard looked at his watch. 'Well, I must be getting on,' he said, 'good afternoon!' He saluted me, and turned back along the path towards Kerrith. 'Come on, Charlie, come and find Daddy,' said the woman.

She nodded to me in friendly fashion, and sauntered off to the edge of the cliff, the little boy running at her heels. A thin man in khaki shorts and a striped blazer waved to her. They sat down by a clump of gorse bushes, and the woman began to undo paper packages.

I wished I could lose my own identity and join them. Eat hard-boiled eggs and potted meat sandwiches, laugh rather loudly, enter their conversation, and then wander back with them during the afternoon to Kerrith and paddle on the beach, run races across the stretch of sand, and so to their lodgings and have shrimps for tea. Instead of which I must go back alone through the woods to Manderley and wait for Maxim. And I did not know what we should say to one another, how he would look at me, what would be his voice. I went on sitting there on the cliff. I was not hungry, I did not think about lunch.

More people came and wandered over the cliffs to look at the ship. It made an excitement for the afternoon. There was nobody I knew. They were all holiday-makers from Kerrith. The sea was glassy calm. The gulls no longer wheeled overhead, they had settled on the water a little distance from the ship. More pleasure-boats appeared during the afternoon. It must be a field day for Kerrith boatmen. The diver came up and then went down again. One of the tugs steamed away while the other still stood by. The harbour-master went back in his grey motor-boat, taking some men with him, and the diver who had come to the surface for the second time. The crew of the ship leant against the side throwing scraps to the gulls, while visitors in pleasure-boats rowed slowly round the ship. Nothing happened at all. It was dead low water now, and the ship was heeled at an angle, the propeller showing clean. Little ridges of white cloud formed in the western sky and the sun became pallid. It was still very hot. The woman in the pink striped frock with the little boy got up and wandered off along the path towards Kerrith, the man in the shorts following with the picnic basket.

I glanced at my watch. It was after three o'clock. I got up and went down the hill to the cove. It was quiet and deserted as always. The shingle was dark and grey. The water in the little harbour was glassy like a mirror. My feet made a queer crunching noise as I crossed the shingle. The ridges of white cloud now covered all the sky above my head, and the sun was hidden. When I came to the further side of the cove I saw Ben crouching by a little pool between two rocks scraping winkles into his hand. My shadow fell upon the water as I passed, and he looked up and saw me.

'G'day,' he said, his mouth opening in a grin.

'Good afternoon,' I said.

He scrambled to his feet and opened a dirty handkerchief he had filled with winkles.

'You eat winkles?' he said.

I did not want to hurt his feelings. 'Thank you,' I said.

He emptied about a dozen winkles into my hand, and I put them in the two pockets of my skirt. 'They'm all right with bread-an-butter,' he said, 'you must boil 'em first.'

'Yes, all right,' I said.

He stood there grinning at me. 'Seen the steamer?' he said.

'Yes,' I said, 'she's gone ashore, hasn't she?'

'Eh?' he said.

'She's run aground,' I repeated. 'I expect she's got a hole in her bottom.'

His face went blank and foolish. 'Aye,' he said, 'she's down there all right. She'll not come back again.'

'Perhaps the tugs will get her off when the tide makes,' I said.

He did not answer. He was staring out towards the stranded ship. I could see her broadside on from here, the red underwater section showing against the black of the top-sides, and the single funnel leaning rakishly towards the cliffs beyond. The crew were still leaning over her side feeding the gulls and staring into the water. The rowing boats were pulling back to Kerrith.

'She's a Dutchman, ain't she?' said Ben.

'I don't know,' I said. 'German or Dutch.'

'She'll break up there where she's to,' he said.

'I'm afraid so,' I said.

He grinned again, and wiped his nose with the back of his hand.

'She'll break up bit by bit,' he said, 'she'll not sink like a stone like the little 'un.' He chuckled to himself, picking his nose. I did not say anything. 'The fishes have eaten her up by now haven't they?' he said.

'Who?' I said.

He jerked his thumb towards the sea. 'Her,' he said, 'the other one.'

'Fishes don't eat steamers, Ben,' I said.

'Eh?' he said. He stared at me, foolish and blank once more.

'I must go home now,' I said; 'good-afternoon.'

I left him and walked towards the path through the woods. I did not look at the cottage. I was aware of it on my right hand; grey and quiet. I went straight to the path and up through the trees. I paused to rest half-way and looking through the trees I could still see the stranded ship leaning towards the shore. The pleasure boats had all gone. Even the crew had disappeared below. The ridges of cloud covered the whole sky. A little wind sprang from nowhere and blew into my face. A leaf fell on to my hand from the tree above. I shivered for no reason. Then the wind went again, it was hot and sultry as before. The ship looked desolate there upon her side, with no one on her decks, and her thin black funnel pointing to the shore. The sea was so calm that when it broke upon the shingle in the cove it was like a whisper, hushed and still. I turned once more to the steep path through the woods, my legs reluctant, my head heavy, a strange sense of foreboding in my heart.

The house looked very peaceful as I came upon it from the woods and crossed the lawns. It seemed sheltered and protected, more beautiful than I had ever seen it. Standing there, looking down upon it from the banks, I realised, perhaps for the first time, with a funny feeling of bewilderment and pride that it was my home, I belonged there, and Manderley belonged to me. The trees and the grass and the flower tubs on the terrace were reflected in the mullioned windows. A thin column of smoke rose in the air from one of the chimneys. The new-cut grass on the lawn smelt sweet as hay. A blackbird was singing on the chestnut-tree. A yellow butterfly winged his foolish way before me to the terrace.

I went into the hall and through to the dining-room. My place was still laid, but Maxim's had been cleared away. The cold meat and salad awaited me on the side board. I hesitated, and then rang the dining-room bell. Robert came in from behind the screen.

'Has Mr. de Winter been in?' I said.

'Yes, Madam,' said Robert; 'he came in just after two, and had a quick lunch, and then went out again. He asked for you and Frith said he thought you must have gone down to see the ship.'

'Did he say when he would be back again?' I asked.

'No, Madam.'

'Perhaps he went to the beach by another way,' I said; 'I may have missed him.'

'Yes, Madam,' said Robert.

I looked at the cold meat and the salad. I felt empty but not hungry. I did not want cold meat now. 'Will you be taking lunch?' said Robert.

'No,' I said. 'No, you might bring me some tea, Robert, in the library. Nothing like cakes or scones. Just tea and bread-and-butter.'

'Yes, Madam.'

I went and sat on the window-seat in the library. It seemed funny without

Jasper. He must have gone with Maxim. The old dog lay asleep in her basket. I picked up *The Times* and turned the pages without reading it. It was queer this feeling of marking time, like sitting in a waiting-room at a dentist's. I knew I should never settle to my knitting or to a book. I was waiting for something to happen, something unforeseen. The horror of my morning and the stranded ship and not having any lunch had all combined to give birth to a latent sense of excitement at the back of my mind that I did not understand. It was as though I had entered into a new phase of my life and nothing would be quite the same again. The girl who had dressed for the fancy dress ball the night before had been left behind. It had all happened a very long time ago. This self who sat on the window-seat was new, was different. . . . Robert brought in my tea, and I ate my bread-and-butter hungrily. He had brought scones as well, and some sandwiches, and an angel cake. He must have thought it improper to bring bread-and-butter alone, nor was it Manderley routine. I was glad of the scones and the angel cake. I remembered I had only had cold tea at half-past eleven, and no breakfast. Just after I had drunk my third cup Robert came in again.

'Mr. de Winter is not back yet is he, Madam?' he said.

'No,' I said. 'Why? Does someone want him?'

'Yes, Madam,' said Robert. 'It's Captain Searle, the harbour-master of Kerrith, on the telephone. He wants to know if he can come up and see Mr. de Winter personally.'

'I don't know what to say,' I said. 'He may not be back for ages.'

'No, Madam.'

'You'd better tell him to ring again at five o'clock,' I said. Robert went out of the room and came back again in a few minutes.

'Captain Searle would like to see you, if it would be convenient, Madam,' said Robert. 'He says the matter is rather urgent. He tried to get Mr. Crawley, but there was no reply.'

'Yes, of course I must see him if it's urgent,' I said. 'Tell him to come along at once if he likes. Has he got a car?'

'Yes, I believe so, Madam.'

Robert went out of the room. I wondered what I should say to Captain Searle. His business must be something to do with the stranded ship. I could not understand what concern it was of Maxim's. It would have been different if the ship had gone ashore in the cove. That was Manderley property. They might have to ask Maxim's permission to blast away rocks or whatever it was that was done to move a ship. But the open bay and the ledge of rock under the water did not belong to Maxim. Captain Searle would waste his time talking to me about it all.

He must have got into his car right away after talking to Robert because in less than quarter-of-an-hour he was shown into the room.

He was still in his uniform as I had seen him through the glasses in the early afternoon. I got up from the window-seat and shook hands with him. 'I'm sorry my husband isn't back yet, Captain Searle,' I said; 'he must have gone down to the cliffs again, and he went into Kerrith before that. I haven't seen him all day.'

'Yes, I heard he'd been to Kerrith but I missed him there,' said the harbour-master. 'He must have walked back across the cliffs when I was in my boat. And I can't get hold of Mr. Crawley either.'

'I'm afraid the ship has disorganised everybody,' I said. 'I was out on the cliffs and went without my lunch, and I know Mr. Crawley was there earlier on. What will happen to her? Will tugs get her off do you think?'

Captain Searle made a great circle with his hands. 'There's a hole that deep in her bottom,' he said, 'she'll not see Hamburg again. Never mind the ship. Her owner and Lloyd's agent will settle that between them. No, Mrs. de Winter, it's not the ship that's brought me here. Indirectly of course she's the cause of my coming. The fact is, I've got some news for Mr. de Winter, and I hardly know how to break it to him.' He looked at me very straight with his bright blue eyes.

'What sort of news, Captain Searle?'

He brought a large white handkerchief out of his pocket and blew his nose. 'Well, Mrs. de Winter, it's not very pleasant for me to tell you either. The last thing I want to do is to cause distress or pain to you and your husband. We're all very fond of Mr. de Winter in Kerrith, you know, and the family has always done a lot of good. It's hard on him and hard on you that we can't let the past lie quiet. But I don't see how we can under the circumstances.' He paused, and put his handkerchief back in his pocket. He lowered his voice, although we were alone in the room.

'We sent the diver down to inspect the ship's bottom,' he said, 'and while he was down there he made a discovery. It appears he found the hole in the ship's bottom and was working round to the other side to see what further damage there was when he came across the hull of a little sailing boat, lying on her side, quite intact and not broken up at all. He's a local man, of course, and he recognised the boat at once. It was the little boat belonging to the late Mrs. de Winter.'

My first feeling was one of thankfulness that Maxim was not there to hear. This fresh blow coming swiftly upon my masquerade of the night before was ironic, and rather horrible.

'I'm so sorry,' I said slowly, 'it's not the sort of thing one expected would happen. Is it necessary to tell Mr. de Winter? Couldn't the boat be left there, as it is, it's not doing any harm is it?'

'It would be left, Mrs. de Winter, in the ordinary way. I'm the last man in the world to want to disturb it. And I'd give anything, as I said before, to spare Mr. de Winter's feelings. But that wasn't all, Mrs. de Winter. My man poked round the little boat and he made another, more important discovery. The cabin door was tightly closed, it was not stove in, and the portlights were closed too. He broke one of the ports with a stone from the sea bed, and looked into the cabin. It was full of water, the sea must have come through some hole in the bottom, there seemed no damage elsewhere. And then he got the fright of his life, Mrs. de Winter.'

Captain Searle paused, he looked over his shoulder as though one of the of the servants might hear him. 'There was a body in there, lying on the cabin floor,' he said quietly. 'It was dissolved of course, there was no flesh on it. But it was a body all right. He saw the head and the limbs. He came up to the surface then and reported it direct to me. And now you understand, Mrs. de Winter, why I've got to see your husband.'

I stared at him, bewildered at first, then shocked, then rather sick.

'She was supposed to be sailing alone?' I whispered. 'There must have been someone with her then, all the time, and no one ever knew?'

'It looks like it,' said the harbour-master.

'Who could it have been?' I said. 'Surely relatives would know if anyone had been missing? There was so much about it at the time, it was all in the papers. Why should one of them be in the cabin and Mrs. de Winter herself be picked up many miles away, months afterwards?'

Captain Searle shook his head. 'I can't tell any more than you,' he said. 'All we know is that the body is there, and it has got to be reported. There'll be publicity, I'm afraid, Mrs. de Winter. I don't know how we're going to avoid it. It's very hard on you and Mr. de Winter. Here you are, settled down quietly, wanting to be happy, and this has to happen.'

I knew now the reason for my sense of foreboding. It was not the stranded ship that was sinister, nor the crying gulls, nor the thin black funnel pointing to the shore. It was the stillness of the black water, and the unknown things that lay beneath. It was the diver going down into those cool quiet depths and stumbling upon Rebecca's boat, and Rebecca's dead companion. He had touched the boat, had looked into the cabin, and all the while I sat on the cliffs and had not known.

'If only we did not have to tell him,' I said. 'If only we could keep the whole thing from him.'

'You know I would if it were possible, Mrs. de Winter,' said the harbour-master, 'but my personal feelings have to go, in a matter like this. I've got to do my duty. I've got to report that body.' He broke off short as the door opened, and Maxim came into the room.

'Hullo,' he said, 'what's happening? I didn't know you were here, Captain Searle? Is anything the matter?'

I could not stand it any longer. I went out of the room like the coward I was and shut the door behind me. I had not even glanced at Maxim's face. I had the vague impression that he looked tired, untidy, hatless.

I went and stood in the hall by the front door. Jasper was drinking noisily from his bowl. He wagged his tail when he saw me and went on drinking. Then he loped towards me, and stood up, pawing at my dress. I kissed the top of his head and went and sat on the terrace. The moment of crisis had come, and I must face it. My old fears, my diffidence, my shyness, my hopeless sense of inferiority, must be conquered now and thrust aside. If I failed now I should fail forever. There would never be another chance. I prayed for courage in a blind despairing way, and dug my nails into my hands. I sat there for five minutes staring at the green lawns and the flower tubs on the terrace. I heard the sound of a car starting up in the drive. It must be Captain Searle. He had broken his news to Maxim and had gone. I got up from the terrace and went slowly through the hall to the library.

I kept turning over in my pockets the winkles that Ben had given me. I clutched them tight in my hands.

Maxim was standing by the window. His back was turned to me. I waited by the door. Still he did not turn round. I took my hands out of my pockets and went and stood beside him. I reached out for his hand and laid it against my cheek. He did not say anything. He went on standing there.

'I'm so sorry,' I whispered, 'so terribly, terribly sorry.' He did not answer. His hand was icy cold. I kissed the back of it, and then the fingers, one by one. 'I don't want you to bear this alone,' I said. 'I want to share it with you. I've grown up, Maxim, in twenty-four hours. I'll never be a child again.'

He put his arm round me and pulled me to him very close. My reserve was broken, and my shyness too. I stood there with my face against his shoulder. 'You've forgiven me, haven't you?' I said.

He spoke to me at last. 'Forgiven you?' he said. 'What have I got to forgive you for?'

'Last night,' I said; 'you thought I did it on purpose.'

'Ah, that,' he said, 'I'd forgotten. I was angry with you, wasn't I?'

'Yes,' I said.

He did not say any more. He went on holding me close to his shoulder. 'Maxim,' I said, 'can't we start all over again? Can't we begin from to-day, and face things together? I don't want you to love me, I won't ask impossible things. I'll be your friend and your companion, a sort of boy. I don't ever want more than that.'

He took my face between his hands and looked at me. For the first time I saw how thin his face was, how lined and drawn. And there were great shadows beneath his eyes.

'How much do you love me?' he said.

I could not answer. I could only stare back at him, at his dark tortured eyes, and his pale drawn face.

'It's too late, my darling, too late,' he said. 'We've lost our little chance of happiness.'

'No, Maxim. No,' I said.

'Yes,' he said. 'It's all over now. The thing has happened.'

'What thing?' I said.

'The thing I've always foreseen. The thing I've dreamt about, day after day, night after night. We're not meant for happiness, you and I.' He sat down on the window-seat, and I knelt in front of him, my hands on his shoulders.

'What are you trying to tell me?' I said.

He put his hands over mine and looked into my face. 'Rebecca has won,' he said.

I stared at him, my heart beating strangely, my hands suddenly cold beneath his hands.

'Her shadow between us all the time,' he said. 'Her damned shadow keeping us from one another. How could I hold you like this, my darling, my little love, with the fear always in my heart that this would happen? I remembered her eyes as she looked at me before she died. I remembered that slow treacherous smile. She knew this would happen even then. She knew she would win in the end.'

'Maxim,' I whispered, 'what are you saying, what are you trying to tell me?'

'Her boat,' he said, 'they've found it. The diver found it this afternoon.'

'Yes,' I said. 'I know. Captain Searle came to tell me. You are thinking about the body, aren't you, the body the diver found in the cabin?'

'Yes,' he said.

'It means she was not alone,' I said. 'It means there was somebody sailing with Rebecca at the time. And you have to find out who it was. That's it, isn't it, Maxim?'

'No,' he said. 'No, you don't understand.'

'I want to share this with you, darling,' I said. 'I want to help you.'

'There was no one with Rebecca, she was alone,' he said.

I knelt there watching his face, watching his eyes.

'It's Rebecca's body lying there on the cabin floor,' he said.

'No,' I said. 'No.'

'The woman buried in the crypt is not Rebecca,' he said. 'It's the body of some unknown woman, unclaimed, belonging nowhere. There never was an accident. Rebecca was not drowned at all. I killed her. I shot Rebecca in the cottage in the cove. I carried her body to the cabin, and took the boat out that night and sank it there, where they found it to-day. It's Rebecca who's lying dead there on the cabin floor. Will you look into my eyes and tell me that you love me now?'

Chapter Twenty

It was very quiet in the library. The only sound was that of Jasper licking his foot. He must have caught a thorn in his pads, for he kept biting and sucking at the skin. Then I heard the watch on Maxim's wrist ticking close to my ear. The little normal sounds of every day. And for no reason the stupid proverb of my school-days ran through my mind, 'Time and Tide wait for no man.' The words repeated themselves over and over again. 'Time and Tide wait for no man.' These were the only sounds then, the ticking of Maxim's watch and Jasper licking his foot on the floor beside me.

When people suffer a great shock, like death, or the loss of a limb, I believe they don't feel it just at first. If your hand is taken from you you don't know, for a few minutes, that your hand is gone. You go on feeling the fingers. You stretch and beat them on the air, one by one, and all the time there is nothing there, no hand, no fingers. I knelt there by Maxim's side, my body against his body, my hands upon his shoulders, and I was aware of no feeling at all, no pain and no fear, there was no horror in my heart. I thought how I must take the thorn out of Jasper's foot and I wondered if Robert would come in and clear the tea-things. It seemed strange to me that I should think of these things, Jasper's foot, Maxim's watch, Robert and the tea-things, I was shocked at my lack of emotion and this queer cold absence of distress. Little by little the feeling will come back to me, I said to myself, little by little I shall understand. What he has told me and all that has happened will tumble into place like pieces of a jig-saw puzzle. They will fit themselves into a pattern. At the moment I am nothing, I have no heart, and no mind, and no senses, I am just a wooden thing in Maxim's arms. Then he began to kiss me. He had not kissed me like this before. I put my hands behind his head and shut my eyes.

'I love you so much,' he whispered. 'So much.'

This is what I have wanted him to say every day and every night, I thought, and now he is saying it at last. This is what I imagined in Monte Carlo, in Italy, here in Manderley. He is saying it now. I opened my eyes and looked at a little patch of curtain above his head. He went on kissing me, hungry, desperate, murmuring my name. I kept on looking at the patch of curtain, and saw where the sun had faded it, making it lighter than the piece above. 'How calm I am,' I thought. 'How cool. Here I am looking at the piece of curtain, and Maxim is kissing me. For the first time he is telling me he loves me.'

Then he stopped suddenly, he pushed me away from him, and got up from the window-seat. 'You see, I was right,' he said. 'It's too late. You don't love me now. Why should you?' He went and stood over by the mantelpiece. 'We'll forget that,' he said, 'it won't happen again.'

Realisation flooded me at once, and my heart jumped in quick and sudden panic. 'It's not too late,' I said swiftly, getting up from the floor and going to him, putting my arms about him; 'you're not to say that, you don't understand. I love you more than anything in the world. But when you kissed me just now I felt stunned and shaken, I could not feel anything. I could not grasp anything. It was just as though I had no more feeling left in me at all.'

'You don't love me,' he said, 'that's why you did not feel anything. I know. I know. I understand. It's come too late for you, hasn't it?'

'No,' I said.

'This ought to have happened four months ago,' he said. 'I should have known. Women are not like men.'

'I want you to kiss me again,' I said, 'please, Maxim.'

'No,' he said, 'it's no use now.'

'We can't lose each other now,' I said. 'We've got to be together always, with no secrets, no shadows. Please, darling, please.'

'There's no time,' he said. 'We may only have a few hours, a few days. How can we be together now that this has happened? I've told you they've found the boat. They've found Rebecca.'

I stared at him stupidly, not understanding. 'What will they do?' I said.

'They'll identify her body,' he said, 'there's everything to tell them, there in the cabin. The clothes she had, the shoes, the rings on her fingers. They'll identify her body; and then they will remember the other one, the woman buried up there, in the crypt.'

'What are you going to do?' I whispered.

'I don't know,' he said. 'I don't know.'

The feeling was coming back to me, little by little, as I knew it would. My hands were cold no longer. They were clammy, warm. I felt a wave of colour come into my face, my throat. My cheeks were burning hot. I thought of Captain Searle, the diver, the Lloyds' agent, all those men on the stranded ship leaning against the side, staring down into the water. I thought of the shop-keepers in Kerrith, of errand boys whistling in the street, of the vicar walking out of church, of Lady Crowan cutting roses in her garden, of the woman in the pink dress and her little boy on the cliffs. Soon they would know. In a few hours. By breakfast time to-morrow. 'They've found Mrs. de Winter's boat, and they say there is a body in the cabin.' A body in the cabin. Rebecca was lying there on the cabin floor. She was not in the crypt at all. Some other woman was lying in the crypt. Maxim had killed Rebecca. Rebecca had not been drowned at all. Maxim had killed her. He had shot her in the cottage in the woods. He had carried her body to the boat, and sunk the boat there in the bay. That grey, silent cottage, with the rain pattering on the roof. The jigsaw pieces came tumbling thick and fast upon me. Disjointed pictures flashed one by one through my bewildered mind. Maxim sitting in the car beside me in the south of France. 'Something happened nearly a year ago that altered my whole life. I had to begin living all over again . . .' Maxim's silence, Maxim's moods. The way he never talked about Rebecca. The way he never mentioned her name. Maxim's dislike of the cove, of the stone cottage. 'If you had my memories you would not go there either.' The way he climbed the path through the woods not looking behind him. Maxim pacing up and down the library after Rebecca died. Up and down. Up and down. 'I came away in rather a hurry,' he said to Mrs. Van Hopper, a line, thin as gossamer, between his brows. 'They say he can't get over his wife's death.' The fancy dress dance last night, and I coming down to the head of the stairs, in Rebecca's dress. 'I killed Rebecca,' Maxim had said. 'I shot Rebecca in the cottage in the woods.' And the diver had found her lying there, on the cabin floor. . . .

'What are we going to do?' I said. 'What are we going to say?'

Maxim did not answer. He stood there by the mantelpiece, his eyes wide and staring, looking in front of him, not seeing anything.

'Does anyone know,' I said, 'anyone at all?'

He shook his head. 'No,' he said.

'No one but you and me?' I asked.

'No one but you and me,' he said.

'Frank,' I said suddenly, 'are you sure Frank does not know?'

'How could he?' said Maxim. 'There was nobody there but myself. It was dark . . .' He stopped. He sat down on a chair, he put his hand up to his forehead. I went and knelt beside him. He sat very still a moment. I took his hands away from his face and looked into his eyes. 'I love you,' I whispered, 'I love you. Will you believe me now?' He kissed my face and my hands. He held my hands very tightly like a child who would gain confidence.

'I thought I should go mad,' he said, 'sitting here, day after day, waiting for something to happen. Sitting down at the desk there, answering those terrible letters of sympathy. The notices in the papers, the interviews, all the little aftermath of death. Eating and drinking, trying to be normal, trying to be sane. Frith, the servants, Mrs. Danvers. Mrs. Danvers, whom I had not the courage to turn away, because with her knowledge of Rebecca she might have suspected, she might have guessed . . . Frank, always by my side, discreet, sympathetic. "Why don't you get away?" he used to say. "I can manage here. You ought to get away." And Giles, and Bee, poor dear tactless Bee. "You're looking frightfully ill, can't you go and see a doctor?" I had to face them, all these people knowing every word I uttered was a lie.'

I went on holding his hands very tight. I leant close to him, quite close.

'I nearly told you, once,' he said, 'that day Jasper ran to the cove, and you went to the cottage for some string. We were sitting here, like this, and then Frith and Robert came in with the tea.'

'Yes,' I said. 'I remember. Why didn't you tell me? The time we've wasted when we might have been together. All these weeks and days.'

'You were so aloof,' he said, 'always wandering into the garden with Jasper, going off on your own. You never came to me like this.'

'Why didn't you tell me?' I whispered. 'Why didn't you tell me?'

'I thought you were unhappy, bored,' he said. 'I'm so much older than you. You seemed to have more to say to Frank than you ever had to me. You were funny with me, awkward, shy.'

'How could I come to you when I knew you were thinking about Rebecca?' I said. 'How could I ask you to love me when I knew you loved Rebecca still?'

He pulled me close to him and searched my eyes.

'What are you talking about, what do you mean?' he said.

I knelt up straight beside him. 'Whenever you touched me I thought you were comparing me to Rebecca,' I said. 'Whenever you spoke to me or looked at me, walked with me in the garden, sat down for dinner, I felt you were saying to yourself, "This I did with Rebecca, and this, and this." ' He stared at me bewildered as though he did not understand.

'It was true, wasn't it?' I said.

'Oh, my God,' he said. He pushed me away, he got up and began walking up and down the room, clasping his hands.

'What is it? What's the matter?' I said.

He whipped round and looked at me as I sat there huddled on the floor. 'You thought I loved Rebecca?' he said. 'You thought I killed her, loving her? I hated her, I tell you, our marriage was a farce from the very first. She was vicious, damnable, rotten through and through. We never loved each other, never had one moment of happiness together. Rebecca was incapable of love, of tenderness, of decency. She was not even normal.'

I sat on the floor, clasping my knees, staring at him.

'She was clever of course,' he said. 'Damnably clever. No one would guess meeting her that she was not the kindest, most generous, most gifted person in the world. She knew exactly what to say to different people, how to match her mood to theirs. Had she met you, she would have walked off into the garden with you, arm-in-arm, calling to Jasper, chatting about flowers, music, painting, whatever she knew to be your particular hobby; and you would have been taken in, like the rest. You would have sat at her feet and worshipped her.'

Up and down he walked, up and down across the library floor.

'When I married her I was told I was the luckiest man in the world,' he said. 'She was so lovely, so accomplished, so amusing. Even Gran, the most difficult person to please in those days, adored her from the first. "She's got the three things that matter in a wife," she told me; "breeding, brains, and beauty." And I believed her, or forced myself to believe her. But all the time I had a seed of doubt at the back of my mind. There was something about her eyes . . .'

The jig-saw pieces came together piece by piece, and the real Rebecca took shape and form before me, stepping from her shadow world like a living figure from a picture frame. Rebecca slashing at her horse; Rebecca seizing life with her two hands; Rebecca, triumphant, leaning down from the minstrel's gallery with a smile on her lips.

Once more I saw myself standing on the beach beside poor startled Ben. 'You're kind,' he said, 'not like the other one. You won't put me to the asylum, will you?' There was someone who walked through the woods by night, someone tall and slim. She gave you the feeling of a snake. . . .

Maxim was talking though. Maxim was walking up and down the library floor. 'I found her out at once,' he was saying, 'five days after we were married. You remember that time I drove you in the car, to the hills above Monte Carlo? I wanted to stand there again, to remember. She sat there, laughing, her black hair blowing in the wind; she told me about herself, told me things I shall never repeat to a living soul. I knew then what I had done, what I had married. Beauty, brains, and breeding. Oh, my God.'

He broke off abruptly. He went and stood by the window, looking out upon the lawns. He began to laugh. He stood there laughing. I could not bear it, it made me frightened, ill. I could not stand it.

'Maxim!' I cried. 'Maxim.'

He lit a cigarette, and stood there smoking, not saying anything. Then he turned away again, and paced up and down the room once more. 'I nearly killed her then,' he said. 'It would have been so easy. One false step, one slip. You remember the precipice. I frightened you, didn't I? You thought I was mad. Perhaps I was. Perhaps I am. It doesn't make for sanity, does it, living with the devil.'

I sat there watching him, up and down, up and down.

'She made a bargain with me up there, on the side of the precipice,' he said. ' "I'll run your house for you," she told me, "I'll look after your precious Manderley for you, make it the most famous show-place in all the country, if you like. And people will visit us, and envy us, and talk about us; they'll say we are the luckiest, happiest, handsomest couple in all England. What a leg-pull, Max," she said, "what a God-damn triumph!" She sat there on the hillside, laughing, tearing a flower to bits in her hands.'

Maxim threw his cigarette away, a quarter smoked, into the empty grate. 'I did not kill her,' he said, 'I watched her, I said nothing, I let her laugh. We got into the car together and drove away. And she knew I would do as she suggested, come here to Manderley, throw the place open, entertain, have our marriage spoken of as the success of the century. She knew I would sacrifice pride, honour, personal feeling, every damned quality on earth, rather than stand before our little world after a week of marriage and have them know the things about her that she told me then. She knew I would never stand in a divorce court and give her away, have fingers pointing at us, mud flung at us in the newspapers, all the people who belong down here whispering when my name was mentioned, all the trippers from Kerrith trooping to the lodge gates, peering into the grounds and saying. "That's where he lives, in there. That's Manderley. That's the place that belongs to the chap who had that divorce case we read about. Do you remember what the judge said about his wife . . .?" '

He came and stood before me. He held out his hands. 'You despise me, don't you?' he said. 'You can't understand my shame, and loathing, and disgust?'

I did not say anything. I held his hands against my heart. I did not care about his shame. None of the things that he had told me mattered to me at all. I clung to one thing only, and repeated it to myself, over and over again. Maxim did not love Rebecca. He had never loved her, never, never. They had never known one moment's happiness together. Maxim was talking, and I listened to him, but his words meant nothing to me. I did not really care. 'I thought about Manderley too much,' he said. 'I put Manderley first, before anything else. And it does not prosper, that sort of love. They don't preach about it in the churches. Christ said nothing about stones, and bricks, and walls, the love that a man can bear for his plot of earth, his soil, his little kingdom. It does not come into the Christian creed.'

'My darling,' I said, 'my Maxim, my love.' I laid his hands against my face, I put my lips against them.

'Do you understand?' he said. 'Do you, do you?'

'Yes,' I said, 'my sweet, my love.' But I looked away from him so he should not see my face. What did it matter whether I understood him or not? My heart was light like a feather floating in the air. He had never loved Rebecca.

'I don't want to look back on those years,' he said slowly. 'I don't want even to tell you about them. The shame and the degradation. The lie we lived, she and I. The shabby, sordid farce we played together. Before friends, before relations, even before the servants, before faithful, trusting creatures like old Frith. They all believed in her down here, they all admired her, they never knew how she laughed at them behind their backs, jeered at them, mimicked them. I can remember days when the place was full for some show or other, a garden party, a pageant, and she walked about with a smile like an angel on her face, her arm through mine, giving prizes afterwards to a little troop of children; and then the day afterwards she would be up at dawn driving to London, streaking to that flat of hers by the river like an animal to its hole in the ditch, coming back here at the end of the week, after five unspeakable days. Oh, I kept to my side of the bargain all right. I never gave her away. Her blasted taste made Manderley the thing it is to-day. The gardens, the shrubs, even the azaleas in the Happy Valley, do you think they existed when my father was alive? God, the place was a wilderness, lovely yes, wild and lonely with a beauty of its own, yes, but crying out for skill and care and the money that he would never give to it, that I would not have thought of giving to it – but for Rebecca. Half the stuff you see here in the rooms was never here originally. The drawing-room as it is to-day, the morning-room – that's all Rebecca. Those chairs that Frith points out so proudly to the visitors on the public day, and that panel of tapestry – Rebecca again. Oh, some of the things were here admittedly, stored away in back rooms, my father knew nothing about furniture or pictures, but the majority was bought by Rebecca. The beauty of Manderley that you see to-day, the Manderley that people talk about and photograph and paint, it's all due to her, to Rebecca.'

I did not say anything. I held him close. I wanted him to go on talking like this, that his bitterness might loosen and come away, carrying with it all the pent-up hatred and disgust and muck of the lost years.

'And so we lived,' he said, 'month after month, year after year. I accepted everything – because of Manderley. What she did in London did not touch me – because it did not hurt Manderley. And she was careful those first years, there was never a murmur about her, never a whisper. Then little by little she began to grow careless. You know how a man starts drinking? He goes easy at first, just a little at a time, a bad bout perhaps every five months or so. And then the period between grows less and less. Soon it's every month, every fortnight, every few days. There's no margin of safety left and all his secret cunning goes. It was like that with Rebecca. She began to ask her friends down here. She would have one or two of them and mix them up at a week-end party so that at first I was not quite sure, not quite certain. She would have picnics down at her cottage in the cove. I came back once, having been away shooting in Scotland, and found her there, with half a dozen of them, people I had never seen before. I warned her, and she shrugged her shoulders. "What the hell's it got to do with you?" she said. I told her she could see her friends in London, but Manderley was mine. She must stick to that part of the bargain. She smiled, she did not say anything. Then she started on Frank, poor shy faithful Frank. He came to me one day and said he wanted to leave Manderley and take another job. We argued for two hours, here in the library, and then I understood. He broke down and told me. She never left him alone, he said, she was always going down to his house, trying to get him to the cottage. Dear, wretched Frank, who had not understood, who had always thought we were the normal happy married couple we pretended to be.

'I accused Rebecca of this, and she flared up at once, cursing me, using every filthy word in her particular vocabulary. We had a sickening, loathsome scene. She went up to London after that and stayed there for a month. When she came back again she was quiet at first, I thought she had learnt her lesson. Bee and Giles came for a week-end, and I realised then what I had sometimes suspected before, that Bee did not like Rebecca. I believe, in her funny, abrupt, downright way she saw through her, guessed something was wrong. It was a tricky, nervy sort of week-end. Giles went out sailing with Rebecca. Bee and I lazed on the lawn. And when they came back I could tell by Giles's rather hearty jovial manner and by a look in Rebecca's eye that she had started on him, as she had done on Frank. I saw Bee watching Giles at dinner, who laughed louder than usual, talked a little too much. And all the while Rebecca sitting there at the head of the table, looking like an angel.'

They were all fitting into place, the jig-saw pieces. The odd strained shapes that I had tried to piece together with my fumbling fingers and they had never fitted. Frank's odd manner when I spoke about Rebecca. Beatrice, and her rather diffident negative attitude. The silence that I had always taken for sympathy and regret was a silence born of shame and embarrassment. It seemed incredible to me now that I had never understood. I wondered how many people there were in the world who suffered, and continued to suffer, because they could not break out from their own web of shyness and reserve, and in their blindness and folly built up a great distorted wall in front of them that hid the truth. This was what I had done. I had built up false pictures in my mind and sat before them. I had never had the courage to demand the truth. Had I made one step forward out of my own shyness, Maxim would have told me these things four months, five months ago.

'That was the last week-end Bee and Giles ever spent at Manderley,' said Maxim. 'I never asked them alone again. They came officially, to garden-parties, and dances. Bee never said a word to me or I to her. But I think she guessed my life, I think she knew. Even as Frank did. Rebecca grew cunning again. Her behaviour was faultless, outwardly. But if I happened to be away when she was here at Manderley I could never be certain what might happen. There had been Frank, and Giles. She might get hold of one of the workmen on the estate, someone from Kerrith, anyone. . . . And then the bomb would have to fall. The gossip, the publicity I dreaded.'

It seemed to me I stood again by the cottage in the woods, and I heard the drip-drip of the rain upon the roof. I saw the dust on the model ships, the rat holes on the divan. I saw Ben with his poor staring idiot's eyes. 'You'll not put me to the asylum, will you?' And I thought of the dark steep path through the woods, and how, if a woman stood there behind the trees, her evening dress would rustle in the thin night breeze.

'She had a cousin,' said Maxim slowly, 'a fellow who had been abroad, and was living in England again. He took to coming here, if ever I was away. Frank used to see him. A fellow called Jack Favell.'

'I know him,' I said, 'he came here the day you went to London.'

'You saw him too?' said Maxim. 'Why didn't you tell me? I heard it from Frank, who saw his car turn in at the lodge gates.'

'I did not like to,' I said, 'I thought it would remind you of Rebecca.'

'Remind me?' whispered Maxim. 'Oh, God, as if I needed reminding.'

He stared in front of him, breaking off from his story, and I wondered if he was thinking, as I was, of that flooded cabin beneath the waters in the bay.

'She used to have this fellow Favell down to the cottage,' said Maxim, 'she would tell the servants she was going to sail, and would not be back before the morning. Then she would spend the night down there with him. Once again I warned her. I said if I found him here, anywhere on the estate, I'd shoot him. He had a black, filthy record. . . . The very thought of him walking about the woods in Manderley, in places like the Happy Valley, made me mad. I told her I would not stand for it. She shrugged her shoulders. She forgot to blaspheme. And I noticed she was looking paler than usual, nervy, rather haggard. I wondered then what the hell would happen to her when she began to look old, feel old. Things drifted on. Nothing very much happened. Then one day she went up to London, and came back again the same day, which she did not do as a rule. I did not expect her. I dined that night with Frank at his house, we had a lot of work on at the time.' He was speaking now in short, jerky sentences. I had his hands very tightly between my two hands.

'I came back after dinner, about half-past ten, and I saw her scarf and gloves lying on a chair in the hall. I wondered what the devil she had come back for. I went into the morning-room but she was not there. I guessed she had gone off there then, down to the cove. And I knew then I could not stand this life of lies and filth and deceit any longer. The thing had got to be settled, one way or the other. I thought I'd take a gun and frighten the fellow, frighten them both. I went down right away to the cottage. The servants never knew I had come back to the house at all. I slipped out into the garden and through the woods. I saw the light in the cottage window, and I went straight in. To my surprise Rebecca was alone. She was lying on the divan with an ash-tray full of cigarette stubs beside her. She looked ill, queer.

'I began at once about Favell and she listened to me without a word. "We've lived this life of degradation long enough, you and I," I said. "This is the end, do you understand? What you do in London does not concern me. You can live with Favell there, or with anyone you like. But not here. Not at Manderley."

'She said nothing for a moment. She stared at me, and then she smiled. "Suppose it suits me better to live here, what then?" she said.

' "You know the conditions," I said, "I've kept my part of our dirty, damnable bargain, haven't I? But you've cheated. You think you can treat my house and my home like your own sink in London. I've stood enough, but my God, Rebecca, this is your last chance."

'I remember she squashed out her cigarette in the tub by the divan, and then she got up, and stretched herself, her arms above her head.

' "You're right, Max," she said. "It's time I turned over a new leaf."

'She looked very pale, very thin. She began walking up and down the room, her hands in the pockets of her trousers. She looked like a boy in her sailing kit, a boy with a face like a Botticelli angel.

' "Have you ever thought," she said, "how damned hard it would be for you to make a case against me? In a court of law, I mean. If you wanted to divorce me. Do you realise that you've never had one shred of proof against me, from the very first? All your friends, even the servants, believe our marriage to be a success?"

' "What about Frank?" I said. "What about Beatrice?"

'She threw back her head and laughed. "What sort of a story could Frank tell against mine?" she said. "Don't you know me well enough for that? As for Beatrice, wouldn't it be the easiest thing in the world for her to stand in a witness-box as the ordinary jealous woman whose husband once lost his head and made a fool of himself? Oh, no, Max, you'd have a hell of a time trying to prove anything against me."

'She stood watching me, rocking on her heels, her hands in her pockets and a smile on her face. "Do you realise that I could get Danny, as my personal maid, to swear anything I asked her to swear in a court of law? And that the rest of the servants, in blind ignorance, would follow her example and swear too? They think we live together at Manderley as husband and wife, don't they? And so does everyone, your friends, all our little world. Well, how are you going to prove that we don't?"

'She sat down on the edge of the table, swinging her legs, watching me.

' "Haven't we acted the parts of a loving husband and wife rather too well?" she said. I remember watching that foot of hers in its striped sandal swinging backwards and forward, and my eyes and my brain began to burn in a strange quick way.

' "We could make you look very foolish, Danny and I," she said softly. "We could make you look so foolish that no one would believe you, Max, nobody at all." Still that foot of hers, swinging to and fro, that damned foot in its blue and white striped sandal.

'Suddenly she slipped off the table and stood in front of me, smiling still, her hands in her pockets.

' "If I had a child, Max," she said, "neither you, nor anyone in the world, would ever prove that it was not yours. It would grow up here in Manderley, bearing your name. There would be nothing you could do. And when you died Manderley would be his. You could not prevent it. The property's entailed. You would like an heir, wouldn't you, for your beloved Manderley? You would enjoy it, wouldn't you, seeing my son lying in his pram under the chestnut tree, playing leap-frog on the lawn, catching butterflies in the Happy Valley? It would give you the biggest thrill of your life, wouldn't it, Max, to watch my son grow bigger day by day, and to know that when you died, all this would be his?"

'She waited a minute, rocking on her heels, and then she lit a cigarette and went and stood by the window. She began to laugh. She went on laughing. I thought she would never stop. "God, how funny," she said, 'how supremely, wonderfully funny. Well, you heard me say I was going to turn over a new leaf, didn't you? Now you know the reason. They'll be happy, won't they, all these smug locals, all your blasted tenants? 'It's what we've always hoped for, Mrs. de Winter,' they will say. I'll be the perfect mother, Max, just as I've been the perfect wife. And none of them will ever guess, none of them will ever know."

'She turned round and faced me, smiling, one hand in her pocket, the other holding her cigarette. When I killed her she was smiling still. I fired at her heart. The bullet passed right through. She did not fall at once. She stood there, looking at me, that slow smile on her face, her eyes wide open. . . .'

Maxim's voice had sunk low, so low, that it was like a whisper. The hand that I held between my own was cold. I did not look at him. I watched Jasper's sleeping body on the carpet beside me, the little thump of his tail, now and then, upon the floor.

'I'd forgotten,' said Maxim, and his voice was slow now, tired, without expression, 'that when you shot a person there was so much blood.'

There was a hole there on the carpet beneath Jasper's tail. The burnt hole from a cigarette. I wondered how long it had been there. Some people said ash was good for the carpets.

'I had to get water from the cove,' said Maxim. 'I had to keep going backwards and forwards to the cove for water. Even by the fireplace, where she had not been, there was a stain. It was all round her where she lay on the floor. It began to blow too. There was no catch on the window. The window kept banging backwards and forwards, while I knelt there on the floor, with that dish-cloth, and the bucket beside me.'

And the rain on the roof, I thought, he does not remember the rain on the roof. It pattered thin and light and very fast.

'I carried her out to the boat,' he said, 'it must have been half-past eleven by then, nearly twelve. It was quite dark. There was no moon. The wind was squally, from the west. I carried her down to the cabin and left her there. Then I had to get under way, with the dinghy astern, and beat out of the little harbour against the tide. The wind was with me but it came in puffs, and I was in the lee there, under cover of the headland. I remember I got the mainsail jammed half-way up the mast. I had not done it, you see, for a long time. I never went out with Rebecca.

'And I thought of the tide, how swift it ran and strong into the little cove. The wind blew down from the headland like a funnel. I got the boat out into the bay. I got her out there, beyond the beacon, and I tried to go about, to clear the ridge of rocks. The little jib fluttered. I could not sheet it in. A puff of wind came and the sheet tore out of my hands, went twisting round the mast. The sail thundered and shook. It cracked like a whip above my head. I could not remember what one had to do. I could not remember. I tried to reach that sheet and it blew above me in the air. Another blast of wind came straight ahead. We began to drift sideways, closer to the ridge. It was dark, so damned dark I couldn't see anything on the black, slippery deck. Somehow I blundered down into the cabin. I had a spike with me. If I didn't do it now it would be too late. We were getting so near to the ridge, and in six or seven minutes, drifting like this, we should be out of deep water. I opened the sea-cocks. The water began to come in. I drove the spike into the bottom boards. One of the planks split right across. I took the spike out and began to drive in another plank. The water came up over my feet. I left Rebecca lying there, on the floor. I fastened both the scuttles. I bolted the door. When I came up on deck I saw we were within twenty yards of the ridge. I threw some of the loose stuff on the deck into the water. There was a life-buoy, a pair of sweeps, a coil of rope. I climbed into the dinghy. I pulled away, and lay back on the paddles, and watched. The boat was drifting still. She was sinking too. Sinking by the head. The jib was still shaking and cracking like a whip. I thought someone must hear it, someone walking the cliffs late at night, some fisherman from Kerrith away beyond me in the bay, whose boat I could not see. The boat was smaller, like a black shadow on the water. The mast began to shiver, began to crack. Suddenly she heeled right over and as she went the mast broke in two, split right down the centre. The life-buoy and the sweeps floated away from me on the water. The boat was not there any more. I remember staring at the place where she had been. Then I pulled back to the cove. It started raining.'

Maxim waited. He stared in front of him still. Then he looked at me, sitting beside him on the floor.

'That's all,' he said, 'there's no more to tell. I left the dinghy on the buoy, as she would have done. I went back and looked at the cottage. The floor was wet with the salt water. She might have done it herself. I walked up the path through the woods. I went into the house. Up the stairs to the dressing-room. I remember undressing. It began to blow and rain very hard. I was sitting there, on the bed, when Mrs. Danvers knocked on the door. I went and opened it, in my dressing-gown, and spoke to her. She was worried about Rebecca. I told her to go back to bed. I shut the door again. I went back and sat by the window in my dressing-gown, watching the rain, listening to the sea as it broke there in the cove.'

We sat there together without saying anything. I went on holding his cold hands. I wondered why Robert did not come to clear the tea.

'She sank too close in,' said Maxim. 'I meant to take her right out in the bay. They would never have found her there. She was too close in.'

'It was the ship,' I said, 'it would not have happened but for the ship. No one would have known.'

'She was too close in,' said Maxim.

We were silent again. I began to feel very tired.

'I knew it would happen one day,' said Maxim, 'even when I went up to Edgecoombe and identified that body as hers, I knew it meant nothing, nothing at all. It was only a question of waiting, of marking time. Rebecca would win in the end. Finding you has not made any difference, has it? Loving you does not alter things at all. Rebecca knew she would win in the end. I saw her smile, when she died.'

'Rebecca is dead,' I said. 'That's what we've got to remember. Rebecca is dead. She can't speak, she can't bear witness. She can't harm you any more.'

'There's her body,' he said, 'the diver has seen it. It's lying there, on the cabin floor.'

'We've got to explain it,' I said. 'We've got to think out a way to explain it. It's got to be the body of someone you don't know. Someone you've never seen before.'

'Her things will be there still,' he said. 'The rings on her fingers. Even if her clothes have rotted in the water there will be something there to tell them. It's not like a body lost at sea, battered against rocks. The cabin is untouched. She must be lying there on the floor as I left her. The boat has been there, all these months. No one has moved anything. There is the boat, lying on the sea-bed where she sank.'

'A body rots in water, doesn't it?' I whispered. 'Even if it's lying there, undisturbed, the water rots it, doesn't it?'

'I don't know,' he said. 'I don't know.'

'How will you find out, how will you know?' I said.

'The diver is going down again at five-thirty to-morrow morning,' said Maxim. 'Searle has made all the arrangements. They are going to try and raise the boat. No one will be about. I'm going with them. He's sending his boat to pick me up in the cove. Five-thirty to-morrow morning.'

'And then?' I said. 'If they get it up, what then?'

'Searle's going to have his big lighter anchored there, just out in the deep water. If the boat's wood has not rotted, if it still holds together, his crane will be able to lift it on to the lighter. They'll go back to Kerrith then. Searle says he will moor the lighter at the head of that disused creek half way up Kerrith harbour. It drives out very easily. It's mud there at low water and the trippers can't row up there. We shall have the place to ourselves. He says we'll have to let the water drain out of the boat, leaving the cabin bare. He's going to get hold of a doctor.'

'What will he do?' I said. 'What will the doctor do?'

'I don't know,' he said.

'If they find out it's Rebecca you must say the other body was a mistake,' I said. 'You must say that body in the crypt was a mistake, a ghastly mistake. You must say that when you went to Edgecoombe you were ill, you did not know what you were doing. You were not sure, even then. You could not tell. It was a mistake, just a mistake. You will say that, won't you?'

'Yes,' he said. 'Yes.'

'They can't prove anything against you,' I said. 'Nobody saw you that night. You had gone to bed. They can't prove anything. No one knows but you and I. No one at all. Not even Frank. We are the only two people in the world to know, Maxim. You and I.'

'Yes,' he said, 'yes.'

'They will think the boat capsized and sank when she was in the cabin,' I said, 'they will think she went below for a rope, for something, and while she was there the wind came from the headland, and the boat heeled over, and Rebecca was trapped. They'll think that, won't they?'

'I don't know,' he said. 'I don't know.'

Suddenly the telephone began ringing in the little room behind the library.

Chapter Twenty-one

Maxim went into the little room and shut the door. Robert came in a few minutes afterwards to clear away the tea. I stood up, my back turned to him so that he should not see my face. I wondered when they would begin to know, on the estate, in the servants' hall, in Kerrith itself. I wondered how long it took for news to trickle through.

I could hear the murmur of Maxim's voice in the little room beyond. I had a sick expectant feeling at the pit of my stomach. The sound of the telephone ringing seemed to have woken every nerve in my body. I had sat there on the floor beside Maxim in a sort of dream, his hand in mine, my face against his shoulder. I had listened to his story and part of me went with him like a shadow in his tracks. I too had killed Rebecca, I too had sunk the boat there in the bay. I had listened beside him to the wind and water. I had waited for Mrs. Danvers' knocking on the door. All this I had suffered with him, all this and more beside. But the rest of me sat there on the carpet, unmoved and detached, thinking and caring for one thing only, repeating a phrase over and over again, 'He did not love Rebecca, he did not love Rebecca.' Now, at the ringing of the telephone, these two selves merged and became one again. I was the self that I had always been, I was not changed. But something new had come upon me that had not been before. My heart, for all its anxiety and doubt, was light and free. I knew then that I was no longer afraid of Rebecca. I did not hate her any more. Now that I knew her to have been evil and vicious and rotten I did not hate her any more. She could not hurt me. I could go to the morning-room and sit down at her desk and touch her pen and look at her writing on the pigeon-holes, and I should not mind. I could go to her room in the west wing, stand by the window even as I had done this morning, and I should not be afraid. Rebecca's power had dissolved into the air, as the mist had done. She would never haunt me again. She would never stand behind me on the stairs, sit beside me in the dining-room, lean down from the gallery and watch me standing in the hall. Maxim had never loved her. I did not hate her any more. Her body had come back, her boat had been found with its queer prophetic name, *Je Reviens*, but I was free of her forever.

I was free now to be with Maxim, to touch him, and hold him, and love him. I would never be a child again. It would not be I, I, I any longer, it would be we, it would be us. We would be together. We would face this trouble together, he and I. Captain Searle, and the diver, and Frank, and Mrs. Danvers, and Beatrice, and the men and women of Kerrith reading their newspapers, could not break us now. Our happiness had not come too late. I was not young any more. I was not shy. I was not afraid. I would fight for Maxim. I would lie and perjure and swear, I could blaspheme and pray. Rebecca had not won. Rebecca had lost.

Robert had taken away the tea and Maxim came back into the room.

'It was Colonel Julyan,' he said, 'he's just been talking to Searle. He's coming out with us to the boat to-morrow. Searle has told him.'

'Why Colonel Julyan, why?' I said.

'He's the magistrate for Kerrith. He has to be present.

'What did he say?'

'He asked me if I had any idea whose body it could be.'

'What did you say?'

'I said I did not know. I said we believed Rebecca to be alone. I said I did not know of any friend.'

'Did he say anything after that?'

'Yes.'

'What did he say?'

'He asked me if I thought it possible that I made a mistake when I went up to Edgecoombe?'

'He said that? He said that already?'

'Yes.'

'And you?'

'I said it might be possible. I did not know.'

'He'll be with you then to-morrow when you look at the boat? He, and Captain Searle, and a doctor.'

'Inspector Welch too.'

'Inspector Welch?'

'Yes.'

'Why? Why Inspector Welch?'

'It's the custom, when a body has been found.'

I did not say anything. We stared at one another. I felt the little pain come again at the pit of my stomach.

'They may not be able to raise the boat,' I said.

'No,' he said.

'They couldn't do anything then about the body, could they?' I said.

'I don't know,' he said.

He glanced out of the window. The sky was white and overcast as it had been when I came away from the cliffs. There was no wind though. It was still and quiet.

'I thought it might blow from the south-west about an hour ago but the wind has died away again,' he said.

'Yes,' I said.

'It will be a flat calm to-morrow for the diver,' he said.

The telephone began ringing again from the little room. There was something sickening about the shrill urgent summons of the bell. Maxim and I looked at one another. Then he went into the room to answer it, shutting the door behind him as he had done before. The queer nagging pain had not left me yet. It returned again in greater force with the ringing of the bell. The feel of it took me back across the years to my childhood. This was the pain I had known when I was very small and the maroons had sounded in the streets of London, and I had sat, shivering, not understanding, under a little cupboard beneath the stairs. It was the same feeling, the same pain.

Maxim came back into the library. 'It's begun,' he said slowly.

'What do you mean, what's happened?' I said, grown suddenly cold.

'It was a reporter,' he said, 'the fellow from the *County Chronicle*. Was it true, he said, that the boat belonging to the late Mrs. de Winter had been found.'

'What did you say?'

'I said, Yes, a boat had been found, but that was all we know. It might not be her boat at all.'

'Was that all he said?'

'No. He asked if I could confirm the rumour that a body had been found in the cabin.'

'No!'

'Yes. Someone must have been talking. Not Searle, I know that. The diver, one of his friends. You can't stop these people. The whole story will be all over Kerrith by breakfast time to-morrow.'

'What did you say, about the body?'

'I said I did not know. I had no statement to make. And I should be obliged if he did not ring me up again.'

'You will irritate them. You will have them against you.'

'I can't help that. I don't make statements to newspapers. I won't have those fellows ringing up and asking questions.'

'We might want them on our side,' I said.

'If it comes to fighting, I'll fight alone,' he said. 'I don't want a newspaper behind me.'

'The reporter will ring up someone else,' I said. 'He will get on to Colonel Julyan or Captain Searle.'

'He won't get much change out of them,' said Maxim.

'If only we could do something,' I said, 'all these hours ahead of us, and we sit here, idle, waiting for to-morrow morning.'

'There's nothing we can do,' said Maxim.

We went on sitting in the library. Maxim picked up a book but I know he did not read. Now and again I saw him lift his head and listen, as though he heard the telephone again. But it did not ring again. No one disturbed us. We dressed for dinner as usual. It seemed incredible to me that this time last night I had been putting on my white dress, sitting before the mirror at my dressing-table, arranging the curled wig. It was like an old forgotten nightmare, something remembered months afterwards with doubts and disbelief. We had dinner. Frith served us, returned from his afternoon. His face was solemn, expressionless. I wondered if he had been in Kerrith, if he had heard anything.

After dinner we went back again to the library. We did not talk much. I sat on the floor at Maxim's feet, my head against his knees. He ran his fingers through my hair. Different from his old abstracted way. It was not like stroking Jasper any more. I felt his finger tips on the scalp of my head. Sometimes he kissed me. Sometimes he said things to me. There were no shadows between us any more, and when we were silent it was because the silence came to us of our own asking. I wondered how it was I could be so happy when our little world about us was so black. It was a strange sort of happiness. Not what I had dreamt about or expected. It was not the sort of happiness I had imagined in the lonely hours. There was nothing feverish or urgent about this. It was a quiet, still happiness. The library windows were open wide, and when we did not talk or touch one another we looked out at the dark dull sky.

It must have rained in the night for when I woke the next morning, just after seven, and got up, and looked out of the window, I saw the roses in the garden below were folded and drooping, and the grass banks leading to the woods were wet and silver. There was a little smell in the air of mist and damp, the smell that comes with the first fall of the leaf. I wondered if autumn would come upon us two months before her time. Maxim had not woken me when he got up at five. He must have crept from his bed and gone through the bathroom to his dressing-room without a sound. He would be down there now, in the bay, with Colonel Julyan, and Captain Searle, and the men from the lighter. The lighter would be there, the crane and the chain, and Rebecca's boat coming to the surface. I thought about it calmly, coolly, without feeling. I pictured them all down there in the bay, and the little dark hull of the boat rising slowly to the surface, sodden, dripping, the grass-green seaweed and the shells clinging to her sides. When they lifted her on to the lighter the water would stream from her sides, back into the sea again. The wood of the little boat would look soft and grey, pulpy in places. She would smell of mud and rust, and that dark black weed that grows deep beneath the sea beside rocks that are never uncovered. Perhaps the name-board still hung upon her stern. *Je Reviens.* The lettering green and faded. The nails rusted through. And Rebecca herself was there, lying on the cabin floor.

I got up and had my bath and dressed, and went down to breakfast at nine o'clock as usual. There were a lot of letters on my plate. Letters from people thanking us for the dance. I skimmed through them, I did not read them all. Frith wanted to know whether to keep the breakfast hot for Maxim. I told him I did not know when he would be back. He had to go out very early, I said. Frith did not say anything. He looked very solemn, very grave. I wondered if he knew.

After breakfast I took my letters along to the morning-room. The room smelt fusty, the windows had not been opened. I flung them wide, letting in the cool fresh air. The flowers on the mantelpiece were drooping, many of them dead. The petals lay on the floor. I rang the bell, and Maud, the under-housemaid, came into the room.

'This room has not been touched this morning,' I said, 'even the windows were shut. And the flowers are dead. Will you please take them away.'

She looked nervous and apologetic. 'I'm very sorry, Madam,' she said. She went to the mantelpiece and took the vases.

'Don't let it happen again,' I said.

'No, Madam,' she said. She went out of the room, taking the flowers with her. I had not thought it would be so easy to be severe. I wondered why it had seemed hard for me before. The menu for the day lay on the writing-desk. Cold salmon and mayonnaise, cutlets in aspic, galantine of chicken, soufflé. I recognised them all from the buffet-supper of the night of the ball. We were evidently still living on the remains. This must be the cold lunch that was put out in the dining-room yesterday and I had not eaten. The staff were taking things easily, it seemed. I put a pencil through the list and rang for Robert. 'Tell Mrs. Danvers to order something hot,' I said. 'If there's still a lot of cold stuff to finish we don't want it in the dining-room.'

'Very good, Madam,' he said.

I followed him out of the room and went to the little flower-room for my scissors. Then I went into the rose-garden and cut some young buds. The chill had worn away from the air. It was going to be as hot and airless as yesterday had been. I wondered if they were still down in the bay or whether they had gone back to the creek in Kerrith harbour. Presently I should hear. Presently Maxim would come back and tell me. Whatever happened I must be calm and quiet. Whatever happened I must not be afraid. I cut my roses and took them back into the morning-room. The carpet had been dusted, and the fallen petals removed. I began to arrange the flowers in the vases that Robert had filled with water. When I had nearly finished there was a knock on the door.

'Come in,' I said.

It was Mrs. Danvers. She had the menu list in her hand. She looked pale and tired. There were great rings round her eyes.

'Good-morning, Mrs. Danvers,' I said.

'I don't understand,' she began, 'why you sent the menu out and the message by Robert. Why did you do it?'

I looked across at her, a rose in my hand.

'Those cutlets and that salmon were sent in yesterday,' I said. 'I saw them on the side-board. I should prefer something hot to-day. If they won't eat the cold in the kitchen you had better throw the stuff away. So much waste goes on in this house anyway that a little more won't make any difference.'

She stared at me. She did not say anything. I put the rose in the vase with the others.

'Don't tell me you can't think of anything to give us, Mrs. Danvers,' I said. 'You must have menus for all occasions in your room.'

'I'm not used to having messages sent to me by Robert,' she said. 'If Mrs. de Winter wanted anything changed she would ring me personally on the house telephone.'

'I'm afraid it does not concern me very much what Mrs. de Winter used to do,' I said. 'I am Mrs. de Winter now, you know. And if I choose to send a message by Robert I shall do so.'

Just then Robert came into the room. 'The *County Chronicle* on the telephone, Madam,' he said.

'Tell the *County Chronicle* I'm not at home,' I said.

'Yes, Madam,' he said. He went out of the room.

'Well, Mrs. Danvers, is there anything else?' I said.

She went on staring at me. Still she did not say anything. 'If you have nothing else to say you had better go and tell the cook about the hot lunch,' I said. 'I'm rather busy.'

'Why did the *County Chronicle* want to speak to you?' she said.

'I haven't the slightest idea, Mrs. Danvers,' I said.

'Is it true,' she said slowly, 'the story Frith brought back with him from Kerrith last night, that Mrs. de Winter's boat has been found?'

'Is there such a story?' I said. 'I'm afraid I don't know anything about it.'

'Captain Searle, the Kerrith harbour-master, called here yesterday, didn't he?' she said. 'Robert told me, Robert showed him in. Frith says the story in Kerrith is that the diver who went down about the ship there in the bay found Mrs. de Winter's boat.'

'Perhaps so,' I said. 'You had better wait until Mr. de Winter himself comes in and ask him about it.'

'Why was Mr. de Winter up so early?' she asked.

'That was Mr. de Winter's business,' I said.

She went on staring at me. 'Frith said the story goes that there was a body in the cabin of the little boat,' she said. 'Why should there be a body there? Mrs. de Winter always sailed alone.'

'It's no use asking me, Mrs. Danvers,' I said. 'I don't know any more than you do.'

'Don't you?' she said slowly. She kept on looking at me. I turned away, I put the vase back on the table by the window.

'I will give the orders about the lunch,' she said. She waited a moment. I did not say anything. Then she went out of the room. She can't frighten me any more, I thought. She has lost her power with Rebecca. Whatever she said or did now it could not matter to me or hurt me. I knew she was my enemy and I did not mind. But if she should learn the truth about the body in the boat and become Maxim's enemy too – what then? I sat down in the chair. I put the scissors on the table. I did not feel like doing any more roses. I kept wondering what Maxim was doing. I wondered why the reporter from the *County Chronicle* had rung us up again. The old sick feeling came back inside me. I went and leant out of the window. It was very hot. There was thunder in the air. The gardeners began to mow the grass again. I could see one of the men with his machine walk backwards and forwards on the top of the bank. I could not go on sitting in the morning-room. I left my scissors and my roses and went out on to the terrace. I began to walk up and down. Jasper padded after me, wondering why I did not take him for a walk. I went on walking up and down the terrace. About half-past eleven Frith came out to me from the hall.

'Mr. de Winter on the telephone, Madam,' he said.

I went through the library to the little room beyond. My hands were shaking as I lifted the receiver.

'Is that you?' he said. 'It's Maxim. I'm speaking from the office. I'm with Frank.'

'Yes?' I said.

There was a pause. 'I shall be bringing Frank and Colonel Julyan back to lunch at one o'clock,' he said.

'Yes,' I said.

I waited. I waited for him to go on. 'They were able to raise the boat,' he said. 'I've just got back from the creek.'

'Yes,' I said.

'Searle was there, and Colonel Julyan, and Frank, and the others,' he said. I wondered if Frank was standing beside him at the telephone, and if that was the reason he was so cool, so distant.

'All right then' he said, 'expect us about one o'clock.'

I put back the receiver. He had not told me anything. I still did not know what had happened. I went back again to the terrace, telling Frith first that we should be four to lunch instead of two.

An hour dragged past, slow, interminable. I went upstairs and changed into a thinner frock. I came down again. I went and sat in the drawing-room and waited. At five minutes to one I heard the sound of a car in the drive, and then voices in the hall. I patted my hair in front of the looking-glass. My face was very white. I pinched some colour into my cheeks and stood up waiting for them to come into the room. Maxim came in, and Frank, and Colonel Julyan. I remembered seeing Colonel Julyan at the ball dressed as Cromwell. He looked shrunken now, different. A smaller man altogether.

'How do you do?' he said. He spoke quietly, gravely, like a doctor.

'Ask Frith to bring the sherry,' said Maxim. 'I'm going to wash.'

'I'll have a wash too,' said Frank. Before I rang the bell Frith appeared with the sherry. Colonel Julyan did not have any. I took some to give me something to hold. Colonel Julyan came and stood beside me by the window.

'This is a most distressing thing, Mrs. de Winter,' he said gently. 'I do feel for you and your husband most acutely.'

'Thank you,' I said. I began to sip my sherry. Then I put the glass back again on the table. I was afraid he would notice that my hand was shaking.

'What makes it so difficult was the fact of your husband identifying that first body, over a year ago,' he said.

'I don't quite understand,' I said.

'You did not hear then, what we found this morning?' he said.

'I knew there was a body. The diver found a body,' I said.

'Yes,' he said. And then, half glancing over his shoulder towards the hall, 'I'm afraid it was her, without a doubt,' he said, lowering his voice. 'I can't go into details with you, but the evidence was sufficient for your husband and Doctor Phillips to identify.'

He stopped suddenly, and moved away from me. Maxim and Frank had come back into the room.

'Lunch is ready, shall we go in?' said Maxim.

I led the way into the hall, my heart like a stone, heavy, numb. Colonel Julyan sat on my right, Frank on my left. I did not look at Maxim. Frith and Robert began to hand the first course. We all talked about the weather. 'I see in *The Times* they had it well over eighty in London yesterday,' said Colonel Julyan.

'Really?' I said.

'Yes. Must be frightful for the poor devils who can't get away.'

'Yes, frightful,' I said.

'Paris can be hotter than London,' said Frank, 'I remember staying a week-end in Paris in the middle of August, and it was quite impossible to sleep. There was not a breath of air in the whole city. The temperature was over ninety.'

'Of course the French always sleep with their windows shut, don't they?' said Colonel Julyan.

'I don't know,' said Frank. 'I was staying in a hotel. The people were mostly Americans.'

'You know France of course, Mrs. de Winter?' said Colonel Julyan.

'Not so very well,' I said.

'Oh, I had the idea you had lived many years out there.'

'No,' I said.

'She was staying in Monte Carlo when I met her,' said Maxim. 'You don't call that France, do you?'

'No, I suppose not,' said Colonel Julyan, 'it must be very cosmopolitan. The coast is pretty though, isn't it?'

'Very pretty,' I said.

'Not so rugged as this, eh? Still, I know which I'd rather have. Give me England every time, when it comes to settling down. You know where you are over here.'

'I dare say the French feel that about France,' said Maxim.

'Oh, no doubt,' said Colonel Julyan.

We went on eating awhile in silence. Frith stood behind my chair. We were all thinking of one thing, but because of Frith we had to keep up our little performance. I supposed Frith was thinking about it too, and I thought how much easier it would be if we cast aside convention and let him join in with us, if he had anything to say. Robert came with the drinks. Our plates were changed. The second course was handed. Mrs. Danvers had not forgotten my wish for hot food. I took something out of a casserole covered in mushroom sauce.

'I think everyone enjoyed your wonderful party the other night,' said Colonel Julyan.

'I'm so glad,' I said.

'Does an immense amount of good locally, that sort of thing,' he said.

'Yes, I suppose it does,' I said.

'It's a universal instinct of the human species, isn't it, that desire to dress up in some sort of disguise?' said Frank.

'I must be very inhuman then,' said Maxim.

'It's natural I suppose,' said Colonel Julyan, 'for all of us to wish to look different. We are all children in some ways.'

I wondered how much pleasure it had given him to disguise himself as Cromwell. I had not seen much of him at the ball. He had spent most of the evening in the morning-room, playing bridge.

'You don't play golf do you, Mrs. de Winter?' said Colonel Julyan.

'No, I'm afraid I don't,' I said.

'You ought to take it up,' he said. 'My eldest girl is very keen, and she can't find many young people to play with her. I gave her a small car for her birthday and she drives herself over to the north coast nearly every day. It gives her something to do.'

'How nice,' I said.

'She ought to have been the boy,' he said. 'My lad is different altogether. No earthly use at games. Always writing poetry. I suppose he'll grow out of it.'

'Oh, rather,' said Frank. 'I used to write poetry myself when I was his age. Awful nonsense too. I never write any now.'

'Good heavens, I should hope not,' said Maxim.

'I don't know where my boy gets it from,' said Colonel Julyan, 'certainly not from his mother or from me.'

There was another long silence. Colonel Julyan had a second dip into the casserole. 'Mrs. Lacy looked very well the other night,' he said.

'Yes,' I said.

'Her dress came adrift as usual,' said Maxim.

'Those Eastern garments must be the devil to manage,' said Colonel Julyan, 'and yet they say, you know, they are far more comfortable and far cooler than anything you ladies wear in England.'

'Really?' I said.

'Yes, so they say. It seems all that loose drapery throws off the hot rays of the sun.'

'How curious,' said Frank, 'you'd think it would have just the opposite effect.'

'No, apparently not,' said Colonel Julyan.

'Do you know the East, sir?' said Frank.

'I know the Far East,' said Colonel Julyan. 'I was in China for five years. Then Singapore.'

'Isn't that where they make curry?' I said.

'Yes, they gave us very good curry in Singapore,' he said.

'I'm fond of curry,' said Frank.

'Ah, it's not curry at all in England, it's hash,' said Colonel Julyan.

The plates were cleared away. A soufflé was handed, and a bowl of fruit salad. 'I suppose you are coming to the end of your raspberries,' said Colonel

Julyan. 'It's been a wonderful summer for them, hasn't it? We've put down pots and pots of jam.'

'I never think raspberry jam is a great success,' said Frank, 'there are always so many pips.'

'You must come and try some of ours,' said Colonel Julyan. 'I don't think we have a great lot of pips.'

'We're going to have a mass of apples this year at Manderley,' said Frank. 'I was saying to Maxim a few days ago we ought to have a record season. We shall be able to send a lot up to London.'

'Do you really find it pays?' said Colonel Julyan. 'By the time you've paid your men for the extra labour, and then the packing, and carting, do you make any sort of profit worth while?'

'Oh, Lord yes,' said Frank.

'How interesting. I must tell my wife,' said Colonel Julyan.

The soufflé and the fruit salad did not take long to finish. Robert appeared with cheese and biscuits, and a few minutes later Frith came with the coffee and cigarettes. Then they both went out of the room and shut the door. We drank our coffee in silence. I gazed steadily at my plate.

'I was saying to your wife before luncheon, de Winter,' began Colonel Julyan, resuming his first quiet confidential tone, 'that the awkward part of this whole distressing business is the fact that you identified the original body.'

'Yes, quite,' said Maxim.

'I think the mistake was very natural under the circumstances,' said Frank quickly. 'The authorities wrote to Maxim, asking him to go up to Edgecoombe, presupposing before he arrived there that the body was hers. And Maxim was not well at the time. I wanted to go with him, but he insisted on going alone. He was not in a fit to state to undertake anything of the sort.'

'That's nonsense,' said Maxim. 'I was perfectly well.'

'Well, it's no use going into all that now,' said Colonel Julyan. 'You made that first identification, and now the only thing to do is to admit the error. There seems to be no doubt about it this time.'

'No,' said Maxim.

'I wish you could be spared the formality and the publicity of an inquest,' said Colonel Julyan, 'but I'm afraid that's quite impossible.'

'Naturally,' said Maxim.

'I don't think it need take very long,' said Colonel Julyan. 'It's just a case of you re-affirming identification, and then getting Tabb, who you say converted the boat when your wife bought her from France, just to give his piece of evidence that the boat was sea-worthy and in good order when he last had her in his yard. It's just red-tape you know. But it has to be done. No, what bothers me is the wretched publicity of the affair. So sad and unpleasant for you and your wife.'

'That's quite all right,' said Maxim. 'We understand.'

'So unfortunate that wretched ship going ashore there,' said Colonel Julyan, 'but for that the whole matter would have rested in peace.'

'Yes,' said Maxim.

'The only consolation is that now we know poor Mrs. de Winter's death must have been swift and sudden, not the dreadful slow lingering affair we all believed it to be. There can have been no question of trying to swim.'

'None,' said Maxim.

'She must have gone down for something, and then the door jammed, and a squall caught the boat without anyone at the helm,' said Colonel Julyan. 'A dreadful thing.'

'Yes,' said Maxim.

'That seems to be the solution, don't you think, Crawley?' said Colonel Julyan, turning to Frank.

'Oh, yes, undoubtedly,' said Frank.

I glanced up and I saw Frank looking at Maxim. He looked away again immediately but not before I had seen and understood the expression in his eyes. Frank knew. And Maxim did not know that he knew. I went on stirring my coffee. My hand was hot, damp.

'I suppose sooner or later we all make a mistake in judgement,' said Colonel Julyan, 'and then we are for it. Mrs. de Winter must have known how the wind comes down like a funnel in that bay, and that it was not safe to leave the helm of a small boat like that. She must have sailed alone over that spot scores of times. And then the moment came, she took a chance – and the chance killed her. It's a lesson to all of us.'

'Accidents happen so easily,' said Frank, 'even to the most experienced people. Think of the number killed out hunting every season.'

'Oh, I know. But then it's the horse falling generally that lets you down. If Mrs. de Winter had not left the helm of her boat the accident would never have happened. An extraordinary thing to do. I must have watched her many times in the handicap race on Saturdays from Kerrith, and I never saw her make an elementary mistake. It's the sort of thing a novice would do. In that particular place too, just by the ridge.'

'It was very squally that night,' said Frank, 'something may have happened to the gear. Something may have jammed. And then she slipped down for a knife.'

'Of course. Of course. Well, we shall never know. And I don't suppose we should be any the better for it if we did. As I said before, I wish I could stop this inquest but I can't. I'm trying to arrange it for Tuesday morning, and it will be as short as possible. Just a formal matter. But I'm afraid we shan't be able to keep the reporters out of it.'

There was another silence. I judged the time had come to push back my chair.

'Shall we go into the garden?' I said.

We all stood up, and then I led the way to the terrace. Colonel Julyan patted Jasper.

'He's grown into a nice-looking dog,' he said.

'Yes,' I said.

'They make nice pets,' he said.

'Yes,' I said.

We stood about for a minute. Then he glanced at his watch.

'Thank you for your most excellent lunch,' he said. 'I have rather a busy afternoon in front of me, and I hope you will excuse me dashing away.'

'Of course,' I said.

'I'm so very sorry this should have happened. You have all my sympathy. I consider it's almost harder for you than for your husband. However, once the inquest is over you must both forget all about it.'

'Yes,' I said, 'yes, we must try to.'

'My car is here in the drive. I wonder whether Crawley would like a lift. Crawley? I can drop you at your office if it's any use.'

'Thank you, sir,' said Frank.

He came and took my hand. 'I shall be seeing you again,' he said.

'Yes,' I said.

I did not look at him. I was afraid he would understand my eyes. I did not want him to know that I knew. Maxim walked with them to the car. When they had gone he came back to me on the terrace. He took my arm. We stood looking down at the green lawns towards the sea and the beacon on the headland.

'It's going to be all right,' he said. 'I'm quite calm, quite confident. You saw how Julyan was at lunch, and Frank. There won't be any difficulty at the inquest. It's going to be all right.'

I did not say anything. I held his arm tightly.

'There was never any question of the body being someone unknown,' he said. 'What we saw was enough for Doctor Phillips even to make the identification alone without me. It was straightforward, simple. There was no trace of what I'd done. The bullet had not touched the bone.'

A butterfly sped past us on the terrace, silly and inconsequent.

'You heard what they said,' he went on, 'they think she was trapped there, in the cabin. The jury will believe that at the inquest too. Phillips will tell them so.' He paused. Still I did not speak.

'I only mind for you,' he said, 'I don't regret anything else. If it had to come all over again I should not do anything different. I'm glad I killed Rebecca, I shall never have any remorse for that, never, never. But you. I can't forget what it has done to you. I was looking at you, thinking of nothing else all through lunch. It's gone forever, that funny, young, lost look that I loved. It won't come back again. I killed that too, when I told you about Rebecca . . . It's gone, in twenty-four hours. You are so much older. . . .'

Chapter Twenty-two

That evening, when Frith brought in the local paper, there were great headlines right across the top of the page. He brought the paper and laid it down on the table. Maxim was not there, he had gone up early to change for dinner. Frith stood a moment, waiting for me to say something, and it seemed to me stupid and insulting to ignore a matter that must mean so much to everyone in the house.

'This is a very dreadful thing, Frith,' I said.

'Yes, Madam, we are all most distressed outside,' he said.

'It's so sad for Mr. de Winter,' I said, 'having to go through it all again.'

'Yes, Madam. Very sad. Such a shocking experience, Madam, having to identify the second body having seen the first. I suppose there is no doubt then, that the remains in the boat are genuinely those of the late Mrs. de Winter?'

'I'm afraid not, Frith. No doubt at all.'

'It seems so odd to us, Madam, that she should have let herself be trapped like that in the cabin. She was so experienced in a boat.'

'Yes, Frith. That's what we all feel. But accidents will happen. And how it happened I don't suppose any of us will ever know.'

'I suppose not, Madam. But it's a great shock, all the same. We are most distressed about it outside. And coming suddenly, just after the party. It doesn't seem right somehow, does it?'

'No, Frith.'

'It seems there is to be an inquest, Madam?'

'Yes. A formality, you know.'

'Of course, Madam. I wonder if any of us will be required to give evidence?'

'I don't think so.'

'I shall be only too pleased to do anything that might help the family, Mr. de Winter knows that.'

'Yes, Frith. I'm sure he does.'

'I've told them outside not to discuss the matter, but it's very difficult to keep an eye on them, especially the girls. I can deal with Robert of course. I'm afraid the news has been a great shock to Mrs. Danvers.'

'Yes, Frith. I rather expected it would.'

'She went up to her room straight after lunch, and has not come down again. Alice took her a cup of tea and the paper a few minutes ago. She said Mrs. Danvers looked very ill indeed.'

'It would be better really if she stayed where she is,' I said. 'It's no use her getting up and seeing to things if she is ill. Perhaps Alice would tell her that. I can very well manage the ordering. The cook and I between us.'

'Yes, Madam. I don't think she is physically ill, Madam, it's just the shock of Mrs. de Winter being found. She was very devoted to Mrs. de Winter.'

'Yes,' I said. 'Yes, I know.'

Frith went out of the room after that, and I glanced quickly at the paper before Maxim came down. There was a great column, all down the front page, and an awful blurred photograph of Maxim that must have been taken at least fifteen years ago. It was dreadful, seeing it there on the front page staring at me. And the little line about myself at the bottom, saying who Maxim had married as his second wife, and how we had just given the fancy dress ball at Manderley. It sounded so crude and callous, in the dark print of the newspaper. Rebecca, whom they described as beautiful, talented, and loved by all who knew her, having been drowned a year ago, and then Maxim marrying again the following spring, bringing his bride straight to Manderley (so it said) and giving the big fancy dress ball in her honour. And then the following morning the body of his first wife being found, trapped in the cabin of her sailing boat, at the bottom of the bay.

It was true of course, though sprinkled with little inaccuracies that added to the story, making it strong meat for the hundreds of readers who wanted value for their pennies. Maxim sounded vile in it, a sort of satyr. Bringing back his 'young bride,' as it described me, to Manderley, and giving the dance, as though we wanted to display ourselves before the world.

I hid the paper under the cushion of the chair so that Maxim should not see it. But I could not keep the morning editions from him. The story was in our London papers too. There was a picture of Manderley, and the story underneath. Manderley was news, and so was Maxim. They talked about him as Max de Winter. It sounded racy, horrible. Each paper made great play of the fact that Rebecca's body had been found the day after the fancy dress ball, as though there was something deliberate about it. Both papers used the same word, 'ironic'. Yes, I supposed it was ironic. It made a good story. I watched Maxim at the breakfast table getting whiter and whiter as he read the papers, one after the other, and then the local one as well. He did not say anything. He just looked across at me, and I stretched out my hand to him. 'Damn them,' he whispered, 'damn them, damn them.'

I thought of all the things they could say, if they knew the truth. Not one column, but five or six. Placards in London. Newsboys shouting in the streets, outside the underground stations. That frightful word of six letters, in the middle of the placard, large and black.

Frank came up after breakfast. He looked pale and tired, as though he had not slept. 'I've told the exchange to put all calls for Manderley, through to the office,' he said to Maxim. 'It doesn't matter who it is. If reporters ring up I can deal with them. And anyone else too. I don't want either of you to be worried at all. We've had several calls already from locals. I gave the same answer to each. Mr. and Mrs. de Winter were grateful for all sympathetic enquiries, and they hoped their friends would understand that they were not receiving calls during the next few days. Mrs. Lacy rang up about eight-thirty. Wanted to come over at once.'

'Oh, my God. . . .' began Maxim.

'It's all right, I prevented her. I told her quite truthfully that I did not think she would do any good by coming over. That you did not want to see anyone but Mrs. de Winter. She wanted to know when they were holding the inquest but I told her it had not been settled. I don't know that we can stop her from coming to that, if she finds it in the papers.'

'Those blasted reporters,' said Maxim.

'I know,' said Frank, 'we all want to wring their necks, but you've got to see their point of view. It's their bread-and-butter, they've got to do the job for their paper. If they don't get a story the editor probably sacks them. If the editor does not produce a saleable edition the proprietor sacks him. And if the paper doesn't sell, the proprietor loses all his money. You won't have to see them or speak to them, Maxim. I'm going to do all that for you. All you have to concentrate on is your statement at the inquest.'

'I know what to say,' said Maxim.

'Of course you do, but don't forget old Horridge is the Coroner. He's a sticky sort of chap, goes into details that are quite irrelevant, just to show the jury how thorough he is at his job. You must not let him rattle you.'

'Why the devil should I be rattled? I have nothing to be rattled about.'

'Of course not. But I've attended these coroner's inquests before, and it's so easy to get nervy and irritable. You don't want to put the fellow's back up.'

'Frank's right,' I said. 'I know just what he means. The swifter and smoother the whole thing goes the easier it will be for everyone. Then, once the wretched thing is over we shall forget all about it, and so will everyone else, won't they, Frank?'

'Yes, of course,' said Frank.

I still avoided his eye, but I was more convinced than ever that he knew the truth. He had always known it. From the very first. I remembered the first time I met him, that first day of mine at Manderley, when he, and Beatrice, and Giles had all been at lunch, and Beatrice had been tactless about Maxim's health. I remembered Frank, his quiet turning of the subject, the way he had come to Maxim's aid in his quiet unobtrusive manner if there was ever any question of difficulty. That strange reluctance of his to talk about Rebecca, his stiff, funny, pompous way of making conversation whenever we had approached anything like intimacy. I understood it all. Frank knew, but Maxim did not know that he knew. And Frank did not want Maxim to know that he knew. And we all stood there, looking at one another, keeping up these little barriers between us.

We were not bothered with the telephone again. All the calls were put through to the office. It was just a question of waiting now. Waiting until the Tuesday.

I saw nothing of Mrs. Danvers. The menu was sent through as usual, and I did not change it. I asked little Clarice about her. She said she was going about her work as usual but she was not speaking to anybody. She had all her meals alone in her sitting-room.

Clarice was wide-eyed, evidently curious, but she did not ask me any questions, and I was not going to discuss it with her. No doubt they talked of nothing else, out in the kitchen, and on the estate too, in the lodge, on the farms. I supposed all Kerrith was full of it. We stayed in Manderley, in the gardens close to the house. We did not even walk in the woods. The weather had not broken yet. It was still hot, oppressive. The air was full of thunder, and there was rain behind the white dull sky, but it did not fall. I could feel it, and smell it, pent up there, behind the clouds. The inquest was to be on the Tuesday afternoon at two o'clock.

We had lunch at a quarter-to-one. Frank came. Thank heaven Beatrice had telephoned that she could not get over. The boy Roger had arrived home with measles; they were all in quarantine. I could not help blessing the measles. I don't think Maxim could have borne it, with Beatrice sitting here, staying in the house, sincere, anxious, and affectionate, but asking questions all the time. Forever asking questions.

Lunch was a hurried, nervous meal. We none of us talked very much. I had that nagging pain again. I did not want anything to eat. I could not swallow. It was a relief when the farce of the meal was over, and I heard Maxim go out on to the drive and start up the car. The sound of the engine steadied me. It means we had to go, we had to be doing something. Not just sitting at Manderley. Frank followed us in his own car. I had my hand on Maxim's knee all the way as he drove. He seemed quite calm. Not nervous in any way. It was like going with someone to a nursing-home, someone who was to have an operation. And not knowing what would happen. Whether the operation would be successful. My hands were very cold. My heart was beating in a funny, jerky way. And all the time that little nagging pain beneath my heart. The inquest was to be held at Lanyon, the market town six miles the other side of Kerrith. We had to park the cars in the big cobbled square by the market-place. Doctor Phillips' car was there already, and also Colonel Julyan's. Other cars too. I saw a passerby stare curiously at Maxim, and then nudge her companion's arm.

'I think I shall stay here,' I said. 'I don't think I'll come in with you after all.'

'I did not want you to come,' said Maxim. 'I was against it from the first. You'd much better have stayed at Manderley.'

'No,' I said. 'No, I'll be all right here, sitting in the car.'

Frank came and looked in at the window. 'Isn't Mrs. de Winter coming?' he said.

'No,' said Maxim. 'She wants to stay in the car.'

'I think she's right,' said Frank, 'there's no earthly reason why she should be present at all. We shan't be long.'

'It's all right,' I said.

'I'll keep a seat for you,' said Frank, 'in case you should change your mind.'

They went off together and left me sitting there. It was early-closing day.

The shops looked drab and dull. There were not many people about. Lanyon was not much of a holiday centre anyway, it was too far inland. I sat looking at the silent shops. The minutes went by. I wondered what they were doing, the Coroner, Frank, Maxim, Colonel Julyan. I got out of the car and began walking up and down the market square. I went and looked in a shop window. Then I walked up and down again. I saw a policeman watching me curiously. I turned up a side-street to avoid him.

Somehow, in spite of myself, I found I was coming to the building where the inquest was being held. There had been little publicity about the actual time, and because of this there was no crowd waiting, as I had feared and expected. The place seemed deserted. I went up the steps and stood just inside the door.

A policeman appeared from nowhere. 'Do you want anything?' he said.

'No,' I said. 'No.'

'You can't wait here,' he said.

'I'm sorry,' I said. I went back towards the steps into the street.

'Excuse me, Madam,' he said, 'aren't you Mrs. de Winter?'

'Yes,' I said.

'Of course that's different,' he said, 'you can wait here if you like. Would you like to take a seat just inside this room?'

'Thank you,' I said.

He showed me into a little bare room with a desk in it. It was like a waiting-room at a station. I sat there, with my hands on my lap. Five minutes passed. Nothing happened. It was worse than being outside, than sitting in the car. I got up and went into the passage. The policeman was still standing there.

'How long will they be?' I said.

'I'll go and enquire if you like,' he said.

He disappeared along the passage. In a moment he came back again. 'I don't think they will be very much longer,' he said. 'Mr. de Winter has just given his evidence. Captain Searle, and the diver, and Doctor Phillips have already given theirs. There's only one more to speak. Mr. Tabb, the boat-builder from Kerrith.'

'Then it's nearly over,' I said.

'I expect so, Madam,' he said. Then he said, on a sudden thought, 'Would you like to hear the remaining evidence? There is a seat there, just inside the door. If you slip in now nobody will notice you.'

'Yes,' I said. 'Yes, I think I will.'

It was nearly over. Maxim had finished giving his evidence. I did not mind hearing the rest. It was Maxim I had not wanted to hear. I had been nervous of listening to his evidence. That was why I had not gone with him and Frank in the first place. Now it did not matter. His part of it was over.

I followed the policeman, and he opened a door at the end of the passage. I slipped in, I sat down just by the door. I kept my head low so that I did not have to look at anybody. The room was smaller than I had imagined. Rather hot and stuffy. I had pictured a great bare room with benches, like a church. Maxim and Frank were sitting down at the other end. The

Coroner was a thin, elderly man in pince-nez. There were people there I did not know. I glanced at them out of the tail of my eye. My heart gave a jump suddenly as I recognised Mrs. Danvers. She was sitting right at the back. And Favell was beside her. Jack Favell, Rebecca's cousin. He was leaning forward, his chin in his hands, his eyes fixed on the Coroner, Mr. Horridge. I had not expected him to be there. I wondered if Maxim had seen him. James Tabb, the boat-builder, was standing up now and the Coroner was asking him a question.

'Yes, sir,' answered Tabb, 'I converted Mrs. de Winter's little boat. She was a French fishing boat originally, and Mrs. de Winter bought her for next to nothing over in Britanny, and had her shipped over. She gave me the job of converting her and doing her up like a little yacht.'

'Was the boat in a fit state to put to sea?' said the Coroner.

'She was when I fitted her out in April of last year,' said Tabb. 'Mrs. de Winter laid her up as usual at my yard in the October, and then in March I had word from her to fit her up as usual, which I did. That would be Mrs. de Winter's fourth season with the boat since I did the conversion job for her.'

'Had the boat ever been known to capsize before?' asked the Coroner.

'No, sir. I should soon have heard of it from Mrs. de Winter had there been any question of it. She was delighted with the boat in every way, according to what she said to me.'

'I suppose great care was needed to handle the boat?' said the Coroner.

'Well, sir, everyone has to have their wits about them, when they go sailing boats, I won't deny it. But Mrs. de Winter's boat wasn't one of those cranky little crafts that you can't leave for a moment, like some of the boats you see in Kerrith. She was a stout sea-worthy boat, and could stand a lot of wind. Mrs. de Winter had sailed her in worse weather than she ever found that night. Why, it was only blowing in fits and starts at the time. That's what I've said all along. I couldn't understand Mrs. de Winter's boat being lost on a night like that.'

'But surely, if Mrs. de Winter went below for a coat, as is supposed, and a sudden puff of wind was to come down from that headland, it would be enough to capsize the boat?' asked the Coroner.

James Tabb shook his head. 'No,' he said stubbornly, 'I don't see that it would.'

'Well, I'm afraid that is what must have happened,' said the Coroner. 'I don't think Mr. de Winter or any of us suggest that your workmanship was to blame for the accident at all. You fitted the boat out at the beginning of the season, you reported her sound and sea-worthy, and that's all I want to know. Unfortunately the late Mrs. de Winter relaxed her watchfulness for a moment and she lost her life, the boat sinking with her aboard. Such accidents have happened before. I repeat again we are not blaming you.'

'Excuse me, sir,' said the boat-builder, 'but there is a little bit more to it than that. And if you would allow me I should like to make a further statement.'

'Very well, go on,' said the Coroner.

'It's like this, sir. After the accident last year a lot of people in Kerrith made unpleasantness about my work. Some said I had let Mrs. de Winter start the season in a leaky, rotten boat. I lost two or three orders because of it. It was very unfair, but the boat had sunk, and there was nothing I could say to clear myself. Then that steamer went ashore, as we all know, and Mrs. de Winter's little boat was found, and brought to the surface. Captain Searle himself gave me permission yesterday to go and look at her, and I did. I wanted to satisfy myself that the work I had put in to her was sound, in spite of the fact that she had been waterlogged for twelve months or more.'

'Well, that was very natural,' said the Coroner, 'and I hope you were satisfied.'

'Yes, sir, I was. There was nothing wrong with that boat as regards the work I did to her. I examined every corner of her there on the lighter up the pill where Captain Searle had put her. She had sunk on sandy bottom, I asked the diver about that, and he told me so. She had not touched the ridge at all. The ridge was a clear five feet away. She was lying on sand, and there wasn't the mark of a rock on her.'

He paused. The Coroner looked at him expectantly.

'Well,' he said, 'is that all you want to say?'

'No, sir,' said Tabb emphatically, 'it's not. What I want to know is this. Who drove the holes in her planking? Rocks didn't do it. The nearest rock was five feet away. Besides, they weren't the sort of marks made by a rock. They were holes. Done with a spike.'

I did not look at him. I was looking at the floor. There was oil-cloth laid on the boards. Green oil-cloth. I looked at it.

I wondered why the Coroner did not say something. Why did the pause last so long? When he spoke at last his voice sounded rather far away.

'What do you mean?' he said. 'What sort of holes?'

'There were three of them altogether,' said the boat-builder, 'one right for'ard, by her chain locker, on her starboard planking, below the water-line. The other two close together amidships, underneath her floor boards, in the bottom. The ballast had been shifted too. It was lying loose. And that's not all. The sea-cocks had been turned on.'

'The sea-cocks? What are they?' asked the Coroner.

'The fitting that plugs the pipes leading from a wash-basin or lavatory, sir. Mrs. de Winter had a little place fitted up right aft. And there was a sink for'ard, where the washing-up was done. There was a sea-cock there, and another in the lavatory. These are always kept tight closed when you're under way, otherwise the water would flow in. When I examined the boat yesterday both sea-cocks were turned full on.'

It was hot, much too hot. Why didn't they open a window? We should be suffocated if we sat here with the air like this, and there were so many people, all breathing the same air, so many people.

'With those holes in her planking, sir, and the sea-cocks not closed, it wouldn't take long for a small boat like her to sink. Not much more than ten minutes, I should say. Those holes weren't there when the boat left my yard. I was proud of my work, and so was Mrs. de Winter. It's my opinion, sir, that the boat never capsized at all. She was deliberately scuttled.'

I must try and get out of the door. I must try and go back to the waiting-room again. There was no air left in this place, and the person next to me was pressing close, close. . . . Someone in front of me was standing up, and they were talking, too, they were talking. I did not know what was happening. I could not see anything. It was hot, so very hot. The Coroner was asking everybody to be silent. And he said something about 'Mr. de Winter.' I could not see. That woman's hat was in front of me. Maxim was standing up now. I could not look at him. I must not look at him. I felt like this once before. When was it? I don't know. I don't know. I don't remember. Oh, yes, with Mrs. Danvers. The time Mrs. Danvers stood with me by the window. Mrs. Danvers was in this place now, listening to the Coroner. Maxim was standing up over there. The heat was coming up at me from the floor, rising in slow waves. It reached my hands, wet and slippery, it touched my neck, my chin, my face.

'Mr. de Winter, you heard the statement from James Tabb, who had the care of Mrs. de Winter's boat? Do you know anything of these holes driven in the planking?'

'Nothing whatever.'

'Can you think of any reason why they should be there?'

'No, of course not.'

'It's the first time you have heard them mentioned?'

'Yes.'

'It's a shock to you, of course?'

'It was shock enough to learn that I made a mistake in identification over twelve months ago, and now I learn that my late wife was not only drowned in the cabin of her boat, but that holes were bored in the boat with the deliberate intent of letting in the water so that the boat should sink. Does it surprise you that I should be shocked?'

No, Maxim. No. You will put his back up. You heard what Frank said. You must not put his back up. Not that voice. Not that angry voice, Maxim. He won't understand. Please, darling, please. Oh, God, don't let Maxim lose his temper. Don't let him lose his temper.

'Mr. de Winter, I want you to believe that we all feel very deeply for you in this matter. No doubt you have suffered a shock, a very severe shock, in learning that your late wife was drowned in her own cabin, and not at sea as you supposed. And I am enquiring into the matter for you. I want, for your sake, to find out exactly how and why she died. I don't conduct this enquiry for my own amusement.'

'That's rather obvious, isn't it?'

'I hope that it is. James Tabb has just told us that the boat which contained the remains of the late Mrs. de Winter had three holes hammered through her bottom. And that the sea-cocks were open. Do you doubt his statement?'

'Of course not. He's a boat-builder, he knows what he is talking about.'

'Who looked after Mrs. de Winter's boat?'

'She looked after it herself.'

'She employed no hand?'

'No, nobody at all.'

'The boat was moored in the private harbour belonging to Manderley?'

'Yes.'

'Any stranger who tried to tamper with the boat would be seen? There is no access to the harbour by public footpath?'

'No, none at all.'

'The harbour is quiet, is it not, and surrounded by trees?'

'Yes.'

'A trespasser might not be noticed?'

'Possibly not.'

'Yet James Tabb has told us, and we have no reason to disbelieve him, that a boat with those holes drilled in her bottom and the sea-cocks open could not float for more than ten or fifteen minutes.'

'Quite.'

'Therefore we can put aside the idea that the boat was tampered with maliciously before Mrs. de Winter went for her evening sail. Had that been the case the boat would have sunk at her moorings.'

'No doubt.'

'Therefore we must assume that whoever took the boat out that night drove in the planking and opened the sea-cocks.'

'I suppose so.'

'You have told us already that the door of the cabin was shut, the port-holes closed, and your wife's remains were on the floor. This was in your statement, and in Doctor Phillips', and in Captain Searle's?'

'Yes.'

'And now added to this is the information that a spike was driven through the bottom, and the sea-cocks were open. Does not this strike you, Mr. de Winter, as being very strange?'

'Certainly.'

'You have no suggestion to make?'

'No, none at all.'

'Mr. de Winter, painful as it may be, it is my duty to ask you a very personal question.'

'Yes.'

'Were relations between you and the late Mrs. de Winter perfectly happy?'

They had to come of course, those black spots in front of my eyes, dancing, flickering, stabbing the hazy air, and it was hot, so hot, with all these people, all these faces, and no open window; the door, from being near to me, was farther away than I had thought, and all the time the ground coming up to meet me.

And then, out of the queer mist around me, Maxim's voice, clear and strong, 'Will someone take my wife outside? She is going to faint.'

Chapter Twenty-three

I was sitting in the little room again. The room like a waiting-room at the station. The policeman was there, bending over me, giving me a glass of water, and someone's hand was on my arm, Frank's hand. I sat quite still, the floor, the walls, the figures of Frank and the policeman taking solid shape before me.

'I'm so sorry,' I said, 'such a stupid thing to do. It was so hot in that room, so very hot.'

'It gets very airless in there,' said the policeman, 'there's been complaints about it often, but nothing's ever done. We've had ladies fainting in there before.'

'Are you feeling better, Mrs. de Winter?' said Frank.

'Yes. Yes, much better. I shall be all right again. Don't wait with me.'

'I'm going to take you back to Manderley.'

'No.'

'Yes. Maxim has asked me to.'

'No. You ought to stay with him.'

'Maxim told me to take you back to Manderley.'

He put his arm through mine and helped me to get up. 'Can you walk as far as the car or shall I bring it round?'

'I can walk. But I'd much rather stay. I want to wait for Maxim.'

'Maxim may be a long time.'

Why did he say that? What did he mean? Why didn't he look at me? He took my arm and walked with me along the passage to the door, and so down the steps into the street. Maxim may be a long time. . . .

We did not speak. We came to the little Morris car belonging to Frank. He opened the door, and helped me in. Then he got in himself and started up the engine. We drove away from the cobbled market-place, through the empty town, and out on to the road to Kerrith.

'Why will they be a long time? What are they going to do?'

'They may have to go over the evidence again.' Frank looked straight in front of him along the hard white road.

'They've had all the evidence,' I said. 'There's nothing more anyone can say.'

'You never know,' said Frank, 'the Coroner may put his questions in a different way. Tabb has altered the whole business. The Coroner will have to approach it now from another angle.'

'What angle? How do you mean?'

'You heard the evidence? You heard what Tabb said about the boat? They won't believe in an accident any more.'

'It's absurd, Frank, it's ridiculous. They should not listen to Tabb. How can he tell, after all these months, how holes came to be in a boat? What are they trying to prove?'

'I don't know.'

'That Coroner will go on and on harping at Maxim, making him lose his temper, making him say things he doesn't mean. He will ask question after question, Frank, and Maxim won't stand it, I know he won't stand it.'

Frank did not answer. He was driving very fast. For the first time since I had known him he was at a loss for the usual conventional phrase. That meant he was worried, very worried. And usually he was such a slow careful driver, stopping dead at every cross-roads, peering to right and left, blowing his horn at every bend in the road.

'That man was there,' I said, 'that man who came once to Manderley to see Mrs. Danvers.'

'You mean Favell?' said Frank. 'Yes, I saw him.'

'He was sitting there, with Mrs. Danvers.'

'Yes, I know.'

'Why was he there? What right had he to go to the inquest?'

'He was her cousin.'

'It's not right that he and Mrs. Danvers should sit there, listening to that evidence. I don't trust them, Frank.'

'No.'

'They might do something; they might make mischief.'

Again Frank did not answer. I realised that his loyalty to Maxim was such that he would not let himself be drawn into a discussion, even with me. He did not know how much I knew. Nor could I tell for certainty how much he knew. We were allies, we travelled the same road, but we could not look at one another. We neither of us dared risk a confession. We were turning in now at the lodge gates, and down the long twisting narrow drive to the house. I noticed for the first time how the hydrangeas were coming into bloom, their blue heads thrusting themselves from the green foliage behind. For all their beauty there was something sombre about them, funereal; they were like the wreaths, stiff and artificial that you see beneath glass cases in a foreign churchyard. There they were, all the way along the drive, on either side of us, blue, monotonous, like spectators lined up in a street to watch us pass.

We came to the house at last and rounded the great sweep before the steps. 'Will you be all right now?' said Frank. 'You can lie down, can't you?'

'Yes.' I said, 'Yes, perhaps.'

'I shall go back to Lanyon,' he said, 'Maxim may want me.'

He did not say anything more. He got quickly back into the car again and drove away. Maxim might want him. Why did he say Maxim might want him? Perhaps the Coroner was going to question Frank as well. Ask him about that evening, over twelve months ago, when Maxim had dined with

Frank. He would want to know the exact time that Maxim left his house. He would want to know if anybody saw Maxim when he returned to the house. Whether the servants knew that he was there. Whether anybody could prove that Maxim went straight up to bed and undressed. Mrs. Danvers might be questioned. They might ask Mrs. Danvers to give evidence. And Maxim beginning to lose his temper, beginning to go white. . . .

I went into the hall. I went upstairs to my room, and lay down upon my bed, even as Frank had suggested. I put my hands over my eyes. I kept seeing that room and all the faces. The lined, painstaking, aggravating face of the Coroner, the gold pince-nez on his nose.

'I don't conduct this enquiry for my own amusement.' His slow, careful mind, easily offended. What were they all saying now? What was happening? Suppose in a little while Frank came back to Manderley, alone?

I did not know what happened. I did not know what people did. I remembered pictures of men in the papers, leaving places like that, and being taken away. Suppose Maxim was taken away? They would not let me go to him. They would not let me see him. I should have to stay here at Manderley day after day, night after night, waiting, as I was waiting now. People like Colonel Julyan being kind. People saying 'You must not be alone. You must come to us.' The telephone, the newspapers, the telephone again. 'No, Mrs. de Winter can't see anyone. Mrs. de Winter has no story to give the *County Chronicle*.' And another day. And another day. Weeks that would be blurred and non-existent. Frank at last taking me to see Maxim. He would look thin, queer, like people in hospital. . . .

Other women had been through this. Women I had read about in papers. They sent letters to the Home Secretary and it was not any good. The Home Secretary always said that justice must take its course. Friends sent petitions too, everybody signed them, but the Home Secretary could never do anything. And the ordinary people who read about it in the papers said why should the fellow get off, he murdered his wife, didn't he? What about the poor, murdered wife? This sentimental business about abolishing the death penalty simply encourages crime. This fellow ought to have thought about that before he killed his wife. It's too late now. He will have to hang for it, like any other murderer. And serve him right too. Let it be a warning to others.

I remember seeing a picture on the back of a paper once, of a little crowd collected outside a prison gate, and just after nine o'clock a policeman came and pinned a notice on the gate for the people to read. The notice said something about the sentence being carried out. 'Sentence of death was carried out this morning at nine o'clock. The Governor, the Prison Doctor, and the Sheriff of the County were present.' Hanging was quick. Hanging did not hurt. It broke your neck at once. No, it did not. Someone said once it did not always work. Someone who had known the Governor of a prison. They put that bag over your head, and you stand on the little platform, and then the floor gives way beneath you. It takes exactly three minutes to go from the cell to the moment you are hanged. No, fifty seconds, someone said. No, that's absurd. It could not be fifty seconds. There's a little flight of steps down the side of the shed, down to the pit. The doctor goes down there to look. They die instantly. No, they don't. The body moves for some time, the neck is not always broken. Yes, but even so they don't feel anything. Someone said they did. Someone who had a brother who was a prison doctor said it was not generally known, because it would be such a scandal, but they did not always die at once. Their eyes are open, they stay open for quite a long time.

God, don't let me go on thinking about this. Let me think about something else. About other things. About Mrs. Van Hopper in America. She must be staying with her daughter now. They had that house on Long Island in the summer. I expect they played a lot of bridge. They went to the races. Mrs. Van Hopper was fond of the races. I wonder if she still wears that little yellow hat. It was too small for her. Much too small on that big face. Mrs. Van Hopper sitting about in the garden of that house on Long Island, with novels, and magazines, and papers on her lap. Mrs. Van Hopper putting up her lorgnette and calling to her daughter. 'Look at this, Helen. They say Max de Winter murdered his first wife. I always did think there was something peculiar about him. I warned that fool of a girl she was making a mistake, but she wouldn't listen to me. Well, she's cooked her goose now all right. I suppose they'll make her a big offer to go on the pictures.'

Something was touching my hand. It was Jasper. It was Jasper, thrusting his cold damp nose in my hands. He had followed me up from the hall. Why did dogs make one want to cry? There was something so quiet and hopeless about their sympathy. Jasper, knowing something was wrong, as dogs always do. Trunks being packed. Cars being brought to the door. Dogs standing with drooping tails, dejected eyes. Wandering back to their baskets in the hall when the sound of the car dies away. . . .

I must have fallen asleep because I woke suddenly with a start, and heard that first crack of thunder in the air. I sat up. The clock said five. I got up and went to the window. There was not a breath of wind. The leaves hung listless on the trees, waiting. The sky was slatey grey. The jagged lightning split the sky. Another rumble in the distance. No rain fell. I went out into the corridor and listened. I could not hear anything. I went to the head of the stairs. There was no sign of anybody. The hall was dark because of the menace of thunder overhead. I went down and stood on the terrace. There was another burst of thunder. One spot of rain fell on my hand. One spot. No more. It was very dark. I could see the sea beyond the dip in the valley like a black lake. Another spot fell on my hands, and another crack of thunder came. One of the housemaids began shutting the windows in the rooms upstairs. Robert appeared and shut the windows of the drawing-room behind me.

'The gentlemen are not back yet, are they, Robert?' I asked.

'No, Madam, not yet. I thought you were with them, Madam.'

'No. No, I've been back some time.'

'Will you have tea, Madam?'

'No, no, I'll wait.'

'It looks as though the weather is going to break at last, Madam.'

'Yes.'

No rain fell. Nothing since those two drops on my hand. I went back and sat in the library. At half-past five Robert came into the room.

'The car has just driven up to the door now, Madam,' he said.

'Which car?' I said.

'Mr. de Winter's car, Madam,' he said.

'Is Mr. de Winter driving it himself?'

'Yes, Madam.'

I tried to get up but my legs were things of straw, they would not bear me. I stood leaning against the sofa. My throat was very dry. After a minute Maxim came into the room. He stood just inside the door.

He looked very tired, old. There were lines at the corner of his mouth I had never noticed before.

'It's all over,' he said.

I waited. Still I could not speak or move towards him.

'Suicide,' he said, 'without sufficient evidence to show the state of mind of the deceased. They were all at sea of course, they did not know what they were doing.'

I sat down on the sofa. 'Suicide,' I said, 'but the motive? Where was the motive?'

'God knows,' he said. 'They did not seem to think a motive was necessary. Old Horridge, peering at me, wanting to know if Rebecca had any money troubles. Money troubles. God in heaven.'

He went and stood by the window, looking out at the green lawns. 'It's going to rain,' he said. 'Thank God it's going to rain at last.'

'What happened?' I said. 'What did the Coroner say? Why have you been there all this time?'

'He went over and over the same ground again,' said Maxim. 'Little details about the boat that no one cared about a damn. Were the sea-cocks hard to turn on? Where exactly was the first hole in relation to the second? What was ballast? What effect upon the stability of the boat would the shifting of the ballast have? Could a woman do this unaided? Did the cabin door shut firmly? What pressure of water was necessary to burst open the door? I thought I should go mad. I kept my temper though. Seeing you there, by the door, made me remember what I had to do. If you had not fainted like that, I should never have done it. It brought me up with a jerk. I knew exactly what I was going to say. I faced Horridge all the time, I never took my eyes off his thin, pernickety, little face and those gold-rimmed pince-nez. I shall remember that face of his to my dying day. I'm tired, darling; so tired I can't see, or hear, or feel anything.'

He sat down on the window-seat. He leant forward, his head in his hands. I went and sat beside him. In a few minutes Frith came in, followed by Robert carrying the table for tea. The solemn ritual went forward as it always did, day after day, the leaves of the table pulled out, the legs adjusted, the laying of the snowy cloth, the putting down of the silver tea-pot and the kettle with the little flame beneath. Scones, sandwiches, three different sorts of cake. Jasper sat close to the table, his tail thumping now and again upon the floor, his eyes fixed expectantly on me. It's funny, I thought, how the routine of life goes on, whatever happens, we do the same things, go through the little performance of eating, sleeping, washing. No crisis can break through the crust of habit. I poured out Maxim's tea, I took it to him on the window-seat, gave him his scones, and buttered one for myself.

'Where's Frank?' I asked.

'He had to go and see the vicar. I would have gone too but I wanted to come straight back to you. I kept thinking of you, waiting here, all by yourself, not knowing what was going to happen.'

'Why the vicar?' I said.

'Something has to happen this evening,' he said. 'Something at the church.'

I stared at him blankly. Then I understood. They were going to bury Rebecca. They were going to bring Rebecca back from the mortuary.

'It's fixed for six-thirty,' he said. 'No one knows but Frank, and Colonel Julyan, and the vicar, and myself. There won't be anyone hanging about. This was arranged yesterday. The verdict doesn't make any difference.'

'What time must you go?'

'I'm meeting them there at the church at twenty-five past six.'

I did not say anything. I went on drinking my tea. Maxim put his sandwich down untasted. 'It's still very hot, isn't it?' he said.

'It's the storm,' I said. 'It won't break. Only little spots at a time. It's there in the air. It won't break.'

'It was thundering when I left Lanyon,' he said, 'the sky was like ink over my head. Why in the name of God doesn't it rain?'

The birds were hushed in the trees: it was still very dark.

'I wish you did not have to go out again,' I said.

He did not answer. He looked tired, so deathly tired.

'We'll talk over things this evening when I get back,' he said presently. 'We've got so much to do together, haven't we? We've got to begin all over again. I've been the worst sort of husband for you.'

'No!' I said. 'No!'

'We'll start again, once this thing is behind us. We can do it, you and I. It's not like being alone. The past can't hurt us if we are together. You'll have children too.' After a while he glanced at his watch. 'It's ten past six,' he said, 'I shall have to be going. It won't take long, not more than half-an-hour. We've got to go down to the crypt.'

I held his hand. 'I'll come with you. I shan't mind. Let me come with you.'

'No,' he said. 'No, I don't want you to come.'

Then he went out of the room. I heard the sound of the car starting up in the drive. Presently the sound died away, and I knew he had gone.

Robert came to clear away the tea. It was like any other day. The routine was unchanged. I wondered if it would have been so had Maxim not come back from Lanyon. I wondered if Robert would have stood there, that wooden expression on his young sheep's face, brushing the crumbs from the snow-white cloth, picking up the table, carrying it from the room.

It seemed very quiet in the library when he had gone. I began to think of them down at the church, going through that door and down the flight of stairs to the crypt. I had never been there. I had only seen the door. I wondered what a crypt was like, if there were coffins standing there. Maxim's father and mother. I wondered what would happen to the coffin of that other woman who had been put there by mistake. I wondered who she was, poor unclaimed soul, washed up by the wind and tide. Now another coffin would stand there. Rebecca would lie there in the crypt as well. Was the vicar reading the burial service there, with Maxim, and Frank, and Colonel Julyan standing by his side? Ashes to ashes. Dust to dust. It seemed to me that Rebecca had no reality any more. She had crumbled away when they had found her on the cabin floor. It was not Rebecca who was lying in that coffin in the crypt, it was dust. Only dust.

Just after seven the rain began to fall. Gently at first, a light pattering in the trees, and so thin I could not see it. Then louder and faster, a driving torrent falling slantways from the slate sky, like water from a sluice. I left the windows open wide. I stood in front of them and breathed the cold clean air. The rain splashed into my face and on my hands. I could not see beyond the lawns, the falling rain came thick and fast. I heard it sputtering in the gutter-pipes above the window, and splashing on the stones of the terrace. There was no more thunder. The rain smelt of moss and earth and of the black bark of trees.

I did not hear Frith come in at the door. I was standing by the window watching the rain. I did not see him until he was beside me.

'Excuse me, Madam,' he said, 'do you know if Mr. de Winter will be long?'

'No,' I said, 'not very long.'

'There's a gentleman to see him, Madam,' said Frith after a moment's hesitation. 'I'm not quite sure what I ought to say. He's so very insistent about seeing Mr. de Winter.'

'Who is it?' I said. 'Is it anyone you know?'

Frith looked uncomfortable. 'Yes, Madam,' he said, 'it's a gentleman who used to come here frequently at one time, when Mrs. de Winter was alive. A gentleman called Mr. Favell.'

I knelt on the window-seat and shut the window. The rain was coming in on to the cushions. Then I turned round and looked at Frith.

'I think perhaps I had better see Mr. Favell,' I said.

'Very good, Madam.'

I went and stood over on the rug beside the empty fireplace. It was just possible that I should be able to get rid of Favell before Maxim came back. I did not know what I was going to say to him, but I was not frightened.

In a few moments Frith returned and showed Favell into the library. He looked much the same as before but a little rougher if possible, a little more untidy. He was the sort of man who invariably went hatless, his hair was bleached from the sun of the last days and his skin was deeply tanned. His eyes were rather blood-shot. I wondered if he had been drinking.

'I'm afraid Maxim is not here,' I said. 'I don't know when he will be back. Wouldn't it be better if you made an appointment to see him at the office in the morning?'

'Waiting doesn't worry me,' said Favell, 'and I don't think I shall have to wait very long, you know. I had a look in the dining-room as I came along, and I see Max's place is laid for dinner all right.'

'Our plans have been changed,' I said. 'It's quite possible Maxim won't be home at all this evening.'

'He's run off has he?' said Favell, with a half smile I did not like. 'I wonder if you really mean it. Of course under the circumstances it's the wisest thing he can do. Gossip is an unpleasant thing to some people. It's more pleasant to avoid it, isn't it?'

'I don't know what you mean,' I said.

'Don't you?' he said. 'Oh, come, you don't expect me to believe that, do you? Tell me, are you feeling better? Too bad fainting like that at the inquest this afternoon. I would have come and helped you out but I saw you had one knight-errant already. I bet Frank Crawley enjoyed himself. Did you let him drive you home? You wouldn't let me drive you five yards when I offered to.'

'What did you want to see Maxim about?' I asked.

Favell leant forward to the table and helped himself to a cigarette. 'You don't mind my smoking, I suppose?' he said. 'It won't make you sick, will it? One never knows with brides.'

He watched me over his lighter. 'You've grown up a bit since I saw you last, haven't you?' he said. 'I wonder what you have been doing. Leading Frank Crawley up the garden-path?' He blew a cloud of smoke in the air. 'I say, do you mind asking old Frith to get me a whisky-and-soda?'

I did not say anything. I went and rang the bell. He sat down on the edge of the sofa, swinging his legs, that half-smile on his lips. Robert answered the bell. 'A whisky-and-soda for Mr. Favell,' I said.

'Well, Robert,' said Favell, 'I haven't seen you for a very long time. Still breaking the hearts of the girls in Kerrith?'

Robert flushed. He glanced at me, horribly embarrassed.

'All right, old chap, I won't give you away. Run along and get me a double whisky, and jump on it.'

Robert disappeared. Favell laughed, dropping ash all over the floor.

'I took Robert out once on his half-day,' he said. 'Rebecca bet me a fiver I wouldn't ask him. I won my fiver all right. Spent one of the funniest evenings of my life. Did I laugh? Oh, boy! Robert on the razzle takes a lot of beating, I tell you. I must say he's got a good eye for a girl. He picked the prettiest of the bunch we saw that night.'

Robert came back again with the whisky and soda on a tray. He still looked very red, very uncomfortable. Favell watched him with a smile as he poured out his drink, and then he began to laugh, leaning back on the arm of the sofa. He whistled the bar of a song, watching Robert all the while.

'That was the one, wasn't it,' he said, 'that was the tune? Do you still like ginger hair, Robert?'

Robert gave him a flat weak smile. He looked miserable. Favell laughed louder still. Robert turned and went out of the room.

'Poor kid,' said Favell. 'I don't suppose he's been on the loose since. That old ass Frith keeps him on a leading string.'

He began drinking his whisky-and-soda, glancing round the room, looking at me every now and again, and smiling.

'I don't think I shall mind very much if Max doesn't get back to dinner,' he said. 'What say you?'

I did not answer. I stood by the fireplace, my hands behind my back. 'You wouldn't waste that place at the dining-room table would you?' he said. He looked at me, smiling still, his head on one side.

'Mr. Favell,' I said, 'I don't want to be rude, but as a matter-of-fact I'm very tired. I've had a long and fairly exhausting day. If you can't tell me what you want to see Maxim about it's not much good your sitting here. You had far better do as I suggest, and go round to the estate office in the morning.'

He slid off the arm of the sofa and came towards me, his glass in his hand. 'No, no,' he said. 'No, no, don't be a brute. I've had an exhausting day too. Don't run away and leave me. I'm quite harmless, really I am. I suppose Max has been telling tales about me to you?'

I did not answer. 'You think I'm the big bad wolf, don't you,' he said 'but I'm not, you know. I'm a perfectly ordinary, harmless bloke. And I think you are behaving splendidly over all this, perfectly splendidly. I take off my hat to you, I really do.' This last speech of his was very slurred and thick. I wished I had never told Frith I would see him.

'You come down here to Manderley,' he said, waving his arm vaguely, 'you take on all this place, meet hundreds of people you've never seen before, you put up with old Max and his moods, you don't give a fig for anyone, you just go your way, I call it a damn good effort, and I don't care who hears me say so. A damn good effort.' He swayed a little as he stood. He steadied himself, and put the empty glass down on the table. 'This business has been a shock to me, you know,' he said. 'A bloody awful shock. Rebecca was my cousin. I was damn fond of her.'

'Yes,' I said. 'I'm very sorry for you.'

'We were brought up together,' he went on. 'Always tremendous pals. Liked the same things, the same people. Laughed at the same jokes. I suppose I was fonder of Rebecca than anyone else in the world. And she was fond of me. All this has been a bloody shock.'

'Yes,' I said. 'Yes of course.'

'And what is Max going to do about it, that's what I want to know? Does he think he can sit back quietly now that sham Inquest is over? Tell me that?' He was not smiling any more. He bent towards me.

'I'm going to see justice is done to Rebecca,' he said, his voice growing louder. 'Suicide . . . God Almighty, that doddering old fool of a Coroner got the jury to say suicide. You and I know it wasn't suicide, don't we?' He leant closer to me still. 'Don't we?' he said slowly.

The door opened and Maxim came into the room, with Frank just behind him. Maxim stood quite still, with the door open, staring at Favell. 'What the hell are you doing here?' he said.

Favell turned round, his hands in his pockets. He waited a moment, and then he began to smile. 'As a matter-of-fact, Max, old chap, I came to congratulate you on the Inquest this afternoon.'

'Do you mind leaving the house,' said Max, 'or do you want Crawley and me to chuck you out?'

'Steady a moment, steady a moment,' said Favell. He lit another cigarette, and sat down once more on the arm of the sofa.

'You don't want Frith to hear what I'm going to say, do you?' he said. 'Well, he will, if you don't shut that door.'

Maxim did not move. I saw Frank close the door very quietly.

'Now listen here, Max,' said Favell, 'you've come very well out of this affair, haven't you? Better than you ever expected. Oh, yes, I was in the court this afternoon, and I dare say you saw me. I was there from start to finish. I saw your wife faint, at a rather critical moment, and I don't blame her. It was touch and go then, wasn't it, Max, what way the enquiry would go? And luckily for you it went the way it did? You hadn't squared those thick-headed fellows who were acting jury, had you? It looked damn like it to me.'

Maxim made a move towards Favell, but Favell held up his hand.

'Wait a bit, can't you?' he said. 'I haven't finished yet. You realise don't you, Max, old man, that I can make things damned unpleasant for you if I choose. Not only unpleasant, but shall I say dangerous?'

I sat down on the chair beside the fireplace. I held the arms of the chair very tight. Frank came over and stood behind the chair. Still Maxim did not move. He never took his eyes off Favell.

'Oh, yes?' he said. 'In what way can you make things dangerous?'

'Look here, Max,' said Favell, 'I suppose there are no secrets between you and your wife, and from the look of things Crawley there just makes the happy trio. I can speak plainly then, and I will. You all know about Rebecca and me. We were lovers, weren't we? I've never denied it, and I never will. Very well then. Up to the present I believed, like every other fool, that Rebecca was drowned sailing in the bay, and that her body was picked up at Edgecoombe weeks afterwards. It was a shock to me then, a bloody shock. But I said to myself, that's the sort of death Rebecca would choose, she'd go out like she lived, fighting.' He paused, he sat there on the edge of the sofa, looking at all of us in turn. 'Then I pick up the evening paper a few days ago and I read that Rebecca's boat had been stumbled on by the local diver and that there was a body in the cabin. I couldn't understand it. Who the hell would Rebecca have as a sailing companion? It didn't make sense. I came down here, and put up at a pub just outside Kerrith. I got in touch with Mrs. Danvers. She told me then that the body in the cabin was Rebecca's. Even so I thought like everyone else that the first body was a mistake and Rebecca had somehow got shut in the cabin when she went to fetch a coat. Well, I attended that inquest to-day, as you know. And everything went smoothly, didn't it, until Tabb gave his evidence? But after that? Well, Max, old man, what have you got to say about those holes in the floor-boards, and those sea-cocks turned full on?'

'Do you think,' said Maxim slowly, 'that after those hours of talk this afternoon I am going into it again – with you? You heard the evidence, and you heard the verdict. It satisfied the Coroner, and it must satisfy you.'

'Suicide, eh?' said Favell. 'Rebecca committing suicide. The sort of thing she would do, wasn't it? Listen, you never knew I had this note, did you? I kept it, because it was the last thing she ever wrote to me. I'll read it to you. I think it will interest you.'

He took a piece of paper out of his pocket. I recognised that thin, pointed, slanting hand. *I tried to ring you from the flat, but could get no answer,* he read. *I'm going down to Manders right away. I shall be at the cottage this evening, and if you get this in time will you get the car and follow me. I'll spend the night at the cottage, and leave the door open for you. I've got something to tell you and I want to see you as soon as possible. Rebecca.*

He put the note back in his pocket. 'That's not the sort of note you write when you're going to commit suicide, is it?' he said. 'It was waiting for me at my flat when I got back about four in the morning. I had no idea Rebecca was to be in London that day or I should have got in touch with her. It happened, by a vile stroke of fortune, I was on a party that night. When I read the note at four in the morning I decided it was too late to go crashing down on a six-hour run to Manderley. I went to bed, determined to put a call through later in the day. I did. About twelve o'clock. And I heard Rebecca had been drowned!'

He sat there, staring at Maxim. None of us spoke.

'Supposing the Coroner this afternoon had read that note, it would have made it a little bit more tricky for you, wouldn't it, Max, old man?' said Favell.

'Well,' said Maxim. 'Why didn't you get up and give it to him?'

'Steady old boy, steady. No need to get rattled. I don't want to smash you, Max. God knows you've never been a friend to me, but I don't bear malice about it. All married men with lovely wives are jealous, aren't they? And some of 'em just can't help playing Othello. They're made that way. I don't blame them. I'm sorry for them. I'm a bit of a Socialist in my way, you know, and I can't think why fellows can't share their women instead of killing them. What difference does it make? You can get your fun just the same. A lovely woman isn't like a motor tyre, she doesn't wear out. The more you use her the better she goes. Now, Max. I've laid all my cards on the table. Why can't we come to some agreement? I'm not a rich man. I'm too fond of gambling for that. But what gets me down is never having any capital to fall back upon. Now if I had a settlement of two or three thousand a year for life I could jog along quite comfortably. And I'd never trouble you again. I swear before God I would not.'

'I've asked you before to leave the house,' said Maxim. 'I'm not going to ask you again. There's the door behind me. You can open it yourself.'

'Half a minute, Maxim,' said Frank, 'it's not quite as easy as all that.' He turned to Favell. 'I see what you're driving at. It happens, very unfortunately, that you could, as you say, twist things round and make it difficult for Maxim. I don't think he sees it as clearly as I do. What is the exact amount you propose Maxim should settle on you?'

I saw Maxim go very white, and a little pulse began to show on his forehead. 'Don't interfere with this, Frank,' he said, 'this is my affair entirely. I'm not going to give way to blackmail.'

'I don't suppose your wife wants to be pointed out as Mrs. de Winter, the widow of a murderer, of a fellow who was hanged,' said Favell. He laughed, and glanced towards me.

'You think you can frighten me, don't you Favell?' said Maxim. 'Well you are wrong. I'm not afraid of anything you can do. There is the telephone, in the next room. Shall I ring up Colonel Julyan and ask him to come over? He's the magistrate. He'll be interested in your story.' Favell stared at him, and laughed.

'Good bluff,' he said, 'but it won't work. You wouldn't dare ring up old Julyan. I've got enough evidence to hang you, Max, old man.' Maxim walked slowly across the room and passed through to the little room beyond. I heard the click of the telephone.

'Stop him!' I said to Frank. 'Stop him, for God's sake.'

Frank glanced at my face, he went swiftly towards the door.

I heard Maxim's voice, very cool, very calm. 'I want Kerrith 17,' he said. Favell was watching the door, his face curiously intense.

'Leave me alone,' I heard Maxim say to Frank. And then, two minutes afterwards. 'Is that Colonel Julyan speaking? It's de Winter here. Yes. Yes, I know. I wonder if you could possibly come over here at once. Yes, to Manderley. It's rather urgent. I can't explain why on the telephone, but you shall hear everything directly you come. I'm very sorry to have to drag you out. Yes. Thank you very much. Good-bye.'

He came back again into the room. 'Julyan is coming right away,' he said. He crossed over and threw open the windows. It was still raining very hard. He stood there, with his back to us, breathing the cold air.

'Maxim,' said Frank quietly. 'Maxim.'

He did not answer. Favell laughed, and helped himself to another cigarette. 'If you want to hang yourself, old fellow, it's all the same to me,' he said. He picked up a paper from the table and flung himself down on the sofa, crossed his legs, and began to turn over the pages. Frank hesitated, glancing from me to Maxim. Then he came beside me.

'Can't you do something?' I whispered. 'Go out and meet Colonel Julyan, prevent him from coming, say it was all a mistake?' Maxim spoke from the window without turning round.

'Frank is not to leave this room,' he said. 'I'm going to manage this thing alone. Colonel Julyan will be here in exactly ten minutes.'

We none of us said anything. Favell went on reading his paper. There was no sound but the steady falling rain. It fell without a break, steady, straight and monotonous. I felt helpless, without strength. There was nothing I could do. Nothing that Frank could do. In a book or in a play I would have found a revolver, and we should have shot Favell, hidden his body in a cupboard. There was no revolver. There was no cupboard. We were

ordinary people. These things did not happen. I could not go to Maxim now
and beg him on my knees to give Favell the money. I had to sit there, with
my hands in my lap, watching the rain, watching Maxim with his back
turned to me, standing by the window.

It was raining too hard to hear the car. The sound of the rain covered all
other sounds. We did not know Colonel Julyan had arrived until the door
opened, and Frith showed him into the room.

Maxim swung round from the window. 'Good evening,' he said. 'We meet
again. You've made very good time.'

'Yes,' said Colonel Julyan, 'you said it was urgent, so I came at once.
Luckily, my man had left the car handy. What an evening.'

He glanced at Favell uncertainly, and then came over and shook hands
with me, nodding to Maxim. 'A good thing the rain has come,' he said. 'It's
been hanging about too long. I hope you're feeling better.'

I murmured something, I don't know what, and he stood there looking
from one to the other of us, rubbing his hands.

'I think you realise,' Maxim said, 'that I haven't brought you out on an
evening like this for a social half-hour before dinner. This is Jack Favell,
my late wife's first cousin. I don't know if you have ever met.'

Colonel Julyan nodded. 'Your face seems familiar. I've probably met you
here in the old days.'

'Quite,' said Maxim. 'Go ahead, Favell.'

Favell got up from the sofa and chucked the paper back on the table. The
ten minutes seemed to have sobered him. He walked quite steadily. He was
not smiling any longer. I had the impression that he was not entirely pleased
with the turn in the events, and he was ill-prepared for the encounter with
Colonel Julyan. He began speaking in a loud, rather domineering voice.
'Look here, Colonel Julyan,' he said, 'there's no sense in beating about the
bush. The reason why I'm here is that I'm not satisfied with the verdict
given at the Inquest this afternoon.'

'Oh?' said Colonel Julyan. 'Isn't that for de Winter to say, not you?'

'No, I don't think it is,' said Favell. 'I have a right to speak, not only as
Rebecca's cousin, but as her prospective husband, had she lived.'

Colonel Julyan looked rather taken aback. 'Oh,' he said. 'Oh, I see. That's
rather different. Is this true, de Winter?'

Maxim shrugged his shoulders. 'It's the first I've heard of it,' he said.

Colonel Julyan looked from one to the other doubtfully. 'Look here,
Favell,' he said, 'what exactly is your trouble?'

Favell stared at him a moment. I could see he was planning something
in his mind, and he was still not sober enough to carry it through. He put
his hand slowly in his waistcoat pocket and brought out Rebecca's note.
'This note was written a few hours before Rebecca was supposed to have
set out on that suicidal sail. Here it is. I want you to read it, and say whether
you think a woman who wrote that note had made up her mind to kill
herself.'

Colonel Julyan took a pair of spectacles from a case in his pocket and
read the note. Then he handed it back to Favell. 'No,' he said, 'on the face

of it, no. But I don't know what the note refers to. Perhaps you do. Or
perhaps de Winter does?'

Maxim did not say anything. Favell twisted the piece of paper in his
fingers, considering Colonel Julyan all the while. 'My cousin made a definite
appointment in that note, didn't she?' he said. 'She deliberately asked me
to drive down to Manderley that night because she had something to tell me.
What it actually was I don't suppose we shall ever know, but that's beside
the point. She made the appointment, and she was to spend the night in the
cottage on purpose to see me alone. The mere fact of her going for a sail
never surprised me. It was the sort of thing she did, for an hour or so, after
a long day in London. But to plug holes in the cabin and deliberately drown
herself, the hysterical impulsive freak of a neurotic girl – oh, no, Colonel
Julyan, by Christ, no!' The colour had flooded into his face, and the last
words were shouted. His manner was not helpful to him, and I could see
by the thin line of Colonel Julyan's mouth that he had not taken to Favell.

'My dear fellow,' he said, 'it's not the slightest use you losing your temper
with me. I'm not the Coroner who conducted the enquiry this afternoon, nor
am I a member of the jury who gave the verdict. I'm merely the magistrate
of the district. Naturally I want to help you all I can, and de Winter, too.
You say you refuse to believe your cousin committed suicide. On the other
hand you heard, as we all did, the evidence of the boat-builder. The sea-
cocks were open, the holes were there. Very well. Suppose we get to the
point. What do you suggest really happened?'

Favell turned his head and looked slowly towards Maxim. He was still
twisting the note between his fingers. 'Rebecca never opened those sea-cocks,
nor split the holes in the planking. Rebecca never committed suicide. You've
asked for my opinion, and by God you shall have it. Rebecca was murdered.
And if you want to know who the murderer is, why there he stands, by the
window there, with that God-damned superior smile on his face. He couldn't
even wait could he, until the year was out, before marrying the first girl he
set eyes on? There he is, there's your murderer for you, Mr. Maximilian
de Winter. Take a good long look at him. He'd look well hanging, wouldn't
he?'

And Favell began to laugh, the laugh of a drunkard, high-pitched, forced
and foolish, and all the while twisting Rebecca's note between his fingers.

Chapter Twenty-four

Thank God for Favell's laugh. Thank God for his pointing finger, his
flushed face, his staring blood-shot eyes. Thank God for the way he stood

there swaying on his two feet. Because it made Colonel Julyan antagonistic, it put him on our side. I saw the disgust on his face, the quick movement of his lips. Colonel Julyan did not believe him. Colonel Julyan was on our side.

'The man's drunk,' he said quietly. 'He doesn't know what he's saying.'

'Drunk, am I?' shouted Favell. 'Oh, no, my fine friend. You may be a magistrate and a colonel into the bargain, but it won't cut any ice with me. I've got the law on my side for a change, and I'm going to use it. There are other magistrates in this bloody country besides you. Fellows with brains in their heads, who understand the meaning of justice. Not soldiers who got the sack years ago for incompetence and walk about with a string of putty medals on their chest. Max de Winter murdered Rebecca and I'm going to prove it.'

'Wait a minute, Mr. Favell,' said Colonel Julyan quietly, 'you were present at the enquiry this afternoon, weren't you? I remember you now. I saw you sitting there. If you felt so deeply about the injustice of the verdict why didn't you say so then, to the jury, to the Coroner himself? Why didn't you produce that letter in court?'

Favell stared at him, and laughed. 'Why?' he said. 'Because I did not choose to, that's why. I preferred to come and tackle de Winter personally.'

'That's why I rang you up,' said Maxim, coming forward from the window; 'we've already heard Favell's accusations. I asked him the same question. Why didn't he tell his suspicions to the Coroner? He said he was not a rich man, and that if I cared to settle two or three thousand on him for life he would never worry me again. Frank was here, and my wife. They both heard him. Ask them.'

'It's perfectly true, sir,' said Frank. 'It's blackmail, pure and simple.'

'Yes, of course,' said Colonel Julyan, 'the trouble is that blackmail is not very pure, nor is it particularly simple. It can make a lot of unpleasantness for a great many people, even if the blackmailer finds himself in gaol at the end of it. Sometimes innocent people find themselves in gaol as well. We want to avoid that, in this case. I don't know whether you are sufficiently sober, Favell, to answer my questions, and if you keep off irrelevant personalities we may get through with the business quicker. You have just made a serious accusation against de Winter. Have you any proof to back that accusation?'

'Proof?' said Favell. 'What the hell do you want with proof? Aren't those holes in the boat proof enough?'

'Certainly not,' said Colonel Julyan, 'unless you can bring a witness who saw him do it. Where's your witness?'

'Witness be damned,' said Favell. 'Of course de Winter did it. Who else would kill Rebecca?'

'Kerrith has a large population,' said Colonel Julyan. 'Why not go from door to door making enquiries? I might have done it myself. You appear to have no more proof against de Winter there than you would have against me.'

'Oh, I see,' said Favell, 'you're going to hold his hand through this. You're going to back de Winter. You won't let him down because you've dined with him, and he's dined with you. He's a big name down here. He's the owner of Manderley. You poor bloody little snob.'

'Take care, Favell, take care.'

'You think you can get the better of me, don't you? You think I've got no case to bring to a court of law. I'll get my proof for you all right. I tell you de Winter killed Rebecca because of me. He knew I was her lover, he was jealous, madly jealous. He knew she was waiting for me at the cottage on the beach, and he went down that night and killed her. Then he put her body in the boat and sank her.'

'Quite a clever story, Favell, in its way, but I repeat again you have no proof. Produce your witness who saw it happen and I might begin to take you seriously. I know that cottage on the beach. A sort of picnic place, isn't it? Mrs. de Winter used to keep the gear there for the boat. It would help your story if you could turn it into a bungalow with fifty replicas alongside of it. There would be a chance then that one of the inhabitants might have seen the whole affair.'

'Hold on,' said Favell slowly, 'hold on. . . . There is a chance de Winter might have been seen that night. Quite a good chance too. It's worth finding out. What would you say if I did produce a witness?'

Colonel Julyan shrugged his shoulders. I saw Frank glance enquiringly at Maxim. Maxim did not say anything. He was watching Favell. I suddenly knew what Favell meant. I knew who he was talking about. And in a flash of fear and horror I knew that he was right. There had been a witness that night. Little sentences came back to me. Words I had not understood, phrases I believed to be the fragments of a poor idiot's mind. 'She's down there isn't she? She won't come back again.' 'I didn't tell no one.' 'They'll find her there, won't they? The fishes have eaten her, haven't they?' 'She'll not come back no more.' Ben knew. Ben had seen. Ben, with his queer crazed brain had been a witness all the time. He had been hiding in the woods that night. He had seen Maxim take the boat from the moorings, and pull back in the dinghy, alone. I knew all the colour was draining away from my face. I leant back against the cushion of the chair.

'There's a local half-wit who spends his time on the beach,' said Favell. 'He was always hanging about, when I used to come down and meet Rebecca. I've often seen him. He used to sleep in the woods, or on the beach, when the nights were hot. The fellow's cracked, he would never have come forward on his own. But I could make him talk, if he did see anything that night. And there's a bloody big chance he did.'

'Who is this? What's he talking about?' said Colonel Julyan.

'He must mean Ben,' said Frank, with another glance at Maxim. 'He's the son of one of our tenants. But the man's not responsible for what he says or does. He's been an idiot since birth.'

'What the hell does that matter?' said Favell. 'He's got eyes, hasn't he? He knows what he sees. He's only got to answer yes or no. You're getting windy now, aren't you? Not so mighty confident?'

'Can we get hold of this fellow and question him?' asked Colonel Julyan.

'Of course,' said Maxim. 'Tell Robert to cut down to his mother's cottage, Frank, and bring him back.'

Frank hesitated. I saw him glance at me out of the tail of his eye.

'Go on, for God's sake,' said Maxim. 'We want to end this thing, don't we?' Frank went out of the room. I began to feel the old nagging pain beneath my heart.

In a few minutes Frank came back again into the room.

'Robert's taken my car,' he said. 'If Ben is at home he won't be more than ten minutes.'

'The rain will keep him at home all right,' said Favell; 'he'll be there. And I think you will find I shall be able to make him talk.' He laughed, and looked at Maxim. His face was still very flushed. Excitement had made him sweat; there were beads of perspiration on his forehead. I noticed how his neck bulged over the back of his collar, and how low his ears were set on his head. Those florid good looks would not last him very long. Already he was out of condition, puffy. He helped himself to another cigarette. 'You're like a little trade union here at Manderley, aren't you?' he said. 'No one going to give anyone else away. Even the local magistrate is on the same racket. We must exempt the bride of course. A wife doesn't give evidence against her husband. Crawley of course has been squared. He knows he would lose his job if he told the truth. And if I guess rightly there's a spice of malice in his soul towards me too. You didn't have much success with Rebecca, did you, Crawley? That garden path wasn't quite long enough, eh? It's a bit easier this time, isn't it? The bride will be grateful for your fraternal arm every time she faints. When she hears the judge sentence her husband to death that arm of yours will come in very handy.'

It happened very quickly. Too quick for me to see how Maxim did it. But I saw Favell stagger and fall against the arm of the sofa, and down on to the floor. And Maxim was standing just beside him. I felt rather sick. There was something degrading in the fact that Maxim had hit Favell. I wished I had not known. I wished I had not been there to see. Colonel Julyan did not say anything. He looked very grim. He turned his back on them and came and stood beside me.

'I think you had better go upstairs,' he said quietly.

I shook my head. 'No,' I whispered. 'No.'

'That fellow is in a state capable of saying anything,' he said. 'What you have just seen was not very attractive, was it? Your husband was right of course, but it's a pity you saw it.'

I did not answer. I was watching Favell who was getting slowly to his feet. He sat down heavily on the sofa and put his handkerchief to his face.

'Get me a drink,' he said, 'get me a drink.'

Maxim looked at Frank. Frank went out of the room. None of us spoke. In a moment Frank came back with the whisky and soda on a tray. He mixed some in a glass and gave it to Favell. Favell drank it greedily, like an animal. There was something sensual and horrible the way he put his mouth to the glass. His lips folded upon the glass in a peculiar way. There was a dark red patch on his jaw where Maxim had hit him. Maxim had turned his back on him again and had returned to the window. I glanced at Colonel Julyan and saw that he was looking at Maxim. His gaze was curious, intent. My heart began beating very quickly. Why did Colonel Julyan look at Maxim in that way?

Did it mean that he was beginning to wonder, to suspect?

Maxim did not see. He was watching the rain. It fell straight and steady as before. The sound filled the room. Favell finished his whisky and soda and put the glass back on the table beside the sofa. He was breathing heavily. He did not look at any of us. He was staring straight in front of him at the floor.

The telephone began ringing in the little room. It struck a shrill, discordant note. Frank went to answer it.

He came back at once and looked at Colonel Julyan. 'It's your daughter,' he said; 'they want to know if they are to keep dinner back.'

Colonel Julyan waved his hand impatiently. 'Tell them to start,' he said, 'tell them I don't know when I shall be back.' He glanced at his watch. 'Fancy ringing up,' he muttered, 'what a moment to choose.'

Frank went back into the little room to give the message. I thought of the daughter at the other end of the telephone. It would be the one who played golf. I could imagine her calling to her sister, 'Dad says we're to start. What on earth can he be doing? The steak will be like leather.' Their little household disorganised because of us. Their evening routine upset. All these foolish inconsequent threads hanging up on one another, because Maxim had killed Rebecca. I looked at Frank. His face was pale and set.

'I heard Robert coming back with the car,' he said to Colonel Julyan. 'The window in there looks on to the drive.'

He went out of the library to the hall. Favell had lifted his head when he spoke. Then he got to his feet once more and stood looking towards the door. There was a queer, ugly smile on his face.

The door opened, and Frank came in. He turned and spoke to someone in the hall outside.

'All right, Ben,' he said quietly, 'Mr. de Winter wants to give you some cigarettes. There's nothing to be frightened of.'

Ben stepped awkwardly into the room. He had his sou'wester in his hands. He looked odd and naked without his hat. I realised for the first time that his head was shaved all over, and he had no hair. He looked different, dreadful.

The light seemed to daze him. He glanced foolishly round the room, blinking his small eyes. He caught sight of me, and I gave him a weak, rather tremulous smile. I don't know if he recognised me or not. He just blinked his eyes. Then Favell walked slowly towards him and stood in front of him.

'Hullo,' he said, 'how's life treated you since we last met?'

Ben stared at him. There was no recognition on his face. He did not answer.

'Well,' said Favell, 'you know who I am, don't you?'

Ben went on twisting his sou'wester. 'Eh?' he said.

'Have a cigarette,' said Favell, handing him the box. Ben glanced at Maxim and Frank.

'All right,' said Maxim, 'take as many as you like.'

Ben took four and stuck two behind each ear. Then he stood twisting his cap again.

'You know who I am, don't you?' repeated Favell.

Still Ben did not answer. Colonel Julyan walked across to him. 'You shall go home in a few moments, Ben,' he said. 'No one is going to hurt you. We just want you to answer one or two questions. You know Mr. Favell, don't you?'

This time Ben shook his head. 'I never seen'un,' he said.

'Don't be a bloody fool,' said Favell roughly; 'you know you've seen me. You've seen me go to the cottage on the beach, Mrs. de Winter's cottage. You've seen me there, haven't you?'

'No,' said Ben. 'I never seen no one.'

'You damned half-witted liar,' said Favell, 'are you going to stand there and say you never saw me, last year, walk through those woods with Mrs. de Winter, and go into the cottage? Didn't we catch you once, peering at us from the window?'

'Eh?' said Ben.

'A convincing witness,' said Colonel Julyan sarcastically.

Favell swung round on him. 'It's a put-up-job,' he said. 'Someone has got at this idiot and bribed him too. I tell you he's seen me scores of times. Here. Will this make you remember?' He fumbled in his hip-pocket and brought out a note-case. He flourished a pound note in front of Ben. 'Now do you remember me?' he said.

Ben shook his head. 'I never seen'un,' he said, and then he took hold of Frank's arm. 'Has he come here to take me to the asylum?' he said.

'No,' said Frank. 'No, of course not, Ben.'

'I don't want to go to the asylum,' said Ben. 'They'm cruel to folk in there. I want to stay home. I done nothing.'

'That's all right, Ben,' said Colonel Julyan. 'No one's going to put you in the asylum. Are you quite sure you've never seen this man before?'

'No,' said Ben, 'I've never seen'un.'

'You remember Mrs. de Winter, don't you?' said Colonel Julyan.

Ben glanced doubtfully towards me.

'No,' said Colonel Julyan gently, 'not this lady. The other lady, who used to go to the cottage.'

'Eh?' said Ben.

'You remember the lady who had the boat?'

Ben blinked his eyes. 'She's gone,' he said.

'Yes, we know that,' said Colonel Julyan. 'She used to sail the boat, didn't she? Were you on the beach when she sailed the boat the last time? One evening, over twelve months ago. When she didn't come back again?'

Ben twisted his sou'wester. He glanced at Frank, and then at Maxim. 'Eh?' he said.

'You were there, weren't you?' said Favell, leaning forward. 'You saw

Mrs. de Winter come down to the cottage, and presently you saw Mr. de Winter too. He went into the cottage after her. What happened then? Go on? What happened?'

Ben shrank back against the wall. 'I seen nothing,' he said. 'I want to stay home. I'm not going to the asylum. I never seen you. Never before. I never seen you and she in the woods.' He began to blubber like a child.

'You crazy little rat,' said Favell slowly, 'you bloody, crazy little rat.'

Ben was wiping his eyes with the sleeve of his coat.

'Your witness does not seem to have helped you,' said Colonel Julyan. 'The performance has been rather a waste of time, hasn't it? Do you want to ask him anything else?'

'It's a plot,' shouted Favell, 'a plot against me. You're all in it, every one of you. Someone's paid this half-wit, I tell you. Paid him to tell his string of dirty lies.'

'I think Ben might be allowed to go home,' said Colonel Julyan.

'All right, Ben,' said Maxim. 'Robert shall take you back. And no one will put you in the asylum, don't be afraid. Tell Robert to find him something in the kitchen,' he added to Frank. 'Some cold meat, whatever he fancies.'

'Payment for services rendered, eh?' said Favell. 'He's done a good day's work for you, Max, hasn't he?'

Frank took Ben out of the room. Colonel Julyan glanced at Maxim. 'The fellow appeared to be scared stiff,' he said, 'he was shaking like a leaf. I was watching him. He's never been ill-treated has he?'

'No,' said Maxim, 'he's perfectly harmless, and I've always let him have the run of the place.'

'He's been frightened at some time,' said Colonel Julyan. 'He was showing the whites of his eyes, just like a dog does, when you're going to whip him.'

'Well, why didn't you?' said Favell. 'He'd have mentioned me all right if you'd whipped him. Oh, no, he's going to be given a good supper for his work to-night. Ben's not going to be whipped.'

'He has not helped your case, has he?' said Colonel Julyan quietly. 'We're still where we were. You can't produce one shred of evidence against de Winter and you know it. The very motive you gave won't stand the test. In a court of law, Favell, you wouldn't have a leg to stand on. You say you were Mrs. de Winter's prospective husband, and that you held clandestine meetings with her in that cottage on the beach. Even the poor idiot we have just had in this room swears he never saw you. You can't even prove your own story, can you?'

'Can't I?' said Favell. I saw him smile. He came across to the fireplace and rang the bell.

'What are you doing?' said Colonel Julyan.

'Wait a moment and you'll see,' said Favell.

I guessed already what was going to happen. Frith answered the bell.

'Ask Mrs. Danvers to come here,' said Favell.

Frith glanced at Maxim. Maxim nodded shortly.

Frith went out of the room. 'Isn't Mrs. Danvers the housekeeper?' said Colonel Julyan.

'She was also Rebecca's personal friend,' said Favell. 'She was with her for years before she married, and practically brought her up. You are going to find Danny a very different sort of witness to Ben.'

Frank came back into the room. 'Packed Ben off to bed?' said Favell. 'Given him his supper and told him he was a good boy? This time it won't be quite so easy for the trade union.'

'Mrs. Danvers is coming down,' said Colonel Julyan. 'Favell seems to think he will get something out of her.'

Frank glanced quickly at Maxim. Colonel Julyan saw the glance. I saw his lips tighten. I did not like it. No, I did not like it. I began biting my nails.

We all waited, watching the door. And Mrs. Danvers came into the room. Perhaps it was because I had generally seen her alone, and beside me she had seemed tall and gaunt, but she looked shrunken now in size, more wizened, and I noticed she had to look up to Favell and to Frank and Maxim. She stood by the door, her hands folded in front of her, looking from one to the other of us.

'Good evening, Mrs. Danvers,' said Colonel Julyan.

'Good evening, sir,' she said.

Her voice was that old, dead, mechanical one I had heard so often.

'First of all, Mrs. Danvers, I want to ask you a question,' said Colonel Julyan, 'and the question is this. Were you aware of the relationship between the late Mrs. de Winter and Mr. Favell here?'

'They were first cousins,' said Mrs. Danvers.

'I was not referring to blood-relationship, Mrs. Danvers,' said Colonel Julyan. 'I mean something closer than that.'

'I'm afraid I don't understand, sir,' said Mrs. Danvers.

'Oh, come off it, Danny,' said Favell, 'you know damn well what he's driving at. I've told Colonel Julyan already, but he doesn't seem to believe me. Rebecca and I had lived together off and on for years, hadn't we? She was in love with me, wasn't she?'

To my surprise Mrs. Danvers considered him a moment without speaking, and there was something of scorn in the glance she gave him.

'She was not,' she said.

'Listen here, you old fool . . .' began Favell, but Mrs. Danvers cut him short.

'She was not in love with you, or with Mr. de Winter. She was not in love with anyone. She despised all men. She was above all that.'

Favell flushed angrily. 'Listen here. Didn't she come down the path through the woods to meet me, night after night. Didn't you wait up for her? Didn't she spend the week-ends with me in London?'

'Well,' said Mrs. Danvers, with sudden passion, 'and what if she did? She had a right to amuse herself, hadn't she? Love-making was a game with her, only a game. She told me so. She did it because it made her laugh. It made her laugh, I tell you. She laughed at you like she did at the rest. I've known her come back and sit upstairs on her bed and rock with laughter at the lot of you.'

There was something horrible in the sudden torrent of words, something horrible and unexpected. It revolted me, even though I knew. Maxim had gone very white. Favell stared at her blankly, as though he had not understood. Colonel Julyan tugged at his small moustache. No one said anything for a few minutes. And there was no sound but that inevitable falling rain. Then Mrs. Danvers began to cry. She cried as she had done that morning in the bedroom. I could not look at her. I had to turn away. No one said anything. There were just the two sounds in the room, the falling rain and Mrs. Danvers crying. It made me want to scream. I wanted to run out of the room and scream and scream.

No one moved towards her, to say anything, or to help her. She went on crying. Then at last, it seemed eternity, she began to control herself. Little by little the crying ceased. She stood quite still, her face working, her hands clutching the black stuff of her frock. At last she was silent again. Then Colonel Julyan spoke, quietly, slowly.

'Mrs. Danvers,' he said, 'can you think of any reason, however remote, why Mrs. de Winter should have taken her own life?'

Mrs. Danvers swallowed. She went on clutching at her frock. She shook her head. 'No,' she said. 'No.'

'There you see?' Favell said swiftly. 'It's impossible. She knows that as well as I do. I've told you already.'

'Be quiet, will you?' said Colonel Julyan. 'Give Mrs. Danvers time to think. We all of us agree that on the face of it the thing's absurd, out of the question. I'm not disputing the truth or veracity of that note of yours. It's plain for us to see. She wrote you that note some time during those hours she spent in London. There was something she wanted to tell you. It's just possible that if we knew what that something was we might have an answer to the whole appalling problem. Let Mrs. Danvers read the note. She may be able to throw light on it.' Favell shrugged his shoulders. He felt in his pocket for the note and threw it on the floor at Mrs. Danvers' feet. She stooped and picked it up. We watched her lips move as she read the words. She read it twice. Then she shook her head. 'It's no use,' she said. 'I don't know what she meant. If there was something important she had to tell Mr. Jack she would have told me first.'

'You never saw her that night?'

'No, I was out. I was spending the afternoon and evening in Kerrith. I shall never forgive myself for that. Never till my dying day.'

'Then you know of nothing on her mind, you can't suggest a solution, Mrs. Danvers? Those words *"I have something to tell you,"* do not convey anything to you at all?'

'No,' she answered. 'No, sir, nothing at all.'

'Does anybody know how she spent that day in London?'

Nobody answered. Maxim shook his head. Favell swore under his breath. 'Look here, she left that note at my flat at three in the afternoon,' he said. 'The porter saw her. She must have driven down here straight after that, and gone like the wind too.'

'Mrs. de Winter had a hair appointment from twelve until one thirty,' said Mrs. Danvers. 'I remember that, because I had to telephone through to London from here earlier in the week and book it for her. I remember doing it. Twelve to one thirty. She always lunched at her club after a hair appointment so that she could leave the pins in her hair. It's almost certain she lunched there that day.'

'Say it took her half-an-hour to have lunch, what was she doing from two until three? We ought to verify that,' said Colonel Julyan.

'Oh, Christ Jesus, who the hell cares what she was doing,' shouted Favell. 'She didn't kill herself, that's the only bloody thing that matters, isn't it?'

'I've got her engagement diary locked in my room,' said Mrs. Danvers slowly. 'I kept all those things. Mr. de Winter never asked me for them. It's just possible she may have noted down her appointments for that day. She was methodical in that way. She used to put everything down and then tick the items off with a cross. If you think it would be helpful I'll go and fetch the diary.'

'Well, de Winter,' said Colonel Julyan, 'what do you say? Do you mind us seeing this diary?'

'Of course not,' said Maxim. 'Why on earth should I?'

Once again I saw Colonel Julyan give him that swift, curious glance. And this time Frank noticed it. I saw Frank look at Maxim too. And then back again to me. This time it was I who got up and went towards the window. It seemed to me that it was no longer raining quite so hard. The fury was spent. The rain that was falling now had a quieter, softer note. The grey light of evening had come into the sky. The lawns were dark and drenched with the heavy rain, and the trees had a shrouded humped appearance. I could hear the housemaid overhead drawing the curtains for the night, shutting down the windows that had not been closed already. The little routine of the day going on inevitably as it had always done. The curtains drawn, shoes taken down to be cleaned, the towel laid out on the chair in the bathroom and the water run for my bath. Beds turned down, slippers put beneath a chair. And here were we in the library, none of us speaking, knowing in our hearts that Maxim was standing trial here for his life.

I turned round when I heard the soft closing of the door. It was Mrs. Danvers. She had come back again with the diary in her hand.

'I was right,' she said quietly. 'She had marked down the engagements as I said she would. Here they are on the date she died.'

She opened the diary, a small, red leather book. She gave it to Colonel Julyan. Once more he brought his spectacles from his case. There was a long pause while he glanced down the page. It seemed to me then that there was something about that particular moment, while he looked at the page of the diary, and we stood waiting, that frightened me more than anything that had happened that evening.

I dug my nails in my hands. I could not look at Maxim. Surely Colonel Julyan must hear my heart beating and thumping in my breast?

'Ah!' he said. His finger was in the middle of the page. Something is going to happen, I thought, something terrible is going to happen. 'Yes,' he said, 'yes, here it is. Hair at twelve, as Mrs. Danvers said. And a cross beside it. She kept her appointment then. Lunch at the club, and a cross beside that. What have we here, though? Baker, two o'clock. Who was Baker?' He looked at Maxim. Maxim shook his head. Then at Mrs. Danvers.

'Baker?' repeated Mrs. Danvers. 'She knew no one called Baker. I've never heard the name before.'

'Well here it is,' said Colonel Julyan, handing her the diary. 'You can see for yourself. Baker. And she's put a great cross beside it as though she wanted to break the pencil. She evidently saw this Baker whoever he may have been.'

Mrs. Danvers was staring at the name written in the diary, and the black cross beside it. 'Baker,' she said. 'Baker.'

'I believe if we knew who Baker was we'd be getting to the bottom of the whole business,' said Colonel Julyan. 'She wasn't in the hands of money-lenders, was she?'

Mrs. Danvers looked at him with scorn. 'Mrs. de Winter?' she said.

'Well, blackmailers perhaps?' said Colonel Julyan, with a glance at Favell.

Mrs. Danvers shook her head. 'Baker,' she repeated. 'Baker.'

'She had no enemy, no one who had ever threatened her, no one she was afraid of?'

'Mrs. de Winter afraid?' said Mrs. Danvers. 'She was afraid of nothing and no one. There was only one thing ever worried her, and that was the idea of getting old, of illness, of dying in her bed. She has said to me a score of times, "When I go, Danny, I want to go quickly, like the snuffing out of a candle". That used to be the only thing that consoled me, after she died. They say drowning is painless, don't they?'

She looked searchingly at Colonel Julyan. He did not answer. He hesitated, tugging at his moustache. I saw him throw another glance at Maxim.

'What the hell's the use of all this?' said Favell, coming forward. 'We're streaking away from the point the whole bloody time. Who cares about this Baker fellow? What's he got to do with it? It was probably some damn merchant who sold stockings, or face-cream. If he had been anyone important Danny here would know him. Rebecca had no secrets from Danny.'

But I was watching Mrs. Danvers. She had the book in her hands and was turning the leaves. Suddenly she gave an exclamation.

'There's something here,' she said, 'right at the back among the telephone numbers. Baker. And there's a number beside it: 0488. But there is no exchange.'

'Brilliant Danny,' said Favell, 'becoming quite a sleuth in your old age, aren't you? But you're just twelve months too late. If you'd done this a year ago there might have been some use in it.'

'That's his number all right,' said Colonel Julyan, '0488, and the name Baker beside it. Why didn't she put the exchange?'

'Try every exchange in London,' jeered Favell. 'It will take you through the night but we don't mind. Max doesn't care if his telephone bill is a hundred pounds, do you, Max? You want to play for time and so should I, if I were in your shoes.'

'There is a mark beside the number but it might mean anything,' said Colonel Julyan, 'take a look at it, Mrs. Danvers. Could it possibly be an M?'

Mrs. Danvers took the diary in her hands again. 'It might be,' she said doubtfully. 'It's not like her usual M, but she may have scribbled it in a hurry. Yes, it might be M.'

'Mayfair 0488,' said Favell, 'what a genius, what a brain!'

'Well,' said Maxim, lighting his first cigarette, 'something had better be done about it. Frank? Go through and ask the exchange for Mayfair 0488'.

The nagging pain was strong beneath my heart. I stood quite still, my hands by my side. Maxim did not look at me.

'Go on, Frank,' he said. 'What are you waiting for?'

Frank went through to the little room beyond. We waited while he called the exchange. In a moment he was back again. 'They're going to ring me,' he said quietly. Colonel Julyan clasped his hands behind his back and began walking up and down the room. No one said anything. After about four minutes the telephone rang shrill and insistent, that irritating, monotonous note of a long-distance call. Frank went through to answer it. 'Is that Mayfair 0488?' he said. 'Can you tell me if anyone of the name of Baker lives there? Oh, I see. I'm so sorry. Yes, I must have got the wrong number. Thank you very much.'

The little click as he replaced the receiver. Then he came back into the room. 'Someone called Lady Eastleigh lives at Mayfair 0488. It's an address in Grosvenor Street. They've never heard of Baker.'

Favell gave a great cackle of laughter. 'The butcher, the baker, the candlestick-maker. They all jumped out of a rotten potato,' he said. 'Carry on, detective Number One, what's the next exchange on the list?'

'Try Museum,' said Mrs. Danvers.

Frank glanced at Maxim. 'Go ahead,' said Maxim.

The farce was repeated all over again. Colonel Julyan repeated his walk up and down the room. Another five minutes went by, and the telephone rang again. Frank went to answer it. He left the door wide open, I could see him lean down to the table where the telephone stood, and bend to the mouth-piece.

'Hullo? Is that Museum 0488? Can you tell me if anyone of the name of Baker lives there? Oh; who is that speaking? A night porter. Yes. Yes, I understand. Not offices. No, no of course. Can you give me the address? Yes, it's rather important.' He paused. He called to us over his shoulder. 'I think we've got him,' he said.

Oh, God, don't let it be true. Don't let Baker be found. Please God make Baker be dead. I knew who Baker was. I had known all along. I watched Frank through the door, I watched him lean forward suddenly, reach for a pencil and a piece of paper. 'Hullo? Yes, I'm still here. Could you spell it? Thank you. Thank you very much. Good-night.' He came back into the room, the piece of paper in his hands. Frank who loved Maxim, who did not know that the piece of paper he held was the one shred of evidence that was worth a damn in the whole nightmare of our evening, and that by producing it he could destroy Maxim as well and truly as though he had a dagger in his hand and stabbed him in the back.

'It was the night porter from an address in Bloomsbury,' he said. 'There are no residents there at all. The place is used during the day as a doctor's consulting rooms. Apparently Baker's given up practice, and left six months ago. But we can get hold of him all right. The night-porter gave me his address. I wrote it down on this piece of paper.'

Chapter Twenty-five

It was then that Maxim looked at me. He looked at me for the first time that evening. And in his eyes I read a message of farewell. It was as though he leant against the side of a ship, and I stood below him on the quay. There would be other people touching his shoulder, and touching mine, but we would not see them. Nor would we speak or call to one another, for the wind and the distance would carry away the sound of our voices. But I should see his eyes and he would see mine before the ship drew away from the side of the quay. Favell, Mrs. Danvers, Colonel Julyan, Frank with the slip of paper in his hands, they were all forgotten at this moment. It was ours, inviolate, a fraction of time suspended between two seconds. And then he turned away and held out his hand to Frank.

'Well done,' he said. 'What's the address?'

'Somewhere near Barnet, north of London,' said Frank, giving him the paper. 'But it's not on the telephone. We can't ring him up.'

'Satisfactory work, Crawley,' said Colonel Julyan, 'and from you too, Mrs. Danvers. Can you throw any light on the matter now?'

Mrs. Danvers shook her head. 'Mrs. de Winter never needed a doctor. Like all strong people she despised them. We only had Doctor Phillips from Kerrith here once, that time she sprained her wrist. I've never heard her speak of this Doctor Baker, she never mentioned his name to me.'

'I tell you the fellow was a face-cream mixer,' said Favell. 'What the hell does it matter who he was? If there was anything to it Danny would know. I tell you it's some fool fellow who had discovered a new way of bleaching her hair or whitening the skin, and Rebecca had probably got the address from her hair-dresser that morning and went along after lunch out of curiosity.'

'No,' said Frank. 'I think you're wrong there. Baker wasn't a quack. The night-porter at Museum 0488 told me he was a very well-known woman's specialist.'

'H'm,' said Colonel Julyan, pulling at his moustache, 'there must have been something wrong with her after all. It seems very curious that she did not say a word to anybody, not even to you, Mrs. Danvers.'

'She was too thin,' said Favell. 'I told her about it, but she only laughed. Said it suited her. Banting I suppose, like all these women. Perhaps she went to this chap Baker for a diet sheet.'

'Do you think that's possible, Mrs. Danvers?' asked Colonel Julyan.

Mrs. Danvers shook her head slowly. She seemed dazed, bewildered by this sudden news about Baker. 'I can't understand it,' she said. 'I don't know what it means. Baker. A Doctor Baker. Why didn't she tell me? Why did she keep it from me? She told me everything.'

'Perhaps she didn't want to worry you,' said Colonel Julyan. 'No doubt she made an appointment with him, and saw him, and then when she came down that night she was going to have told you all about it.'

'And the note to Mr. Jack,' said Mrs. Danvers suddenly. 'That note to Mr. Jack, *"I have something to tell you. I must see you"*; she was going to tell him too?'

'That's true,' said Favell slowly. 'We were forgetting the note.' Once more he pulled it out of his pocket and read it to us aloud. ' *"I've got something to tell you and I want to see you as soon as possible. Rebecca."* '

'Of course, there's no doubt about it,' said Colonel Julyan, turning to Maxim. 'I wouldn't mind betting a thousand pounds on it. She was going to tell Favell the result of that interview with this Doctor Baker.'

'I believe you're right after all,' said Favell. 'The note and that appointment seem to hang together. But what the hell was it all about, that's what I want to know? What was the matter with her?'

The truth screamed in their faces and they did not see. They all stood there, staring at one another, and they did not understand. I dared not look at them. I dared not move lest I betray my knowledge. Maxim said nothing. He had gone back to the window and was looking out into the garden that was hushed and dark and still. The rain had ceased at last, but the spots fell from the dripping leaves and from the gutter above the window.

'It ought to be quite easy to verify,' said Frank. 'Here is the doctor's present address. I can write him a letter and ask him if he remembers an appointment last year with Mrs. de Winter.'

'I don't know if he would take any notice of it,' said Colonel Julyan, 'there is so much of this etiquette in the medical profession. Every case is confidential you know. The only way to get anything out of him would be to get de Winter to see him privately and explain the circumstances. What do you say, de Winter?'

Maxim turned round from the window. 'I'm ready to do whatever you care to suggest,' he said quietly.

'Anything for time, eh?' said Favell. 'A lot can be done in twenty-four hours, can't it? Trains can be caught, ships can sail, aeroplanes can fly?'

I saw Mrs. Danvers look sharply from Favell to Maxim, and I realised then, for the first time, that Mrs. Danvers had not known about Favell's accusation. At last she was beginning to understand. I could tell from the expression on her face. There was doubt written on it, then wonder and hatred mixed, and then conviction. Once again those lean long hands of hers clutched convulsively at her dress, and she passed her tongue over her lips. She went on staring at Maxim. She never took her eyes away from Maxim. It's too late, I thought, she can't do anything to us now, the harm is done. It does not matter what she says to us now, or what she does. The harm is done. She can't hurt us any more. Maxim did not notice her, or if he did he gave no sign. He was talking to Colonel Julyan.

'What do you suggest?' he said. 'Shall I go up in the morning, drive to this address at Barnet? I can write Baker to expect me.'

'He's not going alone,' said Favell, with a short laugh. 'I have a right to insist on that, haven't I? Send him up with Inspector Welch and I won't object.'

If only Mrs. Danvers would take her eyes away from Maxim. Frank had seen her now. He was watching her, puzzled, anxious. I saw him glance once more at the slip of paper in his hands, on which he had written Doctor Baker's address. Then he too glanced at Maxim. I believe then that some faint idea of the truth began to force itself to his conscience, for he went very white and put the paper down on the table.

'I don't think there is any necessity to bring Inspector Welch into the affair – yet,' said Colonel Julyan. His voice was different, harsher. I did not like the way he used the word 'yet'. Why must he use it at all? I did not like it. 'If I go with de Winter, and stay with him the whole time, and bring him back, will that satisfy you?' he said.

Favell looked at Maxim, and then at Colonel Julyan. The expression on his face was ugly, calculating, and there was something of triumph too in his light blue eyes. 'Yes,' he said slowly, 'yes, I suppose so. But for safety's sake do you mind if I come with you too?'

'No,' said Colonel Julyan, 'unfortunately I think you have the right to ask that. But if you do come, I have the right to insist on your being sober.'

'You needn't worry about that,' said Favell, beginning to smile, 'I'll be sober all right. Sober as the judge will be when he sentences Max in three months' time. I rather think this Doctor Baker is going to prove my case, after all.'

He looked around at each one of us and began to laugh. I think he too had understood at last the significance of that visit to the doctor.

'Well,' he said, 'what time are we going to start in the morning?'

Colonel Julyan looked at Maxim. 'How early can you be ready?'

'Any time you say,' said Maxim.

'Nine o'clock?'

'Nine o'clock,' said Maxim.

'How do we know he won't do a bolt in the night?' said Favell. 'He's only got to cut round to the garage and get his car.'

'Is my word enough for you?' said Maxim, turning to Colonel Julyan. And for the first time Colonel Julyan hesitated. I saw him glance at Frank.

And a flush came over Maxim's face. I saw the little pulse beating on his forehead. 'Mrs. Danvers,' he said slowly, 'when Mrs. de Winter and I go to bed to-night will you come up yourself and lock the door on the outside? And call us yourself, at seven in the morning.'

'Yes, sir,' said Mrs. Danvers. Still she kept her eyes on him, still her hands clutched at her dress.

'Very well then,' said Colonel Julyan brusquely. 'I don't think there is anything else we need discuss, to-night. I shall be here sharp at nine in the morning. You will have room for me in your car, de Winter?'

'Yes,' said Maxim.

'And Favell will follow us in his?'

'Right on your tail, my dear fellow, right on your tail,' said Favell.

Colonel Julyan came up to me and took my hand. 'Good-night,' he said. 'You know how I feel for you in all this, there's no need for me to tell you. Get your husband to bed early, if you can. It's going to be a long day.' He held my hand a minute, and then he turned away. It was curious how he avoided my eye. He looked at my chin. Frank held the door for him as he went out. Favell leant forward and filled his case with cigarettes from the box on the table.

'I suppose I'm not going to be asked to stop to dinner?' he said.

Nobody answered. He lit one of the cigarettes, and blew a cloud of smoke into the air. 'It means a quiet evening at the pub on the high-road then,' he said, 'and the barmaid has a squint. What a hell of a night I'm going to spend! Never mind, I'm looking forward to to-morrow. Good night, Danny old lady, don't forget to turn the key on Mr. de Winter, will you?'

He came over to me and held out his hand.

Like a foolish child I put my hands behind my back. He laughed, and bowed.

'It's just too bad, isn't it?' he said. 'A nasty man like me coming and spoiling all your fun. Don't worry, it will be a great thrill for you when the yellow Press gets going with your life story, and you see the headlines "From Monte Carlo to Manderley. Experiences of murderer's girl-bride," written across the top. Better luck next time.'

He strolled across the room to the door, waving his hand to Maxim by the window. 'So long, old man,' he said, 'pleasant dreams. Make the most of your night behind that locked door.' He turned and laughed at me, and then he went out of the room. Mrs. Danvers followed him. Maxim and I were alone. He went on standing by the window. He did not come to me. Jasper came trotting in from the hall. He had been shut outside all the evening. He came fussing up to me, biting the edge of my skirt.

'I'm coming with you in the morning,' I said to Maxim. 'I'm coming up to London with you in the car.'

He did not answer for a moment. He went on looking out of the window. Then 'Yes', he said, his voice without expression. 'Yes, we must go on being together.'

Frank came back into the room. He stood in the entrance, his hand on the door. 'They've gone,' he said, 'Favell and Colonel Julyan. I watched them go.'

'All right, Frank,' said Maxim.

'Is there anything I can do,' said Frank, 'anything at all? Wire to anyone, arrange anything? I'll stay up all night if only there's anything I can do. I'll get that wire off to Baker of course.'

'Don't worry,' said Maxim, 'there's nothing for you to do – yet. There may be plenty – after to-morrow. We can go into all that when the time comes. To-night we want to be together. You understand, don't you?'

'Yes,' said Frank. 'Yes, of course.'

He waited a moment, his hand on the door. 'Good night,' he said.

'Good night,' said Maxim.

When he had gone, and shut the door behind him, Maxim came over to me where I was standing on the fireplace. I held out my arms to him and he came to me like a child. I put my arms round him and held him. We did not say anything for a long time. I held him and comforted him as though he were Jasper. As though Jasper had hurt himself in some way and had come to me to take his pain away.

'We can sit together,' he said, 'driving up in the car.'

'Yes,' I said.

'Julyan won't mind,' he said.

'No,' I said.

'We shall have to-morrow night too,' he said. 'They won't do anything at once, not for twenty-four hours perhaps.'

'No,' I said.

'They aren't so strict now,' he said. 'They let one see people. And it all takes such a long time. If I can I shall try and get hold of Hastings. He's the best. Hastings or Birkett. Hastings used to know my father.'

'Yes,' I said.

'I shall have to tell him the truth,' he said. 'It makes it easier for them. They know where they are.'

'Yes,' I said.

The door opened and Frith came into the room. I pushed Maxim away. I stood up straight and conventional, patting my hair into place.

'Will you be changing, Madam, or shall I serve dinner at once?'

'No, Frith, we won't be changing, not to-night,' I said.

'Very good, Madam,' he said.

He left the door open. Robert came in and began drawing the curtains. He arranged the cushions, straightened the sofa, tidied the books and papers on the table. He took away the whisky and soda and the dirty ash-trays. I had seen him do these things as a ritual every evening I had spent at Manderley, but to-night they seemed to take on a special significance, as though the memory of them would last forever and I should say, long after, in some other time 'I remember this moment.'

Then Frith came in and told us that dinner was served.

I remember every detail of that evening. I remember the ice-cold consommé in the cups, and the fillets of sole, and the hot shoulder of lamb.

I remember the burnt sugar sweet, the sharp savoury that followed.

We had new candles in the silver candlesticks, they looked white and slim and very tall. The curtains had been drawn here too against the dull grey evening. It seemed strange to be sitting in the dining-room and not look out on to the lawns. It was like the beginning of autumn.

It was while we were drinking our coffee in the library that the telephone rang. This time it was I who answered it. I heard Beatrice speaking at the other end. 'Is that you?' she said. 'I've been trying to get through all the evening. Twice it was engaged.'

'I'm so sorry,' I said, 'so very sorry.'

'We had the evening papers about two hours ago,' she said, 'and the verdict was a frightful shock to both Giles and myself. What does Maxim say about it?'

'I think it was a shock to everybody,' I said.

'But my dear, the thing is preposterous. Why on earth should Rebecca have committed suicide? The most unlikely person in the world. There must have been a blunder somewhere.'

'I don't know,' I said.

'What does Maxim say, where is he?' she said.

'People have been here,' I said, 'Colonel Julyan, and others. Maxim is very tired. We're going up to London to-morrow.'

'What on earth for?'

'Something to do with the verdict. I can't very well explain.'

'You ought to get it squashed,' she said. 'It's ridiculous, quite ridiculous. And so bad for Maxim, all this frightful publicity. It's going to reflect on him.'

'Yes,' I said.

'Surely Colonel Julyan can do something?' she said. 'He's a magistrate. What are magistrates for? Old Horridge from Lanyon must have been off his head. What was her motive supposed to be? It's the most idiotic thing I've ever heard in my life. Someone ought to get hold of Tabb. How can he tell whether those holes in the boat were made deliberately or not? Giles said of course it must have been the rocks.'

'They seemed to think not,' I said.

'If only I could have been there,' she said. 'I should have insisted on speaking. No one seems to have made any effort. Is Maxim very upset?'

'He's tired,' I said, 'more tired than anything else.'

'I wish I could come up to London and join you,' she said, 'but I don't see how I can. Roger has a temperature of 103, poor old boy, and the nurse we've got in is a perfect idiot, he loathes her. I can't possibly leave him.'

'Of course not,' I said. 'You mustn't attempt it.'

'Whereabouts in London will you be?'

'I don't know,' I said. 'It's all rather vague.'

'Tell Maxim he must try and do something to get that verdict altered. It's so bad for the family. I'm telling everybody here it's absolutely wicked. Rebecca would never have killed herself, she wasn't the type. I've a good mind to write to the Coroner myself.'

'It's too late,' I said. 'Much better leave it. It won't do any good.'

'The stupidity of it gets my goat,' she said. 'Giles and I think it much more likely that if those holes weren't done by the rocks they were done deliberately, by some tramp or other. A Communist perhaps. There are heaps of them about. Just the sort of thing a Communist would do.'

Maxim called to me from the library. 'Can't you get rid of her? What on earth is she talking about?'

'Beatrice,' I said desperately, 'I'll try and ring you up from London.'

'Is it any good my tackling Dick Godolphin?' she said. 'He's your M.P. I know him very well, much better than Maxim does. He was at Oxford with Giles. Ask Maxim whether he would like me to telephone Dick and see if he can do anything to squash the verdict? Ask Maxim what he thinks of this Communist idea.'

'It's no use,' I said. 'It can't do any good. Please, Beatrice, don't try and do anything. It will make it worse, much worse. Rebecca may have had some motive we don't know anything about. And I don't think Communists go ramming holes in boats, what would be the use? Please, Beatrice, leave it alone.'

Oh, thank God she had not been with us to-day. Thank God for that at least. Something was buzzing in the telephone. I heard Beatrice shouting, 'Hullo, hullo, don't cut us off, exchange,' and then there was a click, and silence.

I went back into the library, limp and exhausted. In a few minutes the telephone began ringing again. I did not do anything. I let it ring. I went and sat down at Maxim's feet. It went on ringing. I did not move. Presently it stopped, as though cut suddenly in exasperation. The clock on the mantelpiece struck ten o'clock. Maxim put his arms round me and lifted me against him. We began to kiss one another, feverishly, desperately, like guilty lovers who have not kissed before.

Chapter Twenty-six

When I awoke the next morning, just after six o'clock, and got up and went to the window there was a foggy dew upon the grass like frost, and the trees were shrouded in a white mist. There was a chill in the air and a little, fresh wind, and the cold, quiet smell of autumn.

As I knelt by the window looking down on to the rose-garden where the flowers themselves drooped upon their stalks, the petals brown and dragging after last night's rain, the happenings of the day before seemed remote and unreal. Here at Manderley a new day was starting, the things of the garden were not concerned with our troubles. A blackbird ran across the rose-garden to the lawns in swift, short rushes, stopping now and again to stab at the earth with his yellow beak. A thrush, too, went about his business, and two stout, little wagtails, following one another, and a little cluster of twittering sparrows. A gull poised himself high in the air, silent and alone, and then spread his wings wide and swooped beyond the lawns to the woods and the Happy Valley. These things continued, our worries and anxieties had no power to alter them. Soon the gardeners would be astir, brushing the first leaves from the lawns and the paths, raking the gravel in the drive. Pails would clank in the courtyard behind the house, the hose would be turned on the car, the little scullery maid would begin to chatter through the open door to the men in the yard. There would be the crisp, hot smell of bacon. The housemaids would open up the house, throw wide the windows, draw back the curtains.

The dogs would crawl from their baskets, yawn and stretch themselves, wander out on to the terrace and blink at the first struggles of the pale sun coming through the mist. Robert would lay the table for breakfast, bring in those piping scones, the clutch of eggs, the glass dishes of honey, jam, and marmalade, the bowl of peaches, the cluster of purple grapes with the bloom upon them still, hot from the greenhouses.

Maids sweeping in the morning-room, the drawing-room, the fresh clean air pouring into the long open windows. Smoke curling from the chimneys, and little by little the autumn mist fading away and the trees and the banks and the woods taking shape, the glimmer of the sea showing with the sun upon it below the valley, the beacon standing tall and straight upon the headland.

The peace of Manderley. The quietude and the grace. Whoever lived within its walls, whatever trouble there was and strife, however much uneasiness and pain, no matter what tears were shed, what sorrows borne, the peace of Manderley could not be broken or the loveliness destroyed. The flowers that died would bloom again another year, the same birds build their nests, the same trees blossom. That old quiet moss smell would linger in the air, and bees would come, and crickets, and herons build their nests in the deep dark woods. The butterflies would dance their merry jig across the lawns, and spiders spin foggy webs and small startled rabbits who had no business to come trespassing poke their faces through the crowded shrubs. There would be lilac, and honeysuckle still, and the white magnolia buds unfolding slow and tight beneath the dining-room windows. No one would ever hurt Manderley. It would lie always in its hollow like an enchanted thing, guarded by the woods, safe, secure, while the sea broke and ran and came again in the little shingle bays below.

Maxim slept on and I did not wake him. The day ahead of us would be a weary thing and long. High-roads, and telegraph poles, and the monotony of passing traffic, the slow crawl into London. We did not know what we should find at the end of our journey. The future was unknown. Somewhere to the north of London lived a man called Baker who had never heard of us, but he held our future in the hollow of his hand. Soon he too would be waking, stretching, yawning, going about the business of his day. I got up, and went into the bathroom, and began to run my bath. These actions held for me the same significance as Robert and his clearing of the library had the night before. I had done these things before mechanically, but now I was aware as I dropped my sponge into the water, as I spread my towel on the chair from the hot rail, as I lay back and let the water run over my body. Every moment was a precious thing, having in it the essence of finality. When I went back to the bedroom and began to dress I heard a soft footstep come and pause outside the door, and the key turn quietly in the lock. There was silence a moment, and then the footsteps went away. It was Mrs. Danvers.

She had not forgotten. I had heard the same sound the night before, after we had come up from the library. She had not knocked upon the door, she had not made herself known; there was just the sound of footsteps and the turning of the key in the lock. It brought me to reality, and the facing of the immediate future.

I finished dressing, and went and turned on Maxim's bath. Presently Clarice came with our tea. I woke Maxim. He stared at me at first like a puzzled child, and then he held out his arms. We drank our tea. He got up and went to his bath and I began putting things methodically in my suit-case. It might be that we should have to stay in London.

I packed the brushes Maxim had given me, a nightdress, my dressing-gown and slippers, and another dress too and a pair of shoes. My dressing-case looked unfamiliar as I dragged it from the back of a wardrobe. It seemed so long since I had used it, and yet it was only four months ago. It still had the Customs mark upon it they had chalked at Calais. In one of the pockets was a concert ticket from the casino in Monte Carlo. I crumpled it and threw it into the waste-paper basket. It might have belonged to another age, another world. My bedroom began to take on the appearance of all rooms when the owner goes away. The dressing-table was bare without my brushes. There was tissue-paper lying on the floor, and an old label. The beds where we had slept had a terrible emptiness about them. The towels lay crumpled on the bathroom floor. The wardrobe doors gaped open. I put on my hat so that I should not have to come up again, and I took my bag and my gloves and my suit-case. I glanced round the room to see if there was anything I had forgotten. The mist was breaking, the sun was forcing its way through and throwing patterns on the carpet. When I was half-way down the passage I had a curious, inexplicable feeling that I must go back and look in my room again. I went without reason, and stood a moment looking at the gaping wardrobe and the empty bed, and the tray of tea upon the table. I stared at them, impressing them for ever on my mind, wondering why they had the power to touch me, to sadden me, as though they were children that did not want me to go away.

Then I turned and went downstairs to breakfast. It was cold in the dining-room, the sun not yet on the windows, and I was grateful for the scalding bitter coffee and heartening bacon. Maxim and I ate in silence. Now and again he glanced at the clock. I heard Robert put the suit-cases in the hall with the rug, and presently there was the sound of the car being brought to the door.

I went out and stood on the terrace. The rain had cleared the air, and the grass smelt fresh and sweet. When the sun was higher it would be a lovely day. I thought how we might have wandered in the valley before lunch, and then sat out afterwards under the chestnut tree with books and papers. I closed my eyes a minute and felt the warmth of the sun on my face and on my hands.

I heard Maxim calling to me from the house. I went back, and Frith helped me into my coat. I heard the sound of another car. It was Frank.

'Colonel Julyan is waiting at the lodge gates,' he said. 'He did not think it worth while to drive right up to the house.'

'No,' said Maxim.

'I'll stand by in the office all day and wait for you to telephone,' said Frank. 'After you've seen Baker you may find you want me, up in London.'

'Yes,' said Maxim. 'Yes, perhaps.'

'It's just nine now,' said Frank. 'You're up to time. It's going to be fine too. You should have a good run.'

'Yes.'

'I hope you won't get over-tired, Mrs. de Winter,' he said to me. 'It's going to be a long day for you.'

'I shall be all right,' I said. I looked at Jasper who was standing by my feet with ears drooping and sad reproachful eyes.

'Take Jasper back with you to the office,' I said. 'He looks so miserable.'

'Yes,' he said. 'Yes, I will.'

'We'd better be off,' said Maxim. 'Old Julyan will be getting impatient. All right, Frank.'

I climbed in the car beside Maxim. Frank slammed the door.

'You will telephone, won't you?' he said.

'Yes, of course,' said Maxim.

I looked back at the house. Frith was standing at the top of the steps, and Robert just behind. My eyes filled with tears for no reason. I turned away and groped with my bag on the floor of the car so that nobody should see. Then Maxim started up the car and we swept round and into the drive and the house was hidden.

We stopped at the lodge-gates and picked up Colonel Julyan. He got in at the back. He looked doubtful when he saw me.

'It's going to be a long day,' he said. 'I don't think you should have attempted it. I would have taken care of your husband you know.'

'I wanted to come,' I said.

He did not say any more about it. He settled himself in the corner. 'It's fine, that's one thing,' he said.

'Yes,' said Maxim.

'That fellow Favell said he would pick us up at the cross-roads. If he's not there don't attempt to wait, we'd do much better without him. I hope the damned fellow has overslept himself.'

When we came to the cross-roads though I saw the long green body of his car, and my heart sank. I had thought he might not be on time. Favell was sitting at the wheel, hatless, a cigarette in his mouth. He grinned when he saw us, and waved us on. I settled down in my seat for the journey ahead, one hand on Maxim's knee. The hours passed, and the miles were covered. I watched the road ahead in a kind of stupor. Colonel Julyan slept at the back from time to time, I turned occasionally and saw his head loll against the cushions, and his mouth open. The green car kept close beside us. Sometimes it shot ahead, sometimes it dropped behind. But we never lost it. At one we stopped for lunch at one of those inevitable old-fashioned hotels in the main street of a county town. Colonel Julyan waded through the whole set lunch, starting with soup and fish, and going on to roast beef and yorkshire pudding. Maxim and I had cold ham and coffee.

I half expected Favell to wander into the dining-room and join us, but when we came out to the car again I saw his car had been drawn up outside a café on the opposite side of the road. He must have seen us from the window, for three minutes after we had started he was on our tail again.

We came to the suburbs of London about three o'clock. It was then that I began to feel tired, the noise and the traffic blocks started a humming in my head. It was warm in London too. The streets had that worn dusty look of August, and the leaves hung listless on dull trees. Our storm must have been local, there had been no rain here.

People were walking about in cotton frocks and the men were hatless. There was a smell of waste-paper, and orange-peel, and feet, and burnt dried grass. Buses lumbered slowly, and taxis crawled. I felt as though my coat and skirt were sticking to me, and my stockings pricked my skin.

Colonel Julyan sat up and looked out through his window. 'They've had no rain here,' he said.

'No,' said Maxim.

'Looks as though the place needed it, too.'

'Yes.'

'We haven't succeeded in shaking Favell off. He's still on our tail.'

'Yes.'

Shopping centres on the outskirts seemed congested. Tired women with crying babies in prams stared into windows, hawkers shouted, small boys hung on to the back of lorries. There were too many people, too much noise. The very air was irritable and exhausted and spent.

The drive through London seemed endless, and by the time we had drawn clear again and were out beyond Hampstead there was a sound in my head like the beating of a drum, and my eyes were burning.

I wondered how tired Maxim was. He was pale, and there were shadows under his eyes, but he did not say anything. Colonel Julyan kept yawning at the back. He opened his mouth very wide and yawned aloud, sighing heavily afterwards. He would do this every few minutes. I felt a senseless stupid irritation come over me, and I did not know how to prevent myself from turning round and screaming to him to stop.

Once we had passed Hampstead he drew out a large-scale map from his coat-pocket and began directing Maxim to Barnet. The way was clear and there were sign-posts to tell us, but he kept pointing out every turn and twist in the road, and if there was any hesitation on Maxim's part Colonel Julyan would turn down the window and call for information from a passer-by.

When we came to Barnet itself he made Maxim stop every few minutes. 'Can you tell us where a house called Roselands is? It belongs to a Doctor Baker, who's retired, and come to live there lately,' and the passer-by would stand frowning a moment, obviously at sea, ignorance written plain upon his face.

'Doctor Baker? I don't know a Doctor Baker. There used to be a house called Rose Cottage near the church, but a Mrs. Wilson lives there.'

'No, it's Roselands we want, Doctor Baker's house,' said Colonel Julyan, and then we would go on and stop again in front of a nurse and a pram. 'Can you tell us where Roselands is?'

'I'm sorry. I'm afraid I've only just come to live here.'

'You don't know a Doctor Baker?'

'Doctor Davidson. I know Doctor Davidson.'

'No, it's Doctor Baker we want.'

I glanced up at Maxim. He was looking very tired. His mouth was set hard. Behind us crawled Favell, his green car covered in dust.

It was a postman who pointed out the house in the end. A square house, ivy covered, with no name on the gate, which we had already passed twice. Mechanically I reached for my bag and dabbed my face with the end of the power puff. Maxim drew up outside at the side of the road. He did not take the car into the short drive. We sat silently for a few minutes.

'Well, here we are,' said Colonel Julyan, 'and it's exactly twelve minutes past five. We shall catch them in the middle of their tea. Better wait for a bit.'

Maxim lit a cigarette, and then stretched out his hand to me. He did not speak. I heard Colonel Julyan crinkling his map.

'We could have come right across without touching London,' he said, 'saved us forty minutes I dare say. We made good time the first two hundred miles. It was from Chiswick on we took the time.'

An errand-boy passed us whistling on his bicycle. A motor-coach stopped at the corner and two women got out. Somewhere a church clock chimed the quarter. I could see Favell leaning back in his car behind us and smoking a cigarette. I seemed to have no feeling in me at all. I just sat and watched the little things that did not matter. The two women from the bus walk along the road. The errand boy disappears round the corner. A sparrow hops about in the middle of the road pecking at dirt.

'This fellow Baker can't be much of a gardener,' said Colonel Julyan. 'Look at those shrubs tumbling over his wall. They ought to have been pruned right back.' He folded up the map and put it back in his pocket. 'Funny sort of place to choose to retire in,' he said. 'Close to the main road and overlooked by other houses. Shouldn't care about it myself. I dare say it was quite pretty once before they started building. No doubt there's a good golf-course somewhere handy.'

He was silent for a while, then he opened the door and stood out on the road. 'Well, de Winter,' he said, 'what do you think about it?'

'I'm ready,' said Maxim.

We got out of the car. Favell strolled up to meet us.

'What were you all waiting for, cold feet?' he said.

Nobody answered him. We walked up the drive to the front door, a strange incongruous little party. I caught sight of a tennis lawn beyond the house, and I heard the thud of balls. A boy's voice shouted 'Forty-fifteen, not thirty all. Don't you remember hitting it out, you silly ass?'

'They must have finished tea,' said Colonel Julyan.

He hesitated a moment, glancing at Maxim. Then he rang the bell.

It tinkled somewhere in the back premises. There was a long pause. A very young maid opened the door to us. She looked startled at the sight of so many of us.

'Doctor Baker?' said Colonel Julyan.

'Yes, sir, will you come in?'

She opened a door on the left of the hall as we went in. It would be the drawing-room, not used much in the summer. There was a portrait of a very plain dark woman on the wall. I wondered if it was Mrs. Baker. The chintz covers on the chairs and on the sofa were new and shiny. On the mantelpiece were photographs of two school-boys with round, smiling faces. There was a very large wireless in the corner of the room by the window. Cords trailed from it, and bits of aerial. Favell examined the portrait on the wall. Colonel Julyan went and stood by the empty fireplace. Maxim and I looked out of the window. I could see a deckchair under a tree, and the back of a woman's head. The tennis court must be round the corner. I could hear the boys shouting to each other. A very old Scotch terrier was scratching himself in the middle of a path. We waited there for about five minutes. It was as though I was living the life of some other person and had come to this house to call for a subscription to a charity. It was unlike anything I had ever known. I had no feeling, no pain.

Then the door opened and a man came into the room. He was medium height, rather long in the face, with a keen chin. His hair was sandy, turning grey. He wore flannels, and a dark blue blazer.

'Forgive me for keeping you waiting,' he said, looking a little surprised, as the maid had done, to see so many of us. 'I had to run up and wash. I was playing tennis when the bell rang. Won't you sit down?' He turned to me. I sat down in the nearest chair and waited.

'You must think this a very unorthodox invasion, Doctor Baker,' said Colonel Julyan, 'and I apologise very humbly for disturbing you like this. My name is Julyan. This is Mr. de Winter, Mrs. de Winter, and Mr. Favell. You may have seen Mr. de Winter's name in the papers recently.'

'Oh,' said Doctor Baker, 'yes, yes I suppose I have. Some inquest or other wasn't there? My wife was reading all about it.'

'The jury brought in a verdict of suicide,' said Favell coming forward, 'which I say is absolutely out of the question. Mrs. de Winter was my cousin, I knew her intimately. She would never have done such a thing, and what's

more she had no motive. What we want to know is what the devil she came
to see you about on the very day she died?'

'You had better leave this to Julyan and myself,' said Maxim quietly.
'Doctor Baker has not the faintest idea what you are driving at.'

He turned to the doctor who was standing between them with a line
between his brows, and his first polite smile frozen on his lips. 'My late
wife's cousin is not satisfied with the verdict,' said Maxim, 'and we've driven
up to see you to-day because we found your name, and the telephone number
of your old consulting-rooms, in my wife's engagement diary. She seems to
have made an appointment with you, and kept it, at two o'clock on the last
day she ever spent in London. Could you possibly verify this for us?'

Doctor Baker was listening with great interest, but when Maxim had
finished he shook his head. 'I'm most awfully sorry,' he said, 'but I think
you've made a mistake. I should have remembered the name de Winter. I've
never attended a Mrs. de Winter in my life.'

Colonel Julyan brought out his note case and gave him the page he had
torn from the engagement diary. 'Here it is, written down,' he said, 'Baker,
two o'clock. And a big cross beside it, to show that the appointment was
kept. And here is the telephone address. Museum 0488.'

Doctor Baker stared at the piece of paper. 'That's very odd, very odd
indeed. Yes, the number is quite correct as you say.'

'Could she have come to see you and given a false name?' said Colonel
Julyan.

'Why, yes, that's possible. She may have done that. It's rather unusual of
course. I've never encouraged that sort of thing. It doesn't do us any good
in the profession if people think they can treat us like that.'

'Would you have any record of the visit in your files?' said Colonel Julyan.
'I know it's not etiquette to ask, but the circumstances are very unusual. We
do feel her appointment with you must have some bearing on the case and
her subsequent – suicide.'

'Murder,' said Favell.

Doctor Baker raised his eyebrows, and looked enquiringly at Maxim. 'I'd
no idea there was any question of that,' he said quietly. 'Of course I
understand, and I'll do anything in my power to help you. If you will excuse
me a few minutes I will go and look up the files. There should be a record
of every appointment booked throughout the year, and a description of the
case. Please help yourself to cigarettes. It's too early to offer you sherry, I
suppose?'

Colonel Julyan and Maxim shook their heads. I thought Favell was going
to say something but Doctor Baker had left the room before he had a chance.

'Seems a decent sort of fellow,' said Colonel Julyan.

'Why didn't he offer us whisky and soda?' said Favell. 'Keeps it locked
up I suppose. I didn't think much of him. I don't believe he's going to help
us now.'

Maxim did not say anything. I could hear the sound of the tennis balls
from the court. The Scotch terrier was barking. A woman's voice shouted
to him to be quiet. The summer holidays. Baker playing with his boys. We

had interrupted their routine. A high-pitched, gold clock in a glass case ticked very fast on the mantelpiece. There was a postcard of the Lake of Geneva leaning against it. The Bakers had friends in Switzerland.

Doctor Baker came back into the room with a large book and a file-case in his hands. He carried them over to the table. 'I've brought the collection for last year,' he said. 'I haven't been through them yet since we moved. I only gave up practice six months ago you know.' He opened the book and began turning the pages. I watched him fascinated. He would find it of course. It was only a question of moments now, of seconds. 'The seventh, eighth, tenth,' he murmured, 'nothing here. The twelfth did you say? At two o'clock? Ah!'

We none of us moved. We all watched his face.

'I saw a Mrs. Danvers on the twelfth at two o'clock,' he said.

'Danny? What on earth . . .' began Favell, but Maxim cut him short.

'She gave a wrong name of course,' he said. 'That was obvious from the first. Do you remember the visit now, Doctor Baker?'

But Doctor Baker was already searching his files. I saw his fingers delve into the pocket marked with D. He found it almost at once. He glanced down rapidly at his own hand-writing. 'Yes,' he said slowly. 'Yes, Mrs. Danvers. I remember now.'

'Tall, slim, dark, very handsome?' said Colonel Julyan quietly.

'Yes,' said Doctor Baker. 'Yes.'

He read through the files, and then replaced them in the case. 'Of course,' he said, glancing at Maxim, 'this is un-professional you know? We treat patients as though they were in the confessional. But your wife is dead, and I quite understand the circumstances are exceptional. You want to know if I can suggest any motive why your wife should have taken her life? I think I can. The woman who called herself Mrs. Danvers was very seriously ill.'

He paused. He looked at every one of us in turn.

'I remember her perfectly well,' he said, and he turned back to the files again. 'She came to me for the first time a week previously to the date you mentioned. She complained of certain symptoms, and I took some X rays of her. The second visit was to find out the result of those X rays. The photographs are not here, but I have the details written down. I remember her standing in my consulting-room and holding out her hand for the photographs. "I want to know the truth," she said, "I don't want soft words and a bedside manner. If I'm for it you can tell me right away." ' He paused, he glanced down at the files once again.

I waited, waited. Why couldn't he get done with it and finish and let us go? Why must we sit there, waiting, our eyes upon his face.

'Well,' he said, 'she asked for the truth, and I let her have it. Some patients are better for it. Shirking the point does them no good. This Mrs. Danvers, or Mrs. de Winter rather, was not the type to accept a lie. You must have known that. She stood it very well. She did not flinch. She said she had suspected it for some time. Then she paid my fee and went out. I never saw her again.'

He shut up the box with a snap, and closed the book. 'The pain was slight as yet but the growth was deep-rooted,' he said, 'and in three or four months' time she would have been under morphia. An operation would have been no earthly use at all. I told her that. The thing had got too firm a hold. There is nothing anyone can do in a case like that, except give morphia, and wait.'

No one said a word. The little clock ticked on the mantelpiece, and the boys played tennis in the garden. An aeroplane hummed overhead.

'Outwardly of course she was a perfectly healthy woman,' he said, 'rather too thin I remember, rather pale, but then that's the fashion nowadays, pity though it is. It's nothing to go upon with a patient. No, the pain would increase week by week, and as I told you, in four or five months' time she would have had to be kept under morphia. The X rays showed a certain malformation of the uterus, I remember, which meant she could never have had a child, but that was quite apart, it had nothing to do with the disease.'

I remember hearing Colonel Julyan speak, saying something about Doctor Baker being very kind to have taken so much trouble. 'You have told us all we want to know,' he said, 'and if we could possibly have a copy of the memoranda in your file it might be very useful.'

'Of course,' said Doctor Baker. 'Of course.'

Everyone was standing up. I got up from my chair too. I shook hands with Doctor Baker. We all shook hands with him. We followed him out into the hall. A woman looked out of the room on the other side of the hall and darted back when she saw us. Someone was running a bath upstairs, the water ran loudly. The Scotch terrier came in from the garden and began sniffing at my heels.

'Shall I send the report to you or to Mr. de Winter?' said Doctor Baker.

'We may not need it at all,' said Colonel Julyan. 'I rather think it won't be necessary. Either de Winter or I will write. Here is my card.'

'I'm so glad to have been of use,' said Doctor Baker; 'it never entered my head for a moment that Mrs. de Winter and Mrs. Danvers could be the same person.'

'No, naturally,' said Colonel Julyan.

'You'll be returning to London I suppose?'

'Yes. Yes, I imagine so.'

'Your best way then is to turn sharp left by that pillar-box, and then right by the church. After that it's a straight road.'

'Thank you. Thank you very much.'

We came out on to the drive and went towards the cars. Doctor Baker pulled the Scotch terrier inside the house. I heard the door shut. A man with one leg and a barrel-organ began playing 'Roses in Picardy' at the end of the road.

Chapter Twenty-seven

We went and stood by the car. No one said anything for a few minutes.
Colonel Julyan handed round his cigarette case. Favell looked grey, rather
shaken. I noticed his hands were trembling as he held the match. The man
with the barrel organ ceased playing for a moment and hobbled towards us,
his cap in his hand. Maxim gave him two shillings. Then he went back to
the barrel organ and started another tune. The church clock struck six
o'clock. Favell began to speak. His voice was diffident, careless, but his face
was still grey. He did not look at any of us, he kept glancing down at his
cigarette and turning it over in his fingers. 'This cancer business,' he said,
'does anybody know if it's contagious?'

No one answered him. Colonel Julyan shrugged his shoulders.

'I never had the remotest idea,' said Favell jerkily. 'She kept it a secret
from everyone, even Danny. What a God-damned appalling thing, eh? Not
the sort of thing one would ever connect with Rebecca. Do you fellows feel
like a drink? I'm all out over this, and I don't mind admitting it. Cancer!
Oh, my God!'

He leant up against the side of the car and shaded his eyes with his hands.
'Tell that bloody fellow with the barrel organ to clear out,' he said. 'I can't
stand that God-damned row.'

'Wouldn't it be simpler if we went ourselves?' said Maxim. 'Can you
manage your own car or do you want Julyan to drive it for you?'

'Give me a minute,' muttered Favell. 'I'll be all right. You don't understand. This thing has been a damned unholy shock to me.'

'Pull yourself together, man, for heaven's sake,' said Colonel Julyan. 'If
you want a drink go back to the house and ask Baker. He knows how to
treat for shock I dare say. Don't make an exhibition of yourself in the street.'

'Oh, you're all right, you're fine,' said Favell, standing straight and looking
at Colonel Julyan and Maxim. 'You've got nothing to worry about any
more. Max is on a good wicket now, isn't he? You've got your motive, and
Baker will supply it in black and white free of cost, whenever you send the
word. You can dine at Manderley once a week on the strength of it and feel
proud of yourself. No doubt Max will ask you to be god-father to his first
child.'

'Shall we get into the car and go?' said Colonel Julyan to Maxim. 'We
can make our plans going along.'

Maxim held open the door of the car, and Colonel Julyan climbed in. I
sat down in my seat in the front. Favell still leant against the car and did

not move. 'I should advise you to get straight back to your flat and go to bed,' said Colonel Julyan shortly, 'and drive slowly, or you will find yourself in gaol for manslaughter. I may as well warn you now, as I shall not be seeing you again, that as a magistrate I have certain powers that will prove effective if you ever turn up in Kerrith or the district. Blackmail is not much of a profession, Mr. Favell. And we know how to deal with it in our part of the world, strange though it may seem to you.'

Favell was watching Maxim. He had lost the grey colour now, and the old unpleasant smile was forming on his lips. 'Yes, it's been a stroke of luck for you, Max, hasn't it?' he said slowly. 'You think you've won, haven't you? The law can get you yet, and so can I, in a different way . . .'

Maxim switched on the engine. 'Have you anything else you want to say?' he said. 'Because if you have you had better say it now.'

'No,' said Favell. 'No, I won't keep you. You can go.' He stepped back on to the pavement, the smile still on his lips. The car slid forward. As we turned the corner I looked back and saw him standing there, watching us, and he waved his hand and he was laughing.

We drove on for a while in silence. Then Colonel Julyan spoke. 'He can't do anything,' he said. 'That smile and that wave was part of his bluff. They're all alike, those fellows. He hasn't a thread of a case to bring now. Baker's evidence would squash it.'

Maxim did not answer. I glanced sideways at his face but it told me nothing. 'I always felt the solution would lie in Baker,' said Colonel Julyan, 'the furtive business of that appointment, and the way she never even told Mrs. Danvers. She had her suspicions you see. She knew something was wrong. A dreadful thing, of course. Very dreadful. Enough to send a young and lovely woman right off her head.'

We drove on along the straight main road. Telegraph poles, motor-coaches, open sports cars, little semi-detached villas with new gardens, they flashed past making patterns in my mind I should always remember.

'I suppose you never had any idea of this, de Winter?' said Colonel Julyan.

'No,' said Maxim. 'No.'

'Of course some people have a morbid dread of it,' said Colonel Julyan. 'Women especially. That must have been the case with your wife. She had courage for every other thing but that. She could not face pain. Well, she was spared that at any rate.'

'Yes,' said Maxim.

'I don't think it would do any harm if I quietly let it be known down in Kerrith and in the county that a London doctor has supplied us with a motive,' said Colonel Julyan. 'Just in case there should be any gossip. You never can tell, you know. People are odd, sometimes. If they knew about Mrs. de Winter it might make it a lot easier for you.'

'Yes,' said Maxim, 'yes, I understand.'

'It's curious and very irritating,' said Colonel Julyan slowly, 'how long stories spread in country districts. I never know why they should but unfortunately they do. Not that I anticipate any trouble over this but it's as well to be prepared. People are inclined to say the wildest things if they are given half a chance.'

'Yes,' said Maxim.

'You and Crawley of course can squash any nonsense in Manderley or the estate, and I can deal with it effectively in Kerrith. I shall say a word to my girl too. She sees a lot of the younger people, who very often are the worst offenders in story-telling. I don't suppose the newspapers will worry you any more, that's one good thing. You'll find they will drop the whole affair in a day or two.'

'Yes,' said Maxim.

We drove on through the northern suburbs and came once more to Finchley and Hampstead.

'Half-past six,' said Colonel Julyan, 'what do you propose doing? I've got a sister living in St. John's Wood, and feel inclined to take her unawares and ask for dinner, and then catch the last train from Paddington. I know she doesn't go away for another week. I'm sure she would be delighted to see you both as well.'

Maxim hesitated, and glanced at me. 'It's very kind of you,' he said, 'but I think we had better be independent. I must ring up Frank, and one thing and another. I dare say we shall have a quiet meal somewhere and start off again afterwards, spending the night at a pub, on the way. I rather think that's what we shall do.'

'Of course,' said Colonel Julyan, 'I quite understand. Could you throw me out at my sister's? It's one of those turnings off the Avenue Road.'

When we came to the house Maxim drew up a little way ahead of the gate. 'It's impossible to thank you,' he said, 'for all you've done to-day. You know what I feel about it without my telling you.'

'My dear fellow,' said Colonel Julyan, 'I've been only too glad. If only we'd known what Baker knew of course there would have been none of this at all. However, never mind about that now. You must put the whole thing behind you as a very unpleasant and unfortunate episode. I'm pretty sure you won't have any more trouble from Favell. If you do, I count on you to tell me at once. I shall know how to deal with him.' He climbed out of the car, collecting his coat and his map. 'I should feel inclined,' he said, not looking directly at us, 'to get away for a bit. Take a short holiday. Go abroad perhaps.'

We did not say anything. Colonel Julyan was fumbling with his map. 'Switzerland is very nice this time of the year,' he said. 'I remember we went once for the girl's holidays, and thoroughly enjoyed ourselves. The walks are delightful.' He hesitated, cleared his throat. 'It is just faintly possible certain little difficulties might arise,' he said, 'not from Favell, but from one or two people in the district. One never knows quite what Tabb has been saying, and repeating, and so on. Absurd of course. But you know the old saying? Out of sight, out of mind. If people aren't there to be talked about the talk dies. It's the way of the world.'

He stood a moment, counting his belongings. 'I've got everything I think.

Map, glasses, stick, coat. Everything complete. Well, good-bye, both of you. Don't get over-tired. It's been a long day.'

He turned in at the gate and went up the steps. I saw a woman come to the window and smile and wave her hand. We drove away down the road and turned the corner. I leant back in my seat and closed my eyes. Now that we were alone again and the strain was over, the sensation was one of almost unbearable relief. It was like the bursting of an abscess. Maxim did not speak. I felt his hand cover mine. We drove on through the traffic and I saw none of it. I heard the rumble of the buses, the hooting of taxis, that inevitable, tireless London roar, but I was not part of it. I rested in some other place that was cool and quiet and still. Nothing could touch us any more. We had come through our crisis.

When Maxim stopped the car I opened my eyes and sat up. We were opposite one of those numerous little restaurants in a narrow street in Soho. I looked about me, dazed and stupid.

'You're tired,' said Maxim briefly. 'Empty and tired and fit for nothing. You'll be better when you've had something to eat. So shall I. We'll go in here and order dinner right away. I can telephone to Frank, too.'

We got out of the car. There was no one in the restaurant but the maître d'hôtel and a waiter and a girl behind a desk. It was dark and cool. We went to a table right in the corner. Maxim began ordering the food. 'Favell was right about wanting a drink,' he said. 'I want one too and so do you. You're going to have some brandy.'

The maître d'hôtel was fat and smiling. He produced long thin rolls in paper envelopes. They were very hard, very crisp. I began to eat one ravenously. My brandy and soda was soft, warming, curiously comforting.

'When we've had dinner we'll drive slowly, very quietly,' said Maxim. 'It will be cool, too, in the evening. We'll find somewhere on the road we can put up for the night. Then we can get along to Manderley in the morning.'

'Yes,' I said.

'You didn't want to dine with Julyan's sister and go down by the late train?'

'No.'

Maxim finished his drink. His eyes looked large and they were ringed with shadows. They seemed very dark against the pallor of his face.

'How much of the truth,' he said, 'do you think Julyan guessed?'

I watched him over the rim of my glass. I did not say anything.

'He knew,' said Maxim slowly, 'of course he knew.'

'If he did,' I said, 'he will never say anything. Never, never.'

'No,' said Maxim. 'No.'

He ordered another drink from the maître d'hôtel. We sat silent and peaceful in our dark corner.

'I believe,' said Maxim, 'that Rebecca lied to me on purpose. The last supreme bluff. She wanted me to kill her. She foresaw the whole thing. That's why she laughed. That's why she stood there laughing when she died.'

I did not say anything. I went on drinking my brandy and soda. It was all over. It was all settled. It did not matter any more. There was no need for Maxim to look white and troubled.

'It was her last practical joke,' said Maxim, 'the best of them all. And I'm not sure if she hasn't won, even now.'

'What do you mean? How can she have won?' I said.

'I don't know,' he said. 'I don't know.' He swallowed his second drink. Then he got up from the table. 'I'm going to ring up Frank,' he said.

I sat there in my corner, and presently the waiter brought me my fish. It was lobster. Very hot and good. I had another brandy and soda, too. It was pleasant and comfortable sitting there and nothing mattered very much. I smiled at the waiter. I asked for some more bread in French for no reason. It was quiet and happy and friendly in the restaurant. Maxim and I were together. Everything was over. Everything was settled. Rebecca was dead. Rebecca could not hurt us. She had played her last joke as Maxim had said. She could do no more to us now. In ten minutes Maxim came back again.

'Well,' I said, my own voice sounding far away, 'how was Frank?'

'Frank was all right,' said Maxim. 'He was at the office, been waiting there for me to telephone him ever since four o'clock. I told him what had happened. He sounded glad, relieved.'

'Yes,' I said.

'Something rather odd though,' said Maxim slowly, a line between his brows. 'He thinks Mrs. Danvers has cleared out. She's gone, disappeared. She said nothing to anyone but apparently she'd been packing up all day, stripping her room of things, and the fellow from the station came for her boxes at about four o'clock. Frith telephoned down to Frank about it, and Frank told Frith to ask Mrs. Danvers to come down to him at the office. He waited, and she never came. About ten minutes before I rang up, Frith telephoned to Frank again and said there had been a long-distance call for Mrs. Danvers which he had switched through to her room, and she had answered. This must have been about ten past six. At a quarter-to-seven he knocked on the door and found her room empty. Her bedroom too. They looked for her and could not find her. They think she's gone. She must have gone straight out of the house and through the woods. She never passed the lodge-gates.'

'Isn't it a good thing?' I said. 'It saves us a lot of trouble. We should have had to send her away, anyway. I believe she guessed, too. There was an expression on her face last night. I kept thinking of it, coming up in the car.'

'I don't like it,' said Maxim. 'I don't like it.'

'She can't do anything,' I argued. 'If she's gone, so much the better. It was Favell who telephoned of course. He must have told her about Baker. He would tell her what Colonel Julyan said. Colonel Julyan said if there was any attempt at blackmail we were to tell him. They won't dare do it. They can't. It's too dangerous.'

'I'm not thinking of blackmail,' said Maxim.

'What else can they do?' I said. 'We've got to do what Colonel Julyan said. We've got to forget it. We must not think about it any more. It's all over, darling, it's finished. We ought to go down on our knees and thank God that it's finished.'

Maxim did not answer. He was staring in front of him at nothing.

'Your lobster will be cold,' I said; 'eat it, darling. It will do you good, you want something inside you. You're tired.' I was using the words he had used to me. I felt better and stronger. It was I now who was taking care of him. He was tired, pale. I had got over my weakness and fatigue and now he was the one to suffer from reaction. It was just because he was empty, because he was tired. There was nothing to worry about at all. Mrs. Danvers had gone. We should praise God for that, too. Everything had been made so easy for us, so very easy. 'Eat up your fish,' I said.

It was going to be very different in the future. I was not going to be nervous and shy of the servants any more. With Mrs. Danvers gone I should learn bit by bit to control the house. I would go and interview the cook in the kitchen. They would like me, respect me. Soon it would be as though Mrs. Danvers had never had command. I would learn more about the estate, too. I should ask Frank to explain things to me. I was sure Frank liked me. I liked him, too. I would go into things, and learn how they were managed. What they did at the farm. How the work in the grounds was planned. I might take to gardening myself, and in time have one or two things altered. That little square lawn outside the morning-room window with the statue of the satyr. I did not like it. We would give the satyr away. There were heaps of things that I could do, little by little. People would come and stay and I should not mind. There would be the interest of seeing to their rooms, having flowers and books put, arranging the food. We would have children. Surely we would have children.

'Have you finished?' said Maxim suddenly. 'I don't think I want any more. Only coffee. Black, very strong, please, and the bill,' he added to the maître d'hôtel.

I wondered why we must go so soon. It was comfortable in the restaurant, and there was nothing to take us away. I liked sitting there, with my head against the sofa back, planning the future idly in a hazy pleasant way. I could have gone on sitting there for a long while.

I followed Maxim out of the restaurant, stumbling a little, and yawning. 'Listen,' he said, when we were on the pavement, 'do you think you could sleep in the car if I wrapped you up with the rug, and tucked you down in the back? There's the cushion there, and my coat as well.'

'I thought we were going to put up somewhere for the night?' I said blankly. 'One of those hotels one passes on the road.'

'I know,' he said, 'but I have this feeling I must get down to-night. Can't you possibly sleep in the back of the car?'

'Yes,' I said doubtfully. 'Yes, I suppose so.'

'If we start now, it's a quarter-to-eight, we ought to be there by half-past two,' he said. 'There won't be much traffic on the road.'

'You'll be so tired,' I said. 'So terribly tired.'

'No,' he shook his head. 'I shall be all right. I want to get home. Something's wrong. I know it is. I want to get home.'

His face was anxious, strange. He pulled open the door and began arranging the rugs and the cushion at the back of the car.

'What can be wrong?' I said. 'It seems so odd to worry now, when everything's over. I can't understand you.'

He did not answer. I climbed into the back of the car and lay down with my legs tucked under me. He covered me with the rug. It was very comfortable. Much better than I imagined. I settled the pillow under my head.

'Are you all right,' he said; 'are you sure you don't mind?'

'No,' I said smiling. 'I'm all right. I shall sleep. I don't want to stay anywhere on the road. It's much better to do this and get home. We'll be at Manderley long before sunrise.'

He got in front and switched on the engine. I shut my eyes. The car drew away and I felt the slight jolting of the springs under my body. I pressed my face against the cushion. The motion of the car was rhythmic, steady, and the pulse of my mind beat with it. A hundred images came to me when I closed my eyes, things seen, things known, and things forgotten. They were jumbled together in a senseless pattern. The quill of Mrs. Van Hopper's hat, the hard straight-backed chairs in Frank's dining-room, the wide window in the west wing at Manderley, the salmon-coloured frock of the smiling lady at the fancy-dress ball, a peasant-girl in a road near Monte Carlo.

Sometimes I saw Jasper chasing butterflies across the lawns; sometimes I saw Doctor Baker's Scotch terrier scratching his ear beside a deck-chair. There was the postman who had pointed out the house to us to-day, and there was Clarice's mother wiping a chair for me in the back parlour. Ben smiled at me, holding winkles in his hands, and the bishop's wife asked me if I would stay to tea. I could feel the cold comfort of my sheets in my own bed, and the gritty shingle in the cove. I could smell the bracken in the woods, the wet moss, and the dead azalea petals. I fell into a strange broken sleep, waking now and again to the reality of my narrow cramped position and the sight of Maxim's back in front of me. The dusk had turned to darkness. There were the lights of passing cars upon the road. There were villages with drawn curtains and little lights behind them. And I would move, and turn upon my back, and sleep again.

I saw the staircase at Manderley, and Mrs. Danvers standing at the top in her black dress, waiting for me to go to her. As I climbed the stairs she backed under the archway and disappeared. I looked for her and I could not find her. Then her face looked at me through a hollow door and I cried out and she had gone again.

'What's the time?' I called. 'What's the time?'

Maxim turned round to me, his face pale and ghostly in the darkness of the car. 'It's half-past eleven,' he said. 'We're over half-way already. Try and sleep again.'

'I'm thirsty,' I said.

He stopped at the next town. The man at the garage said his wife had not gone to bed and she would make us some tea. We got out of the car and stood inside the garage. I stamped up and down to bring the blood back to my hands and feet. Maxim smoked a cigarette. It was cold. A bitter wind blew in through the open garage door, and rattled the corrugated roof. I shivered, and buttoned up my coat.

'Yes, it's nippy to-night,' said the garage man, as he wound the petrol pump. 'The weather seemed to break this afternoon. It's the last of the heat-waves for this summer. We shall be thinking of fires soon.'

'It was hot in London,' I said.

'Was it?' he said. 'Well, they always have the extremes up there, don't they? We get the first of the bad weather down here. It will blow hard on the coast before morning.'

His wife brought us the tea. It tasted of bitter wood, but it was hot. I drank it greedily, thankfully. Already Maxim was glancing at his watch.

'We ought to be going,' he said. 'It's ten minutes to twelve.' I left the shelter of the garage reluctantly. The cold wind blew in my face. The stars raced across the sky. There were threads of cloud too. 'Yes,' said the garage man, 'summer's over for this year.'

We climbed back into the car. I settled myself once more under the rug. The car went on. I shut my eyes. There was the man with the wooden leg winding his barrel organ, and the tune of Roses in Picardy hummed in my head against the jolting of the car. Frith and Robert carried the tea into the library. The woman at the lodge nodded to me abruptly, and called her child into the house. I saw the model boats in the cottage in the cove, and the feathery dust. I saw the cobwebs stretching from the little masts. I heard the rain upon the roof and the sound of the sea. I wanted to get to the Happy Valley and it was not there. There were woods about me, there was no Happy Valley. Only the dark trees and the young bracken. The owls hooted. The moon was shining in the windows of Manderley. There were nettles in the garden, ten foot, twenty foot high.

'Maxim!' I cried. 'Maxim!'

'Yes,' he said. 'It's all right. I'm here.'

'I had a dream,' I said. 'A dream.'

'What was it?' he said.

'I don't know. I don't know.'

Back again into the moving unquiet depths. I was writing letters in the morning-room. I was sending out invitations. I wrote them all myself with a thick black pen. But when I looked down to see what I had written it was not my small square hand-writing at all, it was long, and slanting, with curious pointed strokes. I pushed the cards away from the blotter and hid them. I got up and went to the looking-glass. A face stared back at me that was not my own. It was very pale, very lovely, framed in a cloud of dark hair. The eyes narrowed and smiled. The lips parted. The face in the glass stared back at me and laughed. And I saw then that she was sitting on a chair before the dressing-table in her bedroom, and Maxim was brushing her hair. He held her hair in his hands, and as he brushed it he wound it slowly into a thick long rope. It twisted like a snake, and he took hold of it with both hands and smiled at Rebecca and put it round his neck.

'No,' I screamed. 'No, no. We must go to Switzerland. Colonel Julyan said we must go to Switzerland.'

I felt Maxim's hand upon my face. 'What is it?' he said. 'What's the matter?'

I sat up and pushed my hair away from my face.

'I can't sleep,' I said. 'It's no use.'

'You've been sleeping,' he said. 'You've slept for two hours. It's quarter-past two. We're four miles the other side of Lanyon.'

It was even colder than before. I shuddered in the darkness of the car.

'I'll come beside you,' I said. 'We shall be back by three.'

I climbed over and sat beside him, staring in front of me through the windscreen. I put my hand on his knee. My teeth were chattering.

'You're cold,' he said.

'Yes,' I said.

The hills rose in front of us, and dipped, and rose again. It was quite dark. The stars had gone.

'What time did you say it was?' I asked.

'Twenty-past two,' he said.

'It's funny,' I said. 'It looks almost as though the dawn was breaking over there, beyond those hills. It can't be though, it's too early.'

'It's the wrong direction,' he said, 'you're looking west.'

'I know,' I said. 'It's funny, isn't it?'

He did not answer and I went on watching the sky. It seemed to get lighter even as I stared. Like the first red streaks of sunrise. Little by little it spread across the sky.

'It's in winter you see the northern lights, isn't it?' I said. 'Not in summer?'

'That's not the northern lights,' he said. 'That's Manderley.'

I glanced at him and saw his face. I saw his eyes.

'Maxim,' I said. 'Maxim, what is it?'

He drove faster, much faster. We topped the hill before us and saw Lanyon lying in a hollow at our feet. There to the left of us was the silver streak of the river, widening to the estuary at Kerrith six miles away. The road to Manderley lay ahead. There was no moon. The sky above our heads was inky black. But the sky on the horizon was not dark at all. It was shot with crimson, like a splash of blood. And the ashes blew towards us with the salt wind from the sea.

Jamaica
Inn

Daphne
du Maurier

Chapter One

It was a cold grey day in late November. The weather had changed overnight, when a backing wind brought a granite sky and a mizzling rain with it, and although it was now only a little after two o'clock in the afternoon the pallor of a winter evening seemed to have closed upon the hills, cloaking them in mist. It would be dark by four. The air was clammy cold, and for all the tightly closed windows it penetrated the interior of the coach. The leather seats felt damp to the hands, and there must have been a small crack in the roof, because now and again little drips of rain fell softly through, smudging the leather and leaving a dark-blue stain like a splodge of ink. The wind came in gusts, at times shaking the coach as it travelled round the bend of the road, and in the exposed places on the high ground it blew with such force that the whole body of the coach trembled and swayed, rocking between the high wheels like a drunken man.

The driver, muffled in a greatcoat to his ears, bent almost double in his seat in a faint endeavour to gain shelter from his own shoulders, while the dispirited horses plodded sullenly to his command, too broken by the wind and the rain to feel the whip that now and again cracked above their heads, while it swung between the numb fingers of the driver.

The wheels of the coach creaked and groaned as they sank into the ruts on the road, and sometimes they flung up the soft spattered mud against the windows, where it mingled with the constant driving rain, and whatever view there might have been of the countryside was hopelessly obscured.

The few passengers huddled together for warmth, exclaiming in unison when the coach sank into a heavier rut than usual, and one old fellow, who had kept up a constant complaint ever since he had joined the coach at Truro, rose from his seat in a fury; and, fumbling with the window-sash, let the window down with a crash, bringing a shower of rain in upon himself and his fellow-passengers. He thrust his head out and shouted up to the driver, cursing him in a high petulant voice for a rogue and a murderer; that they would all be dead before they reached Bodmin if he persisted in driving at breakneck speed; they had no breath left in their bodies as it was, and he for one would never travel by coach again.

Whether the driver heard him or not was uncertain; it seemed more likely that the stream of reproaches was carried away in the wind, for the old fellow, after waiting a moment, put up the window again, having thoroughly chilled the interior of the coach, and, settling himself once more in his corner, wrapped his blanket about his knees and muttered in his beard.

His nearest neighbour, a jovial red-faced woman in a blue cloak, sighed heavily in sympathy; and, with a wink to anyone who might be looking and a jerk of her head towards the old man, she remarked for at least the twentieth time that it was the dirtiest night she ever remembered, and she had known some; that it was proper old weather and no mistaking it for summer this time; and, burrowing into the depths of a large basket, she brought out a great hunk of cake and plunged into it with strong white teeth.

Mary Yellan sat in the opposite corner, where the trickle of rain oozed through the crack in the roof. Sometimes a cold drip of moisture fell upon her shoulder, which she brushed away with impatient fingers.

She sat with her chin cupped in her hands, her eyes fixed on the window splashed with mud and rain, hoping with a sort of desperate interest that some ray of light would break the heavy blanket of sky, and but a momentary trace of that lost blue heaven that had mantled Helford yesterday shine for an instant as a forerunner of fortune.

Already, though barely forty miles by road from what had been her home for three and twenty years, the hope within her heart had tired, and that rather gallant courage which was so large a part of her, and had stood her in such stead during the long agony of her mother's illness and death, was now shaken by this first fall of rain and the nagging wind.

The country was alien to her, which was defeat in itself. As she peered through the misty window of the coach she looked out upon a different world from the one she had known only a day's journey back. How remote now and hidden perhaps for ever were the shining waters of Helford, the green hills and the sloping valleys, the white cluster of cottages at the water's edge. It was a gentle rain that fell at Helford, a rain that pattered in the many trees and lost itself in the lush grass, formed into brooks and rivulets that emptied into the broad river, sank into the grateful soil which gave back flowers in payment.

This was a lashing, pitiless rain that stung the windows of the coach, and it soaked into a hard and barren soil. No trees here, save one or two that stretched bare branches to the four winds, bent and twisted from centuries of storm, and so black were they by time and tempest that, even if spring did breathe on such a place, no buds would dare to come to leaf for fear the late frost should kill them. It was a scrubby land, without hedgerow or meadow; a country of stones, black heather, and stunted broom.

There would never be a gentle season here, thought Mary; either grim winter as it was to-day, or else the dry and parching heat of midsummer, with never a valley to give shade or shelter, but grass that turned yellow-brown before May was passed. The country had gone grey with the weather. Even the people on the road and in the villages changed in harmony with their background. At Helston, where she had taken the first coach, she had trodden familiar ground. So many childish memories clung about Helston. The weekly drive to market with her father in the vanished days, and, when he was taken from them, the fortitude with which her mother held his place, driving backwards and forwards, winter and summer, as he had done, with her hens and her eggs and her butter at the back of the cart, while Mary sat at her side, clutching a basket as big as herself, her small chin resting on the handle. Folk were friendly in Helston; the name of Yellan was known and respected in the town, for the widow had had a hard fight against life when her husband died, and there were not many women who would have lived alone as she did with one child and a farm to tend, with never a thought of taking another man. There was a farmer at Manaccan who would have asked her had he dared, and another up the river at Gweek, but they could tell from her eyes she would have neither of them, but belonged in body and mind to the man who had gone. It was the hard work of the farm that told upon her in the end, for she would not spare herself, and, though she had driven and flogged her energy for the seventeen years of her widowhood, she could not stand up to the strain when the last test came, and her heart went from her.

Little by little her stock had decreased, and with times being bad – so she was told in Helston – and prices fallen to nothing, there was no money anywhere. Up-country it was the same. There would be starvation in the farms before long. Then a sickness attacked the ground and killed the livestock in the villages round Helford. There was no name to it, and no cure could be discovered. It was a sickness that came over everything and destroyed, much as a late frost will out of season, coming with the new moon and then departing, leaving no trace of its passage save the little trail of dead things in its path. It was an anxious, weary time for Mary Yellan and her mother. One by one they saw the chickens and the ducklings they had reared sicken and die, and the young calf fell in the meadow where he stood. The most pitiful was the old mare who had served them twenty years, and upon whose broad and sturdy back Mary had first straddled her young legs. She died in the stall one morning, her faithful head in Mary's lap; and when a pit was dug for her under the apple-tree in the orchard, and she was buried, and they knew she would no longer carry them to Helston market-day, Mary's mother turned to her and said, 'There's something of me gone in the grave with poor Nell, Mary. I don't know whether it's my faith or what it is, but my heart feels tired and I can't go on any more.'

She went into the house and sat down in the kitchen, pale as a sheet, and ten years beyond her age. She shrugged her shoulders when Mary said she would fetch the doctor. 'It's too late, child,' she said, 'seventeen years too late.' And she began to cry softly, who had never cried before.

Mary fetched the old doctor who lived in Mawgan and who had brought her into the world, and as he drove her back in his trap he shook his head at her. 'I tell you what it is, Mary,' he said; 'your mother has spared neither her mind nor her body since your father died, and she has broken down at last. I don't like it. It's come at a bad time.'

They drove along the twisting lane to the farmhouse at the top of the village. A neighbour met them at the gate, her face eager to impart bad news. 'Your mother's worse,' she cried. 'She came out of the door just now, staring like a ghost, and she trembled all over, and fell down in the path. Mrs. Hoblyn has gone to her, and Will Searle; they've lifted her inside, poor soul. They say her eyes are shut.'

Firmly the doctor pushed the little gaping crowd away from the door. Together he and the man Searle lifted the still figure from the floor and carried her upstairs to the bedroom.

'It's a stroke,' said the doctor, 'but she's breathing; her pulse is steady. This is what I've been afraid of – that she'd snap suddenly, like this. Why it's come just now, after all these years, is known only to the Lord and herself. You must prove yourself your parents' child now, Mary, and help her through this. You are the only one who can.'

For six long months or more Mary nursed her mother in this her first and last illness, but with all the care she and the doctor gave her it was not the widow's will to recover. She had no wish to fight for her life.

It was as though she longed for release, and prayed silently that it would come quickly. She said to Mary, 'I don't want you to struggle as I have done. It's a breaking of the body and of the spirit. There's no call for you to stay on at Helford after I am gone. It's best for you to go to your Aunt Patience up to Bodmin.'

There was no use in Mary telling her mother that she would not die. It was fixed there in her mind and there was no fighting it.

'I haven't any wish to leave the farm, mother,' she said. 'I was born here and my father before me, and you were a Helford woman. This is where the Yellans belong to be. I'm not afraid of being poor, and the farm falling away. You worked here for seventeen years alone, so why shouldn't I do the same? I'm strong; I can do the work of a man; you know that.'

'It's no life for a girl,' said her mother. 'I did it all these years because of your father, and because of you. Working for someone keeps a woman calm and contented, but it's another thing when you work for yourself. There's no heart in it then.'

'I'd be no use in a town,' said Mary. 'I've never known anything but this life by the river, and I don't want to. Going into Helston is town enough for me. I'm best here, with the few chickens that's left to us, and the green stuff in the garden, and the old pig, and a bit of a boat on the river. What would I do up to Bodmin with my Aunt Patience?'

'A girl can't live alone, Mary, without she goes queer in the head, or comes to evil. It's either one or the other. Have you forgotten poor Sue, who walked the churchyard at midnight with the full moon, and called upon the lover she had never had? And there was one maid, before you were born, left an orphan at sixteen. She ran away to Falmouth and went with the sailors.

'I'd not rest in my grave, nor your father neither, if we didn't leave you safe. You'll like your Aunt Patience; she was always a great one for games and laughing, with a heart as large as life. You remember when she came here, twelve years back? She had ribbons in her bonnet and a silk petticoat. There was a fellow working at Trelowarren had an eye to her, but she thought herself too good for him.'

Yes, Mary remembered Aunt Patience, with her curled fringe and large blue eyes, and how she laughed and chatted, and how she picked up her skirts and tiptoed through the mud in the yard. She was as pretty as a fairy.

'What sort of a man your Uncle Joshua is I cannot say,' said her mother, 'for I've never set eyes on him nor known anyone what has. But when your aunt married him ten years ago last Michaelmas she wrote a pack of giddy nonsense you'd expect a girl to write, and not a woman over thirty.'

'They'd think me rough,' said Mary slowly. 'I haven't the pretty manners they'd expect. We wouldn't have much to say to one another.'

'They'll love you for yourself and not for any airs and graces. I want you to promise me this, child, that when I'm gone you'll write to your Aunt Patience and tell her that it was my last and dearest wish that you should go to her.'

'I promise,' said Mary, but her heart was heavy and distressed at the thought of a future so insecure and changed, with all that she had known and loved gone from her, and not even the comfort of familiar trodden ground to help her through the bad days when they came.

Daily her mother weakened; daily the life ebbed from her. She lingered through harvest-time, and through the fruit-picking, and through the first falling of the leaves. But when the mists came in the morning, and the frosts settled on the ground, and the swollen river ran in flood to meet the boisterous sea, and the waves thundered and broke on the little beaches of Helford, the widow turned restlessly in her bed, plucking at the sheets. She called Mary by her dead husband's name, and spoke of things that were gone, and of people Mary had never known. For three days she lived in a little world of her own, and on the fourth day she died.

One by one Mary saw the things she had loved and understood pass into other hands. The livestock went at Helston market. The furniture was bought by neighbours, stick by stick. A man from Coverack took a fancy to the house and purchased it; with pipe in mouth he straddled the yard and pointed out the changes he would make, the trees he would cut down to clear his view; while Mary watched him in dumb loathing from her window as she packed her small belongings in her father's trunk.

This stranger from Coverack made her an interloper in her own home; she could see from his eye he wanted her to be gone, and she had no other thought now but to be away and out of it all, and her back turned for ever. Once more she read the letter from her aunt, written in a cramped hand, on plain paper. The writer said she was shocked at the blow that had befallen her niece; that she had no idea her sister was ill, it was so many years now since she had been to Helford. And she went on: 'There have been changes with us you would not know. I no longer live in Bodmin, but nearly twelve miles outside, on the road to Launceston. It's a wild and lonely spot, and if you were to come to us I should be glad of your company, winter-time. I have asked your uncle and he does not object, he says, if you are quiet-spoken and not a talker, and will give help when needed. He cannot give you money, or feed you for nothing, as you will understand. He will expect your help in the bar, in return for your board and lodging. You see, your uncle is the landlord of Jamaica Inn.'

Mary folded the letter and put it in her trunk. It was a strange message of welcome from the smiling Aunt Patience she remembered.

A cold, empty letter, giving no word of comfort, and admitting nothing, except that her niece must not ask for money. Aunt Patience, with her silk petticoat and delicate ways, the wife of an innkeeper! Mary decided that this was something her mother had not known. The letter was very different from the one penned by a happy bride ten years ago.

However, Mary had promised, and there was no returning on her word. Her home was sold; there was no place for her here. Whatever her welcome should be, her aunt was her own mother's sister, and that was the one thing to remember. The old life lay behind – the dear familiar farm and the shining Helford waters. Before her lay the future – and Jamaica Inn.

And so it was that Mary Yellan found herself northward bound from Helston in the creaking swaying coach, through Truro town, at the head of the Fal, with its many roofs and spires, its broad cobbled streets, the blue sky overhead still speaking of the south, the people at the doors smiling and waving as the coach rattled past. But when Truro lay behind in the valley, the sky came overcast, and the country on either side of the high road grew rough and untilled. Villages were scattered now, and there were few smiling faces at the cottage doors. Trees were sparse; hedges there were none. Then the wind blew, and the rain came with the wind. And so the coach rumbled into Bodmin, grey and forbidding like the hills that cradled it, and one by one the passengers gathered up their things in preparation for departure – all save Mary, who sat still in her corner. The driver, his face a stream of rain, looked in at the window.

'Are you going on to Launceston?' he said. 'It'll be a wild drive to-night across the moors. You can stay in Bodmin, you know, and go on by coach in the morning. There'll be none in this coach going on but you.'

'My friends will be expecting me,' said Mary. 'I'm not afraid of the drive. And I don't want to go as far as Launceston; will you please put me down at Jamaica Inn?'

The man looked at her curiously. 'Jamaica Inn?' he said. 'What would you be doing at Jamaica Inn? That's no place for a girl. You must have made a mistake, surely.' He stared at her hard, not believing her.

'Oh, I've heard it's lonely enough,' said Mary, 'but I don't belong to a town anyway. It's quiet on Helford river, winter and summer, where I come from, and I never felt lonely there.'

'I never said nothing about loneliness,' answered the man. 'Maybe you don't understand, being a stranger up here. It's not the twenty-odd mile of moor I'm thinking of, though that'd scare most women. Here, wait a minute.' He called over his shoulder to a woman who stood in the doorway of the Royal, lighting the lamp above the porch, for it was already dusk.

'Missus,' he said, 'come here an' reason with this young girl. I was told she was for Launceston, but she's asked me to put her down at Jamaica.'

The woman came down the steps and peered into the coach.

'It's a wild, rough place up there,' she said, 'and if it's work you are looking for, you won't find it on the farms. They don't like strangers on the moors. You'd do better down here in Bodmin.'

Mary smiled at her. 'I shall be all right,' she said. 'I'm going to relatives. My uncle is landlord of Jamaica Inn.'

There was a long silence. In the grey light of the coach Mary could see that the woman and the man were staring at her. She felt chilled suddenly, anxious; she wanted some word of reassurance from the woman, but it did not come. Then the woman drew back from the window. 'I'm sorry,' she said slowly. 'It's none of my business, of course. Good night.'

The driver began to whistle, rather red in the face, as one who wishes to rid himself of an awkward situation. Mary leant forward impulsively and touched his arm. 'Would you tell me?' she said. 'I shan't mind what you say. Is my uncle not liked? Is something the matter?'

The man looked very uncomfortable. He spoke gruffly, and avoided her eyes. 'Jamaica's got a bad name,' he said; 'queer tales get about; you know how it is. But I don't want to make any trouble. Maybe they're not true.'

'What sort of tales?' asked Mary. 'Do you mean there's much drunkenness there? Does my uncle encourage bad company?'

The man would not commit himself. 'I don't want to make trouble,' he repeated, 'and I don't know anything. It's only what people say. Respectable folk don't go to Jamaica any more. That's all I know. In the old days we used to water the horses there, and feed them, and go in for a bit of a bite and drink. But we don't stop there any more. We whip the horses past and wait for nothing, not till we get to Five Lanes, and then we don't bide long.'

'Why don't folk go there? What is their reason?' Mary persisted.

The man hesitated; it was as though he were searching for words.

'They're afraid,' he said at last; and then he shook his head; he would say no more. Perhaps he felt he had been churlish, and was sorry for her, for a moment later he looked in at the window again and spoke to her.

'Will you not take a cup of tea here before we go?' he said. 'It's a long drive before you, and it's cold on the moors.'

Mary shook her head. Desire for food had left her, and, though the tea would have warmed her, she did not wish to descend from the coach and walk into the Royal, where the woman would have stared at her, and people would murmur. Besides, there was a little nagging coward in her that whispered. 'Stay in Bodmin, stay in Bodmin,' and for all she knew she might have given way to it in the shelter of the Royal. She had promised her mother to go to Aunt Patience, and there must be no going back on her given word.

'We'd best be going then,' said the driver. 'You are the only traveller on the road to-night. Here's another rug for your knees. I'll whip the horses on when we've climbed the hill out of Bodmin, for it's no night for the road. I shan't be easy in my mind until I reach my bed in Launceston. There's not many of us likes to cross the moors in winter-time, not when the weather's dirty.' He slammed the door and climbed to his seat.

The coach rumbled away down the street, past the safe and solid houses, the busy winking lights, the scattered people hurrying home for supper, their figures bowed against the wind and rain. Through the shuttered windows Mary could see chinks of friendly candlelight; there would be a fire within the grate, and a cloth spread on the table, a woman and children sitting down to their meal, while the man warmed his hands before the cheerful blaze. She thought of the smiling countrywoman who had been her fellow-passenger; she wondered if she was now sitting at her own table, with her children by her side. How comfortable she had been, with her apple cheeks, her rough, worn hands! What a world of security in her deep voice! And Mary made a little story to herself of how she might have followed her from the coach, and prayed her company, and asked her for a home. Nor would she have been refused, she was certain of that. There would have been a smile for her, and a friendly hand, and a bed for her. She would have served the woman, and grown to love her, shared something of her life, become acquainted with her people.

Now the horses were climbing the steep hill out of the town, and, looking through the window at the back of the coach, Mary could see the lights of Bodmin fast disappearing, one by one, until the last glimmer winked, and flickered, and was gone. She was alone now with the wind and the rain, and twelve long miles of barren moor between her and her destination.

She wondered if this was how a ship felt when the security of harbour was left behind. No vessel could feel more desolate than she did, not even if the wind thundered in the rigging and the sea licked her decks.

It was dark in the coach now, for the torch gave forth a sickly yellow glare, and the draught from the crack in the roof sent the flame wandering hither and thither, to the danger of the leather, and Mary thought it best to extinguish it. She sat huddled in her corner, swaying from side to side as the coach was shaken, and it seemed to her that never before had she known there was malevolence in solitude. The very coach, which all the day had rocked her like a cradle, now held a note of menace in its creaks and groans. The wind tore at the roof, and the showers of rain, increasing in violence now there was no shelter from the hills, spat against the windows with new venom. On either side of the road the country stretched interminably into space. No trees, no lanes, no cluster of cottages or hamlet, but mile upon mile of bleak moorland, dark and untraversed, rolling like a desert land to some unseen horizon. No human being could live in this wasted country, thought Mary, and remain like other people; the very children would be born twisted, like the blackened shrubs of broom, bent by the force of a wind that never ceased, blow as it would from east and west, from north and south. Their minds would be twisted, too, their thoughts evil, dwelling as they must amidst marshland and granite, harsh heather and crumbling stone.

They would be born of strange stock who slept with this earth as a pillow, beneath this black sky. They would have something of the Devil left in them still. On wound the road across the dark and silent land, with never a light to waver for an instant as a message of hope to the traveller within the coach. Perhaps there was no habitation in all the long one-and-twenty miles that stretched between the two towns of Bodmin and Launceston; perhaps there was not even a poor shepherd's hut on the desolate highway: nothing but the one grim landmark that was Jamaica Inn.

Mary lost count of time and space; the miles might have been a hundred and the hour midnight, for all she knew. She began to cling to the safety of the coach; at least it had some remnant of familiarity. She had known it since the early morning, and that was long ago. However great a nightmare was this eternal drive, there were at least the four close walls to protect her, the shabby leaking roof, and, within calling distance, the comfortable presence of the driver. At last it seemed to her that he was driving his horses to an even greater speed; she heard him shout to them, the cry of his voice blown past her window on the wind.

She lifted the sash and looked out. She was met with a blast of wind and rain that blinded her for the moment, and then, shaking clear her hair and pushing it from her eyes, she saw that the coach was topping the breast of a hill at a furious gallop, while on either side of the road was rough moorland, looming ink-black in the mist and rain.

Ahead of her, on the crest, and to the left, was some sort of a building, standing back from the road. She could see tall chimneys, murky dim in the darkness. There was no other house, no other cottage. If this was Jamaica, it stood alone in glory, foursquare to the winds. Mary gathered her cloak around her and fastened the clasp. The horses had been pulled to a standstill and stood sweating under the rain, the steam coming from them in a cloud.

The driver climbed down from his seat, pulling her box down with him. He seemed hurried, and he kept glancing over his shoulder towards the house.

'Here you are,' he said; 'across the yard there yonder. If you hammer on the door they'll let you in. I must be getting on or I'll not reach Launceston to-night.' In a moment he was up on his seat again, and picking up the reins. He shouted at his horses, whipping them in a fever of anxiety. The coach rumbled and shook, and in a moment it was away and down the road, disappearing as though it had never been, lost and swallowed up in the darkness.

Mary stood alone, with the trunk at her feet. She heard a sound of bolts being drawn in the dark house behind her, and the door was flung open. A great figure strode into the yard, swinging a lantern from side to side.

'Who is it?' came the shout. 'What do you want here?'

Mary stepped forward and peered up into the man's face.

The light shone in her eyes, and she could see nothing. He swung the lantern to and fro before her, and suddenly he laughed and took hold of her arm, pulling her roughly inside the porch.

'Oh, it's you, is it?' he said. 'So you've come to us after all? I'm your uncle, Joss Merlyn, and I bid you welcome to Jamaica Inn.' He drew her into the shelter of the house, laughing again, and shut the door, and stood the lantern upon a table in the passage. And they looked upon each other face to face.

Chapter Two

He was a great husk of a man, nearly seven feet high, with a creased black brow and a skin the colour of a gypsy. His thick dark hair fell over his eyes in a fringe and hung about his ears. He looked as if he had the strength of a horse, with immense powerful shoulders, long arms that reached almost to his knees, and large fists like hams. His frame was so big that in a sense his head was dwarfed, and sunk between his shoulders, giving that half-stooping impression of a giant gorilla, with his black eyebrows and his mat of hair. But for all his long limbs and mighty frame there was nothing of the ape about his features, for his nose was hooked, curving to a mouth that might have been perfect once but was now sunken and fallen, and there was still something fine about his great dark eyes, in spite of the lines and pouches and the red blood-flecks.

The best things left to him were his teeth, which were all good still, and very white, so that when he smiled they showed up clearly against the tan of his face, giving him the lean and hungry appearance of a wolf. And, though there should be a world of difference between the smile of a man and the bared fangs of a wolf, with Joss Merlyn they were one and the same.

'So you are Mary Yellan,' he said at length, towering above her, his head bent to observe her more closely, 'and you've come all this way to look after your Uncle Joss. I call it very handsome of you.'

He laughed again, mocking her, his laugh bellowing through the house, acting like a lash on the strung nerves of Mary.

'Where is my Aunt Patience?' she asked, glancing around her in the dimly lit passage, cheerless with its cold stone flags and narrow rickety staircase. 'Is she not expecting me, then?'

'"Where's my Aunt Patience?"' mimicked the man. 'Where's my dear auntie to kiss me and daddle me, and make much of me? Can't you wait an instant without running to her? Haven't you a kiss for your Uncle Joss?'

Mary drew back. The thought of kissing him revolted her. He was either mad or drunk, anyway. Probably both. She did not want to anger him, though; she was too frightened for that.

He saw the question pass through her mind, and he laughed again.

'Oh, no,' he said, 'I'm not going to touch you; you're safe as a church with me. I never did like dark women, my dear, and I've better things to do than to play cat's-cradle with me own niece.'

He jeered down at her contemptuously, treating her like a fool, tired of his joke. Then he lifted his head to the stairs.

'Patience,' he roared, 'what in hell are you doing? Here's the girl arrived, whimpering for you. She's sick of the sight of me already.'

There was a little flutter at the head of the stairs, and a footstep dragged. Then the flicker of a candle, and an exclamation. Down the narrow stairs came a woman, shielding the light from her eyes. She wore a dingy mob-cap on her thin grey hair, which hung in elf-locks to her shoulders. She had turned the edges of her hair in a vain attempt to recapture ringlets, but the curl had gone. Her face had fallen away, and the skin was stretched tight across her cheek-bones. Her eyes were large and staring, as though they asked perpetually a question, and she had a little nervous trick of working her mouth, now pursing the lips and now relaxing them. She wore a faded striped petticoat that had once been cherry-coloured and now a washed-out pink, and over her shoulders was flung a much-mended shawl. She had obviously just strung a new ribbon in her cap in some small attempt to brighten her dress, and it struck a false, incongruous note. It was bright scarlet, and showed up in horrible contrast to the pallor of her face. Mary stared at her dumbly, stricken with sorrow. Was this poor tattered creature the bewitching Aunt Patience of her dreams, dressed now like a slattern, and twenty years her age?

The little woman came down the stairs and into the hall; she took Mary's hands in hers and peered into her face. 'Have you really come?' she whispered. 'It is my niece Mary Yellan, isn't it? My dead sister's child?'

Mary nodded, thanking God that her mother could not see her now. 'Dear Aunt Patience,' she said gently, 'I'm glad to see you again. It's so many long years since you came to us at Helford.'

The woman kept pawing her with her hands, stroking her clothes, feeling her, and suddenly she clung to her, burying her head against her shoulder, and she began to cry, loudly and fearfully, drawing her breath in gasps.

'Ah, stop that,' growled her husband. 'What sort of a welcome is this? What have you got to squark about, you damned fool? Can't you see the girl wants her supper? Get her out to the kitchen and give her some bacon and a drink.'

He bent down and shouldered Mary's box as though it weighed less than a paper packet. 'I'll take this to her room,' he said, 'and if you've not got a bite of supper on the table by the time I'm down again I'll give you something to cry about; and you too, if you like,' he added, thrusting his face into Mary's and laying one great finger across her mouth. 'Are you tame, or do you bite?' he said, and then he laughed once more, bellowing to the roof, and thundered up the narrow stairs with the box swaying on his shoulders.

Aunt Patience controlled herself. She made a tremendous effort and smiled, patting her thin locks into place in an old gesture that Mary half remembered, and then, blinking nervously and working her mouth, she led the way to yet another murky passage, and so into the kitchen, which was lit by three candles, while a low turf fire smouldered on the hearth.

'You musn't mind your Uncle Joss,' she said, her manner changing suddenly, fawning almost, like a whimpering dog that has been trained by constant cruelty to implicit obedience, and who, in spite of kicks and curses,

will fight like a tiger for its master. 'Your uncle must be humoured, you
know; he has his ways, and strangers don't understand him at first. He's a
very good husband to me, and has been so since our wedding-day.'

She pattered on mechanically, going backwards and forwards across the
flagged kitchen as she laid the table for supper, taking bread, cheese, and
dripping from the big cupboard behind the panelling, while Mary crouched
beside the fire in a hopeless attempt to warm her chilled fingers.

The kitchen was heavy with peat-smoke. It crept up to the ceiling and
into the corners, and hung about the air like a thin blue cloud. It stung
Mary's eyes, and explored her nostrils, and lay upon her tongue.

'You'll soon come to like your Uncle Joss, and fit into his ways,' continued
her aunt. 'He's a very fine man, and a very brave one. He has a great name
hereabouts, and is much respected. There's no one will say a word against
Joss Merlyn. We have great company here at times. It's not always as quiet
as this. It's a very busy highway, you know. The coaches pass every day.
And the gentry are most civil to us, most civil. A neighbour was in only
yesterday, and I made him a cake to take home. 'Mrs. Merlyn,' he said,
'you're the only woman in Cornwall can bake a cake.' Those were his very
words. And even the squire himself – that's Squire Bassat, you know, from
North Hill; he owns all the land hereabouts – he passed me on the road the
other day – Tuesday it was – and he took off his hat. 'Good morning,
madam,' he said, and he bowed to me from his horse. They say he was a
great man for the women in his day. Then out comes Joss from the stable,
where he had been mending the wheel of the trap. 'How's life, Mr. Bassat?'
he says. 'As large as yourself, Joss,' answers the squire, and they both fell
to laughing.'

Mary murmured some reply to this little speech, but she was pained and
worried to see how, when speaking, Aunt Patience avoided her eyes, and the
very fluency of her words was in itself suspicious. She spoke much as a child
does who tells herself a story and has a talent for invention. It hurt Mary
to see her act this part, and she longed for her to be done with it, or be silent,
for the flow of words was, in its way, more appalling than her tears had
been. There was a footfall outside the door, and with a sinking heart Mary
realised that Joss Merlyn had come downstairs again, and had in all
possibility listened to his wife's conversation.

Aunt Patience heard him too, for she turned pale, and began to work her
mouth. He came into the room, and looked from one to the other.

'So the hens are clacking already?' he said, the smile and the laugh gone,
his eyes narrow. 'You'll soon stop your tears if you can talk. I heard you,
you blathering fool – gobble, gobble, gobble, like a turkey-hen. Do you think
your precious niece believes a word you say? Why, you wouldn't take in a
child, far less a bunch of petticoats like her.'

He pulled a chair from the wall, and crashed it against the table. He sat
down heavily, the chair creaking beneath him, and, reaching for the loaf, cut
himself off a great hunk of bread, which he slabbed with dripping. He
crammed it into his mouth, the grease running down his chin, and beckoned
Mary to the table. 'You need food, I can see that,' he said, and he proceeded

to cut carefully a thin slice from the loaf, which he quartered in pieces and buttered for her, the whole business very delicately done and in striking contrast to his manner in serving himself – so much so that to Mary there was something almost horrifying in the change from rough brutality to fastidious care. It was as though there was some latent power in his fingers which turned them from bludgeons into deft and cunning servants. Had he cut her a chunk of bread and hurled it at her she would not have minded so much; it would have been in keeping with what she had seen of him. But this sudden coming to grace, this quick and exquisite moving of his hands, was a swift and rather sinister revelation, sinister because it was unexpected and not true to type. She thanked him quietly, and began to eat.

Her aunt, who had not uttered since her husband entered the room, was frying bacon over the fire. No one spoke. Mary was aware of Joss Merlyn watching her across the table, and behind her she could hear her aunt fumbling with ineffectual fingers at the hot handle of the frying-pan. In a minute she had dropped it, uttering a little cry of distress. Mary rose from her place to help her, but Joss thundered at her to sit down.

'One fool is bad enough, without making a couple of them,' he shouted. 'Keep your seat and let your aunt clear up the mess. It won't be for the first time.' He leant back in his chair, and began to pick his teeth with his nails. 'What'll you drink?' he asked her. 'Brandy, wine, or ale? You may starve here but you won't go thirsty. We don't get sore throats at Jamaica.' And he laughed at her, and winked, and put out his tongue.

'I'll have a cup of tea if I may,' said Mary. 'I'm not used to drinking spirits, nor wine neither.'

'Oh, you're not? Well, it's your loss, I'm glad to say. You can have your tea to-night, but, by God, you'll want some brandy in a month or two.'

He reached across the table and took hold of her hand.

'You've a pretty enough paw for one who's worked on a farm,' he said. 'I was afraid it would be rough and red. If there's one thing that makes a man sick it's to have his ale poured out by an ugly hand. Not that my customers are over-particular, but then we've never had a barmaid before at Jamaica Inn.' He gave her a mock bow, and dropped her hand.

'Patience, my dear,' he said, 'here's the key. Go and fetch me a bottle of brandy, for the Lord's sake. I've a thirst on me that all the waters of Dozmary would not slake.' His wife hurried across the room at his word, and disappeared into the passage. Then he fell to picking his teeth again, whistling from time to time, while Mary ate her bread and butter, and drank the tea that he placed before her. Already a splitting headache tightened her brow, and she was ready to drop. Her eyes watered from the peat-smoke. But she was not too tired to watch her uncle, for already she had caught something of the nervousness of her Aunt Patience, and felt that in some sense they were here like mice in a trap, unable to escape, with him playing with them like a monstrous cat.

In a few minutes his wife returned with the brandy, which she put in front of her husband, and while she finished her cooking of the bacon, and served Mary and herself, he fell to drinking, staring moodily before him, kicking the leg of the table. Suddenly he thumped the table with his fist, shaking the plates and cups, while one platter crashed to the floor and broke.

'I tell you what it is, Mary Yellan,' he shouted. 'I'm master in this house, and I'll have you know it. You'll do as you're told, and help in the house and serve my customers, and I'll not lay a finger on you. But, by God, if you open your mouth and squark, I'll break you until you eat out of my hand the same as your aunt yonder.'

Mary faced him across the table. She held her hands in her lap so that he should not see them tremble.

'I understand you,' she said. 'I'm not curious by nature, and I've never gossiped in my life. It doesn't matter to me what you do in the inn, or what company you keep. I'll do my work about the house and you'll have no cause to grumble. But if you hurt my Aunt Patience in any way, I tell you this – I'll leave Jamaica Inn straight away, and I'll find the magistrate, and bring him here, and have the law on you; and then try and break me if you like.'

Mary had turned very pale, and she knew that if he thundered at her now she would break down and cry, and he would have the mastery of her for ever. The torrent of words had come from her in spite of herself, and wrung with pity for the poor broken thing that was her aunt, she could not control them. Had she but known it, she had saved herself, for her little show of spirit impressed the man, and he leant back in his chair and relaxed.

'That's very pretty,' he said; 'very prettily put indeed. Now we know just what sort of lodger we have. Scratch her, and she shows her claws. All right, my dear; you and I are more akin than I thought. If we are going to play, we'll play together. I may have work for you at Jamaica one day, work that you've never done before. Man's work, Mary Yellan, where you play with life and death.' Mary heard her Aunt Patience give a little gasp beside her.

'Oh, Joss,' she whispered. 'Oh, Joss, please?'

There was so much urgency in her voice that Mary stared at her in surprise. She saw her aunt lean forward and motion her husband to be silent, and the very eagerness of her chin and the agony in her eyes frightened Mary more than anything that had happened that night. She felt eerie suddenly, chilled, and rather sick. What had roused Aunt Patience to such panic? What had Joss Merlyn been about to say? She was aware of a fevered and rather terrible curiosity. Her uncle waved his hand impatiently.

'Get up to bed, Patience,' he said. 'I'm tired of your death's head at my supper-table. This girl and I understand one another.'

The woman rose at once and went to the door, with a last ineffectual glance of despair over her shoulder. They heard her patter up the stairs. Joss Merlyn and Mary were alone. He pushed the empty brandy-glass away from him and folded his arms on the table.

'There's been one weakness in my life, and I'll tell you what it is,' he said. 'It's drink. It's a curse, and I know it. I can't stop myself. One day it'll be the end of me, and a good job too. There's days go by and I don't touch more than a drop, same as I've done to-night. And then I'll feel the thirst come on me and I'll soak. Soak for hours. It's power, and glory, and women, and the Kingdom of God, all rolled into one. I feel a king then, Mary. I feel I've got the strings of the world between my two fingers. It's heaven and hell. I talk then, talk until every damned thing I've done is spilt to the four winds. I shut myself in my room and shout my secrets in my pillow. Your aunt turns the key on me, and when I'm sober I hammer on the door and she lets me out. There's no one knows that but she and I, and now I've told you. I've told you because I'm already a little drunk and I can't hold my tongue. But I'm not drunk enough to lose my head. I'm not drunk enough to tell you why I live in this God-forgotten spot, and why I'm the landlord of Jamaica Inn.' His voice was hoarse, and now he scarcely spoke above a whisper. The turf fire had sunk low in the hearth, and dark shadows stretched long fingers on the wall. The candles too had burnt down, and cast a monstrous shadow of Joss Merlyn on the ceiling. He smiled at her, and with a foolish drunken gesture he laid his finger against his nose.

'I've not told you that, Mary Yellan. Oh, no, I've got some sense and cunning left. If you want to know any more you can ask your aunt. She'll pull you a tale. I heard her blathering to-night, telling you we kept fine company here, and the squire takes off his hat to her. It's lies, all lies. I'll tell you that much, for you'll come to know it anyway. Squire Bassat's too mortal scared to shove his nose in here. If he saw me in the road he'd cross his heart and spur his horse. And so would all the precious gentry. The coaches don't stop here now, nor the mails neither. I don't worry; I've customers enough. The wider berth the gentry give to me the better pleased I am. Oh, there's drinking here all right, and plenty of it too. There's some who come to Jamaica Saturday night, and there's some who turn the key of their door and sleep with their fingers in their ears. There are nights when every cottage on the moors is dark and silent, and the only lights for miles are the blazing windows of Jamaica Inn. They say the shouting and the singing can be heard as far down as the farms below Roughtor. You'll be in the bar those nights, if you've a fancy for it, and you'll see what company I keep.'

Mary sat very still, gripping the sides of her chair. She dared not move for fear of that swift changing of his mood which she had observed already, and which would turn him from this sudden intimate tone of confidence to a harsh and coarse brutality.

'They're all afraid of me,' he went on; 'the whole damned lot of 'em. Afraid of me, who's afraid of no man. I tell you, if I'd had learning, I'd have walked the breadth of England beside King George himself. It's drink that's been against me, drink and my hot blood. It's the curse of all of us, Mary. There's never been a Merlyn yet that died peaceful in his bed.

'My father was hanged at Exeter – he had a brawl with a fellow, and killed him. My granddad had his ears cut for thieving; he was sent out to a convict settlement and died raving mad from a snake-bite in the tropics. I'm the eldest of three brothers, all of us born under the shadow of Kilmar, away yonder above Twelve Men's Moor. You walk out over there across the East Moor till you come to Rushyford, and you'll see a great crag of granite like a devil's hand sticking up into the sky. That's Kilmar. If you'd been born under its shadow you'd take to drink, same as I did. My brother Matthew, he was drowned in Trewartha Marsh. We thought he'd gone for a sailor, and had no news of him, and then in the summer there was a drought, and no rain fell for seven months, and there was Matthew sticking up in the bog, with his hands above his head, and the curlews flying round him. My brother Jem, damn him, he was the baby. Hanging on to mother's skirts when Matt and I were grown men. I never did see eye to eye with Jem. Too smart he is, too sharp with his tongue. Oh, they'll catch him in time and hang him, same as they did my father.'

He fell silent a moment, gazing at his empty glass. He picked it up, and put it down again. 'No,' he said, 'I've said enough. I'll have no more to-night. Go up to bed, Mary, before I wring your neck. Here's your candle. You'll find your room over the porch.'

Mary took the candlestick without speaking, and was about to pass him when he seized hold of her shoulder and twisted her round.

'There'll be nights sometimes when you hear wheels on the road,' he said, 'and those wheels will not pass on, but they'll stop outside Jamaica Inn. And you'll hear footsteps in the yard, and voices beneath your window. When that happens, you'll stay in your bed, Mary Yellan, and cover your head with the blankets. Do you understand?'

'Yes, uncle.'

'Very well. Now get out, and if you ever ask me a question again I'll break every bone in your body.'

She went out of the room and into the dark passage, bumping against the settle in the hall, and so upstairs, feeling her way with her hands, judging her whereabouts by turning round and facing the stairs again. Her uncle had told her the room over the porch, and she crept across the dark landing, which was unlit, past two doors on either side – guest-rooms she imagined, waiting for those travellers who never came nowadays, nor sought shelter beneath the roof of Jamaica Inn – and then stumbled against another door and turned the handle, and saw by the flickering flame of her candle that this was her room, for her trunk lay on the floor.

The walls were rough and unpapered, and the floorboards bare. A box turned upside down served as a dressing-table, with a cracked looking-glass on top. There was no jug or basin; she supposed she would wash in the kitchen. The bed creaked when she leant upon it, and the two thin blankets felt damp to her hand. She decided she would not undress, but would lie down upon it in her travelling clothes, dusty as they were, with her cloak wrapped round her. She went to the window and looked out. The wind had dropped, but it was still raining – a thin wretched drizzle that trickled down the side of the house, and smeared the dirt on the window-pane.

A noise came from the far end of the yard, a curious groaning sound like an animal in pain. It was too dark to see clearly, but she could make out a dark shape swinging gently to and fro. For one nightmare of a moment, her imagination on fire with the tales Joss Merlyn had told her, she thought it was a gibbet, and a dead man hanging. And then she realised it was the signboard of the inn, that somehow or other, through neglect, had become insecure upon its nails and now swung backwards, forwards, with the slightest breeze. Nothing but a poor battered board, that had once known prouder days in its first erection, but whose white lettering was now blurred and grey, and whose message was at the mercy of the four winds – Jamaica Inn – Jamaica Inn. Mary pulled down the blind and crept to her bed. Her teeth were chattering, and her feet and hands were numb. For a long while she sat huddled on the bed, a prey to despair. She wondered whether it were possible to break from the house and find her way back the twelve long miles to Bodmin. She wondered whether her weariness would prove too much for her, and if with an agony of fatigue she would drop by the roadside, and fall asleep where she lay, only to be wakened by the morning light and to see the great form of Joss Merlyn towering above her.

She closed her eyes, and at once she saw his face smiling at her, and then the smile changing to a frown, and the frown breaking into a thousand creases as he shook with rage, and she saw his great mat of black hair, his hooked nose, and the long powerful fingers that held such deadly grace.

She felt caught here now, like a bird in a net, and however much she struggled she would never escape. If she wished to be free she must go now, climb from her window and run like a mad thing along the white road that stretched like a snake across the moors. To-morrow it would be too late.

She waited until she heard his footsteps on the stairs. She heard him mutter to himself, and to her relief he turned aside and went along the other passage to the left of the staircase. In the distance a door closed, and there was silence. She decided that she would wait no longer. If she stayed even one night beneath this roof her nerve would go from her, and she would be lost. Lost, and mad, and broken, like Aunt Patience. She opened the door and stole into the passage. She tiptoed to the head of the stairs. She paused and listened. Her hand was on the banister and her foot on the top stair when she heard a sound from the other passage. It was somebody crying. It was someone whose breath came in little gasps and spasms, and who tried to muffle the sound in a pillow. It was Aunt Patience. Mary waited a moment, and then she turned back and went to her own room again, and threw herself on the bed and closed her eyes. Whatever she would have to face in the future, and however frightened she would be, she would not leave Jamaica Inn now. She must stay with Aunt Patience. She was needed here. It might be that Aunt Patience would take comfort from her, and they would come to an understanding, and, in some way which she was now too tired to plan, Mary would act as a protector to Aunt Patience, and stand between her and Joss Merlyn. For seventeen years her mother had lived and worked alone, and known greater hardships than Mary would ever know. She would not have run away because of a half-crazy man. She would not have feared a house that reeked of evil, however lonely it stood on its wind-blown hill, a solitary landmark defying man and storm. Mary's mother would have the courage to fight her enemies. Yes, and conquer them in the end. There would be no giving way for her.

And so Mary lay upon her hard bed, her mind teeming while she prayed for sleep, every sound a fresh stab to her nerves, from the scratching of a mouse in the wall behind her to the creaking of the sign in the yard. She counted the minutes and the hours of an eternal night, and when the first cock crew in a field behind the house she counted no more, but sighed, and slept like a dead thing.

Chapter Three

Mary woke to a high wind from the west, and a thin watery sun. It was the rattling of the window that roused her from her sleep, and she judged from the broad daylight and the colour of the sky that she had slept late, and that it must be past eight o'clock. Looking out of the window and across the yard, she saw that the stable door was open, and there were fresh hoof-marks in the mud outside. With a great sense of relief she realised that the landlord must have gone from home, and she would have Aunt Patience to herself, if only for a little time.

Hurriedly she unpacked her trunk, pulling out her thick skirt and coloured apron, and the heavy shoes she had worn at the farm, and in ten minutes she was down in the kitchen, and washing in the scullery at the back.

Aunt Patience came in from the chicken-run behind the house with some new-laid eggs in her apron, which she produced with a little smile of mystery. 'I thought you'd like one for your breakfast,' she said. 'I saw you were too tired to eat much last night. And I've saved you a spot of cream for your bread.' Her manner was normal enough this morning, and in spite of the red rims round her eyes, which bespoke an anxious night, she was obviously making an effort to be cheerful. Mary decided it was only in the presence of her husband that she went to pieces like a frightened child, and when he was away she had that same child's aptitude for forgetting, and could seize pleasure from little situations such as this of making breakfast for Mary, and boiling her an egg.

They both avoided any reference to the night before, and Joss's name was not mentioned. Where he had gone, and on what business, Mary neither asked nor cared; she was only too relieved to be rid of him.

Mary could see that her aunt was eager to speak of things unconnected with her present life; she seemed afraid of any questions, so Mary spared her, and plunged into a description of the last years at Helford, the strain of the bad times, and her mother's illness and death.

Whether Aunt Patience took it in or not she could not tell; certainly she nodded from time to time, and pursed her lips, and shook her head, and uttered little ejaculations; but it seemed to Mary that years of fear and

anxiety had taken away her powers of concentration, and that some underlying terror prevented her from giving her whole interest to any conversation.

During the morning there was the usual work of the house, and Mary
was thus able to explore the inn more thoroughly.

It was a dark, rambling place, with long passages and unexpected rooms.
There was a separate entrance to the bar, at the side of the house, and,
though the room was empty now, there was something heavy in the atmosphere reminiscent of the last time it was full: a lingering taste of old tobacco,
the sour smell of drink, and an impression of warm, unclean humanity
packed one against the other on the dark stained benches.

For all the unpleasant suggestion that it conjured, it was the one room in
the inn that had vitality, and was not morne and drear. The other rooms
appeared neglected or unused; even the parlour by the entrance-porch had
a solitary air, as though it were many months since an honest traveller had
stepped upon the threshold and warmed his back before a glowing fire. The
guest-rooms upstairs were in an even worse state of repair. One was used
for lumber, with boxes piled against the wall, and old horse-blankets chewed
and torn by families of rats or mice. In the room opposite, potatoes and
turnips had been stored upon a broken-down bed.

Mary guessed that her own small room had been in much the same
condition, and that she owed it to her aunt that it was now furnished at all.
Into their room, along the further passage, she did not venture. Beneath it,
down a passage that ran parallel to the one above, long and in the opposite
direction from the kitchen, was another room, the door of which was locked.
Mary went out into the yard to look at it through the window, but there was
a board nailed up against the frame, and she could not see inside.

The house and outbuildings formed three sides of the little square that
was the yard, in the centre of which was a grass bank and a drinking-trough.
Beyond this lay the road, a thin white ribbon that stretched on either hand
to the horizon, surrounded on each side by moorland, brown and sodden
from the heavy rains. Mary went out on to the road and looked about her,
and as far as her eyes could see there was nothing but the black hills and
the moors. The grey slate inn, with its tall chimneys, forbidding and
uninhabited though it seemed, was the only dwelling-place on the landscape.
To the west of Jamaica high tors reared their heads; some were smooth like
downland, and the grass shone yellow under the fitful winter sun; but others
were sinister and austere, their peaks crowned with granite and great slabs
of stone. Now and again the sun was obscured by cloud, and long shadows
fled over the moors like fingers. Colour came in patches; sometimes the hills
were purple, ink-stained, and mottled, and then a feeble ray of sun would
come from a wisp of cloud, and one hill would be golden-brown while his
neighbour still languished in the dark. The scene was never once the same,
for it would be the glory of high noon to the east, with the moor as motionless
as desert sand; and away to the westward arctic winter fell upon the hills,
brought by a jagged cloud shaped like a highwayman's cloak, that scattered
hail and snow and a sharp spittle rain on to the granite tors. The air was
strong and sweet-smelling, cold as mountain air, and strangely pure. It was

a revelation to Mary, accustomed as she was to the warm and soft climate of Helford, with its high hedges and tall protecting trees. Even the east wind had been no hardship there, for the arm of the headland acted as a defence to those on land, and it was only the river that ran turbulent and green, the wave-crests whipped with foam.

However grim and hateful was this new country, however barren and untilled, with Jamaica Inn standing alone upon the hill as a buffer to the four winds, there was a challenge in the air that spurred Mary Yellan to adventure. It stung her, bringing colour to her cheeks and a sparkle to her eyes; it played with her hair, blowing it about her face; and as she breathed deep she drew it through her nostrils and into her lungs, more quenching and sweeter than a draught of cider. She went to the water-trough, and put her hands under the spring. The water ran clear and icy-cold. She drank some, and it was unlike any water she had drunk before, bitter, queer, with a lingering peat taste like the smoke from the turf fire in the kitchen.

It was deep and satisfying, for her thirst went from her.

She felt strong in her body and emboldened in spirit, and she went back into the house to find Aunt Patience, her appetite sharp for the dinner that she hoped awaited her. She fell to with a will upon stewed mutton and turnips, and, her hunger appeased now for the first time for four-and-twenty hours, she felt her courage return to her, and she was ready to question her aunt and risk the consequences.

'Aunt Patience,' she began, 'why is my uncle the landlord of Jamaica Inn?' The sudden direct attack took the woman by surprise, and for a moment she stared at Mary without reply. Then she flushed scarlet, and began to work her mouth. 'Why,' she faltered, 'it's – it's a very prominent place here, on the road. You can see that. This is the main road from the south. The coaches pass here twice a week. They come from Truro, and Bodmin, and so on, to Launceston. You came yourself yesterday. There's always company on the road. Travellers, and private gentlemen, and sometimes sailors from Falmouth.'

'Yes, Aunt Patience. But why don't they stop at Jamaica?'

'They do. They often ask for a drink in the bar. We've a good custom here.'

'How can you say that when the parlour is never used, and the guest-rooms are stored with lumber, fit only for rats and mice? I've seen them for myself. I've been to inns before, smaller ones than this by far. There was an inn at home, in the village. The landlord was a friend of ours. Many a time mother and I had tea in the parlour; and upstairs, though there were only two rooms, they were furnished and fitted up in style for travellers.'

Her aunt was silent for a moment, working her mouth and twisting her fingers in her lap. 'Your Uncle Joss doesn't encourage folk to stay,' she said at length. 'He says you never know who you are going to get. Why, in a lonely spot like this we might be murdered in our beds. There's all sorts on a road like this. It wouldn't be safe.'

'Aunt Patience, you're talking nonsense. What is the use of an inn that cannot give an honest traveller a bed for the night? For what other purpose was it built? And how do you live, if you have no custom?'

'We have custom,' returned the woman sullenly. 'I've told you that. There's men come in from the farms and outlying places. There are farms and cottages scattered over these moors for miles around, and folk come from there. There are evenings when the bar is full of them.'

'The driver on the coach yesterday told me respectable people did not come to Jamaica any more. He said they were afraid.'

Aunt Patience changed colour. She was pale now, and her eyes roved from side to side. She swallowed, and ran her tongue over her lips.

'Your Uncle Joss has a strong temper,' she said; 'you have seen that for yourself. He is easily roused; he will not have folk interfering with him.'

'Aunt Patience, why should anyone interfere with a landlord of an inn who goes about his rightful business? However hot-tempered a man may be, his temper doesn't scare people away. That's no excuse.'

Her aunt was silent. She had come to the end of her resources, and sat stubborn as a mule. She would not be drawn. Mary tried another question.

'Why did you come here in the first place? My mother knew nothing of this; we believed you to be in Bodmin; you wrote from there when you married.'

'I met your uncle in Bodmin, but we never lived there,' replied Aunt Patience slowly. 'We lived near Padstow for a while, and then we came here. Your uncle bought the inn from Mr. Bassat. It had stood empty a number of years, I believe, and your uncle decided it would suit him. He wanted to settle down. He's travelled a lot in his time; he's been to more places than I can remember the names. I believe he was in America once.'

'It seems a funny thing to come to this place to settle,' said Mary. 'He couldn't have chosen much worse, could he?'

'It's near his old home,' said her aunt. 'Your uncle was born only a few miles away, over on Twelve Men's Moor. His brother Jem lives there now in a bit of a cottage, when he's not roaming the country. He comes here sometimes, but your Uncle Joss does not care for him much.'

'Does Mr. Bassat ever visit the inn?'

'No.'

'Why not, if he sold it to my uncle?'

Aunt Patience fidgeted with her fingers, and worked her mouth.

'There was some misunderstanding,' she replied. 'Your uncle bought it through a friend. Mr. Bassat did not know who Uncle Joss was until we were settled in, and then he was not very pleased.'

'Why did he mind?'

'He had not seen your uncle since he lived at Trewartha as a young man. Your uncle was wild as a lad; he got a name for acting rough. It wasn't his fault, Mary, it was his misfortune. The Merlyns all were wild. His young brother Jem is worse than ever he was, I am sure of that. But Mr. Bassat listened to a pack of lies about Uncle Joss, and was in a great way when he discovered that he'd sold Jamaica to him. There, that's all there is to it.'

She leant back in her chair, exhausted from her cross-examination. Her eyes begged to be excused further questioning and her face was pale and drawn. Mary saw she had suffered enough, but with the rather cruel audacity of youth she ventured one question more.

'Aunt Patience,' she said, 'I want you to look at me and answer me this, and then I won't worry you again. What has the barred room at the end of the passage to do with the wheels that stop outside Jamaica Inn by night?'

As soon as she had spoken she was sorry, and, like many a one before her who has spoken too hastily and too soon, she yearned for the words to be unsaid. It was too late, though now. The damage had been done.

A strange expression crept upon the woman's face, and her great hollow eyes stared across the table in terror. Her mouth trembled, and her hand wandered to her throat. She looked fearful, haunted.

Mary pushed back her chair and knelt by her side. She put her arms round Aunt Patience, and held her close, and kissed her hair.

'I'm sorry,' she said. 'Don't be angry with me; I'm rude and impertinent. It's none of my business, and I've no right to question you, and I'm ashamed of myself. Please, please forget what I said.'

Her aunt buried her face in her hands. She sat motionless, and paid no attention to her niece. For some minutes they sat there in silence, while Mary stroked her shoulder and kissed her hands.

Then Aunt Patience uncovered her face and looked down at her.

The fear had gone from her eyes, and she was calm. She took Mary's hands in hers and gazed into her face.

'Mary,' she said, and her voice was hushed and low, scarcely above a whisper, 'Mary, I can't answer your questions, for there's many I don't know the answer to myself. But because you are my niece, my own sister's child, I must give you a word of warning.'

She glanced over her shoulder, as though she were afraid that Joss himself stood in the shadows behind the door.

'There's things that happen at Jamaica, Mary, that I've never dared to breathe. Bad things. Evil things. I can't never tell you; I can't even admit them to myself. Some of it in time you'll come to know. You can't avoid it, living here. Your Uncle Joss mixes with strange men, who follow a strange trade. Sometimes they come by night, and from your window above the porch you will hear footsteps, and voices, and knocking at the door. Your uncle lets them in, and he takes them along that passage to the room with the locked door. They go inside, and from my bedroom above I can hear the mutter of their voices through the long hours. Before dawn they are away, and no sign left that they have ever been. When they come, Mary, you will say nothing to me or to your Uncle Joss. You must lie in bed, and put your fingers to your ears. You must never question me, nor him, nor anyone, for if you came to guess but half of what I know, you hair would go grey, Mary, as mine has done, and you would tremble in your speech and weep by night, and all that lovely careless youth of yours would die, Mary, as mine has died.'

Then she rose from the table and pushed aside her chair, and Mary heard her climb the staircase with heavy, faltering feet, and so along the landing to her room, and close the door.

Mary sat on the floor beside the empty chair, and she saw through the kitchen window that the sun had already disappeared behind the furthest hill, and that before many hours had passed the grey malevolence of a November dusk would have fallen upon Jamaica once again.

Chapter Four

Joss Merlyn was away from home for nearly a week, and during that time Mary came to know something of the country.

Her presence was not required in the bar, for no one came to it when the landlord was from home, and, after giving her aunt a hand with the housework and in the kitchen, she was free to wander where she pleased. Patience Merlyn was no walker; she had no wish to stir beyond the chicken-run at the back of the inn, and she had no sense of direction. She had a vague idea of the names of the tors, for she had heard them mentioned by her husband, but where they were, and how anyone found them, she did not know. So Mary would strike off on her own at midday, with nothing but the sun to guide her and a certain deep-grained common sense which was her natural inheritance as a countrywoman.

The moors were even wilder than she had at first supposed. Like an immense desert they rolled from east to west, with tracks here and there across the surface and great hills breaking the skyline.

Where was their final boundary she could not tell, except that once, away to the westward, after climbing the highest tor behind Jamaica, she caught the silver shimmer of the sea. It was a silent, desolate country though, vast and untouched by human hand; on the high tors the slabs of stone leant against one another in strange shapes and forms, massive sentinels who had stood there since the hands of God first fashioned them.

Some were shaped like giant furniture, with monstrous chairs and twisted tables; and sometimes the smaller crumbling stones lay on the summit of the hill like a giant himself, his huge, recumbent form darkening the heather and the coarse tufted grass. There were long stones that stood on end, balancing themselves in a queer miraculous way, as though they leant against the wind; and there were flat altar-stones whose smooth and polished faces stared up towards the sky, awaiting a sacrifice that never came. Wild sheep dwelt on the high tors, and there were ravens too, and buzzards; the hills were homing places for all solitary things.

Black cattle grazed on the moors beneath, their careful feet treading the firm ground, and with inborn knowledge they avoided the tufted, tempting grass that was not grass at all, but soggy marsh that sighed and whispered. When the wind blew on the hills it whistled mournfully in the crevices of granite, and sometimes it shuddered like a man in pain.

Strange winds blew from nowhere; they crept along the surface of the grass, and the grass shivered; they breathed upon the little pools of rain in the hollowed stones, and the pools rippled. Sometimes the wind shouted and cried, and the cry echoed in the crevices, and moaned, and was lost again. There was a silence on the tors that belonged to another age; an age that is past and vanished as though it had never been, an age when man did not exist, but pagan footsteps trod upon the hills. And there was a stillness in the air, and a stranger, older peace, that was not the peace of God.

As Mary Yellan walked the moors, climbed the tors, and rested in the low dips beside the springs and streams, she thought about Joss Merlyn and what his boyhood must have been, and how he grew athwart like the stunted broom, with the bloom blown out of him by the north wind.

One day she crossed the East Moor, in the direction he had given her that first evening; and when she had gone some way and stood alone upon a ridge of down, surrounded on all sides by bleak moorland, she saw that the land descended to a deep and treacherous marsh, through which a brook burbled and sang. And rising beyond the marsh, away on the other side, pointing his great fingers to the sky, was a crag like a split hand coming sheer out of the moor, his surface moulded in granite as though sculptured, his slope a venemous grey.

So this was Kilmar Tor; and somewhere amongst that solid mass of stone, where the ridges hid the sun, Joss Merlyn had been born, and his brother lived to-day. Below her in the marsh, Matthew Merlyn had drowned. In her fancy she saw him stride across the high ground, whistling a song, the murmur of the brook in his ears, and somehow evening came upon him before he was aware, and his footsteps faltered as he turned in his tracks. In her fancy she watched him pause, and think a moment, and curse softly, and then with a shrug of his shoulders he plunged down into the mist, his confidence returning; but before he had taken five steps he felt the ground sag under his feet, and he stumbled, and fell, and suddenly he was up above his knees in weed and slime. He reached out for a tuft of grass, and it sank beneath his weight. He kicked with his feet and they would not answer him. He kicked once more, and one foot sucked itself free, but, as he plunged forward, reckless and panic-stricken, he trod deeper water still, and now he floundered helplessly, beating the weed with his hands. She heard him scream in terror, and a curlew rose from the marsh in front of him, flapping his wings and whistling his mournful cry. When the curlew had flown from sight, disappearing behind a ridge of land, the marsh was still again; only a few grass stems shivered in the wind, and there was silence.

Mary turned her back upon Kilmar, and began to run across the moor, stumbling amongst the heather and the stones, nor did she stop until the marsh had sunk beneath the level of the hill, and the crag itself was hidden. She had come further than she intended, and the way home was long. It seemed an eternity before the last hill was conquered and behind her, and the tall chimneys of Jamaica Inn stood out before her above the winding road. As she crossed the yard she noticed with sinking heart that the stable door was open, and the pony was inside. Joss Merlyn had returned.

She opened the door as silently as possible, but it rubbed against the stone flags, and grated in protest. The sound rang in the quiet passage, and in a minute the landlord appeared from the back, bending his head under the beam. His shirt-sleeves were rolled above his elbow, and he had a glass in his hand, and a cloth. He was, it seemed, in high good humour, for he shouted boisterously at Mary, and waved the glass.

'Well,' he roared, 'don't drop your face a mile at the sight of me. Aren't you pleased to see me? Did you miss me much?'

Mary made an effort to smile, and asked him if he had had a pleasant journey. 'Pleasant be damned,' he answered. 'There was money in it, and that's all I care. I've not been staying in the palace with the King, if that's what you mean.' He shouted with laughter at his joke, and his wife appeared behind his shoulder, simpering in harmony.

As soon as his laughter died away the smile faded from Aunt Patience's face, and the strained, haunted expression returned again, the fixed, almost idiot stare that she wore habitually in the presence of her husband.

Mary saw at once that the little freedom from care which her aunt had enjoyed during the past week was now no more, and she had again become the nervy, shattered creature of before.

Mary turned to go up the stairs to her room, when Joss called her. 'Here', he said, 'no skulking up there this evening. There'll be work for you in the bar, alongside of your uncle. Don't you know what day of the week it is?'

Mary paused to think. She was losing count of time. Was it Monday's coach she had taken? That made to-day Saturday. Saturday night. At once she realised what Joss Merlyn meant. To-night there would be company at Jamaica Inn.

They came singly, the people of the moors, crossing the yard swiftly and silently, as though they had no wish to be seen. They lacked substance, in the dim light, and seemed no more than shadows as they skirted the wall and passed under the shelter of the porch to knock upon the door of the bar and gain admittance. Some carried lanterns, the fitful glare of which appeared to worry the bearers, for they attempted to screen the glow by covering it with their coats. One or two rode into the yard on ponies, whose hoofs rang sharply on the stones, and the clatter sounded strangely in the still night, followed as it was by the creaking of the stable door yawning on its hinges, and the low mutter of voices as the men led their ponies to the stalls. Others were yet more furtive, bearing neither flare nor lantern, but flitting across the yard with hats pulled low and coats muffled to the chin, betraying by the very secrecy of their movements their desire to remain unseen. The reason for stealth was not apparent, for any passing traveller upon the road could see that to-night Jamaica Inn gave hospitality. The light streamed from the windows, usually so. shuttered and barred, and, as the evening darkened and the hours went by, the sound of voices rose upon the air. There was singing at times, and shouting, and the rumble of laughter, showing that those visitors to the inn who came so furtively, as if in shame, had lost their fear when under cover of the house, and once packed close to their companions in the bar, with pipes alight and glasses filled, had thrown all caution aside.

They were a strange assortment gathered there, grouped around Joss Merlyn in the bar. Securely separated by the counter itself, and half screened by a barrier of bottles and glasses, Mary could look down upon the company and remain unobserved. They straddled the stools and sprawled upon the benches; they leant against the wall; they slouched beside the tables; and one or two, whose heads or stomachs were weaker than the rest, already lay full length upon the floor. They were dirty for the most part, ragged, ill-kept, with matted hair and broken nails; tramps, vagrants, poachers, thieves, cattle-stealers, and gypsies. There was a farmer who had lost his farm through bad management and dishonesty; a shepherd who had fired his master's rick; a horse-dealer who had been hounded out of Devon. One fellow was a cobbler in Launceston, and under cover of his trade passed stolen goods; he who lay in a drunken stupor on the floor was once mate of a Padstow schooner, and had run his ship ashore. The little man who sat in the far corner, biting his nails, was a Port Isaac fisherman, and rumour had it that he kept a store of gold rolled up in a stocking and hidden in the chimney of his cottage – but where the gold came from no one would say. There were men who lived near by, under the very shadow of the tors, who had known no other country but moorland, marsh and granite; one had come walking without a lantern from the Crowdy Marsh beyond Roughtor, taking Brown Willy in his stride; another came from Cheesewring, and sat now with his face in a mug of ale, his boots on a table, side by side with the poor half-witted fellow who had stumbled up the lane from Dozmary. This last had a birthmark that ran the whole length of his face, blazing it purple, and he kept plucking at it with his hands, and pulling out his cheek, so that Mary, who stood in line with him, for all the bottles that divided them, turned sick and nearly faint at the sight of him; and what with the stale drink smell, and the reek of tobacco, and the foul atmosphere of crowded unwashed bodies, she felt a physical disgust rise up in her, and she knew she would give way to it if she stayed there long. Luckily she did not have to move amongst them; her duty was to stand behind the bar, hidden as much as possible, and then do what washing and cleaning of glasses was required, refilling them from tap or bottle, while Joss Merlyn himself handed them to the customers, or lifted the flap of the bar and strode out into the room, laughing at one, flinging a coarse word at another, patting someone on the shoulder, jerking his head at another. After the first hilarious outburst, the first curious stare, the shrug of the shoulder and the chuckle, the company gathered in the inn ignored Mary. They accepted her as niece of the landlord, a sort of serving-maid of Merlyn's wife, as she was introduced, and, though one or two of the younger men would have spoken to her and plagued her, they were wary of the eye of the landlord himself, fearing that any familiarity on their part might anger him, as he had probably brought her to Jamaica for his own amusement. So Mary was left undisturbed, greatly to her relief, though had she known the reason for their reticence she would have walked out of the bar that night in shame and loathing.

Her aunt did not appear before the company, though Mary was aware of her shadow behind the door at times, and a footstep in the passage, and once she caught sight of her frightened eyes peering through the crack in the door. The evening seemed interminable, and Mary longed for release. The air was so thick with smoke and breath that it was hard to see across the room, and to her weary, half-closed eyes, the faces of the men loomed shapeless and distorted, all hair and teeth, their mouths much too large for their bodies, while those who had drunk their fill and could take no more lay on the benches or the floor like dead men, their faces in their hands.

Those who remained sufficiently sober to stand had crowded round a dirty little blackguard from Redruth, who had established himself wit of the assembly. The mine where he had worked was now in ruins, and he had taken to the road as tinker, pedlar, bagman, and had stored up in consequence a string of loathsome songs, gleaned perhaps from the bowels of the black earth where he had once entombed himself, and with these jewels he now provided entertainment to the company at Jamaica Inn.

The laughter that greeted his sallies nearly shook the roof, topped, of course, by the bellow of the landlord himself, and to Mary there was something appalling in this ugly, screaming laughter, which in some strange way, held not a note of mirth, but echoed down the dark stone passages and into the empty rooms above like a tortured thing. The pedlar was making a bait of the wretched idiot from Dozmary, who, crazy from drink, had no control of himself, and could not rise from the floor, where he squatted like an animal. They lifted him on to a table, and the pedlar made him repeat the words of his songs, complete with actions, amid the frenzy of laughter from the crowd; and the poor beast, excited by the applause that greeted him, jigged up and down on the table, whinnying delight, plucking at his spotted purple birthmark with a broken finger-nail. Mary could bear it no longer. She touched her uncle on the shoulder, and he turned to her, his face blotched with the heat of the room and streaming with perspiration.

'I can't stand this,' she said. 'You'll have to attend to your friends yourself. I'm going upstairs to my room.'

He wiped the sweat from his forehead with his shirt-sleeve and stared down at her. She was surprised to see that, although he had been drinking during the evening, he was himself sober, and even if he was the ringleader of this riotous, crazy company, he knew what he was doing. 'Had enough of it, have you?' he said. 'Think yourself a little bit too good for such as we? I'll tell you this, Mary. You've had an easy time behind the bar, and you ought to go down on your knees and thank me for it. Because you're my niece they've let you alone, my dear, but if you hadn't had that honour – by God, there wouldn't be much left of you now!' He shouted with laughter, and pinched her cheek between his finger and thumb, hurting her. 'Get out, then,' he said; 'it's close on midnight anyway, and I don't want you. You'll lock your door to-night, Mary and pull down your blind. Your aunt's been in bed an hour with the blanket drawn over her head.'

He lowered his voice; bending down to her ear and seizing her wrist, he doubled it behind her back, until she cried out in pain.

'All right,' he said; 'that's like a foretaste of punishment, and you know what to expect. Keep your mouth shut and I'll treat you like a lamb. It doesn't do to be curious at Jamaica Inn, and I'll have you remember that.' He was not laughing now, but stared down at her, frowning, as though he would read her thoughts. 'You're not a fool like your aunt,' he said slowly; 'that's the curse of it. You've got a clever little monkey face, and a ferreting monkey mind, and you're not easily scared. But I tell you this, Mary Yellan; I'll break that mind of yours if you let it go astray, and I'll break your body too. Now go upstairs to bed, and let's hear no more of you to-night.'

He turned away from her, and, frowning still, picked up a glass from the bar in front of him, turning it over and over in his hands, rubbing it slowly with a cloth. The contempt in her eyes must have irritated him, for his good humour had left him in a flash, and he flung aside the glass in a fit of ill temper, splitting it to fragments.

'Strip that damned idiot of his clothes,' he thundered, 'and send him back naked to his mother. Maybe the November air will cool that purple face of his, and cure his dog tricks. We've had enough of him in Jamaica.'

The pedlar and his group yelled in delight, and, throwing the wretched halfwit on his back, began to tear off his coat and breeches, while the bewildered fellow flapped out at them with useless hands, bleating like a sheep.

Mary ran out of the room, slamming the door behind her, and as she went up the rickety stairs, her hands over her ears, she could not keep out that sound of laughter and wild song that echoed down the draughty passage, following her to her room, penetrating through the cracks of the floor-boards.

She felt very sick, and threw herself on her bed, her head in her hands. There was a babel of noise in the yard below, and yells of laughter, while a stream of light from a tossing lantern cast a beam up to her window. She got up, and pulled down the blind, but not before she had seen the outline of a quivering naked form bound across the yard with great loping strides, screaming like a hare, and pursued by a handful of hooting, jeering men, with Joss Merlyn's giant figure in the lead cracking a horse-whip above his head.

Then Mary did as her uncle had told her. She undressed hurriedly and crept into bed, pulling the blanket over her head, stuffing her fingers in her ears, her only thought now to be deaf to the horror and the revelry below; but even with eyes shut and face pressed tight against the pillow, she could see the purple blotched face of the poor idiot man upturned towards his captors, and she could hear the thin echo of his cry as he stumbled into the ditch and fell.

She lay in that half-conscious state that waits on the borderland of sleep, when the events of the past day crowd into the mind and make a jumble of confusion. Images danced before her, and the heads of unknown people, and though at times she seemed to be wandering on the moor, with the great crag of Kilmar dwarfing the neighbouring hills, she was aware of the little path of light made by the moon on her bedroom floor, and the steady rattle of the window-blind. There had been voices, and now there were none; somewhere far away on the high road a horse galloped, and wheels rumbled, but now all was still. She slept; and then, without warning, she heard something snap in the peace of mind that had enfolded her, and she was awake suddenly, sitting up in bed, with the moonlight streaming on her face.

She listened, hearing nothing at first but the thumping of her own heart, but in a few minutes there came another sound, from beneath her room this time – the sound of heavy things being dragged along the stone flags in the passage downstairs, bumping against the walls.

She got out of bed and went to the window, pulling aside an inch of blind. Five waggons were drawn up in the yard outside. Three were covered, each drawn by a pair of horses, and the remaining two were open farm-carts. One of the covered waggons stood directly beneath the porch, and the horses were steaming.

Gathered round the waggons were some of the men who had been drinking in the bar earlier in the evening; the cobbler from Launceston was standing under Mary's window, talking to the horse-dealer; the sailor from Padstow had come to his senses and was patting the head of a horse; the pedlar who had tortured the poor idiot was climbing into one of the open carts and lifting something from the floor. And there were strangers in the yard whom Mary had never seen before. She could see their faces clearly because of the moonlight, the very brightness of which seemed to worry the men, for one of them pointed upwards and shook his head, while his companion shrugged his shoulders, and another man, who had an air of authority about him, waved his arm impatiently, as though urging them to make haste, and the three of them turned at once and passed under the porch into the inn. Meanwhile the heavy dragging sound continued, and Mary could trace the direction of it without difficulty from where she stood. Something was being taken along the passage to the room at the end, the room with the barred windows and the bolted door.

She began to understand. Packages were brought by the waggons and unloaded at Jamaica Inn. They were stored in the locked room. Because the horses were steaming, they had come over a great distance – from the coast perhaps – and as soon as the waggons were unloaded they would take their departure, passing out into the night as swiftly and as silently as they had come.

The men in the yard worked quickly, against time. The contents of one covered waggon were not carried into the inn, but were transferred to one of the open farm-carts drawn up beside the drinking-well across the yard. The packages seemed to vary in size and description; some were large parcels, some were small, and others were long rolls wrapped round about in straw and paper. When the cart was filled, the driver, a stranger to Mary, climbed into the seat and drove away.

The remaining waggons were unloaded one by one, and the packages were either placed in the open carts and driven out of the yard, or were borne by the men into the house. All was done in silence. Those men who had shouted and sung earlier that night, were now sober and quiet, bent on the business in hand. Even the horses appeared to understand the need for silence, for they stood motionless.

Joss Merlyn came out of the porch, the pedlar at his side. Neither wore coat or hat, in spite of the cold air, and both had sleeves rolled up to the elbows.

'Is that the lot?' the landlord called softly, and the driver of the last waggon nodded, and held up his hand. The men began to climb into the carts. Some of those who had come to the inn on foot went with them, saving themselves a mile or two on their long trek home. They did not leave unrewarded; all carried burdens of a sort: boxes strapped over their shoulders, bundles under the arm; while the cobbler from Launceston had not only laden his pony with bursting saddle-bags but had added to his own person as well, being several sizes larger round the waist than when he first arrived.

So the waggons and the carts departed from Jamaica, creaking out of the yard, one after the other in a strange funereal procession, some turning north and some south when they came out on to the high road, until they had all gone, and there was no one left standing in the yard but one man Mary had not seen before, the pedlar, and the landlord of Jamaica Inn himself.

Then they too turned, and went back into the house, and the yard was empty. She heard them go along the passage in the direction of the bar, and then their footsteps died away, and a door slammed.

There was no other sound except the husky wheezing of the clock in the hall and the sudden whirring note preparatory to the strike. It rang the hour – three o'clock – and then ticked on, choking and gasping like a dying man who cannot catch his breath.

Mary came away from the window and sat down upon the bed. The cold air blew in on to her shoulders, and she shivered, and reached for her shawl.

The thought of sleep now was impossible. She was too wide awake, too alive in every nerve, and although the dislike and fear of her uncle was as strong as ever within her, a growing interest and curiosity held the mastery. She understood something of his business now. What she had witnessed here to-night was smuggling on the grand scale. There was no doubt that Jamaica Inn was ideally situated for his purpose, and he must have bought it for that reason alone. All that talk of returning to the home of his boyhood was nonsense, of course. The inn stood alone on the great high road that ran north and south, and Mary could see that it must be easy enough for anyone with a capacity for organisation to work a team of waggons from the coast to the Tamar bank, with the inn itself as halting-place and general store.

Spies were needed about the countryside to make a success of the trade; hence the sailor from Padstow, the cobbler from Launceston, the gypsies and the tramps, the vile little pedlar.

And yet, allowing for his personality, his energy, the very fear which his enormous physical strength must engender in his companions, had Joss

Merlyn the necessary brain and subtlety to lead such an enterprise? Did he plan every move and every departure, and had he been making preparations for to-night's work during the past week, when away from home?

It must be so; Mary could see no alternative, and, although her loathing for the landlord increased, she allowed herself a grudging respect for his management.

The whole business must be controlled, and the agents picked, for all their rough manners and wild appearance, otherwise the law could never have been evaded for so long. A magistrate who suspected smuggling would surely have suspected the inn before now, unless he were an agent himself. Mary frowned, her chin in her hand. If it were not for Aunt Patience she would walk out of the inn now, and find her way to the nearest town, and inform against Joss Merlyn. He would soon be in jail, and the rest of the rogues with him, and there would be an ending of the traffic. It was useless to reckon without Aunt Patience, however, and the fact that she still held a dog-like devotion for her husband made the problem difficult, and at the moment impossible.

Mary kept going over and over the question in her mind, and she was not yet satisfied that all was understood. Jamaica Inn was a nest of thieves and poachers, who, with her uncle as leader apparently, worked a profitable smuggling trade between the coast and Devon. So much was clear. But had she seen only part of the game, and was there still more for her to learn? She remembered the terror in Aunt Patience's eyes, and those words spoken in the hush of that first afternoon, when the shadows of early twilight crept across the kitchen floor: 'There's things happen at Jamaica Inn, Mary, that I've never dared to breathe. Bad things. Evil things. I dare not even admit them to myself.' And she had climbed the staircase to her room, haunted and pale, dragging her feet like a creature old and tired.

Smuggling was dangerous; it was fraught with dishonesty; it was forbidden strictly by the law of the land; but was it evil? Mary could not decide. She needed advice, and there was no one she could ask. She was alone in a grim and rather hateful world, with little prospect of changing it for the better. Had she been a man, she would have gone downstairs and challenged Joss Merlyn to his face, and his friends with him. Yes, and fought them too, and drawn blood, if she were lucky. And then away on a horse from the stable, with Aunt Patience riding pillion, and so down to the south again, to the friendly Helford shore, setting up as a farmer in a small way up Mawgan way, or Gweek, with her aunt to keep house for her.

Well, there was little use in dreaming; the present situation must be faced, and courageously too, if any good were to come of it.

Here she was on her bed, a girl of three-and-twenty, in a petticoat and a shawl, with no weapons but her own brain to oppose a fellow twice her age and eight times her strength, who, if he realised she had watched the scene to-night from her window, would encircle her neck with his hand, and, pressing lightly with finger and thumb, put an end to her questioning.

Then Mary swore; a thing she had only done once before in her life, when chased by a bull at Manaccan, and then it had been for the same purpose as now – to give herself courage and a certain bold pretence.

'I'll not show fear before Joss Merlyn or any man,' she said, 'and, to prove it, I will go down now, in the dark passage, and take a look at them in the bar, and if he kills me it will be my own fault.'

She dressed hurriedly, and pulled on her stockings, leaving her shoes where they were, and then, opening the door, she stood and listened for a moment, hearing nothing but the slow choking tick of the clock in the hall.

She crept out into the passage, and came to the stairs. By now she knew that the third step from the top creaked, and so did the last. She trod gently, one hand resting on the banister and the other against the wall to lighten her weight, and so she came to the dim hall by the entrance-door, empty except for one unsteady chair and the shadowed outline of the grandfather clock. Its husky breathing sounded loud beside her ear, and it jarred upon the silence like a living thing. The hall was as black as a pit, and, although she knew she stood alone there, the very solitude was threatening, the closed door to the unused parlour pregnant with suggestion.

The air was fusty and heavy, in strange contrast to the cold stone flags that struck chill to her stockinged feet. As she hesitated, gathering courage to continue, a sudden beam of light shone into the passage that ran at the back of the hall, and she heard voices. The door of the bar must have swung open, and someone came out, for she heard footsteps pass into the kitchen and in a few minutes return again, but whoever it was still left the door of the bar ajar, as the murmur of voices continued and the beam of light remained. Mary was tempted to climb the stairs again to her bedroom and seek safety in sleep, but at the same time there was a demon of curiosity within her that would not be stilled, and this part of her carried her through to the passage beyond, and so to crouch against the wall a few paces only from the door of the bar. Her hands and her forehead were wet now with perspiration, and at first she could hear nothing but the loud beating of her heart. The door was open enough for her to see the outline of the hinged bar itself, and the collection of bottles and glasses, while directly in front ran a narrow strip of floor. The splintered fragments of the glass her uncle had broken still lay where they had fallen, and beside them was a brown stain of ale, spilt by some unsteady hand. The men must be sitting on the benches against the further wall, for she could not see them; they had fallen to silence, and then suddenly a man's voice rang out, quavering and high, the voice of a stranger.

'No, and no again,' he said. 'I tell you for the final time, I'll not be a party to it. I'll break with you now and for ever, and put an end to the agreement. That's murder you'd have me do, Mr. Merlyn; there's no other name for it – it's common murder.'

The voice was pitched high, trembling on the final note, as though the speaker was carried away by the force of his feelings and had lost command of his tongue. Someone – the landlord himself, no doubt – made reply in a low tone, and Mary could not catch his words, but his speech was broken by a cackle of laughter that she recognised as belonging to the pedlar. The quality of it was unmistakable – insulting and coarse.

He must have hinted a question, for the stranger spoke again swiftly in self-defence. 'Swinging, is it?' he said. 'I've risked swinging before, and I'm not afraid of my neck. No, I'm thinking of my conscience and of Almighty God; and though I'll face any man in a fair fight, and take punishment if need be, when it comes to the killing of innocent folk, and maybe women and children amongst them, that's going straight to hell, Joss Merlyn, and you know it as well as I do.'

Mary heard the scraping of a chair, and the man rise to his feet, but at the same time someone thumped his fist on the table and swore, and her uncle lifted his voice for the first time.

'Not so fast, my friend,' he said, 'not so fast. You're soaked in this business up to your neck, and be damned to your blasted conscience! I tell you there's no going back on it now; it's too late; too late for you and for all of us. I've been doubtful of you from the first, with your gentleman's airs and your clean cuffs, and by God I've proved myself right. Harry, bolt the door over there and put the bar across it.'

There was a sudden scuffle and a cry, and the sound of someone falling, and at the same time the table crashed to the floor, and the door to the yard was slammed. Once more the pedlar laughed, odious and obscene, and he began to whistle one of his songs. 'Shall we tickle him up like Silly Sam?' he said, breaking off in the middle. 'He'd be a little body without his fine clothes. I could do with his watch and chain, too; poor men of the road like myself haven't the money to go buying watches. Tickle him up with the whip, Joss, and let's see the colour of his skin.'

'Shut your mouth, Harry, and do as you're told,' answered the landlord. 'Stand where you are by the door and prick him with your knife if he tries to pass you. Now, look here, Mr. lawyer-clerk, or whatever you are in Truro town, you've made a fool of yourself to-night, but you're not going to make a fool of me. You'd like to walk out of that door, wouldn't you, and get on your horse, and be away to Bodmin? Yes, and by nine in the morning you'd have every magistrate in the country at Jamaica Inn, and a regiment of soldiers into the bargain. That's your fine idea, isn't it?'

Mary could hear the stranger breathe heavily, and he must have been hurt in the scuffle, for when his voice came it was jerky and contracted, as though he were in pain. 'Do your devil's work if you must,' he muttered. 'I can't stop you, and I give you my word I'll not inform against you. But join you I will not, and there's my last word to you both.'

There was a silence, and then Joss Merlyn spoke again. 'Have a care,' he said softly. 'I heard another man say that once, and five minutes later he was treading the air. On the end of a rope it was, my friend, and his big toe missed the floor by half an inch. I asked him if he liked to be so near the ground, but he didn't answer. The rope forced the tongue out of his mouth, and he bit it clean in half. They said afterwards he had taken seven and three-quarter minutes to die.'

Outside in the passage Mary felt her neck and her forehead go clammy with sweat, and her arms and legs were weighted suddenly, as though with lead. Little black specks flickered before her eyes, and with a growing sense of horror she realised that she was probably going to faint.

She had one thought in her mind, and that was to grope her way back to the deserted hall and reach the shadow of the clock; whatever happened she must not fall here and be discovered. Mary backed away from the beam of light, and felt along the wall with her hands. Her knees were shaking now, and she knew that at any moment they would give beneath her. Already a surge of sickness rose inside her, and her head was swimming.

Her uncle's voice came from very far away, as though he spoke with his hands against his mouth. 'Leave me alone with him, Harry,' he said; 'there'll be no more work for you to-night at Jamaica. Take his horse and be off, and cast him loose the other side of Camelford. I'll settle this business by myself.'

Somehow Mary found her way to the hall, and, hardly conscious of what she was doing, she turned the handle of the parlour door and stumbled inside. Then she crumpled in a heap on the floor, her head between her knees.

She must have fainted quite away for a minute or two, because the specks in front of her eyes grouped themselves into one tremendous whole, and her world went black; but the position in which she had fallen brought her to herself quicker than anything else could have done, and in a moment she was sitting up, propped on one elbow, listening to the clatter of a pony's hoofs in the yard outside. She heard a voice curse the animal to stand still – it was Harry the pedlar – and then he must have mounted and driven his heels into the pony's side, for the sound of the hoofs drew away and out of the yard, and disappeared in the distance down the high road, and so was lost beneath the slope of the hill. Her uncle was alone now in the bar with his victim, and Mary wondered whether it would be possible for her to find her way to the nearest dwelling-place on the road to Dozmary and summon help. It meant a walk of two or three miles across a moorland track before the first shepherd's cottage was reached, and somewhere on that same track the poor idiot boy had flown, earlier in the evening, and was even now perhaps wailing and grimacing by the side of the ditch.

She knew nothing of the inhabitants of the cottage; possibly they belonged to her uncle's company, in which case she would be running straight into a trap. Aunt Patience, upstairs in bed, was useless to her, and if anything an encumbrance. It was a hopeless situation, and there seemed no way of escape for the stranger, whoever he should be, unless he himself came to some agreement with Joss Merlyn. If he had any cunning he might be able to overpower her uncle; now that the pedlar had gone they were evenly matched as far as numbers went, though her uncle's physical strength would tell heavily in his favour. Mary began to feel desperate. If only there were a gun somewhere, or a knife, she might be able to wound her uncle, or at least disarm him while the wretched man made his escape from the bar.

She felt careless now for her own safety; it was only a matter of time, anyway, before she was discovered, and there was little sense in crouching here in the empty parlour. That fainting attack had been a momentary affair, and she despised herself for her weakness. She got up from the floor, and, placing both hands on the latch for greater silence, she opened the door a few inches. There was not a sound in the hall but the ticking of the clock, and the beam of light in the back passage shone no more. The door of the bar must be shut. Perhaps at this moment the stranger was fighting for his life, struggling for breath in the great hands of Joss Merlyn, shaken backwards and forwards on the stone floor of the bar. She could hear nothing, though; whatever work there was behind that closed door happened in silence.

Mary was about to step out into the hall once more and creep past the stairs to the further passage, when a sound from above made her pause and lift her head. It was the creaking of a board. There was silence for a minute, and then it happened again: quiet footsteps pacing gently overhead. Aunt Patience slept in the further passage at the other end of the house, and Mary herself had heard Harry the pedlar ride away on his pony nearly ten minutes ago. Her uncle she knew to be in the bar with the stranger, and no one had climbed the stairs since she had descended them. There, the board creaked again, and the soft footsteps continued. Someone was in the empty guest-room on the floor above.

Mary's heart began to thump in her side again, and her breath came quickly. Whoever was in hiding up above must have been there many hours. He must have lain in waiting there since the early evening; stood behind the door when she had gone to bed. Had he gone later she would have heard his footsteps on the stairs. Perhaps he had watched the arrival of the waggons from the window, as she had done, and had seen the idiot boy run screaming down the road to Dozmary. She had been separated from him by a thin partition of wall, and he must have heard her every movement – the falling on to her bed, and later her dressing, and her opening of her door.

Therefore he must wish to remain concealed, otherwise he would have stepped out on to the landing when she had done; had he been one of the company in the bar he would have spoken with her, surely; he would have questioned her movements. Who had admitted him? When could he have gone into the room? He must have hidden there so that he should remain unseen by the smugglers. Therefore he was not one of them; he was enemy to her uncle. The footfalls had ceased now, and, though she held her breath and listened intently, she could hear nothing. She had not been mistaken, though, she was convinced of that. Someone – an ally perhaps – was hiding in the guest-room next to hers, and could help her save the stranger in the bar. She had her foot on the lowest step of the stairs when the beam of light shone forth once more from the back passage, and she heard the door of the bar swing open. Her uncle was coming out into the hall. There was no time for Mary to climb the stairs before he turned the corner, so she was forced to step quickly back into the parlour and stand with her hand against the door. In the blackness of the hall he would never see that the door was not latched.

Trembling with excitement and fear, she waited in the parlour, and she heard the landlord pass across the hall and climb the stairs to the landing above. His footsteps came to a halt above her head, outside the guest-room, and for a second or two he waited, as though he too listened for some alien sound. Then he tapped twice, very softly on the door.

Once more the board creaked, and someone crossed the floor of the room above and the door was opened. Mary's heart sank within her, and her first despair returned. This could be no enemy to her uncle, after all. Probably Joss Merlyn had admitted him in the first place, early in the evening when she and Aunt Patience had been preparing the bar for the company, and he had lain in waiting there until all the men had departed. It was some personal friend of the landlord's, who had no wish to meddle in his evening's business, and would not show himself to the landlord's wife.

Her uncle had known him to be there all the time, and that was why he had sent the pedlar away. He did not wish the pedlar to see his friend. She thanked God then that she had not climbed the stairs and knocked on the door.

Supposing they went into her room to see if she were there and asleep? There would be little hope for her once her absence was discovered. She glanced behind her at the window. It was closed and barred. There was no road of escape. Now they were coming down the stairs; they stopped for an instant outside the parlour door. For one moment Mary thought they were coming inside. They were so close to her that she could have touched her uncle on the shoulder through the crack of the door. As it was, he spoke, and his voice whispered right against her ear.

'It's for you to say,' he breathed; 'it's your judgement now, not mine. I'll do it, or we'll do it between us. It's for you to say the word.'

Screened as she was by the door, Mary could neither see nor hear her uncle's new companion, and whatever gesture or sign he made in return escaped her. They did not linger outside the parlour, but turned back along the hall to the further passage, and so down it to the bar beyond.

Then the door closed, and she heard them no more.

Her first instinct was to unbar the entrance and run out into the road, and so be away from them; but on reflection she realised that by doing this she would gain nothing; for all she knew, there might be other men – the pedlar himself perhaps, and the rest of them – posted at intervals along the high road in the anticipation of trouble.

It seemed as though this new man, who had hidden all evening in the room above, could not have heard her leave her bedroom after all; had he done so he would by now have acquainted her uncle with the fact, and they would search for her; unless they dismissed her as being of no importance whatsoever in the general scheme of things. The man in the bar was their first concern; she could be attended to later.

She must have stood for ten minutes or more waiting for some sound or signal, but everything was still. Only the clock in the hall ticked on, wheezing slowly and impervious to action, a symbol of age and indifference. Once she fancied she heard a cry; but it was gone and lost in an instant, and was so faint and far a thing that it might have been some strange conjuring of her imagination, whipped as it was by all she had seen since midnight.

Then Mary went out into the hall, and so through to the dark passage. No crack of light came under the skirting of the door to the bar. The candles must have been extinguished. Were they sitting there inside the room, all three of them, in darkness? They made an ugly picture in her mind, a silent, sinister group, ruled by some purpose that she did not understand; but the very snuffing out of the light made the quietude more deadly.

She ventured as far as the door, and laid her ear against the panel. There was not even the murmur of a voice, nor that unmistakable suggestion of living, breathing people. The old fusty drink smell that had clung to the passage all evening had cleared, and through the keyhole came a steady draught of air. Mary gave way to a sudden uncontrollable impulse, and, lifting the latch, she opened the door and stepped into the room.

There was nobody there. The door leading to the yard was open, and the room was filled with the fresh November air. It was this that caused the draught in the passage. The benches were empty, and the table that had crashed to the ground in that first scuffle still lay upon the floor, its three legs pointing to the ceiling.

The men had gone, though; they must have turned to the left outside the kitchen and walked straight on to the moor, for she would have heard them had they crossed the road. The air felt cold and sweet upon her face, and now that her uncle and the strangers had left it the room seemed harmless and impersonal once more. The horror was spent.

A last little ray of moonlight made a white circle on the floor, and into the circle moved a dark blob like a finger. It was the reflection of a shadow. Mary looked up to the ceiling and saw that a rope had been slung through a hook in the beam. It was the rope's end that made the blob in the white circle; and it kept moving backwards and forwards, blown by the draught from the open door.

Chapter Five

As the days passed, Mary Yellan settled down to life at Jamaica Inn with a sense of stubborn resolution. It was evident that she could not leave her aunt to face the winter alone, but perhaps, with the coming of spring, Patience Merlyn could be persuaded to see reason, and the pair of them would leave the moors for the peace and quietude of Helford valley.

This was at any rate Mary's hope, and meanwhile she must make the best of the grim six months that lay ahead, and if possible she was determined to have the better of her uncle in the long run, and expose him and his confederates to the law. She would have shrugged her shoulders at smuggling alone, though the flagrant dishonesty of the trade disgusted her, but all she had seen so far went to prove that Joss Merlyn and his friends were not content with this only; they were desperate men, afraid of nothing and no one, and did not stop at murder. The events of that first Saturday night were never far from her mind, and the straggling rope's end hanging from the beam told its own tale. Mary had not a doubt that the stranger had been killed by her uncle and another man, and his body buried somewhere on the moors.

There was nothing to prove it, however, and, considered in the light of day, the very story seemed fantastic. She had returned to her room that night after the discovery of the rope, for the open door of the bar suggested that her uncle would be back at any moment, and, exhausted with all she had seen, she must have fallen asleep, for when she woke the sun was high, and she could hear Aunt Patience pattering about in the hall below.

No sign remained of the evening's work; the bar had been swept and tidied, the furniture replaced and the broken glass taken away, and there was no rope hanging from the beam. The landlord himself spent the morning in the stable and the cow-house, pitchforking filth into the yard, and doing the work that a cowman should have done had he kept one; and when he came into the kitchen at midday, to wolf an enormous meal, he questioned Mary about the farm stock at Helford, and asked for her opinion on a calf that had fallen sick, nor did he make any reference to the events of the preceding night. He seemed in fair good humour, and went so far as to forget to curse his wife, who hovered around him as usual, watching the expression in his eye like a dog who would please his master. Joss Merlyn behaved like a perfectly sober normal man, and it was impossible to believe that he had murdered a fellow-being only a few hours before.

He might be guiltless of this, of course, and the blame rest upon his unknown companion, but at least Mary had seen him with her own eyes chase the naked idiot boy across the yard, and she had heard the boy scream as he felt the lash of the landlord's whip. She had seen him ringleader of that vile company in the bar; she had heard him threaten the stranger who opposed his will; and here he sat before her now, his mouth full of hot stew, shaking his head over a sick calf.

And she answered 'Yes' and 'No' in reply to her uncle, and drank down her tea, watching him over the brim of her cup, her eyes travelling from his great plate of steaming stew to his long, powerful fingers, hideous in their strength and grace.

Two weeks went by and there was no repetition of Saturday night. Perhaps the last haul had satisfied the landlord and his companions, and they were content with that for the while, for Mary did not hear the waggons again, and, though she was sleeping soundly now, she was certain that the noise of wheels would have woken her. Her uncle appeared to have no objection to her wandering on the moors, and day by day she came to know more of the surrounding country, stumbling upon tracks she had not noticed at first and which kept her to the high ground, leading ultimately to the tors, while she learnt to avoid the low soggy grass with tufted tops that by their

very harmless appearance invited inspection, only to reveal themselves as
the borderline of treacherous and dangerous marsh.

Though lonely, she was not actively unhappy, and these rambles in the
grey light of early afternoon kept her healthy at least, and went some way
towards tempering the gloom and depression of the long dark evenings at
Jamaica, when Aunt Patience sat with her hands in her lap, staring at the
turf fire, and Joss Merlyn shut himself up alone in the bar or disappeared
on the back of his pony to some unknown destination.

Companionship there was none, and no one came to the inn for rest or
nourishment. The driver of the coach had spoken the truth when he told
Mary they never stopped now at Jamaica, for she would stand out in the
yard to watch the coaches pass twice in the week, and they were gone by in
a moment, rumbling down the hill and climbing the further one towards
Five Lanes without drawing rein or pausing for breath. Once Mary waved
her hand as she recognised her driver, but he took no notice of her, only
whipping his horses the harder, and she realised with a rather helpless sense
of futility that so far as other people were concerned she must be considered
in the same light as her uncle, and that even if she tried to walk to Bodmin
or Launceston no one would receive her, and the doors would be shut in her
face.

The future loomed very black at times, especially as Aunt Patience made
little effort to be companionable; and though now and again she took hold
of Mary's hand and patted it for a few minutes, telling her how glad she
was to have her in the house, for the most part the poor woman existed in
a dream, pottering about her household duties in a mechanical fashion and
seldom uttering. When she did speak, it was to let forth a torrent of nonsense
about the great man her husband might have been had not ill luck constantly
followed him. Any normal conversation was practically impossible, and
Mary came to humour her and talk gently as she would have done to a
child, all of which was a strain on her nerves and on her patience.

So that it was in a mood of truculence, following upon a day of wind and
rain that had made it impracticable to venture out of doors, that Mary one
morning set herself to clean down the long stone passage that ran the full
width of the back of the house. The hard work, if it strengthened her muscles,
did not improve her temper, and by the time she had finished she was so
disgusted with Jamaica Inn and its inhabitants that for very little she would
have walked out into the patch of garden behind the kitchen, where her
uncle was working, heedless of the rain upon his mat of hair, and thrown
her bucket of dirty soapy water into his very face. The sight of her aunt,
who with bent back poked at the dull peat fire with the end of a stick,
defeated her, and Mary was about to start on the stone flags of the entrance-
hall when she heard a clatter of hoofs in the yard, and in a moment someone
thundered on the closed door of the bar.

No one had approached Jamaica Inn before, and this summons was an
event in itself. Mary went back to the kitchen to warn her aunt, but she had
left the room, and, looking out of the window, Mary could see her pattering
across the garden to her husband, who was loading turf from the stack into

a barrow. They were both out of earshot, and neither could have heard the sound of this new arrival. Mary wiped her hands on her apron and went into the bar. The door must have been unlocked after all, for to her surprise there was a man sitting straddle-legged across a chair, with a glass in his hand filled to the brim with ale, which he had calmly poured out from the tap himself. For a few minutes they considered one another in silence.

Something about him was familiar, and Mary wondered where she had seen him before. The rather drooping lids, the curve of his mouth, and the outline of his jaw, even the bold and decidedly insolent stare with which he favoured her, were things known to her, and definitely disliked.

The sight of him looking her up and down and drinking his ale at the same time irritated her beyond measure.

'What do you think you're doing?' she said sharply. 'You haven't any right to walk in here and help yourself. Besides, the landlord doesn't encourage strangers.' At any other moment she would have laughed to hear herself speak thus, as though in defence of her uncle, but scrubbing the stone flags had done away with her sense of humour, if only for the moment, and she felt she must vent her ill temper on the nearest victim.

The man finished his ale, and held out the glass to be refilled.

'Since when have they kept a barmaid at Jamaica Inn?' he asked her, and, feeling in his pocket for a pipe, he lit it, puffing a great cloud of smoke into her face. His manner infuriated Mary, and she leant forward and pulled the pipe out of his hand, throwing it behind her on to the floor, where it smashed at once. He shrugged his shoulders, and began to whistle, the very tunelessness adding fuel to her flame of irritation.

'Is this how they train you to serve customers?' he said, breaking off in the middle. 'I don't think much of their choice. There are better-mannered maids in Launceston, where I was yesterday, and pretty as paint into the bargain. What have you been doing with yourself? Your hair is coming down at the back, and your face is none too clean.'

Mary turned away and walked towards the door, but he called her back.

'Fill up my glass. That's what you're here for, isn't it?' he said. 'I've ridden twelve miles since breakfast and I'm thirsty.'

'You may had ridden fifty miles for all I care,' said Mary. 'As you seem to know your way about here, you can fill your own glass. I'll tell Mr. Merlyn you are in the bar, and he can serve you himself if he has the mind.'

'Oh, don't worry Joss; he'll be like a bear with a sore head at this time of day,' came the answer. 'Besides, he's never very anxious to see me. What's happened to his wife? Has he turned her out to make room for you? I call that hard on the poor woman. You'll never stay with him ten years, anyway.'

'Mrs. Merlyn is in the garden, if you want to see her,' said Mary. 'You can walk out of the door and turn to the left, and you'll come to the patch of garden and the chicken-run. They were both of them down under, five minutes ago. You can't come through this way because I've just washed the passage, and I don't want to do it all over again.'

'Oh, don't get excited; there's plenty of time,' he replied. She could see he was still looking her up and down, wondering what to make of her, and the familiar, somewhat lazy insolence in his eyes maddened her.

'Do you want to speak to the landlord or not?' she asked at length. 'Because I can't stand here all day awaiting your pleasure. If you don't want to see him, and you've finished your drink, you can put down your money on the counter and go away.'

The man laughed, and his smile and the flash of his teeth struck a chord in her memory, but still she could not name the resemblance.

'Do you order Joss about in that way?' he said. 'He must be a changed man if you do. What a creature of contradictions the fellow is, after all. I never thought he'd run a young woman alongside his other activities. What do you do with poor Patience of an evening? Do you turn her out on the floor, or do you sleep all three abreast?'

Mary flushed scarlet. 'Joss Merlyn is my uncle by marriage,' she said. 'Aunt Patience was my mother's only sister. My name is Mary Yellan, if that means anything to you. Good morning. There's the door behind you.'

She left the bar and walked into the kitchen, straight into the arms of the landlord himself. 'Who in hell's name were you talking to in the bar?' he thundered. 'I thought I'd warned you to keep your mouth shut?'

The loudness of his voice echoed in the passage. 'All right,' called the man from the bar, 'don't beat her. She's broken my pipe and refused to serve me; that sounds like your training, doesn't it? Come in and let's have a look at you. I'm hoping this maid has done you some good.'

Joss Merlyn frowned, and, pushing Mary aside, he stepped into the bar. 'Oh, it's you, Jem, is it?' he said. 'What do you want at Jamaica to-day? I can't buy a horse from you, if that's what you're after. Things are going badly, and I'm as poor as a field-mouse after a wet harvest.' He closed the door, leaving Mary in the passage outside.

She went back to her bucket of water in the front hall, wiping the dirty mark from her face with her apron. So that was Jem Merlyn, her uncle's younger brother. Of course, she had seen the resemblance all the time, and, like a fool, had not been able to place it. He had reminded her of her uncle throughout the conversation, and she had not realised it. He had Joss Merlyn's eyes, without the blood-flecked lines and without the pouches, and he had Joss Merlyn's mouth, firm, though, where the landlord's was weak, and narrow where his lower lip sagged. He was what Joss Merlyn might have been, eighteen, twenty years ago – but smaller in build and height, neater in person.

Mary splashed the water on to the stone flags, and began to scrub furiously, her lips pressed tight together.

What a vile breed they were, then, these Merlyns, with their studied insolence and coarseness, their rough brutality of manner. This Jem had the same streak of cruelty as his brother, she could see it in the shape of his mouth. Aunt Patience had said he was the worst of the family. Although he was a head and shoulders smaller than Joss, and half the breadth, there was a certain strength about him that the elder brother did not possess. He looked hard, and keen. The landlord sagged round the chin, and his shoulders weighed on him like a burden. It was as though his power was wasted in some way, and had run to seed. Drink did that to a man, Mary knew, and for the first time she was able to guess something of the wreck Joss Merlyn had become, in comparison to his former self. It was seeing his brother that had shown her. The landlord had betrayed himself. If the younger one had any sense in his head he would pull himself together before he travelled the same road. Perhaps he did not care, though; there must be a fatality about the Merlyn family that did away with striving forward, and making good in life, and resolution. Their record was too black. 'There's no going against bad blood,' her mother used to say, 'it always comes out in the end. You may fight it as much as you like, but it will have the better of you. If two generations live clean, that may clear the stream sometimes, but likely as not the third will break out and start it going again.' What a waste it all was, what a waste and a pity! And here was poor Aunt Patience dragged in the current with the Merlyns, all her youth and gaiety gone before her, leaving her – if the truth were faced – very little superior to the idiot boy at Dozmary. And Aunt Patience might have been a farmer's wife at Gweek, with sons of her own, and a house and land, and all the little happy trivialities of a normal happy life: gossip with the neighbours, and church on Sundays, and driving into market once a week; fruit-picking, and harvest-time. Things she would have loved, things that had foundation. She would have known placidity, and they would be tranquil years that turned her hair in time to grey – years of solid work and calm enjoyment. All this promise she had thrown away, to live like a slattern with a brute and a drunkard. Why were women such fools, so short-sighted and unwise? wondered Mary; and she scrubbed the last stone flag of the hall with venom, as though by her very action she might cleanse the world and blot out the indiscretions of her kind.

She had worked up her energy to a frenzy, and, turning from the hall, proceeded to sweep the gloomy, dim parlour that had not seen a broom for years. A cloud of dust met her face, and she beat savagely at the wretched threadbare mat. She was so absorbed in her disagreeable occupation that she did not hear the stone flung at the window of the parlour, and it was not until a shower of pebbles made a crack in the glass that her concentration was disturbed, and, looking out of the window, she saw Jem Merlyn standing in the yard beside his pony.

Mary frowned at him, and turned away, but he made answer with another shower of pebbles, this time cracking the glass in earnest, so that a small piece of the pane splintered on to the floor, with a stone beside it.

Mary unbolted the heavy entrance-door and went out into the porch.

'What do you want now?' she asked him, conscious suddenly of her loose hair and rumpled dirty apron.

He still looked down at her with curiosity, but the insolence had gone, and he had the grace to appear the smallest bit ashamed of himself.

'Forgive me if I was rude to you just now,' he said. 'Somehow I didn't expect to see a woman at Jamaica Inn – not a young girl like you, anyway. I thought Joss had found you in one of the towns, and brought you back here for his fancy lady.'

Mary flushed again, and bit her lip in annoyance. 'There's nothing very fanciful about me,' she said scornfully. 'I'd look well in a town, wouldn't I, in my old apron and heavy shoes? I should have thought anyone with eyes in his head could see I was farm-bred.'

'Oh, I don't know,' he said carelessly. 'Put you in a fine gown and a pair of high-heeled shoes, and stick a comb in your hair, I daresay you'd pass for a lady even in a big place like Exeter.'

'I'm meant to be flattered by that, I suppose,' said Mary, 'but, thanking you very much, I'd rather wear my old clothes and look like myself.'

'You could do a lot worse than that, of course,' he agreed; and, looking up, she saw that he was laughing at her. She turned to go back into the house.

'Come, don't go away,' he said. ' I know I deserve black looks for speaking to you as I did, but if you knew my brother as well as I do you'd understand me making the mistake. It looks strange, having a maid at Jamaica Inn. Why did you come here in the first place?'

Mary considered him from the shadow of the porch. He looked serious now, and his likeness to Joss had fled for the moment. She wished he were not a Merlyn.

'I came here to be with my Aunt Patience,' she said. 'My mother died some weeks ago, and I have no other relative. I'll tell you one thing, Mr. Merlyn – I'm thankful my mother isn't alive to see her sister now.'

'I don't suppose marriage with Joss is a bed of roses,' said his brother. 'He always had the temper of the Devil himself, and he drinks like a fish. What did she marry him for? He's been the same as long as I can remember. He used to thrash me when I was a lad, and he'd do the same to-day if he dared.'

'I suppose she was misled by his bright eyes,' said Mary scornfully. 'Aunt Patience was always the butterfly down in Helford, Mother used to say. She wouldn't have the farmer who asked her, but took herself off up-country, where she met your brother. That was the worst day in her life, anyway.'

'You've not much opinion of the landlord, then?' he said, mocking her.

'No, I have not,' she replied. 'He's a bully, and a brute, and many worse things beside. He's turned my aunt from a laughing, happy woman into a miserable drudge, and I'll never forgive him for that as long as I live.'

Jem whistled tunelessly, and patted his horse's neck.

'We Merlyns have never been good to our women,' he said. 'I can remember my father beating my mother till she couldn't stand. She never left him, though, but stood by him all his life. When he was hanged at Exeter, she didn't speak to a soul for three months. Her hair went white with the shock. I can't remember my grandmother, but they say she fought side by side with granddad once near Callington, when the soldiers came to take him, and she bit a fellow's finger right through to the bone. What she had to love in granddad I can't say, for he never as much as asked for her after he'd been taken, and he left all his savings with another woman the other side of Tamar.'

Mary was silent. The indifference in his voice appalled her. He spoke entirely without shame or regret, and she supposed that he had been born, like the rest of his family, lacking the quality of tenderness.

'How long do you mean to stay at Jamaica?' he asked abruptly. 'It's waste for a maid like you, isn't it? There's not much company for you here.'

'I can't help that,' said Mary. 'I'm not going away unless I take my aunt with me. I'd never leave her here alone, not after what I've seen.'

Jem bent down to brush a piece of dirt from his pony's shoe.

'What have you learnt in your short time?' he questioned. 'It's quiet enough here, in all conscience.'

Mary was not easily led. For all she knew, her uncle had prompted his brother to speak to her, hoping in this way to obtain information. No, she was not quite such a fool as that. She shrugged her shoulders, dismissing the subject.

'I helped my uncle in the bar one Saturday night,' she said, 'and I did not think much of the company he kept.'

'I don't suppose you did,' said Jem. 'The fellows who come to Jamaica have never been taught manners. They spend too much time in the county jail. I wonder what they thought of you? Made the same mistake as I did, I suppose, and are now spreading your fame far and wide about the countryside. You'll have Joss throwing dice for you next time, I daresay, and when he loses you'll find yourself riding pillion behind a dirty poacher from the other side of Roughtor.'

'There's not much likelihood of that,' said Mary. 'They'd have to knock me senseless before I rode pillion with anyone.'

'Senseless or conscious, women are pretty much the same when you come down to it,' said Jem. 'The poachers on Bodmin moor would never know the difference, anyway.' And he laughed again, and looked exactly like his brother.

'What do you do for a livelihood?' asked Mary, in sudden curiosity, for during their conversation she became aware that he spoke better than his brother.

'I'm a horse-thief,' he said pleasantly, 'but there's not much money in it really. My pockets are always empty. You ought to ride here. I've got a little pony that would suit you handsomely. He's over at Trewartha now. Why don't you come back with me and look at him?'

'Aren't you afraid of being caught?' said Mary.

'Thieving is an awkward thing to prove,' he told her. 'Supposing a pony strays from his pen, and his owner goes to look for him. Well, you've seen for yourself, these moors are alive with wild horses and cattle. It's not going to be so easy for that owner to find his pony. Say the pony had a long mane, and one white foot, and a diamond mark in his ear – that narrows the field down a bit, doesn't it? And off goes the owner to Launceston fair with his eyes wide open. But he doesn't find his pony. Mark you, the pony is there, right enough, and he's bought by some dealer and sold away up-country. Only his mane is clipped, his four feet are all the same colour, and the mark in his ear is a slit, not a diamond. The owner didn't even look at him twice. That's simple enough, isn't it?'

'So simple that I can't understand why you don't ride past Jamaica in your coach, with a powdered footman on the step,' said Mary swiftly.

'Ah, well, there you are,' he said, shaking his head. 'I've never had the brain for figures. You'd be surprised to learn how quickly money slips through my fingers. Do you know, I had ten pounds in my pocket last week. I've only a shilling piece to-day. That's why I want you to buy that little pony.'

Mary laughed, in spite of herself. He was so frank in his dishonesty that she had not the heart to be angry with him.

'I can't spend my small savings on horses,' she said. 'I'm laying aside for my old age, and if I ever get away from Jamaica I shall need every penny, you may depend on that.'

Jem Merlyn looked at her gravely, and then, on a sudden impulse, he bent towards her, first glancing over her head into the porch beyond.

'Look here,' he said, 'I'm serious now; you can forget all the nonsense I've told you. Jamaica Inn is no place for a maid – nor for any woman, if it comes to that. My brother and I have never been friends, and I can say what I like about him. We go our own ways and be damned to one another. But there's no reason why you should be caught up in his dirty schemes. Why don't you run away? I'd see you on the road to Bodmin all right.'

His tones were persuasive and Mary could almost have trusted him. But she could not forget he was Joss Merlyn's brother, and as such might betray her. She dared not make a confidant of him – not yet, anyway. Time would show whose side he was on.

'I don't need any help,' she said; 'I can look after myself.'

Jem threw his leg over the pony's back and stuck his feet into the leathers.

'All right,' he said, 'I won't worry you. My cottage is across the Withy Brook, if you ever want me. The other side of Trewartha Marsh, at the foot of Twelve Men's Moor. I shall be there until the spring, anyway. Good day to you.' And he was off, and away down the road before she had time to say a word in return.

Mary went slowly back into the house. She would have trusted him had his name been other than Merlyn. She was in urgent need of a friend; but she could not make a friend of the landlord's brother. He was no more than a common horse-thief, a dishonest scoundrel, when all was said and done. He was little better than Harry the pedlar and the rest of them. Because he had a disarming smile and his voice was not unpleasing, she had been ready to believe in him, and he all the time perhaps laughing at her the other side of his face. There was bad blood in him; he broke the law every day of his life, and whatever way she looked at it there was no escaping from that one unredeemable fact – he was Joss Merlyn's brother. He had said there was no bond between them, but even that might be a lie to enlist her sympathy, while the whole of their conversation perhaps had been prompted by the landlord in the bar.

No, whatever happened, she must stand alone in this business and trust no one. The very walls of Jamaica Inn smelt of guilt and deceit, and to speak aloud in earshot of the building courted disaster.

It was dark in the house, and quiet once more. The landlord had returned to the peat-stack at the bottom of the garden, and Aunt Patience was in her kitchen. The surprise of the visit had been a little excitement and a breaking-up of the long, monotonous day. Jem Merlyn had brought something of the outer world with him, a world that was not entirely bounded by the moors and frowned upon by tors of granite; and now that he had departed the early brightness of the day went with him. The sky became overcast, and the inevitable rain came sweeping from the west, topping the hills in mist. The black heather bowed before the wind. The ill-temper that had fastened upon Mary at the beginning of the morning had passed away, and in its place had stolen a numb indifference born of fatigue and despair. Interminably the days and weeks stretched themselves before her, with no other sight but the long white road to tempt her, the stone walls, and the everlasting hills.

She thought of Jem Merlyn riding away with a song on his lips, kicking his heels into his pony's side, and he would ride hatless, careless of the wind and the rain, choosing his own road.

She thought of the lane that led to Helford village, how it twisted and turned and wound suddenly to the water's edge, while the ducks paddled in the mud before the turn of the tide, and a man called to his cows from the field above. All those things were progressive, and part of life, and they went their way without a thought of her, but she was bound here by a promise that she must not break, and the very patter of Aunt Patience's feet as she passed to and fro in the kitchen was a reminder and a warning.

Mary watched the little stinging rain blur the glass of the parlour window, and as she sat there, alone, with her chin in her hand, the tears ran down her cheeks in company with the rain. She let them fall, too indifferent to wipe them away, while the draught from the door she had forgotten to close ruffled a long torn strip of paper on the wall. There had once been a rose pattern, but it was now faded and grey, and the walls themselves were stained deep brown where the damp had turned them. Mary turned away from the window; and the cold, dead atmosphere of Jamaica Inn closed in upon her.

Chapter Six

That night the waggons came again. Mary woke to the sound of the hall clock striking two, and almost at once she was aware of footsteps beneath the porch, and she heard a voice speak soft and low. She crept out of bed and went over to the window. Yes, there they were; only two carts this time, with one horse in harness, and less than half a dozen men standing in the yard.

The waggons looked ghostly in the dim light, like hearses, and the men themselves were phantom figures, having no place in the world of day by day, but moving silently about the yard as some weird pattern in a nightmare fantasy. There was something horrible about them, something sinister in the shrouded waggons themselves, coming as they did in stealth by night. This night, the impression they left upon Mary was even more lasting and profound; for now she understood the significance of their trade.

They were desperate men who worked this road and carried convoys to Jamaica Inn, and last time they brought their waggons to the yard one of their number had been murdered. Perhaps to-night yet another crime would be committed, and the twisted length of rope dangle once again from the beam below.

The scene in the yard held a fatal fascination, and Mary could not leave the window. This time the waggons had arrived empty, and were loaded with the remainder of the cargo deposited at the inn the time before. Mary guessed that this was their method of working. The inn served as a store for a few weeks at a time, and then, when opportunity occurred, the waggons set forth once more, and the cargo was carried to the Tamar bank and so distributed. The organisation must be a big one to cover the ground in the time, and there would be agents scattered far and wide who kept the necessary watch on events. Perhaps there were hundreds implicated in the trade, from Penzance and St. Ives in the south to Launceston on the border of Devon. There had been little talk of smuggling in Helford, and when there had been, it was with a wink and a smile of indulgence, as though a pipe of baccy and a bottle of brandy from a ship in Falmouth port was an occasional harmless luxury, and not a burden on any person's conscience.

This was different, though. This was a grim business, a stern and bloody business, and precious little smiling or winking went with it, from all that Mary had seen. If his conscience pricked a man, he received a rope round his neck in payment. There must be no weak link in the chain that stretched from the coast up to the border, and there was the explanation of the rope on the beam. The stranger had demurred, and the stranger had died. It was with a sudden sting of disappointment that Mary wondered whether the visit of Jem Merlyn to Jamaica Inn this morning had significance. A strange coincidence that the waggons should follow in his train. He had come from Launceston, he said, and Launceston stood on the Tamar bank. Mary was angry with him and with herself. In spite of everything, her last thought before sleeping had been the possibility of his friendship. She would be a fool if she had hopes of it now. The two events ran together in an unmistakable fashion, and it was easy enough to read the purpose of it.

Jem might disagree with his brother, but they were both in the same trade. He had ridden to Jamaica to warn the landlord that he might expect the convoy in the evening. It was simple enough to understand. And then, having something of a heart, he had advised Mary to take herself to Bodmin. It was no place for a maid, he said. No one knew that better than he did himself, being one of the company. It was a wretched, damnable business in every way, without a ray of hope in any direction, and here she was in the midst of it all, with Aunt Patience like a child on her hands.

Now the two waggons were loaded, and the drivers climbed in the seats with their companions. The performance had not been a lengthy one to-night.

Mary could see the great head and shoulders of her uncle on a level with the porch, and he held a lantern in his hand, the light dimmed by a shutter. Then the carts rumbled out of the yard, and turned to the left, as Mary had expected, and so in the direction of Launceston.

She came away from the window, and climbed back into bed. Presently she heard her uncle's footsteps on the stairs, and he went along the further passage to his bedroom. There was no one hiding in the guest-room to-night.

The next few days passed without incident, and the only vehicle on the road was the coach to Launceston, rumbling past Jamaica like a scared blackbeetle. There came a fine crisp morning with frost on the ground, and for once the sun shone in a cloudless sky. The tors stood out boldly against the hard blue heaven, and the moorland grass, usually soggy and brown, glistened stiff and white with the frost. The drinking-well in the yard had a thin layer of ice. The mud had hardened where the cows had trodden, and the marks of their feet were preserved in formed ridges that would not yield until the next fall of rain. The light wind came singing from the north-east, and it was cold.

Mary, whose spirits always rose at the sight of the sun, had turned her morning into washing-day, and, with sleeves rolled well above the elbows, plunged her arms into the tub, the hot soapy water, bubbling with froth, caressing her skin in exquisite contrast to the sharp stinging air.

She felt well in being, and she sang as she worked. Her uncle had ridden away on the moors somewhere, and a sense of freedom possessed her whenever he was gone. At the back here she was sheltered somewhat from the wind, the broad sturdy house acting as a screen, and as she wrung out her linen and spread it on the stunted gorse-bush, she saw that the full force of the sun fell upon it, and it would be dry by noon.

An urgent tapping on the window made her look up, and she saw Aunt Patience beckon to her, very white in the face and evidently frightened.

Mary wiped her hands on her apron and ran to the back door of the house. No sooner had she entered the kitchen than her aunt seized upon her with trembling hands, and began to blabber incoherently.

'Quietly, quietly,' said Mary. 'I cannot understand what you're saying. Here, take this chair and sit down, and drink this glass of water, for mercy's sake. Now, what is it?'

The poor woman rocked backwards and forwards in her chair, her mouth working nervously, and she kept jerking her head towards the door.

'It's Mr. Bassat from North Hill,' she whispered. 'I saw him from the parlour window. He's come on horseback, and another gentleman with him. Oh, my dear, my dear, what are we going to do?'

Even as she spoke there was a loud knock at the entrance-door and then a pause, followed by a thunder of blows.

Aunt Patience groaned aloud, biting the ends of her fingers, and tearing at her nails. 'Why has he come here?' she cried. 'He's never been before. He's always kept away. He's heard something, I know he has. Oh, Mary, what are we going to do? What are we going to say?'

Mary thought quickly. She was in a very difficult position. If this was Mr. Bassat and he represented the law, it was her one chance of betraying her uncle. She could tell him of the waggons and all she had seen since her arrival. She looked down at the trembling woman at her side.

'Mary, Mary, for the sake of the dear Lord, tell me what I am to say?' pleaded Aunt Patience, and she took her niece's hand and held it to her heart.

The hammering on the door was incessant now.

'Listen to me,' said Mary. 'We shall have to let him in or he'll break down the door. Pull yourself together somehow. There's no need to say anything at all. Say Uncle Joss is away from home, and you know nothing. I'll come with you.'

The woman looked at her with haggard, desperate eyes.

'Mary,' she said, 'if Mr. Bassat asks you what you know, you won't answer him, will you? I can trust you, can't I? You'll not tell him of the waggons? If any danger came to Joss I'd kill myself, Mary.'

There was no argument after that. Mary would lie herself into hell rather than let her aunt suffer. The situation must be faced, though, however ironical her position was to be.

'Come with me to the door,' she said; 'we'll not keep Mr. Bassat long. You needn't be afraid of me; I shall say nothing.'

They went into the hall together, and Mary unbolted the heavy entrance-door. There were two men outside the porch. One had dismounted, and it was he who had rained the blows on the door. The other was a big burly fellow, in a heavy top-coat and cape, seated on the back of a fine chestnut horse. His hat was pulled square over his eyes, but Mary could see that his face was heavily lined and weather-beaten, and she judged him to be somewhere about fifty years of age.

'You take your time here, don't you?' he called. 'There doesn't seem to be much of a welcome for travellers. Is the landlord at home?'

Patience Merlyn poked at her niece with her hand, and Mary made answer.

'Mr. Merlyn is from home, sir,' she said. 'Are you in need of refreshment? I will serve you if you will go through to the bar.'

'Damn refreshment!' he returned. 'I know better than to come to Jamaica Inn for that. I want to speak to your master. Here, you, are you the landlord's wife? When do you expect him home?'

Aunt Patience made him a little curtsey. 'If you please, Mr. Bassat,' she said, speaking unnaturally loudly and clearly, like a child who has learnt a lesson, 'my husband went out as soon as he had his breakfast, and whether he will be back before nightfall I really cannot say.'

'H'mph,' growled the squire, 'that's a damned nuisance. I wanted a word or two with Mr. Joss Merlyn. Now look here, my good woman, your precious husband may have bought Jamaica Inn behind my back, in his blackguardly fashion, and we'll not go into that again now, but one thing I won't stand for, and that's having all my land hereabouts made a byword for everything that's damnable and dishonest round the countryside.'

'I'm sure I don't know what you mean, Mr. Bassat,' said Aunt Patience, working her mouth and twisting her hands in her dress. 'We live very quietly here, indeed we do; my niece here will tell you the same.'

'Oh, come, I'm not such a fool as that,' answered the squire. 'I've had my eyes on this place for a long while. A house doesn't get a bad name without reason, Mrs. Merlyn, and Jamaica Inn stinks from here to the coast. Don't you pretend to me. Here, Richards, hold my confounded horse, will you?'

The other man, who by his dress appeared to be a servant, held the bridle, and Mr. Bassat climbed heavily to the ground.

'While I'm here I may as well look round,' he said, 'and I'll tell you here and now that it's useless to refuse me. I'm a magistrate, and I have a warrant.' He pushed his way past the two women, and so through to the little entrance-hall. Aunt Patience made a movement as though to deter him, but Mary shook her head and frowned. 'Let him go,' she murmured. 'If we try and stop him now we shall only anger him the more.'

Mr. Bassat was looking about him in disgust. 'Good God,' he exclaimed, 'the place smells like a tomb. What in the world have you done to it? Jamaica Inn was always rough-cast and plain, and the fare homely, but this is a positive disgrace. Why, the place is as bare as a board; you haven't a stick of furniture.'

He had thrown open the door of the parlour, and pointed to the damp walls with his crop. 'You'll have the roof about your ears if you don't stop that,' he said. 'I've never seen such a thing in my life. Go on, Mrs. Merlyn, lead the way upstairs.' Pale and anxious, Patience Merlyn turned to the staircase, her eyes searching those of her niece for reassurance.

The rooms on the landing were thoroughly explored. The squire peered into the dusty corners, lifted the old sacks, and prodded the potatoes, all the while uttering exclamations of anger and disgust. 'Call this an inn, do you?' he said. 'Why, you haven't even a bed fit to sleep a cat. The place is rotten, rotten right through. What's the idea, eh? Have you lost your tongue, Mrs. Merlyn?'

The poor woman was past replying; she kept shaking her head and working her mouth, and Mary knew that both she and her aunt were wondering what would happen when they came to the barred room in the passage below.

'The landlord's lady appears to be momentarily deaf and dumb,' said the squire drily. 'What about you, young woman? Have you anything to say?'

'It's only lately I've come to stay here,' replied Mary. 'My mother died, and I'm here to look after my aunt. She's not very strong; you can see that for yourself. She's nervous and easily upset.'

'I don't blame her, living in a place like this,' said Mr. Bassat. 'Well, there's nothing more to see up here, so you'll kindly take me downstairs again and show me the room that has barred windows. I noticed it from the yard, and I'd like to see inside.'

Aunt Patience passed her tongue over her lips and looked at Mary. She was incapable of speech.

'I'm very sorry, sir,' Mary replied, 'but if you mean the old lumber-room at the end of the passage, I'm afraid the door is locked. My uncle always keeps the key, and where he puts it I don't know.'

The squire looked from one to the other in suspicion.

'What about you, Mrs. Merlyn? Don't you know where your husband keeps his keys?'

Aunt Patience shook her head. The squire snorted and turned on his heel. 'Well, that's easily settled,' he said. 'We'll have the door down in no time.' And he went out into the yard to call his servant. Mary patted her aunt's hand, and drew her close.

'Try and not tremble so,' she whispered fiercely. 'Anyone can see you have something to hide. Your only chance is to pretend you don't mind, and that he can see anything in the house for all you care.'

In a few minutes Mr. Bassat returned with the man Richards, who, grinning all over his face at the thought of destruction, carried an old bar he had found in the stable, and which he evidently intended using as a battering-ram.

If it had not been for her aunt, Mary would have given herself to the scene with some enjoyment. For the first time she would be permitted a view of the barred room. The fact that her aunt, and herself too for that matter, would be implicated in any discovery that was made, caused her mixed feelings, however, and for the first time she realised that it was going to be a very difficult task to prove their complete and thorough innocence. No one was likely to believe protestations, with Aunt Patience fighting blindly on the landlord's side.

It was with some excitement, then, that Mary watched Mr. Bassat and his servant seize the bar between them and ram it against the lock of the door. For a few minutes it withstood them, and the sound of the blows echoed through the house. Then there was a splitting of wood and a crash, and the door gave way before them. Aunt Patience uttered a little cry of distress, and the squire pushed past her into the room. Richards leant on the bar, wiping the sweat from his forehead, and Mary could see through to the room over his shoulder. It was dark, of course; the barred windows with their lining of sack kept the light from penetrating the room.

'Get me a candle, one of you,' shouted the squire. 'It's as black as a pit in here.' The servant produced a stump of candle from his pocket, and a light was kindled. He handed the candle to the squire, who, lifting it high above his head, stepped into the centre of the room.

For a moment there was silence, as the squire turned, letting the light shine in every corner, and then, clicking his tongue in annoyance and disappointment, he faced the little group behind him.

'Nothing,' he said; 'absolutely nothing. The landlord has made a fool of me again.'

Except for a pile of sacks in one corner the room was completely empty. It was thick with dust, and there were cobwebs on the walls larger than a man's hand. There was no furniture of any sort, the hearth had been blocked up with stones, and the floor itself was flagged like the passage outside.

On the top of the sacks lay a length of twisted rope.

Then the squire shrugged his shoulders, and turned once more into the passage.

'Well, Mr. Joss Merlyn has won this time,' he said; 'there's not enough evidence in that room to kill a cat. I'll admit myself beaten.'

The two women followed him to the outer hall, and so to the porch, while the servant made his way to the stable to fetch the horses.

Mr. Bassat flicked his boot with his whip, and stared moodily in front of him. 'You've been lucky, Mrs. Merlyn,' he said. 'If I'd found what I expected to find in that blasted room of yours, this time to-morrow your husband would be in the county jail. As it is . . .' Once more he clicked his tongue in annoyance, and broke off in the middle of his sentence.

'Stir yourself, Richards, can't you?' he shouted. 'I can't afford to waste any more of my morning. What the hell are you doing?'

The man appeared at the stable door, leading the two horses behind him.

'Now, listen to me,' said Mr. Bassat, pointing his crop at Mary. 'This aunt of yours may have lost her tongue, and her senses with them, but you can understand plain English, I hope. Do you mean to tell me you know nothing of your uncle's business? Does nobody ever call here, by day or by night?'

Mary looked him straight in the eyes. 'I've never seen anyone,' she said.

'Have you ever looked into that barred room before to-day?'

'No, never in my life.'

'Have you any idea why he should keep it locked up?'

'No, none at all.'

'Have you ever heard wheels in the yard by night?'

'I'm a very heavy sleeper. Nothing ever wakes me.'

'Where does your uncle go when he's away from home?'

'I don't know.'

'Don't you think yourself it's very peculiar, to keep an inn on the King's highway, and then bolt and bar your house to every passer-by?'

'My uncle is a very peculiar man.'

'He is indeed. In fact, he's so damned peculiar that half the people in the countryside won't sleep easy in their beds until he's been hanged, like his father before him. You can tell him that from me.'

'I will, Mr. Bassat.'

'Aren't you afraid, living up here, without sound or sight of a neighbour, and only this half-crazy woman for companion?'

'The time passes.'

'You've got a close tongue, haven't you, young woman? Well, I don't envy you your relatives. I'd rather see any daughter of mine in her grave than living at Jamaica Inn with a man like Joss Merlyn.'

He turned away, and climbed on to his horse, gathering the reins in his hands. 'One other thing,' he called from his saddle. 'Have you seen anything of your uncle's younger brother, Jem Merlyn, of Trewartha?'

'No,' said Mary steadily; 'he never comes here.'

'Oh, he doesn't? Well, that's all I want from you this morning. Good day to you both.' And away they clattered from the yard, and so down the road and to the brow of the further hill.

Aunt Patience had already preceded Mary to the kitchen, and was sitting on a chair in a state of collapse.

'Oh, pull yourself together,' said Mary wearily. 'Mr. Bassat has gone, none the wiser for his visit, and as cross as two sticks because of it. If he'd found the room reeking of brandy, then there would be something to cry about. As it is, you and Uncle Joss have scraped out of it very well.'

She poured herself out a tumbler of water and drank it at one breath. Mary was in a fair way to losing her temper. She had lied to save her uncle's skin, when every inch of her longed to proclaim his guilt. She had looked into the barred room, and its emptiness had hardly surprised her when she remembered the visitation of the waggons a few nights back; but to have been faced with that loathsome length of rope, which she recognised immediately as the one she had seen hanging from the beam, was almost more than she could bear. And because of her aunt she had to stand still and say nothing. It was damnable; there was no other word for it. Well, she was committed now, and there was no going back. For better, for worse, she had become one of the company at Jamaica Inn. As she drank down her second glass of water she reflected cynically that in the end she would probably hang beside her uncle. Not only had she lied to save him, she thought with rising anger, but she had lied to help his brother Jem. Jem Merlyn owed her thanks as well. Why she had lied about him she did not know. He would probably never find out anyway, and, if he did, he would take it for granted.

Aunt Patience was still moaning and whimpering before the fire, and Mary was in no mood to comfort her. She felt she had done enough for her family for one day, and her nerves were on edge with the whole business. If she stayed in the kitchen a moment longer she would scream with irritation. She went back to the wash-tub in the patch of garden by the chicken-run, and plunged her hands savagely into the grey soapy water that was now stone-cold.

Joss Merlyn returned just before noon. Mary heard him step into the kitchen from the front of the house, and he was met at once with a babble of words from his wife. Mary stayed where she was by the wash-tub; she was determined to let Aunt Patience explain things in her own way, and, if he called to her for confirmation, there was time enough to go indoors.

She could hear nothing of what passed between them, but the voice of her aunt sounded shrill and high, and now and again her uncle interposed a question sharply. In a little while he beckoned Mary from the window, and she went inside. He was standing on the hearth, his legs straddled wide, and his face as black as thunder.

'Come on!' he shouted. 'Out with it. What's your side of the story? I get nothing but a string of words from your aunt; a magpie makes more sense than she. What in hell's been going on here? That's what I want to know.'

Mary told him calmly, in a few well-chosen words, what had taken place during the morning. She omitted nothing – except the squire's question about his brother – and ended with Mr. Bassat's own words – that people would not sleep easy in their beds until Joss Merlyn was hanged, like his father before him.

The landlord listened in silence, and, when she had finished, he crashed his fist down on the kitchen table and swore, kicking one of the chairs to the other side of the room.

'The damned skulking bastard!' he roared. 'He'd no more right to walk into my house than any other man. His talk of a magistrate's warrant was all bluff, you blithering fools; there's no such thing. By God, if I'd been here, I'd have sent him back to North Hill so as his own wife would never recognise him, and, if she did, she'd have no use for him again. Damn and blast his eyes! I'll teach Mr. Bassat who's got the run of this country, and have him sniffing round my legs, what's more. Scared you, did he? I'll burn his house round his ears if he plays his tricks again.'

Joss Merlyn shouted at the top of his voice, and the noise was deafening. Mary did not fear him like this; the whole thing was bluster and show; it was when he lowered his voice and whispered that she knew him to be deadly. For all his thunder he was frightened; she could see that; and his confidence was rudely shaken.

'Get me something to eat,' he said. 'I must go out again, and there's no time to lose. Stop that yawling, Patience, or I'll smash your face in. You've done well to-day, Mary, and I'll not forget it.'

His niece looked him in the eyes.

'You don't think I did it for you, do you?' she said.

'I don't care a damn why you did it, the result's the same,' he answered. 'Not that a blind fool like Bassat would find anything anyway; he was born with his head in the wrong place. Cut me a hunk of bread, and quit talking, and sit down at the bottom of the table where you belong to be.'

The two women took their seats in silence, and the meal passed without further disturbance. As soon as he had finished, the landlord rose to his feet, and, without another word to either of them, made his way to the stable. Mary expected to hear him lead his pony out once more and ride off down the road, but in a minute or two he was back again, and, passing through the kitchen, he went down to the end of the garden and climbed the stile in the field. Mary watched him strike across the moor, and ascend the steep incline that led to Tolborough Tor and Codda. For a moment she hesitated, debating the wisdom of the sudden plan in her head, and then the sound of her aunt's footsteps overheard appeared to decide her. She waited until she heard the door of the bedroom close, and then, throwing off her apron and seizing her thick shawl from its peg on the wall, she ran down the field after her uncle. When she reached the bottom she crouched beside the stone wall until his figure crossed the skyline and disappeared, and then she leapt up again and followed in his track, picking her way amongst the rough grass and stones. It was a mad and senseless venture, no doubt, but her mood was a reckless one, and she needed an outlet for it after her silence of the morning.

Her idea was to keep Joss Merlyn in view, remaining of course unseen, and in this way perhaps she would learn something of his secret mission. She had no doubt that the squire's visit to Jamaica had altered the landlord's plans, and that this sudden departure on foot across the heart of the West Moor was connected with it. It was not yet half past one, and an ideal afternoon for walking. Mary, with her stout shoes and short skirt to her ankles, cared little for the rough ground. It was dry enough underfoot – the frost had hardened the surface – and, accustomed as she was to the wet shingle of the Helford shore and the thick mud of the farmyard, this scramble over the moor seemed easy enough. Her earlier rambles had taught her some wisdom, and she kept to the high ground as much as possible, following as best she could the tracks taken by her uncle.

Her task was a difficult one, and after a few miles she began to realise it. She was forced to keep a good length between them in order to remain unseen, and the landlord walked at such a pace, and took such tremendous strides, that before long Mary saw she would be left behind. Codda Tor was passed, and he turned west now towards the low ground at the foot of Brown Willy, looking, for all his height, like a little black dot against the brown stretch of moor.

The prospect of climbing some thirteen hundred feet came as something of a shock to Mary, and she paused for a moment, and wiped her streaming face. She let down her hair, for greater comfort, and let it blow about her face. Why the landlord of Jamaica Inn thought it necessary to climb the highest point on Bodmin Moor on a December afternoon she could not tell, but, having come so far, she was determined to have some satisfaction for her pains, and she set off again at a sharper pace.

The ground was now soggy beneath her feet, for here the early frost had thawed and turned to water, and the whole of the low-lying plain before her was soft and yellow from the winter rains. The damp oozed into her shoes with cold and clammy certainty, and the hem of her skirt was bespattered with bog and torn in places. Lifting it up higher, and hitching it round her waist with the ribbon from her hair, Mary plunged on in trail of her uncle, but he had already traversed the worst of the low ground with uncanny quickness born of long custom, and she could just make out his figure amongst the black heather and the great boulders at the foot of Brown Willy. Then he was hidden by a jutting crag of granite, and she saw him no more.

It was impossible to discover the path he had taken across the bog; he had been over and gone in a flash, and Mary followed as best she could, floundering at every step. She was a fool to attempt it, she knew that, but a sort of stubborn stupidity made her continue. Ignorant of the whereabouts of the track that had carried her uncle dry-shod over the bog, Mary had sense enough to make a wide circuit to avoid the treacherous ground, and, by going quite two miles in the wrong direction, she was able to cross in comparative safety. She was now hopelessly left, without a prospect of ever finding her uncle again.

Nevertheless she set herself to climb Brown Willy, slipping and stumbling amongst the wet moss and the stones, scrambling up the great peaks of jagged granite that frustrated her at every turn, while now and again a hill sheep, startled by the sound of her, ran out from behind a boulder to gaze at her and stamp his feet. Clouds were bearing up from the west, casting changing shadows on the plains beneath, and the sun went in behind them.

It was very silent on the hills. Once a raven rose up at her feet and screamed; he went away flapping his great black wings, swooping to the earth below with harsh protesting cries.

When Mary reached the summit of the hill the evening clouds were banked high above her head, and the world was grey. The distant horizon was blotted out in the gathering dusk, and thin white mist rose from the moors beneath. Approaching the tor from its steepest and most difficult side, as she had done, she had wasted nearly an hour out of her time, and darkness would soon be upon her. Her escapade had been to little purpose, for as far as her eyes could see there was no living thing within their range.

Joss Merlyn had long vanished; and for all she knew he might not have climbed the tor at all, but skirted its base amongst the rough heather and the smaller stones, and then made his way alone and unobserved, east or west as his business took him, to be swallowed up in the folds of the further hills.

Mary would never find him now. The best course was to descend the tor by the shortest possible way and in the speediest fashion, otherwise she would be faced with the prospect of a winter's night upon the moors, with dead-black heather for a pillow and no other shelter but frowning crags of granite. She knew herself now for a fool to have ventured so far on a December afternoon, for experience had proved to her that there were no long twilights on Bodmin Moor. When darkness came it was swift and sudden, without warning, and an immediate blotting out of the sun. The mists were dangerous too, rising in a cloud from the damp ground and closing in about the marshes like a white barrier.

Discouraged and depressed, and all excitement gone from her, Mary scrambled down the steep face of the tor, one eye on the marshes below and the other for the darkness that threatened to overtake her. Directly below her there was a pool or well, said to be the source of the river Fowey that ran ultimately to the sea, and this must be avoided at all costs, for the ground around was boggy and treacherous and the well itself of an unknown depth.

She bore to her left to avoid it, but by the time she had reached the level of the plain below, with Brown Willy safely descended and lifting his mighty head in lonely splendour behind her, the mist and the darkness had settled on the moors and all sense of direction was now lost to her.

Whatever happened she must keep her head, and not give way to her growing sense of panic. Apart from the mist the evening was fine, and not too cold, and there was no reason why she should not hit upon some track that would lead ultimately to habitation.

There was no danger from the marshes if she kept to the high ground, so, trussing up her skirt again and wrapping her shawl firmly round her shoulders, Mary walked steadily before her, feeling the ground with some care when in doubt, and avoiding those tufts of grass that felt soft and yielding to her feet. That the direction she was taking was unknown to her was obvious in the first few miles, for her way was barred suddenly by a stream that she had not passed on the outward journey. To travel by its side would only lead her once more to the low-lying ground and the marshes, so she plunged through it recklessly, soaking herself above the knee. Wet shoes and stockings did not worry her; she counted herself fortunate that the stream had not been deeper, which would have meant swimming for it, and a chilled body into the bargain. The ground now seemed to rise in front of her, which was all to the good, as the going was firm, and she struck boldly across the high downland for what seemed to be an interminable distance, coming at length to a rough track bearing ahead and slightly to the right. This at any rate had served for a cart's wheels at one time or other, and where a cart could go Mary could follow. The worst was past; and now that her real anxiety had gone she felt weak and desperately tired.

Her limbs were heavy, dragging things that scarcely belonged to her, and her eyes felt sunken away back in her head. She plodded on, her chin low and her hands at her side, thinking that the tall grey chimneys of Jamaica Inn would be, for the first time perhaps in their existence, a welcome and consoling sight. The track broadened now, and was crossed in turn by another running left and right, and Mary stood uncertainly for a few moments, wondering which to take. It was then that she heard the sound of a horse, blowing as though he had been ridden hard, coming out of the darkness to the left of her.

His hoofs made a dull thudding sound on the turf. Mary waited in the middle of the track, her nerves a-jingle with the suddenness of the approach, and presently the horse appeared out of the mist in front of her, a rider on his back, the pair of ghostly figures lacking reality in the dim light. The horseman swerved as he saw Mary, and pulled up his horse to avoid her.

'Hullo,' he cried, 'who's there? Is anyone in trouble?'

He peered down at her from his saddle, and exclaimed in surprise. 'A woman!' he said. 'What in the world are you doing out here?'

Mary seized hold of his rein and quietened the restive horse.

'Can you put me on the road?' she asked. 'I'm miles from home and hopelessly lost.'

'Steady there,' he said to the horse. 'Stand still, will you? Where have you come from? Of course I will help you if I can.'

His voice was low and gentle, and Mary could see he must be a person of quality.

'I live at Jamaica Inn,' she said, and no sooner were the words out of her mouth than she regretted them. He would not help her now, of course; the very name was enough to make him whip on his horse and leave her to find her own way as best she could. She was a fool to have spoken.

For a moment the man was silent, which was only what she expected, but when he spoke again his voice had not changed, but was quiet and gentle as before.

'Jamaica Inn,' he said. 'You've come a long way out of your road, I'm afraid. You must have been walking in the opposite direction. You're the other side of Hendra Downs here, you know.'

'That means nothing to me,' she told him. 'I've never been this way before; it was very stupid of me to venture so far on a winter's afternoon. I'd be grateful if you could show me to the right path, and, once on the high road, it won't take me long to get home.'

He considered her for a moment, and then he swung himself off the saddle to the ground. 'You're exhausted,' he said, 'you aren't fit to walk another step; and, what's more, I'm not going to let you. We are not far from the village, and you shall ride there. Will you give me your foot, and I'll help you to mount.' In a minute she was up in the saddle, and he stood below her, the bridle in his hand. 'That's better, isn't it?' he said. 'You must have had a long and uncomfortable walk on the moors. Your shoes are soaking wet and so is the hem of your gown. You shall come home with me, and dry those things and rest awhile, and have some supper, before I take you back myself to Jamaica Inn.' He spoke with such solicitude, and yet with such calm authority, that Mary sighed with relief, throwing all responsibility aside for the time being, content to trust herself in his keeping. He arranged the reins to her satisfaction, and, looking up at her, she saw his eyes for the first time from beneath the brim of his hat. They were strange eyes, transparent like glass, and so pale in colour that they seemed near to white; a freak of nature she had never known before. They fastened upon her, and searched her, as though her very thoughts could not be hidden, and Mary felt herself relax before him, and give way; and she did not mind. His hair was white, too, under his black shovel hat, and Mary stared back at him in some perplexity, for his face was unlined, and his voice was not that of an elderly man.

Then, with a little rush of embarrassment, she understood the reason for his abnormality, and she turned away her eyes. He was an albino.

He took off his hat and bared his head before her.

'Perhaps I had better introduce myself,' he said, with a smile. 'However unconventional the meeting, it is, I believe, the usual thing to do. My name is Francis Davey, and I am the vicar of Altarnun.'

Chapter Seven

There was something strangely peaceful about the house, something very rare and difficult to define. It was like a house in an old tale, discovered by the hero one evening in midsummer; there should be a barrier of thorns about it through which he must cut his way with a knife, and then a galaxy of flowers growing in profusion, with monstrous blooms untended by human hand. Giant ferns would mass themselves beneath the windows, and white lilies on tall stems. In the tale there would be strands of ivy clustering the walls, barring the entrance, and the house itself would have slept for a thousand years.

Mary smiled at her fancy, and spread her hands once more to the log fire. The silence was pleasing to her; it soothed her weariness and took away her fear. This was a different world from Jamaica Inn. There the silence was oppressive and heavy with malice; the disused rooms stank of neglect. Here it was different. The room in which she was sitting had the quiet impersonality of a drawing-room visited by night. The furniture, the table in the centre, the pictures on the walls, were without that look of solid familiarity belonging to the day. They were like sleeping things, stumbled upon at midnight by surprise. People had lived here once – happy, placid people; old rectors with musty books beneath their arms; and there by the window a grey-haired woman in a blue gown had stooped to thread her needle. That was all very long ago. They slept now in the churchyard beyond the gate, their names indecipherable on the lichened stone. Since they had gone the house had withdrawn into itself and become silent, and the man who lived there now had suffered the personality of those who had gone before to remain unchanged.

Mary watched him as he laid the table for supper, and she thought how wisely he had allowed himself to become submerged in the atmosphere of the house; for another man would have chatted, perhaps, or made some clatter with the cups, feeling the silence a constraint. Her eyes wandered about the room, and she accepted without question the walls bare of the usual biblical themes, the polished desk empty of papers and books that in her mind were associated with the living-room of a rectory. Standing in the corner was an easel, and on it a half-finished canvas of the pool at Dozmary. It had been painted on a grey day, with the rain-clouds overhead, and the water lacked all brilliance and was slate-coloured, without wind. The scene held Mary's eyes, and fascinated her. She knew nothing of painting, but the picture had power, and she could almost feel the rain in her face. He must have watched the direction of her eyes, for he went to the easel and turned the painting with its back towards her. 'Don't look at that,' he said. 'It was done in a hurry, and I had no time to finish it. If you like pictures, you shall see something better. But first of all I'm going to give you your supper. Don't move from the chair. I'll bring the table to you.'

It was a novelty to be waited upon, but he did it so quietly and made such little show that it seemed a natural, everyday occurrence, and Mary was without embarrassment. 'Hannah lives in the village,' he said; 'she leaves every afternoon at four. I prefer to be by myself. I like getting my own supper, and then I can choose my own time. Luckily she made apple-tart to-day. I hope you can eat it; her pastry is only moderate.'

He poured her out a steaming cup of tea, heaping into it a spoonful of cream. She could not yet accustom herself to his white hair and his eyes; they were such a direct contrast to his voice, and his black clerical dress made them the more remarkable. She was still tired, and a little strange to her surroundings, and he respected her desire for silence. Mary swallowed her supper, and now and again she stole a look at him from behind her cup of tea, but he seemed to sense her glance at once, for he would turn his eyes upon her with their cold white stare – like the impersonal and penetrating stare of a blind man – and she would look away again over her shoulder to the lime-green walls of the room, or to the easel in the corner.

'It was providential that I should come upon you on the moor to-night,' he said at length, when she had pushed away her plate and sunk once more into the chair, her chin in her hand. The warmth of the room and the hot tea had made her drowsy, and his gentle voice came to her from far away.

'My work sometimes takes me to the outlying cottages and farms,' he continued. 'This afternoon I helped to bring a child into the world. It will live, and the mother too. They are hardy and care for nothing, these people of the moors. You may have noticed that for yourself. I have a great respect for them.'

Mary had nothing to say in reply. The company who came to Jamaica Inn had not impressed her with respect. She wondered what was the scent of roses that filled the air, and then she noticed for the first time the bowl of dried petals on the small table behind her chair. Then he spoke again, his voice gentle as ever, but with a new insistence.

'Why did you wander on the moor to-night?' he said.

Mary roused herself and looked into his eyes. They stared down at her in infinite compassion, and she longed to trespass on their mercy.

Scarcely aware of how it happened, she heard her voice reply to his.

'I'm in terrible trouble,' she said. 'Sometimes I think I shall become like my aunt, and go out of my mind. You may have heard rumours down here in Altarnun, and you will have shrugged your shoulders, and not listened to them. I've not been at Jamaica Inn much over a month, but it seems like twenty years. It's my aunt that worries me; if only I could get her away. But she won't leave Uncle Joss, for all his treatment of her. Every night I go to bed wondering if I shall wake up and hear the waggons. The first time they came there were six or seven of them, and they brought great parcels and boxes that the men stored in the barred room at the end of the passage. A man was killed that night; I saw the rope hanging from the beam down-stairs . . .' She broke off, the warm colour flooding her face. 'I've never told anyone before,' she said. 'It had to come out. I couldn't keep it to myself any longer. I shouldn't have said it. I've done something terrible.' For a little while he did not answer; he let her take her time, and then, when she had recovered herself, he spoke gently, and slowly, like a father who reassures a frightened child.

'Don't be afraid,' he said; 'your secret is safe; no one shall know of this but me. You're very tired, you know, and this is all my fault for bringing you into the warm room and making you eat. I ought to have put you to bed. You must have been on the moors for hours, and there are bad places between here and Jamaica; the bogs are at their worst this time of the year. When you are rested, I'll take you back in the trap, and I'll make your excuses myself to the landlord if you wish.'

'Oh, you mustn't do that,' said Mary quickly. 'If he suspects half of what I've done to-night he would kill me, and you too. You don't understand. He's a desperate man, and he'd stop at nothing. No, if the worst comes to the worst I'll try and climb up the porch to my bedroom window, and get in that way. He must never know I have been here, or that I've met you even.'

'Isn't your imagination running away with you a little?' said the vicar. 'I know I must seem unsympathetic and cold, but this is the nineteenth century, you know, and men don't murder one another without reason. I believe I have as much right to drive you on the King's highway as your uncle himself. Having gone so far, don't you think you had better let me hear the rest of your story? What is your name, and how long have you been living at Jamaica Inn?'

Mary looked up at the pale eyes in the colourless face, the halo of cropped white hair, and she thought again how strange a freak of nature was this man, who might be twenty-one, who might be sixty, and who with his soft, persuasive voice would compel her to admit every secret her heart possessed, had he the mind to ask her. She could trust him; that at least was certain. Still she hesitated, turning the words over in her mind.

'Come,' he said with a smile; 'I have heard confession in my time. Not here in Altarnun, but in Ireland and in Spain. Your story will not sound as strange to me as you think. There are other worlds besides Jamaica Inn.'

His speech made her feel humble and a little confused. It was as though he mocked her, for all his tact and kindness, and supposed her, in the back of his mind, to be hysterical and young. She plunged headlong into her story with jerky ill-framed sentences, beginning with that first Saturday night in the bar, and then working backwards to her arrival at the inn. Her tale sounded flat and unconvincing, even to herself who knew the truth of it, and her great fatigue made her labour in the telling of it, so that she was continually at a loss for words, and she kept pausing for reflection, and then going back on her story and repeating herself. He heard her to the end with patience, without comment or question, but all the while she felt his white eyes watching her, and he had a little trick of swallowing at intervals which she came instinctively to recognise, and wait for. The fear she had sustained, the agony and the doubt, sounded to her ears, as she listened, like the worked-up invention of an over-stimulated mind, and the conversation in the bar between her uncle and the stranger had developed into an elaborate piece of nonsense. She sensed, rather than saw, the vicar's unbelief; and in a desperate attempt to tone down her now ridiculous and highly coloured story, her uncle, who had been the villain of it, became the usual hard-drinking bully of a countryman who beat his wife once a week, and the waggons themselves had no more menace than carriers' carts, travelling by night to expedite delivery.

The visit of the squire of North Hill early that day had some conviction, but the empty room struck another note of anti-climax, and the only part of the story that rang with any sense of reality was Mary's losing herself on the moors during the afternoon.

When she had finished, the vicar got up from his chair and began to pace about the room. He whistled softly under his breath and kept playing with a loose button on his coat that was hanging by a thread. Then he came to a standstill on the hearth, with his back to the fire, and looked down upon her – but Mary could read nothing from his eyes.

'I believe you, of course,' he said, after a moment or so. 'You haven't the face of a liar, and I doubt if you know the meaning of hysteria. But your story wouldn't go in a court of law – not as you've told it to-night, anyhow. It's too much of a fairy-tale. And another thing – it's a scandal and an outrage, we all know that, but smuggling is rife all over the county, and half the magistrates do very well out of it. That shocks you, doesn't it? But I can assure you it's the truth. If the law was stricter there would be greater supervision, and your uncle's little nest at Jamaica Inn would have been blotted out long ago. I have met Mr. Bassat once or twice, and I believe him to be an honest, genuine sort of fellow, but, between ourselves, a bit of a fool. He'd bluster and talk, but that's about all. He'll keep this morning's expedition very quiet, unless I'm much mistaken. Actually he had no business to walk into the inn and search the rooms, and if it becomes known that he did so, and found nothing for his pains, he'll become the laughing-stock of the countryside. I can tell you one thing, though: his visit will have scared your uncle, and he'll lie low now for a time. There won't be any more waggons to Jamaica Inn for some while. I think you can be certain of that.'

Mary listened to his reasoning with some misgiving. She had hoped he would be appalled, once admitting the truth of her story, but here he was, apparently quite unmoved, taking it all as a matter of course.

He must have seen the disappointment in her face, for he spoke again.

'I could see Mr. Bassat, if you like,' he said, 'and put your story to him. But unless he can catch your uncle at work, as it were, with the waggons in the yard, there's little chance of convicting him. That's what I must impress upon your mind. I'm afraid I sound very unhelpful, but the position is a difficult one from every point of view. And then again, you don't want your aunt to be implicated in the business, but I don't see how it can be avoided, if it comes to an arrest.'

'What do you suggest I should do, then?' said Mary helplessly.

'If I were you I should play a waiting game,' he replied. 'Keep a close watch on your uncle, and when the waggons do come again you can report at once to me. We can then decide together what is best to be done. That is, if you will honour me again with your confidence.'

'What about the stranger who disappeared?' said Mary. 'He was murdered. I'm certain of that. Do you mean to say that nothing can ever be done about it?'

'I'm afraid not, unless his body is found, which is extremely unlikely,' said the vicar. 'It is quite possible that he was never killed at all, for that matter. Forgive me, but I think you allowed your imagination to run away with you over that. All you saw was a piece of rope, remember. If you had actually seen the man dead, or even wounded – well, that's a different tale altogether.'

'I heard my uncle threaten him,' persisted Mary. 'Isn't that enough?'

'My dear child, people threaten one another every day in the year, but they don't hang for it. Now listen to me. I am your friend, and you can trust me. If you ever become worried or distressed in any way, I want you to come and tell me about it. You are not afraid of walking, judging by your performance this afternoon, and Altarnun is only a few miles by the high road. If you come at any time and I'm not in, Hannah will be here, and she will look after you. Now, that's a bargain between us, isn't it?'

'Thank you very much.'

'Now put on your stockings again, and your shoes, while I go to the stable and get the trap. I'm going to drive you back to Jamaica Inn.'

The thought of returning was hateful to Mary, but it had to be faced. The contrast between this peaceful room with the gently shaded candles, the warm log fire, the deep chair, and the cold grim passages of Jamaica Inn, with her own little cupboard of a room over the porch, must be avoided at all costs. There was one thing to bear in mind, and that was that she could come back here when she wished.

The night was fine; the dark clouds of the early evening had passed away and the sky was ablaze with stars. Mary sat beside Francis Davey on the high seat of the dog-cart, wrapped in a greatcoat with a top collar of velvet. This was not the same horse that he had been riding when she met him on the moor; this was a big grey cob who, fresh from his sojourn in the stable, went like the wind. It was a strange, exhilarating drive. The wind blew in Mary's face, stinging her eyes. The climb from Altarnun had been slow at first, for the hill was steep, but now they were upon the high road, with their faces turned to Bodmin, the vicar pricked the cob with his whip, so that he laid his ears flat to his head and galloped like a mad thing.

His hoofs thundered on the hard white road, raising a cloud of dust, and Mary was flung against her companion. He made no effort to rein in his horse, and, glancing up at him, Mary saw that he was smiling. 'Go on,' he said, 'go on; you can go faster than this'; and his voice was low and excited, as though he were talking to himself. The effect was unnatural, a little startling, and Mary was aware of a feeling of discomfiture, as though he had betaken himself to another world and had forgotten her existence.

Seated where she was, she could observe him for the first time in profile, and she saw how clear-cut were his features, how prominent the thin nose; perhaps it was the peculiarity of nature, creating him white in the beginning, that made him different from any man she had ever seen before.

He looked like a bird. Crouched in his seat, with his black cape-coat blown out by the wind, his arms were like wings. He might be any age, and she could not place him at all. Then he smiled down at her, and was human again.

'I love these moors,' he said. 'You have had a bad introduction to them, of course, so you can't understand me. If you knew them as well as I do, and had seen them in every mood, winter and summer, you would love them too. They have a fascination unlike any other part of the county. They go back a long way in time. Sometimes I think they are the survival of another age. The moors were the first things to be created; afterwards came the forests, and the valleys, and the sea. Climb Roughtor one morning before sunrise, and listen to the wind in the stones. You'll know what I mean then.'

Mary kept thinking of the parson at her home. He was a cheerful little man with a long string of children exactly like himself, and his wife made damson cheese. He preached the same sermon always on Christmas Day, and his parishioners could have prompted him anywhere. She wondered what Francis Davey said in his church at Altarnun. Did he preach about Roughtor, and the light on Dozmary pool? They had come to the dip in the road now, where a cluster of trees made a little valley for the river Fowey, and in front of them stretched the climb to the high, unsheltered ground. Already Mary could see the tall chimneys of Jamaica Inn outlined against the sky.

The drive was ended, and the exhilaration went from her. The old dread and loathing for her uncle returned. The vicar stopped his horse just short of the yard, under the lee of the grass bank.

'There's no sign of anyone,' he said quietly. 'It's like a house of the dead. Would you like me to try the door?'

Mary shook her head. 'It's bolted always,' she whispered, 'and the windows are barred. That's my room, over the porch. I can scramble up there, if you will let me climb on your shoulder. I've managed worse places than that at home. My window is open at the top; once on the porch, it will be easy enough.'

'You'll slip on those slates,' he answered. 'I won't let you do it. It's absurd. Is there no other way of getting in? What about the back?'

'The door of the bar will be bolted, and the kitchen too,' said Mary. 'We can slip round, if you like, and make certain.'

She led the way round to the other side of the house, and she turned to him suddenly, her finger to her lips. 'There's a light in the kitchen,' she whispered. 'That means my uncle is there. Aunt Patience always goes early.

There are no curtains to the window; if we pass by he will see us.' She leant back against the wall of the house. Her companion motioned her to be still.

'Very well,' he said, 'I will take care he does not see me. I am going to look in at the window.'

She watched him to the side of the window, and he stood there for a few minutes gazing into the kitchen. Then he beckoned to her to follow, that same tense smile on his face she had noticed before. His face looked very pale against his black shovel-hat. 'There'll be no argument to-night with the landlord of Jamaica Inn,' he said.

Mary followed the direction of his eyes and pressed forward to the window. The kitchen was lit by a single candle stuck sideways into a bottle. It had already burnt down half way, and great blobs of grease clung to the side of it. The flame itself wavered and spluttered in the draught from the door, which was wide open to the garden. Joss Merlyn sprawled at the table in a drunken stupor, his great legs stretched out on either side of him, his hat on the back of his head. He stared before him at the guttering candle, his eyes glazed and fixed like a dead man. Another bottle lay with its neck smashed on the table, and beside it an empty glass. The peat fire had smouldered itself to nothing.

Francis Davey pointed to the open door. 'You can walk inside and go upstairs to bed,' he said. 'Your uncle will not even see you. Fasten the door after you, and blow out the candle. You don't want a fire on your hands. Good night to you, Mary Yellan. If you are ever in trouble and need me, I shall be waiting for you at Altarnun.'

Then he turned the corner of the house and was gone.

Mary tiptoed into the kitchen, and closed and fastened the door. She could have slammed it had she wished, it would not have roused her uncle.

He had gone to his kingdom of heaven, and the little world was lost to him. She blew out the light beside him and left him alone in the darkness.

Chapter Eight

Joss Merlyn was drunk for five days. He was insensible most of the time, and lay stretched out on a bed in the kitchen that Mary and her aunt had improvised between them. He slept with his mouth wide open, and the sound of his breathing could be heard from the bedrooms above. About five in the evening he would wake for half an hour or so, shouting for brandy and sobbing like a child. His wife went to him at once, and soothed him and settled his pillow. She gave him a little weak brandy-and-water, talking to him gently as she would to a sick child holding the glass to his lips; and he stared around him with glaring blood-shot eyes, muttering to himself and shivering like a dog.

Aunt Patience became another woman, showing a calm coolness and a presence of mind that Mary had not believed her capable of possessing. She gave herself up entirely to this nursing of her husband. She was obliged to do everything for him, and Mary watched her change his blankets and his linen with a sick feeling of disgust in her own heart, for she could not have borne to go near him. Aunt Patience took it as a matter of course, and the oaths and screams with which he greeted her did not appear to frighten her. These were the only times when she had the controlling of him, and he would let her sponge his forehead with a towel and hot water without a protest. Then she would tuck the fresh blanket under him, and smooth his mat of hair, and in a few minutes he would be asleep again, his face purple and his mouth wide open, with his tongue protruding, snoring like a bull. It was impossible to live in the kitchen, and Mary and her aunt turned the little disused parlour into a dwelling-room for themselves. For the first time Aunt Patience became something of a companion. She chatted happily of the old days in Helford, when she and Mary's mother had been girls together; she moved swiftly and lightly about the house, and sometimes Mary would hear her humming snatches of old hymns as she passed backwards and forwards to the kitchen. It seemed that every two months or so Joss Merlyn would have these bouts of drinking. The times used to be further apart, but now they were becoming more frequent, and Aunt Patience was never quite certain when they would occur. This present one had been caused by the visit of Squire Bassat to the inn – the landlord had been very angry and upset, she told Mary – and when he came back from the moors at six in the evening he went straight to the bar. She knew then what would happen.

Aunt Patience accepted without question her niece's explanation of losing herself on the moors. She told her she must beware of the bogs and left it at that. Mary was greatly relieved. She did not want to give details of the adventure, and she was determined to say nothing of her meeting with the vicar of Altarnun. Meanwhile Joss Merlyn lay in his stupor in the kitchen, and the two women spent five comparatively peaceful days.

The weather was cold and grey, and did not tempt Mary from the house, but on the fifth morning the wind dropped and the sun shone, and, in spite of the adventure that had befallen her only a few days before, Mary decided to brave the moors again. The landlord was awake at nine, and began to shout at the top of his voice, and what with the noise he made, and the smell from the kitchen that now pervaded the rest of the house, and the sight of Aunt Patience bustling downstairs with clean blankets over her arm, Mary was seized with a rush of disgust and a loathing for the whole business.

Feeling very ashamed of herself, she slipped out of the house, rolling a crust of bread in a handkerchief, and crossed the high road to the moors. This time she made for the East Moor, striking out towards Kilmar, and with the whole day in front of her there was no fear of being lost. She kept thinking about Francis Davey, her strange vicar of Altarnun, and she realised how little he had told her of himself, while he had from her a life-history in an evening. She thought what an odd figure he must have looked, painting his picture beside the waters of Dozmary, hatless, perhaps, his halo of white hair standing up around his head; and there would be gulls flying inland from the sea, skimming the surface of the lake. He would look like Elijah in the wilderness.

She wondered what had called him to priesthood, and whether he was loved by the people of Altarnun. It was nearly Christmas now, and home at Helford people would be decorating with holly and evergreen and mistletoe. There would be a great baking of pastry and cakes, and a fattening of turkeys and geese. The little parson, wearing a festive air, would beam upon his world, and on Christmas Eve he would ride up after tea to drink sloe gin at Trelowarren. Did Francis Davey decorate his church with holly, and call down a blessing upon the people?

One thing was certain: there would be little gaiety at Jamaica Inn.

Mary had walked for an hour or more before she stopped short in her tracks, her further progress barred by a stream that divided and ran in opposite directions. The stream lay in a valley between the hills, and was encircled by marshes. The country was not unknown to her, and, looking on beyond the smooth green face of the tor ahead, she saw the great split hand of Kilmar pointing his fingers to the sky. She was gazing at Trewartha Marsh once more, where she had wandered that first Saturday, but this time her face was turned to the south-east, and the hills looked different in the brave sunshine. The brook burbled merrily over the stones, and there was a fording gate across the shallow water. The marsh stretched away to the left of her. The soft wind blew the waving strands of grass, that shivered in company, and sighed, and rustled; and planted amidst the pale inviting green were tufts of coarse brown-tipped grass with yellow stocky strands.

These were the treacherous bog islands, suggesting solidity by their breadth, but their weight was of thistledown, and a man's foot planted upon them sank immediately, and the little patches of slate-coloured water that rippled here and there would churn into froth and turn black.

Mary turned her back on the marsh and forded the gate over the stream. She kept to the high ground, with the stream beneath her, and followed its course along the winding valley between the hills. There were few clouds to-day to cast their shadows, and the moors rolled away beyond her, sand-coloured under the sun. A solitary curlew stood pensively beside the stream, watching his reflection in the water; and then his long beak darted with incredible swiftness into the reeds, stabbing at the soft mud, and, turning his head, he tucked his legs under him and rose into the air, calling his plaintive note, and streaking for the south.

Something had disturbed him, and in a few minutes Mary saw what it was. A handful of ponies had clattered down the hill beyond and splashed into the stream to drink. They clod-hopped noisily amongst the stones, pushing into one another, their tails whisking in the wind. They must have come through a gate on the left, a little way ahead, that stood wide open, propped by a jagged stone, and led to a rough farm-track heavy with mud.

Mary leant against the gate and watched the ponies, and out of the tail of her eye she saw a man coming down the track, carrying a bucket in either hand. She was about to move and continue her walk round the bend of the hill when he waved a bucket in the air, and shouted to her.

It was Jem Merlyn. There was no time to escape, and she stood where she was until he came to her. He wore a grimy shirt that had never seen a washtub, and a pair of brown breeches, covered with horsehair and filth from an outhouse. He had neither hat nor coat, and there was rough stubble of beard on his jaw. He laughed at her, showing his teeth, looking for all the world as his brother must have done twenty years ago.

'So you've found your way to me, have you?' he said. 'I didn't expect you so soon or I'd have baked bread in your honour. I haven't washed for three days, and I've been living on potatoes. Here, take hold of this bucket.'

He thrust one of the buckets in her hand before she had time to protest, and was down to the water after the ponies. 'Come out of it!' he shouted. 'Get back, will you, fouling my drinking-water! Go on, you big black devil.'

He hit the largest of the ponies on his hind-quarters with the end of the bucket, and they stampeded up the hill out of the water, kicking their heels in the air. 'My fault for not shutting the gate,' he called to Mary. 'Bring down that other bucket; the water's clear enough the other side of the brook.'

She took it with her to the stream, and he filled them both, grinning at her over his shoulder. 'What would you have done if you hadn't found me at home?' he said, wiping his face on his sleeve. Mary could not help smiling.

'I didn't even know you lived here,' she said, 'and I certainly never walked this way with the intention of finding you. I'd have turned left if I'd known.'

'I don't believe you,' he said. 'You started out with the hope of sighting me, and it's no use pretending any different. Well, you've come in good time to cook my dinner. There's a piece of mutton in the kitchen.'

He led the way up the mud track, and, rounding the corner, they came to a small grey cottage built on the side of the hill. There were some rough outbuildings at the back, and a strip of land for potatoes. A thin stream of smoke rose from the squat chimney. 'The fire's on, and it won't take you long to boil that scrap of mutton. I suppose you can cook?' he said.

Mary looked him up and down. 'Do you always make use of folk this way?' she said.

'I don't often have the chance,' he told her. 'But you may as well stop while you're here. I've done all my own cooking since my mother died, and there's not been a woman in the cottage since. Come in, won't you?'

She followed him in, bending her head as he did under the low door.

The room was small and square, half the size of the kitchen at Jamaica, with a great open fireplace in the corner. The floor was filthy, and littered with rubbish: potato-scrapings, cabbage-stalks, and crumbs of bread. There were odds and ends scattered all over the room, and ashes from the turf fire covered everything. Mary looked about her in dismay.

'Don't you ever do any cleaning?' she asked him. 'You've got this kitchen like a pigsty. You ought to be ashamed of yourself. Leave me that bucket of water, and find me a broom. I'll not eat my dinner in a place like this.'

She set to work at once, all her instincts of cleanliness and order aroused by the dirt and the squalor. In half an hour she had the kitchen scrubbed clean as a pin, the stone floor wet and shining, and all the rubbish cleared away. She had found crockery in the cupboard, and a strip of table-cloth, with which she proceeded to lay the table, and meanwhile the mutton boiled in the saucepan on the fire, surrounded by potato and turnip.

The smell was good, and Jem came in at the door, sniffing the air like a hungry dog. 'I shall have to keep a woman,' he said. 'I can see that. Will you leave your aunt and come and look after me?'

'You'd have to pay me too much,' said Mary. 'You'd never have money enough for what I'd ask.'

'Women are always mean,' he said, sitting down at the table. 'What they do with their money I don't know, for they never spend it. My mother was just the same. She used to keep hers hidden in an old stocking, and I never as much as saw the colour of it. Make haste with the dinner; I'm as empty as a worm.'

'You're impatient, aren't you?' said Mary. 'Not a word of thanks to me that's cooked it. Take your hands away – the plate's hot.'

She put the steaming mutton down in front of him and he smacked his lips. 'They taught you something where you came from, anyway,' he said. 'I always say there's two things women ought to do by instinct, and cooking's one of 'em. Get me a jug of water, will you? You'll find the pitcher outside.'

But Mary had filled a cup for him already, and she passed it to him in silence.

'We were all born here,' said Jem, jerking his head to the ceiling, 'up in the room overhead. But Joss and Matt were grown men when I was still a little lad, clinging to mother's skirt. We never saw much of my father, but when he was home we knew it all right. I remember him throwing a knife at mother once – it cut her above her eye, and the blood ran down her face. I was scared, and ran and hid in that corner by the fire. Mother said nothing; she just bathed her eye in some water, and then she gave my father his supper. She was a brave woman, I'll say that for her, though she spoke little and she never gave us much to eat. She made a bit of a pet of me when I was small, on account of being the youngest, I suppose, and my brothers used to beat me when she wasn't looking. Not that they were as thick as you'd think – we were never much of a loving family – and I've seen Joss thrash Matt until he couldn't stand. Matt was a funny devil; he was quiet, more like my mother. He was drowned down in the marsh yonder. You could shout there until your lungs burst, no one would hear you except a bird or two, and a stray pony. I've been nearly caught there myself in my time.'

'How long has your mother been dead?' said Mary.

'Seven years this Christmas,' he answered, helping himself to more boiled mutton. 'What with my father hanged, and Matt drowned, and Joss gone off to America, and me growing up as wild as a hawk, she turned religious and used to pray here by the hour, calling on the Lord. I couldn't abide that, and I cleared off out of it. I shipped on a Padstow schooner for a time, but the sea didn't suit my stomach, and I came back home. I found Mother gone as thin as a skeleton. "You ought to eat more," I told her, but she wouldn't listen to me, so I went off again, and stayed in Plymouth for a while, picking up a shilling or two in my own way. I came back here to have my Christmas dinner, and I found the place deserted and the door locked up. I was mad. I hadn't eaten for twenty-four hours. I went back to North Hill, and they told me my mother had died. She'd been buried three weeks. I might just as well have stayed in Plymouth for all the dinner I got that Christmas. There's a piece of cheese in the cupboard behind you. Will you eat the half of it? There's maggots in it, but they won't hurt you.'

Mary shook her head, and she let him get up and reach for it himself.

'What's the matter?' he said. 'You look like a sick cow. Has the mutton turned sour on you already?'

Mary watched him return to his seat and spread the hunk of dry cheese on to a scrap of stale bread. 'It will be a good thing when there's not a Merlyn left in Cornwall,' she said. 'It's better to have disease in a country than a family like yours. You and your brother were born twisted and evil. Do you never think of what your mother must have suffered?'

Jem looked at her in surprise, the bread and cheese half way to his mouth.

'Mother was all right,' he said. 'She never complained. She was used to us. Why, she married my father at sixteen; she never had time to suffer. Joss was born the year after, and then Matt. Her time was taken up in rearing them, and by the time they were out of her hands she had to start all over again with me. I was an afterthought, I was. Father got drunk at Launceston fair, after selling three cows that didn't belong to him. If it wasn't for that I wouldn't be sitting here talking to you now. Pass that jug.'

Mary had finished. She got up and began to clear away the plates in silence.

'How's the landlord of Jamaica Inn?' said Jem, tilting back on his chair, and watching her dip the plates in water.

'Drunk, like his father before him,' said Mary shortly.

'That'll be the ruin of Joss,' said his brother seriously. 'He soaks himself insensible, and lies like a log for days. One day he'll kill himself with it. The damned fool! How long has it lasted this time?'

'Five days.'

'Oh, that's nothing to Joss. He'd lie there for a week if you let him. Then he'll come to, staggering on his feet like a new-born calf, with a mouth as black as Trewartha Marsh. When he's rid himself of his surplus liquid, and the rest of the drink has soaked into him – that's when you want to watch him; he's dangerous then. You look out for yourself.'

'He'll not touch me; I'll take good care of that,' said Mary. 'He's got other things to worry him. There's plenty to keep him busy.'

'Don't be mysterious, nodding to yourself with your mouth pursed up. Has anything been happening at Jamaica?'

'It depends how you look at it,' said Mary, watching him over the plate she was wiping. 'We had Mr. Bassat from North Hill last week.'

Jem brought his chair to the ground with a crash. 'The devil you did,' he said. 'And what had the squire to say to you?'

'Uncle Joss was from home,' said Mary, 'and Mr. Bassat insisted on coming into the inn and going through the rooms. He broke down the door at the end of the passage, he and his servant between them, but the room was empty. He seemed disappointed, and very surprised, and he rode away in a fit of temper. He asked after you, as it happened, and I told him I'd never set eyes on you.'

Jem whistled tunelessly, his expression blank as Mary told her tale, but when she came to the end of her sentence, and the mention of his name, his eyes narrowed, and then he laughed. 'Why did you lie to him?' he asked.

'It seemed less trouble at the time,' said Mary. 'If I'd thought longer, no doubt I'd have told him the truth. You've got nothing to hide, have you?'

'Nothing much, except that black pony you saw by the brook belongs to him,' said Jem carelessly. 'He was dapple-grey last week, and worth a small fortune to the squire, who bred him himself. I'll make a few pounds with him at Launceston if I'm lucky. Come down and have a look at him.'

They went out into the sun, Mary wiping her hands on her apron, and she stood for a few moments at the door of the cottage while Jem went off to the horses. The cottage was built on the slope of the hill above Withy Brook, whose course wound away in the valley and was lost in the further hills. Behind the house stretched a wide and level plain, rising to great tors on either hand, and this grassland – like a grazing-place for cattle – with no boundary as far as the eye could reach except the craggy menace of Kilmar, must be the strip of country known as Twelve Men's Moor.

Mary pictured Joss Merlyn running out of the doorway here as a child, his mat of hair falling over his eyes in a fringe, with the gaunt, lonely figure of his mother standing behind him, her arms folded, watching him with a question in her eyes. A world of sorrow and silence, anger and bitterness too, must have passed beneath the roof of this small cottage.

There was a shout and a clatter of hoofs, and Jem rode up to her round the corner of the house, astride the black pony. 'This is the fellow I wanted you to have,' he said, 'but you're so close with your money. He'd carry you well, too; the squire bred him for his wife. Are you sure you won't change your mind?'

Mary shook her head and laughed. 'You'd have me tie him up in the stable at Jamaica, I suppose,' she said, 'and when Mr. Bassat calls again he wouldn't be likely to recognise him, would he? Thanking you for your trouble, but I'd rather not risk it all the same. I've lied enough for your family, Jem Merlyn, for one lifetime.' Jem pulled a long face, and slid to the ground.

'You've refused the best bargain that you'll ever have offered to you,' he said, 'and I won't give you the chance again. He'll go to Launceston on Christmas Eve; the dealers there will swallow him up.' He clapped his hands on the hind-quarters of the pony. 'Get on with you, then'; and the animal made a startled dash for the gap in the bank.

Jem broke off a piece of grass and began to chew it, glancing sideways at his companion. 'What did Squire Bassat expect to see at Jamaica Inn?' he said.

Mary looked him straight in the eyes. 'You ought to know that better than I do,' she answered. Jem chewed his grass thoughtfully, spitting out little bits of it on to the ground.

'How much do you know?' he said suddenly, throwing the stalk away.

Mary shrugged her shoulders. 'I didn't come here to answer questions,' she said. 'I had enough of that with Mr. Bassat.'

'It was lucky for Joss the stuff had been shifted,' said his brother quietly. 'I told him last week he was sailing too close to the wind. It's only a matter of time before they catch him. And all he does in self-defence is to get drunk, the damned fool.'

Mary said nothing. If Jem was trying to tap her by this exhibition of frankness he would be disappointed.

'You must have a good view from that little room over the porch,' he said. 'Do they wake you out of your beauty-sleep?'

'How do you know that's my room?' Mary asked swiftly.

He looked taken aback at her question; she saw the surprise flash through his eyes. Then he laughed, and picked another piece of grass from the bank.

'The window was wide open when I rode into the yard the other morning,' he said, 'and there was a little bit of blind blowing in the wind. I've never seen a window open at Jamaica Inn before.'

The excuse was plausible, but hardly good enough for Mary. A horrible suspicion came into her mind. Could it have been Jem who had hidden in the empty guest-room that Saturday night? Something went cold inside her.

'Why are you so silent about it all?' he continued. 'Do you think I'm going to go to my brother and say, "Here, that niece of yours, she lets her tongue run away with her"? Damn it, Mary, you're not blind or deaf; even a child would smell a rat if he lived a month at Jamaica Inn.'

'What are you trying to make me tell you?' said Mary. 'And what does it matter to you how much I know? All I think about is getting my aunt away from the place as soon as possible. I told you that when you came to the inn. It may take a little time to persuade her, and I'll have to be patient. As for your brother, he can drink himself to death for all I care. His life is his own, and so is his business. It's nothing to do with me.'

Jem whistled, and kicked at a loose stone with his foot.

'So smuggling doesn't appal you after all?' he said. 'You'd let my brother line every room at Jamaica with kegs of brandy and rum, and you'd say nothing, is that it? But supposing he meddled in other things – supposing it was a question of life, and death, and perhaps murder – what then?'

He turned round and faced her, and she could see that this time he was not playing with her; his careless, laughing manner was gone, and his eyes were grave, but she could not read what lay behind them.

'I don't know what you mean,' said Mary.

He looked at her for a long time without speaking. It was as though he debated some problem in his mind and could only find solution in the expression of her face. All his resemblance to his brother vanished. He was harder, older suddenly, and of a different breed.

'Perhaps not,' he said at length, 'but you'll come to know, if you stay long enough. Why does your aunt look like a living ghost – can you tell me that? Ask her, next time the wind blows from the north-west.'

And he began to whistle again softly, his hands in his pockets. Mary stared back at him in silence. He spoke in riddles, but whether it was to frighten her or not she could not say. Jem the horse-stealer with his careless, impecunious manner, she could understand and allow for, but this was a new departure. She was not sure whether she liked it as well.

He laughed shortly, and shrugged his shoulders. 'There'll be trouble between Joss and myself one day, and it's he that'll be sorry for it, not I,' he said. And with that cryptic remark he turned on his heel and went off on to the moor after the pony. Mary watched him thoughtfully, her arms tucked into her shawl. So her first instinct had been right, and there was something behind the smuggling, after all. The stranger in the bar that night had talked of murder, and now Jem himself had echoed his words. She was not a fool, then, nor was she hysterical, whatever she was considered by the vicar of Altarnun.

What part Jem Merlyn played in all this it was hard to say, but that he was concerned in it somewhere she did not doubt for a moment.

And if he was the man who crept so stealthily down the stairs behind her uncle – why, he must know well enough that she had left her room that night, and was in hiding somewhere, and had listened to them. Then he, above all men, must remember the rope on the beam, and guess that she had seen it after he and the landlord had gone out on to the moor.

If Jem was the man, there would be reason enough for all his questions. 'How much do you know?' he had asked her; but she had not told him.

The conversation had cast a shadow on her day. She wanted to be off now, and rid of him, and alone with her own thoughts. She began to walk slowly down the hill towards the Withy Brook. She had reached the gate at the bottom of the track when she heard his running footsteps behind her, and he flung himself first at the gate, looking like a half-bred gypsy with his growth of beard and his filthy breeches.

'Why are you going?' he said. 'It's early yet; it won't be dark till after four. I'll walk back with you then as far as Rushyford Gate. What's the matter with you?' He took her chin in his hands and looked into her face. 'I believe you're frightened of me,' he said. 'You think I've got barrels of brandy and rolls of tobacco in the little old bedrooms up above, and that I'm going to show them to you, and then cut your throat. That's it, isn't it? We're a desperate lot of fellows, we Merlyns, and Jem is the worst of the pack. Is that what you're thinking?'

She smiled back at him in spite of herself. 'Something of the sort,' she confessed, 'but I'm not afraid of you; you needn't think that. I'd even like you if you didn't remind me so much of your brother.'

'I can't help my face,' he said, 'and I'm much better-looking than Joss, you must allow me that.'

'Oh, you've conceit enough to make up for all the other qualities you lack,' agreed Mary, 'and I'll not deprive you of your handsome face. You may break as many hearts as you please. Now let me go; it's a long walk back to Jamaica Inn and I don't fancy losing myself on the moors again.'

'And when did you lose yourself before?' he asked.

Mary frowned slightly. The words had escaped her. 'The other afternoon I was out on the West Moor,' she said, 'and the fog came on early. I wandered some time before I found my way back.'

'You're a fool to go walking,' he said. 'There's places between Jamaica and Roughtor that would swallow a herd of cattle, to say nothing of a slip of a thing like you. It's no pastime for a woman anyhow. What did you do it for?'

'I wanted to stretch my legs. I'd been shut in the house for days.'

'Well, Mary Yellan, next time you want to stretch your legs you can stretch them in this direction. If you come through the gate you can't go wrong, not if you leave the marsh on your left-hand side as you did to-day. Are you coming to Launceston with me on Christmas Eve?'

'What will you be doing over to Launceston, Jem Merlyn?'

'Only selling Mr. Bassat's black pony for him, my dear. You'd be best away from Jamaica Inn that day, if I know anything about my brother. He'll be just recovering from his brandy-bed by then and looking for trouble. If they're used to you gallivanting over the moors they'll not say anything at your absence. I'll bring you home by midnight. Say you're coming, Mary.'

'Supposing you are caught in Launceston with Mr. Bassat's pony? You would look a fool then, wouldn't you? And so would I, if they clapped me into prison alongside of you.'

'No one's going to catch me; not yet awhile, anyway. Take a risk, Mary; don't you like excitement, that you're so careful of your own skin? They must breed you soft down Helford way.'

She rose like a fish to his bait.

'All right then, Jem Merlyn, you needn't think I'm afraid. I'd just as soon be in prison as live at Jamaica Inn anyway. How do we go to Launceston?'

'I'll take you there in the jingle, with Mr. Bassat's black pony behind us. Do you know your way to North Hill, across the moor?'

'No, I do not.'

'You only have to follow your nose. Go a mile along the high road, and you'll come to a gap in the hedge on the top of the hill, bearing to the right. You'll have Carey Tor ahead of you, and Hawk's Tor away on your right, and if you keep straight on you can't miss your way. I'll come half of the distance to meet you. We'll keep to the moor as much as we can. There'll be some travelling on the road Christmas Eve.'

'What time shall I start, then?'

'We'll let the other folk make the pace and get there in the forenoon, and the streets will be thick enough for us by two o'clock. You can leave Jamaica at eleven, if you like.'

'I'll make no promises. If you don't see me you can go on your way. You forget Aunt Patience may need me.'

'That's right. Make your excuses.'

'There's the gate over the stream,' said Mary. 'You don't have to come any further. I can find my own way. I go straight over the brow of that hill, don't I?'

'You can give the landlord my respects, if you like, and tell him I hope his temper has improved, and his tongue also. Ask him if he'd care for me to hang a bunch of mistletoe on the porch of Jamaica Inn! Mind the water. Do you want me to carry you through the gate? You'll wet your feet.'

'If I went up to my waist it wouldn't hurt me. Good afternoon, Jem Merlyn.' And Mary leapt boldly across the running brook, with one hand on the gate to guide her. Her petticoat dipped in the water, and she lifted it up out of the way. She heard Jem laugh from his bank on the other side, and she walked away up the hill without a backward glance or a wave of her hand.

Let him match himself against the men from the south, she thought; against the fellows from Helford, and Gweek, and Manaccan. There was a blacksmith at Constantine who could twist him round his little finger. Jem Merlyn had little to be proud about. A horse-thief, a common smuggler, a rogue and a murderer into the bargain, perhaps. They bred fine men on the moors, it seemed.

Mary was not afraid of him; and to prove it she would ride beside him in his jingle to Launceston on Christmas Eve.

Darkness was falling as she crossed the high road and into the yard. As usual, the inn looked dark and uninhabited, with the door bolted and the windows barred. She went round to the back of the house and tapped on the door of the kitchen. It was opened immediately by her aunt, who seemed pale and anxious.

'Your uncle has been asking for you all day,' she said. 'Where have you been? It's nearly five o'clock; you've been gone since morning.'

'I was walking on the moors,' replied Mary. 'I didn't think it mattered. Why should Uncle Joss ask for me?' She was aware of a little pang of nervousness, and she looked towards his bed in the corner of the kitchen. It was empty. 'Where has he gone?' she said. 'Is he better?'

'He wanted to sit in the parlour,' said her aunt. 'He said he was tired of the kitchen. He's been sitting there all the afternoon at the window, looking out for you. You must humour him now, Mary, and speak fair to him, and not go against him. This is the bad time, when he's recovering . . . he will get a little stronger every day, and he'll be very self-willed, violent perhaps. You'll be careful what you say to him, won't you, Mary?'

This was the old Aunt Patience, with nervous hands and twitching mouth, who glanced over her shoulder as she talked. It was pitiable to see her, and Mary caught something of her agitation.

'Why should he want to see me?' she said. 'He never has anything to say to me. What can he want?'

Aunt Patience blinked, and worked her mouth. 'It's only his fancy,' she said. 'He mutters and talks to himself; you mustn't pay any attention to what he says at times like these. He is not really himself. I'll go and tell him you're home.' She went out of the room and along the passage to the parlour.

Mary crossed to the dresser, and poured herself out a glass of water from the pitcher. Her throat was very dry. The glass trembled in her hands and she cursed herself for a fool. She had been bold enough on the moors just now, and no sooner was she inside the inn than her courage must leave her, quaking and nervous as a child. Aunt Patience came back into the room.

'He's quiet for the moment,' she whispered. 'He's dozed off in the chair. He may sleep now for the evening. We'll have our supper early, and get it finished. There's some cold pie for you here.'

All hunger had gone from Mary, and she had to force her food. She drank two cups of scalding tea, and then pushed her plate away. Neither of the women spoke. Aunt Patience kept looking towards the door. When they had finished supper they cleared the things away silently. Mary threw some turf on the fire and crouched beside it. The bitter blue smoke rose in the air, stinging her eyes, but no warmth came to her from the smouldering turf.

Outside in the hall the clock struck six o'clock with a sudden whirring note. Mary held her breath as she counted the strokes. They broke upon the silence with deliberation; it seemed an eternity before the last note fell, and echoed through the house and died away. The slow ticking of the clock continued. There was no sound from the parlour, and Mary breathed again. Aunt Patience sat at the table, threading a needle and cotton by candlelight. Her lips were pursed and her forehead puckered to a frown as she bent to her task.

The long evening passed; and still there was no call from the landlord in the parlour. Mary nodded her head, her eyes closed in spite of herself, and in that stupid, heavy state between sleeping and waking she heard her aunt move quietly from her chair and put her work away in the cupboard beside the dresser. In a dream she heard her whisper in her ear, 'I'm going to bed. Your uncle won't wake now; he must have settled for the night. I shan't disturb him.' Mary murmured something in reply, and half consciously she heard the light patter of footsteps in the passage outside, and the creaking of the stairs.

On the landing above, a door closed softly. Mary felt the lethargy of sleep steal upon her, and her head sank lower into her hands. The slow ticking of the clock made a pattern in her mind, like footsteps dragging on a high road . . . one . . . two . . . one . . . two . . . they followed one another; she was on the moors beside the running brook and the burden that she carried was heavy, too heavy to bear. If she could lay it aside for a little while, and rest herself beside the bank, and sleep . . .

It was cold, though, much too cold. Her foot was wringing wet from the water. She must pull herself higher up the bank, out of the way . . . The fire was out; there was no more fire . . . Mary opened her eyes, and saw that she was lying on the floor beside the white ashes of the fire. The kitchen was very cold, and the light was dim. The candle had burnt low. She yawned and shivered, and stretched her stiff arms. When she lifted her eyes she saw the door of the kitchen open very slowly, little by little, an inch at a time.

Mary sat without moving, her hands on the cold floor. She waited, and nothing happened. The door moved again, and then was flung wide, crashing against the wall behind it. Joss Merlyn stood on the threshold of the room, his arms outstretched, rocking on his two feet.

At first she thought he had not noticed her; his eyes were fixed on the wall in front of him, and he stood still where he was, without venturing further into the room. She crouched low, her head beneath the level of the table, hearing nothing but the steady thump of her heart. Slowly he turned in her direction, and stared at her a moment or two without speaking. When his voice came, it was strained and hoarse, hardly above a whisper. 'Who's there?' he said. 'What are you doing? Why don't you speak.' His face was a grey mask, drained of its usual colour. His bloodshot eyes fastened themselves upon her without recognition. Mary did not move.

'Put away that knife,' he whispered. 'Put it away, I tell you.'

She stretched her hand along the floor and touched the leg of a chair with the tips of her fingers. She could not hold on to it unless she moved. It was just out of reach. She waited, holding her breath. He stepped forward into the room, his head bent, his two hands feeling the air, and he crept slowly along the floor towards her.

Mary watched his hands until they were within a yard of her and she could feel his breath on her cheek.

'Uncle Joss,' she said softly. 'Uncle Joss ...'

He crouched where he was, staring down at her, and then he leant forward and touched her hair and her lips. 'Mary,' he said, 'is it you, Mary? Why don't you speak to me? Where have they gone? Have you seen them?'

'You've made a mistake, Uncle Joss,' she said; 'there is no one here, only myself. Aunt Patience is upstairs. Are you ill? Can I help you?'

He looked about him in the half-light, searching the corners of the room. 'They can't scare me,' he whispered. 'Dead men don't harm the living. They're blotted out, like a candle ... That's it, isn't it, Mary?'

She nodded, watching his eyes. He pulled himself to a chair and sat down, his hands outstretched on the table. He sighed heavily, and passed his tongue over his lips. 'It's dreams,' he said; 'all dreams. The faces stand out like live things in the darkness, and I wake with the sweat pouring down my back. I'm thirsty, Mary; here's the key; go into the bar and fetch me some brandy.' He fumbled in his pocket and produced a bunch of keys. She took them from him, her hand trembling, and slipped out of the room into the passage. She hesitated for a moment outside, wondering whether she should creep upstairs at once to her room, and lock the door, and leave him to rave alone in the kitchen. She began to tiptoe along the passage to the hall.

Suddenly he shouted to her from the kitchen. 'Where are you going? I told you to fetch the brandy from the bar.' She heard the chair scrape as he pushed it away from the table. She was too late. She opened the door of the bar, and felt in the cupboard amongst the bottles. When she returned to the kitchen he was sprawling at the table, his head in his hands. At first she thought he was asleep again, but at the sound of her footsteps he lifted his head, and stretched his arms, and leant back in the chair. She put the bottle and a glass on the table in front of him. He filled the glass half full, and held it between his two hands, watching her all the while over the rim of it.

'You're a good girl,' he said. 'I'm fond of you, Mary; you've got sense, and you've got pluck; you'd make a good companion to a man. They ought to have made you a boy.' He rolled the brandy around on his tongue, smiling foolishly, and then he winked at her, and pointed his finger.

'They pay gold for this up-country,' he said; 'the best that money can buy. King George himself hasn't better brandy than this in his cellar. And what do I pay? Not one damned bloody sixpence. We drink free at Jamaica Inn.'

He laughed and put out his tongue. 'It's a hard game, Mary, but it's a man's game, for all that. I've risked my neck ten, twenty times. I've had the fellows thundering at my heels, with a pistol-shot whistling through my hair. They can't catch me, Mary; I'm too cunning; I've been at the game too long. Before we came here I was at Padstow, working from the shore. We ran a lugger once a fortnight with the spring tides. There were five of us in it, besides myself. But there's no money working in a small way; you've got to do it big, and you've got to take your orders. There's over a hundred of us now, working inland to the border from the coast. By God, I've seen blood in my time, Mary, and I've seen men killed a score of times, but this game beats all of it – it's running side by side with death.'

He beckoned her to his side, winking again, glancing first over his shoulder to the door. 'Here,' he whispered, 'come close, down here by my side, where I can talk to you. You've got guts in you, I can see that; you're not scared like your aunt. We ought to be partners, you and I.' He seized hold of Mary's arm, and pulled her on the floor beside his chair. 'It's this cursed drink that makes a fool of me,' he said. 'I'm as weak as a rat when it has hold of me, you can see that. And I have dreams, nightmares; I see things that never scare me when I'm sober. Damn it, Mary, I've killed men with my own hands, trampled them under water, beaten them with rocks and stones; and I've never thought no more about it; I've slept in my bed like a child. But when I'm drunk I see them in my dreams; I see their white-green faces staring at me, with their eyes eaten by fish; and some of them are torn, with the flesh hanging on their bones in ribbons, and some of them have seaweed in their hair. . . . There was a woman once, Mary; she was clinging to a raft, and she had a child in her arms; her hair was streaming down her back. The ship was close in on the rocks, you see, and the sea was as flat as your hand; they were all coming in alive, the whole bunch of 'em. Why, the water in places didn't come above your waist. She cried out to me to help her, Mary, and I smashed her face in with a stone; she fell back, her hands beating the raft. She let go of the child and I hit her again; I watched them drown in four feet of water. We were scared then; we were afraid some of them would reach the shore. . . . For the first time we hadn't reckoned on the tide. In half an hour they'd be walking dry-shod on the sand. We had to pelt at 'em all with stones, Mary; we had to break their arms and legs; and they drowned there in front of us, like the woman and her child, with the water not up to their shoulders – they drowned because we smashed them with rocks and stones; they drowned because they couldn't stand. . . .'

His face was close to Mary, his red-flecked eyes staring into hers, and his breath on her cheek. 'Did you never hear of wreckers before?' he whispered.

Outside in the passage the clock struck one o'clock, and the single note rang in the air like a summons. Neither of them moved. The room was very cold, for the fire had sunk away to nothing and a little current of air blew in from the open door. The yellow flame of the candle bowed and flickered. He reached out to her and took her hand; it lay limp in his, like a dead hand. Perhaps he saw something of the frozen horror in her face, for he let her go, and turned away his eyes. He stared straight before him at the empty glass, and he began to drum with his fingers on the table. Crouched on the ground beside him, Mary watched a fly crawl across his hand. She watched it pass through the short black hairs, and over the thick veins to the knuckles, and it ran to the tips of the long slim fingers. She remembered the swift and sudden grace of those fingers when they cut bread for her that first evening, and how if they chose they could be delicate and light; she watched them drumming now on the table, and in her fancy she saw them curl round a block of jagged stone, and fasten upon it; she saw the stone fly through the air. . . .

Once more he turned to her, his whisper hoarse, and he jerked his head towards the ticking of the clock. 'The sound of it rings in my head sometimes,' he said, 'and when it struck one just now, it was like the tolling of a bell-buoy in a bay. I've heard it come travelling down the air on the westerly wind: one-two-one-two, backwards and forwards the clapper goes against the bell, as though it tolled for dead men. I've heard it in my dreams. I heard it tonight. A mournful, weary sound, Mary, is a bell-buoy out in the bay. It rubs on your nerves and you want to scream. When you work on the coast you have to pull out to them in a boat and muffle them; wrap the tongue in flannel. That deadens them. There's silence then. Maybe it's a misty night, with patches of white fog on the water, and outside the bay there'll be a ship casting for scent like a hound. She listens to the buoy, and no sound comes to her. And she comes in then, driving through the fog – she comes straight in to us who are waiting for her, Mary – and we see her shudder suddenly, and strike, and then the surf has her.'

He reached for the bottle of brandy, and let a little liquid trickle slowly into the glass. He smelt it, and rolled it on his tongue.

'Have you ever seen flies caught in a jar of treacle?' he said. 'I've seen men like that; stuck in the rigging like a swarm of flies. They cling there for safety, shouting in terror at the sight of the surf. Just like flies they are, spread out on the yards, little black dots of men. I've seen the ship break up beneath them, and the masts and yards snap like thread, and there they'll be flung into the sea, to swim for their lives. But when they reach the shore they're dead men, Mary.'

He wiped his mouth on the back of his hand, and stared at her. 'Dead men tell no tales, Mary,' he said.

His face nodded at her, and narrowed suddenly, and was blotted out. No longer was she kneeling on the kitchen floor, her hands gripping the table; she was a child again, running beside her father on the cliffs beyond St.

Kevern. He swung her up on his shoulder, and there were other men running with them, who shouted and cried. Somebody pointed to the distant sea, and, clinging to her father's head, she saw a great white ship like a bird rolling helplessly in the trough of the sea, her masts broken short and her sails trailing in the water beside her. 'What are they doing?' asked the child that had been herself; and nobody answered her; they stood where they were, staring in horror at the ship that rolled and plunged. 'God have mercy upon them,' said her father; and the child Mary began to cry, calling for her mother, who came at once from amongst the crowd and took her in her arms, and walked away with her out of sight of the sea. There all memory snapped, and vanished, and there was no ending to the story; but when she grew to understanding, and was no longer a child, her mother would talk of the day they had gone to St. Kevern, when a great barque had sunk with all on board, her back broken on the dreaded Manacles. Mary shivered and sighed, and once more her uncle's face loomed before her in its frame of matted hair, and she was kneeling beside him again in the kitchen at Jamaica Inn. She felt deadly sick, and her hands and feet were icy-cold. She longed only to stumble to her bed and bury her head in her hands, pulling the blanket and pillow over her for greater darkness. Perhaps if she pressed her hands against her eyes she would blot out his face, and the pictures he had painted for her. Perhaps if she thrust her fingers in her ears she would muffle the sound of his voice, and the thunder of the surf upon the shore. Here she could see the pale faces of drowned men, their arms above their heads; she could hear the scream of terror, and the cries; she could hear the mournful clamour of the bell-buoy as it swayed backwards and forwards in the sea. Mary shivered again.

She looked up at her uncle and she saw that he had sloped forward in his chair, and his head had fallen on his chest. His mouth was wide open, and he snorted and spluttered as he slept. His long dark lashes swept his cheeks like a fringe. His arms rested on the table before him, and his hands were clasped as though in prayer.

Chapter Nine

On Christmas Eve the sky was overcast and threatened rain. It had turned mild, too, in the night, and the mud in the yard was churned where the cows had trodden. The walls of Mary's bedroom felt damp to her hand, and there was a great yellow patch in one corner caused by the shrinking plaster.

Mary leant out of the window, and the soft wet wind blew upon her face. In an hour's time Jem Merlyn would be waiting for her on the moor, to take her to Launceston fair. Whether she met him or not depended upon herself, and she could not make up her mind. She had grown older in four days, and the face that looked back at her from the spotted, cracked mirror was drawn and tired.

There were dark rings beneath her eyes, and little hollows in her cheeks. Sleep came late to her at night, and she had no appetite for food. For the first time in her life she saw a resemblance between herself and her Aunt Patience. They had the same pucker of the forehead, and the same mouth. If she pursed up her lips and worked them, biting the edges, it might be Aunt Patience who stood there, with the lank brown hair framing her face. The trick was an easy one to catch, as was the nervous twisting of the hands, and Mary turned away from the tell-tale mirror and began to pace up and down her cramped room. During the past few days she had kept as much as possible to the privacy of her own room, excusing herself on the score of a chill. Mary could not trust herself to speak to her aunt at present – not for any length of time. Her eyes would have betrayed her. They would look at one another with the same dumb horror, the same hidden anguish; and Aunt Patience would have understood. They shared a secret now, a secret that must never be spoken between them. Mary wondered how many years Aunt Patience had kept that knowledge to herself in an agony of silence. No one would ever know how greatly she had suffered. Wherever she should go in the future, the pain of that knowledge would go with her. It could never leave her alone. At last Mary was able to understand the pale, twitching face, the hands that plucked at the dress, the wide, staring eyes. The evidence screamed at her now that she knew.

At first she had felt sick, deadly sick; she had lain on her bed that night, praying for the mercy of sleep, and it had been denied her. There were faces in the darkness that she had not known; the worn and weary faces of drowned people. There was a child with broken wrists; and a woman whose long wet hair clung to her face; and the screaming, frightened faces of men who had never learnt to swim. Sometimes it seemed to her that her own mother and father were amongst them; they looked up at her with wide eyes and pallid lips and they stretched out their hands. Perhaps this was what Aunt Patience suffered, alone in her room at night; the faces came to her too, and pleaded, and she pushed them away. She would not give them release. In her own way Aunt Patience was a murderer too. She had killed them by her silence. Her guilt was as great as Joss Merlyn's himself, for she was a woman and he was a monster. He was bound to her flesh and she let him remain.

Now that it was the third day, and the first horror had passed, Mary felt indifferent, rather old, and very tired. Most of the feeling had gone from her. It seemed to her that she had always known now; that at the back of her mind she had been prepared. The first sight of Joss Merlyn, standing beneath the porch with a lantern in his hands, had been a warning; while the sound of the coach rattling away down the high road and out of her hearing had rung like a farewell.

In the old days at Helford, there had been whispers of these things: little snatches of gossip overheard in the village lanes, a fragment of story, a denial, a shake of the head, but men did not talk much, and the stories were discouraged. Twenty, fifty years ago, perhaps, when her father had been young; but not now, not in the light of the new century. Once more she saw her uncle's face pressed close to hers, and she heard his whisper in her ear, 'Did you never hear of wreckers before?' These were words that she had never heard breathed, but Aunt Patience had lived amongst them for ten years. . . . Mary did not consider her uncle any more. She had lost her fear of him. There was only loathing left in her heart, loathing and disgust. He had lost all hold on humanity. He was a beast that walked by night. Now that she had seen him drunk, and she knew him for what he was, he could not frighten her. Neither he, nor the rest of his company. They were things of evil, rotting the countryside, and she would never rest until they were trodden underfoot, and cleared, and blotted out. Sentiment would not save them again.

There remained Aunt Patience – and Jem Merlyn. He broke into her thoughts against her will, and she did not want him. There was enough on her mind without reckoning with Jem. He was too like his brother. His eyes, and his mouth, and his smile. That was the danger of it. She could see her uncle in his walk, in the turn of his head; and she knew why Aunt Patience had made a fool of herself ten years ago. It would be easy enough to fall in love with Jem Merlyn. Men had not counted for much in her life up to the present; there had been too much to do on the farm at Helford to worry about them. There had been lads who had smiled at her in church and gone with her to picnics harvest-time; once a neighbour had kissed her behind a hayrick after a glass of cider. It was all very foolish, and she had avoided the man ever since; a harmless enough fellow too, who forgot the incident five minutes later. Anyway, she would never marry; it was a long while since she had decided that. She would save money in some way, and do a man's work on a farm. Once she got away from Jamaica Inn and could put it behind her, and make some sort of a home for Aunt Patience, she was not likely to have time on her hands to think of men. And there, in spite of herself, came Jem's face again, with the growth of beard like a tramp, and his dirty shirt, and his bold offensive stare. He lacked tenderness; he was rude; and he had more than a streak of cruelty in him; he was a thief and a liar. He stood for everything she feared and hated and despised; but she knew she could love him. Nature cared nothing for prejudice. Men and women were like the animals on the farm at Helford, she supposed; there was a common law of attraction for all living things, some similarity of skin or touch, and they would go to one another. This was no choice made with the mind. Animals did not reason, neither did the birds in the air. Mary was no hypocrite; she was bred to the soil, and she had lived too long with birds and beasts, had watched them mate, and bear their young, and die. There was precious little romance in nature, and she would not look for it in her own life. She had seen the girls at home walk with the village lads; and there would be a holding of hands, and blushing and confusion, and long-drawn sighs, and a gazing at the moonlight on the water. Mary would see them wander down the grass lane at the back of the farm – Lovers' Lane they called it, though the older men had a better word for it than that – and the lad would have his arm round the waist of his girl, and she with her head on his shoulder. They would look at the stars and the moon, or the flaming sunset if it was summer weather, and Mary, coming out of the cow-shed, wiped the sweat from her face with dripping hands, and thought of the new-born calf she had left beside its mother. She looked after the departing couple, and smiled, and shrugged her shoulders, and going into the kitchen, she told her mother there would be a wedding in Helford before the month was past. And then the bells would ring, and the cake be cut, and the lad in his Sunday clothes would stand on the steps of the church with shining face and shuffling feet with his bride beside him dressed in muslin, her straight hair curled for the occasion; but before the year was out the moon and the stars could shine all night for all they cared, when the lad came home at evening tired from his work in the fields, and calling sharply that his supper was burnt, not fit for a dog, while the girl snapped back at him from the bedroom overhead, her figure sagging and her curls gone, pacing backward and forward with a bundle in her arms that mewed like a cat and would not sleep. There was no talk then of the moonlight on the water. No, Mary had no illusions about romance. Falling in love was a pretty name for it, that was all. Jem Merlyn was a man, and she was a woman, and whether it was his hands or his skin or his smile she did not know, but something inside her responded to him, and the very thought of him was an irritant and a stimulant at the same time. It nagged at her and would not let her be. She knew she would have to see him again.

Once more she looked up at the grey sky and the low-flying clouds. If she were going to Launceston, then it was time to make ready and be away. There would be no excuses to make; she had grown hard in the last four days. Aunt Patience could think what she liked. If she had any intuition, she must guess that Mary did not want to see her. And she would look at her husband, with his bloodshot eyes and his shaking hands, and she would understand. Once more, perhaps for the last time, the drink had loosened his tongue. His secret was spilt; and Mary held his future in her hands. She had not yet determined what use to make of her knowledge, but she would not save him again. To-day she would go to Launceston with Jem Merlyn, and this time it was he who would answer her questions; he would show some humility too when he realised she was no longer afraid of them, but could destroy them when she chose. And to-morrow – well, to-morrow could take care of itself. There was always Francis Davey and his promise; there would be peace and shelter for her at the house in Altarnun.

This was a strange Christmas-tide, she pondered, as she strode across the East Moor with Hawk's Tor as her guide, and the hills rolling away from her on either side. Last year she had knelt beside her mother in church, and prayed that health and strength and courage should be given to them both. She had prayed for peace of mind, and security; she had asked that her mother might be spared to her long, and that the farm should prosper. For answer came sickness, and poverty, and death. She was alone now, caught in a mesh of brutality and crime, living beneath a roof she loathed, amongst people she despised; and she was walking out across a barren, friendless moor to meet a horse-thief and a murderer of men. She would offer no prayers to God this Christmas.

Mary waited on the high ground above Rushyford, and in the distance she saw the little cavalcade approach her: the pony, the jingle, and two horses tethered behind. The driver raised his whip in a signal of welcome. Mary felt the colour flame into her face and drain away. This weakness was a thing of torment to her, and she longed for it to be tangible and alive so that she could tear it from her and trample it underfoot. She thrust her hands into her shawl and waited, her forehead puckered in a frown. He whistled as he approached her, and flung a small package at her feet. 'A happy Christmas to you,' he said. 'I had a silver piece in my pocket yesterday and it burnt a hole. There's a new handkerchief for your head.'

She had meant to be curt and silent on meeting him, but this introduction made it difficult for her. 'That's very kind of you,' she said. 'I'm afraid you've wasted your money all the same.'

'That doesn't worry me, I'm used to it,' he told her, and he looked her up and down in the cool offensive way of his, and whistled a tuneless song. 'You were early here,' he said. 'Were you afraid I'd be going without you?'

She climbed into the cart beside him and gathered the reins in her hands. 'I like to have the feel of them again,' she said, ignoring his remark. 'Mother and I, we would drive into Helston once a week on market-days. It all seems very long ago. I have a pain in my heart when I think of it, and how we used to laugh together, even when times were bad. You wouldn't understand that, of course. You've never cared for anything but yourself.'

He folded his arms and watched her handle the reins.

'That pony would cross the moor blindfold,' he told her. 'Give him his head, can't you? He's never stumbled in his life. That's better. He's taking charge of you, remember, and you can leave him to it. What were you saying?'

Mary held the rein lightly in her hands, and looked at the track ahead of her. 'Nothing very much,' she answered. 'In a way I was talking to myself. So you're going to sell two ponies at the fair, then?'

'Double profit, Mary Yellan, and you shall have a new dress if you help me. Don't smile and shrug your shoulder. I hate ingratitude. What's the matter with you, to-day? Your colour is gone and you've no light in your eyes. Are you feeling sick, or have you a pain in your belly?'

'I've not been out of the house since I saw you last,' she said. 'I stayed up in my room with my thoughts. They didn't make cheerful company. I'm a deal older than I was four days ago.'

'I'm sorry you've lost your looks,' he went on. 'I fancied jogging into Launceston with a pretty girl beside me, and fellows looking up as we passed and winking. You're drab to-day. Don't lie to me, Mary. I'm not as blind as you think. What's happened at Jamaica Inn?'

'Nothing's happened,' she said. 'My aunt patters about in the kitchen, and my uncle sits at the table with his head in his hands and a bottle of brandy in front of him. It's only myself that has changed.'

'You've had no more visitors, have you?'

'None that I know of. Nobody's crossed the yard.'

'Your mouth is set very firm, and there are smudges under your eyes. You're tired. I've seen a woman look like that before, but there was a reason for it. Her husband came back to her at Plymouth after four years at sea. You can't make that excuse. Have you been thinking about me by any chance?'

'Yes, I thought about you once,' she said. 'I wondered who would hang first, you or your brother. There's little in it, from what I can see.'

'If Joss hangs, it will be his own fault,' said Jem. 'If ever a man puts a rope round his own neck, he does. He goes three-quarters of the way to meet trouble. When it does get him it will serve him right, and there'll be no brandy-bottle to save him then. He'll swing sober.'

They jogged along in silence, Jem playing with the thong of the whip, and Mary aware of his hands beside her. She glanced down at them out of the tail of her eye, and she saw they were long and slim; they had the same strength, the same grace, as his brother's. These attracted her; the other repelled her. She realised for the first time that aversion and attraction ran side by side; that the boundary-line was thin between them. The thought was an unpleasant one, and she shrank from it. Supposing this had been Joss beside her, ten, twenty years ago? She shuttered the comparison at the back of her mind, fearing the picture it conjured. She knew now why she hated her uncle.

His voice broke in upon her thoughts. 'What are you looking at?' he said. She lifted her eyes to the scene in front of her. 'I happened to notice your hands,' she said briefly; 'they are like your brother's. How far do we go across the moor? Isn't that the high road winding away yonder?'

'We strike it lower down, and miss two or three miles of it. So you notice a man's hands, do you? I should never have believed it of you. You're a woman after all, then, and not a half-fledged farm-boy. Are you going to tell me why you've sat in your room for four days without speaking, or do you want me to guess? Women love to be mysterious.'

'There's no mystery in it. You asked me last time we met if I knew why my aunt looked like a living ghost. Those were your words, weren't they? Well, I know now, that's all.'

Jem watched her with curious eyes, and then he whistled again.

'Drink's a funny thing,' he said, after a moment or two. 'I got drunk once, in Amsterdam, the time I ran away to sea. I remember hearing a church clock strike half past nine in the evening, and I was sitting on the floor with my arms round a pretty red-haired girl. The next thing I knew, it was seven in the following morning, and I was lying on my back in the gutter, without any boots or breeches. I often wonder what I did during those ten hours. I've thought and thought, but I'm damned if I can remember.'

'That's very fortunate for you,' said Mary. 'Your brother is not so lucky. When he gets drunk he finds his memory instead of losing it.'

The pony slacked in his stride, and she flicked at him with the reins. 'If he's alone he can talk to himself,' she continued; 'it wouldn't have much effect on the walls of Jamaica Inn. This time he was not alone, though. I happened to be there when he woke from his stupor. And he'd been dreaming.'

'And when you heard one of his dreams, you shut yourself up in your bedroom for four days, is that it?' said Jem.

'That's as near as you'll ever get to it,' she replied.

He leant over her suddenly, and took the reins out of her hands.

'You don't look where you're going,' he said. 'I told you this pony never stumbled, but it doesn't mean you have to drive him into a block of granite the size of a cannon-ball. Give him to me.' She sank back in the jingle and allowed him to drive. It was true, she had lacked concentration, and deserved his reproach. The pony picked up his feet and broke into a trot.

'What are you going to do about it?' said Jem.

Mary shrugged her shoulders. 'I haven't made up my mind,' she said. 'I have to consider Aunt Patience. You don't expect me to tell you, do you?'

'Why not? I hold no brief for Joss.'

'You're his brother, and that's enough for me. There are many gaps in the story, and you fit remarkably well into some of them.'

'Do you think I'd waste my time working for my brother?'

'There'd be little waste of time, from what I've seen. There's profit enough and to spare in his business, and no payment in return for his goods. Dead men tell no tales, Jem Merlyn.'

'No, but dead ships do, when they run ashore in a fair wind. It's lights a vessel looks for, Mary, when she's seeking harbour. Have you ever seen a moth flutter to a candle, and singe his wings? A ship will do the same to a false light. It may happen once, twice, three times perhaps; but the fourth time a dead ship stinks to heaven, and the whole country is up in arms, and wants to know the reason why. My brother has lost his own rudder by now, and he's heading for the shore himself.'

'Will you keep him company?'

'I? What have I to do with him? He can run his own head into the noose. I may have helped myself to baccy now and then, and I've run cargoes, but I'll tell you one thing, Mary Yellan, and you can believe it or not, as the mood takes you: I've never killed a man – yet.'

He cracked the whip savagely over his pony's head, and the animal broke into a gallop. 'There's a ford ahead of us, where that hedge runs away to the east. We cross the river, and come out on the Launceston road half a mile on. Then we've seven miles or more before we reach the town. Are you getting tired?'

She shook her head. 'There's bread and cheese in the basket under the seat,' he said, 'and an apple or two, and some pears. You'll be hungry directly. So you think I wreck ships, do you, and stand on the shore and watch men drown? And then put my hands into their pockets afterwards, when they're swollen with water? It makes a pretty picture.'

Whether his anger was pretended or sincere she could not say, but his mouth was set firm, and there was a flaming spot of colour high on his cheekbone.

'You haven't denied it yet, have you?' she said.

He looked down at her with insolence, half contemptuous, half amused, and he laughed as though she were a child without knowledge. She hated him for it, and with a sudden intuition she knew the question that was forming itself, and her hands grew hot.

'If you believe it of me, why do you drive with me to-day to Launceston?' he said.

He was ready to mock her; an evasion or a stammered reply would be a triumph for him, and she steeled herself to gaiety.

'For the sake of your bright eyes, Jem Merlyn,' she said. 'I ride with you for no other reason,' and she met his glance without a tremor.

He laughed at that, and shook his head, and fell to whistling again; and all at once there was ease between them, and a certain boyish familiarity. The very boldness of her words had disarmed him; he suspected nothing of the weakness that lay behind them, and for the moment they were companions without the strain of being man and woman.

They came now to the high road, and the jingle rattled along behind the trotting pony, with the two stolen horses clattering in tow. The rain-clouds swept across the sky, threatening and low, but as yet no drizzle fell from them and the hills that rose in the distance from the moors were clear of mist. Mary thought of Francis Davey in Altarnun away to the left of her, and she wondered what he would say to her when she told him her story. He would not advise a waiting game again. Perhaps he would not thank her if she broke in upon his Christmas; and she pictured the silent vicarage, peaceful and still amongst the cluster of cottages that formed the village, and the tall church tower standing like a guardian above the roofs and chimneys.

There was a haven of rest for her in Altarnun – the very name spelt like a whisper – and the voice of Francis Davey would mean security and a forgetting of trouble. There was a strangeness about him that was disturbing and pleasant. That picture he had painted; and the way he had driven his horse; and how he had waited upon her with deft silence; and strange above all was the grey and sombre stillness of his room that bore no trace of his personality. He was a shadow of a man, and now she was not with him he lacked substance. He had not the male aggression of Jem beside her, he was without flesh and blood. He was no more than two white eyes and a voice in the darkness.

The pony shied suddenly at a gap in the hedge, and Jem's loud curse woke her with a jar from the privacy of her thoughts.

She threw a shot at a venture. 'Are there churches hereabouts?' she asked him. 'I've lived like a heathen these last months, and I hate the feeling.'

'Get out of it, you blasted fool, you!' shouted Jem, stabbing at the pony's mouth. 'Do you want to land us all in the ditch? Churches, do you say? How in the hell should I know about churches? I've only been inside one once, and then I was carried in my mother's arms and I came out Jeremiah.

I can't tell you anything about them. They keep the gold plate locked up, I believe.'

'There's a church at Altarnun, isn't there?' she said. 'That's within walking distance of Jamaica Inn. I might go there to-morrow.'

'Far better eat your Christmas dinner with me. I can't give you turkey, but I can always help myself to a goose from old Farmer Tuckett at North Hill. He's getting so blind he'd never know that she was missing.'

'Do you know who has the living at Altarnun, Jem Merlyn?'

'No, I do not, Mary Yellan. I've never had any truck with parsons, and I'm never likely to. They're a funny breed of man altogether. There was a parson at North Hill when I was a boy; he was very short-sighted, and they say one Sunday he mislaid the sacramental wine and gave the parish brandy instead. The village heard in a body what was happening, and, do you know, that church was so packed, there was scarcely room to kneel; there were people standing up against the walls, waiting for their turn. The parson couldn't make it out at all; there'd never been so many in his church before, and he got up in the pulpit with his eyes shining behind his spectacles, and he preached a sermon about the flock returning to the fold. Brother Matthew it was told me the story; he went up twice to the altar-rails and the parson never noticed. It was a great day in North Hill. Get out the bread and the cheese, Mary; my belly is sinking away to nothing.'

Mary shook her head at him and sighed. 'Have you ever been serious about anything in your life?' she said. 'Do you respect nothing and nobody?'

'I respect my inside,' he told her, 'and it's calling out for food. There's the box, under my feet. You can eat the apple, if you're feeling religious. There's an apple comes in the Bible, I know that much.'

It was a hilarious and rather heated cavalcade that clattered into Launceston at half past two in the afternoon. Mary had thrown trouble and responsibility to the winds, and, in spite of her firm resolution of the early morning, she had melted to Jem's mood and given herself to gaiety.

Away from the shadow of Jamaica Inn her natural youth and her spirits returned, and her companion noticed this in a flash and played upon them.

She laughed because she must, and because he made her; and there was an infection in the air caught from the sound and bustle of the town, a sense of excitement and well-being; a sense of Christmas. The streets were thronged with people, and the little shops were gay. Carriages, and carts, and coaches too, were huddled together in the cobbled square. There was colour, and life, and movement; the cheerful crowd jostled one another before the market stalls, turkeys and geese scratched at the wooden barrier that penned them, and a woman in a green cloak held apples above her head and smiled, the apples shining and red like her cheeks. The scene was familiar and dear; Helston had been like this, year after year at Christmas-time; but there was a brighter, more abandoned spirit about Launceston; the crowd was greater and the voices mixed. There was space here, and a certain sophistication; Devonshire and England were across the river. Farmers from the next county rubbed shoulders with countrywomen from East Cornwall; and there were shopkeepers, and pastrycooks, and little apprentice-boys who pushed in and out amongst the crowd with hot pasties and sausage-meat on trays. A lady in a feathered hat and a blue velvet cape stepped down from her coach and went into the warmth and light of the hospitable White Hart, followed by a gentleman in a padded greatcoat of powder-grey. He lifted his eyeglass to his eyes and strutted after her for all the world like a turkey-cock himself.

This was a gay and happy world to Mary. The town was set on the bosom of a hill, with a castle framed in the centre, like a tale from old history. There were trees clustered here, and sloping fields, and water gleamed in the valley below. The moors were remote; they stretched away out of sight behind the town, and were forgotten. Launceston had reality; these people were alive. Christmas came into its own again in the town and had a place amongst the cobbled streets, the laughing jostling crowd, and the watery sun struggled from his hiding-place behind the grey banked clouds to join festivity. Mary wore the handkerchief Jem had given her. She even unbent so far as to permit him to tie the ends under her chin. They had stabled the pony and jingle at the top of the town, and now Jem pushed his way through the crowd, leading his two stolen horses, Mary following at his heels. He led the way with confidence, making straight for the main square, where the whole of Launceston gathered, and the booths and tents of the Christmas fair stood end to end. There was a place roped off from the fair for the buying and selling of livestock, and the ring was surrounded by farmers and countrymen, gentlemen too, and dealers from Devon and beyond. Mary's heart beat faster as they approached the ring; supposing there was someone from North Hill here, or a farmer from a neighbouring village, surely they would recognise the horses? Jem wore his hat at the back of his head, and he whistled. He looked back at her once, and winked his eye. The crowd parted and made way for him. Mary stood on the outskirts, behind a fat market-woman with a basket, and she saw Jem take his place amongst a group of men with ponies, and he nodded to one or two of them, and ran his eye over their ponies, bending as he did so to a flare to light his pipe. He looked cool and unperturbed. Presently a flashy-looking fellow with a square hat and cream breeches thrust his way through the crowd and crossed over to the horses. His voice was loud and important, and he kept hitting his boot with a crop, and then pointing to the ponies. From his tone, and his air of authority, Mary judged him to be a dealer. Soon he was joined by a little lynx-eyed man in a black coat, who now and again jogged his elbow and whispered in his ear.

Mary saw him stare hard at the black pony that had belonged to Squire Bassat; he went up to him, and bent down and felt his legs. Then he whispered something in the ear of the loud-voiced man. Mary watched him nervously.

'Where did you get this pony?' said the dealer, tapping Jem on the shoulder. 'He was never bred on the moors, not with that head and shoulders.'

'He was foaled at Callington four years ago,' said Jem carelessly, his pipe in the corner of his mouth. 'I bought him as a yearling from old Tim Bray; you remember Tim? He sold up last year and went into Dorset. Tim always told me I'd get my money back on this pony. The dam was Irish bred, and won prizes for him up-country. Have a look at him, won't you? But he's not going cheap, I'll tell you that.'

He puffed at his pipe, while the two men went over the pony carefully. The time seemed endless before they straightened themselves and stood back. 'Had any trouble with his skin?' said the lynx-eyed man. 'It feels very coarse on the surface, and sharp like bristles. There's a taint about him, too, I don't like. You haven't been doping him, have you?'

'There's nothing ailing with that pony,' replied Jem. 'The other one there, he fell away to nothing in the summer, but I've brought him back all right. I'd do better to keep him till the spring now, I believe, but he's costing me money. No, this black pony here, you can't fault him. I'll be frank with you over one thing, and it's only fair to admit it. Old Tim Bray never knew the mare was in foal – he was in Plymouth at the time, and his boy was looking after her – and when he found out he gave the boy a thrashing, but of course it was too late. He had to make the best of a bad job. It's my opinion the sire was a grey; look at the short hair there, close to the skin – that's grey, isn't it? Tim just missed a good bargain with this pony. Look at those shoulders; there's breeding for you. I tell you what, I'll take eighteen guineas for him.'

The lynx-eyed man shook his head, but the dealer hesitated.

'Make it fifteen and we might do business,' he suggested.

'No, eighteen guineas is my sum, and not a penny less,' said Jem.

The two men consulted together and appeared to disagree. Mary heard the word 'fake', and Jem shot a glance at her over the heads of the crowd. A little murmur rose from the group of men beside him. Once more the lynx-eyed man bent and touched the legs of the black pony. 'I'd advise another opinion on this pony,' he said. 'I'm not satisfied about him myself. Where's your mark?'

Jem showed him the narrow slit in the ear and the man examined it closely.

'You're a sharp customer, aren't you?' said Jem. 'Anyone would think I'd stolen the horse. Anything wrong with the mark?'

'No, apparently not. But it's a good thing for you that Tim Bray has gone to Dorset. He'd never own this pony, whatever you like to say. I wouldn't touch him, Stevens, if I were you. You'll find yourself in trouble. Come away, man.'

The loud-voiced dealer looked regretfully at the black pony.

'He's a good-looker,' he said. 'I don't care who bred him, or if his sire was piebald. What makes you so particular, Will?'

Once more the lynx-eyed man plucked at his sleeve and whispered in his ear. The dealer listened, and pulled a face, and then he nodded. 'All right,' he said aloud; 'I've no doubt that you're right. You've got an eye for trouble, haven't you? Perhaps we're better out of it. You can keep your pony,' he added to Jem. 'My partner doesn't fancy him. Take my advice and come down on your price. If you have him for long on your hands you'll be sorry.'

And he elbowed his way through the crowd, with the lynx-eyed man beside him, and they disappeared in the direction of the White Hart. Mary breathed a sigh of relief when she saw the last of them. She could make nothing of Jem's expression; his lips were framed in the inevitable whistle. People came and went; the shaggy moorland ponies were sold for two or three pounds apiece, and their late owners departed satisfied. No one came near the black pony again. He was looked at askance by the crowd. At a quarter to four Jem sold the other horse for six pounds to a cheerful, honest-looking farmer, after a long and very good-humoured argument. The farmer declared he would give five pounds, and Jem stuck out for seven. After twenty minutes' riotous bargaining the sum of six pounds was agreed, and the farmer rode off on the back of his purchase with a grin from ear to ear. Mary began to flag on her feet. Twilight gathered in the market square and the lamps were lit. The town wore an air of mystery. She was thinking of returning to the jingle when she heard a woman's voice behind her, and a high affected laugh. She turned and saw the blue cloak and the plumed hat of the woman who had stepped from the coach earlier in the afternoon. 'Oh, look, James,' she was saying. 'Did you ever see such a delicious pony in your life? He holds his head just like poor Beauty did. The likeness would be quite striking, only this animal of course is black, and has nothing of Beauty's breeding. What a nuisance Roger isn't here. I can't disturb him from his meeting. What do you think of him, James?'

Her companion put up his eyeglass and stared. 'Damn it, Maria,' he drawled, 'I don't know a thing about horses. The pony you lost was a grey, wasn't it? This thing is ebony, positively ebony, my dear. Do you want to buy him?'

The woman gave a little trill of laughter. 'It would be such a good Christmas present for the children,' she said. 'They've plagued poor Roger ever since Beauty disappeared. Ask the price, James, will you?'

The man strutted forward. 'Here, my good fellow,' he called to Jem, 'do you want to sell that black pony of yours?'

Jem shook his head. 'He's promised to a friend,' he said. 'I wouldn't like to go back on my word. Besides, this pony wouldn't carry you. He's been ridden by children.'

'Oh, really. Oh, I see. Oh, thank you. Maria, this fellow says the pony is not for sale.'

'Is he sure? What a shame. I'd set my heart on him. I'll pay him his price, tell him. Ask him again, James.'

Once more the man put up his glass and drawled, 'Look here, my man, this lady has taken a fancy to your pony. She has just lost one, and she wants to replace him. Her children will be most disappointed if they hear about it. Damn your friend, you know. He must wait. What is your price?'

'Twenty-five guineas,' said Jem promptly. 'At least, that's what my friend was going to pay. I'm not anxious to sell him.'

The lady in the plumed hat swept into the ring. 'I'll give you thirty for him,' she said. 'I'm Mrs. Bassat from North Hill, and I want the pony as a Christmas present for my children. Please don't be obstinate. I have half the sum here in my purse, and this gentleman will give you the rest. Mr. Bassat is in Launceston now, and I want the pony to be a surprise to him as well as to my children. My groom shall fetch the pony immediately, and ride him to North Hill before Mr. Bassat leaves the town. Here's the money.'

Jem swept off his hat and bowed low. 'Thank you, madam,' he said. 'I hope Mr. Bassat will be pleased with your bargain. You will find the pony exceedingly safe with children.'

'Oh, I'm certain he will be delighted. Of course the pony is nothing like the one we had stolen. Beauty was a thoroughbred, and worth a great deal of money. This little animal is handsome enough, and will please the children. Come along, James; it's getting quite dark, and I'm chilled to the bone.'

She made her way from the ring towards the coach that waited in the square. The tall footman leapt forward to open the door. 'I've just bought a pony for Master Robert and Master Henry,' she said. 'Will you find Richards and tell him he's to ride it back home? I want it to be a surprise to the squire.' She stepped into the coach, her petticoats fluttering behind her, followed by her companion with the monocle.

Jem looked hastily over his shoulder, and tapped a lad who stood behind him on the arm. 'Here,' he said, 'would you like a five-shilling piece?' The lad nodded, his mouth agape. 'Hang on to this pony, then, and, when the groom comes for him, hand him over for me, will you? I've just had word that my wife has given birth to twins and her life is in danger. I haven't a moment to lose. Here, take the bridle. A happy Christmas to you.'

And he was off in a moment, walking hard across the square, his hands thrust deep in his breeches pockets. Mary followed, a discreet ten paces behind. Her face was scarlet and she kept her eyes on the ground. The laughter bubbled up inside her and she hid her mouth in her shawl. She was near to collapsing when they reached the further side of the square, out of sight of the coach and the group of people, and she stood with her hand to her side, catching her breath. Jem waited for her, his face as grave as a judge.

'Jem Merlyn, you deserve to be hanged,' she said, when she had recovered herself. 'To stand there as you did in the market square and sell that stolen pony back to Mrs. Bassat herself! You have the cheek of the Devil, and the hairs in my head have gone grey from watching you.'

He threw back his head and laughed, and she could not resist him. Their laughter echoed in the street until people turned to look at them, and they too caught the infection, and smiled, and broke into laughter; and Launceston itself seemed to rock in merriment as peal after peal of gaiety echoed in the street, mingling with the bustle and clatter of the fair; and with it all there was shouting, and calling, and a song from somewhere. The torches and the flares cast strange lights on the faces of people, and there was colour, and shadow, and the hum of voices, and a ripple of excitement in the air.

Jem caught at her hand and crumpled the fingers. 'You're glad you came now, aren't you?' he said, and 'Yes,' she said recklessly, and she did not mind.

They plunged into the thick of the fair, with all the warmth and the suggestion of packed humanity about them. Jem bought Mary a crimson shawl, and gold rings for her ears. They sucked oranges beneath a striped tent, and had their fortunes told by a wrinkled gypsy woman. 'Beware of a dark stranger,' she said to Mary, and they looked at one another and laughed again.

'There's blood in your hand, young man,' she told him. 'You'll kill a man one day'; and 'What did I tell you in the jingle this morning?' said Jem. 'I'm innocent as yet. Do you believe it now?' But she shook her head at him; she would not say. Little raindrops splashed on to their faces and they did not care. The wind rose in gusts and billowed the fluttering tents, scattering paper, and ribbons, and silks; and a great striped booth shuddered an instant and crumpled, while apples and oranges rolled in the gutter. Flares streamed in the wind; the rain fell; and people ran hither and thither for shelter, laughing and calling to one another, the rain streaming from them.

Jem dragged Mary under cover of a doorway, his arms around her shoulders, and he turned her face against him, and held her with his hands, and kissed her. 'Beware of the dark stranger,' he said, and he laughed and kissed her again. The night clouds had come up with the rain, and it was black in an instant. The wind blew out the flares, the lanterns glowed dim and yellow, and all the bright colour of the fair was gone. The square was soon deserted; the striped tents and the booths gaped empty and forlorn. The soft rain came in gusts at the open doorway, and Jem stood with his back to the weather, making a screen for Mary. He untied the handkerchief she wore, and played with her hair. She felt the tips of his fingers on her neck, travelling to her shoulders, and she put up her hands and pushed them away. 'I've made a fool of myself long enough for one night, Jem Merlyn,' she said. 'It's time we thought of returning. Let me alone.'

'You don't want to ride in an open jingle in this wind, do you,' he said. 'It's coming from the coast and we'll be blown under on the high ground. We'll have to spend the night together in Launceston.'

'Very likely. Go and fetch the pony, Jem, while this shower lifts for the moment. I'll wait for you here.'

'Don't be a Puritan, Mary. You'll be soaked to the skin on the Bodmin road. Pretend you're in love with me, can't you? You'd stay with me then.'

'Are you talking to me like this because I'm the barmaid at Jamaica Inn?'

'Damn Jamaica Inn! I like the look of you, and the feel of you, and that's enough for any man. It ought to be enough for a woman too.'

'I daresay it is, for some. I don't happen to be made that way.'

'Do they make you different from other women, then, down on Helford river? Stay here with me to-night, Mary, and we can find out. You'd be like the rest by the time morning came, I'd take my oath on that.'

'I haven't a doubt of it. That's why I'd rather risk a soaking in the jingle.'

'God, you're as hard as flint, Mary Yellan. You'll be sorry for it when you're alone again.'

'Better be sorry then than later.'

'If I kissed you again would you change your mind?'

'I would not.'

'I don't wonder my brother took to his bed and his bottle for a week, with you in the house. Did you sing psalms to him?'

'I daresay I did.'

'I've never known a woman so perverse. I'll buy a ring for you if it would make you feel respectable. It's not often I have money enough in my pocket to make the offer.'

'How many wives do you belong to have?'

'Six or seven scattered over Cornwall. I don't count the ones across the Tamar.'

'That's a good number for one man. I'd wait awhile before I took on an eighth, if I were you.'

You're sharp, aren't you? You look like a monkey in that shawl of yours, with your bright eyes. All right, I'll fetch the jingle, and take you home to your aunt, but I'll kiss you first, whether you like it or not.'

He took her face in his hands. '"One for sorrow, two for joy,"' he said. 'I'll give you the rest when you're in a more yielding frame of mind. It wouldn't do to finish the rhyme to-night. Stay where you're to; I'll not be long.'

He bowed his head against the rain and strode across the street. She saw him disappear behind a line of stalls, and so around the corner.

She leant back once more within the shelter of the door. It would be desolate enough on the high road, she knew that; this was a real driving rain, with a venomous wind behind it and there would be little mercy from the moors. It required a certain amount of courage to stand those eleven miles in an open jingle. The thought of staying in Launceston with Jem Merlyn made her heart beat faster perhaps, and it was exciting to think upon it now he was gone and he could not see her face, but for all that she would not lose her head to please him. Once she departed from the line of conduct she had laid down for herself, there would be no returning. There would be no privacy of mind, no independence. She had given too much away as it was, and she would never be entirely free of him again. This weakness would be a drag on her and make the four walls of Jamaica Inn more hateful than they were already. It was better to bear solitude alone. Now the silence of the moors would be a torment because of his presence four miles distant from her. Mary wrapped her shawl around her and folded her arms. She wished that women were not the frail things of straw she believed them to be; then she could stay this night with Jem Merlyn and forget herself as he could forget, and both of them part with a laugh and a shrug of the shoulder in the morning. But she was a woman, and it was impossible. A few kisses had made a fool of her already. She thought of Aunt Patience, trailing like a ghost in the shadow of her master, and she shuddered. That would be Mary Yellan too, but for the grace of God and her own strength of will. A gust of wind tore at her skirt and another shower of rain blew in at the open doorway. It was colder now. Puddles ran on the cobbled stones, and the lights and the people had vanished. Launceston had lost its glamour. It would be a bleak and cheerless Christmas Day to-morrow.

Mary waited, stamping her feet and blowing upon her hands. Jem was taking his own time to fetch the jingle. He was annoyed with her, no doubt, for refusing to stay, and leaving her to become wet and chilled in the open doorway was to be his method of punishment. The long minutes passed and still he did not come. If this was his system of revenge, the plan was without humour and lacked originality. Somewhere a clock struck eight. He had been gone over half an hour, and the place where the pony and jingle were stabled was only five minutes away. Mary was dispirited and tired. She had been on her legs since the early afternoon, and now that the high pitch of excitement had died away she wanted to rest. It would be difficult to recapture the careless, irresponsible mood of the last few hours. Jem had taken his gaiety with him.

At last Mary could stand it no longer, and she set off up the hill in search of him. The long street was deserted, save for a few stragglers, who hung about in the doubtful shelter of doorways as she had done. The rain was pitiless, and the wind came in gusts. There was nothing left now of the Christmas spirit.

In a few minutes she came to the stable where they had left the pony and jingle in the afternoon. The door was locked, and, peering through a crack, she saw that the shed was empty. Jem must have gone, then. She knocked at the little shop next door, in a fever of impatience, and after a while it was opened by the fellow who had admitted them to the shed earlier in the day.

He looked annoyed at being disturbed from the comfort of his fire, and at first he did not recognise her, wild as she was in her wet shawl.

'What do you want?' he said. 'We don't give food to strangers here.'

'I haven't come for food,' Mary replied. 'I'm looking for my companion. We came here together with a pony and jingle, if you remember. I see the stable is empty. Have you seen him?'

The man muttered an apology. 'You'll excuse me, I'm sure. Your friend has been gone twenty minutes or more. He seemed in a great hurry, and there was another man with him. I wouldn't be sure, but he looked like one of the servants from the White Hart. They turned back in that direction at any rate.'

'He left no message, I suppose?'

'No, I'm sorry he did not. Maybe you'll find him at the White Hart. Do you know where it is?'

'Yes, thank you. I'll try there. Good night.'

The man shut the door in her face, glad enough to be rid of her, and Mary retraced her steps in the direction of the town. What should Jem want with one of the servants from the White Hart? The man must have been mistaken. There was nothing for it but to find out the truth for herself. Once more she came to the cobbled square. The White Hart looked hospitable enough, with its lighted windows, but there was no sign of the pony and jingle. Mary's heart sank. Surely Jem had not taken the road without her? She hesitated for a moment, and then she went up to the door and passed inside. The hall seemed to be full of gentlemen, talking and laughing, and once again her country clothes and wet hair caused consternation, for a servant went up to her at once and bade her be gone. 'I've come in search of a Mr. Jem Merlyn,' said Mary firmly. 'He came here with a pony and jingle, and was seen with one of your servants. I'm sorry to trouble you, but I'm anxious to find him. Will you please make some enquiry?'

The man went off with an ill grace, while Mary waited by the entrance, turning her back on the little group of men who stood by the fire and stared. Amongst them she recognised the dealer and the little lynx-eyed man.

She was aware of a sudden sense of foreboding. In a few moments the servant returned with a tray of glasses, which he distributed amongst the company by the fire, and later he appeared again with cake and ham. He took no more notice of Mary, and only when she called to him for the third time did he come towards her. 'I'm sorry,' he said; 'we've plenty here to-night without wasting our time over people from the fair. There's no man here by the name of Merlyn. I've asked outside, and nobody had heard of him.'

Mary turned at once for the door, but the lynx-eyed man was there before her. 'If it's the dark gypsy fellow who tried to sell my partner a pony this afternoon, I can tell you about him,' he said, smiling wide, and showing a row of broken teeth. Laughter broke out from the group by the fire.

She looked from one to the other. 'What have you to say?' she said.

'He was in the company of a gentleman barely ten minutes ago,' returned the lynx-eyed man, still smiling, and looking her up and down, 'and with the help of some of us he was persuaded to enter a carriage that was waiting at the door. He was inclined to resist us at first, but a look from the gentleman appeared to decide him. No doubt you know what became of the black pony? The price he was asking was undoubtedly high.'

His remark brought forth a fresh burst of laughter from the group by the fire. Mary stared steadily at the little lynx-eyed man.

'Do you know where he went?' she asked.

He shrugged his shoulders, and pulled a mock face of pity.

'His destination is unknown to me,' he said, 'and I regret to say that your companion left no message of farewell. However, it is Christmas Eve, the night is young yet, and you can see for yourself it's no weather to remain outside. If you care to wait here until your friend chooses to return, myself and the rest of these gentlemen will be delighted to entertain you.'

He laid a limp hand on her shawl. 'What a blackguard the fellow must be to desert you,' he said smoothly. 'Come in and rest, and forget him.'

Mary turned her back on him without a word and passed out through the door once more. As it closed behind her she caught the echo of his laughter.

She stood in the deserted market square with the gusty wind and scattered showers of rain for company. So the worst had happened, and the theft of the pony had been discovered. There was no other explanation. Jem had gone. Stupidly she stared before her at the dark houses, wondering what was the punishment for theft. Did they hang men for that as well as murder? She felt ill in body, as though someone had beaten her, and her brain was in confusion. She could see nothing clearly, she could make no plans. She supposed that Jem was lost to her now anyway, and she would never see him again. The brief adventure was over. For the moment she was stunned, and, hardly knowing that she did so, she began to walk aimlessly across the square towards the castle hill. If she had consented to stay in Launceston this would never have happened. They would have gone from the shelter of the doorway and found a room in the town somewhere; she would have been beside him, and they would have loved one another.

And, even if he had been caught in the morning, they would have had those hours alone. Now that he was gone from her, mind and body cried out in bitterness and resentment, and she knew how much she had wanted him. It was her fault that he had been taken, and she could do nothing for him. No doubt they would hang him for this; he would die like his father before him. The castle wall frowned down upon her and the rain ran in rivulets beside the road. There was no beauty left in Launceston any more; it was a grim, grey, hateful place, and every bend in the road hinted at disaster. She stumbled along with the mizzling rain driving in her face, caring little where she went, and careless of the fact that eleven long miles lay between her and her bedroom at Jamaica Inn. If loving a man meant this pain and anguish and sickness, she wanted none of it. It did away with sanity and composure, and made havoc of courage. She was a babbling child now when once she had been indifferent and strong. The steep hill rose before her. They had clattered down it in the afternoon; she remembered the gnarled tree-trunk at the gap in the hedge. Jem had whistled, and she had sung snatches of song. Suddenly she came to her senses, and faltered in her steps. It was madness to walk any further; the road stretched like a white ribbon in front of her and two miles of it would bring exhaustion in this wind and rain.

She turned again on the slope of the hill, with the winking lights of the town beneath her. Someone perhaps would give her a bed for the night, or a blanket on the floor. She had no money; they would have to trust her for payment. The wind tore at her hair, and the small stunted trees bowed and curtseyed before it. It would be a wild, wet dawn to Christmas Day.

She went away down the road, driven like a leaf before the wind, and out of the darkness she saw a carriage crawling up the hill towards her. It looked like a beetle, stubby and black, and its progress was slow, with the full force of the weather against it. She watched it with dull eyes; the sight conveyed no message to her brain, except that somewhere on an unknown road Jem Merlyn travelled to his death perhaps by the same manner. The carriage had crept up to her and was passing by, before she ran towards it on an impulse and called to the driver wrapped in a greatcoat on the seat. 'Are you taking the Bodmin road?' she cried. 'Have you a passenger inside?' The driver shook his head and whipped on his horse, but before Mary could step aside an arm came out of the carriage window, and a hand was laid on her shoulder. 'What does Mary Yellan do alone in Launceston on Christmas Eve?' said a voice from within.

The hand was firm, but the voice was gentle. A pale face stared at her from the dark interior of the carriage: white hair and white eyes beneath the black shovel-hat. It was the vicar of Altarnun.

Chapter Ten

She watched his profile in the half-light; sharp it was and clear, the prominent thin nose thrust downward like the curved beak of a bird. His lips were narrow and colourless, pressed firm together, and he leant forward with his chin resting on a long ebony cane that he held between his knees.

For the moment she could see nothing of his eyes; they were veiled by the short white lashes; and then he turned in his seat and considered her, his lashes fluttering, and the eyes that looked upon her were white also, transparent and expressionless as glass.

'So we ride together for the second time,' he said, and his voice was soft and low, like the voice of a woman. 'Once more I have the good fortune to help you by the wayside. You are wet through to the skin; you had better take off your clothes.' He stared at her with cold indifference, and she struggled in some confusion with the pin that clasped her shawl.

'There is a dry rug here that will serve you for the rest of the journey,' he continued. 'As for your feet, they will be better bare. This carriage is comparatively free from draught.'

Without a word she slipped out of her soaking shawl and bodice and wrapped herself in the coarse hair blanket that he held out to her. Her hair fell from its band and hung like a curtain about her bare shoulders. She felt like a child that has been caught on an escapade, and now sat with hands folded meekly together, obedient to the master's word.

'Well?' he said, looking gravely upon her, and she found herself at once stumbling into an explanation of her day. As before at Altarnun, there was something about him that made her untrue to herself, made her sound like a fool and an ignorant country girl, for her story was poor telling and she came out of it badly – just another woman who had cheapened herself at Launceston fair and had been left by the man of her choice to find her way home alone. She was ashamed to mention Jem by name, and she introduced him lamely as a man who lived by breaking horses, and whom she had met once when wandering on the moor. And now there had been some trouble in Launceston over the sale of a pony, and she feared he had been caught in some dishonesty.

She wondered what Francis Davey must think of her, riding to Launceston with a casual acquaintance, and then losing her companion in disgrace and running about the town bedraggled and wet after nightfall, like a woman of the streets. He heard her to the end in silence, and she heard him swallow once or twice, a trick she remembered.

'So you have not been too lonely after all?' he said at length. 'Jamaica Inn was not so isolated as you supposed?'

Mary flushed in the darkness, and, though he could not see her face, she knew that his eyes were upon her, and she felt guilty, as though she had done wrong and this was an accusation.

'What was the name of your companion?' he asked quietly; and she hesitated a moment, awkward and uncomfortable, her sense of guilt stronger than ever.

'He was my uncle's brother,' she replied, aware of the reluctance in her voice, the admission dragging from her like a confession.

Whatever his opinion of her had been hitherto, he was unlikely to raise it after this. Barely a week had passed since she had called Joss Merlyn a murderer, and yet she had ridden from Jamaica Inn with his brother without compunction, a common barmaid who would see the fun of the fair.

'You think ill of me, of course,' she went on hurriedly. 'Mistrusting and loathing my uncle as I do, it was hardly in keeping to make a confidant of his brother. He is dishonest and a thief, I know that; he told me as much at the beginning; but beyond that ...' Her words trailed off with some uncertainty. After all, Jem had denied nothing; he had made little or no attempt to defend himself when she accused him. And now she ranged herself on his side, she defended him instead, without reason and against her sane judgement, bound to him already because of his hands upon her and a kiss in the dark.

'You mean the brother knows nothing of the landlord's trade by night?' continued the gentle voice at her side. 'He is not of the company who bring the waggons to Jamaica Inn?'

Mary made a little gesture of despair. 'I don't know,' she said; 'I have no proof. He admits nothing; he shrugs his shoulders. But he told me one thing; that he had never killed a man. And I believed him. I still believe him. He said also that my uncle was running straight into the hands of the law, and they would catch him before long. He surely would not say that if he was one of the company.'

She spoke now to reassure herself rather than the man at her side, and Jem's innocence became suddenly of vital importance.

'You told me before you had some acquaintance with the squire,' she said quickly. 'Perhaps you have influence with him too. You could no doubt persuade him to deal mercifully with Jem Merlyn when the time comes? After all, he is young; he could start life afresh; it would be easy enough for you in your position.'

His silence was an added humiliation, and, feeling those cold white eyes upon her, she knew what a little graceless fool he must think her, and how feminine. He must see that she was pleading for a man who had kissed her once, and that he despised her went without saying.

'My acquaintance with Mr. Bassat of North Hill is of the slightest,' he told her gently. 'Once or twice we have given one another good afternoon, and we have spoken of matters relating to our respective parishes. It is hardly likely that he should spare a thief because of me, especially if the thief is guilty and happens to be the brother of the landlord of Jamaica Inn.'

Mary said nothing. Once again this strange man of God had spoken words of logic and wisdom, and there was no argument in reply. But she was caught in the sudden fever of love that devastates reason and makes havoc of logic, therefore his words acted as an irritant and created fresh turmoil in her brain.

'You appear anxious for his safety?' he said; and she wondered whether it was mockery she heard in his voice, or reproof, or understanding; but quick as a flash of lightning he continued: 'And if your new friend was guilty of other things, of conspiring with his brother against the belongings and perhaps the lives of his fellow-men, what then, Mary Yellan? Would you still seek to save him?' She felt his hand upon hers, cool and impersonal; and, because she was on edge after the excitement of the day, and was both frightened and frustrated in one, and loved a man against her judgement who was now lost to her through her own fault, she broke down, and began to rave like a child deprived.

'I didn't bargain for this,' she said fiercely. 'I could face the brutality of my uncle, and the pathetic dumb stupidity of Aunt Patience; even the silence and the horror of Jamaica Inn itself could be borne without shrinking and running away. I don't mind being lonely. There's a certain grim satisfaction in this struggle with my uncle that emboldens me at times, and I feel I'll have the better of him in the long run, whatever he says or does. I'd planned to take my aunt away from him, and see justice done, and then, when it was all over, to find work on a farm somewhere, and live a man's life, like I used to do. But now I can't look ahead any more; I can't make plans or think for myself; I go round and round in a trap, all because of a man I despise, who has nothing to do with my brain or my understanding. I don't want to love like a woman or feel like a woman, Mr. Davey; there's pain that way, and suffering, and misery that can last a lifetime. I didn't bargain for this; I don't want it.'

She leant back, her face against the side of the carriage, worn out by her torrent of words and already ashamed of her outburst. She did not care what he thought of her now. He was a priest, and therefore detached from her little world of storm and passion. He could have no knowledge of these things. She felt sullen and unhappy.

'How old are you?' he asked abruptly.

'Twenty-three,' she told him.

She heard him swallow in the darkness, and, taking his hand away from hers, he placed it once more upon the ebony stick and sat in silence.

The carriage had climbed away from the Launceston valley and the shelter of the hedges and was now upon the high ground leading to the open moorland, exposed to the full force of the wind and the rain. The wind was continuous but the showers were intermittent, and now and again a wild star straggled furtively behind a low-sweeping cloud and hung for an instant like a pin-prick of light. Then it would go, obscured and swept away by a black curtain of rain, and from the narrow window of the carriage nothing could be seen but the square dark patch of sky.

In the valley, the rain had fallen with great steadiness, and the wind, though persistent, had been moderate in strength and checked in its passage by the trees and the contour of the hill. Here on the high ground there was no such natural shelter; there was nothing but the moor on either side of the road, and, above, the great black vault of the sky; and there was a scream in the wind that had not been before.

Mary shivered, and edged closer to her companion like a dog to his fellow. Still he said nothing, but she knew that he had turned and was looking down upon her, and for the first time she was aware of his proximity as a person; she could feel his breath on her forehead. She remembered that her wet shawl and bodice lay on the floor at her feet, and she was naked under her rough blanket. When he spoke again she realised how near he was to her, and his voice came as a shock, confusing suddenly, and unexpected.

'You are very young, Mary Yellan,' he said softly; 'you are nothing but a chicken with the broken shell still around you. You'll come through your little crisis. Women like you have no need to shed tears over a man encountered once or twice, and the first kiss is not a thing that is remembered. You will forget your friend with his stolen pony very soon. Come now, dry your eyes; you are not the first to bite your nails over a lost lover.'

He made light of her problem, and counted it as a thing of no account; that was her first reaction to his words. And then she wondered why he had not used the conventional phrases of comfort, said something about the blessing of prayer, the peace of God, and life everlasting. She remembered that last ride with him, when he had whipped his horse into a fever of speed, and how he had crouched in his seat, with the reins in his hands; and he had whispered words under his breath she had not understood. Again she felt something of the same discomfort she had experienced then; a sensation of uneasiness that she connected instinctively with his freak hair and eyes, as though his physical departure from normality was a barrier between him and the rest of the world. In the animal kingdom a freak was a thing of abhorrence, at once hunted and destroyed, or driven out into the wilderness. No sooner had she thought of this than she reproached herself as narrow and un-Christian. He was a fellow-creature and a priest of God; but as she murmured an apology to him for having made a fool of herself before him, and talking like a common girl from the streets, she reached for her clothes and began to draw them on furtively under cover of the blanket.

'So I was right in my surmise, and all has been quiet in Jamaica Inn since I saw you last?' he said after a while, following some train of thought. 'There have been no waggons to disturb your beauty-sleep, and the landlord has played alone with his glass and his bottle?'

Mary, still fretful and anxious, with her mind on the man she had lost, brought herself back to reality with an effort. She had forgotten her uncle for nearly ten hours. At once she remembered the full horror of the past week, and the new knowledge that had come to her. She thought of the interminable sleepless nights, the long days she had spent alone, and the staring bloodshot eyes of her uncle swung before her again, his drunken smile, his groping hands.

'Mr. Davey,' she whispered, 'have you ever heard of wreckers?'

She had never said the word aloud before; she had not considered it even, and now that she heard it from her own lips it sounded fearful and obscene, like a blasphemy. It was too dark in the carriage to see the effect upon his face, but she heard him swallow. His eyes were hidden from her under the black shovel-hat, and she could only see the dim outline of his profile, the sharp chin, the prominent nose.

'Once, years ago, when I was hardly more than a child, I heard a neighbour speak of them,' she said; 'and then later, when I was old enough to understand, there were rumours of these things – snatches of gossip quickly suppressed. One of the men would bring back some wild tale after a visit to the north coast, and he would be silenced at once; such talk was forbidden by the older men; it was an outrage to decency.

'I believed none of these stories; I asked my mother, and she told me they were the horrible inventions of evil-minded people; such things did not and could not exist. She was wrong. I know now she was wrong, Mr. Davey. My uncle is one of them; he told me so himself.'

Still her companion made no reply; he sat motionless, like a stone thing, and she went on again, never raising her voice above a whisper.

'They are in it, every one of them, from the coast to the Tamar bank; all those men I saw that first Saturday in the bar at the inn. The gypsies, poachers, sailors, the pedlar with the broken teeth. They've murdered women and children with their own hands; they've held them under the water; they've killed them with rocks and stones. Those are death waggons that travel the road by night, and the goods they carry are not smuggled casks alone, with brandy for some and tobacco for another, but the full cargoes of wrecked ships bought at the price of blood, the trust and the possession of murdered men. And that's why my uncle is feared and loathed by the timid people in the cottages and farms, and why all doors are barred against him, and why the coaches drive past his house in a cloud of dust. They suspect what they cannot prove. My aunt lives in mortal terror of discovery; and my uncle has only to lose himself in drink before a stranger and his secret is spilt to the four winds. There, Mr. Davey; now you know the truth about Jamaica Inn.'

She leant back, breathless, against the side of the carriage, biting her lips and twisting her hands in an emotion she could not control, exhausted and shaken by the torrent of words that had escaped her; and somewhere in the dark places of her mind an image fought for recognition and found its way into the light, having no mercy on her feelings; and it was the face of Jem Merlyn, the man she loved, grown evil and distorted, merging horribly and finally into that of his brother.

The face beneath the black shovel-hat turned towards her; she caught a sudden flicker of the white lashes, and the lips moved.

'So the landlord talks when he is drunk?' he said, and it seemed to Mary that his voice lacked something of its usual gentle quality; it rang sharper in tone, as though pitched on a higher note; but when she looked up at him his eyes stared back at her, cold and impersonal as ever.

'He talks, yes,' she answered him. 'When my uncle has lived on brandy for five days he'll bare his soul before the world. He told me so himself, the very first evening I arrived. He was not drunk then. But four days ago, when he had woken from his first stupor, and he came out to the kitchen after midnight, swaying on his two feet – he talked then. That's why I know. And that's perhaps why I've lost faith in humanity, and in God, and in myself; and why I acted like a fool to-day in Launceston.'

The gale had increased in force during their conversation, and now with the bend in the road the carriage headed straight into the wind and was brought almost to a standstill. The vehicle rocked on its high wheels, and a sudden shower spattered against the windows like a handful of pebbles. There was no particle of shelter now; the moor on either hand was bare and unprotected, and the scurrying clouds flew fast over the land, tearing themselves asunder on the tors. There was a salt, wet tang in the wind that had come from the sea fifteen miles away.

Francis Davey leant forward in his seat. 'We are approaching Five Lanes and the turning to Altarnun,' he said; 'the driver is bound to Bodmin and will take you to Jamaica Inn. I shall leave you at Five Lanes and walk down into the village. Am I the only man you have honoured with your confidence, or do I share it with the landlord's brother?'

Again Mary could not tell if there was irony or mockery in his voice. 'Jem Merlyn knows,' she said unwillingly. 'We spoke of it this morning. He said little, though, and I know he is not friendly with my uncle. Anyway it doesn't matter now; Jem rides to custody for another crime.'

'And suppose he could save his own skin by betraying his brother, what then, Mary Yellan? There is a consideration for you.'

Mary started. This was a new possibility, and for a moment she clutched at the straw. But the vicar of Altarnun must have read her thoughts, for, glancing up at him for confirmation of her hopes, she saw him smile, the thin line of his mouth breaking for a moment out of passivity, as though his face was a mask and the mask had cracked. She looked away, uncomfortable, feeling like one who stumbles unawares upon a sight forbidden.

'That would be a relief to you and to him, no doubt,' continued the vicar, 'if he had never been involved. But there is always the doubt, isn't there? And neither you nor I know the answer to that question. A guilty man does not usually tie the rope around his own neck.'

Mary made a helpless movement with her hands, and he must have seen the despair in her face, for his voice became gentle again that had been harsh hitherto, and he laid his hand on her knee. 'Our bright days are done, and we are for the dark,' he said softly. 'If it were permitted to take our text from Shakespeare, there would be strange sermons preached in Cornwall to-morrow, Mary Yellan. Your uncle and his companions are not members of my congregation, however, and if they were they would not understand me. You shake your head at me. I speak in riddles. "This man is no comforter," you say; "he is a freak with his white hair and eyes." Don't turn away; I know what you think. I will tell you one thing for consolation, and you can make of it what you will. A week from now will bring the New Year. The false lights have flickered for the last time, and there will be no more wrecks; the candles will be blown.'

'I don't understand you,' said Mary. 'How do you know this, and what has the New Year to do with it?'

He took his hand from her, and began to fasten his coat preparatory to departure. He lifted the sash of the window and called to the driver to rein in his horse, and the cold air rushed into the carriage with a sting of frozen rain. 'I return to-night from a meeting in Launceston,' he said, 'which was but a sequel to many other similar meetings during the past few years. And those of us present were informed at last that His Majesty's Government were prepared to take certain steps during the coming year to patrol the coasts of His Majesty's country. There will be watchers on the cliffs instead of flares, and the paths known only at present to men like your uncle and his companions will be trodden by officers of the law.

'There will be a chain across England, Mary, that will be very hard to break. Now do you understand?' He opened the door of the carriage, and stepped out into the road. He bared his head under the rain, and she saw the thick white hair frame his face like a halo. He smiled again to her, and bowed, and he reached for her hand once more and held it a moment. 'Your troubles are over,' he said; 'the waggon-wheels will rust and the barred room at the end of the passage can be turned into a parlour. Your aunt will sleep in peace again, and your uncle will either drink himself to death and be a riddance to all of you, or he will turn Wesleyan and preach to travellers on the high road. As for you, you will ride south again and find a lover. Sleep well to-night. To-morrow is Christmas Day, and the bells to Altarnun will be ringing for peace and goodwill. I shall think of you.' He waved his hand to the driver, and the carriage went on without him.

Mary leant out of the window to call to him, but he had turned to the right down one of the five lanes, and was already lost to sight.

The carriage rattled on along the Bodmin road. There were still three miles to cover before the tall chimneys of Jamaica Inn broke upon the skyline, and those miles were the wildest and the most exposed of all the long one-and-twenty that stretched between the two towns.

Mary wished now that she had gone with Francis Davey. She would not hear the wind in Altarnun, and the rain would fall silently in the sheltered lane. To-morrow she could have knelt in the church and prayed for the first time since leaving Helford. If what he said was true, then there would be cause for rejoicing after all, and there would be some sense in giving thanks. The day of the wrecker was over; he would be broken by the new law, he and his kind; they would be blotted out and razed from the countryside as the pirates had been twenty, thirty years ago; and there would be no memory of them any more, no record left to poison the minds of those who should come after. A new generation would be born who had never heard their name. Ships would come to England without fear; there would be no harvest with the tide. Coves that had sounded once with the crunch of footsteps on shingle and the whispered voices of men would be silent again, and the scream that broke upon the silence would be the scream of a gull. Beneath the placid surface of the sea, on the ocean-bed, lay skulls without a name, green coins that had once been gold, and the old bones of ships: they would be forgotten for evermore. The terror they had known died with them. It was the dawn of a new age, when men and women would travel without fear, and the land would belong to them. Here, on this stretch of moor, farmers would till their plot of soil and stack the sods of turf to dry under the sun as they did to-day, but the shadow that had been upon them would have vanished. Perhaps the grass would grow, and the heather bloom again, where Jamaica Inn had stood.

She sat in the corner of the carriage, with the vision of the new world before her; and through the open window, travelling down upon the wind, she heard a shot ring out in the silence of the night, and a distant shout, and a cry. The voices of men came out of the darkness, and the padding of feet upon the road. She leant out of the window, the rain blowing in on her face, and she heard the driver of the carriage call out in fear, as his horse shied and stumbled. The road rose steeply from the valley, winding away to the top of the hill, and there in the distance were the lean chimneys of Jamaica Inn crowning the skyline like a gallows. Down the road came a company of men, led by one who leapt like a hare and tossed a lantern before him as he ran. Another shot rang out, and the driver of the carriage crumpled in his seat and fell. The horse stumbled again and headed like a blind thing for the ditch. For a moment the carriage swayed upon its wheels, rocked, and was still. Somebody screamed a blasphemy to the sky; somebody laughed wildly; there was a whistle and a cry.

A face was thrust in at the window of the carriage, a face crowned with matted hair that fell in a fringe above the scarlet, bloodshot eyes. The lips parted, showing the white teeth; and then the lantern was lifted to the window so that the light fell upon the interior of the carriage. One hand held the lantern, and the other clasped the smoking barrel of a pistol; they were long slim hands, with narrow pointed fingers, things of beauty and of grace, the rounded nails crusted with dirt.

Joss Merlyn smiled; the crazy, delirious smile of a man possessed, maddened, and exalted by poison; and he levelled the pistol at Mary, leaning forward into the carriage so that the barrel touched her throat.

Then he laughed, and threw the pistol back over his shoulder, and, wrenching open the door, he reached for her hands and pulled her out beside him on the road, holding the lantern above his head so that all could see her. There were ten or twelve of them standing in the road, ragged and unkempt, half of them drunk as their leader, wild eyes staring out of shaggy bearded faces; and one or two had pistols in their hands, or were armed with broken bottles, knives and stones. Harry the pedlar stood by the horse's head, while face-downwards in the ditch lay the driver of the carriage, his arm crumpled under him, his body limp and still.

Joss Merlyn held Mary to him and tilted her face to the light, and when they saw who she was a howl of laughter broke from the company of men, and the pedlar put his two fingers to his mouth and whistled.

The landlord bent to her, and bowed with drunken gravity; he seized her loose hair in his hand and twisted it in a rope, sniffing at it like a dog.

'So it's you, is it?' he said. 'You've chosen to come back again, like a little whining bitch, with your tail between your legs?'

Mary said nothing. She looked from one to the other of the men in the crowd and they stared back at her, jeering, hemming in upon her and laughing, pointing to her wet clothes, fingering her bodice and her skirt.

'So you're dumb, are you?' cried her uncle, and he hit her across the face with the back of his hand. She called out and put up an arm to protect herself, but he knocked it away and, holding her wrist, he doubled it behind her back. She cried with the pain, and he laughed again.

'You'll come to heel if I kill you first,' he said. 'Do you think you can stand against me, with your monkey face and your damned impudence? And what do you think you do, at midnight, riding on the King's highway in a hired carriage, half naked, with your hair down your back? You're nothing but a common slut, after all.' He jerked at her wrist, and she fell.

'Leave me alone,' she cried; 'you have no right to touch me or speak to me. You're a bloody murderer and a thief, and the law knows it too. The whole of Cornwall knows it. Your reign is over, Uncle Joss. I've been to Launceston to-day to inform against you.'

A hubbub rose amongst the group of men; they pressed forward, shouting at her and questioning, but the landlord roared at them, waving them back.

'Get back, you damned fools! Can't you see she's trying to save her skin by lies?' he thundered. 'How can she inform against me when she knows nothing? She's never walked the eleven miles to Launceston. Look at her feet. She's been with a man somewhere down on the road, and he sent her back on wheels when he'd had enough of her. Get up – or do you want me to rub your nose in the dust?' He pulled her to her feet and held her beside him. Then he pointed to the sky, where the low clouds fled before the scurrying wind and a wet star gleamed.

'Look there,' he yelled. 'There's a break in the sky and the rain's going east. There'll be more wind yet before we're through, and a wild grey dawn on the coast in six hours' time. We'll waste no more of it here. Get your horse, Harry, and put him in the traces here; the carriage will carry half a dozen of us. And bring the pony and the farm-cart from the stable; he's had no work for a week. Come on, you lazy drunken devils, don't you want to feel gold and silver run through your hands? I've lain like a hog for seven crazy days, and, by God, I feel like a child to-night and I want the coast again. Who'll take the road with me through Camelford?'

A shout rose from a dozen voices, and hands were thrust into the air. One fellow burst into a snatch of song, waving a bottle over his head, reeling on his feet as he stood; then he staggered and fell, crumpling on to his face in the ditch. The pedlar kicked him as he lay, and he did not stir; and, snatching the bridle of the horse, he dragged the animal forward, urging him with blows and cries to the steep hill, while the wheels of the carriage passed over the body of the fallen man, who, kicking for an instant like a wounded hare, struggled from the mud with a scream of terror and pain, and then lay still.

The men turned with the carriage and followed it, the sound of their running feet pattering along the road, and Joss Merlyn stood for a moment, looking down upon Mary with a foolish drunken smile; then on a sudden impulse he caught her in his arms and pulled her towards the carriage, wrenching the door once more. He threw her on to the seat in the corner, and then, leaning out of the window, he yelled to the pedlar to whip the horse up the hill.

His cry was echoed by the men who ran beside him, and some of them leapt on to the step and clung to the window, while others mounted the driver's empty seat, and rained at the horse with sticks, and a shower of stones.

The animal quivered, sweating with fear; and he topped the hill at a gallop, with half a dozen madmen clinging to the reins and screaming at his heels.

Jamaica Inn was ablaze with light; the doors were open, and the windows were unbarred. The house gaped out of the night like a live thing.

The landlord placed his hand over Mary's mouth and forced her against the side of the carriage. 'You'd inform against me, would you?' he said. 'You'd run to the law, and have me swinging on a rope's end like a cat? All right, then, you shall have your chance. You shall stand on the shore, Mary, with the wind and the sea in your face, and you shall watch for the dawn and the coming in of the tide. You know what that means, don't you? You know where I'm going to take you?'

She stared back at him in horror; the colour drained from her face, and she tried to speak to him, but his hands forbade her.

'You think you're not afraid of me, don't you?' he said. 'You sneer at me with your pretty white face and your monkey eyes. Yes, I'm drunk; I'm drunk as a king, and heaven and earth can smash for all I care. To-night we shall ride in glory, every man jack of us, maybe for the last time; and you shall come with us, Mary; to the coast. . . .'

He turned away from her, shouting to his companions, and the horse, startled by his cry, started forward again in his stride, dragging the carriage behind him; and the lights of Jamaica Inn vanished in the darkness.

Chapter Eleven

It was a nightmare journey of two hours or more to the coast, and Mary, bruised and shaken by her rough handling, lay exhausted in the corner of the carriage, caring little what became of her. Harry the pedlar and two other men had climbed in beside her uncle, and the air became foul at once with the stink of tobacco and stale drink, and the smell of their bodies.

The landlord had worked himself and his companions into a state of wild excitement, and the presence of a woman amongst them brought a vicious tang to their enjoyment, her weakness and distress acting pleasurably upon them.

At first they talked at her and for her, laughing and singing to win her notice, Harry the pedlar bursting into his lewd songs, which rang with immoderate force in such close quarters and brought howls of appreciation from his audience, stimulating them to greater excitement.

They watched for the effect upon her face, hoping that she would show some sign of shame or discomfort, but Mary was too tired now for any word or song to penetrate her. She heard their voices through a haze of exhaustion; she was aware of her uncle's elbow thrust in her side, bringing another dull ache to add to her pains, and with throbbing head and smarting eyes she saw a sea of grinning faces through the smoke. What they said or did hardly mattered to her any more, and the longing for sleep and forgetfulness became a torment.

When they saw how lifeless she was, and dull, her presence lost its flavour; even the songs lost sting, and Joss Merlyn fumbled in his pocket and produced a pack of cards. They turned from her at once to this new interest, and in the momentary lull that blessed her Mary shrank closer in her corner, away from the hot, animal smell of her uncle, and, closing her eyes, she resigned herself to the movement of the swaying, jolting carriage. Her fatigue was such that full consciousness was no longer part of her; she was swinging in a trance-land across the border. She was aware of pain, and the rocking carriage-wheels, and in the far distance a murmur of voices; but these things moved away from her and not with her; she could not identify them with her own existence. Darkness came upon her like a boon from heaven, and she felt herself slip away into it; and so was lost. Time had nothing to do with her then. It was the cessation of movement that dragged her back to the world; the sudden stillness, and the cold damp air blowing upon her face through the open carriage window.

She was alone in her corner. The men had gone, taking their light with them. She sat motionless at first, fearing to bring them back and uncertain what had befallen her; and then, when she leant forward to the window, the pain and stiffness in her body were intolerable. A weal of pain ran across her shoulders where the cold had numbed her, and her bodice was still damp from the rain that had soaked her early in the evening. She waited a moment, and then leant forward again. It was still blowing hard, but the driving rain had ceased, and only a thin cold mizzle pattered against the window. The carriage had been abandoned in a narrow gully-way with high banks on either side, and the horse had been taken from the traces. The gully appeared to descend sharply, the path becoming rough and broken. Mary could not see more than a few yards in front of her. The night had thickened considerably, and in the gully-way it was black like a pit. There were no

stars now in the sky, and the sharp wind of the moors had become a
boisterous thing of noise and bluster, trailing a wet fog for company. Mary
put her hand out of the window and touched the bank. Her fingers came
upon loose sand and stems of grass, sodden through with the rain. She tried
the handle of the door, but it was locked. Then she listened intently. Her
eyes strained to pierce the darkness ahead of her, down the sharp descent
of the gully-way, and borne up to her on the wind came a sound at once
sullen and familiar, a sound that for the first time in her life she could not
welcome, but must recognise with a leap of her heart and a shiver of
foreboding.

It was the sound of the sea. The gully was a pathway to the shore.

She knew now why a softness had crept upon the air, and why the mizzle
of rain fell on her hand lightly, with a tang of salt. The high banks gave a
false feeling of shelter in contrast to the bleak wilderness of the moors, but
once away from their deceptive shadow the illusion would be lost and the
tearing gale cry louder than before. There could be no stillness where the
sea broke upon a rockbound shore. She heard it again now, and continually;
a murmur and a sigh as the spent water gave itself to the strand and
withdrew reluctantly, and then a pause as the sea gathered itself for a
renewal of effort – a momentary fragment in time – and then once more the
thunder and the crash of fulfilment, the roar of surf upon shingle and the
screaming scatter of stones as they followed the drag of the sea. Mary
shuddered; somewhere in the darkness below, her uncle and his companions
waited for the tide. If she could have heard some sound of them, the waiting
in the empty carriage would have been more bearable. The wild shouting,
the laughter, and the singing with which they had fortified themselves for
the journey would have been a relief, however loathsome; but this deadly
quietude was sinister. Business had sobered them, and they had found work
for their hands. Now that her senses were her own again, and her first
fatigue cast aside, Mary found inactivity impossible. She considered the size
of the window. The door was locked, as she knew, but with straining and
wriggling she might yet attempt to squeeze her body through the narrow
frame.

The endeavour was worth the risk. Whatever happened to-night, her own
life could be counted of little value; her uncle and his companions could find
her and kill her if they wished. This country was known to them, and not
to her. They could trace her in a moment if they wanted, like a pack of
hounds. She worked and strained at the window, leaning backwards through
the gap, the effort made even more difficult because of her stiff shoulder and
her back. The roof of the carriage was slippery and wet, giving no grip to
her fingers, but she struggled and pushed through the gap, and then, with
a sickening squeeze and pressure, her hips were through, the frame of the
window scraping the flesh and turning her faint. She lost foothold and
balance, and fell backwards through the window to the ground below.

The drop was nothing; but the fall shook her, and she felt a little trickle
of blood run down her side where the window had caught her. She gave
herself a moment to recover, and then she dragged herself to her feet and

began to creep uncertainly up the lane, in the dark shelter of the bank. She had not yet formed a plan in her head, but, with her back turned away from the gully and the sea, she would be putting distance between herself and her late companions. There was little doubt that they had descended to the shore. This lane, winding upwards and to the left, would take her at least to the high ground of the cliffs, where in spite of the darkness she would be able to make something of the land. Somewhere there would be a road – the carriage itself must have travelled by one; and if there was a road there would be dwelling-houses before long; there would be honest men and women to whom she could tell her tale, and who would rouse the countryside when they heard her story.

She felt her way along the narrow ditch, stumbling now and again over the stones, her hair blowing into her eyes and troubling her, and, coming suddenly round the sharp corner of the bank, she put up her hands to screw back the loose strands from her eyes, and because of this she did not see the humped figure of a man kneeling in the ditch with his back towards her, his eyes watchful of the winding lane ahead. She came against him, knocking the breath from her body, and he, taken by surprise, fell with her, crying out in mingled terror and rage, smashing at her with his clenched fist.

They fought on the ground, she straining away from him, her hands tearing at his face, but in a moment he was too strong for her, and, rolling her over on her side, he twisted his hands in her hair, pulling at the roots, until the pain forced her to stillness. He leant on her, breathing heavily, for the fall had winded him, and then he peered closely at her, his gaping mouth showing yellow broken teeth.

It was Harry the pedlar. Mary lay motionless; the first move should come from him; and meanwhile she cursed herself for a fool in blundering up the lane the way she had, with never a thought of the outpost that even a child at play would have placed in position.

He expected her to cry or struggle, but when she did neither he shifted his weight to his elbow, and smiled at her slyly, jerking his head in the direction of the shore. 'Didn't think to see me, did you?' he said. 'Thought I was down on the shore with the landlord and the rest, baiting the pots. And so you woke up from your beauty-sleep, and took a walk up the lane. And now you're here I'll make you very welcome.' He grinned at her, touching her cheek with a black finger-nail. 'It's been cold and damp in the ditch,' he said, 'but that's no odds now. They'll be hours down there yet. I can see you've turned against Joss, by the way you spoke to him to-night. He's no right to keep you up at Jamaica like a bird in a cage, with no pretty things to wear. I doubt if he's given you as much as a brooch for your bodice, has he? Don't you mind about that. I'll give you lace for your neck, and bangles for your wrist, and soft silk for your skin. Let's look now. . . .'

He nodded at her, reassuring her, smiling still, smirking and sly, and she felt his furtive hand fasten itself upon her. She moved swiftly, lashing out at him, and her fist caught him underneath the chin, shutting his mouth like a trap, with his tongue caught between his teeth. He squealed like a rabbit, and she struck him again, but this time he grabbed at her and lurched sideways upon her, all pretence of gentle persuasion gone, his strength horrible, his face drained of all colour. He was fighting now for possession, and she knew it, and, aware that his strength was greater than hers and must prevail in the end, she lay limp suddenly, to deceive him, giving him the advantage for the moment. He grunted in triumph, relaxing his weight, which was what she intended, and as he moved his position and lowered his head she jabbed at him swiftly with the full force of her knee, at the same time thrusting her fingers in his eyes. He doubled up at once, rolling on to his side in agony, and in a second she had struggled from under him and pulled herself to her feet, kicking at him once more as he rocked defenceless, his hands clasped to his belly. She grabbed in the ditch for a stone to fling at him, finding nothing but loose earth and sand, and she dug handfuls of this, scattering it in his face and in his eyes, so that he was blinded momentarily and could make no return. Then she turned again, and began to run like a hunted thing up the twisting lane, her mouth open, her hands outstretched, tripping and stumbling over the ruts of the path; and when she heard his shout behind her once more, and the padding of his feet, a sense of panic swamped her reason and she started to climb up the high bank that bordered the lane, her foot slipping at every step in the soft earth, until with the very madness of effort born in terror she reached the top, and crawled, sobbing, through a gap in the thorn hedge that bordered the bank. Her face and her hands were bleeding, but she had no thought for this, and ran along the cliff away from the lane, over tussocks of grass and humped uneven ground, all sense of direction gone from her, her one idea to escape from the thing that was Harry the pedlar.

A wall of fog closed in upon her, obscuring the distant line of hedge for which she had been making, and she stopped at once in her headlong rush, aware of the danger of sea-mist, and how in its deception it might bring her back to the lane again. She fell at once upon hands and knees, and crawled slowly forward, her eyes low to the ground, following a narrow sandy track that wound in the direction she wished to take. Her progress was slow, but instinct told her that the distance was increasing between her and the pedlar, which was the only thing that mattered. She had no reckoning of time; it was three, perhaps four, in the morning, and the darkness would give no sign of breaking for many hours to come. Once more the rain came down through the curtain of mist, and it seemed as though she could hear the sea on every side of her and there was no escape from it; the breakers were muffled no longer; they were louder and clearer than before. She realised that the wind had been no guide to direction, for even now, with it behind her, it might have shifted a point or two, and with her ignorance of the coast-line she had not turned east, as she had meant to do, but was even now upon the brink of a sagging cliff path that, judging by the sound of the sea, was taking her straight to the shore. The breakers, though she could not see them because of the fog, were somewhere beyond her in the darkness, and to her dismay she sensed they were on a level with her, and not beneath her. This meant that the cliffs here descended abruptly to the shore, and, instead of a long and tortuous path to a cove that she had pictured from the

abandoned carriage, the gully-way must have been only a few yards from
the sea itself. The banks of the gully had muffled the sound of the breakers.
Even as she decided this, there was a gap in the mist ahead of her, showing
a patch of sky. She crawled on uncertainly, the path widening and the fog
clearing, and the wind veered in her face once more; and there she knelt
amongst driftwood and seaweed and loose shingle, on a narrow strand, with
the land sloping up on either side of her, while not fifty yards away, and
directly in front of her, were the high combing seas breaking upon the shore.

After a while, when her eyes had accustomed themselves to the shadows,
she made them out, huddled against a jagged rock that broke up the expanse
of the beach: a little knot of men, grouped together for warmth and shelter,
silently peering ahead of them into the darkness. Their very stillness made
them the more menacing who had not been still before; and the attitude of
stealth, the poise of their bodies crouched as they were against the rock, the
tense watchfulness of their heads turned one and all to the incoming sea,
was a sight at once fearful and pregnant with danger.

Had they shouted and sung, called to one another, and made the night
hideous with their clamour, their heavy boots resounding on the crunching
shingle, it would have been in keeping with their character and with what
she expected; but there was something ominous in this silence, which
suggested that the crisis of the night had come upon them. A little jutting
piece of rock stood between Mary and the bare exposed beach, and beyond
this she dared not venture for fear of betraying herself. She crawled as far
as the rock, and lay down on the shingle behind it, while ahead of her, direct
in her line of vision when she moved her head, stood her uncle and his
companions, with their backs turned to her.

She waited. They did not move. There was no sound. Only the sea broke
in its inevitable monotony upon the shore, sweeping the strand and returning
again, the line of breakers showing thin and white against the black night.

The mist began to lift very slowly, disclosing the narrow outline of the
bay. Rocks became more prominent, and the cliffs took on solidity. The
expanse of water widened, opening from a gulf to a bare line of shore that
stretched away interminably. To the right, in the distance, where the highest
part of the cliff sloped to the sea, Mary made out a faint pin-prick of light.
At first she thought it a star, piercing the last curtain of dissolving mist, but
reason told her that no star was white, nor ever swayed with the wind on
the surface of a cliff. She watched it intently, and it moved again; it was like
a small white eye in the darkness. It danced and curtseyed, storm-tossed, as
though kindled and carried by the wind itself, a living flare that would not
be blown. The group of men on the shingle below heeded it not; their eyes
were turned to the dark sea beyond the breakers.

And suddenly Mary was aware of the reason for their indifference, and
the small white eye that had seemed at first a thing of friendliness and
comfort, winking bravely alone in the wild night, became a symbol of horror.

The star was a false light placed there by her uncle and his companions.
The pin-prick gleam was evil now, and the curtsey to the wind became a
mockery. In her imagination the light burnt fiercer, extending its beam to

dominate the cliff, and the colour was white no more, but old and yellow like a scab. Someone watched by the light so that it should not be extinguished. She saw a dark figure pass in front of it, obscuring the gleam for a moment, and then it burnt clear again. The figure became a blot against the grey face of the cliff, moving quickly in the direction of the shore. Whoever it was climbed down the slope to his companions on the shingle. His action was hurried, as though time pressed him, and he was careless in the manner of his coming, for the loose earth and stones slid away from under him, scattering down to the beach below. The sound startled the men beneath, and for the first time since Mary had watched them they withdrew their attention from the incoming tide and looked up to him. Mary saw him put his hands to his mouth and shout, but his words were caught up in the wind and did not come to her. They reached the little group of men waiting on the shingle, who broke up at once in some excitement, some of them starting half way up the cliff to meet him; but when he shouted again and pointed to the sea, they ran down towards the breakers, their stealth and silence gone for the moment, the sound of their footsteps heavy on the shingle, their voices topping one another above the crash of the sea. Then one of them – her uncle it was; she recognised his great loping stride and massive shoulders – held up his hand for silence; and they waited, all of them, standing upon the shingle with the waves breaking beyond their feet; spread out in a thin line they were, like crows, their black forms outlined against the white beach. Mary watched with them; and out of the mist and darkness came another pin-prick of light in answer to the first. This new light did not dance and waver as the one on the cliff had done; it dipped low and was hidden, like a traveller weary of his burden, and then it would rise again, pointing high to the sky, a hand flung into the night in a last and desperate attempt to break through the wall of mist that hitherto had defied penetration. The new light drew nearer to the first. The one compelled the other. Soon they would merge and become two white eyes in the darkness. And still the men crouched motionless upon the narrow strand, waiting for the lights to close with one another.

The second light dipped again; and now Mary could see the shadowed outline of a hull, the black spars like fingers spreading above it, while a white surging sea combed beneath the hull, and hissed, and withdrew again. Closer drew the mast-light to the flare upon the cliff, fascinated and held, like a moth coming to a candle.

Mary could bear no more. She scrambled to her feet and ran down upon the beach, shouting and crying, waving her hands above her head, pitting her voice against the wind and the sea, which tossed it back to her in mockery. Someone caught hold of her and forced her down upon the beach. Hands stifled her. She was trodden upon and kicked. Her cries died away, smothered by the coarse sacking that choked her, and her arms were dragged behind her back and knotted together, the rough cord searing her flesh.

They left her then, with her face in the shingle, the breakers sweeping towards her not twenty yards away; and as she lay there helpless, the breath knocked from her and her scream of warning strangled in her throat, she heard the cry that had been hers become the cry of others, and fill the air with sound. The cry rose above the searing smash of the sea, and was seized and carried by the wind itself; and with the cry came the tearing splinter of wood, the horrible impact of a massive live thing finding resistance, the shuddering groan of twisting, breaking timber.

Drawn by a magnet, the sea hissed away from the strand, and a breaker running high above its fellows flung itself with a crash of thunder upon the lurching ship. Mary saw the black mass that had been a vessel roll slowly upon its side, like a great flat turtle; the masts and spars were threads of cotton, crumpled and fallen. Clinging to the slippery, sloping surface of the turtle were little black dots that would not be thrown; that stuck themselves fast to the splintering wood like limpets; and, when the heaving, shuddering mass beneath them broke monstrously in two, cleaving the air, they fell one by one into the white tongues of the sea, little black dots without life or substance.

A deadly sickness came upon Mary, and she closed her eyes, her face pressed into the shingle. The silence and the stealth were gone; the men who had waited during the cold hours waited no more. They ran like madmen hither and thither upon the beach, yelling and screaming, demented and inhuman. They waded waist-deep into the breakers, careless of danger, all caution spent; snatching at the bobbing, sodden wreckage borne in on the surging tide.

They were animals, fighting and snarling over lengths of splintered wood; they stripped, some of them, and ran naked in the cold December night, the better to fight their way into the sea and plunge their hands amongst the spoil that the breakers tossed to them. They chattered and squabbled like monkeys, tearing things from one another; and one of them kindled a fire in the corner by the cliff, the flame burning strong and fierce in spite of the mizzling rain. The spoils of the sea were dragged up the beach and heaved beside it. The fire cast a ghastly light upon the beach, throwing a yellow brightness that had been black before, and casting long shadows down the beach where the men ran backwards and forwards, industrious and horrible.

When the first body was washed ashore, mercifully spent and gone, they clustered around it, diving amongst the remains with questing, groping hands, picking it clean as a bone; and, when they had stripped it bare, tearing even at the smashed fingers in search of rings, they abandoned it again, leaving it to loll upon its back in the scum where the tide had been.

Whatever had been the practice hitherto, there was no method in their work to-night. They robbed haphazard, each man for himself; crazy they were and drunk, mazed with this success they had not planned – dogs snapping at the heel of their master whose venture had proved a triumph, whose power this was, whose glory. They followed him where he ran naked amongst the breakers, the water streaming from the hair on his body, a giant above them all.

The tide turned, the water receded, and a new chill came upon the air. The light that swung above them on the cliff, still dancing in the wind, like an old mocking man whose joke has long been played, turned pallid now and dim. A grey colour came upon the water and was answered by the sky. At first the men did not notice the change; they were delirious still, intent upon their prey. And then Joss Merlyn himself lifted his great head and sniffed the air, turning about him as he stood, watching the clear contour of the cliffs as the darkness slipped away; and he shouted suddenly, calling the men to silence, pointing to the sky that was leaden now, and pale.

They hesitated, glancing once more at the wreckage that surged and fell in the trough of the sea, unclaimed as yet and waiting to be salved; and then they turned with one accord and began to run up the beach towards the entrance of the gully, silent once more, without words or gesture, their faces grey and scared in the broadening light. They had outstayed their time. Success had made them careless. The dawn had broken upon them unawares, and by lingering overlong they had risked the accusation which daylight would bring to them. The world was waking up around them; night, that had been their ally, covered them no more.

It was Joss Merlyn who pulled the sacking away from her mouth and jerked Mary to her feet. Seeing that her weakness had become part of her now, and could not be withstood, for she could neither stand alone nor help herself in any way, he cursed her furiously, glancing behind him at the cliffs that every minute became harder, more distinct; and then he bent down to her, for she had stumbled to the ground again, and threw her over his shoulder as he would a sack. Her head lolled without support, her arms lifeless, and she felt his hands pressing into her scarred side, bruising it once again, rubbing the numb flesh that had lain upon the shingle. He ran with her up the strand to the entrance of the gully; and his companions, caught up already in a mesh of panic, flung the remnants of spoil they had snatched from the beach upon the backs of the three horses tethered there. Their movements were feverish and clumsy, and they worked without direction, as though unhinged, lacking all sense of order; while the landlord, sober now from necessity and strangely ineffectual, cursed and bullied them to no avail. The carriage, stuck in the bank half way up the gully, resisted their efforts to extract it, and this sudden reverse to their fortune increased the panic and stampede. Some of them began to scatter up the lane, forgetting everything in a blind concentration on personal safety. Dawn was their enemy; and more easily withstood alone, in the comparative security of ditch and hedge, than in the company of five or six upon the road. Suspicion would lie in numbers here on the coast, where every face was known, and strangers were remarkable; but a poacher, or tramp, or gypsy could make his way alone, finding his own cover and his own path. These deserters were cursed by those who remained, struggling with the carriage, and now, through stupidity and panic, the vehicle was wrenched from the bank in so rough a manner that it overturned, falling upon one side and smashing a wheel.

This final disaster let loose pandemonium in the gully-way. There was a wild rush to the remaining farm-cart that had been left further up the lane, and to the already over-burdened horses. Someone, still obedient to the leader and with a sense of necessity, put fire to the broken carriage, whose presence in the lane screamed danger to them all, and the riot that followed – fight between man and man for the possession of the farm-cart that might yet carry them away inland – was a hideous scrap of tooth and nail, of teeth smashed by stones, of eyes cut open by broken glass.

Those who carried pistols now had the advantage, and the landlord, with his remaining ally Harry the pedlar by his side, stood with his back to the cart and let fly amongst the rabble, who, in the sudden terror of pursuit that would follow with the day, looked upon him now as an enemy, a false leader who had brought them to destruction. The first shot went wide, and stubbed the soft bank opposite; but it gave one of the opponents a chance to cut the landlord's eye open with a jagged flint. Joss Merlyn marked his assailant with his second shot, spattering him in mid-stomach, and while the fellow doubled up in the mud amongst his companions, mortally wounded and screaming like a hare, Harry the pedlar caught another in the throat, the bullet ripping the windpipe, the blood spouting jets like a fountain.

It was the blood that won the cart for the landlord; for the remaining rebels, hysterical and lost at the sight of their dying fellows, turned as one man and scuttled like crabs up the twisting lane, intent only on putting a safe distance between themselves and their late leader. The landlord leant against the cart with smoking, murderous pistol, the blood running freely from the cut on his eye. Now that they were alone, he and the pedlar wasted little time. What wreckage had been salved and brought to the gully they threw upon the cart beside Mary – miscellaneous odds and ends, useless and unprofitable, the main store still down on the beach and washed by the tide. They dared not risk the fetching of it, for that would be the work of a dozen men, and already the light of day had followed the early dawn, and made clear the countryside. There was not a moment to spare.

The two men who had been shot sprawled in the lane beside the cart. Whether they still breathed or not was not a matter to be discussed; their bodies bore witness, and must be destroyed. It was Harry the pedlar who dragged them to the fire. It burnt well; much of the carriage was already consumed, while one red wheel stuck out above the charred and splintered wood.

Joss Merlyn led the remaining horse to the traces, and without a word the two men climbed into the cart and jerked the horse to action.

Lying on her back in the cart, Mary watched the low clouds pass across the sky. Darkness had gone; the morning was damp and grey. She could still hear the sound of the sea, more distant and less insistent, a sea that had spent its full fury and now let itself be carried by the tide.

The wind had dropped too; the tall stems of grass on the banks above the gully were still, and a silence had come upon the coast. There was a smell in the air of damp earth and turnips, of a mist that had lain overnight upon the land. The clouds became one with the grey sky. Once again a thin mizzle of rain fell upon Mary's face, and upon her upturned hands.

The wheels of the cart crunched the uneven lane; and, turning right, came out upon a smoothed surface of gravel that was a road, running northwards between low hedges. From far away, across many fields and scattered ploughlands, came the merry peal of bells, odd and discordant, in the morning air.

She remembered suddenly that it was Christmas Day.

Chapter Twelve

The square pane of glass was familiar to her. It was larger than the carriage window, and had a ledge before it, and there was a crack across the pane that she remembered well. She kept her eyes upon it, struggling with memory, and she wondered why she no longer felt the rain on her face and the steady current of wind. There was no movement under her, and her first thought was that the carriage had come to a standstill, thrust against the bank in the gully-way once more, and that circumstance and fate would compel her to react in frightful repetition the things she had already performed. When she climbed through the window she would fall and bruise herself, and, heading yet again up the twisting lane, would come upon Harry the pedlar, squatting in his ditch; but this time she would not have the strength to withstand him. Down on the shingle strand the men waited for the tide, and the great black turtle of a ship rolled flat and monstrous in the trough of the sea. Mary moaned, and turned her head restlessly from side to side; out of the tail of her eyes she saw the brown discoloured wall beside her, and the rusty nail-head where a text had once been hung.

She was lying in her bedroom at Jamaica Inn.

The sight of this room she hated, however cold it was and dreary, was at least protection from the wind and the rain, and from the hands of Harry the pedlar. Nor could she hear the sea. The roar of surf would not disturb her again. If death came now, he would be an ally; existence was not a thing she welcomed any more. Life had been crushed from her anyway, and the body lying on the bed did not belong to her. She had no wish to live. Shock had made a dummy of her, and taken away her strength; tears of self-pity welled into her eyes.

Now there was a face bending down to her, and she shrank back against the pillow, her hands thrust outward and protesting; for the puffy mouth and broken teeth of the pedlar were ever in her mind.

Her hands were held gently, though, and the eyes that peered at her, red-rimmed like her own from weeping, were tremulous and blue.

It was Aunt Patience. They clung to one another, seeking comfort in proximity; and after Mary had wept awhile, easing herself of sorrow and allowing the tide of emotion to carry her to the limit, nature took command

of her again and she was strengthened, something of the old courage and
force coming back to her again.

'You know what has happened?' she asked, and Aunt Patience held her
hands tightly, so that they could not be withdrawn, the blue eyes begging
dumbly for forgiveness, like an animal punished through no fault of his own.

'How long have I lain here?' Mary questioned, and she was told that this
was the second day. For a moment or two Mary was silent, considering the
information, new to her and sudden; two days was a long time to one who
but a few moments ago had watched the dawn break on the coast.

Much could happen in the time, and she had been on her bed here,
helpless.

'You should have woken me,' she said roughly, pushing away the hands
that clung to her. 'I'm not a child, to be mothered and pampered because of
a few bruises. There's work for me to do; you don't understand.'

Aunt Patience stroked her, the caress timid and ineffectual.

'You could not move,' she whimpered. 'Your poor body was bleeding and
broken. I bathed you while you were still unconscious; I thought at first they
had injured you terribly, but thank the dear God no real harm has come to
you. Your bruises will heal, and your long sleep has rested you.'

'You know who did it, don't you? You know where they took me?'

Bitterness had made her cruel. She knew that the words acted like a lash,
and she could not stop herself. She began to talk about the men on the shore.
Now it was the elder woman's turn to whimper, and when Mary saw the
thin mouth working, the vapid blue eyes stare back at her in terror, she
became sickened of herself and could not continue. She sat up in bed, and
swung her legs to the floor, her head swimming with the effort, her temples
throbbing.

'What are you going to do?' Aunt Patience pulled at her nervously, but
her niece shook her aside and began to drag on her clothes.

'I have business of my own,' she said curtly.

'Your uncle is below. He will not let you leave the inn.'

'I'm not afraid of him.'

'Mary, for your sake, for my sake, do not answer him again. You know
what you have suffered already. Ever since he returned with you he has sat
below, white and terrible, a gun across his knees; the doors of the inn are
barred. I know you have seen and endured horrible, unspeakable things;
but, Mary, don't you understand if you go down now he may hurt you
again – he may even kill you? . . . I have never seen him like this. I can't
answer for his mood. Don't go down, Mary. I beg you on my knees not to
go down.'

She began to drag on the floor, clutching at Mary's skirt, clasping at her
hands and kissing them. The sight was miserable, unnerving.

'Aunt Patience, I have gone through enough out of loyalty to you. You
can't expect me to stand any more. Whatever Uncle Joss may have been to
you once, he is inhuman now. All your tears won't save him from justice;
you must realise that. He's a brute, half mad with brandy and blood. Men
were murdered by him on the shore; don't you understand? Men were

drowned in the sea. I can see nothing else. I shall think of nothing else to my dying day.'

Her voice rose, dangerously high; hysteria was not far away. She was still too weak for consecutive thought, and saw herself running out upon the high road, crying loudly for the help that would surely be forthcoming.

Aunt Patience prayed too late for silence; the warning finger was unheeded. The door opened; and the landlord of Jamaica Inn stood on the threshold of the room. He stooped his head under the beam and stared at them. He looked haggard and grey; the cut above his eye was still a vivid scarlet. He was filthy and unwashed, and there were black shadows beneath his eyes.

'I thought I heard voices in the yard,' he said. 'I went to a chink in the shutters, downstairs in the parlour, but I saw no one. Did you hear anything, from this room?'

Nobody answered. Aunt Patience shook her head, the little nervous smile that she conjured for his presence trailing uneasily across her face without her knowledge. He sat down on the bed, his hands plucking at the clothes, his restless eyes roaming from the window to the door.

'He'll come,' he said; 'he's bound to come. I've cut my own throat; I've gone against him. He warned me once, and I laughed at him; I didn't listen. I wanted to play the game on my own. We're as good as dead, all three of us sitting here – you, Patience, and Mary, and I.

'We're finished, I tell you; the game is up. Why did you let me drink? Why didn't you break every blasted bottle in the house, and turn the key on me, and let me lie? I'd not have hurt you; I'd not have touched a hair of your heads, either of you. Now it's too late. The end has come.'

He looked from one to the other of them, his bloodshot eyes hollow, his massive shoulders humped to his neck. They stared back at him without understanding, dumb-founded and awed at the expression on his face they had not seen before.

'What do you mean?' said Mary at length. 'Who are you afraid of? Who warned you?'

He shook his head, and his hands strayed to his mouth, the fingers restless. 'No,' he said slowly, 'I'm not drunk now, Mary Yellan; my secrets are still my own. But I'll tell you one thing – and there's no escape for you; you're in it now as much as Patience there – we have enemies on either side of us now. We have the law on one hand, and on the other . . .' He checked himself, the old cunning in his eyes once more as he glanced at Mary.

'You'd like to know, wouldn't you?' he said. 'You'd like to sneak out of the house with the name on your lips, and betray me. You'd like to see me hanged. All right, I don't blame you for it; I've hurt you enough to make you remember to the rest of your days, haven't I? But I saved you too, didn't I? Have you thought what that rabble would have done to you had I not been there?' He laughed, and spat on the floor, something of his usual self returning to him. 'You can put one good mark against me for that alone,' he said. 'Nobody touched you last night but myself, and I've not spoilt your pretty face. Cuts and bruises mend, don't they? Why, you poor weak thing, you know as well as I do I could have had you your first week at Jamaica

Inn if I'd wanted you. You're a woman after all. Yes, by heaven, and you'd be lying at my feet now, like your Aunt Patience, crushed and contented and clinging, another God-damn bloody fool. Let's get out of here. The room stinks of damp and decay.'

He shambled to his feet, dragging her after him into the passage, and, when they came on to the landing, he thrust her against the wall, beneath the candle stuck in the bracket, so that the light fell upon her bruised, cut face. He took her chin in his hands and held her for a moment, smoothing the scratches with delicate light fingers. She stared back at him in loathing and disgust, the gentle, graceful hands reminding her of all she had lost and renounced; and, when he bent his hated face lower, indifferent of Patience, who stood beside him, and his mouth, so like his brother's, hovered an instant on hers, the illusion was horrible and complete; and she shuddered and closed her eyes. He blew out the light; they followed him down the stairs without a word, their footsteps pattering sharply through the empty house.

He led the way into the kitchen, where even there the door was bolted and the window barred. Two candles were on the table to light the room.

Then he turned and faced the two women, and, reaching for a chair, he straddled his legs across it and considered them, fumbling in his pocket for his pipe meanwhile, and filling it.

'We've got to think out a plan of campaign,' he said; 'we've been sitting here for nigh on two days now, like rats in a trap, waiting to be caught. And I've had enough, I tell you. I never could play that sort of game; it gives me the horrors. If there's going to be a scrap, then, by Almighty God, let's have it in the open.' He puffed awhile at his pipe, staring moodily at the floor, tapping his foot on the stone flags.

'Harry's loyal enough,' he continued, 'but he'd split and have the house about our ears if he thought there'd be profit for himself. As for the rest – they're scattered over the countryside, whining, their tails between their legs, like a blasted pack of curs. This has scared 'em for ever. Yes, and it's scared me too, you can know that. I'm sober now, all right; I can see the damn-fool unholy mess I've landed in, and we'll be lucky, all of us, if we get out of it without swinging. You, Mary, can laugh if you like, with your white contemptuous face; it'll be as bad for you as for Patience and I. You're in it too, up to the neck; you'll not escape. Why didn't you turn the key on me, I say? Why didn't you stop me from drinking?'

His wife stole over to him, and plucked at his jacket, passing her tongue over her lips in preparation for speech.

'Well, what is it?' he said fiercely.

'Why can't we creep away now, before it's too late?' she whispered. 'The trap's in the stable; we'll be in Launceston and across to Devon in a few hours. We could travel by night; we could make for the eastern counties.'

'You damned idiot!' he shouted. 'Don't you realise there are people on the road between here and Launceston who think I'm the Devil himself – who are only waiting their chance to fasten every crime in Cornwall on my head, and get me? The whole country knows by now what happened on the coast on Christmas Eve, and if they see us bolting they'll have the proof. God, don't you think I haven't itched to get away and save my skin? Yes, and by doing so have every man in the country point his finger at us. We'd look fine, wouldn't we, riding in the trap on top of our goods and chattels, like farmers on market-day, waving good-bye in Launceston square? No, we've got one chance, one single chance in a million. We've got to lie quiet; we've got to lie mum. If we sit here tight at Jamaica Inn they may start scratching their heads and rubbing their noses. They've got to look for proof, mind you. They've got to get the sworn proof before they lay hands on us. And unless one of that blasted rabble turns informer they won't get the proof.

'Oh, yes, the ship's there, with her back broken on the rocks, and there's chunks of stuff lying on the beach – piles of it – ready to take away, put there by someone, they'll say. They'll find two bodies, charred to cinders, and a heap of ashes. "What's this?" they'll say. "There's been a fire; there's been a scrap." It'll look dirty, it'll look bad for many of us, but where's proof? Answer me that. I spent my Christmas Eve like a respectable man, in the bosom of my family, playing cat's-cradle and snap-dragon with my niece.' He put his tongue in his cheek and winked.

'You've forgotten one thing, haven't you?' said Mary.

'No, my dear, I have not. The driver of that carriage was shot, and he fell in the ditch, not quarter of a mile down the road outside. You were hoping we'd left the body there, weren't you? Maybe it will shock you, Mary, but the body travelled with us to the coast, and it lies now, if I remember rightly, beneath a ten-foot bank of shingle. Of course, someone is going to miss him; I'm prepared for that; but as they'll never find his carriage it doesn't make much odds. Maybe he was tired of his wife, and has driven to Penzance. They're welcome to look for him there. And now that we've both come to our senses again, you can tell me what you were doing in that carriage, Mary, and where you had been. If you don't answer me, you know me well enough by now. I can find a way of making you talk.'

Mary glanced at her aunt. The woman was shivering like a frightened dog, her blue eyes fixed upon her husband's face. Mary thought rapidly. It was easy enough to lie; time was the all-important factor now, and must be reckoned with and cherished if she and her Aunt Patience were to come out of this alive. She must play upon it and give her uncle rope enough to hang himself. His confidence would go against him in the end. She had one hope of salvation, and he was near, not five miles away, waiting in Altarnun for a signal from her.

'I'll tell you my day, and you can believe it or not,' she said; 'it doesn't matter much to me what you think. I walked to Launceston on Christmas Eve, and went to the fair. I was tired by eight o'clock, and when it came to rain and blow I was wet through and fit for nothing. I hired that carriage, and I told the man I wanted him to take me to Bodmin. I thought if I said the Jamaica Inn he would have refused the journey. There, I've nothing more to tell you than that.'

'Were you alone in Launceston?'

'Of course I was alone.'

'And you spoke to no one?'

'I bought a handkerchief from a woman at a stall.'

Joss Merlyn spat on the floor. 'All right,' he said. 'Whatever I did to you now, you'd tell the same story, wouldn't you? You've got the advantage for once, because I can't prove if you're lying or not. Not many maids your age would spend the day alone in Launceston, I can tell you that. Nor would they drive home by themselves. If your story's true, then our prospects improve. They'll never trace that driver here. God damn it, I shall feel like another drink in a moment.'

He tilted back his chair and pulled at his pipe.

'You shall drive in your own coach yet, Patience,' he said, 'and wear feathers in your bonnet, and a velvet cloak. I'm not beaten yet. I'll see the whole band of 'em in hell first. You wait; we'll start afresh again, we'll live like fighting-cocks. Maybe I'll turn sober, and go to church on Sundays. And you, Mary, you shall hold my hand in my old age and spoon me my food.'

He threw back his head and laughed; but his laugh broke short in the middle, his mouth shut like a trap, and he crashed his chair down on the floor again, and stood up in the middle of the room, his body turned sideways, his face as white as a sheet. 'Listen,' he whispered hoarsely; 'listen. . . .'

They followed the direction of his eyes, fastened as they were upon the chink of light that came through the narrow gap in the shutters.

Something was scraping gently at the kitchen window . . . tapping lightly, softly, scratching furtively at the pane of glass.

It was like the sound made by a branch of ivy when it has broken loose from the trunk and, bending downwards, teases a window or a porch, disturbed and restless with every breath of wind. But there was no ivy on the slate walls of Jamaica Inn, and the shutters were bare.

The scraping continued, persuasive and undaunted, tap . . . tap . . . like the drumming of a beak: tap . . . tap . . . like the four fingers of a hand.

There was no other sound in the kitchen except the frightened breathing of Aunt Patience, whose hand crept out across the table to her niece. Mary watched the landlord as he stood motionless on the kitchen floor, his figure shadowed monstrously on the ceiling, and she saw his lips blue through the dark stubble of his beard. Then he bent forward, crouching on tiptoe like a cat, and, sliding his hand along the floor, his fingers fastened themselves upon his gun that stood against the further chair, never once taking his eyes from the chink of light between the shutters.

Mary swallowed, her throat dry as dust; whether the thing behind the window was friend or enemy to herself made the suspense more poignant, but in spite of her hopes the thumping of her heart told her that fear was infectious, as were the beads of perspiration on her uncle's face. Her hands wandered to her mouth, trembling and clammy.

For a moment he waited beside the closed shutters, and then he sprang forward, tearing at the hinge and pulling them apart, the grey light of afternoon slanting at once into the room. A man stood outside the window, his livid face pressed against the pane, his broken teeth gaping in a grin.

It was Harry the pedlar . . . Joss Merlyn swore, and threw open the window. 'God damn you, come inside, can't you?' he shouted. 'Do you want a bullet in your guts, you blasted fool? You've had me here standing like a deaf-mute for five minutes, with my gun trained on your belly. Unbolt the door, Mary; don't lean against the wall there like a ghost. There's nerves enough in this house without you turning sour.' Like all men who have been badly scared, he threw the blame of his own panic upon the shoulders of another, and now blustered to reassure himself. Mary crossed slowly to the door. The sight of the pedlar brought back a vivid memory of her struggle in the lane, and reaction came swift upon her. Her nausea and disgust returned in force, and she could not look upon him. She opened the door without a word, screening herself behind it, and when he came into the kitchen she turned at once and went to the dull fire, piling the turf upon the embers mechanically, her back towards him. 'Well, have you brought news?' questioned the landlord.

The pedlar smacked his lips in reply, and jerked his thumb over his shoulder.

'The country's gone up in smoke,' he said. 'Every cluttering tongue in Cornwall, from the Tamar to St. Ives. I was in Bodmin this forenoon; the town was ringing with it, and they're hot mad for blood and justice too. Last night I slept at Camelford, every man-jack in the place shaking his fist in the air and blabbing to his neighbour. There'll only be one end to this storm, Joss, and you know the name for it, don't you?'

He made a gesture with his hands across his throat.

'We've got to run for it,' he said; 'it's our only chance. The roads are poison, and Bodmin and Launceston worst of all. I'll keep to the moors and get into Devon above Gunnislake; it'll take me longer, I know that, but what's the odds if you save your skin? Have you got a bite of bread in the house, missus? I've not touched food since yesterday forenoon.'

He threw his question at the landlord's wife, but his glance fell upon Mary. Patience Merlyn fumbled in the cupboard for bread and cheese, her mouth working nervously, her movements clumsy, her mind anywhere but on her mission. As she laid the table she looked beseechingly at her husband.

'You hear what he says,' she pleaded. 'It's madness to stop here; we must go now, at once, before it's too late. You know what this means to the people; they will have no mercy on you; they'll kill you without trial. For God's sake listen to him, Joss. You know I don't care for myself; it's for you. . . .'

'Shut your mouth, can't you?' thundered her husband. 'I've never asked your counsel yet, and I don't ask it now. I can face what's coming to me alone, without you bleating beside me like a sheep. So you'll throw your hand in too, Harry, will you? Run with your tail between your legs because a lot of clerks and Wesleyans are howling to Jesus for your blood? Have they proved it on us? Tell me that. Or has your liver conscience gone against you?'

'Damn my conscience, Joss; it's common sense I'm thinking of. This part of the country has come unhealthy, and I'll go from it while I can. As to proof, we've sailed close enough to the wind these last months to be proof enough, haven't we? I've stuck to you, haven't I? Come out here to-day, risking my neck, to give you warning. I'm not saying anything against you, Joss, but it was your damned stupidity brought us into this mess, wasn't it? You got us mad drunk like yourself, and led us to the shore, on a crazy hare-brained venture that none of us had planned. We took a chance in a million, and the chance came off – too damned bloody well. Because we were drunk we lost our heads, left the stuff and a hundred tracks scattered on the shore. And whose fault was it? Why, yours, I say.' He smashed his fist on the table, his yellow, impudent face thrust close to the landlord, a sneer on his cracked lips.

Joss Merlyn considered him for a moment, and when he spoke his voice was dangerous and low. 'So you accuse me, do you, Harry?' he said. 'You're like the rest of your kind, wriggling like a snake when the luck of the game turns against you. You've done well out of me, haven't you? Had gold to burn you never had before; lived like a prince all these months, instead of at the bottom of a mine, where you belong. And supposing we'd kept our heads the other night, and cleared in order before dawn, as we've done a hundred times before? You'd be sucking up to me now to fill your pockets, wouldn't you? You'd be fawning on me with the rest of the sniffing curs, begging your share of the spoil, calling me God Almighty; you'd lick my boots and lie down in the dust. Run, then, if you like; run to the Tamar bank with your tail between your legs and be damned to you! I'll take the world on alone.'

The pedlar forced a laugh and shrugged his shoulders. 'We can talk, can't we, without cutting each other's throats? I've not gone against you; I'm on your side still. We were all mad drunk on Christmas Eve, I know that; let's leave it alone then: what's done is done. Our lot is scattered, and we needn't reckon with them. They'll be too scared to show their heads and worry us. That leaves you and I, Joss. We've been in this business, the pair of us, deeper than most, I know that, and the more we help each other, the better it'll be for us both. Now then, that's why I'm here, to talk it over and see where we stand.' He laughed again, showing his soft gums, and began to beat a tattoo on the table with his squat black fingers.

The landlord watched him coolly, and reached once more for his pipe.

'Just what would you be driving at, Harry?' he said, leaning against the table, and filling his pipe afresh.

The pedlar sucked his teeth and grinned. 'I'm not driving at anything,' he said. 'I want to make things easier for all of us. We've got to quit, that's evident, unless we want to swing. But it's like this, Joss; I don't see the fun in quitting empty-handed, for all that. There's a mint of stuff we dumped along in the room yonder two days ago, from the shore. That's right, isn't it? And by rights it belongs to all of us who worked for it on Christmas Eve. But there's none of 'em left to claim it but you and I. I'm not saying there's much of value there – it's junk mostly, no doubt – but I don't see why some of it shouldn't help us into Devon, do you?'

The landlord blew a cloud of smoke into his face. 'So you didn't come back to Jamaica Inn because of my sweet smile alone, then?' he said. 'I was thinking you were fond of me, Harry, and wanted to hold my hand.'

The pedlar grinned again, and shifted on his chair. 'All right,' he said; 'we're friends, aren't we? There's no harm done in plain speaking. The stuff's there, and it'll take two men to shift it. The women here can't do it. What's against you and I striking a bargain, and be done with it?'

The landlord puffed thoughtfully at his pipe. 'You're teeming with ideas, all strung out as pretty as the fancy trinkets on your tray, my friend. And supposing the stuff isn't there, after all? Supposing I've disposed of it already? I've been here kicking my heels for two days, you know, and the coaches pass my door. What then, Harry boy?'

The grin faded from the face of the pedlar, and he thrust out his jaw.

'What's the joke?' he snarled. 'Do you play a double game up here at Jamaica Inn? You'll find it hasn't paid you, if you have. You've been mighty silent sometimes, Joss Merlyn, when cargoes were run and when we had the waggons on the road. I've seen things sometimes I haven't understood, and heard things too. You've made a brilliant job of this trade, month in, month out; too brilliant, some of us thought, for the small profit we made out of it, who took most of the risks. And we didn't ask you how you did it, did we? Listen here, Joss Merlyn: do you take your orders from one above you?'

The landlord was on him like a flash. He caught the pedlar on the point of the chin with his clenched fist, and the man went over backwards on to his head, the chair beneath him striking the stone flags with a crash. He recovered instantly, and scrambled to his knees, but the landlord towered above him, the muzzle of his gun pointed at the pedlar's throat.

'Move, and you're a dead man,' he said softly.

Harry the pedlar looked up at his assailant, his little mean eyes half closed, his puffy face yellow. The fall had winded him, and he breathed shortly. At the first sign of a struggle Aunt Patience had flattened herself against the wall, terror-stricken, her eyes searching those of her niece in vain appeal. Mary watched her uncle closely; she had no clue this time to his state of mind. He lowered his gun, and pushed at the pedlar with his foot.

'Now we can talk reason, you and I,' he said. He leant once more against the table, his gun across his arm, while the pedlar sprawled, half kneeling, half crouching, on the floor.

'I'm the leader in this game, and always have been,' said the landlord slowly. 'I've worked it from the beginning three years ago, when we ran cargoes from little twelve-ton luggers to Padstow, and thought ourselves lucky when we were sevenpence-halfpenny in pocket. I've worked it until the trade was the biggest thing in the country, from Hartland to Hayle. I take orders? My God, I'd like to see the man who dared to try me. Well, it's over now. We've run our course, and the day is done. The game is up, for all of us. You didn't come here to-night to warn me; you came to see what you could get out of the smash. The inn was barred, and your little mean heart rejoiced. You scraped at the window there because you knew from experience that the hasp of the shutter is loose, and easy to force. You didn't think to find me here, did you? You thought it would be Patience here, or Mary; and you would scare them easy, wouldn't you, and reach for my gun, where it hangs handy on the wall, as you've often seen? And then to hell with the landlord of Jamaica Inn. You little rat, Harry, do you think I didn't see it in your eye when I flung back the shutter and saw your face at the window? Do you think I never heard your gasp of surprise, nor watched your sudden yellow grin?'

The pedlar passed his tongue over his lips and swallowed. He threw a glance towards Mary, motionless by the fire, the round button of his eye watchful, like a cornered rat. He wondered it she would throw in the dice against him. But she said nothing. She waited for her uncle.

'Very well,' he said; 'we'll strike a bargain, you and I, as you suggested. We'll come to handsome terms. I've changed my mind after all, my loving friend, and with your help we'll take the road to Devon. There's stuff in this place worth taking, as you reminded me, nor can I load alone. To-morrow is Sunday, and a blessed day of rest. Not even the wrecking of fifty ships will drag the people of this country from their knees. There'll be blinds down, and sermons, and long faces, and prayers offered for poor sailor-men who come by misadventure by the Devil's hand; but they'll not go seeking the Devil on the Sabbath.

'Twenty-four hours we have, Harry, my boy, and to-morrow night, when you've broken your back spading turf and turnips over my property in the farm-cart, and kissed me good-bye, and Patience too, and maybe Mary there as well – why, then you can go down on your knees and thank Joss Merlyn for letting you go free with your life, instead of squatting on your scut in a ditch, where you belong to be, with a bullet in your black heart.'

He raised his gun again, edging the cold muzzle close to the man's throat. The pedlar whimpered, showing the whites of his eyes. The landlord laughed.

'You're a pretty marksman in your way, Harry,' he said. 'Isn't that the spot you touched on Ned Santo the other night? You laid his windpipe bare, and the blood whistled out in a stream. He was a good boy, was Ned, but hasty with his tongue. That's where you got him, wasn't it?'

Closer the muzzle pressed against the pedlar's throat. 'If I made a mistake now, Harry, your windpipe would come clean, just like poor Ned's. You don't want me to make a mistake, do you?'

The pedlar could not speak. His eyes rolled up in a squint and his hand opened wide, the four fingers spread square, as though clamped to the floor.

The landlord shifted his gun, and, bending down, he jerked the pedlar to his feet. 'Come on,' he said; 'do you think I'm going to play with you all night? A jest is a jest for five minutes; after that it becomes a burden on the flesh. Open the kitchen door, and turn to the right, and walk down the passage until I tell you to stop. You can't escape through the entrance to the bar; every door and window in this place is barred. Your hands have been itching to explore the wreckage we brought from the shore, haven't they, Harry? You shall spend the night in the store-room amongst it all. Do you know, Patience, my dear, I believe this is the first time we've offered hospitality at Jamaica Inn. I don't count Mary there; she's part of the household.' He laughed, in high good humour, his mood switched round now like a weathercock, and butting his gun into the pedlar's back, he prodded him out of the kitchen and down the dark flagged passage to the store. The door, that had been battered in rough-and-ready manner by Squire Bassat and his servant, had been reinforced with new planking and post, and was now as strong as, if not stronger than, before. Joss Merlyn had not been entirely idle during the past week.

After he had turned the key on his friend, with a parting injunction not to feed the rats, whose numbers had increased, the landlord returned to the kitchen, a rumble of laughter in his chest.

'I thought Harry would turn sour,' he said. 'I've seen it coming in his eyes for weeks, long before this mess landed on us. He'll fight on the winning side, but he'll bite your hand when the luck turns. He's jealous; he's yellow-green with it, rotten through and through. He's jealous of me. They're all jealous of me. They knew I had brains, and hated me for it. What are you staring at me for, Mary? You'd better get your supper and go to bed. You have a long journey before you to-morrow night, and I warn you here and now it won't be an easy one.'

Mary looked at him across the table. The fact that she would not be going with him did not concern her for the moment; he might think as he liked about it. Tired as she was, for the strain of all she had seen and done weighed heavily upon her, her mind was seething with plans.

Some time, somehow, before to-morrow night, she must go to Altarnun. Once there, her responsibility was over. Action would be taken by others. It would be hard for Aunt Patience, hard for herself at first, perhaps; she knew nothing of the jingle and complexities of the law; but at least justice would win. It would be easy enough to clear her own name, and her aunt's. The thought of her uncle, who sat before her now, his mouth full of stale bread and cheese, standing as he would with his hands bound behind him, powerless for the first time and for ever, was something that afforded her exquisite pleasure, and she turned the picture over and over in her mind, improving upon it. Aunt Patience would recover in time; and the years would drain away from her, bringing her peace at last, and quietude. Mary wondered how the capture would be effected when the moment came. Perhaps they would set out upon the journey as he had arranged, and as they turned out upon the road, he laughing in his assurance, they would be surrounded by a band of men, strong in number and in arms, and as he struggled against them hopelessly, borne to the ground by force, she would lean down to him and smile. 'I thought you had brains, uncle,' she would say to him, and he would know.

She dragged her eyes away from him, and turned to the dresser for her candle. 'I'll have no supper to-night,' she said.

Aunt Patience made a little murmur of distress, lifting her eyes from the plain slab of bread on the plate before her, but Joss Merlyn kicked at her for silence. 'Let her stay sulky if she has the mind, can't you?' he said.

'What does it matter to you if she eats or not? Starvation is good for women and beasts; it brings 'em to heel. She'll be humble enough in the morning. Wait, Mary; you shall sleep sounder still if I turn the key on you. I want no prowlers in the passage.'

His eyes strayed to the gun against the wall, and half-consciously back to the shutter, that still gaped open before the kitchen window.

'Fasten that window, Patience,' he said thoughtfully, 'and put the bar across the shutter. When you have finished your supper, you too can go to bed. I shall not leave the kitchen to-night.'

His wife looked up at him in fear, struck by the tone of his voice, and would have spoken, but he cut her short. 'Haven't you learnt by now not to question me?' he shouted. She rose at once and went to the window. Mary, her candle alight, waited by the door. 'All right,' he said. 'Why are you standing there? I told you to go.' Mary went out into the dark passage, her candle throwing her shadow behind her as she walked. No sound came from the store at the end of the passage, and she thought of the pedlar lying there in the darkness, watching and waiting for the day. The thought of him was abhorrent to her; like a rat he was, imprisoned amongst his fellows, and she suddenly pictured him with rat's claws scratching and gnawing at the framework of the door, scraping his way to freedom in the silence of the night.

She shuddered, strangely thankful that her uncle had decided to make a prisoner of her as well. The house was treacherous to-night, her very footsteps sounding hollow on the flags, and there were echoes that came unbidden from the walls. Even the kitchen, the one room in the house to possess some measure of warmth and normality, gaped back at her as she left it, yellow and sinister in the candle-light. Was her uncle going to sit there, then, the candles extinguished, his gun across his knee, waiting for something? . . . for someone? . . . He crossed into the hall as she mounted the stairs, and he followed her along the landing to the bedroom over the porch.

'Give me your key,' he said, and she handed it to him without a word. He lingered for a moment, looking down at her, and then he bent low and laid his fingers on her mouth.

'I've a soft spot for you, Mary,' he said; 'you've got spirit still, and pluck, for all the knocks I've given you. I've seen it in your eyes to-night. If I'd been a younger man I'd have courted you, Mary – aye, and won you too, and ridden away with you to glory. You know that, don't you?'

She said nothing. She stared back at him as he stood beyond the door, and her hand that held the candlestick trembled slightly without her knowledge.

He lowered his voice to a whisper. 'There's danger for me ahead,' he said. 'Never mind the law; I can bluff my way to freedom if it comes to that. The whole of Cornwall can come running at my heels for all I care. It's other game I have to watch for – footsteps, Mary, that come in the night and go again, and a hand that would strike me down.'

His face looked lean and old in the half-light, and there was a flicker of meaning in his eyes that leapt like a flame to tell her, and then dulled again.

'We'll put the Tamar between us and Jamaica Inn,' he said; and then he smiled, the curve of his mouth painfully familiar to her, and known, like an echo from the past. He shut the door upon her and turned the key.

She heard him tramp down the stairs and so down into the passage, and he turned the corner to the kitchen and was gone.

She went then to her bed, and sat down upon it, her hands in her lap; and, for some reason for ever unexplained, thrust away from her later and forgotten, side by side with the little old sins of childhood and those dreams never acknowledged to the sturdy day, she put her fingers to her lips as he had done, and let them stray thence to her cheek and back again.

And she began to cry, softly and secretly, the tears tasting bitter as they fell upon her hand.

Chapter Thirteen

She had fallen asleep where she lay, without undressing, and her first conscious thought was that the storm had come again, bringing with it the rain which streamed against her widow. She opened her eyes, and saw that the night was still, without a tremor of wind from without or the patter of rain. Her senses were alert at once, and she waited for a repetition of the sound that had woken her. It came again in an instant – a shower of earth flung against the pane of glass from the yard outside. She swung her legs to the floor and listened, weighing in her mind the possibility of danger.

If this was a warning signal, the method was a crude one, and better ignored. Someone with little idea of the geography of the inn might have mistaken her window for the landlord's. Her uncle waited below with his gun across his knee in preparation for a visitor; perhaps the visitor had come, and was now standing in the yard. . . . Curiosity gained the better of her in the end, and she crept softly to the window, holding herself in the shadow of the jutting wall. The night was black still, and there were shadows everywhere, but low in the sky a thin line of cloud foretold the dawn.

She had not been mistaken, though; the earth on the floor was real enough, and so was the figure standing directly beneath the porch: the figure of a man. She crouched by the window, waiting for his further movement. He bent again to the ground, fumbling in the barren flower-bed outside the parlour window, and then he raised his hand and threw the little clod of earth at her window, spattering the pane with pebbles and soft mud.

This time she saw his face, and the wonder of it made her cry out in surprise, forgetting the caution to which she had trained herself.

It was Jem Merlyn standing below her in the yard. She leant forward at once, opening her window, and would have called to him, but he lifted his hand for silence. He came close against the wall, skirting the porch which would have hidden her from him, and he cupped his hands to his mouth and whispered up to her, 'Come down to the door here, and unbolt it for me.'

She shook her head at him. 'I cannot do that. I am locked here in my room,' she told him. He stared at her, nonplussed and evidently puzzled, and he looked back at the house as though it might offer some solution of its own. He ran his hands along the slates, testing them, feeling for rusted nails used long ago for creeper, that might afford him foothold of a sort. The low tiles of the porch were within his reach, but they had no gripping surface; he would swing his legs from the ground to no purpose.

'Fetch me the blanket from your bed,' he called softly.

She guessed at once his meaning, and tied one end of her blanket to the foot of her bed, throwing the other out of the window, where it dragged limply above his head. This time he had holding power, and, swinging himself to the low room of the jutting porch, he was able to wedge his body between it and the walls of the house, his feet gripping the slates, and in this manner haul himself up the porch on a level with her window.

He swung his legs over, and straddled the porch, his face close to hers now, the blanket hanging loosely beside him. Mary struggled with the framework of the window, but her efforts were useless. The window opened only a foot or so; he could not enter the room without smashing the glass.

'I shall have to talk to you here,' he said. 'Come closer, where I can see you.' She knelt on the floor of her room, her face at the window gap, and they stared at one another for a moment without speaking. He looked worn, and his eyes were hollow like one who has not slept and has endured fatigue. There were lines about his mouth she had not noticed before, nor did he smile.

'I owe you an apology,' he said at length. 'I deserted you without excuse at Launceston on Christmas Eve. You can forgive me or not, as you feel; but the reason for it – that I can't give you. I'm sorry.'

This attitude of harshness did not suit him; he appeared to have changed much, and the change was unwelcome to her.

'I was anxious for your safety,' she said. 'I traced you to the White Hart and there I was told you had entered a carriage with some gentleman; nothing beyond that, no message, no word of explanation. Those men were there, standing before the fire, the horse-dealer who spoke with you in the market square. They were horrible men, curious, and I mistrusted them. I wondered if the theft of the pony had been discovered. I was wretched and worried. I blame you for nothing. Your business is your own.'

She was hurt by his manner. She had expected anything but this. When she saw him first, in the yard outside her window, she thought of him only as the man she loved, who had come now to her in the night, seeking her presence. His coolness damped her flame, and she withdrew inside herself at once, trusting that he had not seen the blank disappointment in her face.

He did not even ask how she returned that night, and his indifference stunned her. 'Why are you locked in your room?' he questioned.

She shrugged her shoulders, and her voice was flat and dull when she replied.

'My uncle does not care for eavesdroppers. He fears I should wander in the passage and stumble upon his secrets. You appear to have the same dislike of intrusion. To ask you why you are here to-night would be an offence, I suppose?'

'Oh, be as bitter as you like; I deserve it,' he flashed suddenly. 'I know what you think of me. One day I may be able to explain, if you're not out of my reach by then. Be a man for the moment, and send your hurt pride and your curiosity to hell. I'm treading delicate ground, Mary, and one false step will finish me. Where is my brother?'

'He told us he would spend the night in the kitchen. He is afraid of something, or someone; the windows and doors are barred, and he has his gun.'

Jem laughed harshly. 'I don't doubt he's afraid. He'll be more frightened still before many hours are passed, I can tell you that. I came here to see him, but if he sits there with a gun across his knee I can postpone my visit until to-morrow, when the shadows are gone.'

'To-morrow may be too late.'

'What do you mean?'

'He intends to leave Jamaica Inn at nightfall.'

'Are you telling me the truth?'

'Why should I lie to you now?'

Jem was silent. The news had evidently come as a surprise to him, and he was turning it over in his mind. Mary watched him, tortured by doubt and indecision; she was thrown back now upon her old suspicion of him. He was the visitor expected by her uncle, and therefore hated by him and feared. He was the man who held the threads of her uncle's life between his hands. The sneering face of the pedlar returned to her again, and his words, that so provoked the landlord to a flame of fury: 'Listen here, Joss Merlyn, do you take your orders from one above you?' The man whose wits made service of the landlord's strength, the man who had hidden in the empty room.

She thought again of the laughing, care-free Jem who had driven her to Launceston, who had swung hands with her in the market square, who had kissed her and held her. Now he was grave and silent, his face in shadow. The idea of dual personality troubled her, and frightened her as well. He was like a stranger to her to-night, obsessed by some grim purpose she could not understand. Warning him of the landlord's intended flight had been a false move on her part; it might confound the issue of her plans. Whatever Jem had done or intended to do, whether he were false and treacherous and a murderer of men, she loved him, in the weakness of her flesh, and owed him warning.

'You'd best have a care for yourself when you see your brother,' she said. 'His mood is dangerous; whoever interferes with his plans now risks his life. I tell you this for your own safety.'

'I have no fear of Joss, nor ever had.'

'Perhaps not; but what if he is afraid of you?'

To this he said nothing, but, leaning forward suddenly, he looked into her face and touched the scratch that ran from her forehead to her chin.

'Who did this?' he said sharply, turning from the scratch to the bruise on her cheek. She hesitated a moment, and then answered him.

'I got them Christmas Eve.'

The gleam in his eye told her at once that he understood, and had knowledge of the evening, and because of it was here now at Jamaica Inn.

'You were there with them, on the shore?' he whispered.

She nodded, watching him carefully, wary of speech, and for answer he cursed aloud, and, reaching forward, smashed the pane of glass with his fist, careless of the splitting sound of glass and the blood that spouted immediately from his hand. The gap in the window was wide enough now for entrance, and he had climbed into the room and was beside her before she realised what he had done. He lifted her in his arms and carried her to the bed, and laid her down upon it; and, fumbling in the darkness for a candle, he found it at length and lit it, and came back to the bed and knelt beside it, throwing the light upon her face. He traced the bruises with his finger down her neck, and when she winced with the pain he drew in his breath quickly, and again she heard him swear. 'I might have spared you this,' he said; and then, blowing out the light, he sat down beside her on the bed and reached for her hand, which he held a moment, tight, and then gave back to her.

'God Almighty, why did you go with them?' he said.

'They were crazy with drink. I don't think they knew what they were doing. I could no more have stood against them than a child. There were a dozen of them or more, and my uncle . . . he led them. He and the pedlar. If you know about it, why do you ask me? Don't make me remember. I don't want to remember.'

'How much have they hurt you?'

'Bruises, scratches – you can see for yourself. I tried to escape, and I grazed my side. They caught me again, of course. They bound my hands and feet down on the shore, and tied sacking over my mouth so that I could not scream. I saw the ship come through the mist, and I could do nothing – alone there in the wind and the rain. I had to watch them die.'

She broke off, her voice trembling, and she turned on her side, her face in her hands. He made no move towards her; he sat there silently on the bed beside her, and she felt him far from her, wrapped in secrecy.

She was lonelier then than before.

'Was it my brother who hurt you most?' he said presently.

She sighed wearily. It was all too late and did not matter now.

'I've told you he was drunk,' she said. 'You know, better than I perhaps, what he can do then.'

'Yes, I know.' He paused a moment, and then once again he took her hand.

'He shall die for this,' he said.

'His death will not bring back the men he killed.'

'I'm not thinking of them now.'

'If you're thinking of me, don't waste your sympathy. I can revenge myself in my own way. I've learnt one thing at least – to rely on myself.'

'Women are frail things, Mary, for all their courage. You are best out of this business now. The issue lies with me.'

She did not answer him. Her plans were her own and he did not enter into them.

'What do you intend to do?' he asked.

'I have not made up my mind,' she lied.

'If he leaves to-morrow night, you have little to decide,' he said.

'He expects me to go with him, and Aunt Patience as well.'

'And you?'

'That will depend upon to-morrow.'

Whatever she felt for him, she would not hazard her plans into his keeping. He was still an unknown quantity, and above all else an enemy to justice. It came to her then that by betraying her uncle she might also betray him.

'If I ask you to do something, how would you answer me?' she said.

He smiled then for the first time, mocking and indulgent, as he had done in Launceston, and her heart leapt to him at once, encouraged at the change.

'How can I tell?' he said.

'I want you to go away from here.'

'I'm going now.'

'No, I mean away from the moors, away from Jamaica Inn. I want you to tell me you won't return here again. I can stand up against your brother; I'm in no danger from him now. I don't want you to come here to-morrow. Please promise me you'll go away.'

'What have you got in your mind?'

'Something which has no concern with you, but might bring you to danger. I can't say any more. I would rather you trusted me.'

'Trust you? Good God, of course I trust you. It's you who won't trust me, you damned little fool.' He laughed silently, and bent down to her, putting his arms round her, and he kissed her then as he had kissed her in Launceston, but deliberately now, with anger and exasperation.

'Play your own game by yourself, then, and leave me to play mine,' he told her. 'If you must be a boy, I can't stop you, but for the sake of your face, which I have kissed, and shall kiss again, keep away from danger. You don't want to kill yourself, do you? I have to leave you now; it will be daylight within the hour. And if both our plans miscarry, what then? Would you mind if you never saw me again? No, of course you would not care.'

'I have not said so. You hardly understand.'

'Women think differently to men; they travel separate paths. That's why I have no liking for them; they make for trouble and confusion. It was pleasure enough to take you to Launceston, Mary, but when it comes to life and death, like my business now, God knows I wish you a hundred miles away, or sitting primly, your sewing in your lap, in a trim parlour somewhere, where you belong to be.'

'That's never been my life, nor ever will.'

'Why not? You'll wed a farmer one day, or small tradesman, and live respectably among your neighbours. Don't tell them you lived once at Jamaica Inn, and had love made to you by a horse-thief. They'd shut their doors against you. Good-bye, and here's prosperity to you.'

He rose from the bed and went towards the window, climbing through the gap he had broken in the pane; and, swinging his legs over the porch, with one hand on the blanket, he lowered himself to the ground.

She watched him from the window, instinctively waving him farewell, but he had turned and gone without looking back at her, slipping across the yard like a shadow. Slowly she pulled up the blanket and replaced it on the bed. Morning would soon be here; she would not sleep again.

She sat on her bed, waiting until her door should be unlocked; and she made her plans for the evening to come. She must not draw suspicion upon herself during the long day; she must act passively, sullenly perhaps, as though feeling had at last been stifled in her, and she was prepared to undertake the proposed journey with the landlord and Aunt Patience.

Then, later, she would make some excuse – fatigue perhaps, a desire to rest in her room before the strain of the night journey – and then would come the most dangerous moment of her day. She would have to leave Jamaica Inn secretly and unobserved, and run like a hare to Altarnun. This time Francis Davey would understand; time would be against them, and he must act accordingly. She would then return to the inn, with his approval, and trust that her absence had remained unnoticed. This was the gamble. If the landlord went to her room and found her gone, her life would be worth nothing. She must be prepared for that. No excuse would save her then. But if he believed her to be sleeping still, then the game would continue. They would make preparations for the journey; they might even climb into the cart and come out upon the road; after that her responsibility would end. Their fate would be in the hands of the vicar of Altarnun. Beyond this she could not think, nor had she any great desire to look ahead.

So Mary waited for the day; and, when it came, the long hours stretched interminably before her; every minute was an hour, and an hour a particle of eternity itself. The atmosphere of strain was apparent amongst them all. In silence, haggardly, they waited for the night. Little progress could be made during the light of day; intrusion was always possible. Aunt Patience wandered from the kitchen to her room, her footsteps pattering incessantly in the passage and on the stairs, as she made helpless and ineffectual preparations. She would make bundles of what poor clothes remained to her, and then undo them again, when the memory of some forgotten garment jogged her wandering mind. She pottered in the kitchen aimlessly, opening the cupboards, looking into drawers, and she fingered her pots and pans with restless fingers, incapable of deciding which to take and which to leave behind. Mary helped her as best she could, but the unreality of her task made it the more difficult; she knew, while her aunt did not, that all this labour was in vain.

Her heart misgave her at times, when she allowed her thoughts to dwell upon the future. How would Aunt Patience act? How would she look when they came to take her husband from her? She was a child, and must be tended as a child. Again she pattered from the kitchen, climbing the stairs to her room, and Mary would hear her drag her box on the floor, pace up and down, up and down, as she wrapped a single candlestick in a shawl and put it side by side with a cracked teapot and a faded muslin cap, only to unwrap them again and discard them for treasures more ancient.

Joss Merlyn would watch her moodily, cursing her in irritation now and again as she dropped something on the floor, or caught her foot and stumbled. His mood had changed again overnight. His watch in the kitchen had not improved his temper, and the very fact that the hours had been undisturbed and his visitor had not come upon him made him if possible more restless than before. He roamed about the house, nervy and abstracted, muttering to himself at times, peering from the windows as though he expected to see someone come upon him unawares. His nerves reacted upon his wife and Mary. Aunt Patience watched him anxiously, and she too turned her eyes to the window, and would listen, her mouth working, her hands twisting and untwisting her apron.

No sound came from the pedlar in the barred room, nor did the landlord go to him or mention him by name; and this silence was sinister in itself, strange and unnatural. Had the pedlar shouted obscenities, or thundered on the door, it would have been more in keeping with his character; but he lay there in the darkness without sound or movement, and for all her loathing of him Mary shuddered at the possibility of his death.

At the midday meal they sat round the table in the kitchen, eating silently, furtively almost, and the landlord, who usually had the appetite of an ox, drummed moodily with his fingers on the table, the cold meat on his plate untouched. Once Mary lifted her eyes and saw him staring at her beneath shaggy brows. The wild fear ran through her mind that he suspected her, and had some knowledge of her plans. She had counted upon his high humour of the preceding night, and had been prepared to fall in with it, if necessary, answer banter with banter, setting up no opposition to his will. He sat sullen, though, wrapped in gloom, and this was a mood she had experienced before, and, she knew now, led to danger. At length she took courage in both hands and asked him what time he intended to leave Jamaica Inn.

'When I am prepared,' he told her shortly, and would say no more.

She schooled herself to continue, though, and when she had helped to clear the meal away and, at her own suggestion, adding deceit upon deceit, had impressed upon her aunt the necessity of packing a basket of provisions against the journey, she turned to her uncle and spoke again.

'If we are to travel to-night,' she said, 'would it not be better if Aunt Patience and myself rested now during the afternoon, and so could start out fresh upon the journey? There will be no sleep for any of us to-night. Aunt Patience has been upon her feet since daybreak, and I too, for that matter. We do little good, as far as I can see, waiting here for the dusk to fall.' She kept her voice as casual as possible, but the tight band across her heart was a sign that she waited his answer with misgiving, and she could not look into his eyes. He debated the matter a moment, and to control her anxiety she turned away and pretended to fumble in the cupboard.

'You may rest if you will,' he said at length. 'There'll be work for you both, later. You are right when you say there will be no sleep for you to-night. Go then; I shall be well rid of you for the time.'

The first step had been achieved, and Mary lingered awhile with her pretended work in the cupboard, fearing that haste to leave the kitchen should be judged suspicious. Her aunt, who acted always like a dummy to suggestion, followed her meekly upstairs when the time came, and padded along the further passage to her own room as an obedient child would do.

Mary entered her own little room above the porch and closed the door, turning the key. Her heart beat fast at the prospect of adventure, and she could hardly tell whether excitement or fear had the mastery. It was close on four miles to Altarnun by the road, and she could walk the distance in an hour. If she left Jamaica Inn at four o'clock, when the light was failing, she would be back again soon after six; and the landlord would hardly come to rouse her before seven. She had three hours, then, in which to play her part, and she had already determined upon her method of departure. She would climb out on to the porch, and fall to the ground, as Jem had done this morning. The drop was an easy one, and she would escape with little more than a scratch and a jar to her nerves. At any rate, it would be safer to do this than to risk coming upon her uncle in the passage below. The heavy entrance-door would never open noiselessly, and to go through the bar would mean passing the open kitchen.

She put on her warmest dress, and fastened her old shawl across her shoulders with trembling, hot hands. It was the enforced delay that irked her most. Once she was upon the road, the purpose of the walk would bring courage, and the very movement of her limbs would be a stimulant.

She sat by the window, looking out upon the bare yard and the high road where no one ever passed, waiting for the clock in the hall below to strike four. When it sounded at last, the strokes rang out in the silence like an alarm, pounding her nerves; and, unlocking the door, she listened for a moment, hearing footsteps echo the strokes, and whispers in the air.

It was imagination, of course; nothing moved. The clock ticked on into the next hour. Every second was precious to her now, and she must waste no time to be gone. She shut the door, locking it again, and went to the window. She crawled through the gap, as Jem had done, her hands on the sill, and in a moment she was astride the porch, looking down upon the ground.

The distance seemed greater, now that she crouched above it, and she had no blanket to control her fall and let her swing, as he had done. The tiles of the porch were slippery, and gave no grip to hands or feet. She turned, clinging desperately to the security of the window-sill, that seemed desirable suddenly, and a thing well known; then she shut her eyes and launched herself into the air. Her feet found the ground almost immediately – the jump was nothing, as she had already foreseen – but the tiles had grazed her hands and arms and brought back to her again a vivid memory of her last fall, from the carriage in the gully-way beside the shore.

She looked up at Jamaica Inn, sinister and grey in the approaching dusk, the windows barred; she thought of the horrors the house had witnessed, the secrets now embedded in its walls, side by side with the other old memories of feasting and firelight and laughter before her uncle cast his shadow upon it; and she turned away from it, as one turns instinctively from a house of the dead, and went out upon the road.

The evening was fine – that at least favoured her – and she strode out towards her destination with her eyes fixed upon the long white road that lay ahead. Dusk came as she walked, bringing shadows across the moors that lay on either side of her. Away to the left the high tors, shrouded at first in mist, were gathered to the darkness. It was very still. There was no wind. Later, there would be a moon. She wondered if her uncle had reckoned with this force of nature that would shine upon his plans. For herself it would not matter. To-night she had no fear of the moors; they did not concern her. Her business was with the road. The moors lost their significance when unnoticed and untrodden; they loomed beyond her and away from her.

She came at length to the Five Lanes, where the roads branched, and she turned to her left, down the steep hill of Altarnun. Excitement rose high within her now as she passed the twinkling cottage lights, and smelt the friendly smoke of chimneys. Here were neighbourly sounds that had long been lost to her: the barking of a dog, the rustle of trees, the clank of a pail as a man drew water from a well. There were open doors, and voices from within. Chickens clucked beyond a hedge, and a woman called shrilly to a child, who answered with a cry. A cart lumbered past her into the shadows, and the driver gave her good evening. Here was a drowsy movement, a placidity and a peace; here were all the old village smells she knew and understood. She passed them by; and she went to the vicarage beside the church. There were no lights here. The house was shrouded and silent. The trees closed in upon it, and once again she was vividly aware of her first impression that this was a house that lived in its own past, and slept now, with no knowledge of the present. She hammered upon the door and she heard the blows echo through the empty house. She looked in through the windows, and her eyes met nothing but the soft and negative darkness.

Then, cursing her stupidity, she turned back again towards the church. Francis Davey would be there, of course. It was Sunday. She hesitated a moment, uncertain of her movements, and then the gate opened and a woman came out into the road, carrying flowers.

She stared hard at Mary, knowing her a stranger, and would have passed her by with a good night had not Mary turned and followed her.

'Forgive me,' she said; 'I see you have come from the church. Can you tell me if Mr. Davey himself is there?'

'No, he is not,' said the woman; and then, after a moment, 'Were you wishing to see him?'

'Very urgently,' said Mary. 'I have been to his house, and I can get no answer. Can you help me?'

The woman looked at her curiously, and then shook her head.

'I am sorry,' she said. 'The vicar is from home. He went away to-day to preach at another parish, many miles from here. He is not expected back in Altarnun to-night.'

Chapter Fourteen

At first Mary stared at the woman in disbelief. 'Away from home?' she repeated. 'But that is impossible. Surely you are mistaken?'

Her confidence had been such that she rejected instinctively this sudden and fatal blow to her plans. The woman looked offended; she saw no reason why this stranger should doubt her word. 'The vicar left Altarnun yesterday afternoon,' she said. 'He rode away after dinner. I ought to know, for I keep house for him.'

She must have seen something of the agony of disappointment in Mary's face, for she relented and spoke with kindness. 'If there is any message you would like me to give him when he does return—' she began, but Mary shook her head hopelessly, spirit and courage gone from her in a moment with the news.

'It will be too late,' she said in despair. 'This is a matter of life and death. With Mr. Davey gone, I don't know where I can turn.'

Once more a gleam of curiosity came into the woman's eyes. 'Has someone been taken sick?' she enquired. 'I could point you out where our doctor lives, if that would help you. Where have you come from to-night?'

Mary did not answer. She was thinking desperately of some way out of the situation. To come to Altarnun and then return again without help to Jamaica Inn was impossible. She could not place confidence in the village people, nor would they believe her tale. She must find someone in authority – someone who knew something of Joss Merlyn and Jamaica Inn.

'Who is the nearest magistrate?' she said at length.

The woman puckered her brow and considered the question. 'There's no one close by us here in Altarnun,' she said doubtfully. 'Why, the nearest would be Squire Bassat over to North Hill, and that must be over four miles from here – maybe more, maybe less. I cannot say for certain, for I have never been there. You surely would not walk out there to-night?'

'I must,' said Mary; 'there is nothing else for me to do. I must lose no time either. Forgive me for being so mysterious, but I am in great trouble, and only your vicar or a magistrate can help me. Can you tell me if the road to North Hill is hard to find?'

'No, that's easy enough. You go two miles along the Launceston road, and then turn right by the turnpike; but it's scarcely a walk for a maid like you after nightfall, and I'd never go myself. There's rough folk on the moors at times, and you cannot trust them. We dare not venture from our homes these days, with robbery on the high road even, and violence too.'

'Thank you for your sympathy; I am very grateful to you,' said Mary, 'but I have lived all my life in lonely places, and I am not afraid.'

'You must please yourself,' answered the woman, 'but you'd best stay here and wait for the vicar, if you can.'

'That is impossible,' said Mary, 'but when he does return, could you tell him perhaps that . . . Wait, though; if you have pen and paper I will write him a note of explanation; that would be better still.'

'Come into my cottage here, and you may write what you will. When you have gone, I can take the note to his house at once, and leave it on his table, where he will see it as soon as he comes home.'

Mary followed the woman to the cottage, and waited impatiently while she searched her kitchen for a pen. The time was slipping away fast, and the added journey to North Hill had upset every former calculation.

She could hardly return to Jamaica Inn once she had seen Mr. Bassat and still hope her absence had remained unnoticed. Her uncle would take warning from her flight, and leave the inn before the intended time. In which case her mission would have been in vain. . . . Now the woman returned with paper and quill, and Mary wrote desperately, never pausing to choose her words:

'I came here to ask your help, and you were gone,' she scribbled. 'By now you will have heard with horror, as everyone in the country must have done, of the wreck upon the coast on Christmas Eve. It was my uncle's doing, he and the company from Jamaica Inn; that you will have guessed already. He knows that suspicion will fall upon him before long, and because of this he plans to leave the inn to-night, and cross the Tamar into Devon. Finding you absent, I go now with all possible haste to Mr. Bassat at North Hill, to tell everything to him, and warn him of the escape, so that he can send at once to Jamaica Inn to seize my uncle before it is too late. I am giving this note to your housekeeper, who will, I trust, lay it where your eyes will fall upon it directly you return. In haste, then,
Mary Yellan.'

This she folded and gave to the woman by her side, thanking her, and assuring her that she had no fear of the road; and so set out again upon a walk of four miles or more to North Hill. She climbed the hill from Altarnun with a heavy heart and a wretched sense of isolation.

She had placed such faith in Francis Davey that it was hard to realise even yet that by his absence he had failed her. He had not known, of course, that she needed him, and, even if he had, perhaps his plans would have come before her troubles. It was disheartening and bitter to leave the lights of Altarnun behind her, with nothing as yet accomplished. At this moment, perhaps, her uncle was thundering upon her bedroom door, calling her to answer. He would wait a moment, and then force the door. He would find her gone, and the smashed window would tell him the manner of her going. Whether this would play havoc with his plans was a matter for conjecture. She could not know. Aunt Patience was her concern, and the thought of her setting out upon the journey like a shivering dog tethered to its master made Mary run along the bare white road with fists clenched and chin thrust in the air.

She came at last to the turnpike, and turned down the narrow twisting lane as the woman in Altarnun had told her. High hedges screened the country on either side, and the dark moor was thrust away and hidden from her eyes. The road twisted and turned, as the lanes in Helford used to do, and this change of scene, coming so suddenly after the bleak high road, put faith in her once more. She cheered herself by painting a picture of the Bassat family as kindly and courteous, like the Vyvyans at Trelowarren, who would listen to her with sympathy and understanding. She had not seen the squire at his best before; he had come upon Jamaica Inn in high ill-humour and she thought now with regret of the part she had played in his deception. As for his lady, she must know now that a horse-thief had made a fool of her in Launceston market square, and it was lucky for Mary that she had not stood at Jem's side when the pony was sold back to his rightful owner. She continued with her fantasy of the Bassats, but the little incidents came back to her in spite of it, and at the bottom of her heart she looked upon the approaching interview with trepidation.

The contour of the land had changed again, and hills rose away from her, forested and dark, and somewhere beyond her ran a stream singing and breaking over stones. The moorland was no more. The moon came now, topping the further trees, and she walked in confidence with the light blazing a path for her, leading her downwards to the valley, where the trees closed in friendliness upon her. She came at last to lodge gates and the entrance to a drive, while beyond her the lane continued to a village.

That must be North Hill, and this the manor house belonging to the squire. She went down the avenue to the house, and away in the distance a church clock struck seven. She had been about three hours already from Jamaica Inn. Her nervousness returned as she rounded upon the house, large and forbidding in the darkness, with the moon not yet risen high enough to shine kindly upon it. She swung the great bell, and the sound was met at once by the furious baying of hounds. She waited, and presently she heard footsteps from within, and the door was opened by a manservant. He called sharply at the dogs, who thrust their noses at the door, and sniffed at Mary's feet. She felt inferior and small, and was conscious of her old dress and shawl before this man who waited for her to speak. 'I have come to see Mr. Bassat on very urgent business,' she told him. 'He would not know my name, but if he could speak to me for a few minutes I would explain. The matter is of desperate importance, otherwise I would not disturb him at such an hour, and on a Sunday night.'

'Mr. Bassat left for Launceston this morning,' answered the man. 'He was called away hurriedly, and he has not yet returned.'

This time Mary could not control herself, and a cry of despair escaped her.

'I have come some way,' she said, in an agony of feeling, as though by her very distress she could bring the squire to her side. 'If I do not see him within the hour something terrible will happen, and a great criminal escape the hands of the law. You look at me blankly, but I am speaking the truth. If only there was someone I could turn to . . .'

'Mrs. Bassat is at home,' said the man, stung with curiosity. 'Perhaps she will see you, if your business is as urgent as you say. Follow me, will you, to the library. Never mind the dogs; they will not hurt you.'

Mary crossed the hall in a dream, knowing only that her plan had failed again, through chance alone, and that she was powerless now to help herself.

The wide library, with its blazing fire, seemed unreal to her, and, accustomed as she was to the darkness, she blinked at the flood of light that met her eyes. A woman whom she recognised immediately as the fine lady from Launceston market square was sitting in a chair before the fire, reading aloud to two children, and she looked up in surprise when Mary was shown into the room.

The servant began his explanation in some excitement. 'This young woman has very grave news for the squire, madam,' he said. 'I thought it best to show her in to you directly.'

Mrs. Bassat rose to her feet at once, dropping the book from her lap.

'It isn't one of the horses, is it?' she said. 'Richards told me Solomon had been coughing and that Diamond would not take his food. With this undergroom anything may happen.'

Mary shook her head. 'Your household is not in trouble,' she said gravely. 'I bring news of another kind. If I could speak to you alone . . .'

Mrs. Bassat appeared relieved that her horses were not affected, and she spoke quickly to her children, who ran from the room, followed by the manservant.

'What can I do for you?' she said graciously. 'You look pale and fatigued. Won't you sit down?'

Mary shook her head impatiently. 'Thank you, but I must know when Mr. Bassat is returning home.'

'I have no idea,' replied his lady. 'He was obliged to leave this morning at a moment's notice, and, to tell you the truth, I am seriously concerned about him. If this dreadful innkeeper shows fight, as he is certain to do, Mr. Bassat may be wounded, in spite of the soldiers.'

'What do you mean?' said Mary swiftly.

'Why, the squire has set out upon a highly dangerous mission. Your face is new to me, and I conclude you are not from North Hill, otherwise you would have heard of this man Merlyn who keeps an inn upon the Bodmin road. The squire has suspected him for some while of terrible crimes, but it was not until this morning that the full proof came into his hands. He departed at once for Launceston to summon help, and, from what he told me before he went, he intends to surround the inn to-night and seize the inhabitants. He will go well armed, of course, and with a large body of men, but I shall not rest until he returns.'

Something in Mary's face must have warned her, for she turned very pale, and backed towards the fire, reaching out for the heavy bell-pull that hung on the wall. 'You are the girl he spoke about,' she said quickly, 'the girl from the inn, the niece of the landlord. Stay where you are; don't move, or I will summon my servants. You are the girl. I know it; he described you to me. What do you want with me?'

Mary put out her hand, her face as white as the woman's by the fire.

'I won't hurt you,' she said. 'Please do not ring. Let me explain. Yes, I am the girl from Jamaica Inn.' Mrs. Bassat did not trust her. She watched Mary with troubled eyes, and kept her hand upon the bell-rope.

'I have no money here,' she said. 'I can do nothing for you. If you have come to North Hill to plead for your uncle, it is too late.'

'You misunderstand me,' said Mary quietly. 'And the landlord of Jamaica Inn is a relative to me by marriage only. Why I have been living there does not matter now, and the story would take too long in the telling. I fear and detest him more than you or anyone in the country, and with reason. I came here to warn Mr. Bassat that the landlord intended to leave the inn to-night, and so escape justice. I have definite proof of his guilt, which I did not believe Mr. Bassat to possess. You tell me that he has already gone, and perhaps even now is at Jamaica Inn. Therefore I have wasted my time in coming here.'

She sat down then, her hands in her lap, and stared blankly at the fire. She had come to the end of her resources, and for the moment she could not look ahead. All that her weary mind could tell her was that her labour of the evening had been purposeless and in vain. She need never have left her bedroom at Jamaica Inn. Mr. Bassat would have come in any case. And now, by her secret meddling, she had blundered into the very mistake she had wished to avoid. She had stayed away too long; and by now her uncle would have guessed the truth, and in all probability made his escape. Squire Bassat and his men would ride to a deserted inn.

She lifted her eyes once more to the lady of the house. 'I have done a very senseless thing in coming here,' she said hopelessly. 'I thought it clever, and I have only succeeded in making a fool of myself and of everyone else. My uncle will discover my room is empty, and guess at once that I have betrayed him. He will leave Jamaica Inn before Mr. Bassat arrives.'

The squire's lady let go of the bell-rope now, and came towards her.

'You speak sincerely, and you have an honest face,' she said kindly. 'I am sorry if I misjudged you at first, but Jamaica Inn has a terrible name, and I believe anyone would have done the same had they been confronted suddenly with the landlord's niece. You have been placed in a fearful position, and I think you very brave to come here to-night, all those lonely miles, to warn my husband. I should have gone mad with fear. The question is this: what would you have me do now? I am willing to help you in any way you think best.'

'There is nothing we can do,' said Mary, shaking her head. 'I must wait here, I suppose, until Mr. Bassat returns. He won't be over-pleased to see me when he hears how I have blundered. God knows I deserve every reproach. . . .'

'I will speak for you,' replied Mrs. Bassat. 'You could not possibly know my husband had already been informed, and I will soon smooth him down if he needs it. Be thankful you are here in safety meanwhile.'

'How did the squire learn the truth so suddenly?' asked Mary.

'I have not the slightest idea; he was sent for very suddenly this morning, as I have told you already, and he only gave me the barest details before his horse was saddled and he was gone. Now, won't you rest yourself, and forget for the time the whole hateful business? You are probably famished for want of food.' Once more she approached the fireplace, and this time she pulled the bell-rope three or four times. For all her worry and distress, Mary could not help seeing the irony of the situation. Here was the lady of the house offering hospitality, who a moment ago had threatened her with seizure by the same servants who would now bring her food. She thought also of the scene in the market square when this same lady, in velvet cloak and feathered hat, had paid a high price for her own pony, and she wondered whether the trickery had been discovered. If Mary's own part in the deception should come to light, Mrs. Bassat would hardly be so lavish with her hospitality.

Meanwhile the servant appeared, his inquisitive nose in the air, and was told by his mistress to bring a tray of supper for Mary, and the dogs, who had followed him into the room, came now to make friends with the stranger, wagging their tails and pushing their soft noses into her hands, accepting her as a member of the household. Her presence in the manor house at North Hill was still without reality, and, though Mary tried, she could not throw aside anxiety and relax. She felt she had no right to be sitting here before a glowing fire, when outside, in the darkness, life and death fought hand to hand before Jamaica Inn. She ate mechanically, forcing herself to swallow the food she needed, aware of the prattle of her hostess at her side, who in the mistaken kindness of her heart believed that incessant conversation about nothing at all was the only method of alleviating worry. The chatter, had she but realised, increased it, and when Mary had finished her supper and sat once more with her hands on her lap, staring at the fire, Mrs. Bassat, searching in her mind for suitable distraction, fetched an album of her own water-colours and proceeded to turn the pages for the benefit of her guest.

When the clock on the mantelpiece chimed eight o'clock in piercing tones, Mary could bear it no longer. This dragging inactivity was worse than danger and pursuit. 'Forgive me,' she said, rising to her feet; 'you have been so kind, and I can never thank you enough; but I am anxious, desperately anxious. I can think of nothing but my poor aunt, who at this moment may be suffering the tortures of hell. I must know what is happening at Jamaica Inn, if I walk back there myself to-night.'

Mrs. Bassat dropped her album in a flutter of distress. 'Of course you are anxious. I have seen it all along, and tried to take your mind off it. How terrible it is. I am as concerned as you are, for my husband sake. But you cannot possibly walk back there now, alone. Why, it would be after midnight before you arrived, and heaven knows what might not happen to you on the way. I will order the trap, and Richards shall go with you. He is most trustworthy and dependable, and can be armed in case of need. If there is fighting in progress, you would see it from the bottom of the hill, and would

not approach until it was over. I would come with you myself, but my health
is delicate at the moment and . . .'

'Of course you will do nothing of the kind,' said Mary swiftly. 'I am used
to danger and the road by night, and you are not. I shall be putting you to
very great trouble in harnessing your horse at this hour and rousing your
groom. I assure you I'm no longer tired, and I can walk.'

But Mrs. Bassat had already pulled the bell. 'Have word sent to Richards
to bring the trap round immediately,' she said to the astonished servant. 'I
will give him further orders when he arrives. Tell him there must be as little
delay as possible.' She then fitted Mary out with a heavy cloak and hood,
thick rug and foot-warmer, protesting all the while that only her state of
health prevented her from making the journey too, for which Mary was
utterly thankful, Mrs. Bassat being hardly the ideal companion for so
improvident and dangerous an escapade.

In a quarter of an hour the trap drove up to the door, with Richards in
charge, Mary recognising him at once as the servant who had ridden with
Mr. Bassat originally to Jamaica Inn. His reluctance at leaving his fireside
on a Sunday night was soon overcome when he learnt his mission, and with
two large pistols stuck in his belt, and orders to fire at anyone who threatened
the trap, he assumed at once an air of truculence and authority hitherto
unknown to him. Mary climbed in beside him, the dogs baying a chorus of
farewell, and it was only when the drive twisted and the house was out of
sight that Mary realised she had set out on what was probably to be a
foolhardy and dangerous expedition.

Anything might have happened during the five hours she had been absent
from Jamaica Inn, and even with the trap she could scarcely hope to arrive
there before half past ten. She could make no plans, and her action depended
upon the moment when it came. With the moon now high in the sky and
the soft air blowing upon her she felt emboldened to face disaster when it
came, and this ride to the scene of action, however dangerous, was better
than sitting like a helpless child listening to the prattle of Mrs. Bassat. This
man Richards was armed, and she herself would use a gun if necessary. He
was burning with curiosity, of course, but she gave short answers to his
questions, and did not encourage him.

The drive was silent then, for the most part, with no other sound but the
steady clopping of the horse's hoofs upon the road, and now and again an
owl hooted from the still trees. The rustle of hedgerow and the creeping
country whispers were left behind when the trap came out upon the Bodmin
road, and once again the dark moor stretched out on either side, lapping the
road like a desert. The ribbon of the highway shone white under the moon.
It wound and was lost in the fold of the further hill, bare and untrodden.
There were no travellers but themselves upon the road to-night. On Christmas Eve, when Mary had ridden here, the wind had lashed venomously at
the carriage wheels, and the rain hammered the windows: now the air was
still cold and strangely still, and the moor itself lay placid and silver in the
moonlight. The dark tors held their sleeping faces to the sky, the granite

features softened and smoothed by the light that bathed them. Theirs was a peaceful mood, and the old gods slept undisturbed.

Briskly the horse and trap covered the weary miles that Mary had walked alone. She recognised each bend in the road now, and how at times the moor encroached upon it, with high tufts of grass or twisted stem of broom.

There, beyond her in the valley, would be the lights of Altarnun, and already the Five Lanes branched out from the road like fingers from a hand.

The wild stretch to Jamaica lay before them. Even when the night was still the wind played here, bare and open as it was to every compass point, and to-night it hummed from Roughtor in the west, keen as a knife and cold, gathering the marsh smells as it came, over the bitter turf and the running streams. There was still no sign of man or beast upon the road, which rose and dipped again across the moor, and, though Mary strained her eyes and her ears, she could hear nothing. On such a night the slightest sound would be magnified, and the approach of Mr. Bassat's party, numbering, as they would, a dozen men or so, said Richards, would easily be heard two miles or more away.

'We shall find them there before us, as likely as not,' he told Mary, 'and the landlord, with his hands bound, breathing fire at the squire. It will be a good thing for the neighbourhood when he's put out of harm's way, and he would have been before now, if the squire could have had his way. It's a pity we were not here sooner; there'll have been some sport in taking him, I reckon.'

'Little sport if Mr. Bassat finds that his bird has flown,' said Mary quietly. 'Joss Merlyn knows these moors like the back of his hand, and he'll not linger once he has the start of an hour, or less than that.'

'My master was bred here, same as the landlord,' said Richards; 'if it comes to a chase across country, I'd lay odds on the squire every time. He's hunted here, man and boy, for nearly fifty years, I should say, and where a fox will go the squire will follow. But they'll catch this one before he starts to run, if I'm not mistaken.' Mary let him continue; his occasional jerky statements did not worry her as the kindly prattle of his mistress had done, and his broad back and honest rugged face gave her some confidence in this night of strain.

They were approaching the dip in the road and the narrow bridge that spanned the river Fowey; Mary could hear the ripple and play of the stream as it ran swiftly over the stones. The steep hill to Jamaica rose in front of them, white beneath the moon, and as the dark chimneys appeared above the crest, Richards fell silent, fumbling with the pistols in his belt, and he cleared his throat with a little nervous jerk of his head. Mary's heart beat fast now, and she held tight to the side of the trap. The horse bent to the climb, his head low, and it seemed to Mary that the clop of his hoofs rang too loudly on the surface of the road, and she wished they had been more silent.

As they drew near to the summit of the hill, Richards turned and whispered in her ear, 'Would it be best for you to wait here, in the trap, by the side of the road, and I go forward and see if they are there?'

Mary shook her head. 'Better for me to go,' she said, 'and you follow a pace or two behind, or stay here and wait until I call. From the silence, it seems as though the squire and his party are not yet come, after all, and that the landlord has escaped. Should he be there, however – my uncle, I mean – I can risk an encounter with him, when you could not. Give me a pistol; I shall have little to fear from him then.'

'I hardly think it right for you to go alone,' said the man doubtfully. 'You may walk right into him, and I hear no sound from you again. It's strange, as you say, this silence. I'd expected shouting and fighting, and my master's voice topping it all. It's almost unnatural, in a way. They must have been detained in Launceston. I half fancy there'd be more wisdom if we turned aside down that track there, and waited for them to come.'

'I've waited long enough to-night, and gone half mad with it,' said Mary. 'I'd rather come upon my uncle face to face than lie here in the ditch, seeing and hearing nothing. It's my aunt I'm thinking of. She's as innocent as a child in all this business, and I want to care for her if I can. Give me a pistol and let me go. I can tread like a cat, and I'll not run my head into a noose, I promise you.' She threw off the heavy cloak and hood that had protected her from the cold night air, and seized hold of the pistol that he handed down to her reluctantly. 'Don't follow me unless I call or give some signal,' she said. 'Should you hear a shot fired, then perhaps it would be as well to come after me. But come warily, for all that. There's no need for both of us to run like fools into danger. For my part, I believe my uncle to have gone.'

She hoped now that he had, and by driving into Devon made an end to the whole business. The country would be rid of him, and in the cheapest possible way. He might, even as he had said, start life again, or, more likely still, dig himself in somewhere five hundred miles from Cornwall, and drink himself to death. She had no interest now in his capture; she wanted it finished and thrust aside; she wanted above all to lead her own life and forget him, and to put the world between her and Jamaica Inn. Revenge was an empty thing. To see him bound and helpless, surrounded by the squire and his men, would be of little satisfaction. She had spoken to Richards with confidence, but for all that she dreaded an encounter with her uncle, armed as she was; and the thought of coming upon him suddenly in the passage of the inn, with his hands ready to strike, and his bloodshot eyes staring down upon her, made her pause in her stride, before the yard, and glance back to the dark shadow in the ditch that was Richards and the trap. Then she levelled her pistol, her finger upon the trigger, and looked round the corner of the stone wall to the yard.

It was empty. The stable door was shut. The inn was as dark and silent as when she had left it nearly seven hours before, and the windows and the door were barred. She looked up to her window, and the pane of glass gaped empty and wide, unchanged since she had climbed from it that afternoon.

There were no wheel-marks in the yard, no preparations for departure. She crept across to the stable and laid her ear against the door. She waited a moment, and then she heard the pony move restlessly in his stall; she heard his hoofs clink on the cobbles.

Then they had not gone, and her uncle was still at Jamaica Inn.

Her heart sank; and she wondered if she should return to Richards and the trap, and wait, as he had suggested, until Squire Bassat and his men arrived. She glanced once more at the shuttered house. Surely, if her uncle intended to leave, he would have gone before now. The cart alone would take an hour to load, and it must be nearly eleven o'clock. He might have altered his plans, and decided to go on foot, but then Aunt Patience could never accompany him. Mary hesitated; the situation had become odd now, and unreal.

She stood by the porch and listened. She even tried the handle of the door. It was locked, of course. She ventured a little way round the corner of the house, past the entrance to the bar, and so to the patch of garden behind the kitchen. She trod softly now, keeping herself in shadow, and she came to where a chink of candlelight would show through the gap in the kitchen shutter. There was no light. She stepped close now to the shutter, and laid her eye against the slit. The kitchen was black as a pit. She laid her hand on the knob of the door, and slowly turned it. It gave, to her astonishment, and the door opened. This easy entrance, entirely unforeseen, shocked her for the moment, and she was afraid to enter.

Supposing her uncle sat on his chair, waiting for her, his gun across his knee? She had her own pistol, but it gave her no confidence.

Very slowly she laid her face to the gap made by the door. No sound came to her. Out of the tail of her eye she could see the ashes of the fire, but the glow was almost gone. She knew then that nobody was there. Some instinct told her that the kitchen had been empty for hours. She pushed the door wide, and went inside. The room struck cold and damp. She waited until her eyes had become accustomed to the darkness, and she could make out the shape of the kitchen table, and the chair beside it. There was a candle on the table, and she thrust it into the feeble glow of the fire, where it took light, and flickered. When it burnt strong enough, she held it high above her head and looked about her. The kitchen was still strewn with the preparations for departure. There was a bundle belonging to Aunt Patience on the chair, and a heap of blankets lay on the floor ready to be rolled. In the corner of the room, where it always stood, was her uncle's gun. They had decided, then, to wait for another day, and were now abed and asleep in the room upstairs.

The door to the passage was wide open, and the silence became more oppressive than before, strangely and horribly still.

Something was not as it had been; some sound was lacking that must account for the silence. Then Mary realised that she could not hear the clock. The ticking had stopped.

She stepped into the passage and listened again. She was right; the house was silent because the clock had stopped. She went forward slowly, with the candle in one hand and the pistol levelled in the other.

She turned the corner, where the long dark passage branched into the hall, and she saw that the clock, which stood always against the wall beside the door into the parlour had toppled forward and fallen upon its face. The glass was splintered in fragments on the stone flags, and the wood was split. The wall gaped bare where it had stood, very naked now and strange, with the paper marked a deep yellow in contrast to the faded pattern of the wall. The clock had fallen across the narrow hall, and it was not until she came to the foot of the stairs that Mary saw what was beyond.

The landlord of Jamaica Inn lay on his face amongst the wreckage.

The fallen clock had hidden him at first, for he sprawled in the shadow, one arm flung high above his head and the other fastened upon the broken splintered door. Because his legs were stretched out on either side of him, one foot jamming the wainscoting, he looked even larger in death than he did before, his great frame blocking the entrance from wall to wall.

There was blood on the stone floor; and blood between his shoulders, dark now and nearly dry, where the knife had found him.

When he was stabbed from behind he must have stretched out his hands, and stumbled, dragging at the clock; and when he fell upon his face the clock crashed with him to the ground, and he died there, clutching at the door.

Chapter Fifteen

It was a long while before Mary moved away from the stairs. Something of her own strength had ebbed away, leaving her powerless, like the figure on the floor. Her eyes dwelt upon little immaterial things: the fragments of glass from the smashed clock-face that were bloodstained too, and the discoloured patch of wall where the clock had stood.

A spider settled on her uncle's hand; and it seemed strange to her that the hand stayed motionless and did not seek to rid itself of the spider. Her uncle would have shaken it free. Then it crawled from his hand and ran up his arm, working its way beyond the shoulder. When it came to the wound it hesitated, and then made a circuit, returning to it again in curiosity, and there was a lack of fear in its rapidity that was somehow horrible and desecrating to death. The spider knew that the landlord could not harm him. Mary knew this too, but she had not lost her fear, like the spider.

It was the silence that frightened her most. Now that the clock no longer ticked, her nerves strained for the sound of it; the slow wheezing choke had been familiar and a symbol of normality.

The light of her candle played upon the walls, but it did not reach to the top of the stairs, where the darkness gaped at her like a gulf.

She knew she could never climb those stairs again, nor tread that empty landing. Whatever lay beyond her and above must rest there undisturbed.

Death had come upon the house to-night, and its brooding spirit still hovered in the air. She felt now that this was what Jamaica Inn had always waited for and feared. The damp walls, the creaking boards, the whispers in the air, and the footsteps that had no name: these were the warning of a house that had felt itself long threatened.

Mary shivered; and she knew that the quality of this silence had origin in far-off buried and forgotten things.

She dreaded panic, above all things; the scream that forced itself to the lips, the wild stumble of groping feet and hands that beat the air for passage. She was afraid that it might come to her, destroying reason; and, now that the first shock of discovery had lessened, she knew that it might force its way upon her, close in and stifle her. Her fingers might lose their sense of grip and touch, and the candle fall from her hands. Then she would be alone, and covered by the darkness. The tearing desire to run seized hold of her, and she conquered it. She backed away from the hall towards the passage, the candle flickering in the draught of air, and when she came to the kitchen and saw the door still open to the patch of garden, her calm deserted her, and she ran blindly through the door to the cold free air outside, a sob in her throat, her outstretched hands grazing the stone wall as she turned the corner of the house. She ran like a thing pursued across the yard, and came to the open road, where the familiar stalwart figure of the squire's groom confronted her. He put out his hands to save her, and she groped at his belt, feeling for security, her teeth chattering now in the full shock of reaction.

'He's dead,' she said; 'he's dead there on the floor. I saw him'; and, try as she did, she could not stop this chattering of her teeth and the shivering of her body. He led her to the side of the road, back to the trap, and he reached for the cloak and put it around her, and she held it to her close, grateful for the warmth.

'He's dead,' she repeated; 'stabbed in the back; I saw the place where his coat was rent, and there was blood. He lay on his face. The clock had fallen with him. The blood was dry; and he looked as though he had lain there for some time. The inn was dark and silent. No one else was there.'

'Was your aunt gone?' whispered the man.

Mary shook her head. 'I don't know. I did not see. I had to come away.'

He saw by her face that her strength had gone, and she would fall, and he helped her up into the trap and climbed on to the seat beside her.

'All right, then,' he said, 'all right. Sit quiet, then, here. No one shall hurt you. There now. All right, then.' His gruff voice helped her, and she crouched beside him in the trap, the warm cloak muffled to her chin.

'That was no sight for a maid to see,' he told her. 'You should have let me go. I wish now you'd have stayed back here in the trap. That's terrible for you to see him lying dead there, murdered.'

Talking eased her, and his rough sympathy was good. 'The pony was still in the stable,' she said. 'I listened at the door and heard him move. They had never even finished their preparations for going. The kitchen door was unlocked and there were bundles on the floor there; blankets too, ready to load into the cart. It must have happened several hours ago.'

'It puzzles me what the squire is doing,' said Richards. 'He should have been here before this. I'd feel easier if he'd come, and you could tell your story to him. There's been bad work here to-night. You should never have come.'

They fell silent, and both of them watched the road for the coming of the squire.

'Who'd have killed the landlord?' said Richards, puzzled. 'He's a match for most men and should have held his own. There was plenty who might have had a hand in it, though, for all that. If ever a man was hated, he was.'

'There was the pedlar,' said Mary slowly. 'I'd forgotten the pedlar. It must have been him, breaking out from the barred room.'

She fastened upon the idea, to escape from another; and she re-told the story, eagerly now, of how the pedlar had come to the inn the night before. It seemed at once that the crime was proven, and there could be no other explanation.

'He'll not run far before the squire catches him,' said the groom; 'you can be sure of that. No one can hide on these moors, unless he's a local man, and I have never heard of Harry the pedlar before. But, then, they came from every hole and corner in Cornwall, Joss Merlyn's men, by all accounts. They were, as you might say, the dregs of the country.'

He paused, and then: 'I'll go to the inn if you would care for me to, and see for myself if he has left any trace behind him. There might be something . . .'

Mary seized hold of his arm. ' I'll not be alone again,' she said swiftly. 'Think me a coward if you will, but I could not stand it. Had you been inside Jamaica Inn you would understand. There's a brooding quiet about the place to-night that cares nothing for the poor dead body lying there.'

'I can mind the time, before your uncle came there, when the house stood empty,' said the servant, 'and we'd take the dogs there after rats, for sport. We thought nothing of it then; just a lonely shell of a place it seemed, without a soul of its own. But the squire kept it in good repair, mind you, while he waited for a tenant. I'm a St. Neot man myself, and never came here until I served the squire, but I've been told in the old days there was good cheer and good company at Jamaica, with friendly, happy folk living in the house, and always a bed for a passing traveller upon the road. The coaches stayed here then, what never do now, and hounds would meet here once a week in Mr. Bassat's boyhood. Maybe these things will come again.'

Mary shook her head. 'I've only seen the evil,' she said; 'I've only seen the suffering there's been, and the cruelty, and the pain. When my uncle came to Jamaica Inn he must have cast his shadow over the good things, and they died.' Their voices had sunk to a whisper, and they glanced half-consciously over their shoulders to the tall chimneys that stood out against the sky, clear-cut and grey, beneath the moon. They were both thinking of one thing, and neither had the courage to mention it first; the groom from delicacy and tact, Mary from fear alone. Then at last she spoke, her voice husky and low.

'Something has happened to my aunt as well; I know that; I know she is dead. That's why I was afraid to go upstairs. She is lying there in the darkness, on the landing above. Whoever killed my uncle will have killed her too.'

The groom cleared his throat. 'She may have run out on to the moor,' he said; 'she may have run for help along the road. . . .'

'No,' whispered Mary, 'she would never have done that. She would be with him now, down in the hall there, crouching by his side. She is dead. I know she is dead. If I had not left her this would never have happened.'

The man was silent. He could not help her. After all, she was a stranger to him, and what had passed beneath the roof of the inn while she had lived there was no concern of his. The responsibility of the evening lay heavy enough upon his shoulders and he wished that his master would come. Fighting and shouting he understood; there was sense in that; but if there had really been a murder, as she said, and the landlord lying dead there, and his wife too – why, they could do no good in staying here like fugitives themselves, crouching in the ditch, but were better off and away, and so down the road to sight and sound of human habitation.

'I came here by the orders of my mistress,' he began awkwardly; 'but she said the squire would be here. Seeing as he is not . . .'

Mary held up a warning hand. 'Listen,' she said sharply. 'Can you hear something?'

They strained their ears to the north. The faint clop of horses was unmistakable, coming from beyond the valley, over the brow of the further hill.

'It's them,' said Richards excitedly; 'it's the squire; he's come at last. Watch now; we'll see them go down the road into the valley.'

They waited, and when a minute had passed the first horseman appeared like a black smudge against the hard white road, followed by another, and another. They strung out in a line, and closed again, travelling at a gallop; while the cob who waited patiently beside the ditch pricked his ears, and turned an enquiring head. The clatter drew near, and Richards in his relief ran out upon the road to greet them, shouting and waving his arms.

The leader swerved, and drew rein, calling out in surprise at the sight of the groom. 'What the devil do you do here?' he shouted, for it was the squire himself, and he held up his hand to warn his followers behind.

'The landlord is dead, murdered,' cried the groom. 'I have his niece here with me in the trap. It was Mrs. Bassat herself who sent me out here, sir. This young woman had best tell you the story in her own words.'

He held the horse while his master dismounted, answering as well as he could the rapid questions put to him by the squire, and the little band of men gathered around him too, pressing for news; some of them dismounting also, and stamping their feet on the ground, blowing upon their hands for warmth.

'If the fellow has been murdered, as you say, then, by God, it serves him right,' said Mr. Bassat; 'but I'd rather have clapped irons on him myself for all that. You can't pay scores against a dead man. Go on into the yard, the rest of you, while I see if I can get some sense out of the girl yonder.'

Richards, relieved of responsibility was surrounded at once and treated as something of a hero, who had not only discovered the murder, but had tackled the author of it single-handed; until he reluctantly admitted that his part in the adventure had been small. The squire, whose mind worked slowly, did not realise what Mary was doing in the trap, and considered her as his groom's prisoner.

He heard with astonishment how she had walked the long miles to North Hill in the hopes of finding him, and, not content with that, must return again to Jamaica Inn. 'This is altogether beyond me,' he said gruffly. 'I believed you to be in conspiracy with your uncle against the law. Why did you lie to me, then, when I came here earlier in the month? You told me you knew nothing.'

'I lied because of my aunt,' said Mary wearily. 'Whatever I said to you then was for her sake only, nor did I know as much then as I do now. I am willing to explain everything in a court of law should it be necessary; but if I tried to tell you now you would not understand.'

'Nor have I the time to listen,' replied the squire. 'You did a brave thing in walking all that way to Altarnun to warn me, and I shall remember it in your favour; but all this trouble could have been avoided, and the terrible crime of Christmas Eve prevented, had you been frank with me before.

'However, all that for later. My groom tells me that you have found your uncle murdered, but beyond that you know nothing of the crime. Had you been a man you should go with me now to the inn, but I will spare you that. I can see you have endured enough.' He raised his voice and shouted for the servant. 'Take the trap up to the yard, and stay beside it with the young woman while we break into the inn'; and, turning to Mary: 'I must ask you to wait in the yard, if your courage permits you; you are the only one amongst us who knows anything of the matter, and you were the last to see your uncle alive.' Mary nodded her head. She was nothing more now than a passive instrument of the law, and must do as she was bidden. He had at least spared her the ordeal of going once more into the empty inn and looking upon the body of her uncle. The yard, that had lain in shadow when she came, was now the scene of activity; horses stamped on the cobblestones, and there was the shaking, ringing sound of bit and bridle, and there were the footsteps and the voices of the men, topped by the squire's gruff word of command.

He led the way round to the back, at Mary's direction, and presently the bleak and silent house lost its shuttered air. The window in the bar was flung open, and the windows of the parlour; some of the men went upstairs and explored the empty guest-rooms above, for these windows were unbarred also, and opened to the air. Only the heavy entrance-door remained shut; and Mary knew that the landlord's body lay stretched across the threshold.

Someone called sharply from the house, and was answered by a murmur of voices, and a question from the squire. The sounds came plainly now through the open parlour window to the yard outside. Richards glanced across at Mary, and he saw by the pallor of her face that she had heard.

A man who stood by the horses, and who had not gone with the others inside the inn, shouted to the groom. 'Do you hear what they say?' he said in some excitement. 'There's another body there, on the landing upstairs.'

Richards said nothing. Mary drew her cloak further around her shoulders and pulled the hood across her face. They waited in silence. Presently the squire himself came out into the yard, and crossed to the trap.

'I'm sorry,' he said. 'I have bad news for you. Perhaps you expected it.'

'Yes,' said Mary.

'I don't think she suffered at all. She must have died at once. She was lying just inside the bedroom at the end of the passage. Stabbed, like your uncle. She could have known nothing. Believe me, I am very sorry. I wish I could have spared you this.' He stood by her, awkward and distressed, and repeated again that she could not have suffered, that she had not known, but was killed instantly; and then, seeing that Mary was better left alone, and he could not help her, he stamped back across the yard to the inn.

Mary sat motionless, shrouded in her cloak; and she prayed in her own way that Aunt Patience would forgive her, and find peace now, wherever she should be, and that the dragging chains of life would fall away from her, leaving her free. She prayed also that Aunt Patience would understand what she had tried to do; and above all that her mother would be there, and she would not be alone. These were the only thoughts that brought her a measure of consolation, and she knew if she went over in her mind again the story of the last few hours she would come to the one and only accusation: had she not left Jamaica Inn, Aunt Patience might not have died.

Once again, though, there came a murmur of excitement from the house, and this time there was shouting, and the sound of running feet, and several voices raised in unison; so that Richards ran to the open parlour window, forgetting his trust in the excitement of the moment, and thrust his leg over the sill. There was a crash of splintering wood, and the shutters were torn away from the window of the barred room, which no one, apparently, had entered up to now. The men were tearing away the barricade of wood, and someone held a flare to light the room; Mary could see the flame dance in the draught of air.

Then the light vanished, and the voices died away, and she could hear the sound of footsteps tramping to the back of the house; and then round the corner to the yard they came, six or seven of them, led by the squire, holding amongst them something that squirmed and wriggled, and fought for release with hoarse bewildered cries. 'They've got him! It's the murderer!' shouted Richards, calling to Mary; and she turned, brushing aside the hood that covered her face, and looked down upon the group of men who came to the trap. The captive stared up at her, blinking at the light they flashed in his eyes, his clothes cobweb-covered, his face unshaven and black: and it was Harry the pedlar.

'Who is he?' they shouted. 'Do you know him?' And the squire came round in front of the trap and bade them bring the man close, so that she could see him well. 'What do you know of this fellow?' he said to Mary. 'We found him in the barred room yonder lying on some sacks, and he denies all knowledge of the crime.'

'He was of the company,' said Mary slowly, 'and he came to the inn last night and quarrelled with my uncle. My uncle had the better of him, and locked him up in the barred room, threatening him with death. He had every reason to kill my uncle, and no one could have done it but he. He is lying to you.'

'But the door was locked upon him; it took three of us or more to break it down from the outside,' said the squire. 'This fellow had never been from the room at all. Look at his clothes; look at his eyes, dazzled still by the light. He's not your murderer.'

The pedlar glanced furtively from one to the other of his guards, his small mean eyes darting to right and left, and Mary knew at once that what the squire had said was no more than the truth; Harry the pedlar could not have committed the crime. He had lain in the barred room since the landlord put him there, over twenty-four hours ago. He had lain there in the dark, waiting for release, and during the long hours someone had come to Jamaica Inn and gone again, his work completed, in the silence of the night.

'Whoever did it knew nothing of this rascal, locked in the room yonder,' continued the squire, 'and he's no use to us as a witness, as far as I can see, for he heard and saw nothing. But we'll have him in jail for all that, and hang him too, if he deserves it, which I'll be bound he does. But he shall turn King's evidence first, and give us the names of his companions. One of them has killed the landlord for revenge, you may depend on that, and we'll track him down if we set every hound in Cornwall on his heels. Take this fellow to the stable, some of you, and hold him there; the rest come back to the inn with me.'

They dragged the pedlar away, who, realising that some crime had been discovered and suspicion might possibly rest upon him, found his tongue at last and began to blab his innocence, whining for mercy and swearing by the Trinity, until someone cuffed him to silence and threatened him with the rope, there and then, above the stable door. This silenced him, and he fell to muttering blasphemies beneath his breath, turning his rat's eyes now and again to Mary, who sat above him in the trap, a few yards away.

She waited there, her chin in her hands and the hood fallen away from her face, and she neither heard his blasphemies nor saw his furtive narrow eyes, for she remembered other eyes that had looked upon her in the morning, and another voice that had spoken calm and cold, saying of his brother, 'He shall die for this.'

There was the sentence, flung carelessly, on the way to Launceston fair: 'I have never killed a man yet'; and there was the gypsy woman in the market square: 'There's blood on your hand; you'll kill a man one day.' All the little things she would forget rose up again and clamoured against him: his hatred of his brother, his streak of callous cruelty, his lack of tenderness, his tainted Merlyn blood.

That, before all things, would betray him first. Like to like. One of a kind. He had gone to Jamaica Inn as he had promised, and his brother had died, as he had sworn. The whole truth stared up at her in ugliness and horror, and she wished now that she had stayed, and he had killed her too.

He was a thief, in the night he had come and was gone again. She knew that the evidence could be built against him piece by piece, with herself as witness; it would be a fence around him from which there would be no escape. She had only to go now to the squire and say, 'I know who it is that has done this thing', and they would listen to her, all of them; they would crowd around her like a pack of hounds panting for the chase, and the trail would lead them to him, past Rushyford, and through Trewartha Marsh, to Twelve Men's Moor. He slept there now perhaps, forgetful of his crime and caring not at all, stretched on his bed in the lonely cottage where he and his brother had been born. When morning came he would be gone, whistling perhaps, throwing his legs across a horse, and so away and out of Cornwall for ever, a murderer like his father before him.

In her fancy she heard the clop of his horse upon the road, far distant in the quiet night, beating a *tempo* of farewell; but fancy became reason, and reason became certainty, and the sound she heard was not the dream thing of her imagination but the live tapping of a horse upon the highway.

She turned her head and listened, nerves strung now to the limit; and the hands that held the cloak around her were clammy and cold with sweat.

The sound of the horse drew nearer still. He was trotting at a steady, even pace, neither hurried nor slow, and the rhythmic jogging tune that he played on the road had echo in her throbbing heart.

She was not alone now as she listened. The men who guarded the pedlar murmured to one another in low tones, and looked towards the road, and the groom Richards, who was with them, hesitated a moment, and then went swiftly to the inn to call the squire. The beat of the horse's hoofs rang loud now as he climbed the hill, sounding like a challenge to the night so silent and still, and as he topped the summit and rounded the wall into view the squire came out of the inn, followed by his man.

'Stop!' he called. 'In the name of the King. I must ask your business on the road to-night.'

The horseman drew rein, and turned into the yard. The black riding-cape gave no clue to his identity, but when he bowed and bared his head, the thick halo of hair shone white under the moon, and the voice that spoke in answer to the squire was gentle and sweet.

'Mr. Bassat of North Hill, I believe,' he said, and he leant forward in his saddle, with a note in his hand. 'I have a message here from Mary Yellan of Jamaica Inn, who asks my help in trouble; but I see by the company assembled here that I have come too late. You remember me, of course; we have met before. I am the vicar of Altarnun.'

Chapter Sixteen

Mary sat alone in the living-room at the vicarage and watched the smouldering turf fire. She had slept long, and was now rested and refreshed; but the peace for which she craved had not yet come to her.

They had been kind to her and patient; too kind perhaps, coming so sudden and unexpected after the long strain; and Mr. Bassat himself, with clumsy, well-meaning hands, patted her on the shoulder as he would a hurt child, and said to her in his gruff kind way, 'Now you must sleep, and forget all you have gone through, and remember it's behind you now, and over. I can promise you that we shall find the man who killed your aunt soon, very soon, and he shall hang at the next Assizes. And when you are a little recovered from the shock of these last few months, you shall say what you would like to do, and where you would like to go.'

She had no will of her own; they could make decisions for her; and, when Francis Davey offered his home for shelter, she accepted meekly and without feeling, conscious that her listless word of thanks savoured of ingratitude. Once more she knew the humility of being born a woman, when the breaking down of strength and spirit was taken as natural and unquestioned.

Were she a man, now, she would receive rough treatment, or indifference at the best, and be requested to ride at once perhaps to Bodmin or to Launceston to bear witness, with an understanding that she should find her own lodging and betake herself to the world's end if she wished when all questions had been asked. And she would depart, when they had finished with her, and go on a ship somewhere, working her passage before the mast; or tramp the road with one silver penny in her pocket and her heart and soul at liberty. Here she was, with tears ready to the surface and an aching head, being hurried from the scene of action with smooth words and gestures, a nuisance and a factor of delay, like every woman and every child after a tragedy.

The vicar had driven her himself in the trap – with the squire's groom following behind on his horse – and he at least had the gift of silence, for he questioned her not at all, nor murmured sympathy to be both wasted and ignored, but drove swiftly to Altarnun, and arrived there as his church clock struck one.

He roused his housekeeper from the cottage near by, the same woman that Mary had spoken with in the afternoon, and bade her come with him to the vicarage to prepare a room for his guest, which she did at once, without chattering or exclaiming in wonder, bringing the aired linen from her own home to lay on the bed. She kindled a fire in the grate and warmed a rough woollen nightdress before it, while Mary shed her clothes, and when the bed was ready for her, and the smooth sheets turned back, Mary allowed herself to be led to it as a child is led to a cradle.

She would have closed her eyes at once but for an arm suddenly around her shoulders, and a voice in her ear, 'Drink this,' persuasive and cool, and Francis Davey himself stood beside the bed, with a glass in his hand, and his strange eyes looking into hers, pale and expressionless.

'You will sleep now,' he said, and she knew from the bitter taste that he had put some powder in the hot drink which he had brewed for her, and that he had done this in understanding of her restless, tortured mind.

The last that she remembered was his hand upon her forehead and those still white eyes that told her to forget; and then she slept, as he had bidden her.

It was nearly four in the afternoon before she woke, and the fourteen hours of sleep had done the work that he intended, turning the edge of sorrow and blunting her to pain. The sharp grief for Aunt Patience had softened, and the bitterness too. Reason told her that she could not put the blame upon herself; she had done only what her conscience had commanded her to do. Justice had come first. Her dull wit had not foreseen the tragedy; there lay the fault. There remained regret, and regret could not bring Aunt Patience back again.

These were her thoughts on rising; but when she was dressed, and had gone below to the living-room, to find the fire burning and the curtains drawn, and the vicar abroad upon some business, the old nagging sense of insecurity returned to her, and it seemed to her that responsibility for the disaster lay on her shoulders alone. Jem's face was ever present with her as she had seen it last, drawn and haggard in the false grey light, and there had been a purpose in his eyes then, and in the very set of his mouth, that she had wilfully ignored. He had been the unknown factor from the beginning to the end, from that first morning when he had come to the bar in Jamaica Inn, and deliberately she had shut her eyes to the truth. She was a woman, and for no reason in heaven or earth she loved him. He had kissed her, and she was bound to him for ever. She felt herself fallen and degraded, weakened in mind and body, who had been strong before; and her pride had gone with her independence.

One word to the vicar when he returned, and a message to the squire, and Aunt Patience would be avenged. Jem would die with a rope round his neck as his father had done; and she would return to Helford, seeking the threads of her old life, that lay twisted even now and buried in the soil.

She got up from the chair beside the fire and began to walk the length of the room, with some idea that she wrestled now with her ultimate problem, but even as she did so she knew that her very action was a lie, a poor trick to appease her conscience, and that the word would never be given.

Jem was safe from her, and he would ride away with a song on his lips and a laugh at her expense, forgetful of her, and of his brother, and of God; while she dragged through the years, sullen and bitter, the stain of silence marking her, coming in the end to ridicule as a soured spinster who had been kissed once in her life and could not forget it.

Cynicism and sentimentality were two extremes to be avoided, and as Mary prowled about the room, her mind as restless as her body, she felt as though Francis Davey himself was watching her, his cold eyes probing her soul. The room held something of him after all, now that he was not here, and she could imagine him standing in the corner by the easel, his brush in his hand, staring out of the window at things that were dead and gone.

There were canvases with their faces to the wall close to the easel, and Mary turned them to the light in curiosity. Here was an interior of a church – his church, she supposed – painted in the twilight of midsummer it would seem, with the nave in shadow. There was a strange green afterglow upon the arches, stretching to the roof, and this light was something sudden and unexpected that lingered in her memory after she had laid the picture aside, so that she returned to it, and considered it once more.

It might be that this green afterglow was a faithful reproduction, and peculiar to his church at Altarnun, but, for all that, it cast a haunting and uncanny light upon the picture, and Mary knew that had she a home she would not care for it to hang upon her walls.

She could not have put her feeling of discomfort into words, but it was as though some spirit, having no knowledge of the church itself, had groped its way into the interior and breathed an alien atmosphere upon the shadowed nave. As she turned the paintings, one by one, she saw that they were all tainted in the same manner and to the same degree; what might have been a striking study of the moor beneath Brown Willy on a spring day, with the high clouds banked up behind the tor, had been marred by the dark colour and the very contour of the clouds that dwarfed the picture and overwhelmed the scene, with this same green light predominating over all.

She wondered, for the first time, whether by being born albino, and a freak of nature, his colour-sense was therefore in any way impaired, and his sight itself neither normal nor true. This might be the explanation, but, even so, her feeling of discomfort remained after she had replaced the canvases with their faces to the wall. She continued her inspection of the room, which told her little, it being sparsely furnished anyway, and free of ornaments and books. Even his desk was bare of correspondence, and looked seldom used. She drummed with her fingers on the polished surface, wondering if he sat here to write his sermons, and suddenly and unpardonably she opened the narrow drawer beneath the desk. It was empty; and at once she was ashamed. She was about to shut it when she noticed that the paper with which the drawer was laid had one corner turned, and there was some sketch drawn upon the other side. She took hold of the paper and glanced at the drawing. Once again it represented the interior of a church, but this time the congregation was assembled in the pews, and the vicar himself in the pulpit. At first Mary saw nothing unusual in the sketch; it was a subject natural enough for a vicar to choose who had skill with his pen; but when she looked closer she realised what he had done.

This was not a drawing at all, but a caricature, grotesque as it was horrible. The people of the congregation were bonneted and shawled, and in their best clothes as for Sunday, but he had drawn sheep's heads upon their shoulders instead of human faces. The animal jaws gaped foolishly at the preacher, with silly vacant solemnity, and their hoofs were folded in prayer. The features of each sheep had been touched upon with care, as though representing a living soul, but the expression on every one of them was the same – that of an idiot who neither knew nor cared. The preacher, with his black gown and halo of hair, was Francis Davey; but he had given himself a wolf's face, and the wolf was laughing at the flock beneath him.

The thing was a mockery, blasphemous and terrible. Mary covered it quickly and replaced the paper in the drawer, with the white sheet uppermost; then she shut the drawer and went away from the desk, and sat once more in the chair beside the fire. She had stumbled upon a secret, and she would rather that the secret stayed concealed. This was something that concerned her not at all, but rested between the draughtsman and his God.

When she heard his footstep on the path outside, she rose hurriedly, and moved the light away from her chair so that she would be in shadow when he came into the room, and he could not read her face.

Her chair had its back to the door, and she sat there, waiting for him; but he was so long in coming that she turned at last to listen for his step, and then she saw him, standing behind her chair, having entered the room noiselessly from the hall. She started in surprise, and he came forward then into the light, making apology for his appearance.

'Forgive me,' he said; 'you did not expect me so soon, and I have blundered into your dreams.'

She shook her head, and stammered an excuse, and then he asked at once after her health, and how she had slept, stripping himself of his greatcoat as he spoke, and standing before the fire in his black clerical dress.

'Have you eaten to-day?' he said, and, when she told him she had not, he took out his watch and noted the time – a few minutes before six – which he compared with the clock upon his desk. 'You have supped with me before, Mary Yellan, and you shall sup with me again,' he said; 'but this time, if you do not mind and if you are rested enough, you shall lay the table and fetch the tray from the kitchen. Hannah will have left it prepared, and we will not trouble her again. For my part, I have writing to do; that is, if you have no objection.'

She assured him that she was rested, and would like nothing better than to make herself useful, and he nodded his head then and said, 'At a quarter to seven,' turning his back on her; and she gathered she was dismissed.

She made her way to the kitchen, put something out of countenance at his abrupt arrival, and she was glad that he had given her an added half-hour to herself, for she had been ill prepared for conversation when he found her. Perhaps supper would be a brief affair, and, once over, he would turn to his desk again and leave her to her thoughts. She wished she had not opened the drawer. The memory of the caricature lingered with her unpleasantly. She felt much as a child does who acquires knowledge forbidden by his parents, and then hangs his head, guilty and ashamed, fearful that his tongue will betray him. She would have been more comfortable could she have taken her meal alone here in the kitchen and been treated by him as a handmaid rather than a guest. As it was, her position was not defined, for his courtesy and his commands were curiously mingled. She made play then of getting the supper, at home amongst the familiar kitchen smells, and awaited reluctantly the summons of the clock. The church itself chimed the three-quarters and gave her no excuse, so she carried the tray to the living-room, hoping that nothing of her inner feeling showed upon her face.

He was standing with his back to the fire, and he had pulled the table in readiness before it. Although she did not look at him, she felt his scrutiny upon her, and her movements were clumsy. She was aware, too, that he had made some alteration to the room, and out of the tail of her eye she saw that he had taken down his easel, and the canvases were no longer stacked against the wall. The desk, for the first time was in disorder, with papers and correspondence piled upon it, and he had been burning letters too, for the yellow, blackened scraps lay amongst the ashes under the turf.

They sat down together at the table, and he helped her to the cold pie.

'Is curiosity dead in Mary Yellan that she does not ask me what I have done with my day?' he said at length, mocking her gently, and bringing the flush of guilt to her face at once.

'It is no business of mine where you have been,' she answered.

'You are wrong there,' he said, 'and it is your business. I have meddled in your affairs the livelong day. You asked for my help, did you not?'

Mary was ashamed, and hardly knew what to reply. 'I have not thanked you yet for coming so promptly to Jamaica Inn,' she said, 'nor for my bed last night and my sleep to-day. You think me ungrateful.'

'I never said that. I wondered only at your patience. It had not struck two when I bade you sleep this morning, and it is now seven in the evening. Long hours; and things do not stand still by themselves.'

'Did you not sleep, then, after you left me?'

'I slept until eight. And then I breakfasted and was away again. My grey horse was lame and I could not use him, so progress was slow with the cob. He jogged like a snail to Jamaica Inn, and from Jamaica Inn to North Hill.'

'You have been to North Hill?'

'Mr. Bassat entertained me to luncheon. There were eight or ten of us present, I daresay, and each one of us shouting his opinion to the deaf ear of his neighbour. It was a lengthy meal, and I was glad when we came to the end of it. However, we were all of one accord that the murderer of your uncle will not remain at liberty for long.'

'Does Mr. Bassat suspect anyone?' Mary's tone was guarded, and she kept her eyes on her plate. The food tasted like sawdust in her mouth.

'Mr. Bassat is ready to suspect himself. He has questioned every inhabitant within a radius of ten miles, and the number of strange persons who were abroad last night is legion. It will take a week or more to have the truth from every one of them; but no matter. Mr. Bassat is not deterred.'

'What have they done with – with my aunt?'

'They were taken, both of them, to North Hill this morning, and are to be buried there. All that has been arranged, and you need not concern yourself. As for the rest – well, we shall see.'

'And the pedlar? They have not let him go?'

'No, he is safe under lock and key, screaming curses to the air. I do not care for the pedlar. Neither, I think, do you.'

Mary laid aside the fork she had lifted to her lips, and put down the meat again untasted.

'How do you mean?' she said, on the defensive.

'I repeat, you do not care for the pedlar. I can well understand it, for a more unpleasant and disagreeable fellow I have never clapped eyes on. I gather from Richards, groom to Mr. Bassat, that you suspected the pedlar of the murder, and said as much to Mr. Bassat himself. Hence my conclusion that you do not care for him. It is a pity for all of us that the barred room proves him innocent. He would have made an excellent scapegoat, and saved a deal of trouble.'

The vicar continued to make an excellent supper, but Mary was only playing with her food, and when he offered her a second helping she refused.

'What has the pedlar done to incur your displeasure to such an extent?' he enquired, harping upon the subject with persistence.

'He attacked me once.'

'I thought as much. He is true to a particular type. You resisted him, of course?'

'I believe I hurt him. He did not touch me again.'

'No, I do not suppose he did. When did this happen?'

'On Christmas Eve.'

'After I left you at Five Lanes?'

'Yes.'

'I am beginning to understand. You did not return, then, to the inn that night? You fell in with the landlord and his friends upon the road?'

'Yes.'

'And they took you with them to the shore to add to their sport?'

'Please, Mr. Davey, do not ask me any more. I would rather not speak of that night, neither here nor in the future, not ever again. There are some things that are best buried deep.'

'You shall not speak of it, Mary Yellan. I blame myself for having allowed you to continue your journey alone. Looking at you now, with your clear eye and skin, and the way you carry your head, and, above all, the set of your chin, you bear little trace of what you endured. The word of a parish priest may not go for much – but you have shown remarkable fortitude. I admire you.'

She looked up at him, and then away again, and fell to crumbling a piece of bread in her hand.

'When I consider the pedlar,' he continued, after a while, helping himself generously to stewed damsons, 'I feel it very remiss of the murderer not to have looked into the barred room. It may have been that he was pressed for time, but a minute or two could hardly have affected the issue, and he would most certainly have made the whole affair more thorough.'

'In what way, Mr. Davey?'

'Why, by putting paid to the pedlar's account.'

'You mean, he might have killed him too?'

'Precisely. The pedlar is no ornament to the world while he lives, and dead he would at least make food for worms. That is my opinion. What is more, had the murderer known that the pedlar had attacked you, he would have had a motive strong enough to kill twice over.'

Mary cut herself a slice of cake she did not want, and forced it between her lips. By making a pretence of eating she gave herself countenance. The hand shook, though, that held the knife, and she made a poor job of her slice.

'I don't see,' she said, 'what I have to do in the matter.'

'You have too modest an opinion of yourself,' he replied.

They continued to eat in silence, Mary with lowered head and eyes firm fixed upon her plate. Instinct told her that he played her as an angler plays the fish upon his line. At last she could wait no longer, but must blurt him a question. 'So Mr. Bassat and the rest of you have made little headway, after all, and the murderer is still at large?'

'Oh, but we have not moved as slowly as that. Some progress has been made. The pedlar, for instance, in a hopeless attempt to save his own skin, has turned King's evidence to the best of his ability, but he has not helped us much. We have had from him a bald account of the work done on the coast on Christmas Eve – in which, he says, he took no part – and also some patching together of the long months that have gone before. We heard of the waggons that came to Jamaica Inn by night among other things, and we were given the names of his companions. Those he knew, that is to say. The organisation appears to have been far larger than was hitherto supposed.'

Mary said nothing. She shook her head when he offered her the damsons.

'In fact,' continued the vicar, 'he went so far as to suggest that the landlord of Jamaica Inn was their leader in name only, and that your uncle had his orders from one above him. That, of course, puts a new complexion on the matter. The gentlemen became excited, and a little disturbed. What have you to say of the pedlar's theory?'

'It is possible, of course.'

'I believe you once made the same suggestion to me?'

'I may have done. I forget.'

'If this is so, it would seem that the unknown leader and the murderer must be one and the same person. Don't you agree?'

'Why, yes, I suppose so.'

'That should narrow the field considerably. We may disregard the general rabble of the company, and look for someone with a brain and a personality. Did you ever see such person at Jamaica Inn?'

'No, never.'

'He must have gone to and fro in stealth, possibly in the silence of the night when you and your aunt were abed and asleep. He would not have come by the high road, because you would have heard the clatter of his horse's hoofs. But there is always the possibility that he came on foot, is there not?'

'Yes, there is always that possibility, as you say.'

'In which case the man must know the moors, or at least have local knowledge. One of the gentlemen suggested that he lived near by – within walking or riding distance, that is to say. And that is why Mr. Bassat intends to question every inhabitant in the radius of ten miles, as I explained to you at the beginning of supper. So you see the net will close around the murderer, and if he tarries long he will be caught. We are all convinced of that. Have you finished already? You have eaten very little.'

'I am not hungry.'

'I am sorry for that. Hannah will think her cold pie was not appreciated. Did I tell you I saw an acquaintance of yours to-day?'

'No, you did not. I have no friends but yourself.'

'Thank you, Mary Yellan. That is a pretty compliment, and I shall treasure it accordingly. But you are not being strictly truthful, you know. You have an acquaintance; you told me so yourself.'

'I don't know who you mean, Mr. Davey.'

'Come now. Did not the landlord's brother take you to Launceston fair?'

Mary gripped her hands under the table, and dug her nails into her flesh.

'The landlord's brother?' she repeated, playing for time. 'I have not seen him since then. I believed him to be away.'

'No, he has been in the district since Christmas. He told me so himself. As a matter of fact, it had come to his ears that I had given you shelter, and he came up to me with a message for you. 'Tell her how sorry I am.' That is what he said. I presume he referred to your aunt.'

'Was that all he said?'

'I believe he would have said more, but Mr. Bassat interrupted us.'

'Mr. Bassat? Mr. Bassat was there when he spoke to you?'

'Why, of course. There were several of the gentlemen in the room. It was just before I came away from North Hill this evening, when the discussion was closed for the day.'

'Why was Jem Merlyn present at the discussion?'

'He had a right, I suppose, as brother of the deceased. He did not appear much moved by his loss, but perhaps they did not agree.'

'Did – did Mr. Bassat and the gentlemen question him?'

'There was a considerable amount of talk amongst them the whole day. Young Merlyn appears to possess intelligence. His answers were most astute. He must have a far better brain than his brother ever had. You told me he lived somewhat precariously, I remember. He stole horses, I believe.'

Mary nodded. Her fingers traced a pattern on the tablecloth.

'He seems to have done that when there was nothing better to do,' said the vicar, 'but when a chance came for him to use his intelligence he took it, and small blame to him, I suppose. No doubt he was well paid.'

The gentle voice wore away at her nerves, pin-pricking them with every word, and she knew now that he had defeated her, and she could no longer keep up the pretence of indifference. She lifted her face to him, her eyes heavy with the agony of restraint, and she spread out her hands in supplication.

'What will they do to him, Mr. Davey?' she said. 'What will they do to him?'

The pale, expressionless eyes stared back at her, and for the first time she saw a shadow pass across them, and a flicker of surprise.

'Do?' he said, obviously puzzled. 'Why should they do anything? I suppose he has made his peace with Mr. Bassat and has nothing more to fear. They will hardly throw old sins in his face after the service he has done them.'

'I don't understand you. What service has he done?'

'Your mind works slowly to-night, Mary Yellan, and I appear to talk in riddles. Did you not know that it was Jem Merlyn who informed against his brother?'

She stared at him stupidly, her brain clogged and refusing to work. She repeated the words after him like a child who learns a lesson.

'Jem Merlyn informed against his brother?'

The vicar pushed away his plate and began to set the things in order on the tray. 'Why, certainly,' he said; 'so Mr. Bassat gave me to understand. It appears that it was the squire himself who fell in with your friend at Launceston on Christmas Eve, and carried him off to North Hill as an experiment. "You've stolen my horse," said he, "and you're as big a rogue as your brother. I've the power to clap you in jail to-morrow and you wouldn't set eyes on a horse for a dozen years or more. But you can go free if you bring me proof that your brother at Jamaica Inn is the man I believe him to be."

'Your young friend asked for time; and when the time was up he shook his head. "No," said he; "you must catch him yourself if you want him. I'm damned if I'll have truck with the law." But the squire pushed a proclamation under his nose. "Look there, Jem," he said, "and see what you think of that. There's been the bloodiest wreck on Christmas Eve since the *Lady of Gloucester* went ashore above Padstow last winter. Now will you change your mind?" As to the rest of the story, the squire said little in my hearing – people were coming and going all the time, you must remember – but I gather your friend slipped his chain and ran for it in the night, and then came back again yesterday morning, when they thought to have seen the last of him, and went straight to the squire as he came out of church and said, as cool as you please, "Very well, Mr. Bassat, you shall have your proof." And that is why I remarked to you just now that Jem Merlyn had a better brain than his brother.'

The vicar had cleared the table and set the tray in the corner, but he continued to stretch his legs before the fire and take his ease in the narrow high-backed chair. Mary took no account of his movements. She stared before her into space, her whole mind split, as it were, by his information, the evidence she had so fearfully and so painfully built against the man she loved collapsing into nothing like a pack of cards.

'Mr. Davey,' she said slowly, 'I believe I am the biggest fool that ever came out of Cornwall.'

'I believe you are, Mary Yellan,' said the vicar.

His dry tone, so cutting after the gentle voice she knew, was a rebuke in itself, and she accepted it with humility.

'Whatever happens,' she continued, 'I can face the future now, bravely and without shame.'

'I am glad of that,' he said.

She shook her hair back from her face and smiled for the first time since he had known her. The anxiety and the dread had gone from her at last.

'What else did Jem Merlyn say and do?' she asked.

The vicar glanced at his watch, and replaced it with a sigh.

'I wish I had the time to tell you,' he said, 'but it is nearly eight already. The hours go by too fast for both of us. I think we have talked enough about Jem Merlyn for the present.'

'Tell me one thing – was he at North Hill when you left?'

'He was. In fact, it was his last remark that hurried me home.'

'What did he say to you?'

'He did not address himself to me. He announced his intention of riding over to-night to visit the blacksmith at Warleggan.'

'Mr. Davey, you are playing with me now.'

'I most certainly am not. Warleggan is a long trek from North Hill, but I daresay he can find his way in the dark.'

'What has it to do with you if he visits the blacksmith?'

'He will show the nail he picked up in the heather, down in the field below Jamaica Inn. The nail comes from a horse's shoe; the job was carelessly done, of course. The nail was a new one, and Jem Merlyn, being a stealer of horses, knows the work of every blacksmith on the moors. "Look here," he said to the squire. "I found it this morning in the field behind the inn. Now you have had your discussions and want me no more, I'll ride to Warleggan, with your leave, and throw this in Tom Jory's face as bad workmanship."'

'Well, and what then?' said Mary.

'Yesterday was Sunday, was it not? And on Sunday no blacksmith plies his trade unless he has great respect for his customer. Only one traveller passed Tom Jory's smithy yesterday, and begged a new nail for his lame horse, and the time was, I suppose, somewhere near seven o'clock in the evening. After which the traveller continued his journey by way of Jamaica Inn.'

'How do you know this?' said Mary.

'Because the traveller was the vicar of Altarnun,' he said.

Chapter Seventeen

A silence had fallen upon the room. Although the fire burnt steady as ever, there was a chill in the air that had not been there before. Each waited for the other to speak, and Mary heard Francis Davey swallow once. At length she looked into his face, and saw what she expected: the pale, steadfast eyes staring at her across the table, cold no longer, but burning in the white mask of his face like living things at last. She knew now what he would have her know, but still she said nothing; she clung to ignorance as a source of protection, playing for time as the only ally in her favour.

His eyes compelled her to speak, and she continued to warm her hands at the fire, forcing a smile. 'You are pleased to be mysterious to-night, Mr. Davey.'

He did not answer at once; she heard him swallow again, and then he leant forward in his chair, with an abrupt change of subject.

'You lost your confidence in me to-day before I came,' he said. 'You went to my desk and found the drawing; you were disturbed. No, I did not see you; I am no keyhole watcher; but I saw that the paper had been moved. You said to yourself, as you have said before, 'What manner of man is this vicar of Altarnun?' and when you heard my footsteps on the path you crouched in your chair there, before the fire, rather than look upon my face. Don't shrink from me, Mary Yellan; there is no longer any need for pretence between us, and we can be frank with one another, you and I.'

Mary turned to him, and then away again; there was a message in his eyes she feared to read. 'I am very sorry I went to your desk,' she said; 'such an action was unforgivable, and I don't yet know how I came to it. As for the drawing, I am ignorant of such things, and whether it be good or bad I cannot say.'

'Never mind if it be good or bad, the point was that it frightened you?'

'Yes, Mr. Davey, it did.'

'You said to yourself again, 'This man is a freak of nature, and his world is not my world.' You were right there, Mary Yellan. I live in the past, when men were not so humble as they are to-day. Oh, not your heroes of history in doublet and hose and narrow-pointed shoes – they were never my friends – but long ago in the beginning of time, when the rivers and the sea were one, and the old gods walked the hills.'

He rose from his chair and stood before the fire, a lean black figure with white hair and eyes, and his voice was gentle now, as she had known it first.

'Were you a student, you would understand,' he said, 'but you are a woman, living already in the nineteenth century, and because of this my language is strange to you. Yes, I am a freak in nature and a freak in time. I do not belong here, and I was born with a grudge against the age, and a grudge against mankind. Peace is very hard to find in the nineteenth century. The silence is gone, even on the hills. I thought to find it in the Christian Church, but the dogma sickened me, and the whole foundation is built upon a fairy-tale. Christ Himself is a figurehead, a puppet thing created by man himself.

'However, we can talk of these things later, when the heat and turmoil of pursuit is not upon us. We have eternity before us. One thing at least, we have no traps or baggage, but can travel light, as they travelled of old.'

Mary looked up at him, her hands gripping the sides of her chair.

'I don't understand you, Mr. Davey.'

'Why, yes, you understand me very well. You know by now that I killed the landlord of Jamaica Inn, and his wife too; nor would the pedlar have lived had I known of his existence. You have pieced the story together in your own mind while I talked to you just now. You know that it was I who directed every move made by your uncle, and that he was a leader in name alone. I have sat here at night, with him in your chair there and the map of Cornwall spread out on the table before us. Joss Merlyn, the terror of the countryside, twisting his hat in his hands and touching his forelock when I spoke to him. He was like a child in the game, powerless without my orders, a poor blustering bully that hardly knew his right hand from his left. His vanity was like a bond between us, and the greater his notoriety amongst his companions the better was he pleased. We were successful, and he served me well; no other man knew the secret of our partnership.

'You were the block, Mary Yellan, against which we stubbed our toes. With your wide enquiring eyes and your gallant inquisitive head you came amongst us, and I knew that the end was near. In any case, we had played the game to its limit and the time had come to make an end. How you pestered me with your courage and your conscience, and how I admired you for it! Of course you must hear me in the empty guest-room at the inn, and must creep down to the kitchen and see the rope upon the beam: that was your first challenge.

'And when you steal out upon the moor after your uncle, who had tryst with me on Roughtor, and, losing him in the darkness, stumble upon myself and make me confidant. Well, I became your friend, did I not, and gave you good advice? Which, believe me, could not have been bettered by a magistrate himself. Your uncle knew nothing of our strange alliance, nor would he have understood. He brought his own death upon himself, by disobedience. I knew something of your determination, and that you would betray him at the first excuse. Therefore he should give you none, and time alone would quiet your suspicions. But your uncle must drink himself to madness on Christmas Eve, and blundering like a savage and a fool, set the whole country in a blaze. I knew then he had betrayed himself, and with the rope around his neck would play his last card and name me master. Therefore he had to die, Mary Yellan, and your aunt, who was his shadow; and, had you been at Jamaica Inn last night when I passed by, you too – No, you would not have died.'

He leant down to her, and, taking her two hands, he pulled her to her feet, so that she stood level with him, looking in his eyes.

'No,' he repeated, 'you would not have died. You would have come with me then as you will come to-night.'

She stared back at him, watching his eyes. They told her nothing – they were clear and cold as they had been before – but his grip upon her wrists was firm and held no promise of release.

'You are wrong,' she said; 'you would have killed me then as you will kill me now. I am not coming with you, Mr. Davey.'

'Death to dishonour?' he said, smiling, the thin line breaking the mask of his face. 'I face you with no such problem. You have gained your knowledge of the world from old books, Mary, where the bad man wears a tail beneath his cloak and breathes fire through his nostrils. You have proved yourself a dangerous opponent, and I prefer you by my side; there, that is a tribute. You are young, and you have a certain grace which I should hate to destroy. Besides, in time we will take up the threads of our first friendship, which has gone astray to-night.'

'You are right to treat me as a child and a fool, Mr. Davey,' said Mary. 'I have been both since I stumbled against your horse that November evening. Any friendship we may have shared was a mockery and a dishonour, and you gave me counsel with the blood of an innocent man scarce dry upon your hands. My uncle at least was honest; drunk or sober, he blurted his crime to the four winds, and dreamt of them by night – to his terror. But you – you wear the garments of a priest of God to shield you from suspicion; you hide behind the Cross. You talk to me of friendship . . .'

'Your revolt and your disgust please me the more, Mary Yellan,' he replied. 'There is a dash of fire about you that the women of old possessed. Your companionship is not a thing to be thrown aside. Come, let us leave religion out of our discussion. When you know me better we will return to it, and I will tell you how I sought refuge from myself in Christianity, and found it to be built upon hatred, and jealousy, and greed – all the man-made attributes of civilisation, while the old pagan barbarism was naked and clean.

'I have had my soul sickened . . . Poor Mary, with your feet in the nineteenth century and your bewildered faun face looking up to mine, who admit myself a freak of nature and a shame upon your little world. Are you ready? Your cloak hangs in the hall, and I am waiting.'

She backed to the wall, her eyes upon the clock; but he still held her wrists and tightened his grip upon them.

'Understand me,' he said gently, 'the house is empty, you know that, and the pitiful vulgarity of screams would be heard by no one. The good Hannah is in her cottage by her own fireside, the other side of the church. I am stronger than you would suppose. A poor white ferret looks frail enough and misleads you, doesn't he? – but your uncle knew my strength. I don't want to hurt you, Mary Yellan, or spoil that trace of beauty you possess, for the sake of quiet; but that I shall have to do if you withstand me. Come, where is that spirit of adventure which you have made your own? Where is your courage, and your gallantry?'

She saw by the clock that he must have overstepped already his margin of time and had little in reserve. He concealed his impatience well, but it was there, in the flicker of his eye and the tightening of his lips. It was half past eight, and by now Jem would have spoken with the blacksmith at Warleggan. Twelve miles lay between them perhaps, but no more. And Jem was not the fool that Mary herself had been. She thought rapidly, weighing the chances of failure and success. If she went now with Francis Davey she would be a drag upon him, and a brake on his speed: that was inevitable, and he must have gambled upon it. The chase would follow hard upon his heels, and her presence would betray him in the end. Should she refuse to go, why then there would be a knife in her heart at best, for he would not encumber himself with a wounded companion, for all his flattery.

Gallant he had called her, and possessed with the spirit of adventure. Well, he should see what distance her courage took her, and that she could gamble with her life as well as he. If he were insane – and this she believed him to be – why, then his insanity would bring about his destruction; if he were not mad, she would be that same stumbling-block she had been to him from the beginning, with her girl's wits matched against his brains. She had the right upon her side, and faith in God, and he was an outcast in a hell of his own creation.

She smiled then, and looked into his eyes, having made her decision.

'I'll come with you, Mr. Davey,' she said, 'but you'll find me a thorn in the flesh and a stone in your path. You will regret it in the end.'

'Come as enemy or friend, that does not matter to me,' he told her. 'You shall be the millstone round my neck, and I'll like you the better for it. You'll soon cast your mannerisms aside, and all your poor trappings of civilisation that you sucked into your system as a child. I'll teach you to live, Mary Yellan, as men and women have not lived for four thousand years or more.'

'You'll find me no companion on your road, Mr. Davey.'

'Roads? Who spoke of roads? We go by the moors and the hills, and tread granite and heather as the Druids did before us.'

She could have laughed in his face, but he turned to the door and held it open for her, and she bowed to him, mocking, as she passed into the passage. She was filled with the wild spirit of adventure, and she had no fear of him, and no fear of the night. Nothing mattered now, because the man she loved was free and had no stain of blood upon him. She could love him without shame, and cry it aloud had she the mind; she knew what he had done for her, and that he would come to her again. In fancy she heard him ride upon the road in pursuit, and she heard his challenge, and his triumphant cry.

She followed Francis Davey to the stable where the horses were saddled, and this was a sight for which she was ill prepared.

'Do you not mean to take the trap?' she said.

'Are you not great enough encumbrance already, without further baggage?'

he replied. 'No, Mary, we must travel light and free. You can ride; every woman born in a farm can ride; and I shall hold your rein. Speed I cannot promise you, alas, for the cob has been worked to-day and will begrudge us more; as for the grey, he is lame, as you know, and will make poor mileage for us. Ah, Restless, this departure is half your fault, did you but know it; when you cast your nail in the heather you betrayed your master. You must carry a woman on your back as penance.'

The night was dark, with a raw dampness in the air and a chill wind. The sky was overcast with low-flying cloud, and the moon was blotted out. There would be no light upon the way, and the horses would travel unseen. It seemed as though the first cast was against Mary, and the night itself favoured the vicar of Altarnun. She climbed into the saddle, wondering whether a shout and a wild cry for help would rouse the sleeping village, but even as the thought flashed through her mind she felt his hand upon her foot, placing it in the stirrup, and, looking down upon him, she saw the gleam of steel beneath his cape, and he lifted his head and smiled.

'That were a fool's trick, Mary,' he said. 'They go to bed early in Altarnun, and by the time they were astir and rubbing their eyes I should be away on the moor yonder, and you – you would be lying on your face, with the long wet grass for pillow, and your youth and beauty spoilt. Come now; if your hands and feet are cold, the ride will warm them, and Restless will carry you well.'

She said nothing, but took the reins in her hands. She had gone too far now in her game of chance, and must play it to the finish.

He mounted the bay cob, with the grey attached to him by a leading-rein, and they set out upon their fantastic journey like two pilgrims.

As they passed the silent church, shadowed and enclosed, and left it behind them, the vicar flourished his black shovel-hat and bared his head.

'You should have heard me preach,' he said softly. 'They sat there in the stalls like sheep, even as I drew them, with their mouths agape and their souls asleep. The church was a roof above their heads, with four walls of stone, and because it had been blessed at the beginning by human hands they thought it holy. They do not know that beneath the foundation-stone lie the bones of their pagan ancestors, and the old granite altars where sacrifice was held long before Christ died upon His cross. I have stood in the church at midnight, Mary, and listened to the silence; there is a murmur in the air and a whisper of unrest that is bred deep in the soil and has no knowledge of the church and Altarnun.'

His words found echo in her mind, and carried her away, back to the dark passage at Jamaica Inn. She remembered how she had stood there with her uncle dead upon the ground, and there was a sense of horror and fear about the walls that was born of an old cause. His death was nothing, was only a repetition of what had been before, long ago in time, when the hill where Jamaica stood to-day was bare but for heather and stone. She remembered how she had shivered, as though touched by a cold, inhuman hand; and she shivered now, looking at Francis Davey with his white hair and eyes: eyes that had looked upon the past.

They came to the fringe of moor and the rough track leading to the ford, and then beyond this and across the stream to the great black heart of the moor, where there were no tracks and no paths, but only the coarse tufted grass and the dead heather. Ever and again the horses stumbled on the stones, or sank in the soft ground bordering the marshes, but Francis Davey found his way like a hawk in the air, hovering an instant and brooding upon the grass beneath him, then swerving again and plunging to the hard ground.

The tors rose up around them and hid the world behind, and the two horses were lost between the tumbling hills. Side by side they picked their path through the dead bracken with short, uncanny stride.

Mary's hopes began to falter, and she looked over her shoulder at the black hills that dwarfed her. The miles stretched between her and Warleggan, and already North Hill belonged to another world. There was an old magic in these moors that made them inaccessible, spacing them to eternity. Francis Davey knew their secret, and cut through the darkness like a blind man in his home.

'Where are we bound?' she said at length, and he turned to her, smiling beneath his shovel-hat, and pointed to the north.

'The time will come when officers of the law will walk the coasts of Cornwall,' he said. 'I told you that on our last journey, when you rode with me from Launceston. But to-night and to-morrow we shall meet no such interference; only the gulls and the wild birds haunt the cliffs from Boscastle to Hartland. The Atlantic has been my friend before; savage perhaps and more ruthless than I intended, but my friend nevertheless. You have heard of ships, Mary Yellan, I believe, though of late you would not speak of them; and a ship it will be that shall carry us from Cornwall.'

'So we are to leave England, are we, Mr. Davey?'

'What else would you suggest? After to-day the vicar of Altarnun must cast himself adrift from Holy Church and become a fugitive again. You shall see Spain, Mary, and Africa, and learn something of the sun; you shall feel desert sand under your feet, if you will. I care little where we go; you shall make the choice. Why do you smile and shake your head?'

'I smile because everything you say is fantastic, Mr. Davey, and impossible. You know as well as I do that I shall run from you at the first chance, and at the first village perhaps. I came with you to-night because you would have killed me otherwise, but in daylight, within sight and sound of men and women, you will be as powerless as I am now.'

'As you will, Mary Yellan. I am prepared for the risk. You forget, in your happy confidence, that the north coast of Cornwall bears no relation to the south. You come from Helford, you told me, where the pleasant lanes wind by the side of the river, and where your villages touch one another string upon string, and there are cottages upon the road. This north coast is hardly so hospitable, as you will find. It is as lonely and untravelled as these moors themselves, and never a man's face shall you look upon but mine until we come to the haven that I have in mind.'

'Let me grant you that, then,' said Mary, with a bluster born of fear; 'let me grant even that the sea is reached, and we upon your waiting ship, with

the coast behind us. Name any country as you please, Africa or Spain, and
do you think that I should follow you there and not expose you, a murderer
of men?'

'You will have forgotten it by then, Mary Yellan.'

'Forgotten that you killed my mother's sister?'

'Yes, and more besides. Forgotten the moors, and Jamaica Inn, and your
own little blundering feet that stumbled across my path. Forgotten your tears
on the high road from Launceston, and the young man who caused them.'

'You are pleased to be personal, Mr. Davey.'

'I am pleased to have touched you on the raw. Oh, don't bite your lip and
frown. I can guess your thoughts. I told you before, I have heard confessions
in my day, and I know the dreams of women better than you do yourself.
There I have the advantage of the landlord's brother.'

He smiled again, the thin line breaking in his face, and she turned away
so that she could not see the eyes that degraded her.

They rode on in silence, and after a while it seemed to Mary that the
darkness of the night became intensified and the air closer, nor could she see
the hills around her as she had before. The horses picked their way delicately,
and now and again stopped in their tracks and snorted, as though in fear,
uncertain of their steps. The ground was soggy now and treacherous, and,
though Mary could no longer see the land on either side, she knew by the
feel of the soft, yielding grass that they were encompassed by marshes.

This accounted for the horses' fear, and she glanced at her companion to
discover his mood. He leant forward in his saddle, straining his eyes to the
darkness that every moment became thicker and harder to penetrate, and
she saw by his tense profile and his thin mouth tight-closed like a trap that
he was concentrating every nerve upon their passage, fraught suddenly with
a new danger. The nervousness of her horse communicated itself to the rider,
and Mary thought of these same marshes as she had seen them in the broad
light of day, the brown tufted grass swaying to the wind, and, beyond, the
tall, thin reeds quivering and rustling at the merest breath, crowded together
and moving as one force, while beneath them the black water waited in
silence. She knew how the people of the moors themselves could go astray
and falter in their step, so that he who walked with confidence one moment
could stumble the next, and sink without warning. Francis Davey knew the
moors, but even he was not infallible, and might lose his way.

A brook burbled and made song; a brook could be heard running over
stones for a mile or more; but the water of the marshes made no sound. The
first slip could be the last. Her nerves were strung to expectation, and half-
consciously she made preparations to fling herself from the saddle should
her horse stagger suddenly and with sickening plunge grope like a blind
thing in the strangling weeds. She heard her companion swallow, and the
little trick put an edge upon her fear. He peered to right and left, his hat
in his hand to better his sight, and already the moisture glistened in his hair
and clung to his garments. Mary watched the damp mist rise from the low
ground. She smelt the sour and rotting tang of reeds. And then, in front of

them, barring their further progress, rolled a great bank of fog out of the night, a white wall that stifled every scent and sound.

Francis Davey drew rein, and the two horses obeyed him instantly, trembling and snorting, the steam from their flanks merging with the mist.

They waited awhile, for a moorland fog can roll away as suddenly as it comes, but this time there was no thin clearing of the air and no dissolving threads. It hung about them like a spider's web.

Then Francis Davey turned to Mary; like a ghost he looked beside her, with the fog on his lashes and his hair, and his white mask face inscrutable as ever.

'The gods have gone against me after all,' he said. 'I know these fogs of old, and this one will not lift for several hours. To continue now amongst the marshes would be worse madness than to return. We must wait for the dawn.'

She said nothing; her first hopes returning to her again; but even as the thought came to her she remembered that fog baffled pursuit, and was an enemy to the hunter as well as the hunted.

'Where are we?' she asked, and as she spoke he took her rein once more, and urged the horses to the left, away from the low ground, until the yielding grass gave place to firmer heather and loose stones, while the white fog moved with them step by step.

'There will be rest for you after all, Mary Yellan,' he said, 'and a cave for your shelter and granite for your bed. To-morrow may bring the world to you again, but to-night you shall sleep on Roughtor.'

The horses bent to the strain, and they climbed slowly and ponderously out of the mist to the black hills beyond.

Later, Mary sat shrouded in her cloak like a phantom figure, with her back against a hollow stone. Her knees were drawn to her chin, with her arms clasped tight around them, but, even so, the raw air found its way between the folds of her cloak and lapped her skin. The great jagged summit of the tor lifted its face to the sky like a crown above the mist, and below them the clouds hung solid and unchanged, a massive wall defying penetration.

The air was pure here, and crystal-clear, disdaining knowledge of the world below, where living things must grope and stumble in the mist. There was a wind here that whispered in the stones and stirred the heather; there was a breath, keen as a knife and cold, that blew upon the surface of the altar slabs and echoed in the caves. These sounds mingled with one another and became like a little clamour in the air.

Then they would droop again, and fall away, and an old dead silence come upon the place. The horses stood against a boulder for shelter, their heads together for company, but even they were restless and uneasy, turning now and again towards their master. He sat apart, a few yards distant from his companion, and sometimes she felt his eyes upon her in consideration, weighing the chances of success. She was ever watchful, ever ready for attack; and when he moved suddenly, or turned upon his slab of stone, her hands unclasped themselves from her knees and she waited, her fists clenched.

He had bade her sleep, but sleep would never come to her to-night.

Should it creep to her insidiously, she would fight against it, beat it away with her hands and strive to overcome it, even as she must overcome her enemy. She knew that sleep might take her suddenly, before she was aware; and later she would wake with the touch of his cold hands upon her throat and his pale face above her. She would see the short white hair frame his face like a halo, and the still, expressionless eyes glow with a light that she had known before. This was his kingdom here, alone in the silence with the great twisted peaks of granite to shield him and the white mist below to shroud him. Once she heard him clear his throat as though to speak; and she thought how far removed they were from any sphere of life, two beings flung together in eternity, and that this was a nightmare, with no day to follow it, so that soon she must lose herself and merge into his shadow.

He said nothing; and out of the silence came the whisper of the wind again. It rose and fell, making a moan upon the stones. This was a new wind, with a sob and a cry behind it, a wind that came from nowhere, bound from no shore. It rose from the stones themselves, and from the earth beneath the stones; it sang in the hollow caves and in the crevices of rock, at first a sigh and then a lamentation. It played upon the air like a chorus from the dead.

Mary drew her cloak around her, and pulled the hood about her ears to muffle the sound, but even as she did so the wind increased, tugging at her hair, and a little ripple of draught ran screaming to the cave behind her.

There was no source to the disturbance; for below the tor the heavy fog clung to the ground, obstinate as ever, with never a breath of air to roll away the clouds. Here on the summit the wind fretted and wept, whispering of fear, sobbing old memories of bloodshed and despair, and there was a wild, lost note that echoed in the granite high above Mary's head, on the very peak of Roughtor, as though the gods themselves stood there with their great heads lifted to the sky. In her fancy she could hear the whisper of a thousand voices and the tramping of a thousand feet, and she could see the stones turning to men beside her. Their faces were inhuman, older than time, carved and rugged like the granite; and they spoke in a tongue she could not understand, and their hands and feet were curved like the claws of a bird.

They turned their stone eyes upon her, and looked through her and beyond, heeding her not, and she knew she was like a leaf in the wind, tossed hither and thither to no ultimate purpose, while they lived and endured, monsters of antiquity.

They came towards her, shoulder to shoulder, neither seeing nor hearing her, but moving like blind things to her destruction; and she cried suddenly, and started to her feet, every nerve in her body throbbing and alive.

The wind dropped, and was no more than a breath upon her hair; the slabs of granite stood beyond her, dark and immobile, as they had done before, and Francis Davey watched her, his chin upon his hands.

'You fell asleep,' he said; and she told him no, doubting her own statement, her mind still grappling with the dream that was no dream.

'You are tired, yet you persist in watching for the dawn,' he said. 'It is barely midnight now, and there are long hours to wait. Give way to nature, Mary Yellan, and relax. Do you think I want to harm you?'

'I think nothing, but I cannot sleep.'

'You are chilled, crouched there in your cloak with a stone behind your head. I am little better myself, but there is no draught here from a crevice in the rock. We would do well if we gave our warmth to one another.'

'No, I am not cold.'

'I make the suggestion because I understand something of the night,' he said; 'the coldest hour comes before the dawn. You are unwise to sit alone. Come and lean against me, back to back, and sleep then if you will. I have neither the mind nor the desire to touch you.'

She shook her head in reply, and pressed her hands together beneath her cloak. She could not see his face, for he sat in shadow, with his profile turned to her, but she knew that he was smiling in the darkness, and mocked her for her fear. She was cold, as he had said, and her body craved for warmth, but she would not go to him for protection. Her hands were numb now, and her feet had lost all feeling, and it was as though the granite had become part of her and held her close. Her brain kept falling on and off into a dream, and he walked into it, a giant, fantastic figure with white hair and eyes, who touched her throat and whispered in her ear. She came to a new world, peopled with his kind, who barred her progress with outstretched arms; and then she would wake again, stung to reality by the chill wind on her face, and nothing had changed, neither the darkness nor the mist, nor the night itself, and only sixty seconds gone in time.

Sometimes she walked with him in Spain, and he picked her monstrous flowers with purple heads, smiling on her the while; and when she would have thrown them from her they clung about her skirt like tendrils, creeping to her neck, fastening upon her with poisonous, deadly grip.

Or she would ride beside him in a coach, squat and black like a beetle, and the walls closed in upon them both, squeezing them together, pressing the life and the breath from their bodies until they were flat, and broken, and destroyed, and lay against one another, poised into eternity, like two slabs of granite.

She woke from this last dream to certainty, feeling his hand upon her mouth, and this time it was no hallucination of her wandering mind, but grim reality. She would have struggled with him, but he held her fast, speaking harshly in her ear and bidding her be still.

He forced her hands behind her back and bound them, neither hastily nor brutally, but with cool and calm deliberation, using his own belt. The strapping was efficient but not painful, and he ran his finger under the belt to satisfy himself that it would not chafe her skin.

She watched him helplessly, feeling his eyes with her own, as though by doing so she might anticipate a message from his brain.

Then he took a handkerchief from the pocket of his coat and folded it, and placed it in her mouth, knotting it behind her head, so that speech or cry was now impossible, and she must lie there, waiting for the next move in the game. When he had done this he helped her to her feet, for her legs were free and she could walk, and he led her a little way beyond the granite boulders to the slope of the hill. 'I have to do this, Mary, for both our sakes,' he said. 'When we set forth last night upon this expedition I reckoned without the mist. If I lose now, it will be because of it. Listen to this, and you will understand why I have bound you, and why your silence may save us yet.'

He stood on the edge of the hill, holding her arm, and pointed downwards to the white mist below. 'Listen,' he said again. 'Your ears may be sharper than mine.'

She knew now she must have slept longer than she thought, for the darkness had broken above their heads and morning had come. The clouds were low, and straggled across the sky as though interwoven with the mist, while to the east a faint glow heralded the pale, reluctant sun.

The fog was with them still, and hid the moors below like a white blanket. She followed the direction of his hand, and could see nothing but mist and the soaking stems of heather. Then she listened, as he had bade her, and far away, from beneath the mist, there came a sound between a cry and a call, like a summons in the air. It was too faint at first to distinguish, and the tone was strangely pitched, unlike a human voice, unlike the shouting of men. It came nearer, rending the air with some excitement, and Francis Davey turned to Mary, the fog still white on his lashes and his hair.

'Do you know what it is?' he said.

She stared back at him, and shook her head, nor could she have told him had speech been possible. She had never heard the sound before. He smiled then, a slow grim smile that cut into his face like a wound.

'I heard once, and I had forgotten it, that the squire of North Hill keeps bloodhounds in his kennels. It is a pity for both of us, Mary, that I did not remember.'

She understood; and with a sudden comprehension of that distant eager clamour she looked up at her companion, horror in her eyes, and from him to the two horses standing patiently as ever by the slabs of stone.

'Yes,' he said, following her glance, 'we must let them loose and drive them down to the moors below. They can serve us no longer now, and would only bring the pack upon us. Poor Restless, you would betray me once again.'

She watched him, sick at heart, as he released the horses and led them to the steep slope of the hill. Then he bent to the ground, gathering stones in his hands, and rained blow after blow upon their flanks, so that they slipped and stumbled amongst the wet bracken on the hillside; and then, when his onslaught continued and their instinct jogged them to action, they fled, snorting with terror, down the steep slope of the tor, dislodging boulders and earth in their descent, and so plunged out of sight into the white mists below. The baying of the hounds came nearer now, deep-pitched and persistent, and Francis Davey ran to Mary, stripping himself of his long black coat that hung about his knees and throwing his hat into the heather.

'Come,' he said. 'Friend or enemy, we share a common danger now.'

They scrambled up the hill amongst the boulders and the slabs of granite, he with his arm about her, for her bound hands made progress difficult; and they waded in and out of crevice and rock, knee-deep in soaking bracken and black heather, climbing ever higher and higher to the great peak of Roughtor. Here, on the very summit, the granite was monstrously shaped, tortured and twisted into the semblance of a roof; Mary lay beneath the great stone slab, breathless, and bleeding from her scratches, while he climbed above her, gaining foothold in the hollows of the stone. He reached down to her, and, though she shook her head and made sign that she could climb no further, he bent and dragged her to her feet again, cutting at the belt that bound her and tearing the handkerchief from her mouth.

'Save yourself, then, if you can,' he shouted, his eyes burning in his pale face, his white halo of hair blowing in the wind. She clung to a table of stone some ten feet from the ground, panting and exhausted, while he climbed above her and beyond, his lean black figure like a leech on the smooth surface of the rock. The baying of the hounds was unearthly and inhuman, coming as it did from the blanket of fog below, and the chorus was joined now by the cries and the shouting of men, a turmoil of excitement that filled the air with sound and was the more terrible because it was unseen. The clouds moved swiftly across the sky, and the yellow glow of the sun swam into view above a breath of mist. The mist parted and dissolved. It rose from the ground in a twisting column of smoke, to be caught up in the passing clouds, and the land that it had covered for so long stared up at the sky pallid and new-born. Mary looked down upon the sloping hillside; and there were little dots of men standing knee-deep in the heather, the light of the sun shining upon them, while the yelping hounds, crimson-brown against the grey stone, ran before them like rats amongst the boulders.

They came fast upon the trail, fifty men or more, shouting and pointing to the great tablets of stone; and, as they drew near, the clamour of the hounds echoed in the crevices and whined in the caves.

The clouds dissolved as the mist had done, and a patch of sky, larger than a man's hand, showed blue above their heads.

Somebody shouted again, and a man who knelt in the heather, scarcely fifty yards from Mary, lifted his gun to his shoulder and fired.

The shot spat against the granite boulder without touching her, and when he rose to his feet she saw that the man was Jem, and he had not seen her.

He fired again, and this time the shot whistled close to her ear and she felt the breath of its passing upon her face.

The hounds were worming in and out amidst the bracken, and one of them leapt at the jutting rock beneath her, his great muzzle snuffling the stone. Then Jem fired once more; and, looking beyond her, Mary saw the tall black figure of Francis Davey outlined against the sky, standing upon a wide slab like an altar, high above her head. He stood for a moment poised like a statue, his hair blowing in the wind; and then he flung out his arms as a bird throws his wings for flight, and dropped suddenly and fell; down from his granite peak to the wet dank heather and the little crumbling stones.

Chapter Eighteen

It was a hard, bright day in early January. The ruts and holes in the high road, which were generally inches thick in mud or water, were covered with a thin layer of ice, and the wheel-tracks were hoary with frost.

This same frost had laid a white hand upon the moors themselves, and they stretched to the horizon pale and indefinite in colour, a poor contrast to the clear blue sky above. The texture of the ground was crisp, and the short grass crunched beneath the foot like shingle. In a country lane and hedgerow the sun would have shone warmly, with a make-belief of spring, but here the air was sharp and cutting to the cheek, and everywhere upon the land was the rough, glazed touch of winter. Mary walked alone on Twelve Men's Moor, with the keen wind slapping her face, and she wondered why it was that Kilmar, to the left of her, had lost his menace, and was now no more than a black scarred hill under the sky. It might be that anxiety had blinded her to beauty, and she had made confusion in her mind with man and nature; the austerity of the moors had been strangely interwoven with the fear and hatred of her uncle and Jamaica Inn. The moors were bleak still, and the hills were unfriendly, but their old malevolence had vanished and she could walk upon them with indifference.

She was at liberty now to go where she would, and her thoughts turned to Helford and the green valleys of the south. She had a queer, sick longing for home in her heart and the sight of warm familiar faces.

The broad river ran from the sea, and the water lapped the beaches. She remembered with pain every scent and sound that had belonged to her so long, and how the creeks branched away from the parent river like wayward children, to lose themselves in the trees and the narrow whispering streams.

The woods gave sanctuary to the weary, and there was music in the cool rustle of the leaves in summer, and shelter beneath the naked branches even in winter. She was hungry for birds; and for their flight amongst the trees. She yearned for the homely murmurs of a farm: the cluck of hens, the clarion screech of a cock, and the flustered rasp of geese. She wanted to smell again the rich, warm dung in the sheds, and feel the warm breath of cows upon her hands, heavy footsteps treading the yard, and the clank of pails beside the well. She wanted to lean against a gate and look upon a village lane, give good night to a passing friend, and see the blue smoke curl from the chimneys. There would be voices she would know, rough and gentle in her ear, and a laugh somewhere from a kitchen window. She would concern herself with the business of her farm; rise early and draw water from the well, move amongst her little flock with confidence and ease, bend her back to labour and count the strain a joy and an antidote to pain. All seasons would be welcome for the harvest they should bring, and there would be peace and contentment in her mind. She belonged to the soil, and would return to it again, rooted to the earth as her forefathers had been. Helford had given her birth, and when she died she would be part of it once more.

Loneliness was a thing of poor account, and came not into her consideration. A worker paid no heed to solitude, but slept when his day was done. She had determined upon her course, and the way seemed fair and good to follow. She would not linger any more as she had done during the week, faint and indecisive, but make known her project to the Bassats when she returned for the midday meal. They were kind and full of suggestions – overful, perhaps, with their entreaties that she should stay amongst them, for the winter at least – and, rather than she should feel a burden upon them, had put to her, with kindly tact, that they would employ her even in some position in the household – have a care, perhaps, for the children, be companion to Mrs. Bassat herself.

To these conversations she had lent a meek and an unwilling ear, committing nothing, studiously polite, and continually thanking them for what they had already done.

The squire, bluff and good-humoured, twitted her at dinner for her silence. 'Come, Mary, smiles and thanks are well enough in their way, but you must make up your mind. You are too young to live alone, you know, and I'll tell you to your face you're too pretty. There's a home for you here at North Hill, you know that, and my wife joins with me in begging you to stay. Plenty to do, you know, plenty to do. There are flowers to be cut for the house, and letters to write, and the children to scold. Why, you'd have your hands full, I promise you.' And in the library Mrs. Bassat would say much the same, laying a friendly hand on Mary's knee. 'We love to have you in the house; why do you not continue here indefinitely? The children adore you, and Henry told me yesterday you should have his pony if you but said the word! And that is a high tribute from him, I can assure you. We would give you a pleasant, carefree time, with no worries or cares, and you would be a companion to me when Mr. Bassat is away. Do you still fret after your home at Helford?'

Then Mary smiled and thanked her once again, but she could not put into words how much the memory of Helford meant to her.

They guessed that the strain of the past months still had its hand upon her, and in their kindness strove to make amends; but the Bassats kept open house at North Hill, and the neighbours called for many miles around, with, naturally enough, one topic of conversation on their lips. Fifty and a hundred times must Squire Bassat tell his tale, and the names of Altarnun and Jamaica became loathsome to Mary's ear, who would be rid of them for ever.

Here was another reason for departure: she had become too much an object of curiosity and discussion, and the Bassats, with a little show of pride, would point her as a heroine to their friends.

She strove in gratitude to do her best, but she was never at her ease amongst them. They were not her kind. They were another race, another class. She had respect for them, and liking, and goodwill, but she could not love them.

In the kindness of their hearts they would have her enter into conversation when company was present, and strove that she should not sit aside; while she longed the while for the silence of her own bedroom or the homely kitchen of Richards the groom, whose apple-cheeked wife would make her welcome.

And the squire, flogging his humour, would turn to her for advice, laughing heartily at every word he said. 'There'll be the living vacant at Altarnun. Will you turn parson, Mary? I warrant you'd make a better one than the last'; and she must smile at this for his sake, wondering that he should be so dull as not to guess the bitter memories his words aroused.

'Well, there'll be no more smuggling at Jamaica Inn,' he would say, 'and, if I could have my way, no drinking either. I'll sweep the place clean of all those cobwebs, and not a poacher nor a gypsy will dare show his face within the walls when I have done with it. I'll put an honest fellow there who's never smelt brandy in his life, and he shall wear an apron round his waist, and write the word "Welcome" above the door. And do you know who shall call upon him first? Why, Mary, you and I.' And he would burst into a shout of laughter, slapping his thigh, while Mary forced a smile in answer, rather than his joke should fail.

She thought of these things as she walked alone on Twelve Men's Moor, and she knew she must go away from North Hill very soon, for these people were not her people, and only amongst the woods and streams of her own Helford valley would she know peace and contentment again.

There was a cart coming towards her from Kilmar, making tracks in the white frost like a hare. It was the one moving thing upon the silent plain. She watched it in suspicion, for there were no cottages on this moor except Trewartha, away in the valley by the Withy Brook, and Trewartha, she knew, stood empty. Nor had she seen its owner since he had fired at her on Roughtor. 'He's an ungrateful rascal, like the rest of his breed,' said the squire. 'But for me he'd be in jail now, with a long sentence to serve to break his spirit. I forced his hand and he had to knuckle under. I grant he did well after that, and was the means of tracing you, Mary, and that black-coated scoundrel; but he's never as much as thanked me for clearing his name in the business, and has taken himself to the world's end now, for all I know. There's never been a Merlyn yet that came to any good, and he'll go the way of the rest of them.' So Trewartha stood empty, and the horses were gone wild with their fellows and roamed free upon the moors, and their master had ridden away with a song on his lips, as she had known he would.

The cart came nearer to the slope of the hill, and Mary shielded her eyes from the sun to watch its progress. The horse bent to the strain, and she saw that it laboured beneath a strange load of pots and pans, and mattresses, and sticks. Someone was making for the country with his home upon his back.

Even then she did not tumble to the truth, and it was not until the cart was below her and the driver, walking by the side, looked up to her and waved that she recognised him. She went down towards the cart with a fine show of indifference, and turned at once to the horse to pat him and speak to him, while Jem kicked a stone under the wheel and wedged it there for safety.

'Are you better?' he called, from behind the cart. 'I heard you were sick and had taken to your bed.'

'You must have heard wrong,' said Mary. 'I've been about the house there at North Hill, and walking in the grounds; there's never been much the matter with me except a hatred for my neighbourhood.'

'There was a rumour you were to settle there, and be companion to Mrs. Bassat. That's more like the truth, I suppose. Well, you'll lead a soft enough life with them, I daresay. No doubt they're kindly people when you know them.'

'They've been kinder to me than anyone else in Cornwall since my mother died; that's the only thing that matters to me. But I'm not staying in North Hill, for all that.'

'Oh, you're not?'

'No; I'm going back home to Helford.'

'What will you do there?'

'I shall try and start the farm again, or at least work my way to it, for I haven't the money yet. But I've friends there, and friends in Helston too, that will help me at the beginning.'

'Where will you live?'

'There's not a cottage in the village I couldn't call home if I wanted to. We're neighbourly in the south, you know.'

'I've never had neighbours, so I cannot contradict you, but I've had the feeling always it would be like living in a box, to live in a village. You poke your nose over your gate into another man's garden, and if his potatoes are larger than your own there's a talking upon it, and argument; and you know that if you cook a rabbit for your supper he'll have the sniff of it in his kitchen. God damn it, Mary, that's no life for anyone.'

She laughed at him, for his nose was wrinkled in disgust, and then she ran her eyes over his laden cart and the confusion he had there.

'What are you doing with that?' she asked him.

'I've got a hatred for my neighbourhood the same as you,' he said. 'I want to get away from the smell of peat and bog, and the sight of Kilmar yonder, with his ugly face frowning upon me from dusk till dawn. Here's my home, Mary, all I've ever had of it, here in the cart, and I'll take it with me and set it up wherever my fancy takes me. I've been a rover since a boy; never any ties, nor roots, nor fancies for a length of time; and I daresay I'll die a rover too. It's the only life in the world for me.'

'There's no peace, Jem, in wandering, and no quiet. Heaven knows that existence itself is a long enough journey, without adding to the burden. There'll come a time when you'll want your own plot of ground, and your four walls, and your roof, and somewhere to lay your poor tired bones.'

'The whole country belongs to me, Mary, if it comes to that, with the sky for a roof and the earth for a bed. You don't understand. You're a woman, and your home is your kingdom, and all the little familiar things of day to day. I've never lived like that, and never shall. I'll sleep on the hills one night, and in a city the next. I like to seek my fortune here and there and everywhere, with strangers for company and passers-by for friends. To-day I meet a man upon the road, and journey with him for an hour or for a year; and to-morrow he is gone again. We speak a different language, you and I.'

Mary went on with her patting of the horse, the good flesh warm and damp beneath her hand, and Jem watched her, the ghost of a smile on his lips.

'Which way will you go?' she said.

'Somewhere east of Tamar, it doesn't matter to me,' he said. 'I'll never come west again, not until I'm old and grey, and have forgotten a lot of things. I thought of striking north after Gunnislake, and making for the midlands. They're rich up there, and ahead of everyone; there'll be fortune there for a man who goes to find it. Perhaps I'll have money in my pockets one day, and buy horses for pleasure instead of stealing them.'

'It's an ugly black country in the midlands,' said Mary.

'I don't bother about the colour of the soil,' he answered. 'Moorland peat is black, isn't it? And so's the rain when it falls into your pigsties down at Helford. What's the difference?'

'You just talk for argument, Jem; there's no sense in what you say.'

'How can I be sensible when you lean against my horse, with your wild daft hair entangled in his mane, and I know that in five or ten minutes' time I shall be over the hill yonder without you, my face turned towards the Tamar and you walking back to North Hill to drink tea with Squire Bassat?'

'Delay your journey, then, and come to North Hill too.'

'Don't be a damned fool, Mary. Can you see me drinking tea with the squire, and dancing his children on my knee? I don't belong to his class, neither do you.'

'I know that. And I am going back to Helford because of it. I'm homesick, Jem; I want to smell the river again and walk in my own country.'

'Go on, then; turn your back on me and start walking now. You'll come to a road after ten miles or so that will take you to Bodmin, and from Bodmin to Truro, and from Truro to Helston. Once in Helston you will find your friends, and make a home with them until your farm is ready for you.'

'You are very harsh to-day, and cruel.'

'I'm harsh to my horses when they're obstinate and out of hand; but it doesn't mean I love them any the less.'

'You've never loved anything in your life,' said Mary.

'I haven't had much use for the word, that's why,' he told her.

He went round to the back of the cart, and kicked the stone away from the wheel.

'What are you doing?' said Mary.

'It's past noon already, and I ought to be on the road. I've havered here long enough,' he said. 'If you were a man I'd ask you to come with me, and you'd fling your legs over the seat and stick your hands in your pockets and rub shoulders with me for as long as it pleased you.'

'I'd do that now if you'd take me south,' she said.

'Yes, but I'm bound north, and you're not a man, you're only a woman, as you'd know to your cost if you came with me. Move off from the trace there, Mary, and don't twist the rein. I'm going now. Good-bye.'

He took her face in his hands and kissed it, and she saw that he was laughing. 'When you're an old maid in mittens down at Helford, you'll remember that,' he said, 'and it will have to last you to the end of your days. "He stole horses," you'll say to yourself, "and he didn't care for women; and but for my pride I'd have been with him now." '

He climbed into the cart and looked down upon her, flicking his whip and yawning. 'I'll do fifty miles before to-night,' he said, 'and sleep like a puppy at the end of it, in a tent by the side of the road. I'll kindle a fire, and cook bacon for my supper. Will you think of me or not?'

She did not listen, though; she stood with her face towards the south, hesitating and twisting her hands. Beyond those hills the bleak moors turned to pasture, and the pasture to valleys and to streams. The peace and quiet of Helford waited for her beside the running water.

'It's not pride,' she told him; 'you know that it's not pride; there's a sickness in my heart for home and all the things I've lost.'

He said nothing, but drew the reins into his hands and whistled to the horse. 'Wait,' said Mary, 'wait, and hold him still, and give me your hand.'

He laid the whip aside, and reached down to her, and swung her beside him on the driver's seat.

'What now?' he said. 'And where do you want me to take you? You have your back to Helford, do you know that?'

'Yes, I know,' she said.

'If you come with me it will be a hard life, and a wild one at times, Mary, with no biding anywhere, and little rest and comfort. Men are ill companions when the mood takes them, and I, God knows, the worst of them. You'll get a poor exchange for your farm, and small prospect of the peace you crave.'

'I'll take the risk, Jem, and chance your moods.'

'Do you love me, Mary?'

'I believe so, Jem.'

'Better than Helford?'

'I can't ever answer that.'

'Why are you sitting here beside me, then?'

'Because I want to; because I must; because now and for ever more this is where I belong to be,' said Mary.

He laughed then, and took her hand, and gave her the reins; and she did not look back over her shoulder again, but set her face towards the Tamar.

Frenchman's Creek

Daphne du Maurier

Chapter One

When the east wind blows up Helford river the shining waters become troubled and disturbed and the little waves beat angrily upon the sandy shores. The short seas break above the bar at ebb-tide, and the waders fly inland to the mud-flats, their wings skimming the surface, and calling to one another as they go. Only the gulls remain, wheeling and crying above the foam, diving now and again in search of food, their grey feathers glistening with the salt spray.

The long rollers of the Channel, travelling from beyond Lizard point, follow hard upon the steep seas at the river mouth, and mingling with the surge and wash of deep sea water comes the brown tide, swollen with the last rains and brackish from the mud, bearing upon its face dead twigs and straws, and strange forgotten things, leaves too early fallen, young birds, and the buds of flowers.

The open roadstead is deserted, for an east wind makes uneasy anchorage, and but for the few houses scattered here and there above Helford passage, and the group of bungalows about Port Navas, the river would be the same as it was in a century now forgotten, in a time that has left few memories.

In those days the hills and the valleys were alone in splendour, there were no buildings to desecrate the rough fields and cliffs, no chimney pots to peer out of the tall woods. There were a few cottages in Helford hamlet, but they made no impression upon the river itself, which belonged to the birds – curlew and redshank, guillemot and puffin. No yachts rode to the tide then, as they do to-day, and that stretch of placid water where the river divides to Constantine and Gweek was calm and undisturbed.

The river was little known, save to a few mariners who had found shelter there when the south-west gales drove them inshore from their course up-channel, and they found the place lonely and austere, a little frightening because of the silence, and when the wind was fair again were glad to weigh anchor and set sail. Helford hamlet was no inducement to a sailor ashore, the few cottage folk dull-witted and uncommunicative, and the fellow who has been away from warmth and women over-long has little desire to wander in the woods or dabble with the waders in the mud at ebb-tide. So the winding river remained unvisited, the woods and the hills untrodden, and all the drowsy beauty of midsummer that gives Helford river a strange enchantment was never seen and never known.

To-day there are many voices to blunder in upon the silence. The pleasure steamers come and go, leaving a churning wake, and yachtsmen visit one another, and even the day-tripper, his dull eye surfeited with undigested beauty, ploughs in and out amongst the shallows, a prawning net in hand. Sometimes, in a little puffing car, he jerks his way along the uneven, muddy track that leads sharply to the right out of Helford village, and takes his tea with his fellow-trippers in the stone kitchen of the old farm building that once was Navron House. There is something of grandeur about it even now. Part of the original quadrangle still stands, enclosing the farm-yard of to-day, and the two pillars that once formed the entrance to the house, now over-grown with ivy and encrusted with lichen, serve as props to the modern barn with its corrugated roof.

The farm kitchen, where the tripper takes his tea, was part of Navron dining-hall, and the little half-stair, now terminating in a bricked-up wall, was the stair leading to the gallery. The rest of the house must have crumbled away, or been demolished, for the square farm-building, though handsome enough, bears little likeness to the Navron of the old prints, shaped like the letter E, and of the formal garden and the park there is no trace to-day.

The tripper eats his split and drinks his tea, smiling upon the landscape, knowing nothing of the woman who stood there once, long ago, in another summer, who caught the gleam of the river amidst the trees, as he does, and who lifted her head to the sky and felt the sun.

He hears the homely farm-yard noises, the clanking of pails, the lowing of cattle, the rough voices of the farmer and his son as they call to each other across the yard, but his ears are deaf to the echoes of that other time, when someone whistled softly from the dark belt of trees, his hands cupped to his mouth, and was swiftly answered by the thin, stooping figure crouching beneath the walls of the silent house, while above them the casement opened, and Dona watched and listened, her hands playing a little nameless melody upon the sill, her ringlets falling forward over her face.

The river flows on, the trees rustle in the summer wind, and down on the mud flats the oyster-catchers stand at ebb-tide scanning the shallows for food, and the curlews cry, but the men and women of that other time are forgotten, their headstones encrusted with lichen and moss, their names indecipherable.

To-day the cattle stamp and churn the earth over the vanished porch of Navron House, where once a man stood as the clock struck midnight, his face smiling in the dim candle-light, his drawn sword in his hand.

In spring the farmer's children gather primroses and snowdrops in the banks above the creek, their muddy boots snapping the dead twigs and the fallen leaves of a spent summer, and the creek itself, swollen with the rains of a long winter, looks desolate and grey.

The trees still crowd thick and darkly to the water's edge, and the moss is succulent and green upon the little quay where Dona built her fire and looked across the flames and laughed at her lover, but to-day no ship lies at anchor in the pool, with rakish masts pointing to the skies, there is no rattle of chain through the hawse hole, no rich tobacco smell upon the air, no echo of voices coming across the water in a lilting foreign tongue.

The solitary yachtsman who leaves his yacht in the open roadstead of Helford, and goes exploring up river in his dinghy on a night in midsummer, when the night-jars call, hesitates when he comes upon the mouth of the creek, for there is something of mystery about it even now, something of enchantment. Being a stranger, the yachtsman looks back over his shoulder to the safe yacht in the roadstead, and to the broad waters of the river, and he pauses, resting on his paddles, aware suddenly of the deep silence of the creek, of its narrow twisting channel, and he feels – for no reason known to him – that he is an interloper, a trespasser in time. He ventures a little way along the left bank of the creek, the sound of the blades upon the water seeming over-loud and echoing oddly amongst the trees on the farther bank, and as he creeps forward the creek narrows, the trees crowd yet more thickly to the water's edge, and he feels a spell upon him, fascinating, strange, a thing of queer excitement not fully understood.

He is alone, and yet – can that be a whisper, in the shallows, close to the bank, and does a figure stand there, the moonlight glinting upon his buckled shoes and the cutlass in his hand, and is that a woman by his side, a cloak around her shoulders, her dark ringlets drawn back behind her ears? He is wrong, of course, those are only the shadows of the trees, and the whispers are no more than the rustle of the leaves and the stir of a sleeping bird, but he is baffled suddenly, and a little scared, he feels he must go no farther, and that the head of the creek beyond the farther bank is barred to him and must remain unvisited. And so he turns to go, heading the dinghy's nose for the roadstead, and as he pulls away the sounds and the whispers become more insistent to his ears, there comes the patter of footsteps, a call, and a cry in the night, a far faint whistle, and a curious lilting song. He strains his eyes in the darkness, and the massed shadows before him loom hard and clear like the outline of a ship. A thing of grace and beauty, born in another time, a painted phantom ship. And now his heart begins to beat, and he strains at his paddles, and the little dinghy shoots swiftly over the dark water away from enchantment, for what he has seen is not of his world, and what he has heard is beyond his understanding.

Once more he reaches the security of his own ship, and looking back for the last time to the entrance of the creek, he sees the full moon white and shining in all its summer glory rise above the tall trees, bathing the creek in loveliness and light.

A night-jar churrs from the bracken on the hills, a fish breaks the surface of the water with a little plopping sound, and slowly his ship turns to meet the incoming tide, and the creek is hidden from him.

The yachtsman goes below to the snug security of his cabin, and browsing amongst his books he finds at last the thing for which he has been searching. It is a map of Cornwall, ill-drawn and inaccurate, picked up in an idle moment in a Truro bookshop. The parchment is faded and yellow, the markings indistinct. The spelling belongs to another century. Helford river is traced fairly enough, and so are the hamlets of Constantine and Gweek. But the yachtsman looks away from them to the marking of a narrow inlet, branching from the parent river, its short, twisting course running westward into a valley. Someone has scratched the name in thin faded characters – Frenchman's Creek.

The yachtsman puzzles awhile over the name, then shrugs his shoulders and rolls away the map. Presently he sleeps. The anchorage is still. No wind blows upon the water, and the night-jars are silent. The yachtsman dreams – and as the tide surges gently about his ship and the moon shines on the quiet river, soft murmurs come to him, and the past becomes the present.

A forgotten century peers out of dust and cobwebs and he walks in another time. He hears the sound of hoof-beats galloping along the drive to Navron House, he sees the great door swing open and the white, startled face of the manservant stare upward at the cloaked horseman. He sees Dona come to the head of the stairs, dressed in her old gown, with a shawl about her head, while down in the silent hidden creek a man walks the deck of his ship, his hands behind his back, and on his lips a curious secret smile. The farm kitchen of Navron House is a dining-hall once more, and someone crouches on the stairs, a knife in his hand, while from above there rings suddenly the startled cry of a child, and down upon the crouching figure a shield crashes from the walls of the gallery, and two little King Charles spaniels, perfumed and curled, run yapping and screaming to the body on the floor.

On Midsummer Eve a wood fire burns on a deserted quay, and a man and a woman look at one another and smile and acknowledge their secret, and at dawn a ship sails with the tide, and the sun shines fiercely from a bright blue sky, and the sea-gulls cry.

All the whispers and echoes from a past that is gone teem into the sleeper's brain, and he is with them, and part of them; part of the sea, the ship, the walls of Navron House, part of a carriage that rumbles and lurches in the rough roads of Cornwall, part even of that lost forgotten London, artificial, painted, where link-boys carried flares, and tipsy gallants laughed at the corner of a cobbled mud-splashed street. He sees Harry in his satin coat, his spaniels at his heels, blundering into Dona's bedroom, as she places the rubies in her ears. He sees William with his button mouth, his small inscrutable face. And last he sees *La Mouette* at anchor in a narrow twisting stream, he sees the trees at the water's edge, he hears the heron and the curlew cry, and lying on his back asleep he breathes and lives the lovely folly of that lost mid-summer which first made the creek a refuge, and a symbol of escape.

Chapter Two

The church clock struck the half-hour just as the coach clattered into Launceston and drew up at the Inn. The driver grunted, and his companion swung himself to the ground and ran to the horses' heads. The driver put two fingers to his mouth and whistled. Presently an ostler came from the Inn on to the square, rubbing his sleepy eyes in astonishment.

'No time to linger. Bring water at once, and a feed for the horses,' said the driver and he rose in his seat, and stretched himself, glancing sourly about him, while his companion stamped his numbed feet on the ground and grinned back at him in sympathy.

'Their backs are not yet broken, that's one blessing,' he called softly; 'perhaps they are worth all the guineas Sir Harry paid for them after all.' The driver shrugged his shoulders. He was too tired and too stiff to argue. The roads were damnation, and if the wheels were broken and the horses destroyed he would be to blame, not his companion. If they could have travelled quietly, taking a week over the journey, but this devilish break-neck speed, sparing neither man nor beast, all because of my lady's damned ill-humour. Anyway, thank God, she was asleep for the moment, and all was quiet within the coach. His wishes had misled him, however, for as the ostler returned, bearing a pail of water in either hand, and the horses began to drink greedily, the window of the coach was flung open and his mistress leant out, no trace of sleep about her, her eyes wide and clear, and that cool, imperious voice, which he had grown to dread during these last days, as commanding as ever.

'Why the devil this delay?' she said. 'Did you not stop to water the horses three hours ago?'

The driver muttered a prayer for patience, and climbing down from his seat he approached the open window of the coach.

'The horses are not accustomed to the pace, my lady,' he said; 'you forget that during the last two days we have covered nearly two hundred miles – besides,these roads are not fit for animals so highly bred as yours.'

'Nonsense,' came the reply, 'the higher the breeding the greater the endurance. In future you will halt the horses only when I give the command. Pay the fellow here what we owe him, and continue the journey.'

'Yes, my lady.' The man turned away, his mouth set in weary obstinate lines, and with a nod to his companion, and muttering under his breath, he climbed back again to his seat.

The pails of water were removed, the thick-headed ostler gaped without understanding, and once more the horses pawed at the ground and snorted, the steam rising from their hot flesh, and so away out of the cobbled square and the little sleepy town and out again on to the rough and jolting road.

Dona stared moodily out of the window, her chin cupped in her hands. The children were still asleep, that was one blessing, and even Prue, their nurse, her mouth open and her face flushed, had not stirred for two hours or more. Poor Henrietta had been sick for the fourth time, and now lay pale and wan, a tiny edition of Harry, her golden head against the nurse's shoulder. James never stirred; his was the true deep sleep of babyhood, he would not wake perhaps until they reached their destination. And then – what pitiful anticlimax awaited them! Damp beds no doubt, and closed shutters, the mouldy, stifling smell of unused rooms, the irritation of surprised, disgruntled servants. And all because of an impulse blindly obeyed, a sudden boiling up of resentment against the futility of her life, those endless suppers, dinners, card-parties, those foolish pranks worthy only of an apprentice boy on holiday, that stupid flirtation with Rockingham, and Harry himself, so lazy, so easy-going, fulfilling too well the part of perfect husband with his tolerance, his yawn before midnight, his placid and sleepy adoration. This sense of futility had been growing upon her for many months, nagging at her now and again like dormant toothache, but it had taken Friday night to arouse in her that full sense of self-loathing and exasperation, and because of Friday night she was jolting backwards and forwards now in this damnable coach, bound on a ridiculous journey to a house she had seen once in her life and knew nothing about, carrying with her, in anger and irritation, the two surprised children and their reluctant nurse.

She was obeying an impulse, of course, as she always had done, from the beginning, throughout her life, following a whisper, a suggestion, that sprang into being from nowhere and mocked at her afterwards. She had married Harry on impulse, because of his laugh – its funny lazy quality had attracted her – and because she had thought that the expression in his blue eyes meant much more than it did – and now she realised that after all . . . but then those were things one did not admit, not even to oneself, and what was the use, the thing was done, and here she was with her two great children, and next month anyway she would be thirty.

No, it was not poor Harry who was to blame, nor even the senseless life they led, nor the foolish escapades, nor their friends, nor the stifling atmosphere of a too early summer falling upon the caked mud and dust of London, nor the silly chatter in the playhouse, the froth, the frivolity, the bawdy nonsense Rockingham whispered in her ear. It was herself who was at fault.

She had played too long a part unworthy of her. She had consented to be the Dona her world had demanded – a superficial, lovely creature, who walked, and talked, and laughed, accepting praise and admiration with a shrug of the shoulder as natural homage to her beauty, careless, insolent, deliberately indifferent, and all the while another Dona, a strange, phantom Dona, peered at her from a dark mirror and was ashamed.

This other self knew that life need not be bitter, nor worthless, nor bounded by a narrow casement, but could be limitless, infinite – that it meant suffering, and love, and danger, and sweetness, and more than this even, much more. Yes, the full force of her self-loathing had come upon her that Friday evening, so that even now, sitting in the coach, with the soft country air bathing her face, she could conjure up once more the hot street smell that came from the London gutters, a smell of exhaustion and decay, that had emerged in some inexplicable way with the heavy, sultry sky, with Harry's yawn as he dusted the skirt of his coat, with Rockingham's pointed smile – as though they all typified a weary, dying world from which she must free herself and escape, before the sky fell in upon her and she was trapped. She remembered the blind hawker at the corner, his ears pricked for the tinkle of a coin, and the apprentice boy from the Haymarket who ambled along with his tray on his head, shouting his wares in a shrill, disconsolate voice, and how he had fallen over some garbage in the gutter and spilled the contents on the dusty cobbled stones. And oh, heaven – the crowded playhouse, the stench of perfume upon heated bodies, the silly laughter and the clatter, the party in the Royal box – the King himself present – the impatient crowd in the cheap seats stamping and shouting for the play to begin while they threw orange peel on to the stage. Then Harry, laughing at nothing in particular as was his custom, became fuddled with the wit of the play, or possibly he had drunk too much before they had set out. Anyway he had started snoring in his seat, and Rockingham, seizing his chance to make a diversion, pressed against her with his foot and whispered in her ear. Damn his impudence, his air of possession, of familiarity, all because she had permitted him to kiss her once in an idle moment, because the night was fine. And they had proceeded to supper at the Swan, which she had grown to detest, her amusement at its novelty having ceased – for it was no longer a stimulant to be the only wife amongst a crowd of mistresses.

Once it had held a certain attraction, it had sharpened her sense of fun to sup with Harry in these places where no other husband took his wife, to sit cheek by jowl with the ladies of the town and to see Harry's friends first scandalised, then fascinated, and finally whipped into a fever, like curious schoolboys who tread forbidden ground. And yet even then, even at the beginning, she had felt a little prick of shame, a curious sense of degradation, as though she had dressed up for a masquerade and the clothes had not fitted her well.

While Harry's lovable and slightly stupid laugh, his expression of half-shocked dismay: 'You've made yourself the talk of the town, you know, the fellows are gossiping about you in the taverns,' had not served as a rebuke but as an irritant. She had wished that he would be angry, would shout at her, insult her even – but he only laughed, shrugging his shoulders, and fondled her in heavy, clumsy fashion, so that she knew her folly had not touched him, that inwardly he was really quite pleased that men were gossiping about his wife and admiring her, because it made him a person of importance in their eyes. The coach lurched over a deep rut in the road, and James stirred in his sleep. His little face puckered as though to cry, and Dona reached for the toy that had slipped from his grasp, and he cuddled it to his mouth, and so slept once more. He looked as Harry did when demanding a reassurance of her affection, and she wondered why it was that a quality so attractive and touching in James should seem to her, in Harry, more than a little absurd and a secret source of irritation.

Dressing that Friday night, placing the rubies in her ears to match the pendant round her throat, she had been reminded suddenly of James snatching the pendant, and stuffing it in his mouth, and she had smiled to herself, thinking of him, and Harry, standing beside her, dusting the lace at his wrists, had caught the smile and turned it into an invitation. 'Damn it, Dona,' he had said, 'why do you look at me like that? Don't let's go to the play, hang Rockingham, hang the world, why the devil don't we stay at home?' Poor Harry, how vain, how typical, provoked by a smile that was not for him into instant adoration. She had said: 'How ridiculous you are,' turning from him, so that he should not touch her bare shoulder with his clumsy hands, and at once his mouth set in that grumpy, obstinate line she knew so well, so that they set out to the play, as they had done to other plays and to other suppers, times without number, with moods ill-tuned and tempers frayed, putting an edge upon the evening before it had begun.

Then he had called to his spaniels, Duke and Duchess, and they had yapped up at him for sweetmeats, filling the room with their shrill barking, leaping and jumping at his hands.

'Hey, Dúke, hey, Duchess,' he had said, 'go seek, go find,' throwing a sweetmeat across the room and on to her bed, so that they clawed at the curtains, and tried to spring upon it, yapping horribly the while, and Dona, her fingers in her ears to thrust out the sound, swept from the room and downstairs to her waiting chair, white, and cold, and angry, to be met with the hot street smells and the breathless vapid sky.

Once more the coach shook and trembled in the deep ruts of the country road, and this time it was the nurse who stirred – poor, wretched Prue, her foolish, honest face all heavy and mottled with fatigue, how she must grudge her mistress this sudden inexplicable journey – and Dona wondered whether she had left some young man forlorn in London who would prove false in all probability and marry somebody else and Prue's life would be blighted, all because of her, Dona, and her whim and fancies and savage ill-humour. What would poor Prue find to do at Navron House, but parade the children up and down the avenue and through the gardens, sighing for the streets of London hundreds of miles away? Were there gardens at Navron? She could not remember. It all seemed so long ago, that brief visit after she had married. There were trees surely, and a shining river, and great windows that peered from a long room, but more than this she had forgotten, because she had felt so ill during those days, with Henrietta on the way, and life one endless business of sofas, and sickness, and smelling-bottles. Suddenly Dona felt hungry, the coach had just rumbled past an orchard and the apple trees were in blossom, and she knew she must eat now, at once, without more ado, on the side of the road in the sunshine, they must all eat – so she thrust her head out of the window and called up to her coachman: 'We will halt here for a while, and eat. Come and help me spread the rugs beneath the hedge.'

The man stared down at her in bewilderment. 'But my lady, the ground may be damp, you will take cold.'

'Nonsense, Thomas, I am hungry, we are all hungry, we must eat.'

He climbed down from his seat, his face red with embarrassment, and his companion turned away also, coughing behind his hand.

'There is a hostelry in Bodmin, my lady,' the coachman ventured, 'there you could eat in comfort, and rest perhaps; surely it would be more fitting. If anyone should pass this way, and see you by the side of the road, I hardly think Sir Harry would like . . .'

'Damn it, Thomas, can't you obey orders?' said his mistress, and she opened the door of the coach herself, and stepped down into the muddy road, lifting her gown above her ankles in a most brazen way. Poor Sir Harry, thought the coachman, this was the sort of thing he had to contend with every day, and in less than five minutes she had them all assembled on the grass by the side of the road, the nurse barely awake blinking her round eyes, and the children staring in astonishment. 'Let us all drink ale,' said Dona, 'we have some in the basket beneath the seat. I have a mad desire for ale. Yes, James, you shall have some.' And there she sat, her petticoats tucked beneath her and her hood falling away from her face, quaffing her ale like any beggaring gipsy, handing some on the tip of her finger for her baby son to taste, smiling the while at the coachman to show him that she bore no malice for his rough driving and his obstinacy. 'You must both drink, too, there is plenty for all,' she said, and the men were obliged to drink with her, avoiding the eye of the nurse. She thought the whole proceeding unseemly, as they did, and was wishing for a quiet parlour in a hostelry, and fresh warm water where she could bathe the children's hands and faces.

'Where are we going?' asked Henrietta for the twelfth time, looking about her in distaste, holding her dress close to her so that the mud should not stain it. 'Is the drive nearly finished, and shall we soon be home?'

'We are going to another home,' said Dona, 'a new home, a much nicer home. You will be able to run free in the woods and dirty your clothes, and Prue will not scold you because it will not matter.'

'I don't want to dirty my clothes. I want to go home,' said Henrietta, and her lip trembled; she looked up at Dona in reproach, and then – she was tired, perhaps, it was all strange, this journey, this sitting by the roadside, she missed her monotonous routine – she began to cry, and James, placid and happy until then, opened his mouth wide, and roared in sympathy. 'There, my pets, there my treasures, did they hate the nasty ditch and the prickly hedge,' said Prue, folding them both in her arms, a world of meaning in her voice for her mistress, the cause of all the upset, so that Dona, her conscience stung, rose to her feet, kicking at the remains of the feast. 'Come then, let us continue the journey by all means, but without tears, for pity's sake,' and she stood for a moment, while the nurse, and the food, and the children packed themselves in the coach. Yes, there was apple blossom on the air, and the scent of gorse as well, and the tang of moss and peat from the moors away in the distance, and surely somewhere, not too distant, over the farther hills, a wet sea smell.

Forget the children's tears, forget Prue's grievance, forget the pursed-up mouth of the coachman, forget Harry and his troubled distressed blue eyes when she announced her decision. 'But damn it, Dona, what have I done, what have I said, don't you know that I adore you?' Forget all these things, because this was freedom, to stand here for one minute with her face to the sun and the wind, this was living, to smile and to be alone.

She had tried to explain it to Harry on the Friday night, after that foolish idiotic escapade at Hampton Court; she had tried to tell him what she meant, how the ridiculous prank on the Countess was only a thwarted, bastard idea of fun, a betrayal of her real mood; that in reality it was escape she wanted, escape from her own self, from the life they led together; that she had reached a crisis in her particular span of time and existence, and must travel through that crisis, alone.

'Go to Navron by all means if you wish it,' he said sulkily. 'I will send word at once that preparation is made for you, that the house is opened up, the servants are ready. But I don't understand. Why suddenly, and why have you never expressed the desire before, and why do you not want me to come with you?'

'Because I would be alone, because my humour is such that if I am not alone I shall drive you mad, and myself as well,' she said.

'I don't understand,' he went on, his mouth set, his eyes sullen, and she, in despair, tried to paint a picture of her mood.

'Do you remember my father's aviary in Hampshire,' she said, 'and how the birds there were well fed, and could fly about their cage? And one day I set a linnet free, and it flew straight out of my hands towards the sun?'

'What of it?' he said, clasping his hands behind his back.

'Because I feel like that. Like the linnet before it flew,' she said, and then she turned away, smiling in spite of her sincerity, because he looked so puzzled, so hopelessly out of his depth, staring at her in his white nightshirt, and he shrugged his shoulders, poor dear, she could well understand it, he shrugged his shoulders, and climbed into bed, and turned his face to the wall away from her and said: 'Oh, hell and damnation, Dona, why must you be so confounded tricky?'

Chapter Three

She fumbled for a moment with the catch, it had jammed of course, through lack of use, probably it had not been touched for months, and then she flung the windows wide and let in the fresh air and the sun. 'Faugh! The room smells like a tomb,' she said, and as a shaft of sunlight struck the pane she caught the reflection of the manservant looking at her, she could have sworn he was smiling, but when she turned he was still and solemn as he had been from the first moment of their arrival, a thin, spare little man, with a button mouth and a curiously white face.

'I don't remember you,' she said, 'you were not here when we came before.'

'No my lady,' he said.

'There was an old man – I forget his name – but he had rheumatism in all his joints, and could scarcely walk, where is he now?'

'In his grave, my lady.'

'I see.' She bit her lip, and turned again to the window. Was the fellow laughing at her or not?

'And you replaced him then?' she said, over her shoulder, looking out towards the trees.

'Yes, my lady.'

'And your name?'

'William, my lady.'

She had forgotten the Cornish people spoke in so strange a way, foreign almost, a curious accent, at least she supposed it was Cornish, and when she turned to look at him again he wore that same slow smile she had noticed in the reflected window.

'I fear we must have caused a good deal of trouble,' she said, 'our sudden arrival, the opening up of the house. The place has been closed far too long, of course. There is dust everywhere, I wonder you have not noticed it.'

'I had noticed it, my lady,' he said 'but as your ladyship never came to Navron it scarcely seemed worth my while to see that the rooms were cleaned. It is difficult to take pride in work that is neither seen nor appreciated.'

'In fact,' said Dona, stung to amusement, 'the idle mistress makes the idle servant?'

'Naturally, my lady,' he said gravely.

Dona paced up and down the long room, fingering the stuff of the chairs, which was dull and faded. She touched the carving on the mantel, and looked up at the portraits on the wall – Harry's father, painted by Van Dyck, what a tedious face he had – and surely this was Harry himself, this miniature in a case, taken the year they were married. She remembered it now; how youthful he looked and how pompous. She laid it aside, aware of the manservant's eyes upon her – what an odd creature he was – and then she pulled herself together; no servant had ever got the better of her before.

'Will you please see that every room in the house is swept and dusted,' she said, 'that all the silver is cleaned, that flowers are placed in the rooms, that everything takes place, in short, as though the mistress of the house had not been idle, but had been in residence here for many years?'

'It will be my personal pleasure, my lady,' he said, and then he bowed, and left the room, and Dona, vexed, realised that he had laughed at her once again, not openly, not with familiarity, but as it were secretly, behind his eyes.

She stepped out of the window and on to the grass lawns in front of the house. The gardeners had done their work at least, the grass was fresh trimmed, and the formal hedges clipped, perhaps all in a rush yesterday, or the day before, when the word had come that their mistress was returning; poor devils, she understood their slackness, what a pest she must seem to them, upsetting the quiet tenor of their lives, breaking into their idle routine, intruding upon this queer fellow William – was it really Cornish, that accent of his? – and upsetting the slack disorder he had made for himself.

Somewhere, from an open window in another part of the house, she could

hear Prue's scolding voice, demanding hot water for the children, and a lusty
roar from James – poor sweet, why must he be washed, and bathed, and
undressed, why not tossed, just as he was, into a blanket in any dark corner
and left to sleep – and then she walked across to the gap in the trees that
she remembered from the last time, and yes – she had been right, it was the
river down there, shining and still and soundless. The sun still upon it,
dappled green and gold, and a little breeze ruffled the surface, there should
be a boat somewhere – she must remember to ask William if there was a
boat – and she would embark on it, let it carry her to the sea. How absurd,
what an adventure. James must come too, they would both dip their hands
and faces in the water and become soaked with the spray, and fishes would
jump out of the water and the sea-birds would scream at them. Oh, heaven,
to have got away at last, to have escaped, to have broken free, it could not
be possible, to know that she was at least three hundred miles away from
St. James's Street, and dressing for dinner, and the Swan, and the smells in
the Haymarket, and Rockingham's odious meaning smile, and Harry's
yawn, and his blue reproachful eyes. Hundreds of miles too from the Dona
she despised, the Dona who from devilry or from boredom, or from a spice
of both, had played that idiotic prank on the Countess in Hampton Court,
had dressed up in Rockingham's breeches and cloaked and masked herself,
and ridden with him and the others, leaving Harry at the Swan (too fuddled
with drink to know what was happening), and had played at foot-pads,
surrounding the Countess's carriage and forcing her to step down into the
highroad.

'Who are you, what do you want?' the poor little old woman had cried,
trembling with fear, while Rockingham had been obliged to bury his face
in his horse's neck, choking with silent laughter, and she, Dona, had played
the leader, calling out in a clear cold voice:

'A hundred guineas or your honour.'

And the Countess, poor wretch, sixty if she were a day, with her husband
some twenty years in the grave, fumbled and felt in her purse for sovereigns,
terrified that this young rip from the town should throw her down in the
ditch – and when she handed over the money and looked up into Dona's
masked face, there was a pitiful tremor at the corner of her mouth, and she
said:

'For God's sake spare me, I am very old, and very tired.'

So that Dona, swept in an instant by a wave of shame and degradation,
had handed back the purse, and turned her horse's head, and ridden back
to town, hot with self-loathing, blinded by tears and abasement, while
Rockingham pursued her with shouts and cries of 'What the devil now, and
what has happened?' and Harry, who had been told the adventure would
be nothing but a ride to Hampton Court by moonlight, walked home to bed,
not too certain of his direction, to be confronted by his wife on the doorstep
dressed up in his best friend's breeches.

'I had forgotten – was there a masquerade – was the King present?' he
said, staring at her stupidly, rubbing his eyes, and 'No, damn you,' said

Dona, 'what masquerade there was is over and done with, finished now for ever more. I'm going away.'

And so upstairs, and that interminable argument in the bedroom, followed by a sleepless night, and more arguments in the morning, then Rockingham calling and Dona refusing him admittance, then someone riding to Navron to give warning, the preparations for the journey, the journey itself, and so here at last to silence, and solitude, and still unbelievable freedom.

Now the sun was setting behind the trees, leaving a dull red glow upon the river below, the rooks rose in the air and clustered above their nests, the smoke from the chimneys curled upwards in thin blue lines, and William was lighting the candles in the hall. She supped late, making her own time – early dinner, thank heaven, was now a thing of the past – and she ate with a new and guilty enjoyment, sitting all alone at the head of the long table, while William stood behind her chair and waited silently.

They made a strange contrast, he in his sober dark clothes, his small inscrutable face, his little eyes, his button mouth, and she in her white gown, the ruby pendant round her throat, her hair caught back behind her ears in the fashionable ringlets.

Tall candles stood on the table, and a draught from the open window caused a tremor in their flame, and the flame played a shadow on her features. Yes, thought the man-servant, my mistress is beautiful, but petulant too, and a little sad. There is something of discontent about the mouth, and a faint trace of a line between the eyebrows. He filled her glass once more, comparing the reality before him to the likeness that hung on the wall in the bedroom upstairs. Was it only last week that he had stood there, with someone beside him, and the someone had said jokingly, glancing up at the likness: 'Shall we ever see her, William, or will she remain forever a symbol of the unknown?' and looking closer, smiling a little, he had added: 'The eyes are large and very lovely, William, but they hold shadows too. There are smudges beneath the lids as though someone had touched them with a dirty finger.'

'Are there grapes?' said his mistress suddenly, breaking in upon the silence. 'I have a fancy for grapes, black and succulent, with the bloom on them, all dusty.' 'Yes, my lady,' said the servant, dragged back into the present, and he fetched her grapes, cutting a bunch with the silver scissors and putting them on her plate, his button mouth twisted as he thought of the news he would have to carry to-morrow, or the next day, when the spring tides were due again and the ship returned.

'William,' she said.

'My lady?'

'My nurse tells me that the servant girls upstairs are new to the house, that you sent for them when you heard I was arriving? She says one comes from Constantine, another from Gweek, even the cook himself is new, a fellow from Penzance.'

'That is perfectly true, my lady.'

'What was the reason, William? I understood always, and I think Sir Harry thought the same, that Navron was fully staffed?'

'It seemed to me, my lady, possibly wrongly, that is for you to say, that one idle servant was sufficient about the house. For the last year I have lived here entirely alone.'

She glanced at him over her shoulder, biting her bunch of grapes.

'I could dismiss you for that, William.'

'Yes, my lady.'

'I shall probably do so in the morning.'

'Yes, my lady.'

She went on eating her grapes, considering him as she did so, irritated and a little intrigued that a servant could be so baffling a person. Yet she knew she was not going to send him away.

'Supposing I do not dismiss you, William, what then?'

'I will serve you faithfully, my lady.'

'How can I be sure of that?'

'I have always served faithfully the people I love, my lady.'

And to this she could make no answer, for his small button mouth was as impassive as ever, and his eyes said nothing, but she felt in her heart that he was not laughing at her now, he was speaking the truth. 'Am I to take that as a compliment then, William?' she said at last, rising to her feet, as he pulled away her chair.

'It was intended as one, my lady,' he said, and she swept from the room without a word, knowing that in this odd little man with his funny half-familiar manner she had found an ally, a friend. She laughed secretly to herself, thinking of Harry and how he would stare without comprehension: 'What damned impertinence, the fellow needs whipping.'

It was all wrong of course, William had behaved disgracefully, he had no business to live alone in the house, and no wonder there was dust everywhere, and a graveyard smell. But she understood it for all that, because had she not come here to do the same thing herself? Perhaps William had a nagging wife, and an existence in another part of Cornwall too full of cares; perhaps he too had wished to escape? She wondered, as she rested in the salon, staring at the wood fire he had kindled, on her lap a book that she did not read, whether he had sat here amongst the sheets and coverlets before she came, and whether he begrudged her the use of the room now. Oh, the lovely luxury of stillness, to live alone like this, a cushion behind her head, a draught of air from the open window ruffling her hair, and to rest secure in the knowledge that no one would come blundering in upon her presence with loud laugh, with a voice that grated – that all those things belonged to another world, a world of dusty cobbled stones, of street smells, of apprentice boys, of ugly music, of taverns, of false friendships and futility. Poor Harry, he would be supping now with Rockingham probably, bemoaning his fate at the Swan, dozing over cards, drinking a little too much, saying: 'Damn it, she kept talking about a bird, saying she felt like a bird, what the devil did she mean?' And Rockingham, with his pointed, malicious smile and those narrow eyes that understood, or thought they understood, her baser qualities, would murmur: 'I wonder – I very much wonder.'

Presently, when the fire had sunk, and the room cooled, she went upstairs to her bedroom, first passing through the children's rooms to see if all was well. Henrietta looked like a waxen doll, her fair curls framing her face, her mouth slightly pouted, while James in his cot frowned in his sleep, chubby and truculent, like a little pug-dog. She tucked his fist inside the cover, kissing it as she did so, and he opened one eye and smiled. She stole away, ashamed of her furtive tenderness for him – so primitive, so despicable, to be moved to folly, simply because he was male. He would no doubt grow up to be fat, and gross, and unattractive, making some woman miserable.

Someone – William she supposed – had cut a sprig of lilac and placed it in her room, on the mantelshelf, beneath the portrait of herself. It filled the room with scent, heady and sweet. Thank God, she thought, as she undressed, there will be no pattering feet of spaniels, no scratching noises, no doggy smells, and the great deep bed is mine alone. Her own portrait looked down at her with interest. Have I that sulky mouth, she thought, that petulant frown? Did I look like that six, seven years ago? Do I look like it still?

She pulled on her nightgown, silken and white, and cool, and stretched her arms above her head, and leant from the casement. The branches stirred against the sky. Below the garden, away down in the valley, the river ran to meet the tide. She pictured the fresh water, bubbling with the spring rains, surging against the salt waves, and how the two would mingle and become one, and break upon the beaches. She pulled the curtains back, so that the light should flood the room, and she turned to her bed, placing her candlestick on the table at her side.

Then drowsing, half asleep, watching the moon play patterns on the floor, she wondered what other scent it was that mingled itself with the lilac, a stronger, harsher smell, something whose name eluded her. It stung her nostrils even now, as she turned her head on the pillow. It seemed to come from the drawer beneath the table, and stretching out her arm she opened the drawer, and looked inside. There was a book there, and a jar of tobacco. It was the tobacco she had smelt of course. She picked up the jar, the stuff was brown and strong and freshly cut. Surely William had not the audacity to sleep in her bed, to lie there, smoking, looking at her portrait? That was a little too much, that was really unforgivable. There was something so personal about this tobacco, so very unlike William, that surely she must be mistaken – and yet – if William had lived here at Navron, for a year, alone?

She opened the book – was he then a reader as well? And now she was more baffled than before, for the book was a volume of poetry, French poetry, by the poet Ronsard, and on the flyleaf someone had scribbled the initials 'J.B.A. – Finistère' and underneath had drawn a tiny picture of a gull.

Chapter Four

When she woke, the next morning, her first thought was to send for William, and, confronting him with the jar of tobacco and the volume of poetry, to enquire whether he had slept ill on his new mattress, and whether he had missed the comfort of her bed. She played with the idea, amusing herself at the picture of his small inscrutable face colouring up at last, and his button mouth dropping in dismay, and then, when the heavy-footed maid brought her breakfast, stumbling and blushing in her awkwardness, raw country girl that she was, she decided to bide her time, to wait a few days, for something seemed to warn her that any admission of her discovery would be premature, out of place.

So she left the tobacco jar, and the poetry, in the table drawer beside her bed, and when she rose, and dressed, and went downstairs, she found the dining-hall and the salon had been swept and cleaned, as she had commanded, there were fresh flowers in the rooms, the windows were opened wide, and William himself was polishing the tall candlesticks on the wall.

He enquired at once if she had slept well, and she answered, 'Yes,' thinking instantly that this would be the moment, and could not prevent herself from adding, 'And you too, I hope, were not fatigued by our arrival?' At which he permitted himself a smile, saying, 'You are very thoughtful, my lady. No, I slept well, as always. I heard Master James cry once in the night, but the nurse soothed him. It seemed strange to hear a child's cry in the house, after the long silence.'

'You did not mind?' she said.

'No my lady. The sound took me back to my own childhood. I was the eldest in a family of thirteen. There were always little ones arriving.'

'Is your home near here, William?'

'No, my lady.' And now there was a new quality in his voice, a note of finality. As though he said: 'A servant's life is his own. Do not intrude upon it,' and she had the insight to leave it, to question him no more. She glanced at his hands. They were clean and waxen white, no tobacco stains upon them, and there was an impersonal soapy texture about the whole of him, vastly different from that male tobacco smell, so harsh and brown, in the jar upstairs.

Perhaps she maligned him, perhaps the jar had stood there for three years – since Harry's last visit to the estate, when she had not accompanied him. And yet Harry did not smoke strong tobacco. She wandered to the shelves where great leather-bound volumes stood in rows, books that nobody ever read, and she made a pretext of taking a volume down and glancing through it, while the servant continued to polish the candlesticks.

'Are you a reader, William?' she said suddenly.

'You have gathered I am not, my lady,' he said, 'because the books in those shelves are coated with dust. No, I have never handled them. But I will do so to-morrow. I will take them all down and dust them well.'

'You have no hobby then?'

'Moths interest me, my lady. I have quite a fine collection in my room. The woods round Navron are excellent for moths.' And with that she left him. She wandered out into the garden, hearing the children's voices. Really the little man was an oddity, she could not fathom him out, and surely if it was he who read Ronsard in the night watches he would have browsed amongst these books, at least once or twice, out of curiosity.

The children called her with delight, Henrietta dancing like a fairy, and James, still very unsteady, rolling after her like a drunken sailor, and the three wandered into the woods to gather bluebells. The flowers were just appearing in the young green, short and stubby and blue; next week or the week after there would be a carpet for them to lie upon.

So the first day passed, and the next, and the one after, Dona exulting in her new-found freedom. Now she could live without a plan, without a decision, taking the days as they came, rising at noon if she had the mind or at six in the morning, it did not matter, eating when hunger came upon her, sleeping when she wished, in the day or at midnight. Her mood was one of lovely laziness. She would lie out in her garden hour after hour, her hands behind her head, watching the butterflies as they frolicked in the sun, and chased one another, and had their moment; listening to the birds intent upon domestic life among the branches, so busy, so ardent, like newly-wed couples proud of their first home polished as a pin. And all the while the bright sun shone down upon her, and little mackerel clouds scurried across the sky, and away in the valley beneath the woods there was the river, the river which she had not found yet, because she was too idle, because there was so much time; one day, quite soon, she would go down to it, early one morning, and stand in the shallows barefoot and let the water splash upon her, and smell the muddied river smell, pungent and sweet.

The days were glorious and long, the children were browning like little gypsies. Even Henrietta was losing her town ways, and consented to run with naked feet upon the grass, to play leap-frog, to roll on the ground as James did, like a puppy.

They were playing thus one afternoon, tumbling and falling upon Dona, who lay on her back with her gown anyhow and her ringlets in mad disorder (the disapproving Prue safely within the house) and as they pelted one another with daisy heads and honeysuckle there came to Dona, warm and drugged, and foolish with the sun, the ominous sound of hoof-beats in the avenue, and presently a clatter into the court-yard before the house, and the jangle of the great bell. And horror upon horror there was William advancing towards her on the grass, and a stranger following him, a large, burly creature with a florid face and bulbous eyes, his wig over-curled, slashing at his boots as he walked with a gold-knobbed cane.

'Lord Godolphin to see you, my lady,' said William gravely, no whit abashed at her appearance, so tattered, so disgraceful. She rose to her feet at once, pulling at her gown, patting her ringlets: how infuriating, how embarrassing, and what a damnable intrusion. The creature stared at her in dismay, no wonder; well, he must endure it, perhaps he would go the sooner. And then she curtsied, and said: 'I am enchanted to see you,' at which he bowed solemnly and made no reply. She led the way into the house, catching sight of herself in the mirror on the wall; there was honeysuckle behind her ear, she left it there obstinately, she did not care. And then they sat down on stiff chairs, and stared at each other, while Lord Godolphin nibbled his gold-knobbed cane.

'I had heard you were in residence,' he said at length, 'and I considered it a duty, or rather a pleasure, to pay my respects as soon as possible. It is many years since you and your husband condescended to visit Navron. In fact, I may say you have become strangers. I knew Harry very well when he lived here as a boy.'

'Indeed,' said Dona, fascinated suddenly by the growth at the side of his nose; she had only just noticed it. How unfortunate, poor man. And then she glanced away quickly, for fear he should realise she was looking, and 'Yes,' he continued, 'I may say that I used to count Harry as among my dearest friends. But since his marriage we have seen so little of him, he spends his time in Town.'

A reproach to me, she thought, very natural of course, and 'I am sorry to say Harry is not with me,' she told him, 'I am here alone, with my children.'

'That is a great pity,' he said, and she answered nothing, for what was there to say?

'My wife would have accompanied me,' he continued, 'but she does not enjoy very good health at the moment. In short . . .' He paused, uncertain how to continue, and Dona smiled. 'I quite understand, I have two small children myself,' at which he looked a little abashed, and bowed. 'We hope for an heir,' he said, and 'Of course,' said Dona, fascinated once again by that growth at the end of his nose. How distressing for his wife, how did she endure it. But Godolphin was talking again, saying something about his wife being very glad to welcome her at any time, there were so few neighbours, and so on, and so forth. How boring and heavy he was, thought Dona, was there no middle course between this solemn pompous pretentiousness and the vicious frivolity of Rockingham? Would Harry become like this if he lived at Navron? A great turnip, with eyes that said nothing, and a mouth like a slit in a suet pudding. 'I was hoping,' Godolphin was saying, 'that Harry would have given some assistance in the county. You have heard of our troubles, no doubt.'

'I have heard nothing,' said Dona.

'No? Perhaps you are too remote here for the news to reach you, though the talk and chatter has been rife for miles around. We have been vexed and harried, almost at our wits' end, in fact, with acts of piracy. Goods of considerable value have been lost at Penryn, and along the coast. An estate of my neighbour's was sacked a week or so ago.'

'How distressing,' said Dona.

'It is more than distressing, it is a positive outrage!' declared Godolphin, his face reddening, his eyes more bulbous than ever, 'and no one knows how to deal with it. I have sent up complaints to London, and get no reply. They send us a handful of soldiers from the garrison at Bristol, but they are worse than useless. No, I can see that I and the rest of the land-owners in the county will have to band ourselves together and deal with the menace. It is very unfortunate that Harry is not at Navron, very unfortunate.'

'Can I do anything to help you?' asked Dona, digging her nails into her hands to stop herself from smiling: he looked so provoked, so highly indignant, almost as though he blamed her for the acts of piracy.

'My dear lady,' he said, 'there is nothing you can do, except ask your husband to come down, and rally round his friends, so that we can fight this damned Frenchman.'

'Frenchman?' she said.

'Why, yes, that's the plague of it,' he said, almost shouting in his anger; 'this fellow's a low sneaking foreigner, who for some reason or other seems to know our coast like the back of his hand, and slips away to the other side, to Brittany, before we can lay our hands on him. His craft is like quicksilver, none of our ships down here can catch him. He'll creep into our harbours by night, land silently like the stealthy rat he is, seize our goods, break open our stores and merchandise, and be away on the morning tide while our fellows are rubbing the sleep out of their eyes.'

'In fact, he is too clever for you,' said Dona.

'Why, yes, Madam – if you like to put it that way,' he answered haughtily, at once taking offence.

'I'm afraid Harry would never catch him, he is far too lazy,' she said.

'I do not for a moment suggest that he could,' said Godolphin, 'but we need heads in this business, the more the better. And we have to catch this fellow if it means spending all the time and money at our disposal. You perhaps do not realise how serious the matter is. Down here we are constantly robbed, our womenfolk sleep in terror of their lives, and not only their lives.'

'Oh, he is that sort of pirate, then?' murmured Dona.

'No lives have been lost as yet, and none of our women have been taken,' said Godolphin stiffly, 'but as this fellow is a Frenchman we all realise that it is only a question of time before something dastardly occurs.'

'Oh, quite,' said Dona, and seized with sudden laughter she rose to her feet and walked towards the window, for his gravity and pomposity were beyond bearing, she could stand it no longer, her laughter would win control. But, thank heaven, he took her rising as a gesture of dismissal, for he bowed solemnly, and kissed the hand she gave him.

'When you next send messages to your husband I trust you will remember me to him, and give him some account of our troubles,' he said, and 'Yes, of course,' answered Dona, determined that whatever happened Harry should not come hot-foot down to Navron to deal with elusive pirates, breaking in upon her privacy and lovely freedom. When she had promised that she would call upon his wife, and he had uttered a few more formalities, she summoned William, and he withdrew, and she heard the steady trot of his horse as he vanished down the drive.

She hoped he would be the last visitor, for this sort of thing was not what she intended; this solemn sitting around on chairs exchanging small conversation with a turnip-head was one degree worse than supping at the Swan. William must be warned, in future she would not be at home to callers. He must make an excuse; she would be out walking, or asleep, or ill, or mad even – confined to her room in chains – anything, rather than face the Godolphins of the county, in all their grandeur and pomposity.

How dull-witted they must be, these local gentry, to be robbed in this way, their goods and merchandise seized in the night, and unable to prevent it, even with the help of soldiers. How slow they must be, how inefficient. Surely if they kept a watch, were constantly on the alert, it would be possible to lay some trap for the foreigner as he crept into their harbours. A ship was not a phantom thing, it depended on wind and tide, nor were men soundless, their feet must echo on the quays, their voices fall upon the air. That day she dined early, at six, and talked to William as he stood behind her chair, bidding him close the door to visitors in future.

'You see, William,' she said, 'I came to Navron to avoid people, to be alone. My mood is to play the hermit, while I am here.'

'Yes, my lady,' he said, 'I made a mistake about this afternoon. It shall not occur again. You shall enjoy your solitude, and make good your escape.'

'Escape?' she said.

'Yes, my lady,' he answered, 'I have rather gathered that is why you are here. You are a fugitive from your London self, and Navron is your sanctuary.'

She was silent a minute, astonished, a little dismayed, and then: 'You have uncanny intuition, William,' she said, 'where does it come from?'

'My late master talked to me long and often, my lady,' he said. 'Many of my ideas and much of my philosophy are borrowed from him. I have made a practice of observing people even as he does. And I rather think that he would term your ladyship's arrival here as an escape.'

'And why did you leave your master, William?'

'His life is such, at the moment, my lady, that my services are of little use to him. We decided I would do better elsewhere.'

'And so you came to Navron?'

'Yes, my lady.'

'And lived alone and hunted moths?'

'Your ladyship is correct.'

'So that Navron is also, possibly, an escape for you as well?'

'Possibly, my lady.'

'And your late master, what does he do with himself?'

'He travels, my lady.'

'He makes voyages from place to place?'

'Exactly, my lady.'

'Then he also, William, is a fugitive. People who travel are always fugitives.'

'My master has often made the same observation, my lady. In fact I may say his life is one continual escape.'

'How pleasant for him,' said Dona, peeling her fruit; 'the rest of us can only run away from time to time, and however much we pretend to be free, we know it is only for a little while – our hands and our feet are tied.'

'Just so, my lady.'

'And your master – he has no ties at all?'

'None whatever, my lady.'

'I would like to meet your master, William.'

'I think you would have much in common, my lady.'

'Perhaps one day he will pass this way, on his travels?'

'Perhaps, my lady.'

'In fact, I will withdraw my command about visitors, William. Should your late master ever call, I will not feign illness or madness or any other disease, I will receive him.'

'Very good, my lady.'

And looking round – for she was standing now, and he had pulled away her chair – she saw that he was smiling, but instantly his smile was gone, when he met her eyes, and his mouth was pursed in its usual button. She wandered into the garden. The air was soft and languid and warm, and away to the west the sun flung great patterns across the sky. She could hear the voices of the children as Prue put them to bed. It was a time for going forth alone, a time for walking. And fetching a shawl and throwing it across her shoulders she went out of the garden and across the park-land to a stile, and a field, and a muddied lane, and the lane brought her to a cart-track, and the cart-track to a great stretch of rough wild grass, of uncultivated heathland, leading to the cliffs and the sea.

She had the urge within her to walk then to the sea, to the open sea itself, not the river even, and as the evening cooled and the sun sank in the sky, she came at length to a sloping headland where the gulls clamoured furiously at her approach, for it was the nesting season, and flinging herself down on the tussocky earth and the scrubby stones of the headland she looked out upon the sea. There was the river, away to the left, wide and shining as it met the sea, and the sea itself was still and very calm, while the setting sun dappled the water with copper and crimson. Down below, far and deep, the little waves splashed upon the rocks.

The setting sun behind her made a pathway on the sea, stretching to the far horizon, and as Dona lay and watched, her mind all drowsy and content, her heart at peace, she saw a smudge on the horizon, and presently the smudge took shape and form, and she saw the white sails of a ship. For a while it made no progress, for there was no breath upon the water, and it seemed to hang there, between sea and sky, like a painted toy. She could see the high poop-deck, and the fo'c'sle head, and the curious raking masts, and the men upon her must have had luck with their fishing for a crowd of gulls clustered around the ship, wheeling and crying, and diving to the water.

Presently a little tremor of a breeze came off the headland where Dona lay, and she saw the breeze ruffle the waves below her, and travel out across the sea towards the waiting ship. Suddenly the sails caught the breeze and filled, they bellied out in the wind, lovely and white and free, the gulls rose in a mass, screaming above the masts, the setting sun caught the painted ship in a gleam of gold, and silently, stealthily, leaving a long dark ripple behind her, the ship stole in towards the land. And a feeling came upon Dona, as though a hand touched her heart, and a voice whispered in her brain, 'I shall remember this.' A premonition of wonder, of fear, of sudden strange elation. She turned swiftly, smiling to herself for no reason, humming a little tune, and strode back across the hills to Navron House, skirting the mud and jumping the ditches like a child, while the sky darkened, and the moon rose, and the night wind whispered in the tall trees.

Chapter Five

She went to bed as soon as she returned, for the walk had tired her, and she fell asleep almost at once, in spite of the curtains drawn wide, and the shining moon. And then, just after midnight it must have been, for subconsciously she had heard the stable clock strike the hour, she was awake, aware of a footstep that had crunched the gravel beneath her window. She was instantly alert, the household should be sleeping at such an hour, she was suspicious of footsteps in the night. She rose from bed then, and went to the casement, and looked out into the garden. She could see nothing beneath her, the house was in shadow, and whoever had stood there, beneath the casement, must have passed on. She waited and watched, and suddenly, from the belt of trees beyond the lawn, a figure stole into a square patch of moonlight and looked up towards the house. She saw him cup his hands to his mouth and give a soft low whistle. At once another figure crept out from the shadowed house, he must have been sheltering just inside the window of the salon, and this second figure ran swiftly across the lawn to the man by the belt of trees, his hand raised as though in warning, and she saw that the running figure was William. Dona leant forward, screened by the curtain, her ringlets falling over her face, and she breathed quicker than usual, and her heart beat fast, for there was excitement in what she saw, there was danger – her fingers beat a little nameless tune upon the sill. The two men stood together in the patch of moonlight, and Dona saw William gesticulate with his hands, and point towards the house, at which she drew back into the shadow for fear of being observed. The two continued talking, the strange man looking upward at the house also, and presently he shrugged his shoulders, spreading out his hands, as though the matter were beyond his powers of settlement, and then they both withdrew into the belt of trees, and disappeared. Dona waited, and listened, but they did not return. Then she shivered, for the breeze was cool blowing upon her thin nightgown, and she returned to bed, but could not sleep, for this new departure of William's was a mystery that must be solved.

Had she seen him walk by moonlight into the trees, alone, she would have thought little of it, there might have been a woman in Helford hamlet by the river who was not unpleasing to him, or his silent expedition might have been more innocent still, a moth-hunt at midnight. But that stealthy tread, as though he waited for a signal, and that dark figure with his cupped hands and the soft whistle, William's run across the lawn with his warning hand, these were graver problems, giving cause for worry.

She wondered if she had been a very great fool in trusting William. Anyone but herself would have dismissed him that first evening, on learning of his stewardship, how he had lived there in the house alone, without orders to do so. And that manner of his, so unlike the usual servant, that manner which intrigued and amused her, would no doubt have caused offence to most mistresses, to a Lady Godolphin. Harry would have sent him away at once – except that no doubt his manner would have been different with Harry, she felt that instinctively. And then the tobacco jar, the volume of poetry – it was mystifying, beyond her comprehension, but in the morning she must do something, take the matter in hand, and so without having decided anything, her mind in disorder, she fell asleep at length, just as the grey morning light broke into the room.

The day was hot and shining, like its predecessor, a high golden sun in a cloudless sky, and when Dona came down her first movement was towards the belt of trees where the stranger and William had talked, and disappeared, the night before. Yes, it was as she had expected, their footsteps had made a little track through the bluebells, easy to follow, they led straight across the main pathway of the woods and down deep amongst the thickest trees. She continued for a while, the track leading downwards always, twisting, uneven, very hard to follow, and suddenly she realised that this way would lead her in time towards the river, or a branch of the river, because in the distance she caught the gleam of water that she had not suspected could be so close, for surely the river itself must be away behind her, to the left, and this thread of water she was coming to was something unknown, a discovery. She hesitated a moment, uncertain whether to continue, and then remembering the hour, and how the children would be looking for her, and William himself perhaps, for orders, she turned back, and climbed up through the woods once more, and so on to the lawns of Navron House. The matter must be postponed to a better time, later perhaps in the afternoon.

So she played with the children, and wrote a duty letter to Harry – the groom was riding back to London in a day or so, to bear him news. She sat in the salon by the wide open window, nibbling the end of her pen, for what was there to say except that she was happy in her freedom, absurdly happy, and that would be hurtful; poor Harry, he would never understand.

'That friend of your youth called upon me, one Godolphin,' she wrote, 'whom I found ill-favoured and pompous, and could not picture you together romping in the fields as little boys. But perhaps you did not romp, but sat upon gilt chairs and played cat's cradle. He has a growth on the end of his nose, and his wife is expecting a baby, at which I expressed sympathy. And he was in a great fuss and pother about pirates, or rather one pirate, a Frenchman, who comes by night and robs his house, and the houses of his neighbours, and all the soldiers of the west cannot catch him, which seems to me not very clever of them. So I propose setting forth myself, with a cutlass between my teeth, and when I have entrapped the rogue, who according to Godolphin is a very fierce fellow indeed, a slayer of men and a ravisher of women, I will bind him with strong cords and send him to you as a present.' She yawned, and tapped her teeth with her pen, it was easy to write this sort of letter, making a jest of everything, and she must be careful not to be tender, because Harry would take horse at once and ride to her, nor must she be too cold, for that would fret him, and would also bring him.

So 'Amuse yourself as you wish, and think of your figure when you take that fifth glass,' she wrote, 'and address yourself, if you should have the desire, to any lovely lady your sleepy eye should fall upon, I will not play the scold when I see you again.

'Your children are well, and send their love, and I send you – whatever you would wish me to send.

'Your affectionate wife

'Dona.'

She folded the letter, and sealed it. Now she was free once more, and began to think how she could rid herself of William for the afternoon, for she wished him well away before she started on her expedition. At one o'clock, over her cold meat, she knew how she would do it.

'William,' she said.

'My lady?'

She glanced up at him, and there was no night-hawk look about him, he was the same as always, attentive to her commands.

'William,' she said, 'I would like you to ride to my Lord Godolphin's manor this afternoon, bearing flowers for his lady who is unwell.'

Was that a flicker of annoyance in his eye, a momentary unwillingness, a hesitation?

'You wish me to take the flowers to-day, my lady?'

'If you please, William.'

'I believe the groom is doing nothing, my lady.'

'I wish the groom to take Miss Henrietta and Master James and the nurse for a picnic, in the carriage.'

'Very well, my lady.'

'You will tell the gardener to cut the flowers?'

'Yes, my lady.'

She said no more, and he too was silent, and she smiled to herself, for she guessed he did not want to go. Perhaps he had another assignation with his friend, down through the woods. Well, she would keep it for him.

'Tell one of the maids to turn back my bed and draw the curtains, I shall rest this afternoon,' she said, as she went from the room, and William bowed without reply.

This was a ruse to dull any fears he might have, but she was certain he was without suspicion. And so, playing her part, she went upstairs and lay down on her bed. Later she heard the carriage draw up in the courtyard, and the children's voices chattering excitedly at the sudden picnic, and then the carriage bowled away down the avenue. After a short while she heard a single horse clatter on the cobbled stones, and leaving her room, and going out on the passage where the window looked out upon the yard, she saw William mount one of the horses, a great bunch of flowers before him on the saddle, and so ride away.

How successful the strategy, she thought, laughing to herself like a silly child on an adventure. She put on a faded gown which she would not mind tearing, and a silken handkerchief around her head, and slipped out of her own house like a thief.

She followed the track that she had found in the morning, but this time plunging down deep into the woods without hesitation. The birds were astir again, after their noonday silence, and the silent butterflies danced and fluttered, while drowsy bumble bees hummed in the warm air, winging their way to the topmost branches of the trees. Yes, there once again was the glimmer of water that had surprised her. The trees were thinning, she was coming to the bank – and there, suddenly before her for the first time, was the creek, still and soundless, shrouded by the trees, hidden from the eyes of men. She stared at it in wonder, for she had had no knowledge of its existence, this stealthy branch of the parent river creeping into her own property, so sheltered, so concealed by the woods themselves. The tide was ebbing, the water oozing away from the mud flats, and here where she stood was the head of the creek itself, for the stream ended in a trickle, and the trickle in a spring. The creek twisted round a belt of trees, and she began to walk along the bank, happy, fascinated, forgetting her mission, for this discovery was a pleasure quite unexpected, this creek was a source of enchantment, a new escape, better than Navron itself, a place to drowse and sleep, a lotus-land. There was a heron, standing in the shallows, solemn and grey, his head sunk in his hooded shoulders, and beyond him a little oyster-catcher pattered in the mud, and then, weird and lovely, a curlew called, and rising from the bank, flew away from her down the creek. Something, not herself, disturbed the birds, for the heron rose slowly, flapping his slow wings, and followed the curlew, and Dona paused a moment, for she too had heard a sound, a sound of tapping, of hammering.

She went on, coming to the corner where the creek turned, and then she paused, withdrawing instinctively to the cover of the trees, for there before her, where the creek suddenly widened, forming a pool, lay a ship at anchor – so close that she could have tossed a biscuit to the decks. She recognised it at once. This was the ship she had seen the night before, the painted ship on the horizon, red and golden in the setting sun. There were two men slung over the side, chipping at the paint, this was the sound of hammering she had heard. It must be deep water where the ship lay, a perfect anchorage, for on either side the mud banks rose steeply and the tide ran away, frothing and bubbling, while the creek itself twisted again and turned, running towards the parent river out of sight. A few yards from where she stood was a little quay. There was tackle there, and blocks, and ropes; they must be making repairs. A boat was tied alongside, but no one was in it.

But for the two men chipping at the side of the ship all was still, the drowsy stillness of a summer afternoon. No one would know, thought Dona, no one could tell, unless they had walked as she had done, down from Navron House, that a ship lay at anchor in this pool, shrouded as it was by the trees, and hidden from the open river.

Another man crossed the deck and leant over the bulwark, gazing down at his fellows. A little smiling man, like a monkey, and he carried a lute in his hands. He swung himself up on the bulwark, and sat cross-legged, and began to play the strings. The two men looked up at him, and laughed, as he strummed a careless, lilting air, and then he began to sing, softly at first, then a little louder, and Dona, straining to catch the words, realised with a sudden wave of understanding, and her heart thumping, that the man was singing in French.

Then she knew, then she understood – her hands went clammy, her mouth felt parched, and she felt, for the first time in her life, a funny strange spasm of fear.

This was the Frenchman's hiding-place – that was his ship.

She must think rapidly, make a plan, make some use of her knowledge; how obvious it was now, this silent creek, this perfect hiding-place, no one would ever know, so remote, so silent, so still – something must be done, she would have to say something, tell someone.

Or need she? Could she go away now, pretend she had not seen the ship, forget about it, or pretend to forget it – anything so that she need not be involved, for that would mean a breaking up of her peace, a disturbance, soldiers tramping through the woods, people arriving, Harry from London – endless complications, and Navron no more a sanctuary. No, she would say nothing, she would creep away now, back to the woods and the house, clinging to her guilty knowledge, telling no one, letting the robberies continue – what did it matter – Godolphin and his turnip friends must put up with it, the country must suffer, she did not care.

And then, even as she turned to slip away amongst the trees, a figure stepped out from behind her, from the woods, and throwing his coat over her head blinded her, pinning her hands to her sides, so that she could not move, could not struggle, and she fell down at his feet, suffocated, helpless, knowing she was lost.

Chapter Six

Her first feeling was one of anger, of blind unreasoning anger. How dare anyone treat her thus, she thought, truss her up like a fowl and carry her to the quay. She was thrown roughly on to the bottom boards of the boat, and the man who had knocked her down took the paddles and pushed out towards the ship. He gave a cry – a sea-gull's cry – and called something in a patois which she could not understand to his companions on the ship. She heard them laugh in reply, and the fellow with the lute struck up a merry little jig, as though in mockery.

She had freed herself now from the strangling coat, and looked up at the man who had struck her. He spoke to her in French and grinned. He had a merry twinkle in his eye, as though her capture were a game, an amusing jest of a summer's afternoon, and when she frowned at him haughtily, determined to be dignified, he pulled a solemn face, feigning fear, and pretended to tremble.

She wondered what would happen if she raised her voice and shouted for help – would anyone hear her, would it be useless?

Somehow she knew she could not do this, women like herself did not scream. They waited, they planned escape. She could swim, it would be possible later perhaps to get away from the ship, lower herself over the side, perhaps when it was dark. What a fool she had been, she thought, to linger there an instant, when she knew that the ship was the Frenchman. How deserving of capture she was, after all, and how infuriating to be placed in such a position – ridiculous, absurd – when a quiet withdrawal to the trees and back to Navron would have been so easy. They were passing now under the stern of the ship, beneath the high poop-deck and the scrolled windows, and there was the name written with a flourish, in gold letters *La Mouette*. She wondered what it meant, she could not remember, her French was hazy suddenly, and now he was pointing to the ladder over the side of the ship, and the men on deck were crowding round, grinning, familiar – damn their eyes – to watch her mount. She managed the ladder well, determined to give them no cause for mockery, and shaking her head she swung herself down on the deck, refusing their offers of assistance.

They began to chatter to her in this patois she could not follow – it must be Breton, had not Godolphin said something about the ship slipping across to the opposite coast – and they kept smiling and laughing at her in a familiar, idiotic way that she found infuriating, for it went ill with the heroic dignified part she wished to play. She folded her arms, and looked away from them, saying nothing. Then the first man appeared again – he had gone to warn their leader she supposed, the captain of this fantastic vessel – and beckoned her to follow him.

It was all different from what she had expected. These men were like children, enchanted with her appearance, smiling and whistling, and she had believed pirates to be desperate creatures, with rings in their ears and knives between their teeth.

The ship was clean – she had imagined a craft filthy and stained, and evil-smelling – there was no disorder about it, the paint was fresh and gay, the decks scrubbed like a man-o'-war and from the forward part of the ship, where the men lived she supposed, came the good hunger-making smell of vegetable soup. And now the man was leading her through a swinging door and down some steps, and he knocked on a further door, and a quiet voice bade him enter. Dona stood on the threshold, blinking a little, for the sun was streaming through the windows in the stern, making water patterns on the light wood panelling. Once again she felt foolish, disconcerted, for the cabin was not the dark hole she had imagined, full of empty bottles and cutlasses, but a room – like a room in a house – with chairs, and a polished table, and little paintings of birds upon the bulkheads. There was something restful about it, restful yet austere, the room of someone who was sufficient to himself. The man who had taken her to the cabin withdrew, closing the door quietly, and the figure at the polished table continued with his writing, taking no notice of her entrance. She watched him furtively, aware of sudden shyness and hating herself for it, she, Dona, who was never shy, who cared for nothing and for no one. She wondered how long he would keep her standing there; it was unmannerly, churlish, and yet she knew she could not be the first to speak. She thought of Godolphin suddenly, Godolphin with his bulbous eyes and the growth on the end of his nose, and his fears for his women-folk; what would he say if he could see her now, alone in the cabin with the terrible Frenchman?

And the Frenchman continued writing, and Dona went on standing by the door. She realised now what made him different from other men. He wore his own hair as men used to do, instead of the ridiculous curled wigs that had become the fashion, and she saw at once how suited it was to him, how impossible it would be for him to wear it in any other way.

How remote he was, how detached, like some student in college studying for an examination; he had not even bothered to raise his head when she came into his presence, and what was he scribbling there anyway that was so important? She ventured to step forward closer to the table, so that she could see, and now she realised he was not writing at all, he was drawing, he was sketching, finely, with great care, a heron standing on the mud-flats, as she had seen a heron stand, ten minutes before.

Then she was baffled, then she was at a loss for words, for thought even, for pirates were not like this, at least not the pirates of her imagination, and why could he not play the part she had assigned to him, become an evil, leering fellow, full of strange oaths, dirty, greasy-handed, not this grave figure seated at the polished table, holding her in contempt?

Then he spoke at last, only the very faintest trace of accent marking his voice, and still he did not look at her, but went on with his drawing of the heron.

'It seems you have been spying upon my ship,' he said.

Immediately she was stung to anger – she spying! Good God, what an accusation? 'On the contrary,' she said, speaking coldly, clearly, in the boyish voice she used to servants. 'On the contrary, it seems your men have been trespassing upon my land.'

He glanced up at once, and rose to his feet – he was tall, much taller than she had imagined – and into his dark eyes came a look, surely of recognition, like a sudden flame, and he smiled slowly, as if in secret.

'My very humble apologies,' he said. 'I had not realised that the lady of the manor had come to visit me in person.'

He reached forward for a chair, and she sat down, without a word. He went on looking at her, that glance of recognition, of secret amusement in his eyes, and he leant back in his chair, crossing his legs, biting the end of his quill.

'Was it by your orders that I was seized and brought here?' she said, because surely something must be said, and he would do nothing but look her up and down in this singular fashion.

'My men are told to bind anyone who ventures to the creek,' he said. 'As a rule we have no trouble. You have been more bold than the inhabitants, and alas, have suffered from that boldness. You are not hurt are you, or bruised?'

'No,' she said shortly.

'What are you complaining about then?'

'I am not used to being treated in such a manner,' she said, angry again, for he was making her look like a fool.

'No, of course not,' he said quietly, 'but it will do you no harm.'

God almighty, what insolence, what damned impertinence. Her anger only amused him though, for he went on tilting his chair and smiling, biting the end of his quill.

'What do you propose to do with me?' she said.

'Ah! there you have me,' he replied, putting down his pen. 'I must look up my book of rules.' And he opened a drawer in the table and took out a volume, the pages of which he proceeded to turn slowly, with great gravity.

'Prisoners – method of capture – questioning – detainment – their treatment – etc., etc.,' he read aloud, 'h'm, yes, it is all here, but unfortunately these notes relate to the capture and treatment of male prisoners. I have made no arrangements apparently to deal with females. It is really most remiss of me.'

She thought of Godolphin again, and his fears, and in spite of her annoyance she found herself smiling, remembering his words: 'As the fellow is a Frenchman it is only a matter of time.'

His voice broke in upon her thoughts. 'That is better,' he said. 'Anger does not become you, you know. Now you are beginning to look more like yourself.'

'What do you know of me?' she said.

He smiled again, tilting forward on his chair. 'The Lady St. Columb,' he said, 'the spoilt darling of the Court. The Lady Dona who drinks in the London taverns with her husband's friends. You are quite a celebrity, you know.'

She found herself flushing scarlet, stung by the irony of his words, his quiet contempt.

'That's over,' she said, 'finished and done with.'

'For the time being, you mean.'

'No, for ever.'

He began whistling softly to himself, and reaching for his drawing continued to play with it, sketching in the background.

'When you have been at Navron a little while you will tire of it,' he said, 'and the smells and sounds of London will call to you again. You will remember this mood as a passing thing.'

'No,' she said.

But he did not answer, he went on with his drawing.

She watched him, stung with curiosity, for he drew well, and she began to forget that she was his prisoner and that they should be at enmity with one another.

'That heron was standing on the mud, by the head of the creek,' she said, 'I saw him, just now, before I came to the ship.'

'Yes,' answered, 'he is always there, when the tide ebbs. It is one of his feeding grounds. He nests some distance away though, nearer to Gweek, up the main channel. What else did you see?'

'An oyster-catcher, and another bird, a curlew I think it was.'

'Oh, yes,' he said, 'they would be there too. I expect the hammering drove them away.'

'Yes,' she said.

He continued his little tuneless whistle, drawing the while, and she watched him, thinking how natural it was, how effortless and easy, to be sitting here, in this cabin, on this ship, side by side with the Frenchman, while the sun streamed in through the windows and the ebb-tide bubbled round the stern. It was funny, like a dream, like something she had always known would happen, as though this was a scene in a play, in which she must act a part, and the curtain had now lifted, and someone had whispered: 'Here – this is where you go on.'

'The night-jars have started now, in the evenings,' he said, 'they crouch in the hillside, farther down the creek. They are so wary though, it's almost impossible to get really close.'

'Yes,' she said.

'The creek is my refuge, you know,' he said, glancing up at her, and then away again. 'I come here to do nothing. And then, just before idleness gets the better of me, I have the strength of mind to tear myself away, to set sail again.'

'And commit acts of piracy against my countrymen?' she said.

'And commit acts of piracy against your countrymen,' he echoed.

He finished his drawing, and put it away, and then rose to his feet, stretching his arms above his head.

'One day they will catch you,' she said.

'One day ... perhaps,' he said, and he wandered to the window in the stern, and looked out, his back turned to her.

'Come and look,' he said, and she got up from her chair and went and stood beside him, and they looked down to the water, where there floated a great cluster of gulls, nosing for scraps.

'They come in dozens, always,' he told her; 'they seem to know at once when we return, and they come in here from the headlands. My men will feed them, I can't prevent them. And I am as bad myself. I am always throwing crumbs to them, from the windows here.' He laughed, and reaching for a crust of bread, he tossed it to them, and the gulls leapt upon it screaming and fighting.

'Perhaps they have a fellow feeling for the ship,' he said; 'it is my fault for naming her *La Mouette*.'

'*La Mouette* – the Sea-gull – why, of course,' she said. 'I had forgotten what it meant,' and they went on watching the gulls, leaning against the window.

'This is absurd,' Dona thought, 'why am I doing this, it is not what I intended. By now surely I should be bound with ropes and thrust into the dark hold of the ship, gagged and bruised, and here we are throwing bread to the seagulls, and I have forgotten to go on being angry.'

'Why are you a pirate?' she said at last, breaking the silence.

'Why do you ride horses that are too spirited?' he answered.

'Because of the danger, because of the speed, because I might fall,' she said.

'That is why I am a pirate,' he said.

'Yes, but ...'

'There are no "buts". It is all very simple really. There are no dark problems about it. I have no grudge against society, no bitter hatred of my fellow-men. It just happens that the problems of piracy interest me, suit my particular bent of thought. It is not just a matter of brutality and bloodshed, you know. The organisation takes many hours of many days, every detail of a landing has to be thought out, and prepared. I hate disorder, or any slipshod method of attack. The whole thing is very much like a geometrical problem, it is food for the brain. And then – well – then I have my fun, my spice of excitement, my beating of the other fellow. It is very satisfying, very absorbing.'

'Yes,' she said. 'Yes, I understand.'

'You are puzzled, aren't you,' he said, laughing down at her, 'because you expected to find me drunk here on the floor, surrounded by blood and knives and bottles and shrieking women.'

She smiled back at him; she did not answer.

Someone knocked at the door, and when the Frenchman called 'Enter' one of his men came in, bearing a great bowl of soup on a tray. It smelt rich and good. The hot steam rose in the air. The man proceeded to lay the table, spreading a white cloth on the farther end. He went to a locker in the bulkhead and brought out a bottle of wine. Dona watched. The smell of the soup was very tempting, and she was hungry. The wine looked cool, in its slim bottle. The man withdrew, and looking up she saw that the master of the ship was watching her, with laughter in his eyes.

'Will you have some?' he said.

She nodded, feeling foolish once again: why did he read her thoughts? And he fetched another plate and spoon, and another glass from the cupboard. Then he pulled up two chairs to the table. She saw that there was new bread too, freshly baked in the French fashion, the crust dark and brown, and little pats of very yellow butter.

They ate their meal in silence, and then he poured out the wine. It was cold and clear, and not too sweet. And all the while she kept thinking how like a dream it was, a remembered dream that she had had once; a quiet, familiar thing, a dream she recognised.

'I have done this before,' she thought, 'this is not the first time.' Yet that was absurd, for of course it was the first time, and he was a stranger to her. She wondered what hour it was. The children would have returned from their picnic. Prue would be putting them to bed. They would run and knock upon her door and she would not answer. 'It does not matter,' she thought, 'I don't care,' and she went on drinking her wine, looking at the bird pictures on the bulkhead, and now and again stealing a glance at him when she knew that his head was turned from her.

Then he reached out an arm towards a tobacco-jar on a shelf, and began to shake the mixture into his hand. It was close cut, very dark and brown. And suddenly, the truth striking at her like a blow, she saw the tobacco-jar in her bedroom, and the volume of French poetry, with the drawing of a seagull on the title-page. She saw William running to the belt of trees – William – his master, his master who made voyages from place to place – whose life was one continual escape. She got up from her chair, staring at him.

'Good God!' she said.

He looked up. 'What is the matter?'

'It's you,' she said, 'you who left the tobacco-jar in my bedroom, and the volume of Ronsard. It's you have been sleeping in my bed.'

He smiled at her, amused at her choice of words, smiling too at her astonishment, her confusion and dismay.

'Did I leave them there?' he said. 'I had forgotten. How very remiss and careless of William not to have noticed.'

'It was for you that William stayed at Navron,' she said; 'it was for your sake that he sent the servants away. All these months, while we were in London, you have been at Navron.'

'No,' he said, 'not continually. From time to time, when it suited my plans. And in the winter, you know, it can be damp here in the creek. It made a change, a luxurious change, to seek the comfort of your bedroom. Somehow, I always felt you would not mind.'

He went on looking at her, and always that glimmer of secret amusement in his eyes.

'I consulted your portrait, you know,' he said. 'I addressed myself to it several times. My lady, I said (for I was most subservient), would you grant a very weary Frenchman the courtesy of your bed? And it seemed to me that you bowed gracefully, and gave me permission. Sometimes you even smiled.'

'It was very wrong of you,' she said, 'very irregular.'

'I know,' he said.

'Besides being dangerous.'

'That was the fun of it.'

'And if I had known for one moment . . .'

'What would you have done?'

'I should have come down to Navron at once.'

'And then?'

'I should have barred the house. I should have dismissed William. I should have set a watch on the estate.'

'All that?'

'Yes.'

'I don't believe you.'

'Why not?'

'Because when I lay in your bed, looking up at your portrait on the wall, that was not how you behaved.'

'How did I behave?'

'Very differently.'

'What did I do?'

'Many things.'

'What sort of things?'

'You joined my ship's company, for one thing. You signed your name amongst the faithful. You were the first, and the last, woman to do so.'

And saying this, he rose from the table, and went to a drawer, and fetched out a book. This he opened, and on the page she saw the words *La Mouette*, followed by a string of names. Edmond Vacquier . . . Jules Thomas . . . Pierre Blanc . . . Luc Dumont . . . and so on. And he reached then for his pen, and dipped it in the ink, and handed it to her.

'Well,' she said, 'what about it?'

She took it from him, balancing it in her hand a moment, as though weighing the question, and she did not know whether it was the thought of Harry in London, yawning over his cards, or Godolphin with his bulbous eyes, or the good soup she had taken and the wine she had drunk, making her drowsy and warm, and a little careless, like a butterfly in the sun, or whether it was because he was standing there beside her, but she looked up at him, laughing suddenly, and signed her name in the centre of the page, beneath the others, Dona St. Columb.

'And now you must go back, your children will wonder what has happened to you,' he said.

'Yes,' she said.

He led the way out of his cabin, and on to the deck. He leant over the rail, and called down to the men amidships.

'First you must be introduced,' he said, and he called out an order, in the Breton patois she could not understand, and in a moment his company assembled themselves, glancing up at her in curiosity.

'I am going to tell them that from henceforth you come to the creek unchallenged,' he said; 'that you are free to come and go as you please. The creek is yours. The ship is yours. You are one of us.' He spoke to them briefly, and then one by one they came up to her, and bowed, and kissed her hand, and she laughed back at them, saying 'Thank you' – and there was a madness about it, a frivolity, like a dream under the sun. Below, in the water, one of the men waited for her in the boat. She climbed the bulwark, and swung herself over the side on to the ladder. The Frenchman did not help her. He leant against the bulwark and watched her.

'And Navron House?' he said. 'Is it barred and bolted, is William to be dismissed?'

'No,' she said.

'I must return your call, then,' he said, 'as a matter of courtesy.'

'Of course.'

'What is the correct hour? In the afternoon, I believe, between three and four, and you offer me a dish of tea?'

She looked at him, laughing, and shook her head.

'No,' she said, 'that is for Lord Godolphin and the gentry. Pirates do not call upon ladies in the afternoon. They come stealthily, by night, knocking upon a window – and the lady of the manor, fearful for her safety, gives him supper, by candlelight.'

'As you will,' he said, 'to-morrow then, at ten o'clock?'

'Yes,' she said.

'Good night.'

'Good night.'

He went on standing against the bulwark watching her, as she was pulled ashore in the little boat. The sun had gone behind the trees, and the creek was in shadow. The last of the ebb had run away from the flats, and the water was still. A curlew called once, out of sight, round the bend of the river. The ship, with its bold colouring, its raking masts, looked remote, unreal, a thing of fantasy. She turned, and sped through the trees towards the house, smiling guiltily to herself, like a child hugging a secret.

Chapter Seven

When she came to the house she saw that William was standing by the window of the salon, making a pretence of putting the room in order, but she knew at once he had been watching for her.

She did not tell him immediately, for the fun of teasing him, and coming into the room, casting her kerchief from her head, she said, 'I have been walking, William, my head is better.'

'So I observe, my lady,' he said, his eyes upon her.

'I walked by the river, where it is quiet and cool.'

'Indeed, my lady.'

'I have no knowledge of the creek before. It is enchanting, like a fairy-tale. A good hiding-place, William, for fugitives like myself.'

'Very probably, my lady.'

'And my Lord Godolphin, did you see him?'

'His lordship was not at home, my lady. I bade his servant give your flowers and the message to his lady.'

'Thank you, William.' She paused a moment, pretending to arrange the sprigs of lilac in their vase, and then, 'Oh, William, before I forget. I am giving a small supper party to-morrow night. The hour is rather late, ten o'clock.'

'Very well, my lady. How many will you be?'

'Only two, William. Myself and one other – a gentleman.'

'Yes, my lady.'

'The gentleman will be coming on foot, so there is no need for the groom to stay up and mind a horse.'

'No, my lady.'

'Can you cook, William?'

'I am not entirely ignorant of the art, my lady.'

'Then you shall send the servants to bed, and cook supper for the gentleman and myself, William.'

'Yes, my lady.'

'And you need not mention the visit to anyone in the house, William.'

'No, my lady.'

'In fact, William, I propose to behave outrageously.'

'So it would seem, my lady.'

'And you are dreadfully shocked, William?'

'No, my lady.'

'Why not, William?'

'Because nothing you or my master ever did could possibly shock me, my lady.'

And at this she burst out laughing, and clasped her hands together.

'Oh, William, my solemn William, then you guessed all the time! How did you know, how could you tell?'

'There was something about your walk, as you entered just now, my lady, that gave you away. And your eyes were – if I may say so without giving offence – very much alive. And coming as you did from the direction of the river I put two and two together, as it were, and said to myself: "It has happened. They have met at last".'

'Why "at last", William?'

'Because, my lady, I am a fatalist by nature, and I have always known that, sooner or later, the meeting was bound to come about.'

'Although I am a lady of the manor, married and respectable, with two children, and your master a lawless Frenchman, and a pirate?'

'In spite of all those things, my lady.'

'It is very wrong, William. I am acting against the interests of my country, I could be imprisoned for it.'

'Yes, my lady.'

But this time he hid his smile no longer, his small button mouth relaxed, and she knew he would no longer be inscrutable and silent, but was her friend, her ally, and she could trust him to the last.

'Do you approve of your master's profession, William?' she said.

'Approve and disapprove are two words that are not in my vocabulary, my lady. Piracy suits my master, and that is all there is to it. His ship is his kingdom, he comes and goes as he pleases, and no man can command him. He is a law unto himself.'

'Would it not be possible to be free, to do as he pleases, and yet not be a pirate?'

'My master thinks not, my lady. He has it that those who live a normal life, in this world of ours, are forced into habits, into customs, into a rule of life that eventually kills all initiative, all spontaneity. A man becomes a cog in the wheel, part of a system. But because a pirate is a rebel, and an outcast, he escapes from the world. He is without ties, without man-made principles.'

'He has the time, in fact, to be himself.'

'Yes, my lady.'

'And the idea that piracy is wrong, that does not worry him?'

'He robs those who can afford to be robbed, my lady. He gives away much of what he takes. The poorer people in Brittany benefit very often. No, the moral issue does not concern him.'

'He is not married, I suppose?'

'No, my lady. Marriage and piracy do not go together.'

'What if his wife should love the sea?'

'Women are apt to obey the laws of nature, my lady, and produce babies.'

'Ah, very true, William.'

'And women who produce babies have a liking for their own fireside, they no longer want to roam. So a man is faced at once with a choice. He must either stay at home and be bored, or go away and be miserable. He is lost in either case. No, to be really free, a man must sail alone.'

'That is your master's philosophy?'

'Yes, my lady.'

'I wish I were a man, William.'

'Why so, my lady?'

'Because I too would find my ship, and go forth, a law unto myself.'

As she spoke there came a loud cry from upstairs, followed by a wail, and the sound of Prue's scolding voice. Dona smiled, and shook her head. 'Your master is right, William,' she said. 'We are all cogs in a wheel, and mothers most especially. It is only the pirates who are free.' And she went upstairs to her children, to soothe them, and wipe away their tears. That night, as she lay in bed, she reached for the volume of Ronsard on the table by her side, and thought how strange it was that the Frenchman had lain there, his head upon her pillow, this same volume in his hands, his pipe of tobacco in his mouth. She pictured him laying aside the book when he had read enough, even as she did now, and blowing out the candle, and then turning on his side to sleep. She wondered if he slept now, in that cool, quiet cabin of his ship, with the water lapping against the side, the creek itself mysterious and hushed. Or whether he lay on his back as she did, eyes open in the darkness and sleep far distant, brooding on the future, his hands behind his head.

Next morning, when she leant from her bedroom and felt the sun on her face, and saw the clear bright sky with a sharp gloss about it because of the east wind, her first thought was for the ship in the creek. Then she remembered how snug was the anchorage, tucked away in the valley, shrouded by the trees, and how they could scarce have knowledge there of the turbulent tide ripping up the parent river, the short waves curling, while the steep seas at the mouth of the estuary reared and broke themselves into spray.

She remembered the evening that was to come, and the supper party, and began to smile, with all the guilty excitement of a conspirator. The day itself seemed like a prelude, a foretaste of things to come, and she wandered out into the garden to cut flowers, although those in the house were not yet faded.

The cutting of flowers was a peaceful thing, soothing to her unquiet mind, and the very sensation of touching the petals, fingering the long green stalks, laying them in a basket, and later placing them one by one in the vases that William had filled for her, banished her first restlessness. William too was a conspirator. She had observed him in the dining hall, cleaning the silver, and he had glanced up at her in understanding, for she knew why he worked with such ardour.

'Let us do full justice to Navron,' she said; 'bring out all the silver, William, and light every candle. And we will use that dinner service with the rose border that is shut away for banquets.' It was exciting, it was amusing – she fetched the dinner service herself and washed the plates, dusty with disuse, and she made a little decoration in the centre of the table with the young buds of fresh-cut roses. Then she and William descended together to the cellar, and peered by candle-light at the cobweb-covered bottles, and he brought forth a wine greatly prized by his master, which they had not known was there. They exchanged smiles, they whispered furtively, and Dona felt all the lovely wickedness of a child who does something wrong, something forbidden, and chokes with secret laughter behind his parent's back.

'What are we going to eat?' she said, and he shook his head, he would not tell. 'Rest easy, my lady,' he said, 'I will not disappoint you,' and she went out into the garden once more, singing, her heart absurdly gay. The hot noon passed, hazy with the high east wind, and the long hours of afternoon, and tea with the children under the mulberry tree, and so round to early evening once again, and their bed-time, and a ceasing of the wind, while the sun set, the sky glowed, and the first stars shone.

The house was silent once more, and the servants, believing her to be weary, to be retiring supperless to bed, congratulated themselves on the easiness of their mistress, and took themselves to their own quarters. Somewhere, alone in his room no doubt, William prepared the supper. Dona did not ask. It did not matter.

She went to her own room, and stood before her wardrobe, pondering which gown to wear. She chose one cream-coloured, which she had worn often, and which she knew became her well, and she placed in her ears the ruby earrings that had belonged to Harry's mother, and round her throat the ruby pendant.

'He will not notice,' she thought, 'he is not that sort of person, he does not care about women, or their clothes, or their jewels,' and yet she found herself dressing with great care, combing her ringlets round her fingers and setting them behind her ears. Suddenly she heard the stable clock strike ten, and in a panic she laid the comb aside, and went downstairs. The staircase led direct into the dining-hall, and she saw that William had lighted every candle, even as she had told him, and the bright silver shone on the long table. William himself was standing there, arranging dishes on the sideboard, and she went to see what it was he had prepared. Then she smiled. 'Oh, William, now I know why you went down to Helford this afternoon, returning with a basket.' For there on the sideboard was crab, dressed and prepared in the French fashion, and there were small new potatoes too, cooked in their skins, and a fresh green salad sprinkled with garlic, and tiny scarlet radishes. He had found time too to make pastry. Thin, narrow wafers, interlaid with cream, while next to them, alone in a glass bowl, was a gathering of the first wild strawberries of the year.

'William, you are a genius,' she said, and he bowed, permitting himself a smile. 'I am pleased you are glad, my lady.'

'How do I look? Will your master approve?' she asked him, turning on her heels. 'He will make no comment, my lady,' replied the servant, 'but I do not think he will be entirely indifferent to your appearance.'

'Thank you, William,' she said gravely, and went out into the salon to await her guest. William had drawn the curtains for greater safety, but she pulled them back, letting in the summer night, and as she did so the Frenchman came towards her across the lawn, a tall, dark figure, walking silently.

She saw at once that he had fallen in with her mood, and knowing that she would play the lady of the manor he had dressed himself, even as she had done, as though for a party. The moonlight touched his white stockings, and glimmered on his silver-buckled shoes. His long coat was wine-coloured, and his sash the same, though in a deeper tone, and there was lace at his throat, and at his wrists. He still disdained the curled wigs of fashion, and wore his own hair, like a cavalier. Dona held out her hand to him, and this time he bent over it, as a guest should do, brushing it with his lips, and then stood on the threshold of the salon, by the long window, lookind down upon her with a smile.

'Supper awaits you,' she said, shy suddenly, for no reason, and he did not answer, but followed her to the dining-hall, where William stood waiting behind her chair.

The guest stood a moment, looking about him at the blaze of candles, at the bright silver, at the shining plates with the rose border, and then he turned to the hostess, with that same slow mocking smile she had grown to expect: 'Is it wise of you, do you think, to put all this temptation before a pirate?'

'It is William's fault,' said Dona, 'it is all William's doing.'

'I don't believe you,' he said; 'William never made these preparations for me before, did you, William? You cooked me a chop and served it to me on a chipped plate, and you brushed away one of the covers of the chairs, and told me I must be content.'

'Yes, sir,' said William, his eyes glowing in his small round face, and Dona sat down, shy no longer, for the presence of William broke constraint between them.

He understood his role, playing the butt to perfection, laying himself open purposely to shafts of wit from his mistress, accepting with a smile and a shrug of the shoulder the mockeries of his master. And the crab was good, the salad excellent, the pastries light as air, the strawberries nectar, the wine perfection.

'I am a better cook than William, for all that,' pronounced his master, 'and one day you shall taste my spring chicken, roasted on a spit.'

'I will not believe it,' she said, 'chickens were never roasted in that cabin of yours, like a hermit's cell. Cooking and philosophy do not go together.'

'On the contrary, they go very well,' he said, 'but I will not roast your chicken in my cell. We will build a wood fire in the open, on the shores of the creek, and I will roast your chicken for you there. But you must eat it with your fingers. And there will be no candle-light, only the light of the fire.'

'And perhaps the night-jar you told me about will not be silent,' she said.

'Perhaps!'

He smiled at her across the table, and she had a sudden vision of the fire they would build, on the shore beside the water, and how the flames would hiss and crackle in the air, and how the good burnt smell of roasting chicken would come to their nostrils. The cooking would absorb him, even as his drawing of the heron absorbed him yesterday, and his planning of piracy would to-morrow. She noticed, for the first time, that William had left them, and rising from the table she blew the candles, and led the way into the salon.

'Smoke, if you wish,' she said, and there, on the mantelpiece before him, he recognised his jar of tobacco.

'The perfect hostess,' he said.

She sat down, but he went on standing by the mantelpiece, filling his pipe, looking about the room as he did so.

'It is very different from the winter,' he said. 'When I came then, the covers shrouded the furniture, and there were no flowers. There was something austere about the room. You have changed all that.'

'All empty houses are like sepulchres,' she said.

'Ah, yes – but I don't mean that. Navron would have remained a sepulchre, had anyone else broken the silence.'

She did not answer. She was not sure what he meant.

For a while there was silence between them, and then he said, 'What brought you to Navron, in the end?'

She played with a tassel of the cushion behind her head.

'You told me yesterday that Lady St. Columb was something of a celebrity,' she said, 'that you had heard gossip of her escapades. Perhaps I was tired of Lady St. Columb, and wanted to become somebody else.'

'In other words – you wished to escape?'

'That is what William told me you would say.'

'William has experience. He has seen me do the same sort of thing. Once there was a man called Jean-Benoit Aubéry, who had estates in Brittany, money, friends, responsibilities, and William was his servant. And William's master became weary of Jean-Benoit Aubéry, and so he turned into a pirate, and built *La Mouette*.'

'And is it really possible to become somebody else?'

'I have found it so.'

'And are you happy?'

'I am content.'

'What is the difference?'

'Between happiness and contentment? Ah, there you have me. It is not easy to put into words. Contentment is a state of mind and body when the two work in harmony, and there is no friction. The mind is at peace, and the body also. The two are sufficient to themselves. Happiness is elusive – coming perhaps once in a life-time – and approaching ecstasy.'

'Not a continuous thing, like contentment?'

'No, not a continuous thing. But there are, after all, degrees of happiness. I remember, for instance, one particular moment after I became a pirate, and I fought my first action, against one of your merchant ships. I was successful, towed my prize into port. That was a good moment, exhilarating, happy. I had achieved the thing I had set myself to do, of which I had been uncertain.'

'Yes,' she said. 'Yes – I understand that.'

'And there have been other moments too. The pleasure felt after I have made a drawing, and I look at the drawing, and it has the shape and form of what I meant. That is another degree of happiness.'

'It is easier then, for a man,' she said, 'a man is a creator, his happiness comes in the things that he achieves. What he makes with his hands, with his brains, with his talents.'

'Possibly,' he said. 'But women are not idle. Women have babies. That is a greater achievement than the making of a drawing, or the planning of an action.'

'Do you think so?'

'Of course.'

'I never considered it before.'

'You have children, have you not?'

'Yes – two.'

'And when you handled them for the first time, were you not conscious of achievement? Did you not say to yourself, "This is something I have done – myself"? And was not that near to happiness?'

She thought for a moment, and then smiled at him.

'Perhaps,' she said.

He turned away from her, and began touching the things on the mantel-piece. 'You must not forget I am a pirate,' he said; 'here you are leaving your treasures about in careless fashion. This little casket, for instance, is worth several hundred pounds.'

'Ah, but then I trust you.'

'That is unwise.'

'I throw myself upon your mercy.'

'I am known to be merciless.'

He replaced the casket, and picked up the miniature of Harry. He considered it a moment, whistling softly.

'Your husband?' he said.

'Yes.'

He made no comment, but put the miniature back into its place, and the fashion in which he did so, saying nothing of Harry, of the likeness, of the miniature itself, gave to her a curious sense of embarrassment. She felt instinctively that he thought little of Harry, considered him a dolt, and she wished suddenly that the miniature had not been there, or that Harry was in some way different.

'It was taken many years ago,' she found herself saying, as though in defence, 'before we were married.'

'Oh, yes,' he said. There was a pause, and then –

'That portrait of you,' he said, 'upstairs in your room, was that done about the same time?'

'Yes,' she said, 'at least – it was done soon after I became betrothed to Harry.'

'And you have been married – how long?'

'Six years. Henrietta is five.'

'And what decided you upon marriage?'

She stared back at him, at a loss for a moment; his question was so unexpected. And then, because he spoke so quietly, with such composure, as though he were asking why she had chosen a certain dish for dinner, caring little about the answer, she told him the truth, not realising that she had never admitted it before.

'Harry was amusing,' she said, 'and I liked his eyes.'

As she spoke it seemed to her that her voice sounded very far distant, as though it were not herself who spoke, but somebody else.

He did not answer. He had moved away from the mantelpiece, and had sat down on a chair, and was pulling out a piece of paper from the great pocket of his coat. She went on staring in front of her, brooding suddenly upon Harry, upon the past, thinking of their marriage, in London, the vast assembly of people, and how poor Harry, very youthful, scared possibly at the responsibilities before him and having little imagination, drank too much on their wedding-night, so as to appear bolder than he was, and only succeeded in seeming a very great sot and a fool. And they had journeyed about England, to meet his friends, for ever staying in other people's houses in an atmosphere strained and artificial, and she – starting Henrietta almost immediately – became irritable, fretful, entirely unlike herself, so unaccustomed to ill-health of any kind. The impossibility of riding, of walking, of doing all the things she wished to do, increased her irritation. It would have helped could she have talked to Harry, asked for his understanding, but understanding, to him, meant neither silence, nor tenderness, nor quiet, but a rather hearty boisterousness, a forced jollity, a making of noise in an endeavour to cheer her, and on top of it all great lavish caresses that helped her not at all.

She looked up suddenly, and saw that her guest was drawing her.

'Do you mind?' he said.

'No,' she said, 'of course not,' wondering what sort of drawing he would make, and she watched his hands, skilful and quick, but she could not see the paper, for it rested against his knee.

'How did William come to be your servant?' she asked.

'His mother was a Breton – you did not know that, I suppose?' he answered.

'No,' she said.

'His father was a mercenary, a soldier of fortune, who somehow or other found his way to France, and married. You must have noticed William's accent.'

'I thought it Cornish.'

'Cornishmen and Bretons are very much alike. Both are Celts. I discovered William first running bare-foot, with torn breeches, about the streets of Quimper. He was in some scrape or other, which I managed to save him from. From then he became one of the faithful. He learnt English, of course, from his father. I believe he lived in Paris for many years, before I fell in with him. I have never delved into William's life history. His past is his own.'

'And why did William decline to become a pirate?'

'Alas! For a reason most prosaic, and unromantic. William has an uneasy stomach. The channel that separates the coast of Cornwall from the coast of Brittany is too much for him.'

'And so he finds his way to Navron, which makes a most excellent hiding-place for his master?'

'Precisely.'

'And Cornish men are robbed, and Cornish women go in fear of their lives, and more than their lives, so Lord Godolphin tells me?'

'The Cornish women flatter themselves.'

'That is what I wanted to tell Lord Godolphin.'

'And why did you not?'

'Because I had not the heart to shock him.'

'Frenchmen have a reputation for gallantry which is entirely without foundation. We are shyer than you give us credit for. Here – I have finished your portrait.'

He gave her the drawing, and leant back in his chair, his hands in the pockets of his coat. Dona stared at the drawing in silence. She saw that the face that looked up at her from the torn scrap of paper belonged to the other Dona – the Dona she would not admit, even to herself. The features were unchanged, the eyes, the texture of the hair, but the expression in the eyes was the one she had seen sometimes reflected in her mirror, when she was alone. Here was someone with illusions lost, someone who looked out upon the world from a too narrow casement, finding it other than she had hoped, bitter, and a little worthless.

'It is not very flattering,' she said, at length.

'That was not my intention,' he replied.

'You have made me appear older than I am.'

'Possibly.'

'And there is something petulant about the mouth.'

'I dare say.'

'And – and a curious frown between the brows.'

'Yes.'

'I don't think I like it very much.'

'No, I feared you would not. A pity. I might have turned from piracy to portraiture.'

She gave it back to him, and she saw he was smiling.

'Women do not like to hear the truth about themselves,' she said.

'Does anyone?' he asked.

She would not continue the discussion. 'I see now why you are a successful pirate,' she told him, 'you are thorough in your work. The same quality shows itself in your drawings. You go to the heart of your subject.'

'Perhaps I was unfair,' he said. 'I caught this particular subject unawares, when a mood was reflected in her face. Now if I drew you at another time, when you were playing with your children, for example, or simply when you were giving yourself up to the delight of having escaped – the drawing would be entirely different. Then you might accuse me of flattering you.'

'Am I really as changeable as that?'

'I did not say you were changeable. It just happens that you reflect upon your face what is passing through your mind, which is exactly what an artist desires.'

'How very unfeeling of the artist.'

'How so?'

'To make a copy of emotion, at the expense of the sitter. To catch a mood, and place it on paper, and so shame the possessor of the mood.'

'Possibly. But on the other hand the owner of the mood might decide, on seeing herself reflected for the first time, to discard the mood altogether as being unworthy, and a waste of time.' As he spoke he tore the drawing across, and then again into small pieces. 'There,' he said, 'we will forget about it. And anyway it was an unpardonable thing to do. You told me yesterday that I had been trespassing upon your land. It is a fault of mine, in more ways than one. Piracy leads one into evil habits.'

He stood up, and she saw that he had it in his mind to go.

'Forgive me,' she said, 'I must have seemed querulous, and rather spoilt. The truth is – when I looked upon your drawing – I was ashamed, because for the first time someone else had seen me as I too often see myself. It was as though I had some blemish on my body and you had drawn me, naked.'

'Yes. But supposing the artist bears a similar blemish himself, only more disfiguring, need the sitter still feel ashamed?'

'You mean, there would be a bond between them?'

'Exactly.' Once more he smiled, and then he turned, and went towards the window. 'When the east wind starts blowing on this coast it continues for several days,' he said. 'My ship will be weather-bound and I can be idle, and make many drawings. Perhaps you will let me draw you again?'

'With a different expression?'

'That is for you to say. Do not forget you have signed your name in my book, and when the mood comes upon you to make your escape even more complete, the creek is accustomed to fugitives.'

'I shall not forget.'

'There are birds to watch, too, and fishes to catch, and streams to be explored. All these are methods of escape.'

'Which you have found successful?'

'Which I have found successful. Thank you for my supper. Good night.'

'Good night.'

This time the Frenchman did not touch her hand, but went out through the window, without looking back, and she watched him disappear amongst the trees, his hands thrust deep into the pockets of his coat.

Chapter Eight

The air was stifling inside the house, and because of his lady's condition Lord Godolphin had commanded that the windows should be shut, and the curtains drawn across them to screen her from the sun. The brightness of midsummer would fatigue her, the soft air might bring a greater pallor to her already languid cheeks. But lying on the sofa, backed with cushions, exchanging small civilities with her friends, the half darkened room humming with heavy chatter and the warm smell of humanity eating crumbling cake – that could tire nobody. It was both Lord Godolphin's and his lady's idea of relaxation.

'Never again,' thought Dona, 'never again will I be persuaded forth, whether for Harry's or for conscience's sake, to meet my neighbours,' and bending down, feigning an interest in a little lap-dog crouching at her gown, she gave him the damp chunk of cake forced upon her by Godolphin himself. Out of the tail of her eye she saw that her action had been observed, and horror upon horror, here was her host bearing down upon her once again, a fresh assortment in his hands, and she must smile her false, brilliant smile, and bow her thanks and place yet another dripping morsel between her reluctant lips.

'If you could only persuade Harry to forsake the pleasures of the Town,' observed Godolphin, 'we could have many of these small informal gatherings. With my wife in her present state, a large assembly would be prejudicial to her health, but a few friends, such as we have to-day, can do her nothing but good. I greatly regret that Harry is not here.' He looked about him, satisfied with his hospitality, and Dona, drooping upon her chair, counted once again the fifteen or sixteen persons in the room, who, weary of each other's company over too great a span of years, watched her with apathetic interest. The ladies observed her gown, the new long gloves she played with on her lap, and the hat with the sweeping feather that concealed her right cheek. The men stared dumbly, as though in the front seats at a playhouse, and one or two, with heavy jovial humour, questioned her about the life at Court, and the pleasures of the King, as though the very fact of her coming from London gave her full knowledge of his life and of his habits. She hated gossip for gossip's sake, and though she might have told them much, had she the mind, of the froth and frivolity from which she had escaped, the artificial painted London, the link-boys with their flares tip-toeing through the dusty cobbled streets, the swaggering gallants standing at the doors of the taverns laughing a little too loudly and singing over-much, that roystering, rather tipsy atmosphere presided over by someone with a brain he would not use, a dark roving eye and a sardonic smile, she kept silent, saying instead how much she loved the country. 'It is a great pity that Navron is so isolated,' said someone, 'you must find it wretchedly lonely after town. If only we were all a little nearer to you, we could meet more often.'

'How kind of you,' said Dona, 'Harry would greatly appreciate the thought. But, alas, the road is exceedingly bad to Navron. I had great difficulty in coming here to-day. And then, you see, I am a most devoted mother. My children absorb nearly all my time.'

She smiled upon the company, her eyes large and very innocent, and even as she spoke there came a sudden vision to her mind of the boat that would be waiting for her at Gweek, the fishing lines coiled on the bottom boards, and the man who would be idling there, with coat thrown aside, and sleeves rolled up above the elbows.

'I consider you show remarkable courage,' sighed her ladyship, 'in living there all alone, and your husband absent. I find I become uneasy if mine is away for a few hours in the day-time.'

'That is perhaps excusable, under the circumstances,' murmured Dona, quelling an insane desire to laugh, to say something monstrous, for the thought of Lady Godolphin languishing here upon her sofa, and aching for her lord, with that distressing growth upon his nose so wretchedly conspicuous, moved her to wickedness.

'You are, I trust, amply protected at Navron,' said Godolphin, turning to her, solemnly. 'There is much licence and lawlessness abroad these days. You have servants you can trust?'

'Implicitly.'

'It is as well. Had it been otherwise I should have presumed upon my old friendship with Harry, and sent you two or three of my own people.'

'I assure you it would be entirely unnecessary.'

'So you may think. Some of us believe differently.'

He looked across at his nearest neighbour, Thomas Eustick, who owned a large estate beyond Penryn – a thin-lipped man with narrow eyes – who had been watching Dona from the other side of the room. He now came forward, and with him also was Robert Penrose, from Tregony. 'Godolphin has told you, I think, how we are menaced from the sea,' he said abruptly.

'By an elusive Frenchman,' smiled Dona.

'Who may not remain elusive very much longer,' replied Eustick.

'Indeed? Have you summoned more soldiers from Bristol?'

He flushed, glancing at Godolphin in irritation.

'This time there will be no question of hired mercenaries,' he said. 'I was against that idea from the first, but as usual was overruled. No, we propose dealing with the foreigner ourselves, and I consider our methods will be effective.'

'Providing enough of us join together,' said Godolphin drily.

'And the most capable amongst us takes the lead,' said Penrose, of Tregony. There was a pause, the three men eyeing one another in suspicion. Had the atmosphere, for some reason or other, become a little strained?

'A house divided against itself will not stand,' murmured Dona.

'I beg your pardon?' said Thomas Eustick.

'Nothing. I was reminded suddenly of a line from the Scriptures. But you were talking about the pirate. One against so many. He will be caught, of course. And what is the plan of capture?'

'It is as yet in embryo, madam, and naturally enough cannot be unfolded. But I would warn you, and I rather think that is what Godolphin meant just now when he enquired about your servants, I would warn you that we suspect some of the country people in the district to be in the Frenchman's pay.'

'You astound me.'

'It is unpardonable, of course, and if our suspicions are verified they will all of them hang, as he will. The fact is we believe the Frenchman to have a hiding-place along the coast, and we believe one or two of the inhabitants must know of this, and are holding their tongues.'

'Have you not made a thorough search?'

'My dear Lady St. Columb, we are forever combing the district. But, as you must have heard, the fellow is as slippery as an eel, like all Frenchmen, and he appears to know our coast better than we do ourselves. You have, I suppose, seen nothing of a suspicious nature around Navron?'

'Nothing whatever.'

'The manor commands a view of the river, does it not?'

'A most excellent view.'

'So that you would have seen any strange craft entering or leaving the estuary?'

'Most assuredly.'

'I have no wish to alarm you, but it is possible, you know, that the Frenchman has used Helford in the past, and may yet do so again.'

'You terrify me.'

'And I must warn you that he is the type of man who would have little respect for your person.'

'You mean – he is quite unscrupulous?'

'I fear so.'

'And his men are most desperate and savage?'

'They are pirates, madam, and Frenchmen at that.'

'Then I will take the greatest possible care of my household. Are they, do you think, cannibals also? My baby son is not yet two.'

Lady Godolphin gave a little shriek of horror, and began fanning herself rapidly. Her husband clicked his tongue in annoyance.

'Calm yourself, Lucy, Lady St. Columb was jesting, of course. I would assure you, though,' he added, turning to Dona once again, 'that the matter is not a trifling one, nor to be treated with levity. I feel myself responsible for the safety of the people in the district around, and as Harry is not with you at Navron I must admit that I am concerned about you.'

Dona rose to her feet, holding out her hand. 'It is very good of you,' she said, treating him to her special smile, the one she reserved for difficult occasions. 'I shall not forget your kindness, but I assure you there is no need for anxiety. I can, if necessary, bar and bolt my house. And with neighbours such as yourselves' – as she glanced from Godolphin to Eustick and to Penrose – 'I am aware that no harm can come to me. You are all three so reliable, so stalwart, so very – if I may say so – English, in your ways.'

The three men bowed over her hand in turn, and she smiled at each of them. 'Perhaps,' she said, 'the Frenchman has left our coasts for good, and you need concern yourselves no more about him.'

'I wish we could think so,' said Eustick, 'but we flatter ourselves we are beginning to know the scoundrel. He is always most dangerous when he is most quiet. We shall hear of him again, and that before very long.'

'And,' added Penrose, 'he will strike just where we least expect him, under our very noses. But it will be the last time.'

'It will be my very special pleasure,' said Eustick slowly, 'to hang him from the tallest tree in Godolphin's park, just before sundown. And invite the company here present to attend the ceremony.'

'Sir, you are very bloodthirsty,' said Dona.

'So would you be, madam, if you had been robbed of your possessions. Pictures, silver, plate – all of considerable value.'

'But think what joy you will have replacing them.'

'I fear I consider the matter in a very different light.' He bowed and turned away, his cheek flushing once again in annoyance.

Godolphin accompanied Dona to her carriage. 'Your remark was somewhat unfortunate,' he said. 'Eustick is very near with his money.'

'I am notorious,' said Dona, 'for making unfortunate remarks.'

'No doubt in London they are understood.'

'I think not. That was one of the reasons I came away from London.'

He stared at her without understanding, and handed her into her carriage. 'Your coachman is competent?' he asked, glancing up at William, who alone, and unattended by a footman, held the reins in his hands. 'Very competent,' said Dona. 'I would trust him with my life.'

'He has an obstinate face.'

'Yes – but so amusing, and I adore his mouth.'

Godolphin stiffened, and stepped away from the door of the carriage. 'I am sending letters to town within the week,' he said coldly, 'have you any message for Harry?'

'Only that I am well, and exceedingly happy.'

'I shall take it upon myself to tell him of my anxiety concerning you.'

'Please do not bother.'

'I consider it a duty. Also Harry's presence in the neighbourhood would be of enormous assistance.'

'I cannot believe it.'

'Eustick is apt to be obstructive, and Penrose dictatorial, I am constantly having to make the peace.'

'And you see Harry in the role of peacemaker?'

'I see Harry wasting his time in London, when he should be looking after his property in Cornwall.'

'The property has looked after itself for a number of years.'

'That is beside the point. The fact of the matter is we need all the help we can get. And when Harry knows that piracy is rampant on the coast. . . .'

'I have already mentioned it to him.'

'But not with sufficient force, I am persuaded. If Harry thought for one moment that Navron House itself might be menaced, his possessions stolen, his wife threatened – he would hardly stay in town. Were I in his shoes. . . .'

'Yes, but you are not.'

'Were I in his shoes I would never have permitted you to travel west, alone. Women, without their husbands, have been known to lose their heads.'

'Only their heads?'

'I repeat, they have been known to lose their heads in a moment of crisis. You think yourself brave enough now, no doubt, but if you came face to face with a pirate I dare swear you would shiver and swoon, like the rest of your sex.'

'I would certainly shiver.'

'I could not say much in front of my wife, her nerves are very bad at the moment, but one or two ugly rumours have come to my ears, and Eustick's also.'

'What sort of rumours?'

'Women – er – distressed, and so on.'

'Distressed about what?'

'The country people are dumb, they give nothing away. But it looks to us as if some of the women in the hamlets hereabouts have suffered at the hands of these damned scoundrels.'

'Is it not rather unwise to probe into the matter?'

'Why so?'

'You may find they did not suffer at all, but on the contrary, enjoyed themselves immensely. Drive on, will you, William.' And bowing and smiling from her open carriage the Lady St. Columb waved her gloved hand to Lord Godolphin.

Down the long avenue they sped, past the peacocks on the smooth lawns, and the deer in the park, and so out on to the highway, and Dona, taking off her hat and fanning herself with it, glanced up at William's stiff back and laughed silently.

'William, I have behaved very badly.'

'So I gathered, my lady.'

'It was exceedingly hot in Lord Godolphin's house, and his lady had all the windows shut.'

'Very trying, my lady.'

'And I found none of the company particularly to my taste.'

'No, my lady.'

'And for two pins I would have said something perfectly terrible.'

'Just as well you had no pins upon you, my lady.'

'There was a man called Eustick, and another called Penrose.'

'Yes, my lady.'

'I disliked both equally.'

'Yes, my lady.'

'The fact of the matter is, William, these people are beginning to wake up. There was much talk of piracy.'

'I overheard his lordship just now, my lady.'

'Talk also of plans of capture, of banding themselves together, of hangings from the tallest tree. And they have their suspicions of the river.'

'I knew it was only a matter of time, my lady.'

'Do you think your master is aware of the danger?'

'I rather think so, my lady.'

'And yet he continues to anchor in the creek.'

'Yes, my lady.'

'He has been here nearly a month. Does he always stay as long as this?'

'No, my lady.'

'What is his usual visit?'

'Five or six days, my lady.'

'The time has gone very quickly. Possibly he does not realise he has been here so long.'

'Possibly not.'

'I am becoming quite knowledgeable about birds, William.'

'So I have noticed, my lady.'

'I am beginning to recognise the many differences in song, and the variations in flight, William.'

'Indeed, my lady.'

'Also I am quite an expert with rod and line.'

'That I have observed, my lady.'

'Your master is an excellent instructor.'

'So it would appear, my lady.'

'It is rather strange, is it not, William, that before I came to Navron I thought very little about birds, and even less of fishing?'

'It is rather strange, my lady.'

'I suppose that – that the desire to know about these things was always present, but lying dormant, if you understand what I mean.'

'I understand your meaning perfectly, my lady.'

'It is difficult for a woman to acquire knowledge of birds and of fishing alone, don't you think?'

'Almost impossible, my lady.'

'An instructor is really necessary.'

'Quite imperative, my lady.'

'But of course the instructor must be sympathetic.'

'That is important, my lady.'

'And fond of – imparting his knowledge to his pupil.'

'That goes without saying, my lady.'

'And possibly, through the pupil, the instructor's own knowledge becomes more perfect. He gains something he did not have before. In a sense, they learn from one another.'

'You have put the matter in a nutshell, my lady.'

Dear William, he was most companionable. He always understood. It was like having a confessor who never reproved or condemned.

'What story did you tell at Navron, William?'

'I said that you were staying to dine at his lordship's, and would be late, my lady.'

'And where will you stable the horses?'

'That is all arranged for. I have friends at Gweek, my lady.'

'To whom you have also spun a story?'

'Yes, my lady.'

'And where shall I change my gown?'

'I thought your ladyship would not be averse to changing behind a tree.'

'How very considerate of you, William. Have you chosen the tree?'

'I have gone so far as to mark one down, my lady.'

The road turned sharply to the left, and they were beside the river once again. The gleam of water shimmered between the trees. William pulled the horses to a standstill. He paused a moment, then put his hand to his mouth and gave a seagull's cry. It was echoed immediately from the river bank, just out of sight, and the servant turned to his mistress.

'He is waiting for you, my lady.'

Dona pulled out an old gown from behind the cushion in the carriage, and threw it over her arm. 'Which is the tree you mean, William?'

'The wide one, my lady, the oak with the spreading branches.'

'Do you think me mad, William?'

'Shall we say – not entirely sane, my lady?'

'It is rather a lovely feeling, William.'

'So I have always understood, my lady.'

'One is absurdly happy for no reason – rather like a butterfly.'

'Exactly, my lady.'

'What do you know of the habits of butterflies?'

Dona turned, and William's master stood before her, his hands busy with a line which he was knotting, and which he slipped through the eye of a hook, breaking the loose end between his teeth.

'You walk very silently,' she said.

'A habit of long practice.'

'I was merely making an observation to William.'

'About butterflies I gather. And what makes you so sure of their happiness?'

'One has only to look at them.'

'Their fashion of dancing in the sun, you mean?'

'Yes.'

'And you feel like doing the same?'

'Yes.'

'You had better change your gown then. Ladies of the manor who drink tea with Lord Godolphin know nothing of butterflies. I will wait for you in the boat. The river is alive with fish.' He turned his back on her, and went off again to the river bank, and Dona, sheltered by the spreading oak, stripped herself of her silk gown, and put on the other, laughing to herself, while her ringlets escaped from the clasp that held them, and fell forward over her face. When she was ready she gave her silk gown to William, who was standing with his face averted by his horses' heads.

'We shall go down river with the tide, William, and I will walk up to Navron from the creek.'

'Very good, my lady.'

'I shall be in the avenue shortly after ten o'clock, William.'

'Yes, my lady.'

'And you can drive me to the house as though we were just returning from Lord Godolphin's.'

'Yes, my lady.'

'What are you smiling at?'

'I was not aware, my lady, that my features were in any way relaxed.'

'You are a liar. Good-bye.'

'Good-bye, my lady.'

She lifted her old muslin gown above her ankles, tightening the sash at her waist to keep it in place, and then ran bare-foot through the trees to the boat that was waiting beneath the bank.

Chapter Nine

The Frenchman was fixing the worm on to the line, and looked up with a smile. 'You have not been long.'

'I had no mirror to delay me.'

'You understand now,' he said, 'how simple life becomes when things like mirrors are forgotten.' She stepped down into the boat beside him.

'Let me fix the worm on the hook,' she said.

He gave her the line, and taking the long paddles he pushed down stream, watching her as she sat in the bows of the boat. She frowned, concentrating on her task, and because the worm wriggled she jabbed her fingers with the hook. She swore under her breath, and glancing up, saw that he was laughing at her.

'I can't do it,' she said angrily, 'why must a woman be so useless at these things?'

'I will do it directly,' he said, 'when we are farther down stream.'

'But that is beside the point,' she said. 'I wish to do it myself. I will not be beaten.'

He did not answer, but began whistling softly to himself, and because he took his eye from her, watching a bird flying overhead, saying nothing to her, she settled once again to her task, and presently cried out in triumph, 'I have done it, look, I have done it,'·and held up her line for him to see.

'Very good,' he said, 'you are making progress,' and resting on the paddles, he let the boat drift with the tide.

Presently, when they had gone some distance, he reached for a large stone under her feet, and fastening this to a long length of rope he threw it overboard, so that they came to anchor, and they sat there together, she in the bows of the boat and he on the centre thwart, each with a fishing-line.

There was a faint ripple on the water, and down with the ebbing tide came little wisps of grass, and a fallen leaf or two. It was very still. The thin wet line between Dona's fingers pulled gently with the tide, and now and again, from impatience, she pulled it in to examine the hook, but the worm remained untouched, save for a dark ribbon of seaweed that clung to the end of the line. 'You are letting it touch the bottom,' he said. She pulled in a length or so, watching him out of the tail of her eye, and when she saw that he did not criticise her method of fishing, or intrude upon her in any way, but continued with his own fishing, quietly content, she let the length of line slip once more between her fingers, and began to consider the line of his jaw, the set of his shoulders, the shape of his hands. He had been drawing as usual, while he waited for her, she supposed, for in the stern of the boat, under some fishing tackle, was a sheet of paper, bedraggled now and wet, and a rough sketch of a flight of sanderling, rising from the mud.

She thought of the drawing he had made of her, a day or so ago, and how different it was from that first one he had done, the one he had torn in fragments, for the new drawing had caught her in a laughing mood, leaning over the rail of the ship and watching the comic Pierre Blanc sing one of his outrageous songs, and later he had nailed it up on the bulkhead of his cabin, over the fireplace, scrawling the date at the bottom of the paper.

'Why do you not tear it up, as you did the first?' she had asked.

'Because this is the mood I would capture, and remember,' he had said.

'As being more fitting to a member of the crew of *La Mouette*?'

'Perhaps,' he answered, but he would say nothing more. And here he was now, forgetful of his drawing, intent only upon this business of fishing, while only a few miles away there were men who planned his capture, his death, and even at this moment possibly the servants of Eustick, and Penrose and Godolphin were asking questions along the coast, and in the scattered hamlets of the countryside.

'What is the matter?' he said quietly, breaking in upon her thoughts. 'Do you not want to fish any more?'

'I was thinking about this afternoon,' she said.

'Yes, I know, I could see that by your face. Tell me about it.'

'You should not stay here any more. They are beginning to suspect. They were all talking about it, gloating over the possibilities of your capture.'

'That does not worry me.'

'I believe them to be serious. Eustick had a hard, obstinate look about him. He is not a pompous dunderhead like Godolphin. He means to hang you from the tallest tree in Godolphin's park.'

'Which is something of a compliment after all.'

'Now you are laughing at me. You think that, like all women, I am afire with rumours and gossip.'

'Like all women you like to dramatise events.'

'And you to ignore them.'

'What would you have me do then?'

'First I would beg you to be cautious. Eustick said that the country people know you have a hiding-place.'

'Very possibly.'

'And one day someone will betray you, and the creek will be surrounded.'

'I am quite prepared for that.'

'How are you prepared?'

'Did Eustick and Godolphin tell you how they proposed to capture me?'

'No.'

'Neither shall I tell you how I propose to evade them.'

'Do you think for one moment I should . . .'

'I think nothing – but I believe you have a fish on your line.'

'You are being deliberately provoking.'

'Not at all. If you don't want to land the fish give the line to me.'

'I do want to land it.'

She proceeded to do so, reluctantly, a little sulky, and then – feeling suddenly the tug and the pull upon the hook – she began to haul faster, the wet line falling upon her lap and down to her bare feet; and laughing at him over her shoulder she said, 'He's there, I can feel him, he's there, on the end of the hook.'

'Not quite so fast,' he said quietly, 'you may lose him. Gently now, bring him to the side of the boat.'

But she would not listen. She stood up in her excitement, letting the line slip for a moment, and then pulled harder than ever, and just as she caught the white gleam of the fish streaking to the surface it jerked the line, flashing sideways, and was gone.

Dona gave a cry of disappointment, turning to him with reproachful eyes. 'I have lost him,' she said, 'he has got away.'

He looked up at her, laughing, shaking the hair out of his eyes.

'You were too excited.'

'I can't help it. It was such a lovely feeling – that tug on the line. And I wanted to catch him so much.'

'Never mind. Perhaps you will catch another.'

'My line is all in a tangle.'

'Give it to me.'

'No – I can do it myself.'

He took up his own line once again, and she bent down in the boat, gathering the hopeless tangle of wet line into her lap. It had twisted itself into countless loops and knots, and as she strove to unwind it with her fingers it became more tangled than before. She glanced at him, frowning with vexation, and he stretched out his hand, without looking at her, and took the tangle from her. She thought he would mock her, but he said nothing, and she leant back in the bows of the boat and watched his hands as he unravelled the loops and turns of the long wet line.

The sun, away in the west, was flinging ribbons across the sky, and there were little pools of golden light upon the water. The tide was ebbing fast, gurgling past the bows of the boat.

Farther down the stream a solitary curlew paddled in the mud, and presently he rose in the air, and whistled softly, and was gone.

'When shall we build our fire?' said Dona.

'When we have caught our supper,' he answered.

'And supposing we catch no supper?'

'Then we cannot build a fire.'

She went on watching his hands, and miraculously, it seemed to her, the line became straight again, and loosely coiled, and he threw it once more over the side and gave her the end to hold.

'Thank you,' she said, her voice small, rather subdued, and looking across at him she saw that his eyes were smiling in the secret fashion she had grown to expect from him, and she knew, in some strange way, that the smile was connected with her although he said nothing, and she felt light-hearted suddenly, and curiously gay.

They continued with their fishing, while a single blackbird hidden in the woods the other side of the river sang his intermittent song, meditative and sweet.

It seemed to her, as they sat there side by side, without a word, that she had never known peace before, until this moment, that all the restless devils inside her who fought and struggled so often for release were, because of this silence and his presence, now appeased. She felt, in a sense, like someone who had fallen under a spell, under some strange enchantment, because this sensation of quietude was foreign to her, who had lived hitherto in a turmoil of sound and movement. And yet at the same time the spell awoke echoes within her that she recognised, as though she had come to a place she had known always, and deeply desired, but had lost, through her own carelessness, or through circumstances, or the blunting of her own perception.

She knew that it was this peace that she had wanted when she came away from London, and had come to Navron to find, but she knew also that she had found only part of it alone, through the woods, and the sky, and the river, it became full and complete when she was with him, as at the moment, or when he stole into her thoughts.

She would be playing with the children at Navron, or wandering about the garden, filling the vases with flowers, and he away down in his ship in the creek, and because she had knowledge of him there her mind and her body became filled with life and warmth, a bewildering sensation she had never known before.

'It is because we are both fugitives,' she thought, 'there is a bond between us,' and she remembered what he had said that first evening, when he supped at Navron, about bearing the same blemish. Suddenly she saw that he was pulling in his line, and she leaned forward in the boat, her shoulder touching his shoulder, and she called excitedly, 'Have you caught something?'

'Yes,' he said, 'do you want to pull it in?'

'It would not be fair,' she said longingly, 'he is your fish.' Laughing, he gave her the line, and she brought the struggling fish to the side of the boat, and landed it on the bottom boards, where it jumped and flapped, coiling itself in the twisted line. She knelt down and seized it between her hands, her dress all wet and muddied from the river, her ringlets falling over her face.

'He is not so big as the one I lost,' she said.

'They never are,' he answered.

'But I caught him, I brought him in all right, did I not?'

'Yes, you did very well.'

She was still kneeling, trying to take the hook out of the mouth of the fish. 'Oh, poor little thing, he is dying,' she said. 'I am hurting him, what shall I do?' she turned to him in great distress, and he came and knelt beside her, taking the fish from her hands and releasing the hook with a sudden jerk. Then he put his fingers in the mouth and bent back the head, so that the fish struggled an instant, and lay dead.

'You have killed him,' she said sadly.

'Yes,' he said, 'was that not what you wanted me to do?'

She did not answer, aware for the first time, now the excitement was over, how close he was to her, their shoulders touching, his hands beside her hands, and that he was smiling again in his silent secret way, and she was filled suddenly with a glow hitherto unknown to her, a brazen, shameless longing to be closer still, with his lips touching hers and his hands beneath her back. She looked away from him, out across the river, dumb and stricken with the new flame that had arisen within her, fearful that he might read the message in her eyes and so despise her, as Harry and Rockingham despised the women at the Swan, and began to pat her ringlets into place again, and smooth her dress, silly little mechanical gestures she felt could not deceive him, but gave her some measure of protection from her own naked self.

When she was calm again, she threw a glance at him over her shoulder, and saw that he had wound in the lines, and was taking the paddles in his hands.

'Hungry?' he said.

'Yes,' she answered, her voice a little uncertain, not quite her own.

'Then we will build our fire and cook our supper,' he said. The sun had gone now, and the shadows were beginning to creep over the water. The tide was running fast, and he pushed the boat out into the channel so that the current helped to carry them down stream. She curled herself up in the bows and sat with her legs crossed beneath her, her chin cupped in her hands.

The golden lights had gone, and the sky was paler now, mysterious and soft, while the water itself seemed darker than before. There was a smell of moss about the air, and the young green from the woods, and the bitter tang of bluebells. Once, in mid-stream, he paused, and listened, and turning her head towards the shore she heard, for the first time, a curious churring sound, low and rather harsh, fascinating in its quiet monotony.

'Night-jar,' he said, looking at her an instant, and then away again, and she knew, at that moment, that he had read the message in her eyes a little while before, and he did not despise her for it, he knew and understood, because he felt as she did, the same flame, the same longing. But because she was a woman and he a man these things would never be admitted to one another; they were both bound by a strange reserve until their moment came, which might be to-morrow, or the day after, or never – the matter was not of their own choosing.

He pushed on down stream without a word, and presently they came to the entrance of the creek, where the trees crowded to the water's edge, and edging up close inshore into the narrow channel they came to a little clearing in the woods where there had once been a quay, and he rested on his paddles and said, 'This?'

'Yes,' she answered, and he pushed the nose of the boat into the soft mud, and they climbed ashore.

He pulled the boat out of the tide, and then reached for his knife, and kneeling beside the water cleaned the fish, calling over his shoulder for Dona to build the fire.

She found some dry twigs, under the trees, and broke them across her knee, her dress torn now and hopelessly crumpled, and she thought, laughing to herself, of Lord Godolphin and his lady, and their stare of bewilderment could they see her now, no better than a travelling gypsy woman, with all a gypsy's primitive feelings too, and a traitor to her country into the bargain.

She built the sticks, one against the other. He came up from the water's edge, having cleaned the fish, and knelt beside the fire, with his flint and tinder, and slowly kindled the flame, which came in a little flash at first, and then burnt brighter. Presently the long sticks crackled and flared, and they looked across the flames and laughed at one another.

'Have you ever cooked fish, in the open?' he asked.

She shook her head, and he cleared a little place in the ashes beneath the sticks, and laid a flat stone in the centre, and placed the fish upon it. He cleaned his knife on his breeches, and then, crouching beside the fire, he waited a few minutes until the fish began to brown, when he turned it with his knife, so that the heat came to it more easily. It was darker here in the creek than it had been in the open river, and the trees threw long shadows down to the quay. There was a radiance in the deepening sky belonging only to those nights of midsummer, brief and lovely, that whisper for a moment in time and go forever. Dona watched his hands, busy with the fish, and glanced up at his face, intent upon his cooking, the brows frowning a little in concentration, and his skin reddened by the glow of the fire. The good food smell came to her nostrils and to his at the same moment, and he looked at her and smiled, saying not a word, but turned the fish once again to the crackling flame.

Then when he had judged it brown enough, he lifted it with his knife on to a leaf, the fish all sizzling and bubbling with the heat, and slicing it down the middle he pushed one half of the fish on to the edge of the leaf, giving her the knife, and taking the other half between his fingers began to eat, laughing at her as he did so. 'It is a pity,' said Dona, spearing her fish with the knife, 'that we have nothing to drink.' In answer he rose to his feet, and went down to the boat at the water's edge, coming back in a moment with a long slim bottle in his hands.

'I had forgotten,' he said, 'that you were used to supping at the Swan.'

She did not reply at once, stung momentarily by his words, and then, as he poured the wine into the glass he had brought for her, she asked, 'What do you know of my suppers at the Swan?' He licked his fingers, sticky with the fish, and poured some wine into a second glass for himself.

'The Lady St. Columb sups cheek by jowl with the ladies of the town,' he said, 'and later roysters about the streets and highways like a boy with his breeches down, returning home as the night-watchman seeks his bed.'

She held her glass between her hands, not drinking, staring down at the dark water, and into her mind suddenly came the thought that he believed her bawdy, promiscuous, like the women in the tavern, and considered that her behaviour now, sitting beside him in the open air at night, cross-legged, like a gypsy, was but another brief interlude in a series of escapades, that she had, in a similar fashion, behaved thus with countless others, with Rockingham, with all Harry's friends and acquaintances, that she was nothing but a spoilt whore, lusting after new sensations, without even a whore's excuse of poverty. She wondered why the thought that he might believe this of her should cause her such intolerable pain, and it seemed to her that the light had gone out of the evening, and all the lovely pleasure was no more. She wished suddenly she was back at Navron, at home, in her own room, with James coming in to her, staggering on fat unsteady legs, so that she could pick him up in her arms, and hold him tight, and bury her face in his smooth fat cheek and forget this new strange anguish that filled her heart, this feeling of sorrow, of lost bewilderment.

'Are you not thirsty after all?' he said, and she turned to him, her eyes tormented, 'No,' she said. 'No, I believe not,' and fell silent again, playing with the ends of her sash.

It seemed to her that the peace of their being together was broken, and a constraint had come between them. His words had hurt her, and he knew that they had hurt her, and as they stared into the fire without a word all the unspoken hidden things flamed in the air, creating a brittle atmosphere of unrest.

At last he broke the silence, his voice very low and quiet.

'In the winter,' he said, 'when I used to lie in your room at Navron, and look at your picture, I made my own pictures of you in my mind. I would see you fishing perhaps, as we did this afternoon, or watching the sea from the decks of *La Mouette*. And somehow, the pictures would not fit with the servants' gossip I had heard from time to time. The two were not in keeping.'

'How unwise of you,' she said slowly, 'to make pictures of someone you had never seen.'

'Possibly,' he said, 'but it was unwise of you to leave your portrait in your bedroom, untended and alone, when pirates such as myself made landings on the English coast.'

'You might have turned it,' she said, 'with its face to the wall – or even put another in its place, of the true Dona St. Columb, roistering at the Swan, and dressing up in the breeches of her husband's friends, and riding at midnight with a mask on her face to frighten old solitary women.'

'Was that one of your pastimes?'

'It was the last one, before I became a fugitive. I wonder you did not hear it, with the rest of the servants' gossip.'

Suddenly he laughed, and reaching to the little pile of wood behind him, he threw fresh fuel on to the fire, and the flames crackled and leapt into the air.

'It is a pity you were not born a boy,' he said, 'you would have discovered then what danger meant. Like myself, you are an outlaw at heart, and dressing up in breeches and frightening old women was the nearest thing to piracy you could imagine.'

'Yes,' she said, 'but you – when you have captured your prize or made your landing – sail away with a sense of achievement, whereas I, in my pitiful little attempt at piracy, was filled with self-hatred, and a feeling of degradation.'

'You are a woman,' he said, 'and you do not care for killing fishes either.'

This time, looking across the fire, she saw that he was smiling at her in a mocking way, and it seemed as though the constraint between them vanished, they were themselves again, and she could lean back on her elbow and relax.

'When I was a lad,' he said, 'I used to play at soldiers, and fight for my king. And then, in a thunderstorm, when the lightning came and the thunder clapped, I would hide my head in my mother's lap and put my fingers in my ears. Also, to make my soldiering more realistic, I would paint my hands red and pretend to be wounded – but when I saw blood for the first time on a dog that was dying, I ran away and was sick.'

'That was like me,' she said, 'that was how I felt, after my masquerade.'

'Yes,' he said, 'that is why I told you.'

'And now,' she said, 'you don't mind blood any more, you are a pirate, and fighting is your life – robbing, and killing, and hurting. All the things you pretended to do and were afraid to do – now you don't mind them any longer.'

'On the contrary,' he said, 'I am often very frightened.'

'Yes,' she said, 'but not in the same way. Not frightened of yourself. Not frightened of being afraid.'

'No,' he said. 'No, that has gone for ever. That went when I became a pirate.'

The long twigs in the fire began to crumple and fall, and to break into fragments. The flames burnt low, and the ashes were white.

'To-morrow,' he said, 'I must begin to plan again.'

She glanced across at him, but the firelight no longer shone upon him, and his face was in shadow.

'You mean – you must go away?' she said.

'I have been idle too long,' he answered, 'the fault lies in the creek. I have allowed it to take a hold on me. No, your friends Eustick and Godolphin shall have a run for their money. I shall see if I can bring them into the open.'

'You are going to do something dangerous?'

'Of course.'

'Will you make another landing along the coast?'

'Very probably.'

'And risk capture, and possibly death?'

'Yes.'

'Why – and for what reason?'

'Because I want the satisfaction of proving to myself that my brain is better than theirs.'

'But that is a ridiculous reason.'

'It is my reason, nevertheless.'

'It is an egotistical thing to say. A sublime form of conceit.'

'I know that.'

'It would be wiser to sail back to Brittany.'

'Far wiser.'

'And you will be leading your men into something very desperate.'

'They will not mind.'

'And *La Mouette* may be wrecked, instead of lying peacefully at anchor in a port across the channel.'

'*La Mouette* was not built to lie peacefully in a port.'

They looked at each other across the ashes, and his eyes held her for a long instant, with a light in them like the flame that had spent itself in the fire, and at last he stretched himself, and yawned, and said: 'It is a pity indeed you are not a boy, you could have come with me.'

'Why must I be a boy to do that?'

'Because women who are afraid of killing fishes are too delicate and precious for pirate ships.'

She watched him a moment, biting the end of her finger, and then she said, 'Do you really believe that?'

'Naturally.'

'Will you let me come this once, to prove to you that you are wrong?'

'You would be sea-sick,' he said.

'No.'

'You would be cold, and uncomfortable, and frightened.'

'No.'

'You would beg me to put you ashore just as my plans were about to work successfully.'

'No.'

She stared at him, antagonistic, angry, and he rose to his feet suddenly, and laughed, kicking the last embers of the fire, so that the glow was gone, and the night became dark.

'How much,' she said, 'will you wager that I am sick, and cold, and frightened?'

'It depends,' he said, 'what we have to offer each other.'

'My ear-rings,' she said, 'you can have my ruby ear-rings. The ones I wore when you supped with me at Navron.'

'Yes,' he said, 'they would be a prize indeed. There would be little excuse for piracy if I possessed them. And what will you demand of me, should you win your wager?'

'Wait,' she said, 'let me think,' and standing silently a moment beside him, looking down into the water, she said, seized with amusement, with devilry: 'A lock from Godolphin's wig.'

'You shall have the wig itself,' he said.

'Very good,' she said, turning, and making her way down to the boat, 'then we need discuss the matter no further. It is all arranged. When do we sail?'

'When I have made my plans.'

'And you start work to-morrow?'

'I start work to-morrow.'

'I will take care not to disturb you. I too must lay my plans. I think I shall have to become indisposed, and take to my bed, and my malady will be of a feverish sort, so that the nurse and the children are denied my room. Only William will attend me. And each day dear faithful William will bear food and drink to the patient who – will not be there.'

'You have an ingenious mind.'

She stepped into the boat, and seizing the paddles he rowed silently up the creek, until the hull of the pirate ship loomed before them in the soft grey light. A voice hailed them from the ship, and he answered in Breton, and passing on brought the boat to the landing place at the head of the creek.

They walked up through the woods without a word, and as they came to the gardens of the house, the clock in the courtyard struck the half-hour. Down the avenue William would be waiting with the carriage, so that she could drive up to the house as she had planned.

'I trust you enjoyed your dinner with Lord Godolphin?' said the Frenchman.

'Very much so,' she answered.

'And the fish was not too indifferently cooked?'

'The fish was delicious.'

'You will lose your appetite when you go to sea.'

'On the contrary, the sea air will make me ravenous.'

'I shall have to sail with the wind and the tide, you realise that? It will mean leaving before dawn.'

'The best time of the day.'

'I may have to send for you suddenly – without warning.'

'I shall be ready.'

They walked on through the trees, and coming to the avenue, saw the carriage waiting, and William standing beside the horses.

'I shall leave you now,' he said, and then stood for a moment under the shadow of the trees, looking down at her.

'So you will really come?'

'Yes,' she said.

They smiled at one another, aware suddenly of a new intensity of feeling between them, a new excitement, as though the future, which was still unknown to them both, held a secret and a promise. Then the Frenchman turned, and went away through the woods, while Dona came out upon the avenue, under the tall beech trees, that stood gaunt and naked in the summer night, the branches stirring softly, like a whisper of things to come.

Chapter Ten

It was William who awoke her, William shaking her arm and whispering in her ear. 'Forgive me, my lady, but Monsieur has just sent word, the ship sails within the hour.' Dona sat up in bed at once, all wish for sleep vanishing with his words, and 'Thank you, William,' she said, 'I shall be ready in twenty minutes' time. What hour is it?'

'A quarter to four, my lady.'

He left the room, and Dona, pulling aside the curtains, saw that it was yet dark, the white dawn had not broken. She began to dress hurriedly, her heart beating with excitement and her hands unnaturally clumsy, feeling all the while like a naughty child proceeding to a forbidden venture. It was five days since she had supped with the Frenchman in the creek, and she had not seen him since. Instinct had told her that when he worked he would be alone, and she had let the days go by without walking through the woods to the river, without sending messages even by William, for she knew that when he had laid his plans he would send for her. The wager was not a momentary thing of folly, broached on a summer's night and forgotten before morning, it was a pact by which he would abide, a testing of her strength, a challenge to her courage. Sometimes she thought of Harry, continuing with his life in London, his riding, his gaming, the visits to the taverns, the play-houses, the card-parties with Rockingham, and the images she conjured seemed to her those of another world, a world which concerned her not at all. It belonged, in its strange fashion, to a past that was dead and gone, while Harry himself had become a kind of ghost, a phantom figure walking in another time.

The other Dona was dead too, and this woman who had taken her place was someone who lived with greater intensity, with greater depth, bringing to every thought and every action a new richness of feeling, and an appreciation, half sensuous in its quality, of all the little things that came to make her day.

The summer was a joy and a glory in itself, the bright mornings picking flowers with the children, and wandering with them in the fields and the woods, and the long afternoons, lazy and complete, when she would lie on her back under the trees, aware of the scent of whin, of broom, of bluebells. Even the simple things, the basic acts of eating, drinking, sleeping, had become, since she had been at Navron, a source of pleasure, of lazy still enjoyment.

No, the Dona of London had gone for ever, the wife who lay beside her husband in that great canopied bed in their house in St. James's Street, with the two spaniels scratching in their baskets on the floor, the window opened to the stuffy laden air and the harsh street cries of chair-menders and apprentice boys – that Dona belonged to another existence.

The clock in the courtyard struck four, and the new Dona, in an old gown long laid aside to be bestowed upon a cottager, with a shawl about her shoulders, and a bundle in her hands, crept down the stairway to the dining hall, where William awaited her, a taper in his hand.

'Pierre Blanc is outside, in the woods, my lady.'

'Yes, William.'

'I will supervise the house in your absence, my lady, and see that Prue does not neglect the children.'

'I have every confidence in you, William.'

'My intention is to announce to the household this morning that your ladyship is indisposed – a trifle feverish, and that for fear of infection you would prefer that the children did not come to your room, or the maidservants, and that you have bidden me wait upon you myself.'

'Excellent, William. And your face, so solemn, will be exactly right for the occasion. You are, if I may so so, a born deceiver.'

'Women have occasionally informed me so, my lady.'

'I believe you to be heartless, William, after all. Are you sure I can trust you all alone amongst a pack of scatterbrained females?'

'I will be a father to them, my lady.'

'You may reprimand Prue if you wish, she is inclined to be idle.'

'I will do so.'

'And frown upon Miss Henrietta if she talks too much.'

'Yes, my lady.'

'And should Master James very much desire a second helping of strawberries – '

'I am to give them to him, my lady.'

'Yes, William. But not when Prue is looking . . . afterwards in the pantry, by yourself.'

'I understand the situation perfectly, my lady.'

'Now I must go. Do you wish you were coming with me?'

'Unfortunately, my lady, I possess an interior that does not take kindly to the motion of a ship upon the water. Your ladyship follows my meaning?'

'In other words, William, you are horridly sick.'

'Your ladyship has a happy turn of phrase. In fact, since we are discussing the matter I am taking the liberty to suggest, my lady, that you should take with you this little box of pills, which I have found invaluable in the past, and which may be of help to you should some unhappy sensation come upon you.'

'How very kind of you, William. Give them to me, and I will put them in my bundle. I have a wager with your master that I shall not succumb. Do you think I shall win?'

'It's depends upon what your ladyship is alluding to.'

'That I shall not succumb to the motion of the ship, of course. What did you think I meant?'

'Forgive me, my lady. My mind, for the moment, had strayed to other things. Yes, I think you will win that wager.'

'It is the only wager we have, William.'

'Indeed, my lady.'

'You sound doubtful.'

'When two people make a voyage, my lady, and of one of them a man like my master, and the other a woman like my mistress, the situation strikes me as being pregnant with possibilities.'

'William, you are very presumptuous.'

'I am sorry, my lady.'

'And – French in your ideas.'

'You must blame my mother, my lady.'

'You are forgetting that I have been married to Sir Harry for six years, and am the mother of two children, and that next month I shall be thirty.'

'On the contrary, my lady, it was these three things that I was most remembering.'

'Then I am inexpressibly shocked at you. Open the door at once, and let me into the garden.'

'Yes, my lady.'

He pulled back the shutters, and threw aside the long heavy curtains. Something fluttered against the window, seeking an outlet, and as William flung open the door a butterfly, that had become imprisoned in the folds of the curtains, winged its way into the air.

'Another fugitive seeking escape, my lady.'

'Yes, William.' She smiled at him an instant, and standing upon the threshold sniffed the cool morning air, and looking up saw the first pale streak of the day creep into the sky. 'Goodbye, William.'

'Au revoir, my lady.'

She went across the grass, clutching her bundle, her shawl over her head, and looking back once saw the grey outline of the house, solid and safe, and sleeping, with William standing sentinel by the window. Waving her hand to him in farewell she followed Pierre Blanc, with his merry eyes and his dark monkey face and his ear-rings, down through the woods to the pirate ship in the creek.

Somehow she had expected bustle and noise, the confusion of departure, but when they came alongside *La Mouette* there was the usual silence. It was only when she had climbed the ladder to the deck and looked about her that she realised that the ship was ready for sea, the decks were clear, the men standing at their appointed places.

One of the men came forward and bowed, bending his head low.

'Monsieur wishes you to go to the quarter-deck.'

She climbed the ladder to the high poop deck, and as she did so she heard the rattle of the cable in the hawser, the grind of the capstan, and the stamping of feet. Pierre Blanc, the songmaker, began his chant, and the voices of the men, low and soft, rose in the air, so that she turned, leaning over the rail to watch them. Their steady treading upon the deck, the creak of the capstan, and the monotony of their chant made a kind of poetry in the air, a lovely thing of rhythm, all seeming part of the fresh morning and part of the adventure.

Suddenly she heard an order called out behind her, clear and decisive, and for the first time she saw the Frenchman, standing beside the helmsman at the wheel, his face tense and alert, his hands behind his back. This was a different being from the companion of the river who had sat beside her in the little boat and mended her line, and later built a wood fire on the quay and cooked the fish, his sleeves rolled above his elbows, his hair falling into his eyes.

She felt an intruder, a silly woman amongst a lot of men who had work to do, and without a word she went and stood at a distance, against the rail, where she could not bother him, and he continued with his orders, glancing aloft, at the sky, at the water, at the banks of the river.

Slowly the ship gathered way, and the wind of the morning, coming across the hills, filled the great sails. She crept down the creek like a ghost upon the still water, now and again almost brushing the trees where the channel ran inshore, and all the while he stood beside the helmsman, giving the course, watching the curving banks of the creek. The wide parent river opened up before them, and now the wind came full and true from the west, sending a ripple on the surface, and as *La Mouette* met the strength of it she heeled slightly, her decks aslant, and a little whipping spray came over the bulwark. The dawn was breaking in the east, and the sky had a dull haze about it and a glow that promised fine weather. There was a salty tang in the air, a freshness that came from the open sea beyond the estuary, and as the ship entered the main channel of the river the sea-gulls rose in the air and followed them.

The men had ceased their chanting, and now stood, looking towards the sea, an air of expectancy about them, as though they were men who had idled and lazed too long and were suddenly thirsty, suddenly aflame. Once again the spray rose from the top of a high-crested sea, as the ship crossed the bar at the mouth of the estuary, and Dona, smiling, tasted it on her lips, and looking up, saw that the Frenchman had left the helmsman and was standing beside her, and the spray must have caught him too, for there was salt upon his lips and his hair was wet.

'Do you like it?' he said, and she nodded, laughing up at him, so that he smiled an instant, looking towards the sea. As he did so she was filled with a great triumph and a sudden ecstasy, for she knew then that he was hers, and she loved him, and that it was something she had known from the very beginning, from the first moment when she had walked into his cabin and found him sitting at the table drawing the heron. Or before that even, when she had seen the ship on the horizon stealing in towards the land, she had known then that this thing was to happen, that nothing could prevent it; she was part of his body and part of his mind, they belonged to each other, both wanderers, both fugitives, cast in the same mould.

Chapter Eleven

It was about seven o'clock in the evening, and Dona, coming up on deck, found that the ship had altered course again, and was now standing in once more towards the coast.

The land was a blur as yet upon the horizon, no clearer than a wisp of cloud. All day they had remained at sea, and in mid-channel, with never a sight of another vessel, while a spanking breeze had held for the full twelve hours, causing *La Mouette* to jump and dance like a live thing. Dona understood that the plan was to stay out of sight of land until dusk, and when evening came to creep inshore under cover of darkness. The day therefore had been little more than a filling up of time, with the added chance, of course, of meeting with some merchant vessel carrying cargo up-channel, which might offer itself for plunder, but such a ship had not been encountered, and the crew, enlivened by the long day at sea, found their appetites whipped now for the adventure that lay before them, and the unknown hazard of the night. One and all seemed possessed by a sense of excitement, a spirit of devilry, they were like boys setting forth upon some foolhardy venture, and Dona, leaning over the rail of the poop deck to watch them, would hear them laugh and sing, cracking jokes with one another, and now and again glancing up in her direction, throwing her a look, a smile, all with a conscious air of gallantry, intensely aware of the presence on board of a woman, who had never sailed with them before.

Even the day was infectious, the hot sun, the fresh westerly breeze, the blue water, and Dona had a ridiculous longing to be a man amongst them, to handle ropes and blocks, to climb aloft to the tall raking spars and trim the sails, to handle the spokes of the great wheel. Now and again the spray broke on the deck, splashing her hands, soaking her gown, but she did not care, the sun would soon dry her clothes, and she found a little patch of dry deck to leeward of the wheel where she sat cross-legged like a gypsy, her shawl tucked into her sash, and the wind playing havoc with her hair. By noon, she was prodigiously hungry, and there came to her, from the bows of the ship, the smell of hot burnt bread and bitter black coffee, and presently she saw Pierre Blanc climb the ladder to the poop, bearing in his hands a tray.

She took it from him, almost ashamed of her eagerness, and he, winking at her with an absurd familiarity which made her laugh, rolled his eyes to heaven and rubbed his stomach.

'Monsieur will join you directly,' he said, smiling, like an accomplice, and she thought how like William they all were in their linking of two together, and how they accepted it as natural, light-hearted and lovely.

She fell upon the loaf of bread like a creature ravenous for food, cutting a chunk off the black crust, and there was butter too, and cheese, and the heart of a lettuce. Presently she heard a step behind her and glancing up she saw the captain of *La Mouette* looking down upon her. He sat by her side and reached for the loaf of bread.

'The ship can take care of herself,' he said, 'and anyway this is her weather, she would keep to her course all day, with a finger to the wheel now and again. Give me some coffee.'

She poured out the steaming brew into two cups, and they drank greedily, watching each other over the rims.

'What do you think of my ship?' he asked.

'I think she is bewitched, and is not a ship at all, for I feel as though I had never been alive before.'

'That is the effect she first had upon me, when I turned to piracy. What is the cheese like?'

'The cheese is also enchanted.'

'And you do not feel sick?'

'I have not felt better in my life.'

'Eat all you can now, because to-night there will be little time for food. Do you want another crust of bread?'

'Please.'

'This wind will hold all day, but this evening it will fall light, and we shall have to creep along the coast, taking full advantage of the tide. Are you happy?'

'Yes . . . Why do you ask?'

'Because I am happy too. Give me some more coffee.'

'The men are very gay to-day,' she said, reaching for the jug, 'is it because of tonight, or because they are at sea again?'

'A mixture of both. And they are gay too, because of you.'

'Why should I make any difference?'

'You are an added stimulation. They will work all the better to-night because of you.'

'Why did you not have a woman on board before?'

He smiled, his mouth full of bread and cheese, but he did not answer.

'I forgot to tell you,' she said, 'what Godolphin said the other day.'

'And what did he say?'

'He told me that there were ugly rumours about the countryside, because of the men belonging to your ship. He said that he had heard cases of women in distress.'

'In distress about what?'

'The very thing I asked him. And he replied, to my choking delight, that he feared some of the country-women had suffered at the hands of your damned scoundrels.'

'I doubt if they suffered.'

'So do I.'

He went on munching bread and cheese, glancing aloft now and again at the trim of the sails.

'My fellows never force their attentions upon your women,' he said, 'the trouble generally is that your women won't leave them alone. They creep out of their cottages, and stray upon the hills, if they think *La Mouette* is at anchor near their shores. Even our faithful William has trouble that way, I understand.'

'William is very – Gallic.'

'So am I, so are we all, but pursuit can sometimes be embarrassing.'

'You forget,' she said, 'that the country-women find their husbands very dull.'

'They should teach their husbands better manners.'

'The English yokel is not at his best when he makes love.'

'So I have heard. But surely he can improve, upon instruction.'

'How can a woman instruct her husband in the things she does not know herself, in which she has had no tuition?'

'Surely she has instinct?'

'Instinct is not always enough.'

'Then I am very sorry for your country-women.'

He leant on his elbow, feeling in the pocket of his long coat for a pipe, and she watched him fill the bowl with the dark harsh tobacco that had lain once in the jar in her bedroom, and in a minute or two he began to smoke, holding the bowl in his hand.

'I told you once before,' he observed, his eyes aloft at his spars, 'that Frenchmen have a reputation for gallantry that is not merited. We cannot all be brilliant our side of the channel, while the blunderers remain on yours.'

'Perhaps there is something in our English climate that is chilling to the imagination?'

'Climate has nothing to do with it, nor racial differences. A man, or a woman for that matter, is either born with a natural understanding of these things or he is not.'

'And supposing, in marriage for example, one partner has the understanding and the other has not?'

'Then the marriage is doubtless very monotonous, which I believe most marriages to be.' A wisp of smoke blew across her face, and looking up she saw that he was laughing at her.

'Why are you laughing?' she said.

'Because your face was so serious, as though you were considering writing a treatise on incompatibility.'

'Perhaps I may do so, in my old age.'

'The Lady St. Columb must write with knowledge of her subject, that is essential to all treaties.'

'Possibly I have that knowledge.'

'Possibly you have. But to make the treatise complete you must add a final word on compatibility. It does happen, you know, from time to time, that a man finds a woman who is the answer to all his more searching dreams. And the two have understanding of each other, from the lightest moment to the darkest mood.'

'But it does not happen very often?'

'No, not very often.'

'Then my treatise will have to remain incomplete.'

'Which will be unfortunate for your readers, but even more unfortunate for yourself.'

'Ah, but instead of a word on – compatibility, as you phrase it, I could write a page or two on motherhood. I am an excellent mother.'

'Are you?'

'Yes. Ask William. He knows all about it.'

'If you are so excellent a mother, what are you doing on the deck of *La Mouette* with your legs tucked up under you and your hair blowing about your face, discussing the intimacies of marriage with a pirate?'

This time it was Dona who laughed, and putting her hands to her hair she tried to arrange the disordered ringlets, tying them behind her ears with a ribbon from her bodice.

'Do you know what Lady St. Columb is doing now?' she asked.

'I should love to know.'

'She is lying in bed with a feverish headache and a chill on the stomach, and she will receive no one in her room except William, her faithful servant, who now and again brings her grapes to soothe her fever.'

'I am sorry for her ladyship, especially if she browses on incompatibility as she lies there.'

'She does no such thing, she is far too level-headed.'

'If Lady St. Columb is level-headed, why did she masquerade as a highwayman in London, and dress herself in breeches?'

'Because she was angry.'

'Why was she angry?'

'Because she had not made a success of her life.'

'And finding she had not made a success, she tried to escape?'

'Yes.'

'And if Lady St. Columb tosses on a bed of fever now, regretting her past, who is this woman sitting on the deck beside me?'

'She is a cabin-boy, the most insignificant member of your crew.'

'The cabin-boy has a monstrous appetite, he has eaten up all the cheese, and three-quarters of the loaf.'

'I am sorry. I thought you had finished.'

'So I have.'

He smiled at her, and she looked away, lest he should read her eyes and think her wanton, which she knew herself to be, and did not care. Then, emptying his pipe on the deck, he said: 'Would you like to sail the ship?'

She looked at him once again, her eyes dancing.

'May I? Will she not sink?'

He laughed and rose to his feet, pulling her up beside him, and they went together to the great wheel, where he said a word to the helmsman.

'What do I do?' asked Dona.

'You hold the spokes in your two hands – thus. You keep the ship steady on her course – thus. Do not let her come up too much, or you will catch the big foresail aback. Do you feel the wind on the back of your head?'

'Yes.'

'Keep it there then, and do not let it come forward of your right cheek.'

Dona stood by the wheel, with the spokes in her hands, and after a moment she felt the lifting of the ship, she sensed the movement of the lively hull, and the surge of the vessel as she swept over the long seas. The wind whistled in the rigging and the spars, and there was a sound of humming, too, in the narrow triangular sails above her head, while the great square foresail pulled and strained upon its ropes like a live thing.

Down in the waist of the ship the men had perceived the change of helmsman, and nudging one another, and pointing, they laughed up at her, calling to one another in the Breton patois she could not understand, while their captain stood beside her, his hands deep in the pockets of his long coat, his lips framed in a whistle, his eyes searching the seas ahead.

'So there is one thing,' he said at last, 'that my cabin-boy can do by instinct.'

'What is it?' she asked, her hair blowing over her face.

'He can sail a ship.'

And laughing, he walked away, leaving her alone with *La Mouette*.

For an hour Dona stood her trick at the wheel, as happy, she thought to herself, as James would be with a new toy, and finally, her arms tiring, she looked over her shoulders to the helmsman she had relieved, who stood by the wheel watching her with a grin on his face, and coming forward he took the wheel from her again, and she went below to the master's cabin and lay down upon his bunk and slept.

Once, opening an eye, she saw him come in and lean over the charts on the table, jotting calculations on a piece of paper, and then she must have fallen asleep again, for when she woke the cabin was empty, and rising and stretching herself she went on deck, aware, with a certain sense of shame, that she was hungry again.

It was seven then, and the ship was drawing near the coast with the Frenchman himself at the wheel. She said nothing, but went and stood by him, watching the blur of the coast on the horizon.

Presently he called out an order to his men, and they began to climb the rigging, little lithe figures, hand over hand, like monkeys, and then Dona saw the great square topsail sag and fall into folds as they furled it upon the yard.

'When a ship comes in sight of land,' he said to her, 'the topsail is the first thing that shows to a landsman ashore. It is still two hours to dusk and we do not wish to be seen.'

She looked towards the distant coast, her heart beating with a strange excitement, and she was seized, even as he and his men were seized, with the spirit of superb adventure.

'I believe you are going to do something very mad and very foolish,' she said.

'You told me you wanted Godolphin's wig,' he answered.

She watched him out of the tail of her eye, intrigued by his coolness, his quiet steady voice, just the same as it was when he went with her fishing on the river. 'What is going to happen?' she said. 'What are you going to do?'

He did not answer immediately. He called a fresh order to his men, and another sail was furled.

'Do you know Philip Rashleigh?' he said after a while.

'I have heard Harry speak of him.'

'He married Godolphin's sister – but that is by-the-way. Philip Rashleigh is expecting a ship from the Indies, a fact which came to my ears too late, otherwise I should have taken steps to meet her. As it is, I presume her to have arrived at her destination within the last two days. My intention is to seize her, as she lies at anchor, put a prize crew on board, and have them sail her to the opposite coast.'

'But supposing her men outnumbered yours?'

'That is one of the risks I take continuously. The essential thing is the element of surprise, which has never failed me yet.'

He looked down at her, amused by her frown of perplexity, and her shrug of the shoulder, as though she considered him crazy indeed.

'What do you suppose I do,' he said, 'when I shut myself in my cabin and make my plans? Do I stake everything on a turn of luck? My men are not idle, you know, when I seek relaxation in the creek. Some of them move about the country, as Godolphin told you, but not with the intention of causing women to be distressed. This distress is a minor detail.'

'Do they speak English?'

'Of course. That is why I choose them for this particular work.'

'You are exceedingly thorough,' she said.

'I dislike inefficiency,' he countered.

Little by little the line of the coast became distinct, and they were entering a great sweeping bay. Away to the west she could see white stretches of sand, turning to shadowed grey now in the gathering dusk. The ship was heading north, sailing towards a dark headland, and as yet there seemed to be no creek or inlet where a vessel could lie at anchor.

'You don't know where we are going?' he asked.

'No,' she answered.

He smiled, saying nothing, and began to whistle softly under his breath, watching her as he did so, so that at last she looked away, knowing that her eyes betrayed her, and his also; they were speaking to each other without words. She looked out over the smooth sea towards the land, the smell of it came to her with the evening breeze, warm cliff grass, and moss, and trees, hot sand where the sun had shone all day, and she knew that this was happiness, this was living as she had always wished to live. Soon there would be danger, and excitement, and reality perhaps of fighting, and through it all and afterwards they would be together, making their own world where nothing mattered but the things they could give to one another, the loveliness, the silence, and the peace. And then, stretching her arms above her head and smiling, and glancing back to him over her shoulder she said to him, 'Where are we bound then?'

'We are bound for Fowey Haven,' he told her.

Chapter Twelve

The night was dark, and very still. What breeze there was came from the north, but here, under the lee of the headland, there was none of it. Only a sudden whistle in the rigging now and again and a ripple across the face of the black water told that a mile or two offshore the breeze still held. *La Mouette* lay at anchor on the fringe of a little bay, and close at hand – so close that you could toss a pebble on to the rocks – rose the great cliffs, shadowy and indistinct in the darkness. The ship had come stealthily to her appointed place, no voices were raised, no commands given as she bore up into the wind to drop anchor, and the cable that dropped through the padded hawser gave a hollow muffled sound. For a moment or so the colony of gulls, nesting in hundreds in the cliffs above, became restive and disturbed, and their uneasy cries echoed against the cliff face and travelled across the water, and then, because there was no further movement, they settled again, and the silence was unbroken. Dona stood against the rail on the poop deck watching the headland, and it seemed to her that there was something eerie in the stillness, something strange, as though they had come unwittingly to a land asleep, whose dwellers lay under a spell, and these gulls that had risen at their approach were sentinels, placed there to give warning. She remembered then, that this country and these cliffs which were another part of her own coast must be for her, this night at any rate, a hostile place. She had come to enemy territory, and the townsfolk of Fowey Haven, who at this moment were sleeping in their beds, were alien too.

The crew of *La Mouette* were gathered in the waist of the ship, she could see them standing shoulder to shoulder, motionless and silent, and for the first time since she had started on the adventure she was aware of a tiny prick of misgiving, a feminine chill of fear. She was Dona St. Columb, wife of an English landowner and baronet, and because of impulsive madness she had thrown in her lot with a pack of Bretons, of whom she knew nothing but that they were pirates and outlaws, unscrupulous and dangerous, led by a man who had never told her anything of himself, whom she loved ridiculously without rhyme or reason, a thing which – if she stayed to consider it in cold blood – would make her hot with shame. It might be that the plan would fail, that he and his men would be captured, and she with them, and the whole band of them would be brought ignominiously to justice, and then it would not be long before her identity would be established, Harry brought hot-foot from London. She could see in a flash the whole story blazed over the country, the horror and the scandal it would cause. A sordid, tarnished air would cling upon it, there would be smutty laughter in London amongst Harry's friends, and Harry himself would probably blow his brains out, and the children be orphaned, forbidden to speak her name, their mother who had run away after a French pirate like a kitchen-maid after a groom. The thoughts chased themselves round her head, as she gazed down at the silent crew of *La Mouette*, seeing, in her mind, her comfortable bed at Navron, the peaceful garden, the safety and normality of life with the children. And then, looking up, she saw that the Frenchman was standing beside her, and she wondered how much he could read in her face.

'Come below,' he said quietly, and she followed him, feeling subdued suddenly like a pupil who was to receive chastisement from his master, and she wondered how she would answer him should he chide her for her fear. It was dark in the cabin, two candles gave a feeble glow, and he sat down on the edge of the table considering her, while she stood in front of him, her hands behind her back.

'You have remembered that you are Dona St. Columb,' he said.

'Yes,' she answered.

'And you have been wishing, up there on the deck, that you were safe home again, and had never set eyes on *La Mouette*.'

There was no reply to this, the first part of his sentence might be true, but the last could never be. There was silence between them for a moment, and she wondered if all women, when in love, were torn between two impulses, a longing to throw modesty and reserve to the winds and confess everything, and an equal determination to conceal the love forever, to be cool, aloof, utterly detached, to die rather than admit a thing so personal, so intimate.

She wished she were somewhere else, whistling carelessly, hands stuck into breeches pockets, discussing with the captain of the ship the schemes and possibilities of the coming night, or that he was different, another personality, someone for whom she felt no concern, instead of being the one man in the world she loved and wanted.

And there was a flame of anger in her suddenly, that she, who had laughed at love and scorned the sentimental, should be brought, in so few weeks, to such shaming degradation, to such despicable weakness. He got up from the table and opened the locker in the bulkhead, and brought out a bottle and two glasses.

'It is always unwise,' he said, 'to set forth upon an adventure with a cold heart and an empty stomach, that is, if one is untrained to adventure.' He poured the wine into a glass, leaving the other empty, and gave the full one to her.

'I shall drink afterwards,' he said, 'when we return.'

She noticed, for the first time, that there was a tray on the sideboard by the door covered with a napkin, and he went now and brought it to the table. There was cold meat, and bread upon it, and a slice of cheese. 'This is for you,' he said, 'eat it quickly, for time is getting short.' He turned his back on her, busying himself with a chart on the side table, and she began to eat and drink, despising herself already for the reluctance that had come upon her on the deck, and when she had eaten some of the meat, and cut herself a slice of bread and cheese, and had finished the glass of wine he had poured for her, she felt that the doubts and fears would not return, they had been, after all, the outcome of chilled feet and an empty stomach, and he had realised this from the beginning, understanding her mood in his strange incalculable way.

She pushed back her chair, and he turned, hearing the sound, and he was smiling at her, and she laughed at him in return, flushing guiltily, like a spoilt child.

'That is better, is it not?' he said.

'Yes,' she answered, 'how did you know?'

'Because the master of the ship makes it his business to know these things,' he said, 'and a cabin boy must be broken in to piracy rather more gently than the rest of my crew. And now to business.' He picked up the chart he had been studying and she saw that it was a plan of Fowey Haven, and he placed it before her on the table.

'The main anchorage is there, in deep water, opposite the town,' he said, putting his finger on the plan, 'and Rashleigh's vessel will be lying about here, where his vessels always lie, moored to a buoy at the entrance of this creek.'

There was a cross in red upon the plan to indicate the buoy.

'I am leaving part of the crew on board *La Mouette*,' he said, 'and if you wish to, you know, you can stay here with them.'

'No,' she said, 'a quarter of an hour ago I should have said yes, but not now, not any more.'

'Are you certain about that?'

'I have never been more certain about anything in my life.'

He looked down at her in the flickering candle-light, and she felt gay suddenly, and absurdly light-hearted, as though nothing mattered, nothing at all, and even if they were caught and brought to justice and both hanged from the tallest tree in Godolphin's park, it would be worth it, for first there would be this adventure they would have together.

'So Lady St. Columb has returned to her sick-bed?' he said.

'Yes,' said Dona, and she looked away from him, down to the plan of Fowey Haven.

'You will remark,' he said, 'there is a fort at the entrance of the haven, which is manned, and there are two castles, one on either side of the channel, but these will not be guarded. In spite of the dark night it would be unwise to attempt the passage by boat. Although I have a fair knowledge of your Cornishman by now, and he is a great fellow for sleeping, I cannot guarantee that every man within the fort will have his eyes shut for my benefit. So there is nothing for it but to go overland.'

He paused, and fell to whistling under his breath, considering the plan as he did so. 'This is where we are lying,' he said, pointing to a small bay a mile or so to the eastward of the haven, 'and I propose going ashore here, on this beach. There is a rough path up the cliffs, and then we strike inshore and come to a creek – something similar to the creek we have left at Helford but possibly less enchanting – and at the entrance to the creek, in face of the town of Fowey, we shall find Rashleigh's ship.'

'You are very sure of yourself,' she said.

'I could not be a pirate if I were not. Can you climb cliffs?' he said.

'If you would lend me a pair of your breeches I could climb better,' she said.

'That is what I thought,' he told her, 'there is a pair belonging to Pierre Blanc on the bunk there, he keeps them for Saints' days and confession, so they should be clean enough. You can try them on directly He can lend you a shirt too and stockings and shoes. You will not need a jacket, the night is too warm.'

'Shall I cut off my hair with a pair of scissors?' she said.

'You would look more like a cabin-boy perhaps, but I would rather risk capture than have you do it,' he answered.

She said nothing for a moment, for he was looking at her, and then, 'When we reach the shores of the creek, how do we get to the ship?' she asked him.

'We will get to the creek first and then I will tell you,' he said.

He reached down for the plan, and folded it up throwing it back in the locker, and she saw he was smiling to himself in his secret way.

'How long will it take you to change your clothes?' he asked.

'Five minutes or longer,' she said.

'I will leave you then. Come up on deck when you are ready. You will want something to tie up those ringlets.' He opened a locker drawer, and ruffling there a moment, drew out the crimson sash he had worn round his waist the night he had supped with her at Navron. 'Lady St. Columb becomes a highwayman and a mountebank for the second time in her life,' he said, 'but this time there won't be any old lady for you to frighten.'

Then he went out of the cabin, Shutting the door behind him. When she joined him, some ten minutes later, he was standing by the ladder that had been thrown over the ship's side. The first party had already gone ashore, while the rest were now assembled in the boat below. She went towards him a little nervously, feeling small and rather lost in Pierre Blanc's breeches, while his shoes cut her heels, a secret she must keep to herself. He ran his eye over her and then nodded briefly. 'You will do,' he said, 'but you would not pass in moonlight,' and she laughed up at him, and climbed down into the boat with the rest of the men. Pierre Blanc himself was crouching in the bows of the boat like a monkey, and when he saw her he closed one eye, and put one hand over his heart. There was a ripple of laughter in the boat, and one and all they smiled at her with a mingled admiration and familiarity that could not offend, and she smiled back at them, leaning back in the stern thwart and clasping her knees with a lovely freedom, no longer hampered by petticoats and ribbons.

The captain of *La Mouette* descended last, and he took his seat beside her, holding the tiller, and the men bent to their oars and the boat sped across the little bay to the shingle beach beyond. Dona trailed her hand a moment in the water, which was warm, with a velvet softness about it, the phosphorescence gleaming like a shower of stars, and she thought, smiling to herself in the darkness that at last she was playing the part of a boy, which as a child she had so often longed to be, watching her brothers ride off with her father, and she gazing after them with resentful eyes, a doll thrown aside on the floor in disgust. The bows of the boat touched the shingle, and the first group of men, waiting there on the beach, laid their hands on either side of the gunwale and pulled the boat out of the wash. They had disturbed the gulls again, and two or three pairs rose with a wailing cry, and a flapping of wings.

Dona felt the shingle crunch under her heavy shoes, and she could smell the turf on the cliffs above. Then the men turned to the narrow path that skirted the cliff face like a snake, and they began to climb. Dona set her teeth, for the climb would be a hard one in these shoes that did not fit, and then she saw the Frenchman beside her, and he took her hand, and they climbed the cliff together, she holding on to him for all the world like a small boy clasping his parent. Once they paused for breath, and looking back over her shoulder, she could see the dim outline of *La Mouette* anchored in the bay, and the sound of muffled oars as the boat that had put them ashore crept back across the water. The gulls had settled again, and now there was no sound but the small scraping noises of the men's feet as they climbed the path ahead, and away below the wash of the sea as it broke upon the shore.

'Can you go on again now?' the Frenchman said, and she nodded, and his grasp on her hand tightened; so she felt little strain on her back or her shoulders, and she thought to herself, happily, brazenly, that this was the first time he had touched her, and the strength of his hand was good to feel. When the cliff was scaled there was still much climbing to be done, for the going was rough, and the young bracken already knee-high, and he continued to lead her after him, while his men spread themselves fan-wise across country, so that she could no longer count their numbers. He had studied his map carefully, of course, and they, too, she supposed, for there was no faltering in their steps or his, and no pause to reconnoitre, and all the while her clumsy shoes rubbed the sides of her feet, and she knew there was a blister on her right heel the size of a gold piece.

Now they were descending again, having crossed a cart track that no doubt served as a road, and at last he dropped her hand, and struck off a little in front, she following close behind like a shadow. Once away to the left, she fancied she caught a glimpse of a river, but soon it was lost again, they were walking under cover of a hedge, and then down once more, through bracken and undergrowth and gorse – the smell of it warm in the air like honey – and so at last to thick stunted trees crouching by the water's edge, and there was a narrow strip of beach, and a creek in front of them, opening out into a harbour with a little town beyond.

They sat down under cover of the trees, and waited; and presently, one by one, came the ship's company, silent figures slipping towards them out of the darkness.

The captain of *La Mouette* called their names softly, and when they had answered, each one in turn, and he knew they were all together, he began to speak to them in the Breton that Dona could not understand. Once he looked out across the creek and pointed, and Dona saw the dim outline of a ship at anchor; she was swinging now, the bows pointing up-stream towards them as the first of ebb-tide bubbled down the channel.

There was a riding-light high in the rigging, but otherwise no sign of life, and now and again there came a hollow creaking sound across the water as the ship swerved at the buoy to which it was moored. There was something desolate in this sound, something mournful, as though the ship had been abandoned and was a lost thing, and then with the sound came a little ripple of wind down the creek from the harbour, and the Frenchman, raising his head sharply and looking west towards the little town, frowned a moment, and turned his cheek to the breeze.

'What is it?' whispered Dona, for she felt instinctively that suddenly, for some reason, all was not well, and he waited a second or two before replying, still sniffing the air like an animal for scent, and then, 'The wind has backed to the south-west,' he said briefly.

Dona turned her cheek in the direction of the wind, and she, too, saw that the breeze that had blown off the land for the past twenty-four hours was now coming from the sea, and there was a tang about it that was different, a wet salt smell, and it came in gusts. She thought of *La Mouette* lying at anchor in the little bay, and she thought too of this other ship, moored here in the creek, and how the tide now was their only ally, for the wind had changed sides and had become a hostile force.

'What are you going to do?' she asked, but he did not answer, he had risen to his feet, and was making his way down over the slippery rocks and the dank sea-weed to the strip of beach beside the creek, and the men followed him without a word, each in turn looking upwards at the sky, and to the south-west where the wind blew.

They all stood there on the beach, looking out across the creek to the silent vessel, and now there was a strong ripple upon the water, for the wind was blowing against the ebb-tide, and the sound of the hollow cable straining against the buoy became louder than before. Then the captain of *La Mouette* walked a little way apart, and he beckoned to Pierre Blanc, who went to him, and stood listening to his master, his monkey-head nodding now and again in understanding. When they had finished the Frenchman came to Dona, and stood beside her, and he said, 'I have just told Pierre Blanc to take you back to *La Mouette.*'

She felt her heart suddenly in her breast, and a chill feeling come over her, and 'Why?' she said. 'Why do you want me to go?' Once more he looked up at the sky, and this time a spot of rain fell on to his cheek.

'The weather is going to play us false,' he said. '*La Mouette* is now on a lee-shore, and the men I left on board will be making ready to beat out of the bay. You and Pierre Blanc will have time to return and hail her before they get sail on her.'

'I understand,' she said, 'about the weather. It is going to be difficult for you to get the ship away. Not *La Mouette* I mean, but this ship. You no longer have the wind and the tide with you. That is why you want me to go back to *La Mouette*, is it not? In case there is trouble.'

'Yes,' he said.

'I am not going,' she said.

He did not answer, and she could not see the expression on his face for he was looking out once more towards the harbour.

'Why do you want to stay?' he said at last, and there was something in his voice that made her heart beat afresh, but for another reason, and she remembered the evening they had gone fishing on the river and he had said the word 'Night-jar' to her, in the same voice, with the same softness.

A wave of recklessness came upon her, and 'What does it matter?' she thought, 'why do we go on pretending, we may both die to-night, or to-morrow, and there will be so much that we shall not have had together.' And digging her nails in her hand and looking out with him across the harbour she said with sudden passion, 'Oh, death and damnation, you know why I want to stay.'

She felt him turn and look at her, and away again, and then he said, 'I wanted you to go, for the same reason.'

Once more there was silence between them, each one searching for words, and if they had been alone there would have been no need for speaking, for the shyness that had been a barrier between them had dissolved suddenly, as though it had never been, and he laughed, and reached for her hand, and kissed the palm of it, saying, 'Stay then, and we will make a fight for it, and hang together from the same tree, you and I.'

Once more he left her, and beckoned again to Pierre Blanc, who grinned all over his face because the orders were changed. But now the spots of rain increased, the clouds had gathered in the sky, and the south-west wind was blowing in gusts down the creek from the harbour.

'Dona,' he called, using her name for the first time, but carelessly, easily, as though he had always done so, and 'Yes,' she answered, 'what is it, what do you want me to do?'

'There is no time to lose,' he said, 'we must get the ship under way before the wind strengthens. But first we must have the owner on board.'

She stared at him as though he was crazy.

'What do you mean?' she said.

'When the wind was off the land,' he told her briefly, 'we could have sailed her out of Fowey Haven before the lazy fellows ashore had rubbed the sleep out of their eyes. Now we shall have to beat out, or even warp her through the narrow channel between the castles. Philip Rashleigh will be safer on board his own vessel than raising the devil ashore, and sending a cannon-ball across our bows as we pass the fort.'

'Are those not rather desperate measures?' she said.

'No more desperate than the undertaking itself,' he answered.

He was smiling down at her as though nothing mattered and he did not care. 'Would you like to do something with a spice of danger in it?' he asked.

'Yes,' she said, 'tell me what to do.'

'I want you to go with Pierre Blanc and find a boat,' he said. 'If you walk a little way along the shores of the creek here, towards the harbour entrance, you will come to some cottages on the hillside and a quay. There will be boats moored there by the quay. I want you and Pierre Blanc to take the nearest boat you find and cross over to Fowey town, and go ashore and call on Philip Rashleigh.'

'Yes,' she said.

'You won't mistake his house,' he said, 'it is hard by the church, facing the quay. You can see the quayside from here. There is a light upon it now.'

'Yes,' she said.

'I want you to tell him that his presence is urgently required on board his ship. Make up any story you like, play any part you have a fancy for. But keep in the shadow. You are a passable enough cabin-boy in·darkness, but a woman under the light.'

'Suppose he refuses to come?'

'He will not refuse, not if you are clever.'

'And if he suspects me, and keeps me there?'

'I shall deal with him then.'

He walked to the water's edge, and the men followed him. Suddenly she knew why they none of them wore jackets, why one and all were hatless, and why they now kicked off their shoes, tying them round their necks with a cord through the buckle. She looked out towards the ship, straining at her moorings there in the creek, the riding-light swaying to the freshening wind, while the men on board her slept soundly; and she thought of those silent trespassers who would come upon her out of the darkness. No creaking of oars in the night, no shadow of boats, but a wet hand stretching from the water upon the chain, and a wet footmark upon the fo'c'sle head, and lithe dripping figures dropping down upon her decks, a whisper, and a whistle, and a strangled smothered cry.

She shivered for no reason, except that she was a woman, and turning to her from the water he smiled at her and said, 'Go now, turn your back on us, and go,' and she obeyed him, stumbling once more across the rocks and the seaweed, with little Pierre Blanc trotting at her heels like a dog. Not once did she look back over her shoulder to the river, but she knew that they were all swimming now to the ship, that the wind was blowing stronger every moment, and the tide was running swiftly. She lifted her face, and then the rain began to fall, hard and fast, from the south-west.

Chapter Thirteen

Dona crouched in the stern of the little boat, the rain beating on her shoulders, and Pierre Blanc fumbled in the darkness for the paddles. Already there was a run in the pool where the boats were anchored, and a white wash was breaking against the steps of the quay. There was no sign of life from the cottages on the side of the hill, and they had taken the first boat to hand without difficulty. Pierre Blanc pulled out into mid-channel, and as soon as they opened up the harbour entrance they met the full force of the rising wind, which, with the strong ebb-tide, set up a short cross-sea that splashed over the low gunwale of the small boat. The rain came fiercely, blotting out the hills, and Dona, shivering in her thin shirt, felt something of hopelessness in her heart, and she wondered if perhaps it was all her fault, she had broken the luck, and this was to be the last adventure of *La Mouette*, which had never before sailed with a woman on board.

She looked at Pierre Blanc as he strained at the paddles, and now he was no longer smiling, he kept glancing across his shoulder at the harbour mouth. They were coming closer to the town of Fowey, she could see a group of cottages by the side of the quay, and above them rose the tower of a church.

The whole adventure had become suddenly like an evil dream from which there could be no waking, and little Pierre Blanc with his monkey face was the partner of it.

She leant forward to him, and he rested a moment on his paddles, the boat rocking in the trough of a short sea.

'I shall find the house alone,' she said, 'and you must wait for me in the boat, by the side of the quay.'

He glanced at her doubtfully, but she spoke with urgency, laying her hand on his knee. 'It is the only way,' she said, 'and then if I do not return in half-an-hour, you must go at once to the ship.'

He seemed to turn her words over in his mind, and then he nodded, but still he did not smile, poor Pierre Blanc who had never been serious before, and she guessed that he too sensed the hopelessness of the adventure. They drew close to the quay, and the sickly lantern light shone down upon their faces. The water surged round the ladder, and Dona stood up in the stern of the boat, and seized the rungs in her hand. 'Do not forget, Pierre Blanc,' she said, 'you are not to wait for me. Give me a half-hour only,' and she turned swiftly, so that she should not see his anxious troubled face. She went past the few cottages towards the church, and came to the one house standing in the street, by the side of the hill.

There was a light in the lower casement, she could see the glow of it through the drawn curtains, but the street itself was deserted. She stood beneath the casement uncertainly, blowing on her cold fingers, and it seemed to her, not for the first time, that this scheme of summoning Philip Rashleigh was the most foolhardy of the whole enterprise, for surely he would soon be abed and asleep and therefore would give them no trouble. The rain beat down upon her, and she had never felt more lonely, never more helpless and more lost to action.

Suddenly she heard the casement above her head open, and in panic she flattened herself against the wall. She could hear someone lean his elbows on the sill, and the sound of heavy breathing, and then there was a scattering of ashes from a pipe, they fell upon her shoulder, and a yawn and a sigh. There was a scraping of a chair in the room within, and whoever had moved the chair asked a question and he by the window made reply in a voice that was startlingly familiar. 'There is a gale of wind blowing up from the southwest,' said Godolphin, 'it is a pity now that you did not moor the ship up the river after all. They may have trouble with her in the morning if this weather holds.'

There was silence, and Dona could feel her heart thumping in her side. She had forgotten Godolphin, and that he was brother-in-law to Philip Rashleigh. Godolphin, in whose house she had taken tea less than a week before. And here he was, within three feet of her, dropping the ash from his pipe on to her shoulder.

The foolish wager of the wig came to her mind, and she realised then that the Frenchman must have known that Godolphin would be staying with Philip Rashleigh in Fowey that night, and that side by side with the capture of the ship he had planned the seizing of Godolphin's wig.

In spite of her fear and her anxiety she smiled to herself, for surely this was sublime folly if anything was, that a man could so risk his life for the sake of a crazy wager. The thought of it made her love him the more, that beside those qualities of silence and understanding that had drawn her to him in the beginning, he should have this total indifference to the values of the world, this irrepressible madness.

Godolphin was still leaning at the open casement, she could hear his heavy breathing and his yawns, and the words he had just spoken lingered in her mind, his reference to the ship, and the moving of her up river. An idea began to shape in her brain, whereby the summoning of the owner on board would seem legitimate; then the other voice spoke abruptly from the room inside, and the casement was suddenly closed. Dona thought rapidly, reckless now of capture, the whole crazy folly of the night rousing in her the old choking sensation of delight she had known months ago when superbly indifferent to gossip and more than a little drunk she had roistered in the streets of London.

Only this time the adventure was real, and not a practical joke, trumped up to alleviate the boredom of the small hours when the London air was stifling, and Harry too insistent in his claims. She turned away from the window, and went to the door, and without hesitation jangled the great bell that hung outside.

The sound was greeted by the immediate barking of dogs, and then footsteps, and the drawing of bolts, and to her consternation Godolphin himself stood there, a taper in his hand, his great bulk filling the doorway. 'What do you want?' he said angrily. 'Don't you know the hour, it's close on midnight, and everyone abed.'

Dona crouched back out of the light, as though timid at the reception he gave her. 'Mr. Rashleigh is wanted,' she said, 'they sent me for him. The master is anxious to move the ship now, before the gale worsens.'

'Who is it?' called Philip Rashleigh from within, and all the while the dogs were barking and scratching at her legs, and Godolphin was kicking them back, 'Down, Ranger, you devil, get back, Tancred,' and then, 'Come inside, boy, can't you?'

'No, sir, I'm wet through to the skin, if you would please tell Mr. Rashleigh they have sent for him, from the ship,' and already she began to edge away, for he was staring down at her, his brows drawn together in perplexity, as though there was something about her appearance that he did not understand, that was irregular. Once more Philip Rashleigh called out in irritation from the room within: 'Who the devil is it then, is it Dan Thomas's boy, from Polruan, is it young Jim?'

'Not so fast, then,' called Godolphin, laying a hand upon Dona's shoulder. 'Mr. Rashleigh would talk to you, is your name Jim Thomas?'

'Yes, sir,' said Dona, snatching insanely at the straw he offered her, 'and the matter is urgent, the master says would Mr. Rashleigh go on board at once, there is no time to lose, the ship is in danger. Let me go, sir, I have another message to deliver, my mother is desperately ill, I must run now for the physician.'

But still Godolphin kept his hand on her shoulder, and now he brought the taper close to her face. 'What have you round your head?' he said. 'Are you ill, also, as well as your mother?'

'What is all this nonsense?' shouted Rashleigh, coming into the hall, 'Jim Thomas's mother has been in her grave these ten years. Who is it? What is wrong with the ship?' and now Dona shook herself clear from the hand that held her, and calling to them over her shoulder to make haste, the gale was freshening all the while, she ran across the square and down to the quay, hysterical laughter rising in her throat, with one of Rashleigh's dogs barking at her heels.

She pulled up sharply just short of the quay, taking refuge in the doorway of a cottage, for there was someone standing there by the ladder who had not been there before, and he was staring out across the harbour towards the entrance of the creek. He carried a lantern in his hand, and she guessed that he must be the night-watchman of the town, making his rounds, and now, through very cussedness it seemed to her, had taken up a position on the quay. She dared not venture forward until he had gone, and anyway Pierre

Blanc would have taken the boat some little distance away, at sight of the night-watchman.

She sheltered there in the doorway, watching the man, and biting at her finger-nails in anxiety, and still he stared out across the harbour towards the creek, as though there was something there which engaged his attention, some movement. A little sick feeling stole over her, for perhaps after all the boarding of the ship had not gone according to plan, and even now the crew of *La Mouette* were struggling in the water, and their leader with them, or the resistance had been stronger than they had expected, and they were fighting now on the decks of Rashleigh's ship, and it was these sounds that the night-watchman could hear, straining his eyes across the water. She could do nothing to help them; as it was she had probably drawn suspicion upon herself, and even as she stood there helpless in the doorway she heard the sound of voices, and footsteps, and round the corner of the street came Rashleigh himself and Godolphin, clad in great-coats against the weather, and Rashleigh with a lantern in his hand.

'Ho, there,' he called, and the night-watchman turned at his voice and hurried to meet him.

'Have you seen a lad run this way?' said Rashleigh, but the watchman shook his head. 'I have seen no one,' he said, 'but there is something amiss yonder, sir, it looks as though your vessel has broken from the buoy.'

'What's that?' said Rashleigh, making towards the quay, and Godolphin, following him, said, 'Then the lad did not lie after all.' Dona crouched back in the doorway. They were past her now, and on to the quay, never once looking in the direction of the cottage. She watched them from the cover of the door, and they were standing with their backs to her, staring across the harbour as the watchman had done, and Godolphin's cape was billowing in the gusty wind, while the rain streamed down upon their heads.

'Look, sir,' called the watchman, 'they are getting sail on her, the master must be going to take her up river.'

'The fellow is crazy,' shouted Rashleigh, 'there are not a dozen men on board, three-quarters of the fellows are sleeping ashore, they'll have her aground before they've finished. Go rouse some of 'em, Joe, we must get all hands on to her. Blast that incompetent fool Dan Thomas, what in the name of the Almighty does he think he is doing?'

He put his hands to his mouth and bellowed across the harbour.

'Ahoy, there! *Merry Fortune*, ahoy!' and the night-watchman sped across the quay, and seized the rope of a ship's bell that was hanging there beside the lantern, and the sound of it clanged in the air, loud and insistent, compelling enough to waken every sleeping soul in Fowey. Almost at once a window was thrust open in a cottage up the street, and a head looked out and said, 'What ails you, Joe, is anything wrong?' and Rashleigh, stamping up and down in a blind fury, shouted back, 'Put your breeches on, damn you, and get your brother too, the *Merry Fortune* is adrift there in the harbour.'

A figure came out from a doorway in another cottage, struggling into a coat as he emerged, and another man came running down the street, and all the while the ship's bell clanged, and Rashleigh shouted, and the rain and the wind tore at his cloak and the swaying lantern he carried in his hand.

Lights appeared now in the windows of the cottages beneath the church and voices shouted, and voices called, and men appeared from nowhere, running on to the quay. 'Get me a boat, can't you?' yelled Rashleigh. 'Put me aboard, one of you, put me aboard.'

Someone was astir in the cottage where Dona had been hiding, she heard the patter of footsteps on the stairs, and she left the doorway and came out upon the quay. In the darkness and confusion, in the whistling wind and the streaming rain, she was only another figure mixing with the rest, staring out towards the ship that with sails hoisted on her yards was bearing down now towards the centre of the channel, her bows pointing to the harbour mouth.

'Look, she's helpless,' cried a voice, 'the tide is taking her to the rocks, they must be mad aboard, or dead drunk, all of them.'

'Why doesn't he wear ship and get up, out of it,' shouted another, and 'Look, the tide has her,' came the answer, and someone else, shrieking in Dona's ear, 'The tide is stronger than the wind yet, the tide has her every time.'

Some of the men were struggling now with the boats moored beneath the quay, she could hear them swear as they fumbled with a frape, and Rashleigh and Godolphin, peering down from the side of the quay, cursed them for the delay. 'Someone's monkey'd here with the frape,' shouted one of the men, 'the rope is parting, someone must have cut it with a knife,' and suddenly Dona had a vision of little Pierre Blanc, grinning to himself in the darkness while the great bell clanged and jangled on the quay.

'Swim, one of you,' yelled Rashleigh, 'swim and bring me a boat. By God, I'll thrash the fellow who played the trick, I'll have him hanged.'

Now the ship was coming closer, Dona could see the men on the yards, and the great topsail shaking out, and someone was at the wheel there giving orders, someone with head thrown back, watching the sail draw taut.

'Ahoy, there! Ahoy!' yelled Rashleigh, and Godolphin too added his cry, 'Wear ship, man, wear ship before you lose your chance.'

And still the *Merry Fortune* held to her course; straight down channel and across the harbour she came, the ebb-tide ripping under her keel. 'He's crazy,' screamed someone, 'he's making for the harbour mouth, look there, all of you, look there.' For now that the ship was within hail Dona could see that there were three boats out in a line abreast, with a warp from the ship to each of them, and every man in them bent double to his oars, and still the topsail filled and pulled, and the courses too, and the ship heeled to a great puff of wind that came from the hills behind the town.

'He is going to sea,' shouted Rashleigh, 'by God, he is taking her to sea,' and suddenly Godolphin turned, and his great bulbous eyes fell upon Dona, who in her excitement had crept close to the edge of the quay. 'There's that boy,' he called, 'he is to blame for this, catch him, one of you, catch that boy there.' Dona turned, ducking swiftly under the arm of an old man who stared at her blankly, and she began to run, blindly, away from the quay and straight up the lane past Rashleigh's house, away from the church, and the town, towards the cover of the hills, while behind her she could hear a man shouting, and the sound of running feet, and a voice calling 'Come back, will you, come back, I say.'

There was a path to her left, winding amongst the gorse and the young bracken, and she took it, stumbling on the rough ground in her clumsy shoes, the rain streaming in her face, and down below her she caught a gleam of the harbour water and could hear the wash of the tide against the cliff wall.

Her only thought was to escape, to hide herself from those questing, bulbous eyes of Godolphin, for Pierre Blanc was lost to her now, and the *Merry Fortune* fighting her own battle in mid-harbour.

She ran on in the wind and the darkness, the path taking her along the side of the hill to the harbour mouth, and even now it seemed to her that she could hear the hideous clanging of the ship's bell on that quay, rousing the people of the town, and could see the angry figure of Philip Rashleigh hurling curses upon the men who struggled with the frape. The path began to descend at last, and pausing in her head-long flight, and wiping the rain from her face, she saw that it led down to a cove by the harbour mouth, and then wound upwards again to the fort on the headland. She stared in front of her, listening to the sound of the breakers below, and straining her eyes for a glimpse of the *Merry Fortune,* and then, glancing back over her shoulder, she saw a pin-prick of light advancing towards her down the path, and she heard the crunch of footsteps.

She flung herself down among the bracken, and the footsteps drew nearer, and she saw it was a man bearing a lantern in his hand. He walked swiftly, looking neither to the right nor left of him, and he went straight past her, down to the cove, and then up again towards the headland; she could see the glimmer of his lantern as he climbed the hill. She knew then that he was going to the fort, Rashleigh had sent him to warn the soldiers on duty at the fort. Whether suspicion had crossed his mind at last, or whether he still thought that the master of the *Merry Fortune* had lost his wits and was taking his ship to disaster, she could not tell, nor did it matter very much. The result would be the same. The men who guarded the entrance to the harbour would fire on the *Merry Fortune.*

And now she ran down the path to the cove, but instead of climbing to the headland as the man with the lantern was doing, she turned left along the beach, scrambling over the wet rocks and the sea-weed to the harbour mouth itself. It seemed to her that she was looking once again at the plan of Fowey Haven. She saw the narrow entrance, and the fort, and the ridge of rocks jutting out from the cove where she now found herself, and in her mind was the one thought that she must reach those rocks before the ship came to the harbour mouth, and in some way warn the Frenchman that the alarm had been sent to the fort.

She was sheltering momentarily, under the lee of the head-land, and no longer had to fight her way against the wind and the rain, but her feet slipped and stumbled on the slippery rocks, still running wet where the tide had left them, and there were cuts on her hands and her chin where she had fallen, while the hair that had come loose from the sash that bound it blew about her face.

Somewhere a gull was screaming. Its persistent cry echoed in the cliffs above her head, and she began to curse it, savagely and uselessly, for it seemed to her that every gull now was a sentinel, hostile to herself and to her companions, and this bird who wailed in the darkness was mocking her, crying that all her attempts to reach the ship were useless.

In a moment or two the ridges of rocks would be within reach, she could hear the breakers, and then, raising herself on her hands and looking forward, she saw the *Merry Fortune* bearing down towards the harbour mouth, the short seas breaking over her bows. The boats that had towed her were hoisted now on deck, and the men that had manned them were thronging the ship's side, for suddenly and miraculously the wind had shifted a point or two to the west, and with the strong ebb under her the *Merry Fortune* was sailing her way sea-ward. There were other boats upon the water now, little craft coming in pursuit, and men who shouted and men who swore, and surely that was Godolphin himself in one of them, with Rashleigh by his side. Dona laughed, wiping her hair out of her eyes, for nothing mattered now, neither Rashleigh's anger nor Godolphin's recognition of her should it come, for the *Merry Fortune* was sailing away from them, recklessly and joyfully, into the summer gale. Once again the gull screamed, and this time he was close to her; she looked about for a stone to throw at him, and instead she saw a small boat shoot past the ridge of rocks ahead of her, and there was Pierre Blanc, his small face upturned towards the cliffs, and once again he gave his sea-gull's cry.

Dona stood then, laughing still, and raised her arms above her head, and shouted to him, and he saw her and brought his boat in to the rocks beside her, and she scrambled down into the boat beside him, asking no question, nor he either, for he was pulling now into the short breaking seas towards the ship. The blood was running from the cut on her chin, and she was soaked to the waist, but she did not care. The little boat leapt into the steep seas, and the salt spray blew in her face with the wind and the rain. There was a flash of light, and the crash of a cannon, and something splashed into the water ten yards ahead of them, but Pierre Blanc, grinning like a monkey, pulled on into mid-channel, and here was the *Merry Fortune* herself, thrashing through the sea towards them, the wind thundering in her crowded sails.

Another flash, another deafening report, and this time there was a tearing sound of splintering wood, but Dona could see nothing, she only knew that someone had thrown a rope down into the boat, and someone was pulling them close to the side of the ship, and there were faces laughing down at her, and hands that lifted her, and away beneath her was the black swirl of water and the little boat upside down, disappearing in the darkness.

The Frenchman was standing at the wheel of the *Merry Fortune*, and he too had a cut on his chin, and his hair was blowing about his face, and the water streamed from his shirt, but for one moment his eyes held hers and they smiled at each other, and then 'Throw yourself on your face, Dona,' he said, 'they'll be firing again,' and she lay beside him on the deck, exhausted, aching, shivering with the rain and the spray, but nothing mattered, and she did not mind.

This time the shot fell short. 'Save your powder, boys,' he laughed, 'you'll not catch us this time,' while little Pierre Blanc, streaming wet and shaking himself like a dog, leant over the ship's side, his finger to his nose. And now the *Merry Fortune* reared and fell into the trough of the seas, and the sails thundered and shook, while someone shouted from the pursuing boats behind, and someone with a musket in his hand let fly at the rigging.

'There is your friend, Dona,' called the Frenchman, 'do you know if he shoots straight?' She crawled aft, looking over the stern rail, and there was the leading boat almost beneath them with Rashleigh's face glaring up at them, and Godolphin raising a musket to his shoulder.

'There's a woman aboard,' shouted Rashleigh, 'look there!' But as he spoke Godolphin fired again, the ball whistling harmlessly over her head, and as the *Merry Fortune* heeled over in a sudden gust of wind Dona saw the Frenchman leave the wheel a moment to Pierre Blanc at his side. Laughing, he swung himself over the lee rail of the ship as it dipped in the sea, and Dona saw that he had a sword in his hand.

'Greetings to you, gentlemen,' he called, 'and a safe passage back to Fowey quay, but first of all we would like something to remember you by,' and reaching out with his sword he knocked Godolphin's hat off into the water, and pricking the great curled periwig with the point of his sword, he bore it aloft triumphantly, waving it in the air. Godolphin, bald as a naked baby, his bulbous eyes starting out of his scarlet face, fell backwards into the stern of the boat, his musket clattering beside him.

Then a squall of rain came, blotting them from sight, and the sea broke over the rail of the ship, knocking Dona down into the scuppers. When she could stand again and get her breath, wiping the hair from her face, there was the fort on the headland away astern of them, and the boats were out of sight, and the Frenchman was standing with his hand on the wheel of the *Merry Fortune*, laughing at her, with Godolphin's wig dangling from the spokes.

Chapter Fourteen

There were two ships in mid-channel, sailing in company about three miles distant from each other, and the leading ship had a curious rakish air about her, with her slanting masts and her coloured paintwork, as though she were

leading the sober merchantman that followed her to uncharted waters beyond
the far horizon.

The summer gale that had thrashed the sea for twenty-four hours without
ceasing had now blown itself out, and the sky was hard and blue without
a single cloud. The swell too had died away, leaving the sea quiet and
curiously still, so that the two ships, with only the breath of a northerly
breeze to drive them, stayed almost motionless in the channel, their sails
hanging uselessly upon the yards. A smell of cooking came from the galley
of the *Merry Fortune*, the warm brown smell of roasting chicken, and the
fragrance of it crept into the open port-hole of the cabin, mingling with the
fresh salt air and the warm sun. Dona opened her eyes, and she became
aware for the first time that the ship was no longer pitching and tossing in
the trough of the Atlantic swell, the sickness that had overtaken her was
gone, and above all she was hungry, hungrier than she had been in her life.
She yawned, stretching her arms above her head, smiling to herself because
she was no longer sea-sick, and then she swore softly, using one of Harry's
more stable-sounding oaths, for she remembered that by being sea-sick she
had forfeited her wager. She put her hands up to her ears, fingering her
ruby ear-rings reluctantly, and as she did so she realised with full consciousness that she was stark naked under the blanket, and there was no trace of
her clothes upon the cabin floor.

It seemed eternity since she had stumbled down the companion-way in
the dark, drenched, and exhausted, and sick, and flinging off her shirt and
her breeches, and those lumping blistering shoes, had crept into the warmth
of those comforting blankets, longing only for stillness and for sleep.

Someone must have come into the cabin while she was sleeping, for the
port-hole was wide open that had been closed before against the weather,
her clothes had been taken away, and in their place was a ewer of boiling
water and a towel.

She climbed from the spacious bunk where she had lain for a day and a
night, thinking, as she stood naked upon the floor of the cabin and washed,
that whoever had been master of the *Merry Fortune* believed in comfort
before vigilance. Glancing out of the port-hole as she parted her hair she
saw away on the starboard bow the spars of *La Mouette*, gleaming scarlet
in the sun. Once more the smell of chicken came to her nostrils, and then,
hearing the sound of footsteps on the deck outside, she climbed back into her
berth, dragging the blanket to her chin.

'Are you awake yet?' called the Frenchman. She bade him come in,
leaning back against the pillow, her heart beating foolishly, and he stood
there in the doorway smiling down at her, and he had a tray in his hands.

'I have lost my ear-rings after all,' she said.

'Yes, I know," he said.

'How do you know?'

'Because I came below once to see how you were, and you threw a pillow
at my head and damned me to hell,' he answered.

She laughed, shaking her head. 'You are lying,' she said, 'you never came,
I never saw a soul.'

'You were too far gone to remember anything about it,' he said, 'but we will not argue. Are you hungry?'

'Yes.'

'So am I. I thought we might have dinner together.'

He began to lay the table, and she watched him from under cover of her blanket.

'What is the time?' she asked.

'About three o'clock in the afternoon,' he told her.

'And what day would it be?'

'Sunday. Your friend Godolphin will have missed his morning in church, unless there is a good barber in Fowey.'

He glanced up at the bulkhead, and following his eyes she saw the curled periwig hanging upon a nail over her head.

'When did you put it there?' she laughed.

'When you were sick,' he said.

And now she was silent, hating the thought that he had seen her at such a moment, so shaming, so grossly undignified, and she pulled the blanket yet more closely round her, watching his hands busy with the chicken.

'Can you eat a wing?' he asked.

'Yes,' she nodded, wondering how she could sit up without a stitch upon her body, and when he had turned his back to uncork the wine she sat up swiftly, and draped the blanket about her shoulders.

He brought her a plate of chicken, looking her up and down as he did so. 'We can do better for you than that,' he said, 'you forget the *Merry Fortune* had been to the Indies,' and going outside for a moment he stooped to a large wooden box that stood beside the companion-way, and lifting the top he brought out a gaily-coloured shawl, all scarlet and gold, with a silken fringe. 'Perhaps Godolphin had this in mind for his wife,' he said. 'There are plenty more down in the hold if you want them.'

He sat down at the table, tearing off a drumstick from the chicken, and eating it in his hand. She drank her wine, watching him over the rim of the glass.

'We might have been hanging from that tree in Godolphin's park,' she said.

'We would have been, but for that slant of wind from the west,' he answered.

'And what are we going to do now?'

'I never make plans on a Sunday,' he told her.

She went on eating her chicken, seizing the wing in her hands as he was doing, and from the bows of the ship came the sound of Pierre Blanc's lute, and the men's voices singing softly.

'Do you always have the devil's own luck, Frenchman?' she said.

'Always,' he answered, throwing his drumstick out of the port-hole, and taking the fellow.

The sun streamed in upon the table, while the lazy sea lapped against the side of the ship, and they went on eating, each aware of the other, and the hours that stretched before them.

'Rashleigh makes his seamen comfortable,' said the Frenchman presently, looking about him, 'perhaps that was why they were all asleep when we climbed on board.'

'How many were there then?'

'Half-a-dozen, that is all.'

'And what did you do with them?'

'Oh, we bound them back to back and gagged them, and cast them adrift in a boat. They were picked up by Rashleigh himself I dare say.'

'Will the sea be rough again?'

'No, that is all finished.'

She leant back on her pillow, watching the pattern that the sun made on the bulkhead.

'I am glad I had it, the danger and the excitement,' she said, 'but I am glad it is over too. I do not want to do it again, not that waiting outside Rashleigh's house, and hiding on the quay, and running across the hills to the cove until I thought my heart would burst.'

'You did not do too badly, for a cabin-boy,' he said.

He looked across at her, and then away again, and she began to plait the silk fringe of the shawl he had given her. Pierre Blanc was still playing his lute, playing the little rippling song she had heard when she saw *La Mouette* for the first time anchored in the creek below Navron.

'How long shall we stay in the *Merry Fortune?*' she said.

'Why, do you want to go home?' he asked.

'No – No, I just wondered,' she said.

He got up from the table, and crossing to the port-hole looked out at *La Mouette* where she lay almost becalmed some two miles distant.

'That's the way of it at sea,' he said, 'always too much wind or too little. We'd be at the French coast by now with a capful of breeze. Perhaps we shall get it, to-night.'

He stood there with his hands deep in his breeches pockets, his lips framing the song that Pierre Blanc was playing on the lute.

'What will you do when the wind does come?' she asked.

'Sail within sight of land, and then leave a handful of men to take the *Merry Fortune* into port. As for ourselves, we shall return on board *La Mouette.*'

She went on playing with the tassel of the shawl.

'And then where do we go?' she said.

'Back to Helford of course. Do you not want to see your children?'

She did not answer. She was watching the back of his head, and the set of his shoulders.

'Perhaps the night-jar is still calling in the creek at midnight,' he said. 'We could go and find him, and the heron too. I never finished the drawing of the heron, did I?'

'I do not know.'

'There are many fish too in the river waiting to be caught,' he said.

Pierre Blanc's song dwindled and died, and there was no sound but the lapping of water against the side of the ship. The *Merry Fortune's* bell struck the half-hour, and this was echoed by *La Mouette*, away in the distance. The sun blazed down upon the placid sea. Everything was peaceful. Everything was still.

He turned away then from the port-hole, and came and sat down on the bunk beside her, still whistling the song under his breath.

'This is the best moment for a pirate,' he said. 'The planning is over and done with, and the game a success. Looking back on it one can remember only the good moments, and the bad are put aside until next time. And so, as the wind will not blow before night-fall, we may do as we please.'

Dona listened to the lapping of the sea against the hull.

'We might swim,' she said, 'in the cool of the evening, before the sun goes down.'

'We might,' he said.

There was silence between them, and she went on watching the reflection of the sun above her head.

'I cannot get up until my clothes are dry,' she said.

'No, I know.'

'Will they be very long, out there, in the sun?'

'At least three hours more, I should say.'

Dona sighed, and settled herself down against her pillow.

'Perhaps you could lower a boat,' she said, 'and send Pierre Blanc off to *La Mouette* for my gown.'

'He is asleep by now,' said the captain of the ship, 'they are all asleep. Didn't you know that Frenchmen like to be idle between one and five in the afternoon?'

'No,' she said, 'I did not.'

She put her arms behind her head, and closed her eyes.

'In England,' she said, 'people never sleep in the afternoon. It must be a custom peculiar to your countrymen. But in the meanwhile, what are we going to do until my clothes are dry?'

He watched her, the ghost of a smile on his lips.

'In France,' he said, 'they would tell you there is only one thing we could do. But perhaps that also is a custom peculiar to my countrymen.'

She did not answer. Then leaning forward he stretched out his hand, and very gently he began to unscrew the ruby from her left ear.

Chapter Fifteen

Dona stood at the wheel of *La Mouette*, and the ship plunged into the long green seas, tossing the spray back upon the deck towards her. The white

sails stretched and sang above her head, and all the sounds that she had
grown to love came to her ears now in beauty and in strength. The creaking
of the great blocks, the straining of ropes, the thud of the wind in the rigging,
and down in the waist of the ship the voices of the men, laughing and
chaffing one another, now and again looking up to see if she observed them,
showing off like children to win a glance from her. The hot sun shone upon
her bare head, and when the spray blew back upon the deck the taste came
to her lips, and even the deck itself had a warm pungent smell, an odour of
tar, and rope, and blue salt water.

And all this, she thought, is only momentary, is only a fragment in time
that will never come again, for yesterday already belongs to the past and is
ours no longer, and tomorrow is an unknown thing that may be hostile.
This is our day, our moment, the sun belongs to us, and the wind, and the
sea, and the men for'ard there singing on the deck. This day is forever a day
to be held and cherished, because in it we shall have lived, and loved, and
nothing else matters but that in this world of our own making to which we
have escaped. She looked down at him, as he lay on the deck against the
bulwark, his hands behind his head, and his pipe in his mouth. Now and
again he smiled to himself as he slept there in the sun, and she remembered
the feel of his back that had lain against hers all the night, and she thought
with pity for all the men and women who were not light-hearted when they
loved, who were cold, who were reluctant, who were shy, who imagined that
passion and tenderness were two things separate from one another, and not
the one, gloriously intermingled, so that to be fierce was also to be gentle,
so that silence was a speaking without words. For love, as she knew it now,
was something without shame and without reserve, the possession of two
people who had no barrier between them, and no pride; whatever happened
to him would happen to her too, all feeling, all movement, all sensation of
body and of mind.

The wheel of *La Mouette* lifted under her hands, and the ship heeled over
in the freshening breeze, and all this, she thought, is part of what we feel
for each other, and part of the loveliness of living, the strength that lies in
the hull of a ship, the beauty of sails, the surge of water, the taste of the sea,
the touch of the wind on our faces, and even the little simple pleasures of
eating, and drinking, and sleeping, all these we share with delight and
understanding, because of the happiness we have in one another.

He opened his eyes and looked at her, and taking the pipe out of his
mouth he shook the ashes on the deck, and they blew away, scattering in the
wind, and then he rose and stretched himself, yawning in idleness and peace
and contentment, and he came and stood beside her at the wheel, putting his
hands on the spokes above her hands, and they stood there, watching the sky
and the sea and the sails, and never speaking.

The coast of Cornwall was a thin line on the far horizon, and the first
gulls came to greet them, wheeling and crying above the masts, and they
knew that presently the land smell would drift towards them from the distant
hills, and the sun would lose its strength, and later the wide estuary of

Helford would open to them with the setting sun shining red and gold upon the water.

The beeches would be warm where the sun shone all day, and the river itself full and limpid with the tide. There would be sanderling skimming the rocks, and oyster-catchers brooding on one leg by the little pools, while higher up the river, near the creek, the heron would stand motionless, like a sleeping thing, only to rise at their approach and glide away over the trees with his great soundless wings.

The creek itself would seem still and silent after the boisterous sun and the lifting sea, and the trees, crowding by the water's edge, would be kindly and gentle. The night-jar would call as he had said, and the fishes plop suddenly in the water, and all the scents and sounds of midsummer would come to them, as they walked in the twilight under the trees, amongst the young green bracken and the moss.

'Shall we build a fire again, and cook supper, in the creek?' he said to her, reading her thoughts. 'Yes,' she said, 'on the quay there, as we did before,' and leaning against him, watching the thin line of the coast becoming harder and more distinct, she thought of the other supper they had cooked together, and of the little shyness and restraint between them then that could never come again, for love was a thing of such simplicity once it was shared, and admitted, and done, with all the joy intensified and all the fever gone.

So *La Mouette* stole in once more towards the land, as she had done that first evening that seemed so long ago now, when Dona had stood on the cliffs and watched her, premonition already in her heart. The sun went down, and the gulls came out to greet them, and the rising tide and the little evening wind brought the ship gently and in silence up the channel of the estuary. Even in the few days they had been absent a depth of colour had come to the trees that had not been before, and there was a richness in the green of the hills, and the still warm fragrance of midsummer hovered in the air like the touch of a hand. As *La Mouette* drifted with the tide a curlew rose with a whistle and sped away up the river, and then, the ship losing way with the lack of wind as they came to the creek, the boats were lowered, and the warps made fast, and the ship was brought to her secret anchorage as the first shadows fell upon the water.

The cable rattled with a hollow sound in the deep pool beneath the trees, and the ship swung round to meet the last of the flood tide, and suddenly from nowhere came a swan and his mate, like two white barges sailing in company, and following them three cygnets, soft and brown. They went away down the creek, leaving a wake behind them as a vessel would, and presently when all was snugged down for the night and the decks deserted, the smell of cooking came from the galley forward, and the low murmur of voices as the men talked in the fo'c'sle.

The captain's boat waited beneath the ladder, and coming up from the cabin he called to Dona, who was leaning against the rail on the poop deck watching the first star above the dark tree, and they pulled away down the creek where the swans had gone, the little boat lapping against the water.

Soon the fire glowed in the clearing, the dried sticks snapping and breaking, and this night they cooked bacon, curling and streaky and crisp, with bread that was burnt also by the fire and was toasted and black. They broke the bacon in their hands, and then brewed coffee, strong and bitter, in a saucepan with a bent handle, and afterwards he reached for his pipe and his tobacco, and Dona leant against his knee, her hands behind her head.

'And this,' she said, watching the fire, 'could be forever, if we wished. Could be to-morrow, and the next day, and a year ahead. And not only here, but in other countries, on other rivers, in lands of our own choosing.'

'Yes,' he said, 'if we so wished. But Dona St. Columb is not Dona the cabin-boy. She is someone who has a life in another world, and even at this moment she is waking in the bedroom at Navron, with her fever gone, remembering only very faintly the dream she had. And she rises, and dresses, and sees to her household and her children.'

'No,' she said, 'she has not woken yet, and the fever is still heavy upon her, and her dreams are of a loveliness that she never knew in her life before.'

'For all that,' he told her, 'they are still dreams. And in the morning she will wake.'

'No,' she said. 'No, no. Always this. Always the fire, and the dark night, and the supper we have cooked, and your hand here against my heart.'

'You forget,' he said, 'that women are more primitive than men. For a time they will wander, yes, and play at love, and play at adventure. And then, like the birds, they must make their nest. Instinct is too strong for them. Birds build the home they crave, and settle down into it, warm and safe, and have their babies.'

'But the babies grow up,' she said, 'and fly away, and then the parent birds fly away too, and are free once more.'

He laughed at her, staring into the fire, watching the flames.

'There is no answer, Dona,' he said, 'for I could sail away now in *La Mouette* and come back to you in twenty years' time, and what should I find but a placid, comfortable woman in place of my cabin-boy, with her dreams long forgotten, and I myself a weather-beaten mariner, stiff in the joints, with bearded face, and my taste for piracy gone with the spent years.'

'My Frenchman paints a dismal picture of the future,' she said.

'Your Frenchman is a realist,' he answered.

'And if I sailed with you now, and never returned to Navron?' she asked.

'Who can tell? Regret perhaps, and disillusion, and a looking back over your shoulder.'

'Not with you,' she said, 'never with you.'

'Well then, perhaps no regrets. But more building of nests, and more rearing of broods, and I having to sail alone again, and so a losing once more of adventure. So you see, my Dona, there is no escape for a woman, only for a night and for a day.'

'No, you are right,' she said, 'there is no escape for a woman. Therefore if I sail with you again I shall be a cabin-boy, and borrow Pierre Blanc's breeches once and for always, and there will be no complications of a primitive nature, so that our hearts and our minds can be easy, and you can seize ships and make your landings on the coast, and I, the humble cabin-boy, will brew your supper for you in the cabin, and ask no questions, and hold no conversation with you.'

'And how long would we endure that, you and I?'

'For as long as we pleased.'

'You mean, for as long as I pleased. Which would be neither for a night nor an hour, and anyway, not this night and not this hour, my Dona.'

The fire burnt low, and sank away to nothing, and later she said to him, 'Do you know what day this is?'

'Yes,' he said, 'midsummer day. The longest in the year.'

'Therefore,' she said, 'to-night we should sleep here, instead of in the ship. Because it will never happen again. Not for us. Not in this way, in the creek here.'

'I know,' he said, 'that is why I brought the blankets in the boat. And the pillow for your head. Did you not see them?'

She looked up at him, but she could not see his face any longer, for it was in shadow, the fire-light being gone, and then without a word he got up and went down to the boat, and then came back to her with the bedding and pillow in his arms, and he spread them out in the clearing under the trees, close to the water's edge. The tide was ebbing now, and the mud flats showing. The trees shivered in a little wind, and then were still again. The night-jars were silent and the sea-birds slept. There was no moon, only the dark sky above their heads, and beside them the black waters of the creek.

'To-morrow, very early, I shall go to Navron,' she told him, 'at sunrise, before you are awake.'

'Yes,' he said.

'I will call William before the household is astir, and then if all is well with the children, and there is no need for me to stay, I will return to the creek.'

'And then?'

'Well, I do not know. That is for you to say. It is unwise to plan. Planning so often goes astray.'

'We will make a pretence of planning,' he said, 'we will make a pretence that you come back to breakfast with me, and afterwards we take the boat and go down the river, and you shall fish again, but this time perhaps more successfully than the last.'

'We will catch many fish?'

'That we will not decide to-night. We will leave that until the moment comes.'

'And when we have done with fishing,' she went on, 'we will swim. At noon, when the sun is hottest upon the water. And afterwards, we will eat, and then sleep on our backs on a little beach. And the heron will come down to feed with the turn of the tide, so that you can draw him again.'

'No, I shall not draw the heron,' he said, 'it is time I made another drawing of the cabin-boy of *La Mouette*.'

'And so another day,' she said, 'and another, and another. And no past and no future, only the present.'

'But to-day,' he said, 'is the longest day. To-day is midsummer. Have you forgotten that?'

'No,' she said. 'No, I have not forgotten.'

And somewhere, she thought, before she slept, somewhere there is another Dona, lying in that great canopied bed in London, restless and lonely and knowing nothing of this night beside the creek, or of *La Mouette* at anchor there in the pool, or of his back against mine here in the darkness. She belongs to yesterday. She has no part in this. And somewhere too there is a Dona of to-morrow, a Dona of the future, of ten years away, to whom all this will be a thing to cherish, a thing to remember. Much will be forgotten then, perhaps, the sound of the tide on the mud-flats, the dark sky, the dark water, the shiver of the trees behind us and the shadows they cast before them, and the smell of the young bracken and the moss. Even the things we said will be forgotten, the touch of hands, the warmth, the loveliness, but never the peace that we have given to each other, never the stillness and the silence.

When she woke there was a grey light upon the trees and a mist upon the water, and the two swans were coming back up the creek like ghosts of the morning. The ashes of the fire were white as dust. She looked at him beside her, as he lay sleeping, and she wondered why it was that men seemed children when they slept. All lines were smoothed away, all knowledge too, they became again the small boys they had been long ago. She shivered a little in the first chill of the day, and then, throwing aside the blanket, she stood with bare feet upon the ashes of the fire, and watched the swans disappear into the mist.

Then she leaned down for her cloak, and wrapped it about her, and turned away from the quay towards the trees, and the narrow twisting path that would bring her to Navron.

She tried to pick up the threads of her normal life. The children in their beds. James in his cot, with face flushed and fists clenched; Henrietta lying upon her pillow; Prue, with open mouth, sleeping beside them. While William, faithful William, kept watch upon the house, and lied for her sake and his master's.

Soon the mist would clear, and the sun would come up over the trees beyond the river, and even now, as she came out of the woods and stood upon the lawn, the morning light laid a finger upon Navron, as it slept, still and shuttered, while she stood there watching it. She crept across the lawn, silver with dew, and tried the door. It was locked, of course. She waited a moment, and then went round to the courtyard behind the house, for William's window looked upon it, and it might be that she could make him hear, if she called softly. She listened beneath his window. It was open, and the curtain was not drawn.

'William?' she said softly. 'William, are you there?'

There was no answer, and stooping, she picked up a little pebble and threw it against the pane. In a moment his face appeared, and he stared at her as though she were a phantom, and then he put his finger to his lips and disappeared. She waited, anxiety in her heart, for his face was white and haggard, the face of a man who had not slept. James is ill, she thought, James is dead. He is going to tell me that James is dead. Then she heard him draw the bolts gently in the great door, and the door itself open a small space to admit her. 'The children,' she said, laying her hand on his sleeve, 'the children, are they ill?' He shook his head, still motioning her to silence, glancing over his shoulder to the stairway in the hall.

She entered the house, looking about her as she did so, and then, her heart leaping in sudden understanding, she saw the great-coat on the chair, the riding-whip, the usual disorder of arrival, and there was a hat flung carelessly upon the stone floor, and a second riding-whip, and a thick plaided rug.

'Sir Harry has come, my lady,' said William. 'He came just before sundown, he had ridden from London. And Lord Rockingham is with him.' She said nothing. She went on staring at the great-coat on the chair. And suddenly, from above, she heard the shrill yapping of a little spaniel dog.

Chapter Sixteen

Once again William glanced up the stairway, his small eyes gleaming in his pale face, but Dona shook her head silently, and crossing the hall on tip-toe she led the way into the salon. William lit two candles, and then stood before her, waiting for her to speak.

'What reason did he give?' she said. 'Why have they come?'

'I gather that Sir Harry was becoming restless in London without you, my lady,' said William, 'and a word from Lord Rockingham decided him. It seems that his lordship met a relative of Lord Godolphin's at Whitehall, who told him that Sir Harry's presence in Cornwall was urgently needed at the present time. That is all I could discover from their conversation at supper, my lady.'

'Yes,' said Dona, as though she had not heard him. 'Yes, it would be Rockingham. Harry is too lazy to come without persuasion.'

William stood motionless before her, the candle in his hand.

'What did you tell Sir Harry?' she asked. 'How did you keep him from my room?'

For the first time a trace of a smile appeared on William's face, and he looked at his mistress with understanding.

'Sir Harry would not have passed into your room, my lady,' he said, 'he must have slain me first. I explained to the gentlemen, as soon as they had dismounted, that you had been in bed for several days with a high fever, that at last you were obtaining some measure of sleep, and that it would be extremely prejudicial to your health if Sir Harry as much as ventured into the room. Absolute quiet was essential.'

'And he accepted your story?'

'Like a lamb, my lady. He swore a trifle at first, and cursed me for not having sent for him, but I explained that it was your ladyship's strict orders that he was not to be told. And then Miss Henrietta and Master James came running to meet Sir Harry, telling the same tale, that your ladyship was poorly and confined to your bed, and Prue of course came too, with a woebegone face, saying that your ladyship would not even admit her to tend upon you. So after having played with the children and supped, and taken a turn round the gardens, my lady, Sir Harry and Lord Rockingham retired. Sir Harry is in the blue room, my lady.'

Dona smiled at him, and put her hand on his arm.

'Faithful-one,' she said, 'and then you did not sleep yourself for thinking of the morning that was to come. And supposing I had not returned?'

'No doubt I would have arrived at some decision, my lady, although the problem was a little hard.'

'And my Lord Rockingham? What did he say to all this?'

'His lordship appeared disappointed, my lady, that you were not down to receive them, but he said very little. It seemed to interest him when Prue told Sir Harry that no one was looking after you but myself. I observed that his lordship looked upon me with curiosity, my lady, and if I might venture to say so, with new eyes.'

'He would, William, Lord Rockingham has that sort of mind. He is a person to watch for he has a long nose like a terrier dog.'

'Yes, my lady.'

'It is strange, William, what fatality lies in the making of plans. I thought to breakfast with your master in the creek, and to fish with him, and to swim, and to cook our supper under the stars again as we did last night, and now that is finished and done with.'

'But not for long, my lady.'

'That we cannot tell. At all costs word must be sent to *La Mouette*, and she must leave the creek with the next tide.'

'It would be more prudent to wait until night-fall, my lady.'

'Your master will decide of course. Ah, William.'

'My lady?'

But she shook her head, shrugging her shoulders, telling him with her eyes the things that she could never say in speech, and suddenly he bent down, patting her shoulder as though she were Henrietta, his funny button mouth twisted.

'I know, my lady,' he said, 'but it will come all right. You will be together again,' and then because of the anti-climax of home-coming, because she was tired, because he patted her shoulder in his kind ridiculous way, she felt the tears running down her cheeks, and she could not stop them. 'Forgive me, William,' she said.

'My lady.'

'So foolish, so unutterably foolish and weak. It is something to do with having been so happy.'

'I know, my lady.'

'Because we were happy, William. And there was the sun, and the wind, and the sea, and – loveliness such as has never been.'

'I can imagine it, my lady.'

'It does not happen often, does it.'

'Once in a million years, my lady.'

'Therefore I will shed no more tears, like a spoilt child. For whatever happens we have had what we have had. No one can take that from us. And I have been alive, who was never alive before. Now, William, I shall go to my room, and undress, and get into bed. And later in the morning you shall call me, with my breakfast, and when I am sufficiently prepared for the ordeal, I will see Sir Harry, and find out how long he intends to stay.'

'Very good, my lady.'

'And somehow, in some way, word must be sent to your master in the creek.'

'Yes, my lady.'

And so, with the daylight coming through the chinks in the shutters, they left the room, and Dona, her shoes in her hands and her cloak about her shoulders, crept up the stairway she had descended some five days earlier, and it seemed to her that a year and a life-time had passed since then. She listened for a moment outside Harry's room, and yes, there were the familiar snuffling snores of Duke and Duchess, the spaniels, and the heavy slow breathing of Harry himself. Those things, she thought, were part of the pattern that irritated me once, that drove me to absurdities, and now they no longer have any power to touch me, for they are not of my world now, I have escaped.

She went to her own room, and closed the door. It smelt cool and sweet, for the window was open on to the garden, and William had put lilies-of-the-valley beside her bed. She pulled aside the curtains and undressed, and lay down with her hands over her eyes, and now, she thought, now he is waking beside the creek, putting out his hand for me beside him and finding me gone, and then he remembers and smiles, and stretches, and yawns, and watches the sun come up over the trees. And later he will get up and sniff the day, as I have seen him do, whistling under his breath, scratching his left ear, and then walk down to the creek and swim. He will call up to the men on *La Mouette*, as they scrub the decks, and one of them will lower the rope ladder for him to climb, and another launch a dinghy to bring back the little boat and the supper things and the blankets. Then he will go to the cabin, and rub himself dry with a towel, glancing out of the port-hole on to the water as he does so, and presently, when he has dressed, Pierre Blanc will bring breakfast, and he will wait a little, but then because he will be hungry he will eat it without me. Later he will come up on deck and watch the path through the trees. She could see him fill his pipe, and lean against the poop rail, looking down into the water, and perhaps the swans would come back, and he would throw bread to them, idle, contented, filled with

a warm laziness after his morning swim, thinking perhaps of the day's
fishing to come, and the hot sun, and the sea. She knew how he would glance
up towards her, if she came through the trees down to the creek, and how
he would smile, saying nothing, never moving from the rail on the deck,
throwing the bread down to the swans as though he did not see her. And
what is the use, thought Dona, of going over this in my mind, for all that
is finished, and done with, and will not happen again, for the ship must sail
before she is discovered. And here am I, lying on my bed at Navron, and
there is he, down in the creek, and we are not together any more, and this
then, that I am feeling now, is the hell that comes with love, the hell and
the damnation and the agony beyond all enduring, because after the beauty
and the loveliness comes the sorrow and the pain. So she lay on her back,
her arms across her eyes, never sleeping, and the sun came up and streamed
into the room.

It was after nine o'clock that William came in with her breakfast, and put
the tray down on the table beside her bed, and 'Are you rested, my lady?'
he asked. 'Yes, William,' she lied, breaking off a grape from the bunch he
had brought her.

'The gentlemen are below breakfasting, my lady,' he told her. 'Sir Harry
bade me enquire whether you were sufficiently recovered for him to see you.'

'Yes, I shall have to see him, William.'

'If I might suggest it, my lady, it would be prudent to draw the curtains
a trifle, so that your face is in shadow. Sir Harry might think it peculiar
that you look so well.'

'Do I look well, William?'

'Suspiciously well, my lady.'

'And yet my head is aching intolerably.'

'From other causes, my lady.'

'And I have shadows beneath my eyes, and I am exceedingly weary.'

'Quite, my lady.'

'I think you had better leave the room, William, before I throw something
at you.'

'Very good, my lady.'

He went away, closing the door softly behind him, and Dona, rising,
washed and then arranged her hair, and after drawing the curtains as he
had suggested, she went back to her bed, and presently she heard the shrill
yapping of the spaniels, and their scratching against the door, followed by
a heavy footstep, and in a moment Harry was in the room, and the dogs
with delighted barking hurled themselves upon her bed.

'Get down, now, will you, you little devils,' he shouted. 'Hi, Duke, hi,
Duchess, can't you see your mistress is ill, come here, will you, you rascals,'
making, as was his wont, more ado than the dogs themselves, and then,
sitting heavily upon the bed in place of them, he brushed away the marks
of their feet with his scented handkerchief, puffing and blowing as he did
so.

'God dammit, it's warm this morning,' he said, 'here I am sweating
through my shirt already, and it's not ten o'clock. How are you, are you

better, where did you get this confounded fever? Have you a kiss for me?'
He bent over her, the smell of scent strong upon him, and his curled wig
scratched her chin, while his clumsy fingers prodded her cheek. 'You do not
look very ill, my beautiful, even in this light, and here was I expecting to
find you at death's door itself, from what the fellow told me. What sort of
a servant is he, anyway? I'll dismiss him if you don't like him, you know.'

'William is a treasure,' she said, 'the best servant I have ever had.'

'Ah, well, as long as he pleases you, that's all that matters. So you've been
ill, have you? You should never have left London. London always suits you.
Although I admit it's been damned dull without you. Not a play worth
seeing, and I nearly lost a fortune at piquet the other night. The King has
a new mistress, they tell me, but I haven't seen her yet. Some actress or
other. Rockingham's here, you know, and all agog to see you. God dammit,
he said to me, in town, let's go down to Navron and see what Dona is up
to, and here we are, and you a confounded invalid in bed.'

'I am much better, Harry. It was only a passing thing.'

'Well, I'm glad to hear that. As I say, you look well enough. You have
a tan on you, haven't you? You're as dark as a gypsy.'

'The illness must have made me yellow.'

'And your eyes are larger than ever they were, dammit.'

'The result of the fever, Harry.'

'Queer sort of fever. Must be something to do with the climate down here.
Would you like the dogs up on your bed?'

'No, I think not.'

'Hi, Duke, give your mistress a kiss, and then get down. Here Duchess,
here's your mistress. Duchess has a sore patch on her back, and she's nearly
scratched herself raw, look at that now, what would you do to her? I've
rubbed in some pomade, but it does her no good. I've bought a new horse,
by-the-way, she's down there in the stable. A chestnut, with a deuce of a
temper, but she covers the ground quick enough. "I'll give you a thousand
for her," says Rockingham, and "Make it five thousand," I tell him, "and
I might bite," but he won't play. So the county's infested with pirates, is it,
and robbery, rape and violence causing havoc amongst people?'

'Where did you hear that?'

'Well, Rockingham brought back a story in town one day. Met a cousin
of George Godolphin's. How is Godolphin?'

'A little out of temper when I last saw him.'

'So I should think. He sent me a letter a while back, which I forgot to
answer. And now his brother-in-law has lost a ship, it seems. Do you know
Philip Rashleigh?'

'Not to speak to, Harry.'

'Well, you'll meet him soon. I invited him over here. We met him in
Helston yesterday. He was in a devil of a temper, and so was Eustick, who
was with him. It seems this infernal Frenchman sailed the vessel straight
out of Fowey harbour, right under the nose of Rashleigh and Godolphin.
What infernal impudence, eh? And then off to the French coast, of course,

with not a damned ship in pursuit. God knows what the vessel was worth, she was just home from the Indies.'

'Why did you invite Philip Rashleigh here?'

'Well, it was Rockingham's idea really. "Let's take a hand in the game," he said to me, "you're an authority, you know, in this part of the world. And we might have some sport out of it." "Sport?" says Rashleigh, "you'd think it sport no doubt if you'd lost a fortune like I've done." "Ah," says Rockingham, "you're all asleep down here. We'll catch the fellow for you, and then you'll have sport enough." So we'll hold a meeting, I thought, and collect Godolphin and one or two others, and set a trap for the Frenchman, and when we've caught him we'll string him up somewhere, and give you a laugh.'

'So you think you'll succeed, Harry, where others have failed?'

'Oh, Rockingham will think of something. He's the fellow to tackle the job. I know I'm no damn use, I haven't got a brain in my head, thank God. Here, Dona, when are you going to get up?'

'When you have left the room.'

'Still aloof, eh, and keeping yourself to yourself? I don't get much fun out of my wife, do I, Duke? Hi, then, fetch a slipper, where is it, boy, go seek, go find,' and throwing Dona's shoe across the room he sent the dogs after it, and they fought for it, yapping and scratching, and returning, hurled themselves upon the bed.

'All right then, we'll go, we're not wanted, dogs, we're in the way. I'll go and tell Rockingham you're getting up, he'll be as pleased as a cat with two tails. I'll send the children to you, shall I?'

And he stamped out of the room, singing loudly, the dogs barking at his heels.

So Philip Rashleigh had been in Helston yesterday, and Eustick with him. And Godolphin too must have returned by now. She thought of Rashleigh's face as she had seen it last, scarlet with rage and helplessness, and his cry, 'There's a woman aboard, look there,' as he stared up at her from the boat in Fowey Haven, and she, with the sash gone from her head, and her curls blowing loose, had laughed down at him, waving her hand.

He would not recognise her. It would be impossible. For then she was in shirt and breeches, her face and hair streaming with the rain. She got up, and began to dress, her mind still busy with the news that Harry had given her. The thought of Rockingham here at Navron, bent on mischief, was a continual pin-prick of irritation, for Rockingham was no fool. Besides, he belonged to London, to the cobbled streets, and the play-houses, to the over-heated, over-scented atmosphere that was St. James's, and at Navron, her Navron, he was an interloper, a breaker of the peace. The serenity of the place was gone already, she could hear his voice in the garden beneath her window, and Harry's too, they were laughing together, throwing stones for the dogs. No, it was done with and finished. Escape was a thing of yesterday. And *La Mouette* might never have returned after all. The ship might still have lain becalmed and quiet off the coast of France, while her crew took the *Merry Fortune* into port. The breakers on the white still beach, the green sea golden under the sun, the water cold and clean on her naked body, and after swimming, the warmth of the dry deck under her back, as she looked up at the tall, raffish spars of *La Mouette* stabbing the sky.

Then there were knockings on the door, and the children came in, Henrietta with a new doll that Harry had brought her, and James stuffing a rabbit into his mouth, and they flung themselves upon her with small hot hands and generous kisses, Prue curtsying in the background with anxious enquiries for her health, and somewhere, thought Dona, as she held them to her, somewhere there is a woman who cares for none of these things, but lies upon the deck of a ship and laughs with her lover, and the taste of salt is on their lips, and the warmth of the sun and the sea. 'My doll is nicer than James's rabbit,' said Henrietta, and James, jigging up and down on Dona's knee, his fat cheek pressed against hers, shouted 'No, no, mine, mine,' and taking his rabbit from his mouth hurled it in his sister's face. So then there were tears, and scoldings, and reconciliations, and more kisses, and a finding of chocolate, and much fuss and chatter, and the ship was no more, and the sea was no more, but Lady St. Columb of Navron, with her hair dressed high off her forehead, and clad in a soft blue gown, descended the stairs to the garden below, a child in either hand.

'So you have had a fever, Dona?' said Rockingham, advancing towards her, and kissing the hand she gave him. 'At all events,' he added, drawing back to look at her, 'it was a most becoming fever.'

'That's what I say,' said Harry. 'I told her so upstairs, she's got a tan on her like a gypsy,' and bending down he seized the children, bearing them high on his shoulder, and they screamed delightedly, the dogs joining in the clamour.

Dona sat down on the seat on the terrace, and Rockingham, standing before her, played with the lace at his wrists.

'You don't appear very delighted to see me,' he said.

'Why should I?' she answered.

'It's some weeks since I saw you,' he said, 'and you went off in such an extraordinary way, after the escapade at Hampton Court. I suppose I did something to offend you.'

'You did nothing,' she said.

He looked at her out of the corners of his eyes, and shrugged his shoulders. 'What have you been doing with yourself down here?' he asked. Dona yawned, watching Harry and the children as they played on the lawn with the dogs. 'I have been very happy,' she said, 'alone here, with the children. I told Harry, when I left London, that I wanted to be alone. I am angry with both of you for breaking my peace.'

'We have not come entirely for pleasure,' said Rockingham, 'we are here on business as well. We propose catching the pirate who seems to be giving you all so much trouble.'

'And how do you propose doing that?'

'Ah, well . . . we shall see. Harry is quite excited at the idea. He's been getting bored with nothing to do. And London in midsummer stinks too much even for me. The country will do us both good.'

'How long do you propose to stay?'

'Until we have caught the Frenchman.'

Dona laughed, and picking a daisy from the grass, began tearing off the petals. 'He has gone back to France,' she said.

'I think not,' said Rockingham.

'Why so?'

'Because of something that fellow Eustick was saying yesterday.'

'The surly Thomas Eustick? What had he to say?' said Dona.

'Only that a fishing craft from St. Michael's Mount had reported seeing a vessel in the early hours of yesterday morning, making towards the English coast.'

'Slender evidence. Some merchantman returning from abroad.'

'The fisherman thought not.'

'The coast of England goes a long way, my dear Rockingham. From the Land's End to the Wight is a precious stretch to watch.'

'Yes, but the Frenchman leaves the Wight alone. It seems he leaves everything alone, but for this narrow strip of Cornwall. Rashleigh will have it that he has even visited your Helford river here.'

'He must do it by night then, when I am in bed and asleep.'

'Possibly he does. At any rate, he will not dare to do it much longer. It will be vastly amusing to stop his little game. I suppose there are many creeks and inlets round your coast here?'

'No doubt, Harry could tell you better than I.'

'And the country hereabouts is sparsely inhabited. Navron is the only big house in the district I understand.'

'Yes, I suppose it is.'

'How ideal for a law-breaker. I almost wish I were a pirate myself. And if I knew the house was without masculine protection, and that the lady of the manor was as beautiful as you, Dona . . .'

'Yes, Rockingham?'

'If I were a pirate, I repeat, knowing all these things, I should be most tempted to return to the district again and again.'

Dona yawned once more, and threw away the mutilated daisy.

'But you are not a pirate, my dear Rockingham, you are only a grossly spoilt, over-dressed, exceedingly decadent member of the aristocracy, with too great a fondness for women and for alcohol. So shall we leave the subject alone? I am becoming rather bored.'

She got up from the seat, and began to wander towards the house.

'Time was,' he said casually, 'when you were not bored either by me or by my conversation.'

'You flatter yourself.'

'Do you remember a certain evening at Vauxhall?'

'I remember many evenings at Vauxhall, and one in particular, when because I had drunk two glasses of wine and was feeling intolerably sleepy, you had the audacity to kiss me and I was too idle to protest. I disliked you ever afterwards, and myself more so.'

They stopped at the long window, and he gazed at her, a flush on his face. 'What a delightful speech,' he said. 'The Cornish air has made you almost venomous. Or possibly it is the result of the fever.'

'Possibly it is.'

'Were you as churlish as this to the curious-looking manservant who attended you?'

'You had better ask him.'

'I think I shall. If I were Harry I should ask many questions, and all of an extremely personal nature.'

'Who's this, what's this all about?' and Harry himself joined them, flinging himself down in a chair in the salon, wiping his forehead with a lace handkerchief. 'What are you discussing, both of you?'

'We were discussing your manservant,' said Rockingham, with a brilliant smile, 'so strange that Dona would permit no one else to attend her while she was ill.'

'Yes, by heaven, he's a rum-looking devil, and no mistake. Wouldn't trust him too far, if I were you, Dona. What d'you see in the fellow?'

'He is quiet, he is discreet, he walks soundlessly, and nobody else in the house does those things. Therefore I determined I should be nursed by him and by no one else.'

'Extremely pleasant for the manservant,' said Rockingham, polishing his nails.

'Yes, hang it,' blustered Harry, 'Rock's quite right, you know, Dona. The fellow might have taken infernal liberties. It was a damned risky thing to do. You lying weak and helpless in bed, and the fellow creeping about round you. He's not like an old retainer either, I know very little about him.'

'Oh, so he has not been in your service long?' said Rockingham.

'No. Hang it, Rock, we never come to Navron, as you know. And I'm so confounded idle I never know half the time who my servants are. I've a mind to dismiss him.'

'You will do nothing of the kind,' said Dona; 'William shall remain in my service for as long as it pleases me.'

'All right, all right, no need to be tricky about it,' said Harry, picking up Duchess and fondling her, 'but it looks a trifle queer to have the fellow hanging about your bedroom. Here he is anyway, bringing a letter from someone. He looks as if he were sickening for some fever himself.' Dona glanced at the door, and there was William, with a note in his hand, and his face paler than usual, and there was something of strain in his eyes.

'What's this, eh?' said Harry.

'A letter from Lord Godolphin, Sir Harry,' answered William. 'His man has just brought it, and waits for an answer.'

Harry tore open the letter, and then threw it across to Rockingham with a laugh. 'The hounds are gathering, Rock,' he said, 'we shall have some fun out of this.'

Rockingham read the note with a smile, and then tore it into fragments.

'What answer will you give?' he said.

Harry examined the back of his spaniel, pulling aside the dog's coat. 'She has another patch of eczema here, confound it,' he said, 'that pomade I'm trying is no use at all. What d'you say? Oh, yes, an answer for Godolphin. Tell the man, will you, William, that her ladyship and I will be delighted to receive his lordship and the other gentlemen this evening for supper.'

'Very good, sir,' said William.

'And what invitation is this?' asked Dona, patting her curls in the mirror, 'and who shall I be delighted to receive?'

'George Godolphin, Tommy Eustick, Philip Rashleigh, and half-a-dozen others,' said Harry, flinging the dog off his knee, 'and they're going to catch the froggie at last, aren't they, Duchess, and we shall be in at the kill.'

Dona said nothing, and looking back into the room through the mirror she saw that Rockingham was watching her.

'It will be an amusing party, do you not think?' he said.

'I rather doubt it,' said Dona, 'knowing Harry as a host, you will all be under the table by midnight.'

She went out of the room and when she had closed the door she called to William softly, and he came to her at once, his eyes troubled.

'What is it?' she said. 'You are anxious. Lord Godolphin and his friends, they can't do anything, it will be too late, *La Mouette* will have sailed.'

'No, my lady,' said William, 'she will not have sailed. I have been down to the creek to warn my master. And I found the ship had grounded with the morning's tide, a rock piercing her planking under-water. They were working on her when I went to the creek. And she will not be fit to sail for twenty-four hours.'

His eyes wandered from her face, he moved away, and Dona, glancing over her shoulder, saw that the door she had just closed had been opened again, and Rockingham was standing in the entrance, playing with the lace at his wrists.

Chapter Seventeen

The long day dragged to its close. The hands of the stable clock seemed reluctant to move, and the chimes every half-hour had a sombre tone. The afternoon was sultry and grey, with that heavy look about the sky that comes when thunder brews but does not break.

Harry had lain out upon the lawns with a handkerchief over his face, snoring loudly, with his two dogs snuffling by his side, and Rockingham sat with a book open in his hands, the pages of which he seldom turned and when Dona glanced across at him from time to time she would be aware of his gaze upon her, curious and hungry.

He knew nothing, of course, but some uncanny intuition, almost feminine in quality, had observed the change in her, and he was suspicious, suspicious of the weeks she had spent here at Navron, of her familiarity with the manservant William, and of this more than ordinary aloofness toward Harry and himself, which he could swear came not from boredom but from something more vital, more dangerous. She was more silent than of old, she did not chatter, tease, and gibe at Harry as she was wont to do, but sat plucking the stems of grass with her hands, her eyes half-closed, like one who dreams in secret. All this he observed, and she knew that he was watching her, and the tension between them became more marked as the hours passed. It seemed to her that he had the brooding watchfulness of a cat, crouching beneath a tree, and she was the bird, silent amongst the long grass, waiting her chance to escape.

And Harry, oblivious to all atmospheres, slumbered and sighed.

Dona knew that the men would be working on the planking of the ship. She pictured them at low tide, with bare feet, stripped to the waist, the sweat pouring off their backs, and *La Mouette*, with the wound in her hull exposed, heeling slightly, her planking grey with the mud.

He would be working with them, his forehead wrinkled, his lips compressed, with that look of concentration upon his face that she had grown to love and to respect, for the repairing of his ship would be a thing of life and of death even as the landing at Fowey had been, and there would be no time now for idleness, for dreams.

Somehow, before to-night, she must go to the creek, and beg him to sail with the next tide, although *La Mouette* might still be taking in water, for the net was drawing in upon him, and to linger even one night longer must be fatal for him and for his crew.

The ship had been seen drawing towards the coast, so Rockingham had told her, and now nearly twenty-four hours had come and gone, and much might have been achieved in that time by his enemies, much might have been foreseen and planned. There would be watchers perhaps upon the headlands, and spies on the hills and in the woods, and to-night Rashleigh, Godolphin, and Eustick would themselves be seated at Navron, with God knows what purpose in their minds.

'You are thoughtful, Dona,' said Rockingham, and she, looking across at him, saw that he had laid his book aside and was considering her, his head upon one side, his narrow eyes unsmiling. 'It must be the fever that has altered you so,' he continued, 'for in town you were never silent for five minutes at a time.'

'I am getting old,' she said lightly, chewing a stem of grass, 'in a few weeks I shall be thirty.'

'A curious fever,' he said, ignoring her words, 'that leaves the patient with gipsy colouring and eyes so large. You did not see a physician, it seems?'

'I was my own physician.'

'With the advice of the excellent William. What an unusual accent he has, by-the-way. Quite a foreign intonation.'

'All Cornishmen speak likewise.'

'But I understand he is not a Cornishman at all, at least so the groom informed me in the stable this morning.'

'Perhaps he is from Devon then. I have never questioned William about his ancestry.'

'And it seems that the house was entirely empty until you came? The unusual William took the responsibility of Navron upon his shoulders with no other servants to help him.'

'I did not realise you engaged in stable gossip, Rockingham.'

'Did you not, Dona? But it is one of my favourite pastimes. I always learn the latest scandals in town from the servants of my friends. The chatter of back-stairs is invariably true, and so extremely entertaining.'

'And what have you learnt from the back-stairs at Navron?'

'Sufficient, dear Dona, to pique the curiosity.'

'Indeed?'

'Her ladyship, I understand, has a passion for long walks in the heat of the day. She takes a joy, it seems in wearing the oldest clothes, and returning, sometimes, be-splashed with mud and river water.'

'Very true.'

'Her ladyship's appetite is fitful, it appears. Sometimes she will sleep until nearly midday, and then demand her breakfast. Or she will taste nothing from noon until ten o'clock at night, and then, when her servants are abed, the faithful William brings her supper.'

'True again.'

'And then, after having been in the rudest of health, she unaccountably takes to her bed, and shuts her doors upon her household, even upon her children, it seems she suffers from a fever, although no physician is sent for, and once again the unusual William is the only person admitted within her door.'

'And what more, Rockingham?'

'Oh, nothing more, dear Dona. Only that you seem to have recovered very quickly from your fever, and show not the slightest pleasure in seeing your husband or his closest friend.'

There was a sigh, and a yawn, and a stretching of limbs, and Harry threw his handkerchief from his face and scratched his wig.

'God knows that last remark you made was true enough,' he said, 'but then Dona always was an iceberg, Rock, old fellow; I have not been married to her for close on six years without discovering that! Damn these flies! Hi, Duchess, catch a fly. Stop 'em from plaguing your master, can't you?' And sitting up he waved his handkerchief in the air, and the dogs woke up and jumped and yapped, and then the children appeared round the corner of the terrace for their half-hour's romp before bed-time.

It was just after six when a shower sent them indoors, and Harry, still yawning and grumbling about the heat, sat down with Rockingham to play piquet. Three hours and a half yet until supper, and *La Mouette* still at anchor in the creek.

Dona stood by the window, tapping her fingers on the pane, and the summer shower fell heavy and fast. The room was close, smelling already of the dogs, and the scent that Harry sprinkled on his clothes. Now and again he burst into a laugh, gibing at Rockingham for some mistake or other in the game. The hands of the clock crept faster than she wished, making up now for the slowness of the day, and she began to pace up and down the room, unable to control her growing premonition of defeat.

'Our Dona seems restless,' observed Rockingham, glancing up at her from his cards, 'perhaps the mysterious fever has not entirely left her?'

She gave him no answer, pausing once more by the long window.

'Can you beat the knave,' laughed Harry, throwing a card down upon the table, 'or have you lost again? Leave my wife alone, Rock, and attend to the game. Look you there, there's another sovereign gone into my pocket. Come and sit down, Dona, you are worrying the dogs with your infernal pacing up and down.'

'Look over Harry's shoulder, and see if he is cheating,' said Rockingham, 'time was when you could beat the pair of us at piquet.'

Dona glanced down at them, Harry loud and cheerful, already a little flushed with the drink he had taken, oblivious to everything but the game he was playing, and Rockingham humouring him as he was wont to do, but watchful still, like a sleek cat, his narrow eyes turned upon Dona in greed and curiosity.

They were set there though, for another hour at least, she knew Harry well enough for that, and so yawning, and turning from the window, she began to walk towards the door.

'I shall lie down until supper,' she said. 'I have a headache. There must be thunder in the air.'

'Go ahead, Rock, old boy,' said Harry, leaning back in his chair, 'I'll wager you don't hold a heart in your hand. Will you increase your bid? There's a sportsman for you. Fill up my glass, Dona, as you're up. I'm as thirsty as a crow.'

'Don't forget,' said Rockingham smiling, 'that we may have work to do before midnight.'

'No, by the Lord, I have not forgotten. We're going to catch the froggie, aren't we? What are you staring at me for, my beautiful?'

He looked up at his wife, his wig a little askew, his blue eyes filmy in his handsome florid face.

'I was thinking, Harry, that you will probably look like Godolphin in about ten years' time.'

'Were you, damme? Well, and what of it? He's a stout fellow, is George Godolphin, one of my oldest friends. Is that the ace you're holding in front of my face? Now God damn you for a blasted cheat and a robber of innocent men.'

Dona slipped from the room, and going upstairs to her bedroom she shut the door, and then pulled the heavy bell-rope that hung beside the fireplace. A few minutes later someone knocked, and a little maidservant came into the room.

'Will you please send William to me,' said Dona.

'I am sorry, my lady,' said the girl, with a curtsy, 'but William is not in the house. He went out just after five o'clock and he has not returned.'

'Where has he gone?'

'I have no idea, my lady.'

'It does not matter then, thank you.'

The girl left the room, and Dona threw herself down on her bed, her hands behind her head. William must have had the same idea as herself. He had gone to see what progress had been made upon the ship, and to warn his master that his enemies would be supping at Navron this very night. Why did he delay though? He had left the house at five and it was now nearly seven.

She closed her eyes, aware in the stillness of her quiet room that her heart was thumping now as it had done once before, when, standing on the deck of *La Mouette*, she had waited to go ashore in Lantic bay. She remembered the chilled cold feeling she had had, and how, when she had gone below to the cabin, and eaten and drunk a little, the fear and the anxiety left her, and she had been filled with the glow of adventure. To-night though it was different. To-night she was alone, and his hand was not in hers, and his eyes had not spoken to her. She was alone, and must play hostess to his enemies.

She went on lying there on her bed, and outside the rain fell away to a drizzle and ceased, and the birds began to sing, but still William did not come. She got up and went to the door and listened. She could hear the low murmur of the men's voices from the salon, and once Harry laughed and Rockingham too, and then they must have continued with their playing of piquet, for there came only the murmur again, and Harry swearing at one of the dogs for scratching. Dona could wait no longer. She wrapped a cloak around her, and stole downstairs into the great hall on tiptoe, and went out by the side-door into the garden.

The grass was wet after the rain, there was a silver sheen upon it, and there was a warm damp smell in the air like an autumn mist.

The trees dripped in the wood, and the little straggling path that led to the creek was muddied and churned. It was dark in the wood too, for the sun would not return now after the rain, and the heavy green foliage of midsummer made a pall over her head. She came to the point where the path broke off and descended rapidly, and she was about to turn leftwards as usual down the creek when some sound made her pause suddenly, and hesitate, and she waited a moment, her hand touching the low branch of a tree. The sound was that of a twig snapping under a foot, and of someone moving through the bracken. She stood still, never moving, and presently, when all was silent again, she looked over the branch that concealed her, and there, some twenty yards away, a man was standing, with his back to a tree, and a musket in his hands.

She could see the profile under the three-cornered hat, and the face was one she did not recognise, and did not know, but he stood there, waiting, peering down towards the creek.

A heavy rain-drop fell upon him from the tree above, and taking off his hat he wiped his face with his handkerchief, turning his back to her as he did so, and at once she moved away from the place where she had stood, and ran homewards along the path by which she had come. Her hands were chilled, and she drew her cloak more closely about her shoulders, and that, she thought, that is the reason why William has not returned, for either he has been caught and held, or he is hiding in the woods, even as I hid just now. For where there is one man there will be others, and the man I have just seen is not a native of Helford, but belongs to Godolphin, to Rashleigh, or to Eustick. And so there is nothing I can do, she thought, nothing but return to the house, and dress myself, and put on my ear-rings and my pendants and my bracelets, and descend to the dining-hall with a smile on my lips, and sit at the head of the table with Godolphin on my right and Rashleigh on my left, while their men keep a watch here in the woods.

She sped back along the path to the house, the rain-drops falling from the clustered trees, and the blackbirds were silent now, and the evening curiously still.

When she came to the clearing in the trees in front of the green lawns, and looked towards the house, she saw that the long window of the salon was open on to the terrace, and Rockingham was standing there gazing up into the sky, while the dogs, Duke and Duchess, pattered at his heels. Dona drew back under cover, and then one of the dogs, snuffling at the lawn, came upon her footprints in the wet grass, and followed them, wagging his tail. She saw Rockingham watch the dog, and then he glanced up at the window above his head, and after a moment or two he advanced cautiously, stepping to the edge of the lawn and looking down upon the tell-tale footprints where they crossed the grass and disappeared amongst the trees.

Dona slipped back into the woods, and she heard Rockingham call the dog softly by her name, 'Duchess . . . Duchess,' and a little to the left of her she could hear the dog nosing amongst the bracken. She turned now amongst the trees, making her way towards the drive which would bring her back to the front of the house, and to the courtyard, and Duchess must have followed her track through the wood towards the creek, for Dona could hear her no longer, and she came to the courtyard without discovery.

She let herself into the house through the great door, and luckily the dining-hall was still in shadow, the candles not being lit, for at the farther side a maid-servant was carrying plates and piling them on a side-table, while Harry's man from London assisted her. And still no sign of William.

Dona waited in the shadows, and after a moment the servants withdrew through the opposite door to the kitchens at the back, and swiftly she climbed the stairs and so along the passage to her bedroom.

'Who's that?' called Harry from his room. She did not answer, but slipped into her room, shutting the door, and in a few moments she heard his footsteps outside her door, and only just in time she flung her cloak aside and lay down on her bed, throwing her coverlet over her knees, for he burst in without knocking, as was his custom, clad only in his shirt and breeches.

'Where the devil has that fellow William gone to?' he said. 'He has the key of the cellar hidden somewhere, and Thomas came to me about the wine. He tells me William is nowhere to be found.'

Dona lay still, her eyes shut, and then she turned on her side and looked up at Harry yawning, as though he had woken her from sleep.

'How should I know where William is?' she said. 'Perhaps he is chatting with the grooms in the stables. Why don't they search for him?'

'They have searched,' fumed Harry; 'the fellow has simply disappeared, and here we are with George Godolphin and the rest coming to supper and no wine. I tell you, Dona, I won't stand for it. I shall sack him, you know.'

'He will come back directly,' said Dona wearily, 'there is plenty of time.'

'Confounded impudence,' said Harry, 'that's what happens to a servant when there's no man about the place. You have let him do exactly as he pleases.'

'On the contrary, he does exactly what pleases me.'

'Well, I don't like it, I tell you. Rock's quite right. The fellow has a familiar impudent manner about him. Rock's always right about these things.' He stood in the middle of the room, looking moodily down at Dona, his face flushed, his blue eyes choleric, and she recognised at once his usual manner when a little drunk, and that in a moment or two he would become abusive.

'Did you win at piquet?' asked Dona, seeking to distract him, and he shrugged his shoulders, and walked over to the mirror and stared at himself, smoothing the pouches under his eyes with his fingers. 'Do I ever win for ten minutes at a time playing with Rock?' he grumbled. 'No, it always ends with my losing twenty or thirty sovereigns, which I can ill afford. Look here, Dona, am I going to be allowed in here to-night?'

'I thought you were to be employed in catching pirates.'

'Oh, that will be over by midnight, or soon afterwards. If the fellow's in hiding on the river somewhere, as Godolphin and Eustick seem to think, he won't stand a dog's chance. There are men to be posted everywhere from here to the headland, and on either side of the river to boot. He won't slip away from the net this time.'

'And what part do you propose to take yourself?'

'Oh, I shall be a looker-on, and come in at the kill. And we'll all have a drink, and have no end of fun. But you haven't answered my question, Dona.'

'Shall we leave it until the time comes? Knowing what you are usually like after midnight you won't be caring very much if you lie down in my room or under the dining-table.'

'That's only because you're always so damned hard on me, Dona. I tell you it's a bit thick, this business of you running off here to Navron and leaving me to kick my heels in town, and then catching some Tom-fool fever when I do come after you.'

'Shut the door, Harry. I want to sleep.'

'Sleep my foot. You're always wanting to sleep. It's been your answer to me under every circumstance now for God knows how long,' and he stamped out of the room, banging the door, and she heard him stand a moment on the staircase and bawl out to the servant below whether that scoundrel William had returned.

And Dona, getting up from her bed and looking out of the window, saw Rockingham come back across the lawn, with the little dog Duchess pattering at his heels.

She began to dress, slowly and with great care, curling her dark ringlets round her fingers and placing them behind her ears, and into the ears themselves she screwed the rubies and round her neck she clasped the ruby pendant. For Dona St. Columb in her cream satin gown, with her ringlets and her jewels, must bear no resemblance to that bedraggled cabin-boy of *La Mouette*, who with the rain streaming down his thin shirt, had stood beneath Philip Rashleigh's window only five days ago. She looked at herself in the mirror, and then up at the portrait on the wall, and she saw how she had changed, even in the short while she had been at Navron, for her face had filled out, and the sulky look had gone from her mouth, and there was something different about her eyes, as Rockingham had said. As for her gypsy tan, there was no concealing it, and her hands and throat were burnt too by the sun. Who in the world will believe, she thought of herself, that this is the result of a fever, that the sunburn is a jaundice – Harry perhaps, he has so little imagination, but Rockingham, never.

Presently she heard the jangle of the stable bell in the courtyard, and this was the first of the guests arriving, his carriage driving to the steps. Then, after a few minutes' grace, the clatter of horses' hoofs, and once again the jangle of the bell, and now she could hear the sound of voices come from the dining-hall below, and Harry's voice booming out above the others, and the barking of Duke and Duchess. It was nearly dark, the garden was in shadow outside her window, and the trees were still. Down there in the woods, she thought, that sentinel is standing, peering down towards the creek, and perhaps he has been joined now by others, and they are all waiting there, with their backs to the trees, in silence, until we have finished our supper here in the house, and Eustick looks across at Godolphin, and Godolphin at Harry, and Harry at Rockingham, and then they will push back their chairs and smile at one another, and fingering their swords, go down into the woods. And if this were a hundred years ago, she thought, I would be prepared for this, and there would be sleeping draughts to put in their wine, or I would have sold myself to the devil and placed them under a spell, but it is not a hundred years ago, it is my own time, and such things do not happen any more, and all I can do is to sit at the table and smile upon them, and encourage them to drink.

She opened the door, and the sound of voices rose from the dining-hall. There were the pompous tones of Godolphin, and that scratchy querulous cough of Philip Rashleigh, and a question from Rockingham, silken and smooth. She turned along the corridor to the children's room before descending, and kissed them as they slept, pulling aside the curtain so that the cool night air should come to them from the open casement, and then, as she walked once more to the head of the stairs, she heard a sound behind her, slow and dragging, as though someone uncertain of his way in the darkness, shuffled in the passage.

'Who is there?' she whispered, and there was no answer. She waited a moment, a chill of fear upon her, while the loud voices of the guests came from below, and then once again there was the dragging shuffling sound in the dark passage, and a faint whisper, and a sigh.

She brought a candle from the children's room, and holding it high above her head, looked down into the long corridor whence the sound had come, and there, half-crouching, half-lying against the wall, was William, his face ashen pale, his left-arm hanging useless at his side. She knelt down beside him, but he pushed her back, his small button mouth twisted with pain. 'Don't touch me, my lady,' he whispered, 'you will soil your gown, there is blood on my sleeve.'

'William, dear William, are you badly hurt?' she said, and he shook his head, his right hand clasping his shoulder.

'It is nothing, my lady,' he said, 'only somewhat unfortunate . . . to-night of all nights.' And he closed his eyes, weak with pain, and she knew he was lying to her.

'How did it happen?' she asked.

'Coming back through the woods, my lady,' he said, 'I saw one of Lord Godolphin's men, and he challenged me. I managed to evade him, but received this scratch.'

'You shall come to my room, and I will bathe your wound, and bind it for you,' she whispered, and because he was barely conscious now, he protested no longer, but suffered her to lead him along the passage to her room, and once there she closed the door and bolted it, and helped him to her bed. Then she brought water and a towel, and in some fashion cleansed the cut in his shoulder, and bound it for him, and he turned his eyes up to her and said, 'My lady, you should not do this for me,' and 'Lie still,' she whispered, 'lie still and rest.'

His face was deadly white still, and she, knowing little of the depth of the wound or what she could do to ease his pain, felt helpless suddenly, and despairing, and he must have sensed it for he said 'Do not worry, my lady, I shall be all right. And at least my mission was successful, I went to *La Mouette* and saw my master.'

'You told him?' she asked. 'You told him that Godolphin, and Eustick, and the others were supping here to-night?'

'Yes, my lady, and he smiled in that way of his, my lady, and he said to me, "Tell your mistress I am in no way disturbed, and that *La Mouette* has need of a cabin-boy".' As William spoke there was a footstep outside, and someone knocked at the door. 'Who is there?' called Dona, and the voice of the little maidservant answered, 'Sir Harry sends word to your ladyship, that he and the gentlemen are awaiting supper.'

'Tell Sir Harry to start, I will be with them directly,' said Dona, and bending down again to William she whispered, 'And the ship herself, is all well with the ship, and will she sail to-night?' But he stared back at her now without recognition, and then closed his eyes, and she saw that he had fainted.

She covered him with her blankets, scarcely knowing what she did, and washed the blood from her hands in the water, and then, glancing in the mirror and seeing that the colour had drained away from her face too, she dabbed rouge high on her cheek-bones with unsteady fingers. Then she left her room, leaving William unconscious on her bed, and walking down the stairs into the dining-hall she heard the scraping of the chairs on the stone floor as the guests rose to their feet and waited for her. She held her head high in the air, and there was a smile on her lips, but she saw nothing, not the blaze of the candles, nor the long tables piled with dishes, nor Godolphin in his plum-coloured coat, nor Rashleigh with his grey wig, nor Eustick fingering his sword, nor all the eyes of the men who stared at her and bowed low as she passed to her seat at the head of the table, but only one man, who stood on the deck of his ship in the silent creek, saying farewell to her in thought as he waited for the tide.

Chapter Eighteen

So, for the first time for many years, there was a banquet in the great dining-hall of Navron House. The candles shone down upon the guests as they sat shoulder to shoulder, six a side, at the long table, and the table itself was splendid with silver and rose-bordered plate and large bowls piled high with fruit. At one end the host, blue-eyed and flushed, his blond wig a little askew, laughed a shade too loudly and too long at every jest that passed. At the other end the hostess toyed with the dishes set before her, cool, unperturbed, throwing glances now and again at the guests beside her as though he on her right hand and he on her left were the only men who mattered in the world, she was theirs for this evening, or longer if so desired. Never before, thought Harry St. Columb, kicking at one of the dogs under the table, never before had Dona flirted so blatantly, made eyes so outrageously. If this was the result of that confounded fever, God help all the fellows present. Never before, thought Rockingham, watching her across the table, never before had Dona looked so provocative; what was passing through her head that moment, and why had she walked through the woods towards the river at seven o'clock that evening, when he thought her asleep in her bed?

And this, thought every guest who sat at her table, this is the famous Lady St. Columb, of whom, from time to time, we hear so much gossip, so much scandal; who sups in London taverns with the ladies of the town, who rides bareback in the streets at midnight in her husband's breeches, who has given something of herself, no doubt, to every philanderer at St. James's, not to mention His Majesty himself.

So at first the guests were suspicious, inarticulate, and shy, but when she talked, and looked across at them with a word and a smile, and asked them about their homes, their hobbies and pursuits, and who was married and who was not, and gave them, in turn, to understand that every word they uttered had importance to her, had charm, and that given the opportunity she would understand them as they had never been understood before, then they relaxed, then they melted, and to hell, thought young Penrose, with all the people who have maligned her, the jealous chit-chat of plain women of course, and God's truth, what a wife to have and to keep, thought Eustick, under lock and key, and never let out of your sight. There was Tremayne from beyond Probus, and red-wigged Carnethick who owned all the land on the west coast, and the first had no wife and no mistress and so watched her dumbly, in sulky adoration, and the second had a wife ten years older than himself, and wondered, when Dona flashed him a glance across the table, whether there was any possibility of seeing her alone, later, when supper was over. Even Godolphin, the pompous Godolphin with his protruding eyes and his bulbous nose, admitted to himself, somewhat grudgingly, that Harry's wife had charm, although of course he did not approve of her and never would, and somehow he could not see Lucy taking to her as a companion, there was something bold about her eyes that made him feel uncomfortable. Philip Rashleigh, always taciturn with women, always gruff and silent, suddenly began to tell her about his boyhood, and how fond he had been of his mother, who had died when he was ten.

'And it's now nearly eleven o'clock,' thought Dona, 'and we are still eating, and drinking, and talking, and if I can go on like this, even for a little longer, it will give him time down there in the creek, for the tide must be making all the while, and no matter whether *La Mouette* has a gap in her hull or not, what repairs they have done to her must hold, and the ship must sail.'

She signalled with her eyes to the servants waiting, the glasses were filled once more, and while the hum and chatter of voices rang in her ear, and she glanced at her left-hand neighbour with a smile, she wondered if William had woken from his faint, or if he still lay upon her bed, ashen pale, with his eyes closed and that dark red stain on his shoulder. 'We should have music,' said Harry, his eyes half-closed, 'we should have music like my grandfather used to, up there in the gallery you know, when the old Queen was still alive, damn it, why does nobody have minstrels nowadays? I suppose the confounded Puritans killed 'em all.' He is well away, thought Dona, watching him, knowing the signs, he will give little trouble this evening. 'I consider that sort of foolery better dead,' said Eustick frowning, the gibe at the Puritans pricking him, for his father had fought for Parliament.

'Is there much dancing then at Court?' questioned young Tremayne, flushing all over his face, looking up at her eagerly. 'Why, yes,' she answered him, 'you should come to town you know, when Harry and I return, I will find a wife for you.' But he shook his head, stammering a refusal, a dog-like appeal in his eyes. 'James will be his age in twenty years' time,' she thought, 'creeping into my room at three in the morning to tell me of his latest scrape, and all this will be forgotten, and put aside, and perhaps I shall remember it suddenly, seeing James's eyes and his eager face, and I shall tell him how I kept twelve men at supper until nearly midnight, so that the only man I have ever loved should escape to France and out of my life for ever.'

What was Rockingham saying, out of the corner of his mouth to Harry? 'Yes, by thunder,' called Harry down the table, 'that rascal of a servant of yours has never come back, do you know that, Dona?' And he thumped the table with his fist, the glasses shaking, and Godolphin frowned, for he had spilt his wine down his lace cravat. 'I know,' smiled Dona, 'but it has made no difference, we have done very well without him.'

'What would you do, George,' shouted Harry, determined to air his grievance, 'with a servant who takes the night off when his master has guests for supper?'

'Dismiss him, naturally, my dear Harry,' said Godolphin.

'Thrash him into the bargain,' added Eustick.

'Yes, but that's all very well,' said Harry, hiccoughing, 'the blasted fellow is a pet of Dona's. When she was ill he was in and out of her bedroom all hours of the day and night. Would you put up with that, George? Does your wife have a manservant hanging about her bedroom, eh?'

'Certainly not,' replied Godolphin. 'Lady Godolphin is in a very delicate state of health at the moment, and can't abide anyone but her old nurse with her, excepting of course myself.'

'How charming,' said Rockingham, 'how rural and touching. Lady St. Columb, on the contrary, seems to have no women servants about her at all,' and he smiled across at Dona, raising his glass, and, 'How did you enjoy your walk, Dona,' he said, 'did you find it wet there in the woods?'

Dona did not answer. Godolphin looked upon her with suspicion, for really if Harry permitted his wife to dally with servants, he would soon be the talk of the countryside, and now he came to think of it he remembered an impertinent scrap of a groom driving the carriage the day Harry's wife had taken tea with them. 'How is your wife bearing with the heat?' Dona enquired. 'I think of her so often,' but she did not hear his reply, for Philip Rashleigh was talking in her left ear. 'I swear I have seen you before, dear lady,' he was saying, 'but I cannot for the life of me recollect the time or the place.'

And he stared at his plate, wrinkling his brows, as though by force of concentration he would bring back the scene.

'Some more wine for Mr. Rashleigh,' said Dona, smiling graciously, pushing his glass towards him. 'Yes, I also feel that we have met, but it must have been six years ago, when I came here as a bride.'

'No, I'll take my oath on that,' said Rashleigh, shaking his head. 'It is an inflection in your voice, I believe, and I have heard it not so long ago either.'

'But Dona has that effect on every man,' said Rockingham; 'they always feel, after seeing her, that they have known her before. You will find, my dear Rashleigh, that it will keep you awake at night.'

'I gather you speak from experience?' said Carnethick, and they exchanged glances, and Rockingham smiled, adjusting the lace at his wrists.

'How I detest him,' thought Dona; 'those narrow cat-like eyes, that meaning smile. He would like every man at this table to believe he makes love to me.'

'Were you ever in Fowey?' asked Philip Rashleigh.

'Never, to my certain knowledge,' she answered, and he drank down his wine, still shaking his head doubtfully.

'You have heard how I was robbed?' he said.

'Yes, indeed,' she answered, 'so very distressing for you. And you have never had news of your ship since?'

'Never a word,' he said bitterly. 'Ah, she's snug in a French port by now, with no legal means of extracting her. That's what comes of having a Court packed with foreigners, and a King who speaks better French, by all accounts, than he does English. However, I hope to settle accounts to-night, once and for all.'

Dona glanced up at the clock above the stairs. It wanted twenty minutes to midnight. 'And you, my lord,' she said, smiling upon Godolphin, 'were you also involved in the loss of Mr. Rashleigh's ship?'

'I was, madam,' he replied stiffly.

'But I trust you received no hurt?'

'Luckily none. The rascals were too glad to show us their heels. Like every Frenchman, they preferred to run for it rather than face up to an honest fight.'

'And was their leader really the desperate man you have led me to believe?'

'Twenty times worse, madam. The most impudent, bloodthirsty, evil-looking rogue I've ever clapped eyes upon. We have heard since that his own ship carries a full complement of women, on every voyage, and most of them, poor wretches, kidnapped from our villages. Needless to say, I have told nothing of this to my wife.'

'Naturally not, it might precipitate matters unduly,' murmured Dona.

'He had a woman aboard the *Merry Fortune*,' said Philip Rashleigh. 'I could see her there on the deck above me, as plain as I see you now. A bold-faced baggage if ever there was one, with a cut on her chin, and her hair all over her eyes. Some harlot from the French docks, no doubt.'

'And there was a boy,' added Godolphin, 'a wretched scrap of a boy who came knocking on Philip's door; I'll take my oath he had a hand in it. He had a whining way of speaking, and a womanish cut about him that was most unpleasing.'

'These Frenchmen are so decadent,' said Dona.

'They'd never have slipped away from us, but for that wind,' snorted Rashleigh; 'down came a puff from Readymoney Cove, and her sails filled. You'd say it was the work of the devil himself. George here had the villain covered with his musket, but he missed him.'

'And how was that, my lord?'

'I was temporarily at a disadvantage, madam,' began Godolphin, the colour mounting to his face, and Harry, looking down from the opposite end of the table, slapped his hand on his knee and shouted, 'We've heard all about it, never fear, George. You lost your wig, didn't you? The rascal of a froggie pinched your wig?' and immediately all eyes turned on Godolphin, who sat stiff as a ramrod, staring at the glass in front of him.

'Take no notice of them, dear Lord Godolphin,' smiled Dona, 'only have a little more to drink. For what, after all, is the loss of a wig? It might have been something so much more precious, and what would Lady Godolphin do then?' And Rashleigh's neighbour Carnethick, on her left, choked suddenly over his wine.

A quarter to midnight, ten minutes, five minutes to midnight, and there was young Tremayne discussing cock-fighting with Penrose of Tregony, and a man from Bodmin whose name she had not heard was digging Rockingham in the ribs, whispering some bawdy story behind his hand, and Carnethick was leering at her across the table, and Philip Rashleigh was picking off grapes with a wrinkled hairy hand, and Harry, half lolling in his chair, was singing a song to himself that had no tune, one hand caressing his glass and the other fondling the spaniel on his lap. But suddenly, Eustick, glancing at the clock. leapt to his feet and called in a voice of thunder, 'Gentlemen, we have wasted time enough. Have you all forgotten we have met to-night on very desperate business?'

There was silence at once. Tremayne looked down at his plate, blushing, and Carnethick wiped his mouth with a lace handkerchief, gazing straight in front of him. Someone coughed awkwardly, someone shuffled with his feet under the table, and only Harry continued smiling, humming his tuneless drunken song, and out in the courtyard the stable clock struck midnight. Eustick looked meaningly at his hostess. Dona rose to her feet at once, and 'You wish me to go?' she said.

'Nonsense,' called Harry, opening one eye, 'let my wife stay at her own table, damme. The party will fall flat without her, parties always do. Here's your health, my beautiful, even if you do permit servants in and out of your bedroom.'

'Harry, the time for jesting is over,' said Godolphin, and turning to Dona, 'We could talk more freely if you were not here. As Eustick has just observed, we have all become a little forgetful of our purpose.'

'But of course I understand,' said Dona, 'I would not dream of hindering in any way,' and as they stood to let her pass, the great bell jangled in the court outside.

'Who the devil's that?' yawned Harry. 'Someone two-and-a-half hours late for supper? Let's open another bottle of wine.'

'We are all here,' said Eustick, 'we expect none other. What about you, Godolphin?'

'No, I have warned no one else,' frowned Godolphin. 'The meeting was a secret one in any case.'

Once again the bell jangled. 'Go and open the door, someone,' shouted Harry. 'Where the deuce are all the servants?'

The dog jumped from his knees, and ran barking to the door.

'Thomas, one of you, what are you doing?' called Harry, over his shoulder, and Rockingham, rising, went to the door at the back of the hall that led to the kitchen, and flung it open, 'Hullo, there,' he cried, 'are you all asleep?' but no answer came to him, and the passage was dark and silent.

'Someone has blown the candles,' he said. 'It's as black as pitch here in the passage. Hullo, there, Thomas.'

'What orders did you give your servants, Harry?' said Godolphin, pushing back his chair. 'Did you tell them to go to bed?'

'To bed, no,' said Harry, rising unsteadily, 'the fellows are waiting in the kitchen somewhere. Give 'em another call, Rock, can't you?'

'I tell you there's no answer,' said Rockingham, 'and there's not a light anywhere. The kitchen itself yonder is as black as a pit.'

The bell jangled for the third time, and Eustick, with an oath, strode towards the door, and began to draw back the bolts.

'It must be one of our people come to report,' said Rashleigh, 'one of the men we have posted in the woods. Someone has given us away, and the fight's begun.'

The door swung open, and Eustick stood on the threshold, calling into the darkness, 'Who asks for Navron House?'

'Jean-Benoit Aubéry, at the service of all you gentlemen,' came the answer, and into the hall walked the Frenchman, a sword in his hand, and a smile on his lips. 'Don't move, Eustick,' he said, 'and the rest of you, stay where you are. I have you covered, all of you. The first man who moves will have a bullet through his brains.'

And Dona, looking up the staircase to the gallery above, saw Pierre Blanc with a pistol in his hands, and Edmund Vacquier beside him, while at the door leading to the kitchen stood William, white and inscrutable, one arm hanging useless by his side, the other with a naked cutlass pointing at Rockingham's throat.

'I pray you be seated, gentlemen,' said the Frenchman, 'and I will not keep you long. As for her ladyship, she may please herself, but first she must give me the rubies she wears in her ears, for I have had a wager about them with my cabin boy.'

And he stood before her, bowing, playing with his sword, while twelve men stared at him in hatred and in fear.

Chapter Nineteen

They might have all been dead men, frozen in their seats at the table. No one spoke a word, but every man watched the Frenchman as he stood there smiling, his hand outstretched for the jewels.

Five against twelve, but the five were armed, and the twelve had supped unwisely and too well, and the swords by their sides were sheathed. Eustick still had his hand upon the door, but Luc Dumont from *La Mouette* stood beside him, pointing a pistol to his ribs, and slowly Eustick closed the door, and drew the bolts into their sockets. Down the staircase from the gallery above came Pierre Blanc and his companion, and they took up positions at either end of the long hall, so that if any man's hand strayed to his sword that man would have fallen, even as their master said. Rockingham leant against the wall, watching the point of William's cutlass, and he passed his tongue over his lips and did not speak. Only the host, who had sunk once again into his chair, surveyed the scene with bland bewilderment, a glass half-filled with wine, raised to his lips.

Dona unscrewed the rubies from her ears, and laid them in the outstretched hand before her.

'Is that all?' she said.

He pointed with his sword to the pendant around her throat.

'Won't you spare me that as well?' he said, one eyebrow raised. 'My cabin-boy will curse me otherwise. And the bracelet on your arm, I must ask you for that too.'

She unfastened the bracelet and the pendant, and without a word and without a smile she placed them in his hand.

'Thank you,' he said, 'I trust you are recovered from your fever?'

'I thought so,' she answered, 'but your presence here will doubtless bring it back again.'

'That would be a pity,' he said gravely. 'My conscience would be uneasy. My cabin-boy suffers from fever from time to time, but the sea air does wonders for him. You ought to try it.' And bowing he placed the jewels in his pocket, and turned away from her.

'Lord Godolphin I believe,' he said, standing before his lordship. 'Last time we met I relieved you of your wig. That also was the fault of a wager. This time, perhaps, I might take something a little more substantial.' He reached for the decoration on Godolphin's breast, a ribbon and a star, and cut it away with his sword.

'Your weapon also, I regret to say, is something I cannot leave upon your person,' and Godolphin's sheath clattered upon the ground. The Frenchman bowed again, and passed on to Philip Rashleigh. 'Good evening, sir,' he said, 'you are looking a trifle less warm than when I saw you last. I must thank you for the gift of the *Merry Fortune*. She is a splendid vessel. You would not recognise her now, I swear. They have given her a new rig on my side of the channel, and a coat of paint into the bargain. Your sword, sir, if you please. And what have you in your pockets?'

The veins stood out in Rashleigh's forehead, and his breath came quick and fast. 'You'll pay for this, God damn you,' he said.

'Possibly,' said the Frenchman, 'but in the meanwhile, it is you who are paying,' and he emptied Rashleigh's sovereigns into a bag tied at his waist.

Slowly he made the circuit of the table, and each guest in turn lost the weapon at his side, and the money from his pockets, with the rings from his

fingers, and the pin from his cravat. And as the Frenchman strolled round
the table, whistling a tune under his breath, he would lean, now and again,
to the bowl of fruit, and pluck a grape, and once, while waiting for the stout
guest from Bodmin to divest himself of the many rings on his fingers, swollen
with gout, he sat on the edge of the table, amongst the silver and the dishes,
and poured himself a glass of wine from a carafe.

'You have a good cellar, Sir Harry,' he said. 'I should advise you to keep
this a year or so longer; it is a wine that will improve. I had some half-dozen
bottles of the same vintage in my own house in Brittany, and like a fool I
drank it all too soon.'

'Death and damnation,' spluttered Harry, 'of all the confounded . . .'

'Don't worry,' smiled the Frenchman, 'I could have the key of the cellar
from William if I wanted it, but I would not deprive you of the fun of
drinking this in four or five year's time.' He scratched his ear, and glanced
down at the ring on Harry's finger.

'That is a very fine emerald,' he said.

For answer Harry tore it from his finger and threw it at the Frenchman's
face, but he caught it in his hands, and held it to the light.

'Not a single flaw,' he said, 'which is rare in an emerald. However, I will
not take it. On second thoughts, Sir Harry, I have robbed you enough.' And
bowing, he handed the ring back to Dona's husband. 'And now, gentlemen,'
he said, 'I have a last request to make. It is, perhaps, a little crude, but
under the circumstances, very necessary. You see, I wish to return to my
ship, and to have you join your fellows in the woods and give chase to me
would, I fear, somewhat prejudice my plans. In short, I must ask you to take
off your breeches and hand them over to my men here. Likewise your
stockings and your shoes.' One and all they stared at him in rage, and 'By
heaven, no,' shouted Eustick, 'have you not made game of us enough?'

'I am sorry,' smiled the Frenchman, 'but really I must insist. The night
is warm, you know, and yesterday was mid-summer. Lady St. Columb,
perhaps you would be good enough to go into the salon? These gentlemen
will not care to undress themselves before you in public, however much they
may desire to do so in private.'

And he held open the door for her to pass, and looking over his shoulder
to the guests he called, 'I will give you five minutes, but no more. Pierre
Blanc, Jules, Luc, William – keep a close watch upon the gentlemen, and
while they are disrobing, her ladyship and I will discuss the affairs of the
day.'

He followed her into the salon and shut the door.

'And you,' he said, 'with your proud smile, standing at the head of the
table, shall I make you do the same, my cabin-boy?' and he threw his sword
on the chair, and laughed and held out his arms. She went to him, and put
her hands on his shoulders.

'Why are you so reckless,' she asked, 'so shameless, and so wicked? Do
you know that the woods and the hills are black with men?'

'Yes,' he said.

'Why did you come here then?'

'Because, as in all my undertakings, the most hazardous performance is usually the most successful. Besides, I had not kissed you for nearly twenty-four hours.' And he bent his head, and took her face in his hands.

'What did you think,' she said, 'when I did not come for breakfast?'

'There was little time to think,' he answered, 'because I was woken just after sunrise by Pierre Blanc, to tell me *La Mouette* was aground, and taking in water. We have had the devil's own time with her, as you can imagine. And then, later on, when we were all stripped to the waist and working on her, William came down with your news.'

'But you did not know then, what was being planned for – to-night?'

'No, but I soon had a shrewd suspicion. One of my men saw a figure on the beach, up the river, and another in the hills opposite. And we knew then, that we were working against time. Even so, they had not found *La Mouette*. They were guarding the river and the woods, but they had not come down to the creek.'

'And then William came the second time?'

'Yes, between five and six this evening. He warned me of your party here at Navron, and I decided then what I should do. I told him of course, but that cut he received from the fellow in the woods on his way back to you did not help much.'

'I kept thinking of him, during supper, lying wounded and fainting on my bed.'

'Yes, but he dragged himself to the window, all the same, to admit us, just as we had planned. Your servants, by-the-way, are all shut up in your game larder, tied back-to-back, like the fellows we found on the *Merry Fortune*. Do you want your trinkets back again?' He felt in his pocket for her jewels, but she shook her head.

'You had better keep them,' she said, 'to remember me by.'

He said nothing, but looked over her head, stroking her curls.

'*La Mouette* will sail within two hours, if all goes well,' he said. 'The patch in her side is rough, but it must hold until she reaches the French coast.'

'What of the weather?' she asked.

'The wind is fair, and steady enough. We should reach Brittany in eighteen hours or less.'

Dona was silent, and he went on touching her hair.

'I have no cabin boy,' he said. 'Do you know of a likely lad who would sail with me?' She looked at him then, but he was not smiling any more, and he moved away from her, and picked up his sword.

'I shall have to take William, I'm afraid,' he said. 'He has played his part at Navron, and your household will know him no longer. He has served you well, has he not?'

'Very well,' she answered.

'If it were not for the scrap he had to-night with Eustick's man, I would have left him,' he said, 'but recognition would come swift and fast, and Eustick would have hanged him without scruple. Besides, I hardly think he would have stayed to serve your husband.'

He glanced about the room, his eyes alighting for a moment on Harry's portrait, and then he walked to the long window, and flung it open, drawing back the curtains. 'Do you remember the first night I supped with you,' he said, 'and afterwards you stared into the fire, and I drew your picture. You were angry with me, were you not?'

'No,' she said, 'not angry. Only ashamed, because you guessed too much.'

'I will tell you one thing,' he said, 'you will never make a fisherman. You are too impatient. You will keep getting tangled up in your line.'

Someone knocked at the door, and 'Yes?' he called in French. 'Have the gentlemen done what I commanded them?'

'They have, Monsieur,' answered William, through the door.

'Very well then. Tell Pierre Blanc to tie their hands behind their backs, and escort them to the bedrooms above. Close the doors upon them and turn the keys. They will not trouble us for two hours, which will give me the time we need.'

'Very good, Monsieur.'

'And William?'

'Monsieur?'

'How is your arm?'

'A trifle painful, Monsieur, but not seriously so.'

'That is good. Because I want you to take her ladyship by carriage to that spit of sand three miles this side of Coverack.'

'Yes, Monsieur.'

'And there await my further orders.'

'I understand, Monsieur.'

She stared at him, puzzled, and he came and stood before her, his sword in hand. 'What are you going to do?' she said.

He waited a moment before he answered, and he was not smiling any more, and his eyes were dark.

'You remember how we talked together last night by the creek?'

'Yes,' she said.

'And we arranged that it was impossible for a woman to escape, except for an hour and a day?'

'Yes.'

'This morning,' he said, 'when I was working on the ship, and William brought me the news that you were alone no longer, I realised that our make-believe was over, and the creek was our sanctuary no more. From this time forward *La Mouette* must sail other waters, and find different hiding-places. And although she will be free, and the men on board her free, her master will remain captive.'

'What do you mean?' said Dona.

'I mean that I am bound to you, even as you are bound to me. From the very first, I knew that it would be so. When I came here, in the winter, and lay upstairs in your room, my hands behind my head, and looked at your sullen portrait on the wall, I smiled to myself, and said, "That – and none other." And I waited, and I did nothing, for I knew that our time would come.'

'What else?' she said.

'You, too,' he said, 'my careless indifferent Dona, so hard, so disillusioned, playing the boy in London with your husband and his friends, you guessed that somewhere, in heaven knew what country and what guise, there was someone who was part of your body and your brain, and that without him you were lost, a straw blown by the wind.'

She went to him, and put her hand over his eyes.

'All that,' she said, 'all that you feel, I feel. Every thought, every wish, every changing mood. But it's too late, there is nothing we can do. You have told me so already.'

'I told you so last night,' he said, 'when we had no cares, and we were together, and the morning was many hours away. At those times a man can afford to shrug his shoulders at the future, because he holds the present in his arms, and the very cruelty of the thought adds, in some desperate fashion, to the delight of the moment. And when a man makes love, my Dona, he escapes from the burden of that love, and from himself as well.'

'Yes,' she said, 'I know that. I have always known it. But not every woman.'

'No,' he said, 'not every woman.' He took the bracelet from his pocket and clasped it on her wrist. 'And so,' he went on, 'when the morning came and I saw the mist on the creek, and you were gone from my side, there came also, not disillusion, but realisation. I knew that escape, for me too, was impossible. I had become like a prisoner in chains, and the dungeon was deep.'

She took his hand, and laid it against her cheek.

'And all day long you worked upon your ship,' she said, 'and you sweated, and toiled, and said nothing, and frowned that frown of concentration I have come to understand, and then – when you had finished - what was your answer?'

He looked away from her, towards the open window.

'My answer,' he said slowly, 'was still the same. That you were Dona St. Columb, wife of an English baronet, and mother of two children, and I was a Frenchman, and an outlaw, a robber of your country, an enemy to your friends. If there is an answer, Dona, you must make it and not me.'

He crossed to the window once more, and looked back at her over his shoulder.

'That is why I have asked William to take you to the cove near Coverack,' he said, 'so that you can decide what you wish to do. If I, and Pierre Blanc and the rest of us, return safely to the ship through this cordon in the wood, and hoist sail without delay, and leave with the tide, we shall be abreast of Coverack by sunrise. I will put off in a boat to have your answer. Should there be no sign of *La Mouette* by day-light, you will know that something has gone amiss with my plan. And Godolphin perhaps will have at last the satisfaction of hanging that hated Frenchman from the tallest tree in his park.'

He smiled, and stepped out on to the terrace. 'I have loved you, Dona,' he said, 'in almost every mood. But mostly, I think, when you threw yourself down on the deck of the *Merry Fortune,* in Pierre Blanc's breeches, with blood on your face, and the rain streaming down your torn shirt, and I looked at you and laughed, and a bullet whistled over your head.'

Then he turned, and vanished in the darkness.

She stood still, without moving, her hands clasped in front of her, while the minutes sped. Then at last she realised, like someone who has woken from a dream, that she was alone, and the house was silent, and that she held her ruby earrings and her pendant in her hands. A draught came from the open window, blowing the candles on the wall, and hardly aware of what she did she went to it, and closed and bolted it, and then went to the door leading to the dining-hall, and opened it wide.

There were the plates and the dishes on the table, and the bowls piled high with fruit, and the silver goblets and the glasses. The chairs were pushed back, as though the guests had risen from their supper, and withdrawn, and there was a strange forlorn air about the table, like a still-life picture drawn by an amateur brush, in which the food, and the fruit, and the spilt wine lack life and reality. The two spaniels crouched on the floor, and Duchess, lifting her nose from between her paws. looked up at Dona, and whined uncertainly. One of the men from *La Mouette* must have snuffed the candles, and then left, in haste, before extinguishing them all; for there were three that remained burning, the grease dripping on the floor, and the light they gave was sinister and queer.

One of them went out, and only two stayed now to flicker and dance upon the wall. The men of *La Mouette* had done their work and departed. They were creeping through the woods now to the ship in the creek, and their master was with them, his sword in his hand. The clock in the stable yard struck one; a high thin note, like the echo of a bell. Upstairs, unclothed and with their wrists tied, the guests of Navron House would be lying helpless and enraged upon the floor. All except Harry, and he would be asleep, on his back, and snoring, his wig askew and his mouth wide open, for not all the ill-treatment in the world would keep a St. Columb from his bed, when he had supped too well. William must be attending to his own hurt, in his own room, and her conscience reproached her, for she had been forgetting him. So she turned then, to the great staircase, and placed her hand on the rail, when a sound from above made her look upwards to the gallery. And there, staring down at her with narrow, unsmiling eyes, stood Rockingham with a gash across his face, and a knife in his hand.

Chapter Twenty

For eternity it seemed he stood there staring down at her, and then slowly he descended, never taking his eyes from her face, and she backed away from him, feeling for the table, and sat down in her chair, and watched him. He was clad only in his shirt and breeches, and she saw now that there was blood upon the shirt, and on the knife that he held in his hand. She knew then what had happened. Somewhere in one of the dark passages above, a man lay mortally wounded, or even dead, and it might be one of the crew from *La Mouette*, or it might be William. This struggle had taken place in silence and in darkness, while she had sat in the salon alone and dreaming, her rubies in her hands. Now he stood at the bottom of the stairs, and still he said nothing, but he went on watching her with his narrow catlike eyes, and then he sat himself in Harry's chair at the far end of the table, and put the knife down on the plate before him.

When at last he spoke the familiarity of his voice sounded odd in contrast to his altered looks, for the man who faced her was not the Rockingham she had jested with in London, ridden beside at Hampton Court, and despised as a degenerate and a rake. This man had something cold about him, something evil, and from henceforward he was her enemy, wishing her suffering and pain.

'I see,' he said, 'that your jewels have been returned to you.'

She shrugged her shoulders without answering, for how much he had guessed was of little consequence. The only thing that mattered was to know the plan in his head, and what movement he would make.

'And what,' he said, 'did you give in place of your jewels?'

She began to replace the rubies in her ears, watching him over her arm as she did so. And then, because his gaze was something that she hated now, and could even grow to fear, she said to him, 'We have become very serious, Rockingham, all of a sudden. I should have thought this evening's jest would have amused you well.'

'You are right,' he answered, 'it has amused me much. That twelve men could be disarmed and unbreeched in so short a time by so few jesters bears a curious likeness to the pranks we used to play at Hampton Court. But that Dona St. Columb should look upon the leader of the jesters in the way she did – in a way that could mean one thing only – no, that I did not find amusing.'

She leant her elbows on the table, and cupped her chin in her hands.

'And so?' she asked.

'And so in a flash I understood much that had puzzled me since my arrival here last night. That servant of yours, a spy of course of the Frenchman's. The friendliness between you, and you knew he was a spy. And those walks of yours, those wanderings in the woods, that elusive look in your eye that I had never seen before, yes, indeed, elusive to me, to Harry, to all men but one man, and I have seen that man to-night.' His voice was low now, scarcely above a whisper, and all the time he looked at her with hatred.

'Well,' he said, 'do you deny it?'

'I deny nothing,' she answered.

He picked up the knife from his plate, and began tracing lines with it upon the table, as though abstracted.

'You know,' he said, 'that you could be imprisoned for this, and possibly hanged, should the truth come out?'

Once again she shrugged her shoulders, and did not answer.

'Not a very pleasant ending, for Dona St. Columb,' he said. 'You have never been inside a jail, have you? You have never smelt the heat and the filth, you have never tasted the black broken bread, or drunk the water, thick with scum. And the feeling of a rope about your neck, as it tightens, and chokes you. How would you like that, Dona?'

'My poor Rockingham,' she said slowly, 'I can imagine all these things far better than you can describe them. What is your object? Do you wish to frighten me? Because you are not succeeding.'

'I thought it only wise,' he said, 'to remind you of what may happen.'

'And all this,' she said, 'because my lord Rockingham fancies I smiled upon a pirate when he asked me for my jewels. Tell your story to Godolphin, to Rashleigh and to Eustick, to Harry even – they will say that you are mad.'

'Possibly,' he said, 'with your Frenchman on the high seas, and yourself sitting at your ease in Navron House. But supposing your Frenchman was not on the high seas, supposing he was caught, and bound and brought before you, and we played with him a little, as they played with prisoners some hundred years ago, Dona, with you for audience. I rather believe you would give yourself away.'

Once again she saw him as she had seen him earlier in the day, a sleek cat crouching in the long grass, a bird between his claws, so padded, so soft, and she realised, her memory streaking back to the past, how she had always suspected in him some quality of deliberate and cruel depravity which, because of the foolhardy lightness of the age in which they lived, was well concealed.

'It pleases you to be dramatic,' she said, 'but the days of the thumb-screw and the rack are over. We no longer burn our heretics at the stake.'

'Not our heretics perhaps,' he said, 'but our pirates are hanged, and drawn, and quartered, and their accomplices suffer the same fate.'

'Very well,' she said, 'since you believe me an accomplice, do what you wish. Go upstairs, and unbind the guests who supped here to-night. Wake Harry from his drunken slumbers. Call the servants. Fetch horses, fetch soldiers and weapons. And then when you have caught your pirate, you may hang us both side by side from the same tree.'

He did not answer. He stared at her across the table, balancing the knife in his hand.

'Yes,' he said, 'you would suffer that, would you not, and be proud and glad. You would not mind dying now, because you have had, at last, the thing you wanted all your life. Is not that true?'

She looked back at him, and then she laughed.

'Yes,' she said, 'it is true.'

He turned very white, and the gash on his face showed vivid red in contrast, altering the shape of his mouth, like a strange grimace.

'And it might have been me,' he said, 'it might have been me.'

'Never,' she said, 'that I swear. Never in this world.'

'If you had not left London, if you had not come down here to Navron, it would have been me. Yes, though it were from boredom, from idleness, from indifference, even from disgust, it would have been me.'

'No, Rockingham . . . never. . . '

He got up slowly from his chair, still balancing the knife in his hands, and he kicked the spaniel away from under his feet, and he rolled his sleeves above his elbows.

She rose too, gripping the sides of her chair, and the murky light from the two candles on the wall flickered down upon his face.

'What is it, Rockingham?' she asked.

Then for the first time he smiled, and he pushed back his chair, and laid one hand on the corner of the table.

'I believe,' he whispered, 'that I am going to kill you.'

In a moment she had flung a glass of wine, close to her hand, straight in his face, and for half a second it blinded him, while the glass shivered to fragments on the floor. Then he made a lunge towards her across the table, but she eluded him, reaching for one of the heavy chairs beside her, and she lifted it, and sent it crashing amongst the silver and the fruit on the table, the leg of it striking his shoulder. He breathed quickly, with the pain of it, and hurling the chair from the table to the ground, he held his knife poised an instant, high above his shoulder, and threw it from him, straight at her throat. It struck the ruby pendant around her neck, cracking it in two, and she felt the cold steel slip away from her, pricking her skin, catching itself in the folds of her gown. She fumbled for it, sick with horror and with pain, but before she could seize it he was upon her, one hand doubling her wrist behind her back, and the other pressing her mouth in suffocation. She felt herself falling back against the table, the glasses and the plates crashing to the ground, and somewhere beneath her was the knife which he wished to find. The dogs were barking now, furiously excited, imagining this was some new sport designed for their amusement, and they leapt up at him, scratching with their paws, so that he was forced to turn a moment, and kick them from under him, releasing the pressure of his hand upon her mouth.

She bit through the palm of his hand, and drove her left fist into his eyes, and now he released her wrist, doubled up beneath her back, so that he could have two hands on her throat, and she felt the pressure of his thumbs on her wind-pipe, choking her. Her right hand struggled for the knife, and suddenly her fingers closed upon it, and gripping the cold hasp she drove it upwards, under his arm-pit, and she felt the horrid yielding of his soft flesh to the blade, surprisingly easy, surprisingly warm, with the blood running thick and fast on her hand. He sighed, long-drawn and strange, his hand no longer pressing upon her throat, and fell sideways on the table amongst the glass, and she pushed him from her and stood once more on her feet, her knees trembling, with the dogs barking madly about her legs. And now he was dragging himself from the table, too, his glazed eyes turned upon her, one hand pressed to the wound under his arm, and with the other he reached for a great silver carafe that still stood upon the table, and with this he would have smashed her face and trodden her to the ground, but even as he moved towards her the last candle flickered on the wall and was gutted, and they were in darkness.

She felt the edge of the table with her hands, and worked her way round it, out of his reach, and she heard him groping for her in the black hall, stumbling over a chair that stood in his way. Now she was making for the staircase, she could see a glimmer of pale light from the window in the gallery, and here were the stairs themselves, and the rail, and she was climbing the stairs, with the two dogs barking at her heels. Somewhere from above she could hear shouts and cries, and the thumping of fists upon a door, but all this was confusion, was a dream having no connection with the battle that was hers alone. Looking back over her shoulder, sobbing, she saw Rockingham at the foot of the stairs, and he was not standing upright as he had before, but was climbing towards her on all fours like the dogs at her heels. She reached the top of the stairs, and the shouts and thumps were louder now. There was Godolphin's voice amongst them, and Harry's too, while the barking of the dogs joined the clamour, and from the direction of the nurseries came the high-pitched frightened scream of a child, woken from his sleep. Then she knew anger at last, and not fear. Then she was resolute, and calm, and cold.

The grey light from the window, where the moon struggled through the clouds, shone feebly upon a shield hanging on the wall, some trophy of a dead St. Columb, and she tore it from its place on the wall, heavy and dusty with age, and the weight of it dragged her to her knees. Still Rockingham came. She could see his back, humped against the rail, as he paused for breath, and she could hear the scratching of his hands upon the stairs and the quick sound of his breathing. When he turned the corner of the stair and stood a moment, turning his head, looking for her in the darkness, she hurled the shield at him, driving it full in his face, and he staggered and fell, turning over and over on the stairs, crashing with the shield on top of him to the stone floor below. And the dogs went down after him, excited and barking, scampering in play, nosing his body as it lay there on the floor. Dona stood motionless, all feeling spent, a great ache behind her eyes, the sound of James's cry still ringing in her ears, and somewhere now there were footsteps, and a voice calling in anxiety and fear, and the splintering tearing noise of breaking wood. It would be Harry perhaps, or Eustick, or Godolphin, beating down the locked door of the bedroom where they were imprisoned, and it seemed to her that these things mattered little, for she was too weary now to care. She wanted to lie down in the darkness, and to sleep with her face between her hands, and she remembered that somewhere along this passage was her room, and her own bed, where she could hide and be forgotten. Somewhere, in the river, there was a ship called *La Mouette*, and the man she loved stood at the wheel now, taking his ship to the sea. She had promised to give him her answer at day-break, and to wait for him on the little spit of sand that jutted out into the sea. William would take her to him, William the faithful, somehow they would find their way across the country in the darkness. and when they reached the cove the boat would put off from the ship towards them, even as he had said. She thought of the coast of Brittany as she had seen it once before, golden at sunrise with the rocks about it jagged and crimson, like the coast of Devon. The white breakers hurled themselves upon the sand, and the spray threw a fine mist on to the cliffs, the smell of it mingling with the warm earth and the grass.

Somewhere there was a house which she had never seen, but he would take her to it, and she would feel the grey walls with her hands. She wanted to sleep now, and dream of these things, and remember no more the guttering candles in the dining-hall below, with the smashed glass and the broken chairs, and Rockingham's face when the knife touched his flesh. She wanted to sleep, and it seemed to her suddenly that she stood no longer, that she was falling too, as Rockingham had done, and the blackness came about her and covered her, and there was a rushing of wind in her ears. . . .

Surely it was long afterwards that people came and bent over her, and hands lifted her and carried her. And someone bathed her face, and her throat, and laid pillows under her head. There were many voices in the distance, men's voices, and the coming and going of heavy footsteps, and there must have been horses in the courtyard outside the house; she could hear their hoofs on the cobbles. Once too she heard the stable clock strike three.

And dimly, in the back of her mind, something whispered, 'He will be waiting for me on the spit of sand, and I am lying here, and I cannot move, and I cannot go to him,' and she tried to raise herself from her bed, but she had no strength. It was still dark, while outside her window she could hear a little thin trickle of rain. Then she must have slept, the heavy dull sleep of exhaustion, for when she opened her eyes it was daylight, and the curtains had been drawn, and there was Harry kneeling by her side, fondling her hair with his great clumsy hands. He was peering into her face, his blue eyes troubled, and he was blubbing like a child.

'Are you all right, Dona?' he said. 'Are you better, are you well?'

She stared at him without understanding, the dull ache still behind her eyes, and she thought how ridiculous it was that he should kneel there, in so foolish a manner, and she felt a sort of shame upon her that he should do so.

'Rock's dead,' he said. 'We found him dead there, on the floor, with his poor neck broken. Rock, the best friend I have ever had.' And the tears rolled down his cheeks, and she went on staring at him. 'He saved your life, you know,' said Harry; 'he must have fought that devil single-handed, alone there in the darkness, while you fled up here to warn us. My poor beautiful, my poor sweet.'

She did not listen to him any more, she sat up, looking at the daylight as it streamed into her window. 'What is the time,' she said, 'how long has the sun been risen?'

'The sun?' he said blankly. 'Why, it's nearly noon I believe. What of it? You are going to rest, are you not? You must, after all you have suffered last night.'

She put her hands over her eyes and tried to think. It was noon then, and the ship would have sailed, for he could not have waited for her after the day had broken. She had lain here sleeping on her bed, while the little boat put in to the spit of sand and found it empty.

'Try and rest again, my lovely,' said Harry, 'try and forget the confounded God-damned night. I'll never drink again, I swear it. It's my fault, I ought to have stopped it all. But you shall have your revenge, I promise you that. We've caught him, you know, we've got the blasted fellow.'

'What do you mean,' she said slowly, 'what are you talking about?'

'Why, the Frenchman of course,' he said, 'the devil who killed Rock, and would have killed you too. The ship's gone, and the rest of his battered crew, but we've got him, the leader, the damned pirate.'

She went on staring at him without understanding, dazed, as though he had struck her, and he, seeing her eyes, was troubled, and began once more to fondle her hair and to kiss her fingers, murmuring, 'My poor girl, what a confounded to-do, eh, what a night, what a devilish thing.' And then, pausing a moment he looked at her, and flushed, a little confused, still holding her fingers, and because the despair in her eyes was something dark and new, was a thing he did not understand, he said to her awkwardly, like a shy and clumsy boy: 'That Frenchman, that pirate, he didn't molest you in any way, did he, Dona?'

Chapter Twenty-one

Two days came and went, things without hours or minutes in which she dressed herself, and ate, and went out into the garden, and all the while she was possessed by a strange sense of unreality as though it was not she who moved, but some other woman, whose very words she did not understand. No thoughts came to her mind: it was as though part of her slept still, and the numbness spread from her mind to her body, so that she felt nothing of the sun when it came from two clouds and shone a moment, and when a little chill wind blew she was not cold.

At one time the children ran out to greet her, and James climbed on her knee, and Henrietta, dancing before her, said 'A wicked pirate has been caught, and Prue says he will be hanged.' She was aware of Prue's face, pale, rather subdued, and with an effort she remembered that there had been death, of course, at Navron, that at this moment Rockingham would be lying in a darkened church awaiting burial. There was a dull greyness about these days, like the Sundays she remembered as a child, when the Puritans forbade dancing on the green. There was a moment when the rector of Helford Church appeared and spoke to her gravely, condoling with her on the loss of so great a friend. And afterwards he rode away, and Harry was beside her again, blowing his nose, and speaking in a hushed voice, entirely unlike himself. He stayed by her continually, humble and anxious to please, and kept asking her whether she needed anything, a cloak, or a coverlet for her knees, and when she shook her head, wishing he would leave her quietly, so that she could sit, staring at nothing, he began protesting once more how much he loved her, and that he would never drink again: it was all because he had drunk too much that fatal night that they had let themselves be trapped in such a way, and but for his carelessness and sloth poor Rockingham would be alive.

'I'll cut out gambling too,' he said. 'I'll never touch another card, and I'll sell the town house, and we'll go and live in Hampshire, Dona, near your old home where we first met. I'll live the life of a country gentleman at last, with you and the children, and I'll teach young James to ride and to hawk. How would you like that, eh?'

Still she did not answer, but went on staring in front of her.

'There's always been something baleful about Navron,' he said, 'I remember thinking so as a boy. I never felt well here: the air is so soft. It doesn't suit me. It doesn't suit you, either. We'll go away as soon as this business is over and done with. If only we could lay our hands on that damned spy of a servant, and hang 'em both at the same time. God, when I think of the danger you were in, you know, trusting that fellow.' And he began to blow his nose again, shaking his head. One of the spaniels came fawning up to her, licking her hands, and suddenly she remembered the furious barking of the night, the yapping, the excitement, and in a flash her darkened mind became alive again, awake and horribly aware. Her heart beat loudly, for no reason, and the house, and the trees, and the figure of Harry sitting beside her took shape and form. He was talking, and she knew now that every word he uttered might be of importance, and that she must miss nothing, for there were plans to make, and time itself was now of desperate value.

'Poor Rock must have outwitted the servant from the first,' he was saying. 'There were signs of the struggle in his room, you know, and a trail of blood leading along the passage, and then it stopped suddenly, and we found no trace of the fellow. Somehow he must have got away, and perhaps have joined those other rascals on the ship, though I think it doubtful. They must have used some part of the river time and again as a sneak-hole. By thunder, Dona, if we'd only known.'

He smote his fist in the palm of his hand, and then, remembering that Navron had been a house of death and that to talk loudly, or to swear, was to show irreverence towards the dead, he lowered his voice, and sighed, and said 'Poor Rock. I hardly know how we shall do without him, you know.'

She spoke at last, her voice sounding strange to her own ears, because her words were careful, like a lesson learnt by heart.

'How was he caught?' she said, and the dog was licking her hand again, but she did not feel it.

'You mean that damned Frenchman?' said Harry, 'well, we – we rather hoped you could tell us a bit about it, the first part, because you were with him, weren't you, in the salon there. But I don't know, Dona, you seemed so stunned and strange when I asked you. I said to Eustick and the others, "Hell, no, she's been through too much," and if you'd rather not tell me about it, that's all there is to it, you know.'

She folded her hands on her lap and said, 'He gave me back my ear-rings and then he went.'

'Oh, well,' said Harry, 'if that was all. But then he must have come back, you know, and tried to follow you upstairs. Perhaps you don't remember fainting there, in the passage by your room. Anyway, Rock must have been there by then, and guessing what the scoundrel was after, threw himself on the fellow, and in the fight that followed – for your safety Dona, you must always remember that – he lost his life, dear staunch friend that he was.'

Dona waited a moment, watching Harry's hand as he stroked the dog.

'And then?' she said, looking away from him, across the lawn.

'Ah, the rest we owe to Rock too. It was his plan, from the first. He suggested it to Eustick and George Godolphin when we met them at Helston. "Have your men posted on the beaches," he said, "and boats in readiness, and if there is a vessel hiding up the river, you'll get her as she comes down by night, on the top of the tide." But instead of getting the ship, we got the leader instead.'

And he laughed, pulling at the dog's ears, and tickling her back.

'Yes, Duchess, we got the leader, and he'll hang for piracy and murder, won't he? And the people will sleep easy in their beds once more.'

Dona heard herself saying sharply in a clear cold voice 'Was he wounded at all? I don't understand.'

'Wounded? God bless me, no. He'll hang without a scratch on him, and he'll know what it feels like. The devilry up here had delayed him, you see, and those three other scoundrels, and they were making for a point below Helford to join their vessel in mid-river. He must have told the rest of his crew to get the ship under way when he was up at the house. God knows how they managed it, but they did. When Eustick and the others got down to the point agreed upon, there was the ship in midstream, and the fellows swimming out to her, all but their leader, and he was standing on the beach, as cool as a blade of steel, fighting two of our people at once, while his men got away. He kept shouting over his shoulder to them in his damned lingo as they swam to the ship, and though the boats were launched from the beaches, as we arranged, they were too late to catch the scoundrels or the ship. She sailed out of Helford with a roaring tide under her, and a fair wind on her quarter, and the Frenchman watched her go, and God damn it, he was laughing, Eustick said.'

As Harry spoke it seemed to Dona that she could see the river where it broadened, and met the sea, and she could hear the wind in the rigging of *La Mouette* as she had heard it once, and the escape would be a repetition of all the escapes that had gone before, but this time they sailed without their captain, this time they went alone. Pierre Blanc, Edmond Vacquier, and the rest, they had left him there on the beach because he had bid them to do so, and she guessed what his words must have been, as he stood there, facing his enemies, while they swam to the ship. He had saved his crew, and he had saved his ship, and even now, in whatever prison he found himself, that calm unfettered brain of his would be working and planning some new method of escape, and she realised now that she was stunned and afraid no longer, for the manner of his capture had killed all fear within her.

'Where have they taken him then?' she asked, rising now, throwing on the ground the wrap that Harry had put round her shoulders. He told her, 'George Godolphin has him, in the keep, strongly guarded, and they're for moving him up to Exeter or Bristol when an escort comes down for him in forty-eight hours.'

'And what then?'

'Why, they'll hang him, Dona, unless George and Eustick and the rest of us save His Majesty's servants the trouble of doing so, and hang him on Saturday midday, as a treat to the people.'

They entered the house, and she stood now on the spot where he had bidden her farewell, and she said, 'Would that be within the law?' 'No, perhaps not,' said Harry, 'but I don't think His Majesty would trouble us for a reason.'

So there was little time to lose, she thought, and much to be done. She remembered the words he had spoken: how the most hazardous performance was often the most successful. That was a piece of advice she would repeat to herself continually during the next hours, for if any situation appeared beyond all saving and all hope, the saving of him did so at this moment.

'You are all right again, are you not?' said Harry anxiously, putting an arm about her. 'It was the shock of poor Rock's death that made you so strange these two days. That was it, wasn't it?'

'Perhaps,' she said. 'I don't know. It does not matter. But I am well again now. There is no need for you to be anxious.'

'I want to see you well,' he repeated. 'That's all I care about, damn it, to see you well and happy.' And he stared down at her, his blue eyes humble with adoration, and he reached clumsily for her hand.

'We'll go to Hampshire then, shall we?' he said.

'Yes,' she answered, 'yes, Harry, we'll go to Hampshire.' And she sat down on the low seat before the fireplace where no fire burnt because it was mid-summer, and she stared at the place where the flames should have been while Harry, forgetting that Navron had been a house of death called, 'Hi Duke . . . Hi, Duchess, your mistress says she'll come with us to Hampshire. Find it, then, go seek.'

It was imperative of course that she should see Godolphin, and talk to him, and persuade him into granting her an interview alone with his prisoner. That part of it should be easy, because Godolphin was a fool. She would flatter him, and during the interview she could pass weapons, a knife or a pistol if she could procure one, and so far, so good, because the actual method of escape could not be of her choosing. They supped quietly, she and Harry, in the salon before the open window, and soon afterwards Dona went up to her room, pleading weariness, and he had the intuition to say nothing, and to let her go alone.

When she was undressed, and lying in her bed, her mind full of her visit to Godolphin, and how she should achieve it, she heard a gentle tapping at her door. 'Surely,' she thought, her heart sinking, 'it is not Harry, in this new wistful penitent mood, not to-night.' But when she did not answer, hoping he would think her asleep, the tapping came again. Then the latch lifted, and it was Prue standing there in her nightgown, a candle in her hand, and Dona saw that her eyes were red and swollen with crying.

'What is it?' said Dona, sitting up at once. 'Is it James?'

'No, my lady,' whispered Prue, 'the children are asleep. It's only – it's only that I have something to tell you, my lady.' And she began weeping again, rubbing her eyes with her hand.

'Come in, and shut the door,' said Dona. 'What is the matter, then, why are you crying? Have you broken something? I shall not scold you.'

The girl continued to weep, and glancing about her, as though afraid that Harry himself might be there, and would hear her, she whispered between her tears, 'It's about William, my lady, I have done something very wicked.'

'Oh heaven,' thought Dona, 'she has been seduced by William while I was away in *La Mouette*, and now because he has gone, she is afraid and ashamed, and thinks she will have a baby, and that I will send her away,' and 'Don't be afraid, Prue,' she said softly, 'I won't be angry. What is it about William? You can tell me, you know. I shall understand.'

'He was always very good to me,' said Prue, 'and most attentive to me and the children, when you were ill, my lady. He could not do too much for us. And after the children were asleep, he used to come and sit with me, while I did my sewing, and he used to tell me about the countries he had visited, and I found it very pleasant.'

'I expect you did,' said Dona, 'I should have found it pleasant too.'

'I never thought,' said the girl, sobbing afresh, 'that he had anything to do with foreigners, or with these terrible pirates we had heard about. He was not rough in his ways at all, with me.'

'No,' said Dona, 'I hardly suppose he was.'

'And I know it was very wrong of me, my lady, not to have told Sir Harry and the other gentlemen that night, when there was all that terrible to-do, and they came bursting out of their rooms, and poor Lord Rockingham was killed, but I had not the heart to give him up, my lady. So faint he was with loss of blood, and as white as a ghost, I just could not do it. If it's found out I shall be beaten and sent to prison, but he said I must tell you whatever happened.'

And she stood there, twisting her hands, with tears running down her cheeks.

'Prue,' said Dona, swiftly, 'what are you trying to tell me?'

'Only that I hid William in the nursery that night, my lady, when I found him lying in the passage, with a cut on his arm, and another on the back of his head. And he told me then that Sir Harry and the other gentlemen would kill him if he was found, that the French pirate was his master, and there had been fighting at Navron that night. So, instead of giving him up, my lady, I bathed and dressed his wounds, and I made him up a bed on the floor beside the children, and after breakfast, when the gentlemen were all away searching for him and the other pirates, I let him out, my lady, by the side door, and no one knows anything about it but you and me.'

She blew her nose noisily on her handkerchief, and would have cried again. But Dona smiled at her, and leaning forward patted her shoulder, and said, 'It's all right, Prue. You are a good and faithful girl to tell me this, and I shall keep it to myself. I am fond of William, too, and should be greatly distressed if any harm came to him. But I want you to tell me something. Where is William now?'

'He said something about Coverack when he woke, my lady, and asked for you, and I told him you were in bed, very shocked and exhausted, as Lord Rockingham had been killed in the night. At that he seemed to think a while, my lady, and then when I had bathed and dressed his wounds afresh he said he had friends at Gweek who would shelter him, and would not betray him, and that he would be there if you wished to send word to him, my lady.'

'At Gweek?' said Dona. 'Very well then, Prue. I want you to go back to bed, and think no more of this, and say nothing of it ever again, to anyone, not even to me. Go on as you have always done, won't you Prue, and look after the children, and love them well.'

'Yes, my lady,' said Prue, and she curtsied, her tears still near the surface, and left the room, and went back to the nursery. And Dona smiled to herself in the darkness, for William the faithful was still at hand, her ally and her friend, and his master's escape from the keep had become a thing of possibility.

So she slept, her mind easier than it had been, and when she woke she saw that the listless sky had become blue again and the clouds were gone, and there was something in the air of that midsummer that would not come again, a warmth and a brilliance belonging to the days when, careless and enraptured, she had gone fishing in the creek.

While she dressed she made her plans, and when she had breakfasted she sent word for Harry to come to her. Already he had recovered something of his former spirits, and as he came into the room he called to his dogs in his usual voice, hearty and well content with himself, and he kissed her on the back of her neck as she sat before her mirror.

'Harry,' she said, 'I want you to do something for me.'

'Anything in the world,' he promised eagerly, 'what is it?'

'I want you to leave Navron to-day,' she said, 'and take Prue and the children with you.'

His face fell, and he stared at her in dismay.

'But you,' he said, 'why will you not come with us?'

'I shall follow you,' she said, 'to-morrow.'

He began to pace up and down the room.

'I imagined we could all travel together, when this business is over,' he protested. 'They'll be hanging that fellow to-morrow in all probability. I thought of going over to see Godolphin and Eustick about it to-day. You'd like to see him hanged, would you not? We could fix it for nine in the morning, perhaps, and then start our journey afterwards.'

'Have you ever seen a man hanged?' she said.

'Why, yes, there's little to it, I admit. But this is rather different. Damn it, Dona, the fellow murdered poor Rock, and would have killed you too. Do you mean to say you have no wish for revenge?'

She did not answer, and he could not see her face, for her back was turned to him.

'George Godolphin would think it very cool of me,' he said, 'to slip away without a word of explanation.'

'I would do the explaining,' she said. 'I propose calling on him myself this afternoon, after you have gone.'

'Do you mean that I should deliberately set off on the journey, without you, taking the children and the nurse, and leaving you here, all alone, with a handful of half-witted servants?'

'Exactly that, Harry.'

'And if I take the carriage for the children, and ride myself, how would you travel to-morrow?'

'I should hire a post-chaise from Helston.'

'And join with us at Okehampton you mean, in the evening?'

'And join with you at Okehampton, in the evening.'

He stood by the window, staring moodily out on to the garden.

'Oh, God damn it, Dona, shall I ever understand you?'

'No, Harry,' she said, 'but it does not matter very much.'

'It does matter,' he said, 'it makes life most confounded hell for both of us.'

She glanced up at him standing there with his hands behind his back.

'Do you really think that?' she said.

He shrugged his shoulders. 'Oh, damme,' he said, 'I don't know what I think. I only know I'd give everything in the world to make you happy, but the cursed trouble is I don't know how to, and you are fonder of James's fingernail than you are of me. What's a fellow to do when his wife doesn't love him but drink and play cards? Will you tell me that?'

She stood beside him a moment, and put her hand on his shoulder. 'I shall be thirty in three weeks' time,' she said. 'Perhaps as I grow older, Harry, I shall grow wiser.'

'I don't want you any wiser,' he said sullenly, 'I want you as you are.'

She did not answer, and playing with her sleeve he said to her, 'Do you remember, before you came to Navron, you said some nonsense or other about feeling like that bird in your father's aviary. I couldn't make head or tail of it, and I still can't. It sounded such gibberish, you know. I wish I knew what you were driving at.'

'Don't think about it,' she said, patting his cheek, 'because the linnet found its way to the sky. And now, Harry, are you going to do what I asked you?'

'Yes, I suppose so,' he said, 'but I warn you, I don't like it, and I shall put up at Okehampton and wait for you. You won't delay your journey for any reason, will you?'

'No,' she said. 'No, I won't delay.'

And he went downstairs to make the necessary arrangements for departure, while she summoned Prue and told her of the sudden change of plans. At once all was bustle and confusion, the strapping up of bedding and boxes, the packing of food and clothing for the journey, while the children ran about like puppies, delighted in all movement, any sort of change for the variety it gave, and 'They don't mind leaving Navron,' thought Dona; 'in a month's time they will be playing in Hampshire fields, and Cornwall will be forgotten. Children forget places so easily, and faces even faster.'

They had cold meat at one o'clock, the children eating with herself and Harry for a treat. Henrietta danced about the table like a fairy, white with excitement because he was to ride beside their carriage. James sat on Dona's lap, endeavouring to put his feet up on the table, and when Dona permitted him, he looked about him with an air of triumph, and she kissed his fat cheek and held him to her. Harry caught something of his children's excitement, and he began to tell them about Hampshire, and how they would go there in all probability, for the rest of the summer. 'You shall have a pony, Henrietta,' he said, 'and James too, later on,' and he began to throw pieces of meat across the floor to the dogs, and the children clapped their hands and shouted.

The carriage came to the door, and they were bundled inside with packages, rugs, pillows, and the baskets for the two dogs, while Harry's horse champed at his bit, and pawed the ground.

'You must make my peace with George Godolphin,' said Harry, bending down to Dona, flicking his boots with his whip. 'He won't understand it, you know, my tearing off in this way.'

'Leave everything to me,' she answered, 'I shall know what to say.'

'I still don't know why you won't come with us,' he said, staring at her, 'but we'll be waiting for you, to-morrow evening, at Okehampton. When we pass through Helston to-day I will order your chaise for the morning.'

'Thank you, Harry.'

He went on flicking the toe of his boot. 'Stand still, will you, you brute?' he said to his horse; and then to Dona, 'I believe you've still got that damned fever on you, and you won't admit it.'

'No,' she said, 'I have no fever.'

'Your eyes are strange,' he said; 'they looked different to me the first moment I saw you, lying in bed there, up in your room. The expression has changed. God damn it, I don't know what it is.'

'I told you this morning,' she said, 'I'm getting older, and shall be thirty in three weeks' time. It's my age you can see in my eyes.'

'Damn it, it's not,' he said. 'Ah, well, I suppose I'm a fool and a blockhead, and will have to spend the rest of my days wondering what the hell has happened to you.'

'I rather think you will, Harry,' she said.

Then he waved his whip, and wheeled his horse about, and cantered away down the drive, while the carriage followed soberly, the two children smiling from the window and blowing kisses, until they turned the corner of the avenue and could see her no more.

Dona went through the empy dining-hall and into the garden. It seemed to her that the house already had a strange, deserted appearance, as though it knew in its old bones that soon the covers would be placed upon the chairs, and the shutters drawn, and the doors bolted, and nothing would be there any longer but its own secret darkness: no sunshine, no voices, no laughter, only the quiet memories of the things that had been.

Here, beneath this tree, she had lain on her back in the sun and watched the butterflies, and Godolphin had called upon her for the first time, surprising her with her ringlets in disorder and the flowers behind her ears. And in the woods there had been bluebells, where there were bluebells no more, and the bracken had been young which was now waist-high and darkly green. So much loveliness, swiftly come and swiftly gone, and she knew in her heart that this was the last time of looking upon it all, and that she would never come to Navron again. Part of her would linger there for ever: a footstep running tip-toe to the creek, the touch of her hand on a tree, the imprint of her body in the long grass. And perhaps one day, in after years, someone would wander there and listen to the silence, as she had done, and catch the whisper of the dreams that she had dreamt there, in midsummer, under the hot sun and the white sky.

Then she turned her back on the garden, and calling to the stable-boy in the courtyard she bade him catch the cob who was in the meadow, and put a saddle on him, for she was going riding.

Chapter Twenty-two

When Dona came to Gweek she made straight for a little cottage almost buried in the woods, a hundred yards or so from the road, which she knew instinctively to be the place she sought. Passing there once before she had seen a woman at the doorway, young and pretty, and William, driving the carriage, had saluted her with his whip.

'There have been ugly rumours,' Godolphin had said, 'of young women in distress,' and Dona smiled to herself, thinking of the girl's blush as she remembered it, and William's expression, his gallant bow, little guessing that his mistress had observed him.

The cottage appeared deserted, and Dona, dismounting, and knocking on the door, wondered for one moment if she had been mistaken after all. Then she heard a movement from the scrap of garden at the back, and she caught the glimpse of a petticoat disappearing into a door, and that door suddenly shutting, and the bolt being drawn. She knocked gently, and getting no answer called, 'Don't be afraid. It is Lady St. Columb from Navron.'

In a minute or two the bolt was pulled back, and the door was opened, and on the threshold stood William himself, with the flushed face of the young woman peering behind his shoulder.

'My lady,' he said, staring at her, with his button mouth twisted. She feared for one moment he was going to break down and cry. Then he stiffened, and held the door open wide. 'Run upstairs, Grace,' he said to the girl, 'her ladyship wishes to speak to me alone.'

The girl obeyed him, and Dona preceded William into the little kitchen, and sat down by the low hearth, and looked at him.

He still wore his right arm in a sling, and his head was bandaged, but he was the same William, standing before her as though he awaited her instructions for the ordering of supper.

'Prue gave me your message, William,' she said, and because he stood there so stiffly, without expression, she smiled at him with understanding. He said humbly, his eyes downcast, 'My lady, what can I say to you? I would have died for you that night, and instead I proved false, and lay like a sick child on the floor of the nursery.'

'You could not help it,' she said. 'You were weak and faint from loss of blood, and your prisoner proved too swift and cunning for you. But I have not come to talk about that, William.'

For a moment his eyes entreated her, but she shook her head. 'No questions,' she said, 'for I know what you would ask me. I am well, and strong, and quite unhurt, and what happened that night does not concern you. It is all over and put aside. Do you understand?'

'Yes, my lady, since you insist.'

'Sir Harry and Prue and the children left Navron just after noon to-day. The only thing that matters now is that we help your master. You know what happened?'

'I know, my lady, that the ship was lucky enough to escape with the crew safe aboard, but that my master lies a prisoner in the care of Lord Godolphin.'

'And time is short, William, for his lordship and the others may take the law into their own hands, and do what they would do to him – before the escort comes from Bristol. We may have a few hours only, and therefore we must work to-night.'

She made him sit down on the stool beside the hearth, and she showed the pistol she had secreted in her habit, and the knife as well. 'The pistol is loaded,' she said, 'and when I leave you now, I shall proceed to his lordship's, and somehow gain admittance to the keep. It should not prove difficult, for his lordship is a fool.'

'And then, my lady?' he asked.

'And then I shall assume that your master already has a plan prepared, and we will act upon it. He will realise the desperate importance of time, and may wish us to have horses waiting, at an hour to be decided upon.'

'That should not prove impossible, my lady. There are ways and means of procuring horses.'

'I can believe it, William.'

'The young woman who is giving me hospitality. . . .'

'A very charming young woman, William.'

'Your ladyship is gracious. The young woman who is giving me hospitality may prove helpful over the matter of horses. You can safely leave the matter in my hands.'

'And the young woman also, as I did Prue, when I went away with your master.'

'My lady, I declare to you most solemnly that I never touched a hair of Prue's head.'

'Probably not, William, we will not discuss it. Very well then. The first move in the game is understood. I shall return here, after my visit to Lord Godolphin, and tell you what has been arranged.'

'Very good, my lady.'

He opened the door for her, and she stood a moment, smiling at him, before she passed into the little overgrown garden.

'We are not going to fail, William,' she said. 'In three days' time, or less than that perhaps, you will see the cliffs of Brittany. It will please you, will it not, to smell France again?'

And he would have asked her a question, but she walked swiftly down the path, and to her horse, tethered to the bough of a tree. Now that she was employed, and action was demanded of her, she felt resolute and strong, and the strange wistfulness that had come upon her as she stood alone in the garden at Navron had gone with the moment that brought it. All that belonged to the past. She rode swiftly, the sturdy cob striding out well along the muddy lane, and soon she came to the park gates of Godolphin's estate, and in the distance she saw the grey outline of his house, and the squat tower and strong walls of the keep that formed part of the mansion. There was one narrow slit in the tower, midway between the battlement and the ground, and as she passed beneath it her heart beat strongly, with sudden excitement: that must be his prison, and he might have heard the sound of her horse and, climbing to the slit, be looking down upon her.

A servant ran forward to take her horse, glancing at her in surprise, and wondering, she thought, what the Lady St. Columb of Navron could be doing in the heat of the afternoon upon a rough country cob, alone, and unattended by husband or groom.

She passed into the long hall, enquiring whether his lordship would see her, and while she waited she looked out of the long windows on to the park, and she saw, roped apart from its fellows in the centre of the grass, a tall tree, far taller than its fellows, and there was a man upon one of the wide branches, working with a saw, calling down to a little group of men beneath.

She turned away, feeling cold suddenly, a little sick, and then she heard a footstep coming across the hall, and Lord Godolphin advanced towards her, his usual composure somewhat ruffled. 'My very humble apologies, madam,' he said, kissing her hand, 'I fear I kept you waiting, the truth is that your visit is somewhat inopportune – we are all rather concerned – the fact of the matter is that my wife is in labour, and we await the physician.'

'My dear Lord Godolphin, you must forgive me,' said Dona, 'and had I known I would never have disturbed you. But I bring messages from Harry, you see, and his apologies. Something in London necessitated his immediate return, he left at noon to-day with the children, and . . .'

'Harry left for town?' he said, in astonishment. 'But it was all arranged that he should come to-morrow. Half the countryside will be gathered here for the occasion. The men are preparing the tree, as you can see. Harry was most insistent that he must see the Frenchman hang.'

'He asked most humbly for your forgiveness,' she said, 'but the matter was really pressing. His Majesty himself, I believe, is concerned in it.'

'Oh, well, naturally madam, under such circumstances, I understand. But it is a pity, a very great pity. The occasion is so unusual, and such a triumph. And as things are turning out, it looks as though we may celebrate something else at the same time.' He coughed, bridling with self-esteem and importance, and then, as the sound of carriage wheels came to their ears, he looked away from her, towards the door. 'This will be the physician,' he said quickly, 'you will, I am sure, excuse me a moment.'

'But of course, Lord Godolphin,' she smiled, and turning away, wandered into the small salon and stood thinking rapidly, while from the hall she heard voices, and murmurs, and heavy footsteps, and 'He is so agitated,' she thought, 'that if we seized his wig again, he could not notice it.'

The footsteps and the voices disappeared up the broad staircase, and Dona, looking from the window, saw that there were no guards outside the keep, or in the avenue; they must be within the keep itself. After five minutes

Godolphin returned, looking if possible more flushed and concerned than before.

'The physician is with her ladyship now,' he said, 'but he seems to think nothing is likely to occur until late this evening. It seems rather remarkable, I had no idea, indeed I considered that any minute . . .'

'Wait,' she said, 'until you have been a father a dozen times, and then perhaps you will understand that babies are leisurely creatures, and like to linger over this business of entering the world. Dear Lord Godolphin, I wish I could distract you. I'm sure your wife is in no danger at all. Is that where the Frenchman is imprisoned?'

'Yes, madam, and spends his time, so his jailers tell me, in drawing birds upon a sheet of paper. The fellow is mad, of course.'

'Of course.'

'Congratulations are pouring in upon me from all over the county. I flatter myself that I have earned them. It was I, you know, who disarmed the scoundrel.'

'How courageous of you.'

'It is true he gave his sword into my hands, but nevertheless it was to me he gave it.'

'I shall make a great story of it at Court, Lord Godolphin, when I am next at St. James's. His Majesty will be very impressed with your handling of the whole affair. You were the genius of it all.'

'Ah, you flatter me, madam.'

'No, indeed. Harry would agree with me I know. I wish I had some souvenir of the Frenchman to show His Majesty. Do you think, as he is a draughtsman, he would give me one of his drawings?'

'The easiest thing in the world. They are scattered all over his cell.'

'I have forgotten so much, heaven be praised, of that fearful night,' sighed Dona, 'that I cannot now recollect his appearance, except that he was extremely large and black and fierce, and appallingly ugly.'

'You are somewhat at fault, madam, I should not describe him so. He is not so large a man as myself, for instance, and, like all Frenchmen, has a sly rather than an ugly face.'

'What a pity it is that I cannot see him, and so give a strictly accurate description of him to His Majesty.'

'You will not come then to-morrow?'

'Alas, no. I go to rejoin Harry and the children.'

'I suppose,' said Lord Godolphin, 'that I could permit you a glimpse of the rascal in his cell. But I understand from Harry that after the tragedy the other night you could scarcely abide to speak of the fellow – that he had so terrified you in short, that . . .'

'To-day, Lord Godolphin, is so different from the other night. I have you to protect me, and the Frenchman is unarmed. I would like to paint a picture to His Majesty of the notorious pirate, caught and put to death by the most faithful of his Cornish subjects.'

'Then you shall, madam, you shall. When I think what you might have endured at his hands, I would willingly hang him three times over. I believe it was the excitement and alarm of the whole affair that precipitated her ladyship's confinement.'

'Most probably,' said Dona gravely, and seeing that he still would talk of the matter, and might even yet plunge into domestic details which she understood more thoroughly than he did himself, she added, 'Let us go now, then, while the physician is with your wife.' Before he could protest, she walked out of the salon into the hall, and so to the steps before the house, and he was forced to accompany her, glancing up at the windows of the house as he did so.

'My poor Lucy,' he said, 'if only I could have spared her this ordeal.'

'You should have thought of that nine months ago, my lord,' she answered, and he stared at her, greatly embarrassed and shocked, and murmured something about having hoped for years for a son and heir.

'Which I am sure she will give you,' smiled Dona, 'even if you have ten daughters first.' And here they were at the keep, standing in the small stone entrance, where two men were standing, armed with muskets, and another was seated on a bench before a table. 'I have promised Lady St. Columb a glance at our prisoner,' said Godolphin, and the man at the table looked up and grinned.

'He won't be fit for a lady to see this time to-morrow, my lord,' he said and Godolphin laughed loudly. 'No, that is why her ladyship has come to-day.' The guard led the way up the narrow stone stairway, taking a key from his chain, and 'There is no other door,' thought Dona, 'no other stair. And the men below there, always on guard.' The key turned in the lock, and once again her heart began to beat, foolishly, ridiculously, as it always did whenever she was about to look on him. The jailer threw open the door, and she stepped inside, with Godolphin behind her, and then the jailer withdrew, locking the door upon them. He was sitting at a table, as he had done the first time she had seen him, and on his face was the same absorbed expression that he had worn then, intent upon his occupation, thinking of nothing else, so that Godolphin, put out of countenance by his prisoner's indifference, thumped his hand on the table and said sharply, 'Stand up, can't you, when I choose to visit you?'

The indifference was no play, as Dona knew, for so intent was the Frenchman upon his drawing, that he had not known the footstep of Godolphin from the jailer. He pushed the drawing aside – it was a curlew, Dona saw, flying across an estuary towards the open sea – and then for the first time he saw her, and making no sign of recognition, he stood up, and bowed, and said nothing.

'This is Lady St. Columb,' said Godolphin stiffly, 'who, disappointed that she cannot see you hanged to-morrow, wishes to take one of your drawings back to town with her, so that His Majesty may have a souvenir of one of the biggest blackguards that ever troubled his faithful subjects.'

'Lady St. Columb is very welcome,' said the prisoner. 'Having had little else to do during the last few days, I can offer her a fair selection. What is your favourite bird, madam?'

'That,' answered Dona, 'is something I can never decide. Sometimes I think it is a night-jar.'

'I regret I cannot offer you a night-jar,' he said, rummaging amongst the papers on the table. 'You see, when I last heard one, I was so intent upon another occupation that I did not observe the night-jar as clearly as I might have done.'

'You mean,' said Godolphin sternly, 'that you were so intent upon robbing one of my friends of his possessions for your personal gratification that you gave no thought to any other distraction.'

'My lord,' bowed the captain of *La Mouette*, 'I have never before heard the occupation in question so delicately described.'

Dona turned over the drawings on the table. 'Here is a herring-gull,' she said, 'but I think you have not given him his full plumage.'

'The drawing is unfinished, madam,' he replied, 'this particular sea-gull dropped one of its feathers in flight. If you know anything about the species you will remember, however, that they seldom venture far to sea. This particular gull, for instance, is probably only ten miles from the coast at the present moment.'

'No doubt,' said Dona, 'and then to-night he will return again to the shore in search of the feather he has lost.'

'Your ladyship knows little of ornithology,' said Godolphin. 'For my part I have never heard of a sea-gull or any other bird picking up feathers.'

'I had a feather mattress as a child,' said Dona, talking rather quickly, and smiling at Godolphin, 'and I remember the feathers became loose after a while, and one of them fluttered from the window of my bedroom and fell into the garden below. Of course the window was a large one, not like the slit that gives light to this cell.'

'Oh, of course,' answered his lordship, a little puzzled, and he glanced at her doubtfully, wondering if she still had a touch of fever, for surely she sounded a little light in the head.

'Did they ever blow under the door?' enquired the prisoner.

'Ah, that I can't remember,' said Dona, 'I think that even a feather would have difficulty in passing beneath a door . . . unless of course it was given assistance, like a strong breath of air, you know, say the draught from a barrel of a pistol. But I have not chosen my drawing. Here is a sanderling, I wonder if this would please His Majesty. My lord, do I hear wheels upon the drive? If so, it must be that the physician is departing.'

Lord Godolphin clicked his tongue in annoyance, and looked towards the door. 'He surely would not leave without consulting me first,' he said. 'Are you certain you hear wheels? I am a little deaf.'

'I could not be more certain in the world,' answered Dona.

His lordship strode to the door, and thumped upon it.

'Ho, there,' he called, 'unlock the door, will you, immediately?'

The jailer called in answer, and they could hear his footstep mount the narrow stair. In a moment Dona had passed the pistol and the knife from her riding-habit on to the table, and the prisoner had seized them from her, and covered them with a mass of his drawings. The jailer unlocked the door, and Godolphin turned, and looked at Dona.

'Well, madam,' he said, 'have you chosen your drawing?'

Dona fluttered the drawings in distraction, wrinkling her brow.

'It is really most monstrously difficult,' she said. 'I cannot decide between the sea-gull and the sanderling. Do not wait for me, my lord, you must know by this time that a woman can never make up her mind. I will follow you in a moment or two.'

'It is really imperative that I see the physician,' said Godolphin, 'so that if you will excuse me, madam. You remain here with her ladyship,' he added to the guard, as he left the cell.

Once again the guard closed the door, and this time stood against it, his arms folded and he smiled across at Dona with understanding.

'We shall have two celebrations to-morrow, my lady,' he said.

'Yes,' she said, 'I hope for your sake that it proves to be a boy. There will be more ale for all of you.'

'Am I not the only cause for excitement?' asked the prisoner.

The guard laughed, and jerked his head towards the slit in the cell.

'You'll be forgotten by midday,' he said, 'you'll be dangling from the tree, while the rest of us drink to the future Lord Godolphin.'

'It seems rather hard that neither the prisoner nor myself will be here to drink the health of the son and heir,' smiled Dona, and she drew her purse from her pocket, and threw it to the jailer. 'I wager,' she said, 'that you would rather do so now, than keeping watch below, hour after hour. Supposing we drink now, the three of us, while his lordship is with the physician?'

The jailer grinned and winked at his prisoner.

'If we do, it won't be the first time I've drunk ale before an execution,' he said. 'But I will say one thing, and that is that I've never seen a Frenchman hang yet. They tell me they die quicker than we do. The bones in their neck are more brittle,' and winking again, he unlocked the door, and called down to his assistant.

'Bring three glasses, and a jug of ale.'

While his back was turned Dona questioned the prisoner with her eyes, and his lips moved soundlessly.

'To-night at eleven.'

She nodded, and whispered 'William and I.'

The jailer looked over his shoulder. 'If his lordship catches us there'll be the devil to pay,' he said.

'I would absolve you,' said Dona, 'this is the sort of jest that will please His Majesty when I see him at Court. What is your name?'

'Zachariah Smith, my lady.'

'Very well, then, Zachariah, if trouble come of this, I will plead your case to the king himself.'

The jailer laughed, and his assistant coming this moment with the ale, he closed the door, and carried the tray to the table.

'Long life then to your ladyship,' he said, 'a full purse and a good appetite to myself, and to you, sir, a speedy death.'

He poured the ale into the glasses, and Dona, clicking hers against the jailer's, said, 'Long life, then, to the future Lord Godolphin.'

The jailer smacked his lips, and tilted his head.

The prisoner raised his glass and smiled at Dona.

'Should we not also drink to Lady Godolphin, at this moment, I imagine, suffering somewhat of discomfort?'

'And,' replied Dona, 'to the physician also, who will be rather heated.' As she drank, an idea flashed suddenly to her mind, and glancing at the Frenchman, she knew instinctively that the same thought had come to him, for he was looking at her.

'Zachariah Smith, are you a married man?' she said.

The jailer laughed. 'Twice married,' he said, 'and the father of fourteen.'

'Then you know what his lordship is enduring at this moment,' she smiled, 'but with so able a physician as Doctor Williams there is little cause for anxiety. You know the doctor well, I suppose?'

'No, my lady. I come from the north coast. I am not a Helston man.'

'Doctor Williams,' said Dona dreamily, 'is a funny little fellow, with a round solemn face, and a mouth like a button. I have heard it said that he is as good a judge of ale as any man living.'

'Then it's a great pity,' said the prisoner, laying down his glass, 'that he does not drink with us now. Perhaps he will do so later, when his day's work is finished, and he has made a father of Lord Godolphin.'

'Which will not be much before midnight, what do you say, Zachariah Smith, and father of fourteen?' asked Dona.

'Midnight is generally the hour, your ladyship,' laughed the jailer, 'all nine of my boys were born as the clock struck twelve.'

'Very well, then,' said Dona, 'when I see Doctor Williams directly I will tell him that in honour of the occasion, Zachariah Smith who can boast of more than a baker's dozen, will be pleased to drink a glass of ale with him before he goes on duty for the night.'

'Zachariah, you will remember this evening for the rest of your life,' said the prisoner.

The jailer replaced the glasses on the tray. 'If Lord Godolphin has a son,' he said, winking an eye, 'there'll be so much rejoicing on the estate that we'll be forgetting to hang you in the morning.'

Dona took up the drawing of the sea-gull from the table. 'Well,' she said, 'I have chosen my drawing. And rather than his lordship should see you with the tray, Zachariah, I will descend with you, and we will leave the prisoner with his pen and his birds. Good-bye, Frenchman, and may you slip away to-morrow as easily as the feather did from my mattress.'

The prisoner bowed. 'It will depend,' he said, 'upon the quantity of ale that my jailer consumes to-night with Doctor Williams.'

'He'll have to boast a stout head if he can beat mine,' said the jailer, and he unlocked the door, and held it open for her to pass.

'Good-bye, Lady St. Columb,' said the prisoner, and she stood for a

moment looking at him, realising that the plan they had in mind was more
hazardous and more foolhardy than any that he had yet attempted, and that
if it should fail there would be no further chance of escape, for to-morrow
he would hang from the tree there in the park. Then he smiled, as though
in secret, and it seemed to her that his smile was the personification of
himself, it was the thing in him that she had first loved, and would always
cherish, and it conjured the picture in her mind of *La Mouette*, and the sun,
and the wind upon the sea, and with it too the dark shadows of the creek,
the wood fire and the silence. She went out of the cell without looking at
him, her head in the air, and her drawing in her hand, and 'He will never
know,' she thought, 'at what moment I have loved him best.'

She followed the jailer down the narrow stair, her heart heavy, her body
suddenly tired with all the weariness of anti-climax. The jailer, grinning at
her, put the tray under the steps, and said, 'Cold-blooded, isn't he, for a man
about to die? They say these Frenchmen have no feelings.'

She summoned a smile, and held out her hand. 'You are a good fellow,
Zachariah,' she said, 'and may you drink many glasses of ale in the future,
and some of them to-night. I won't forget to tell the physician to call upon
you. A little man, remember, with a mouth like a button.'

'But a throat like a well,' laughed the jailer. 'Very good, your ladyship,
I will look out for him, and he shall quench his thirst. Not a word to his
lordship, though.'

'Not a word, Zachariah,' said Dona solemnly, and she went out of the
dark keep into the sunshine, and there was Godolphin himself coming down
the drive to meet her.

'You were wrong, madam,' he said, wiping his forehead, 'the carriage has
not moved, and the physician is still with my wife. He has decided after all
that he will remain for the present, as poor Lucy is in some distress. Your
ears must have played you false.'

'And I sent you back to the house, all to no purpose,' said Dona. 'So very
stupid of me, dear Lord Godolphin, but then women, you know, are very
stupid creatures. Here is the picture of a sea-gull. Do you think it will please
His Majesty?'

'You are a better judge of his taste than I, madam,' said Godolphin, 'or
so I presume. Well, did you find the pirate as ruthless as you expected?'

'Prison has softened him, my lord, or perhaps it is not prison, but the
realisation that in your keeping, escape is impossible. It seemed to me that
when he looked at you he knew that he had at last met a better, and a more
cunning brain than his own.'

'Ah, he gave you that impression, did he? Strange, I have sometimes
thought the opposite. But these foreigners are half women, you know. You
never know what they are thinking.'

'Very true, my lord.' They stood before the steps of the house, and there
was the physician's carriage, and the servant still holding Dona's cob. 'You
will take some refreshment, madam, before you go?' enquired Godolphin,
and 'No,' she answered, 'no, I have stayed too long as it is, for I have much
to do to-night before my journey in the morning. My respects to your wife,

when she is in a state to receive them, and I hope that before the evening is out, she will have presented you with a replica of yourself, dear Lord Godolphin.'

'That, madam,' he said gravely, 'is in the hands of the Almighty.'

'But very soon,' she said, mounting her horse, 'in the equally capable hands of the physician. Good-bye.' She waved her hand to him, and was gone, striking the cob into a startled canter with her whip, and as she drew rein past the keep and looked up at the slit in the tower she whistled a bar of the song that Pierre Blanc played on his lute, and slowly, like a snow-flake, a feather drifted down in the air towards her, a feather torn from the quill of a pen. She caught it, caring not a whit if Godolphin saw her from the steps of his house, and she waved her hand again, and rode out on to the high-road laughing, with the feather in her hat.

Chapter Twenty-three

Dona leaned from the casement of her bedroom at Navron, and as she looked up into the sky she saw, for the first time, the little gold crescent of the new moon high above the dark trees.

'That is for luck,' she thought, and she waited a moment, watching the shadows in the still garden, and breathing the heavy sweet scent of the magnolia tree that climbed the wall beneath her. These things must be stored and remembered in her heart with all the other beauty that had gone, for she would never look upon them again.

Already the room itself wore the appearance of desertion, like the rest of the house, and her boxes were strapped upon the floor, her clothes folded and packed by the maid-servant, according to instruction. When she had returned, late in the afternoon, hot and dusty from her ride, and the groom had taken the cob from her in the courtyard, the ostler from the Inn at Helston was waiting to speak to her.

'Sir Harry left word with us, your ladyship,' he said, 'that you would be hiring a chaise to-morrow, to follow him to Okehampton.'

'Yes,' she said.

'And the landlord sent me to tell you, your ladyship, that the chaise will be available, and will be here for you at noon to-morrow.'

'Thank you,' she had said, staring away from him towards the trees in the avenue, and the woods that led to the creek, for everything he said to her lacked reality, the future was something with which she had no concern. As she left him and went into the house he looked after her, puzzled, scratching his head, for she seemed to him like a sleep-walker, and he did not believe she had fully understood what he had told her. She wandered then to the nursery, and stared down at the stripped beds, and the bare boards, for the carpets had been taken up. The curtains were drawn too, and the air was already hot and unused. Beneath one of the beds lay the arm of a stuffed rabbit that James had sucked, and then torn from the rabbit's body in a tantrum.

She picked it up and held it, turning it over in her hands. There was something forlorn about it, like a relic of bygone days. She could not leave it lying there on the floor, so she opened the great wardrobe in the corner, and threw it inside, and shut the door upon it, and then left the room and did not go into it again.

At seven her supper was brought to her on a tray, and she ate little of it, not being hungry. Then she gave orders to the servant not to disturb her again during the evening, for she was tired, and not to call her in the morning, for she would sleep late in all probability, before the tedium of the journey.

When she was alone, she undid the bundle that William had given her on her return from Lord Godolphin. Smiling to herself she drew out the rough stockings, the worn breeches, and the patched though gaily coloured shirt. She remembered his look of embarrassment as he had given them to her, and his words: 'These are the best Grace can do for you, my lady, they belong to her brother.' 'They are perfect, William,' she had replied, 'and Pierre Blanc himself could have done no better.' For she must play the boy again, for the last time, and escape from her woman's clothes for this night at least. 'I will be able to run better without petticoats,' she said to William, 'and I can ride astride my horse, like I used to as a child.' He had procured the horses, as he had promised, and was to meet her with them on the road from Navron to Gweek just after nine o'clock.

'You must not forget, my William,' she said, 'that you are a physician, and that I am your groom, and it were better that you should drop "my lady" and call me Tom.'

He had looked away from her in embarrassment. 'My lady,' he said, 'my lips could not frame the word, it would be too distressing.' She had laughed, and told him that physicians must never be embarrassed, especially when they had just brought sons and heirs into the world. And now she was dressing herself in the lad's clothes, and they fitted her well, even the shoes, unlike the clumsy clogs belonging to Pierre Blanc; there was a handkerchief too, which she wound about her head, and a leather strap for her waist. She looked at herself in the mirror, her dark curls concealed, her skin a gipsy brown, and 'I am a cabin-boy again,' she thought, 'and Dona St. Columb is asleep and dreaming.'

She listened at her door, and all was still; the servants were safe in their own quarters. She braced herself for the ordeal of descending the stairway to the dining-hall, for this was what she dreaded most, in the darkness, with the candles unlit, and flooding her mind with sharp intensity was the memory of Rockingham crouching there, his knife in his hands. It was better, she thought, to shut her eyes, and feel her way along the landing to the stairs, for then she would not see the great shield on the wall, nor the outline of the stairs themselves. So she went down, her hands before her and her eyes tight shut, and all the while her heart was beating, and it seemed to her that Rockingham still waited for her in the darkest corner of the hall. With a sudden panic she flung herself upon the door, wrenching back the bolts, and ran out into the gathering dusk to the safety and stillness of the avenue. Once she was free of the house she was no longer afraid, the air was soft and warm, and the gravel crunched under her feet, while high in the pale sky the new moon gleamed like a sickle.

She walked swiftly, for there was freedom in her boy's clothes, and her spirits rose, and once again she fell to whistling Pierre Blanc's song, and she thought of him too, with his merry monkey face and his white teeth, waiting now on the deck of *La Mouette* somewhere in mid-channel, for the master he had left behind.

She saw a shadow move towards her, round the bend of the road, and there was William with the horses, and there was a lad with him, Grace's brother she presumed, and the owner of the clothes she wore.

William left the boy with the horses, and came towards her, and she saw, the laughter rising within her, that he had borrowed a black suit of clothes, and white stockings, and he wore a dark curled wig.

'Was it a son or a daughter, Doctor Williams?' she asked and he looked at her with confusion, not entirely happy at the part he had to play: for that he should be the gentleman and she the groom seemed to him shocking, who was shocked at nothing else.

'How much does he know?' she whispered, pointing to the lad.

'Nothing, my lady,' he whispered, 'only that I am a friend of Grace's, and am in hiding, and that you are a companion who would help me to escape.'

'Then Tom I will be,' she insisted, 'and Tom I will remain.' And she went on whistling Pierre Blanc's song, to discomfort William, and going to one of the horses she swung herself up into the saddle, and smiled at the lad, and digging her heels into the side of the horse, she clattered ahead of them along the road, laughing at them over her shoulder. When they came to the wall of Godolphin's estate they dismounted, and left the lad there with the horses, under cover of the trees. She and William went on foot the half-mile to the park-gates, for so they had arranged earlier in the evening.

It was dark now, with the first stars in the sky, and they said nothing to one another as they walked, for all had been planned and put in readiness. They felt like actors who must appear upon the boards for the first time, with an audience who might be hostile. The gates were shut, and they turned aside, and climbed the wall into the park, and crept towards the drive under shadow of the trees. In the distance they could see the outline of the house, and there was a light still in the line of windows above the door.

'The son and heir still tarries,' whispered Dona. She went on ahead of William to the house, and there, at the entrance to the stables, she could see the physician's carriage drawn up on the cobbled stones, and the coachman was seated with one of Godolphin's grooms on an upturned seat beneath a lantern, thumbing a pack of cards. She could hear the low murmur of the voices, and their laughter. She turned back again, and went to William. He was standing beside the drive, his small white face dwarfed by his borrowed wig and his hat. She could see the butt of his pistol beneath his coat, and his mouth was set in a firm thin line.

'Are you ready?' she said, and he nodded, his eyes fixed upon her, and he followed her along the drive to the keep. She had a moment of misgiving, for she realised suddenly that perhaps, like other actors, he lacked confidence in his part, and would stumble over his words, and the game would be lost because William, upon whom so much depended, had no skill. As they stood before the closed door of the keep she looked at him, and tapped him on the shoulder, and for the first time that evening he smiled, his small eyes twinkling in his round face, and her faith in him returned, for he would not fail.

He had become, in a moment, the physician, and as he knocked upon the door of the keep, he called, in full round tones surprisingly unlike the William she knew at Navron: 'Is there one Zachariah Smith within, and may Doctor Williams from Helston have a word with him?'

Dona could hear an answering shout from the keep, and in a moment the door swung open, and there was her friend the guard standing on the threshold, his jacket thrown aside because of the heat, his sleeves rolled high above his elbows, and a grin on his face from ear to ear.

'So her ladyship didn't forget her promise?' he said. 'Well, come inside, sir, you are very welcome, and we have enough ale here, I tell you, to christen the baby and yourself into the bargain. Was it a boy?'

'It was indeed, my friend,' said William, 'a fine boy, and the image of his lordship.' He rubbed his hands together, as though in satisfaction, and followed the jailer within, while the door was left ajar, so that Dona, crouching beside the wall of the keep, could hear them move about the entrance, and she could hear too the clink of glasses, and the laughter of the guard. 'Well, sir,' he was saying, 'I've fathered fourteen and I may say I know the business as well as you. What was the weight of the child?'

'Ah,' said William, 'the weight now . . . let me see,' and Dona, choking back her laughter, could picture him standing there, his brows drawn together in perplexity, ignorant as a baby himself would be at such a question. 'Round about four pounds I should say, though I cannot recollect the exact figure . . .' he began, and there came a whistle of astonishment from the jailer, and a burst of laughter from his assistant.

'Do you call that a fine boy?' he said, 'why, curse me, sir, the child will never live. My youngest turned the scale at eleven pounds when he was born, and he looked a shrimp at that.'

'Did I say four?' broke in William hastily. 'A mistake of course. I meant fourteen. Nay, now I come to remember, it was somewhere around fifteen or sixteen pounds.'

The jailer whistled again.

'God save you, sir, but that's something over the odds. It's her ladyship you must look to, and not the child. Is she well?'

'Very well,' said William, 'and in excellent spirits. When I left she was discussing with his lordship what names she would bestow upon her son.'

'Then she's a pluckier woman than I'd ever give her credit for,' answered the jailer. 'Well, sir, it seems to me you deserve three glasses after that. To bring a child of sixteen pounds into the world is a hard evening's work. Here's luck, sir, to you, and the child, and to the lady who drank with us here this evening, for she's worth twenty Lady Godolphins if I'm not mistaken.'

There was silence a moment, and the clinking of glasses, and Dona heard a great sigh from the jailer, and a smacking of lips.

'I warrant they don't brew stuff like that in France,' he said, 'it's all grapes and frogs over there, isn't it, and snails, and such-like? I took a glass just now to my prisoner above, and you'll scarcely credit me, sir, but he's a cold-blooded fish for a dying man, as you might say. He quaffed his ale in one draught and he slapped me on the shoulder, laughing.'

'It's the foreign blood,' broke in the second guard. 'They're all alike, Frenchmen, Dutchmen, Spaniards, no matter what they are. Women and drink is all they think about, and when you're not looking it's a stab in the back.'

'And what does he do his last day,' continued Zachariah, 'but cover sheets of paper with birds, and sit there smoking and smiling to himself. You'd think he'd send for a priest, for they're all papists, these fellows; it's robbery and rape one minute and confession and crucifixes the next. But not our Frenchman. He's a law to himself, I reckon. Will you have another glass, doctor?'

'Thank you, my man,' said William. Dona could hear the sound of the ale as it was poured in to the tankard, and she wondered, for the first time, how strong a head William had, and whether it was altogether wise to accept the jailer's invitation with so good a grace.

William coughed, dry and hard, a little signal to herself.

'I should be interested to see the man,' he said, 'after what I have heard. A very desperate person, by all accounts. The country will be well rid of him. He's asleep now, I suppose, if a man can sleep on his last night?'

'Asleep? Bless you, no, sir. He's had two glasses of ale, and he said you'd pay me for them, and that if you did turn up at the keep here before midnight he'd join you in another glass, and drink to the son and heir.' The jailer laughed, and then lowering his voice he added, 'It's irregular, sir, of course, but then, when a man is going to be hanged in the morning, even if he is a pirate and a Frenchman, you can't exactly wish him ill, can you, sir?' Dona could not catch William's reply, but she heard the chink of coins, and the scrape of feet. The jailer laughed again and said, 'Thank you, sir, you're a true gentleman, and when my wife's expecting again, I shall think of you.'

Now she could hear their feet climbing the stair to the room above, and she swallowed, her nails digging into the palms of her hands. For this was the moment now she feared above all others, when a slip might cause disaster, when recognition might come and all be lost. She waited until she judged them outside his cell above, and going close to the door she listened, and heard the sound of voices and the turning of a key in the lock. Then, when she heard the heavy clanging of the door upon them, she ventured to the entrance of the keep and stepped inside, and saw the two remaining guards with their backs towards her. One was sitting on a bench against the wall, yawning and stretching himself, and the other stood looking up the stair.

The light was dim, for only one lantern swung from the beam. Keeping in the shadow of the door she knocked, and said, 'Is Doctor Williams within?' The men turned at the sound of her voice, and the one on the bench blinked at her and said, 'What do you want with him?'

'They've sent word from the house,' she answered. 'Her ladyship's been taken worse.'

'Small wonder,' said the man by the stair, 'after carrying sixteen pounds. All right, lad, I'll tell him.' He began to mount the stair, calling as he did so, 'Zachariah, they want the doctor up at the house yonder.' Dona watched him turn the corner of the stair, and beat upon the door, and as he did so she kicked the door of the entrance with her foot, and slammed it, and shot the bolt and closed the grill, before the guard on the bench could rise to his feet and shout, 'Hi, there, what the devil are you doing?'

The table was between them, and as he came towards her she leant against it, putting all her weight upon it, and the table crashed on the floor with him sprawling upon it, and as he fell she heard a stifled cry from the stair above, and the sound of a blow. Then, seizing the jug of ale beside her, she threw it at the lantern and the light was extinguished. The man on the floor scrambled from beneath the table, shouting for Zachariah, and as he raised his voice, cursing and stumbling in the darkness, Dona heard the Frenchman call to her from the stair, 'Are you there, Dona?' and 'Yes,' she panted, half dazed with laughter and excitement and fear, and he sprang over the rail of the stone stair to the ground beneath, and found the man in the darkness. She heard them fighting there, close to the steps. He was using the butt end of the pistol; she could hear the blow. The man fell against the table, groaning, and 'Give me your handkerchief, Dona, for a gag,' said the Frenchman, and she tore it from her head.

In a moment he had done what he wished. 'Watch him,' he said swiftly, 'he cannot move,' and Dona heard the Frenchman slip away from her in the darkness, and climb the stair again to the cell above. 'Have you got him, William?' he said, and there was a funny strangled sob from the room above, and the sound of something heavy being dragged along the floor. She could hear the gagged man gasping for breath beside her, and all the while the heavy dragging sound from above, and a sudden desire to laugh rose in her throat, a terrible strained feeling of hysteria, and she knew if she gave way to it she would never stop, it would swell up within her like a scream.

Then the Frenchman called to her from above, 'Open the door, Dona, and see if the road is clear,' and she felt her way to it in the darkness, her hands fumbling with the heavy bolts. She wrenched it open, and looked out, and from the direction of the house she heard the sound of wheels, and down the drive towards the keep came the physician's carriage: she could hear the driver crack his whip and call to his horse.

She turned back inside the keep to warn them, but already the Frenchman was at her side, and she looked up into his face, and in his eyes she saw the reckless laughter that she had seen before when he had pricked the curled wig from Godolphin's head, and 'By heaven,' he said softly, 'it's the physician going home at last.'

He stepped out bare-headed into the drive, holding up his hand. 'What are you doing?' she whispered, 'are you mad, are you crazy?' But he laughed, taking no notice. The driver pulled up his horse at the entrance to the keep, and the long thin face of the physician appeared at the carriage window.

'Who are you, what do you want?' he said in querulous tones, and the Frenchman put his hands on the window, and smiled, and 'Did you give his lordship an heir then, and is he pleased with his baby?' he said.

'Pleased my foot,' swore the physician. 'There are twin daughters up there at the hall, and I'll thank you to take your hands off my carriage window and to let me pass, for all I want is my supper and my bed.'

'Ah, but you'll give us a ride first, won't you?' said the Frenchman, and in a moment he had knocked the driver from his seat, tumbling him down into the drive below, and 'Climb beside me, Dona,' he said; 'we'll ride in style if we ride at all.' She did as he bade her, shaking with laughter. And there was William, in his strange black coat, without wig and without his hat, slamming the door of the keep behind him, a pistol in his hands pointing in the face of the startled physician. 'Get inside, William,' called the Frenchman, 'and give the doctor a glass of ale, if you have any left, for by the lord, he's had a harder time to-night than we have had these last few minutes.'

Down the drive sped the carriage, the physician's horse breaking into a gallop, who had never galloped before, and they came abreast the park gates, firmly shut. 'Open them wide!' called the Frenchman, as a sleepy head appeared at the window of the lodge. 'Your master has twin daughters, and the physician wants his supper, and as for me and my cabin-boy, we've had ale enough this night to last us for thirty years.'

The gates were flung back, the lodge-keeper staring at them in astonishment, his mouth wide open, while from within the carriage came the protesting cries of the physician.

'Where are we bound, William?' called the Frenchman, and William thrust his round face through the window of the carriage. 'There are horses a mile up the road, m'sieu,' he said, 'but we are bound for Portleven on the coast.'

'We are bound for perdition, for all I care,' he answered, and he put his arm round Dona, and kissed her. 'Don't you know,' he said, 'that this is my last night in the world, and I'm going to be hanged in the morning?'

And with the horse galloping like a mad thing, and the white dust flying from the wheels, the carriage swung out on to the hard high-road.

Chapter Twenty-four

The adventure was over now, and the madness, and the laughter. Somewhere back on the road lay a carriage tumbled in a ditch, and a horse without bridle or rein grazed beside a hedge. There was a physician who walked along the high-road in search of his supper, and there were guards who lay bound and gagged upon a dungeon floor.

These things belonged to the evening, and had no place in the night that had come. For it was long past midnight now, and darker than it would ever be again. The stars were clustered thick like little pin-pricks of light, and the crescent moon had gone.

Dona stood beside her horse, looking down upon the lake, and she saw that it was separated from the sea by a bank of high shingle, and while the waves broke upon the shore the lake itself was still and undisturbed. There was no wind, and the sky for all its darkness had the strange clarity and radiance of midsummer. Now and again a wave a little larger than its fellows would spend itself upon the shingle beach, and murmur, and sigh, and the lake, catching a tremor from the sea would bear a ripple upon its surface of glass, and shiver an instant, while the ripple washed away into the bent reeds. Now and again there were bird noises from the pool, the startled cry of a moor-hen as it paddled amongst the reeds and hid itself, furtively rustling the tall stems, and there were whispers and stealthy movements from all the unknown nameless things that come out into the silent world at night, and live for a while, and breathe, and have their moment.

Beyond the woods and the hill lay the village of Portleven where the fishing boats were moored against the quay, and William looked up into his master's face, and then over his shoulder again towards the hill.

'It would be wise, m'sieu,' he said, 'if I went now, before the day breaks, and found a boat. I will bring it round to the beach here, and we can leave as the sun rises.'

'Do you think you will find a boat?' said the Frenchman.

'Yes, m'sieu,' he answered, 'there will be a small boat at the harbour entrance. I made enquiries, m'sieu, before I left Gweek.'

'William is resourceful,' said Dona. 'He forgets nothing. And because of him there will be no hanging in the morning, but only a small boat putting out to sea.'

The Frenchman looked at his servant, and the servant looked at Dona, as she stood beside the lake, and suddenly he went from them, over the ridge of shingle to the hill beyond, a curious little figure in his long black coat and his large three-cornered hat. He disappeared into the darkness, and they were alone. The horses grazed on to the grass beside the lake, and their soft mouths made a quiet crunching sound, and from the woods opposite the tall trees rustled and whispered and were still.

There was a hollow beside the lake, of smooth white sand, and there it was they built their fire, and presently a tongue of flame leapt upwards into the air, and the dry sticks crackled and broke.

He knelt close to the fire, the flame lighting his face and his throat and his hands, and 'Do you remember,' said Dona, 'that once you told me you would cook chicken for me on a spit?'

'Yes,' he answered, 'but to-night I have no chicken, and I have no spit, and my cabin-boy must be content with burnt bread instead.'

He frowned, concentrating upon his task, and because the heat of the fire was great he shook his head, and wiped his forehead with the sleeve of his shirt, and she knew that this was a picture of him that could never be lost, the fire, the lake, the dark sky studded with stars, and the sea breaking upon the shingle behind them.

'And so,' he said later, as they ate their supper, with the fire smaller than before and the bitter smell of wood smoke lingering in the air, 'you fought a man, my Dona, and he died, on the floor of Navron House.'

She stared across at him, but he was not looking at her; he was crunching the bread between his teeth. 'How did you know?' she asked.

'Because I was accused of his murder,' he answered, 'and when I was accused I remembered the companion of Hampton Court, and the face of a man who looked on me with hatred as I robbed him of his rings, and I knew then what happened, Dona, when I left you that night.'

She clasped her hands round her knees, and looked out upon the lake. 'When we went fishing, you and I,' she said, 'I could not take the hook out of the fish, do you remember? But it was different, what I did that night. At first I was afraid, and then I was angry, and when I was angry I took the shield down from the wall, and afterwards – he died.'

'What made you angry?' he asked.

She thought a moment, trying to remember, and then, 'It was James,' she said, 'it was James who woke and cried.'

He said nothing, and glancing across at him she saw that he had finished his supper, and was sitting now as she did, with hands around his knees, and he was staring at the lake.

'Ah,' he said, 'so it was James who woke and cried, and you and I, Dona, we meet at the Loe pool instead of Coverack, and your answer is the same as mine.'

He threw a pebble into the lake, and a ripple formed and spread across the surface of the water, and vanished as though it had never been, and then he lay on his back on the strip of sand, and put out his hand to her, and she went and lay beside him.

'I think,' he said, 'that Lady St. Columb will never more roister in the streets of London, for she has had her measure of adventure.'

'The Lady St. Columb,' she said, 'will became a gracious matron, and smile upon her servants, and her tenants, and the village folk, and one day she will have grandchildren about her knee, and will tell them the story of a pirate who escaped.'

'And what will happen to the cabin-boy?' he asked.

'The cabin-boy will vigil sometimes in the night, and tear his nails, and beat his pillow, and then he will fall asleep perhaps, and dream again.'

The pool lay dark and silent at their feet, and from behind them came the sound of the sea as it broke upon the shingle.

'There is a house in Brittany,' he said, 'where once a man lived called Jean-Benoit Aubéry. It may be that he will go back there again, and cover the bare walls from floor to ceiling with pictures of birds and portraits of his cabin-boy. But as the years go by the portraits of the cabin-boy will become blurred and indistinct.'

'In what part of Brittany does Jean-Benoit Aubéry have his house?' she asked.

'In Finistère,' he said, 'which means, my Dona, the land's end.'

It seemed to her that she could see the rugged cliffs and the scarred face of the headland, and she could hear the sea crash against the rocks, and the gulls cry, and she knew how sometimes the sun would beat upon the cliffs so that the grass became parched, and thirsty, and dry, and how sometimes a soft wind would blow from the west and there would be mist and rain.

'There is a jagged piece of rock,' he said, 'and it runs out into the Atlantic and we call it la Pointe du Raz. No tree can live upon it, and no blade of grass, for it is swept all day and all night by the west wind. And out in the sea, beyond the point, two tides meet, and surge together, and all the time forever there is a roughness and a boiling of surf and foam, and the spray rises fifty feet into the air.'

A little cold wind rose from the centre of the lake and blew upon them, and the stars went misty suddenly and dim, and it was that hour of night when all is silent and still: no movement of bird or beast, no whisper in the reeds, and nothing sounding but the breaking of the sea upon the shingle.

'Do you think,' she said, 'that *La Mouette* is waiting for you, out there, on the sea, and that you will find her in the morning?'

'Yes,' he said.

'And you will climb aboard and be master of her again, and hold the wheel in your hand, and feel the deck under your feet?'

'Yes,' he said.

'And William,' she said, 'William who does not like the sea, he will be ill and wish himself back at Navron again.'

'No,' he said, 'William will feel the salt on his lips, and the wind in his hair, and before night-fall perhaps, if the breeze is steady, he will look upon the land again, and smell the warm grass on the headland, and it will mean Brittany and home.'

She lay on her back as he did, with her hands behind her head, and now there was a change in the sky, a pallor of false dawn, and the little wind blew stronger than before.

'I wonder,' he said, 'when it was that the world first went amiss, and men forgot how to live and to love and to be happy. For once, my Dona, there was a lake like this one in the life of every man.'

'Perhaps there was a woman,' she said, 'and the woman told her man to build a house of reeds, and after that a house of wood, and after that a house of stone, and there came other men and other women, and soon there were no more hills and no more lakes, nothing but little round stone houses all alike.'

'And you and I,' he said, 'we have our lake and our hills, for this night only, and we have only three hours now to sunrise.'

It seemed to them, when the day came, that there was a whiteness and a cold clarity about it that they had never known before. The sky was hard and bright, and the lake lay at their feet like a sheet of silver. They got up from the spit of sand, and he bathed in the chill water, which was cold like the frozen water of the north. Presently the birds began to murmur and whisper in the woods, and he left the lake and dressed, and walked out on to the shingle beach where the tide was high, and a ridge of foam lapped against the stones. A hundred yards away from the beach a little fishing boat rocked at anchor, and when William saw the figures on the beach he drew out the long paddles and pulled towards them.

They stood there together on the beach, waiting for the boat, and suddenly on the far horizon Dona saw the white topsail of a ship, and the ship was drawing in towards the land. And the ship took shape and form, and she had raking crimson masts, and her sails were full.

La Mouette was returning for her master, and as he climbed into the waiting fishing boat, and hoisted the little sail on to the single mast, it seemed to Dona that this moment was part of another moment, long ago, when she had stood upon a headland and looked out across the sea. The ship drifted on the horizon like a symbol of escape, and there was something strange about her in the morning light, as though she had no part in the breaking of the day, but belonged to another age and to another world.

She seemed a painted ship upon the still white sea, and Dona shivered suddenly, for the shingle felt cold and chill on her bare feet, while a little wave splashed upon them, and sighed, and was no more. Then out of the sea, like a ball of fire, the sun came hard and red.

My Cousin Rachel

Daphne du Maurier

Chapter One

They used to hang men at Four Turnings in the old days.

Not any more, though. Now, when a murderer pays the penalty for his crime, he does so up at Bodmin, after fair trial at the Assizes. That is, if the law convicts him, before his own conscience kills him. It is better so. Like a surgical operation. And the body has decent burial, though a nameless grave. When I was a child it was otherwise. I can remember as a little lad seeing a fellow hang in chains where the four roads meet. His face and body were blackened with tar for preservation. He hung there for five weeks before they cut him down, and it was the fourth week that I saw him.

He swung between earth and sky upon his gibbet, or, as my cousin Ambrose told me, betwixt heaven and hell. Heaven he would never achieve, and the hell that he had known was lost to him. Ambrose prodded at the body with his stick. I can see it now, moving with the wind like a weather-vane on a rusty pivot, a poor scarecrow of what had been a man. The rain had rotted his breeches, if not his body, and strips of worsted drooped from his swollen limbs like pulpy paper.

It was winter, and some passing joker had placed a sprig of holly in the torn vest for celebration. Somehow, at seven years old, that seemed to me the final outrage, but I said nothing. Ambrose must have taken me there for a purpose, perhaps to test my nerve, to see if I would run away, or laugh, or cry. As my guardian, father, brother, counsellor, as in fact my whole world, he was forever testing me. We walked around the gibbet, I remember, with Ambrose prodding and poking with his stick; and then he paused and lit his pipe, and laid his hand upon my shoulder.

'There you are, Philip,' he said, 'it's what we all come to in the end. Some upon a battlefield, some in bed, others according to their destiny. There's no escape. You can't learn the lesson too young. But this is how a felon dies. A warning to you and me to lead the sober life.' We stood there side by side, watching the body swing, as though we were on a jaunt to Bodmin fair, and the corpse was old Sally to be hit for coconuts. 'See what a moment of passion can bring upon a fellow,' said Ambrose. 'Here is Tom Jenkyn, honest and dull, except when he drank too much. It's true his wife was a scold, but that was no excuse to kill her. If we killed women for their tongues all men would be murderers.'

I wished he had not named the man. Up to that moment the body had been a dead thing, without identity. It would come into my dreams, lifeless and horrible, I knew that very well from the first instant I had set my eyes upon the gibbet. Now it would have connection with reality, and with the

man with watery eyes who sold lobsters on the town quay. He used to stand
by the steps in the summer months, his basket beside him, and he would set
his live lobsters to crawl along the quay in a fantastic race, to make the
children laugh. It was not so long ago that I had seen him.

'Well,' said Ambrose, watching my face, 'what do you make of him?'

I shrugged my shoulders, and kicked the base of the gibbet with my foot.
Ambrose must never know I cared, that I felt sick at heart, and terrified. He
would despise me. Ambrose at twenty-seven was god of all creation, certainly
god of my own narrow world, and the whole object of my life was to resemble
him.

'Tom had a brighter face when I saw him last,' I answered. 'Now he isn't
fresh enough to become bait for his own lobsters.'

Ambrose laughed, and pulled my ears. 'That's my boy,' he said. 'Spoken
like a true philosopher.' And then he added, with a sudden flash of perception,
'If you feel squeamish, go and be sick behind the hedge there, and remember
I have not seen you.'

He turned his back upon the gibbet and the four roads, and went striding
away down the new avenue he was planting at the time, which cut through
the woods and was to serve as a second carriage-way to the house. I was
glad to see him go because I did not reach the hedge in time. I felt better
afterwards, though my teeth chattered and I was very cold. Tom Jenkyn lost
identity again, and became a lifeless thing, like an old sack. He was even a
target for the stone I threw. Greatly daring, I watched to see the body move.
But nothing happened. The stone hit the sodden clothing with a plonk, then
shied away. Ashamed of my action I sped off down the new avenue in search
of Ambrose.

Well, that was all of eighteen years ago, and to the best of my recollection
I have not thought much of it since. Until these last few days. It is strange
how in moments of great crisis the mind whips back to childhood. Somehow
I keep thinking of poor Tom, and how he hung there in his chains. I never
heard his story, and few people would remember it now. He killed his wife,
so Ambrose said. And that was all. She was a scold, but that was no excuse
for murder. Possibly, being over-fond of drink, he killed her in his cups. But
how? And with what weapon? With a knife, or with his bare hands?
Perhaps Tom staggered forth from the inn upon the quay, that winter's
night, all lit with love and fever. And the tide was high, splashing upon the
steps, and the moon was also full, shining on the water. Who knows what
dreams of conquest filled his unquiet mind, what sudden burst of fantasy?

He may have groped his way home to his cottage behind the church, a
pale rheumy-eyed fellow stinking of lobster, and his wife lashed out at him
for bringing his damp feet inside the door, which broke his dream, and so
he killed her. That well might be his story. If there is survival after death,
as we are taught to believe, I shall seek out poor Tom and question him. We
will dream in purgatory together. But he was a middle-aged man of some
sixty years or more, and I am five-and-twenty. Our dreams would not be
the same. So go back into your shadows, Tom, and leave me some measure

of peace. That gibbet has long since gone, and you with it. I threw a stone at you in ignorance. Forgive me.

The point is, life has to be endured, and lived. But how to live it is the problem. The work of day by day presents no difficulties. I shall become a Justice of the Peace, as Ambrose was, and also be returned, one day, to Parliament. I shall continue to be honoured and respected, like all my family before me. Farm the land well, look after the people. No one will ever guess the burden of blame I carry on my shoulders; nor will they know that every day, haunted still by doubt, I ask myself a question which I cannot answer. Was Rachel innocent or guilty? Maybe I shall learn that too, in purgatory.

How soft and gentle her name sounds when I whisper it. It lingers on the tongue, insidious and slow, almost like poison, which is apt indeed. It passes from the tongue to the parched lips, and from the lips back to the heart. And the heart controls the body, and the mind also. Shall I be free of it one day? In forty, in fifty years? Or will some lingering trace of matter in the brain stay pallid and diseased? Some minuscule cell in the blood stream fail to race with its fellows to the fountain heart? Perhaps, when all is said and done, I shall have no wish to be free. As yet, I cannot tell.

I still have the house to cherish, which Ambrose would have me do. I can reface the walls where the damp enters, and keep all sound and well and in repair. Continue to plant trees and shrubs, cover the bare hills where the wind comes roaring from the east. Leave some legacy of beauty when I go, if nothing else. But a lonely man is an unnatural man, and soon comes to perplexity. From perplexity to fantasy. From fantasy to madness. And so I swing back again to Tom Jenkyn, hanging in his chains. Perhaps he suffered too.

Ambrose, those eighteen years ago, went striding down the avenue, and I in wake of him. He may well have worn the jacket I am wearing now. This old green shooting jacket, with the leather padding on the elbows. I have become so like him that I might be his ghost. My eyes are his eyes, my features his features. The man who whistled to his dogs and turned his back upon the four roads and the gibbet could be myself. Well, it was what I always wanted. To be like him. To have his height, his shoulders, his way of stooping, even his long arms, his rather clumsy looking hands, his sudden smile, his shyness at first meeting with a stranger, his dislike of fuss, of ceremony. His ease of manner with those who served and loved him – they flatter me, who say I have that too. And the strength which proved to be illusion, so that we fell into the same disaster. I have wondered lately if, when he died, his mind clouded and tortured by doubt and fear, feeling himself forsaken and alone in that damned villa where I could not reach him, whether his spirit left his body and came home here to mine, taking possession, so that he lived again in me, repeating his own mistakes, caught the disease once more and perished twice. It may be so. All I know is that my likeness to him, of which I was so proud, proved my undoing. Because of it, there came defeat. Had I been another man, agile and quick, with a deft tongue and a shrewd head for business, the past year would have been no more than another twelve months come and gone. I should be settling down to a brisk contented future. To marriage, possibly, and to a young family.

But I was none of these things, nor was Ambrose. We were dreamers, both of us, unpractical, reserved, full of great theories never put to test, and, like all dreamers, asleep to the waking world. Disliking our fellow men, we craved affection; but shyness kept impulse dormant until the heart was touched. When that happened the heavens opened, and we felt, the pair of us, that we had the whole wealth of the universe to give. We would have both survived, had we been other men. Rachel would have come here just the same. Spent a night or two, and gone her way. Matters of business would have been discussed, some settlement arranged, the will read formally with lawyers round a table, and I – summing up the position in a glance – have given her an annuity for life, and so been quit of her.

It did not happen that way because I looked like Ambrose. It did not happen that way because I felt like Ambrose. When I went up to her room, that first evening she arrived, and after knocking stood within the door, my head bent slightly because of the low lintel, and she got up from the chair where she had been sitting by the window and looked up at me, I should have known then, from the glance of recognition in her eyes, that it was not I she saw, but Ambrose. Not Philip, but a phantom. She should have gone then. Packed up her trunks and left. Travelled back to the place where she belonged, back to that shuttered villa, musty with memories, the formal terraced garden and the dripping fountain in the little court. Returned to her own country, parched in mid-summer and hazy with heat, austere in winter under the cold and brilliant sky. Some instinct should have warned her that to stay with me would bring destruction, not only to the phantom she encountered, but finally to her also.

Did she, I wonder, when she saw me standing there diffident and awkward, smarting with sullen resentment at her presence yet hotly conscious of being host and master, and all too angrily aware of my big feet and arms and legs, sprawling, angular, an unbroken colt – did she, I wonder, think swiftly to herself, 'Ambrose must have been thus when he was young. Before my time. I did not know him when he looked like this' – and therefore stayed?

Perhaps that was the reason why, when I had that brief meeting with Rainaldi, the Italian, for the first time also, he too looked at me with the same shock of recognition quickly veiled, and playing with a pen upon his desk thought for a moment, and then softly said to me, 'You have only arrived to-day? Then your cousin Rachel has not seen you.' Instinct had warned him also. But too late.

There is no going back in life. There is no return. No second chance. I cannot call back the spoken word or the accomplished deed, sitting here, alive and in my own home, any more than poor Tom Jenkyn could, swinging in his chains.

It was my godfather Nick Kendall who, in his bluff straightforward fashion, said to me on the eve of my twenty-fifth birthday – a few months ago only, yet God! how long in time – 'There are some women, Philip, good women very possibly, who through no fault of their own impel disaster.

Whatever they touch somehow turns to tragedy. I don't know why I say this to you, but I feel I must.' And then he witnessed my signature on the document that I had put before him.

No, there is no return. The boy who stood under her window on his birthday eve, the boy who stood within the doorway of her room the evening that she came, he has gone, just as the child has gone who threw a stone at a dead man on a gibbet to give himself false courage. Tom Jenkyn, battered specimen of humanity, unrecognisable and unlamented, did you, all those years ago, stare after me in pity as I went running down the woods into the future?

Had I looked back at you, over my shoulder, I should not have seen you swinging in your chains, but my own shadow.

Chapter Two

I had no sense of foreboding, when we sat talking together that last evening, before Ambrose set out on his final journey. No premonition that we would never be together again. It was now the third autumn that the doctors had ordered him to winter abroad, and I had become used to his absence and to looking after the estate while he was away. The first winter that he went I had been up at Oxford still, so his going had made very little difference to me, but the second winter I came down for good and remained the whole time at home, which was what he wanted me to do. I did not miss the gregarious life at Oxford, in fact I was glad to be quit of it.

I never had any desire to be anywhere but at home. Apart from my schooldays at Harrow, and afterwards at Oxford, I had never lived in any place but this house, where I had come at the age of eighteen months after my young parents died. Ambrose, in his queer generous way, was seized with pity for his small orphaned cousin, and so brought me up himself, as he might have done a puppy, or a kitten, or any frail and lonely thing needing protection.

Ours was a strange sort of household from the first. He sent my nurse packing when I was three years old, because she smacked my bottom with a hairbrush. I don't remember the incident, but he told me later.

'It made me so damnably angry,' he said to me, 'to see that woman belabouring your small person with her great coarse hands for some trifling misdemeanour that she was too unintelligent to comprehend. After that, I corrected you myself.'

I never had reason to regret it. There could not be a man more fair, more just, more lovable, more full of understanding. He taught me my alphabet in the simplest possible way by using the initial letters of every swearword – twenty-six of them took some finding, but he achieved it somehow, and warned me at the same time not to use the words in company. Although invariably courteous he was shy of women, and mistrustful too, saying they made mischief in a household. Therefore he would employ only menservants, and the tribe was controlled by old Seecombe, who had been my uncle's steward.

Eccentric perhaps, unorthodox – the west country has always been known for its odd characters – but despite his idiosyncratic opinions on women, and the upbringing of small boys, Ambrose was no crank. He was liked and respected by his neighbours, and loved by his tenants. He shot and hunted in the winter, before rheumatism got a grip on him, fished in the summer from a small sailing boat he kept anchored in the estuary, dined out and entertained when he had the mind to do so, went twice to church on a Sunday even though he did pull a face at me across the family pew when the sermon was too long, and endeavoured to induce in me his passion for the planting of rare shrubs.

'It's a form of creation,' he used to say, 'like anything else. Some men go in for breeding. I prefer growing things from the soil. It takes less out of you, and the result is far more satisfying.'

It shocked my godfather, Nick Kendall, and Hubert Pascoe, the vicar, and others of his friends who used to urge him to settle down to domestic bliss and rear a family instead of rhododendrons.

'I've reared one cub,' he would make reply, pulling my ears, 'and that has taken twenty years off my span of life, or put them on, whichever way I care to look at it. Philip is a ready-made heir, what's more, so there is no question of having to do my duty. He'll do it for me when the time comes. And now sit back in your chairs and be comfortable, gentlemen. As there is no woman in the house we can put our boots on the table and spit on the carpet.'

Naturally we did no such thing. Ambrose was nothing if not fastidious, but it delighted him to make these remarks before the new vicar, hen-pecked, poor fellow, with a great tribe of daughters, and round the dining-room table would go the port after Sunday dinner, with Ambrose winking at me from his end of the table.

I can see him now, half hunched, half sprawling in his chair – I caught the habit from him – shaking with silent laughter when the vicar made his timid ineffectual remonstrance, and then, fearing he might have hurt the man's feelings, intuitively changing the tone of the conversation, passing on to matters where the vicar would be at ease, and putting himself to the utmost trouble to make the little fellow feel at home. I came to appreciate his qualities the more when I went to Harrow. The holidays passed all too swiftly, as I compared his manners and his company with the urchins who were my schoolmates, and the masters, stiff and sober, lacking to my mind all humanity.

'Never mind,' he used to say, patting my shoulder before I started off, white-faced, a trifle tearful, to catch the coach to London. 'It's just a training process, like breaking in a horse; we have to face it. Once your schooldays are behind you, and they will be before you've even counted, I'll bring you home here for good, and train you myself.'

'Train me for what?' I asked.

'Well, you're my heir, aren't you? That's a profession in itself.'

And away I would go, driven by Wellington the coachman to pick up the London coach at Bodmin, turning for a last glimpse of Ambrose as he stood leaning on his stick with the dogs beside him, his eyes wrinkled in sure and certain understanding, his thick curling hair already turning grey; and as he whistled to the dogs and went back into the house I would swallow the lump in my throat and feel the carriage wheels bear me away, inevitably and fatally, along the crunching gravel drive across the park and through the white gate, past the lodge, to school and separation.

He reckoned without his health, though, and when school and university lay behind me it was then his turn to go.

'They tell me if I spend another winter being rained on every day I shall end my days crippled in a bath-chair,' he said to me. 'I must go off and search for the sun. The shores of Spain or Egypt, anywhere on the Mediterranean where it is dry, and warm. I don't particularly want to go, but on the other hand I'm damned if I'll end my life a cripple. There is one advantage in the plan. I shall bring back plants that nobody else has got. We'll see how the demons thrive in Cornish soil.'

The first winter came and went, likewise the second. He enjoyed himself well enough, and I don't think he was lonely. He returned with heaven knows how many trees, shrubs, flowers, plants of every form and colour. Camellias were his passion. We started a plantation for them alone, and whether he had green fingers or a wizard's touch I do not know, but they flourished from the first, and we lost none of them.

So the months passed, until the third winter. This time he had decided upon Italy. He wanted to see some of the gardens in Florence and Rome. Neither town would be warm in winter, but that did not worry him. Someone had assured him that the air would be dry, if cold, and that he need not have any fear of rain. We talked late, that evening. He was never one for early bed, and often we would sit together in the library until one or two in the morning, sometimes silent, sometimes talking, both of us with our long legs stretched out before the fire, the dogs curled round our feet. I have said before that I felt no premonition, but now I wonder, thinking back, if it was otherwise for him. He kept looking at me in a puzzled, reflective sort of way, and from me to the panelled walls of the room and the familiar pictures, and so to the fire, and from the fire to the sleeping dogs.

'I wish you were coming with me,' he said suddenly.

'It wouldn't take me long to pack,' I answered.

He shook his head, and smiled. 'No,' he said, 'I was joking. We can't both be away for months at a time. It's a responsibility, you know, being a landowner, though not everybody feels as I do.'

'I could travel with you down to Rome,' I said, excited at the idea. 'Then, granting the weather did not hold me back, I'd still be home by Christmas.'

'No,' he said slowly, 'no, it was just a whim. Forget it.'

'You're feeling well enough, aren't you?' I said. 'No aches or pains?'

'Good God, no,' he laughed, 'what do you take me for, an invalid? I haven't had a twinge of rheumatism for months. The trouble is, Philip boy, I'm too much of a fool about my home. When you reach my age, perhaps you'll feel about it the way I do.'

He got up from his chair and went over to the window. He drew back the heavy curtains and stood for a few moments, staring out across the grass. It was a quiet, still evening. The jackdaws had gone to roost, and for once even the owls were silent.

'I'm glad we did away with the paths and brought the turf close to the house,' he said. 'It would look better still if the grass went sloping right to the end there, by the pony's paddock. One day you must cut away the undergrowth to give a view of the sea.'

'How do you mean,' I said, '*I* must do it? Why not you?'

He did not answer at once. 'Same thing,' he said at last, 'same thing. It makes no odds. Remember though.'

My old retriever, Don, raised his head and looked across at him. He had seen the corded boxes in the hall, and sensed departure. He struggled to his feet, and went and stood beside Ambrose, his tail drooping. I called softly to him, but he did not come to me. I knocked out the ashes of my pipe into the hearth. The clock in the belfry struck the hour. From the servants' quarters I could hear Seecombe's grumbling voice scolding the pantry boy.

'Ambrose,' I said, 'Ambrose, let me come with you.'

'Don't be a damn fool, Philip, go to bed,' he answered.

That was all. We did not discuss the matter any more. Next morning at breakfast he gave me some last instructions about the spring planting, and various things he had in mind for me to do before his return. He had a sudden fancy to make a small pool where the ground was marshy in the park by the entrance to the east drive, and this would have to be cut out and banked if we got some passable weather in the winter months. The time for departure came all too soon. Breakfast was over by seven, for he was obliged to make an early start. He would pass the night at Plymouth, and sail from there on the morning tide. The vessel, a trader, would take him to Marseilles, and from there he would travel into Italy at his leisure; he enjoyed a long sea trip. It was a raw damp morning. Wellington brought the carriage to the door, and it was soon piled high with baggage. The horses were restless and eager to be off. Ambrose turned to me, and laid his hand upon my shoulder. 'Take care of things,' he said, 'don't fail me.'

'That's a hit below the belt,' I answered. 'I've never failed you yet.'

'You're very young,' he said. 'I put a great deal on your shoulders. Anyway, everything I have is yours, you know that.'

I believe then if I had pressed the matter he would have let me go with him. But I said nothing. Seecombe and I put him in the carriage with his rugs and sticks, and he smiled at us from the open window.

'All right, Wellington,' he said, 'drive on.'

And they went away down the drive just as the rain began.

The weeks passed much as they had done during the two previous winters.

I missed him as I always did, but there was plenty to occupy me. If I wished for company I rode over to visit my godfather, Nick Kendall, whose only daughter, Louise, was a few years younger than myself, and a playmate from childhood days. She was a staunch girl, with no fancy ways, and pretty enough. Ambrose used to jest at times and say she would make me a wife one day, but I confess I never thought of her as such.

It was mid-November when his first letter came, brought back in the same vessel that had landed him at Marseilles. The voyage had been uneventful, the weather good, despite a bit of a tossing in the Bay of Biscay. He was well, and in good spirits, and looking forward to the journey into Italy. He was not trusting himself to a diligence, which would have meant going up to Lyons anyway, but had hired himself horses and a conveyance, and proposed driving along the coast into Italy, and then turning towards Florence. Wellington shook his head at the news, and foretold an accident. He was of the firm opinion that no Frenchman could drive, and that all Italians were robbers. Ambrose survived, however, and the next letter came from Florence. I kept all his letters, and I have the bunch of them before me now. How often I read them during the next months; they were thumbed, and turned, and read again, as though by the very pressure of my hands upon them more could be gleaned from the pages than the written words gave of themselves.

It was towards the close of this first letter from Florence, where he had apparently spent Christmas, that he first spoke of cousin Rachel.

'I have made the acquaintance of a connection of ours,' he wrote. 'You have heard me talk about the Coryns, who used to have a place on the Tamar, now sold up and changed to other hands. A Coryn married an Ashley two generations ago, as you will find on the family tree. A descendant of that branch was born and brought up in Italy by an impecunious father and an Italian mother, and married off at an early age to an Italian nobleman called Sangalletti, who departed this life by fighting a duel, it appears, when half-seas over, leaving his wife with a load of debts and a great empty villa. No children. The Contessa Sangalletti, or, as she insists on calling herself, my cousin Rachel, is a sensible woman, good company, and has taken it upon her shoulders to show me the gardens in Florence, and in Rome later, as we shall both be there at the same time.'

I was glad that Ambrose had found a friend, and someone who could share his passion for gardens. Knowing nothing of Florentine or Roman society, I had feared English acquaintances would be few, but here at least was a person whose family had hailed from Cornwall in the first place, so they would have that in common too.

The next letter consisted almost entirely of lists of gardens, which, though not at their best at this season in the year, seemed to have made a great impression upon Ambrose. So had our relative.

'I am beginning to have a real regard for our cousin Rachel,' wrote Ambrose in early spring, 'and feel quite distressed to think what she must have suffered from that fellow Sangalletti. These Italians are treacherous blackguards, there's no denying it. She is just as English as you or I in her ways and outlook, and might have been living beside the Tamar yesterday. Can't hear enough about home and all I have to tell her. She is extremely intelligent but, thank the Lord, knows when to hold her tongue. None of that endless yattering, so common in women. She has found me excellent rooms in Fiesole, not far from her own villa, and as the weather becomes milder I shall spend a good deal of my time at her place, sitting on the terrace, or pottering in the gardens which are famous, it seems, for their design, and for the statuary, which I don't know much about. How she exists I hardly know, but I gather she has had to sell much of the valuable stuff in the villa to pay off the husband's debts.'

I asked my godfather, Nick Kendall, if he remembered the Coryns. He did, and had not much opinion of them. 'They were a feckless lot, when I was a boy,' he said. 'Gambled away their money and estates, and now the house, on Tamar-side, is nothing much more than a tumbled-down farm. Fell into decay some forty years ago. This woman's father must have been Alexander Coryn – I believe he did disappear to the continent. He was second son of a second son. Don't know what happened to him though. Does Ambrose give this Contessa's age?'

'No,' I said, 'he only told me she had been married very young, but he did not say how long ago. I suppose she is middle-aged.'

'She must be very charming for Mr. Ashley to take notice of her,' remarked Louise. 'I have never heard him admire a woman yet.'

'That's probably the secret,' I said. 'She's plain and homely, and he doesn't feel forced to pay her compliments. I'm delighted.'

One or two more letters came, scrappy, without much news. He was just back from dining with our cousin Rachel, or on his way there to dinner. He said how few people there were in Florence amongst her friends who could really give her disinterested advice on her affairs. He flattered himself, he said, that he could do this. And she was so very grateful. In spite of her many interests, she seemed strangely lonely. She could never have had anything in common with Sangalletti, and confessed she had been hungry all her life for English friends. 'I feel I have accomplished something,' he said, 'besides acquiring hundreds of new plants to bring back home with me.'

Then came a space of time. He had said nothing of the date of his return, but it was usually towards the end of April. Winter had seemed long with us, and frost, seldom keen in the west country, unexpectedly severe. Some of his young camellias had been affected by it, and I hoped he would not return too soon and find hard winds and driving rains with us still.

Shortly after Easter his letter came. 'Dear boy,' he said, 'you will wonder at my silence. The truth is, I never thought I should, one day, write such a letter to you. Providence works in strange ways. You have always been so close to me that possibly you have guessed something of the turmoil that has been going on in my mind during the past weeks. Turmoil is the wrong word. Perhaps I should say happy bewilderment, turning to certainty. I have made no quick decision. As you know, I am too much a man of habit to change my way of living for a whim. But I knew, some weeks back, that no other course was possible. I had found something I had never found before, and did not think existed. Even now, I can hardly believe it has happened. My thoughts have gone to you very often, but somehow I have not felt calm and steady enough to write, until today. You must know that your cousin Rachel and I were married a fortnight ago. We are now together in Naples, on our honeymoon, and intend returning to Florence shortly. Further than that I cannot say. We have made no plans, and neither of us have any wish, at the present time, to live beyond the moment.

'One day, Philip, not too far distant, I hope, you will know her. I could write much of personal description that would weary you, and of her goodness too, her real and loving tenderness. These things you will see for yourself. Why she has chosen me of all men, a crusty cynical woman-hater if ever there was one, I cannot say. She teases me about it, and I admit defeat. To be defeated by someone like herself is, in a sense, a victory. I might call myself victor, not vanquished, if it were not so damnably conceited a statement.

'Break the news to everyone, give them all my blessings, and hers too, and remember, my dearest boy and pup, that this marriage, late in life, cannot belittle one jot my deep affection for you, rather it will increase it, and now that I think of myself as the happiest of men I shall endeavour to do more for you than ever before, and will have her to help me. Write soon, and if you can bring yourself to do so add a word of welcome to your cousin Rachel.

'Always, your devoted Ambrose.'

The letter came about half-past five, just after I had dined. Luckily, I was alone. Seecombe had brought in the post-bag, and left it with me. I put the letter in my pocket and walked out across the fields down to the sea. Seecombe's nephew, who had the mill cottage on the beach, said good-day to me. He had his nets spread on the stone wall, drying in the last of the sun. I barely answered him, and he must have thought me curt. I climbed over the rocks to a narrow ledge, jutting into the little bay, where I used to swim in summer. Ambrose would anchor some fifty yards out in his boat, and I would swim to him. I sat down, and taking the letter from my pocket read it again. If I could have felt one spark of sympathy, of gladness, one single ray of warmth towards those two who were sharing happiness together down in Naples, it would have eased my conscience. Ashamed of myself, bitterly angry at my selfishness, I could raise no feeling in my heart at all. I sat there, numb with misery, staring at the flat calm sea. I had just turned twenty-three, and yet I felt as lonely and as lost as I had done years before, sitting on a bench in Fourth Form, at Harrow, with no one to befriend me, and nothing before me, only a new world of strange experience that I did not want.

Chapter Three

I think what shamed me most was the delight of his friends, their real pleasure and true thought for his welfare. Congratulations were showered upon me, as a sort of messenger to Ambrose, and in the midst of it all I had to smile, and nod my head, and make out to them that I had known it would happen all along. I felt double-faced, a traitor. Ambrose had so tutored me to hate falsity, in man or beast, that suddenly to find myself pretending to be other than I was came near to agony.

'The best thing that could have happened.' How often I heard the words and had to echo them. I began to shun my neighbours, and skulk at home around the woods, rather than meet the eager faces and the wagging tongues. If I rode out about the farmlands, or into town, there was no escape. Tenants on the estate, or acquaintances from here and there, had but to catch a glimpse of me and I was doomed to conversation. An indifferent actor, I forced a smile on to my face, feeling the skin stretch in protest as I did so, and was obliged to answer questions with a kind of heartiness I hated, a heartiness that the world expects when there is mention of a wedding. 'When will they be coming home?' For this there was one answer. 'I don't know. Ambrose has not told me.'

There would be much speculation upon the looks, the age, the general appearance of his bride, to which I would make reply, 'She is a widow, and she shares his love for gardens.'

Very suitable, the heads would nod, could not be better, the very thing for Ambrose. And then would follow jocularity, and jesting and much amusement at the breaking in of a confirmed bachelor to wedlock. That shrew Mrs. Pascoe, the vicar's lady, ground away upon this subject as if by doing so she won revenge for past insults upon the holy state.

'What a change there will be now, Mr. Ashley,' she said on every possible occasion. 'No more go-as-you-please for *your* household. And a very good thing too. Some organisation will at last be brought to bear upon the servants, and I don't imagine Seecombe being too well pleased. He has had things his own way long enough.'

In this she spoke the truth. I think Seecombe was my one ally, but I was careful not to side with him, and stopped him when he tried to feel his way with me.

'I don't know what to say, Mr. Philip,' he murmured, gloomy and resigned. 'A mistress in the house will have everything upside down, and we shan't know where we are. There will first be one thing, then another, and probably no pleasing the lady whatever is done for her. I think the time has come for me to retire and give way to a younger man. Perhaps you had better mention the matter to Mr. Ambrose when you write.'

I told him not to be foolish, and that Ambrose and I would be lost without him, but he shook his head and continued to go about the place with a long face, and never let an opportunity pass without making some sad allusion to the future, how the hours of the meals would no doubt be changed, the furniture altered, and an interminable cleaning be ordered from dawn till dusk with no repose for anybody, and, as a final thrust, even the poor dogs destroyed. This prophecy, uttered in sepulchral tones, brought back to me some measure of my own lost sense of humour, and I laughed for the first time since reading Ambrose's letter.

What a picture Seecombe painted! I had a vision of a regiment of serving girls with mops, sweeping the house free from cobwebs, and the old steward, his underlip jutting in the familiar way, watching them in stony disapproval. His gloom amused me, but when much the same thing was foretold by others – even by Louise Kendall, who knowing me well might have had perception enough to hold her tongue – the remarks brought irritation.

'Thank goodness you will have fresh covers in the library,' she said gaily. 'They have gone quite grey with age and wear, but I dare say you never noticed it. And flowers in the house, what an improvement! The drawing-room will come into its own at last. I always thought it a waste that it was not used. Mrs. Ashley will furnish it, no doubt, with books and pictures from her Italian villa.'

She ran on and on, going over in her mind a whole list of improvements, until I lost patience with her and said roughly, 'For heaven's sake, Louise, leave the subject alone. I'm sick and tired of it.'

She stopped short then, and looked at me shrewdly.

'You aren't jealous, are you, by any chance?' she said.

'Don't be a fool,' I told her.

It was an ugly thing to call her, but we knew each other so well that I thought of her as a younger sister, and had small respect for her.

After that she was silent, and I noticed when the well-worn theme came up again in conversation she glanced across at me, and tried to change it. I was grateful, and liked her the more.

It was my godfather and her father, Nick Kendall, who made the final thrust, unaware of course that he was doing so, and speaking bluntly in his plain straightforward way.

'Have you made any plans for the future, Philip?' he said to me one evening, after I had ridden over to take dinner with them.

'Plans, sir? No,' I said, uncertain of his meaning.

'Early yet, of course,' he answered, 'and I suppose you cannot very well do so until Ambrose and his wife return home. I wondered whether you had considered looking around the neighbourhood for some small property of your own.'

I was slow to grasp his meaning. 'Why should I do that?' I asked.

'Well, the position is somewhat changed, isn't it?' he said in matter-of-fact tones. 'Ambrose and his wife will want most naturally to be together. And if there should be a family, a son, things won't be the same for you, will they? I am certain Ambrose won't let you suffer from the change, and will buy you any property you fancy. Of course it is possible they will have no children, but on the other hand there is no reason to suppose they won't. You might prefer to build. It is sometimes more satisfactory to build your own place than take over a property for sale.'

He continued talking, mentioning places within twenty miles or so of home that I might care to own, and I was thankful that he did not seem to expect a reply to anything he said. The fact was that my heart was too full to answer him. What he suggested was so new and unexpected that I could barely think straight, and shortly afterwards made an excuse to go. Jealous, yes. Louise was right about that, I supposed. The jealousy of a child who must suddenly share the one person in his life with a stranger.

Like Seecombe, I had seen myself doing my utmost to settle down to new uncomfortable ways. Putting out my pipe, rising to my feet, making an effort at conversation, drilling myself to the rigours and tedium of feminine society. And watching Ambrose, my god, behaving like a ninny, so that I should have to leave the room from sheer embarrassment. I had never once seen myself an outcast. No longer wanted, put out of my home and pensioned like a servant. A child arriving, who would call Ambrose father, so that I should be no longer needed.

Had it been Mrs. Pascoe who had drawn my attention to this possibility I should have put it down as malice, and forgotten it. But my own godfather, quiet and calm, making a statement of fact, was different. I rode home, sick with uncertainty and sadness. I hardly knew what to do, or how to act. Should I make plans, as my godfather had said? Find myself a home? Make preparations for departure? I did not want to live anywhere else, or possess another property. Ambrose had brought me up and trained me for this one alone. It was mine. It was his. It belonged to both of us. But now no longer, everything had changed. I can remember wandering about the house, when I came home from visiting the Kendalls, looking upon it with new eyes, and the dogs, seeing my restlessness, followed me, as uneasy as myself. My old nursery, uninhabited for so long, and now the room where Seecombe's niece came once a week to mend and sort the linen, took on new meaning. I saw it freshly painted, and my small cricket bat that still stood, cobweb-covered on a shelf amongst a pile of dusty books, thrown out for rubbish. I had not thought before what memories the room held for me, going in and out of it once in two months perhaps, with a shirt to be repaired, or socks to be darned. Now I wanted it for my own again, a haven of refuge from the outer world. Instead of which it would become an alien place, stuffy, smelling of boiled milk and blankets put to dry, like the living-rooms of cottages that I so often visited, where there lived young children. In my imagination I could see them crawling with fretful cries upon the floor, forever bumping heads or bruising elbows; or worse, dragging themselves up upon one's knees, their faces puckering like monkeys if denied. Oh God, was all this in store for Ambrose?

Hitherto, when I had thought of my cousin Rachel – which I did but sparingly, brushing her name from my mind as one does all things unpleasant – I had pictured to myself a woman resembling Mrs. Pascoe, only more so. Large-featured and angular, with a hawk's eyes for dust as Seecombe prophesied, and far too loud a laugh when there was company for dinner, so that one winced for Ambrose. Now she took on new proportions. One moment monstrous, like poor Molly Bate at the West Lodge, obliging one to avert the eyes from sheer delicacy, and the next pale and drawn, shawl-covered in a chair, with an invalidish petulance about her, while a nurse hovered in the background, mixing medicines with a spoon. One moment middle-aged and forceful, the next simpering and younger than Louise, my cousin Rachel had a dozen personalities or more and each one more hateful than the last. I saw her forcing Ambrose to his knees to play at bears, the children astride his back, and Ambrose consenting with a humble grace, having lost all dignity. Yet again, decked out in muslin, with a ribbon in her hair, I saw her pout and toss her curls, a curving mass of affection, while Ambrose sat back in his chair surveying her, the bland smile of an idiot on his face.

When in mid-May the letter came, saying that after all they had decided to remain abroad throughout the summer, my relief was so intense that I could have shouted aloud. I felt more traitorous than ever, but I could not help it.

'Your cousin Rachel is still so bothered by the tangle of business that must be settled before coming to England,' wrote Ambrose, 'that we have decided, although with bitter disappointment, as you may imagine, to defer our return home for the present. I do the best I can, but Italian law is one thing and ours another, and it's the deuce of a job to reconcile the two. I seem to be spending a mint of money, but it's in a good cause and I don't begrudge it. We talk of you often, dear boy, and I wish you could be with us.' And so on to enquiries about the work at home and the state of the gardens, with his usual fervour of interest, so that it seemed to me I must be mad to have thought for a moment he could change.

Disappointment was of course intense throughout the neighbourhood that they would not be home this summer.

'Perhaps,' said Mrs. Pascoe, with a meaning smile, 'Mrs. Ashley's state of health forbids her travelling?'

'As to that I cannot say,' I answered. 'Ambrose mentioned in his letter that they had spent a week in Venice, and both of them came back with rheumatism.'

Her face fell. 'Rheumatism? His wife also?' she said. 'How very unfortunate.' And then, reflectively: 'She must be older than I thought.'

Vacuous woman, her mind running upon one single train of thought. I had rheumatics in my knees at two years old. Growing pains, my elders told me. Sometimes, after rain, I have them still. For all that, there was some similarity between my mind and Mrs. Pascoe's. My cousin Rachel aged some twenty years. She had grey hair once more, she even leant upon a stick, and I saw her, when she wasn't planting roses in that Italian garden

which I could not picture, seated at a table, thumping with her stick on the
floor, surrounded by some half-dozen lawyers all jabbering Italian, while
my poor Ambrose sat patient at her side.

Why did he not come home and leave her to it?

My spirits rose, though, as the simpering bride gave place to the ageing
matron, racked with lumbago where it catches most. The nursery receded,
and I saw the drawing-room become a lady's boudoir, hedged about with
screens, huge fires burning even in midsummer, and someone calling to
Seecombe in a testy voice to bring more coal, the draught was killing her.
I took to singing once again when I went riding, urged the dogs after young
rabbits, swam before breakfast, sailed Ambrose's little boat about the estuary
when the wind favoured, and teased Louise about the London fashions when
she went to spend the season there. At twenty-three it takes very little to
make the spirits soar. My home was still my home. No one had taken it
from me.

Then, in the winter, the tone of his letters changed. Imperceptible at first,
I scarcely noticed it, yet on re-reading his words I became aware of a sense
of strain in all he said, some underlying note of anxiety creeping in upon
him. Nostalgia for home in part, I could see that. A longing for his own
country and his own possessions, but above all a kind of loneliness that
struck me as strange in a man but ten months married. He admitted that
the long summer and autumn had been very trying, and now the winter was
unusually close. Although the villa was high, there was no air in it; he said
he used to move about from room to room like a dog before a thunderstorm,
but no thunder came. There was no clearing of the air, and he would have
given his soul for drenching rain, even if it crippled him. 'I was never one
for headaches,' he said, 'but now I have them frequently. Almost blinding
at times. I am sick of the sight of the sun. I miss you more than I can say.
So much to talk about, difficult in a letter. My wife is in town today, hence
my opportunity to write.' It was the first time that he had used the words
'my wife'. Always before he had said Rachel or 'your cousin Rachel', and
the words 'my wife' looked formal to me, and cold.

In these winter letters there was no talk of coming home, but always a
passionate desire to know the news, and he would comment upon any little
trifle I had told him in my letters, as though he held no other interest.

Nothing came at Easter, or at Whitsun, and I grew worried. I told my
godfather, who said no doubt the weather was holding up the mails. Late
snow was reported in Europe, and I could not expect to hear from Florence
before the end of May. It was over a year now since Ambrose had been
married, eighteen months since he had been home. My first relief at his
absence, after his marriage, turned to anxiety that he would not return at
all. One summer had obviously tried his health. What would a second do?
At last, in July, a letter came, short and incoherent, totally unlike himself.
Even his writing, usually so clear, sprawled across the page as if he had had
difficulty in holding his pen.

'All is not well with me,' he said, 'you must have seen that when I wrote
you last. Better keep silent though. She watches me all the time. I have

written to you several times, but there is no one I can trust, and unless I can get out myself to mail the letters they may not reach you. Since my illness I have not been able to go far. As for the doctors, I have no belief in any of them. They are liars, the whole bunch. The new one, recommended by Rainaldi, is a cut-throat, but then he would be, coming from that quarter. However, they have taken on a dangerous proposition with me, and I will beat them yet.' Then there was a gap, and something scratched out which I could not decipher, followed by his signature.

I had the groom saddle my horse and rode over to my godfather to show him the letter. He was as much concerned as I was myself. 'Sounds like a mental breakdown,' he said at once. 'I don't like it at all. That's not the letter of a man in his right senses. I hope to heaven . . .' He broke off, and pursed his lips.

'Hope what?' I asked.

'Your uncle Philip, Ambrose's father, died of a tumour on the brain. You know that, don't you?' he said shortly.

I had never heard it before, and told him so.

'Before you were born, of course,' he said. 'It was never a matter much discussed in the family. Whether these things are hereditary or not I can't say, nor can the doctors. Medical science isn't far enough advanced.' He read the letter again, putting on his spectacles to do so. 'There is, of course, another possibility, extremely unlikely, but which I would prefer,' he said.

'And that is?'

'That Ambrose was drunk when he wrote the letter.'

If he had not been over sixty years, and my godfather, I would have hit him for the bare suggestion.

'I have never seen Ambrose drunk in my life,' I told him.

'Nor I either,' he said drily. 'I am merely trying to choose the better of two evils. I think you had better make up your mind to go to Italy.'

'That,' I remarked, 'I had already decided upon before I came to see you,' and I rode home again, without the remotest idea how to set about the journey.

There was no vessel sailing from Plymouth that would help me. I was obliged to travel up to London, and thence to Dover, catch the packet to Boulogne, and then cross France into Italy by the usual diligence. Granted no delay, I should be in Florence within three weeks or so. My French was poor, my Italian non-existent, but none of this bothered me as long as I could get to Ambrose. I bade a short farewell to Seecombe and the servants, telling them only that I intended paying a hurried visit to their master but saying nothing of his illness, and so set forth for London on a fine morning in July, with the prospect of nearly three weeks' travelling in a strange country ahead of me.

As the carriage turned on to the Bodmin road I saw the groom riding towards us with the post-bag. I told Wellington to rein the horses, and the boy handed me the bag. The chance was one in a thousand that there would be a further letter from Ambrose, but it so happened that the chance was there. I took the envelope from the bag and sent the boy on home. As

Wellington whipped up the horses I drew out the scrap of paper and held it to the window for light.

The words were scrawled, almost illegible.

'For God's sake come to me quickly. She has done for me at last, Rachel my torment. If you delay, it may be too late. Ambrose.'

That was all. There was no date upon the paper, no mark upon the envelope, which was sealed with his own ring.

I sat in the carriage, the scrap of paper in my hand, knowing that no power on heaven or earth could bring me to him before mid-August.

Chapter Four

When the conveyance brought me and the other passengers to Florence and dumped us down at the hostelry beside the Arno, I felt I had been a lifetime upon the road. It was now the fifteenth of August. No traveller, setting his foot upon the continent of Europe for the first time, was ever less impressed than I. The roads we traversed, the hills and valleys, the cities, French or Italian, where we halted for the night, seemed all alike to me. Everywhere was dirty, verminous, and I was nearly deafened by the noise. Used to the silence of a well-nigh empty house – for the servants slept away in their own quarters beneath the clock tower – where I heard no sound at night but the wind in the trees and the lash of rain when it blew from the south-west, the ceaseless clatter and turmoil of foreign cities came near to stupefying me.

I slept, yes, who does not sleep at twenty-four, after long hours upon the road, but into my dreams came all the alien sounds; the banging of doors, the screech of voices, footsteps beneath the window, cart-wheels on the cobbled stones, and always, every quarter, the chime of a church bell. Perhaps, had I come abroad upon some other errand, it would have been different. Then, I might have leant from my window in the early mornings with a lighter heart, watched the bare-footed children playing in the gutter and thrown coins to them, heard all the new sounds and voices with fascination, wandered at night amongst the narrow twisting streets and come to like them. As it was, I looked upon what I saw with indifference, passing to hostility. My need was to reach Ambrose, and because I knew him to be ill in a foreign country my anxiety turned to loathing of all things alien, even of the very soil itself.

It grew hotter every day. The sky was a glazed hard blue, and it seemed to me, twisting and turning along those dusty roads in Tuscany, that the sun had drawn all moisture from the land. The valleys were baked brown, and the little villages hung parched and yellow on the hills with the haze of heat upon them. Oxen lumbered by, thin-looking, bony, searching for water, goats scuffed by the wayside, tended by little children who screamed and shouted as the coach rolled by, and it seemed to me, in my anxiety and fear for Ambrose, that all living things were thirsty in this country, and when water was denied they fell into decay and died.

My first instinct, on climbing from the coach in Florence, as the dusty baggage was unloaded and carried within the hostelry, was to cross the cobbled street and stand beside the river. I was travel-stained and weary, covered from head to foot with dust. For the past two days I had sat beside the driver rather than die from suffocation within, and like the poor beasts upon the road I longed for water. There it was before me. Not the blue estuary of home, rippling, and salty fresh, whipped with sea spray, but a slow-moving turgid stream, brown like the river bed beneath it, oozing and sucking its way under the arches of the bridge, and ever and again its flat smooth surface breaking into bubbles. Waste matter was borne away upon this river, wisps of straw, and vegetation, yet to my imagination, fevered almost with fatigue and thirst, it was something to be tasted, swallowed, poured down the throat as one might pour a draught of poison.

I stood watching the moving water, fascinated, and the sun beat down upon the bridge, and suddenly, from behind me in the city, a great bell chimed four o'clock, deep-sounding, solemn. The chime was taken up by other bells from other churches, and the sound mingled with the surging river as it passed, brown and slimy, over the stones.

A woman stood by my side, a whimpering child in her arms, another dragging at her torn skirt, and she stretched out her hand to me for alms, her dark eyes lifted to mine in supplication. I gave her a coin and turned away, but she continued to touch my elbow, whispering, until one of the passengers, still standing by the coach, let forth a string of words at her in Italian, and she shrank back again to the corner of the bridge whence she had come. She was young, not more than nineteen or so, but the expression on her face was ageless, haunting, as though she possessed in her lithe body an old soul that could not die; centuries in time looked out from those two eyes, she had contemplated life so long it had become indifferent to her. Later, when I had mounted to the room they showed me, and stood out upon the little balcony that gave upon the square, I saw her creep away between the horses and the carrozzas waiting there, stealthy as a cat that slinks by night, its belly to the ground.

I washed and changed my clothes with a strange apathy. Now that I had reached my journey's end a sort of dullness came upon me, and the self which had set forth upon his journey excited, keyed to a high pitch and ready for any battle, existed no longer. In his place a stranger stood, dispirited and weary. Excitement had long since vanished. Even the reality of the torn scrap of paper in my pocket had lost substance. It had been written many weeks ago; so much could have happened since. She might have taken him away from Florence; they might have gone to Rome, to Venice, and I saw myself dragged back to that lumbering coach again, in their wake. Swaying through city after city, traversing the length and breadth of the accursed country, and never finding them, always defeated by time and the hot dusty roads.

Or yet again, the whole thing might be an error, the letters scribbled as a crazy jest, one of those leg-pulls loved by Ambrose in days gone by, when as a child I would fall into some trap he set for me. And I might go now to seek him at the villa and find some celebration, dinner in progress, guests invited, lights and music; and I would be shown in upon the company with no excuse to offer, Ambrose in good health turned astounded eyes upon me.

I went downstairs and out into the square. The carrozzas that had been waiting there had driven off. The siesta hour was over, and the streets were crowded once again. I plunged into them and was lost at once. About me were dark courts and alleyways, tall houses touching one another, jutting balconies, and as I walked, and turned, and walked again, faces peered at me from the doorways, passing figures paused and stared, all wearing upon them that same age-old look of suffering and passion long since spent which I had first noticed on the beggar girl. Some of them followed me, whispering as she had done, stretching out their hands, and when I spoke roughly, remembering my fellow passenger from the coach, they drew back again, flattening themselves against the walls of the tall houses, and watched me pass on, with a strange smouldering pride. The church bells began to clamour once again, and I came to a great piazza where the people stood thickly, clustered together in groups, talking, gesticulating, having, so it seemed to my alien eyes, no connection with the buildings fringing the square, austere and beautiful, nor with the statues remotely staring with blind eyes upon them, nor with the sound of the bells themselves, echoing loud and fateful to the sky.

I hailed a passing carrozza, and when I said doubtfully the words 'Villa Sangalletti' the driver answered something which I could not understand, but I caught the word 'Fiesole' as he nodded and pointed with his whip. We drove through the narrow crowded streets, and he shouted to the horse, the reins jingling, the people falling back from us as we passed amongst them. The bells ceased and died away, yet the echo seemed to sound still in my ears, solemn, sonorous, tolling not for my mission, insignificant and small, nor for the lives of the people in the streets, but for the souls of men and women long since dead, and for eternity.

We climbed a long twisting road towards the distant hills, and Florence lay behind us. The buildings fell away. It was peaceful, silent, and the hot staring sun that had beaten down upon the city all day, glazing the sky, turned gentle suddenly, and soft. The glare was gone. The yellow houses and the yellow walls, even the brown dust itself, were not so parched as they had been before. Colour came back to the houses, faded perhaps, subdued, but with an afterglow more tender now that the full force of the sun was spent. Cypress trees, shrouded and still, turned inky green.

The driver drew up his carrozza before a closed gate set in a long high wall. He turned in his seat and looked down at me over his shoulder. 'Villa Sangalletti,' he said. The end of my journey.

I made signs to him to wait, and getting out, walked up to the gate and pulled at the bell that hung there on the wall. I could hear it jangle from within. My driver coaxed his horse into the side of the road, and climbing from his seat stood by the ditch, waving the flies away from his face with his hat. The horse drooped, poor half-starved brute, between his shafts; he had not spirit enough after his climb to crop the wayside, and dozed, with twitching ears. There was no sound from within the gate, and I rang the bell again. This time there was a muffled barking of a dog, becoming suddenly louder as some door was opened; the fretful cry of a child was hushed shrilly, with irritation, by a woman's voice, and I could hear footsteps approaching the gate from the other side. There was a heavy dragging sound of bolts being withdrawn, and then the grind of the gate itself, as it scraped the stone beneath and was opened. A peasant woman stood peering at me. Advancing upon her, I said: 'Villa Sangalletti? Signor Ashley?'

The dog, chained inside the lodge where the woman lived, barked more furiously than before. An avenue stretched in front of me, and at the far end I could see the villa itself, shuttered and lifeless. The woman made as though to shut the gate against me, as the dog continued barking and the child cried. Her face was puffed and swollen on one side, as though with toothache, and she kept the fringe of her shawl to it to ease the pain.

I pushed past her through the gate and repeated the words 'Signor Ashley.' This time she started, as though for the first time she saw my features, and began to talk rapidly, with a sort of nervous agitation, gesturing with her hands towards the villa. Then she turned swiftly and called over her shoulder, to the lodge. A man, presumably her husband, appeared at the open door, a child on his shoulder. He silenced the dog and came towards me, questioning his wife. She continued her torrent of words to him, and I caught the words 'Ashley,' and then 'Inglese,' and now it was his turn to stand and stare at me. He looked a better type than the woman, cleaner, with honest eyes, and as he stared at me an expression of deep concern came upon his face and he murmured a few words to his wife, who withdrew with the child to the entrance of the lodge and stood watching us, her shawl still held to her swollen face.

'I speak a little English, signore,' he said. 'Can I help you?'

'I have come to see Mr. Ashley,' I said. 'Are he and Mrs. Ashley at the villa?'

The concern on his face became greater. He swallowed nervously. 'You are Mr. Ashley's son, signore?' he said.

'No,' I said impatiently, 'his cousin. Are they at home?'

He shook his head, distressed. 'You have come from England then, signore, and have not heard the news? What can I say? It is very sad, I do not know what to say. Signor Ashley, he died three weeks ago. Very sudden. Very sad. As soon as he is buried, the contessa she shut up the villa, she went away. Nearly two weeks she has been gone. We do not know if she will come back again.'

The dog began to bark again and he turned to quieten it.

I felt all the colour drain away from my face. I stood there, stunned. The

man watched me, in sympathy, and said something to his wife, who dragged
forward a stool, and he placed it beside me.

'Sit, signore,' he said. 'I am sorry. So very sorry.'

I shook my head. I could not speak. There was nothing I could say. The
man, distressed, spoke roughly to his wife to relieve his feelings. Then he
turned again to me. 'Signore,' he said, 'if you would like to go to the villa
I will open it for you. You can see where the signor Ashley died.' I did not
care where I went or what I did. My mind was still too numbed to
concentrate. He began to walk up the drive, drawing some keys from his
pocket, and I walked beside him, my legs heavy suddenly, like lead. The
woman and the child followed behind us.

The cypress trees closed in upon us, and the shuttered villa, like a
sepulchre, waited at the further end. As we drew closer I saw that it was
large, with many windows, all of them blank and closed, and before the
entrance the drive swept in a circle, for carriages to turn. Statues, on their
pedestals, stood between the shrouded cypresses. The man opened the huge
door with his key, and motioned me inside. The woman and the child came
too, and the pair of them began to fling open the shutters, letting the daylight
into the silent hall. They went before me, passing from room to room,
opening the shutters as they did so, believing, in the goodness of their hearts,
that by doing this they somehow eased my pain. The rooms all led into each
other, large and sparse, with frescoed ceilings and stone floors, and the air
was heavy with a medieval musty smell. In some of the rooms the walls
were plain, in others tapestried, and in one, darker and more oppressive
than the rest, there was a long refectory table flanked with carved monastic
chairs, and great wrought iron candlesticks stood on either end.

'The villa Sangalletti very beautiful, signore, very old,' said the man. 'The
signor Ashley, this is where he would sit, when the sun was too strong for
him outside. This was his chair.'

He pointed, almost with reverence, to a tall high-backed chair beside the
table. I watched him in a dream. None of this held reality. I could not see
Ambrose in this house, or in this room. He could never have walked here
with familiar tread, whistling, talking, throwing his stick down beside this
chair, this table. Relentlessly, monotonously, the pair went round the room,
throwing wide the shutters. Outside was a little court, a sort of cloistered
quadrangle, open to the sky but shaded from the sun. In the centre of the
court stood a fountain, and the bronze statue of a boy, holding a shell in his
two hands. Beyond the fountain a laburnum tree grew between the paving
stones, making its own canopy of shade. The golden flowers had long since
drooped and died, and now the pods lay scattered on the ground, dusty and
grey. The man whispered to the woman, and she went to a corner of the
quadrangle and turned a handle. Slowly, gently, the water trickled from the
shell between the bronze boy's hands. It fell down and splashed into the pool
beneath.

'The signor Ashley,' said the man, 'he sat here every day, watching the
fountain. He liked to see the water. He sat there, under the tree. It is very

beautiful, in spring. The contessa, she would call down to him from her room above.'

He pointed to the stone columns of the balustrade. The woman disappeared within the house, and after a moment or two appeared on the balcony where he had pointed, throwing open the shutters of the room. The water went on dripping from the shell. Never fast, never flowing, just splashing softly into the little pool.

'In summer, always they sit here,' went on the man, 'signor Ashley and the contessa. They take their meals, they hear the fountain play. I wait upon them, you understand. I bring out two trays and set them here, on this table.' He pointed to the stone table and two chairs that stood there still. 'They take their tisana here after dinner,' he continued, 'day after day, always the same.'

He paused, and touched the chair with his hand. A sense of oppression grew upon me. It was cool in the quadrangle, cold almost as a grave, and yet the air was stagnant like the shuttered rooms before he opened them.

I thought of Ambrose as he had been at home. He would walk about the grounds in summer time without a coat, an old straw hat upon his head against the sun. I could see the hat now, tilted forward over his face, and I could see him, his shirtsleeves rolled above the elbow, standing in his boat, pointing at something far away at sea. I remembered how he would reach down with his long arms, and pull me into the boat when I swam alongside.

'Yes,' said the man, as though speaking to himself, 'the signor Ashley sat in the chair here, looking at the water.'

The woman came back and, crossing the quadrangle, turned the handle. The dripping ceased. The bronze boy looked down at an empty shell. Everything was silent, still. The child, who had stared with round eyes at the fountain, bent suddenly to the ground and began grubbing amongst the paving stones, picking up the laburnum pods in his small hands and throwing them into the pool. The woman scolded him, pushing him back against the wall, and seizing a broom that stood there began to sweep the court. Her action broke the stillness, and her husband touched my arm.

'Do you wish to see the room where the signore died?' he said softly.

Possessed with the same sense of unreality, I followed him up the wide stairway to the landing above. We passed through rooms more sparsely furnished than the apartments below, and one, looking northwards over the avenue of cypress trees, was plain and bare like a monk's cell. A simple iron bedstead was pushed against the wall. There was a pitcher, a ewer, and a screen beside the bed. Tapestries hung over the fireplace, and in a niche in the wall was the small statuette of a kneeling madonna, her hands clasped in prayer.

I looked at the bed. The blankets were folded neatly at the foot. Two pillows, stripped of their linen, were placed on top of one another at the head.

'The end,' said the man in a hushed voice, 'was very sudden, you understand. He was weak, yes, very weak from the fever, but even the day before he had dragged himself down to sit by the fountain. No, no, said the contessa, you will become more ill, you must rest, but he is very obstinate, he will not listen to her. And there is coming and going all the time with the doctors. Signor Rainaldi, he is here too, talking, persuading, but never will he listen, he shouts, he is violent, and then, like a little child, falls silent. It was pitiful, to see a strong man so. Then, in the early morning, the contessa she comes quickly to my room, calling for me. I was sleeping in the house, signore. She says, her face white as the wall there, "He is dying, Giuseppe, I know it, he is dying," and I follow her to his room, and there he is, lying in bed, his eyes closed, breathing still, but heavily, you understand, not a true sleep. We send away for the doctor, but the signor Ashley he never wakes again, it was the coma, the sleep of death. I myself lit the candles with the contessa, and when the nuns had been I came to look at him. The violence had all gone, he had a peaceful face. I wish you could have seen it, signore.'

Tears stood in the fellow's eyes. I looked away from him, back to the empty bed. Somehow I felt nothing. The numbness had passed away, leaving me cold and hard.

'What do you mean,' I said, 'by violence?'

'The violence that came with the fever,' said the man. 'Twice, three times I had to hold him down in bed, after his attacks. And with the violence came the weakness inside, here.' He pressed his hand against his stomach. 'He suffered much with pain. And when the pain went he would be dazed and heavy, his mind wandering. I tell you, signore, it was pitiful. Pitiful, to see so large a man helpless.'

I turned away from that bare room like an empty tomb, and I heard the man close the shutters once again, and close the door. 'Why was nothing done?' I said. 'The doctors, could they not ease the pain? And Mrs. Ashley, did she just let him die?'

He looked puzzled. 'Please, signore?' he said.

'What was this illness, how long did it last?' I asked.

'I have told you, at the end, very sudden,' said the man, 'but one, two attacks before then. And all winter the signore not so well, sad somehow, not himself. Very different from the year before. When the signor Ashley first came to the villa, he was happy, gay.'

He threw open more windows as he spoke, and we walked outside on to a great terrace, spaced here and there with statues. At the far end a long stone balustrade. We crossed the terrace and stood by the balustrade, looking down upon a lower garden, clipped and formal, from which the scent of roses came, and summer jasmine, and in the distance was another fountain, and yet another, wide stone steps leading to each garden, the whole laid out, tier upon tier, until at the far end came that same high wall flanked with cypress trees, surrounding the whole property.

We looked westward towards the setting sun, and there was a glow upon the terrace and the hushed gardens; even the statues were held in the one rose-coloured light, and it seemed to me, standing there with my hand upon the balustrade, that a strange serenity had come upon the place that was not there before.

The stone was still warm under my hand, and a lizard ran away from a crevice and wriggled down on to the wall below.

'On a still evening,' said the man, standing a pace or so behind me, as though in deference, 'it is very beautiful, signore, here in the gardens of the villa Sangalletti. Sometimes the contessa gave orders for the fountains to be played, and when the moon was full she and the signor Ashley used to come out on to the terrace here, after dinner. Last year, before his illness.'

I went on standing there, looking down upon the fountains, and the pools beneath them with the water lilies.

'I think,' said the man slowly, 'that the contessa will not come back again. Too sad for her. Too many memories. Signor Rainaldi told us that the villa is to be let, possibly sold.'

His words jerked me back into reality. The spell of the hushed garden had held me for a brief moment only, the scent of roses and the glow of the setting sun, but it was over now.

'Who is Signor Rainaldi?' I asked.

The man turned back with me towards the villa. 'The signor Rainaldi he arrange all things for the contessa,' he answered, 'matters of business, matters of money, many things. He knows the contessa a long time.' He frowned, and waved his hand at his wife who with the child in her arms was walking on the terrace. The sight offended him, it was not right for them to be there. She disappeared within the villa, and began fastening the shutters.

'I want to see him, Signor Rainaldi,' I said.

'I give you his address,' he answered. 'He speak English very well.'

We went back into the villa, and as I passed through the rooms to the hall the shutters were closed, one by one, behind me. I felt in my pockets for some money. I might have been anyone, a casual traveller upon the continent, visiting a villa from curiosity with a view to purchase. Not myself. Not looking for the first and last time on the place where Ambrose had lived and died.

'Thank you for all you did for Mr. Ashley,' I said, putting the coins into the fellow's hand.

Once again the tears came in his eyes. 'I am so sorry, signore,' he said, 'so very sorry.'

The last shutters were closed. The woman and the child stood beside us in the hall, and the archway to the empty rooms beyond and to the stairway grew dark again, like the entrance to a vault.

'What happened to his clothes,' I asked, 'his belongings, his books, his papers?'

The man looked troubled. He turned to his wife, and they spoke to one another for a moment. Questions and answers passed between them. Her face went blank, she shrugged her shoulders.

'Signore,' said the man, 'my wife gave some help to the contessa when she went away. But she says the contessa took everything. All the signor Ashley's clothes were put in a big trunk, all his books, everything was packed. Nothing left behind.'

I looked into both their eyes. They did not falter. I knew they were speaking the truth. 'And you have no idea,' I asked, 'where Mrs. Ashley went?'

The man shook his head. 'She has left Florence, that is all we know,' he said. 'The day after the funeral, the contessa went away.'

He opened the heavy front door and I stepped outside.

'Where is he buried?' I asked, impersonal, a stranger.

'In Florence, signore, in the new Protestant cemetery. Many English buried there. Signor Ashley, he is not alone.'

It was as if he wished to reassure me that Ambrose would have company, and that in the dark world beyond the grave his own countrymen would bring him consolation.

For the first time I could not bear to meet the fellow's eyes. They were like a dog's eyes, honest and devoted.

I turned away, and as I did so I heard the woman exclaim suddenly to her husband, and before he had time to shut the door she had darted back into the villa once again, and opened a great oak chest that was standing against the wall. She came back carrying something in her hand which she gave to her husband, and he in turn to me. His puckered face relaxed, broadening to relief.

'The contessa,' he said, 'one thing she has forgotten. Take it with you, signore, it is for you alone.'

It was Ambrose's hat, wide-brimmed and bent. The hat that he used to wear at home against the sun. It would never fit any other man, it was too big. I could feel their anxious eyes upon me, waiting for me to say something, as I turned the hat over and over in my hands.

Chapter Five

I remember nothing of the return drive to Florence except that the sun had set and it grew quickly dark. There was no twilight as we had at home. From the ditches by the wayside insects, crickets maybe, set up their monotonous chanting, and now and again barefooted peasants passed us, carrying baskets on their backs.

When we came into the city we lost the cooler cleaner air of the surrounding hills, and it was hot once more. Not like the day-time, burning and dusty white, but the flat stale heat of evening, buried too many hours in the walls and roofs of houses. The lassitude of noon, and the activity of those hours between siesta and sunset, had given place to a deeper animation, more alive, more tense. The men and women who thronged the piazzas and the narrow streets strolled with another purpose, as if all day they had lain hidden, sleeping, in their silent houses, and now came out like cats to prowl the town. The market-stalls were lit by flares and candles and besieged by customers, delving with questing hands amongst the proffered goods. Shawled women pressed one another, chattering, scolding, and vendors shouting their wares to make their voices heard. The clanging bells began again, and it seemed to me this time that their clamour was more personal. The doors of the churches were pushed open so that I could see the candlelight within, and the groups of people broke up a little, scattered, and pressed inside at the summons of the bells.

I paid off my driver in the piazza by the cathedral, and the sound of that great bell, compelling, insistent, rang like a challenge in the still and vapid air. Scarcely aware of what I did, I passed into the cathedral with the people, and straining my eyes into the gloom stood for a brief moment by a column. An old lame peasant stood beside me, leaning on a crutch. He turned one sightless eye towards the altar, his lips moving, his hands trembling, while about me and before me knelt women, shawled and secret, intoning with shrill voices after the priest, their gnarled hands busy with their beads.

I still held Ambrose's hat in my left hand, and as I stood there in the great cathedral, dwarfed into insignificance, a stranger in that city of cold beauty and spilt blood, seeing the priest's obeisance to the altar, hearing his lips intone words, centuries old and solemn, that I could not understand, I realised suddenly and sharply the full measure of my loss. Ambrose was dead. I would never see him again. He was gone from me forever. Never more that smile, that chuckle, those hands upon my shoulder. Never more his strength, his understanding. Never more that known figure, honoured and loved, hunched in his library chair, or standing, leaning on his stick, looking down towards the sea. I thought of the bare room where he had died, in the villa Sangalletti, and of the madonna in her niche; and something told me that when he went he was not part of that room, or of that house, or of this country, but that his spirit went back where it belonged, to be amongst his own hills and his own woods, in the garden that he loved, within sound of the sea.

I turned and went out of the cathedral and on to the piazza, and looking up at that great dome and the tower beside me, remote and slender, carved against the sky, I remembered for the first time, with the sudden recollection that comes after great shock and stress, that I had not eaten for the day. I turned my thoughts away from the dead, back to the living; and having found a place to eat and drink, close to the cathedral, I went, with hunger satisfied, in search of Signor Rainaldi. The good servant at the villa had written down his address for me, and after one or two enquiries, pointing at the piece of paper and struggling lamely with the pronunciation, I found his house, over the bridge from my hostelry, on the left bank of the Arno. This side of the river was darker and more silent than in the heart of Florence. Few people wandered in the streets. Doors were closed and windows shuttered. Even my footsteps sounded hollow on the cobbled stones.

I came at last to the house, and rang the bell. A servant opened the door within a moment, and without enquiring my name led me upstairs and along a passage, and knocking upon a door showed me into a room. I stood blinking at the sudden light, and saw a man seated in a chair beside a table, looking through a pile of papers. He rose as I came into the room, and stared at me. He was a little less than my own height, and of some forty years perhaps, with a pale, almost colourless face, and lean aquiline features. There was something proud, disdainful about his cast of countenance, like that of someone who would have small mercy for fools, or for his enemies; but I think I noticed most his eyes, dark and deep-set, which at first sight of me startled into a flash of recognition that in one second vanished.

'Signor Rainaldi?' I said. 'My name is Ashley. Philip Ashley.'

'Yes,' he said, 'will you sit down?'

His voice had a cold hard quality, and his Italian accent was not strongly marked. He pushed forward a chair for me.

'You are surprised to see me, no doubt?' I said, watching him carefully. 'You were not aware I was in Florence?'

'No,' he answered. 'No, I was not aware that you were here.'

The words were guarded, but it may have been that his command of the English language was small, so that he spoke carefully.

'You know who I am?' I asked.

'I think I am clear as to the exact relationship,' he said. 'You are cousin, are you not, or nephew to the late Ambrose Ashley?'

'Cousin,' I said, 'and heir.'

He took up a pen between his fingers, and tapped with it on the table, as if he played for time, or for distraction.

'I have been to the villa Sangalletti,' I said, 'I have seen the room where he died. The servant Giuseppe was very helpful. He gave me all the details, but referred me to you.'

Was it my fancy, or did a veiled look come over those dark eyes?

'How long have you been in Florence?' he asked.

'A few hours. Since afternoon.'

'You have only arrived to-day? Then your cousin Rachel has not seen you.' The hand that held the pen relaxed.

'No,' I said, 'the servant at the villa gave me to understand that she had left Florence the day after the funeral.'

'She left the villa Sangalletti,' he said, 'she did not leave Florence.'

'Is she still here, in the city?'

'No,' he said, 'no, she has now gone away. She wishes me to let the villa. Sell it possibly.'

His manner was oddly stiff and unbending, as if any information that he gave me must be considered first, and sorted in his mind.

'Do you know where she is now?' I asked.

'I am afraid not,' he said. 'She left very suddenly, she had made no plans. She told me she would write, when she had come to some decision about the future.'

'She is with friends perhaps?' I ventured.

'Perhaps,' he said. 'I do not think so.'

I had the feeling that only to-day, or even yesterday, she had been with him in this room, that he knew much more than he admitted.

'You will understand, Signor Rainaldi,' I said, 'that this sudden hearing of my cousin's death, from the lips of servants, was a very great shock to me. The whole thing has been like a nightmare. What happened? Why was I not informed that he was ill?'

He watched me carefully, he did not take his eyes from my face. 'Your cousin's death was sudden too,' he said, 'it was a great shock to us all. He had been ill, yes, but not, as we thought, dangerously so. The usual fever that attacks many foreigners here in the summer had brought about a certain weakness, and he complained too of a violent headache. The contessa – I should say Mrs. Ashley – was much concerned, but he was not an easy patient. He took an instant dislike to our doctors, for what reason it was hard to discover. Every day Mrs. Ashley hoped for some improvement, and certainly she had no desire to make you and his friends in England anxious.'

'But we were anxious,' I said, 'that was why I came to Florence. I received these letters from him.'

It was a bold move perhaps, and reckless, but I did not care. I handed across the table the two last letters Ambrose had written me. He read them carefully. His expression did not change. Then he passed them back to me.

'Yes,' he said, his voice quite calm, without surprise, 'Mrs. Ashley feared he might have written something of the sort. It was not until those last weeks, when he became so secretive and strange, that the doctors feared the worst, and warned her.'

'Warned her?' I said. 'Warned her of what?'

'That there might be something pressing on his brain,' he answered, 'a tumour, or growth, of rapidly increasing size, which would account for his condition.'

A lost feeling came over me. A tumour? Then my godfather's surmise was right after all. First uncle Philip, and then Ambrose. And yet. . . . Why did this Italian watch my eyes?

'Did the doctors say that it was a tumour that killed him?'

'Unquestionably,' he answered. 'That, and a certain flare-up of after-fever weakness. There were two doctors present. My own, and another. I can send for them, and you can ask any question you care to put. One speaks a little English.'

'No,' I said slowly, 'no, it is not necessary.'

He opened a drawer and pulled out a piece of paper.

'I have here a copy of the certificate of death,' he said, 'signed by them both. Read it. One copy has already been posted to you in Cornwall, and a second to the trustee of your cousin's will, Mr. Nicholas Kendall, near Lostwithiel, in Cornwall.'

I looked down at the certificate. I did not bother to read it.

'How did you know,' I asked, 'that Nicholas Kendall is trustee to my cousin's will?'

'Because your cousin Ambrose had a copy of the will with him,' replied Signor Rainaldi. 'I read it many times.'

'You read my cousin's will?' I asked, incredulous.

'Naturally,' he replied. 'As trustee myself to the contessa, to Mrs. Ashley, it was my business to see her husband's will. There is nothing strange about it. Your cousin showed me the will himself, soon after they were married. I have a copy of it, in fact. But it is not my business to show it to you. It is the business of your guardian, Mr. Kendall. No doubt he will do so, on your return home.'

He knew my godfather was my guardian also, which was more than I did. Unless he spoke in error. Surely no man past twenty-one possessed a guardian, and I was twenty-four? This did not matter, though. What mattered was Ambrose and his illness, Ambrose and his death.

'These two letters,' I said stubbornly, 'are not the letters of a sick man, of a person ill. They are the letters of a man who has enemies, who is surrounded by people he cannot trust.'

Signor Rainaldi watched me steadily.

'They are the letters of a man who was sick in mind, Mr. Ashley,' he answered me. 'Forgive my bluntness, but I saw him those last weeks, and you did not. The experience was not a pleasant one for any of us, least of all for his wife. You see what he says in the first letter there, that she did not leave him. I can vouchsafe for that. She did not leave him night or day. Another woman would have had nuns to tend him. She nursed him alone, she spared herself nothing.'

'Yet it did not help him,' I said. 'Look at the letters, and this last line, "She has done for me at last, Rachel my torment. . . ." What do you make of that, Signor Rainaldi?'

I suppose I had raised my voice in my excitement. He got up from his chair, and pulled a bell. When his servant appeared he gave an order, and the man returned with a glass, and some wine and water. He poured some out for me, but I did not want it.

'Well?' I said.

He did not go back to his seat. He went over to the side of the room where books lined the wall and took down a volume.

'Are you any sort of a student of medical history, Mr. Ashley?' he asked.

'No,' I said.

'You will find it here,' he said, 'the sort of information you are seeking, or you can question those doctors, whose address I am only too willing to give you. There is a particular affliction of the brain, present above all when there is a growth, or tumour, when the sufferer becomes troubled by delusions. He fancies, for instance, that he is being watched. That the person nearest to him, such as a wife, has either turned against him, or is unfaithful, or seeks to take his money. No amount of love or persuasion can allay this suspicion, once it takes hold. If you don't believe me, or the doctors here, ask your own countrymen, or read this book.'

How plausible he was, how cold, how confident. I thought of Ambrose lying on that iron bedstead in the villa Sangalletti, tortured, bewildered, with this man observing him, analysing his symptoms one by one, watching perhaps from over that three-fold screen. Whether he was right or wrong I did not know. All I knew was that I hated Rainaldi.

'Why didn't she send for me?' I asked. 'If Ambrose had lost faith in her, why not send for me? I knew him best.'

Rainaldi closed the book with a snap, and replaced it on the shelf.

'You are very young, are you not, Mr. Ashley?' he said.

I stared at him. I did not know what he meant.

'What do you mean by that?' I asked.

'A woman of feeling does not easily give way,' he said. 'You may call it pride, or tenacity, call it what you will. In spite of all evidence to the contrary, their emotions are more primitive than ours. They hold to the thing they want, and never surrender. We have our wars and battles, Mr. Ashley. But women can fight too.'

He looked at me, with his cold deep-set eyes, and I knew I had no more to say to him.

'If I had been here,' I said, 'he would not have died.'

I rose from my chair and went towards the door. Once again Rainaldi pulled the bell, and the servant came to show me out.

'I have written,' he said, 'to your guardian, Mr. Kendall. I have explained to him very fully, in great detail, everything that has happened. Is there anything more I can do for you? Will you be staying long in Florence?'

'No,' I said, 'why should I stay? There is nothing to keep me.'

'If you wish to see the grave,' he said, 'I will give you a note to the guardian, in the Protestant cemetery. The site is quite simple and plain. No stone as yet, of course. That will be erected presently.'

He turned to the table, and scribbled a note which he gave me.

'What will be written on the stone?' I said.

He paused a moment, as though reflecting, while the servant waiting by the open door handed me Ambrose's hat.

'I believe,' he said, 'that my instructions were to put "In Memory of Ambrose Ashley, beloved husband of Rachel Coryn Ashley", and then of course the date.'

I knew then that I did not want to go to the cemetery or visit the grave. That I had no wish to see the place where they had buried him. They could put up the stone, and later take flowers there if they wished, but Ambrose would never know, and never care. He would be with me in that west country, under his own soil, in his own land.

'When Mrs. Ashley returns,' I said slowly, 'tell her that I came to Florence. That I went to the villa Sangalletti, and that I saw where Ambrose died. You can tell her too about the letters Ambrose wrote to me.'

He held out his hand to me, cold and hard like himself, and still he watched me with those veiled, deep-set eyes.

'Your cousin Rachel is a woman of impulse,' he said. 'When she left Florence she took all her possessions with her. I very much fear that she will never return.'

I left the house and went out into the dark street. It was almost as if his eyes still followed me from behind his shuttered windows. I walked back

along the cobbled streets and crossed the bridge, and before turning into the
hostelry to seek what sleep I could before the morning I went and stood once
more beside the Arno.

The city slept. I was the only loiterer. Even the solemn bells were silent,
and the only sound was the river, sucking its way under the bridge. It ran
more swiftly now, it seemed, than in the day, as though the water had been
pent up and idle during the long hours of heat and sun and now, because
of night, because of silence, found release.

I stared down at the river, watched it surge and flow and lose itself in the
darkness, and by the single flickering lantern light upon the bridge I saw the
bubbles forming, frothy brown. Then borne upon the current, stiff and
slowly turning, with its four legs in the air, came the body of a dog. It
passed under the bridge and went its way.

I made a vow there, to myself, beside the Arno.

I swore that, whatever it had cost Ambrose in pain and suffering before
he died, I would return it, in full measure, upon the woman who had caused
it. Because I did not believe Rainaldi's story. I believed in the truth of those
two letters that I held in my right hand. The last Ambrose had ever written
to me.

Someday, somehow, I would repay my cousin Rachel.

Chapter Six

I arrived home the first week in September. The news had preceded me –
the Italian had not lied when he told me he had written to Nick Kendall.
My godfather had broken the news to the servants and to the tenants on the
estate. Wellington was waiting for me at Bodmin with the carriage. The
horses were decked in crepe, as were Wellington and the groom, their faces
long and solemn.

My relief at being back in my own country was so great that for the
moment grief was dormant, or possibly that long homeward trek across
Europe had dulled all feeling; but I remember my first instinct was to smile
at sight of Wellington and the boy, to pat the horses, to enquire if all was
well. It was almost as though I were a lad again, returned from school. The
old coachman's manner was stiff, however, with a new formality, and the
young groom opened the carriage door to me with deference. 'A sad home-
coming, Mr. Philip,' said Wellington, and when I asked after Seecombe and
the household he shook his head and told me that they and all the tenants
were sorely grieved. The whole neighbourhood, he said, had talked of nothing
else since the news became known. The church had been draped in black

all Sunday, likewise the chapel on the estate, but the greatest blow of all, Wellington said, was when Mr. Kendall told them that the master had been buried in Italy and would not be brought home to lie in the vault amongst his family.

'It doesn't seem right to any of us, Mr. Philip,' he said, 'and we don't think Mr. Ashley would have liked it either.'

There was nothing I could say in answer. I got into the carriage and let them drive me home.

It was strange how the emotion and the fatigue of the past weeks vanished at sight of the house. All sense of strain left me, and in spite of the long hours on the road I felt rested and at peace. It was afternoon, and the sun shone on the windows of the west wing, and on the grey walls, as the carriage passed through the second gate up the slope to the house. The dogs were there, waiting to greet me, and poor Seecombe, wearing a crepe band on his arm like the rest of the servants, broke down when I wrung him by the hand.

'It's been so long, Mr. Philip,' he said, 'so very long. And how were we to know that you might not take the fever too, like Mr. Ashley?'

He waited upon me while I dined, solicitous, anxious for my welfare, and I was thankful that he did not press me with questions about my journey or about his master's illness and death, but was full of the effect upon himself and the household; how the bells had tolled for a whole day, how the vicar had spoken, how wreaths had been brought in offering. And all his words were punctuated with a new formality of address. I was 'Mr.' Philip. No longer 'Master' Philip. I had noticed the same with the coachman and the groom. It was unexpected, yet strangely warming to the heart.

When I had dined I went up to my room and looked about me, and then down into the library, and so out into the grounds, and I was filled with a queer feeling of happiness that I had not thought ever to possess with Ambrose dead; for when I left Florence I had reached the lowest ebb of loneliness, and hoped for nothing. Across Italy and France I was possessed with images which I could not drive away. I saw Ambrose sitting in that shaded court of the villa Sangalletti, beside the laburnum tree, watching the dripping fountain. I saw him in that bare monk's cell above, propped on two pillows, struggling for breath. And always within earshot, always within sight, was the shadowy hated figure of that woman I had never seen. She had so many faces, so many guises, and that name contessa, used by the servant Giuseppe and by Rainaldi too, in preference for Mrs. Ashley, gave to her a kind of aura she had never had with me at first, when I had seen her as another Mrs. Pascoe.

Since my journey to the villa she had become a monster, larger than life itself. Her eyes were black as sloes, her features aquiline like Rainaldi's, and she moved about those musty villa rooms sinuous and silent, like a snake. I saw her, when there was no longer breath left in his body, packing his clothes in trunks, reaching for his books, his last possessions, and then creeping away, thin-lipped, to Rome perhaps, to Naples, or even lying concealed in that house beside the Arno, smiling, behind the shutters. These images remained with me until I crossed the sea and came to Dover. And now, now that I had returned home, they vanished as nightmares do at break of day. My bitterness went too. Ambrose was with me once again and he was not tortured, he no longer suffered. He had never been to Florence or to Italy at all. It was as though he had died here, in his own home, and lay buried with his father and his mother and my own parents, and my grief was now something I could overcome; sorrow was with me still, but not tragedy. I too was back where I belonged, and the smell of home was all about me.

I went out across the fields, and the men were harvesting. The shocks of corn were being lifted into the waggons. They ceased work at the sight of me, and I went and spoke to all of them. Old Billy Rowe, who had been tenant of the Barton ever since I could remember and had never called me anything but Master Philip, touched his forehead when I came up to him, and his wife and daughter, helping with the rest of the men, dropped me a curtsey. 'We've missed you, sir,' he said, 'it hasn't seemed right to start carrying the corn without you. We're glad you're home.' A year ago I would have rolled up my sleeves like the rest of the hinds, and seized a fork, but something stayed me now, a realisation that they would not think it fit.

'I'm glad to be home,' I said. 'Mr. Ashley's death has been a great sadness to me, and to you too, but now we all have to carry on as he would have wished us to do.'

'Yes, sir,' he said, and touched his forelock once again.

I stayed a few moments talking, then called to the dogs and went my way. He waited until I reached the hedge before telling the men to resume their work. When I came to the pony paddock, midway between the house and the sloping fields, I paused and looked back over the sunken fence. The waggons were silhouetted on the further hill, and the waiting horses and the moving figures black dots on the skyline. The shocks of corn were golden in the last rays of the sun. The sea was very blue, almost purple where it covered the rocks, and had that deep full look about it that always comes with the flood tide. The fishing fleet had put out, and were standing eastward to catch the shore breeze. Back at home the house was in shadow now, only the weathervane on the top of the clock tower catching a loose shaft of light. I walked slowly across the grass to the open door.

The windows were still unshuttered, for Seecombe had not yet sent the servants to close them down. There was something welcome in the sight of those raised sashes, with the curtains softly moving, and the thought of all the rooms behind the windows, known to me and loved. The smoke rose from the chimneys, tall and straight. Old Don, the retriever, too ancient and stiff to walk with me and the younger dogs, scratched on the gravel under the library windows, and then turning his head towards me slowly wagged his tail as I drew near.

It came upon me strongly and with force, and for the first time since I had learnt of Ambrose's death, that everything I now saw and looked upon belonged to me. I need never share it with anyone living. Those walls and windows, that roof, the bell that struck seven as I approached, the whole living entity of the house was mine, and mine alone. The grass beneath my feet, the trees surrounding me, the hills behind me, the meadows, the woods, even the men and women farming the land yonder, were all part of my inheritance; they all belonged.

I went indoors and stood in the library, my back to the open fireplace, my hands in my pockets. The dogs came in as was their custom, and lay down at my feet. Seecombe came to ask me if there were any orders for Wellington, for the morning. Did I want the horses and the carriage, or should he saddle Gypsy for me? No, I told him, I would give no orders to-night. I would see Wellington myself after breakfast. I wished to be called at my usual time. He answered, 'Yes, sir,' and left the room. Master Philip had gone forever. Mr. Ashley had come home. It was a strange feeling. In a sense it made me humble, and at the same time oddly proud. I was aware of a sort of confidence and of a strength that I had not known before, and a new elation. It seemed to me that I felt as a soldier might feel on being given command of a battalion; this sense of ownership, of pride, and of possession too, came to me, as it might do to a senior major, after having deputised for many months and years in second place. But, unlike a soldier, I would never have to give up my command. It was mine for life. I believe that when I had this realisation, standing there before the library fire, I knew a moment of happiness that I have never had in life, before or since. Like all such moments it came swiftly, and as swiftly passed again. Some sound of day by day broke the spell: perhaps a dog stirred, an ember fell from the fire, or a servant moved overhead as he went to close the windows – I don't remember what it was. All I remember is the feeling of confidence which I had that night, as though something long sleeping had stirred inside me and now come to life. I went early to bed, and slept without once dreaming.

My godfather, Nick Kendall, came over the following day, bringing Louise with him. As there were no close relatives to summon, and only bequests to Seecombe and the other servants, with the customary donations to the poor in the parish, the widows, and the orphans, and the whole of his estate and property was left to me, Nick Kendall read the will alone to me, in the library. Louise took herself off for a walk in the grounds. In spite of the legal language, the business seemed simple and straightforward. Except for one thing. The Italian Rainaldi had been right. Nick Kendall *was* appointed my guardian, because the estate did not become virtually mine until I was twenty-five.

'It was a belief of Ambrose's,' said my godfather, taking off his spectacles as he handed me the document to read for myself, 'that no young man knows his own mind until he turns twenty-five. You might have grown up with a weakness for drink or gambling or women, and this twenty-five-year clause made a safeguard. I helped him to draw the will when you were still at Harrow, and though we both knew that none of these tendencies had developed yet Ambrose preferred to keep the clause. "It can't hurt Philip," he always said, "and will teach him caution." Well, there we are, and there's nothing to be done about it. In point of fact it won't affect you, except that you will have to call upon me for money, as you always have done, for the estate accounts and for your personal use, for a further seven months. Your birthday is in April, isn't it?'

'You should know,' I said, 'you were my sponsor.'

'A funny little worm you were too,' he said with a smile, 'staring with puzzled eyes at the parson. Ambrose was just down from Oxford. He pinched your nose to make you cry, shocking his aunt, your mother. Afterwards he challenged your poor father to a pulling race, and they rowed from the castle to Lostwithiel, getting drenched to the skin the pair of them. Ever felt the lack of parents, Philip? It's been hard on you, I often think, without your mother.'

'I don't know,' I said, 'I've never thought about it much. I never wanted anyone but Ambrose.'

'It was wrong, all the same,' he said. 'I used to tell Ambrose so, but he never listened to me. There should have been someone in the house, a housekeeper, a distant relative, anyone. You have grown up ignorant of women, and if you ever marry it will be hard on your wife. I was saying so to Louise at breakfast.'

He broke off then, looking – if my godfather could look such a thing – a little uncomfortable, as if he said more than he meant.

'That's all right,' I said, 'my wife can take care of all the difficulties when the time comes. If it ever does come, which is unlikely. I think I am too much like Ambrose, and I know now what marriage must have done to him.'

My godfather was silent. Then I told him of my visit to the villa and of my meeting with Rainaldi, and he showed me in turn the letter that the Italian had written him. It was much as I expected, giving in cold stilted words his story of Ambrose's illness and death, of his own personal regret, and of the shock and grief to the widow, who was, according to Rainaldi, inconsolable.

'So inconsolable,' I said to my godfather, 'that the day after the funeral she goes off, like a thief, taking all Ambrose's possessions with her, except his old hat, which she forgot. Because, no doubt, it was torn and had no value.'

My godfather coughed. His bushy eyebrows knitted.

'Surely,' he said, 'you don't begrudge her the books and clothes? Hang it all, Philip, it's all she has.'

'How do you mean,' I asked, 'it's all she has?'

'Well, I've read the will to you,' he answered, 'and there it is before you. It's the same will that I drew up ten years ago. No codicil, you know, upon his marriage. There is no provision in it for a wife. All this past year I rather expected word from him, at some time or other, about a settlement at least. It's usual. But I suppose his absence abroad made him neglectful of such a necessity, and he kept hoping to return. Then his illness put a stop to any business. I am a little surprised that this Italian, Signor Rainaldi, whom you seem so much to dislike, makes no mention of any sort of claim on the part of Mrs. Ashley. It shows great delicacy on his part.'

'Claim?' I said. 'Good God, you talk of a claim when we know perfectly well she drove him to his death?'

'We don't know anything of the sort,' returned my godfather, 'and if that is the way you are going to talk about your cousin's widow I don't care to listen.' He got up and began to put his papers together.

'So you believe the story of the tumour?' I said.

'Naturally I believe it,' he replied. 'Here is the letter from this Italian, Rainaldi, and the death certificate, signed by two doctors. I remember your uncle Philip's death, which you do not. The symptoms were very similar. It is exactly what I feared, when the letter came from Ambrose and you left for Florence. The fact that you arrived too late to be of any assistance is one of those calamities that nobody can help. It is possible, now I think of it, that it was not a calamity after all, but a mercy. You would not have wished to see him suffer.'

I could have hit him, the old fool, for being so obstinate, so blind.

'You never saw the second letter,' I said, 'the note that came the morning I went away. Look at this.'

I had it still. I kept it always in my breast pocket. I gave it to him. He put on his spectacles again, and read it.

'I'm sorry, Philip,' he said, 'but even that poor heartbreak of a scribble cannot alter my opinion. You must face facts. You loved Ambrose, so did I. When he died I lost my greatest friend. I am as distressed as you when I think of his mental suffering, perhaps even more so, because I have seen it in another. Your trouble is that you will not reconcile yourself to the fact that the man we knew and admired and loved was not his true self before he died. He was mentally and physically sick, and not responsible for what he wrote or said.'

'I don't believe it,' I said. 'I can't believe it.'

'You mean you won't believe it,' said my godfather, 'in which case there is nothing more to be said. But for Ambrose's sake, and for the sake of everybody who knew and loved him, here on the estate and in the county, I must ask you not to spread your views to others. It would cause distress and pain to all of them, and if such a whisper ever got to his widow, wherever she may be, you would cut a miserable figure in her eyes, and she would be well within her rights to bring a case against you for slander. If I were her man of business, as that Italian seems to be, I would not hesitate to do so.'

I had never heard my godfather speak with such force. He was right in saying there was no more to be said on the subject. I had learnt my lesson. I would not broach it again.

'Shall we call Louise?' I said pointedly. 'I think she has been wandering about the gardens long enough. You had both better stay and dine with me.'

My godfather was silent during dinner. I could tell he was still shocked by what I had said to him. Louise questioned me about my travels, what had I thought of Paris, the French countryside, the Alps and Florence itself, and my very inadequate replies filled up the gaps in conversation. She was quickwitted, though, and saw something was wrong. And after dinner, when my godfather summoned Seecombe and the servants to tell them of the various bequests, I went and sat with her in the drawing-room.

'My godfather is displeased with me,' I said, and told her the story. She watched me in that rather critical enquiring way she always had, to which I was well accustomed, her head a little on one side, her chin lifted. 'You know,' she said, when I had finished, 'I think you are probably right. I dare say poor Mr. Ashley and his wife were not happy, and he was too proud to write and tell you so before he fell ill, and then perhaps they had a quarrel, and everything happened at once, and so he wrote you those letters. What did those servants say about her? Was she young, was she old?'

'I never asked,' I said. 'I don't see that it matters. The only thing that matters is that he did not trust her when he died.'

She nodded. 'That was terrible,' she agreed, 'he must have felt so lonely.' My heart warmed to Louise. Perhaps it was because she was young, my own age, that she seemed to have so much more perception than her father. He was getting old, I thought to myself, losing his judgement. 'You should have asked that Italian, Rainaldi, what she looked like,' said Louise. 'I should have done. It would have been my first question. And what had happened to the Count, her first husband. Didn't you tell me once he had been killed in a duel? You see, that speaks badly for her, too. She probably had several lovers.'

This aspect of my cousin Rachel had not occurred to me. I only saw her as malevolent, like a spider. In spite of my hatred, I could not help smiling. 'How like a girl,' I said to Louise, 'to picture lovers. Stilettos in a shadowed doorway. Secret staircases. I ought to have taken you to Florence with me. You would have learnt much more than I did.'

She flushed deeply when I said this, and I thought how odd girls were; even Louise, whom I had known my whole life, failed to understand a joke. 'At any rate,' I said, 'whether that woman had a hundred lovers or not doesn't concern me. She can lie low in Rome or Naples or wherever she is for the present. But one day I shall hunt her out, and she'll be sorry for it.'

At that moment my godfather came to find us, and I said no more. He seemed in a better humour. No doubt Seecombe and Wellington and the others had been grateful for their little bequests and he, in benign fashion, felt himself in part the author of them.

'Ride over and see me soon,' I told Louise, as I helped her into the dog-cart beside her father. 'You're good for me. I like your company.' And she flushed again, silly girl, glancing up at her father to see how he would take it, as though we had not ridden backwards and forwards visiting one another before, times without number. Perhaps she also was impressed by my new status, and before I knew where I was I would become Mr. Ashley to her too, instead of Philip. I went back into the house, smiling at the idea of Louise Kendall, whose hair I used to pull only a few years back, now looking upon me with respect, and the next instant I forgot her, and my godfather as well, for on coming home there was much to do after two months' absence.

I did not think to see my godfather again for at least a fortnight, what with the harvest and other things upon my hands; but scarcely a week had passed before his groom rode over one morning, soon after midday, with a verbal message from his master, asking me to go and see him; he was unable to come himself, he was confined to the house with a slight chill, but he had news for me.

I did not think the matter urgent – we carried the last of the corn that day – and the following afternoon I rode to see him.

I found him in his study, alone. Louise was absent somewhere. He had a curious look upon his face, baffled, ill at ease. I could see he was disturbed.

'Well,' he said, 'now something has got to be done, and you have to decide exactly what, and when. She has arrived by boat in Plymouth.'

'Who has arrived?' I asked. But I think I knew.

He showed me a piece of paper in his hand.

'I have a letter here,' he said, 'from your cousin Rachel.'

Chapter Seven

He gave me the letter. I looked at the handwriting on the folded paper. I don't know what I thought to see. Something bold, perhaps, with loops and flourishes; or its reverse, darkly scrawled and mean. This was just hand-writing, much like any other, except that the ends of the words tailed off in little dashes, making the words themselves not altogether easy to decipher.

'She does not appear to know that we have heard the news,' said my godfather. 'She must have left Florence before Signor Rainaldi wrote his letter. Well, see what you make of it. I will give you my opinion afterwards.'

I opened up the letter. It was dated from a hostelry in Plymouth, on the thirteenth of September.

Dear Mr. Kendall,
   When Ambrose spoke of you, as he so often did, I little thought my first communication with you would be fraught with so much sadness. I arrived in Plymouth, from Genoa, this morning, in a state of great distress, and alas alone.
   My dear one died in Florence on the 20th of July, after a short illness but violent in its attack. Everything was done that could be done, but the best doctors I could summon were not able to save him. There was a recurrence of some fever that had seized him earlier in the spring, but the last was due to pressure on the brain which the doctors think had lain dormant for some months, then rapidly increased its hold upon him. He lies in the Protestant cemetery in Florence, in a site chosen by myself, quiet, and a little apart from the other English graves, with trees surrounding it, which is what he would have wished. Of my personal sorrow and great emptiness I will say nothing; you do not know me, and I have no desire to inflict my grief upon you.

My first thought has been for Philip, whom Ambrose loved so dearly, and whose grief will be equal to my own. My good friend and counsellor, Signor Rainaldi of Florence, assured me that he would write to you and break the news, so that you in turn could tell Philip, but I have little faith in those mails from Italy to England, and was fearful either that the news should come to you by hearsay, through a stranger, or that it would not come at all. Hence my arrival in this country. I have brought with me all Ambrose's possessions; his books, his clothes, everything that Philip would wish to have and keep, which now, by right, belong to him. If you will tell me what to do with them, how to send them, and whether or not I should write to Philip myself, I shall be deeply grateful.

I left Florence very suddenly, on impulse and without regret. I could not bear to stay with Ambrose gone. As to further plans, I have none. After so great a shock time for reflection is, I think, most necessary. I had hoped to be in England before this, but was held up at Genoa, for the ship that brought me was not ready to sail. I believe I still have members of my own family, the Coryns, scattered about Cornwall, but knowing none of them I have no wish to intrude upon them. I would much prefer to be alone. Possibly, after I have rested here a little, I may travel up to London, and then make further plans.

I will await instruction from you what to do with my husband's possessions.

Most sincerely yours,
Rachel Ashley.

I read the letter once, twice, perhaps three times, then gave it back to my godfather. He waited for me to speak. I did not say a word.

'You see,' he said at length, 'that after all she has kept nothing. Not so much as one book, or a pair of gloves. They are all for you.'

I did not answer.

'She doesn't even ask to see the house,' he went on, 'the house that would have been her home had Ambrose lived. That voyage she has just made, you realise, of course, that if things had been otherwise they would have made it together? This would have been her homecoming. What a difference, eh? All the people on the estate to welcome her, the servants agog with excitement, the neighbours calling – instead of which, a lonely hostelry in Plymouth. She may be pleasant or unpleasant – how can I tell, I have not met her. But the point is, she asks nothing, she demands nothing. Yet she is Mrs. Ashley. I'm sorry, Philip. I know your views, and you won't be shaken. But as Ambrose's friend, as his trustee, I cannot sit here and do nothing when his widow arrives alone and friendless in this country. We have a guest-room in this house. She is welcome to it until her plans are formed.'

I went and stood by the window. Louise was not absent after all. She had a basket on her arm, and was snipping off the heads of the dead flowers in the border. She raised her head and saw me, waving her hand. I wondered if my godfather had read the letter to her.

'Well, Philip?' he said. 'You can write to her or not, just as you wish. I don't suppose you want to see her, and if she accepts my invitation I shall not ask you over whilst she is here. But some sort of message at least is due from you, an acknowledgement of the things she has brought back for you. I can put that in a postscript when I write.'

I turned away from the window, and looked back at him.

'Why should you imagine I don't wish to see her?' I asked. 'I do wish to see her, very much. If she is a woman of impulse, which she appears to be from that letter – I recollect Rainaldi telling me the same thing – then I can also act on impulse, which I propose to do. It was impulse that took me to Florence in the first place, wasn't it?'

'Well?' asked my godfather, his brows knitting, staring at me suspiciously.

'When you write to Plymouth,' I said, 'say that Philip Ashley has already heard the news of Ambrose's death. That he went to Florence on receipt of two letters, went to the villa Sangalletti, saw her servants, saw her friend and adviser, Signor Rainaldi, and is now returned. Say that he is a plain man, and lives in a plain fashion. That he has no fine manners, no conversation, and is little used to the society of women, or indeed of anyone. If, however, she wishes to see him and her late husband's home – Philip Ashley's house is at the disposal of his cousin Rachel, when she cares to visit it.' And I placed my hand upon my heart, and bowed.

'I never thought,' said my godfather slowly, 'to see you grow so hard. What has happened to you?'

'Nothing has happened to me,' I said, 'save that, like a young war-horse, I smell blood. Have you forgotten my father was a soldier?'

Then I went out into the garden to find Louise. Her concern at the news was greater than my own. I took her hand and dragged her to the summer-house beside the lawn. We sat there together, like conspirators.

'Your house isn't fit to receive anyone,' she said at once, 'let alone a woman like the contessa – like Mrs. Ashley. You see, I can't help calling her contessa too, it comes more naturally. Why, Philip, there hasn't been a woman staying there for twenty years. What room will you put her in? And think of the dust! Not only upstairs but in the drawing-room too. I noticed it last week.'

'None of that matters,' I said impatiently. 'She can dust the place herself, if she minds so much. The worse she finds it, the better pleased I shall be. Let her know at last the happy care-free life we led, Ambrose and I. Unlike that villa . . .'

'Oh, but you're wrong,' exclaimed Louise. 'You don't want to seem a boor, an ignoramus, like one of the hinds on the estate. That would be putting yourself at a disadvantage before you even spoke to her. You must remember she has lived on the continent all her life, has been used to great refinement, many servants – they say foreign ones are much better than ours – and she is certain to have brought a quantity of clothes, and jewels too, perhaps, besides Mr. Ashley's things. She will have heard so much about the house from him that she will expect something very fine, like her own villa. And to have it all untidy, dusty, smelling like a kennel – why, you would not want her to find it so, Philip, for his sake, surely?'

God damn it, I was angry. 'What the devil do you mean,' I said, 'by my house smelling like a kennel? It's a man's house, plain and homely, and please God it always will be. Neither Ambrose nor I went in for fancy furnishings and little ornaments on tables that come crashing to the ground if you brush your knee against them.'

She had the grace to look contrite, if not ashamed.

'I'm sorry,' she said, 'I did not mean to offend you. You know I love your house, I have a great affection for it and always will. But I can't help saying what I think, as to the way it's kept. Nothing new for so long, no real warmth about it, and lacking – well, lacking comfort, if you'll forgive that too.'

I thought of the bright trim parlour where she made my godfather sit of an evening, and I knew which I would prefer to have, and he too in all probability, faced with the choice of that and my library.

'All right,' I said, 'forget my lack of comfort. It suited Ambrose, and it suits me, and for the space of a few days – however long she chooses so to honour me with her presence – it can suit my cousin Rachel too.'

Louise shook her head at me.

'You're quite incorrigible,' she said. 'If Mrs. Ashley is the woman I believe her to be she will take one look at the house and then seek refuge in St. Austell, or with us.'

'You're very welcome,' I replied, 'when I have done with her.'

Louise looked at me curiously. 'Will you really dare to question her?' she asked. 'Where will you begin?'

I shrugged my shoulders. 'I can't say until I have seen her. She'll try to bluster her way out, I have no doubt. Or maybe make a great play of emotion, swoon and have hysterics. That won't worry me. I shall watch her, and enjoy it.'

'I don't think she will bluster,' said Louise, 'nor have hysterics. She will merely sweep into the house and take command. Don't forget, she must be used to giving orders.'

'She won't give them in my house.'

'Poor Seecombe! What I would give to see his face. She will throw things at him, if he fails to come when she pulls her bell. Italians are very passionate, you know, very quick-tempered. I have always heard so.'

'She's only half Italian,' I reminded her, 'and I think Seecombe is well able to take care of himself. Perhaps it will rain for three days, and she will be confined to bed with rheumatism.'

We laughed together in the summer-house, like a pair of children, but for all that I was not so light of heart as I pretended. The invitation had been flung on to the air like a challenge, and already I think I had regretted it, though I did not say so to Louise. I regretted it more when I went home and looked about me. Dear heaven, it was a foolhardy thing to go and do, and had it not been for pride I think I would have ridden back to my godfather and told him to send no message from me, when he wrote to Plymouth.

What in the world was I to do with that woman in my house? What indeed should I say to her, what action should I take? If Rainaldi had been plausible, she would be ten times more so. Direct attack might not succeed, and what was it the Italian had said anyway about tenacity, and women fighting battles? If she should be loud-mouthed, vulgar, I thought I knew how to shut her up. A fellow from one of the farms became entangled with such a one, who would have sued him for breach of promise, and I soon had her packing back to Devon, where she belonged. But sugary, insidious, with heaving bosom and sheep's eyes, could I deal with that? I believed so. I had met with some of these in Oxford, and I always found extreme bluntness of speech, amounting to brutality, sent them back to their holes in the ground with no bones broken. No, all things considered, I was pretty cock-sure, pretty confident, that when I had actual speech with my cousin Rachel I should find my tongue. But preparations for the visit, that was the deuce, the façade of courtesy before the salute to arms.

To my great surprise, Seecombe received the idea without dismay. It was almost as if he had expected it. I told him briefly that Mrs. Ashley had arrived in England, bringing with her Mr. Ambrose's effects, and that it was possible she would arrive for a short visit within the week. His under-lip did not jut forward, as it usually did when faced with any problem, and he listened to me with gravity.

'Yes, sir,' he said, 'very right and very proper. We shall all be glad to welcome Mrs. Ashley.'

I glanced at him over my pipe, amused at his pomposity.

'I thought,' I said, 'you were like me, and did not care for women in the house. You sang a different tune when I told you Mr. Ambrose had been married, and she would be mistress here.'

He looked shocked. This time the nether lip went forward.

'That was not the same, sir,' he said; 'there has been tragedy since then. The poor lady is widowed. Mr. Ambrose would have wished us to do what we can for her, especially as it seems' – he coughed discreetly – 'that Mrs. Ashley has not benefited in any way from the decease.'

I wondered how the devil he knew that, and asked him.

'It's common talk, sir,' he said, 'all around the place. Everything left to you, Mr. Philip, nothing to the widow. It is not usual, you see. In every family, big or small, there is always provision for the widow.'

'I'm surprised at you, Seecombe,' I said, 'lending your ear to gossip.'

'Not gossip, sir,' he said with dignity; 'what concerns the Ashley family concerns us all. We, the servants, were not forgotten.'

I had a vision of him sitting out at the back there, in his room, the steward's room as it was called from long custom, and coming in to chat and drink a glass of bitter with him would be Wellington, the old coachman, Tamlyn, the head gardener, and the first woodman – none of the young servants, of course, would be permitted to join them – and the affairs of the will, which I had thought most secret, would be discussed and puzzled over and discussed again with pursed lips and shaking heads.

'It was not a question of forgetfulness,' I said shortly. 'The fact that Mr. Ashley was abroad, and not at home, made matters of business out of the question. He did not expect to die there. Had he come home things would have been otherwise.'

'Yes, sir,' he said, 'that is what we thought.'

Oh, well, they could cluck their tongues about the will, it makes no odds. But I wondered, with a sudden flash of bitterness, what their manner would have been to me if, after all, I had not inherited the property. Would the deference be there? The respect? The loyalty? Or would I have been young Master Philip, a poor relative, with a room of my own stuck away somewhere at the back of the house? I knocked out my pipe, the taste was dry and dusty. How many people were there, I wondered, who liked me and served me for myself alone?

'That is all, Seecombe,' I said. 'I will let you know if Mrs. Ashley decides to visit us. I don't know about a room. I leave that side of the business to you.'

'Why surely, Mr. Philip, sir,' said Seecombe in surprise, 'it will be correct to put Mrs. Ashley into Mr. Ashley's own room?'

I stared at him, shocked into sudden silence. Then fearing my feelings showed in my face, I turned away.

'No,' I said, 'that won't be possible. I shall be moving into Mr. Ashley's room myself. I meant to tell you so before. I decided upon the change some days ago.'

It was a lie. I had not thought of such a thing until that moment.

'Very well, sir,' he said, 'in that case the blue room and the dressing-room will be more suitable for Mrs. Ashley.' And he left the room.

Good God, I thought, to put that woman into Ambrose's room, what sacrilege. I flung myself down in my chair, biting the stem of my pipe. I felt angry, unsettled, sick of the whole concern. It was madness to have sent that message through my godfather, madness to have her in the house at all. What in the name of the devil had I let myself in for? That idiot, Seecombe, with his ideas of what was right and what was wrong.

The invitation was accepted. She wrote a letter back to my godfather, not to me. Which, as no doubt Seecombe would have thought, was duly right and proper. The invitation had not come direct from me, therefore it must be returned through the correct channel. She would be ready, she said, whenever it was convenient to send for her, or if not convenient she would come by post-chaise. I replied, again through my godfather, that I would send the carriage for her on the Friday. And that was that.

Friday came all too soon. A moody, fitful sort of day, with gusts of wind. We often had them thus, the third week in September, with the big tides of the year. The clouds were low, scudding across the sky from the south-west, threatening rain before the evening. I hoped it would rain. One of our true downpours, with maybe a gale thrown in for further measure. A west country welcome. No Italian skies. I had sent Wellington off with the horses the day before. He would stay overnight in Plymouth and return with her. Ever since I had told the servants that Mrs. Ashley was expected a sort of unrest had come upon the house. Even the dogs were aware of it and followed me about from room to room. Seecombe reminded me of some old priest who, after years of abstinence from any form of religious celebration, suddenly conforms again to forgotten ritual. He moved about, mysterious and solemn, with hushed footsteps – he had even bought himself a pair of soft-soled slippers – and bits of silver I had never seen in my life before were borne into the dining-room and placed on the table, or on the sideboard. Relics, I suppose, of my uncle Philip's day. Great candlesticks, sugar-castors, goblets, and a silver bowl filled – great Joshua – with roses placed as a centre piece.

'Since when,' I said to him, 'have you turned acolyte? What about the incense, and the holy water?'

He did not move a muscle of his face. He stood back, surveying the relics. 'I have asked Tamlyn to bring cut flowers from the walled garden,' he said. 'The boys are sorting them now, out at the back. We shall need flowers in the drawing-room, and in the blue bedroom, in the dressing-room and boudoir.' He frowned at the pantry boy, young John, who slipped and nearly fell, staggering under the load of yet another pair of candlesticks.

The dogs gazed up at me, dejected. One of them crept and hid under the settle in the hall. I went upstairs. Heaven knows when last I had trespassed into the blue room. We never had visitors, and it was connected in my mind with some game of hide-and-seek, long since, when Louise had come over with my godfather one Christmas. I could remember creeping into the silent room and hiding beneath the bed, amongst the dust. I had a dim recollection that Ambrose had once said it was aunt Phoebe's room, and aunt Phoebe had gone away to live in Kent, and later died.

No trace of her remained to-day. The boys, under Seecombe's direction, had worked hard, and aunt Phoebe had been swept away with the dust of years. The windows were open, looking out on the grounds, and the morning sun shone on the well-beaten rugs. Fresh linen, of a quality unknown to me, had been put upon the bed. Had that wash-stand and ewer always been there, I wondered, in the dressing-room adjoining? Did that easy chair belong? I remembered none of them, but then I remembered nothing of aunt Phoebe, who had taken herself to Kent before I was even born. Well, what had done for her would do for my cousin Rachel.

The third room, under the arch, making up the suite, had been aunt Phoebe's boudoir. This too had been dusted, and the windows opened. I dare say I had not entered this room either since those days of hide-and-seek. There was a portrait of Ambrose hanging on the wall above the fireplace, painted when he was a young man. I did not even know of its existence, and he had probably forgotten it. Had it been done by some well-known painter it would have been below with the other family portraits, but sent up here, to a room never used, suggested no one had thought much of it. It was painted three-quarter length, and he had his gun under his arm and carried a dead partridge in his left hand. The eyes looked ahead, into my eyes, and the mouth smiled a little. His hair was longer than I remembered it. There was nothing very striking in the portrait, or in the face. Only one thing. It was strangely like myself. I looked into the mirror, and back again to the portrait, and the only difference lay in the slant of his eyes, something narrower than mine, and in his darker colouring of hair. We could be brothers, though, almost twin brothers, that young man in the portrait and myself. This sudden realisation of our likeness gave an uplift to my spirits. It was as if the young Ambrose was smiling at me saying 'I am with you.' And the older Ambrose, too, felt very close. I shut the door behind me and, passing back once more through the dressing-room and the blue bedroom, went downstairs.

I heard the sound of wheels out on the drive. It was Louise, in the dog-cart, and she had great bunches of michaelmas daisies and dahlias on the seat beside her.

'For the drawing-room,' she called, on sight of me. 'I thought that Seecombe might be glad of them.'

Seecombe, passing that moment through the hall with his drove of minions, looked offended. He stood stiffly, as Louise passed into the house carrying the flowers. 'You should not have troubled, Miss Louise,' he said, 'I had made all arrangements with Tamlyn. Sufficient flowers were brought in first thing from the walled garden.'

'I can arrange them, then,' said Louise; 'your men will only break the vases. I suppose you have vases. Or have they been cramming the flowers into jam-pots?'

Seecombe's face was a study in pained dignity. I pushed Louise into the library hurriedly and shut the door.

'I wondered,' said Louise, in an undertone, 'whether you would have liked me to stay and see to things, and be here when Mrs. Ashley comes. Father would have accompanied me, but he is still rather unwell, and with this threatening rain I thought it best he remained indoors. What do you say? Shall I stay? These flowers were only an excuse.'

I felt vaguely irritated that both she and my godfather should think me so incapable, and poor old Seecombe too, who had worked like a slave-driver for the past three days.

'Good of you to suggest it,' I said, 'but quite unnecessary. We can manage very well.'

She looked disappointed. She was evidently afire with curiosity to see my visitor. I did not tell her that I had no intention of being in the house myself when she arrived.

Louise looked critically about the room, but made no comment. No doubt she saw many faults, but had the tact to hold her tongue.

'You can go upstairs, if you like, and see the blue room,' I told her, as a sop to disappointment.

'The blue room?' said Louise. 'That's the one facing east, over the drawing-room, isn't it? Then you have not put her in Mr. Ashley's room?'

'I have not,' I said. 'I use Ambrose's room myself.'

This insistence that she, and everybody else, should put upon the placing of Ambrose's room at the disposal of his widow added fresh fuel to my rising irritation.

'If you really wish to arrange the flowers, ask Seecombe for some vases,' I said, going towards the door. 'I have a mass of things to do outside, and shall be away about the estate most of the day.'

She picked up the flowers, glancing at me as she did so.

'I believe you're nervous,' she said.

'I am not nervous,' I said, 'I merely want to be alone.'

She flushed and turned away, and I felt the prick of conscience that always came to me after wounding anyone.

'Sorry, Louise,' I said, patting her shoulder, 'don't take any notice of me. And bless you for coming, and bringing the flowers, and for offering to stay.'

'When shall I see you again,' she asked, 'to hear about Mrs. Ashley? You know I shall be longing to know everything. Of course, if father is better we shall come down to Church on Sunday, but all to-morrow I shall be thinking and wondering . . .'

'Wondering what?' I said. 'If I have thrown my cousin Rachel over the headland? I might do that, if she goads me hard enough. Listen – just to satisfy you – I will ride over to-morrow afternoon to Pelyn, and paint a vivid picture for you. Does that content you?'

'That will do very well,' she answered, smiling, and went off to find Seecombe and the vases.

I was out all morning and returned about two, hungry and thirsty after my ride, and had some cold meat and a glass of ale. Louise had gone. Seecombe and the servants were in their own quarters, sitting down to their midday dinner. I stood alone in the library, munching my sandwich of meat and bread. Alone, I thought, for the last time. To-night she would be here, either in this room or in the drawing-room, an unknown hostile presence, stamping her personality upon my rooms, my house. She came as an intruder to my home. I did not want her. I did not want her or any woman, with peering eyes and questing fingers, forcing herself into the atmosphere, intimate and personal, that was mine alone. The house was still and silent, and I was part of it, belonging, as Ambrose had done and still did, somewhere in the shadows. We needed no one else to break the silence.

I looked about the room, almost in farewell, and then went out of the house and plunged into the woods.

I judged that Wellington would be home with the carriage not earlier than five o'clock, so I determined to remain without until after six. They could wait dinner for me. Seecombe already had his instructions. If she was hungry, she must hold her hunger until the master of the house returned. It gave me satisfaction to think of her sitting alone in the drawing-room, dressed to the nines, full of self-importance, and no one to receive her.

I went on walking in the wind and rain. Up the avenue to where the four roads met, and eastwards to the boundary of our land; then back through the woods again and northwards to the outlying farms, where I made a point of dallying and talking with the tenants, thus spacing out the time. Across the park and over the westward hills, and home at last by the Barton, just as it grew dusk. I was wet nearly to the skin but I did not care.

I opened the hall door and went into the house. I expected to see the signs of arrival, boxes and trunks, travel rugs and baskets; but all was as usual, there was nothing there.

A fire was burning in the library, but the room was empty. In the dining-room a place was laid for one. I pulled the bell for Seecombe. 'Well?' I said.

He wore his new-found look of self-importance, and his voice was hushed.

'Madam has come,' he said.

'So I would suppose,' I answered, 'it must be nearly seven. Did she bring luggage? What have you done with it?'

'Madam brought little of her own,' he said. 'The boxes and trunks belonged to Mr. Ambrose. They have all been put in your old room, sir.'

'Oh,' I said. I walked over to the fire and kicked a log. I would not have him notice for the world that my hands were trembling.

'Where is Mrs. Ashley now?' I said.

'Madam has gone to her room, sir,' he said. 'She seemed tired, and she asked you to excuse her for dinner. I had a tray taken up to her about an hour ago.'

His words came as a relief. Yet in a sense it was an anti-climax.

'What sort of journey did she have?' I asked.

'Wellington said the road after Liskeard was rough sir,' he answered, 'and it was blowing hard. One of the horses cast a shoe, and they had to turn in at the smithy before Lostwithiel.'

'H'm.' I turned my back upon the fire and warmed my legs.

'You're very wet, sir,' said Seecombe. 'Better change your things, or you'll take cold.'

'I will directly,' I answered him, and then, glancing about the room, 'Where are the dogs?'

'I think they followed madam upstairs,' he said, 'at least old Don did, I am not certain of the others.'

I went on warming my legs before the fire. Seecombe still hovered by the door, as if expecting me to draw him in conversation.

'All right,' I said, 'I'll bath and change. Tell one of the boys to take up the hot water. And I'll dine in half an hour.'

I sat down that evening alone to my dinner before the newly polished candlesticks and the silver rose bowl. Seecombe stood behind my chair, but we did not speak. Silence must have been torture to him, on this night of nights, for I knew how much he longed to comment on the new arrival. Well, he could bide his time, and then let forth to his heart's content in the steward's room.

Just as I finished dinner, John came into the room and whispered to him. Seecombe came and bent over my shoulder.

'Madam has sent word that if you should wish to see her, when you have dined, she will be pleased to receive you,' he said.

'Thank you, Seecombe.'

When they had left the room I did something that I very rarely did. Only after extreme exhaustion, after riding perhaps, or a hard day's shoot, or buffeting about in a summer gale in the sailing boat with Ambrose. I went to the sideboard and poured myself a glass of brandy. Then I went upstairs, and knocked upon the door of the little boudoir.

Chapter Eight

A low voice, almost inaudible, bade me come in. Although it was now dark, and the candles had been lit, the curtains were not drawn, and she was sitting on the window-seat looking out on to the garden. Her back was turned to me, her hands were clasped in her lap. She must have thought me one of the servants, for she did not move when I entered the room. Don lay before the fire, his muzzle in his paws and the two young dogs beside him. Nothing had been moved in the room, no drawers opened in the small secretaire, no clothes flung down; there was none of the litter of arrival.

'Good evening,' I said, and my voice sounded strained and unnatural in the little room. She turned, and rose at once and came towards me. It was happening so quickly that I had no time, no moment for reflection back upon the hundred images I had formed of her during the past eighteen months. The woman who had pursued me through the nights and days, haunted my waking hours, disturbing my dreams, was now beside me. My first feeling was one of shock, almost of stupefaction, that she should be so small. She barely reached my shoulder. She had nothing like the height or the figure of Louise.

She was dressed in deep black, which took the colour from her hair, and there was lace at her throat and at her wrists. Her hair was brown, parted in the centre with a low knot behind, her features neat and regular. The only things large about her were the eyes, which at first sight of me widened in sudden recognition, startled, like the eyes of a deer, and from recognition to bewilderment, from bewilderment to pain, almost to apprehension. I saw the colour come into her face and go again, and I think I was as great a shock to her as she was to me. It would be hazardous to say which of us was the more nervous, which the more ill-at-ease.

I stared down at her and she looked up at me, and it was a moment before either of us spoke. When we did, it was to speak together.

'I hope you are rested,' was my stiff contribution, and hers, 'I owe you an apology.' She followed up my opening swiftly with 'Thank you, Philip, yes,' and moving towards the fire she sat down on a low stool beside it and motioned me to the chair opposite. Don, the old retriever, stretched and yawned, and pulling himself on to his haunches placed his head upon her lap.

'This is Don, isn't it?' she said, putting her hand on his nose. 'Was he really fourteen last birthday?'

'Yes,' I said, 'his birthday is a week before my own.'

'You found him in a pie-crust with your breakfast,' she said. 'Ambrose was hiding behind the screen in the dining-room, and watched you open up the pie. He told me he would never forget the look of amazement on your face when you lifted the crust and Don struggled out. You were ten years old, and it was the first of April.'

She looked up from patting Don, and smiled at me; and to my great discomfiture I saw tears in her eyes, gone upon the instant.

'I owe you an apology for not coming down to dinner,' she said. 'You had made so much preparation, just for me, and must have come hurrying home long before you wanted. But I was very tired. I would have made a poor sort of companion. It seemed to me that it would be easier for you if you dined alone.'

I thought of how I had tramped about the estate from east to west so as to keep her waiting, and I said nothing. One of the younger dogs woke up and licked my hand. I pulled his ears to give myself employment.

'Seecombe told me how busy you were, and how much there is to do,' she said. 'I don't want you to feel hampered in any way by my sudden unexpected visit. I can find my way about alone, and shall be happy doing so. You mustn't make any sort of alteration in your day to-morrow because of me. I just want to say one thing, which is thank you, Philip, for letting me come. It can't have been easy for you.'

She rose then, and crossed over to the window to draw the curtains. The rain was beating against the panes. Perhaps I should have drawn the curtains for her, I did not know. I stood up, awkwardly, in an attempt to do so, but it was too late anyway. She came back beside the fire, and we both sat down again.

'It was such a strange feeling,' she said, 'driving through the park and up to the house, with Seecombe standing by the door to welcome me. I've done it so many times, you know, in fancy. Everything was just as I had imagined it. The hall, the library, the pictures on the walls. The clock struck four as the carriage drove up to the door; I even knew the sound of it.' I went on pulling at the puppy's ears. I did not look at her. 'In the evenings, in Florence,' she said, 'last summer and winter before Ambrose became ill, we used to talk about the journey home. It was his happiest time. He would tell me about the gardens, and the woods, and the path down to the sea. We always intended to return by the route I came; that's why I did it. Genoa, and so to Plymouth. And the carriage coming there with Wellington to bring us back. It was good of you to do that, to know how I would feel.'

I felt something of a fool, but found my tongue.

'I fear the drive was rather rough,' I said, 'and Seecombe told me you were obliged to stop at the smithy to shoe one of the horses. I'm sorry about that.'

'It did not worry me,' she said. 'I was quite happy, sitting beside the fire there, watching the work and chatting to Wellington.'

Her manner was quite easy now. That first nervousness had gone, if it had been nervousness at all. I could not tell. I found now that if anyone was at fault it was myself, for I felt oddly large and clumsy in so small a room, and the chair in which I was sitting might have been made for a dwarf. There is nothing so defeating to ease of manner as being uncomfortably seated, and I wondered what sort of a figure I must cut, hunched there in the damnable little chair, with my large feet tucked awkwardly beneath it and my long arms hanging down on either side of it.

'Wellington pointed out to me the entrance to Mr. Kendall's house,' she said, 'and for a moment I wondered if it would be right, and polite, to go and pay him my respects. But it was late, and the horses had been far, and very selfishly I was longing to be – here.' She had paused a moment before saying the word 'here', and it came to me that she had been on the point of saying 'home' but checked herself. 'Ambrose had described it all so well to me,' she said, 'from the entrance hall to every room in the house. He even sketched them for me, so that to-day, I well believe, I could find my way blindfold.' She paused a moment, and then she said, 'It was perceptive of you to let me have these rooms. They were the ones we meant to use, had we been together. Ambrose always intended you to have his room, and Seecombe told me you had moved into it. Ambrose would be glad.'

'I hope you'll be comfortable,' I said. 'Nobody seems to have been in here since someone called aunt Phoebe.'

'Aunt Phoebe fell love-sick of a curate, and went away to Tonbridge to mend a broken heart,' she said, 'but the heart proved stubborn, and aunt Phoebe took a chill that lasted twenty years. Did you never hear the story?'

'No,' I said, and glanced across at her, under my eyes. She was looking into the fire, smiling. I suppose at the thought of aunt Phoebe. Her hands were clasped on her lap in front of her. I had never seen hands so small before on an adult person. They were very slender, very narrow, like the hands of someone in a portrait painted by an old master and left unfinished.

'Well,' I said, 'what happened to aunt Phoebe?'

'The chill left her, after twenty years, at sight of another curate. But by then aunt Phoebe was five and forty, and her heart was not so brittle. She married the second curate.'

'Was the marriage a success?'

'No,' said my cousin Rachel, 'she died on her wedding night – of shock.'

She turned and looked at me, her mouth twitching, yet her eyes still solemn, and suddenly I had a vision of Ambrose telling the story, as he must have done, hunched in his chair, his shoulders shaking, with her looking up at him in just this way, concealing laughter. I could not help myself. I smiled at cousin Rachel, and something happened to her eyes and she smiled back at me.

'I think you made it up upon this instant,' I said to her, instantly regretting my smile.

'I did nothing of the sort,' she said. 'Seecombe will know the story. Ask him.'

I shook my head. 'He would not think it fitting. And he would be deeply shocked if he thought you had told it to me. I forgot to ask you if he brought you anything for dinner?'

'Yes. A cup of soup, a wing of chicken, and a devilled kidney. All were excellent.'

'You realise, of course, there are no women servants in the house? No one to look after you, to hang your gowns, only young John or Arthur to fill your bath?'

'I much prefer it. Women chatter so. As to my gowns, all mourning is the same. I have only brought this and one other. I have strong shoes for walking in the grounds.'

'If it rains like this tomorrow you will have to stay indoors,' I said. 'There are plenty of books in the library. I don't read much myself, but you might find something to your taste.'

Her mouth twitched again and she looked at me gravely. 'I could always polish the silver,' she said. 'I had not thought to see so much of it. Ambrose used to say it turned to mildew by the sea.' I could swear from her expression that she had guessed the array of relics came from a long-locked cupboard, and that behind her large eyes she was laughing at me.

I looked away. I had smiled at her once, I was damned if I would smile at her again.

'At the villa,' she said, 'when it was very hot, we would sit out in a little court there, with a fountain. Ambrose would tell me to close my eyes, and listen to the water, making believe that it was the rain falling at home. He had a great theory, you know, that I should shrink and shiver in the English climate, especially the damp Cornish one; he called me a green-house plant, fit only for expert cultivation, quite useless in the common soil. I was city-bred, he said, and over-civilised. Once I remember I came down to dinner wearing a new gown, and he told me I reeked of old Rome. "You'll freeze in that at home," he said; "it will be flannel next the skin, and a woollen shawl." I haven't forgotten his advice. I brought the shawl.' I glanced up. Indeed she had one, black like her dress, lying on the stool beside her.

'In England,' I said, 'especially down here, we lay great stress upon the weather. We have to, by the sea. Our land isn't very rich, you see, for farming, not as it is up-country. The soil is poor, and with four days out of seven wet we're very dependent on the sun when it does shine. This will take off to-morrow, I dare say, and you'll get your walk.'

' 'Bove town and Bawden's meadow,' she said, 'Kemp's close and Beef Park, Kilmoor and beacon field, the Twenty Acres, and the West Hills.'

I looked at her astonished. 'You know the names of the Barton lands?' I said.

'Why yes, I've known them by heart now for near two years,' she answered.

I was silent. There seemed nothing I could say in answer. Then, 'It's rough walking for a woman,' I told her gruffly.

'But I have strong shoes,' she answered me.

The foot she thrust out from beneath her gown seemed to me woefully inadequate for walking, clad as it was in a black velvet slipper.

'That?' I asked.

'Of course not, something stronger,' she replied.

I could not picture her tramping about the fields, however much she saw herself. And my ploughman boots would drown her.

'Can you ride?' I asked her.

'No.'

'Can you sit upon a horse if you were led?'

'I might do that,' she answered, 'but I would have to hold on to the saddle with both hands. And isn't there something called a pommel on which one balances?'

She put the question with great earnestness, her eyes solemn, yet once more I was certain there was laughter hidden there and she wished to draw me. 'I'm not sure,' I said stiffly, 'if we have a lady's saddle. I'll ask Wellington, but I have never seen one in the harness room.'

'Perhaps aunt Phoebe used to ride,' she said, 'when she lost her curate. It may have been her only consolation.'

It was useless. Something bubbled in her voice, and I was lost. She saw me laughing, that was the devil of it. I looked away.

'All right,' I said, 'I'll see about it in the morning. Do you think I should ask Seecombe to search the closets and see if aunt Phoebe left a riding-habit too?'

'I shan't need a habit,' she said, 'not if you lead me gently and I balance on that pommel.'

At that moment Seecombe knocked upon the door and entered, bearing in his hands a silver kettle upon a monstrous tray, likewise a silver tea-pot and a canister. I had never set eyes upon the things before, and I wondered from what labyrinth in the steward's room he had come upon them. And for what purpose did he bring them? My cousin Rachel saw the amazement in my eyes. Not for the world would I hurt Seecombe, who placed his offering upon the table with great dignity, but a rising tide of something near hysteria rose in my chest, and I got up from my chair and went over to the window in pretence of looking out upon the rain.

'Tea is served, madam,' said Seecombe.

'Thank you, Seecombe,' she answered solemnly.

The dogs rose, sniffing, thrusting their noses at the tray. They were as amazed as I. Seecombe clicked at them with his tongue.

'Come, Don,' he said, 'come on, all three of you. I think, madam, I had better remove the dogs. They might upset the tray.'

'Yes, Seecombe,' she said, 'perhaps they might.'

Again that laughter in the voice. I was thankful my back was turned to her. 'What about breakfast, madam?' asked Seecombe. 'Mr. Philip has his in the dining-room at eight o'clock.'

'I should like mine in my room,' she said. 'Mr. Ashley used to say no woman was fit to look upon before eleven. Will that give trouble?'

'Certainly not, madam.'

'Then thank you, Seecombe, and good night.'

'Good night, madam. Good night, sir. Come, dogs.'

He snapped his fingers and they followed him reluctantly. There was silence in the room for a few moments and then she said softly: 'Would you like some tea? I understand it is a Cornish custom.'

My dignity vanished. Holding to it had become too great a strain. I went back to the fire and sat on the stool beside the table.

'I'll tell you something,' I said. 'I have never seen this tray before, nor the kettle, nor the tea-pot.'

'I didn't think you had,' she said. 'I saw the look in your eyes when Seecombe brought them into the room. I don't believe he has seen them before either. They're buried treasure. He has dug for them in the cellars.'

'Is it really the thing to do,' I asked, 'to drink tea after dinner?'

'Of course,' she said, 'in high society, when ladies are present.'

'We never have it on Sundays,' I said, 'when the Kendalls and the Pascoes come to dinner.'

'Perhaps Seecombe doesn't consider them high society,' she said. 'I'm very flattered. I like my tea. You can eat the bread and butter.'

This too was an innovation. Pieces of thin bread, rolled like small sausages. 'I'm surprised they knew how to do this in the kitchen,' I said, swallowing them down, 'but they're very good.'

'A sudden inspiration,' said cousin Rachel, 'and no doubt you will have what is left for breakfast. That butter is melting, you had better suck your fingers.'

She drank her tea, watching me over her cup.

'If you want to smoke your pipe, you can,' she said.

I stared at her surprised.

'In a lady's boudoir?' I said. 'Are you sure? Why, on Sundays, when Mrs. Pascoe comes with the vicar, we never smoke in the drawing-room.'

'It's not the drawing-room, and I'm not Mrs. Pascoe,' she answered me.

I shrugged my shoulders and felt in my pocket for my pipe.

'Seecombe will think it very wrong,' I said. 'He'll smell it in the morning.'

'I'll open the window before I go to bed,' she said. 'It will all blow out, with the rain.'

'The rain will come in and spoil the carpet,' I said, 'then that will be worse than the smell of the pipe.'

'It can be rubbed down with a cloth,' she said. 'How pernickety you are, like an old gentleman.'

'I thought women minded about such things.'

'They do, when they have nothing else to worry them,' she said.

It struck me suddenly as I smoked my pipe, sitting there in aunt Phoebe's boudoir, that this was not at all the way I had intended to spend the evening. I had planned a few words of icy courtesy and an abrupt farewell, leaving the interloper snubbed, dismissed.

I glanced up at her. She had finished her tea, and put the cup and saucer back on the tray. Once again I was aware of her hands, narrow and small and very white, and I wondered if Ambrose had called them city-bred. She wore two rings, fine stones both of them, on her fingers, yet they seemed to clash in no way with her mourning, nor be out of keeping with her person. I was glad I had the bowl of my pipe to hold, and the stem to bite upon; it made me feel more like myself and less like a sleep-walker, muddled by a dream. There were things I should be doing, things I should be saying, and here was I sitting like a fool before the fire, unable to collect my thoughts or my impressions. The day, so long-drawn-out and anxious, was now over, and I could not for the life of me decide whether it had turned to my advantage or gone against me. If only she had borne some resemblance to the image I had created I would know better what to do, but now that she was here, beside me, in the flesh, the images seemed fantastic crazy things that all turned into one another and then faded into darkness.

Somewhere there was a bitter creature, crabbed and old, hemmed about with lawyers; somewhere a larger Mrs. Pascoe, loud-voiced, arrogant; somewhere a petulant spoilt doll, with corkscrew curls; somewhere a viper, sinuous and silent. But none of them was with me in this room. Anger seemed futile now, and hatred too, and as for fear – how could I fear anyone who did not measure up to my shoulder, and had nothing remarkable about her save a sense of humour and small hands? Was it for this that one man had fought a duel, and another, dying, written to me and said, 'She's done for me at last, Rachel my torment?' It was as though I had blown a bubble in the air, and stood by to watch it dance; and the bubble had now burst.

I must remember, I thought to myself, nearly nodding by the flickering fire, not to drink brandy another time after a ten-mile walk in the rain; it dulls the senses and it does not ease the tongue. I had come to fight this woman and I had not even started. What was it she had said about aunt Phoebe's saddle?

'Philip,' said the voice, very quiet, very low, 'Philip, you're nearly asleep. Will you please get up and go to bed?'

I opened my eyes with a jerk. She was sitting watching me, her hands in her lap. I stumbled to my feet, and nearly crashed the tray.

'I'm sorry,' I said, 'it must have been because I was sitting cramped there on that stool, it made me sleepy. I usually stretch my legs out in the library.'

'You took a lot of exercise to-day too, didn't you?' she said.

Her voice was innocent enough and yet . . . What did she mean? I frowned, and stood staring down at her, determined to say nothing. 'If it's fine then to-morrow morning,' she said, 'will you really find a horse for me that will be steady and quiet, so that I can sit up on him and go and see the Barton acres?'

'Yes,' I said, 'if you want to go.'

'I needn't bother you; Wellington shall lead me.'

'No, I can take you. I have nothing else to do.'

'Wait though,' she said, 'you forget it will be Saturday. That's the morning you pay the wages. We'll wait till afternoon.'

I looked down at her, nonplussed. 'Great heavens,' I said, 'how in the world do you know that I pay the wages on Saturday?'

To my dismay and great embarrassment, her eyes grew bright suddenly, and wet, as they had done earlier when she talked of my tenth birthday. And her voice became much harder than before.

'If you don't know,' she said, 'you have less understanding than I thought. Stay here a moment, I have a present for you.'

She opened the door and passed into the blue bedroom opposite, and returned within a moment carrying a stick in her hand.

'Here,' she said, 'take it, it's yours. Everything else you can sort out and see another time, but I wanted to give you this myself, tonight.'

It was Ambrose's walking stick. The one he always used, and leant upon. The one with the gold band, and the dog's head on the top carved in ivory.

'Thank you,' I said awkwardly, 'thank you very much.'

'Now go,' she said, 'please go, quickly.'

And she pushed me from the room, and shut the door.

I stood outside, holding the stick in my hands. She had not given me time even to wish her good night. No sound came from the boudoir, and I walked slowly down the corridor to my own room. I thought of the expression in her eyes as she gave me the stick. Once, not so long ago, I had seen other eyes with that same age-old look of suffering. Those eyes too had held reserve and pride, coupled with the same abasement, the same agony of supplication. It must be, I thought, as I came to my room, Ambrose's room, and examined the well-remembered walking stick, it must be because the eyes are the same colour and they belong to the same race. Otherwise they could have nothing in common, the beggar woman beside the Arno and my cousin Rachel.

Chapter Nine

I was down early the following morning, and immediately after breakfast walked across to the stables and summoned Wellington, and we went together to the harness room.

Yes, there were some half-dozen side-saddles amongst the rest. I suppose the fact was that I had never noticed them.

'Mrs. Ashley cannot ride,' I told him. 'All she wants is something to sit upon and to cling on to.'

'We'd better put her up on Solomon,' said the old coachman. 'He may never have carried a lady but he won't let her down, that's certain. I couldn't be sure, sir, of any of the other horses.'

Solomon had been hunted years back, by Ambrose, but now took his ease chiefly in the meadow, unless exercised on the high road by Wellington. The side-saddles were high up on the wall of the harness room, and he had to send for the groom, and a short ladder, to bring them down. It caused quite a pother and excitement, the choice of the saddle; this one was too worn, the next too narrow for Solomon's broad back, and the lad was scolded because the third had a cobweb across it. I laughed inwardly, guessing that neither Wellington nor anybody else had thought about those saddles for a quarter of a century, and told Wellington that a good polish with a leather would set it to rights, and Mrs. Ashley would think the saddle had come down from London yesterday.

'What time does the mistress wish to start?' he asked, and I stared at him a moment, taken aback by his choice of words.

'Some time after noon,' I said shortly. 'You can bring Solomon round to the front door, and I shall be leading Mrs. Ashley myself.'

Then I turned back to the estate room, in the house, to reckon up the weekly books and check the accounts before the men came for their wages. The mistress indeed. Was that how they looked upon her, Wellington and Seecombe and the rest? I supposed in a sense it was natural of them, yet I thought how swiftly men, especially men-servants, became fools when in the presence of a woman. That look of reverence in Seecombe's eye when he had brought in the tea last night, and his respectful manner as he placed the tray before her, and this morning at breakfast it was young John, if you please, who waited by the side-board and lifted the covers from my bacon, because 'Mr. Seecombe,' he said, 'has gone upstairs with the tray for the boudoir.' And now here was Wellington, in a state of excitement, polishing and rubbing at the old side-saddle, and shouting over his shoulder to the boy to see to Solomon. I worked away at my accounts, glad to be so unmoved by the fact that a woman had slept under the roof for the first time since Ambrose had sent my nurse packing; and now I came to think of it her treatment of me as I nearly fell asleep, her words, 'Philip, go to bed,' were what my nurse might have said to me, over twenty years ago.

At noon the servants came, and the men who worked outside in the stables, woods, and gardens, and I gave them their money; then I noticed that Tamlyn, the head gardener, was not amongst them. I enquired the reason, and was told that he was somewhere about the grounds with 'the mistress'. I made no observation as to this, but paid the rest their wages and dismissed them. Some instinct told me where I should find Tamlyn and my cousin Rachel. I was right. They were in the forcing ground, where we had brought on the camellias, and the oleanders, and the other young trees that Ambrose had carried back from his travels.

I had never been an expert – I had left that to Tamlyn – and now as I rounded the corner and came upon them I could hear her talking about cuttings, and layers, and a north aspect, and the feeding of the soil, and Tamlyn listening to it all with his hat in his hand and the same look of reverence in the eye that Seecombe had, and Wellington. She smiled at the sight of me and rose to her feet. She had been kneeling on a piece of sacking, examining the shoots of a young tree.

'I've been out since half-past ten,' she said. 'I looked for you to ask permission but could not find you, so I did a bold thing and went down myself to Tamlyn's cottage to make myself known to him, didn't I, Tamlyn?'

'You did, ma'am,' said Tamlyn, with a sheep's look in his eye.

'You see, Philip,' she continued, 'I brought with me to Plymouth – I could not get them in the carriage, they will follow on by carrier – all the plants and shrubs that we had collected, Ambrose and I, during the past two years. I have the lists here with me, and where he wished them to go, and I thought it would save time if I talked over the list with Tamlyn, and explained what everything was. I may be gone when the carrier brings the load.'

'That's all right,' I said. 'You both of you understand these things better than I do. Please continue.'

'We've finished, haven't we, Tamlyn?' she said. 'And will you please thank Mrs. Tamlyn for that cup of tea she gave me, and tell her that I do so hope her sore throat will be better by this evening? Oil of eucalyptus is the remedy, I will send some down to her.'

'Thank you, ma'am,' said Tamlyn (it was the first I had heard of his wife's sore throat), and looking at me he added, with a little awkward air of diffidence, 'I've learnt some things this morning, Mr. Philip, sir, that I never thought to learn from a lady. I always believed I knew my work, but Mrs. Ashley knows more about gardening than I do, or ever will for that matter. Proper ignorant she's made me feel.'

'Nonsense, Tamlyn,' said my cousin Rachel, 'I only know about trees and shrubs. As to fruit – I haven't the least idea how to set about growing a peach, and remember, you haven't yet taken me round the walled garden. You shall do so to-morrow.'

'Whenever you wish, ma'am,' said Tamlyn, and she bade him good morning and we set back towards the house.

'If you have been out since after ten,' I said to her, 'you will want to rest now. I will tell Wellington not to saddle the horse after all.'

'Rest?' she said. 'Who talks of resting? I have been looking forward to my ride all morning. Look, the sun. You said it would break through. Are you going to lead me, or will Wellington?'

'No,' I said, 'I'll take you. And I warn you, you may be able to teach Tamlyn about camellias, but you won't be able to do the same with me and farming.'

'I know oats from barley,' she said. 'Doesn't that impress you?'

'Not a jot,' I said, 'and anyway, you won't find either out on the acres, they're all harvested.'

When we came to the house I discovered that Seecombe had laid out a cold luncheon of meat and salad in the dining-room, complete with pies and puddings as though we were to sit for dinner. My cousin Rachel glanced at me, her face quite solemn, yet that look of laughter behind her eyes.

'You are a young man, and you have not finished growing,' she said. 'Eat, and be thankful. Put a piece of that pie in your pocket and I will ask you for it when we are on the west hills. I am going upstairs now to dress myself suitably for riding.'

At least, I thought to myself as I tucked into the cold meat with hearty appetite, she does not expect waiting upon or other niceties, she has a certain independence of spirit that would seem, thank the Lord, unfeminine. The only irritation was that my manner with her, which I hoped was cutting, she apparently took in good part and enjoyed. My sarcasm was misread as joviality.

I had scarcely finished eating when Solomon was brought round to the door. The sturdy old horse had undergone the grooming of his lifetime. Even his hoofs were polished, an attention that was never paid to my Gypsy. The two young dogs pranced around his heels. Don watched them undisturbed; his running days were over, like his old friend Solomon's.

I went to tell Seecombe we would be out till after four, and when I returned my cousin Rachel had come downstairs and was already mounted upon Solomon. Wellington was adjusting her stirrup. She had changed into another mourning gown, cut somewhat fuller than the other, and instead of a hat she had wound her black lace shawl about her hair for covering. She was talking to Wellington, her profile turned to me, and for some reason or other I remembered what she had said the night before about Ambrose teasing her, how he had told her once that she reeked of old Rome. I think I knew now what he meant. Her features were like those stamped on a Roman coin, definite, yet small; and now with that lace shawl wound about her hair I was reminded of the women I had seen kneeling in that cathedral in Florence, or lurking in the doorways of the silent houses. As she sat up on Solomon you could not tell that she was so small in stature when she stood upon the ground. The woman whom I considered unremarkable, save for her hands and her changing eyes and the bubble of laughter in her voice upon occasion, looked different now that she sat above me. She seemed more distant, more remote, and more – Italian.

She heard my footstep and turned towards me; and it went swiftly, the distant look, the foreign look, that had come upon her features in repose. She looked now as she had before.

'Ready?' I said. 'Or are you fearful of falling?'

'I put my trust in you and Solomon,' she answered.

'Very well, then. Come on. We shall be about two hours, Wellington.' And taking the bridle I set off with her to tour the Barton acres.

The wind of the day before had bown itself up-country, taking the rain with it, and at noon the sun had broken through and the sky was clear. There was a salty brightness in the air, lending a zest to walking, and you could hear the running swell of the sea as it broke upon the rocks fringing the bay. We had these days often in the fall of the year. Belonging to no season they had a freshness all their own, yet with a hint of cooler hours to come and tasting still the aftermath of summer.

Ours was a strange pilgrimage. We started off by visiting the Barton, and it was as much as I could do to prevent Billy Rowe and his wife from inviting us inside the farmhouse to sit down to cakes and cream; in fact it was only by the promise of doing so on Monday that I got Solomon and my cousin Rachel past the byre and the midden and through the gates at all, up on the stubble of the west hills.

The Barton lands form a peninsula, the beacon fields forming the further end of it and the sea running into bays, east and west, on either side. As I had told her, the corn had all been carried, and I could lead old Solomon wherever I pleased, for he could do no damage on the stubble. The larger part of the Barton land is grazing land anyway, and to make a thorough tour of it all we kept close to the sea, and finally brought up by the beacon itself, so that looking back she could see the whole run of the estate, bounded on the western side by the great stretch of sandy bay and three miles to the eastward by the estuary. The Barton farm, and the house itself – the mansion, as Seecombe always called it – lay in a sort of saucer, but already the trees planted by Ambrose and my uncle Philip grew thick and fast to give the house more shelter, and to the north the new avenue wound through the woods and up the rise to where the four roads met.

Remembering her talk of the night before, I tried to test my cousin Rachel on the names of the Barton fields, but could not fault her; she knew them all. Her memory did not mislead her when she came to mention the various beaches, the headlands, and the other farms on the estate; she knew the names of the tenants, the size of their families, that Seecombe's nephew lived in the fish house on the beach, and that his brother had the mill. She did not throw her information at me, it was rather I, my curiosity piqued, who led her on to disclose it, and when she gave me the names, and spoke of the people, it was as a matter of course and with something of wonder that I should think it strange.

'What do you suppose we talked of, Ambrose and I?' she said to me at last, as we came down from the beacon hill to the eastward fields. 'His home was his passion, therefore I made it mine. Would you not expect a wife of yours to do the same?'

'Not possessing a wife I cannot say,' I answered her, 'but I should have thought that having lived on the continent all your life your interests would have been entirely different.'

'So they were,' she said, 'until I met Ambrose.'

'Except for gardens, I gather.'

'Except for gardens,' she agreed, 'which was how it started, as he must have told you. My garden at the villa was very lovely, but this' – she paused a moment, reining in Solomon, and I stood with my hand on the bridle – 'but this is what I have always wanted to see. This is different.' She said nothing for a moment or two, as she looked down on the bay. 'At the villa,' she went on, 'when I was young and first married – I am not referring to Ambrose – I was not very happy, so I distracted myself by designing afresh the gardens there, replanting much of them and terracing the walls. I sought advice, and shut myself up with books, and the results were very pleasing; at least I thought so, and was told so. I wonder what you would think of them.'

I glanced up at her. Her profile was turned towards the sea and she did not know that I was looking at her. What did she mean? Had not my godfather told her I had been to the villa?

A sudden misgiving came upon me. I remembered her composure of the night before, after the first nervousness on meeting, and also the easiness of our conversation, which, on thinking it over at breakfast, I had put down to her own social sense and my dullness after drinking brandy. It struck me

now that it was odd she had said nothing last night about my visit to
Florence, odder still that she had made no reference to the manner in which
I had learnt of Ambrose's death. Could it be that my godfather had shirked
that issue and left it to me to break it to her? I cursed him to myself for an
old blunderer and a coward, and yet as I did so I knew that it was I myself
who was the coward now. Last night, had I only told her last night, when
I had the brandy inside me; but now, now it was not so easy. She would
wonder why I had said nothing of it sooner. This was the moment, of course.
This was the moment to say, 'I have seen the gardens at your villa Sangalletti.
Didn't you know?' But she made a coaxing sound to Solomon and he moved
on.

'Can we go past the mill, and up through the woods the other side?' she
asked.

I had lost my opportunity, and we went on back towards home. As we
progressed through the woods she made remarks from time to time about
the trees, or the set of the hills, or some other feature; but for me the ease
of the afternoon had gone, for somehow or other I had got to tell her about
my visit to Florence. If I said nothing of it she would hear of it from
Seecombe, or from my godfather himself when he came to dinner on Sunday.
I became more and more silent as we drew towards the house.

'I've exhausted you,' she said. 'Here I have been, riding like a queen on
Solomon, and you walking all the while, pilgrim fashion. Forgive me, Philip.
I've been so very happy. You can never guess how happy.'

'No, I'm not tired,' I said, 'I'm – I'm delighted that you enjoyed your
ride.' Somehow I could not look into those eyes, direct and questioning.

Wellington was waiting at the house to help her dismount. She went
upstairs to rest before she changed for dinner, and I sat down in the library,
frowning over my pipe and wondering how the devil I was to tell her about
Florence. The worst of the business was that had my godfather told her of
it in his letter it would have been for her to open the subject, and for me to
relax and wait for what she said. As things stood at present, the move must
come from me. Even this would not have mattered had she been the woman
I expected. Why, in heaven's name, did she have to be so different and play
such havoc with my plans?

I washed my hands, and changed my coat for dinner, and put into my
pocket the two last letters Ambrose had written me, but when I went into
the drawing-room, expecting to see her seated there, the room was empty.
Seecombe, passing that moment through the hall, told me that 'Madam' had
gone into the library.

Now that she no longer sat on Solomon, above me, and had taken off the
head-shawl and smoothed her hair, she seemed even smaller than before,
and more defenceless. Paler too by candlelight, and her mourning gown
darker in comparison.

'Do you mind my sitting here?' she said. 'The drawing-room is lovely in
the daytime, but somehow now, at evening, with the curtains drawn and the
candles lit, this room seems the best. Besides, it was where you and Ambrose
always sat together.'

Now perhaps was my chance. Now to say, 'Yes. You have nothing like this at the villa.' I was silent, and the dogs came in to make distraction. After dinner, I said to myself, after dinner is the time. And I will drink neither port nor brandy.

At dinner Seecombe placed her on my right hand, and both he and John waited upon us. She admired the rose bowl and the candlesticks, and talked to Seecombe as he handed the courses, and all the while I was in a sweat that he should say, 'That happened, madam, or this occurred, when Mr. Philip was away in Italy.'

I could hardly wait for dinner to be over and for the pair of us to be alone again, though it brought me nearer to my task. We sat down together before the library fire, and she brought out some piece of embroidery and began to work upon it. I watched the small deft hands and wondered at them.

'Tell me what it is that is bothering you,' she said, after a while. 'Don't deny there is something, because I shall know you are not speaking the truth. Ambrose used to tell me I had an animal's instinct for sensing trouble, and I sense it with you, to-night. In fact, since late afternoon. I have not said anything to hurt you, have I?'

Well, here it was. At least she had opened a way clear for me.

'You've said nothing to hurt me,' I replied, 'but a chance remark of yours confounded me a little. Could you tell me what Nick Kendall said to you in the letter he wrote to Plymouth?'

'Why, certainly,' she said. 'He thanked me for my letter, he told me that you both of you knew already the facts of Ambrose's death, that Signor Rainaldi had written to him sending copies of the death certificate and other particulars, and that you invited me here for a short visit until my plans were formed. Indeed, he suggested that I should go on to Pelyn after leaving you, which was very kind of him.'

'That was all he said?'

'Yes, it was quite a brief letter.'

'He said nothing about my having been away?'

'No.'

'I see.' I felt myself grow hot, and she went on sitting there so calm and still, working at the piece of embroidery.

Then I said, 'My godfather was correct in telling you that he and the servants learnt of Ambrose's death through Signor Rainaldi. But it was not so for me. You see, I learnt of it in Florence, at the villa, from your servants.'

She lifted her head and looked at me; and this time there were no tears in her eyes, no hint of laughter either; the gaze was long and searching and it seemed to me I read in her eyes both compassion and reproach.

Chapter Ten

'You went to Florence?' she said. 'When, how long ago?'

'I have been home a little under three weeks,' I said. 'I went there and returned through France. I spent one night in Florence only. The night of the fifteenth of August.'

'The fifteenth of August?' I heard the new inflection in her voice, I saw her eyes flash back in memory. 'But I had only left for Genoa the day before. It isn't possible.'

'It is both possible and true,' I said; 'it happened.'

The embroidery had fallen from her hands, and that strange look, almost of apprehension, came back into her eyes.

'Why didn't you tell me?' she said. 'Why have you let me stay here in the house, four-and-twenty hours, and never breathed a word of it? Last night, you should have told me last night.'

'I thought you knew,' I said. 'I had asked my godfather to write it in his letter. Anyway, there it is. You know now.'

Some coward steak in me hoped that we could let the matter rest, that she would pick up the embroidery once again. But it was not to be.

'You went to the villa,' she said, as though talking to herself. 'Giuseppe must have let you in. He would open up the gates and see you standing there, and he would think . . .' She broke off, a cloud came over her eyes, she looked away from me to the fire.

'I want you to tell me what happened, Philip,' she said.

I put my hand in my pocket. I felt the letters there.

'I had not heard from Ambrose in a long while,' I said, 'not since Easter, or perhaps Whitsun – I don't recall the date, but I have all his letters upstairs. I grew worried. And the weeks went by. Then, in July, the letter came. Only a page. Unlike himself, a sort of scrawl. I showed it to my godfather, Nick Kendall, and he agreed that I should start at once for Florence, which I did within a day or two. As I left another letter came, a few sentences only. I have both these letters in my pocket now. Do you want to see them?'

She did not answer immediately. She had turned back from the fire and was looking at me once again. There was something of compulsion in those eyes, neither forceful nor commanding, but strangely deep, strangely tender, as if she had the power to read and understand my reluctance to continue, knowing the reason for it, and so urged me on.

'Not just yet,' she said, 'afterwards.'

I shifted my gaze from her eyes down to her hands. They were clasped in front of her, small and very still. It was easier to speak somehow if I did not look directly at her, but at her hands.

'I arrived in Florence,' I said, 'I hired a carrozza and drove to your villa. The servant, the woman, opened the gate, and I asked for Ambrose. She seemed frightened and called to her husband. He came, and then he told me Ambrose was dead and you had gone away. He showed me the villa. I saw the room where he had died. Just before I left the woman opened a chest and gave me Ambrose's hat. It was the only thing you had forgotten to take with you.'

I paused, and went on looking at the hands. The right fingers were touching the ring on the left hand. I watched them tighten upon it.

'Go on,' she said.

'I went down into Florence,' I said. 'The servant had given me the address of Signor Rainaldi. I went and called upon him. He looked startled at sight of me, but soon recovered. He gave me the particulars of Ambrose's illness and death, also a note to the guardian at the Protestant cemetery should I care to visit the grave, which I did not. I enquired of your whereabouts, but he professed not to know. That was all. The following day I started back on my journey home.'

There was another pause. The fingers relaxed their hold upon the ring. 'Can I see the letters?' she said.

I took them from my pocket and gave them to her. I looked back again at the fire, and I heard the crinkle of the paper as she opened the letters. There was a long silence. Then she said, 'Only these two?'

'Only those two,' I answered.

'Nothing after Easter, or Whitsun, did you say, until these came?'

'No, nothing.'

She must have been reading them over and over, learning the words by heart as I had done. At last she gave them back to me.

'How you have hated me,' she said slowly.

I looked up, startled, and it seemed to me, as we stared at one another, that she knew now all my fantasies, my dreams, that she saw one by one the faces of the women I had conjured all those months. Denial was no use, protestation absurd. The barriers were down. It was a queer feeling, as though I sat naked in my chair.

'Yes,' I said.

It was easier, once said. Perhaps, I thought to myself, this is how a Catholic feels in the confessional. This is what it means to be purged. A burden lifted. Emptiness instead.

'Why did you ask me here?' she said.

'To accuse you.'

'Accuse me of what?'

'I am not sure. Perhaps of breaking his heart, which would be murder, wouldn't it?'

'And then?'

'I had not planned so far. I wanted, more than anything in the world, to make you suffer. To watch you suffer. Then, I suppose, to let you go.'

'That was generous. More generous than I should deserve. Still, you have been successful. You have got what you wanted. Go on watching me, until you've had your fill.'

Something was happening to the eyes that looked at me. The face was very white and still; that did not change. Had I ground the face to powder with my heel, the eyes would have remained, with the tears that never ran down upon the cheeks, and never fell.

I rose from my chair and walked across the room.

'It's no use,' I said. 'Ambrose always told me I would make a rotten soldier. I can't shoot in cold blood. Please go upstairs, or anywhere but here. My mother died before I can remember, and I have never seen a woman cry.' I opened the door for her. But she went on sitting there by the fire, she did not move.

'Cousin Rachel, go upstairs,' I said.

I don't know how my voice sounded, whether it was harsh, or loud, but old Don, lying on the floor, lifted his head and looked up at me, fixing me in his old-wise doggy fashion, and then stretching himself, and yawning, went and laid his head on her feet, beside the fire. Then she moved. She put down her hand and touched his head. I shut the door and came back to the hearth. I took the two letters and threw them in the fire.

'That's no use either,' she said, 'when we both of us remember what he said.'

'I can forget,' I said, 'if you will too. There's something clean about a fire. Nothing remains. Ashes don't count.'

'If you were a little older,' she said, 'or your life had been different, if you were anyone but yourself and had not loved him quite so much, I could talk to you about those letters, and about Ambrose. I won't, though; I would rather you condemned me. It makes it easier in the long run for both of us. If you will let me stay until Monday I will go away after that, and you need never think about me again. Although you did not intend it to be so, last night and today were deeply happy. Bless you, Philip.'

I stirred the fire with my foot, and the embers fell.

'I don't condemn you,' I said. 'Nothing has worked out as I thought or planned. I can't go on hating a woman who doesn't exist.'

'But I do exist.'

'You are not the woman I hated. There's no more to it than that.'

She went on stroking Don's head, and now he lifted it and leant it against her knee.

'This woman,' she said, 'that you pictured in your mind. Did she take shape when you read the letters, or before?'

I thought about it for a moment. Then I let it all come, with a rush of words. Why hold back anything to rot?

'Before,' I said slowly. 'In a sense I was relieved when the letters came. They gave me a reason for hating you. Up till then there was nothing I could go upon, and I was ashamed.'

'Why were you ashamed?'

'Because I believe there is nothing so self-destroying, and no emotion quite so despicable, as jealousy.'

'You were jealous . . .'

'Yes. I can say it now, oddly enough. Right from the start, when he wrote and told me he was married. Perhaps even before there may have been a sort of shadow, I don't know. Everyone expected me to be as delighted as they were themselves, and it wasn't possible. It must sound highly emotional and absurd to you that I should have been jealous. Like a spoilt child. Perhaps that's what I was, and am. The trouble is that I have never known anyone or loved anyone in the world but Ambrose.'

Now I was thinking aloud, not caring what she thought of me. I was putting things into words I had not acknowledged to myself before.

'Was not that his trouble too?' she said.

'How do you mean?'

She took her hand off Don's head, and cupping her chin in her hands, her elbows on her knee, she stared into the fire.

'You are only twenty-four, Philip,' she said, 'you have all your life before you, many years probably of happiness, married no doubt, with a wife you love, and children of your own. Your love for Ambrose will never grow less, but it will slip back into place where it belongs. The love of any son for any father. It was not so for him. Marriage came too late.'

I knelt on one knee before the fire and lit my pipe. I did not think to ask permission. I knew she did not mind.

'Why too late?' I asked.

'He was forty-three,' she said, 'when he came out to Florence just two years ago, and I saw him for the first time. You know how he looked, how he spoke, his ways, his smile. It was your life since babyhood. But you would not know the effect it had upon a woman whose life had not been happy, who had known men – very different.'

I said nothing, but I think I understood.

'I don't know why he turned to me, but he did,' she said. 'Those things can never be explained, they happen. Why this man should love that woman, what queer chemical mix-up in our blood draws us to one another, who can tell? To me, lonely, anxious, and a survivor of too many emotional shipwrecks, he came almost as a saviour, as an answer to prayer. To be strong as he was, and tender too, lacking all personal conceit, I had not met with that. It was a revelation. I know what he was to me. But I to him . . .'

She paused, and drawing her brows together, frowned into the fire. Once again her fingers played with the ring on her left hand.

'He was like someone sleeping who woke suddenly and found the world,' she said, 'all the beauty of it, and the sadness too. The hunger and the thirst. Everything he had never thought about or known was there before him, and magnified themselves into one person who by chance, or fate, call it what you will, happened to be me. Rainaldi – whom he detested by the way, as you probably did too – told me once that Ambrose had woken to me just as some men wake to religion. He became obsessed, in the same fashion. But a man who gets religion can go into a monastery and pray all day before Our Lady on an altar. She is made of plaster anyway, and does not change. Women are not so, Philip. Their moods vary with the days and nights, sometimes even with the hours, just as a man's can do. We are human, that is our failing.'

I did not understand what she meant about religion. I could only think of old Isaiah, down at St. Blazey, who turned Methodist and went about bareheaded preaching in the lanes. He called upon Jehovah, and said he and all of us were miserable sinners in the eyes of the Lord, and we must go knocking at the gates of a new Jerusalem. I did not see how this state of things applied to Ambrose. Catholics were different, of course. She must mean that Ambrose had thought of her like a graven image in the Ten Commandments. Thou shalt not bow down to them, nor worship them.

'You mean,' I said, 'that he expected too much of you? He put you on a sort of pedestal?'

'No,' she said, 'I would have welcomed a pedestal, after my rough life. A halo can be a lovely thing, providing you can take it off, now and again and become human.'

'What then?'

She sighed, and her hands dropped to her side. She suddenly looked very tired. She leant back in her chair, and resting her head against the cushion closed her eyes.

'Finding religion does not always improve a person,' she said, 'waking to the world did not help Ambrose. His nature changed.'

Her voice sounded tired too, and oddly flat. Perhaps if I had been speaking in the confessional, so had she. She lay back in the chair pressing her eyes with the palms of her hands.

'Change?' I said. 'How did his nature change?'

I felt a queer sort of shock in my heart, like the shock that comes to you as a child when you suddenly learn of death, or of evil, or of cruelty.

'The doctors told me later that it was his illness,' she said, 'that he could not help himself, that qualities lying dormant all his life came to the surface at long last, through pain, and fear. But I shall never be sure. Never be certain that it need have happened. Something in me brought out those qualities. Finding me was ecstasy to him for one brief moment, and then catastrophe. You were right to hate me. If he had not come to Italy he would have been living here with you now. He would not have died.'

I felt ashamed, embarrassed. I did not know what to say. 'He might have become ill just the same,' I said, as though to help her. 'Then I would have borne the brunt of it, not you.'

She took her hands away from her face, and without moving looked across at me and smiled.

'He loved you so much,' she said. 'You might have been his son, he was so proud of you. Always my Philip would do this, my boy would do that. Why, Philip, if you have been jealous of me these eighteen months, I think we are quits. Heaven knows I could have done with less of you at times.'

I looked back at her, and slowly smiled.

'Did you make pictures too?' I asked her.

'I never stopped,' she said. 'That spoilt boy, I told myself, always writing letters to him, which I may say he would read extracts from, but never show. That boy who has no faults, but all the virtues. That boy who understands him, when I fail. That boy who holds three-quarters of his heart, and all the best of him. While I hold one-third, and all the worst. Oh, Philip . . .' She broke off, and smiled again at me. 'Good God,' she said, 'you talk of jealousy. A man's jealousy is like a child's, fitful and foolish, without depth. A woman's jealousy is adult, which is very different.' Then she put back the cushion from behind her head, and patted it. She straightened her gown, and sat upright in her chair. 'I would say that, for this night, I have talked to you enough,' she said. She bent forward, and picked up the piece of embroidery that had fallen on the floor.

'I'm not tired,' I said. 'I could go on longer, much longer. That is to say, not speaking perhaps myself, but listening to you.'

'We still have tomorrow,' she said.

'Why only tomorrow?'

'Because I go on Monday. I came for the week-end only. Your godfather, Nick Kendall, has invited me to Pelyn.'

It seemed to me absurd, and altogether pointless, that she should shift her quarters quite so soon.

'There's no need to go there,' I said, 'when you have only just arrived. You have plenty of time to visit Pelyn. You have not seen the half of this yet. I don't know what the servants would think, or the people on the estate. They would be deeply offended.'

'Would they?' she asked.

'Besides,' I said, 'there is the carrier coming from Plymouth, with all the plants and cuttings. You have to discuss it with Tamlyn. And there are Ambrose's things to go through and sort.'

'I thought you could do that by yourself,' she said.

'Why,' I said, 'when we could do it both of us together?'

I stood up from my chair and stretched my arms above my head. I kicked Don with my foot. 'Wake up,' I said, 'it's time you stopped that snoring and went out with the others to the kennels.' He stirred himself, and grunted. 'Lazy old devil,' I said. I glanced down at her, and she was looking up at me with such a strange expression in her eyes, almost as though she saw right through me into someone else.

'What is it?' I asked.

'Nothing,' she answered, 'nothing at all. . . . Can you find me a candle, Philip, and light me up to bed?'

'Very well,' I said. 'I'll take Don to his kennel afterwards.'

The candlesticks were waiting on the table by the door. She took hers, and I lighted the candle for her. It was dark in the hall but above, on the landing, Seecombe had left a light to the further corridor.

'That will do,' she said. 'I can find my way alone.'

She stood a moment on one step of the staircase, her face in the shadow. One hand held the candlestick, the other held her dress.

'You don't hate me any more?' she asked.

'No,' I said, 'I told you it was not you. It was another woman.'

'Are you sure it was another woman?'

'Quite sure.'

'Good night, then. And sleep well.'

She turned to go, but I put my hand on her arm and held her back.

'Wait,' I said, 'it's my turn to ask you a question.'

'What is it, Philip?'

'Are you still jealous of me, or was that also some other man, and never me at all?'

She laughed and gave me her hand, and because she stood above me on the stairs there seemed a new sort of grace about her that I had not realised before. Her eyes looked large in the flickering candlelight.

'That horrid boy, so spoilt and prim?' she said. 'Why, he went yesterday, as soon as you walked into aunt Phoebe's boudoir.'

Suddenly she bent, and kissed my cheek.

'The first you have ever had,' she said, 'and if you don't like it, you can pretend I did not give it to you, but that it came from the other woman.'

She walked up the stairs away from me, and the light of the candle threw a shadow, dark and distant, on the wall.

Chapter Eleven

We always carried out a strict routine upon a Sunday. Breakfast was later, at nine o'clock, and at a quarter past ten the carriage came to take Ambrose and me to church. The servants followed in the waggonette. When church was over, they returned to eat their midday dinner, later again, at one; and then at four we dined ourselves, with the vicar and Mrs. Pascoe, possibly one or two of the unmarried daughters, and generally my godfather and Louise. Since Ambrose had gone abroad I had not used the carriage but had ridden down to church on Gypsy, causing, I believe, some small amount of talk, I know not why.

This Sunday, in honour of my visitor, I gave orders for the carriage to come as of old custom, and my cousin Rachel, prepared for the event by Seecombe when he took her breakfast, descended to the hall upon the stroke of ten. A kind of ease had come upon me since the night before, and it seemed to me, as I looked upon her, that I could in future say to her what I pleased. Nothing need hold me back, neither anxiety, nor resentment, nor even common courtesy.

'A word of warning,' I said, after I had wished her a good morning. 'All eyes will be upon you in the church. Even the laggards, who sometimes make excuse to stay in bed, will not remain at home to-day. They will be standing in the aisles, maybe on tip-toe.'

'You terrify me,' she said. 'I shall not go at all.'

'That would be disgrace,' I said, 'for which neither you nor I would ever be forgiven.'

She looked at me with solemn eyes.

'I am not sure,' she said, 'that I know how to behave. I was bred a Catholic.'

'Keep it to yourself,' I told her. 'Papists, in this part of the world, are fit only for hellfire. Or so they tell me. Watch everything I do. I won't mislead you.'

The carriage came to the door. Wellington, with brushed hat and trim cockade, the groom beside him, was swollen with importance like a pouter pigeon. Seecombe, in starched clean stock and his Sunday coat, stood at the front door with no less dignity. It was the occasion of a lifetime.

I handed my cousin Rachel into the carriage and took my place beside her. She had a dark mantle around her shoulders, and the veil from her hat concealed her face.

'The people will want to see your face,' I said to her.

'Then they must want,' she answered.

'You don't understand,' I said. 'Nothing like this has happened in their lives. Not for nearly thirty years. The old people remember my aunt, I suppose, and my mother, but for the younger ones there has never been a Mrs. Ashley come to church before. Besides, you must enlighten their ignorance. They know you come from what they term outlandish parts. For all they know Italians may be black.'

'Will you please be quiet?' she whispered. 'I can tell from Wellington's back there, up on the box, that he can hear what you are saying.'

'I shall not be quiet,' I said, 'the matter is of grave importance. I know how rumour spreads. All the countryside will go back to Sunday dinner shaking their heads and saying Mrs. Ashley is a negress.'

'I will lift my veil in church, but not before,' she said, 'when I am kneeling. They can look then, if they have the mind, but by rights they should do no such thing. Their eyes should be on their prayer-books.'

'A high bench surrounds the pew, with curtains to it,' I told her. 'Once kneeling there you will be concealed from view. You can even play marbles if you want to. I used to, as a child.'

'Your childhood,' she said; 'don't speak of it. I know every detail. How Ambrose dismissed your nurse when you were three. How he took you out of petticoats and put you into breeches. The monstrous way in which you learnt your alphabet. I am not surprised you played at marbles in the church pew. I wonder you did no worse.'

'I did once,' I said. 'I brought white mice in my pocket and they ran under the seat. They scampered up the petticoat of an old lady in the pew behind. She had the vapours, and had to be removed.'

'Didn't Ambrose beat you for it?'

'Why, no. It was he who set them loose upon the floor.'

My cousin Rachel pointed to Wellington's back. His shoulders had stiffened, and his ears were red.

'You will behave yourself to-day, or I shall walk out of the church,' she said to me.

'Then everyone would think *you* had the vapours,' I said, 'and my godfather and Louise would come rushing to your assistance. Oh, great heaven . . .' I broke off, and clapped my hand on my knee in consternation.

'What's the matter?'

'I've only just remembered. I promised to ride over yesterday to Pelyn to see Louise, and I forgot all about it. She may have waited for me all afternoon.'

'That,' said my cousin Rachel, 'was not very gallant of you. I hope she snubs you well.'

'I shall blame it upon you,' I said, 'which will be the truth. I shall say you demanded to be taken round the Barton.'

'I would not have asked you to do so,' she said, 'had I known you were supposed to be elsewhere. Why did you not tell me?'

'Because I had forgotten all about it.'

'If I were Louise,' she said, 'I would take that in bad part. You could not offer a woman a worse excuse.'

'Louise isn't a woman,' I said, 'she's younger than myself, and I have known her since she ran around in petticoats.'

'That's no answer. She has feelings just the same.'

'Ah well, she will get over them. She will sit next to me at dinner, and I shall tell her how well she arranged the flowers.'

'What flowers?'

'The flowers in the house. The flowers in your boudoir, and in the bedroom. She drove over especially to do them.'

'How very thoughtful'

'She did not trust Seecombe to do them properly.'

'I don't blame her for that. She showed great delicacy and taste. I liked best of all the bowl on the mantelpiece in the boudoir, and the autumn crocus beside the window.'

'Was there a bowl on the mantelpiece,' I said, 'and another by the window? I did not notice either. But I will compliment her just the same, and hope she does not ask for a description.'

I looked at her, and laughed, and I saw the eyes smile back at me under the veil, but she shook her head.

We had descended the steep hill and turned along the lane, and were now come to the village and the church. As I had thought, there was a gathering of people by the rails. I knew most of them, but there were many besides drawn there by curiosity. There was a sort of pressure amongst them as the carriage drew up before the gate and we alighted. I took off my hat and offered my cousin Rachel my arm. I had seen my godfather do this to Louise a score of times. We walked up the path to the church door, the people staring at us. I had expected to feel myself a fool, and out of my own character, but it was quite otherwise. I felt confident and proud, and oddly pleased. I stared ahead of me, looking neither to right nor to left, and as we passed the men took their hats off to us and the women curtsied. I could not remember them doing this to me alone. It was, after all, a great occasion.

As we entered the church, and the bells were ringing, those people who were already seated in their pews turned round to look at us. There was a scraping of feet amongst the men, and a rustle of skirts amongst the women. We walked up the aisle past the Kendall pew to our own. I caught sight of my godfather, his bushy brows drawn straight together, a thoughtful expression on his face. No doubt he was wondering how I had conducted myself during the past forty-eight hours. Good breeding forbade him to look at either of us. Louise sat beside him, very stiff and straight. She had a haughty air about her, and I supposed I had given her offence. But as I stepped aside to let my cousin Rachel enter the pew first, curiosity proved too much for Louise. She glanced up, stared at my visitor, and then caught my eye. She raised her eyebrows in a question. I pretended not to see, and closed the door of the pew behind me. The congregation knelt in prayer.

It was a queer sensation having a woman in the pew beside me. My memory went right back to childhood, when Ambrose took me first, and I had to stand on a footstool to look over the bench in front of me. I would copy Ambrose, holding the prayer-book in my hands, but very often upside down; and when it came to murmuring the responses I would echo the mumble he made, with no thought as to meaning. As I grew taller I would pull the curtains aside and look out upon the people, watch the parson and the choir boys in their stalls, and later, on holiday from Harrow, sit back with folded arms as Ambrose did, and doze if the sermon proved too long. Now I had come to manhood church had become a period for reflection. Not, I regret to say, upon my failings and omissions, but upon my plans for the forthcoming week; what must be done upon the farmlands or in the woods, what I must say to Seecombe's nephew at the fish-house in the bay, what forgotten order must be passed on to Tamlyn. I had sat in the pew alone, locked in myself, with nothing and no one to distract me. I sang the psalms and gave the responses from long habit. This Sunday was different. I was aware of her beside me all the time. There was no question of her not knowing what to do. She might have attended a Church of England service every Sunday of her life. She sat very still, her eyes fixed gravely upon the vicar, and when she knelt I noticed that she knelt full upon her knees, and did not sit half upon the seat as Ambrose and I were wont to do. Nor did she rustle, turn her head, or stare about her, as Mrs. Pascoe and her daughters always did, from their pew in the side aisle where the vicar could not see them. When we came to sing the hymns she put up her veil, and I saw her lips follow the words, but I did not hear her sing. She lowered the veil again when we sat down to listen to the sermon.

I wondered who had been the last women to sit here in the Ashley pew. Aunt Phoebe possibly, sighing for her curate; or uncle Philip's wife, Ambrose's mother, whom I had never seen. Perhaps my father had sat here, before he went away to fight the French and lose his life, and my own mother, young and delicate, who survived my father, Ambrose told me, a bare five months. I had never thought much about them, or felt the lack of them, Ambrose had answered for them both. But now, looking at my cousin Rachel, I wondered about my mother. Had she knelt there, on that footstool beside my father; had she sat back, and clasped her hands on her lap in front of her, and listened to the sermon? And afterwards, did she drive back home and go to pick me from my cradle? I wondered, sitting there as Mr. Pascoe's voice droned on, what it had felt like as a child, being held in my mother's arms. Had she touched my hair and kissed my cheek, and then, smiling, put me back into the cradle? I wished suddenly that I could remember her. Why was it that a child's mind could not return beyond a certain limit? I had been a little boy, staggering after Ambrose, shouting to him to wait for me. Nothing before that. Nothing at all. . . .

'And now to God the Father, God the Son, and God the Holy Ghost.' The vicar's words brought me to my feet. I had not heard a word of his sermon. Nor had I planned my week to come. I had sat there dreaming, and watching my cousin Rachel.

I reached for my hat, and touched her arm. 'You did very well,' I whispered, 'but your real ordeal is now before you.'

'Thank you,' she whispered back, 'so is yours. You have to make amends for your broken promise.'

We went out of the church into the sun, and there waiting for us was a little crowd of people, tenants, acquaintances and friends, and amongst them Mrs. Pascoe, the vicar's wife, and her daughters, as well as my godfather and Louise. One by one they came up to be presented. We might have been at Court. My cousin Rachel put up her veil, and I made a mental note to tease her about it when we were alone again.

As we walked down the path to the waiting carriages she said to me before the others, so that I could not remonstrate – and I could tell by the look in her eye and the bubble in her voice that she did it purposely – 'Philip, would you not like to conduct Miss Kendall in your carriage, and I will go with Mr. Kendall in his?'

'Why certainly, if you prefer it,' I said.

'That seems to me a very happy arrangement,' she said, smiling at my godfather, who, bowing in his turn, offered her his arm. They turned with one accord to the Kendall carriage, and there was nothing for it but to climb into the first one with Louise. I felt like a schoolboy who has been slapped. Wellington whipped up the horses and we were off.

'Look here, Louise, I'm sorry,' I began at once, 'it was quite impossible to get away yesterday afternoon after all. My cousin Rachel wished to see the Barton acres, so I accompanied her. There was no time to let you know, or I would have sent the boy over with a note.'

'Oh, don't apologise,' she said. 'I waited about two hours, but it did not matter. The day was luckily fine, and I passed the time by picking a basket of late blackberries.'

'It was most unfortunate,' I said, 'I'm really very sorry.'

'I guessed something of the sort had kept you,' she said, 'but I am thankful it was nothing serious. I know how you felt about the whole visit, and I was rather fearful that you might do something violent, perhaps have some terrible disagreement, and we would suddenly find her arriving on our doorstep. Well, what happened? Have you really survived so far without a clash? Tell me all.'

I tilted my hat over my eyes and folded my arms.

'All? What do you mean by "all"?'

'Why, everything. What did you say to her, how did she take it. Was she very much aghast by all you said, or did she show no sign of guilt at all?'

Her voice was low, and Wellington could not hear, but for all that I felt irritated, and altogether out of humour. What a place and time to choose for such a conversation, and anyway, why must she catechise me at all?'

'We've had little time for talking,' I said. 'The first evening she was tired, and went early to bed. Yesterday was taken up by walking about the place. The gardens in the morning, and the Barton lands in the afternoon.'

'Then you've had no serious discussion whatsoever?'

'It depends what you mean by serious. All I know is that she is a very different sort of person from what I thought she would be. You can see that for yourself, in the brief glimpse you've had of her.'

Louise was silent. She did not lean back against the carriage seat as I did. She sat bolt upright, her hands in her muff.

'She's very beautiful,' she said at last.

I took my legs down from the seat opposite and turned round to stare at her.

'Beautiful?' I said, amazed. 'My dear Louise, you must be mad.'

'Oh, no, I'm not,' replied Louise. 'Ask my father, ask anyone. Didn't you notice how the people stared when she put up her veil? It's only because you are so blind to women that you have not noticed it.'

'I've never heard such nonsense in my life,' I said. 'Perhaps she has fine eyes, but otherwise she is quite ordinary. The most ordinary person I have ever met. Why, I can say what I like to her, I can talk of anything, I don't have to put on any sort of special manner of behaviour in front of her, it is the easiest thing in the whole world merely to sit down in a chair in front of her and light my pipe.'

'I thought you said you had no time to talk to her?'

'Don't quibble. Of course we talked at dinner, and out upon the acres. The point I wish to make is that it required no effort.'

'Evidently.'

'As to being beautiful, I shall have to tell her. She will laugh at that. Naturally the people stared at her. They stared at her because she was Mrs. Ashley.'

'That as well. But not entirely. Anyway, whether she be ordinary or not, she seems to have made a great impression on you. Of course she is middle-aged. Quite thirty-five I should say, wouldn't you? Or do you think her less?'

'I haven't the remotest idea, nor do I care, Louise. I'm not interested in people's ages. She could be ninety-nine for all I know.'

'Don't be ridiculous. Women don't have eyes like that at ninety-nine, nor that complexion. She dresses well. That gown was excellently cut, so was the mantle. Mourning certainly does not appear drab on her.'

'Great heavens, Louise, you might be Mrs. Pascoe. I've never before in my life heard such woman-ish sort of gossip come from you.'

'Nor I such enthusiasm from you, so it's tit-for-tat. What a change in forty-eight hours. Well, one person will be relieved and that's my father. He feared bloodshed, after you saw him last, and who shall blame him?'

I was thankful the long hill had come, so that I could get out of the carriage and walk up it, with the groom, to ease the horses as was our custom. What an extraordinary attitude for Louise to take. Instead of being relieved that my cousin Rachel's visit was passing off so well she appeared quite put out, almost angry. It seemed to me a poor way to show her friendship. When we came to the top of the hill I climbed in again and sat beside her, and we did not say a word to one another the whole way. It was quite ridiculous, but if she made no attempt to break the silence I was damned if I would either. I could not help reflecting how much more pleasant had been the drive going down to church than the return.

I wondered how the other pair had fared in the second carriage. Pretty well, it seemed. When we descended from our carriage and Wellington had turned round to make way for them, Louise and I stood by the door and waited for my godfather and my cousin Rachel. They were chattering like old friends, and my godfather, generally rather blunt and taciturn, was holding forth upon some subject with unusual warmth. I caught the words 'disgraceful' and 'the country won't stand for it.' I knew then that he was launched upon his favourite subject, the Government and the Opposition. I wagered to myself that he, for his part, had probably not eased the horses by walking up the hill.

'Did you have a pleasant drive?' enquired my cousin Rachel, searching my eye, a tremor at her mouth, and I could swear she knew from our stiff faces how the drive had been.

'Thank you, yes,' said Louise, standing back, allowing her to pass first, in courtesy; but my cousin Rachel took her arm and said, 'Come with me to my room, and take off your coat and hat. I want to thank you for the lovely flowers.'

My godfather and I had barely had time to wash our hands and exchange greetings before the entire family of Pascoe was upon us, and it devolved upon me to escort the vicar and his daughters round the gardens. The vicar was harmless enough, but I could have dispensed with the daughters. As to the vicar's wife, Mrs. Pascoe, she had gone upstairs to join the ladies like a hound after quarry. She had never seen the blue room out of dust covers. . . . The daughters were loud in praise of my cousin Rachel, and like Louise professed to find her beautiful. It delighted me to tell them that I found her small and entirely unremarkable, and they uttered little squeals of protestation. 'Not unremarkable,' said Mr. Pascoe, flipping the head of a hortensia with his cane, 'certainly not unremarkable. Nor would I say, as the girls do, beautiful. But feminine, that is the word, most decidedly feminine.'

'But, father,' said one of the daughters, 'surely you would not expect Mrs. Ashley to be anything else?'

'My dear,' said the vicar, 'you would be surprised how many women lack that very quality.'

I thought of Mrs. Pascoe and her horselike head, and swiftly pointed out the young palms that Ambrose had brought back from Egypt, which they must have seen a score of times before, thus turning, it seemed to me with tact, the conversation.

When we returned to the house, and entered the drawing-room, we discovered Mrs. Pascoe telling my cousin Rachel in loud tones about her kitchen-maid, brought to trouble by the garden boy.

'What I cannot understand, Mrs. Ashley, is where it happened? She shared a room with my cook and as far as we know never left the house.'

'How about the cellar?' said my cousin Rachel.

The conversation was instantly stifled as we came into the room. Not since Ambrose had been home two years before had I ever known a Sunday pass as swiftly. And even when he was there it had dragged many times. Disliking Mrs. Pascoe, indifferent to the daughters, and merely suffering Louise because she was the daughter of his oldest friend, he had always angled for the vicar's company alone, with my godfather's. Then the four of us had been able to relax. When the women came the hours had seemed like days. This day was different.

Dinner, when it was served, with the meats upon the table and the silver polished, seemed to spread itself before us like a banquet. I sat at the head of the table, where Ambrose had always sat, and my cousin Rachel at the further end. It gave me Mrs. Pascoe as a neighbour, but for once she did not goad me to a fury. Three-quarters of the time her large enquiring face was turned to the other end; she laughed, she ate, she forgot even to snap her jaws at her husband, the vicar, who, drawn out of his shell for possibly the first time in his life, flushed and with eyes afire, proceeded to quote poetry. The entire Pascoe family blossomed like the rose, and I had never seen my godfather enjoy himself so much.

Only Louise seemed silent, and withdrawn. I did my best with her, but she did not, or would not, respond. She sat stiffly on my left hand, eating little and crumbling bits of bread, with a fixed expression on her face as if she had swallowed a marble. Well, if she wanted to sulk, then sulk she must. I was too much entertained myself to worry with her. I sat hunched in my chair, resting my arms on the sides of it, laughing at my cousin Rachel, who kept encouraging the vicar with his verse. This, I thought to myself, is the most fantastic Sunday dinner I have ever sat through, eaten, and enjoyed, and I would have given the whole world for Ambrose to be there, sharing it with us. When we had finished dessert, and the port was put upon the table, I did not know whether I should rise, as I usually did, to open the door, or if, now I had a hostess opposite me, it would be her place to give some signal. There was a pause in the conversation. Suddenly she looked at me and smiled. I smiled back at her in answer. We seemed to hold each other for a moment. It was queer, strange. The feeling went right through me, never before known.

Then my godfather remarked in his gruff deep voice. 'Tell me, Mrs. Ashley, does not Philip remind you very much of Ambrose?'

There was a moment's silence. She put down her napkin on the table. 'So much so,' she said, 'that I have wondered, sitting here at dinner, if there is any difference.'

She rose to her feet, the other women too, and I went across the dining-room and opened the door. But when they were gone, and I had returned to my chair, the feeling was with me still.

Chapter Twelve

They all went off about six o'clock, as the vicar had to take even-song in another parish. I heard Mrs. Pascoe engage my cousin Rachel to pass an afternoon with her during the week, and each of the Pascoe daughters pressed their claims upon her too. One wanted advice upon a water-colour, another had a set of covers to be worked in tapestry and could not decide upon the wools, a third always read aloud to a sick woman in the village every Thursday, could my cousin Rachel possibly accompany her, the poor soul had such a wish to see her. 'Indeed,' said Mrs. Pascoe, as we advanced through the hall to the front door, 'there are so many people who desire to make your acquaintance, Mrs. Ashley, that I think you can reckon upon engagements every afternoon for the next four weeks.'

'She can do that very well from Pelyn,' said my godfather; 'we are situated handily for visiting. More so than here. And I rather believe we are to have the pleasure of her company within a day or two.'

He glanced at me, and I made haste to reply and squash the idea before further entanglement was possible.

'Not so, sir,' I said, 'my cousin Rachel remains here for the present. Before she becomes involved in any outside invitations she has the whole of the estate to visit. We begin to-morrow by taking tea at the Barton. The rest of the farms must be taken in their turn. Great offence will be given if she does not pay her respects to every one of the tenants in strict precedence.'

I saw Louise look at me wide-eyed, but I took no notice.

'Oh, well, yes of course,' said my godfather, in his turn surprised, 'very right, very proper. I would have suggested conducting Mrs. Ashley myself, but if you are prepared to do so that is quite another matter. And if,' he went on, turning to my cousin Rachel, 'you find yourself uncomfortable here – Philip will forgive me, I know, for saying this, but they have not been used to entertaining ladies here for many years, as you doubtless know, and things may be a little rough – or if you would like a woman's company, I know my daughter will only be too ready to receive you.'

'We have a guest-room at the vicarage,' said Mrs. Pascoe. 'If at any time you should be lonely, Mrs. Ashley, always remember it is at your disposal. We should be so happy to have you with us.'

'Indeed, indeed,' echoed the vicar; and I wondered if another tag of poetry was ready on his lips.

'You are all very kind and more than generous,' said my cousin Rachel. 'When I have done my duty here, on the estate, we will talk about it again, shall we? Meanwhile, believe me grateful.'

There was much clatter and chatter and saying of good-byes, and the carriages drove away down the drive.

We went back into the drawing-room. The evening had passed pleasantly enough, heaven knows, but I was glad that they had gone and the house was silent once again. She must have had the same thought, for as she stood a moment, looking around her in the drawing-room, she said, 'I love the stillness of a room, after a party. The chairs are moved, the cushions disarranged, everything is there to show that people enjoyed themselves; and one comes back to the empty room happy that it's over, happy to relax and say, "Now we are alone again." Ambrose used to say to me in Florence that it was worth the tedium of visitors to experience the pleasure of their going. He was so right.'

I watched her as she smoothed the covering of a chair, and touched a cushion. 'You don't have to do that,' I told her. 'Seecombe and John and the rest will see to it to-morrow.'

'A woman's instinct,' she said to me. 'Don't look at me; sit down and fill your pipe. Have you enjoyed yourself?'

'I have.' I lay sideways, sprawling on a stool. 'I don't know why,' I added, 'usually I find Sundays a great bore. It's because I'm not a conversationalist. All I had to do to-day was to sit back in my chair and let you do the talking for me.'

'That's where a woman can be useful,' she said; 'it's part of their training. Instinct warns them what to do if conversation flags.'

'Yes, but you don't make it obvious,' I said. 'Mrs. Pascoe is very different. She goes on and on until one wants to scream. No man ever got a chance to talk on other Sundays. I can't think what it is you did to make it all so pleasant.'

'So it was pleasant?'

'Why, yes, I've told you so.'

'Then you had better hurry up and marry your Louise, and have a real hostess, not just a bird of passage.'

I sat up on the stool, and stared at her. She was smoothing her hair before the mirror.

'Marry Louise?' I said. 'Don't be absurd. I don't want to marry anyone. And she isn't "my" Louise.'

'Oh!' said my cousin Rachel. 'I rather thought she was. At least, your godfather gave me that impression.'

She sat down on one of the chairs and took up her embroidery. Just then young John came in to draw the curtains, so I was silent. I was fuming, though. By what right did my godfather make such an assumption? I waited until John had gone.

'What did my godfather say?' I asked.

'I don't remember, specifically,' she said; 'I just think he felt it was an understood thing. He mentioned, driving back from church in the carriage, that his daughter had come over here to do the flowers, and that it had been such a handicap for you, brought up in a household of men; the sooner you married and had a wife to look after you the better. He said Louise understood you very well, as you did her. I hope you apologised for your bad manners on Saturday.'

'Yes, I apologised,' I said, 'but it did not seem to make much difference. I have never met Louise in so vile a humour. By the way, she thinks you are beautiful. And so do the Miss Pascoes.'

'How very flattering.'

'And the vicar does not agree with them.'

'How distressing.'

'But he finds you feminine. Decidedly feminine.'

'I wonder in what way?'

'I suppose in a way different from Mrs. Pascoe.'

A bubble of laughter escaped from her, and she glanced up from her embroidery. 'How would you define it, Philip?'

'Define what?'

'The difference in our femininity, Mrs. Pascoe's and mine.'

'Oh, heaven knows,' I said, kicking the leg of the stool, 'I don't know anything about the subject. All I know is that I like looking at you, and I don't like looking at Mrs. Pascoe.'

'That's a nice simple answer, thank you, Philip.'

I might have said the same about her hands. I liked watching them too. Mrs. Pascoe's hands were like boiled hams.

'It's all nonsense about Louise, anyway,' I said, 'so please forget it. I have never considered her as a wife, and don't intend to.'

'Poor Louise.'

'Ridiculous of my godfather to have got such an idea into his head.'

'Not really. When two young people are of the same age, and thrown much together, and like each other's company, it is very natural that onlookers should think of marriage. Besides, she is a nice, good-looking girl, and very capable. She would make you an excellent wife.'

'Cousin Rachel, will you be quiet?'

She looked up at me again, and smiled.

'And another thing you can be quiet about is this nonsense of visiting everybody,' I said, 'staying at the vicarage, staying at Pelyn. What is wrong with this house, and with my company?'

'Nothing, as yet.'

'Well, then . . .'

'I will stay until Seecombe becomes tired of me.'

'Seecombe has nothing to do with it,' I said, 'nor Wellington nor Tamlyn, nor anyone at all. I am the master here, and it has to do with me.'

'Then I must do as I am bid,' she answered; 'that is part of a woman's training too.'

I glanced at her suspiciously to see if she was laughing, but she was looking at her work and I could not see her eyes.

'To-morrow,' I said, 'I shall draw up a list of the tenants, in order of seniority. The ones who have served the family longest will be the first to be visited. We will start with the Barton, as arranged on Saturday. We will set forth at two o'clock every afternoon until there is not a single individual on the estate that you have not met.'

'Yes, Philip.'

'You will have to write a note of explanation to Mrs. Pascoe and those girls, explaining you are otherwise engaged.'

'I will do so to-morrow morning.'

'When we have finished with our own people, you will have to stay in the house three afternoons a week, I believe it is Tuesdays, Thursdays, and Fridays, in case you are called upon by the County.'

'How do you know the days?'

'Because I have heard them discussed often enough by the Pascoes and Louise.'

'I see. And do I sit alone here in the drawing-room, or do you sit with me, Philip?'

'You sit alone. They will call upon you, not me. Receiving the County is not part of a man's work.'

'Supposing I am invited out to dinner, may I accept?'

'You will not be invited. You are in mourning. If there is any question of entertaining, we shall do it here. But never more than two couples at a time.'

'Is that etiquette in this part of the world?' she asked.

'Etiquette be blowed,' I answered her, 'Ambrose and I never followed etiquette; we made our own.'

I saw her bend her head lower over her work, and I had a shrewd suspicion it was to hide laughter, though what she was laughing at I could not say. I was not trying to be funny.

'I suppose,' she said, after a moment, 'you would not care to draw up for me a little list of rules? A code of conduct? I could study it here, while I am waiting to be called upon. It would be very unfortunate if I made some social *faux pas*, according to your lights, and so disgraced myself.'

'You can say what you please, to whom you please,' I said; 'all I ask is that you say it here, in the drawing-room. Never allow anyone to enter the library, under any pretext whatsoever.'

'Why? What will be happening in the library?'

'*I* shall be sitting there. With my feet upon the mantel.'

'On Tuesdays, Thursdays, and on Fridays too?'

'Not on Thursdays. On Thursdays I go into town to the bank.'

She held her skeins of silk closer to the candlesticks to examine the colour, and then folded them and wrapped them in her work. She rolled the work into a bundle, and put it aside.

I glanced at the clock. It was early yet. Did she think of going upstairs so soon? I had a sense of disappointment.

'And when the County have finished calling upon me,' she said, 'what happens then?'

'Why, then, you are obliged to return their calls, every single one of them. I will order the carriage every afternoon for two o'clock. I beg your pardon. Not every afternoon. But every Tuesday, Thursday and Friday.'

'And I go alone?'

'You go alone.'

'And what do I have to do on Mondays and on Wednesdays?'

'On Mondays and on Wednesdays, let me see . . .' I considered rapidly, invention failing me. 'Do you sketch at all, or sing? Like the Miss Pascoes? You could practise singing on the Mondays, and draw or paint upon the Wednesdays.'

'I neither sketch nor sing,' said my cousin Rachel, 'and I am afraid you are drawing up for me a programme of leisure for which I am entirely unsuited. If, instead of waiting for the County to call upon me, I call upon them for the purpose of giving them lessons in Italian, that would suit me much better.'

She rose to her feet, having snuffed the candles in the tall stand beside her. I stood up from my stool.

'Mrs. Ashley give lessons in Italian?' I said, in mock horror. 'What a disgrace upon the name. Only spinsters give lessons, when they have no one to support them.'

'And what do widows do who find themselves in similar circumstances?' she asked.

'Widows?' I said, not thinking. 'Oh, widows marry again as fast as possible, or sell their rings.'

'I see. Well, I intend doing neither. I prefer giving lessons in Italian.' She patted me on the shoulder and left the room, calling good night over her shoulder.

I felt myself go scarlet. Good God, what had I said? I had spoken without a thought of her condition, forgetting who she was and what had happened. I had fallen into the fun of conversation with her as I might have done with Ambrose in the past, and had let my tongue run away with me in consequence. Remarry. Sell her rings. What in heaven's name could she have thought of me?

How blundering, how unfeeling, how altogether oafish and ill-bred I must have seemed. I could feel the colour mount right up the back of my neck to the roots of my hair. Hell and damnation. No use apologising. It would make too big a business of it. Better to let it go, and hope and pray she would forget. I was thankful nobody else had been present, my godfather, say, to draw me aside and frown at such breach of manners. Or suppose it

had been at table, and Seecombe waiting, and young John? Remarry. Sell
her rings. Oh, Lord . . . Oh, Lord. . . . What on earth could have possessed
me? I should not sleep now for the night, I should lie awake and toss and
turn, and all the while hear that reply of hers, swift as lightning, 'I intend
doing neither. I prefer giving lessons in Italian.'

I called Don, and letting myself out by the side-door I walked out in the
grounds. As I walked it seemed to me that my offence grew worse instead
of better. Coarse, unthinking, empty-headed lout. . . . And what had she
meant anyway? Was it possible that she had so little money that she was
really serious in what she said? Mrs. Ashley give lessons in Italian? I
remembered her letter to my godfather from Plymouth. That she planned,
after a short rest, to go to London. I remembered what that man Rainaldi
had said, that she was obliged to sell the villa in Florence. I remembered,
or rather I realised, with the full force of its application, that in Ambrose's
will he had left her nothing, nothing at all. Every penny of his property
belonged to me. I remembered, once again, the servants' gossip. No provision
made for Mrs. Ashley. What in the world would they think, in the servants'
hall, on the estate, in the neighbourhood, in the county, if Mrs. Ashley went
about giving lessons in Italian?

Two days ago, three days ago, I would not have cared. She could have
starved, that other woman of my fancy, and deserved it. But not now. Now
it was different. The whole situation had entirely changed. Something would
have to be done about it, and I did not know what. I could not possibly
discuss it with her. The very thought made me go scarlet again with shame
and embarrassment too. Then, with a sensation of relief, I suddenly remembered that the money and the property were not yet legally mine, and would
not become so until my birthday in six months' time. Therefore it was out
of my hands. It was the responsibility of my godfather. He was trustee to
the estate, and my guardian. Therefore it was for him to approach my cousin
Rachel and make some sort of provision for her out of the estate. I would
go to see him about it at the first opportunity. My name need not come into
the matter. It could seem as though it was just a piece of legal business that
would have happened anyway, the custom in this country. Yes, that was the
solution. Thank heaven I had thought of it. Italian lessons . . . How shaming,
how appalling.

Feeling easier in mind I came back to the house, but I still had not
forgotten the original blunder. Remarry, sell the rings. . . . I came to the
edge of the grass by the east front and whistled softly to Don, who was
sniffing in the undergrowth. My footsteps crunched slightly on the gravel
path. I heard a voice call down to me, 'Do you often go walking in the
woods at night?' It was my cousin Rachel. She was sitting, without a light,
at the open window of the blue bedroom. My blunder came upon me with
full force, and I thanked heaven she could not see my face.

'At times,' I said, 'when I have something on my mind.'

'Does that mean you have something on your mind to-night?'

'Why, yes,' I answered. 'I came to a serious conclusion walking in the
woods.'

'What was it?'

'I came to the conclusion that you were perfectly right to dislike the sound of me, before you saw me, and to consider me, as you did, conceited, pert and spoilt. I am all three, and worse than that besides.'

She leant forward, her arms upon the window-sill.

'Then walking in the woods is bad for you,' she said, 'and your conclusions very stupid.'

'Cousin Rachel . . .'

'Yes?'

But I did not know how to make my apology. The words that had strung themselves so easily to make a blunder in the drawing-room would not come now that I wished the blunder remedied. I stood there below her window, tongue-tied and ashamed. Suddenly I saw her turn and stretch behind her, and then she leaned forward once again and threw something at me from the window. It struck me on the cheek and fell to the ground. I stooped to pick it up. It was one of the flowers from her bowl, an autumn crocus.

'Don't be so foolish, Philip; go to bed,' she said.

She closed her window and drew the curtains; and somehow my shame went from me, and the blunder too, and I felt light of heart.

It was not possible to ride over to Pelyn in the early part of the week, because of the programme I had drawn up for visiting the tenants. Besides, I could hardly have made the excuse of seeing my godfather without taking my cousin Rachel to call upon Louise. On Thursday my opportunity arrived. The carrier came from Plymouth with all the shrubs and plants that she had brought with her from Italy, and as soon as Seecombe gave her the news of this – I was just finishing my breakfast at the time – my cousin Rachel was dressed and downstairs, her lace shawl wound about her head, prepared to go out into the garden. The door of the dining-room was open to the hall and I saw her pass. I went out to say good morning.

'I understood,' I said, 'that Ambrose told you no woman was fit to look upon before eleven. What are you doing downstairs at half-past eight?'

'The carrier has come,' she said, 'and at half-past eight on the last morning of September I am not a woman; I am a gardener. Tamlyn and I have work to do.'

She looked gay and happy as a child might do at the prospect of a treat.

'Are you going to count the plants?' I asked her.

'Count them? No,' she answered, 'I have to see how many have survived the journey and which are worth putting in the soil at once. Tamlyn will not know, but I shall. No hurry for the trees, we can do that at our leisure, but I would like to see the plants in right away.' I noticed that she wore upon her hands an old rough pair of gloves, most incongruous on her neat small person.

'You are not going to grub about the soil yourself?' I asked her.

'But of course I am. You'll see. I shall work faster than Tamlyn and his men. Do not expect me home for any midday meal.'

'But this afternoon,' I protested. 'We were expected at Lankelly and at Coombe. The farm kitchens will be scrubbed, and tea prepared.'

'You must send a note postponing the visit,' she said. 'I commit myself to nothing when there is planting to be done. Good-bye.' And she waved her hand at me and passed through the front door on to the gravel drive.

'Cousin Rachel?' I called at her from the dining-room window.

'What is it?' she said over her shoulder.

'Ambrose was wrong in what he said of women,' I shouted. 'At half-past eight in the morning they look very well indeed.'

'Ambrose was not referring to half-past eight,' she called back to me; 'he was referring to half-past six, and he did not mean downstairs.'

I turned back laughing into the dining-room, and saw Seecombe standing at my elbow, his lips pursed. He moved, with disapproval, to the sideboard, and motioned to young John to remove the breakfast dishes. One thing at least about this day of planting, I should not be wanted. I altered my arrangements for the morning, and giving orders for Gypsy to be saddled I was away on the road to Pelyn by ten o'clock. I found my godfather at home and in his study, and without any preamble I broached the subject of my visit.

'So you understand,' I said to him, 'something will have to be done, and right away. Why, if it should reach Mrs. Pascoe's ears that Mrs. Ashley considers giving lessons in Italian it would be about the county in twenty-four hours.'

My godfather, as I had expected, looked most shocked and pained.

'Oh, disgraceful,' he agreed, 'quite out of the question. It would never do at all. The matter is a delicate one, of course. I must have time to think this out, how to approach the business.'

I became impatient. I knew his cautious legal frame of mind. He would fiddle-faddle with the job for days.

'We have no time to waste,' I said. 'You don't know my cousin Rachel as well as I do. She is quite capable of saying to one of the tenants, in her easy way, "Do you know of anyone who would like to learn Italian?" And where should we be then? Besides, I have heard gossip already, through Seecombe. Everyone knows that she has been left nothing in the will. All that must be rectified, and at once.'

He looked thoughtful, and bit his pen.

'That Italian adviser said nothing of her circumstances,' he said. 'It is unfortunate that I cannot discuss the matter with him. We have no means of knowing the extent of her private income, or what settlement was made upon her by her previous marriage.'

'I believe everything went to pay Sangalletti's debts,' I said. 'I remember Ambrose said as much in his letters to me. It was one of the reasons why they did not come home last year, her financial affairs were so involved. No doubt that is why she has to sell that villa. Why, she may scarcely have a penny to her name. We must do something for her, and to-day.'

My godfather sorted his papers spread upon the desk.

'I am very glad, Philip,' he said, glancing at me over his spectacles, 'that you have changed your attitude. I was most uncomfortable before your cousin Rachel came. You were prepared to be very unpleasantly rude, and do absolutely nothing for her, which would have caused a scandal. At least you now see reason.'

'I was mistaken,' I said shortly; 'we can forget all that.'

'Well then,' he answered, 'I will write a letter to Mrs. Ashley, and to the bank. I will explain to her, and to the bank, what the estate is prepared to do. The best plan will be to pay a quarterly cheque, from the estate, into an account which I will open for her. When she moves to London, or elsewhere, the branch there will have instructions from us here. In six months' time, when you become twenty-five, you will be able to handle the business yourself. Now, as to the sum of money every quarter. What do you suggest?'

I thought a moment, and named a figure.

'That is generous, Philip,' he said, 'rather over-generous. She will hardly need as much as that. Not at the moment, at least.'

'Oh, for God's sake, don't let's be niggardly,' I said. 'If we do this thing, let us do it as Ambrose would have done it, or not at all.'

'H'm,' he said. He scribbled a figure or two on his blotter.

'Well, she should be pleased by this,' he said; 'it should atone for any disappointment with the will.'

How hard and cold-blooded was the legal mind. Scratching away there with his pen at sums and figures, reckoning up shillings and pence, how much the estate could afford. Lord! how I hated money.

'Hurry, sir,' I said, 'and write your letter. Then I can take it back with me. I can ride to the bank also, so that they have your letter too. My cousin Rachel can then draw from them at once.'

'My dear fellow, Mrs. Ashley will hardly be as pushed as that. You are going from one extreme to the other.'

He sighed, and drew a sheet of paper before him on the blotter.

'She was correct when she said you were like Ambrose,' he replied.

This time, when he wrote his letter, I stood over him, so that I could be certain what he said to her. He did not mention my name. He talked of the estate. It was the wish of the estate that provision should be made for her. The estate had decided upon the sum to be paid quarterly. I watched him like a hawk.

'If you do not wish to seem mixed up in the affair,' he said to me, 'you had better not take the letter. Dobson has to go your way this afternoon. He can take the letter for me. It will look better.'

'Excellent,' I said, 'and I will go to the bank. Thank you, uncle.'

'Don't forget to see Louise before you go,' he said; 'I think she is somewhere in the house.'

I could have done without Louise, in my impatience to be off, but I could not say so. She was in the parlour, as it happened, and I was obliged to pass the open door from my godfather's study.

'I thought I heard your voice,' she said. 'Have you come to spend the day? Let me give you some cake and fruit. You must be hungry.'

'I have to go at once,' I said, 'thank you, Louise. I only rode over to see my godfather on a business matter.'

'Oh,' she said, 'I see.' Her expression, that had been cheerful and natural at sight of me, turned back to the stiff look of Sunday. 'And how is Mrs. Ashley?' she said.

'My cousin Rachel is well, and exceedingly busy,' I said. 'All the shrubs she brought home from Italy have arrived this morning, and she is planting them out with Tamlyn in the forcing ground.'

'I should have thought you would have stayed at home to help her,' said Louise.

I don't know what it was about the girl, but this new inflection in her voice was strangely irritating. I was reminded suddenly of her behaviour in old days, when we would be running races in the garden, and just as I would be happily employed she would for no reason shake her curls and say to me, 'I don't think, after all, I want to play,' and would stand looking at me with this same stubborn face.

'You know perfectly well I am a fool at gardening,' I said, and then, from devilry, I added, 'Haven't you got over your ill-humour yet?'

She drew herself up, and flushed, 'Ill-humour? I don't know what you mean,' she said quickly.

'Oh yes, you do,' I answered. 'You were in a vile humour the whole of Sunday. It was most noticeable. I wonder the Pascoe girls did not remark upon it.'

'The Pascoe girls,' she said, 'like everyone else, were probably far too busy remarking something else.'

'And what was that?' I asked.

'How simple it must be for a woman of the world, like Mrs. Ashley, to twist a young man like yourself around her finger,' said Louise.

I turned on my heel and left the room. I could have struck her.

Chapter Thirteen

By the time I had ridden back along the high road from Pelyn, and across country down into town, and so home again, I must have covered near on twenty miles. I had paused for a draught of cider at the inn on the town quay, but had eaten nothing, and was well-nigh famished by four o'clock.

The clock struck the hour from the belfry on the house and I rode straight to the stables, where as ill luck had it Wellington was waiting instead of the groom.

He clucked his tongue at sight of Gypsy in a lather. 'This won't do at all, Mr. Philip, sir,' he said, as I dismounted, and I felt as guilty as I used to do when on holiday from Harrow. 'You know the mare catches cold when overheated, and here you've been and brought her back steaming. She's in no condition to follow hounds, if that's what you've been doing.'

'If I'd been following hounds I'd be away on Bodmin moor,' I said. 'Don't be an ass, Wellington. I've been over to see Mr. Kendall on business, and then went into town. I'm sorry about Gypsy, but it can't be helped. I don't think she'll come to harm.'

'I hope not, sir,' said Wellington, and he began running his hands over poor Gypsy's flanks as though I had put her to a steeplechase.

I walked back to the house, and went into the library. The fire was burning brightly, but there was no sign of my cousin Rachel. I rang the bell for Seecombe.

'Where is Mrs. Ashley?' I asked, as he entered the room.

'Madame came in a little after three, sir,' he said. 'She and the gardeners have been working in the grounds ever since you left. Tamlyn is in the steward's room with me now. He says he has never seen anything like it, the manner in which the mistress sets about it. He says she's a wonder.'

'She must be exhausted,' I said.

'I was afraid of that, sir. I suggested she should go to bed, but she would not hear of it. "Tell the boys to bring me up cans of hot water. I'll take a bath, Seecombe," she said to me, "and I'll wash my hair as well." I was about to send for my niece, it seems hardly right for a lady to wash her own hair, but she would not hear of that either.'

'The boys had better do the same for me,' I told him; 'I've had a hard day too. And I'm devilish hungry. I want my dinner early.'

'Very well, sir. At a quarter to five?'

'Please, Seecombe, if you can manage it.'

I went upstairs, whistling, to throw my clothes off and sit in the steaming tub before my bedroom fire. The dogs came along the corridor from my cousin Rachel's room. They had become quite accustomed to the visitor, and followed her everywhere. Old Don thumped his tail at me from the top of the stairs.

'Hullo, old fellow,' I said; 'you're faithless, you know. You've left me for a lady.' He licked my hand with his long furry tongue, and made big eyes at me.

The boy came with the can and filled the bath, and it was pleasant to sit there in the tub, cross-legged, and scrub myself, whistling a tuneless song above the steam. As I rubbed myself dry with the towel I noticed that on the table beside my bed was a bowl of flowers. Sprigs from the woods, orchis and cyclamen amongst them. No one had ever put flowers in my room before. Seecombe would not have thought of it, or the boys either. It must have been my cousin Rachel. The sight of the flowers added to my mood of high good humour. She may have been messing with the plants and shrubs all day, but she had found the time to fill the bowl with flowers as well. I tied my cravat and put on my dinner coat, still humming my tuneless song. Then I went along the corridor, and knocked upon the door of the boudoir.

'Who is it?' she called from within.

'It is me, Philip,' I answered. 'I have come to tell you that dinner will be early to-night. I'm starving, and so I should think are you, after the tales I've heard. What in the world have you and Tamlyn been up to, that you have to take a bath and wash your hair?'

That bubble of laughter, so infectious, was her answer.

'We've been burrowing underground, like moles,' she called.

'Have you earth up to your eyebrows?'

'Earth everywhere,' she answered. 'I've had my bath, and now I am drying my hair. I am pinned up and presentable, and look exactly like aunt Phoebe. You may come in.'

I opened the door and went into the boudoir. She was sitting on the stool before the fire, and for a moment I scarcely recognised her, she looked so different out of mourning. She had a white dressing wrapper around her, tied at the throat and at the wrists with ribbon, and her hair was pinned on the top of her head, instead of parted smoothly in the centre.

I had never seen anything less like aunt Phoebe, or aunt anyone. I stood blinking at her in the doorway.

'Come and sit down. Don't look so startled,' she said to me.

I shut the door behind me, and went and sat down on a chair.

'Forgive me,' I said, 'but the point is that I have never seen a woman in undress before.'

'This isn't undress,' she said, 'it's what I wear at breakfast. Ambrose used to call it my nun's robe.'

She raised her arms, and began to jab pins into her hair.

'At twenty-four,' she said, 'it is high time you saw a pleasant homely sight such as aunt Phoebe doing up her hair. Are you embarrassed?'

I folded my arms and crossed my legs, and continued to look at her. 'Not in the slightest,' I said, 'merely stunned.'

She laughed, and holding the pins in her mouth took them one by one, and winding her hair into a roll placed it the way it should go, in the low knot behind. The whole matter only took a few seconds, or so it seemed to me.

'Do you do that every day in so short a time?' I asked, amazed.

'Oh, Philip, what a lot you have to learn,' she said to me; 'have you never seen your Louise pin up her hair?'

'No, and I wouldn't want to,' I answered swiftly, with a sudden memory of Louise's parting remark as I left Pelyn. My cousin Rachel laughed, and dropped a hair-pin on my knee.

'A keepsake,' she said. 'Put it under your pillow, and watch Seecombe's face at breakfast in the morning.'

She passed from the boudoir into the bedroom opposite, leaving the door wide open.

'You can sit there and shout through to me while I dress,' she called.

I looked furtively at the little bureau to see if there was any sign of my godfather's letter, but could see nothing. I wondered what had happened. Perhaps she had it with her in the bedroom. It might be that she would say nothing to me, that she would treat the matter as a private one between my godfather and herself. I hoped so.

'Where have you been all day?' she called to me.

'I had to go into town,' I said, 'there were people there I was obliged to see.' I need not say a word about the bank.

'I was so happy with Tamlyn and the gardeners,' she called. 'There were only very few of the plants to be thrown away. There is so much, Philip, you know, still to be done in that plantation; the undergrowth bordering the meadow should be cleared, and a walk laid down, and the whole ground there given up to camellias, so that in less than twenty years you could have a spring garden there that the whole of Cornwall would come to see.'

'I know,' I said; 'that was what Ambrose intended.'

'It needs careful planning,' she said, 'and not just left to chance and Tamlyn. He is a dear, but his knowledge is limited. Why do you not take more interest in it yourself?'

'I don't know enough,' I said, 'it was never my department anyway. Ambrose knew that.'

'There must be people who could help you,' she said. 'You could have a designer down from London to lay it out.'

I did not answer. I did not want a designer down from London. I was pretty sure she knew more about it than any designer.

Just then Seecombe appeared and hovered in the passage.

'What is it, Seecombe, is dinner ready?' I asked.

'No, sir,' he replied. 'Mr. Kendall's man, Dobson, has ridden over with a note for madam.'

My heart sank. The wretched fellow must have stayed somewhere drinking on the road to be so late. Now I should be caught for the business of her reading it. How wretchedly ill-timed. I heard Seecombe knock on her open door, and give in the letter.

'I think I will go below and wait for you in the library,' I said.

'No, don't go,' she called, 'I'm ready dressed. We can go down together. Here is a letter from Mr. Kendall. Perhaps he invites us both to Pelyn.'

Seecombe disappeared along the corridor. I stood up and wished that I could follow him. Suddenly I felt uneasy, nervous. No sound came from the blue bedroom. She must be reading the letter. Ages seemed to pass. At last she came out of the bedroom, and she stood in the doorway, the letter open in her hand. She was dressed for dinner. Perhaps it was the contrast of her skin against the mourning that made her look so white.

'What have you been doing?' she said.

Her voice sounded quite different. Oddly strained.

'Doing?' I said. 'Nothing. Why?'

'Don't lie, Philip. You don't know how.'

I stood most wretchedly before the fire, staring anywhere but in those searching accusing eyes.

'You have been to Pelyn,' she said; 'you rode over there to-day to see your guardian.'

She was right. I was the most hopeless useless liar. At any rate, to her.

'I may have done,' I said. 'What if I did?'

'You made him write this letter,' she said.

'No,' I said, swallowing, 'I did nothing of the sort. He wrote it of his own accord. There was business to discuss, and it so happened that in talking various legal matters came to the fore, and . . .'

'And you told him your cousin Rachel proposed giving lessons in Italian, isn't that the truth?' she said.

I felt hot and cold and miserably ill at ease.

'Not exactly,' I said.

'Surely you realised I was only joking when I told you that?' she said. If she was joking, I thought, why then must she be so angry with me now?

'You don't realise what you have done,' she said; 'you make me feel utterly ashamed.' She went and stood by the window, with her back to me. 'If you wish to humiliate me,' she said, 'by heaven you have gone the right way about it.'

'I don't see,' I said, 'why you have to be so proud.'

'Proud?' She turned round, her eyes very dark and large, and looked at me in fury. 'How dare you call me proud?' she said. I stared back at her. I think I was amazed that anyone who a moment or two before had been laughing with me could suddenly become so angry. Then, to my own very great surprise, my nervousness went from me. I walked towards her, and stood beside her.

'I shall call you proud,' I said, 'I shall go further, and I shall call you damnably proud. It is not you who is likely to be humiliated but me. It was not a joke, when you said that about giving lessons in Italian. Your answer came far too swiftly for it to be a joke. You said it, because you meant it.'

'And if I did mean it?' she said. 'Is there anything shameful in giving lessons in Italian?'

'In the ordinary sense, no,' I said, 'but in your case, yes. For Mrs. Ambrose Ashley to give lessons in Italian is shameful; it reflects upon the husband who neglected to make provision for her in his will. And I, Philip Ashley, his heir, won't permit it. You will take that allowance every quarter, cousin Rachel, and when you draw the money from the bank, please remember that it does not come from the estate, nor from the heir to the estate, but from your husband, Ambrose Ashley.'

A wave of anger, as great as hers, had come over me as I spoke. I was damned if any creature, small and frail, should stand there and accuse me of humiliating her; and I was damned furthermore if she should refuse the money that belonged to her by right.

'Well? Do you understand what I have been saying to you?' I said.

For one moment I thought she was going to hit me. She stood quite still, staring up at me. Then her eyes filled with tears, and pushing past me she went into the bedroom and slammed the door. I walked downstairs. I went to the dining-room and rang the bell and told Seecombe that I thought Mrs. Ashley would not be down for dinner. I poured myself out a glass of claret, and sat down alone at the head of the table. Christ! I thought, so that's how women behave. I had never felt so angry, nor so spent. Long days in the open, working with the men at harvest time; arguments with tenants behindhand with their rent or involved in some quarrel with a neighbour which I had to settle; nothing of this could compare to five minutes with a woman whose mood of gaiety had turned in a single instant to hostility. And was the final weapon always tears? Because they knew full well the effect upon the watcher? I had another glass of claret. As to Seecombe, who hovered at my elbow, I could have wished him a world away.

'Is Madam indisposed, sir, do you think?' he asked me.

I might have told him that Madam was not so much indisposed as in a fury, and would probably ring her bell in a moment and demand Wellington and the carriage to take her back to Plymouth.

'No,' I said, 'her hair is not yet dry. You had better tell John to take a tray up to the boudoir.'

This, I supposed, was what men faced when they were married. Slammed doors, and silence. Dinner alone. So that appetite, whipped up by the long day's outing, and the relaxation of the bath-tub, and the pleasure of a tranquil evening by the fire passed in intermittent conversation, watching with lazy ease hands that were white and small against embroidery, had to simmer down. With what cheerfulness had I dressed for dinner and walked along the corridor, knocked on the boudoir door and found her sitting on the stool in that white wrapper, with her hair pinned on top of her head. How easy the mood we shared, making a kind of intimacy that gave a glow to the whole prospect of the evening. And now, alone at the table, with a beefsteak that might have been shoe-leather for all I cared. And what was she doing? Lying on her bed? Were the candles snuffed, the curtains drawn, and the room in darkness? Or was the mood over now, and did she sit sedately in the boudoir, dry-eyed, eating her dinner off the tray, to make a show for Seecombe? I did not know. I did not care. Ambrose had been so right when he used to say that women were a race apart. One thing was certain now. I should never marry. . . .

Dinner over, I went and sat in the library. I lit my pipe, and put my feet up on the fire-irons, and composed myself to that after dinner slumber that can be sweet and consoling upon occasion, but to-night lacked every charm. I had become used to the sight of her in the chair opposite my own, her shoulders turned so that the light fell upon her work, and Don at her feet; now the chair looked strangely empty. Well, to hell with it, that a woman could so disturb the close of day. I got up and found a book upon the shelves, and turned the pages. Then I must have dozed, because when I looked up again the hands of the clock in the corner were a little short of nine. To bed then, and to sleep. No sense in sitting on, with the fire gone out. I took the dogs round to the kennels – the weather had changed, it was blowing and spitting rain – and then bolted up and went to my room. I was just about to throw my coat off on the chair when I saw a note, placed beside the bowl of flowers on the table next to my bed. I went over to the table, and picked up the note and read it. It was from my cousin Rachel.

'Dear Philip,' it said, 'if you can bring yourself to do so, please forgive me for my rudeness to you to-night. It was unpardonable of me to behave so in your house. I have no excuse, except that I am not entirely myself these days; emotion lies too near the surface. I have written to your guardian, thanking him for his letter and accepting the allowance. It was generous and dear of you both to think of me. Good night. Rachel.'

I read the letter twice, and then put it in my pocket. Was her pride spent then, and the anger too? Did these feelings dissolve with the tears? A load went from me, that she had accepted the allowance. I had visualised another visit to the bank, and further explanations, countermanding my first orders; and then interviews with my godfather, and arguments, and the whole business ending most wretchedly with my cousin Rachel sweeping out of the house and taking herself to London, there to live in lodgings giving Italian lessons.

Had it cost her much to write that note, I wondered? The swing from pride to humility? I hated the fact that she had to do so. For the first time since he had died, I found myself blaming Ambrose for what had happened. Surely he might have taken some thought for the future. Illness and sudden death can come to anyone. He must have known that by making no provision he left his wife to our mercy, to our charity. A letter home to my godfather would have spared all this. I had a vision of her sitting down in aunt Phoebe's boudoir and writing me this note. I wondered if she had left the boudoir yet and gone to bed. I hesitated for a moment, and then went along the corridor and stood under the archway by her rooms.

The door of the boudoir was open, the door of the bedroom shut. I knocked upon the bedroom door. For a moment no answer came, and then she said, 'Who is it?'

I did not answer 'Philip.' I opened the door, and went inside. The room was in darkness, and the light from my candle showed the curtains of the bed to be partly drawn. I could see the outline of her form under the coverlet.

'I have just read your note,' I said. 'I wanted to thank you for it, and to say good night.'

I thought she might sit up and light her candle, but she did not do so. She lay just as she was, on her pillows, behind the curtains.

'I wanted you to know also,' I said, 'that I had no idea of patronising you. Please believe that.'

The voice that came from the curtains was strangely quiet and subdued.

'I never thought you had,' she answered.

We were both silent an instant, and then she said, 'It would not worry me to give Italian lessons. I have no pride about that sort of thing. What I could not bear was when you said my doing so would reflect badly upon Ambrose.'

'It was true,' I said, 'but forget it now. We need not think of it again.'

'It was dear of you, and very like you,' she said, 'to go riding over to Pelyn to see your guardian. I must have seemed so ungracious, so completely lacking in gratitude. I can't forgive myself.' The voice, so near to tears again, did something to me. A kind of tightness came to my throat and to my belly.

'I would much rather that you hit me,' I told her, 'than that you cried.'

I heard her move in her bed, and feel for a handkerchief and blow her nose. The gesture and the sound, so commonplace and simple, happening there in the darkness behind the curtains, made me even weaker in the belly than before.

Presently she said, 'I will take the allowance, Philip, but I must not trespass on your hospitality after this week. I think next Monday, if it will suit you, I should leave here and move elsewhere, perhaps to London.'

A blank feeling came over me at her words.

'Go to London?' I said. 'But why? What for?'

'I only came for a few days,' she answered. 'I have already stayed longer than I intended.'

'But you have not met everybody yet,' I said, 'you have not done everything you are supposed to do.'

'Does it matter?' she said. 'After all – it seems so pointless.'

How unlike her it sounded, that lack of spirit in her voice.

'I thought you liked it,' I said, 'going about the estate, and visiting the tenants. Each day we went about it together you seemed so happy. And today, putting in those shrubs with Tamlyn. Was it all show, and were you just being polite?'

She did not answer for a moment, and then she said, 'Sometimes, Philip, I think you lack all understanding.'

Probably I did. I felt sullen and hurt and I did not care.

'All right,' I said; 'if you want to go, do so. It will cause a lot of talk, but no matter.'

'I should have thought,' she said, 'that it would cause more talk if I stayed.'

'Talk if you stayed?' I said. 'What do you mean? Don't you realise that by rights you belong here, that if Ambrose had not been such a lunatic this would have been your home?'

'Oh, God,' she flared out at me in sudden anger, 'why else do you think I came?'

I had put my foot in it again. Blundering and tactless, I had said all the wrong things. I felt suddenly hopeless and inadequate. I went up to the bed, and pulled aside the curtains, and looked down at her. She was lying propped against her pillows, her hands clasped in front of her. She was wearing something white, frilled at the neck like a choir-boy's surplice, and her hair was loose, tied behind with a piece of ribbon, as I remembered Louise's as a child. It shook me, and surprised me, that she should look so young.

'Listen,' I said, 'I don't know why you came, or what were your motives in doing all you have done. I don't know anything about you, or about any woman. All I know is that I like it now you are here. And I don't want you to go. Is that complicated?'

She had put her hands up to her face, almost in defence, as if she thought I meant to harm her.

'Yes,' she said, 'very.'

'Then it is you who make it so,' I said, 'not I.'

I folded my arms and looked at her, assuming an ease of manner I was far from feeling. Yet in a sense by standing there, while she lay in bed, I had her at a disadvantage. I did not see how a woman with her hair loose, becoming a girl again without a woman's status, could be angry.

I saw her eyes waver. She was searching in her mind for some excuse, some new reason why she should be gone, and in a sudden flash I hit upon a master stroke of strategy.

'You told me this evening,' I said, 'that I should have a designer down from London, to lay out the gardens, I know that was what Ambrose always intended to do. The fact remains that I don't know of one, and should go mad with irritation anyway, if I had to have such a fellow about me. If you have any feeling for the place, knowing what it meant to Ambrose, you would remain here for a few months and do it for me.'

The shaft struck home. She stared in front of her, playing with her ring. I had remarked before that when preoccupied this was a trick of hers. I pushed on with my advantage.

'I never could follow the plans that Ambrose used to draw,' I said to her, 'nor Tamlyn either, for that matter. He works wonders, I know, but only under direction. Time and again he has come to me this past year and asked for advice which I have been quite at a loss to give him. If you remained here – just for the autumn, when so much planting needs to be done – it would help us all.'

She twisted the ring back and forth upon her finger. 'I think I should ask your godfather what he feels,' she said to me.

'It does not concern my godfather,' I said. 'What do you take me for, a schoolboy under age? There is only one consideration, whether you yourself desire to stay. If you really want to go, I cannot keep you.'

She said, surprisingly, in a still small voice, 'Why do you ask that? You know I want to stay.'

Sweet heaven, how could I know? She had intimated the exact opposite.

'Then you will remain, for a little while,' I said, 'to do the garden? That is settled, and you won't go back on your word?'

'I will remain,' she said, 'for a little while.'

I had difficulty in not smiling. Her eyes were serious, and I had the feeling that if I smiled she would change her mind. Inwardly, I triumphed.

'Very well, then,' I said, 'I will bid you good night and leave you. What about your letter to my godfather? Do you want me to put it in the post-bag?'

'Seecombe has taken it,' she said.

'Then you will sleep now, and not be angry with me any more?'

'I wasn't angry, Philip.'

'But you were. I thought you were going to hit me.'

She looked up at me. 'Sometimes you are so stupid,' she said, 'that I think one day I shall. Come here.'

I drew closer, my knee touched the coverlet.

'Bend down,' she said.

She took my face between her hands and kissed me.

'Now go to bed,' she said, 'like a good boy, and sleep well.' She pushed me away, and drew her curtains.

I stumbled out of the blue bedroom with my candlestick, light-headed and somehow dazed, as though I had drunk brandy, and it seemed to me that the advantage I had thought to have over her, as I stood above her and she lay on her pillows, was now completely lost. The last word, and the last gesture too, had been with her. The little girl look and the choir-boy surplice had misled me. She was a woman all the time. For all that, I was happy. The misunderstanding was now over, and she had promised to remain. There had been no more tears.

Instead of going immediately to bed I went down to the library once again, to write a line to my godfather and to reassure him that all had gone off well. He need never know of the troublous evening spent by the pair of us. I scribbled my letter, and went into the hall to place it in the post-bag for the morning.

Seecombe had left the bag for me, as was his custom, upon the table in the hall, with the key beside it. When I opened up the bag two other letters fell into my hand, both written by my cousin Rachel. One was addressed to my godfather Nick Kendall, as she had told me. The second letter was addressed to Signor Rainaldi in Florence. I stared at it a moment, then put it back with the other in the post-bag. It was foolish of me, perhaps, senseless and absurd; the man was her friend, why should she not write a letter to him? Yet, as I went upstairs to bed, I felt exactly as if she had hit me after all.

Chapter Fourteen

The following day when she came downstairs, and I joined her in the garden, my cousin Rachel was as happy and unconcerned as though there had never been a rift between us. The only difference in her manner to me was that she seemed more gentle, and more tender; she teased me less, laughed with me and not at me, and kept asking my opinion as to the planting of the shrubs, not for the sake of my knowledge but for my future pleasure when I should look upon them.

'Do what you want to do,' I told her; 'bid the men cut the hedge-rows, fell the trees, heap up the banks yonder with shrubs, whatever you fancy will do well, I have no eye for line.'

'But I want the result to please you, Philip,' she said. 'All this belongs to you, and one day will belong to your children. What if I make changes in the grounds, and when it is done you are displeased?'

'I shan't be displeased,' I said; 'and stop talking about my children. I am quite resolved to remain a bachelor.'

'Which is essentially selfish,' she said, 'and very stupid of you.'

'I think not,' I answered. 'I think by remaining a bachelor I shall be spared much distress and anxiety of mind.'

'Have you ever thought what you would lose?'

'I have a shrewd guess,' I told her, 'that the blessings of married bliss are not all they are claimed to be. If it's warmth and comfort that a man wants, and something beautiful to look upon, he can get all that from his own house, if he loves it well.'

To my astonishment she laughed so much at my remark that Tamlyn and the gardeners, working at the far end of the plantation, raised their heads to look at us.

'One day,' she said to me, 'when you fall in love, I shall remind you of those words. Warmth and comfort from stone walls, at twenty-four. Oh, Philip!' And the bubble of laughter came from her again.

I could not see that it was so very funny.

'I know quite well what you mean,' I said; 'it just happens that I have never been moved that way.'

'That's very evident,' she said. 'You must be a heartbreak to the neighbourhood. That poor Louise. . . .'

But I was not going to be led into a discussion on Louise, nor again a dissertation upon love and matrimony. I was much more interested to watch her work upon the garden.

October set in fine and mild, and for the first three weeks of it we had barely no rain at all, so that Tamlyn and the men, under the supervision of my cousin Rachel, were able to go far ahead with the work in the plantation. We managed also to visit in succession all the tenants upon the estate, which gave great satisfaction, as I knew it would. I had known every one of them since boyhood, and had been used to calling in upon them every so often, for it was part of my work to do so. But it was a new experience for my cousin Rachel, brought up in Italy to a very different life. Her manner with the people could not have been more right or proper, and it was a fascination to watch her with them. The blend of graciousness and cameraderie made them immediately look up to her, yet put them at their ease. She asked all the right questions, replied with the right answers. Also – and this endeared her to many of them – there was the understanding she seemed to have of all their ailments, and the remedies she produced. 'With my love for gardening,' she told them, 'goes a knowledge of herbs. In Italy we always made a study of these things.' And she would produce balm, from some plant, to rub upon wheezing chests, and oil from another, as a measure against burns; and she would instruct them too how to make tisana, as a remedy for indigestion and for sleeplessness – the best nightcap in the world, she said to them – and tell them how the juice of certain fruits could cure almost any ill from a sore throat to a stye on the eyelid.

'You know what will happen,' I told her; 'you will take the place of midwife in the district. They will send for you in the night to deliver babies, and once that starts there will be no peace for you at all.'

'There is a tisana for that too,' she said, 'made from the leaves of raspberries and of nettles. If a woman drinks that for six months before the birth, she has her baby without pain.'

'That's witchcraft,' I said. 'They wouldn't think it right to do so.'

'What nonsense! Why should women suffer?' said my cousin Rachel.

Sometimes, in the afternoons, she would be called upon by the county, as I had warned her. And she was as successful with the 'gentry', as Seecombe called them, as she was with the humbler folk. Seecombe, I soon came to realise, now lived in a seventh heaven. When the carriages drove up to the door upon a Tuesday or a Thursday, at three o'clock of an afternoon, he would be waiting in the hall. He still wore mourning, but his coat was new, kept only for these occasions. The luckless John would have the task of opening the front door to the visitors, then of passing them on to his superior, who with slow and stately step (I would have it all from John afterwards) preceded the visitors through the hall to the drawing-room. Throwing the door open with a flourish (this from my cousin Rachel) he would announce the names like the toast-master at a banquet. Beforehand, she told me, he would discuss with her the likelihood of this or that visitor appearing, and give her a brief resumé of their family history up to date. He was generally right in his prophecy of who would appear, and we wondered whether there was some method of sending messages from household to household through the servants' hall to give due warning, even as savages beat tom-toms in a jungle. For instance, Seecombe would tell my cousin Rachel that he had it for certain that Mrs. Tremayne had ordered her carriage for Thursday afternoon, and that she would bring with her the married daughter Mrs. Gough, and the unmarried daughter Miss Isobel; and that my cousin Rachel must beware when she talked to Miss Isobel, as the young lady suffered from an affliction of the speech. Or again, that upon a Tuesday old Lady Penryn would be likely to appear, because she always visited her grand-daughter upon that day, who lived only ten miles distant from us; and my cousin Rachel must remember on no account to mention foxes before her, as Lady Penryn had been frightened by a fox before her eldest son was born, and he carried the stigma as a birth-mark upon his left shoulder to this day.

'And Philip,' said my cousin Rachel afterwards, 'the whole time she was with me I had to head the conversation away from hunting. It was no use, she came back to it like a mouse sniffing at cheese. And finally, to keep her quiet, I had to invent a tale of chasing wild cats in the Alps, which is an impossibility, and something no one has done.'

There was always some story of the callers with which she greeted me when I returned home, slinking by the back way through the woods when the last carriage had bowled safely down the drive; and we would laugh together, and she would smooth her hair before the mirror and straighten the cushions, while I polished off the last of the sweet cakes that had been put before the visitors. The whole thing would seem like a game, like a conspiracy; yet I think she was happy there, sitting in the drawing-room making conversation. People and their lives had interest for her, how they thought, and what they did; and she used to say to me, 'But you don't understand, Philip, this is all so new after the very different society in Florence. I have always wondered about life in England, in the country. Now I am beginning to know. And I love every minute of it.'

I would take a lump out of the sugar bowl, and crunch it, and cut myself a slice from the seed cake.

'I can think of nothing more monotonous,' I told her, 'than discussing generalities with anyone, in Florence or in Cornwall.'

'Ah, but you are hopeless,' she said, 'and will end up very narrow-minded, thinking of nothing but turnips and of kale.'

I would fling myself down in the chair, and on purpose to try her put my muddy boots up on the stool, watching her with one eye. She never reproved me, and if she had noticed did not appear to do so.

'Go on,' I would say, 'tell me the latest scandal in the county.'

'But if you are not interested,' she would answer, 'why should I do so?'

'Because I like to hear you talk.'

So before going upstairs to change for dinner she would regale me with county gossip, what there was of it – the latest betrothals, marriages, and deaths, the new babies on the way; she appeared to glean more from twenty minutes' conversation with a stranger than I would from an acquaintance after a lifetime.

'As I suspected,' she told me, 'you are the despair of every mother within fifty miles.'

'Why so?'

'Because you do not choose to look at any of their daughters. So tall, so presentable, so eligible in every way. Pray, Mrs. Ashley, do prevail upon your cousin to go out more.'

'And what is your answer?'

'That you find all the warmth and entertainment that you need within these four walls. On second thoughts,' she added, 'that might be misconstrued. I must watch my tongue.'

'I don't mind what you tell them,' I said, 'as long as you do not involve me in an invitation. I have no desire to look at anybody's daughter.'

'There is heavy betting upon Louise,' she said; 'quite a number say that she will get you in the end. And the third Miss Pascoe has a sporting chance.'

'Great heaven!' I exclaimed. 'Belinda Pascoe? I'd as soon marry Katie Searle, who does the washing. Really, cousin Rachel, you might protect me. Why not tell these gossips I'm a recluse and spend all my spare time scribbling Latin verses? That might shake them.'

'Nothing will shake them,' she answered. 'The thought that a good-looking young bachelor should like solitude and verse would make you sound all the more romantic. These things whet appetite.'

'Then they'll feed elsewhere,' I replied. 'What staggers me is the way in which the minds of women in this part of the world – perhaps it's the same everywhere – run perpetually upon marriage.'

'They haven't much else to think about,' she said; 'the choice of fare is small. I do not escape discussion, I can tell you. A list of eligible widowers has been given me. There is a peer down in west Cornwall declared to be the very thing. Fifty, an heir, and both daughters married.'

'Not old St. Ives?' I said in tones of outrage.

'Why, yes, I believe that is the name. They say he's charming.'

'Charming, is he?' I said to her. 'He's always drunk by midday, and creeps around the passages after the maids. Billy Rowe, from the Barton, had a niece in service there. She had to come back home, she grew so scared.'

'Who's talking gossip now?' said cousin Rachel. 'Poor Lord St. Ives, perhaps if he had a wife he wouldn't creep about the passages. It would, of course, depend upon the wife.'

'Well, you're not going to marry him,' I said with firmness.

'You could at least invite him here to dinner?' she suggested, her eyes full of that solemnity that I had learnt now spelt mischief. 'We could have a party, Philip. The prettiest young women for you, and the best-favoured widowers for me. But I think I have made my choice. I think, if I am ever put to it, I will take your godfather, Mr. Kendall. He has a fair direct way of speaking, which I much admire.'

Maybe she did it on purpose, but I rose to the bait, exploding.

'You cannot seriously mean it?' I said. 'Marry my godfather? Why damn it, cousin Rachel, he's nearing sixty; and he's never without a chill or some complaint.'

'That means he doesn't find warmth or comfort inside his house as you do,' she answered me.

I knew then that she was laughing, so laughed with her; but afterwards I wondered about it with mistrust. Certainly my godfather was most courteous when he came on Sundays, and they got on capitally together. We had dined there once or twice, and my godfather had sparkled in a way unknown to me. But he had been a widower for ten years. Surely he could not entertain so incredible an idea as to fancy his chance with my cousin Rachel? And surely she would not accept? I went hot at the thought. My cousin Rachel at Pelyn, Mrs. Ashley, becoming Mrs. Kendall. How monstrous! If anything so presumptuous was passing through the old man's mind I was damned if I would continue inviting him to Sunday dinner. Yet to break the invitation would be to break the routine of years. It was not possible. Therefore I must continue as we had always done, but the next Sunday, when my godfather on the right of my cousin Rachel bent his deaf ear to her, and suddenly sat back, laughing and saying, 'Oh, capital, capital,' I wondered sulkily what it portended and why it was that they laughed so much together. This, I thought to myself, is another trick of women, to throw a jest in the air that left a sting behind it.

She sat there, at Sunday dinner, looking remarkably well and in high good humour, with my godfather on her right and the vicar on her left, none of them at a loss for conversation, and for no good reason I turned sulky and silent, just as Louise had done that first Sunday, and our end of the table had all the appearance of a Quaker meeting. Louise sat looking at her plate, and I at mine, and I suddenly lifted my eyes and saw Belinda Pascoe, with round eyes, gaping at me; and remembering the gossip of the countryside I became more dumb than ever. Our silence spurred my cousin Rachel to greater effort, in order, I suppose, to cover it; and she and my godfather and the vicar tried to cap each other, quoting verse, while I became more and more sulky, and thankful for the absence of Mrs. Pascoe through indisposition. Louise did not matter. I was not obliged to talk to Louise.

But when they had all gone my cousin Rachel took me to task. 'When,' she said, 'I entertain your friends, I look to have a little support from you. What was wrong, Philip? You sat there scowling, with a mulish face, and never addressed a word to either neighbour. Those poor girls...' And she shook her head at me, displeased.

'There was so much gaiety at your end,' I answered her, 'that I saw no point in contributing to it. All that nonsense about "I love you" in Greek. And the vicar telling you that "my heart's delight" sounded very well in Hebrew.'

'Well, so it did,' she said. 'It came rolling off his tongue, and I was most impressed. And your godfather wants to show me the beacon head by moonlight. Once seen, he tells me, never forgotten.'

'Well, he's not showing it to you,' I replied. 'The beacon is my property. There is some old earth-work that belongs to the Pelyn estate. Let him show you that. It's covered thick in brambles.' And I threw a lump of coal upon the fire, hoping the clatter bothered her.

'I don't know what's come over you,' she said; 'you are losing your sense of humour.' And she patted me on the shoulder and went upstairs. That was the infuriating thing about a woman. Always the last word. Leaving one to grapple with ill-temper, and she herself serene. A woman, it seemed, was never in the wrong. Or if she was, she twisted the fault to her advantage, making it seem otherwise. She would fling these pin-pricks in the air, these hints of moonlight strolls with my godfather, or some other expedition, a visit to Lostwithiel market, and ask me in all seriousness whether she should wear the new bonnet that had come by parcel post from London – the veil had a wider mesh and did not shroud her, and my godfather had told her it became her well. And when I fell to sulking, saying I did not care whether she concealed her features with a mask, her mood soared to serenity yet higher – the conversation was at dinner on the Monday – and while I sat frowning she carried on her talk with Seecombe, making me seem more sulky than I was.

Then in the library afterwards, with no observer present, she would relent; the serenity was with her still, but a kind of tenderness came too. She neither laughed at me for lack of humour, nor chided me for sullenness. She asked me to hold her silks for her, to choose the colours I liked best, because she wanted to work a covering for me to use on the chair in the estate office. And quietly, without irritating, without probing, she asked me questions about my day, whom I had seen, what I had done, so that all sulkiness went from me and I was eased and rested, and I wondered, watching her hands with the silks, smoothing them and touching them, why it could not have been thus in the first place; why first the pin-prick, the barb of irritation to disturb the atmosphere, giving herself the trouble to make it calm again? It was as if my change of mood afforded her delight, but why it should do so I had no remote idea. I only knew that when she teased me I disliked it, and it hurt. And when she was tender I was happy and at peace. .

By the end of the month the fine weather broke. It rained for three days without stopping, and there was no gardening to be done, no work for me on the estate, riding to and fro to be soaked to the skin, and all callers from the county were kept within their doors, like the rest of us. It was Seecombe who suggested, what I think the pair of us had both been shirking, that the time was opportune to go through Ambrose's effects. He broached it one morning as my cousin Rachel and I stood by the library window, staring out at the driving rain.

'The office for me,' I had just observed, 'and a day in the boudoir for you. What about those boxes down from London? More gowns to sort, and try upon your person, and return again?'

'Not gowns,' she said, 'but coverings for curtains. I think aunt Phoebe's eye lacked lustre. The blue bedroom should live up to its name. At present it is grey, not blue at all. And the quilting to the bed has moth, but don't tell Seecombe. The moth of years. I have chosen you new curtains and new quilting.'

It was then that Seecombe entered, and seeing us apparently without employment said, 'The weather being so inclement, sir, I had thought the boys might be put to extra cleaning within doors. Your room needs attention. But they cannot dust there while Mr. Ashley's trunks and boxes cover the floor.'

I glanced at her, fearing this lack of tact might wound her, that she might turn away, but to my surprise she took it well.

'You are quite right, Seecombe,' she said; 'the boys cannot clean the room until the boxes are unpacked. We have left it far too long. Well, Philip, what about it?'

'Very well,' I said, 'if you are agreeable. Let us have the fire lit, and when the room is warm we'll go upstairs.'

I think that both of us tried to conceal our feelings from the other. We forced a sort of brightness into our behaviour and into our conversation. For my sake, she was determined not to show distress. And I, wishing to spare the same for her, assumed a heartiness utterly foreign to my nature. The rain was lashing at the windows of my old room, and a patch of damp had appeared upon the ceiling. The fire, that had not been lit since last winter, burnt with a false crackle. The boxes stood in a line upon the floor, waiting to be opened; and on top of one was the well remembered travel rug of dark blue, with the yellow monogram 'A.A.' in large letters in one corner. I had the sudden recollection of putting it over his knees that last day, when he drove away.

My cousin Rachel broke the silence. 'Come,' she said, 'shall we open the clothes trunk first?'

Her voice was purposely hard and practical. I handed her the keys, which she had left in Seecombe's charge on her arrival.

'Just as you will,' I said.

She put the key in the lock, and turned it, and threw open the lid. His old dressing-gown was on the top. I knew it well. It was of heavy silk in a dark red colour. His slippers were there too, long and flat. I stood there staring at them, and it was like walking back into the past. I remembered him passing into my room while he was shaving of a morning, the lather on his face. 'Look, boy, I've been thinking . . .' Into this room, where we were standing now. Wearing that dressing-gown, wearing those slippers. My cousin Rachel took them from the trunk.

'What shall we do with them?' she said, and the voice that had been hard was lower now, subdued.

'I don't know,' I said; 'it's for you to say.'

'Would you wear them, if I gave them to you?' she asked.

It was strange. I had taken his hat. I had taken his stick. His old shooting coat with the leather at the elbows that he had left behind when he went upon his last journey, that I wore constantly. Yet these things, the dressing-gown, the slippers – it was almost as though we had opened up his coffin and looked upon him dead.

'No,' I said, 'no, I don't think so.'

She said nothing. She put them on the bed. She came next to a suit of clothing. A light-weight suit – he must have worn it in hot weather. It was not familiar to me, but she must have known it well. It was creased from lying in the trunk. She took it out and placed it with the dressing-gown upon the bed. 'It should be pressed,' she said. Suddenly she began lifting the things from the trunk very swiftly and putting them in a pile, one on top of the other, barely touching them.

'I think,' she said, 'that if you don't want them, Philip, the people on the estate here, who loved him, might like to have them. You will know best what to give, and to whom.'

I think she did not see what she was doing. She took them from the trunk in a sort of frenzy, while I stood by and watched her.

'The trunk?' she said. 'A trunk is always useful. You could do with the trunk?' She looked up at me, and her voice faltered.

Suddenly she was in my arms, her head against my chest.

'Oh, Philip,' she said, 'forgive me. I should have let you and Seecombe do it. I was a fool to come upstairs.'

It was queer. Like holding a child. Like holding a wounded animal. I touched her hair, and put my cheek against her head.

'It's all right,' I said, 'don't cry. Go back to the library. I can finish it alone.'

'No,' she said, 'it's so weak of me, so stupid. It's just as bad for you as it is for me. You loved him so. . . .'

I kept moving my lips against her hair. It was a strange feeling. And she was very small, standing there against me.

'I don't mind,' I said; 'a man can do these things. It's not easy for a woman. Let me do it, Rachel, go downstairs.'

She stood a little way apart and wiped her eyes with her handkerchief.

'No,' she said, 'I'm better now. It won't happen again. And I have unpacked the clothes. But if you will give them to the people on the estate, I shall be grateful. And anything you want for yourself, wear it. Never be afraid to wear it. I shan't mind, I shall be glad.'

The boxes of books were nearer to the fire. I brought a chair and placed it for her, close to the warmth, and knelt beside the other trunks and opened them, one by one.

I hoped she had not noticed – I had barely noticed it myself – that for the first time I had not called her cousin, but Rachel. I don't know how it happened. I think it must have been because standing there, with my arms about her, she had been so much smaller than myself.

The books did not have the personal touch about them that the clothes had done. There were old favourites that I knew, with which he always travelled, and these she gave to me to keep beside my bed. There were his cuff-links, too, his studs, his watch, his pen – all these she pressed upon me, and I was glad of them. Some of the books I did not know at all. She explained them to me, picking up first one volume, then another, and now no longer was the task so sad; this book, she said, he had picked up in Rome, it was a bargain, he was pleased, and that one there, with the old binding, and the other beside it, came from Florence. She described the place where he had bought them, and the old man who had sold them to him, and it seemed, as she chatted to me, that the strain had lifted, it had gone with the tears she had wiped away. We laid the books, one after the other, upon the floor, and I fetched a duster for her and she dusted them. Sometimes she read a passage out to me and told me how this paragraph had pleased Ambrose; or she showed me a picture, an engraving, and I saw her smiling at some well-remembered page.

She came upon a volume of drawings of the lay-out of gardens. 'This will be very useful to us,' she said, and rising from her chair took it to the window to see it better in the light.

I opened another book at random. A piece of paper fell from between the leaves. It had Ambrose's handwriting upon it. It seemed like the middle scrap of a letter, torn from its context and forgotten. *'It's a disease, of course, I have often heard of it, like kleptomania or some other malady, and has no doubt been handed down to her from her spendthrift father, Alexander Coryn. How long she has been a victim of it I cannot say, perhaps always; certainly it explains much of what has disturbed me hitherto in all this business. This much I do know, dear boy, that I cannot any longer, nay I dare not, let her have command over my purse, or I shall be ruined, and the estate will suffer. It is imperative that you warn Kendall, if by any chance . . .'* The sentence broke off. There was no end to it. The scrap of paper was not dated. The handwriting was normal. Just then she came back from the window, and I crumpled the piece of paper in my hand.

'What have you there?' she said.

'Nothing,' I said.

I threw the piece of paper on the fire. She saw it burn. She saw the handwriting on the paper curl and flicker in the flame.

'That was Ambrose's writing,' she said. 'What was it? Was it a letter?'

'It was just some note he had made,' I said, 'on an old scrap of paper.' I felt my face burn in the light of the fire.

Then I reached for another volume from the trunk. She did the same. We continued sorting the books, side by side, together; but the silence had come between us.

Chapter Fifteen

We had finished sorting the books by midday. Seecombe sent John up to us, and young Arthur, to know if anything needed carrying downstairs before they went off to their dinner.

'Leave the clothes on the bed, John,' I said, 'and put a covering on top of them. I shall want Seecombe to help me make packages of them by and by. Take this pile of books down to the library.'

'And these to the boudoir, Arthur, please,' said my cousin Rachel.

It was her first utterance since I had burnt the scrap of paper.

'It will be all right, will it, Philip,' she asked, 'if I keep the books on gardens in my room?'

'Why, yes, of course,' I answered. 'All the books are yours, you know that.'

'No,' she said, 'no, Ambrose would have wanted the others in the library.' She stood up, and smoothed her dress, and gave John the duster.

'Some cold luncheon is laid below, madam,' he said.

'Thank you, John. I am not hungry.'

I hesitated, standing by the open door, after the boys had disappeared carrying the books.

'Will you not come down to the library,' I asked, 'and help me put away the books?'

'I think not,' she said, then paused a moment, as if to add something, but did not do so. Then she walked along the corridor to her room.

I ate my lunch alone, staring out of the dining-room windows. It was still raining fast. No use attempting to go out of doors, there was nothing to be done. I had better finish the task of sorting the clothes, with Seecombe to help me. It would please him to be asked advice. What should go to the Barton, what to Trenant, what to the East Lodge; everything to be carefully chosen so that no one should take offence at what he had. It would employ the pair of us all afternoon. I tried to keep my mind upon the business; yet, nagging like a pain in the tooth that flares up suddenly and dies again, my thoughts would be wrenched back to the scrap of paper. What had it been doing between the pages of that book, and how long had it lain there, torn, forgotten? Six months, a year, or longer? Had Ambrose started upon a letter to me which never reached its destination; or were there other bits of paper, part of the same letter, which for some unknown reason were still lying between the pages of a book? The letter must have been written before his illness. The writing was firm and clear. Therefore last winter, last autumn possibly. . . . I was swept by a kind of shame. What business was it of mine to probe back into that past, to wonder about a letter that had never reached me? It was not my affair. I wished to heaven I had not come upon it.

All afternoon Seecombe and I sorted the clothes, and he put them into packages while I wrote notes of explanation to go with them. He suggested that the parcels should be given out at Christmas, which seemed to me a sound idea, and one that would appeal to the tenants. When we had finished I went downstairs again to the library, and put the books into the shelves. I found myself shaking the leaves of each volume, before I placed it on the shelf; and as I did so I felt furtive, like someone guilty of a petty crime.

'. . . *a disease, of course, like kleptomania, or some other malady* . . .' Why did I have to remember those words? What did Ambrose mean?

I reached for a dictionary, and looked up kleptomania. 'An irresistible tendency to theft in persons not tempted to do it by needy circumstances.' That was not his accusation. His accusation was one of prodigality, of extravagance. How could extravagance be a malady? It was totally unlike Ambrose, the most generous of men, to accuse anyone of such a habit. As I put the dictionary back upon the shelf the door opened, and my cousin Rachel came into the room.

I felt as guilty as if she had caught me in deceit. 'I have just finished putting away the books,' I said, and I wondered if my voice sounded as false to her as it did to me.

'So I see,' she answered, and she went and sat down by the fire. She was ready changed for dinner. I had not realised it was so late.

'We have sorted the clothes,' I said. 'Seecombe was very helpful. We think it a good plan, if you approve, that the things should be given out at Christmas.'

'Yes,' she said, 'so he told me just now. I think it most appropriate.'

I did not know if it was my manner, or hers, but there was a kind of constraint between us.

'It hasn't ceased raining for the day,' I said.

'No,' she answered.

I glanced at my hands, dusty from the books. 'If you will excuse me,' I said, 'I will go and wash, and change for dinner.' I went upstairs, and dressed, and when I came down again dinner was upon the table. We took our places in silence. Seecombe, from long habit, would break in upon our conversation very often, at dinner-time, when he had something that he wished to say, and tonight, when we had nearly finished, he said to my cousin Rachel, 'Have you shown Mr. Philip the new coverings, madam?'

'No, Seecombe,' she answered, 'there hasn't yet been time. But if he cares to see them I can do so after dinner. Perhaps John would carry them down to the library.'

'Coverings?' I said, puzzled. 'What covers are they?'

'Don't you remember?' she answered. 'I told you I had ordered coverings for the blue bedroom. Seecombe has seen them, and is very much impressed.'

'Oh, yes,' I said, 'yes, I remember now.'

'I have seen nothing like them in my life, sir,' said Seecombe, 'certainly no mansion in these parts has any furnishings to touch them.'

'Ah, but then the stuff is imported from Italy, Seecombe,' said my cousin Rachel. 'There is only one place in London where it is procurable. I was told of it in Florence. Would you like to see the coverings, Philip, or does it not interest you?'

She put the question to me half hopefully, half anxiously, as though wishing for my opinion, yet fearing I should be bored.

I don't know how it was, but I felt myself go scarlet. 'Why, yes,' I said, 'I shall be pleased to look at them.'

We rose from dinner and went into the library. Seecombe followed us, and in a moment or two he and John brought down the coverings and spread them out.

Seecombe was right. There could be no other furnishings like these in Cornwall. I had seen none like them anywhere, either in Oxford or in London. There were many of them. Rich brocades, and heavy silken hangings. They were the kind of stuffs you might see in a museum.

'There is quality for you, sir,' said Seecombe. His voice was hushed. He might have been in church.

'I thought this blue for the bed-hangings,' said my cousin Rachel, 'and the deeper blue and gold for the curtains, and the quilting for the coverlet. What do you say, Philip?'

She looked up at me, anxiously. I did not know how to answer her.

'Do you not like them?' she said to me.

'I like them very much,' I said, 'but' – I felt myself go red again – 'are they not very dear?'

'Oh, yes, they are dear,' she answered, 'any stuff like this is dear, but it will last for years, Philip. Why, your grandson, and great grandson, will be able to sleep in the blue bedroom, with these coverings upon the bed and these hangings for the curtains. Isn't that so, Seecombe?'

'Yes, madam,' said Seecombe.

'The only thing that matters is whether you like them, Philip,' she asked again.

'Why yes,' I said, 'who could help but like them?'

'Then they are yours,' she told me, 'they are a present to you, from me. Take them away, Seecombe. I will write to the place in London in the morning and say we will keep them.'

Seecombe and John folded the coverings and took them from the room. I had the feeling that her eyes were upon me, and rather than meet them I took out my pipe and lit it, taking longer over the job than usual.

'Something's the matter,' she said. 'What is it?'

I was not sure how to answer her. I did not want to hurt her.

'You should not give me a present like that,' I said awkwardly, 'it will cost you far too much.'

'But I want to give them to you,' she said, 'you have done so much for me. It's such a little gift to give, in return.'

Her voice was soft and pleading, and when I glanced up at her there was quite a wounded look about her eyes.

'It's very sweet of you,' I said, 'but I don't think you should do it, all the same.'

'Let me be the judge of that,' she answered, 'and I know, when you see the room finished, you will be pleased.'

I felt wretched, and uncomfortable; not that she should wish to give me a present, which was generous of her and impulsive, and which I would have accepted without thought had it been yesterday. But this evening, since I had read that infernal scrap of letter, I was haunted by the doubt that what she wanted to do for me might turn in some way to her disadvantage; and that in giving way to her I was giving way to something that I did not fully understand.

Presently she said to me, 'That book of gardens is going to be very helpful for our planning here. I had forgotten I had given it to Ambrose. You must look at the engravings. Of course they are not right for this place, but certain features would work in well. A terraced walk, for instance, looking down to the sea across the fields, and on the other side of it a sunken water garden – as they have in one of the villas in Rome where I used to stay. There's an engraving of it in the book. I know just the spot for it, where that old wall used to stand.'

I hardly know how I did it, but I found myself asking her, in a voice at once casual and off-hand, 'Have you always lived in Italy, since you were born?'

'Yes,' she answered, 'did Ambrose never tell you? My mother's people came from Rome, and my father Alexander Coryn was one of those men who find it difficult to settle anywhere. He never could bear England, I think he did not get on very well with his family here, in Cornwall. He liked the life in Rome, and he and my mother suited each other well. But they led a precarious sort of existence, never any money, you know. I was used to it as a child, but as I grew up it was most unsettling.'

'Are they both dead?' I asked.

'Oh, yes, my father died when I was sixteen. Mother and I were alone for five years. Until I married Cosimo Sangalletti. Five fearful years they were too, moving from city to city, not always certain where our next meal would come from. Mine was not a sheltered girlhood, Philip. I was thinking only last Sunday how different from Louise.'

So she had been twenty-one when she married first. The same age as Louise. I wondered how they had lived, she and her mother, until she met Sangalletti. Perhaps they had given lessons in Italian, as she had suggested doing here. Perhaps that was what had made her think of it.

'My mother was very beautiful,' she said, 'quite different from me, except for colouring. Tall, almost massive. And like many women of her type she

went suddenly to pieces, lost her looks, grew fat and careless; I was glad my
father did not live to see it. I was glad he did not live to see many things she
did, or myself either, for that matter.'

Her voice was matter-of-fact and simple, she spoke without bitterness; yet
I thought, looking at her there as she sat by my library fire, how little of her
I really knew, and how little of that past life of hers I would ever know. She
had called Louise sheltered, which was true. And I thought suddenly that
the same held good for me. Here I was, twenty-four, and apart from the
conventional years at Harrow and Oxford I knew nothing of the world but
my own five hundred acres. When a person like my cousin Rachel moved
from one place to another, left one home for a second, and then a third;
married once, then twice; how did it feel? Did she shut the past behind her
like a door and never think of it again, or was she beset with memories from
day to day?

'Was he much older than you?' I said to her.

'Cosimo?' she said. 'Why no, only a year or so. My mother was introduced
to him in Florence, she had always wanted to know the Sangallettis. He
took nearly a year before he made up his mind between my mother and
myself. Then she lost her looks, poor dear, and lost him too. The bargain
I picked up proved a liability. But of course Ambrose must have written you
the whole story. It is not a happy one.'

I was about to say, 'No, Ambrose was more reserved than you ever knew.
If there was something that hurt him, that shocked him, he would pretend
it was not there, that it had not happened. He never told me anything about
your life before you married him, except that Sangalletti was killed fighting,
in a duel.' Instead, I said none of this. I knew suddenly that I did not want
to know either. Not about Sangalletti, nor about her mother and her life in
Florence. I wanted to shut the door on it. And lock it too.

'Yes,' I said, 'yes, Ambrose wrote and told me.'

She sighed, and patted the cushion behind her head.

'Ah, well,' she said, 'it all seems very long ago now. The girl who endured
those years was another person. I had nearly ten years of it, you know,
married to Cosimo Sangalletti. I would not be young again, if you offered
me the world. But then I'm prejudiced.'

'You talk,' I said, 'as if you were ninety-nine.'

'For a woman I very nearly am,' she said. 'I'm thirty-five.'

She looked at me and smiled.

'Oh?' I said. 'I thought you more.'

'Which most women would take as an insult, but I as a compliment,' she
said. 'Thank you, Philip.' And then, before I had time to frame an answer,
she went on, 'What was really on that piece of paper you threw on the fire
this morning?'

The suddenness of the attack caught me unprepared. I stared at her and
swallowed hard.

'The paper?' I hedged. 'What paper?'

'You know perfectly well,' she said; 'the piece of paper with Ambrose's
handwriting upon it, which you burnt so that I should not see.'

I made up my mind then that a half-truth was better than a lie. Although I felt the colour flame into my face, I met her eyes.

'It was a piece torn from a letter,' I said, 'a letter, I think, that he must have been writing to me. He simply expressed himself as worried about expenditure. There was only a line or two, I don't even remember how it went. I threw it in the fire because coming upon it, just at that moment, might have saddened you.'

Rather to my surprise, but to my relief also, the eyes, watching me so intently, relaxed. The hands, holding the rings, fell on her lap.

'Was that all?' she said. 'I wondered so much. . . . I could not understand.'

Thank heaven, though, she accepted my explanation.

'Poor Ambrose,' she said, 'it was a constant source of worry to him, what he considered my extravagance; I wonder that you did not hear of it more often. The life out there was so entirely different from the one he knew at home. He never could bring himself to accept it. And then – good heaven, I cannot blame him – I know at the bottom of his heart he bore resentment against the life I had been obliged to lead before I met him. Those frightful debts, he paid them all.'

I was silent, but as I sat watching her, and smoking, I felt easier in my mind, no longer anxious. The half-truth had been successful, and she was speaking to me now without strain.

'He was so generous,' she said, 'those first months. You cannot imagine, Philip, what it meant to me; at last someone I could trust, and, what was more wonderful still, someone I could love as well. I think if I had asked him for anything on earth he would have given it to me. That was why, when he became ill . . .' She broke off, and her eyes were troubled. 'That was why it was so hard to understand, the way he changed.'

'You mean,' I said, 'that he wasn't generous any more?'

'He was generous, yes,' she said, 'but not in the same way. He would buy me things, presents, pieces of jewellery, almost as though he tried to test me in some way; I can't explain it. And if I asked him for any money, some little necessity for the house, something we had to have – he would not give me the money. He used to look at me, with a strange brooding sort of suspicion; he would ask me why I wanted the money, how I intended to use it, was I going to give it to anyone. . . . Eventually I had to go to Rainaldi, I had to ask Rainaldi, Philip, for money to pay the servants' wages.'

She broke off again, and looked at me.

'Did Ambrose find out that you did that?' I asked.

'Yes,' she said. 'He had never cared for Rainaldi, I believe I told you so before. But when he knew I went to him for money . . . that was the finish, he could not bear him to come to the villa any more. You would hardly credit it, Philip, but I had to go out furtively, when Ambrose was resting, and meet Rainaldi in order to get money for the house.' Suddenly she gestured with her hands, and got up from her chair.

'Oh, God,' she said, 'I did not mean to tell you all this.'

She went over to the window, and pulled aside the curtain, and looked out at the driving rain.

'Why not?' I asked.

'Because I want you to remember him as you knew him here,' she said. 'You have your picture of him, in this house. He was your Ambrose then. Let it stay like that. The last months were mine, and I want no one to share them with me. You, least of all.'

I did not want to share them with her. I wanted her to close all those doors belonging to the past, one by one.

'You know what has happened?' she said, turning round from the window and looking at me. 'We did wrong when we opened those boxes in the room upstairs. We should have let them stay there. We were wrong to touch his things. I felt it from the first moment, when I opened the trunk and saw his dressing-gown and the slippers. We have let something loose that was not with us before. Some sort of bitter feeling.' She had become very white. Her hands were clasped in front of her. 'I have not forgotten,' she said, 'those letters that you threw into the fire, and burnt. I pushed the thought of them away, but to-day, since we opened up the trunks, it is just as though I had read them once again.'

I got up from my chair and stood with my back to the fire. I did not know what to say to her as she paced up and down the room.

'He said, in his letter, that I watched him,' she went on. 'Of course I watched him, lest he should do himself some damage. Rainaldi wanted me to have the nuns in from the convent to help me, but I would not; had I done that, Ambrose would have said they were keepers, brought in by me to spy upon him. He trusted no one. The doctors were good and patient men, but more often than not he refused to see them. One by one, he asked me to dismiss the servants. In the end, only Giuseppe remained. He trusted him. He said he had dog's eyes. . . .'

She broke off, and turned away. I thought of the servant from the lodge by the villa gate, and his desire to spare me pain. It was strange that Ambrose too had believed in those honest, faithful eyes. And I had only looked upon the servant once.

'There is no need to talk of all that now,' I said to her: 'it does no good to Ambrose, and it only tortures you. As to myself, what happened between you and him is no concern of mine. That is all over and done with and forgotten. The villa was not his home. Nor, when you married Ambrose, was it yours either. This is your home.'

She turned and looked at me. 'Sometimes,' she said slowly, 'you are so like him that I become afraid. I see your eyes, with that same expression, turned upon me; and it is as though, after all, he had not died, and everything that was endured must be endured once more. I could not bear it again, not that suspicion, not that bitterness, going on and on, day after day, night after night.'

As she spoke, I had a clear picture of the villa Sangalletti. I saw the little court, and the laburnum tree as it would be in spring, with yellow blossom. I saw the chair there, with Ambrose sitting in it and his stick beside him. I felt the whole dark silence of the place. I smelt the musty air, I watched the dripping fountain. And for the first time the woman who looked down from the balcony above was not a figment of my imagination, but was Rachel. She looked at Ambrose with the same pleading look, that look of suffering, of supplication. Suddenly, I felt very old, and very wise, and full of a new strength I did not understand. I held out my hands to her.

'Rachel. Come here,' I said.

She came across the room to me, and she put her hands in mine.

'There is no bitter feeling in this house,' I said to her. 'The house is mine. Bitterness goes with people when they die. Those clothes are all packed up and put away. They have nothing any more to do with either of us. From now on you are going to remember Ambrose as I remember him. We'll keep his old hat there, on the settle in the hall. And the stick, with the others, in the stand. You belong here now, just as he did, just as I do. We are all three of us part of the place together. Do you understand?'

She looked up at me. She did not take away her hands.

'Yes,' she said.

I felt strangely moved, as if all that I did and said was laid down for me and planned, while at the same time a small still voice whispered to me in some dark cell of matter, 'You can never go back upon this moment. Never . . . never . . .' We stood, holding each other's hands, and she said to me, 'Why are you so good to me, Philip?'

I remembered that in the morning, when she cried, she had rested her head against my heart. I had put my arms about her, for a moment, and laid my face against her hair. I wanted it to happen again. More than anything I had ever known. But to-night she did not cry. To-night she did not come and rest her head against my heart. She just stood there, holding my hands.

'I'm not good to you,' I said; 'I only want you to be happy.'

She moved away and picked up her candlestick to take to bed, and as she went from the room she said to me, 'Good night, Philip, and God bless you. One day you may come to know some of the happiness that I knew once.'

I heard her go upstairs, and I sat down and stared into the library fire. It seemed to me that if there was any bitterness left in the house it did not come from her, nor from Ambrose, but was a seed deep in my own heart, which I should never tell her of and she need never know. The old sin of jealousy I thought buried and forgotten was with me once again. But this time I was jealous, not of Rachel, but of Ambrose, whom hitherto I had known and loved best in the whole world.

Chapter Sixteen

November and December passed very swiftly, or so it seemed to me. Usually, as the days shortened and the weather worsened, when there would be little to do outside and it grew dark by half-past four, I had found the long evenings in the house monotonous. Never a great reader, and unsociable, so that I did not care to shoot with my neighbours or go out and dine with them, I used to be champing for the turn of the year, when with Christmas behind me and the shortest day gone I could look forward to the spring. And spring comes early, in the west. Even before New Year's Day the first shrubs are in bloom. Yet this autumn passed without monotony. The leaves fell, and the trees were bare, and all the Barton acres lay brown and soggy with the rain, while a chill wind nipped the sea and turned it grey. But I did not look upon it with despondency.

We settled down to a routine, my cousin Rachel and myself, which seldom varied, and it seemed to suit us well. When the weather permitted it, she would spend the morning in the grounds directing Tamlyn and the gardeners about the planting, or watching the progress of the terraced walk we had decided upon, which had necessitated the employment of extra men, besides those who worked in the woods; while I did my usual business about the estate, riding to and fro amongst the farms, or visiting others in the outlying districts, where I held land also. We met at half-past twelve for a brief meal, cold usually, a ham, or pie, with cake. It was the servants' dinner hour, and we waited on ourselves. It would be my first sight of her for the day, for she always took breakfast in her room.

When I was out and about on the estate, or in my office, and heard the clock on the belfry strike noon, followed almost at once by the great clanging bell that summoned the men to their dinner, I would be aware of a rising excitement within me, a quick lifting of the heart.

What I was employed upon would seem, all of a sudden, to lack interest. If I was riding out of doors, in the park, say, or in the woods or the nearby acres, and the sound of the clock and the bell echoed through the air – for it travelled far, and I have heard it three miles distant when the wind was with it – I would turn Gypsy's head for home with impatience, almost as if I feared, by delaying any longer without doors, I might miss one moment of the luncheon hour. And in my office it would be the same. I would stare at the papers on the desk before me, bite on my pen, tilt backwards on my chair; and what I had been writing would become, of a sudden, of no importance whatsoever. That letter could wait, those figures need not be reckoned, that piece of business over in Bodmin could be decided upon another time; and pushing everything aside I would leave the office, and pass through the court-yard to the house and so the dining-room.

She was usually there before me, to give me welcome and wish me a good morning. Often she laid a sprig beside my plate, as a sort of offering, which I would put into my button-hole; or there would be some new cordial for me to taste, one of those herb brews of which she seemed to have a hundred recipes and was forever giving to the cook to try. She had been several weeks with me in the house before Seecombe told me, in deadly secret, behind his hand, that the cook had been going to her every day to ask for orders, and that was the reason why we now fed so well.

'The mistress,' Seecombe said, 'had not wished Mr. Ashley to know, lest it should be thought presumptuous of her.'

I laughed, and did not tell her that I knew; but sometimes, for the fun of it, I would remark upon some dish that we were having, and exclaim, 'I cannot think what has come over them in the kitchen. The boys are turning into chefs from France,' and she would answer me in innocence, 'Do you like it? Is it something better than you had before?'

One and all called her 'the mistress' now, and I did not mind it. I think it pleased me and gave me, too, a sort of pride.

When we had eaten luncheon she would go upstairs to rest, or if it was a Tuesday or a Thursday I might order the carriage for her, and Wellington would drive her about the neighbourhood to return the calls that had been made upon her. Sometimes, if I had business on the way, I would ride with her for a mile or so, and then get out of the carriage and let her go her way. She would take great care about her person, when she went calling. Her best mantle, and her new veil and bonnet. I would sit with my back to the horses, in the carriage, so that I could look at her; and, I think to tease me, she would not lift her veil.

'Now to your gossip,' I would say, 'now to your little shocks and scandals. I would give much to become a fly upon the wall.'

'Come with me,' she would answer; 'it would be very good for you.'

'Not on your life. You can tell me all, at dinner.'

And I would stand in the road and watch the carriage bowl away, while from the window blew the wisp of a handkerchief to taunt me. I would not see her again until we dined at five, and the intervening hours became something to be gone through for the evening's sake. Whether I was on business, or about the estate, or talking with people, all the time I had a sense of urgency, an impatience to be done. How was the time? I looked at Ambrose's watch. Still only half-past four? How the hours dragged. And coming back to the house, by way of the stables, I would know at once if she had returned, for I would see the carriage in the coach-house and the horses being fed and watered. Going into the house, passing into the library and the drawing-room, I would see both rooms were empty, and this would mean she had gone up to her rooms to rest. She always rested before dinner. Then I would take a bath, or wash, and change, and go down into the library below to wait for her. My impatience mounted as the hands of the clock drew nearer to five. I would leave the door of the library open, so that I could hear her step.

First would come the patter of the dogs – I counted for nothing with them now, they followed her like shadows – and then the rustle of her gown as it swept the stairs. It was, I think, the moment I loved best in the whole day. There was something in the sound that gave me such a shock of anticipation, such a feeling of expectancy, that I hardly knew what to do or what to say when she came into the room. I don't know what stuff her gowns were made of, whether of stiff silk, or satin, or brocade, but they seemed to sweep the floor, and lift, and sweep again; and whether it was the gown itself that floated, or she wearing it and moving forward with such grace, but the library, that had seemed dark and austere before she entered, would be suddenly alive.

A new softness came to her by candlelight that was not with her in the day. It was as if the brightness of morning and the duller shades of afternoon were given up to purposes of work, of practicality, making a briskness of movement that was definite and cool; and now with evening closed in, the shutters fastened, the weather banished, and the house withdrawn into itself, she shone with a radiance that had lain concealed about her person until now. There was more colour to her cheeks and to her hair, great depth to her eyes, and whether she turned her head to speak, or moved to the bookcase to pick up a volume, or bent to pat Don as he lay stretched out before the fire, there was an easy grace in all she did which gave to every movement fascination. I wondered, in these moments, how I could ever have thought her unremarkable.

Seecombe would announce dinner, and we would pass into the dining-room and take our places, I at the head of the table, she at my right hand, and it seemed to me this had always happened, there was nothing new in it, and nothing strange, and I had never sat there alone, in my old jacket, unchanged, with a book propped up in front of me so that I did not have to talk to Seecombe. Yet, if it had always happened, it would not have seemed stimulating to me, as it did now, with the mere process of eating and drinking becoming, in a sense, a new adventure.

The excitement did not lessen with the passing weeks, rather it increased, so that I would find myself making excuses to be about the house, for the sake of five minutes or so, when I might catch a glimpse of her, thus making an addition to the regular time of midday and evening when we would be together.

She might be in the library, or passing through the hall upon some business, or waiting in the drawing-room for her callers, and she would smile at me and say, in some surprise, 'Philip, what brings you home at such an hour?' causing me to think up some invention. As to the gardens, I who had yawned and kicked my heels in the old days when Ambrose had tried to interest me, I now made a point of being present whenever there should be a consultation in the plantation or upon the terrace walk, and again after dinner, in the evenings, we would look through her Italian books together, compare the engravings and debate, with much argument, what could best be copied. I think if she had suggested we should build a replica of the Roman Forum itself, above the Barton acres, I would have agreed with her. I said yes, and no, and very fine indeed, and shook my head, but I never really listened. It was watching her interest in the business that gave me pleasure, watching her consider thoughtfully between one picture and another, her brows knit, a pen in her hand to mark the page, and then to watch the hands themselves that turned from one volume to another.

We did not always sit below in the library. Sometimes she would ask me to go with her upstairs, to aunt Phoebe's boudoir, and we would spread out the books and plans of gardens upon the floor. I was host in the library down below, but here, in her boudoir, she was hostess. I am not sure I did not like it better. We lost formality. Seecombe did not bother us – by some great measure of tact she had got him to dispense with the solemnity of the silver tea tray – and she would brew tisana for us both instead, which she said was a continental custom and much better for the eyes and skin.

These after-dinner hours passed all too swiftly, and I would hope that she would forget to ask the time, but the wretched clock in the belfry, far too close to our heads to strike ten o'clock and not be noticed, always shattered the peace.

'I had no idea it was so late,' she used to say, rising to her feet and closing the books. I knew this was the signal for dismissal. Even the trick of lingering by the door in conversation did not pass with her. Ten o'clock had struck, and I must go. Sometimes she gave me her hand to kiss. Sometimes she offered me a cheek. Sometimes she patted me upon the shoulder, as she might have done a puppy. Never again did she come close to me, or take my face between her hands as she had done that evening when she lay in bed. I did not look for it, I did not hope for it; but when I had said goodnight and gone back along the corridor to my own room, opened up my shutters and stared out at the silent garden, and heard the distant murmur of the sea breaking in the little bay beneath the woods, I would feel oddly lonely, as a child does when holiday is done.

The evening, which had built itself up, hour by hour throughout the day in fevered fancy, was over now. It would seem long before it came again. And neither my mind nor my body was ready for repose. In the old days, before she had come to the house, I used to doze before the fire in winter after dining, and then, stretching and yawning, clump my way upstairs, happy to roll into my bed and sleep till seven. Now, it was otherwise. I could have walked all night. I could have talked till dawn. To do the first was foolish. To do the second, an impossibility. Therefore I flung myself down in a chair before the open window, and smoked, and stared out across the lawn; and sometimes it was one or two in the morning before I undressed and went to bed, and all I had done was to sit there brooding in my chair, thinking of nothing, wasting the silent hours.

In December the first frosts came with the full moon, and then my nights of vigil held a quality harder to bear. There was a sort of beauty to them, cold and clear, that caught at the heart and made me stare in wonder. From my windows the long lawns dipped to the meadows, and the meadows to the

sea, and all of them were white with frost, and white too under the moon.
The trees that fringed the lawns were black and still. Rabbits came out and
pricked about the grass, then scattered to their burrows; and suddenly, from
the hush and stillness, I heard that high sharp bark of a vixen, with the little
sob that follows it, eerie, unmistakable, unlike any other call that comes by
night, and out of the woods I saw the lean low body creep and run out upon
the lawn, and hide again where the trees would cover it. Later I heard the
call again, away in the distance, in the open park, and now the full moon
topped the trees and held the sky, and nothing stirred on the lawns beneath
my window. I wondered if Rachel slept, in the blue bedroom; or if, like me,
she left her curtains wide. The clock that had driven me to bed at ten struck
one, struck two, and I thought that here about me was a wealth of beauty
that we might have shared.

People who mattered not could take the humdrum world. But this was
not the world, it was enchantment; and all of it was mine. I did not want
it for myself alone.

So like a weather-glass I swung, from moods of exultation and excitement
to a low level sometimes of dullness and depression, when, remembering her
promise to remain with me for a brief time only, I wondered how much
longer she would stay. If, after Christmas, she would turn to me and say,
'Well, Philip, next week I go to London.' The spell of hard weather put a
stop to all the planting, and little more could be done now till the spring.
The terrace might be completed, for this was better done when dry, but with
the plan to follow the men could work without her very well. Any day she
might decide to go, and I would not be able to think of an excuse to hold her
back.

In old days, at Christmas, when Ambrose had been home, he had given
dinner to the tenants on Christmas Eve. I had let it lapse, the last winters
of his absence, because when he had returned from travelling he held the
dinner on mid-summer day. Now I decided to give the dinner once again,
as of long custom, if only for the reason that Rachel would be there.

When I was a child it had been the highlight of my Christmas. The men
used to bring in a tall fir tree about a week before Christmas Eve, and put
it in the long room over the coach houses, where we held the dinner. I was
not supposed to know that it was there. But when no one was about,
generally at midday, when the servants would be eating, I used to go round
by the back and climb up the steps to the side-door leading into the long
room, and there I would see the great tree, standing in its tub at the far end,
and stacked against the wall, ready to place in rows, were the long trestle
tables for the dinner. I never helped to decorate until my first holiday from
Harrow. The promotion was tremendous. I had never felt so proud. As a
little lad I had sat beside Ambrose at the top table, but on my promotion I
headed a table of my own.

Now, once again, I gave my orders to the woodmen, in fact I went out
myself into the woods to choose the tree. Rachel was all delight. No
celebration could have pleased her better. She held earnest consultation with
Seecombe and the cook, she visited the larders, and the storage chambers,

and the game-house; she even prevailed upon my male household to allow two girls from the Barton to come up and make French pastry under her supervision. All was excitement, and mystery too; because I would have it that she should not see the tree, and she insisted that I must not know what would be put before us for the dinner.

Packages arrived for her, and were whisked away upstairs. When I knocked upon her boudoir door I would hear crackling of paper, and then, an age afterwards it seemed, her voice would answer me, 'Come in.' And she would be kneeling on the floor, her eyes bright, her cheeks flushed, with a covering flung over several objects strewn about the carpet, and she would tell me not to look.

I was back to childhood once again, back to the old fever of standing in my nightshirt tip-toe on the stairs, hearing the murmur of voices from below, and Ambrose coming suddenly from the library and laughing at me, 'Go up to bed, you rascal, I'll flay the hide off you.'

One thing gave me anxiety. What could I give Rachel for a present? I took a day in Truro, browsing in the bookshops for a book on gardens, but could find nothing. And what was more, the books from Italy she had brought with her were finer than any I could give her. I had no idea what present pleased a woman. My godfather used to buy stuff to make a gown, when he gave anything to Louise, but Rachel wore mourning only. I could not give her that. Once, I remember, Louise had been much delighted with a locket that he had brought from London. She used to wear it of an evening, when she ate Sunday dinner with us. And then the solution came to me.

There must be something, amongst the jewels belonging to my family, that I could give to Rachel. They were not kept at home in the safe, with the Ashley documents and papers, but at the bank. Ambrose had thought it best, in case of fire. I had no knowledge what was there. I had a hazy recollection of going to the bank one day with Ambrose, when I was very young, and of his picking up some necklace and telling me, smiling, that it had belonged to our grandmother, and that my mother had worn it on her wedding-day, but for the day only, as a loan, my father not being in the direct line of succession, and that one day, if I behaved myself well, Ambrose would permit me to give it to my wife. I realised, now, that whatever there was in the bank belonged to me. Or would do, in three months' time; but that was quibbling.

My godfather would know, of course, what jewels there were, but he had gone up to Exeter on business and would not be home until Christmas Eve, when he and Louise were invited to the dinner. I determined to go to the bank myself and demand to see the jewels.

Mr. Couch received me with his usual courtesy, and taking me into his private room, facing the harbour, he listened to my request.

'I take it Mr. Kendall would have no objection?' he asked.

'Of course not,' I said impatiently, 'the matter is quite understood.' Which was untruthful, but at twenty-four, within a few months of my birthday, to have to ask my godfather for permission to do every little thing was quite ridiculous. And it riled me.

Mr. Couch sent to the vaults for the jewels. They came up, in sealed boxes. He broke the seal, and, placing a cloth on the desk in front of him, laid the jewels out upon it, one by one.

I had no idea the collection was so fine. There were rings, bracelets, ear-rings, brooches; and many of the pieces went together, such as a ruby head-piece for the hair and ruby ear-rings to go with it, likewise a sapphire bracelet and pendant and ring. Yet as I looked at them, not liking to touch them even with my finger, I remembered, with disappointment, that Rachel was in mourning and wore no coloured stones. If I presented her with these, it would be pointless; she would have no use for them.

Then Mr. Couch opened the last box, and drew from it a collar of pearls. There were four strands. They fastened round the neck like a band, with a single diamond clasp. I recognised it instantly. It was the necklace that Ambrose had shown me as a child.

'I like this,' I said, 'this is the finest thing in the whole collection. I remember my cousin Ambrose showing it to me.'

'Why, there might be a difference of opinion,' said Mr. Couch; 'for my part, I would price the rubies highest. But there is family feeling about the pearl collar. Your grandmother, Mrs Ambrose Ashley, wore it first as a bride, at the Court of St. James. Then your aunt, Mrs. Philip, had it given to her, as a matter of course, when the estate passed down to your uncle. Various members of the family have worn it on their wedding-day. Your own mother was amongst them; in point of fact, I think she was the last to do so. Your cousin, Mrs. Ambrose Ashley, would never permit it to go out of the country, when there were weddings elsewhere.' He held the collar in his hand, and the light from the window fell upon the smooth round pearls.

'Yes,' he said, 'it is a beautiful thing. And no woman has put it on for five-and-twenty years. I attended your mother's wedding. She was a pretty creature. It became her well.'

I put out my hand and took the collar from him.

'Well, I want to keep it now,' I said, and I placed the collar with its wrappings in the box. He looked a little taken aback.

'I do not know if that is wise, Mr. Ashley,' he said. 'If this should be lost or mislaid it would be a terrible thing.'

'It won't be lost,' I answered briefly.

He did not seem happy, and I made haste to go, lest he should produce some argument more forceful.

'If you are worried what my guardian will say,' I told him, 'please rest assured. I will make it right with him when he returns from Exeter.'

'I hope so,' said Mr. Couch, 'but I had preferred it had he been present. Of course in April, when you come into the property legally, it would not matter if you took the whole collection, and did as you wished with them. I should not advise such a step, but it would be strictly legal.'

I held out my hand to him and wished him a pleasant Christmas and rode home, much elated. If I had searched the whole country I could not have found a better present for her. Thank heaven pearls were white. And it made a bond to think that the last woman to wear them had been my mother.

I would tell her that. Now I could face the prospect of Christmas Eve with a lighter heart.

Two days to wait. . . . The weather was fine, the frost was light, and there was all the promise of a clear dry evening for the dinner. The servants were much excited, and on the morning of Christmas Eve, when the trestle tables and the benches had been set down the room, and the knives and forks and platters all laid ready, with evergreen hanging from the beams, I asked Seecombe and the lads to come with me and decorate the tree. Seecombe made himself master of the ceremony. He stood a little apart from the rest of us, to give himself a longer view, and as we turned the tree this way and that, and lifted one branch and then another, to balance the frosty fir cones on it and the holly berries, he waved his hands at us, looking for all the world like the conductor of a string sextet.

'The angle does not please me, Mr. Philip,' he said, 'the tree would appear to better advantage if moved a trifle to the left. Ah! too far . . . Yes, that is better. John, the fourth branch on the right is bent. Raise it somewhat. Tch, tch . . . your touch is heavy. Spread out the branches, Arthur, spread them. The tree must seem to be standing as nature placed it. Don't stamp upon the berries, Jim. Mr. Philip, let it stay now as it is. One further movement, and the whole is wrecked.'

I had never thought him to possess such a sense of artistry.

He stood back, his hands under his coat-tails, his eyes near closed. 'Mr. Philip,' he said to me, 'we have attained perfection.' I saw young John nudge Arthur in the ribs and turn away.

Dinner was set to start at five. The Kendalls and the Pascoes would be the only 'carriage folk,' as the expression had it. The rest would come by wagonette or trap, or even on their own feet, those who lived near by. I had written out all the names on pieces of paper, and placed them on the appropriate platters. Those who had difficulty in reading, or who could not read at all, had neighbours who could do so. There were three tables. I was to head one, with Rachel at the further end. The second was headed by Billy Rowe from the Barton, and the third by Peter Johns, from Coombe.

The custom was for all the company to be assembled in the long room, ready seated, soon after five; and when everyone was in place we would walk into the room. When dinner was over, Ambrose and I used to give the people their presents from the tree, always money for the men, and new shawls for the women, and hampers of food for all of them. The presents never varied. Any change of routine would have shocked them, every one. This Christmas, though, I had asked Rachel to give out the presents with me.

Before dressing for dinner, I had sent along to Rachel's room the collar of pearls. I had left it in its wrappings, but had placed a note inside. On the note I had written these words, 'My mother wore this last. Now it belongs to you. I want you to wear it tonight, and always. Philip.'

I had my bath, and dressed, and was ready before a quarter to five.

The Kendalls and the Pascoes would not call for us at the house; the custom was for them to go straight to the long room, where they chatted with the tenants and helped to break the ice. Ambrose had always considered this a sound idea. The servants would be in the long room also, and Ambrose and I used to walk though the stone passages at the back of the house, and across the court, and out and up the flight of steps to the long room above the coach-houses. Tonight, Rachel and I would walk the passages alone.

I came downstairs and waited in the drawing-room. I felt some trepidation, as I stood there, for never in my life had I given a present to a woman. It might be that it was a breach of etiquette, that flowers only were acceptable, or books, or pictures. What if she should be angry, as she had been over that business of the quarterly allowance, and should imagine, in some queer fashion, that I did this to insult her? It was a desperate thought. The passing minutes were slow torture. At last I heard her footstep on the stairs. No dogs preceded her to-night. They had all been locked early in their kennels.

She came slowly; the familiar rustle of her gown drew near. The door was open, and she came into the room and stood before me. She wore deep black, as I had expected, but I had not see the gown before. It stood out, away from her, clinging only about the bodice and the waist, and the stuff had a sheen to it as though the light was upon it. Her shoulders were bare. She had dressed her hair higher than usual, the roll of it was looped up and drawn back, showing her ears. Around her neck was the collar of pearls. It was the only piece of jewellery upon her person. It glowed soft and white against her skin. I had never seen her look so radiant, or so happy. Louise and the Pascoes had been right after all. Rachel was beautiful.

She stood there a moment watching me, and then she put out her hands to me and said, 'Philip.' I walked towards her. I stood in front of her. She put her arms about me and held me to her. There were tears in her eyes, but tonight I did not mind. She took her arms from my shoulders, and raised them to the back of my head, and touched my hair.

Then she kissed me. Not as she had done before. And as I stood there, holding her, I thought to myself, 'It was not yearning for home, nor sickness of the blood, nor fever of the brain – but for this, that Ambrose died.'

I kissed her in return. In the belfry the clock struck five. She said nothing to me, nor I to her. She gave me her hand. We went down the dark kitchen passages together, across the court, and so to the long room above the coach-house, where the windows were brightly lit. To the laughing surge of voices and the bright expectant faces.

Chapter Seventeen

The whole company stood up as we came into the room. The tables were pushed back, there was shuffling of feet, the murmur of voices hushed; the heads of one and all turned round to look at us. Rachel paused a moment on the threshold; I think she had not expected such a sea of faces. Then she saw the Christmas tree at the far end, and gave a cry of pleasure. The pause was broken, and a murmur of sympathy and gladness at her surprise arose from everyone.

We took our places at our respective ends of the top table, and Rachel sat down. The rest of us did the same, and at once a clamour of chat and talk began, with clattering of knives, and moving of platters, and each man jostling his neighbour in laughter and apology. I had for partner on my right Mrs. Bill Rowe, from the Barton, sprigged out to beat all comers in her muslins, and I noticed that Mrs. Johns of Coombe, upon my left, looked at her in disfavour. I had forgotten, in my desire for protocol, that neither of them 'spoke' to the other. Some rift, dating back to a misunderstanding about eggs on market day, had lasted fifteen years. No matter, I would be gallant to the pair of them and cover all distress. Flagons of cider would come to my assistance, and seizing the nearest jug I helped them, and myself, most liberally, then turned to the bill of fare. The kitchens had done us well. Never, in my long memories of Christmas dinners, had we been offered plenty such as this. Roast goose, roast turkey, sides of beef and mutton, great smoked hams decorated with a frill, pastries and pies of all shapes and sizes, puddings bulging with dried fruits; and between the heavier fare were platters of that delicate fragile pastry, airy as thistledown, that Rachel had concocted with the Barton maids.

Smiles of anticipation and of greed wreathed the faces of the hungry guests, my own amongst them, and already great gusts of laughter came from the other tables, where, undaunted by the immediate presence of the 'master', the broader-tongued among my tenants let themselves go with loosening of belts and collars. I heard Jack Libby, of bibulous eye, utter hoarsely to his neighbour – I think he had already had a glass or two of cider on the road – 'By Gor . . . after this lot they could feed us to the crows and we wouldn't feel et.' Little thin-lipped Mrs. Johns upon my left pricked at her wing of goose with a fork poised between her fingers like a quill, and the fellow whispered to her, with a wink in my direction, 'Go to it 'm'dear, with thumb and finger. Tear 'un asunder.'

It was then I noticed that each one of us had a small package put beside his plate, the packages addressed in Rachel's handwriting. Everybody seemed to perceive this at the same time, and for a brief moment the food was forgotten, in the excited tearing of the paper. I watched, and waited, before opening my own. I realised, with a sudden ache in my heart, what she had done. She had given every man and woman assembled there a present. She had wrapped them up herself, and enclosed with each a note. Nothing big, or fine, but a little trifle that would please them well. So that was the reason for the mysterious wrappings behind the boudoir door. I understood it all.

When each of my neighbours had fallen to their food again I opened my own. I unwrapped it on my knees, beneath the table, determined that only I myself should see what had been given me. It was a gold chain for my keys, with a disk upon it bearing our initials, P.A.R.A., and the date beneath. I held it for a moment in my hands, then put it, furtively, into my waistcoat pocket. I looked up at her and smiled. She was watching me. I raised my glass to her, she raised hers in reply. God! I was happy.

Dinner proceeded, uproarious and gay. Greasy platters, heaped with food, were emptied, I know not how. Glasses were filled, and filled again. Someone, halfway down the table, began to sing, and the song was taken up and joined by those from the other tables. Boots hummed a measure on the floor, knives and forks beat time upon the platters, bodies swayed to and fro in rollicking rhythmic fashion; and thin-lipped Mrs. Johns of Coombe told me that, for a man, my lashes were far too long. I helped her to more cider.

At last, remembering how Ambrose timed his moment to perfection, I rapped long and loud upon the table. The voices died away. 'Those who desire to do so,' I said, 'may go outside, and then return again. In five minutes' time Mrs. Ashley and I will give the presents from the tree. Thank you, ladies and gentlemen.'

The pressure to the doors was precisely what I had expected. And with a smile on my lips I watched Seecombe, walking stiff and straight yet treading the ground lest it should give way beneath his feet, bring up the rear. Those who remained pushed the benches and the trestles against the wall. After the presents had been given from the tree, and we had departed, those who were able to do so would take their partners in a dance. High revelry would last until midnight. I used to listen to the stamping, as a boy, from my nursery window. To-night I made my way over to the little group standing by the tree. The vicar was there, and Mrs. Pascoe, three daughters and a curate. Likewise my godfather and Louise. Louise looked well, but a trifle pale. I shook hands with them. Mrs. Pascoe gushed at me, all teeth, 'You have surpassed yourself. Never have we enjoyed ourselves so much. The girls are quite in ecstasy.'

They looked it, with one curate between three of them.

'I'm glad you thought it went off well,' I said, and, turning to Rachel, 'Have you been happy?'

Her eyes met mine and smiled. 'What do you think?' she said. 'So happy, I could cry.'

I saluted my godfather, 'Good evening to you, sir, and happy Christmas,' I said. 'How did you find Exeter?'

'Cold,' he said shortly, 'cold and drear.'

His manner was abrupt. He stood with one hand behind his back, the other tugged at his white moustache. I wondered if something about the dinner had upset him. Had the cider flowed too freely for his liking? Then I saw him stare at Rachel. His eyes were fixed upon the collar of pearls around her throat. He saw me staring, and he turned away. For a moment I felt back again in the Fourth Form at Harrow, with the master discovering the crib hidden under my Latin book. Then I shrugged my shoulders. I was Philip Ashley, aged four-and-twenty years. And no one in the world, certainly not my godfather, could dictate to me to whom I should, or should not, give Christmas presents. I wondered if Mrs. Pascoe had already dropped some fell remark. Possibly good manners would prevent her. And anyway, she could not know the collar. My mother had been dead before Mr. Pascoe held the living. Louise had noticed it. That was already plain. I saw her blue eyes waver towards Rachel, and then drop again.

The people came stumping back into the room. Laughing, murmuring, pressing together, they came nearer to the tree, as Rachel and I took our stand before it. Then I bent to the presents, and, reading out the names, gave the parcels to Rachel; and one by one they came to take their gifts. She stood there, before the tree, flushed, and gay, and smiling. It was all I could do to read the names instead of looking at her. 'Thank you, God bless you, sir,' they said to me; and passing on to her, 'Thank you, m'am. God bless you, too.'

It took us the best part of half an hour to give the presents and to say a word to each. When it was over and done with, the last present accepted with a curtsey, a sudden silence fell. The people, standing all together in a great group against the wall, waited for me. 'A happy Christmas to you, one and all,' I said. And back came the shout from the whole lot of them as one, 'A happy Christmas to you, sir, and to Mrs. Ashley.'

Then Billy Rowe, his one lock plastered down upon his brow for the occasion, piped up in a high reedy voice, 'Three cheers, then, for the pair of 'en.' And the cheers that echoed through the rafters of the long room nearly shook the boards and brought us all down upon the carriages below. I glanced at Rachel. There were tears now. I shook my head at her. She smiled, and blinked them back, and gave her hand to me. I saw my godfather looking at us with a stiff nipped face. I thought, most unpardonably, of that retort, passed from one schoolboy to another, to silence criticism. 'If you don't like it, you can go. . . .' The blast would be appropriate. Instead of which I smiled, and drawing Rachel's hand inside my arm I led her back from the long room to the house.

Someone, young John I should imagine, for Seecombe had been moving as though to a distant drum, had bolted back to the drawing-room between present giving and placed cake and wine in the drawing-room. We were too well-filled. Both remained untouched, though I saw the curate crumble a sugared bun. Perhaps he eats for three. Then Mrs. Pascoe, who was surely born into this world, heaven save her, to wreck all harmony with her blabbing tongue, turned to Rachel and said, 'Mrs. Ashley, forgive me, I really must comment upon it. What a beautiful pearl collar you are wearing. I have had eyes for nothing else all evening.'

Rachel smiled at her, and touched the collar with her fingers. 'Yes,' she said, 'it is a very proud possession.'

'Proud indeed,' said my godfather drily; 'it's worth a small fortune.'

I think only Rachel and myself noticed his tone of voice. She glanced at my godfather, puzzled, and from him to me, and was about to speak when I moved forward. 'I think the carriages have come,' I said.

I went and stood by the drawing-room door. Even Mrs. Pascoe, usually deaf to suggestions of departure, saw by my manner that her evening had reached its climax. 'Come, girls,' she said, 'you must all be tired, and we have a busy day before us. No rest for a clergyman's family, Mr. Ashley, on Christmas Day.' I escorted the Pascoe family to the door. Luckily, I had been right in my surmise. Their carriage was ready waiting. They took the curate with them. He crouched like a small bird between two daughters, fully fledged. As they drove away the Kendall carriage drew forward in its turn. I turned back to the drawing-room and found it empty, save for my godfather.

'Where are the others?' I asked.

'Louise and Mrs. Ashley went upstairs,' he said; 'they will be down in a moment or two. I am glad of the opportunity to have a word with you, Philip.'

I crossed over to the fireplace and stood there, with my hands behind my back.

'Yes?' I said. 'What is it?'

He did not answer for a moment. He was plainly embarrassed.

'I had no chance to see you before I left for Exeter,' he said, 'or I would have spoken of this before. The fact is, Philip, I have had a communication from the bank that I find decidedly disturbing.'

The collar, of course, I thought. Well, that was my affair.

'From Mr. Couch, I suppose?' I said to him.

'Yes,' he answered. 'He advises me, as is very right and proper, that Mrs. Ashley is already several hundred pounds overdrawn on her account.'

I felt myself go cold. I stared back at him; then the tension snapped, and the colour flamed into my face.

'Oh?' I said.

'I don't understand it,' he continued, pacing the floor. 'She can have few expenses here. She is living as your guest, and her wants must be few. The only thing that occurs to me is that she is sending the money out of the country.'

I went on standing by the fire and my heart was beating against my ribs. 'She is very generous,' I said, 'you must have noticed that, to-night. A present for each one of us. That cannot be done on a few shillings.'

'Several hundred pounds would pay for them a dozen times over,' he replied. 'I don't doubt her generosity, but presents alone cannot account for an overdraft.'

'She has taken it upon herself to spend money on the house,' I said. 'There have been furnishings bought for the blue bedroom. You can take all that into consideration.'

'Possibly,' said my godfather, 'but nevertheless the fact remains that the sum we decided to give her quarterly has already been doubled, nearly trebled, by the amount she has withdrawn. What are we to decide for the future?'

'Double, treble, the amount we give her now,' I said. 'Obviously what we gave was not sufficient.'

'But that is preposterous, Philip,' he exclaimed. 'No woman, living as she does here, could possibly desire to spend so much. A lady of quality in London would be hard put to it to fritter so much away.'

'There may be debts,' I said, ' of which we know nothing. There may be creditors, pressing for money, back in Florence. It is not our business. I want you to increase the allowance and cover that overdraft.'

He stood before me, with pursed lips. I wanted the matter over, done with. My ears were awake for the sound of footsteps on the stairs.

'Another thing,' he said, uneasily. 'You had no right, Philip, to take that collar from the bank. You realise, don't you, that it is part of the collection, part of the estate, and you have not the right to remove it?'

'It is mine,' I said; 'I can do what I like with my property.'

'The property is not yet yours,' he said, 'for a further three months.'

'What of it?' I gestured. 'Three months pass quickly. No harm can come to the collar in her keeping.'

He glanced up at me.

'I am not so sure,' he said.

The implication in his words drove me to fury.

'Good God!' I said. 'What are you suggesting? That she might take that collar and sell it?'

For a moment he did not reply. He tugged at his moustache.

'Since going to Exeter,' he said, 'I have come to learn a little more about your cousin Rachel.'

'What the devil do you mean?' I asked.

His eyes went from me to the door, then back again.

'It happened that I came across old friends,' he said, 'people you would not know, who are great travellers. They have wintered in Italy and France over a period of years. It seems that they met your cousin when she was married to her first husband, Sangalletti.'

'Well?'

'Both were notorious. For unbridled extravagance, and, I must add, for loose living also. The duel in which Sangalletti died was fought because of another man. These people said that when they learnt of Ambrose Ashley's marriage to the countess Sangalletti they were horrified. They predicted that she would run through his entire fortune within a few months. Luckily, it was not so. Ambrose died before it was possible for her to do it. I am sorry, Philip. But this news has much disturbed me.' Once again he paced the floor.

'I did not think that you would fall so low as to listen to travellers' tales,'

I said to him. 'Who are these people, anyway? How dare they have the mischief to repeat gossip of over ten years past? They would not dare to do so before my cousin Rachel.'

'Never mind that now,' he replied. 'My concern now is with those pearls. I am sorry, but as your guardian for another three months I must ask you to desire her to return the collar. I will have it placed in the bank again, with the rest of the jewellery.'

Now it was my turn to pace the floor. I hardly knew what I did.

'Return the collar?' I said. 'But how can I possibly ask her to do that? I gave it to her, tonight, as a Christmas present. It is the last thing in the whole world that I could do.'

'Then I must do it for you,' he answered.

I suddenly hated his stiff stubborn face, his rigid way of standing, his stolid indifference to all feeling.

'I'll be damned if you will,' I said to him.

I wished him a thousand miles away. I wished him dead.

'Come, Philip,' he said, altering his tone, 'you are very young, very impressionable, and I quite understand that you wanted to give your cousin some token of esteem. But family jewels are rather more than that.'

'She has a right to them,' I said. 'God knows if anyone has a right to wear the jewels it is she.'

'Had Ambrose lived, yes,' he answered, 'but not now. Those jewels remain in trust for your wife, Philip, when you marry. And that's another thing. That collar has a significance of its own, which some of the older among the tenants at dinner tonight may remark upon. An Ashley, on his marriage, allows his bride to wear the collar on her wedding day, as sole adornment. That is the kind of family superstition which the people about here delight in, and, as I have told you, the older amongst them know the tale. It is unfortunate, and the sort of thing that causes gossip. I am sure that Mrs. Ashley, in her situation, is the last person to wish that.'

'The people here tonight,' I said impatiently, 'will think, if they were in a state to think at all, that the collar is my cousin's own possession. I have never heard such rubbish in my life, that her wearing of it might cause gossip.'

'That,' he said, 'is not for me to say. I shall doubtless know only too soon if there is talk. One thing I must be firm upon, Philip. And that is, that the collar is returned to the safety of the bank. It is not yet yours to give, and you had no right whatsoever to go to the bank, without my permission, and bring it from safe custody. I repeat, if you will not ask Mrs. Ashley to return it, I shall.'

In the intensity of our discussion we had not heard the rustle of the gowns upon the stairs. Now it was too late, Rachel, followed by Louise, stood in the doorway.

She stood there, her head turned towards my godfather, who was planted in the centre of the drawing-room, confronting me.

'I am sorry,' she said, 'I could not help but overhear what you have said. Please, I don't want either of you to embarrass yourselves on my account.

It was dear of Philip to let me wear the pearls tonight, and quite right, Mr. Kendall, of you to ask for their return. Here they are.' She raised her hands and unfastened them from her neck.

'No,' I said, 'why the devil should you do so?'

'Please, Philip,' she said.

She took off the collar and gave it to my godfather. He had the grace to look uncomfortable, yet relieved too.

I saw Louise look at me with pity. I turned away.

'Thank you, Mrs. Ashley,' said my godfather in his gruff way. 'You understand that this collar is really part of the estate trust, and Philip had no business to take it from the bank. It was a foolish, thoughtless action. But young men are headstrong.'

'I perfectly understand,' she said, 'let us say no more about it. Do you need wrapping for it?'

'Thank you, no,' he answered, 'my handkerchief will do.'

He took a handkerchief from his breast pocket, and placed the collar in the middle of it, with great care.

'And now,' he said, 'I think that Louise and I will say good night. Thank you for a delightful and successful dinner, Philip, and I wish you both a happy Christmas.'

I did not answer. I went out into the hall, and stood by the front door, and handed Louise into the carriage without a word. She pressed my hand in sign of sympathy, but I was too much moved to answer her. My godfather climbed in beside her, and they went away.

I walked slowly back to the drawing-room. Rachel was standing there, gazing down into the fire. Her neck seemed naked without the collar. I stood looking at her without speaking, angry, miserable. At sight of me she put out her arms and I went to her. My heart was too full to speak. I felt like a little lad of ten years old, and it would not have taken much to make me cry.

'No,' she said, her voice tender with the warmth that was so much part of her, 'you must not mind. Please, Philip, please. I am so proud to have worn it for that once.'

'I wanted you to wear it,' I said, 'I wanted you to keep it always. God damn him, and send him to hell.'

'Hush,' she said, 'dear, don't say those things.'

I was so bitter and angry I could have ridden to the bank upon the instant, and gone to the vaults, and brought back every piece of jewellery there, every stone, every gem, and given them to her, and all the gold and silver in the bank as well. I could have given her the world.

'Well, it's spoilt now,' I said, 'the whole evening, the whole of Christmas. Everything is wasted.'

She held me close, and laughed. 'You are like a child,' she said, 'running to me with empty hands. Poor Philip.' I stood away, and looked down upon her.

'I am no child,' I said, 'I am five-and-twenty years, all but three blasted months. My mother wore those pearls on her wedding day, and before that my aunt, and before that my grandmother. Don't you realise why I wanted you to wear them too?'

She put her hands on my shoulders, and kissed me once again.

'Why, yes,' she answered, 'that was why I was so happy, and so proud. You wanted me to wear them because you knew that had I been married here, and not in Florence. Ambrose would have given them to me on our wedding day.'

I said nothing. She had told me, some weeks back, that I lacked perception. Tonight, I might have said the same of her. A few moments later, she patted me on the shoulder, and went upstairs to bed.

I felt in my pocket for the gold chain she had given me. That, if nothing else, was mine alone.

Chapter Eighteen

Our Christmas was a happy one. She saw to that. We rode to the farms on the estate, and to the cottages and lodges, and distributed the clothes that had belonged to Ambrose. And under each roof we were obliged to eat a pie, or taste a pudding, so that when evening came again we were too full to sit ourselves to dinner, but, surfeited, left the servants to finish all the remaining geese and turkey of the night before, while she and I roasted chestnuts before the drawing-room fire.

Then, as though I had gone back in time some twenty years, she bade me shut my eyes, and, laughing, went up to her boudoir and came down again and put into my hands a little tree. This she had dressed in gay fantastic fashion, with presents wrapped in brightly coloured paper, each present an absurdity; and I knew she did this for me because she wanted me to forget the drama of Christmas Eve and the fiasco of the pearls. I could not forget. Nor could I forgive. And from Christmas onwards a coolness came between my godfather and myself. That he should have listened to petty lying gossip was bad enough, but even more I resented his sticking to the quibble in the will which left me under his jurisdiction for three more months. What if Rachel had spent more than we had foreseen? We had not known her needs. Neither Ambrose nor my godfather had understood the way of life in Florence. Extravagant she well might be, but was it so great a crime? As to society there, we could not judge it. My godfather had lived all his life in careful niggardly fashion, and, because Ambrose had never bothered to spend much upon himself, my godfather had taken it for granted that this state of things would continue once the property was mine. My wants were few, and I had no more desire for personal spending than had Ambrose, in his time, but this cheeseparing on the part of my godfather induced in me a sort of fury that made me determined to have my way and use the money that was mine.

He had accused Rachel of frittering away her allowance. Well, he could accuse me of wanton waste about my house. I decided, after the New Year, that I wished to make improvements to the property that would be mine. But not only to the gardens. The terracing of the walk above the Barton fields proceeded, also the hollowing away and preparation of the ground beside it that was to become the sunken water-garden, copied from the engraving in Rachel's book.

I was determined to repair the house as well. Too long, I considered, we had made do with the monthly visitations of Nat Dunn, the estate mason, who crept from ladder to ladder upon the roof and replaced slates, swept off by a gale of wind, smoking his pipe up there the while, his back against a chimney. Now was the time to set the whole roof in order, have new tiles, new slates, new guttering, strengthening also those walls damaged by long years of wind and rain. Too little had been done about the place since the old days, two hundred years ago, when the men of Parliament had wrought such havoc, and my ancestors had been hard put to it to keep the house from falling into ruin. I would make amends for past neglect, and if my godfather pulled a face and drew sums upon his blotter he could go hang himself.

So I went my own way about the business, and before January was out some fifteen to twenty men were working on my roof, or about the building, and inside the house as well, decorating ceilings and walls to my orders. It gave me the greatest satisfaction to picture my godfather's expression when the bills for the work should be submitted to him.

I made the repairs about the house serve as an excuse for not entertaining visitors, thereby putting an end, for the time being, to Sunday dinner. Therefore I was spared the regular visit of the Pascoes and the Kendalls, and saw nothing of my godfather, which was part of my intention. I also had Seecombe spread it, in his jungle fashion, below stairs, that Mrs. Ashley found it difficult to receive callers at the moment, owing to there being workmen in the drawing-room. We lived therefore, during those days of winter and early spring, in hermit fashion, greatly to my liking. Aunt Phoebe's boudoir, as Rachel would still insist in naming it, became our place of habitation. There, at the close of day, Rachel would sit, and sew or read, and I would watch her. A new gentleness had come to her manner, since the incident of the pearls on Christmas Eve, which, though warming beyond belief, was sometimes hard to bear.

I think she had no knowledge what it did to me. Those hands, resting for a moment on my shoulder, or touching my head in a caress, as she passed by the chair where I was sitting, talking all the while about the garden or some practical matter, would set my heart beating so that it would not be stilled. To watch her move was a delight, and sometimes I even wondered if she rose from her chair on purpose, to go to the window, to reach upwards to the curtain, to stand there with her hand upon it looking outwards on to the lawn, because she knew my eyes were watching her. She said my name

Philip in a manner quite her own. To others, it had always been a short, clipped word, with some emphasis on the final letter, but she lingered on the 'l' slowly, deliberately, in a way that somehow, to my ear, gave it a new sound I liked well. As a lad I had always wished to be called Ambrose, and the wish had remained with me, I think, until the present. Now I was glad that my name went back even farther into the past than his had done. When the men brought the new lead piping to be placed against the walls, to serve as guttering from the roof to the ground, and the bucket heads were in position, I had a strange feeling of pride as I looked up at the little plaque beneath them stamped with my initials P.A. and the date beneath, and lower down the lion that was my mother's crest. It was as though I gave something of myself into the future. And Rachel, standing beside me, took my arm and said, 'I never thought you proud, Philip, until now. I love you the better for it.'

Yes, I was proud . . . but emptiness went with it all the same.

So the work proceeded, in the house and in the grounds; and the first days of spring came, being in themselves a blend of torment and delight. Blackbird and chaffinch sang beneath our windows on first waking, rousing both Rachel and myself from sleep. We talked of it at midday when we met. The sun came to her first, on the eastern side of the house, and with her windows wide drove a slant of light on to her pillow. I had it later, as I dressed. Leaning out, looking over the meadows to the sea, I would see the horses and the plough climb the further hill, with the gulls wheeling about them, and in the pasture lands closer to the house were the ewes and the young lambs, back to back for comfort. Lapwings, on passage bent, came in a little cloud, with fluttering wings. Soon they would pair, and the male soar and tumble in his flight of rapture. Down on the shore the curlews whistled, and the oyster-catchers, black and white like parsons, poked in the seaweed solemnly, for breakfast. The air had a zest to it, salt-tasting, under the sun.

It was on a morning such as this that Seecombe came to me and told me that Sam Bate, up at the East Lodge, who was in bed, poorly, wished very much that I would go and see him, as he had something of importance to give me. He inferred that whatever it was he had was too precious to deliver to his son or to his daughter. I thought little of it. It is always a pleasure amongst country folk to make much mystery over small matters. Nevertheless, in the afternoon, I walked up the avenue to the gates there where the four roads meet, and turned in at the lodge to have a word with him. Sam was sitting up in bed, and lying on the blanket before him was one of the coats that had belonged to Ambrose, which had been given to him on Christmas Day. I recognised it as the light-coloured one I had not known, which Ambrose must have bought for the hot weather on the continent.

'Well, Sam,' I said, 'I am sorry to find you in bed. What is the matter?'

'The same old cough, Mr. Philip, sir, that catches me aback every spring,' replied the man. 'My father had it before me, and one spring t'will carry me to the grave, the same as it did him.'

'Nonsense, Sam,' I told him, 'those are old tales they spread, that what a man's father had will kill the son.'

Sam Bate shook his head. 'There's truth in it, sir,' he said, 'and you know it, too. How about Mr. Ambrose and his father, the old gentleman your uncle? Brain sickness did for the pair of them. There's no going agin the ways of nature. I've seen the same in cattle.'

I said nothing, wondering, at the same time, how Sam should know what illness it was of which Ambrose had died. I had told no one. It was incredible how rumour spread about our countryside.

'You must send your daughter to ask Mrs. Ashley for some cordial to cure your cough,' I said to him. 'She has great knowledge of such things. Oil of eucalyptus is one of her remedies.'

'I will, Mr. Philip, I will,' he answered me, 'but first I felt it right to ask you to come yourself, concerning the matter of the letter.'

He lowered his voice, and looked suitably concerned and solemn.

'What letter, Sam?' I asked.

'Mr. Philip,' he replied, 'on Christmas Day, you and Mrs. Ambrose kindly gave some of us clothes and the like belonging to the late master. And very proud we are, all of us, to have the same. Now this coat that you see here, on the bed, was given to me.' He paused, and touched the coat, with some of the same awe about him still with which he had received it on Christmas Day. 'Now I brought the coat up here, sir, that same night,' Sam continued, 'and I said to my daughter if we had a glass case to put it in we'd do so, but she told me to get along with such nonsense, the coat was meant to wear, but wear it I would not, Mr. Philip. T'would have seemed presuming on my part, if you follow me, sir. So I put the coat away in the press, yonder, and took him out now and agin and had a look at it. Then, when this cough seized me, and I lay up here abed, I don't know how it was, but the fancy came upon me to wear the coat. Just sitting up in bed, like, as you see me now. The coat being lightish weight, and easy on my back. Which I did, Mr. Philip, for the first time yesterday. It was then I found the letter.'

He paused, and, fumbling under his pillow, drew forth a packet. 'What had happened, Mr. Philip, was this,' he said. 'The letter must have slipped down inside the material of the coat and the lining. T'wouldn't have been noticed in the folding of it, or in packing. Only by someone such as me smoothing the coat with my hands for wonder at having it around me. I felt the crackling of it, and made so bold as to open up the lining with a knife. And here it is, sir. A letter, plain as day. Sealed, and addressed to you by Mr. Ambrose himself. I know his hand, of old. It shook me, sir, to come upon it. It seemed, if you understand, as though I had come upon a message from the dead.'

He gave the letter to me. Yes, he was right. It was addressed to me, and by Ambrose. I looked down at the familiar handwriting, and felt a sudden wrench at my heart.

'That was wise of you, Sam, to act as you have done,' I said, 'and very proper to send for me in person. Thank you.'

'No thanks, Mr. Philip, no thanks at all,' he answered, 'but I thought how maybe that letter had laid there all these months, and should have been in your hands a long time since. But the poor master being dead, made it so wisht, to come upon it. And the same to you on reading it, maybe. And so I thought it best to tell you of it myself, rather than send my daughter to the mansion.'

I thanked him again, and after putting the letter away in my breast pocket talked for a few minutes or so, before I left him. Some intuition, I don't know what it was, made me tell him to say nothing of the business to anyone, not even to his daughter. The reason I gave him was the same that he had given me, respect for the dead. He promised, and I left the lodge.

I did not return at once to the house. I climbed up through the woods to a path that runs above that part of the estate, bordering the Trenant acres and the wooded avenue. Ambrose had been fonder of this walk than any other. It was our highest point of land, saving the beacon to the south, and had a fine view over the woods and the valley to the open sea. The trees fringing the path, planted by Ambrose and his father before him, gave shelter, although not high enough as yet to dim the view, and in May month the bluebells made a cover to the ground. At the end of the path, topping the woods, before plunging to descent and the keeper's cottage in the gully, Ambrose had set up a piece of granite. 'This,' he said to me, half joking, half in earnest, 'can serve me for tombstone when I die. Think of me here, rather than in the family vault with the other Ashleys.'

He little thought, when he had it put in place, that he would not lie in the family vault ever, but in the Protestant cemetery, in Florence. Upon the slab of granite he had scrolled some mention of the lands where he had travelled, and a line of doggerel at the end to make us laugh when we looked at it together. For all the nonsense, though, I believe his heart intended it; and during that last winter, when he was from home, I had often climbed the path up through the woods to stand beside the granite stone, and look down upon the prospect that he loved so well.

When I came to it today I stood for a moment with my hands upon the slab, and I could not bring myself to a decision. Below me the smoke curled from the keeper's cottage, and his dog, left upon a chain while he was absent, barked now and again, at nothing, or maybe because the sound of his own yelps gave him company. The glory of the day had gone, and it was colder. Clouds had come across the sky. In the distance I could see the cattle coming down from the Lankelly hills to water in the marshes under the woods, and beyond the marshes, in the bay, the sea had lost the sun and was slatey grey. A little wind blew shoreward, rustling the trees below me.

I sat down beside the slab, and taking Ambrose's letter from my pocket placed it face downwards, on my knee. The red seal stared up at me, imprinted with his ring and the chough's head. The packet was not thick. It contained nothing. Nothing but a letter, which I did not want to open. I cannot say what misgiving held me back, what cowardly instinct drove me to hide my head like an ostrich in the sand. Ambrose was dead, and the past went with him when he died. I had my own life to make, and my own will to follow. It might be that in this letter there would be some further mention of that other matter I had chosen to forget. If Ambrose had accused Rachel of extravagance, he could now use the same epithet, with more reason perhaps, to me. I should have dispensed more upon the house itself in a few months than he had done in years. I did not feel it was betrayal.

But not to read the letter . . . what would he say to that? If I tore it now to shreds, and scattered the pieces, and never learnt the contents, would he condemn me? I balanced the letter in my hand, this way and that. To read, or not to read; I wished to heaven the choice was not before me. Back in the house, my loyalty was with her. In the boudoir, with my eyes upon her face, watching those hands, that smile, hearing her voice, no letter would have haunted me. Yet here, in the woods beside the slab of granite where we had so often stood together, he and I, Ambrose holding the very stick I carried now, wearing the same coat, here his power was strongest. Like a small boy who prays that the weather shall be fine upon his birthday I prayed God now that the letter should contain nothing to disturb me, and so opened it. It was dated April of the preceding year, and was therefore written three months before he died.

Dearest boy,
'If my letters have been infrequent, it is not because I have not thought of you. You have been in my mind, these past months, perhaps more than ever before. But a letter can miscarry, or be read by others, and I would not wish either of those things to happen; therefore I have not written, or when I have done so I know there has been little in anything I have said. I have been ill, with fever and bad headache. Better now. But for how long, I cannot tell. The fever may come again, and the headaches too, and when in the grip of them I am not responsible for what I say or do. This much is certain.

'But I am not yet certain of the cause. Philip, dear boy, I am much disturbed. That is lightly said. I am in agony of mind. I wrote to you, during the winter I think it was, but was ill shortly afterwards and have no recollection what happened to the letter, I may very well have destroyed it in the mood that possessed me. In it, I believe I told you of her fault that caused me so much concern. Whether hereditary or not I cannot say, but I believe so, and believe also that the loss of our child, only a few months on its way, did her irreparable harm.

'This, by the way, I had kept from you in my letters; we were both much shaken at the time. For my part, I have you, and am consoled. But with a woman it goes deeper. She had made plans and projects, as you can imagine, and when, after but four-and-a-half months, it went for nothing, and she was told by her doctor there could not be another, her distress was very great, profounder than my own. I could swear her manner altered from that time. The recklessness with money became progressive, and I perceived in her a tendency to evasion, to lies, to withdrawal from me, that was completely contrary to the warm nature that was hers when we first married. As the months passed I noticed more and more that she turned to this man I have mentioned before in my letters, signor Rainaldi, a friend and I gather a lawyer of Sangalletti's, for advice, rather than to me. I believe this man to have a pernicious influence upon her. I suspect him of having been in love with her for years, even when Sangalletti was alive, and although I do not for an instant believe that she ever thought of him in such a connection up to a short while ago, now, since she has altered in her manner to me, I cannot be so sure. There is a shadow in her eye, a tone in her voice, when his name is said that awakens in my mind the most terrible suspicion.

'Brought up as she was by feckless parents, living a life, before and even during her first marriage, about which both of us have had reserve, I have often felt that her code of behaviour is different to ours at home. The tie of marriage may not be so sacred. I suspect, in fact I have proof, that he gives her money. Money, God forgive me for saying so, is at the present time the one way to her heart. I believe, if the child had not been lost, none of this would be; and I wish with all my heart that I had not listened to the doctor at the time when he dissuaded travel, but had brought her home. We would have been with you now, and all of us content.

'At times she seems like her true self, and all is well, so well that I feel I have been through some nightmare and wake again to the happiness of the first months of our marriage. Then, with a word or an action, all is lost again. I will come down to the terrace and find Rainaldi there. At sight of me, both fall silent. I cannot but wonder what it is they have been discussing. Once, when she had gone into the villa and Rainaldi and I were left alone, he asked an abrupt question as to my will. This he had seen, incidentally, when we married. He told me that as it stood, and should I die, I would leave my wife without provision. This I knew, and had anyway drawn up a will myself that would correct the error, and would have put my signature to it, and had it witnessed, could I be certain that her fault of spending was a temporary passing thing, and not deep-rooted.

'This new will, by the way, would give her the house and the estate for her lifetime only, and so to you upon her death, with the proviso that the running of the estate be left in your hands entirely.

'It still remains unsigned, and for the reason I have told you.

'Mark you, it is Rainaldi who asked questions on the will, Rainaldi who drew my attention to the omissions of the one that stands at present. She does not speak of it, to me. But do they speak of it together? What is it that they say to one another, when I am not there?

'This matter of the will occurred in March. Admittedly, I was unwell, and nearly blinded with my head, and Rainaldi bringing up the matter may have done so in that cold calculating way of his, thinking that I might die. Possibly it is so. Possibly it is not discussed between them. I have no means of finding out. Too often now I find her eyes upon me, watchful and strange. And when I hold her, it is as though she were afraid. Afraid of what, of whom?

'Two days ago, which brings me to the reason for this letter, I had another attack of this same fever, which laid me low in March. The onset is sudden. I am seized with pains and sickness, which passes swiftly to great excitation of my brain, driving me near to violence, and I can hardly stand upon my feet for dizziness of mind and body. This, in its turn, passes, and an intolerable desire for sleep comes upon me, so that I fall upon the floor, or upon my bed, with no power over my limbs. I do not recollect my father being thus. The headaches, yes, and some difficulty of temperament, but not the other symptoms.

'Philip, my boy, the only being in the world whom I can trust, tell me what it means, and if you can, come out to me. Say nothing to Nick Kendall. Say no word to any single soul. Above all, write not a word in answer, merely come.

'One thought possesses me, leaving me no peace. Are they trying to poison me?
'Ambrose.'

I folded the letter back into its creases. The dog stopped barking in the cottage garden below. I heard the keeper open his gate and the dog yelp at him in welcome. I heard voices from the cottage, the clank of a pail, the shutting of a door. From the trees on the hill opposite the jackdaws rose in flight, and circled, cawing, and moved in a black cloud to the tops of other trees, beside the marshes.

I did not tear the letter. I dug a hole for it, beneath the slab of granite. I put it inside my pocket-book, and buried the pocket-book, deep in the dark earth. Then I smoothed the place with my hands. I walked away down the hill, and through the woods to the avenue below. As I climbed again, up the back way to the house, I heard laughter and the chatter of the men as they went home from work. I stood a moment and watched them trudge off across the park. The scaffolding placed against the walls where they had been working all the day looked bleak and bare.

I went in, through the back entrance across the court, and as my feet sounded on the flags Seecombe came out to me from the steward's room, with consternation on his face.

'I am glad you have come, sir,' he said. 'The mistress has been asking for you this long while. Poor Don has had an accident. She is much concerned.'

'An accident?' I said. 'What happened?'

'A great slate from the roof fell on him, sir,' he answered. 'You know how deaf he has become of late, and how loath to leave his place in the sun, outside the library window. The slate must have fallen on his back. He cannot move.'

I went to the library. Rachel was kneeling there on the floor, with Don's head pillowed in her lap. She raised her eyes when I came into the room. 'They have killed him,' she said, 'he is dying. Why did you stay away so long? If you had been here, it would not have happened.'

Her words sounded like an echo to something long forgotten in my mind. But what it was I could not now remember. Seecombe went from the library, leaving us alone. The tears that filled her eyes ran down her face. 'Don was your possession,' she said, 'your very own. You grew up together. I can't bear to see him die.'

I went and knelt beside her on the floor, and I realised that I was thinking, not of the letter buried deep beneath the granite slab, nor of poor Don so soon to die, stretched out there between us, his body limp and still. I was thinking of one thing only. It was the first time since she had come to my house that her sorrow was not for Ambrose, but for me.

Chapter Nineteen

We sat with Don, through the long evening. I had my dinner, but Rachel would eat nothing. Shortly before midnight he died. I carried him away and covered him, and tomorrow we would bury him in the plantation. When I returned the library was empty, and Rachel had gone upstairs. I walked along the corridor to the boudoir and she was sitting there, with wet eyes, staring into the fire.

I sat beside her and took her hands. 'I think he did not suffer,' I said to her. 'I think he had no pain.'

'Fifteen long years,' she said, 'the little boy of ten, who opened his birthday pie. I kept remembering the story, as he lay there with his head in my lap.'

'In three weeks' time,' I said, 'it will be the birthday once again. I shall be twenty-five. Do you know what happens on that day?'

'All wishes should be granted,' she answered, 'or so my mother used to say, when I was young. What will you wish for, Philip?'

I did not answer her at once. I stared, with her, into the fire.

'I shall not know,' I said, 'until the day comes.'

Her hand, with rings upon it, lay white and still upon my own.

'When I am twenty-five,' I said, 'my godfather has no further control over the property. It is mine, to do with what I will. The pearl collar, the other jewels there in the bank, I can give them all to you.'

'No,' she said, 'I would not take them, Philip. They should remain in trust for your wife, when you marry. I know you have no desire to marry yet, but one day you may change your mind.'

I knew well what I longed to say to her, yet dared not. Instead, I bent down and kissed her hand, then moved away.

It is only through error,' I said, 'that those jewels are not yours today. And not only the jewels, but everything. This house, the money, the estate. You know that perfectly.'

She looked distressed. She turned from the fire, and leant back in her chair. Her hand began playing with her rings.

'There is no need to discuss that,' she said. 'If there was error, I am used to it.'

'You may be,' I said, 'but I am not.'

I stood up, my back to the fire, looking down upon her. I knew now what I could do, and no one could prevent me.

'What do you mean?' she said, with that same shadow of distress still in her eyes.

'It does not matter,' I answered; 'you shall know, in three weeks' time.'

'In three weeks' time,' she said, 'after your birthday, I must leave you, Philip.'

She had said them at last, the words I had expected. But now that I had a plan formed in my mind they might not matter.

'Why?' I asked.

'I have stayed too long,' she answered.

'Tell me,' I said, 'supposing that Ambrose had made a will leaving the property to you for your lifetime, with the proviso that during that lifetime I looked after the estate and ran it for you, what would you have done?'

Her eyes flickered away from me, back to the fire again.

'How do you mean,' she asked, 'what would I have done?'

'Would you have lived here?' I said. 'Would you have turned me out?'

'Turned you out?' she exclaimed. 'From your own home? Why, Philip, how could you ask me such a thing?'

'You would have stayed then?' I replied. 'You would have lived here in the house, and, in a sense, employed me in your business? We should be living here together, just as we are doing now?'

'Yes,' she said, 'yes, I suppose so. I have never thought. It would be so different, though, you cannot make comparison.'

'How different?'

She gestured with her hands. 'How can I explain to you?' she said. 'Don't you understand that my position, as it is, is untenable, simply because I am a woman? Your godfather would be the first to agree with me. He has said nothing, but I am sure he feels that the time has come for me to go. It would have been quite otherwise, had the house been mine and you, in the sense you put it, in my employ. I should be Mrs. Ashley, you my heir. But now, as it has turned out, you are Philip Ashley, and I, a woman relative, living on your bounty. There is a world of difference, dear, between the two.'

'Exactly,' I replied.

'Well then,' she said, 'let's talk of it no further.'

'We will talk of it further,' I said, 'because the matter is of supreme importance. What happened to the will?'

'What will?'

'The will that Ambrose made, and never signed, in which he left the property to you?'

I saw the anxiety deepen in her eyes.

'How do you know of such a will? I never told you of it,' she said.

A lie would serve as an excuse, and I gave it her.

'I have always known there must be one,' I answered, 'but possibly it was left unsigned, and so invalid, from a legal point of view. I go even further, and suggest you have it here amongst your things.'

This was a shot at venture, but it told. Her eyes flashed instinctively towards the little bureau, against the wall, then back to me.

'What are you trying to make me say?' she asked.

'Only confirm that it exists,' I said.

She hesitated, then shrugged her shoulders.

'Very well, yes,' she replied, 'but it alters nothing. The will was never signed.'

'Can I see it?' I asked.

'For what purpose, Philip?'

'For a purpose of my own. I think you can trust me.'

She looked at me a long while. She was clearly bewildered, and I think anxious too. She rose from her chair and went towards the bureau, then, hesitant, glanced back at me again.

'Why suddenly all this?' she said. 'Why can't we leave the past alone? You promised we should do so, that evening in the library.'

'You promised you would stay,' I answered her.

To give it me or not, the choice was hers. I thought of the choice that I had made that afternoon beside the granite slab. I had chosen, for better or for worse, to read the letter. Now she must come to a decision too. She went to the bureau, and, taking a small key, opened up a drawer. Out of the drawer she took a piece of paper, and gave it to me.

'Read it, if you wish,' she said.

I took the paper to the candlelight. The writing was in Ambrose's hand, clear and firm, a stronger hand than in the letter I had read that afternoon. The date was November, of a year ago, when he and Rachel had been married seven months. The paper was headed 'Last Will and Testament of Ambrose Ashley.' The contents were just as he had told me. The property was left to Rachel, for her lifetime, passing at her death to the eldest of any children that might be born to both of them, and failing the birth of children, then to me, with the proviso that I should have the running of the same while she should live.

'May I make a copy of this?' I said to her.

'Do what you want,' she said. She looked pale and listless, as if she did not care. 'It's over and done with, Philip, there is no sense in talking of it now.'

'I will keep it for the moment, and make a copy of it too,' I said, and sitting at the bureau I took pen and paper and did so, while she lay in her chair, her cheek resting in her hand.

I knew that I must have confirmation of everything that Ambrose had told me in his letter, and though I hated every word I had to say I forced myself to question her. I scratched away with the pen: copying the will was more a pretext than anything else, and served its purpose so that I did not have to look at her.

'I see that Ambrose dated this November,' I said. 'Have you any idea why he should choose that month to make a new will? You were married the preceding April.'

Her answer was slow in coming; and I thought suddenly how a surgeon must feel, when he probes about the scar of a wound but lately healed.

'I don't know why he wrote it in November,' she said. 'We were neither of us thinking of death at that time. Rather the reverse. It was the happiest time of all the eighteen months we were together.'

'Yes,' I said, seizing a fresh piece of paper, 'he wrote and told me of it.' I heard her move in her chair, and turn to look at me. But I went on writing at the bureau.

'Ambrose told you?' she said. 'But I asked him not to, I feared you might misunderstand and feel, in some way, slighted; it would be very natural if you had. He promised to keep it secret. And then, as it turned out, it made no odds.'

The voice was flat, without expression. Perhaps, after all, when a surgeon probed a scar the sufferer would say dully that he felt no pain. In the letter, buried beneath the granite, Ambrose had said, 'With a woman, these things go deeper.' As I scratched upon the piece of paper I saw that I had written the words, 'It made no odds . . . it made no odds.' I tore up the piece of paper, and began afresh.

'And finally,' I said, 'in the long run, the will was never signed.'

'No,' she said, 'Ambrose left it as you see it now.'

I had done with writing. I folded the will and the copy I had made, and put both of them in my breast pocket, where earlier in the afternoon I had carried his letter. Then I went and knelt beside her chair, and putting my arms about her held her fast; not as I would a woman, but as a child.

'Rachel,' I said, 'why did not Ambrose sign the will?'

She lay quite still, and did not move away. Only the hand that rested on my shoulder tightened suddenly.

'Tell me,' I said, 'tell me, Rachel.'

The voice that answered me was faint and far away, not more than a whisper in my ear.

'I never knew,' she said; 'we did not speak of it again. But I think when he realised that I could not, after all, have children, he lost belief in me. Some sort of faith went, though he never knew it.'

As I knelt there, with my arms about her, I thought of the letter in the pocket book beneath the granite slab, with this same accusation said in other words, and I wondered how it could be that two people who had loved could yet have such a misconception of each other and, with a common grief, grow far apart. There must be something in the nature of love between a man and a woman that drove them to torment and suspicion. 'You were unhappy then?' I asked.

'Unhappy?' she said. 'What do you suppose? I was almost out of my mind.'

And I could see them sitting on the terrace of the villa, with this strange shadow between them, built out of nothing but their own doubts and fears, and it seemed to me that the seeds of this same shadow went back beyond all reckoning and could never more be traced. Perhaps, unconscious of his grudge, he brooded about her past with Sangalletti and before, blaming her for the life he had not shared, and she, with resentment likewise, feared loss of love must go with loss of child-bearing. How little she had understood of Ambrose after all. And what small knowledge he had had of her. I might tell her of the contents of the letter under the slab, but it would do no good. The misunderstanding went too deep.

'So it was all through error that the will was never signed, and put aside?' I said to her.

'Call it error if you like,' she answered, 'it cannot matter now. But soon afterwards, his manner altered and he himself changed. Those headaches, almost blinding him, began. They drove him near to violence, once or twice. I wondered how much could be my fault, and was afraid.'

'And you had no friend?'

'Only Rainaldi. And he never knew what I have told you tonight.'

That cold hard face, those narrow searching eyes, I did not blame Ambrose for mistrusting him. Yet how could Ambrose, who was her husband, have been so uncertain of himself? Surely a man must know when a woman loved him? Yet possibly one could not always tell.

'And when Ambrose fell ill,' I said, 'you no longer asked Rainaldi to the house?'

'I dared not,' she said. 'You will never understand how Ambrose became, and I don't want to tell you. Please, Philip, you must not ask me any more.'

'Ambrose suspected you – of what?'

'Of everything. Of infidelity, and worse than that.'

'What can be worse than infidelity?'

Suddenly she pushed me away, and rising from her chair went to the door and opened it. 'Nothing,' she said, 'nothing in the world. Now go away, and leave me to myself.'

I stood up slowly, and went to the door beside her.

'I am sorry,' I said, 'I did not mean to make you angry.'

'I am not angry,' she answered me.

'Never again,' I said, 'will I ask you questions. These were the last. I give you my solemn promise.'

'Thank you,' she said.

Her face was strained and white. Her voice was cold.

'I had a reason for asking them,' I said. 'You will know it in three weeks' time.'

'I don't ask the reason, Philip,' she said, 'all I ask of you is, go.'

She did not kiss me, or give me her hand. I bowed to her, and went. Yet a moment just before she had permitted me to kneel beside her with my arms about her. Why, in a sudden, had she changed? If Ambrose had known little about women, I knew less. That warmth so unexpected, catching a man unaware and lifting him to rapture, then swiftly, for no reason, the changing mood, casting him back where he had stood before. What trail of thought, confused and indirect, drove through those minds of theirs, to cloud their judgment? What waves of impulse swept about their being, moving them to anger and withdrawal, or else to sudden generosity? We were surely different, with our blunter comprehension, moving more slowly to the compass points, while they, erratic and unstable, were blown about their course by winds of fancy.

Next morning, when she came downstairs, her manner was as usual, kind and gentle; she made no reference to our conversation of the night before. We buried poor Don in the plantation, in a piece of ground apart, where the camellia walk began, and I made a small circle round his grave with stones. We did not talk of that tenth birthday when Ambrose gave him to me, nor yet of the twenty-fifth that was to come. But the following day I rose early, and, giving orders for Gypsy to be saddled, rode to Bodmin. I called upon an attorney there, a man named Wilfred Tewin, who did much of the business for the county but had not hitherto handled Ashley affairs, my godfather dealing with his own people in St. Austell. I explained to him that I had come upon a matter of great urgency and privacy, and that I desired him to draw up a document in legal form and language that would enable me to dispose of my entire property to my cousin, Mrs. Rachel Ashley, upon the first day of April, when it became mine by law.

I showed him the will that Ambrose had not signed, and I explained to him that it was only through sudden illness, followed by death, that Ambrose had omitted to sign it. I told him to incorporate, in the document, much of what Ambrose had written in the will, that on Rachel's decease the property passed back again to me, and that I should have the running of it in her lifetime. Should I die first the property would go, as matter of course, to my second cousins in Kent, but only at her death, and not before. Tewin was quick to understand what it was I wanted, and I think, being no great friend of my godfather – which was partly the reason I had gone to him – he was gratified to have so important a business entrusted to his care.

'You wish,' he said, 'to put in some clause safeguarding the land? As the draft stands at present, Mrs. Ashley could sell what acreage she pleased, which seems to me unwise if you desire to pass it on to your heirs in its entirety.'

'Yes,' I said slowly, 'there had better be a clause forbidding sale. That goes, most naturally, for the house too.'

'There are family jewels, are there not,' he said, 'and other personal possessions? What of them?'

'They,' I replied, 'are hers, to do with as she pleases.'

He read the draft through to me, and I did not think it could be faulted.

'One thing,' he said. 'We have no proviso should Mrs. Ashley marry again.'

'That,' I said, 'is not likely to happen.'

'Possibly not,' he answered, 'but the point should be covered just the same.'

He looked at me enquiringly, his pen poised in the air.

'Your cousin is still comparatively a young woman, is she not?' he said. 'It should certainly be taken into account.'

I thought suddenly, most monstrously, of old St. Ives in the far end of the county, and the remarks that Rachel had made to me in jest.

'In the case of her re-marriage,' I said quickly, 'the property reverts again to me. That is most definite.'

He made a note upon the paper, and read the draft again.

'And you desire this ready and drawn up, in legal form, by the first of April, Mr. Ashley?' he said.

'Please. That is my birthday. On that day the property becomes mine, absolutely. No objection can be put forward from any quarter.'

He folded the paper, and smiled at me.

'You are doing a very generous thing,' he said, 'giving everything away the moment it is yours.'

'It would never have been mine to begin with, I said, 'if my cousin Ambrose Ashley had put his signature to that will.'

'All the same,' he said, 'I doubt if such a thing has ever been done before. Certainly not to my knowledge, or in my lifetime of experience. I gather you want nothing said of this until the day?'

'Nothing at all. The matter is most secret.'

'Very well, then, Mr. Ashley. And I thank you for entrusting me with your confidence. I am at your disposal at any time in the future should you wish to call upon me regarding any matter whatsoever.'

He bowed me from the building, promising that the full document should be delivered to me on the thirty-first day of March.

I rode home with a reckless feeling in my heart. I wondered if my godfather would have an attack of apoplexy when he heard the news. I did not care. I wished him no ill, once I was rid of his jurisdiction, but for all that I had turned the tables on him to perfection. As for Rachel, she could not go to London now and leave her property. Her argument of the preceding night would not hold good. If she objected to me in the house, very well, I would take myself to the lodge, and call upon her every day for orders. I would be with Wellington and Tamlyn and the rest, and wait upon her bidding, cap in hand. I think had I been a little lad, I would have cut a caper from sheer love of living. As it was, I set Gypsy at a bank, and nearly took a toss in doing so when I landed with a bump the other side. The March winds made a fool of me; I would have sung aloud, but I could not for the life of me keep to a single tune. The hedgerows were green, and the willows were in bud, and all the honeyed mass of golden gorse in bloom. It was a day for folly and high fever.

When I returned, mid-afternoon, and rode up the carriage-way to the house, I saw a post-chaise drawn up before the door. It was an unusual sight, for always, when people called upon Rachel, they came in their own carriage. The wheels and the coach were dusty, as if from a long journey on the road, and certainly neither the vehicle nor the driver was known to me. I turned back at sight of them, and rode round to the stables, but the lad who came to take Gypsy knew no more than I did of the visitors, and Wellington was absent.

I saw no one in the hall but when I advanced softly towards the drawing-room I heard voices from within, behind the closed door. I decided not to mount the stairs, but to go up to my room by the servants' stairway at the back. Just as I turned the drawing-room door opened, and Rachel, laughing over her shoulder, came out into the hall. She looked well and happy, and wore that radiance about her that was so much part of her when her mood was gay.

'Philip, you are home,' she said. 'Come into the drawing-room – this visitor of mine you shall not escape. He has travelled very far to see us both.' Smiling, she took my arm, and drew me, most reluctantly, into the room. A man was seated there, who at sight of me rose from his chair, and came towards me with his hand outstretched.

'You did not expect me,' he said, 'and I make my apology. But then neither did I expect you, when I saw you first.'

It was Rainaldi.

Chapter Twenty

I do not know if I showed my feelings in my face as plainly as I felt them in my heart, but I think I must have done; for Rachel passed swiftly on in conversation, telling Rainaldi that I was always without doors, riding or walking, she never knew where, nor had I fixed hours for my return. 'Philip works harder than his own labourers,' she said, 'and knows every inch of his estate far more than they do.'

She still kept her hand upon my arm, as though to show me off before her visitor, much as a teacher would a sullen child.

'I congratulate you upon your fine property,' said Rainaldi. 'I do not wonder that your cousin Rachel has become so much attached to it. I have never seen her look so well.'

His eyes, the eyes that I remembered clearly, heavy-lidded and expressionless, dwelt upon her for a moment, then turned again to me.

'The air here,' he said, 'must be more conducive to repose of mind and body than our keener air in Florence.'

'My cousin,' I said, 'has her origin in the west country. She has merely returned where she belonged.'

He smiled, if the slight movement of his face could be so called, and addressed himself to Rachel. 'It depends what tie of blood is strongest, does it not?' he said. 'Your young relative forgets your mother came from Rome. And, I may add, you grow more like her every day.'

'In face alone, I hope,' said Rachel, 'not in her figure nor in her character. Philip, Rainaldi declares that he will put up in a hostelry, whatever we can recommend, he is not particular, but I have told him it is nonsense. Surely we can place a room at his disposal here?'

My heart sank at the suggestion but I could not refuse it.

'Of course,' I said. 'I will give orders at once, and send away the post-chaise too, as you won't want it further.'

'It brought me from Exeter,' said Rainaldi. 'I will pay the man, and then hire again when I return to London.'

'There is plenty of time to decide upon that,' said Rachel. 'Now that you are here you must stay a few days at least, so that you can see everything. Besides, we have so much to discuss.'

I went from the drawing-room to give orders for a room to be prepared – there was a large bare one on the west side of the house that would do him well – and went slowly upstairs to my own room to bath myself and change for dinner. From my window I saw Rainaldi come out and pay the fellow with the post-chaise, and then with an air of appraisal he stood a moment in the carriage-way, to look about him. I had the feeling that in one glance he priced the timber, reckoned the value of the trees and shrubs, and I saw him, too, examine the carving on the front door and run his hand over the scrolled figures. Rachel must have joined him, and I heard her laugh, and then the pair of them began talking in Italian. The front door closed. They came inside.

I had half a mind to stay up in my room and not descend, to send word to John to bring me my dinner on a tray. If they had so much to talk about they could do it better with me absent. Yet I was host, and could not show discourtesy. Slowly I bathed, reluctantly I dressed, and came downstairs to find Seecombe and John busy in the dining-room, which we had not used since the men had cleaned the panelling and done some repairs about the ceiling. The best silver was laid upon the table, and all the paraphernalia for visitors displayed.

'No need for all this pother,' I said to Seecombe, 'we could have eaten in the library very well.'

'The mistress gave orders, sir,' said Seecombe, on his dignity, and I heard him order John to fetch the lace-edged napery from the pantry, that we did not even use for Sunday dinner.

I lit my pipe, and went out into the grounds. The spring evening was still bright, and twilight would not come for an hour or more. The candles were lighted in the drawing-room, though, and the curtains not yet drawn. The candles were lighted too in the blue bedroom, and I saw Rachel pass to and fro before the windows as she dressed. It would have been an evening for the boudoir had we been alone, I hugging to myself the knowledge of what I had done in Bodmin, and she in gentle mood, telling me of her day. Now there would be none of this. Brightness in the drawing-room, animation in the dining-room, talk between the two of them about things that concerned me not; and over and above this the instinctive feeling of revulsion that I had about the man, that he came on no idle errand, to pass the time of day, but for some other purpose. Had Rachel known that he had arrived in England and would visit her? All the pleasure of my jaunt to Bodmin had left me. The schoolboy prank was over. I went into the house in low spirits, full of misgiving. Rainaldi was alone in the drawing-room standing by the fire. He had changed from travelling clothes to dinner dress, and was examining the portrait of my grandmother which hung upon one of the panels.

'A charming face,' he said, commenting on it, 'fine eyes, and complexion. You come of a handsome family. The portrait in itself of no great value.'

'Probably not,' I said, 'the Lelys and the Knellers are on the stairs, if you care to look at them.'

'I noticed them as I came down,' he answered. 'The Lely is well placed but not the Kneller. The latter, I would say, is not in his best style, but executed in one of his more florid moments. Possibly finished by a pupil.' I said nothing, I was listening for Rachel's step upon the stair. 'In Florence, before I came away,' he said, 'I was able to sell an early Furini for your cousin, part of the Sangalletti collection, now unfortunately dispersed. An exquisite thing. It used to hang upon the stairs at the villa, where the light caught it to its greatest advantage. You possibly would not have noticed it when you went to the villa.'

'Very possibly not,' I answered him.

Rachel came into the room. She was wearing the gown she had worn on Christmas Eve, but I saw she had a shawl about her shoulders. I was glad of it. She glanced from one to the other of us, as though to glean from our expressions how we were doing in conversation.

'I was just telling your cousin Philip,' said Rainaldi, 'how fortunate I was to sell the Furini madonna. But what a tragedy that it had to go.'

'We are used to that, though, aren't we?' she answered him. 'So many treasures that could not be saved.' I found myself resenting the use of the word 'we' in such a connection.

'Have you succeeded in selling the villa?' I asked bluntly.

'Not as yet,' answered Rainaldi, 'in fact – that is partly why I came here to see your cousin Rachel – we are practically decided upon letting it instead, for a term of some three or four years. It would be more advantageous, and to let it not so final as to sell. Your cousin may wish to return to Florence, one of these days. It was her home for so many years.'

'I have no intention of going back as yet,' said Rachel.

'No, possibly not,' he replied, 'but we shall see.'

His eyes followed her as she moved about the room, and I wished to heaven she would sit down so that he could not do so. The chair where she always sat stood back a little distance from the candlelight, leaving her face in shadow. There was no reason for her to move about the room unless to show her gown. I pulled a chair forward, but she did not sit.

'Imagine, Rainaldi has been in London for over a week, and did not tell me of it,' she said. 'I have never been more surprised in my life than when Seecombe announced that he was here. I think it was very remiss of him not to give me warning.' She smiled over her shoulder at him, and he shrugged his shoulders.

'I hoped the surprise of a sudden arrival would give you greater pleasure,' he said, 'the unexpected can be delightful or the reverse, it all depends upon the circumstances. Do you remember that time you were in Rome, and Cosimo and I turned up just as you were dressing for a party at the Casteluccis? You were distinctly annoyed with both of us.'

'Ah, but I had reason for that,' she laughed. 'If you have forgotten, I won't remind you of it.'

'I have not forgotten,' he said. 'I remember too the colour of your gown. It was like amber. Also Benito Castelucci had presented you with flowers. I saw his card, and Cosimo did not.'

Seecombe came in to announce dinner, and Rachel led the way across the hall into the dining-room, still laughing and reminding Rainaldi of happenings in Rome. I had never felt more glum or out of place. They went on talking personalities, and places, and now and again Rachel would put out her hand to me across the table, as she would do to a child, and say, 'You must forgive us, Philip dear. It is so long since I have seen Rainaldi,' while he watched me with those dark hooded eyes, and slowly smiled.

Once or twice they broke into Italian. He would be telling her something, and suddenly search for a word that would not come, and with a bow of apology to me speak in his own language. She would answer him, and as she spoke and I heard the unfamiliar words pour from her lips, so much faster surely than when we talked together in English, it was as though her whole cast of countenance was changed; she became more animated and more vivid, yet harder in a sense, and with a new brilliance that I did not like so well.

It seemed to me that the pair of them were ill-placed at my table, in the panelled dining-room; they should have been elsewhere, in Florence or in Rome, with smooth dark servants waiting on them and all the glitter of a society foreign to me chattering and smiling in these phrases I did not know. They should not be here, with Seecombe padding round in his leather slippers and one of the young dogs scratching under the table. I sat hunched in my chair, damping, discouraging, a death's head at my own dinner, and, reaching for the walnuts, cracked them between my hands to relieve my feelings. Rachel sat with us while we passed the port and brandy. Or rather I passed it, for I took neither, while he drank both.

He lit a cigar, taking one from a case he carried with him, and surveyed me, as I lit my pipe, with an air of tolerance.

'All young Englishmen smoke pipes, it seems to me,' he observed. 'The idea is that it helps digestion, but I am told it fouls the breath.'

'Like drinking brandy,' I answered, 'which can foul the judgement too.'

I was reminded suddenly of poor Don, dead now in the plantation, and how in his younger days, when he had come upon a dog he much disliked, his hackles rose, tail stood stiff and straight, and with a bound he seized him by the throat. I knew now how he must have felt.

'If you will excuse us, Philip,' said Rachel, rising from her chair, 'Rainaldi and I have much we must discuss, and he has papers with him that I have to sign. It will be best to do it upstairs, in the boudoir. Will you join us presently?'

'I think not,' I said. 'I have been out all day and have letters in the office. I will wish you both good night.'

She went from the dining-room, and he followed her. I heard them go upstairs. I was still sitting there when John came to clear the table.

I went out then, and walked about the grounds. I saw the light in the boudoir, but the curtains were drawn. Now they were together they would speak Italian. She would be sitting in the low chair by the fire, and he beside her. I wondered if she would tell him about our conversation of the preceding night, and how I had taken away the will and made a copy of it. I wondered what advice he gave to her, what words of counsel, and what papers he too brought from his file to show her that she must sign. When they had finished business, did they return again to personalities, to the discussing of people and of places they both knew? And would she brew tisana for him, as she did for me, and move about the room so that he could watch her? I wondered at what time he would take his leave of her and go to bed, and when he did so would she give him her hand? Would he stay awhile, lingering by the door, making an excuse to dally, as I did myself? Or knowing him so well, would she permit him to stay late?

I went on walking in the grounds, up to the new terrace walk, down the pathway nearly to the beach and back, up again along the walk where the young cedar trees were planted, and so round and back and round again, until I heard the clock in the belfry strike ten. That was my hour of dismissal: would it be his, as well? I went and stood at the edge of the lawn, and watched her window. The light was still burning in her boudoir. I watched, and waited. It continued burning. I had been warm from walking but now the air was chill, under the trees. My hands and feet grew cold. The night was dark and utterly without music. No frosty moon this evening topped the trees. At eleven, just after the clock struck, the light in the boudoir was extinguished and the light in the blue bedroom came instead. I paused a moment and then, on a sudden, walked round the back of the house and past the kitchens, and so to the west front, and looked up at the window of Rainaldi's room. Relief came to me. A light burnt there as well. I could see the chink of it, though he kept his shutters closed. The window was tight shut as well. I felt certain, with a sense of insular satisfaction, that he would open neither for the night.

I went into the house and up the staircase to my room. I had just taken off my coat and my cravat, and flung them on the chair, when I heard the rustle of her gown in the corridor, and then a soft tapping on the door. I went and opened it. She stood there, not yet undressed, with that same shawl about her shoulders still.

'I came to wish you good night,' she said.

'Thank you,' I answered, 'I wish you the same.'

She looked down at me, and saw the mud upon my shoes.

'Where have you been all evening?' she asked.

'Out walking in the grounds,' I answered her.

'Why did you not come to the boudoir for your tisana?' she asked.

'I did not care to do so,' I replied.

'You are very ridiculous,' she said. 'You behaved at dinner like a sulky schoolboy in need of a whipping.'

'I am sorry,' I said.

'Rainaldi is a very old friend, you know that well,' she said. 'We had much to talk about, surely you understand?'

'Is it because he is such an older friend than I that you permit him to linger in the boudoir until eleven?' I asked.

'Was it eleven?' she said. 'I really did not realise it.'

'How long is he going to stay?' I asked.

'That depends on you. If you are civil, and will invite him, he will stay for perhaps three days. More is not possible. He has to return to London.'

'Since you ask me to invite him, I must do so.'

'Thank you, Philip.' Suddenly she looked up at me, her eyes softened, and I saw the trace of a smile at the corner of her mouth. 'What is the

matter,' she said, 'why are you so foolish? What were you thinking of, as
you paced about the grounds?'

I might have answered her a hundred things. How I distrusted Rainaldi,
how I hated his presence in my house, how I wanted it to be as it was
before, and she alone with me. Instead, for no reason save that I loathed all
that had been discussed that evening, I said to her, 'Who was Benito
Castelucci that he had to give you flowers?'

The bubble of laughter rose within her, and, reaching up, she put her
arms about me. 'He was old, and very fat, and his breath smelt of cigars –
and I love you much too much,' she said, and went.

I have no doubt she was asleep within twenty minutes of leaving me,
while I heard the clock in the belfry chime every hour until four; and falling
into that uneasy morning slumber that becomes heaviest at seven was woken
ruthlessly by John at my usual hour.

Rainaldi stayed, not for three days but for seven, and in those seven days
I found no reason to alter my opinion of him. I think what I disliked most
was his air of tolerance towards me. A kind of half-smile played upon his
lips whenever he looked on me, as though I were a child to be humoured,
and whatever business I had been upon during the day was enquired about
and treated like a schoolboy escapade. I made a point of not returning for
any midday luncheon, and when I came home and entered the drawing-
room in the afternoon, a little after four, I would find the pair of them
together, talking their inevitable Italian, which would be broken off at my
entrance.

'Ah, the worker returns,' Rainaldi would say, seated, God damn him, in
the chair I always used when we had been alone. 'And while he has been
tramping about his acres and seeing, no doubt, that his ploughs make the
necessary furrows in the soil, you and I, Rachel, have been many hundred
miles away in thought and fancy. We have not stirred for the day, except
to wander on the new terrace walk. Middle age has many compensations.'

'You are bad for me, Rainaldi,' she would answer; 'since you have been
here I have neglected all my duties. Paid no visits, supervised no planting.
Philip will scold me for idleness.'

'You have not been idle intellectually,' came his reply. 'We have covered
as much ground in that sense as your young cousin has in actual fact upon
his feet. Or was it not upon feet today, but in the saddle? Young Englishmen
are forever driving their bodies to fatigue.'

I could sense his mockery of me, a cart-horse with a turnip head, and the
way Rachel came to my rescue, once more the teacher with her pupil, made
me more angry still.

'Surely it is Wednesday,' she said, 'and on Wednesday Philip does not
ride or walk, he does his accounts, in the office. He has a good head for
figures, and knows exactly what he spends, don't you, Philip?'

'Not always,' I answered, 'and in point of fact today I attended Petty
Sessions for a neighbour, and sat in judgement upon a fellow accused of
theft. He was let off with a fine, and not imprisoned.'

Rainaldi watched me, with his same air of tolerance.

'A young Solomon as well as a young farmer,' he said. 'I am continually hearing of new talents. Rachel, does not your cousin remind you very much of Del Sarto's portrait of the Baptist? He has much the same arrogance and innocence so charmingly blended.'

'Perhaps,' said Rachel, 'I had not thought of it before. He resembles one person only, to my mind.'

'Ah, that of course,' answered Rainaldi, 'but there is also quite definitely a Del Sarto touch about him. Some time you will have to wean him from his acres here, and show him our country. Travel broadens the mind, and I would like to see him wander in a gallery or a church.'

'Ambrose was bored by both,' said Rachel, 'I doubt if Philip would be any more impressed. Well, did you see your godfather at Petty Sessions? I would like to take Rainaldi to call upon him at Pelyn.'

'Yes, he was there,' I said, 'and sent you his respects.'

'Mr. Kendall has a very charming daughter,' said Rachel to Rainaldi, 'a little younger than Philip.'

'A daughter? H'm, indeed,' observed Rainaldi, 'then your young cousin is not entirely cut off from youthful feminine society?'

'Far from it,' laughed Rachel. 'Every mother has her eye upon him within a distance of forty miles.'

I remember glaring at her, and she laughed the more; and passing by me on her way to dress for dinner, she patted my shoulder in the infuriating habit that was hers – aunt Phoebe's gesture, I had called it before now, which delighted her as though I told her so for compliment.

It was upon this occasion that Rainaldi said to me, when she had gone upstairs, 'It was generous of you and your guardian to give your cousin Rachel the allowance. She wrote and told me of it. She was deeply touched.'

'It was the very least the estate owed to her,' I said, and hoped my tone of voice was discouraging to further conversation. I would not tell him what was going to happen in three weeks' time.

'You perhaps know,' said Rainaldi, 'that apart from the allowance she has no personal means whatsoever, except what I can sell for her from time to time. This change of air has done wonders for her, but I think before long she will feel the need of society, such as she has been used to in Florence. That is the real reason I do not get rid of the villa. The ties are very strong.'

I did not answer. If the ties were strong, it was only because he made them so. She had spoken of no ties until he came. I wondered what was the extent of his own personal wealth, and if he gave her money from his own possession, not only what he sold from Sangalletti's estate. How right Ambrose had been to distrust him. But what weakness in Rachel made her keep him as her counsellor and friend?

'Of course,' continued Rainaldi, 'it would possibly be wiser to sell the villa eventually, and for Rachel to have a small apartment in Florence, or else to build something small, up in Fiesole. She has so many friends who have no wish to lose her, I among them.'

'You told me, when we first met,' I said, 'that my cousin Rachel was a woman of impulse. No doubt she will continue to be so, and live where she pleases.'

'No doubt,' answered Rainaldi. 'But the nature of her impulses has not always led her into happiness.'

I suppose by this he wanted to infer that her marriage with Ambrose had been on impulse, and unhappy likewise, and that her coming to England was also impulse, and he was uncertain of the outcome of it. He had power over her, because he had the management of her affairs, and it was this power that might take her back to Florence. I believed that was the purpose of his visit, so to drum it into her, and possibly to tell her also that the allowance the estate paid to her would not be sufficient to maintain her indefinitely. I had the trump card, and he did not know it. In three weeks' time she would be independent of Rainaldi for the rest of her life. I could have smiled, but for the fact that I disliked him too intensely to do so in his presence.

'It must be very strange, with your upbringing, suddenly to entertain a woman in the house, and for many months, as you have done,' said Rainaldi, with his hooded eyes upon me. 'Has it put you out at all?'

'On the contrary,' I said, 'I find it very pleasant.'

'Strong medicine, all the same,' he answered, 'for one young and inexperienced like yourself. Taken in so large a dose, it could do damage.'

'At nearly five-and-twenty,' I replied, 'I think I know pretty well what medicine suits me.'

'Your cousin Ambrose thought so too, at forty-three,' answered Rainaldi, 'but as it turned out he was wrong.'

'Is that a word of warning, or of advice?' I asked.

'Of both,' he said, 'if you will take it the right way. And now, if you will excuse me, I must go dress for dinner.'

I suppose this was his method to drive a wedge between me and Rachel, to drop a word, hardly venomous in itself, yet with sufficient sting to foul the air. If he suggested I should beware of her, what did he hint of me? Did he dismiss me with a shrug, as they sat together in the drawing-room when I was absent, saying how inevitable it was for young Englishmen to be long of limb and lacking in brain, or would that be too easy an approach? He certainly had a store of personal remarks, always ready to his tongue, to cast aspersion.

'The trouble with very tall men,' he said, on one occasion, 'is the fatal tendency to stoop.' (I was standing under the lintel of the doorway when he said this, bending my head to say a word to Seecombe.) 'Also, the more muscular amongst them turn to fat.'

'Ambrose was never fat,' said Rachel swiftly.

'He did not take the exercise that this lad takes. It is the violent walking, riding and swimming that develops the wrong portions of the body. I have noticed it very often, and nearly always amongst Englishmen. Now, in Italy we are smaller boned, and lead more sedentary lives. Therefore we keep our figures. Our diet, too, is easier on the liver and the blood. Not so much heavy beef and mutton. As to pastry . . .' He gestured with his hands in deprecation. 'This boy is forever eating pastry. I saw him demolish a whole pie for dinner yesterday.'

'Do you hear that, Philip?' said Rachel. 'Rainaldi considers that you eat too much. Seecombe, we shall have to cut down on Mr. Philip's food.'

'Surely not, madam,' said Seecombe, greatly shocked. 'To eat less than he does would be injurious to health. We have to remember, madam, that in all probability Mr. Philip is still growing.'

'Heaven forbid,' murmured Rainaldi. 'If he is growing still at twenty-four one would fear some serious glandular disturbance.'

He sipped his brandy, which she permitted him to take into the drawing-room, with a meditative air, his eyes upon me, until I felt for all the world that I was nearly seven foot, like poor dull-witted Jack Trevose who was hawked about Bodmin fair by his mother for the people to stare at him and give him pennies.

'I suppose,' said Rainaldi, 'that you do enjoy good health? No serious illness as a child that would account for growth?'

'I don't remember,' I answered, 'ever having been ill in my life.'

'That in itself is bad,' he said; 'those who have never suffered from disease are the first to be struck down, when nature attacks them. Am I not right in saying so, Seecombe?'

'Very possibly, sir. I hardly know,' said Seecombe; but as he went from the room I noticed him glance at me in doubt, as if I already sickened for the smallpox. 'This brandy,' said Rainaldi, 'should have been kept for at least another thirty years. It will be drinkable when young Philip's children come of age. Do you remember, Rachel, that evening at the villa when you and Cosimo entertained the whole of Florence, or so it seemed, and he insisted that all of us should be in dominoes and masks, like a Venetian carnival? And your dear lamented mother behaved so badly with prince someone-or-other, I think it was Lorenzo Ammanati, wasn't it?'

'It could have been with anyone,' said Rachel, 'but it was not Lorenzo, he was too busy running after me.'

'What nights of folly,' mused Rainaldi. 'We were all of us absurdly young, and entirely irresponsible. Far better to be staid and peaceful as we are today. I think they never give such parties here in England? The climate, of course, would be against it. But for that, young Philip here might find it amusing to dress himself up in mask and domino and search about the bushes for Miss Kendall.'

'I am sure Louise would ask for nothing better,' answered Rachel, and I saw her eye upon me and her mouth twitch.

I went out of the room and left them, and almost at once I heard them break into Italian, his voice interrogatory, and hers laughing in answer to his question, and I knew they were discussing me, and possibly Louise also, and the whole damned story of the rumours that were supposed to go about the countryside concerning some future betrothal between the pair of us. God! How much longer was he going to stay? How many more days and nights of this must I endure?

Eventually, on the last evening of his visit, my godfather, with Louise, came to dine. The evening passed off well, or so it seemed. I saw Rainaldi putting himself to infinite trouble to be courteous to my godfather, and the three of them, he, Rainaldi, and Rachel, somehow formed themselves into a group for conversation, leaving Louise and me to entertain ourselves. Now and again I noticed Rainaldi look towards us, smiling with a sort of amiable indulgence, and once I even heard him say, *sotto voce*, to my godfather, 'All my compliments upon your daughter and your godson. They make a very charming couple.' Louise heard it too. The poor girl flushed crimson. And at once I began asking her when she was next due to visit London, which I hoped would ease her feelings, but for all I know it may have made it worse. After dinner the subject of London came up once again, and Rachel said, 'I hope to visit London myself before very long. If we are there at the same time' – this to Louise – 'you must show me all the sights, because I have never been there.'

My godfather pricked up his ears at her remark.

'So you are thinking of leaving the country?' he said. 'Well, you have certainly endured the rigours of a winter visit to us in Cornwall very well. You will find London more amusing.' He turned to Rainaldi. 'You will still be there?'

'I have business there for some weeks yet,' replied Rainaldi, 'but if Rachel decides to come up I shall very naturally put myself at her disposal. I am no stranger to your capital. I know it very well. I hope that you and your daughter will give us the pleasure of dining with us, when you are there.'

'We shall be very happy to,' said my godfather. 'London in the spring can be delightful.'

I could have hit the whole bunch of heads together for the calm assumption of their meeting, but Rainaldi's use of the word 'us' maddened me the most. I could see his plan. Lure her to London, entertain her there while he conducted his other business, and then prevail upon her to return to Italy. And my godfather, for his own reasons, would further such a plan.

They little knew I had a plot to fox them all. So the evening passed, with much expression of good-will on every side, and with Rainaldi even drawing my godfather apart for the last twenty minutes or more, to drop more venom of some sort or other, I well imagined.

I did not return to the drawing-room, after the Kendalls had gone. I went up to bed, leaving my door ajar so that I could hear Rachel and Rainaldi as they came upstairs. They were long in doing so. Midnight struck, and they were still below. I went and stood out on the landing, listening. The drawing-room door was open a little, and I could hear the murmur of their voices. Resting my hand upon the banister, to bear my weight, I went halfway down the stairs in my bare feet. Memory flashed back to childhood. I had done this as a lad, when I knew Ambrose was below and had company for dinner. The same sense of guilt was with me now. The voices went on and on. But listening to Rachel and Rainaldi was of no purpose, for they spoke together in Italian. Now and again I caught mention of my name, Philip, and several times that of my godfather, Kendall. They were discussing me or him, or both of us. Rachel had an urgency to her voice that sounded strange, and he, Rainaldi, spoke as though he questioned her. I wondered, with sudden revulsion, if my godfather had told Rainaldi about his travelling friends from Florence, and if, in his turn, Rainaldi talked of this to Rachel. How useless had been by Harrow education, and the study of Latin and Greek. Here were two persons talking Italian in my own house, discussing perhaps matters that might be of great importance to me, and I could gather nothing from it, save the mention of my own name.

There fell a sudden silence. Neither of them spoke. I heard no movement. What if he had gone towards her, and had put his arms about her, and she kissed him now as she had kissed me on Christmas Eve? Such a wave of hatred for him came to me at the thought that I nearly lost all caution and went running down the stairs to fling the door open wide. Then I heard her voice once more, and the rustle of her gown, drawing nearer to the door. I saw the flicker of her lighted candle. The long session was over at last. They were coming up to bed. Like that child of long ago, I stole back to my room.

I heard Rachel pass along the corridor to her own suite of rooms, and he turn the other way to his. I would never know, in all probability, what they had discussed together all those hours, but at least this was his last night under my roof, and tomorrow I should sleep with an easy heart. I could hardly swallow my breakfast, the next morning, in haste to hurry him away. The wheels of the post-chaise that was to carry him to London sounded on the drive, and Rachel, who I had thought must have said farewell the night before, came down, ready dressed for gardening, to bid him goodbye.

He took her hand, and kissed it. This time, for the sake of common courtesy to me, his host, he spoke his adieus in English. 'So you will write me your plans?' he said to her. 'Remember, when you are ready to come, I shall await you there, in London.'

'I shall make no plans,' she said, 'before the first of April.' And, looking over his shoulder, she smiled at me.

'Isn't that your cousin's birthday?' said Rainaldi, climbing into the post-chaise. 'I hope he enjoys it, and does not eat too large a pie.' And then, looking from the window, said as a parting shot to me, 'It must be odd to have a birthday on so singular a date. All Fools Day, is it not? But perhaps, at twenty-five, you will think yourself too old to be reminded of it.' Then he was gone, the post-chaise passing down the drive to the park-gates. I looked across at Rachel.

'Perhaps,' she said, 'I should have asked him to return upon that day, for celebration?' Then, with the sudden smile that touched my heart, she took the primrose she had been wearing in her gown and put it in my button-hole. 'You have been very good,' she murmured, 'for seven days. And I, neglectful of my duties. Are you glad we are alone again?' Without waiting for my answer she went off to the plantation after Tamlyn.

Chapter Twenty-one

The remaining weeks of March passed very swiftly. Each day that came I felt a greater confidence in the future, and grew more light of heart. Rachel seemed to sense my mood, and shared it with me.

'I have never,' she said, 'seen anyone so absurd about a birthday. You are like a child, who finds the world magic when he wakes. Does it mean so much to you to be free of poor Mr. Kendall and his care? I am sure you could not have a guardian more kind. What plan, anyway, do you intend to make for the day itself?'

'No plan at all,' I answered, 'except that you have to remember what you said to me the other day. The celebrator of a birthday must be granted every wish.'

'Only up to the age of ten years old,' she said, 'never afterwards.'

'That is not fair,' I said; 'you made no stipulation about age.'

'If we are to picnic by the sea, or sail a boat,' she told me, 'I will not come with you. It is too early in the year to sit upon a beach, and as for climbing in a boat, I know even less about that than I do about a horse. You must take Louise instead.'

'I will not take Louise,' I said, 'and we will go nowhere not fitting to your dignity.' In point of fact, I had not thought about the events of the day itself, I only planned that she should have the document upon her breakfast tray, and the rest I would leave to chance. When the day of the thirty-first of March came, however, I knew that there was something else I wished to do. I remembered the jewels in the bank, and thought what a fool I was not to have recollected them before. So I had two encounters before me, on that day. One with Mr. Couch, and the other with my godfather.

I made certain first of Mr. Couch. I thought the packages might be too bulky to carry upon Gypsy, and I did not wish to order the carriage for fear Rachel might hear of it and express a desire to come into town upon some errand. Besides, it was an unusual thing for me to do, to go anywhere by carriage. So on some unnecessary pretext I walked into town, and had the groom fetch me in the dog-cart. As ill-luck had it, the whole neighbourhood appeared to be on shopping bent upon that morning, and as a person must either dodge into a doorway or fall into the harbour if he wishes to avoid his neighbour in our port, I was forever skulking behind corners so that I might not come face to face with Mrs. Pascoe and her brood of daughters. My very furtiveness must have drawn all eyes upon me, and word gone about the place that Mr. Ashley was behaving in singular fashion, running in one door of the fishmarket and out the other, and bobbing into the Rose and Crown before eleven in the morning, just as the vicar's lady from the neighbouring parish came walking down the street. No doubt it would be spread abroad that Mr. Ashley drank.

I got myself inside sanctuary at last, within the safe walls of the bank. Mr. Couch received me as pleasantly as he had done before.

'This time,' I told him, 'I have come to take all away.' He looked at me in pained surprise.

'You are not, Mr. Ashley,' he said, 'intending to remove your banking account to another establishment?'

'No,' I said, 'I was speaking about the family jewels. Tomorrow I shall be twenty-five, and they become my legal property. I wish to have them in my custody when I awake upon my birthday.'

He must have thought me an eccentric, or at best a little odd.

'You mean,' he answered, 'you wish to indulge yourself in a whim for the day only? You did something of the sort, did you not, on Christmas Eve. Mr. Kendall, your guardian, brought the collar back immediately.'

'Not a whim, Mr. Couch,' I said. 'I want the jewels at home, in my possession. I do not know how I can make it still more clear.'

'I understand,' he said. 'Well, I trust that you have a safe in the house, or at least some place of security where you can keep them.'

'That, Mr. Couch,' I said, 'is really my affair. I would be much obliged if you would fetch the jewels right away. Not only the collar this time. The whole collection.'

I might have been robbing him of his own possessions.

'Very good,' he said reluctantly, 'it will take a little time to fetch them from the vaults, and wrap them with even greater care. If you have any other business in the town . . .'

'I have none,' I interrupted. 'I will wait here, and take them with me.' He saw there was no use in delay and, sending word to his clerk, instructed the packages to be brought. I had a carrier for the purpose, which was luckily just large enough to take the whole – as a matter of fact it was a wicker basket that we used at home for carting cabbages, and Mr. Couch winced as he put the precious boxes into it, one by one.

'It would have been far better, Mr. Ashley,' he said, 'had I sent the packages to the house, in proper fashion. We have a brougham, you know, belonging to the bank, more suitable for the purpose.'

Yes, I thought, and what a clatter of tongues there would have been then. The bank brougham, driving to Mr. Ashley's residence, with a top-hatted manager within. Far better the vegetable basket in a dog-cart.

'That is all right, Mr. Couch,' I said, 'I can manage very well.'

I staggered from the bank in triumph, bearing the basket upon my shoulder, and ran full tilt into Mrs. Pascoe, a daughter on either side.

'Good gracious, Mr. Ashley,' she remarked, 'you appear well loaded.'

Holding the basket with one hand, I swept off my hat with a flourish.

'You observe me fallen on evil days,' I said to her, 'I am sunk so low that I needs must sell cabbages to Mr. Couch and his clerks. Repairing the roof at home has well nigh ruined me, and I am obliged to hawk my produce about the town.'

She stared at me, her mouth agape, and the two daughters opened their eyes wide. 'Unfortunately,' I said, 'this basketful that I have here is due to another customer. Otherwise I would have pleasure in selling you some carrots. But in future, when you lack vegetables at the rectory, remember me.'

I went off to find the waiting dog-cart, and as I heaved the carrier into it, and climbed up and took the reins, while the groom jumped up beside me, I saw her still staring at me, at the street corner, her face dumbfounded. Now the story would go round that Philip Ashley was not only eccentric, drunk, and mad, but a pauper in the bargain.

We drove home by the long avenue from Four Turnings, and while the boy put away the dog-cart I went into the house the back way – the servants were at dinner – and, going upstairs by their staircase, I tip-toed through to the front and to my room. I locked the vegetable basket in my wardrobe, and went downstairs to eat some lunch.

Rainaldi would have closed his eyes and shuddered. I wrought havoc upon a pigeon pie, and washed it down with a great tankard of ale.

Rachel had been in and waited – she left a note to say so – and, thinking I would not return, had gone up to her room. For this once I did not mind her absence. I think my guilty delight would have shown too plainly on my face.

No sooner had I swallowed my meal than I was off again, this time on horseback, to Pelyn. Safe in my pocket I had the document, which the attorney, Mr. Trewin, had sent to me, as he had promised, by special messenger. I also had the will. The prospect of this interview was not as pleasing as that of the morning had been; nevertheless, I was undaunted.

My godfather was at home, and in his study.

'Well, Philip,' he said, 'if I am a few hours premature, no matter. Let me wish you a happy birthday.'

'Thank you,' I said, 'and I would also thank you, in return, for your affection for me and for Ambrose, and for your guardianship over these past years.'

'Which,' he said smiling, 'ends tomorrow.'

'Yes,' I said, 'or rather, tonight, at midnight. And as I do not want to rouse you from your sleep at such an hour, I would like you to witness my signature to a document I wish to sign, which will come into effect at that precise moment.'

'H'm,' he said, reaching for his spectacles, 'a document, what document?'

I brought the will from my breast pocket.

'First,' I said, 'I would like you to read this. It was not given to me willingly, but only after much argument and discussion. I had long felt such a paper must be in existence, and here it is.'

I passed it to him. He placed his spectacles on his nose and read it through. 'It is dated, Philip,' he said, 'but it is not signed.'

'Quite so,' I answered, 'but it is in Ambrose's hand, is it not?'

'Why, yes,' he replied, 'undoubtedly. What I do not understand is why he never had it witnessed and sent to me. I had expected such a will as this from the first days he was married, and told you so.'

'It would have been signed,' I said, 'but for his illness, and for the fact that he expected, any month, to be home here and give it to you in person. That I know.'

He laid it down on his desk.

'Well, there it is,' he said. 'These things have happened in other families. Unfortunate for his widow, but we can do no more for her than we have done. A will without a signature is invalid.'

'I know,' I said, 'and she did not expect otherwise. As I told you just now, it was only by dint of much persuasion that I retrieved this paper from her. I must return it, but here is a copy.'

I pocketed the will, and gave him the copy I had made.

'What now?' he said, 'Has anything else come to light as well?'

'No,' I answered, 'only that my conscience tells me I have been enjoying something that is not mine by right. Ambrose intended to sign that will, and death, or rather illness in the first place, prevented him. I want you to read this document that I have had prepared.'

And I handed him the scroll that had been drawn up by Trewin at Bodmin.

He read it slowly, carefully, his face becoming grave as he did so, and it was only after a long while that he removed his spectacles and looked at me.

'Your cousin Rachel,' he said, 'has no knowledge of this document?'

'No knowledge whatsoever,' I answered, 'never by word or intimation has she expressed any thought of what I have had put there, and what I intend to do. She is utterly and entirely innocent of my purpose. She does not even know that I am here, or that I have shown you the will. As you heard her say a few weeks ago, she intends to leave for London shortly.'

He sat at his desk, his eyes upon my face.

'You are quite determined upon this course?' he said to me.

'Quite,' I answered him.

'You realise that it may lead to abuse, that there are few safeguards, and that the whole of the fortune due to you eventually, and to your heirs, may be dispersed?'

'Yes,' I said, 'and I am willing to take the risk.'

He shook his head, and sighed. He rose from his chair, looked out of the window, and returned to it again.

'Does her adviser, Signor Rainaldi, know of this document?' he asked.

'Most certainly not,' I said.

'I wish you had told me of it, Philip,' he said. 'I could have discussed it with him. He seemed to me a man of sense. I had a word with him that evening. I went so far as to tell him about my uneasiness as to that overdraft. He admitted that extravagance was a fault, and always had been. That it had led to trouble, not only with Ambrose, but also with her first husband, Sangalletti. He gave me to understand that he, Signor Rainaldi, is the only person who knows how to deal with her.'

'I don't care a jot what he told you,' I said. 'I dislike the man, and believe he uses this argument for his own purpose. He hopes to entice her back to Florence.'

My godfather regarded me once more.

'Philip,' he said, 'forgive me asking you this question, personal I know, but I have known you since birth. You are completely infatuated with your cousin, are you not?'

I felt my cheeks burn, but I went on looking at him.

'I don't know what you mean,' I said. 'Infatuation is a futile and most ugly word. I respect and honour my cousin Rachel more than anyone I know.'

'I have meant to say this to you before,' he said. 'There is much talk, you know, about her being so long a visitor to your house. I go further and say the whole of the county whispers of little else.'

'Let them continue,' I said. 'After tomorrow they will have something else to discuss. The transfer of property and fortune can hardly be kept secret.'

'If your cousin Rachel has any wisdom, and wishes to keep her self-respect,' he said, 'she will either go to London, or ask you to live elsewhere. The present situation is very wrong for you both.'

I was silent. Only one thing mattered, that he should sign the paper.

'Of course,' he said, 'there is, in the long run, only one way out of gossip. And, according to this document, only one way out of the transfer of this property. And that is, that she should marry again.'

'I believe it most unlikely,' I said.

'I suppose,' he said, 'you have not thought of asking her yourself?'

Once again the colour flamed in my face.

'I would not dare to do so,' I said; 'she would not have me.'

'I am not happy about any of this, Philip,' he said. 'I wish now that she had never come to England. However, it is too late to regret that. Very well then, sign. And take the consequences of your action.'

I seized a pen, and put my name to the deed. He watched me with his still, grave face.

'There are some women, Philip,' he observed, 'good women very possibly, who through no fault of their own impel disaster. Whatever they touch, somehow turns to tragedy. I don't know why I say this to you, but I feel I must.' And then he witnessed my signature on the long scroll of paper.

'I suppose,' he said, 'you will not wait to see Louise?'

'I think not,' I replied, and then relenting, 'If you are both at liberty to-morrow evening, why not come and dine, and drink my health upon my birthday?'

He paused. 'I am not certain if we are free,' he said. 'I will at any rate send word to you by noon.' I could see plainly he had little wish to come and see us, and had some embarrassment in refusing my invitation. He had taken the whole matter of the transfer better than I had expected, there had been no violent expostulation, no interminable lecture, but possibly he knew me too well by now to imagine anything of the sort would have had effect. That he was greatly shaken and distressed I knew by his grave manner. I was glad that no mention had been made of the family jewels. The knowledge that they were concealed in the cabbage basket in my wardrobe might have proved the final straw.

I rode home, remembering my mood of high elation the last time I had done so, after visiting the attorney Trewin in Bodmin, only to find Rainaldi on arriving home. There would be no such visitor to-day. In three weeks full spring had come about the countryside and it was warm like May. Like all weather prophets, my farmers shook their heads and prophesied calamity. Late frost would come, and nip the buds in bloom and wither the growing corn beneath the surface of the drying soil. I think, on that last day of March, I would not have greatly cared if famine came, or flood, or earthquake.

The sun was sinking beyond the westward bay, flaming the quiet sky, darkening the water, and the rounded face of the near full moon showed plain over the eastern hills. This, I thought to myself, is how a man must feel when in a state of high intoxication, this complete abandon to the passing hour. I saw things, not in hazy fashion, but with the clarity of the very drunk. The park, as I entered it, had all the grace of fairy tale; even the cattle, plodding down to drink at their trough beside the pool, were beasts of enchantment, lending themselves to beauty. The jackdaws were building high, they flapped and straddled their untidy nests in the tall trees near to the avenue, and from the house and the stables I could see the blue smoke curling from the chimneys, and I could sense the clatter of pails about the yard, the whistling of the men, the barking of the puppies from their kennels. All this was old to me, long-known and loved, possessed from babyhood; yet now it held new magic.

I had eaten too fully at midday to be hungry, but I was thirsty, and drank deep of the cool clear water from the well in the courtyard.

I joked with the boys as they bolted the back doors and closed the shutters. They knew to-morrow was my birthday. They whispered to me how Seecombe had had his likeness painted for me, as a deadly secret, and that he had told them I was bound to hang it upon a panel in the hall with the ancestral portraits. I gave them a solemn promise that it was exactly what I would do. And then the three of them, with much head-nodding amongst themselves and muttering in corners, disappeared into the servants' hall and then returned again, bearing a package. John, as spokesman, gave it me and said, ''Tis from us all, Mr. Philip, sir, we none of us can bear wait to give it you.'

It was a case of pipes. It must have cost them all of a month's wages. I shook hands with them, and clapped them on the back, and vowed to each that I had been planning to get the very same myself next time I went to Bodmin or to Truro, and they gazed back at me in great delight, so that like an idiot I could have wept to see their pleasure. In truth, I never smoked any pipe but the one Ambrose had given me when I was seventeen, but in the future I must make a point of smoking all of theirs, for fear of disappointing them.

I bathed and changed, and Rachel was waiting for me in the dining-room.

'I smell mischief,' she said at once. 'You have not been home for the day. What have you been at?'

'That, Mrs. Ashley,' I said to her, 'is no concern of yours.'

'No one has set eyes upon you since early morning,' she said. 'I came home to luncheon, and had no companion.'

'You should have lunched with Tamlyn,' I told her. 'His wife is a most excellent cook, and would have done you well.'

'Did you go to town?' she asked.

'Why, yes, I went to town.'

'And did you see anyone of our acquaintance?'

'Why, yes,' I answered, nearly bursting into laughter. 'I saw Mrs. Pascoe and the girls, and they were greatly shocked at my appearance.'

'Why so?'

'Because I was carrying a basket on my shoulder, and told them I had been selling cabbages.'

'Were you telling them the truth, or had you been to the Rose and Crown and drunk too much cider?'

'I was not telling them the truth, nor had I been to the Rose and Crown for cider.'

'Then what was it all about?'

I would not answer her. I sat in my chair and smiled.

'I think,' I said, 'that when the moon is fully risen I shall go swimming after dinner. I feel all the energy of the world in myself to-night, and all the folly.'

She looked at me over her glass of wine with solemn eyes.

'If,' she said, 'you desire to spend your birthday in your bed with a poultice on your chest, drinking black currant every hour, nursed – not by me, I warn you, but by Seecombe – go swimming, if you please. I shall not stop you.'

I stretched my arms above my head, and sighed for pure enjoyment. I asked permission to smoke, which she granted.

I produced my case of pipes. 'Look,' I said, 'what the boys have given me. They could not wait till morning.'

'You are as great a baby as they,' she said, and then, in a half-whisper, 'You do not know what Seecombe has in store for you.'

'But I do,' I whispered back, 'the boys have told me. I am flattered beyond measure. Have you seen it?'

She nodded. 'It is perfect,' she said; 'his best coat, the green one, his underlip, and all. It was painted by his son-in-law, from Bath.'

When we had dined we went into the library, but I had not been telling her an untruth when I said I had all the energy of the world. I was in such a state of exultation that I could not rest in my chair, with longing for the night to pass and for the day to come.

'Philip,' she said at last, 'for the sake of pity, go and take your walk. Run to the beacon and back again, if that will cure you. I think you have gone mad, in any case.'

'If this is madness,' I said, 'then I would want to stay that way for always. I did not know lunacy could give such delight.'

I kissed her hand and went out into the grounds. It was a night for walking, still and clear. I did not run, as she had bidden me, but for all that I achieved the beacon hill. The moon, so nearly full, hovered, with swollen cheek, above the bay, and wore about his face the look of a wizard man who shared my secret. The bullocks, sheltering for the night in the lea of the stone wall in the valley's dip, stumbled to their feet at my approach, and scattered.

I could see a light from the Barton, above the meadow, and when I reached the beacon head, and the bays stretched out on either side of me, there were the flickering lights of the little towns along the western coast, and our own harbour lights to the east as well. Yet presently they dimmed, as the candlelight did within the Barton, and there was nothing about me but that light from the pale moon, making a silver track across the sea. If it was a night for walking it was a night for swimming too. No threat of poultices or cordials would keep me from it. I climbed down, to my favourite point where the rocks jutted, and, laughing to myself at this folly most sublime, plunged into the water. God! It was icy cold. I shook myself like a dog, with chattering teeth, and struck out across the bay, returning, after a bare four minutes, back to the rocks to dress.

Madness. Worse than madness. But still I did not care, and still my mood of exultation held me in thrall.

I dried myself, as best I could, upon my shirt, and walked up through the woods, back to the house. The moonlight made a ghostly path for me, and shadows, eerie and fantastic, lurked behind the trees. Where my path divided into two, one taking me to the cedar walk and the other to the new terrace above, I heard a rustle where the trees grew thickest, and suddenly to my nostrils came that rank vixen smell about me in the air, tainting the very leaves under my feet; yet I saw nothing, and all the daffodils, leaning from the banks on either side of me, stayed poised and still, without a breath to stir them.

I came to the house at last, and looked up at her window. It was open wide, and I could not tell if her candle burnt still or if she had blown it out. I looked at my watch. It wanted five minutes to midnight. I knew suddenly that if the boys had not been able to wait to give me my present, neither could I wait to give Rachel hers. I thought of Mrs. Pascoe, and the cabbages, and my mood of folly swept me in full force. I went and stood under the window of the blue bedroom, and called up to her. I called her name three times before I had an answer. She came to the open window, dressed in that white nun's robe, with the full sleeves and the lace collar.

'What do you want?' she said. 'I was three parts asleep, and you have woken me.'

'Will you wait there,' I said, 'just a few moments? I want to give you something. The package that Mrs. Pascoe saw me carry.'

'I have not Mrs. Pascoe's curiosity,' she said. 'Let it wait until the morning.'

'It cannot wait until the morning,' I said, 'it has to happen now.'

I let myself in by the side door, and went upstairs to my room and came down again, carrying the cabbage basket. Round the handles I knotted a great piece of string. I had with me, also, the document, which I placed in my jacket pocket. She was still waiting there, beside the window.

'What in the world,' she called softly, 'have you got carried in that basket? Now, Philip, if this is one of your practical jokes, I will not share it. Have you got crabs hidden there, or lobsters?'

'Mrs. Pascoe believes they are cabbages,' I said. 'At any rate, I give you my promise they won't bite. Now, catch the string.'

I threw up the end of the long string to the window.

'Haul away,' I told her, 'with both hands, mind. The basket is some weight.' She pulled, as she was bidden, and the basket bumped and crashed against the wall, and against the wire that was there to hold the creeper, and I stood below, watching her, shaking with silent laughter.

She pulled the basket on to her window-sill, and there was silence.

After a moment she looked out again. 'I don't trust you Philip,' she said. 'These packages have odd shapes. I know they are going to bite.'

For answer I began to climb up the creeper wire, hand over hand, until I reached her window.

'Be careful,' she called, 'you will fall and break your neck.'

In a moment I was inside the room, one leg upon the floor, the other on the sill.

'Why is your head so wet?' she said. 'It is not raining.'

'I've been swimming,' I answered. 'I told you I would do so. Now, open up the packages, or shall I do it for you?'

One candle was burning in the room. She stood with bare feet upon the floor and shivered.

'For heaven's sake,' I said, 'put something round you.'

I seized the coverlet from the bed and threw it about her, then lifted her and put her amongst her blankets.

'I think,' she said, 'that you have gone raving mad.'

'Not mad,' I said, 'it's only that I have become, at this minute, twenty-five. Listen.' I held up my hand. The clock struck midnight. I put my hand into my pocket. 'This,' I said, laying the document upon the table, by the candlestick, 'you can read at your leisure. But the rest I want to give you now.'

I emptied the packages upon the bed and cast the wicker basket on the floor. I tore away the paper, scattering the boxes, flinging the soft wrappings anywhere. Out fell the ruby headpiece and the ring. Out came the sapphires and the emeralds. Here were the pearl collar and the bracelets, all tumbling in mad confusion on the sheets. 'This,' I said, 'is yours. And this, and this . . .' And in an ecstasy of folly I heaped them all upon her, pressing them on her hands, her arms, her person.

'Philip,' she cried, 'you are out of your mind, what have you done?'

I did not answer. I took the collar, and put it about her neck. 'I'm twenty-five,' I said; 'you heard the clock strike twelve. Nothing matters any more. All this for you. If I possessed the world, you should have it also.'

I have never seen eyes more bewildered or amazed. She looked up at me, and down to the scattered necklaces and bracelets and back to me again, and then, I think because I was laughing, she put her arms suddenly about me and was laughing too. We held one another, and it was as though she caught my madness, shared my folly, and all the wild delight of lunacy belonged to both of us.

'Is this,' she said, 'what you have been planning all these weeks?'

'Yes,' I said, 'they should have come with your breakfast. But like the boys and the case of pipes, I could not wait.'

'And I have nothing for you,' she said, 'but a gold pin for your cravat. Your birthday, and you shame me. Is there nothing else you want? Tell me, and you shall have it. Anything you ask.'

I looked down at her, with all the rubies and the emeralds spread about her, and the pearl collar around her neck, and all of a sudden I was serious and remembered what the collar meant.

'One thing, yes,' I said, 'but it isn't any use my asking it.'

'Why not?' she said.

'Because,' I answered, 'you would box my ears, and send me straight to bed.'

She stared up at me, touching my cheek with her hand.

'Tell me,' she said. And her voice was gentle.

I did not know how a man asks a woman to become his wife. There is generally a parent, whose consent must first be given. Or if no parent, then there is courtship, there is all the give and take of some preceding conversation. None of this applied to her and me. And it was midnight, and talk of love and marriage had never passed between us. I could say to her, bluntly, plainly, 'Rachel, I love you, will you be my wife?' I remembered that morning in the garden, when we had jested about my dislike of the whole business, and I had told her that I asked for nothing better than my own house to comfort me. I wondered if she could understand, and remember too.

'I told you once,' I said, 'that I had all the warmth and the comfort that I needed within four walls. Have your forgotten?'

'No,' she said, 'I have not forgotten.'

'I spoke in error,' I said, 'I know now what I lack '

She touched my head, and the tip of my ear, and the end of my chin.

'Do you?' she said. 'Are you so very sure?'

'More sure,' I answered, 'than of anything on earth.'

She looked at me. Her eyes seemed darker in the candlelight.

'You were very certain of yourself upon that morning,' she said, 'and stubborn too. The warmth of houses . . .'

She put out her hand to snuff the candle, and she was laughing still.

When I stood upon the grass at sunrise, before the servants had wakened and come down to open the shutters and let in the day, I wondered if any man before me had been accepted in marriage in quite so straight a fashion.

It would save many a weary courtship if it was always so. Love, and all its trappings, had not concerned me hitherto; men and women must do as best they pleased, I had not cared. I had been blind, and deaf, and sleeping; now, no longer.

What happened on those first hours of my birthday will remain. If there was passion, I have forgotten it. If there was tenderness, it is with me still. Wonder is mine forever, that a woman, accepting love, has no defence. Perhaps this is the secret that they hold to bind us to them. Making reserve of it, until the last.

I would not know, having no other for comparison. She was my first, and last.

Chapter Twenty-two

I remember the house waking to the sunlight, and seeing the round ball of it appear over the trees that fringed the lawn. The dew had been heavy, and the grass was silver, as though touched with frost. A blackbird starting singing, and a chaffinch followed, and soon the whole spring chorus was in song. The weather-vane was the first to catch the sun, and gleaming gold against the sky, poised above the belfry tower, it swung to the nor'west and there remained, while the grey walls of the house, dark and sombre at first sight, mellowed to the morning light with a new radiance.

I went indoors and up to my room, and dragging a chair beside the open window sat down in it, and looked towards the sea. My mind was empty, without thought. My body calm and still. No problems came swimming to the surface, no anxieties itched their way through from the hidden depths to ruffle the blessed peace. It was as though everything in life was now resolved, and the way before me plain. The years behind me counted for nothing. The years to come were no more than a continuation of all I now knew and held, possessing; it would be so, forever and ever, like the amen to a litany. In the future only this; Rachel and I. A man and his wife living within themselves, the house containing us, the world outside our doors passing unheeded. Day after day, night after night, as long as we both should live. That much I remembered from the prayer-book.

I shut my eyes, and she was with me still; and then I must have slept upon the instant, because when I woke the sun was streaming into the open window, and John had come in and laid out my clothes upon the chair and brought me my hot water and gone again, and I had not heard him. I shaved and dressed and went down to my breakfast, which was now cold upon the sideboard – Seecombe thinking I had long descended – but hard-boiled eggs and ham made easy fare. I could have eaten anything that day. Afterwards I whistled to the dogs and went out into the grounds, and, caring nothing for Tamlyn and his cherished blooms, I picked every budding camellia I set eyes upon and laid them in the carrier, the same that had done duty for the jewels the day before, and went back into the house and up the stairs and along the corridor to her room.

She was sitting up in bed, eating her breakfast, and before she had time to call out in protest and draw her curtains, I had showered the camellias down upon the sheets and covered her.

'Good morning once again,' I said, 'and I would remind you that it is still my birthday.'

'Birthday or not,' she said, 'it is customary to knock upon a door before you enter. Go away.'

Dignity was difficult, with the camellias in her hair, and on her shoulders, and falling into the tea-cup and the bread-and-butter, but I straightened my face and withdrew to the end of the room.

'I am sorry,' I said. 'Since entering by window I have grown casual about doors. In fact, my manners have forsaken me.'

'You had better go,' she said, 'before Seecombe comes up to take my tray. I think he would be shocked to see you here, for all your birthday.'

Her cool voice was a damper to my spirits, but I supposed there was logic in her remark. It was a trifle bold, perhaps, to burst in on a woman at her breakfast, even if she was to be my wife – which was something that Seecombe did not know as yet.

'I will go,' I said. 'Forgive me. I only want to say one thing to you. I love you.'

I turned to the door and went, and I remember noticing that she no longer wore the collar of pearls. She must have taken it off after I left her in the early morning, and the jewels were not lying on the floor, all had been tidied away.

But on the breakfast tray, beside her, was the document that I had signed the day before.

Downstairs Seecombe awaited me, a package in his hand bound up in paper.

'Mr. Philip, sir,' he said, 'this is a very great occasion. May I take the liberty of wishing you many, many happy returns of your birthday?'

'You may, Seecombe,' I answered, 'and thank you.'

'This, sir,' he said, 'is only a trifle. A small memento of many years of devoted service to the family. I hope you will not be offended, and that I have not taken any liberty in assuming you might be pleased to accept it as a gift.'

I unwrapped the paper and the visage of Seecombe himself, in profile, was before me; unflattering perhaps, but unmistakable.

'This,' I said gravely, 'is very fine indeed. So fine, in fact, that it shall hang in place of honour near the stairs. Bring me a hammer and a nail.' He pulled the bell, with dignity, for John to do his errand.

Between us we fixed the portrait upon the panel outside the dining-room.

'Do you consider, sir,' said Seecombe, 'that the likeness does me justice? Or has the artist given something of harshness to the features, especially the nose? I am not altogether satisfied.'

'Perfection in a portrait is impossible, Seecombe,' I answered. 'This is as near to it as we shall get. Speaking for myself, I could not be more delighted.'

'Then that is all that matters,' he replied.

I wanted to tell him there and then that Rachel and I were to be married, I was so bursting with delight and happiness, but a certain hesitation held me back; the matter was too solemn and too delicate to thrust upon him unawares, and maybe we should tell him together.

I went round the back to the office, in pretence of work, but all I did when I got there was to sit before my desk and stare in front of me. I kept seeing her, in my mind's eye, propped up against the pillows, eating her breakfast, with the camellia buds scattered on the tray. The peace of early morning had gone from me, and all the fever of last night was with me once again. When we were married, I mused, tilting back my chair and biting the end of my pen, she would not dismiss me from her presence with such ease. I would breakfast with her. No more descending to the dining-room alone. We would start upon a new routine.

The clock struck ten, and I heard the men moving in the court and in the yard outside the office window, and I looked at a sheaf of bills, and put them back again, and started a letter to a fellow magistrate upon the bench and tore it up again. For no words came and nothing that I wrote made any sense, and it was still two hours to noon, when Rachel would come downstairs. Nat Bray, the farmer from Penhale, came in to see me, with a long tale about some cattle that had strayed into Trenant and how the fault was with his neighbour for not seeing to his fences, and I nodded and agreed, hearing little of his argument, for surely by now Rachel might be dressed, and out about the grounds, talking to Tamlyn.

I cut the luckless fellow short and bid him good day, and, seeing his look of hurt discomfiture, took him to seek the steward's room and have a glass of ale with Seecombe. 'To-day, Nat,' I said, 'I do no business, it's my birthday, I am the happiest of men,' and clapping him on the shoulder left him open-mouthed to make what he would of my remark.

Then I thrust my head out of the window, and called across the court to the kitchen, and asked them to pack a luncheon basket for a picnic, for suddenly I wanted to be alone with her under the sun, with no formality of house or dining-room or silver upon a table, and this order given I walked to the stables to tell Wellington that I wished to have Solomon saddled for the mistress.

He was not there. The coach-house door was wide and the carriage gone. The stable lad was sweeping the cobbles. He looked blank at my enquiry.

'The mistress ordered the carriage soon after ten,' he said. 'Where she has gone I cannot say. Perhaps to town.'

I went back to the house and rang for Seecombe, but he could tell me nothing, except that Wellington had brought the carriage to the door at a little after ten, and Rachel was ready waiting in the hall. She had never before gone driving in the morning. My spirits, pitched so high, flagged suddenly and dropped. The day was all before us and this was not what I had planned.

I sat about, and waited. Noon came and the bell clanged out for the servants' dinner. The picnic basket was beside me, Solomon was saddled. But the carriage did not come. Finally, at two, I took Solomon round to the stable myself and bade the boy unsaddle him. I walked down the woods to the new avenue, and the excitement of the morning had turned to apathy. Even if she came now it would be too late to picnic. The warmth of an April sun would be gone by four o'clock.

I was nearly at the top of the avenue, at Four Turnings, when I saw the groom open the lodge gates and the carriage pass through. I stood waiting, in the middle of the drive, for the horses to approach, and at sight of me Wellington drew rein and halted them. The weight of disappointment, so heavy during the past hours, went at the glimpse of her, sitting in the carriage, and telling Wellington to drive on I climbed in and sat opposite her, on the hard narrow seat.

She was wrapped in her dark mantle, and she wore her veil down, so that I could not see her face.

'I have looked for you since eleven,' I said. 'Where in the world have you been?'

'To Pelyn,' she said, 'to see your godfather.'

All the worries and perplexities, safely buried in the depths, came rushing to the fore-front of my mind, and with a sharp misgiving I wondered what they could do, between them, to make havoc of my plans.

'Why so?' I asked. 'What need to go find him in such a hurry? Everything has been settled long since.'

'I am not sure,' she answered, 'what you mean by everything.'

The carriage jolted in a rut beside the avenue, and she put out her hand in its dark glove to the strap for steadiness. How remote she seemed, sitting there in her mourning clothes, behind her veil, a world away from the Rachel who had held me against her heart.

'The document,' I said, 'you are thinking of the document. You cannot go against it. I am legally of age. My godfather can do nothing. It is signed, and sealed and witnessed. Everything is yours.'

'Yes,' she said, 'I understand it now. The wording was a little obscure, that was all. So I wished to make certain what it meant.'

Still that distant voice, cool and unattached, while in my ears and in my memory was the other, that had whispered in my ear at midnight.

'Is it clear to you now?' I said.

'Quite clear,' she answered.

'Then there is nothing more to be said on the matter?'

'Nothing,' she replied.

Yet there was a kind of nagging at my heart, and a strange mistrust. All spontaneity was gone, the joy and laughter we had shared together when I gave her the jewels. God damn my godfather if he had said anything to hurt her.

'Put up your veil,' I said.

For a moment she did not move. Then she glanced up at Wellington's broad back and the groom beside him on the box. He whipped the horses to a brisker pace as the twisting avenue turned into the straight.

She lifted her veil, and the eyes that looked into mine were not smiling as I had hoped, or tearful as I had feared, but steady and serene and quite unmoved, the eyes of someone who has been out upon a matter of business and settled it in satisfaction.

For no great reason I felt blank, and in some sense cheated. I wanted the eyes to be as I remembered them at sunrise. I had thought, foolishly perhaps, that it was because her eyes were still the same that she had hidden them behind her veil. Not so, however. She must have sat facing my godfather thus, across the desk in his study, purposeful and practical and cool, no whit dismayed, while I sat waiting for her, in torment, on the front door step at home.

'I would have been back before now,' she said, 'but they pressed me to remain for luncheon, and I could not well refuse. Had you made a plan?' She turned her face to watch the passing scene, and I wondered how it was that she could sit there, as if we were two people of casual acquaintance, while it was as much as I could do not to put out my hands to her and hold her. Since yesterday, everything was changed. Yet she gave no sign of it.

'I had a plan,' I said, 'but it does not matter now.'

'The Kendalls dine tonight in town,' she said, 'but will look in upon us afterwards, before returning home. I fancy I made some progress with Louise. Her manner was not quite so frozen.'

'I am glad of that,' I said, 'I would like you to be friends.'

'In fact,' she went on, 'I am coming back again to my original way of thinking. She would suit you well.'

She laughed, but I did not laugh with her. It was unkind, I thought, to make a joke of poor Louise. Heaven only knew, I wished the girl no harm, and that she might find herself a husband.

'I think,' she said, 'that your godfather disapproves of me, which he has a perfect right to do, but by the end of luncheon I think we understood one another very well. The tension eased, and conversation was not difficult. We made more plans to meet in London.'

'In London?' I asked. 'You don't still intend to go to London?'

'Why, yes,' she said, 'why ever not?'

I said nothing. Certainly she had a right to go to London if she pleased. There might be shops she wished to visit, purchases to make, especially now that she had money to command, and yet . . . surely she could wait awhile, until we could go together? There were so many things we must discuss, but I was hesitant to do so. It struck me with full force, suddenly and sharply, what I had not thought of until now. Ambrose was but nine months dead. The world would think it wrong for us to marry before midsummer. Somehow there were problems to the day that had not been at midnight, and I wanted none of them.

'Don't let's go home immediately.' I said to her. 'Walk with me in the woods.'

'Very well,' she answered.

We stopped by the keeper's cottage in the valley, and descending from the carriage let Wellington drive on. We took one of the paths beside the stream, which twisted upward to the hill above, and here and there were primroses, in clumps, beneath the trees, which she must stoop and pick, returning again to the subject of Louise as she did so, saying the girl had quite an eye for gardens and with instruction would learn more, in time. Louise could go to the ends of the earth for all I cared, and garden there to her heart's content; I had not brought Rachel in the woods to talk about Louise.

I took the primroses from her hands and put them on the ground, and spreading my coat under a tree I asked her to sit down upon it.

'I am not tired,' she said. 'I have been sitting in the carriage this past hour or more.'

'And I also,' I said, 'these four hours, by the front door, waiting for you.'

I took off her gloves, and kissed her hands, and put the bonnet and the veil amongst the primroses, and kissed the rest of her as I had wanted to do for long hours past, and once again she was without defence. 'This,' I said, 'was my plan, which you have spoilt by lunching with the Kendalls.'

'I rather thought it might be,' she answered, 'which was one of the reasons why I went.'

'You promised to deny me nothing on my birthday, Rachel.'

'There is,' she said, 'a limit to indulgence.'

'I could see none. I was happy once again, with all anxiety gone.

'If,' she remarked, 'this is a path frequented by the keeper we would look a little foolish.'

'And he more foolish still,' I replied, 'when I pay his wages on Saturday. Or will you take that over with the rest? I am your servant now, you know, another Seecombe, and await your further orders.'

I lay there, with my head in her lap, and she ran her fingers through my hair. I shut my eyes, and wished it might continue. To the end of time, nothing but that moment.

'You are wondering why I had not thanked you,' she said. 'I saw your puzzled eyes in the carriage. There is nothing I can say. I always believed myself impulsive, but you are more so. It will take me a little time, you know, to grasp the full measure of your generosity.'

'I have not been generous,' I answered, 'it was your due. Let me kiss you once again. I have to make up for those hours upon the doorstep.'

Presently she said, 'I have learnt one thing at least. Never to go walking with you in the woods again. Philip, let me rise.'

I helped her to her feet, and, with a bow, handed her the gloves and bonnet. She fumbled in her purse, and brought out a small package, which she unwrapped. 'Here,' she said, 'is your birthday present, which I should have given you before. Had I known that I was coming into a fortune, the pearl head would have been larger.' She took the pin and put it in my cravat.

'Now will you permit me to go home? she said.

She gave me her hand, and I remembered that I had eaten no lunch that day and had now a prodigious appetite for dinner. We turned along the pathway, I thinking of boiled fowl and bacon and the night to come, and suddenly we were upon the granite stone above the valley, which I had forgotten awaited us at the termination of the path. I turned swiftly into the trees, so as to avoid it, but too late. She had already seen it, dark and square among the trees, and letting go my hand stood still and stared at it.

'What is it, Philip,' she asked, 'that shape there, like a tombstone, rising so suddenly out of the ground?'

'It is nothing,' I said swiftly, 'just a piece of granite. A sort of landmark. There is a path here, through the trees, where the walking is less steep. This way, to the left. Not past the stone.'

'Wait a moment,' she said, 'I want to look at it. I have never been this way before.'

She went up to the slab and stood before it. I saw her lips move as she read the words, and I watched her in apprehension. Perhaps it was my fancy, yet it seemed to me that her body stiffened, and she paused there longer than she need have done. She must have read the words twice over. Then she came back and joined me, but this time she did not take my hand, she walked alone. She made no comment on the monument, nor did I, but somehow that great slab of granite was with us as we walked. I saw the lines of doggerel, and the date beneath, and his initials A.A. cut into the stone, and I saw also, which she could not, the pocket-book with the letter buried deep beneath the stone, in the dank earth. And I felt, in some vile fashion, that I had betrayed them both. Her very silence showed that she was moved. Unless, I thought to myself, I speak now, at this moment, the slab of granite will be a barrier between us, and will grow in magnitude.

'I meant to take you there before,' I said, my voice sounding loud and unnatural after so long an interval. 'It was the view Ambrose liked best, on the whole estate. That is why the stone is there.'

'But it was not,' she answered, 'part of your birthday plan to show it to me.' The words were clipped and hard, the words of a stranger.

'No,' I said quietly, 'not part of the plan.' And we walked along the drive without further conversation, and on entering the house she went straight to her room.

I took my bath and changed my clothes, no longer light of heart but dull, despondent. What demon took us to that granite stone, what lapse of memory? She did not know, as I did, how often Ambrose had stood there, smiling and leaning on his stick, but the silly doggerel lines would conjure up the mood that prompted them, half-jesting, half nostalgic, the tender thought behind his mocking eyes. The slab of granite, tall and proud, would have taken on the substance of the man himself, whom, through fault of circumstance, she had not permitted to return to die at home, but who lay many hundred miles away, in that Protestant cemetery in Florence.

Here was a shadow for my birthday night.

At least she knew nothing of the letter, nor would she ever know, and I wondered, as I dressed for dinner, what other demon had prompted me to bury it there, rather than burn it in the fire, as though I had the instinct of an animal, that would one day return to dig it up. I had forgotten all that it contained. His illness had been upon him as he wrote. Brooding, suspicious, with the hand of death so close, he had not reckoned on his words. And suddenly, as though it danced before me on the wall, I saw the sentence, 'Money, God forgive me for saying so, is, at the present time, the one way to her heart.'

The words jumped on to the mirror, as I stood before it brushing my hair. They were there as I placed her pin in my cravat. They followed me down the stairs and into the drawing-room, and they turned from the written words into his voice itself, the voice of Ambrose, deep, well-loved, long known, remembered always – 'The one way to her heart.'

When she came down to dinner she wore the pearl collar round her neck, as though in forgiveness, as though in tribute to my birthday; yet somehow, to my mind, the fact that she wore it made her not closer to me, but more distant. To-night, if only for to-night, I had rather that her neck had been left bare.

We sat down to dinner, with John and Seecombe waiting on us, and the full regalia of the candlesticks and the silver upon the table, and the lace napery too, in honour of my birthday, and there was boiled fowl and bacon as of long custom, from my school-boy days, which Seecombe bore in with great pride, his eye upon me. We laughed and smiled, and toasted them and ourselves, and the five-and-twenty years that lay behind me; but all the while I felt that we forced our spirits into jollity for the sake of Seecombe and for John, and left to ouselves would fall to silence.

A kind of desperation came upon me, that it was imperative to feast, imperative to make merry, and the solution therefore was to drink more wine, and fill her glass as well, so that the sharper edge of feeling could be dulled and both of us forget the granite slab and what it stood for in our inner selves. Last night I had walked to the beacon head under the full moon, in exultation, sleep-walking, in a dream. To-night, though in the intervening hours I had woken to the wealth of the whole world, I had woken to shadows too.

Muzzy-eyed, I watched her across the table; she was laughing over her shoulder to Seecombe, and it seemed to me she had never looked more lovely. If I could recapture my mood of early morning, the stillness and the peace, and blend it with the folly of the afternoon among the primroses under the tall beech trees, then I would be happy once again. She would be happy too. And we would hold the mood for ever, precious and sacred, carrying it into the future.

Seecombe filled my glass again and something of the shadow slipped away, the doubts were eased; when we are alone together, I thought, all will be well, and I shall ask her this very evening, this very night, if we can be married soon, but soon, in a few weeks perhaps, in a month, for I wanted everyone to know, Seecombe, John, the Kendalls, everyone, that Rachel would bear her name because of me.

She would be Mrs. Ashley; Philip Ashley's wife.

We must have sat late, for we had not left the table when there came the sound of carriage wheels upon the drive. The bell pealed and the Kendalls were shown in to the dining-room where we were still seated amidst the confusion of crumbs and dessert and half-empty glasses, and all the aftermath of dinner. I rose, unsteadily I recollect, and dragged two chairs to the table, with my godfather protesting that they had already dined, and only came in for a moment to wish me good health.

Seecombe brought fresh glasses and I saw Louise, in a blue gown, look at me, a question in her eyes, thinking, I felt instinctively, that I had drunk too much. She was right, but it did not happen often, it was my birthday, and time she knew, once and for all, that she would never have the right to criticise me, except as a childhood friend. My godfather should know too. It would put an end to all his plans for her, and put an end to gossip also, and ease the mind of anyone who cared to worry on the subject.

We all sat down again, with buzz of conversation, my godfather, Rachel and Louise already eased to each other's company through the hours spent at luncheon; while I sat silent at my end of the table, scarce taking in a word, but turning over in my mind the announcement I had resolved to make.

At length my godfather, leaning towards me glass in hand and smiling. said, 'To your five-and-twenty years, Philip. Long life and happiness.'

The three of them looked at me, and whether it was the wine I had taken, or my own full heart within me, but I felt that both my godfather and Louise were dear and trusted friends, I liked them well, and Rachel, my love, with tears already in her eyes, was surely nodding her head and smiling her encouragement.

This was the moment then, opportune and fit. The servants were from the room, so the secret could be held amongst the four of us.

I stood up and thanked them, and then with my own glass filled I said, 'I too have a toast I wish you to drink to-night. Since this morning I have been the happiest of men. I want you, godfather, and you Louise, to drink to Rachel, who is to be my wife.'

I drained my glass, and looked down upon them, smiling. No one answered, no one moved, I saw perplexity in my godfather's expression and turning to Rachel I saw that her smile had gone, and that she was staring at me, her face a frozen mask.

'Have you quite lost your senses, Philip?' she said.

I put my glass down upon the table. I was uncertain of my hand, and placed it too near the edge. It toppled over, and shivered in fragments on the floor. My heart was thumping. I could not take my eyes away from her still white face.

'I am sorry,' I said, 'if it was premature to break the news. Remember it is my birthday, and they are both my oldest friends.'

I gripped the table with my hands for steadiness, and there was a sound of drumming in my ears. She did not seem to understand. She looked away from me, back to my godfather and Louise.

'I think,' she said, 'that the birthday and the wine have gone to Philip's head. Forgive this piece of school-boy folly, and forget it, if you can. He will apologise when he is himself again. Shall we go to the drawing-room?'

She rose to her feet and led the way from the room. I went on standing there, staring at the debris of the dinner table, the crumbs of bread, the spilt wine on the napery, the chairs pushed back, and there was no feeling in me, none at all, but a kind of vacuum where my heart had been. I waited awhile, and then, stumbling from the dining-room before John and Seecombe should come to clear the table, I went into the library, and sat there in the darkness, beside the empty grate. The candles had not been lighted, and the logs had fallen into ash. Through the half-open door I could hear the murmur of the voices in the drawing-room. I pressed my hands to my reeling head, and the taste of the wine was sour on my tongue. Perhaps if I sat still there, in the darkness, I would recover my sense of balance, and the numb emptiness would go. It was the fault of the wine that I had blundered. Yet why should she mind so much what I had said? We could have sworn the pair of them to secrecy. They would have understood. I went on sitting there, waiting for them to go. Presently – the time seemed endless but it may not have been more than ten minutes or so – the voices grew louder and they passed into the hall, and I heard Seecombe opening the front door, bidding them good night, and the wheels drive away, and the clanging and bolting of the door.

My brain was clearer now. I sat and listened. I heard the rustle of her gown. It came near to the half-open door of the library, paused an instant, then passed away; and then her footstep on the stair. I got up from my chair and followed her. I came upon her at the turn of the corridor, where she had paused to snuff the candles at the stair-head. We stood staring at one another in the flickering light.

'I thought you were gone to bed,' she said. 'You had better go, at once, before you do more damage.'

'Now that they are gone,' I said, 'will you forgive me? Believe me, you can trust the Kendalls. They won't give away our secret.'

'Good God, I should hope not, since they know nothing of it,' she replied. 'You make me feel like a backstairs servant, creeping to some attic with a groom. I have known shame before, but this is the worst.'

Still the white frozen face that was not hers.

'You were not ashamed last night at midnight,' I said, 'you gave your promise then, and were not angry. I would have gone at once if you had bidden me.'

'My promise?' she said. 'What promise?'

'To marry me, Rachel,' I answered.

She had her candlestick in her hand. She raised it, so that the naked flame showed on my face. 'You dare to stand there, Philip,' she said, 'and bluster to me that I promised to marry you last night? I said at dinner, before the Kendalls, that you had lost your senses, and so you have. You know very well I gave you no such promise.'

I stared back at her. It was not I who was out of mind, but she. I felt the colour flame into my face.

'You asked me what I wanted,' I said, 'as a birthday wish. Then, and now, there was only one thing in the world I could ever ask, that you should marry me. What else could I mean?'

She did not answer. She went on looking at me, incredulous, baffled, like someone listening to words in a foreign language that cannot be translated or comprehended, and I realised suddenly, with anguish and despair, that so it was, in fact, between us both; all that had passed had been in error. She had not understood what it was I asked of her at midnight, nor I, in my blind wonder, what she had given, therefore what I had believed to be a pledge of love was something different, without meaning, on which she had put her own interpretation.

If she was ashamed then I was doubly so, that she could have been mistaken in me.

'Let me put it in plain language now,' I said. 'When will you marry me?'

'But never, Philip,' she said, with a gesture of her hand, as if dismissing me. 'Take that as final, and forever. If you hoped otherwise, I am sorry. I had no intention to mislead you. Now, good night.'

She turned to go, but I seized hold of her hand, and held it fast.

'Do you not love me then?' I asked. 'Was it pretence? Why, for God's sake, did you not tell me the truth last night and bid me go?'

Once again her eyes were baffled; she did not understand. We were strangers, with no link between us. She came from another land, another race.

'Do you dare to reproach me for what happened?' she said. 'I wanted to thank you, that was all. You had given me the jewels.'

I think I knew, upon that instant, all that Ambrose had known too. I knew what he had seen in her, and longed for, but had never had. I knew the torment, and the pain, and the great gulf between them, ever widening. Her eyes, so dark and different from our own, stared at both of us, uncomprehending. Ambrose stood beside me in the shadows, under the flickering candlelight. We looked at her, tortured, without hope, while she looked back at us in accusation. Her face was foreign too, in the half light. Small and narrow, a face upon a coin. The hand I held was warm no longer. Cold and brittle, the fingers struggled for release, and the rings scratched, cutting at my palm. I let it go, and as I did so wanted it again.

'Why do you stare at me?' she whispered. 'What have I done to you? Your face has changed.'

I tried to think what else I had to give. She had the property, the money, and the jewels. She had my mind, my body, and my heart. There was only my name, and that she bore already. Nothing remained. Unless it should be fear. I took the candle from her hand and placed it on the ledge, above the stairs. I put my hands about her throat, encircling it; and now she could not move, but watched me, her eyes wide. And it was as though I held a frightened bird in my two hands, which, with added pressure, would flutter awhile, and die, and with release would fly away to freedom.

'Never leave me,' I said, 'swear it, never, never.'

She tried to move her lips in answer, but could not do so, because of the pressure of my hands. I loosened my grasp. She backed away from me, her fingers to her throat. There were two red weals where my hands had been, on either side of the pearl collar.

'Will you marry me now?' I said to her.

She gave no answer, but walked backwards from me, down the corridor, her eyes upon my face, her fingers still to her throat. I saw my own shadow on the wall, a monstrous thing, without shape or substance. I saw her disappear under the archway. I heard the door shut, and the key turn in the lock. I went to my room, and catching sight of my reflection in the mirror paused, and stared. Surely it was Ambrose who stood there, with the sweat upon his forehead, the face drained of all colour? Then I moved and was myself again; with stooping shoulders, limbs that were clumsy and too long, hesitant, untutored, the Philip who had indulged in school-boy folly. Rachel had told the Kendalls to forgive me, and forget.

I flung open the window, but there was no moon to-night and it was raining hard. The wind blew the curtain, and ruffling the almanack upon the mantelpiece brought it to the door. I stooped to pick it up, and tearing off the page crumpled it, and flung it in the fire. The end of my birthday. All Fools Day was over.

Chapter Twenty-three

In the morning when I sat to breakfast, looking out upon the blustering windy day with eyes that saw nothing, Seecombe came into the dining-room with a note upon the salver. My heart jumped at the sight of it. It might be that she asked me to call upon her in her room. But it was not from Rachel. The handwriting was larger, rounder. The note was from Louise. 'Mr. Kendall's groom has just brought this, sir,' said Seecombe, 'he is waiting for an answer.'

I read it through. 'Dear Philip, I have been so much distressed by what occurred last night. I think I understand what you felt, more so than my father. Please remember I am your friend, and always will be. I have to go to town this morning. If you want someone to talk to, I could meet you outside the church a little before noon. Louise.'

I put the note in my pocket and asked Seecombe to bring me a piece of paper and a pen. My first instinct, as always at the suggestion of any encounter with no matter whom, but more especially upon this morning, was to scribble a word of thanks, and then refuse. When Seecombe brought the pen and paper, though, I had decided otherwise. A sleepless night, an agony of loneliness made me of a sudden yearn for company. Louise was better known to me than anyone. I wrote therefore, telling her I would be in the town that morning, and would look for her outside the church.

'Give this to Mr. Kendall's groom,' I said, 'and tell Wellington I shall want Gypsy saddled at eleven.'

After breakfast I went to the office, and cleared up the bills, and wrote the letter that I had started yesterday. Somehow it was simpler to-day. A part of my brain worked in a dull fashion, took note of facts and figures, and jotted them down as if compelled by force of habit. My work accomplished I walked round to the stable, in a haste to get away from the house and all it meant to me. I did not ride by the avenue through the woods, with its memories of yesterday, but straight across the park and to the high road. My mare was very fresh, and nervous as a fawn; starting at nothing she pricked and shied, and backed into the hedgerows, and the tearing wind did its worst to both of us.

The bluster that should have been in February and March had come at last. Gone was the mellow warmth of the past weeks, the smooth sea, and the sun. Great clouds with dragging tails, black-edged and filled with rain, came scudding from the west, and now and again with sudden bursting fury emptied themselves as hail. The sea was a turmoil in the western bay. In the fields on either side of the road the gulls screamed and dipped in the flesh ploughed earth, seeking the green shoots fostered by the early spring. Nat Bray, whom I had dismissed so swiftly the preceding morning, stood by his gate as I passed it, a wet sack hanging about his shoulders to protect him from the hail, and he put up his hand and shouted me good morning, but the sound of his voice carried beyond me, and away.

Even from the high road I could hear the sea. To the west, where it ran shallow over the sands, it was short and steep, turned backwards on itself and curling into foam, but to the east, before the estuary, the great long rollers came, spending themselves upon the rocks at the harbour entrance, and the roar of the breakers mingled with the biting wind that swept the hedgerows and forced back the budding trees.

There were few people about as I descended the hill into the town, and those I saw went about their business bent sideways with the wind, their faces nipped with the sudden cold. I left Gypsy at the Rose and Crown, and walked up the path to the church. Louise was sheltering beneath the porch. I opened the heavy door and we went in together, to the church itself. It seemed dark and peaceful, after the bluster of the day without, yet with it too that chill so unmistakable, oppressive, heavy, and the mouldering churchy smell. We went and sat by the marble recumbent figure of my ancestor, his sons and daughters weeping at his feet, and I thought how many Ashleys were scattered about the countryside, some here, others in my own parish, and how they had loved, and suffered, and then gone upon their way.

Instinct hushed us both, in the silent church, and we spoke in whispers.

'I have been unhappy about you for so long,' said Louise, 'since Christmas, and before. But I could not tell you. You would not have listened.'

'There was no need,' I answered, 'all had gone very well until last night. The fault was mine, in saying what I did.'

'You would not have said it,' she replied, 'unless you had believed it to be the truth. There has been deception from the first, and you were prepared for it, in the beginning, before she came.'

'There was no deception,' I said, 'until the last few hours. If I was mistaken there is no one but myself to blame.'

A sudden shower stung the church windows southward, and the long aisle with the tall pillars turned darker than before.

'Why did she come here last September?' said Louise. 'Why did she travel all this way to seek you out? It was not sentiment that brought her here, or idle curiosity. She came to England, and to Cornwall, for a purpose, which she has now accomplished.'

I turned and looked at her. Her blue eyes were simple and direct.

'What do you mean?' I asked.

'She has the money,' said Louise. 'That was the plan she had in mind before she took her journey.'

My tutor at Harrow, when teaching in Fifth Form, told us once that truth was something intangible, unseen, which sometimes we stumbled upon and did not recognise, but was found, and held, and understood only by old people near their death, or sometimes by the very pure, the very young.

'You are mistaken,' I said, 'you know nothing about her. She is a woman of impulse and emotion, and her moods are unpredictable and strange, God knows, but it is not in her nature to be otherwise. Impulse drove her from Florence. Emotion brought her here. She stayed because she was happy, and because she had a right to stay.'

Louise looked at me in pity. She put her hand upon my knee.

'Had you been less vulnerable,' she said, 'Mrs. Ashley would not have stayed. She would have called upon my father, struck a close fair bargain, and then departed. You have misunderstood her motives from the first.'

I could have stood it better, I thought, as I stumbled from the pew into the aisle, if Louise had struck Rachel with her hands, or spat upon her, torn her hair, her gown. That would be primitive and animal. That would be fighting fair. But this, in the quietude of the church, with Rachel absent, was slander, almost blasphemy.

'I can't sit here and listen to you,' I said. 'I wanted your comfort and your sympathy. If you have none to give, no matter.'

She stood up beside me, catching at my arm.

'Don't you see I am trying to help you?' she pleaded. 'But you are so blind to everything, it's no use. If it's not in Mrs. Ashley's nature to plan the months ahead, why has she been sending her allowance out of the country week by week, month by month, throughout the winter?'

'How do you know,' I said, 'that she has done that?'

'My father had means of knowing,' she answered. 'These things could not be hidden, between Mr. Couch and my father, acting as your guardian.'

'Well, what if she did?' I said. 'There were debts in Florence, I have known that all along. Creditors were pressing to be paid.'

'From one country to another?' she said. 'Is it possible? I would not have thought so. Isn't it more likely that Mrs. Ashley hoped to build up something for her return, and that she spent the winter here only because she knew you came legally into your money and your property on your twenty-fifth birthday, which was yesterday? Then, with my father no longer guardian, she could bleed you as she chose. But there was suddenly no need. You made her a present of everything you had.'

I could not believe it possible that a girl I knew and trusted could have so damnable a mind, and speak – that was the greatest hell – with so much logic and plain common sense, to tear apart another woman like herself.

'Is it your father's legal mind speaking in you, or you yourself?' I said to her.

'Not my father,' she said; 'you know his reserve. He has said little to me. I have a judgement of my own.'

'You set yourself against her from the day you met,' I said. 'A Sunday, wasn't it, in church? You came back to dinner and did not say a word, but sat there at the table, with your face all stiff and proud. You had made up your mind to dislike her.'

'And you?' she said. 'Do you remember what you said about her before she came? I can't forget the enmity you had for her. And with good reason.' There was a creaking movement from the side door near to the choir stalls. It opened, and the cleaner, a little mousy woman, Alice Tabb, crept in with broom in hand to sweep the aisles. She glanced at us furtively, and went away behind the pulpit; but her presence was with us, and solitude had gone.

'It's no use, Louise,' I said, 'you can't help me. I am fond of you, and you of me. If we continue talking we shall hate each other.'

Louise looked at me, her hand dropped from my arm.

'Do you love her, then, so much?' she said.

I turned away. She was younger than myself, a girl, and she could not understand. No one could ever understand, save Ambrose, who was dead.

'What does the future hold now for either of you?' asked Louise.

Our footsteps sounded hollow down the aisle. The shower, that had spat upon the windows, ceased. A gleam of fitful sun lit the halo on St. Peter's head in the south window, then left it dim once more.

'I asked her to marry me,' I said; 'I have asked her once, and twice. I shall continue asking her. That's my future for you.'

We came to the church door. I opened it and we stood in the porch again. A blackbird, heedless of the rain, was singing from the tree by the church gate, and a butcher's boy, his tray upon his shoulder, went past it whistling for company, his apron over his head.

'When was the first time that you asked her?' said Louise.

The warmth was with me once again, the candlelight, the laughter. And suddenly no light, and suddenly no laughter. Only Rachel and myself. Almost in mockery of midnight, the church clock struck twelve of noon.

'On the morning of my birthday,' I told Louise.

She waited for the final stroke of the bell that sounded so loud above our heads.

'What did she answer you?' she said.

'We spoke at cross purposes,' I answered; 'I thought that she meant yes, when she meant no.'

'Had she read the document at that time?'

'No. She read that later. Later, the same morning.'

Below the church gate I saw the Kendall groom and the dog-cart. He raised his whip, at sight of his master's daughter, and climbed down from the trap. Louise fastened her mantle and pulled the hood over her hair. 'She lost little time in reading it, then, and driving out to Pelyn to see my father,' said Louise.

'She did not understand it very well,' I said.

'She understood it when she drove away from Pelyn,' said Louise. 'I remember perfectly, as the carriage waited and we stood upon the steps, my father said to her "The re-marriage clause may strike a little hard. You must remain a widow if you wish to keep your fortune." And Mrs. Ashley smiled at him, and answered, "That suits me very well." '

The groom came up the path, bearing the big umbrella. Louise fastened her gloves. A fresh black squall came scudding across the sky.

'The clause was inserted to safeguard the estate,' I said, 'to prevent any squander by a stranger. If she were my wife it would not apply.'

'That is where you are wrong,' said Louise. 'If she married you, the whole would revert to you again. You had not thought of that.'

'But even so?' I said. 'I would share very penny of it with her. She would not refuse to marry me because of that one clause. Is that what you are trying to suggest?'

The hood concealed her face, but the blue eyes looked out at me, though the rest was hidden.

'A wife,' said Louise, 'cannot send her husband's money from the country, nor return to the place where she belongs. I suggest nothing.'

The groom touched his hat, and held the umbrella over her head. I followed her down the path and to the trap, and helped her to her seat.

'I have done you no good,' she said, 'and you think me merciless and hard. Sometimes a woman sees more clearly than a man. Forgive me for hurting you. I only want you to be yourself again.' She leant to the groom. 'Very well, Thomas,' she said, 'we will go back to Pelyn,' and he turned the horse and they went away up the hill to the high road.

I went and sat in the little parlour of the Rose and Crown. Louise had spoken true when she told me she had done me no good. I had come for comfort, and found none. Only cold hard facts, twisted to distortion. All of what she said would make sense to a lawyer's mind. I knew how my godfather weighed things in the balance, without allowance for the human heart. Louise could not help it if she had inherited his shrewd strict outlook and reasoned accordingly.

I knew better than she did what had come between Rachel and myself. The granite slab, above the valley in the woods, and all the months that I had never shared. 'Your cousin Rachel,' Rainaldi said, 'is a woman of impulse.' Because of impulse she had let me love her. Because of impulse she had let me go again. Ambrose had known these things. Ambrose had understood. And neither for him, nor for me, could there ever be another woman, or another wife.

I sat a long while in the chill parlour of the Rose and Crown. The landlord brought me cold mutton and some ale, though I was not hungry. Later I went out and stood upon the quay and watched the high tide splashing on the steps. The fishing vessels rocked at their buoys, and one old fellow, seated across a thwart, baled out the water from the bottom boards of his boat, his back turned to the spray that filled it again with every breaking sea.

The clouds came lower than they had before, turning to mist, cloaking the trees on the opposite shore. If I wished to return home without a soaking, and Gypsy without a chill, I had best return before the weather worsened. No one remained now without doors. I mounted Gypsy and climbed the hill, and to spare myself the further mileage of the high road turned down where the four roads met, and into the avenue. We were more sheltered here, but scarce had gone a hundred yards before Gypsy suddenly hobbled and went lame, and rather than go into the lodge and have the business of removing the stone that had cut into her shoe, and having gossip there, I decided to dismount and lead her gently home. The gale had brought down branches that lay strewn across our path, and the trees that yesterday had been so still tossed now, and swayed, and shivered with the misty rain.

The vapour from the boggy valley rose in a white cloud, and I realised, with a shudder, how cold I had been the livelong day, since I had sat with Louise in the church, and all the while in the fireless parlour at the Rose and Crown. This was another world from yesterday.

I led Gypsy past the path that Rachel and I had taken. Our footmarks were still there, where we had trodden in around the beeches for the primroses. Clumps of them nestled still, dejected, in the moss. The avenue seemed endless, with Gypsy hobbling, my hand upon her bridle guiding her, and the dripping rain found its way down the collar of my coat to chill my back.

When I reached home I was too tired to say good afternoon to Wellington, but threw him the reins without a word, leaving him staring after me. God knows, after the night before, I had little desire to drink anything but water, but being cold and wet I thought a taste of brandy might bring some sort of warmth to me, however raw. I went into the dining-room and John was there, laying the table for dinner. He went to fetch me a glass from the pantry, and while I waited I saw he had laid three places on the table.

On his return I pointed to them. 'Why three?' I said.

'Miss Pascoe,' he replied, 'she's been here since one o'clock. The mistress went calling there this morning, not long after you had gone. She brought Miss Pascoe back with her. She's come to stay.'

I stared at him, bewildered. 'Miss Pascoe come to stay?' I said.

'That's so,' he answered, 'Miss Mary Pascoe, the one that teaches in the Sunday school. We have been busy getting the pink room ready for her. She and the mistress are in the boudoir now.'

He went on with his laying of the table, and leaving the glass upon the side-board, without bothering to pour the brandy, I went upstairs. There was a note upon the table in my room, Rachel's hand upon it. I tore it open. There was no beginning, only the day, and the date. 'I have asked Mary Pascoe to stay here with me in the house as a companion. After last night, I cannot be alone with you again. You may join us in the boudoir, if you wish, before and after dinner. I must ask you to be courteous. Rachel.'

She could not mean it. It could not be true. How often we had laughed about the Pascoe daughters, and more especially about chattering Mary, forever working samplers, visiting those poor who had rather be left alone, Mary, a stouter, even a plainer edition of her mother. As a joke, yes, Rachel could have invited her as a joke, merely for dinner, so as to watch my glum face at the end of the table – but the note was not written as a joke.

I went out on to the landing from my room, and saw that the door of the pink bedroom was open. There was no mistake. A fire burnt in the grate, shoes and a wrapper were laid out upon a chair, there were brushes, books, the personel paraphernalia of a stranger all about the room, and the further door, usually kept locked, which communicated with Rachel's suite of rooms, was locked no longer, but wide open too. I could even hear the distant murmur of voices from the boudoir beyond. This, then, was my punishment. This my disgrace. Mary Pascoe had been invited to make a division between Rachel and myself, that we might no longer be alone together, even as she had written in her note.

My first feeling was one of such intense anger that I hardly knew how to contain myself from walking along the corridor to the boudoir, seizing Mary Pascoe by the shoulders and telling her to pack and begone, that I would have Wellington take her home in the carriage without delay. How had Rachel dared to invite her to my house on such a pretext, miserable, flimsy, and insulting, that she could no longer be alone with me? Was I then doomed to Mary Pascoe at every meal, Mary Pascoe in the library and the drawing-room, Mary Pascoe walking in the grounds, Mary Pascoe in the boudoir, for evermore the interminable chatter between women that I had only endured through force of habit over Sunday dinner?

I went along the corridor – I did not change, I was still in my wet things. I opened the boudoir door. Rachel was seated in her chair, with Mary Pascoe beside her on the stool, the pair of them looking at the great volume with the illustrations of Italian gardens.

'So you are back?' said Rachel. 'It was an odd day to choose to go out riding. The carriage was nearly blown from the road when I went down to call at the Rectory. As you see, we have the good fortune to have Mary here as visitor. She is already quite at home. I am delighted.'

Mary Pascoe gave a trill of laughter.

'Such a surprise, Mr. Ashley,' she said, 'when your cousin came to fetch me. The others were green with envy. I can hardly believe yet I am here. And how pleasant and snug it is to sit here in the boudoir. Nicer even than below. Your cousin says it is your habit to sit here of an evening. Do you play cribbage? I am wild for cribbage. If you cannot play I shall be pleased to teach you both.'

'Philip,' said Rachel, 'has little use for games of chance. He prefers to sit and smoke in silence. You and I, Mary, will play together.'

She looked across at me, over Mary Pascoe's head. No, it was no joke. I could see by her hard eyes that she had done this thing with great deliberation.

'Can I speak to you alone?' I said bluntly.

'I see no need for that,' she answered. 'You are at liberty to say anything you please in front of Mary.'

The vicar's daughter rose hurriedly to her feet. 'Oh, please,' she said, 'I don't wish to make intrusion. I can easily go to my room.'

'Leave the doors wide open, Mary,' said Rachel, 'so that you can hear me if I call.' Her eyes, so hostile, remained fixed on me.

'Yes, certainly, Mrs. Ashley,' said Mary Pascoe. She brushed past me, her eyes goggling, leaving all the doors ajar.

'Why have you done this?' I said to Rachel.

'You know perfectly well,' she answered; 'I told you in my note.'

'How long is she to stay?'

'As long as I choose.'

'You will not be able to stand her company for more than one day. You will drive yourself mad, as well as me.'

'You are mistaken,' she said. 'Mary Pascoe is a good harmless girl. I shall not talk to her if I do not wish for conversation. At least I feel some measure of security with her in the house. Also, it was time. Things could not have continued as they had been, not after your outburst at the table. Your godfather said as much before he left.'

'What did he say?'

'That there was gossip about my being here, which your boast of marriage will have done little to improve. I don't know what other people you have chatted to. Mary Pascoe will silence further gossip. I shall take good care of that.'

Was it possible that my action of the night before could bring about such change, such terrible antagonism?

'Rachel,' I said, 'this can't be settled in a moment's conversation, with the doors open. I beg of you, listen to me, let me talk to you alone, after dinner, when Mary Pascoe goes to bed.'

'You threatened me last night,' she said. 'Once was enough. There is nothing to settle. You can go now, if you wish. Or stay and play cribbage here with Mary Pascoe.' She turned again to the book of gardens.

I went from the room. There was nothing else to do. This then was my punishment, for that brief moment of the night before, when I had put my hands about her neck. The action, instantly repented and regretted, was unforgivable. This, then, the reward. As quickly as my anger had come, it went, turning, with heavy dullness, to despair. Oh, God, what had I done?

Such a little while ago, so few hours in time, we had been happy. The exultation of my birthday eve, and all the magic, was now gone, frittered away by my own fault. Sitting in the cold parlour of the Rose and Crown it had seemed to me that perhaps, in a few weeks, her reluctance to become my wife might be overcome. If not immediately, then later; if not later, then what matter, so long as we could be together, in love, as on my birthday morning. Hers the decision, hers the choice, yet surely she would not refuse? I had been almost hopeful when I had come into the house. But now the stranger, the third person, misunderstanding all about us still. Presently as I stood in my room, I heard their voices approach the stair, and then the sweep of gowns descending. It was later than I thought, they must be ready dressed for dinner. I knew I could not face the business of sitting with them. They must dine alone. Anyway, I was not hungry; I felt cold and stiff, probably I had taken chill, and would be better in my room. I rang the bell and told John to make my apologies, but I would not be down to dinner, I was going straight to bed. This made a pother, as I feared it might, and Seecombe came up, concern upon his face.

'Unwell, Mr. Philip, sir?' he said. 'May I suggest a mustard bath, and a hot grog? It comes of riding out in such weather.'

'Nothing, thank you, Seecombe,' I replied. 'I'm a little tired, that's all.'

'No dinner, Mr. Philip? We have venison, and apple pie. It is all ready to serve. Both the ladies are in the drawing-room now.'

'No, Seecombe. I slept badly last night. I shall be better in the morning.'

'I will tell the mistress,' he said, 'she will be much concerned.'

At least by remaining in my room it might give me a chance to see Rachel alone. After dinner, perhaps, she would come up and enquire about me.

I undressed and got into my bed. Undoubtedly I must have caught some sort of chill. The sheets seemed bitter cold, and I threw them off and got between the blankets. I felt stiff and numb and my head throbbed, things most unusual and unknown. I lay there, waiting for them to finish dinner. I heard them pass from the hall into the dining-room, the chatter ceaseless – I was spared that, at any rate – and then, after a long interval, back again to the drawing-room.

Some time after eight o'clock I heard them come upstairs. I sat up in bed and put my jacket round my shoulders. This, perhaps, was the moment she would choose. In spite of the rough blankets I was still cold, and the stiff pain that was about my legs and neck shifted in full measure to my head, so that it seemed on fire.

I waited, but she did not come. They must be sitting in the boudoir. I heard the clock strike nine, then ten, then eleven. After eleven, I knew that she did not intend to come and see me that night at all. Ignoring me, then, was but a continuation of my punishment.

I got out of bed and stood in the passage. They had retired for the night, for I could hear Mary Pascoe moving about in the pink bedroom, and now and then an irritating little cough to clear her throat – another habit she had taken from her mother.

I went along the corridor to Rachel's room. I put my hand upon the handle of the door, and turned it. But it did not open. The door was locked. I knocked, very softly. She did not answer. I went slowly back to my own room and to my bed, and lay there, icy cold.

I remember in the morning that I dressed, but I have no recollection of John coming in to call me, nor that I breakfasted, nor of anything at all, but

...ge stiffness in my neck and the agonising pain in my head. I
... chair in the office. I wrote no letters, I saw no one. Some
... Seecombe came to find me to tell me that the ladies were
...eon. I said I wanted none. He came near to me and looked

...lip,' he said, 'you are ill. What is it?'
... know,' I said. He took my hand and felt it. He went out of the
... I heard him hurry across the courtyard.
...ently the door opened once again. Rachel stood there, with Mary
...be behind her and Seecombe also. She came towards me.
'Seecombe says you are ill,' she said to me. 'What is the matter?'

I stared up at her. Nothing of what was happening was real at all. I
hardly knew that I was sitting there, in my office chair, but thought myself
to be upstairs in my room cold in my bed, as I had been the night before.

'When will you send her home?' I said. 'I won't do anything to harm you.
I give you my word of honour.'

She put her hand on my head. She looked into my eyes. She turned swiftly
to Seecombe. 'Get John,' she said. 'Both of you, help Mr. Ashley to bed.
Tell Wellington to send the groom quickly for the doctor . . .'

I saw nothing but her white face and her eyes; and then over her shoulder,
ludicrous somehow, out of place and foolish, the started, shocked gaze of
Mary Pascoe fixed upon me. Then nothing. Only the stiffness, and the pain.

Back in my bed again, I was aware that Seecombe stood by the windows,
closing the shutters, drawing the curtains, bringing the room to darkness
which I craved. Possibly the darkness would ease the blinding pain. I could
not move my head upon the pillow, it was as though the muscles of my neck
were taut and rigid. I felt her hand in mine. I said again, 'I promise not to
harm you. Send Mary Pascoe home.'

She answered, 'Don't talk now. Only lie still.'

The room was full of whispers. The door opening, shutting, opening once
again. Soft footsteps creeping on the floor. Chinks of light coming from the
landing, and always this furtiveness of whispers, so that it seemed to me, in
the sudden sharp delirium that must be sweeping me, that the house was
filled with people, a guest in every room, and that the house itself was not
large enough to contain them, they stood shoulder to shoulder in the drawing-
room and in the library, with Rachel moving in the midst of them, smiling,
talking, holding out her hands. I kept repeating, over and over again, 'Send
them away.'

Then I saw the round spectacled face of Dr. Gilbert looking down on me;
he too, then, was of the company. When I was a lad he had come to treat
me for the chickenpox, I had scarce seen him since.

'So you went swimming in the sea at midnight?' he said to me. 'That was
a very foolish thing to do.' He shook his head at me as if I were still a child,
and stroked his beard. I closed my eyes against the light. I heard Rachel say
to him, 'I know too much about this kind of fever to be mistaken. I have seen
children die of it in Florence. It attacks the spine, and then the brain. Do
something, for God's sake . . .'

They went away. And once again the whispering began. This was followed by the sound of wheels on the drive, and a departing carriage. Later, I heard someone breathing, close to the curtains of my bed. I knew then what had happened. Rachel had gone. She had driven to Bodmin, to take the coach for London. She had left Mary Pascoe in the house to watch me. The servants, Seecombe, John, they had all departed; no one was left but Mary Pascoe.

'Please go,' I said, 'I need no one.'

A hand came out to touch my forehead. Mary Pascoe's hand. I shook it off. But it returned again, stealthy, cold, and I shouted loud to her to go, but it pressed down upon me, hard, gripping like ice, and so to ice it turned, on my forehead, on my neck, clamping me close, a prisoner. Then I heard Rachel whisper in my ear, 'Dear, lie still. This will help your head. It will be better, by-and-by.'

I tried to turn, but could not. Had she not gone to London after all?

I said, 'Don't leave me. Promise not to leave me.'

She said, 'I promise. I will be with you all the time.'

I opened my eyes but I could not see her, the room was in darkness. The shape of it was different, not the bedroom that I knew. It was long and narrow, like a cell. The bedstead hard, like iron. There was one candle burning somewhere, behind a screen. In a niche, on the wall opposite, knelt a madonna. I called loudly 'Rachel . . . Rachel . . .'

I heard footsteps running, and a door opening, and then her hand in mine and she was saying, 'I am with you.' I closed my eyes again.

I was standing on a bridge, beside the Arno, making a vow to destroy a woman I had never seen. The swollen water passed under the bridge, bubbling brown, and Rachel, the beggar girl, came up to me with empty hands. She was naked, save for the pearl collar round her throat. Suddenly she pointed at the water and Ambrose went past us, under the bridge, his hands folded on his breast. He floated away down the river out of sight, and slowly, majestically, his paws raised stiff and straight, went the body of the dead dog after him.

Chapter Twenty-four

The first thing that I noticed was that the tree outside my window was in leaf. I looked at it, puzzled. When I had gone to bed the buds were barely formed. It was very strange. True, the curtains had been drawn, but I well remembered noticing how tight they were upon my birthday morning, when I leant out of the window and looked across the lawn. There was no pain now in my head and the stiffness had all gone. I must have slept for many hours, possibly a day or more. There was no reckoning with time, when anyone fell ill.

Surely I had seen him many times, though, old Doctor Gilbert with his beard, and another man as well, a stranger. The room in darkness always. Now it was light. My face felt scrubby – I must be in great need of a shave. I put my hand up to my chin. Now this was madness, for I too had a beard. I stared at my hand. It did not look like mine. It was white and thin, the nails grown to a fine length; too often I broke them, riding. I turned my head and saw Rachel sitting in a chair, near to my bed – her own chair, from the boudoir. She did not know I saw her. She was working upon a piece of embroidery, and wore a gown I did not recognise. It was dark, like all her gowns, but the sleeves were short, above the elbow, and the stuff was light, as though for coolness' sake. Was the room so warm? The windows were wide open. There was no fire in the grate.

I put my hand up to my chin again and felt the beard. It had a pleasant touch to it. Suddenly I laughed, and at the sound she raised her head and looked at me.

'Philip,' she said, and smiled; and suddenly she was kneeling by my side, with her arms about me.

'I have grown a beard,' I said.

I could not stop myself from laughing, for the folly of it, and then, from laughing, turned to coughing, and at once she had a glass with some ill-tasting stuff inside it which she made me drink, holding it to my lips, then putting me back again upon the pillows.

This gesture struck a chord in memory. Surely, for a long while, there had been a hand, with a glass, making me drink, that had come into my dreams, and gone again? I had believed it to be Mary Pascoe, and kept pushing it away. I lay staring at Rachel, and put out my hand to her. She took it and held it fast. I ran my thumb along the pale blue veins that showed always on the back of hers, and turned the rings. I continued thus for quite a time, and did not talk.

Presently I said, 'Did you send her away?'

'Send who?' she asked.

'Why, Mary Pascoe,' I replied.

I heard her catch her breath, and glancing up I saw that her smile had gone and a shadow had come to her eyes.

'She has been gone these five weeks,' she said. 'Never mind that now. Are you thirsty? I have made you a cool drink with fresh limes, sent down from London.' I drank, and it tasted good after the bitter medicine she had given me.

'I think I must have been ill,' I said to her.

'You nearly died,' she answered.

She moved, as though to go, but I would not have it.

'Tell me about it,' I said. I had all the curiosity of someone who has been asleep for years, like Rip van Winkle, to find the world had gone along without him.

'If you want to revive in me all those weeks of anxiety I will tell you,' she answered, 'not otherwise. You have been very ill. Let that be enough.'

'What was the matter with me?'

'I have small regard to your English doctors,' she replied. 'On the continent we call that illness meningite, which here no one knew anything about. That you are alive to-day is little short of a miracle.'

'What pulled me through?'

She smiled, and held my hand the tighter. 'I think your own horse strength,' she answered me, 'and certain things I bade them do. Making a puncture on your spine to take the fluid was but one. Also letting into your blood stream a serum made from the juice of herbs. They called it poison. But you have survived.'

I remembered the cordials that she had made for some of the tenants who had been sick during the winter, and how I had teased her about it, calling her midwife and apothecary.

'How do you know about these things?' I said to her.

'I learnt them from my mother,' she said. 'We are very old, and very wise, who come from Florence.'

The words struck some chord in memory, but I could not recollect just what it was. To think was still an effort. And I was content to lie there in my bed, her hand in mine.

'Why is the tree in leaf outside my window?' I asked.

'It should be, in the second week of May,' she said.

That I had lain there knowing nothing all those weeks was hard to understand. Nor could I remember the events that had brought me to my bed. Rachel had been angry with me, for some reason that escaped me, and had invited Mary Pascoe to the house, I knew not why. That we had been married the day before my birthday was very certain, though I had no clear vision of the church, or of the ceremony; except that I believed my godfather and Louise had been the only witnesses, with little Alice Tabb, the church cleaner. I remembered being very happy. And suddenly, for no reason, in despair. Then falling ill. No matter, all was well again. I had not died, and it was the month of May.

'I think I am strong enough to get up,' I said to her.

'You are no such thing,' she answered. 'In a week, perhaps, you shall sit in a chair, by the window there, to feel your feet. And later, walk as far as the boudoir. By the end of the month we may get you below, and sitting out-of-doors. But we shall see.'

Indeed, my rate of progress was much as she had said. I have never in my life felt such a ninny as the first time I sat sideways on the bed, and put my feet upon the floor. The whole room rocked. Seecombe was one side of me, and John the other, and I as weak as a baby newly born.

'Great heavens, madam, he has grown again,' said Seecombe, with the consternation on his face so great I had to sit down again for laughter.

'You can show me for a freak at Bodmin Fair after all,' I said, and then saw myself in the mirror, gaunt and pale, with the brown beard on my chin, for all the world like an apostle.

'I've half a mind,' I said, 'to go preaching about the countryside. Thousands would follow me. What do you think?' I turned to Rachel.

'I prefer you shaved,' she said gravely.

'Bring me a razor, John,' I said; but when the work was done, and my face bare again, I felt I had lost some sort of dignity and was reduced again to school-boy status.

Those days of convalescence were pleasant indeed. Rachel was always with me. We did not talk much, because I found conversation tired me sooner than anything else, and brought back some shadow of that aching head. I liked, more than anything, to sit by my open window, and to make diversion Wellington would bring the horses and exercise them round and round the gravel sweep in front of me, like show beasts in a ring. Then, when my legs were stronger, I walked to the boudoir and our meals were taken there, Rachel waiting upon me and caring for me like a nurse with a child; indeed, I said to her on one occasion, if she was doomed to a sick husband for the rest of her life, she had no one to blame but herself. She looked at me strangely when I said this, and was about to speak, then paused, and passed on to something else.

I remembered that for some reason or other our marriage had been kept secret from the servants, I think to allow the full twelve months to lapse since Ambrose died before announcing it; perhaps she was afraid I might be indiscreet in front of Seecombe, so I held my tongue. In two months' time we could declare it to the world; until then, I would be patient. Each day I think I loved her more; and she, more gentle and more tender than ever in the past months of winter.

I was amazed, when I came downstairs for the first time and went out into the grounds, to see how much had been achieved about the place during my sickness. The terrace walk was now completed, and the sunken garden beside it had been hollowed away to a great depth, and was ready to be paved with stone and the banks faced. At the moment it yawned, dark and ominous, a deep wide chasm, and the fellows digging there looked up at me, grinning, as I stared down at them from the terrace above.

Tamlyn escorted me with pride to the plantation – Rachel had called in to see his wife, at the nearby cottage – and though the camellias were over, the rhododendrons were still in bloom, and the orange berberis, and leaning to the field below the soft yellow flowers of the laburnum trees hung in clusters, scattering their petals.

'We'll have to shift them though, another year,' said Tamlyn. 'At the rate they're growing the branches lean down too far to the field, and the seeds will kill the cattle.' He reached up to a branch, and where the flowers had fallen the pods were already forming, with the little seeds within. 'There was a fellow the other side of St. Austell who died eating these,' said Tamlyn, and he threw the pod away, over his shoulder.

I had forgotten how brief was their flowering time, like every other blossom, also how beautiful; and suddenly I remembered the drooping tree in the little courtyard in the Italian villa, and the woman from the lodge taking her broom, sweeping the pods away.

'There was a fine tree of this kind,' I said, 'in Florence, where Mrs. Ashley had her villa.'

'Yes, sir?' he said. 'Well, they grow most things in that climate, I understand. It must be a wonderful place. I can understand the mistress wishing to return.'

'I don't think she has any intention of returning,' I replied.

'I'm glad of that, sir,' he said, 'but we heard different. That she was only waiting to see you restored to health before she went.'

It was incredible what stories were made up from scraps of gossip, and I thought how the announcement of our marriage would be the only means to stop it. Yet I was hesitant to broach the matter to her. It seemed to me that once before there had been discussion on that point, which had made her angry, before I was taken ill.

That evening, when we were sitting in the boudoir and I was drinking my tisana, as had become my custom before going to bed, I said to her, 'There is fresh gossip round the countryside.'

'What now?' she asked, lifting her head to look at me.

'Why, that you are going back to Florence,' I replied.

She did not answer me at once, but bent her head again to her embroidery.

'There is plenty of time to decide about these things,' she said. 'First, you must get well and strong.'

I looked at her, puzzled. Then Tamlyn had not been entirely in error. The idea of going to Florence was there, somewhere in her mind.

'Have you not sold the villa yet?' I asked.

'Not yet,' she answered, 'nor do I intend to sell it after all, or even let it. Now things are changed and I can afford to keep it.'

I was silent. I did not want to hurt her, but the thought of having the two homes was not one that pleased me very well. In fact, I hated the very image of that villa which I held still in my mind, and which I thought by now she hated too.

'Do you mean you would want to spend the winter there?' I asked.

'Possibly,' she said, 'or the late summer; but there is no necessity to talk of it.'

'I have been idle too long,' I said. 'I don't think I should leave this place without attention for the winter, or, in fact, be absent from it at all.'

'Probably not,' she said, 'in fact, I would not care to leave the property unless you were in charge. You might like to pay me a visit in the spring, and I could show you Florence.'

The illness I had suffered had left me very slow of understanding; nothing of what she said made any sense.

'Pay you a visit?' I said. 'Is that how you propose that we should live? Absent from one another for long months at a time?'

She laid down her work and looked at me. There was something of anxiety in her eyes, a shadow on her face.

'Philip dear,' she said, 'I have said, I don't wish to talk about the future now. You have only just recovered from a dangerous illness, and it is bad to start planning the time ahead. I give you my promise I will not leave you until you are well.'

'But why,' I demanded, 'is there any need to go at all? You belong here now. This is your home.'

'I have my villa too,' she said, 'and many friends, and a life out there – different from this, I know, but none the less I am accustomed to it. I have been in England for eight months, and now feel the need for change again. Be reasonable, and try to understand.'

'I suppose,' I said slowly, 'I am very selfish. I had not thought of it.' I must make up my mind, then, to the fact that she would want to divide her time between England and Italy, in which case I must do the same, and start looking about for a bailiff to put in charge of the estate. The idea of separation was of course preposterous.

'My godfather may know of someone,' I said, speaking my thoughts aloud.

'Someone for what?' she asked.

'Why, to take over here, when we are absent,' I replied.

'I think it hardly necessary,' she said. 'You would not be in Florence more than a few weeks, if you came. Though you might like it so much that you would decide to stay longer. It is very lovely in the spring.'

'Spring be damned,' I said. 'Whatever date you decide upon to go, I shall go too.'.

Again the shadow on her face, the apprehension in her eye.

'Never mind that now,' she said, 'and look, past nine o'clock, later than you have been as yet. Shall I ring for John, or can you manage alone?'

'Ring for no one,' I said. I got up slowly from my chair, for my limbs were still most damnably weak, and I went and knelt beside her, and put my arms about her.

'I find it very hard,' I said, 'the solitude of my own room, and you so close, along the corridor. Can we not tell them soon?'

'Tell them what?' she said.

'That we are married,' I replied.

She sat very still in my arms, and did not move. It was almost as if she turned rigid, like something without life.

'Oh, God . . .' she whispered. Then she put her hands upon my shoulders, and looked into my face. 'What do you mean, Philip?' she said.

A pulse somewhere in my head began to beat, like an echo to the pain that had been there the past weeks. It throbbed deeper, ever deeper, and with it came a sense of fear.

'Tell the servants,' I said. 'Then it will be right and natural for me to stay with you, because we are married . . .' But my voice sank away to nothing, because of the expression in her eyes.

'But we are not married, Philip dear,' she said.

Something seemed to burst inside my head.

'We are married,' I said, 'of course we are married. It happened on my birthday. Have you forgotten?'

But when had it happened? Where was the church? Who was the

minister? All the throbbing pain returned again, and the room swung round about me.

'Tell me it's true?' I said to her.

Then suddenly I knew that all was fantasy, that the happiness which had been mine for the past weeks was imagination. The dream was broken.

I buried my head against her, sobbing; tears had never come from me like this before, not even as a child. She held me close, her hand stroking my hair, and never speaking. Presently I won command over myself again, and lay down in the chair, exhausted. She brought me something to drink, then sat down on the stool beside me. The shadows of the summer evening played about the room. The bats crept forth from their hiding places in the eaves, and circled in the twilight outside the window.

'It would have been better,' I said, 'had you let me die.'

She sighed, and laid her hand against my cheek. 'If you say that,' she answered, 'you destoy me too. You are unhappy now because you are still weak. But presently, when you are stronger, none of this will seem important. You will go about your work again, on the estate – there will be so much to see to that, from your illness, has been allowed to lapse. The full summer will be here. You can swim again, go sailing in the bay.'

I knew from her voice that she was talking to convince herself, not me.

'What else?' I asked.

'You know very well that you are happy here,' she said; 'it is your life, and will continue to be so. You have given me the property, but I shall always look on it as yours. It will be a sort of trust between us.'

'You mean,' I said, 'that letters will pass between us, from Italy to England, month after month, throughout the year. I shall say to you, "Dear Rachel, The camellias are in bloom." And you will reply to me, "Dear Philip, I am glad to hear it. My rose-garden is doing very well." Is that to be our future?'

I could see myself hanging about the gravel sweep of a morning after breakfast, waiting for the boy to bring the post-bag, knowing full well there would be no letter in it, except some bill from Bodmin.

'I would be back again each summer, very probably,' she said, 'to see that all went well.'

'Like the swallows, who come only for the season,' I replied, 'then take wing again the first week in September.'

'I have already suggested,' she said, 'that you visit me in spring. There is much that you would like in Italy. You have not travelled, save the once. You know very little of the world.'

She might have been a teacher, soothing a fractious child. Perhaps it was thus she looked upon me.

'What I have seen,' I answered, 'gives me a distaste for all the rest. What would you have me do? Potter about a church or a museum, guide-book in hand? Converse with strangers, to broaden my ideas? I would rather brood at home and watch the rain.'

My voice was harsh and bitter, but I could not help it. She sighed again, and it was as though she searched about for some argument to prove to me that all was well.

'I tell you again,' she insisted, 'that when you are better the whole of the future will seem different to you. Nothing is so much changed from what it was. As to the money . . .' she paused, looking at me.

'What money?' I said.

'The money for the property,' she went on. 'All that will be placed on a proper footing, and you shall have enough to run the estate without loss, while I take what I need out of the country. It is all in process of arrangement now.'

She could take every farthing for all I cared. What had any of this to do with what I felt for her? But she went on talking.

'You must continue to make what improvements you feel justified in doing,' she said rapidly. 'You know I shall query nothing, you need not even send me the bills, I can trust your judgement. Your godfather will always be near to give advice. In a little while everything will seem to you just the same as it was before I came.'

The room was deep in twilight now. I could not even see her face for the shadows all about us.

'Do you really believe that?' I said to her.

She did not answer at once. She searched for some excuse for my existence, to pile upon those that she had given me already. There were none, and she knew it well. She turned towards me, giving me her hand. 'I must believe it,' she said, 'or I would have no peace of mind.'

In all the months I had known her she had given me many answers to the questions, serious or otherwise, that I had put to her. Some had been laughing, some evasive, yet each one had some feminine twist to make adornment. This was direct at last, straight from the heart. She must believe me happy, to have peace of mind. I had left the land of fantasy, to her to enter into it. Two persons therefore could not share a dream. Except in darkness, as in make-believe. Each figure, then, a phantom.

'Go back if you will.' I said, 'but not just yet. Give me a few weeks more to hold in memory. I am no traveller, you are my world.'

I sought to evade the future and escape. But when I held her it was not the same; faith was gone, and the first ecstasy.

Chapter Twenty-five

We did not speak again of her departure. It was a bogey, thrust into the background by us both. For her sake I strove to appear light-hearted, without

care. She did the same, for me. The summer weather was about us, and I
soon grew strong again, at least to all appearance; but sometimes the pain
in my head returned again, not with its full force, but stabbing, without
warning, and for no good reason.

I did not tell her of it – what was the use? It did not come from physical
exertion, or when I was outdoors, but only if I put my mind to thinking.
Simple problems brought to me in the estate office by the tenants could even
do it, so that a fog would seem to settle on me and I be unable to give them
a decision.

More often, though, it would happen because of her. I would be looking
at her, as we sat perhaps after dinner outside the drawing-room window,
for the June weather enabled us to sit without of an evening until past nine
o'clock; and suddenly I would wonder what went on there, in her mind, as
she sat drinking her tisana, watching the dusk creep closer to the trees that
fringed the lawn. Did she ponder, in her secret self, how much longer she
must endure this life of solitude? Did she think, secretively, 'Next week,
now he is well, I can safely go?'

That villa Sangalletti, back in Florence, had for me now another shape
and atmosphere. Instead of the shuttered darkness I had seen on that one
visit I saw it now as brightly lit, with all the windows wide. Those unknown
people whom she called her friends wandered from room to room; there was
gaiety and laughter, much noise of conversation. A sort of brilliance hung
above the place, and all the fountains played. She would move from guest
to guest, smiling and at ease, mistress of her domain. This, then, was the life
she knew, and loved, and understood. Her months with me were an interlude.
Thankfully, she would return to the home where she belonged. I could
picture the first arrival, with the man Giuseppe and his wife flinging wide
the iron gates to admit her carrozza, and then her happy eager pacing
through the rooms she knew so well and had not seen for long, asking her
servants questions, receiving their replies, opening the many letters there
awaiting her, content, serene, with all the myriad threads of an existence to
pick up again and hold that I could never know and never share. So many
days and nights, no longer mine.

Presently she would feel my eyes upon her, and would say, 'What is the
matter, Philip?'

'Nothing,' I would reply.

And as the shadow passed across her face, doubtful, distressed, I felt
myself a burden on her shoulders. She would be better quit of me. I tried
to lose my energies, as of old, in the running of the place, in the common
tasks of day by day; but it no longer meant the same to me. What if the
Barton acres were all dried through lack of rain? I could not greatly care.
And if our stock won prizes at the Show, and so were the champions of the
country, was this glory? Last year, it might have been. But now, what an
empty triumph.

I could see myself losing favour in the eyes of all who looked upon me as
their master. 'You are still weak, Mr. Ashley, after that sickness,' said Billy
Rowe, the farmer at the Barton; and there was a world of disappointment

in his voice that I had failed to show enthusiasm for his achievements. It was the same with all the rest. Even Seecombe took me to task.

'You don't seem to pick up as you should, Mr. Philip,' he said. 'We were talking of it, in the steward's room, last evening. "What's come to the master?" Tamlyn said to me. "He's whisht as a ghost on Hallowe'en, and looks at nothing." I would advise marsala in the morning. There is nothing like a wine-glass of marsala to restore the blood.'

'Tell Tamlyn,' I said to Seecombe, 'to go about his business. I am perfectly well.'

The routine of Sunday dinner, with the Pascoes and the Kendalls, had not yet been restored, which was a mercy. I think poor Mary Pascoe had returned to the rectory, after I fell ill, with tales that I was mad. I saw her look at me askance, in church, the first morning that I went when I was well; and the whole family eyed me with a sort of pity, enquiring for me with low voices and averted gaze.

My godfather came to see me, also Louise. They too assumed an unaccustomed manner, a blend of cheerfulness and sympathy, suited to a child who had been sick; and I felt they had been warned not to touch upon any subject that might cause me concern. The four of us sat like strangers in the drawing-room. My godfather, I thought, is ill at ease, and wishing he had not come, but feels it to be his duty to call upon me; while Louise, with some odd instinct possessed by women, always knows what has happened here and shrinks at thought of it. Rachel, as always, was in command of the situation, and kept the tenor of the conversation on the level that was required. The county Show, the betrothal of the second Pascoe daughter, the warmth of the present weather, the prospect of a change in Government – all these were easy matters. But what if we spoke the things we really thought?

'Get out of England soon, before you destroy yourself and this boy with you,' thus my godfather.

'You love her more than ever. I can see it, by your eyes,' from Louise.

'I must prevent them from making Philip anxious, at all costs,' so Rachel. And myself, 'Leave me alone with her, and go. . . .'

Instead, we clung to courtesy, and lied. Each one of us breathed the easier at the termination of the visit, and as I watched them drive to the park gates, no doubt thankful to be away, I wished I could erect a fence about the property, as in the old enchanted tales of childhood, to keep away all callers, and disaster too.

It seemed to me, though she said nothing, that she planned the first steps towards departure. I would find her, of an evening, sorting through her books, arranging them as people do who wish to make a choice between the volumes they take with them and those they leave behind. Another time she would be sitting at the bureau, putting her papers into order, filling the waste-paper basket with torn scraps and discarded letters, and tying up the rest with bands of tape. All this would stop, once I came into the boudoir, and going to her chair she would take up her work, or sit beside the window;

but I was not deceived. Why the sudden desire for making all things straight, unless she was soon to leave the boudoir empty?

It seemed to me the room looked barer than it had before. Trifles were missing. A work-basket that had stood through the spring and winter in one corner, a shawl that had lain over the elbow of a chair, a crayon sketch of the house, presented to her by a caller one winter's day, that used to be on the mantelpiece – all were there no more. It took me back to my boyhood, before I went away for the first time, to school. Seecombe had made a clearance in the nursery, tying my books in bundles that would go with me, and the rest, that were not favourites, were placed in a separate box for the children on the estate. There were coats I had outgrown, which were sadly worn; and I remember he insisted that I should hand them down to smaller boys less fortunate than I, which I resented. It was as though he took the happy past away from me. Now something of the same atmosphere clung to Rachel's boudoir. That shawl, had she given it away because she would not need it in a warmer climate? The work-box, was it dismantled, and now reposing at the bottom of a trunk? No sign, as yet, of actual trunks themselves. That would be the final warning. The heavy footsteps in the attic, the boys descending, boxes borne between them, and a kind of dusty cobweb smell, woven about with camphor. Then I would know the worst, and like the dogs with uncanny sense of change, await the end. Another thing was that she started to go out driving in the morning, which she had not done before. She would tell me she had shopping she wished to do, and business at the bank. These things were possible. I should have thought one journey would have settled them. But three mornings in one week followed upon each other, with one day spaced between, and now yet again, in the week that was upon us, twice she had driven into town. The first time it was a morning. The second, afternoon. 'You have,' I said to her, 'the devil of a lot of shopping of a sudden, and business too. . . .'

'I would have done it all before,' she answered, 'but could not do so all the weeks that you were ill.'

'Do you meet anyone as you go about the town?'

'Why, no, not in particular. Yes, now I think of it. I saw Belinda Pascoe and the curate to whom she is engaged. They sent you their respects.'

'But,' I insisted, 'you were away all afternoon. Did you buy up all the contents of the drapers?'

'No,' she said. 'You are really very curious, and prying. Can I not order the carriage when I please, or do you fear to tire the horses?'

'Drive to Bodmin or to Truro if you please,' I said, 'you will find better shopping there, and more to see.'

She did not care for it, then, when I questioned her. Her business must be very personal and private, that she was so reserved.

The next time she ordered the carriage the groom did not go with them. Wellington drove her alone. It seemed that Jimmy had the ear-ache. I had been in the office, and I found him sitting in the stable, nursing his injured ear.

'You must ask the mistress for some oil,' I said to him. 'I'm told that is the remedy.'

'Yes, sir,' he said, disconsolate, 'she promised to see to it for me, by and by on her return. I think I caught cold in it yesterday. There was a fresh wind blowing on the quay.'

'What were you doing on the quay?' I asked.

'We were waiting a long while for the mistress,' he answered, 'so Mr. Wellington thought best to bait the horses in the Rose and Crown, and he let me go off and watch the boats in the harbour.'

'Was the mistress shopping then all afternoon?' I asked.

'No, sir,' he replied, 'she didn't shop at all. She was in the parlour at the Rose and Crown, the same as always.'

I stared at him in disbelief. Rachel in the parlour of the Rose and Crown? Did she sit taking tea with the landlord and his wife? For a moment I thought to question him further, then decided against it. It might be he was speaking out of turn, and would be scolded by Wellington for blabbing. All things were kept from me these days, it seemed. The whole household was in league against me, in a conspiracy of silence. 'Well, Jim,' I said, 'I hope your ear will soon be better,' and left him in the stable. But here was mystery. Had Rachel grown so desirous of company that she had to seek it in the town inn? Knowing my dislike of visitors, did she hire the parlour for a morning, or an afternoon, and bid people visit her there? I said nothing of the matter, on her return, but merely asked her if she had passed a pleasant afternoon, and she replied she had.

The following day she did not order her carriage. She told me, at luncheon, that she had letters to write, and went up to her boudoir. I said I had to walk to Coombe, to see the farmer there, which was true enough, and so I did. But I went further. Into the town itself. It was a Saturday, and because of the fine weather many folk were out about the streets, people from the neighbouring market towns, who did not know me by sight, so that I passed amongst them unobserved. I saw no one I knew. The 'quality', as Seecombe termed them, never went into the town of an afternoon, and never on a Saturday.

I leant over the harbour wall, near to the quay, and saw some boys fishing from a boat, getting themselves entangled in their lines. Presently they sculled towards the steps and clambered out. One of them I recognised. It was the lad who helped behind the bar in the Rose and Crown. He had three or four fine bass on a piece of string.

'You've done well,' I said. 'Are they for supper?'

'Not for me, sir,' he grinned, 'they'll be welcome at the inn though, I'll be bound.'

'Do you serve bass now with the cider?' I asked.

'No,' he said, 'this fish is for the gentleman in the parlour. He had a piece of salmon yesterday, from up the river.'

A gentleman in the parlour. I pulled some silver from my pocket.

'Well,' I said, 'I hope he pays you well. Here's this for luck. Who is your visitor?'

He screwed his face into another grin. 'Don't know his name, sir,' he replied, 'Italian, they say he is. From foreign parts.'

And he ran off across the quay, with his fish dangling from the string over his shoulder. I glanced at my watch. It was after three o'clock. No doubt the gentleman from foreign parts would dine at five. I walked through the town, and down the narrow alleyway to the boathouse where Ambrose had kept his sails and gear for the sailing boat he used to use. The small pram was made fast to the frape. I pulled in the pram, and climbed down into it; then paddled out into the harbour and lay off, a little distance from the quay.

There were several fellows pulling to and from the vessels anchored in the channel, to the town steps; and they did not notice me, or if they did cared little, and took me for a fisherman. I threw the weight into the water and rested on my paddles, and watched the entrance of the Rose and Crown. The bar entrance was in the side-street. He would not enter that way. If he came at all, it would be by the front. An hour passed. The church clock struck four. Still I waited. At a quarter before five I saw the landlord's wife come out of the parlour entrance and look about her, as though in search of someone. Her visitor was late for supper. The fish was cooked. I heard her call out to a fellow standing by the boats that were fastened to the steps, but I did not catch her words. He shouted back at her and, turning, pointed out towards the harbour. She nodded her head, and went back inside the inn. Then, ten minutes after five, I saw a boat approaching the town steps. Pulled by a lusty fellow in the bows, the boat itself new varnished, it had all the air of one hired out for strangers, who cared to be rowed about the harbour for their pleasure.

A man, with a broad-brimmed hat upon his head, was seated in the stern. They came to the steps. The man climbed out and gave the fellow money, after slight argument, then turned towards the inn. As he stood for a moment on the steps, before entering the Rose and Crown, he took off his hat and looked about him, with that air of putting a price on all he saw that I could not mistake. I was so near, I could have tossed a biscuit at him. Then he went inside. It was Rainaldi.

I hauled up the weight and pulled back to the boathouse, made the boat fast, walked through the town, and up the rope walk to the cliffs. I think I covered the four miles to home in forty minutes. Rachel was in the library waiting for me. Dinner had been put back because I had not come. She came towards me, anxious.

'At last you have returned,' she said. 'I have been very worried. Where were you, then?'

'Out rowing, in the harbour,' I answered her. 'Fine weather for excursions. Far better on the water than inside the Rose and Crown.'

The startled shock that came into her eyes was all I needed for the final proof.

'All right, I know your secret,' I continued. 'Don't think up any lies.'

Seecombe came in to ask if he should serve dinner.

'Do so, at once,' I said, 'I shall not change.'

I stared at her, saying no more, and we went in to dinner. Seecombe was all concern, sensing something wrong. He hovered at my elbow like a doctor, tempting me to taste the dishes that he proffered.

'You have overtaxed your strength, sir,' he said, 'this will not do at all. We shall have you ill again.'

He looked at Rachel for confirmation, and for backing. She said nothing. As soon as dinner was over, which each of us had barely tasted, Rachel rose to her feet and went straight upstairs. I followed her. When she came to the door of the boudoir she would have closed it against me, but I was too quick for her and stood inside the room, with my back against it. The look of apprehension came to her eyes again. She went away from me, and stood by the mantelpiece.

'How long has Rainaldi been staying at the Rose and Crown?' I said.

'That is my business,' she replied.

'Mine also. Answer me,' I said.

I think she saw there was no hope to keep me quiet, or fob me off with fables. 'Very well then, for the past two weeks,' she answered.

'Why is he here?' I said.

'Because I asked him. Because he is my friend. Because I needed his advice, and, knowing your dislike, could not ask him to this house.'

'Why should you need his advice?'

'That, again, is my business. Not yours. Stop behaving like a child, Philip, and have some understanding.'

I was glad to see her so distressed. It showed she was at fault.

'You ask me to have understanding,' I said. 'Do you expect me to understand deceit? You have been lying every day to me for the past two weeks, and cannot deny it.'

'If I have deceived you, it was not willingly,' she said. 'I did it for your sake only. You hate Rainaldi. If you had known that I was meeting him, this scene would have come the sooner, and you would have been ill in consequence. Oh, God – must I go through all again? First with Ambrose, and now with you?'

Her face was white and strained, but whether from fear or anger was hard to tell. I stood with my back against the door and watched her.

'Yes,' I said, 'I hate Rainaldi, as did Ambrose. And with reason.'

'What reason, for pity's sake?'

'He is in love with you. And has been, now, for years.'

'What utter nonsense . . .' She paced up and down the little room, from the fireplace to the window, her hands clasped in front of her. 'Here is a man who has stood beside me through every trial and trouble. Who has never misjudged me, or tried to see me as other than I am. He knows my faults, my weaknesses, and does not condemn them, but accepts me at my own value. Without his help, through all the years that I have known him – years of which you know nothing – I would have been lost indeed. Rainaldi is my friend. My only friend.'

She paused, and looked at me. No doubt it was the truth, or so distorted in her mind that, to her, it became so. It made no difference to my judging of Rainaldi. Some of his reward he held already. The years of which, so she just told me, I knew nothing. The rest would come in time. Next month, perhaps, next year – but finally. He had a wealth of patience. But not I, nor Ambrose.

'Send him away, back where he belongs,' I said.

'He will go, when he is ready,' she replied, 'but if I need him he will stay. Indeed, if you try and threaten me again I will have him in this house, as my protector.'

'You would not dare,' I said.

'Dare? Why not? The house is mine.'

So we had come to battle. Her words were a challenge that I could not meet. Her woman's brain worked differently from mine. All argument was fair, all blows were foul. Physical strength alone disarmed a woman. I made one step towards her, but she was at the fireplace, with her hand upon the bell-rope.

'Stay where you are,' she cried, 'or I shall ring for Seecombe. Do you want to be shamed in front of him, when I tell him that you tried to strike me?'

'I was not going to strike you,' I replied. I turned, and opened wide the door. 'All right,' I said, 'call for Seecombe, if you wish. Tell him all that has happened here, between us. If we must have violence and shame, let us have it in full measure.'

She stood by the bell-rope, I by the open door. She let the bell-rope fall. I did not move. Then, tears coming to her eyes, she looked at me and said, 'A woman can't suffer twice. I have had all this before.' And lifting her fingers to her throat she added, 'Even the hands around my neck. That too. Now will you understand?'

I looked over her head, straight at the portrait above the mantelpiece, and the young face of Ambrose staring at me was my own. She had defeated both of us.

'Yes,' I said, 'I understand. If you want to see Rainaldi, ask him here. I would rather that, than that you crept to meet him at the Rose and Crown.'

And I left her in the boudoir, and went back to my room.

Next day he came to dinner. She had sent a note to me at breakfast, asking permission to invite him, her challenge of the night before forgotten no doubt, or expediently put aside, to restore me to position. I sent a note back in return, saying I would give orders for Wellington to fetch him in the carriage. He arrived at half-past four.

It happened that I was alone in the library when he came, and by some error on the part of Seecombe he was shown in to me, and not into the drawing-room. I rose from my chair, and bade him good afternoon. He seemed greatly at his ease, and offered me his hand.

'I hope you are recovered,' he said, in greeting me. 'In fact, I think you look better than I expected. All the reports I had of you were bad. Rachel was much concerned.'

'Indeed, I am very well,' I said to him.

'The fortune of youth,' he said. 'What it is to have good lungs, and good digestion, so that in the space of a few weeks all traces of sickness leave you. No doubt you are already galloping about the countryside on horseback. Whereas we older people, like your cousin and myself, go carefully, to avoid all strain. Personally, I consider a nap in the immediate afternoon essential to middle age.'

I asked him to sit down and he did so, smiling a little as he looked about him. 'No alterations to this room as yet?' he said. 'Perhaps Rachel intends to leave it so, as giving atmosphere. Just as well. The money can be better spent on other things. She tells me much has been already done about the grounds, since my last visit. Knowing Rachel, I can well believe it. But I must see first, before I give approval. I regard myself as a trustee, to hold a balance.'

He took a thin cigar from his case, and lit it, still smiling as he did so. 'I had a letter to you, written in London,' he said, 'after you made over your estate, and would have sent it, but that I had the news of your illness. There was little in the letter that I can't say now to your face. It was merely thanking you, for Rachel's sake, and assuring you that I would take great care to see there was no great loss to you in the transaction. I shall watch all expenditure.' He puffed a cloud of smoke into the air, and gazed up at the ceiling. 'That candelabra,' he said, 'was not chosen with great taste. We could do better for you than that, in Italy. I must remember to tell Rachel to make a note of these things. Good pictures, good furniture and fittings, are all sound investments. Eventually, you will find we shall hand the property back to you with double value. However, that's in the distant future. And you by that time, no doubt, with grown sons of your own. Rachel and myself, old people in wheeled chairs.' He laughed, and smiled at me again. 'And how is the charming Miss Louise?' he said to me.

I told him I believed that she was well. I watched him smoking his cigar, and thought how smooth his hands were for a man. They had a kind of feminine quality that did not fit in with the rest of him, and the great ring, on his little finger, was out of place.

'When do you go back to Florence?' I asked him.

He flicked the ash that had fallen on his coat down to the grate.

'It depends on Rachel,' he said. 'I return to London to settle my business there, and then shall either go home ahead of her, to prepare the villa and the servants for her reception, or wait and travel with her. You know, of course, that she intends to go?'

'Yes,' I answered.

'I am relieved that you have not put any pressure upon her to remain,' he said. 'I quite understand, that with your illness you became greatly dependent on her; she told me as much. And she has been anxious to spare your feelings in every way. But. as I explained to her, this cousin of yours is now a man, and not a child. If he cannot stand upon his own feet, he must learn to do so. Am I not right?' he asked me.

'Perfectly.'

'Women, especially Rachel, act always from emotion. We men, more usually though not always so, with reason. I am glad to see you sensible.

Perhaps in spring, when you visit us in Florence, you will allow me to show you some of the treasures there. You will not be disappointed.' He blew another cloud of smoke up to the ceiling.

'When you say "we",' I ventured, 'do you use it in the royal sense, as if you owned the city, or is it a legal phrase?'

'Forgive me,' he said, 'but I am so accustomed to acting for Rachel, even to thinking for her, in so many ways, that I can never entirely dissociate myself from her and so fall to using that particular pronoun personal.' He looked across at me. 'In time,' he said, 'I have good reason to believe that I shall come to use it in a sense more intimate. But that' – he gestured, his cigar in hand – 'is in the laps of the gods. Ah, here she comes.'

He stood up, and so did I, when Rachel came into the room; and as she gave her hand to him, which he took and kissed, she made him welcome in Italian. Perhaps it was watching them at dinner, I do not know – his eyes, that never left her face, her smile, her change of manner with him – but I felt, rising within me, a sort of nausea. The food I ate tasted of dust. Even the tisana, which she made for the three of us to drink when dinner was over, had a bitter unaccustomed tang. I left them, sitting in the garden, and went up to my room. As soon as I had gone I heard their voices break into Italian. I sat in the chair by my window, where I had sat during those first days and weeks of convalescence, and she beside me; and it was as though the whole world had turned evil, and of a sudden, sour. I could not bring myself to descend and say good night to him. I heard the carriage come, I heard the carriage drive away. I went on sitting in my chair. Presently Rachel came up and tapped upon my door. I did not answer. She opened it, and entering the room came to my side, and put her hand upon my shoulder.

'What is it now?' she asked. There was a sort of sigh about her voice, as if she had reached the limit of endurance. 'He could not have been more courteous, or kind,' she said to me. 'What fault was there to-night?'

'None,' I answered.

'He speaks so well of you to me,' she said, 'if you could only hear him, you would realise that he has a great regard for you. This evening you surely could not take exception to anything he said? If only you could be less difficult, less jealous. . . .'

She drew the curtains of my room, for dusk was nearly come. Even in her gesture, the way she touched the curtain, there was impatience.

'Are you going to sit there, hunched in that chair, till midnight?' she asked. 'If so, put a wrap about you, or you will take cold. For my part, I am exhausted and shall go to bed.'

She touched my head, and went. Not a caress. The quick gesture of someone patting a child who has misbehaved, the adult finding herself too lost in tedium to continue scolding, but brushing the whole aside. 'There . . . there . . . For heaven's sake, have done.'

That night fever returned to me again. Not with the old force, but something similar. Whether it was chill or not, caught from sitting in the boat in the harbour twenty-four hours before, I do not know, but in the morning I was too giddy to stand upright upon the floor, and fell to retching and to shuddering, and was obliged to go back to bed again. The doctor was sent for, and with my aching head I wondered if the whole miserable business of my illness was to set in with repetition. He pronounced my liver out of order, and left medicine. But when Rachel came to sit with me, in the afternoon, it seemed to me she had upon her face that same expression of the night before, a kind of weariness. I could imagine she thought within her, 'It is going to start again? Am I doomed to sit here as a nurse to all eternity?' She was more brusque with me, as she handed me my medicine; and when later I was thirsty, and wished to drink, I did not ask her for the glass, for fear of giving trouble.

She had a book in her hands, which she did not read, and her presence in the chair beside me seemed to hold a mute reproach.

'If you have other things to do,' I said at last, 'don't sit with me.'

'What else do you suppose I have to do?' she answered.

'You might wish to see Rainaldi.'

'He has gone,' she said.

My heart was the lighter for the news. I was almost well.

'He has returned to London?' I enquired.

'No,' she answered, 'he sailed from Plymouth yesterday.'

My relief was so intense that I had to turn away my head lest I showed it in my face, and so increased her irritation.

'I thought he had business still to do in England?'

'So he had; but we decided it could be done just as well by correspondence. Matters of greater urgency attended him at home. He had news of a vessel due to sail at midnight, and so went. Now are you satisfied?'

Rainaldi had left the country, I was satisfied with that. But not with the pronoun 'we'; nor that she spoke of home. I knew why he had gone – to warn the servants at the villa to make ready for their mistress. There was the urgency attending him. My sands were running out.

'When will you follow him?'

'It depends on you,' she answered.

I supposed, if I wished, I could continue to feel ill. Complain of pain, and make excuse of sickness. Drag on, pretending, for a few weeks more. And then? The boxes packed, the boudoir bare, her bed in the blue room covered with the dust-sheet that had been upon it all the years before she came, and silence.

'If,' she sighed, 'you would only be less bitter and less cruel, these last days could be happy.'

Was I bitter? Was I cruel? I had not thought so. It seemed to me the hardness was in her. There was no remedy. I reached out for her hand, and she gave it me. Yet as I kissed it I kept thinking of Rainaldi . . .

That night I dreamt I climbed to the granite stone and read the letter once again, buried beneath it. The dream was so vivid that it did not fade with waking, but remained throughout the morning. I got up, and was well enough to go downstairs, as usual, by midday. Try as I would, I could not shake off the desire within me to read the letter once again. I could not remember what it said about Rainaldi. I must know, for certainty, what it was Ambrose had said of him. In the afternoon Rachel went to her room to rest, and as soon as she had gone I slipped away through the woods and down to the avenue, and climbed the path above the keeper's cottage, filled with loathing for what I meant to do. I came to the granite slab. I knelt beside it and, digging with my hands, felt suddenly the soggy leather of my pocket-book. A slug had made its home there for the winter. The trail across the front was sticky. I knocked it off, and opened the pocket-book took out the crumpled letter. The paper was damp and limp, the lettering more faded than before, but still decipherable. I read the letter through. The first part more hastily, though it was strange that his illness, from another cause, could have been, in symptoms, so much similar to mine. But to Rainaldi . . .

'As the months passed,' wrote Ambrose, 'I noticed more and more how she turned to this man I have mentioned before in my letters, Signor Rainaldi, a friend and I gather a lawyer of Sangalletti's, for advice, rather than to me. I believe this man to have a pernicious influence upon her. I suspect him of having been in love with her for years, even when Sangalletti was alive, and although I do not for an instant believe she ever thought of him in such a connection up to a short while ago, now, since she has altered in her manner to me, I cannot be so sure. There is a shadow in her eye, a tone in her voice, when his name is said, that awakens in my mind the most terrible suspicion.

'Brought up as she was by feckless parents, living a life, before and even during her first marriage, about which both of us have had reserve, I have often felt her code of behaviour is different to ours at home. The tie of marriage may not be so sacred. I suspect, in fact I have proof, that he gives her money. Money, God forgive me for saying so, is at the present time the one way to her heart.'

There it was, the sentence I had not forgotten, which had haunted me. Where the paper folded the words were indistinct, until I caught again the word 'Rainaldi.' 'I will come down to the terrace,' Ambrose said, 'and find Rainaldi there. At sight of me, both fall silent. I cannot but wonder what it is they have been discussing. Once, when she had gone into the villa and Rainaldi and I were left alone, he asked an abrupt question as to my will. This he had seen, incidentally, when we married. He told me that as it stood, and should I die, I would leave my wife without provision. This I knew, and had anyway drawn up a will myself that would correct the error, and would have put my signature to it, and had it witnessed, could I be certain that her fault of spending was a temporary passing thing, and not deep-rooted.

'This new will, by the way, would give her the house and the estate for her lifetime only, and so to you upon her death, with the proviso that the running of the estate be left in your hands entirely.

'It still remains unsigned, and for the reason I have told you.

'Mark you, it is Rainaldi who asked questions on the will, Rainaldi who drew my attention to the omissions of the one that stands at present. She does not speak of it, to me. But do they speak of it, together? What is it that they say to one another, when I am not there?

'This matter of the will occurred in March. Admittedly, I was unwell, and nearly blinded with my head, and Rainaldi bringing up the matter may have done so in that cold calculating way of his, thinking that I might die. Possibly it is so. Possibly it is not discussed between them. I have no means of finding out. Too often now I find her eyes upon me, watchful and strange. And when I hold her, it is as though she were afraid. Afraid of what, of whom?

'Two days ago, which brings me to the reason for this letter, I had another attack of this same fever, which laid me low in March. The onset is sudden. I am seized with pain and sickness, which passes swiftly to great excitation of my brain, driving me near to violence, and I can hardly stand upon my feet for dizziness of mind and body. This, in its turn, passes, and an intolerable desire for sleep comes upon me, so that I fall upon the floor, or upon my bed, with no power over my limbs. I do not recollect my father being thus. The headaches, yes, and some difficulty of temperament, but not the other symptoms.

'Philip, my boy, the only being in the world whom I can trust, tell me what it means, and if you can, come out to me. Say nothing to Nick Kendall. Say no word to any single soul. Above all, write not a word in answer, only come.

'One thought possesses me, leaving me no peace. Are they trying to poison me? – Ambrose.'

This time I did not put the letter back into the pocket book. I tore it piece by piece into tiny shreds, and ground the shreds into the earth with my heel. Each shred was scattered, and then ground, in a separate place. The pocket book, soggy from its sojourn in the earth, I was able to wrench in two with a single twist. I flung each half over my shoulder, and they fell amongst the bracken. Then I walked home. It seemed like a postscript to the letter, that when I entered the hall Seecombe was just bringing in the post-bag, that the boy had fetched from town. He waited while I unlocked it, and there, amidst the few there were for me, was one to Rachel, with the Plymouth mark upon it. I needed but to glance at the thin spidery hand to know that it was from Rainaldi. I think, if Seecombe had not been there, I would have kept it. As it was, there was nothing for it but to give it him to take up to Rachel.

It was ironic, too, that when I went up to her a little later, saying nothing of my walk or where I had been, all her sharpness with me seemed to have gone. The old tenderness had returned. She held out her arms to me, and smiled, and asked me how I felt and if I was rested. She said nothing of the letter she had received. I wondered, during dinner, whether the news it had contained had made her happy; and, as I sat eating, I pictured to myself the framework of his letter, what he had said to her, how he addressed her – if, in short, it were a letter of love. It would be written in Italian. But here and there, though, there might be words I should understand. She had taught me a few phrases. I would know, at any rate, with the first words, the relationship they bore to one another.

'You are very silent. Are you well?' she said.

'Yes,' I answered, 'I am well,' and flushed, lest she should read my mind and guess what I meant to do.

After dinner we went up to her boudoir. She prepared the tisana, as usual, and set it down in its cup on the table by my side, and hers as well. On the bureau lay Rainaldi's letter, half covered by her handkerchief. My eyes were drawn towards it, fascinated. Would an Italian, writing to the woman he loved, keep to formality? Or setting sail from Plymouth, with the prospect of a few weeks' separation, and having dined well, drunk his brandy and smoked his cigar, and smiling in complaisance, would he turn to indiscretion and permit himself the licence of spilling love on paper?

'Philip,' said Rachel, 'you keep your eyes fixed on one corner of the room as though you saw a ghost. What is the matter?'

'I tell you nothing,' I said. And for the first time lied, as I knelt beside her pretending an urgency of longing and of love, so that her questions might be stilled, and that she would forget the letter lying on the desk and leave it there.

Late that night, long after midnight, when I knew she slept – for standing in her room with a lighted candle I looked down on her and saw that it was so – I went back into the boudoir. The handkerchief was still there, the letter gone. I looked in the fire, no ashes in the grate. I opened the drawers of the bureau, and there were her papers all in order, but not the letter. It was not in the pigeon-holes, nor the little drawers beside it. There remained only one drawer, and that was locked. I took my knife and edged it in the crack. Something white showed, from inside the drawer. I went back to the bedroom, took the bunch of keys from the bedside table, and tried the smallest. It fitted. The drawer opened. I put in my hand and pulled out an envelope, but as I did so my tense excitement turned to disappointment, for it was not Rainaldi's letter that I held in my hands. It was just an envelope, containing pods, with seeds. The seeds ran from the pods on to my hands, and spilt upon the floor. They were very small, and green. I stared at them, and remembered that I had seen pods and seeds like these before. They were the same as those that Tamlyn had thrown over his shoulder in the plantation, and that had also covered the court in the villa Sangalletti, which the servants there had swept away.

They were laburnum seeds, poisonous to cattle, and to men.

Chapter Twenty-six

I put the envelope back in the drawer. I turned the key. I took the bunch of keys and replaced it on the dressing-table. I did not look at her, as she lay sleeping in her bed. I went to my room.

I think I was more calm than I had been for many weeks. I went to my washing-stand, and standing there beside the jug and basin were the two bottles of medicine that the doctor had prescribed for me. I emptied the contents from the window. Then I went downstairs, with a lighted candle, and into the pantry. The servants had all gone to their quarters long ago. On the table near the washing-sink stood the tray with the two cups upon it from which we had drunk our tisana. I knew that John was sometimes idle of an evening, and might leave the cups till morning to be washed, as indeed he had. The dregs of the tisana lay in both the cups. I examined both of them by candlelight. They looked the same. I put my little finger into the dregs, first hers, then mine, and tasted. Was there a difference? It was hard to tell. It might be that the dregs from my cup were just a little thicker, but I could not swear to it. I left the pantry, and went again upstairs to my room.

I undressed and went to bed. As I lay there in the darkness I was not aware of anger, or of fear. Only compassion. I saw her as someone not responsible for what she did, besmirched by evil. Compelled and driven by the man who had power over her, lacking, through fault of circumstance and birth, in some deep moral sense, she was capable by instinct and by impulse of this final act. I wanted to save her from herself, and knew not how. It seemed to me that Ambrose was beside me, and I lived again in him, or he in me. The letter he had written, which I had torn in shreds, was now fulfilled.

I believed, in her strange way, that she had loved us both, but we had become dispensable. Something other than blind emotion directed her actions after all. Perhaps she was two persons, torn in two, first one having sway and then the other. I did not know. Louise would say that she had been the second always. That from the very first every thought, every move, had some premeditation. In Florence with her mother, after her father died, had it started then, or even before, the way of living? Sangalletti, dying in a duel, who had never been to Ambrose or myself other than a shadow without substance, had he suffered too? Louise, no doubt, would tell me that he had. Louise would insist that from the first encounter with Ambrose, two years before, she planned to marry him, for money. And when he did not give her what she wanted, planned his death. There was the legal mind. And she had not read the letter I had torn to shreds. What would be her judgement if she had?

What a woman has done once without detection, she can do twice. And rid herself of yet another burden.

Well, the letter was torn; neither Louise nor any one else would ever read it. The contents mattered little to me now. I did not think so much of them as of the last scrap that Ambrose wrote, dismissed by Rainaldi, and by Nick Kendall too, as being the final utterance of a brain diseased. 'She has done for me at last, Rachel my torment.'

I was the only one to know he spoke the truth.

I was back again, then, where I had been before. I had returned to the bridge beside the Arno, where I had sworn an oath. Perhaps, after all, an oath was something that could not be foresworn, that had to be fulfilled, in its own time. And the time was come . . .

Next day was Sunday. Like all the Sundays past, since she had been a visitor to the house, the carriage came to take us both to church. The day was fine and warm. It was full summer. She wore a new dark gown of thin light stuff, and a straw bonnet, and carried a parasol. She smiled good morning at Wellington, and at Jim, and I helped her into the carriage. When I took my seat beside her, and we drove off through the park, she put her hand in mine.

I had held it many times, in love, before. Felt the small size of it, turned the rings upon the fingers, seen the blue veins upon the back, touched the small close-filed nails. Now, as it rested in my hand, I saw it, for the first time, put to another purpose. I saw it take the laburnum pods, in deft fashion, and empty out the seeds; then crush the seeds, and rub them in her palm. I remembered once I had told her that her hands were beautiful, and she had answered, with a laugh, that I was the first to tell her so. 'They have their uses,' she said. 'Ambrose used to say, when I was gardening, that they were workmen's hands.'

Now we had come to the steep hill, and the drag was put upon the rear wheel of the carriage. She touched my shoulder with her shoulder, and putting up her parasol against the sun she said to me, 'I slept so sound last night, I never heard you go,' and she looked at me, and smiled. Though she had deceived me for so long, I felt the greater liar. I could not even answer her, but to keep up the lie held her hand the firmer, and turned away my head.

The sands were golden in the westward bay, the tide far out, the water sparkling in the sun. We turned along the lane that led to the village, and to church. The bells were ringing out across the air, and the people stood around the gate and waited for us to alight from the carriage and pass in before them. Rachel smiled and bowed to all of them. We saw the Kendalls, and the Pascoes, and the many tenants from the estate, and we walked up the aisle to our pew as the organ played.

We knelt in prayer for a brief moment, our faces buried in our hands. 'And what,' I thought to myself, for I did not pray, 'is she saying to her God, if she acknowledges one? Does she give thanks for success in all she has achieved? Or does she ask for mercy?'

She rose from her knees and sat back on the cushioned seat, opening her prayer-book. Her face was serene and happy. I wished that I could hate her, as I had hated her for many months, unseen. Yet I could feel nothing now but this strange, terrible compassion.

We stood up as the vicar entered, and the service began. I remember the psalm we sang upon that morning. 'He that worketh deceit shall not dwell within my house: he that telleth lies shall not tarry in my sight.' Her lips moved with the words, her voice was soft and low as she sang. And when the vicar mounted the pulpit to preach his sermon, she folded her hands upon her lap and composed herself to listen, and her eyes, serious and intent, lifted to watch his face as he gave out his text, 'It is a fearful thing to fall into the hands of the living God.'

The sun came through the stained glass of the windows and shone upon her. I could see, from my seat, the round rosy faces of the village children, yawning a little as they waited for the sermon to finish, and I could hear the shuffle of their feet, pinched into Sunday boots, longing to be barefoot on the green in play. I wished passionately, for one brief moment, that I might be young again, and innocent, with Ambrose, and not Rachel, beside me in the pew.

'There is a green hill far away, beneath a city wall.' I don't know why we sang that hymn this day; perhaps there had been some festival in connection with the village children. Our voices rose loud and clear in the parish church, and I did not think of Jerusalem, as I was no doubt supposed to do, but only of a plain grave in its corner of the Protestant cemetery in Florence.

When the choir had departed and the congregation were stepping out into the aisles, Rachel whispered to me, 'I believe we should ask the Kendalls and the Pascoes to dine to-day, as we used to do. It has been so long, and they will grow offended.'

I thought a moment, and then nodded briefly. It would be better so. Their company would help to bridge the gulf between us, and occupied in conversation with the guests, used to my silence on these occasions, she would have no time to look at me, and wonder. Outside the church, the Pascoes needed no persuasion, the Kendalls rather more. 'I shall be obliged to leave you,' said my godfather, 'immediately we have dined, but the carriage can return again to fetch Louise.'

'Mr. Pascoe has to preach again at evensong,' interrupted the vicar's wife, 'we can take you back with us.' They fell into elaborate plans of transportation, and while they were thus arguing, and arranging how it could best be done, I noticed that the foreman in charge of the workmen who were employed upon the building of the terrace walk and the future sunken garden stood at the side of the path to speak to me, his hat in his hand.

'What is it?' I said to him.

'Excuse me, Mr. Ashley sir,' he said, 'I looked for you yesterday, when we were done work for the day, but did not see you, just to warn you, if you should go on the terrace walk, not to stand on the bridgeway we are building across the sunken garden.'

'Why, what is wrong with it?'

'It's only a framework, sir, until we can get working on it Monday morning. The planking looks firm enough to the eye, but it doesn't bear no weight upon it. Anyone stepping on it, thinking to cross to the further side, could fall and break their neck.'

'Thank you,' I said, 'I will remember.'

I turned to find my party had come to their agreement, and as on that first Sunday, which now seemed so long ago, we split into three groups, Rachel and my godfather driving in his carriage, and Louise and I in mine. The Pascoes, in their brougham, followed third. No doubt it had come about like this many times between; yet as we climbed the hill, and I got out and walked, I kept thinking of the first time, nearly ten months before, on that Sunday in September. I had been irritated by Louise that morning, sitting so stiff and proud, and had neglected her from that day forward. She had not wavered, but had stayed my friend. When we topped the hill, and I stepped once more into the carriage, I said to her, 'Did you know that laburnum seeds are poisonous?'

She looked at me, surprised. 'Yes, I believe so,' she said; 'I know that if cattle eat them they die. And children too. What makes you ask? Have you lost cattle at the Barton?'

'No, not yet,' I said, 'but Tamlyn spoke to me the other day about moving the trees that lean from the plantation to the field beneath, because of the seeds falling to the ground.'

'It might be wise to do so,' she replied. 'Father lost a horse once, years ago, eating yew berries. It can come about so quickly, and there is nothing one can do.'

We came along the lane, and to the park gates, and I wondered what she would say if I told her of my discovery of the night before. Would she stare at me in horror, telling me I was mad? I doubted it. I thought she would believe me. This was not the place, though, with Wellington seated on the box and Jim beside him.

I turned my head; the other carriages were following behind. 'I want to talk to you, Louise,' I said to her. 'When your father leaves, after dinner, make some excuse to stay.'

She stared at me, a question in her eyes, but I said no more.

Wellington pulled up before the house. I got out and gave Louise my hand. We stood waiting for the others. Yes, it might have been that other Sunday, in September. Rachel was smiling now, as she smiled then. She was looking up at my godfather, talking as she did so; and I believe they were at politics again. That Sunday, though drawn towards her, she had been a stranger to me still. And now? Now, no part of her was strange. I knew the best, I knew the worst. Even the motives for all she did, baffling perhaps even to herself, I guessed them too. She hid nothing for me now, Rachel my torment . . .

'This,' she said smiling, as we all assembled in the hall, 'is like old times again. I am so happy you have come.'

She embraced the party in a glance, and led the way to the drawing-room. The room, as always, looked its best in summer. The windows were flung wide open, it was cool. The Japanese hortensias, feathery blue, stood long and slender in the vases, and reflected in the mirrors on the walls. Outside the sun beat down upon the lawns. It was very warm. A lazy bumble-bee droned against one of the windows. The visitors sat down, languid, and content to rest. Seecombe brought cake and wine.

'You are all overcome because of a little sun,' laughed Rachel. 'To me, it is nothing. In Italy we have it thus for nine months in the year. I thrive upon it. Here, I will wait upon you all. Philip, remain seated. You are still my patient.'

She poured the wine into the glasses and brought it to us. My godfather and the vicar both stood up, protesting, but she waved them aside. When she came last to me, I was the only one who did not drink.

'Not thirsty?' she said.

I shook my head. I would take nothing from her hands again. She put the glass back upon the tray, and with her own went and sat beside Mrs. Pascoe and Louise upon the sofa.

'I suppose,' said the vicar, 'that in Florence now the heat is well-nigh unbearable, even to you?'

'I never found it so,' said Rachel. 'The shutters would be closed early in the morning, which kept the villa cool throughout the day. We adapt ourselves to the climate. Anyone who stirs without in the middle of the day asks for disaster; so we stay within, and sleep. I am lucky, at the villa Sangalletti, in having a little court beside the house that faces north and never has the sun upon it. There is a pool there, and a fountain; and when the air feels used I turn on the fountain; the water dripping has a soothing sound. In spring and summer I never sit anywhere else.'

In spring, indeed, she could watch the buds upon the laburnum tree swell and turn to flower, and the flowers themselves, with drooping golden heads, make a canopy for the naked boy who stood above the pool, holding the shell between his hands. In their turn the flowers would fade and fall, and when high summer came to the villa, as it had come here, in less intensity, the pods upon the branches of the tree would burst and scatter, and the green seeds tumble to the ground. All this she would have watched, sitting in the little court, with Ambrose at her side.

'I would dearly love to visit Florence,' said Mary Pascoe, her eyes round, and dreaming of God knew what strange magnificence, and Rachel turned to her, and said, 'Then you must do so, next year, and come and stay with me. You must all come and stay with me, in turn.' At once we were in the midst of exclamations, questions and expressions of dismay. Must she go soon? When would she return? What were her plans? She shook her head in answer. 'Presently I shall go,' she said, 'and presently return. I act on impulse, and will not confine myself to dates.' Nor would she be drawn into further detail.

I saw my godfather glance at me, out of the corner of his eye; then, tugging his moustache, stare at his feet. I could imagine the thought that was passing through his head. 'Once she has gone, he will be himself again.' The afternoon wore on. At four, we sat to dinner. Once more I was seated at the head of the table and Rachel at the foot, my godfather and the vicar on either hand. Once more there was talk and laughter, even poetry. I sat, much with the same silence that I had at first, and watched her face. Then, it had been with fascination, because unknown. The continuation of conversation, the change of topic, the inclusion of each person at the table, was something that I had never seen a woman do, so it was magic. Now, I knew all the tricks. The starting of the subject, the whisper behind her hand to the vicar, and the laughter of both followed at once by my godfather leaning forward asking, 'Now what was that, Mrs. Ashley, what did you say?' and her immediate reply, quick and mocking. 'The vicar will inform you,' with the vicar, blushing red and proud, thinking himself a wit, embarking on a story that his family had not heard. It was a little game that she enjoyed, and we were all of us, with our dull Cornish ways, so easy to handle, and to fool.

I wondered if in Italy her task was harder. I did not think so. Only her company there was more suited to her mettle. And with Rainaldi at her hand to help her, speaking the language she knew best, the talk would sparkle at the villa Sangelletti with greater brilliance than it had ever done at my dull table. Sometimes she gestured with her hands, as though to clarify her rapid speech. When she talked to Rainaldi in Italian, I had noticed she did it even more. To-day, interrupting my godfather in some statement, she did it once again; both hands, so quick and deft, brushing aside the air. Then, waiting for his answer, her elbows resting lightly on the table, the hands folded themselves, were still. Her head was turned to him as she listened, so that from the head of the table, where I sat, I looked on her in profile. She was always a stranger, thus. Those neat clipped features on a coin. Dark and withdrawn, a foreign woman standing in a doorway, a shawl about her head, her hand outstretched. But full-face, when she smiled, a stranger never. The Rachel that I knew, that I had loved.

My godfather finished his story. There was a pause, and silence. Trained now to all her movements, I watched her eyes. They looked to Mrs. Pascoe, then to me. 'Shall we go into the garden?' she said. We all rose from our chairs, and the vicar, pulling out his watch, sighed and observed, 'Much as I regret it, I must tear myself away.'

'I too,' remarked my godfather. 'I have a brother sick at Luxilyan, and promised to call and see him. But Louise may stay.'

'Surely you have time to drink your tea?' said Rachel; but it seemed the hour was later than they thought, and at length, after some pother, Nick Kendall and the Pascoes departed in the brougham. Louise alone remained.

'Since there are only the three of us,' said Rachel, 'let us be informal. Come to the boudoir.' And smiling at Louise she led the way upstairs. 'Louise shall drink tisana,' she called, over her shoulder. 'I will show her my method. When her father suffers from insomnia, if ever, this is the remedy.'

We all came to the boudoir and sat down, I by the open window, Louise upon the stool. Rachel busied herself with her preparations.

'The English way,' said Rachel, 'if there can be an English way, which I rather doubt, is to take peeled barley. I brought my own dried herbs from Florence. If you like the taste, I will leave some with you when I go.'

Louise rose from the stool, and stood beside her. 'I heard from Mary Pascoe that you know the name of every herb,' she said, 'and have doctored the tenants here on the estate for many ailments. In old days, the people knew more about these things than they do now. Yet some of the old folk can still charm away warts and rashes.'

'I can charm more than warts,' laughed Rachel. 'Call in at their cottages, and ask them. Herb-lore is very ancient. I learnt it from my mother. Thank you, John.' John had brought up the kettle of steaming water. 'In Florence,' said Rachel, 'I used to brew the tisana in my room, and let it stand. It is better thus. Then we would go out into the court, and sit, and I would turn on the fountain, and while we sipped our tisana the water dripped into the pool. Ambrose would sit there, watching it, for hours.' She poured the water that John had brought into the teapot. 'I have a mind,' she said 'to bring back from Florence, next time I come to Cornwall, a little statue, like the one above my pool. It will take some finding, but I shall be successful in the end. Then we can put him to stand in the middle of the new sunken garden we are building here, and make a fountain too. What do you think?' She turned to me, smiling, and she was stirring the tisana with a spoon in her left hand.

'If you like,' I answered.

'Philip lacks all enthusiasm,' she said to Louise; 'either he agrees to all I say, or does not care. Sometimes I think my labours here are wasted, the terrace walk, the shrubs in the plantation. He would have been content with rough grass, and a muddied path. Here, take your cup.'

She gave the cup to Louise, who sat down on the stool. Then she brought me mine, where I was sitting on the window-sill.

I shook my head. 'No tisana, Philip?' she said. 'But it is good for you, and makes you sleep. You have never refused before. This is a special brew. I have made it double strength.'

'You drink it for me,' I replied.

She shrugged her shoulders, 'Mine is already poured. I like it to stand longer. This must be wasted. What a pity.' She leant over me, and poured it from the window. Drawing back, she put her hand on my shoulder, and from her came the scent I knew so well. No perfume, but the essence of her own person, the texture of her skin.

'Are you not well?' she whispered, so that Louise could not hear.

If all knowledge, and all feeling, could be blotted out, I would have asked it then, and that she should remain, her hand upon my shoulder. No letter torn to shreds, no secret packet locked in a little drawer, no evil, no duplicity. Her hand moved from my shoulder to my chin, and stayed there for a moment in a brief caress, which, because she stood between me and Louise, passed unseen.

'My sullen one,' she said.

I looked above her head, and saw the portrait of Ambrose above the mantelpiece. His eyes stared straight into mine, in youth and innocence. I answered nothing; and moving from me she put back my empty cup on to the tray.

'What do you think of it?' she asked Louise.

'I am afraid,' apologised Louise, 'that it would take me a little time to like it well.'

'Perhaps,' said Rachel; 'the musty flavour does not suit all persons. Never mind. It is a sedative to unquiet minds. To-night we shall all sleep well.' She smiled, and drank slowly from her own cup.

We chatted a little while, for perhaps half an hour or more, or rather she did with Louise; then rising, and putting back her cup upon the tray, she said, 'Now it is cooler, who will walk with me in the garden?' I glanced across at Louise, who, looking at me, stayed silent.

'I have promised Louise,' I said, 'to show her an old plan of the Pelyn estate that I came across the other day. The boundaries are strongly marked, and show the old hill fortress being part of it.'

'Very well,' said Rachel, 'take her to the drawing-room, or remain here, as you please. I shall take my walk alone.'

She went, humming a song, into the blue bedroom.

'Stay where you are,' I said softly, to Louise.

I went downstairs, and to the office, for in truth there was an old plan that I had somewhere, among my papers. I found it, in a file, and went back across the court. As I came to the side door, that led from near the drawing-room to the garden, Rachel was setting forth upon her walk. She wore no hat, but had her sunshade, open, in her hand. 'I shall not be long,' she said, 'I'm going up to the terrace – I want to see if a little statue would look well in the sunken garden.'

'Have a care,' I said to her.

'Why, of what?' she asked.

She stood beside me, her sunshade resting on her shoulder. She wore a dark gown, of some thin muslin stuff, with white lace about the neck. She looked much as I had seen her first, ten months ago, except that it was summer. The scent of the new cut grass was in the air. A butterfly flew past in happy flight. The pigeons cooed from the great trees beyond the lawn.

'Have a care,' I said slowly, 'of walking beneath the sun.'

She laughed, and went from me. I watched her cross the lawn and climb the steps towards the terrace.

I turned back into the house, and going swiftly up the stairs came to the boudoir. Louise was waiting there.

'I want your help,' I said briefly, 'I have little time to lose.'

She rose from the stool, her eyes a question. 'What is it?'

'You remember the conversation that we had those weeks ago, in the church?' I said to her. She nodded.

'Well, you were right, and I was wrong,' I answered, 'but never mind that now. I have suspicions of worse beside, but I must have final proof. I

think she has tried to poison me, and that she did the same to Ambrose.'
Louise said nothing. Her eyes widened in horror.

'It does not matter now how I discovered it,' I said, 'but the clue may lie
in a letter from that man Rainaldi. I am going to search her bureau here,
to find it. You learnt a smattering of Italian, with your French. Between us,
we can reach some translation.'

Already I was looking through the bureau, more thoroughly than I was
able to do the night before by candlelight.

'Why did you not warn my father?' said Louise. 'If she is guilty, he could
accuse her with greater force than you?'

'I must have proof,' I answered her.

Here were papers, envelopes, stacked neatly in a pile. Here were receipts
and bills that might have alarmed my godfather had he seen them but meant
little to me, in my fever to discover what I sought. I tried again the little
drawer that held the packet. This time it was not locked. I pulled it open,
and the drawer was empty. The envelope had gone. This might be an added
proof, but my tisana had been poured away. I went on opening the drawers,
and Louise stood beside me, her brows knit with anxiety. 'You should have
waited,' she said. 'It is not wise. You should have waited for my father, who
could take legal action. What you are doing now is what anyone might do,
a common thief.'

'Life and death,' I said, 'do not wait for legal action. Here, what is this?'
I tossed her a long paper, with names upon it. Some of them in English,
some Latin, some Italian.

'I am not sure,' she answered, 'but I think it is a list of plants, and herbs.
The writing is not clear.'

She puzzled over it, as I turned out the drawers.

'Yes,' she said, 'these must be her herbs and remedies. But the second
sheet is in English, and would seem to be notes on the propagation of plants;
species after species, dozens of them.'

'Look for laburnum,' I said.

Her eyes held mine an instant, in sudden understanding. Then she looked
down once more to the page she held in her hands.

'Yes, it is here,' she said, 'but it tells you nothing.'

I tore it from her hands and read, where her finger pointed. 'Laburnum
Cytisus. A native of south Europe. These plants are all capable of being
increased by seeds, and many of them by cuttings and layers. In the first
mode, the seeds should be sown, either in beds or where the plants are to
remain. In spring, as about March, and when of sufficient growth, trans-
planted into nursery rows, to remain till of a proper size of being planted
in the situations where they are to grow.' Beneath was an added note of the
source from where she had taken the information: *The New Botanic Garden.*
Printed for John Stockdale and Company, by T. Bousley, Bold Court. Fleet
Street. 1812.

'There is nothing here about poison,' said Louise.

I continued searching the desk. I found a letter from the bank. I recognised
the handwriting of Mr. Couch. Ruthless and careless now, I opened it. 'Dear

Madam, We thank you for the return of the Ashley collection of jewels, which, according to your instruction, as you are shortly to leave the country, will remain with us in custody until such time as your heir, Mr. Philip Ashley, may take possession of them. Yours faithfully, HERBERT COUCH.'

I put the letter back, in sudden anguish. Whatever Rainaldi's influence, some impulse of her own directed this action.

There was nothing else of any matter. I had searched thoroughly each drawer, raked every pigeon-hole. Either she had destroyed the letter, or carried it upon her. Baffled, frustrated, I turned again to Louise. 'It is not here,' I said.

'Have you looked through the blotter?' she asked, in doubt.

Like a fool, I had laid it on the chair, never thinking that so obvious a place could hide a secret letter. I took it up, and there, in the centre, between two clean white sheets, fell out the envelope from Plymouth. The letter was still inside. I pulled it from its cover, and gave it to Louise. 'This is it,' I said, 'see if you can decipher it.'

She looked down at the piece of paper, then gave it back to me. 'But it isn't in Italian,' she said to me. 'Read it yourself.'

I read the note. There were only a few, brief lines. He had dispensed with formality, as I had thought he might; but not in the manner I had pictured. The time was eleven of the evening, but there was no beginning. 'Since you have become more English than Italian, I write to you in your language of adoption. It is after eleven, and we weigh anchor at midnight. I will do all you ask of me in Florence, and perhaps more beside, though I am not sure you deserve any of it. At least, the villa will be waiting for you, and the servants, when you at last decide to tear yourself away. Do not delay too long. I have never had great faith in those impulses of your heart, and your emotions. If, in the end, you cannot bring yourself to leave that boy behind, then bring him with you. I warn you though, against my better judgement. Have a care to yourself, and believe me, your friend Rainaldi.'

I read it once, then twice. I gave it to Louise.

'Does it give you the proof you wanted?' she asked.

'No,' I said.

Something must be missing. Some postscript, on a further scrap of paper, that she had thrust into another sheet of the blotter. I looked once more, but there was nothing. The blotter was clean, save for one folded packet lying on the top. I seized it, and tore away the wrapping. This time it was not a letter, nor a list of herbs or plants. It was a drawing of Ambrose. The initials in the corner were indistinct, but I supposed it was by some Italian friend, or artist, for Florence was scribbled after the initials, and the date was the month of June, of the year he died. As I stared at it, I realised it must be the last likeness ever taken. He had aged much, then, after leaving home. There were lines about his mouth I did not know, and at the corners of his eyes. The eyes themselves had a haunted look about them, as though some shadow stood close to his shoulder and he feared to look behind. There was something lost about the face, and lonely too. He seemed to know disaster was in store. Though the eyes asked for devotion, they pleaded for pity too.

Underneath the drawing, Ambrose himself had scribbled some quotation in Italian. 'To Rachel. Non ramentare che le ore felici. Ambrose.'

I gave the drawing to Louise. 'There is only this,' I said. 'What does it mean?'

She read the words aloud, then thought a moment. 'Remember only the happy hours,' she said slowly. She gave it back to me, and the letter from Rainaldi too. 'Did she not show it you before?' she asked.

'No,' I answered.

We looked at one another in silence for a moment. Then Louise said, 'Can we have misjudged her, do you think? About the poison? You see yourself, there is not any proof.'

'There never will be any proof,' I said. 'Not now. Not ever.'

I put the drawing back upon the bureau, and the letter too.

'If there is no proof,' said Louise, 'you cannot condemn her. She may be innocent. She may be guilty. You can do nothing. If she be innocent, and you accused her, you could never forgive yourself. You would be guilty then, not her at all. Let's leave this room, and go down into the drawing-room. I wish now we had not meddled with her things.'

I stood by the open window of the boudoir staring out across the lawn.

'Is she there?' asked Louise.

'No,' I said, 'she has been gone nearly half an hour, and has not returned.'

Louise crossed the room and stood by my side. She looked into my face. 'Why is your voice so strange?' she said. 'Why do you keep your eyes fixed there, on those steps leading to the terrace walk? Is anything the matter?'

I brushed her aside and went towards the door.

'Do you know the bell rope on the landing beneath the belfry,' I said to her, 'the one that is used at noon to summon the men to dinner? Go now, and pull it hard.'

She looked at me, puzzled. 'What for?' she asked.

'Because it is Sunday,' I said, 'and everyone is out, or sleeping, or scattered somewhere; and I may need help.'

'Help?' she repeated.

'Yes,' I said, 'there may have been an accident, to Rachel.'

Louise stared at me. Her eyes, so blue and candid, searched my face.

'What have you done?' she said; and apprehension came upon her, conviction too. I turned, and left the room.

I ran downstairs, and out across the lawn and up the path to the terrace walk. There was no sign of Rachel.

Near to the stones and mortar and the stack of timber above the sunken garden the two dogs were standing. One of them, the younger, came towards me. The other stayed where he was, close to the heap of mortar. I saw her footsteps in the sand and lime, and her sunshade, still open, tipped upon its side. Suddenly the bell rang out from the clock-tower on the house. It went on and on, and the day being still and calm the sound of it must have travelled across the field, down to the sea, so that men fishing in the bay would have heard it too.

I came to the edge of the wall above the sunken garden, and saw where the men had started work upon the bridge. Part of the bridge still remained and hung suspended, grotesque and horrible, like a swinging ladder. The rest had fallen to the depths below.

I climbed down to where she lay amongst the timber and the stones. I took her hands and held them. They were cold.

'Rachel,' I said to her, and 'Rachel' once again.

The dogs began barking up above, and louder still came the sound of the clanging bell. She opened her eyes, and looked at me. At first, I think in pain. Then in bewilderment. Then finally, so I thought, in recognition. Yet I was in error, even then. She called me Ambrose. I went on holding her hands until she died.

They used to hang men at Four Turnings in the old days.
Not any more, though.